Praise for *Europe Central* by V

"His most welcoming work, possibly his
stories, virtuoso historical remembrance a

—

"In *Europe Central,* Vollmann may have written the
the stories, told by several narrators, including a high-ranking Russian secret service operative and a phone operator, weave a remarkable tapestry of mid-twentieth century continental history. . . . *Europe Central* resembles *War and Peace* not merely in its scope, but in its perception of history as a determining force that individual lives merely illustrate. . . . He has created a book that aspires to the highest possible potential of literature. *Europe Central* is more than physically enormous; it is morally significant."

—*Los Angeles Times*

"The former Soviet Union and Nazi Germany are the settings for Vollmann's new novel, a grimly magnificent dramatization of the impossible moral choices forced on individuals by those totalitarian regimes. . . . Vollmann's language beautifully captures these warring conflicts, moving from lyricism to military strategy to hallucination to erotic longing as his characters navigate their way through a landscape of atrocities. . . . If you have been following Vollmann's extraordinary career, *Europe Central* may be his best novel ever. . . . His willingness to go against the preferred social realism of our day, enabled by his publisher's willingness to allow him to unfold his Wagnerian epics at full length, make him a hero of our time."

—*The Washington Post*

"Vollmann seems to write long because what he wants us to understand is broad and deeply complex, deeply resistant to simplification. . . . With this profound and fully realized new work of fiction, Vollmann asks us to put aside what we think we know of history and immerse ourselves in it once again."

—*The Boston Globe*

"It's neither an exaggeration nor an insult to say that William T. Vollmann's throbbing, twitching, exasperating—and brilliant—*Europe Central* might put a few readers toward madness. No, that's too tame: *Europe Central,* angry and vivid, claustrophobic and consuming, mesmerizing and meandering, has an emotional force capable of ripping almost any reader from his moorings, or at the very least, inspiring a strange and overpowering urge to sit sobbing over Shostakovitch's heartbreaking, dead-man-walking Opus 110 for days on end. . . . Vollmann has done as much as anyone in recent memory to return moral seriousness to American fiction, and here's hoping that this jarring, haunting, absurdly ambitious symphony of a book will inspire other writers to batter down mental barriers, the way that Shostakovich's music did."

—*San Francisco Chronicle*

"The plagues of Nazism and Stalinism were carried by Idea and Symbol. Vollmann's achievement in *Europe Central* is to bring the power of these ideas and symbols to life—while also giving flesh to those who resisted sleepwalking through the tragedy. . . . *Europe Central* is easily Vollmann's greatest work, and it deserves a central place in what must be our continuous imagining of the horrors we are all too capable of reliving."

—*Star Tribune* (Minneapolis)

"Wide reaching and hugely ambitious, this work tells the stories of major and minor figures on the German and Russian fronts. . . . Vollmann intends the reading of his works to be an emotionally traumatic experience, and *Europe Central* is harrowing, in part because of its depressing subject, but also because of the raw and often sadistically insightful way the material is treated. . . . Vollmann is a master storyteller and bravura stylist, and he sustains and constantly reignites interest over the course of this lengthy book. . . . That he has turned to the historical novel and made it his own, fashioning a work which is cinematic in scope, epic in ambition and continuously engaging, shows that he is one of the most important and fascinating writers of our time."

—*The Times Literary Supplement*

"An epic, fever dream fusion of fiction and fact. . . . Vollmann, calling to mind Pynchon's view of history as 'a great disorderly tangle of lines,' attempts and largely succeeds in *Europe Central* in synthesizing and reconciling varied factual, cultural, and imaginative strands. . . . With minute attention to detail and psychological probing, Vollmann traces the evolution of events and the differing fates with dramatic and compelling effect. . . . He conveys it all with great insights as always, punctuating his incisive analysis with masterful prose in a style and in a passion and commitment all his own."

—*The San Diego Union-Tribune*

PENGUIN BOOKS

EUROPE CENTRAL

William T. Vollmann was born in Los Angeles in 1959. He attended Deep Springs College and Cornell University, where he graduated *summa cum laude* in comparative literature. Vollmann's novels include *You Bright and Risen Angels, Whores for Gloria, The Butterfly Stories, The Royal Family,* and four of a projected series of seven novels dealing with the repeated collisions between Native Americans and their European colonizers and oppressors: *The Ice-Shirt, Fathers and Crows, The Rifles,* and *Argall.* Vollmann is also the author of three short story collections (*The Rainbow Stories, Thirteen Stories and Thirteen Epitaphs,* and *The Atlas,* winner of the PEN Center USA West Award for Fiction), and two works of nonfiction, *An Afghanistan Picture Show* and *Rising Up and Rising Down,* which was a finalist for the 2003 National Book Critics Circle Award in nonfiction. Vollmann won a 1988 Whiting Award and the Shiva Naipaul Memorial Award in 1989. His journalism and fiction have appeared in such magazines as *The New Yorker, Harper's, Esquire, Outside, Granta,* and *Conjunctions.* He lives in California.

WILLIAM T. VOLLMANN

EUROPE CENTRAL

PENGUIN BOOKS

PENGUIN BOOKS

Published by the Penguin Group
Penguin Group (USA) Inc., 375 Hudson Street, New York, New York 10014, U.S.A.
Penguin Group (Canada), 90 Eglinton Avenue East, Suite 700, Toronto,
Ontario, Canada M4P 2Y3 (a division of Pearson Penguin Canada Inc.)
Penguin Books Ltd, 80 Strand, London WC2R 0RL, England
Penguin Ireland, 25 St Stephen's Green, Dublin 2, Ireland (a division of Penguin Books Ltd)
Penguin Group (Australia), 250 Camberwell Road, Camberwell,
Victoria 3124, Australia (a division of Pearson Australia Group Pty Ltd)
Penguin Books India Pvt Ltd, 11 Community Centre, Panchsheel Park, New Delhi – 110 017, India
Penguin Group (NZ), cnr Airborne and Rosedale Roads, Albany,
Auckland 1310, New Zealand (a division of Pearson New Zealand Ltd)
Penguin Books (South Africa) (Pty) Ltd, 24 Sturdee Avenue,
Rosebank, Johannesburg 2196, South Africa

Penguin Books Ltd, Registered Offices:
80 Strand, London WC2R 0RL, England

First published in the United States of America by Viking Penguin,
a member of Penguin Group (USA) Inc. 2005
Published in Penguin Books 2006

10 9 8 7 6 5 4 3 2

Portions of this work first appeared in *Conjunctions, Grand Street, Film Comment, The New Yorker, The Paris Review*, and *Expelled from Eden: A William T. Vollmann Reader*, edited by William T. Vollmann, Larry McCaffery, and Michael Hemmingson (Thunder's Mouth Press, 2005).

PUBLISHER'S NOTE
This is a work of fiction. Names, characters, places, and incidents either are the product of the author's imagination or are used fictitiously, and any resemblance to actual persons, living or dead, business establishments, events, or locales is entirely coincidental.

THE LIBRARY OF CONGRESS HAS CATALOGED THE HARDCOVER EDITION AS FOLLOWS:
Vollmann, William T.
Europe Central / by William T. Vollmann.
p. cm.
ISBN 0-670-03392-8 (hc.)
ISBN 0 14 30.3659 9 (pbk.)
1. Germany—Social life and customs—Fiction.
2. Soviet Union—Social life and customs—Fiction. I. Title.
PS3572.O395E97 2005
813'.54—dc22 2004061170

Printed in the United States of America
Map by the author
Designed by Carla Bolte Set in Scala and Futura, with additional fonts

This book is dedicated to the memory of Danilo Kiš, whose masterpiece *A Tomb for Boris Davidovich* kept me company for many years while I was preparing to write this book.

The majority of my symphonies are tombstones.

—D. D. Shostakovich

CONTENTS

PATRONYMICS

For the convenience of my countrymen who lose their way in Russian novels.

Akhmatova [Gorenko], Anna Andreyevna
Arnshtam, Leo Oskarovich
Danchenko, Natalya Kovalova
Denisov, Edison Vasiliyevich. *Nickname:* Edik.
Glikman, Isaak Davidovich
Glivenko, Tatyana Ivanovna
Kainova, Margarita Andreyevna
Karmen, Roman Lazarevich
Konstantinovskaya, Elena [Yelena] Evseyevna. *Nicknames:* Elenka, Elenochka, Lyalya, Lyalka, Lyalotchka.
Krupskaya, Nadezhda Konstantinovna
Lebedinsky, Lev Nikolayevich
Lenin [Ulyanov], Vladimir Ilyich. Often called Ilyich.
Litvinova, Flora Pavlovna
Nikolayevna, Tatyana Petrovna
Rostropovich, Mstislav Leopoldovich
Shebalina, Alisa Maximova
Shostakovich, Dimitri Dimitriyevich. *Nicknames:* Mitya, Mitenka, etc.
Shostakovich, Galina Dimitriyevich. *Nicknames:* Galya, Galisha, Galotchka.
Shostakovich, Mariya Dimitriyevna. *Nickname:* Mariyusha.
Shostakovich, Zoya Dimitriyevna
Supinskaya [later Shostakovich], Irina Antonova. *Nicknames:* Irinotchka, Irinka.
Ustvolskaya, Galina Ivanovna
Varzar [later Shostakovich], Nina Vasilyevna. *Nicknames:* Ninotchka, Ninusha, Ninka, Nita.
Vlasov, Andrei Andreyevich

Operation Barbarossa
London
Paris
Berlin
DRESDEN
Prague
MÜNCHEN
Wien
Rome
РОМАН КАРМЕН
Madrid
Operation Magic Fire

ARCTIC CIRCLE
White Sea
Operation Northern Lights
Operation Citadel
Leningrad
Operation Ring
Operation Little Saturn
Moscow
Operation Reinhard
VORONEZH
Stalingrad
KHARKOV
OREL
POLTAVA
LVOV
LEMBERG
VINNITSA
Operation Blau
Caspian Sea
Bucharest
Sebastopol
Black Sea
Constantinople

VIEW FROM A RUINED ROMANIAN FORT

(1945)

STEEL IN MOTION

As often as not, the things that attract us to another person are quite trivial, and what always delighted me about Blumentritt was his fanatical attachment to the telephone.

—Field-Marshal Erich von Manstein (1958)

1

A squat black telephone, I mean an octopus, the god of our Signal Corps, owns a recess in Berlin (more probably Moscow, which one German general has named *the core of the enemy's whole being*). Somewhere between steel reefs, a wire wrapped in gutta-percha vibrates: *I hereby . . . zzZZZZ . . . the critical situation . . . a crushing blow.* But because these phrases remain unauthenticated (and because the penalty for eavesdropping is death), it's not recommended to press one's ear to the wire, which bristles anyhow with electrified barbs; better to sit obedient, for the wait can't be long; negotiations have failed. Away flees Chamberlain, crying: *Peace in our time.* France obligingly disinterests herself in the Prague government. Motorized columns roll into snowy Pilsen and keep rolling. Italy foresees adventurism's reward, from which she would rather save herself, but, enthralled by the telephone, she somnambulates straight to the balcony to declare: *We cannot change our policy now. We are not prostitutes.* The ever-wakeful sleepwalker in Berlin and the soon-to-be-duped realist in the Kremlin get married. *This will strike like a bomb!* laughs the sleepwalker. All over Europe, telephones begin to ring.

In the round room with the fan-shaped skylight, with Greek gods ranked behind the dais, the Austrian deputies sit woodenly at their wooden desks, whose black rectangular inlays enhance the elegance; they were the first to accept our future; their telephone rang back in '38. Bulgaria, denied the British credits which wouldn't have preserved her anyway, receives the sleepwalker's forty-five million Reichsmarks. The realist offers credits to no one but the sleepwalker. Shuffling icons like playing cards, Romania reiterates her neutrality in hopes of being overlooked. Yugoslavia wheedles airplanes from Germany and money from France. Warsaw's humid shade is already scented with panic-gasps. The wire vibrates: *Fanatical determination . . . ready for anything.*

According to the telephone (for perhaps I did listen in once, treasonously), Europe Central's not a nest of countries at all, but a blank zone of black icons and gold-rimmed clocks whose accidental, endlessly contested territorial divisions (essentially old walls from Roman times) can be overwritten as we like, Gauleiters and commissars blanching them down to grey dotted lines of permeability convenient to police troops. Now's the time to gaze across all those red-grooved roof-waves oceaning around, all the green-tarnished tower-islands rising above white facades which grin with windows and sink below us into not yet completely telephone-wired reefs; now's the time to enjoy Europe Central's café umbrellas like anemones, her old grime-darkened roofs like kelp, her hoofbeats clattering up and bellnotes rising, her shadows of people so far below in the narrow streets. Now's the time, because tomorrow everything will have to be, as the telephone announces, *obliterated without warning, destroyed, razed,* Germanified, Sovietized, *utterly smashed.* It's an order. It's a necessity. We won't fight like those soft cowards who get held back by their consciences; we'll liquidate Europe Central! But it's still not too late for negotiation. If you give us everything we want within twenty-four hours, we'll compensate you with land in the infinite East.

In Mecklenburg, we've prepared a demonstration of the world's first rocket-powered plane. Serving the sleepwalker's rapture, Göring promises that five hundred more rocket-powered planes will be ready within a lightning-flash. Then he runs out for a tryst with the film star Lida Baarova. In Moscow, Marshal Tukhachevsky announces that *operations in a future war will unfold as broad maneuver undertakings on a massive scale.* He'll be shot right away. And Europe Central's ministers, who will also be shot, appear on balconies supported by nude marble girls, where they utter dreamy speeches, all the while listening for the ring of the telephone. Europe Central will resist, they say, at least until the commencement of Case White. Every man will be issued a sweaty black machine-carbine, probably hand-forged, along with ten round lead bullets, three black pineapple grenades each not much larger than a pistol grip, and a forked powder horn of yellowed ivory adorned with circle-inscribed stars . . .

The telephone gloats: *Liberating advance . . . shock armies . . . ratio of mechanized forces.*

Across the next frontier, where each line of fenceposts leans away from the other, our shared victim's proud military poets dull all apprehensions by equating Warsaw 1939 with Smolensk 1634. While they dispose their hopeless echelons, we draw the Ribbentrop-Molotov Line, on which we stamp GEHEIM, which means *secret.* And why stop there? The sleepwalker gets Lithuania, the realist Finland. Our creed's a lamp whose calibrated radiance bows down into its zone. *It was and is Jews who bring the Negroes into the Rhineland. That is precisely why the Party affirms that Trotskyism is a Social-Democratic deviation in our Party.* The telephone rings; General Guderian receives his instructions to activate Case Yellow. We'll whirl away Europe Central's wine-tinted maple leaves and pale hexagonal church towers.

2

You won't get to watch it happen; they don't allow windows in this office, so you may feel a trifle dull at times, but at least you'll never be alone, since on the steel desk, deep within arm's length, hunches that octopus whose ten round eyes, each inscribed with a number, glare through you at the world. *The Pact of Steel . . . a correct decision . . . my unalterable will . . . rally round the Party of Lenin and Stalin.* In the bottom righthand drawer's a codebook whose invocations control the speeds and payloads of steel, but the octopus seems to be watching. Take the gamble if you dare; how well can those ten eyes see? The sleepwalker in the Reich Chancellery could tell you (not that he would): they're *his* eyes, lidless, oval, which imparts to them a monotonously idiotic or hysterical appearance; in the ditch outside, a hundred other open-eyed heads revert to clay, not that they have anything in common with the octopus, whose glare remains eternally sentient.

What about the mouthpiece? Is it true that it can hear your every breath through its black holes? In his underground headquarters with its many guards, the realist sits tired behind a large desk, awaiting the telephone's demands. Although he's good at hanging up on people with as much force as the soldier who slams another shell into our antitank gun, he's hanging up on *them,* not on the telephone itself, which he can't live without. He subsumes himself in it, all-hearing; he knows when Shostakovich takes his name in vain. At the first ring he'll summon his generals to attend him at that conference table with its green cloth.

The sleepwalker's all eyes; the realist is all ears; their mating forms the telephone.

3

This consciousness may indeed derive, as the American victors will assert, from entirely mechanical factors: Within the bakelite* skull of the entity hangs, either nestled or strangled in a latticework of scarlet-colored wires, a malignantly complex brain not much larger than a walnut. Its cortex consists of two brown-and-yellow lobes filamented with fine copper wire. It owns ideas as neatly, numerously arrayed as Poland's faded yellow eagle standards: *The camp of counterrevolution . . . German straightforwardness . . . the slanders of the opposition . . . the soundness of the Volkish theory.* It knows how to get everyone, from Akhmatova (who, visionary that she is, mistakes it for a heart of rose coral), to Zhykov (who fools himself that it can be played with), from Gerstein to Guderian, those twin freethinkers who dance alone within their soaring bullet-prisons in obedience to the telephone-brain's involution at the center of the shell.

Don't trust any technicians who assure you that this brain is "neutral"—soon you'll hear how angrily the receiver jitters in its cradle. Kollwitz, Krupskaya and the rest—it will dispose of them all, magically. It's got their number. (As the sleepwalker admonishes Colonel-General Paulus: *One has to be on the watch, like a spider in its web . . .*) In short, it will enforce the principle of unified command.

It makes the connection. It rings.

From the receiver, now clattering like a dispatch rider's motorcycle across the cobblestones of Prague, to the black cold body, runs a coil whose elasticity draws out the process of strangulation. (Thanks to this telephone, General Vlasov will perish in a noose of piano wire.) From the anus-mouth behind the dial extrudes another strand of black gut thinner and less elastic than the re-

---

*If this organism does in fact reside in Moscow, then I presume that the cranial casing partakes of Soviet duralumin—an excellent variety, called *kol'chugaliuminii,* which was developed by Iu. G. Muzalevskii and S. M. Voronov.

ceiver's coil, and this pulses all the way to the wall socket. *Since this morning our troops have been . . .* Some frowning little Romanian blonde's in the way; we've got to shoot her. Now into the deep green forests of Europe Central! *The relationship of forces in the Stalingrad sector . . . ferro-concrete defense installations.* Can rubberoid sinews feel? How do I make them bleed? *Ruthless fanaticism . . . we'll find a way to deal with him.* They undulate now, as the telephone rings.

The telephone rings. It squats like an idol. How could I have mistaken it for an octopus?

Behind the wall, rubberized black tentacles spread across Europe. Military maps depict them as fronts, trenches, salients and pincer movements. Politicians encode them as borders (*destroyed, razed, utterly smashed*). Administrators imagine that they're roads and rivers. Public health officials see them as the black trickles of people dwindling day by day on Leningrad's frozen streets. Poets know them as the veins of Partisan Zoya's martyred body. They're anything. They can do anything.

4

In a moment steel will begin to move, slowly at first, like troop trains pulling out of their stations, then more quickly and ubiquitously, the square crowds of steel-helmed men moving forward, flanked by rows of shiny planes; then tanks, planes and other projectiles will accelerate beyond recall. Polish soldiers feebly camouflage their helmets with netting. Germans go to the cinema to fall in love with film stars; when Operation Citadel fails, they'll be swooning over Lisca Malbran. Russian cavalry charge into action against German tanks; German schoolgirls try to neutralize Russian tanks by pouring boiling water down the turrets. Barrage balloons swim in the air, finned and fat like children's renderings of fish. Don't worry; Europe Central's troops will stand fast, at least until Operation Barbarossa! (Their strategic dispositions are foxed and grimed like a centuries-old Bible.) Steel finds them all.

Steel, imbued with the sleepwalker's magic sight, illuminates itself as it comes murdering. (Amidst the cemetery snowdrifts of Leningrad lie the coffined and the coffinless. Steel did this.) The broad rays of light as a *Nebelwerfer* gets launched from its half track, those inform steel's gaze, mark steel's reach.

From the heavy, pleated metal of a DShK machine-gunsight, a soldier's gaze travels so that his bullet may speed true. Steel needs him to launch it on its way, but don't the gods always need their worshipers? From the telephone's brain, thoughts shoot down insulated copper conductors. It's time to commence Operation Blau. The Signal Corps prepares to receive and retransmit the dispatch: *Defend the achievements of Soviet power . . . a severe but just punishment . . .* And already the telephone is ringing again! Who will answer? Maybe no one except the Signal Corps, whose flags, attached to arms evolved from human, can transform any command into a series of articulated colors. The telephone rings!

The telephone rings. The receiver clamps itself to a mouth and an ear. (Where did *those* come from? I thought they were mine.) Another order flies up the black cable, down the elastic coil, and into the ear: *Under no circumstances will we agree to artillery preparation, which squanders time and the advantage of surprise.*

The V-phone rings; the S-phone rings. Jackboots ring on Warsaw's uneven sidewalks. The Tyrvakians have mined their bridges with Turkish dynamite. *We believe, on the contrary, that the combination of the internal combustion engine and armor plate enable us to take our fire to the enemy without any artillery preparation . . .*

All across Europe, telephones ring, teleprinters begin to click their hungry teeth, a Signal Corps functionary waves the first planes forward, and velocity infuses steel-plated monsters whose rivets and scales shimmer more blindingly than Akhmatova's poems. Within each monster, men sit on jumpseats, waiting to kill and die.

Just in case, shouldn't we now call up our rectangles of knobbly reptile-flesh, each knob a helmeted Red Army man, the rectangles marching across the snow toward the Kremlin domes while chilly purple sky-stripes rush in the same direction, white cloud-stripes in between? They're dark icons, almost black. The telephone rings: Commence Operation Little Saturn. Everything becomes a mobile entity comprised of articulated segments. Don't worry. In the cinema palaces, Lisca Malbran will help us pretend that it isn't happening.

Here come the guns like needles on round bases, and the guns which protrude from between two grey shields, and the guns which grow out of steel mushrooms, and the guns as long as houses, anchored by chassis large enough for a crew of twenty, the guns whose barrels are as long as torpedoes and the wheeled guns with fat snouts and long flare suppressors. It's only a question of time and manpower. And so the mechanized hordes go rushing east and west across Europe.

5

Guarding itself against posterity's blame, the telephone has qualified itself: *Provided always that the operation obeys the following conditions: appropriate terrain, surprise and mass commitment.* Moreover, it warns, each component must be metallic, replaceable, reliable, rapid and lethal—In spite of mass commitment, there were not enough components. The operation will fail.

Someday, bereft of propellants, steel must fall to rest and rust. (The telephone pleads: *Mechanical reinforcement.*) Smiling wearers of the starred helmet will raise high the red banner, as filmed by R. L. Karmen. *Hold fast to the last bullet.* Then, in the shellshocked silence of Europe, *which squanders time and the advantage of surprise,* morgues and institutes will blossom through the snow. In one of them, in a windowless, telephoned recess, I sit at a desk, playing with a Geco 7.65 shell.

6

What once impelled millions of manned and unmanned bullets into motion? You say *Germany*. They say *Russia*. It certainly couldn't have been Europe herself, much less Europe Central, who's always such a good docile girl. I repeat: Europe's a mild heifer, a plump virgin, an R-maiden or P-girl ripe for loving, an angel, a submissive prize. Europe is Lisca Malbran. Europe's never burned a witch or laid hands on a Jew! How can one catalogue her jewels? In Prague, for instance, one sees dawn sky through the arched windows of bell-towers, and that sky becomes more desirable by being set in that verdigrised frame whose underpinning, the finger of the tower itself, emerges from the city's flesh, the floral-reliefed, cartouched and lionheaded facades of it whose walled and winding streets have ever so many eyes; Europe's watchful since she's already been raped so many times, which may be why some of her eyes still shine with lamplight even now, but what good does it do to see them coming? The first metal lice already scuttle over her skin, which is cobblestoned with dark grey and light grey follicles. Europe feels all, bears all, raising her sky-ringed church-fingers up to heaven so that she can be married.

What set steel in motion? The late ϟϟ-Obersturmführer Kurt Gerstein has counseled me to seek the answers in Scripture, meaning Europe Central's old Greek Bibles with their red majiscules and black woodcut engravings of terrifying mummies bursting up from narrow sarcophagi; a few dozen of those volumes survived the war. To Gerstein, *elucidation* became even more magical a solvent than xylol, into which our forensicists immerse the identity documents dug up from Katyń Forest. (In that bath, inks bleached away by cadaveric fluid come back to life.) Have you ever seen a railroad tank car of fuel shot up by incendiary bullets? *Elucidation* must be even brighter than that! He asked himself what he dared not ask his strict father: Why, why all the death? His blood-red Bibles told him why.

The telephone rings. It informs me that Gerstein's answer has been rejected, that Gerstein has been hanged, obliterated, ruthlessly crushed. It puts the former Field-Marshal Paulus on the line.

Paulus advises me that the solution to any problem is simply a matter of time and manpower.

So I apply myself now, on this dark winter night, preparing to invade the meaning of Europe; I can do it; I can almost do it, just as when coming to a gap in the wall of some ruined Romanian fort, one can peer down upon thriving linden treetops; you can see them waving and massing, then far away dropping abruptly down to the fields. ▸

PINCER MOVEMENTS

(1914–1975)

THE SAVIORS: A KABBALISTIC TALE

1

The tale of Fanya Kaplan, that darkhaired, pale-faced, slender idealist, tells itself with grim brevity in keeping with her times. For just as tyrannicides spurn slow justice, so likewise with tyrants. Between exploit and recompense lay only four days, which in most histories would comprise but an ellipsis between words, a quartet of periods, thus: . . . .—but which, if through close reading we magnify them into spheres, prove to contain in each case a huddle of twenty-four grey subterranean hours like orphaned mice; and in the flesh of every hour a swarm of useless moments like ants whose queen has perished; and within each moment an uncountable multitude of instants resembling starpointed syllables shaken out of words—which at the close of this interval, Fanya Kaplan was carried beyond *Tau,* final letter of the magic alphabet. Her attempt took place on 30 August 1918. It is written that after Lenin fell, the young assassin hysterically fled, but then, remembering that the moral code of the Social Revolutionaries required her to give up her life in exchange for her victim's, stopped running, turned back, and in trembling silence surrendered to our security forces. On 3 September, Fanya Kaplan, who happened to be noted for her "Jewish features," was led into a narrow courtyard of the Lubyanka and there shot from behind by the commandant of the Kremlin himself, P. D. Malkov. (That luminary I. M. Sverdlov, who'd already played so indispensable a role in the liquidation of the Romanov family, instructed Malkov: *Her remains are to be destroyed without a trace.*) Thus the life and works of the blackhaired woman.

The tale of Lenin's bride, N. K. Krupskaya, makes for a happier parable.

And doesn't the parable possess greater integrity, greater righteousness we might almost say, than any other literary form? For its many conventions weave a holy covenant between the reader, who gets the mystification he craves in a bonbon-sized dose, and the writer, whose absence renders him divine. Granted, those very stringencies sometimes telescope events into dreamlike absurdity. In Krupskaya's case, were it not for her nearly accidental marriage she'd surely have remained as hidden to history as the silent letter *Aleph*. What was she then in her maiden days? We don't want to call her a cipher; we can't deny that her parable, like ours, began with birth. But in this genre (as in the lyric poem) there can be no random causes. Every death must occur for good reason. Every *word*, right down to its gaping letters *o* and grinning letters *e*, must offer resonance with sentences before and beyond—not predictability, mind you, for that would be tedious, but after each comma the hindsighted reader needs to be in the position of saying: Why didn't I see that coming? Fanya Kaplan, for example, was never notified that she'd been condemned to death. And yet when Malkov's very first bullet exploded between her shoulderblades, she experienced coherence, and screamed not with surprise, but with desperate fear and outrage against inevitability.—As for Krupskaya, call her the darling of parable-mongers; introduce her as *the perfect personification of convention*. (This is why her collected works are so deadly dull.) Trotsky patronized her; Stalin by the end commanded her; Lenin himself merely used her. Historians regard her as a faithful mediocrity. I myself have always read in her a striving toward kindliness, for which I offer praise. Unutterably typical of her epoch—and thus perhaps curiously akin to Fanya Kaplan—she was agitated all her life by *fervor*. Just as the same letter may appear in two words of contrary meaning, so the lives of those two women write themselves in nearly identical characters. Who am I to find in Krupskaya's enthusiasms anything alien to Fanya Kaplan's? One loved the Revolution; the other hated it. What force transformed them into opposites, if they *were* opposites?

2

We read that Krupskaya was first (that is, before her parable is supposed to begin) a pious little girl who prayed to the icon in her bedroom, then a rapturous Tolstoyan. In company with her friends she attacked a wealthy factory owner with snowballs. We find her cutting hay to help hostile and uncomprehending peasants at age fifteen, then teaching night classes in literacy to factory workers at twenty-two. She was one of those souls who long more than anything to be of use in this world. Unknowingly she found herself drawn to the letter *Cheth,* which resembles the Greek letter *pi* and which, thus visually representing a gate, refers to ownership. She yearned to give herself, to be possessed, to know where she stood.

By the time she was twenty-six, she was receiving, materializing and carrying to underground printers the invisible-inked manifestoes which Lenin sent from prison. The legend says that one of her greatest joys was to watch the magic letters appear in the boiling water, as if they comprised a secret message written expressly for her, instead of being merely another metallically impersonal appeal to the workers. (After all, reader, don't you prefer to believe that this story which you're taking the trouble to read has something to say to you?) But for just the same reason that she shunned fashionable clothes, chocolates and other frivolous pleasures, Krupskaya strove to persuade herself that in the self-abnegation of *transcription* lay her destiny.

When she reached the age of twenty-seven, N. K. Krupskaya was arrested for the first time. After two months in preliminary detention, they released her, thinking her to be a shy nobody who'd gotten mixed up in illegal activity only by mistake, but so brazen and exalted were her actions on behalf of the Kostroma strikers that she was arrested again after only eighteen days.

Here again I seem to see that pallid, protuberant-featured Social Revolutionary woman who sought to kill Lenin. It's said that Fanya Kaplan had already become a committed anarcho-terrorist by the time she was sixteen. When the gendarmes burst in, she and her comrades were arrayed around the bed, carefully assembling the components of a bomb, like those Kabbalists who in their circle-beset diagrams arrange into bristling molecules the various emanations and manifestations of God. It's even said that the police themselves were moved by the perfection of the urchin-spined grey spheres laid out upon the young girl's white sheets. Fearing for the Tsar's safety, the court at first condemned her to death, but in view of her youth and sex the sentence was commuted to hard labor for life in Siberia. There she dwelled between the river-ice and the celestial alphabets of constellations until the October Revolution amnestied her. By then Fanya Kaplan was more determined than ever to redeem all Russia from centralist abomination.

As for Comrade Krupskaya, who proved equally unrepentant, they kept her in the blankness of the cells for five months, until a convict named M. F. Vetrova burned herself to death to protest her own fate. So in garments of flame this woman (otherwise almost unknown) dictated her tale of righteousness. Who says that tales are only words? Embarrassed by Vetrova's propaganda triumph, the authorities felt compelled to exercise upon their remaining female prisoners the same leniency which they would grant Fanya Kaplan. In March of 1897, not long after her twenty-eighth birthday, they freed Krupskaya on grounds of failing health. (Fanya Kaplan for her part was also twenty-eight when she was freed forever by Malkov's bullets.)

A photograph from this period reveals Krupskaya's pale, stern beauty. Her smooth forehead glows like winter sunshine on a snowy field, her clenched lips cannot entirely deny their own sensuousness, and her eyes gaze with painful sincerity into the ideal—dark eyes these, longing eyes from which a craving for meaning steadfastly bleeds. Her high and proper collar hides her almost to the chin, so she's but a face, closed but promising something, like a flower-bud. She's combed her hair severely back, and cropped it short; she's a recruit, a fighter, a militant.

3

Knowing that Lenin needed a copyist in his Siberian exile, and learning that she too would be exiled (the police themselves being not entirely illiterate readers of dangerousness), she accepted her leader's proposal for a marriage of convenience, replying in those famous words, meant to show her imperviousness to bourgeois institutions: *Well, so what. If as a wife, then as a wife.*—In fact there is every reason to believe that beneath this bravado lived an idolatrous passion.—Upon her arrival the following year, when Fanya Kaplan was celebrating her tenth birthday, the reunited atheists submitted to a full church wedding in Shushenskoe, which is wistfully called "the Siberian Italy."

The law required an exchange of rings; and devotees of that most Kabbalistic genre, the parable-within-a-parable, might well concentrate on this most pathetic episode of the ceremony, unable to resist dissecting the ironic symbolism of those two copper wedding bands lying side by side on the black velvet cushion.* It's said that when the eternally virginal Krupskaya first saw

*Exegesis easily uncovers other ironies: The purple-cloaked priest, it is written, was as exasperated as his victims, because this marriage prevented him from renting the extra room of Lenin's house which the bride and her mother would now occupy. (Had she remained unmarried, Krupskaya would have been remanded to the locality of Ufa.) And perhaps he scented the godlessness of the convict spouses. What must he have made of Krupskaya's abashedness, Lenin's sarcastic smiles? How might he have proceeded, had he understood that this church of his, by sealing the union of these two helpmeets, was hastening its own destruction, and his?

them, she blushed. Freshly worked copper has a peculiar brightness, like bloody gold. We need not detain ourselves here with mystic correlations and analogies, God being ineffable anyway; it seems that the raw luminosity of the rings exposed her unacknowledged feelings in their revelatory glare. They'd been fashioned by a Finnish comrade who was still learning the jeweler's craft—indeed, he was indebted to Krupskaya for his tools, so he'd taken special pains, inscribing them with the names of the bride and groom in characters which in their squat angularity might well have graced some seventeenth-century diagram of astrology's nested spheres. In their shape the rings are said to have resembled the letter *Samekh*—a sort of *o* which tapers as it rejoins its starting point, and which sports a tiny bud on top, imagined by dreamy brides to be a precious stone. Need I add that this character of the mystical alphabet symbolizes both *help* and *sleep*? (Recall Marx's ambiguous proverb: Religion is the opium of the masses.)

Who knows the fate of those shining circlets? The ring which Krupskaya slipped upon Lenin's finger was never seen again. As for the one he slid onto hers, she removed it immediately, for the sake of revolutionary convention. Then the ceremony was over, and they walked home by separate ways.

So she became both drudge and disciple, the good soldier, the bedfellow (or occasional bedfellow as I should say, for in their Kremlin suite each spouse had a private room and a single-width metal-framed bed*), the harmless mediocrity, the liquidator of pessimism, the amateur who transcribed Lenin's essays and sewed his nightshirts. (That German Communist Clara Zetkin, more glamorous than Krupskaya by far, visited the happy couple before and after the Revolution; her memoirs indulgently commend the wife's "frankness, simplicity and rather puritanic modesty.")

He called her Nadya. She called him Volodya.

4

On that August day two decades later, when the darkhaired, pale-faced, slender woman approached Lenin's Rolls-Royce, then took shaky aim with her little Browning as a line of hysterical determination sank from each corner of

---

*Upon his own escape from Siberia to England in 1902, Trotsky had likewise found them working in separate quarters. "Nadyezhda Konstantinovna Krupskaya . . . was at the very centre of all the organization work," he writes in his memoirs. "In her room there was always a smell of burned paper from the secret letters she heated over the fire to read."

her tight-compressed lips, the supreme deity of the Soviet Union ought to have been gathered in, rising to the heart of heaven just as letters of the Hebrew alphabet are said to take wing during the course of certain Kabbalistic raptures. Certainly Fanya Kaplan (alias Dora) was banking on that when she gave herself up in observance of the covenant *a life for a life*. But the black-haired woman, member in good standing of the Social Revolutionary Combat Organization though she was (which is to say, self-spendthrift), lacked competence. One cannot forbear to recall the half-built bomb on her girlhood's bed. Was the premature ending of that story mere bad luck, or had she and her accomplices forgotten to post sentries? (In this connection we'd do well to invoke the letter *Daleth*, whose shape—the upper righthand angle of a square—implies both knowledge and unenlightenment, being a door which can open and close. The young anarchists had faith* that the door would stay closed until they'd completed their preparations to murder the Minister of the Interior. The police forced it open. Either way, the tale would have gone on, and the door remained.) What else should we expect? So many revolutionaries are intellectuals, a class of people whose aspirations tend to run ahead of their capabilities. Just think of that Paris Communard of the previous century who used to sit in cafés, constructing such beautiful little barricades out of breadcrumbs that everyone admired him; come the uprising, he built a perfect barricade out of stones—and the troops marched around it. (Shall we interject here that Krupskaya was perfectly useless with a gun, and that her attempts at cryptography brought smiles to the lips of Tsarist police spies?)

With typically hysterical exoticism, Fanya Kaplan had incised her bullets with dum-dum crosses so that they represented magic atoms, then dipped them in a substance which she believed to be curare poison, but which would prove to exert no effect whatsoever. Then she set out to try her luck. As soon as Lenin had completed his Friday address to the workers, she fired three shots which hummed like the letter *Mem*. One pierced a woman who was complaining about the confiscation of bread at railroad stations. The second shot struck Lenin in the upper arm, injuring his shoulder. The third soared upward through his lung into his neck, coming to rest in a

---

*Blind faith, one might say. In Siberia she went literally and mysteriously blind for three years, but upon her blindness was engraved the secret alphabet of her cause. Under the influence of the terrorist Spiridovna, she swore to be patient, and someday to execute justice. And then, as if by magic, the world revealed itself once more to her sight.

fortuitous spot (if any bullet wound can be considered such). Lenin's face paled, and he sank to the running board, bleeding, unconscious.

5

The Cheka sent a car for Krupskaya without telling her anything. She was in terror; that day the leading Chekist Uritsky had already been assassinated. At such moments, when we find ourselves in danger of losing the protagonist we love, the tale of our marriage begins to glow, and the letters tremble on the page as once did our own souls when we realized the inevitability of the first kiss. Later, if he lives, those same words will go dry and stale. But for now the beloved Name trembles in every constituent, and we feel weak and sick. Krupskaya had already begun to suffer from the heart condition which would underline the remaining chapters of her life. She felt half suffocated. Her vision doubled; the streets of Moscow shimmered with tears. When, penetrating the magic circle of Latvian Riflemen, she found her husband apparently dying,* she composed herself and gripped his hand in silence. (Years later, she'd be dry-eyed at his funeral.) He was lying on his right side. They said he'd opened his eyes when the car pulled up; he'd wanted to ascend the stairs himself. In the secret pocket of her dress, her fingers clasped the copper ring he'd given her in Shushenskoe.

The doctors had already cut his suit off. Lenin's eyes would not open. He breathed with the desperate, shallow gasps of a lover nearing orgasm; and, as if to reinforce this impression, a curl of blood had dried upon his paper-white chest in the shape of the letter *Lamed,* whose snaky shape has Kabbalistic associations with sexual intercourse.

At dawn his breaths deepened, and then he looked at her. Krupskaya whispered: We have no one but you. Stay with us; save us . . .

To comfort her, one of the nurses (who herself was weeping) said: He needs you, Nadezhda Konstantinovna.

Then they all began to heal him, giving him injections with a squat glass syringe whose shape was reminiscent of the letter *Qoph,* emblem of inner sight.

---

*Arguably Fanya Kaplan had, as exegetes like to say, "wrought better than she knew," since the bullet remaining in Volodya's neck proved to be a time bomb. Nearly three years later, the doctors finally decided to remove it, and although the operation was a success, scarcely two days later he suffered the first of the cerebral hemorrhages which were to carry him off.

As soon as he came back into his mind, he became impatient. He had many things to do to insure that his Revolution would be irreversible. Krupskaya rarely found herself alone with him. First it was the doctors, then Trotsky, Stalin and the rest, come to congratulate him on his survival. He gazed at her half-humorously, rolling his eyes. She knew he longed to be at work by himself, preparing new commandments and testimonies. What could she do to aid him? How could she prevent him from tiring himself into a relapse? Shyly clearing her throat, she said: Pretend this convalescence is only another term in prison, Volodya. You know you can deal with that!—He laughed delightedly.

On 14 September she took him to somebody's confiscated estate in the pleasant village of Gorki. He recovered secretly behind those walls. Krupskaya remained at his side as often as he would let her. While he slept, she sat in her room, repeating his name with such whispered fervor that the nurses said: It's almost as if she believes he'll fade away if she closes her eyes for one minute!—They tried to get her to rest, but she burst into tears.

In another week Volodya's bandages came off. Before October he began to walk again without her help, although he'd lost much blood and there were circles under his eyes. She brought him home to the Kremlin just before the end of that month, sleeping with her door open in case he should call for her. He'd already reverted to his habit of pacing his office on tiptoe throughout the night hours, muttering, searching for clear policies; these well-known sounds soothed her. By November he was almost entirely restored. And in celebration, the Bolsheviks everywhere replicated his graven images.

6

Fanya Kaplan was executed on the same day that the Commissar of the Interior released the infamous "Order Concerning Hostages," which decreed that all Right Social Revolutionaries be arrested at once and reserved for mass liquidation as needed. In Perm alone they shot thirty-six captives to avenge Lenin and Uritsky. Thus the terrorists were requited to their faces. Less than twenty-four hours later, the Red Terror was born. The birth announcement went hissing across telegraph lines like the letter *Shin,* whose three vertical arms culminate in poppy-heads of flame. Meanwhile the press kept calling for more blood, more blood. In the ever timely words of Comrade N. V. Krylenko (whose own destiny would be death by shooting): *We must execute not only the guilty. Execution of the innocent will impress the masses even more.*

But unlike the assassin herself, whose sweat had reeked of anger and fear, Krupskaya could not believe that a fellow revolutionary ought to be put to death.

The Central Committee will have to decide, her husband said. He knew that Fanya Kaplan's corpse had already been burned, and the ashes buried in an unmarked grave.

Volodya, don't think I'm a conciliationist. During all these thirty years my attitude has not changed.

I shall consider it.

I'm so sorry to disturb you about this. I've only taken her case to heart because—

Slowly raising his bald crown from the outspread *Pravda* (upside down to her) which it was his habit to grip in both of his hands, he gazed at her across the neutral zone of his desk, guarded from her by his two inkwells, whose brass caps shone like the domes of Orthodox churches, by his lamp and telephone, by his long narrow scissors whose point faced her, and his eyes were very sorrowful as he said: Where's Makarov's dictionary? I think I'll study it. The alphabetical arrangement of words creates such a refreshing sort of chaos. Ah—look here. In a row we find *sleepy, never-drying, truancy, obscurity, bliss,* then *inharmoniousness.* What unlike ideas! And all because they begin with the letters **HE**. In English or in Hebrew, for instance, I fancy they'd be arranged quite differently. And what if there's some perfect ordering that's never been thought of before? But my opinions on linguistics are not important . . .

Promise me you won't let them do this, pleaded Krupskaya, who thanks to her thyroid condition had already developed the protuberant eyes which would give her the nickname "The Fish." (Strangely enough, in her youth, one of her revolutionary aliases had been "The Lamprey.")

Lenin blinked and said: Nadya, you know very well that right now our Revolution faces so many dangers.

I never asked you for anything. I married you; I mended your clothes; I let you have your mistress and even collaborated with her. Save this woman, Volodya, I beg you!

Lenin said to her: Nadya, you need to control your emotions.

Trembling, breathing heavily, she sat down. She was overweight, unhealthy; not long afterward she'd suffer her first heart attack.

Lenin was not undevoted. He'd carried milk to his wife with his own hands when she'd lain in a sanatorium. (On one such mission, bandits had robbed him of his coat. On another, they expropriated one of his cars.) He'd granted her political power in accordance with her abilities. He'd given her a small, ornate desk in the Kremlin, a window view, a sofa flanked by bookcases, a personal library of twenty thousand volumes; these were her luxuries. This was the first and last time she'd ever ask him for anything. And so Lenin called to him Comrade J. V. Stalin, who was so useful in matters of this kind. Stalin smiled angrily and said that it would be done.

Just because she fucks Lenin doesn't mean I have to get up on my hind legs for her, he said to his understudy, Molotov, who quickly agreed: She understands nothing about politics. Nothing.

A week later, Lenin told his wife: It's all right. I've made inquiries. You can talk with her tomorrow. But it's all got to stay top secret. Right now the whole world is against us.

Krupskaya knelt and kissed his hand.

7

Typically enough, she set out for the prison alone, in her stained and dirty peasant dress, with her hair tucked up in a bun. It was snowing, and the streets remained dangerous with ice. In those days it was the custom for every pass to be scrutinized in turn by dozens of menacing, half-literate faces, none of whom could grant the bearer absolution from fear, but any one of whom possessed full authority to shoot. Under the stipulations of the Red Terror, mistaken ruthlessness would be forgiven; mistaken mercy might not be. By virtue of her special association with Lenin, Krupskaya possessed the security of the elect, but even she must expect inconveniences, particularly when seeking out a convicted enemy of the people. And yet, strange to say, the sentry, whose cap was pulled low over his eyes, opened the squeaking gate without demur, and when she descended the stairs, she found in a labyrinth of brickwork corridors another guard already waiting for her, although of him she never saw anything but his back. Silently he led her down another staircase, darkness oozing from his boots. Through the walls came rhythmic screams, sometimes muffled by the earth of those deep-sunk grave-wells, sometimes amplified by the ventilation pipes, just as they say in classical times the cries of Sicilian victims echoed from the throat of a hollow brazen bull inside which the condemned were slowly roasted. As we know, Krupskaya was a sentimentalist (who secretly among all her books preferred Louisa May Alcott's *Little Women*), and these sounds horrified her. But from childhood it had been impossible to unsettle her heavy, melancholy steadiness, which disguised itself as optimism.

She trudged on behind the guard, who finally stopped to unlock an ancient iron door with three keys. He stood aside, his face in the shadows, and as soon as she had entered closed the door upon her.

8

In regard to this cell, it should have been observable to Krupskaya that the walls were incised with Hebrew letters which seemed almost to flutter in the luminescence of the guttering lantern. Of course she was so long past her religious days as to be blind to the uncanny. And yet anyone can read in her memoirs that her heart had literally pounded with joy when she first read *Das Kapital,* because Marx had proven there, with scientific infallibility, that capitalism was doomed. Well, what might constitute uncanniness to a devout Bolshevik? The presence of a Social Revolutionary? But why seek the uncanny out? Motivations lie nested in motivations, like the numerological values of the letters of Hebrew parables. If, as the Kabbalah posits, the most secret meaning is also the most precious, then we must sink into hermeneutic darkness. Krupskaya needed to prove herself to be so excellent, so above vindictive personalism, that she could forgive even the one who would have killed her husband-god. And forgiveness need not exclude contempt. Within the coils of this rationale hid a second craving which she hardly dared read, a lust for reassurance about her Revolution. But even this did not explain the intensity of Krupskaya's attraction to Fanya Kaplan.

In her girlhood there had been an eighteen-year-old teacher named Timofeika who preached socialism to the peasants. Krupskaya adored her, and expressed that adoration through emulation. Her desire to give up her own self and become Timofeika hung between them like a glowing letter *Tsae,* which is Y-shaped like the female pudendum but which terminates in a fishhook, symbolizing attachment, penetration and parasitism. (Don't mistake me; they never so much as touched one another. The key words of their tale are not lascivious, but have as usual to do with honor, worship, burnt offerings.) In any event, Timofeika soon got arrested; Krupskaya never saw her again. Very likely she became a Social Revolutionary like Fanya Kaplan. So Krupskaya would have had to break off with her in any event, to avoid compromising Volodya, who in Siberia had refused to allow her to color Easter eggs, because that would have been falling into religious superstition.) In her curiosity regarding Fanya Kaplan there lurked perhaps a shade of longing for

Timofeika's purity. And yet, as had increasingly become the case with all she loved, her yearning was polluted by repulsion and rage.

And so Krupskaya sat with her hand upon the table, wearing the white blouse and grubby striped vest which she so often affected, gazing drearily upon the prisoner and blinking her tired, protuberant eyes. Her face was tanned almost to griminess, thanks to all her propaganda work in the open air. Her stringy hair and the two vertical creases between her eyes gave her an urgent, almost crazed expression.

9

As for the convict, she scarcely deigned to turn upon Krupskaya her half-closed gaze. The visitor took this unceasing coldness, or at least guardedness, to be evidence of guilt. But in her socialist faith, as in her private relations with her husband, she had been so long accustomed to consider individual peculiarities to be irrelevant that this reticence scarcely affected her. Questions could be answered without "personality" coloring any words. The neat ranks of book-spines behind Volodya's desk offered statistics, errors, energy, fertilization. What mattered the gaze of their authors? She was interested in Fanya Kaplan only insofar as she embodied a force which threatened her interpretation of history.

At last the other woman, half turning away, brushed her hair out of her eyes with a long, pallid hand, cleared her throat, and huskily said: Well, why did you come?

Krupskaya replied: I did not come to save you. I came to understand you. I came to lift a stone from my soul.

Ah! You speak like a true Russian—so mystical, so emotional . . .

And you? You're not Russian?

I'm a Jewess.

What has that to do with anything? Trotsky's a Jew, and Sverdlov, Litvinov, Chicherin, Radek, Zinoviev, Kamenev, Krestinsky—

When I was alive I was a Social Revolutionary, but now that I'm dead I've become quite the little Jewess. When they arrested me they continually spoke of my Jewish features—

That's all cant, Krupskaya insisted. You know that national origins mean nothing. Don't tell me you committed *that crime* because you're a Jew.

She'd found herself saying *that crime* because she did not want to utter her husband's name in front of this wretch. To call him *Lenin* would be to deny her relationship to him, which felt almost like a betrayal; whereas *Volodya* would be too intimate; she certainly desired no intimacy with F. D. Kaplan. In public, she frequently used the familiar yet still somewhat official *Ilyich,* which might be thinkable here, but somehow she preferred that the victim's presence loom unnamably between them like the blade of a giant guillotine.

But why not just call what I did a religious act? asked the woman with a nervously goading smile. Why not call it a mystery?

Her lips pressed together, her chin thrust ever so slightly forward, Krupskaya said: So you acted out of some fanatical superstition—

I shot Lenin because I believe him to be a traitor.

Then you do deserve death. At a time like this, when Russia is—

Of course I'm a fanatic. The fewer possibilities I have, the more urgently I must imagine.

I cannot understand you.

The brooding mouth said: Nadezhda Konstantinovna, you know very well what we demand: Universal suffrage, freedom of the press, peasant power, a representative people's government—

But those pseudo-democratic phrases of yours are printed in the constitutions of capitalist republics all over the world! Don't you see that they mean nothing? How can you support universal suffrage when the richest people control the vote? Freedom of the press—who owns that press? A people's government—of which people? You've let yourself become a pawn of the White Guard clique—

Even a pawn sometimes controls destiny, replied the woman with a beautiful smile.

You S.R.s want to stand in the middle; that's your error. You're trying to persuade the people that it's possible to refrain from choosing between the capitalists and us. That's a crime for which you all deserve to be shot like mad dogs . . .

But at these counterarguments the criminal merely smiled again. Something almost inexpressible did find expression in her. What was it? Krupskaya's indignation and hatred were beginning to be supplanted by sensations of murky confusion.

10

Lenin's eyes had taken on the famous ironic twinkle when he'd said to Stalin: She'd better be good. You know that Nadya is not stupid.

Stalin grinned rudely back, thinking: Her intelligence may not lie beyond honest controversy.

More weird word-consonance: Nadya also happened to be the name of Stalin's brown-eyed wife, twenty-two years younger than he, whom he'd just wed and who was already giving him trouble. Of course she was as beautiful as a perfect story. The tresses curled round her ear in imitation of the letter *Pe*; one of the few in the Hebrew alphabet which are not angular, it relates not only to the ear, but also to submission (and, of course, to its opposite), and coincidentally to that dream of all politicians, eternally perfect speech. During her lifetime, Comrade N. A. Stalin was indeed but a subjugated ear. More acute than Krupskaya, or at least more sensitive, she was characterized by friends and relatives in that hackneyed phrase *a trembling doe*. Her future was suicide. Beside her bleeding corpse she left a note denouncing her husband's crimes. Thus in the end she did dominate him, that letter *Pe* hanging forever now above his head, condemning him unreachably. But in 1918 their final quarrel still lay fourteen years away. Stalin had deciphered a few characters of the threatening message upon her forehead, but, mistaking her silence for blankness, convinced himself that he'd read nothing there—a pathetic reversal of his paranoia toward all other human beings. Upon his face God wrote: *For the thing that I fear comes across me, and what I dread befalls me.** Doubtless that slogan colored his own reading of Krupskaya. Her wifely solicitude had sometimes interposed itself between Lenin and himself, which was unforgivable. And in the present case, her compulsive attachment to a traitor she'd never met constituted no less than an assault upon the Party. She'd embarrassed Lenin. Here was a chance to do Lenin a favor, but also to put that fat old hag in her place. Moreover, he now had perfect means to blackmail Lenin should he ever need to.

And so, when the actress was brought to his office and stood before him as straight as the letter *Vau,* which resembles a nail, Stalin lit his pipe, looked her over, then said: Well, comrade, do you understand that you've been given a gigantic *moral* responsibility?

Yes, Comrade Stalin, I—

I have my doubts that you do. Listen, you. We don't want the old cunt to put us to this trouble again. Just because she shares the same bathroom with Lenin is no reason why I have to respect her. Hey! Did you hear what I said? You're not sick, are you?

No, Comrade Stalin.

---

*Job 3:25.

Make her hate you, and don't let her pin you down on anything. Mystification is in order, get it? *Nu,* you're a Yid, so act like a Yid.

Stalin's will, if the black-clad woman had correctly deciphered it, was that she punish and terrify Krupskaya. Each syllable departing her mouth must become a ravening animal to attack the grand lady's soul.

Unlike most inmates of that epoch, the woman could see the future as brightly as if it were a six-pointed star of violet fire around which whirled all the signs of the heavens. Until she ceased to exist, Lenin and Stalin would worry that the trick might be exposed. And therefore she must take refuge in gnomic utterances.—Her apprehension now ascended higher, until she realized that even so obscure a course, mystification as he'd called it, would profit her nothing. No matter what she said or did, she was doomed.

And so she felt herself even more pinned to silence, like Fanya Kaplan herself, who'd done nothing, it is said, but stare out the window of her cell, waiting for the bullet in the back. It was all hopeless.

But as soon as Krupskaya had entered her cell, the woman had pitied her. She would be true to the text whose letters crawled around her so uneasily. *The lot is cast into the lap, but the decision is wholly from the Lord.**

11

Most literary critics agree that fiction cannot be reduced to mere falsehood. Well-crafted protagonists come to life, pornography causes orgasms, and the pretense that life is what we want it to be may conceivably bring about the desired condition. Hence religious parables, socialist realism, Nazi propaganda. And if this story likewise crawls with reactionary supernaturalism, that might be because its author longs to see letters scuttling across ceilings, cautiously beginning to reify themselves into angels. For if they could only do that, then why not us?

A kindred longing for autonomy doubtless animated the prisoner when in her low and leaden voice she whispered: Nadezhda Konstantinovna, have you ever read the Kabbalah?

I haven't time for that trash. Say what you like . . .

It's written that man is the moving hand, and God is the shadow. Only man can save God. And now you and Lenin are the two gods of Russia. Don't

*Proverbs 16:33.

deny it, Nadezhda Konstantinovna! You yourself are *God.** And only I can save you. Only I can repair your glory.

Krupskaya half rose, staring at her in astonishment.—So that's the kind you are, she said. You're not even intelligent.

Not at all. But at least *I am real.* I tried to kill Lenin because he wanted to be God, but now that he's achieved his aim he's become my shadow, so I must worship him. And you, too, with your tremors, your isolation and your silliness, you're my shadow, too! If it weren't for me, you wouldn't be here . . .

You should be in an asylum. I'm leaving.

I seek hidden worlds, the woman said into Krupskaya's staring, steadfast face. And then, in a very low voice (since Stalin was undoubtedly listening behind the wall), she whispered: Are you true to yourself?

I beg your pardon! Why should I answer to you, murderess?

I don't ask for justifications, Nadezhda Konstantinovna. I ask only for your pity.

Krupskaya's heart was pounding. Rubbing her forehead, rapidly gasping, she wondered when a stroke would finish her off.

Will you pity me? the woman was demanding.

I—

Look at me. Look at where I am. *Will you pity me?*

Krupskaya wanted to weep, but dared not. Clearing her throat, she haltingly said: I remember when I was in prison and I felt so passionately that armed struggle was necessary. And I—I think that you, too, must feel passionately.

The woman's face swelled then with a dull ecstasy, and she knelt before Krupskaya on the flagstones of the cell, flinging back her head, offering her throat, so that in her shape she resembled the letter *Beth,* which means both wisdom and madness.

But you're deranged! You need a doctor. I'll tell Ilyich . . .

Don't trouble yourself, Nadezhda Konstantinovna—

Then Krupskaya began to tremble, and she said: You're not Fanya Kaplan, are you?

If I'm not who I say I am, draw your own conclusions—

Is she dead?

---

*Literally, SHEKHINAH, the female aspect of Jehovah.

Rising, the woman said: In other words, you wish to know whether I am the assassin in herself, or the manifestation of an assassin.

Who are you?

I am your revelation.

Then the woman (who unlike both Krupskaya and Fanya Kaplan sought to delay her own doom) knelt down once more and began to murmur these words: *Suryah, Prince of the Presence, I have fasted with my head between my knees; now I adjure You one hundred and twelve times with the Name of God. I adjure You with the name NADEZHDA KONSTANTINOVNA KRUPSKAYA HA-SHEM ELOHEI YISRA'EL.*

Paling more and more in the darkness until her flesh was as a white flame, one hundred and eleven times (each time in a single long breath) she repeated this clandestine Name, nodding her head with each syllable, counting on the fingers of her ecstatically outstretched hands.

Krupskaya sat paralyzed. Afterward she could scarcely remember her sensations. It was as if she hadn't been there at all, or been there only in some insubstantial sense, like a wisp of smoke . . . And then, whispering *LE'ARSIY IEHOLE MEHS-AN AYAKSPURK ANVONITNATSNOK ADHZEDAN,* the woman trembled and fell upon the floor foaming at the mouth, and in her eyes was darkness like the darkness within Krupskaya's nostrils. At that moment the writhing Hebrew letters upon the wall became as red as fire, and took wing, gathering into a circular swarm about the woman's face, so that her features were obscured just as Fanya Kaplan's execution had been veiled in the mysterious roaring of an automobile engine (Malkov had been afraid that bystanders might otherwise hear the screams). Then the letters disappeared into the woman's mouth. Krupskaya was speechless. The woman began to glow more and more, until the light from her was as white and pure as a page of the Torah.

She stood and approached Krupskaya, who, overcome by a mysterious impulse, kissed her upon the mouth so that those two drank from each other at last.

Then, in a voice as soft as the lace in Russian shopwindows before the Revolution stripped them, the woman said: I have beheld you, I have prayed to you, and I have repaired your glory with the power of righteousness. You stand guiltless. But as for me, now that I have beheld you, I shall surely die.

Who are you? said Krupskaya, squeezing the woman's hand.

And if I told you, would you be swept aside by the telling?

Who are you?

I am you. I have become you. I have given myself utterly to you. And now what will you do? You are innocent and perfect, so you can do anything.

Who are you?

I am unknowable, the woman whispered. I am nothing.

12

Brushing past the fixed bayonets of ironically polite Chekists outside the Kremlin wall, she ascended the three long, steep flights of stairs, clenching her trembling hands. Her worshiper had drunk from her the kiss of enlightenment, but who can enlighten God Herself? Krupskaya felt as if she were trapped within a circle of fire.

Yesterday we talked about legalizing them; today we are arresting them! she heard Volodya say with that cheerful chuckle of his. That's the way to cut off counterrevolution . . .

Not long afterward, Comrade Angelica Balabanoff came to visit. When the latter raised the subject of Fanya Kaplan's execution, Krupskaya is said to have wept many tears.*

13

Here, perhaps, the parable should end, because in her last years Krupskaya shared scant sisterhood with either of the two Fanya Kaplans. She preached, lectured, traveled, set up schools, ever remaining enchanted, though she could not admit it, by the old Narodnik slogan *Go to the people.*—Well, and so she did still resemble her husband's assassins! How can we end yet?—She wrote austere essays on pedagogy. (Krupskaya loved children and would have been so happy to bear her own. But Volodya was embalmed now in the Mausoleum she'd opposed.†) In her writings recurred this phrase: *The task before us . . .* In the years when her Party was murdering Ukrainians by the millions, a certain comrade otherwise unrecorded told her the tale of a poor lit-

---

*R. H. McNeal in his drily reliable *Bride of the Revolution* goes so far as to write that *very likely Krupskaya lived out her life in the consoling belief that Fanya Kaplan was alive in jail.*

†In the last photographs taken before her widowhood one already finds a dourly *absent* expression upon her heavyset features, even when everyone else is smiling.

tle boy who liked to draw pictures of flowers, but had been born paralyzed from the waist down, so he had to remain indoors and scarcely ever saw real plants; as usual, Krupskaya wept; she wanted to do something. And what right have I to belittle weeping? Were not her goodness and her judgment laid up in store against all adversaries?—Kabbalistically she now possessed affinity for the letter *Yod,* which resembles a deformed bullet dug out of a corpse and which means, above all, *praxis.* In short, she followed the correct line, remaining worthy of the supreme experience. Convicts told her: I am well treated . . . —Before Volodya's death she was already transmitting directives requiring libraries to suppress undesirable books, including the harmfully superficial ecstasies of Tolstoyans. Blame Volodya if you want to. It was upon his instructions that she had long ago broken off with the Narodniks whose printers once set in illegal type his invisible-inked prison essays. Had Volodya then been the key to her submission? Or was it simply her lack of intellectual self-confidence, which left her convinced throughout life that she still knew too little to render any unguided sacrifice?

When the new wave of "repressions" began in 1928, the peasants, who worshiped her, sent her many letters begging her to save their families from dekulakization, exile and imprisonment. It was impossible even to answer them all. She said to herself: My personal reading of these words is irrelevant. The Revolution must be saved.—The rapture was gone. She no longer hoped to write in the Book of Life, or even to be Lenin's copy-editor; all that remained to her was to read aloud whatever might be set before her. In 1936 we find her writing in support of Stalin's show trials that many of her own former comrades-in-arms deserved to be shot like mad dogs (a stilted commonplace of the time). By then she'd become a sad, round-faced babushka, a good *Kommunistka* who stared slowly at the world. Sometimes it was whispered to her that Fanya Kaplan was still alive. She credulously gobbled such rumors, which were presented to her like offerings.

Superior in her destiny to the murdered murderess, she escaped even the show trials. The rumor that Stalin poisoned her need not be credited. She died of arterial sclerosis in 1939, and this seems to me a strangely appropriate disease for one whose vitality and spontaneity had been gradually clogged. Stalin was prominent among those who carried her funeral urn to its waiting niche in the Kremlin wall. ▸

MOBILIZATION

I have often observed in myself that my will has decided even before my thinking is over.

—Bismarck (*ca.* 1878)

1

In the Kaiser's time, iron crosses hung from the Brandenburg Gate, and there were processions of white horses and of Prussian officers whose immense brass buttons gleamed fiercely. (The Russians didn't mind at first; the Tsar and the Kaiser were cousins.) After our spectacular adventures in France, we had begun to overcome the human fearfulness of death, and even (on certain very hot nights) to speak to each other of destiny. A man leaped up in the beerhall and cried out that this would be the year when our century finally began, fourteen years late; never mind those fourteen lost years because we had a thousand more ahead of us! And nobody laughed. Pretty soon we were all in the streets. The July breath of linden trees, the sheen of rivers, the Kaiser's promises and the perfumed humidity rising up from between women's breasts now dissolved one another into a supersaturated solution whose molecules swarmed apart, perched in the lindens, opened their wings, then, unable to remain alone beyond the saturation limit, rejoined the Kaiser's newly crystalline slogans.

A generation before, the Iron Chancellor had observed: *I've always found the word* Europe *on the lips of those statesmen who want something from a foreign power which they would never venture to ask for in their own name.* And so the Kaiser, inaugurating a century of perfect honesty, divorced the word *Europe*. He said *Germany*. At once, Berlin's department stores became as airy and multi-windowed as hothouses. The clockfaces which crowned them opened gilded hands to embrace a futurity of undying summer.

The Kaiser shouted: *Germany!* On the outer walls of the Zeughaus, stone helmets which had obediently overshadowed stone collars for nearly two centuries came alive. Within each helmet-darkness, drops of excited moisture strove to become eagles.

2

The winged figures on the bridges of Berlin are now mostly flown, for certain things went wrong in Europe, which was supposed to become Germany; indeed, the wrongnesses ripened into bombs, so our angels had to flee or go smash. But even now (I'm writing in the year 2002), Berlin remains the city of eagles; and in 1914, when everything began to happen, we were, if I may say so, graced to perfection by those kingly war-birds, who inspired us as much as they guarded us, sometimes disguising themselves as winged deities on columns—I'm thinking of the gilded Victory who still flexes her wings atop the Siegessäule's triumphal phallus—sometimes protecting our dead, as does, for instance, the black eagle in gold upon the ancient pall of Anna Elisabeth Louise, the Margrave's daughter.

In the Hitler years we still believed in books enough to burn them. Imagine, then, how much life our faith could impart to stone effigies of eagles back in the Kaiser's day, when belief really meant something! The Brandenburg Gate had not yet been time-scorched to the color of earth. None of the people in the old photographs were dead—not one! Berlin's pale green willow trees bent over the water, craving to marry their own reflections and thereby complete eternity's circle; several succeeded. On the bridges and columns, eagles shrieked. New atoms of humidity flew up to become eagles.

3

Here came our Kaiser, jaunty and true; he was sterner than a Bismarck statue in a crypt; his soul was a sarcophagus of gilded lizard-dragons and gaping faces eternally melded to black bronze. He came in uniform, with his Iron Cross and dark sash, emerging from a crypt-gate between pillars crowned by a pair of eagle-angels. He'd been communing with the white grave-effigy of Kaiser Friedrich III, the gilded bier of Friedrich I. He'd rested his ear against the marble and heard a voice groan: *Germany.*

Do you want to know more? Beneath that bier, the marble was cunningly tunneled through. That's where it got secret; farther down, it got top secret.

That was where the stone always sweated and the tunnels stopped forking; there was only one choice. The deep passage ended in a niche into whose wall a medallion had been set forever (which is to say, until 1945). Whose likeness did it carry? Whose could it have been, but his, the one who won the Pope's kiss of peace even when all Europe stood against us, the one who sent our first iron tentacles into the Slavic East, the one who launched the Third Crusade? Oh, yes, it was Barbarossa's round, cruelly birdlike face beneath that squat crown; he was bulging-eyed; he clutched floral spearheads; he glared at us all from within his heavy round money-disk. And so the Kaiser came down to him. He knelt and placed his ear against the face of Barbarossa, as we do with telephones. And Barbarossa sighed in a voice neither gravelly nor liquid: *Germany.*

The Kaiser rose up. *Germany* was on his lips now. *Germany* would come out.

Awaiting his words, we beerhall men got our hats ready to throw up in the air. We'd brought our martial-looking mothers, wives and children, all of whom were blank-eyed, tranquil and strong, the children protected by their mothers' hands, the mothers guarded by the gilded profile of Friedrich I, which was in turn upheld by gruesome, menacing eagles.

Our Kaiser began to speak. Clenching his hand in the white glove, he said that like the bravely honest people that we were, we must honor our promise to the Austrians and punish the Serbs; that this meant war against England and France; that because Russia refused to disinterest herself in the Serbian question, the only correct thing was to declare war on Russia also.

Then the Kaiser shouted: *Germany!* and before we could even wave our hats, all the Medusa-faces which had glared somnolently on stone shields since the creation of Berlin, which was the creation of the world, woke up. They wanted war games and adventures. Soon our white-clad girls would be waving goodbye to troop trains.

On the Schlossbrücke, a winged goddess held a dying naked warrior above an eagle who was about to eat a snake. Their flesh was stone, but now the snake writhed, the warrior groaned, the goddess laughed, and the eagle shrieked! In the Berliner Dom, an immense white eagle, blocky and menacing, with a fantail, had masqueraded as an angel for centuries. Now it too began to scream, flapping its wings until all the picture postcards blew out of the little kiosk outside. The church's stained-glass windows glowed yellow. Then the silver gunbarrels of the organ began to fire; gold and silver music-notes rained up into the air; and right beside me a pale little man, probably a tramp, with disheveled hair and a dark trapezoidal moustache, began to caper, smiling at the world with a sleepwalker's eyes. He was the one who'd leaped up in the beer-hall that time. He gripped my hand and cried: I saw them! I saw them come to life! It happened when the Kaiser said *Germany* . . .

He was a ridiculous little man. But he threw back his head to yell: *Germany!* and his shout drowned out the Kaiser's; moreover, it grew louder the farther it traveled, and by the time it passed beyond the Egyptian Museum and the Schloss Charlottenburg, it was so loud that our ears burst and we could no longer hear it. And then creepers and vines of fire began rising up to hide Europe, just as they did in Wagner's Magic Fire music. ▸

WOMAN WITH DEAD CHILD

◩

A new bride cries until sunrise; a sister cries until she gets a golden ring; a mother cries until the end of her life.

—Russian Proverb

1

Berlin 1914, crowds shouting and waving their hats when mobilization was announced, that was her epoch, the epoch of eagles. She'd once met Rodin. That fact alone proves how old she already was in this terrible new Europe.

At the Kaiser's word they'd overruled themselves, declining to award her the gold medal after all; she was a woman, you see, and with leftist views besides. She stood there whitehaired but still young-looking in her pale smock, her white-sleeved wrists crossed against the darkness, proud and angry in defeat. Karl raged for her, then brought flowers. And now the Kaiser had fled and would never come back. Her familiar, hated, hero-worshiping Germany had died with its heroes, after which the eagles stopped screaming, pretending once again to be stone. What would become of us now? Her only hope was world socialism.

Russian children played with the fallen head of Alexander II's statue; German children longed for a savior. As for her, she kept making her quick, crude placard drawings of sick men, despairing mothers, children huddled in terror as the skeleton prepared to strike. In a sense, the Weavers' Series had been her life's work. In another sense, her life's work was the iteration and reiteration of a single image, which achieved its final expression where she stood before a woman whom she'd made out of stone, gazing at the woman's face—her own face—as she wept and stroked the granite woman's cheeks. That wasn't yet. Just now she couldn't stop thinking about Karl's patient, Frau Becker, who kept losing her children; five out of eleven were already in the ground. Frau Becker used to talk about it as if it had nothing to do with her: The big ones died off, and the little ones were always coming back.—In her honor, Käthe made another etching of a mother with a dead child. Strange to think that she'd once felt at loose ends . . .

Look! Red flags on Unter den Linden! Soldiers were shouting; who knew what they might do? Karl had begged her to stay home, but she couldn't have borne to miss this. She was at the Brandenburg Gate when they threw their cockades into the dust. Peter would have joined them in that, she was sure.

Then from the window of the Reich Chancellery Herr Scheidemann proclaimed a Republic. Never mind that all he wanted was to forestall Liebknecht from spreading Lenin's revolution; God be thanked for the result! Of course it made the eagles scream, but the cheering crowds drowned them out. She came running to witness this, still wearing the pale smock she wore in her atelier; the idea of human brotherhood drew her here. A Republic in Germany! She was so happy now. And then, enraged with herself for having felt happy, she remembered the first victory of Peter's war, 11.8.14 it was, when we regained Alsace-Lorraine for the Reich: even the Social Democrats had been hypnotized by 11.8.14; we rained roses on our soldiers as they marched through the Brandenburg Gate, and even the family of Dr. Karl Kollwitz hung the Imperial flag from the balcony; they'd never done that in their lives, and never would again. Who celebrated 11.8.14 now? Alsace-Lorraine had long since gone French again, and our soldiers who'd won it were hungry now or maimed or else they were a closepacked line of corpses in a groove of dirt. A moment ago she'd felt happy about Scheidemann's republic, and for what? Across the street, a crazy little man with a moustache was shaking his fist in a rage, stamping like Rumpelstilzchen, while at her side a crowd of workers kept singing the Internationale.

The fact remained that last year, when news came of the Russian Revolution, she'd wept for joy. She wasn't ashamed of her tears and never would be.

And now a Republic! Surely there was something fine about that . . .

She ran home to tell Karl that we had a Republic. He lifted her up in the air in his joy. Then the electricity went out.

The railroad workers struck again; troops guarded the bridges, every soldier with his hand grenade. Here with a hollow clap of horse-hooves came the police; a line of Green Minnas waited to take the prisoners away. And the Spartacists got beaten down; it was the old story; people were singing *Deutschland, Deutschland über alles.*

They'd sung that when Peter and Hans marched off with their regiments. She remembered Peter's flag hanging from the balcony, hymns coming from the tower, and then *Deutschland, Deutschland über alles*. How young they'd all been then! And before that, when he was little, Peter used to shout *hurrah!* at the zeppelins.

She asked Hans if he remembered, and he nodded silently. He lived separately on the fourth floor.

She heard shooting in the streets. Karl was in the city; she didn't know where Hans was.

The day she voted for the first time in her life should have been joyous; but the day before that, she found herself writing in her diary: *Vile, outrageous murder of Liebknecht and Luxemburg*. Everything changed in her Republic forever, just as it already had within her heart once she received the news about Peter. Living over Karl's office all those years and sometimes hearing the groans of his patients through the floor, she found that the suffering of others pressed upon her ever more tightly; as an artist, as a leftist, as a German and a human being, above all, as Peter's mother, she couldn't avoid feeling even had she wanted to. And so she didn't simply imagine the last moments of the two martyrs; she experienced them. (Karl had likewise wept when he heard.) Nine days later, Liebknecht was buried, along with thirty-eight others. *For Rosa Luxemburg an empty coffin near Liebknecht*. They'd thrown Rosa in the Landwehrkanal.

The tale of Easter's empty tomb used to haunt her. If we could only leave death behind! Oh, all those dreams she used to have! She wrote them in her diary; she told them to Karl and to her sister Lise. She tried not to torture Hans with them; that wouldn't have been fair. The occupied grave was worse, far worse; on the other hand, how many times in her life had she found the stone rolled aside, the skeleton bereft of his prey? The best one could hope for was Scheidemann's republic. Under those conditions, wasn't a hollow monument worst of all? Rosa Luxemburg's coffin wasn't void because she'd been resurrected, but because she'd disappeared. That was what assassins did nowadays, when they . . .

She carved the mourners light on dark over Liebknecht's snow-white bier, her chisel-strokes in each woodblocked face resembling muscles beneath flayed flesh. The Communists told her that she had no right, because she wasn't one of them. But the family had asked her to come. They'd laid red roses on his forehead, to hide the bullet holes. Outside, the rightists were singing *Heil Dir im Siegerkranz*.

Liebknecht wasn't the last. It got almost unbearable, but of course it couldn't compare with the World War. To get right down to it, what could she do but work, and sometimes catnap in Peter's room when Karl wasn't there to be hurt? What he'd always wanted of her was intimacy increasing without limit. She knew now that she'd never desire that, not ever. There wasn't space.

Berlin's trains kept shooting over the steel bridges; Berlin's boats kept boring underneath them. Our exhausted front-line veterans kept gathering; now they called themselves Old Fighters although most were only in their twenties. Rightists and leftists, they killed each other in their rage.

She visited the morgue and counted up to two hundred and forty-four murdered corpses, naked behind glass, with their clothes rolled up on their bellies. She heard the people who loved those dead ones weeping. She said to herself: Oh, what a dismal, dismal place this is . . . —Then she went home to Weissenbürgerstrasse, to etch in tears and paint in blood what she had seen. Of course in the World War it had been worse; she must never forget that.

Another of Frau Becker's children had died. Karl said that nothing could have been done, given the conditions in which that family had to live. He got emotional, actually. Even the living ones didn't seem to grow very much. She remembered the way that Peter had suddenly grown so large at age fourteen . . .

She could hear Frau Becker sobbing in Karl's office. Karl must be giving her a sedative. Then that grocer's apprentice came back, although by now it was practically the middle of the night; she could hear him coughing; and the atmosphere of Karl's office, humid with tears and sputum, began to seep up around her. She'd do another woodcut of Frau Becker, but not now, because she didn't have the strength. Sometimes she felt numb, and then her work wasn't any good; she longed to feel. But when feeling came back, it often overcame her, and then she could do nothing but weep or stare at the floor. She went into Peter's room and closed the door. Here she felt at peace.

Many years ago, she and Karl had been quarreling, and so she had slept alone. Then Peter, who had been very little, had a nightmare and came scurrying into bed with her. As soon she pressed him against herself, all the desolation she'd been feeling went away. Of course it was not quite like that anymore. Oh, she felt tired, so tired! She wasn't yet so old that she had any right to be tired. She said to herself: Work.

She worked without reference to the fiery proto-Cubism of those years, the representational, classical past as dead as the Second Reich itself, dead, dead!—as dead as the Tsarist officers who'd now sunk beneath their own weedy mucky parade grounds so that the Party of Lenin and Stalin could march across their moldering faces. Since 1912 she had kept a room on Siegmundshof for her plastic arts. That was where she would create the mourning woman out of stone. Mostly she carved, etched, and painted in that flat on Weissenbürgerstrasse. Those were the years when the figures in other people's paintings began to go ever flatter, more garish, more distorted, the colors hurtful to her although she liked some of the galloping calligraphic riders in Kandinsky. Grosz's desperately angry caricatures, the X-ray bitterness of Otto Dix, not to mention abstract constructivism; she didn't swim with that tide. Käthe Kollwitz kept painting poor people, starving people (white figures in dark fields, dark chalk on brown Ingres paper), raped women, mothers with dying children, mothers with dead children. In the end she depicted mainly herself, her stricken, simian face thinking and grieving. She too was a mother with a dead child.

2

The child had died quickly. He'd been the very first of his regiment to die. He'd died innocently, like our German hero Siegfried, who in Latin chronicles, Norse epics, German poems and songs dies over and over again, invincible from the front, stabbed in the back. (Goethe was her favorite writer, very possibly because he was not happy.) He'd never seen his death coming because it was sent to him by machine; how could he have fought it?

(People forget that Hagen, the man who murdered Siegfried, was also a German. He had his reasons. This war was Siegfried's war. The next war would be Hagen's.)

After the first anguish, the stretch of loneliness which she, too strong or weak for suicide, had yet to cross remained as immense as the entry on the war in our 1935 *Grosser Brockhaus*: forty-seven pages, ten charts, twelve full-color maps, inset photoportraits of our German heroes.

3

As I've said, she lived on Weissenbürgerstrasse with Karl in a neighborhood whose red-roofed, multistoreyed pillars enclosed humid courtyards for the working poor. She lived there for fifty-two years, accomplishing such works as the lithograph "Fallen" (1921), which depicts a mother clapping her hands to her face in utter grief, her children gathered around her, bewildered, anxious, distressed, reaching up toward her for the reassurance which just then she cannot give. The little girl at her back, who seems to be clutching a doll, stares up at her with the same black-dots-on-white-domino face as so many of the dead children.—Then came widows, more bereaved mothers; it might have been a theme. That was inside. Outside, the police kept taking strikers away in Green Minnas. The workers kept striking. It was in their honor that on a sheet of copper she drypointed the wrinkles, threads and shadows of prisoners' trousers as they crowded together behind the wire. She printed it, and it wept forever and ever in shiny trembling tears of ink. The birds in the Tiergarten, the green summer light in the Tiergarten, she didn't have those. She had blackness.

Sometimes she bought her hope from the small newspaper kiosks which stationed themselves between flower stands; she wanted to keep up with developments in Russia. Why not still hope?

But the Kapp Putsch, when Berlin went utterly dark, and then the street battles between strikers and swastika'd Freikorpsmen, the shooting and the shouting, it went on and on. After the World War you'd think that people could have learned something. Naturally, how could they? She'd been four years old when Germans raised their swords to victory in the Mirror-Hall of Versailles; that was what Germans still wanted. Sometimes she felt so tired; there was neither beginning nor end. Karl had turned Social Democrat; after the murder of Luxemburg and Liebknecht he'd said that it was time to be realistic, especially in Scheidemann's republic. Käthe hadn't argued. She felt herself more Communist than Social Democrat, and made lithographs for the Communists, because they were more active and lively. Anyhow, Karl had always been a "realistic" sort of person. A few weeks after they'd received the telegram about Peter, Hans's regiment got sent into a zone of typhus. Karl proposed to write the Ministry of War to advise against this on medical grounds. When Käthe, pleased but surprised that he would even attempt so vain an errand, asked what on earth he was thinking of, he told her, almost spitefully, she later thought: You have strength only for sacrifice and letting go of things, not for keeping track of trifles.—Although his face was bonier and he had less hair, he had scarcely aged much. Of course Käthe's hair was now entirely white.

In the early winter hours, when she heard fighting in the street, her grief for Germany got mixed up somehow with those recurring dreams she used to have that Peter was still alive; sometimes he and Hans were on the battlefield together; she tried to help him discover what he should do to avoid being shot again.

4

He had fallen on 22.10.14, in Flanders, ten days after his war began. He was the first of his regiment to die.

Peter was the volunteer. The other son Hans, the one she hardly knew, of course survived. Hans saw through the war to its skeleton of politics. He later became a doctor like Karl. He was always realistic.

5

Karl had refused Peter permission to go, so he had turned to his mother. She never knew exactly how he succeeded in getting her to overcome her fear, but he did, after which the father, as usual, obeyed the mother.

Then came the telegram: IHR SOHN IST GEFALLEN.

Her friend Liebermann gave her this advice: Work.

6

Having been raised by a perfect, untouchable mother, she was fated—indeed, she had been brought into the world—to be the same, all the while exuding a secret lavish maternality. And then, from a jet-black cloud, death's long grey arms reached to pick her child from amidst a harvest of wide-eyed children. How many women have we all seen wilting away, because they were prevented from fully giving the love which was in them to give? The *Great Soviet Encyclopedia,* which criticizes her favorably, explains that she *perceived World War I through the prism of personal tragedy, which imparted a gloomy, sacrificial tone to her creative work.* Hence her crazed figures dancing open-mouthed around the guillotine; hence those elongated, muscle-striated arms reaching up at the sky in grief and anger.

Throughout most of the following decade she created posters for the German Communist Party. Meanwhile she continued her mournful, simian self-portraits; she woodblock-printed her hundredth screaming mother bearing her dead child in her arms, other mothers crowding around her in the procession to the grave.

7

The myth that her son's death was the inspiration for this work is easily exploded. For instance, "Death, Mother and Child" dates from 1910, when Peter still had four years left to live. It formally resembles the previous year's chalk sketch, entitled "Goodbye": the child's face, lovely, stark-white and realistic, clutched by the mother against her own larger, greyer face, which seemed in its grief to be decaying into the black, black smudge beneath it. In 1903, in both her "Pietà" and her "Mother with Dead Child," the positions had been reversed, the mother clutching the little corpse from above, resting her head on the breast while the child's head dangled in space, the lips slightly parted in the white face. There had been another "Mother with Dead Child" in that same year, this one almost Blakean in the foregrounding of the leg, foot and toes; the mother was sitting cross-legged with one knee up, bowing her head down against the child, whose form, shrouded into a phallic blur, blended into hers; her ear, wrinkled forehead and one sunken eye were there, but only in that furred, decomposed fashion common to embryos and unfinished art; the Kaiser would not have seen any virtue in this.

In 1911, Peter was growing rapidly but remained underweight; he read his New Testament in Greek and ran to see zeppelins; meanwhile, his mother completed her "Mother in the Bed of a Dead Child," again the white, white face, this time almost resembling a skull, the crudely cross-hatched sheets, and then the mother's face, dark-hatched against the black hinterground, with a single candle-flame shining forlornly behind her; her dark heavy fingers reach forward to caress the white cheek; her deep dark eye-sockets seem to contain fibers of muscle, like those of a thoroughly anatomized cadaver. The slow love and grief, upon which Kollwitz has superimposed the living body's almost reptilian grossness, combine into something quite simply horrifying. Soon enough she etched another version of "Mother and Dead Child," this time entitled "Tod und Frau um das Kind ringend" (1911), the child's mouth blackly gaping in a face gone slightly darker, the mother's correspondingly lighter so that the two black slits of her clenched mouth and eye leap out at us; here too is death, a white skeleton whose round eye-socket gazes at the pair with something between curiosity and glee; shreds of flesh, perhaps hiding ribs, join it to the two forms which it has now begun to sever. We'll ignore such variations as "Death and Woman," in which the little child fights with all its feeble strength to save Mother from being raped away by death; I suppose you get the picture.

Four years before the World War and two years before the Kaiser ordered the removal of her poster demanding playgrounds in tenement housing (a sad girl stands by a wall, clasping a sick baby; behind them, the sign reads **PLAYING FORBIDDEN**) we find her writing in her daybook: *Today started work on the sculpture "Woman with Dead Child."*

8

For years she looked out her window at the same gaunt man who grimaced under his tophat. She never learned his name, but she learned to recognize his footsteps on the cobblestones. For awhile he used to be accompanied by a little blond boy with sunken eyes, but the blond boy died of tuberculosis, and then the man came down with it, too; he was one of Karl's patients, but he wouldn't give his name; he felt very ashamed because he couldn't pay. No doubt that was why he then stopped being Karl's patient. Perhaps Karl had saved him; he lived on year after year. Käthe, newly a mother, was still at work on her Weavers' Series when she first came to know him; she was still scratching the dark fine lines of anguish on brown paper, bringing to life the pale children, the weak figures in black, the death. Once, in about 1895 it must have been, the gaunt man removed his tophat to scratch at his hair, and then, right then, when his eyes almost met hers, she caught him, sketching his head for three or four seconds of passionate struggle; yes, she'd possessed him; now he was hers; his agony wasn't in vain anymore; he became one of her weavers.

In 1921 she drew a poster for the Russenhilfe; she wanted to do what she could to help the Communists fight that terrible hunger in their country. But she didn't care to join the Party, because their tactics didn't suit her. She made two pairs of hands respectfully reaching to support the swaying head of someone Slavic, someone with dark hair whose eyes were closed in extreme weakness. All the sick proletarians Karl treated, whose stories were so sad and who all too often lived and died beyond anyone's power to help, she remembered them when she made that Russian face.—No, not all of them. That man in the tophat, when he passed beneath her window he conveyed so dramatic an impression that she took up her graphite stick, but there was too much anger and not enough weakness in him. Frau Becker's son, the dark one who'd died last year, she remembered his drooping eyes when he was dying. She worked him into the Slavic face. She looked it over and said to herself: It's good, thank God.—Karl agreed, as he always did.

She sat herself down in Peter's room and considered doing a series of very straightforward posters about Lenin. But when she and Hans came by some accident to be discussing politics, she said: There are other problems that interest me now, essential human problems like death.

But your woodcut about Liebknecht—

A little sternly, she said to him: I'm not the old hating, fighting Käthe Kollwitz.

In fact, she remained as unchanging as Berlin's pale green summer weeds and trees along the water, because her anguish was as dependable as the ocherish brownstones.

9

In 1922 she rendered death's skull-moon in the darkness above bowed children who spasm in concert with our century's millions of enchained volunteers; the title is "Hunger," and I've read that this image, badly reproduced in a secondhand monograph, lay in wait for decades like an antipersonnel mine for the specific purpose of horrifying Shostakovich's daughter Galina; one day when she, still unmarried and presumably in Leningrad to attend the premiere of her father's Eleventh Symphony, was browsing the book-kiosks along the Nevsky, the mine exploded: Galina, who was actually trying to find a present for her brother's name day, opened the volume by accident—well, isn't that a tautology? Isn't every accident an accident? I won't exaggerate; I won't claim that the young woman screamed; after all, she'd lived through the Great Patriotic War, even if she couldn't remember all of it; she'd seen real skulls enough! All the same, such was the power of this image that she had a nightmare, and in the morning her famous father, who was himself feeling a bit anxious just then, saw some peculiar wretchedness in her face which he experienced like a punch in his stomach; this sensation, suitably translated into the chord *D-D-Sch,* later found its way into both his Fifteenth Symphony and the unholy Opus 110.

Meanwhile, the man in the tophat promenaded sadly under Käthe Kollwitz's window.

10

In 1926, A. Lunacharsky, who was then our People's Commissar of Culture, paid her this compliment: *She aims at an immediate effect, so that at the very first glance one's heart is wrung. She is a great agitator.* That was the year she went to Roggevelde with Karl, to visit Peter's grave for the first time.

In 1927, she stood amidst the jury of the Prussian Academy, those short-haired, dark-suited old men with canes and tophats, with both hands gripping the mat of one of her woodcuts as the man beside her, resting his hat against his large belly, gazed respectfully down at Art. Perhaps they regretted that the Kaiser had not permitted them to give her the gold medal twenty-nine years ago. They reminded her of Hans and Peter when they were little, the two pairs of eyes staring at her above the white collars they hated. Their hall glowed with the light of heavenly privilege. They presented her with a prize.

After the ceremony, a gentleman from the National Front tried to talk to her about the mystical role of motherhood, and Professor Moholy-Nagy, fresh from the Bauhaus, scolded her that her latest composition, another white-on-black woodcut of a woman and child going into death, was both too static and too dark.

After all, she said wearily, it's a representation of death.

It is an elementary biological necessity, Moholy-Nagy sternly said, for human beings to absorb color, to extract color.

What do you mean, a biological necessity?

We live in a colorless age.

So you're sad, like me.

Don't say that! I reject emotion unconditionally.

As gently as she could (there were many people in the room), she said to him: We've all been injured by the war years. In your case, perhaps you're afraid to feel, because—

Professor Moholy-Nagy vindictively interrupted: The traditional painting has become a historical relic and is finished with.

She smiled at him. Then slowly she turned away to receive more congratulations from elitists and militarists, the ones who had killed Peter, and not just Peter, but all the brave young men in helmets who toiled white-faced through zigzag trenches and marched through hellscapes, falling a dozen at a time, the smokeskinned young men with daggers who crept through tunnels to murder one another, the brave young men who rushed against barbed wire, got impaled, and hung there until the bullet-wind blew through them; or else if they were lucky they became squinting prisoners, marched away between lines of Frenchmen on horseback; then they could look forward to coming home years later, bitter, poor and hateful, ripe for the next war. When she couldn't bear any more of it, she caught the tram for Weissenbürgerstrasse. She went home to her nervously overworked husband whose patients had so often modeled poverty's face to her.

The man in the tophat stood outside. This time she spied him in conversation with that tubercular young grocer's apprentice who was in ecstasies about Hitler; Karl said that little could be done for him; he'd be in the grave in six months. Käthe had once asked the boy why, what he had against Jews, how he could possibly wish on Germany more hate and war. He replied: Excuse me, Frau Kollwitz, but I would like to stand for something. I would like to be there for something.—Now both of them wore swastika armbands. They looked more cheerful than she had ever seen them.

They didn't even notice her at first. Then they did see her. The man in the tophat said: Well, well, it's Frau Kollwitz again.

And she realized that all these years he had also been watching her.

She'd put up with enough at the Prussian Academy. She had nothing to say to him.

But the man in the tophat had something to say. Taking two steps closer, while the ashen-faced grocer's apprentice gazed at him with shining eyes, he said: You know the difference between you and us, Frau Kollwitz? We're *optimists.*

This shocked her so much that she could scarcely breathe, because it was true.

The dying apprentice chimed in: We never gave up. Even at the end we still believed in victory.

She looked them in the face and said: Do you believe in it now?

Yes, Frau Kollwitz; *we* at least will keep our faith.

She rushed upstairs to Karl's office; the door was closed and a man was groaning. She needed Karl right then, but so be it. The last flight of stairs exhausted her. She unlocked the flat and went straight to Peter's room.

That was the night when she dreamed that the man in the tophat had come two steps closer, and two steps closer, until suddenly he turned into a drawing she did once, of a mother catching her dead soldier-boy as he tumbles gruesomely into her arms; it was early next morning, when she awoke in Karl's arms, sobbing, that she realized that death had now become a friend; and there would be one famous self-portrait (catalogue number 157) where death kindly leads her away. (As the sleepwalker laughed to Colonel Hagen: Don't you think there's something Jewish about that?) *Ruf des Todes,* she entitled it. That hand descending in the fullness of time to touch the artist's shoulder, whose was it? Not a skeleton's but also not Peter's. His hand was eternally frail and little to her now, just as he was no grown man but a beautiful naked little boy. The hand in *Ruf des Todes* was heavy and old; perhaps it was Karl's; its touch was domestic; it called her to herself so that she, weary and not at all surprised, could go with its owner to lie down in peace. But even if the hand wasn't Peter's, it was Peter's bed she lay down upon.

11

In that same year 1927, the fraternal peoples of the USSR prepared to celebrate the achievements of Soviet power. In spite of Trotsky, the kulaks and the bourgeois monopolists, we'd built socialist democracy! Specifically, the emiseration of the masses under capitalism, which our dear friend K. Kollwitz has depicted so powerfully in her graphic work, was forever *vanished,* like the prewar prostitutes of the Nevsky. Moreover, we'd carried out this feat of humanism without giving ground to the capitalist anaconda which encircled us. By 1927, we could show the world an unbroken and unbreakable chain of victories. This was the year when an airplane of our R-3 series accomplished the first Moscow–Tokyo–Moscow flight. On the musical front, Shostakovich had not yet been disgraced. Photographically and metallurgically we held our own; on the educational front, we'd nearly liquidated illiteracy.

Therefore, to mark our Revolution's tenth birthday, it was decided to invite nine hundred and forty-seven foreign delegates, among whom K. Kollwitz came quickly to mind:* K. Kollwitz, who empathized so sincerely with the working class—the Kaiser had called her a gutter artist—K. Kollwitz, who had never joined the Party and whose presence in our land would thereby prove the broadmindedness of our goodwill; K. Kollwitz, whose grief-hued tableaux of worker-martyrs, by being set in Germany, showed the superiority of our own system—I myself especially admire her lithograph of a proletarian woman in profile (1903), whose tired old hands clasp one another uncertainly, and whose pale face bows submissively in the darkness; Kollwitz has done the hair in stipples rather than in lines, so that this worker resembles a shaved convict—K. Kollwitz, who offered good odds of dying before she could turn against us; she was sixty years old, tired, worried she was done.—Retrospection proves that we gambled well; in 1944, the second to last year of her life, with the sleepwalker's war against us obviously lost, we find her writ-

---

*In 1924 our fellow traveler Otto Nagel had opened the first German arts exhibition in the Soviet Union. Käthe Kollwitz was represented. No one came out against her.

ing her children, advising that little Arne be taught Russian: *With the two countries bound to be so linked . . . so let him learn the language while there is still time.* That same month she wrote: *My only hope is in world socialism.* (Needless to say, she also wrote: *The desire, the unquenchable longing for death remains.—I shall close now, dear children. I thank you with all my heart.*) In other words, she remained as reliable as our Polikarpov-Grigorovich I-5 biplane fighter of 1930 (two hundred and eighty kilometers per hour).

So Dr. Kollwitz and his wife boarded the tramcar which carried them past a boarded up window in a four-storey flat, trees and birds, shadows near the river bridge; then came a flag battalion whose fourteen crimson banners spoke out against the big financiers who headed the Jewish hydra, and she thought she saw that man, that gaunt man who'd stood below her window grimacing under his tophat for all these years, but he wore a brown uniform now and his right arm touched the sky and he was shouting in ecstasy. Sounding its bell, the tram turned the corner, and before they even knew it they'd arrived at the Ostbahn Station. Leaning, hunched figures were begging on the steps; they could have crawled out of one of her etchings. Käthe gave them all the coins she had in her pockets, while Karl, smiling patiently and stroking his iron-grey beard, guarded the luggage.

They had one valise each. They bought their tickets knowing that we'd reimburse them. Then they went upstairs to the platform. The train came. Their seats were reserved. They stowed their luggage and sat down. And the train began to move. She'd never forget that slow-departing troop train, Peter waving to her from the window. The Kaiser had called merrily to the departing troops: *Back home when the leaves fall!*

A young girl with reddish-blonde bangs lowered the train window until she could rest her chin on it; she leaned, gazed, stretched and turned as fluidly as a newt. Karl adjusted the reading lamp for her. Käthe sat writing in her diary: *And I must do the prints on Death. Must, must, must!* She had always wanted to visit Russia.

The German boy who'd shared their compartment on the train, his slender legs crossed as he plucked half-consciously at his long raven hair, read Hölderlin, with a flask of water wedged beneath his arm. He suddenly realized that this doctor's wife was somebody important; but by then it was too late.—Well, well, we think that Hölderlin or Kollwitz is a "choice," but what is culture but a historically determined form of social organization?

The farther east they went, the colder it grew. By the time they crossed the border it was actually snowing.—It's another world, said Karl.—Changing trains, waiting for their documents to be inspected, they arrived at the Byelorussian-Baltic Station three hours late, but a man in raspberry-colored boots was waiting for them on the platform. He led them into one of our black, flat-topped Russian automobiles whose chests sloped doubly down over the wheels, like the clasped mandibles of praying mantises; Karl helped her in, and although the car proceeded very slowly, on account of the ice, before they knew it, they found themselves exactly where they were supposed to be. The luggage got sent on to the hotel.

Karl had been hoping to stretch his legs; he'd been looking forward to a promenade on the Tverskaia, but was told that there wasn't time, on account of the delay with the train. He looked sadly across the street into the window of a pastry-shop. Now here stood the curator, shivering and waiting. Here stood the pretty interpreter, who had long dark hair. The man in raspberry-colored boots, who seemed much taken with some private joke, waved goodbye and rode away with the driver. Then Käthe and Karl had to check their overcoats. Käthe was feeling a bit dizzy; she didn't know quite why; Karl had to help her out of her coat. She had longed so much to be here, and now she hardly even felt curious. And she worried about doing something wrong, of leaving something important in her coat pocket, or somehow offending these Russians although they seemed so jolly—this interpreter, for instance, who must be nervous, for she kept trying so fervently to be welcoming that Käthe couldn't think. The interpreter's name might have been Elena; Käthe couldn't remember anything the way she used to. Karl would certainly remember it, but how could she ask him when the girl stood right here? Never mind. The curator was twittering and beckoning. This husband who used to bring her red roses in bed, who wept when he saw her completed work, and who used to examine Peter in the consulting room, then share with her his every worry about the boy's fragility, what a fine man he was! He murmured sweetly in her ear: I'm completely proud of you, Käthe.—She took his hand.

On the walls of the exhibition hall, her grief was already in place, framed and captioned: woodcuts in the main gallery, lithographs on the left, important etchings on the right, drawings in the other gallery; this was perhaps not exactly the way she would have done it, but the nervously ecstatic curator, who kept biting her nails, gazed on her so worshipfully that she had to express total satisfaction with the organization, selection and illumination of Käthe Kollwitz's uncountable roundeyed, upgazing children, pallid figures leaning on their hands, pale and grimy women whose faces were lit by exploitation's arc lamp. They were all real people whose tragedies were tied as much to life itself as to anything else: Grete, whose insanity had a strong sexual component and who at thirty was married and remained a virgin; Anna, who'd experienced bleeding and pain from constant sexual intercourse and who had considered suicide; that old Proletariarfrau who'd stood grim and angry outside the morgue after those two hundred and forty-four Communists were shot. In the midst of other agony-angled, grief-distorted compositions, her woodcuts loomed largest, with their gaunt pseudo-realism.

And here was an enlarged photoportrait of her from long ago. In her twenties she had strangely resembled Lenin's wife, Nadezhda Krupskaya, who as it happened was only two years younger than she. Both women had the same intense eyes, the same lips clenched as if to hide their fullness. Käthe stared at her youthful self for a long time. For some reason, she knew not why, she dared not look at Karl.

They introduced her to the Soviet people, explaining: *Her family was involved in the workers' movement.* So densely was the hall ornamented with her life's work, and in such a loving fashion did all these Russians regard her, that she hardly knew who she was. They photographed her seated in the center of a gathering of our Soviet artists, her ancient eyelids drooping, young women leaning lovingly against her, light shining on the spectacles of painters, photographers and actors, a fellow from Meyerhold's theater standing stiffly or ironically to one side, as if he knew that he wouldn't be aboveground much longer. Karl stood self-deprecatingly out of the picture except when they called him. About him his poor patients remembered: *The doctor came immediately, and his invoice never.*

Another man in raspberry-colored boots who said he was an art critic pointed to one of her etchings and brusquely demanded that she explain it.

Well, Käthe said, that's the typical misfortune of a worker's family: A man drinks or gets sick, then he becomes a parasite or goes crazy, or kills himself. And then, you know, the woman's misery is always the same.

But here that doesn't happen anymore, because we're all part of the collective.

I'm so glad, she said. It's very, very good to be in a place where there's actually hope!

The man nodded unsmiling and wrote something in a notebook.

They'd devoted an entire room to her Weavers' Series, whose every wrinkle was dark, the ground made of fine lines, everything marching or progressing or fissuring: outstretched hands, bent bodies, fists grasping stones, dark houses with corpses on the floor, crazed widows reaching at nothing. This was the work whose gold medal had been vetoed by the Kaiser himself.

A proletarian woman cried out, very vigorously, but through the dark-haired interpreter, that since Frau Kollwitz had lost her son in the last war, she doubtless was at one with us in our unflinching class hatred.

I have experienced those feelings, yes.

It's really true about your child? inquired the intrepreter. Frau Kollwitz, I am so very very sorry! And also in my family . . .

And the curator fluttered excitedly about, exclaiming over everything.

Käthe knew that these new friends of hers, with their soulful Slavic natures, saw at least as deeply into her work as her compatriots, and indeed, their comments, particularly regarding the Weavers' Series, lacked for neither passion nor intellect. All the same, the interpreter, who'd known nothing of the most important event in her life, not to mention the poor curator, who like many of her peers throughout this world found herself so burdened by the necessity that this event be successful that she had no time to communicate with the creator of the work; the woman who thought to substitute hatred for sorrow; these people began to infect her with disappointment, which she battled as desperately as any Old Fighter ever fought an enemy.

Frau Kollwitz, is it true that the rightists call you an enemy of the nation?

Karl laughed proudly, and with a half-smile she agreed that it was.

Several of her new colleagues—such clever, frail young theoreticians! it goes without saying that all but one of them were doomed—opined that since revolution was a dynamic and ultimately all-embracing process, art ought to be dynamic, too; they pointed out to her that paintings and etchings could depict only moments, whereas a film could actually unscroll time when the projectionist plucked it out of its jar. Furthermore, so one young man insisted in excellent German (he wore small oval spectacles as Hans had done when he was a student), the temporal sequence of a movement could be more effectively conveyed through acoustical than through optical articulation.

That's all beyond me, she replied calmly. She was hardly listening to him. There was a woman she'd seen in the street that morning, an old woman who obviously knew nothing but hard work; she could have been one of her husband's patients. She kept wishing she'd embraced that woman.

Your "Woman with Dead Child" is superb propaganda, the young man was saying. With great effectiveness it mobilizes us against the bloodbaths and massacres which will remain inevitable as long as capital dominates the world.

Thank you, she said.

You think I have no compassion. I can see that now. To you I'm just a fool in love with an idea.

It's a beautiful idea, she said, as politely as she could. (How tired she was!)

That seemed to encourage him. Coming a little closer, he confessed: I used to believe that if I lived out my life without making anybody feel compassion for me, I would have done well. And I loved the masses because they didn't excite my compassion, even when they perished.—I see your disappointment and disapproval (or is that compassion in your eyes?) Maybe I can't explain it. At that time I'd simply made up my mind: To hell with personal feelings! I wanted to live only as part of a collective.

She had to laugh a little. She liked him now.

And is that still what you want?

Of course.

The young man, whose name was Comrade Alexandrov, offered to escort her and her husband to a Shostakovich concert. This Shostakovich was apparently the darling of the Soviet Union just then. His Second Symphony would soon premiere in Leningrad, the young man said. Karl was happy because now he'd finally get his promenade. He'd lived with her for all these years, and the Weavers' Series was not exactly novel to him. In point of fact, she herself had lived with it for so many years that it was almost dead to her; when she'd seen it again tonight, all she could think of was that there were a few details which should have been done differently; for the rest, it was what it was. As for the promenade, Käthe would rather have gone home.—I think the concert would be wonderful, she said, stroking her husband's grey hair.

Look, Käthe! he cried out in astonishment. That store sells nothing but butter! And everyone's queuing up for it!

Correct, said the young man, shooting him a long look. The Romanovs left our country in a shambles.

Karl grew silent. As for Käthe, she hadn't even seen the store he was talking about. The sidewalk was so icy and the night so dark that all she could do was watch her footing. Actually, there was quite a bit to see. The Museum of Atheism was open. The tapering metal lacework of the Shukhov Radio Tower wasn't quite finished; the windowed bays of Zholtovsky's electric power station wouldn't glow for two years yet; but no one could deny that we were ahead of Berlin. (Red Kiel, Red Leipzig, Red Munich, Red Frankfurt, Red Stuttgart, all fallen like Alexander II's statue!) A shivering old lady stood in a doorway, trying to sell dough-and-sugar figurines. Käthe would have bought one, simply for pity, but Comrade Alexandrov, who reminded her more and more of her son Hans, said they hadn't time. She didn't look at Karl's face.

The composition which they attended, the Scherzo in E-flat Major, had the flavor of something modern, but not quite new. Her husband, as she could see quite well from the vagueness of his smile, did not like it at all. How much he had to endure for her! She for her part preferred Schnabel, whose music she called *clear-consoling-good.* Whenever she listened to Beethoven on the gramophone, the heavens opened. This scherzo was like a peek into hell. The stench of grief rose up from its grey and lifeless earth. As Shostakovich's notes wailed out, the great hall seemed to get so cold that she wouldn't have been surprised to see icicles on the ceiling. All the same, there was something about the music which haunted her, not simply its acoustic color, which beneath the greyness resembled a gruesome aurora borealis, but a desperate encoded message which baffled her. She said as much to Comrade Alexandrov, who suavely replied: Why then, if he's incomprehensible then he's failed.—She thought that rather harsh. At the end she saw this Shostakovich, for they called him onstage to take his bow. She thought him a nice-looking boy, somewhat nervously high-spirited. Everything in Russia was so strange . . .

You look tired, Frau Kollwitz. If you wish, we can go back to your hotel by sleigh. You might enjoy the lights of Tverskoi Boulevard.

Truth to tell, she certainly *was* very, very tired, but she found herself saying: Thank you, that sounds beautiful, but I'm all right.

As you wish.

They walked and walked, with Russia curving ecstatically all around her like the Soviet trams swerving in double tracks through the mosaic of pavingstones, the intersection almost empty, a few sparse stragglers crossing behind the tram, then nothing but stone blankness and concrete blankness flat and eternal.

And now I think we'll take a tram, Frau Kollwitz. Herr Doktor Kollwitz, don't you agree? Your wife looks done in.

Hands folded, the tram driver watched her through his round mirror.

The janitress and her little boy were sleeping on a mattress under the stairs, the child's plump cheek pressed against the mother's weary mouth, her workworn hand around his neck. Karl's observant old face, rendered pseudo-enthusiastic by the lenses of his spectacles, turned itself upon the sleepers, and then he sighed.

The next morning, while Comrade Alexandrov took her husband to see Red Square, which bored him, and Saint Basil's Cathedral, whose domes, variously patterned in balloon-stripes, pinecone-knurls, ice cream swirls and ocean-waves, he reported to be quite fairytale-like, she stayed in; she was old; she wanted only to sleep. Karl, who was so devoted to her, and who always told her how much good and luck she brought him—how she loved him; how she hated him! *Marriage is a kind of work,* she'd once told her friend Lene Bloch. He'd never understood why she needed to be alone. It hurt him. It wasn't that she didn't love him! She'd learned to conceal from him how happy she became when she withdrew alone into Peter's room. Even Russia stifled her today; she must be really, really old.

Then there was a parade on Red Square, with Lenin's Mausoleum always in the background, so she went to see that: a military parade, then armed workers, followed by demonstrations. In its own way it was as lovely as a service in the Marienkirche. Karl, the empathetic Social Democrat, hurrahed with the rest of them, although he didn't understand a word. It was then and there that she made the pencil drawing entitled "Listening," which would be lithographed the following year with the title translated into its Russian equivalent, *Slushayuoshchie,* the eyes rendered more bright and innocent still, and the contrast increased. (Otto Nagel: *Out of Moscow, Käthe Kollwitz brought with her a beautiful page which was later worked in stone.)* At that time, "Listening" was simply a pencil drawing of three rapt young heads gazing upwards, the farthest with its mouth agape like the dead child—but there is life in this young man's eyes, amazement and inspiration, for he hears the words of Comrade Stalin! Next comes a head with closed lips; he is lost in the speech; then in the foreground, seated on his lap, snuggling in against his right arm, with its head on his shoulder, is the child, white-faced, wide-eyed, the mouth open, utterly curious and surprised but in the same position as so many of Kollwitz's dead children, head back lifelessly. But what am I saying? It wasn't lifeless at all! When they used to drink coffee or hot chocolate with the children in some café under the trees, the little ones sometimes gripped the backs of the chairs, peering over them at the world just like that! And Peter had said . . .

Her husband said: I keep dreaming of elaborate Russian cakes.

12

This story, like this book itself, is derivative. In his unsurpassable *A Tomb for Boris Davidovich,* the Serbian writer Danilo Kiš relates a fable: Édouard Herriot, highest-ranking French Radical Socialist, charismatic orator, effective politician (thanks in part to him, France recognized the Soviet government), has come to pay a visit to Odessa. Monsieur Herriot, Comrade Herriot I can almost call him, has one weakness: He's squeamish about the persecution of priests. Unfortunately, he's due to arrive in four hours, and we've long since converted Saint Sophia Cathedral into a brewery! What to do? Steady now! Take down the antireligious banner outside. *Under my personal supervision a hundred and twenty inmates of the nearby regional prison camp carried out another restoration of the church, in less than four hours.* And Herriot is tricked.

What about Käthe Kollwitz? Didn't she also want to be tricked? If nothing else, didn't she crave to feel just once the antithesis of that morbid grief she'd been condemned so long to tunnel through? So what if it were false light? At the end of that year, back in Berlin, she took up her diary and commended *Moscow with its different atmosphere, so that Karl and I came back as if we had both had a good airing.* It would be a simple matter to write this story as a parable of the heart which through its very empathy was duped. But she saw the janitress even though they wouldn't have wanted her to. She sensed secret meanings in Comrade Alexandrov's tone. The speeches on Red Square meant less to her than the rapt children who listened. She was all too well aware that the jury of the Prussian Academy, like their predecessors in the Kaiser's day, would have preferred to insert her somewhere within the list *Frauensport, Frauenheim, Frauenhaus* (obsolete for bordello), *Frauenkauf,* rather than recognizing her as an artist. Why not give her the credit of supposing that she also saw through their Soviet equivalents? For example, when Comrade Alexandrov, perhaps genuinely wanting to know, but more likely wishing to determine the extent of her cooperation, requested her views on the emiseration of the German proletariat, she looked steadily into the man's face, then replied: When the man and the woman are healthy, a worker's life is not unbearable.

In retrospect, what *should* she have thought or understood? Joy in others, being in harmony with them, had always been one of the deepest pleasures in her life; shouldn't that be everyone's? Given the limitation of her bourgeois origins, shouldn't the fact of her empathy for the working class have counted sufficiently in her favor for "posterity" not to expect anything else of her? It may well be that her impressions of Russia are of a piece with the memorial to Peter, which once depicted Peter himself, but now depicts his parents. I sometimes fear that this is the case with everyone's impressions of everything. (Danilo Kiš would say all this much better in his trademark ironic style; unfortunately, he's now in the same place as Peter.) Perhaps she really did continue working without illusions. It would be too cheap to write that someone eavesdropped on her while she drew "Listening." But even if that were true, and even if she didn't notice, what then?

I've read, not in her daybooks, but in the account of Comrade Alexandrov, to whom I am very close, that at one point when he uttered a remark which she might have construed as sinister, for it seemed to call on her to praise Comrade Stalin's portrait (darkhaired, dark-moustached, not quite Asian, almost smiling), she simply replied: We each must fulfill our own obligation.

It's fair to say that this new Red Russia of dog-nosed, sprawling trucks and flat-roofed trams literally intoxicated her, and that for this pretty, darkhaired Elena—yes, her name actually was Elena—who explained to everyone that the reason Frau Kollwitz had taken up etching was in order to distribute the maximum number of prints to the working class, Käthe suddenly felt a surge of physical feeling, such as she had not felt for any woman since she was much, much younger. She heard a ringing in her ears. Gamely, she tried to sing the "Propeller Song . . ."

13

When it was time for her to go they made another party for her, of course, and when she arrived at the train station she found some people spontaneously organized in her honor; some of them even had banners. Among them stood a young photojournalist from Odessa; he asked permission to take her picture with his dead father's camera; in a low shy voice he informed her that he was hoping that an editor he knew would agree to publish a portrait of the great artist K. Kollwitz in *Vsyermirnaya Ilustratsia*. She was feeling very tired by then, really, really tired; but she also felt sorry for him, so she nodded.

He was very sincere and very quick. She ended up liking him. He asked if she would be willing to pose right there on the station platform with her latest masterpiece, "Listening," which had been drawn from life in our own Soviet Union, but she explained that it was already packed away. He smiled understandingly.

She asked him what he aimed to do with his life, and he said that he wanted to document the progress of the Communist Revolution here and throughout the world. He was considering attending the State School of Photography if he could find somebody to help him. He wanted to go into films.

Käthe nodded, leaning against Karl's shoulder. All she wanted to do was take her seat on the train and rest. If she never answered another question again, except from her grandchildren, that would be so perfect! At the same time, she couldn't bring herself to be rude to the young man. If she could only keep Karl from realizing how tired she was! Trying to rescue her, he would surely hurt the young man's feelings.

Excuse me, my dear, she said to him, but could you kindly repeat your name? We elderly people find ourselves becoming a bit stupid, unfortunately.

Of course, Frau Kollwitz! My name is Karmen, Roman Lazarevich. Perhaps someday I'll make a name for myself.

And where did you say you come from?

Odessa. This camera is actually my late father's. It's all he was able to leave me. The White Guards tortured him because he'd published a few articles in the Communist press. Later they released him, but he never recovered. He died quite young.

You poor, poor child, said Käthe, shaking her head. She hoped that her husband hadn't heard. Karl, who'd lost his own father and mother early, was easily upset by such cases.

It's a common story, unfortunately. Your expression is perfect; could you hold still for just a moment?

And the handsome young Karmen in his corduroy cap, smoothfaced, sighted through the camera, whose bellows were part way extended and locked in position by the steel X across the top; she saw that the metal lens board of the front standard was armored, and so was everything else.

(Shall I describe that perfect expression of hers? She conveyed an impression most of all of sad steadiness; not only did she no longer need any model but herself, but she'd turned into one of her own sculptures. Her eyes were not unlike Shostakovich's in that grief seemed almost ready to explode out of them, like corpses flying into the air when a stray shell hits a mass grave.)

He didn't seem at all bitter. There was something in him of Peter's, of that mobilized idealism we all had in Germany during that first week (although old Reschke in the Café Monopol had probably got it right when he said to her: God be thanked that mobilization is happening; the suspense wouldn't have been bearable anymore . . .)—when Peter joined the colors she'd thought him still a child; he was eighteen and a half; but his enthusiasm moved her almost to tears; as for Karl, he'd said: This noble young generation, we must work so that we can measure up to them.—That was at the beginning, of course, when even she had believed the Kaiser, and Peter still lived.

How old were you when your father died?

Fourteen, he replied with his quick smile. That was when the Poles took Kiev—

He clicked the shutter; the magnesium powder flashed.

Thank you, Frau Kollwitz. I'll send you a copy. Well, this camera gave me my start, but I'm now becoming bored with still photography. I don't think it represents the dynamism of our new age. Have you seen the Rodchenko exhibit?

Yes, I have, she said politely. Comrade Alexandrov had arranged to take her. She had hated it.

Well, those strange angles, those distortions, I love that! And he's useful, too; he does billboards which catch people's interest and educate them. Only I want to go farther! I want to animate everything! At the same time, it's important to remain true to life, as you've always been. I won't make escapist films; I'll make documentaries.

He now reminded her so much of Peter that she could hardly bear it; specifically, he reminded her of Peter in the last month of his life, smiling in his dark uniform with its column of big shiny buttons; he wore his new cap as often as he could and he kept gazing off into what he thought was the future.

That sounds very admirable, said Käthe, smiling at him. And now I must board my train.

May I please ask you for one bit of advice? said the young man.

It's time to go, said Karl.

I'll gladly help you, Roman Lazarevich. But only if you don't cause me to miss my train!

Where was Karl now? Oh, God be thanked, he'd gotten all the luggage on board . . .

This young Roman Lazarevich flashed her one of his quick smiles and said to her: How terrible it must seem to be a mother who weeps over her dead child, and a man to see it and film it! At least that's how I imagine it. I haven't made any films yet, but I know that it's going to be my task to seek out misery and hopefully to reveal its causes and solutions. So in a sense I want to become the next Käthe Kollwitz. I want to devote my life to women and dead children. But it seems wrong to *use* them for any purpose, even for the universal good.

Karl, whose smallish eyes seemed ever in retreat behind his glasses, was back now and had slipped his arm around her. He murmured: You're not obliged to answer that if you don't wish it, Käthe.

What should she have said? Should she have confessed that without ever asking she'd caught that gaunt man who grimaced under his tophat and imprisoned him forever in her Weavers' Series? That was true, but how much more often she'd hunted down her own ancient, exhausted face!

All at once she thought she was going to cry again. She would have hated that more than anything.

She said: Roman Lazarevich, with me it's very simple. The woman with the dead child is me, myself. And the child is also myself.

14

And so they came back through the arch-shaped door at number twenty-five Weissenbürgerstrasse. Peter's room remained the same as it had been thirteen years ago, with his white bed made up just so, his framed silhouette on the wall, the glass panes closed on his cabinet of boyish curiosities; flowers in the vase, clothes on the hooks.

A commentator notes that *in the diaries one finds almost nothing about this journey, and even her son in Berlin, to whom she so often reported in such detail on all her trips, seems to have received only one letter from her.* All the same, she must have been contented with her experience, because the following year, while the sleepwalker, wearing a business suit and a fancy hat, was giving another speech in Hamburg, striding back and forth in a frenzy, with a short riding-whip in his hand, Käthe finished chiseling out a woodcut of Elisabeth pregnant with Johannes and Maria pregnant with Jesus, took off her apron, sat down at the wide wooden table in the living room, then wrote Gorki: *All that I saw in Russia I saw in the light of the Soviet star.* Coming from a German, her next sentence now seems ironic, to say the least: *And I have a longing to go again, deep into the land, to the Volga.* Fourteen years later her grandson, who was also named Peter, would die there, drowned in an eddy of bullets and bombs near the great whirlpool called Stalingrad.

She didn't gaze out the window so much nowadays, so I can't report whether or not she saw the man in the tophat parading up and down the cobblestones of Weissenbürgerstrasse with his fellow Brownshirts; perhaps, he'd died by then; the grocer's apprentice was long in the grave. She was much too busy to take in the late summer light, let alone the mist on the Wannsee; she was too encumbered with honors. By the time the Great Depression stabbed her Republic in the back, they had promoted her to department head of the Prussian Academy of Arts. When Shostakovich's Second Symphony premiered, she was making another dark woodcut, the mother's face blurred like a shrouded mummy's, the little one apparently dead; she called it "Sleeping with Child."

In 1931 her huge lithograph "We Protect the Soviet Union!" showed bitterly stern proletarian men locking arms with one determined proletarian woman; they were all in a line, walling away evil; coincidentally, they remind me of the rows of figures in Roman Karmen's documentaries. *Her creative work, which is devoted to the German proletariat and its liberation struggle, is one of the high points of European revolutionary realistic art.*

In the following year, while S. Korolev's RP-1 rocket plane first flew through the Soviet sky and the sleepwalker summoned his lieutenants to headquarters at the Kaiserhof Hotel, demanding speechless obedience, she arrived at the cemetery where Peter was buried. It was July. She spent two days grieving alone, shrugging off Karl's touch. (When after years of hesitation she finally decided to marry, her mother had promised her that she would never be without his love.) The cemetery looked more pleasant to her each time she saw it. The first time she had come, it had been walled in with barbed wire. A Belgian soldier helped her get in and led her to Peter's grave. She had been grateful for his silence and his lack of surprise. Oh, but everything had seemed so dreary then! Now she was quite accustomed to it.

Hans came on the twenty-fifth.—And in an instant the bullet struck him! she kept explaining over and over, while Hans stared at her, slowly shaking his head. Keim and the others put him in the trench, she said, because they thought he was only wounded when he was actually dead in that moment . . .

That dull or guarded look, she could never be quite sure which, had came into Hans's eyes during the war years; perhaps it was only when he was with her; it would have been natural for him to believe that she loved Peter best, simply because she'd never stop mourning him. For his sixteenth birthday she'd made Hans a bookplate of a blond and naked angel, whose genitals were neither overstated nor hidden in the American manner; and the angel stood on the edge of a white island, with his wings and fists raised as he gazed down into a grey sea, the whole scene illuminated by the riches of futurity, which, as it proved, Hans would be able to spend and his brother would not. Hadn't she sensed that? She knew both their bodies so well; first Hans used to model for her, then Peter. And Karl used to worry about Peter's lungs, his lack of weight. Well, poor Hans was going grey now.

The figures were installed on the twenty-eighth, not at the grave itself, which would have been too small, but across from the cemetery's entrance: the kneeling father, his arms folded rigidly inward as he stares straight ahead, or pretends to; really he's gazing down into the earth, which is nowhere; his face is frozen; he bites back his grief.—Such is our life, she said to Karl.—The mother for her part bows frankly forward and down; she seems about to pitch into the grave at any moment. Indeed, in the course of its placement this female figure began tipping forward in the mucky ground; the workmen had to correct the pedestal and then lower the mother back onto her vigil-stone a second time.—I'm not sure that the World Congress of Friends of the Soviet Union would have been interested in such details.

All the same, that was the year of her second and more extensive Soviet exhibition, the one in Leningrad. Framed prints, one or two high, depending on size, wound round the walls of a rococco salon whose carved ceiling-flowers and molding-flowers the Revolution had not yet removed. Slender Otto Nagel put on his striped suit and went there for the opening; many Leningraders attended; in the photograph, eleventh from the left, I see a young girl with dark, dark hair; I think her name is Elena Konstantinovskaya. Two rows behind her, and not looking in her direction at all, because they hadn't noticed each other yet, I definitely see D. D. Shostakovich; his new wife Nina is away at work.—But Käthe stayed home, which is to say at Peter's grave, with yellow wooden crosses all around her.

Then everything in Germany became black, white and red—the colors of the Third Reich.* She thought of something that Professor Moholy-Nagy used to say: I don't care to participate in this sort of optical event.

15

In the end, her art got supplanted in both zones. A grief-stricken mother holding her dead child is all very well, but perhaps a trifle too universal—or, as Comrade Stalin would say, *incorrect*. For how could our ends be served by implying that everybody, even the enemy herself, grieves over dead children?

---

*Surprisingly, as late as 1939 they'll allow her a tiny entry in *Meyers Lexikon:* She was born; she received a German education; she's been a wife since 1891. *Her expressive pages are not free from the class-battle standpoint used for Communist propaganda.* That knock on the door, when will it come? When it does, three years after her enforced resignation from the Prussian Academy, the Gestapo command her to disavow certain pro-Russian statements she's made in an interview with *Isvestiya*. She submits. Afterward, she'll make halfhearted plans with Karl to have poison ready. Karl, his practice already banned, will die of old age just as the sleepwalker's tanks glide into Paris. On 23.10.43, the family flat will be destroyed by American bombers. Käthe will die in Saxony, shortly after the firebombing of Dresden. I quote from one of her very last letters: *Oh, Lise, being dead must be good, but I am much too much afraid of dying, of being terribly afraid at the moment of death.*

Better by far that famous poster of the Red Army woman with one hand on her hip, another on her bemedaled breast, standing sentry-straight before a bullet-pocked German wall, her red-starred cap at an angle to show off her hair (short, yet feminine) as she smiles into the sideways future! Thus runs the Russian view. On the other side we merely need to quote our Führer's dictum that *the Germans—this is essential—will have to constitute amongst themselves a closed society, like a fortress.* ▸

YOU HAVE SHUT THE DANUBE'S GATES

At the very point when death becomes visible behind everything, it disrupts the imaginative process. The menace is more stimulating when you are not confronting it from close up.

—Käthe Kollwitz (1932)

1

In our Soviet literature of today (nationalist in form, socialist in content), there is scant room for epics and suchlike old trash. However, the twelfth-century *Song of Igor's Campaign* does contain a passage which I find relevant to my context. Addressing *eight-minded Yaroslav of Galich,* whom I myself couldn't care less about, the anonymous bard sings:

You reign high upon your throne of gold;
you have locked closed Hungary's mountains,
bolting them with your iron troops;
you have barred the King's way;
you have shut the Danube's gates.

It's true; he had shut the Danube's gates, and you know who I mean; you understand what the Danube stands for.

The king he'd barred the way against was presently gazing down a long tree-lined gunbarrel whose steel was comprised of angled cobblestones; the rifle's mouth gleamed gold; and through that gunbarrel roofed with trees came the Condor Legion straight ahead, bearing arms and standards as they marched like bullets through the gunbarrel's mouth. It was their victory parade.—I wasn't there. I was guarding the Danube's gates.

I did have observers in place by the swastika-buntinged Brandenburg Gate when the Condor Legion came marching through; that night the black telephone rang, and when I lifted the receiver, my Red Orchestra began to play me a song, not Shostakovich but Hindemith: closing my eyes, translating program music into pictures, I got to see it all: First came that trio of scowling young warriors in canted berets and shiny calf-length boots. The center man bore the standard, which was topped by an eagle and swastika. All three of them were decorated. At a discreet distance behind them strode the columns with their upraised rifles. *Prestissimo,* now! The Condor Legion came goose-stepping forward with bayonet-fixed rifles pointing straight up, passing a line of drummers in uniforms and steel helmets.

2

Call me a Kirov made of bronze, burly in my worker's jacket, broad, smiling and hatted. Elderly women are susceptible to me. My duties are as tedious as Leningrad's dogs, snow, horses. I wander amidst the booksellers on Nevsky Prospect, making sure that all's well with our Danube's gates. Yezhov rings me up on the big black telephone: *Send me more little ballerinas!* That's not my job, but I'll do it. My job's everything long and low.

Have you been to the neutral countries? Not I. To me there are no neutral countries. That's why listening to foreign broadcasts in Leningrad will soon be a capital offense.

I turned in my report on Operation Magic Fire and went home. Yezhov's ballerinas were already whispering to me about Operation Barbarossa, but Case White hadn't even been opened yet; we still had infinite time. The future doesn't exist until it happens.

I live alone, and that's by choice. My one desire is to aggravate the contradictions of capitalist culture.—Are you stupid enough to believe that?—What I really like to do is listen to the Red Orchestra. And whenever they tell me to, I'll drive over to listen in at Akhmatova's. I'll bet that Lidiya Chukovskaya's over there again tonight. No one's ever caught them doing it, but I know they're both lesbians. If it were up to me, they'd both be shot.

The humble secretary on his throne of gold had shut the Danube's gates.

I know what I know, so I didn't argue. The Red Orchestra said that the King would sign a treaty with us first, so he didn't have to fight a two-front war. Well, that would be logical.

The King could never get through. We were safe. You-know-who would reign forever on his throne of gold.

3

Pyotr Alexeev, with whom I sometimes do wet work, told me a funny one yesterday. It seems that a herd of kolkhozniks with fresh manure on their shoes get to Moscow; you know; they're shock workers; they've won the prize! Think of them as Rodchenko's robotlike abstract paper cutouts painted with dark oil and mounted on circular wooden bases. The guide explains that they are now in the world capital of progress, abundance, freedom, you name it. Eventually one of the farmers comes up timidly and says: Comrade Leader, yesterday I walked all over the city and didn't see any of those things! The guide has just the right answer. He replies: You should spend less time walking around and more time reading newspapers!

That's what I tell myself. He's shut the Danube's gates, so all's well. It doesn't feel that way to me, but I should spend less time walking around and more time reading newspapers. Unfortunately, my job is to walk around.

Tukhachevsky informs Comrade Stalin that the next war will be fought with tanks. Very good—let's experiment with tanks in Spain. Straightaway sixty of our tanks get captured by the Condor Legion, mostly with the assistance of Moors to whom the Fascists paid five hundred pesetas each. To this provocation, Comrade Stalin has an answer: Shoot Tukhachevsky. Tukhachevsky should have spent more time reading the newspapers. Then he would have known that tanks will never be any threat. And the Condor Legion goose-steps forward.

I lift the big black telephone. All the better to listen in, my dears! Chukovskaya is saying, in that peculiarly arch tone she adopts whenever she's trying to impress Akhmatova: The streets are so wet and gloomy now . . .

I'm thinking: Lidiya Korneeva, you don't know the half of it!

Akhmatova says: One might say that Leningrad is particularly suited to catastrophes . . .

I'm thinking to myself: What horseshit! It offends me that such a person ever got published.

Akhmatova's running on: That cold river, those menacing sunsets, that operatic, terrifying moon . . .

Chukovskaya whispers: The black water with yellow flecks of light . . .

Under the black water's where you deserve to be. That's what I thought. Of course, nobody gives a shit about *my* opinions.

4

The Danube's gates are safely frozen, just as the sleepwalker's frozen with his left hand on his belt and his right arm up and out, the fingers slightly open, while facing him, Generalmajor Freiherr von Richthofen mirrors him, and the Condor Legion is frozen in its multiple goosestep, one leg up in the air, its hydra-faces grimacing; this is a sailor's dance. ▸

ELENA'S ROCKETS

◩

The children invented a game for themselves that involved hurling a stocking, which has been tightly packed with dust, through the air like a rocket, and as it falls it creates an entire cloud of dust. The youngsters play this game a lot, although it has been forbidden by the management.

—Anonymous, Memorandum to Deputy Chairman of Moscow City Children's Commission, re: Children's Commune, Barybino (1936)

1

Even then there was something about Elena Konstantinovskaya which rendered her an object of obsessive desire. In the fantasies of Shostakovich, whom she was not to meet for several years yet, she occasionally resembled a certain Rodchenko angel whose long dress was a tipi-like construction of electric-blue slats; atop this triangle, which is to say right at her infinitesimally narrow waist, she outstretched pure white skeleton-arms which resembled picket fences; these blessed the world with their triangular golden hands. (For the sake of completeness I want to tell you that this particular angel also possessed a crimson scapula, not to mention a triangular crimson head whose only feature was a single strawlike white protrusion.) Elena might not have looked much like that to anyone but Shostakovich, and even to him only on certain days, when the music she inspired achieved its extreme limit of formalism. As has been written about the rocket scientist F. Zander, *one of the tragedies of this outstanding intellect was that his engineering solutions, however mature, did not correspond to the technical possibilities of his time.*

Well, what did Elena *really* look like? Akhmatova, who met her briefly, compared her to a church—specifically, to one of the *forty times forty* churches in Marina Tsvetaeva's poems about Moscow.* Remember that in those days it was unwise even to mention churches; they were getting demolished or converted into museums of atheism all over our Soviet land. *Church times church, all those forty times forty,* Akhmatova couldn't stop chanting that nursery rhyme, which certainly cost Tsvetaeva dearly and may have helped bring about Akhmatova's own punishment later on, but at this point in the story the fact of the untrustworthiness of those three people—Shostakovich, Akhmatova and Tsvetaeva, I mean—feels less important to me than the fact that they couldn't stop comparing one thing with another. Rodchenko made avant-garde "constructions"—an act which also seems slightly untrustworthy, now that I come to think of it, but all right; let's suppose that they were correctly conceived—why did Shostakovich have to distort her into one of them? What was wrong with Elena just being Elena? Why did she have to be a church? One theory I have—this is Comrade Alexandrov speaking—is that Akhmatova had so many women in her life that they might as well have been the forty times forty churches of prerevolutionary Moscow! This gets to the root of what makes intellectuals dangerous. We use them to add *newness* to life, which is what keeps it bearable, but newness shouldn't mutate into utter alienation; a woman never ought to become a church. And now I beg your pardon and will get out of the story.

Shostakovich, Akhmatova, Tsvetaeva were all, insofar as it was possible to be without getting liquidated (Tsvetaeva liquidated herself), rebels. Elena Konstantinovskaya was more the good girl. I see here that her parents applied on her behalf for membership in the Little Octobrists, but she was a few months too old. In the Young Pioneers ("Carpenter" link, N. K. Krupskaya Brigade) she became a leading force among the other children, thanks to her enthusiasm for making floats and banners. Her excuse for not immediately entering the Komsomol, namely dedication to her schoolwork, strikes me as plausible. When she did join, at age fifteen, her marks continued to be excellent. One of her professors, the widow Liadova, seems to have been responsible for the girl's decision to take up linguistics. In the course of preparing this summary I have reviewed Elena's translations of German military docu-

---

*In fact, she is said to have resembled Tsvetaeva, especially around the mouth, although her long, dark hair, which she so often wore in bangs reaching nearly to the eyebrow, also reminded some people of that doomed poet.

ments, for in 1941 I myself had unfortunate occasion to learn that other language; in spite of the adverse report of Lieutenant N. K. Danchenko, which I also happen to have here, I can testify to her literalness and neutrality. Such qualities cannot be taken for granted, particularly in translators of the front echelon, whose perfectionistic quest for exactly the right word sometimes gets corrupted into expression of self.

Konstantinovskaya's work reassures me with its touch of stiltedness: Here is a professional who is more concerned with correctness than with style. Furthermore, she lived the quiet life. I am creditably informed that when Shostakovich uttered rash, irreverent and at times even provocative speeches against Soviet power, she urged him to be more pleasant. She disapproved of his more extremist acquaintances, and in the course of a quarrel informed him: I'm glad that your friends aren't my friends! which I myself will always count in her favor. Her expressions of support for his formalist-individualist Opus 40 may be excused, since he dedicated it to her. When we sent her north in '35, it was simply to put pressure on Shostakovich, to *remind* him. Take it from me: We had nothing against her. We arrested Akhmatova's son and boyfriend in the same year and for equivalent reasons. It was my pleasure to help her get an early release, not that she ever knew about my help. My work tends to leave me with the worst thoughts about people. I'm left with only good thoughts about Elena Konstantinovskaya.

Nonetheless, and this may have been one of the qualities which attracted Shostakovich, she bore her own not so secret deviation—a harmless one, to be sure. How should I say it? (I've said it more bluntly about Akhmatova, but that's because I never liked that woman.) In 1928, when rocket projectiles were first launched from our Soviet land, Elena was abnormally close to her schoolmate Vera Ivanovna. A report on those two stated that *we noticed two black and blue marks on the neck of Elena Konstantinovskaya. First Elena did not want to explain the reason for those marks, but then with embarrassment she said that Vera Ivanova had kissed her in the woods, which resulted in the blue marks on her neck.* This incident impels me to reconsider the girl's relationship with Professor Liadova, who by the way introduced her to the poems of the bisexual Tsvetaeva.

After Vera, a whole year later in fact, the year that Shostakovich married Nina Varzar and Comrade Stalin's wife shot herself; the year after Hitler's niece shot herself and the year before Hitler became Chancellor, there would take place a conference in international linguistics, one of whose delegates would be a German comrade named Lina, a woman with brown eyes and brown bangs who that very first time would sit on the soft red armchair of that hotel room in Leningrad, watching Elena and pushing the collar of her sweater up around her throat with both hands; for the previous half hour Lina and Elena would have been engaged in a fervent discussion as to the best Russian rendering of the following thirteenth-century verse: *Isolde's secret song was her marvelous beauty, whose invisible music crept through the windows of the eyes.* Aside from the sweater, Lina would be naked with her white knees drawn up almost to her shoulders and her white thighs shining and the long white lips of her vulva as irresistible as candy to Elena, and her anus was a white star. In a moment, Elena was going to kneel down and bury her face in the German girl's flesh; she knew it and so did Lina. Just before that happened, Lina was going to say: We have almost the same name, don't we? and Elena, hardly able to bear her desire for the other woman, would nod rapidly while Lina let go of her sweater with her right hand and slowly reached out, rested her fingers in Elena's hair, twisted it in a knot, and forced her head down; no, no, it wouldn't be that way at all; Elena, who had won a prize in the Komsomol fencing competition, would be lunging for Lina's cunt like a pikefish striking at bait; then Lina would be stroking the top of Elena's head, murmuring: We're both so white, aren't we?—And *then* Lina would wrap her hand in Elena's hair and pull her head more firmly against her, whispering: Oh, baby, but you're white like snow and I'm white like a cloud . . . —and before she'd even finished uttering these words, Elena would begin to melt from the heat of Lina, while Lina would turn to rain in Elena's mouth. There would be a second time and a third (by which point Elena would be ready to die for Lina), then a fourth and a fifth, all in the space of a long white night. At midmorning Lina would set out sleepless to Berlin and Elena would never even know what happened to her.

Do you want to know the difference between Vera Ivanova and Lina? Elena did the same thing, performed the same sexual act, with both of them. But with Lina, because she was now more adult and more experienced, she did it in much the way that von Karajan conducts Shostakovich's Tenth Symphony: more smooth, rounded, polished, elegant (one hears this especially in the brasses), less harsh and desperate than as André Previn does it. The ferocious second movement especially, although Karajan's tempo is actually faster than Previn's, sounds richer, more modulated than his. (I myself prefer Previn's starkness here.) In the third movement all irony is lost, resulting in what I consider to be a serious misinterpretation of Shostakovich; but in exchange Karajan imparts a haunting sweetness to the music quite unlike what Previn achieved. Uncanny how different the same notes can sound!

(By the way, Karajan got his Nazi Party card in April 1933, less than two months after the sleepwalker became Chancellor.)

By the time she'd become Shostakovich's mistress, which is to say the muse of his Cello Sonata in D Minor, she'd learned to make love even more smoothly and perfectly than she had with Lina. There was something about her—Akhmatova was correct!—something akin to entering an ancient church. It wasn't just that she knew how to hold and how to tease *vibrato,* how to *manipulate* (thus she later summed up sex for her husband Roman Karmen); there was something about her that made her lovers cry.

But the strangest thing of all about her was that she knew how to disguise herself in plainness (I suppose so that she wouldn't get hurt). Once she'd put on her round glasses and tied her hair into a bun, hardly anybody looked at her when she walked down the street. And in school she was likewise inconspicuous—a highly adaptive trait in her time and place. I've read that those who were lucky enough to see her literally let her hair down could never forget her for the rest of their lives. In 1927, the year of A Ya. Fedorov's rocket-powered automobile, a girl committed suicide over her.

Shostakovich in a moment of curiosity once asked her whether she might ever stop being attracted to women, and she gravely, proudly replied: I'll never change.

And why should she? As I said before, why should Elena be compelled to be anything other than Elena? I think that the reason she loved him above all others was that to him, who and what she was was perfect. An E-sharp cannot be improved; nor can it be replaced by a B-flat. It is what it is. She loved women, and he loved her for it.

2

In 1931, when construction of the first Soviet rocket-glider commenced, Elena seriously considered applying to the S. Ordzhonikidze Moscow Aviation Institute. She could have done anything; she was good at becoming part of the collective. That must have been why she kept dreaming that in every room there was a big black telephone which buzzed when she walked by. She'd saved last year's newspaper about the Seventh All-Union Glider Rally, when S. M. Korolev's "Red Star" glider proved capable of spectacular acrobatics; Elena imagined falling in love with Korolev. In 1934, when she was having her affair with Shostakovich, Roman Karmen stood young and handsome in a flier's suit and a warm beret, everything buttoned up around his throat as, holding up a snow-white camera, he filmed the flier W. S. Molokov, Hero of the Soviet Union, who was also young and handsome but covered up, wearing a thick round fur cap so you couldn't really tell who either of them were; Molokov had goggles pushed up against his hat, and Karmen didn't; it was when she saw that photograph of Karmen that Elena fell in love with him. By then our first liquid-propellant rocket, a rather small one, had succeeded in leaving the launching rig. It would soon be superseded by a rocket as tall as the spire of the Fortress of Peter and Paul! Elena read all about it in *Izvestiya*. And just when she had definitively resolved to marry Roman Karmen, she received a card from Vera Ivanova, who would not get expelled from the Komsomol until 1937, a year after Elena, who as she opened it remembered the mud on Vera's shoes as Vera leaned forward naked in the chair with her long, beloved, slightly greasy hair falling over her eyes, shadow in her cleavage, shadow between her legs.

3

Elena would most certainly have been there, gazing up through the flags and streamers, when the AHT-20 "Maxim Gorki" plane flew overhead in 1935, but that was when we locked her away. I remember when we arrested her; I was there, and she stood before us with her eyes half-closed like the blacked-out headlights of a tramcar in wartime; that was when I *knew* that this was her "intimate look," that Shostakovich and Vera and Lina and those other boys and girls alike in love with her, always throwing rockets, they'd all seen this; this made me crazy; it was right then that I fell in love with her; I became another of her victims.

Squares of Red Army men marched along the base of a wall of airplanes whose propellers had all been oriented perfectly parallel to the ground, but Elena wasn't there; she was with us.

I repeat: What did Elena *really* look like? Not like a Rodchenko angel at all, not any more than she resembled the KPIR-3 glider of 1925: wings like squared-off banana fronds, a skeletal body of hollow triangles. In her own interest, I freely confess to altering certain details of her appearance throughout this book. For instance, Elena Konstantinovskaya was blonde, and it was as a blonde that Shostakovich, the protagonist of these stories, would certainly have thought of her, but to me, and what I say goes, she will always be *the darkhaired woman*, or, if you prefer, *the woman with the dark, dark hair.*

4

In 1930, People's Commissar Voroshilov was present at the maiden voyage of the TB-5 bomber, but Elena was too young. (Her Komsomol report for that year reports her as being extremely proficient in sharpshooting and first aid—two skills which would serve her well in Spain.) How happy she would have been to watch the takeoff of the TB-5! I'll write her in if I care to; I'll give her a front row spot in front of what they still liked to call the cosmodrome. Can't I be allowed my amusements? After all, the great aviator V. Chkalov was grounded for prankishly flying under a bridge in Leningrad.

In proof of my deservingness, let me remind you that I never touched Elena Konstantinovskaya. I never even introduced myself, not even when I arrested her.—Vera Ivanova was another matter.—So it's not from personal experience but from personal *observation* that I can so accurately describe the way that Elena could be so distant and angry with those who loved her, so sweet to win back those who were slipping away. I didn't lean on Roman Karmen, nor even on that bastard Shostakovich until Elena had definitively moved on. From 1953 on I resisted checking up on her more than once a week, no matter how tempted I felt. (I remember on one winter morning in Leningrad watching her flicker between each of the eight white columns, formerly yellow, of the Smolny Institute.) When she died in 1975, I respectfully refrained from attending her funeral. Establishing that code of behavior for myself didn't require me to own a degree in rocket science (an endeavor of great importance to our Soviet land, and accordingly always supported by Marshal M. N. Tukhachevsky). As a matter of fact, most rocket scientists end up being traitors. I wish it weren't that way. But since it is, why not imagine that there's one loyal rocket scientist? And who would that be but Elena Konstantinovskaya, who is pure and perfect and good? Shall I make her an astrophysicist right now? Don't tell me I don't have the nerve! Why, if I felt like it, I could anoint her with those crimson rhomboids which we find exclusively on the shoulders of our Red Army commanders!

B. N. Yuriev was the very first to construct a rigid theoretical proof that helicopter flight was possible. What could you do to me if I corrected history so that the name of that theoretician became E. E. Konstantinovskaya? At the very least, can't I place her within one of those blue and green Soviet biplanes which used to be all the time buzzing in the slipstream above our heads?

I know everything, I really do. I could tell you precisely which two of Akhmatova's lines it was that Vera Ivanova murmured in Elena's ear on that last day by the riverbank when she understood that it was truly over between her and Elena. I've read Elena's diary (which is now in our archive) and I'm more aware than she ever was, thanks not only to the gift of distance but also to my own professional training, why she dreamed what she did the night after she first met Shostakovich. These temptations I'm likewise proof against; surely you're not interested in biochemical accidents of personality. But another of her dreams I'll report to you, because it was a dream that all of us had in those years, thanks to the deteriorating international situation, which resulted inevitably from the struggle between capitalists to devour the hugest profits. Over and over, Elena Konstantinovskaya woke up sweating from a dream she hated almost as much as her dream of the black telephone; she dreamed of a long finned bomb slowly flying through darkness above a glowing pyramid. ▸

MAIDEN VOYAGE

What child is there that lives, as I did, midway between Reality and Fairyland, that does not long sometimes to leave altogether the familiar world and set off in search of new and fabulous realms?

—Hanna Reitsch, German pilot, *ca.* 1947

1

The telephone rang. Then it was agreed: Krakow to us, Lwow to them, Warsaw to us, Brest-Litovsk to them. That was how we established the Ribbentrop-Molotov Line.—Not another inch! the sleepwalker shouted into the heavy black mouthpiece, but that obedient buzz of assent might have concealed something. He longed to smash open the telephone's bakelite shell and peer within, but dreaded what he might find. Never mind; he'd win with commands and arguments.

He told the telephone: Get somebody over here with the order of battle.

Trudl, he said to his favorite secretary, would you be so good as to bring me that white Barbarossa folder? Thank you, child.

He instructed the telephone: That makes absolutely no difference. Over there they've got nothing but low-quality Slavic formations.

Then it was time to confirm with Göring that our rocket-planes were ready.

As a matter of fact, we weren't even supposed to have tanks. Even armored scout cars had been forbidden us by the Anglo-American plutocrats. Well, what about rockets? Our enemies had overlooked those. I myself was already a fervent rocket man and had been ever since the Rhön Gliding Contests of 1933. How else were we going to get the Polish Corridor back?

If we could only go to the moon! sighed Herr Doktor von Braun.—I met him once—a certified genuis. He died in America, long after the war. Imagine! He'd sold himself to the victors, just so somebody could get to the moon.

But in the sleepwalker's time, our moon-wooers were flying inside of bombs powered by intermittent propulsive duct engines.

You probably don't even remember your first rocket, for the same reason that I forget my first telephone. The first rocket I ever saw was a long grey-green monster with a helmeted, goggled man in the cockpit, black crosses on each wing, screaming engines and fat little bombs, not to mention a pair of machine-guns on the upper deck. You wouldn't call it a rocket at all; you live in the future, when the Americans stand on the verge of conquering Saturn. That first rocket was actually nothing but a fighter with a rocket engine, its bomblets only for show. Doktor von Braun hadn't started working on our V-weapons; the Russians hadn't yet stolen a march on us with Sputnik. Still, why not call it a rocket? By the way, it happened to be equipped with a quintuplicator to record five pieces of aerial data; that I can swear to, because I invented the quintuplicator myself! Oh, yes, I was there; I was *there* at the very beginning; even before the Heinkel-Hirth turbojet experiments. I'd always wanted to visit the moon myself, you see.

Of course I was also practical. As Heidegger writes: *The upward glance passes aloft toward the sky, and yet it remains below on the earth.* You're too young to understand the spiritual nature of flight because rockets and planes are everywhere now; flying's debased. When I was a boy, we'd all run out into the streets to watch our fire-red biplanes pass over us! Just take it from me: You'll never understand.

I don't mind telling you that we cheered when that rocket-plane took off on its maiden voyage, rising up a ladder of speeding flames! Where did it go? That's top secret, but we all saw it, everyone who mattered saw it as it sped over villages decked with flags and flowers; I'm reliably informed that it made a soft landing in the sand dunes of East Prussia. You're probably sneering, but that was an achievement in those days, especially given the political limitations imposed by our adversaries; East Prussia might as well have been the moon, and yet we got there! I'll never stop believing that this was a triumph for the human race.

Before 1934 was half over, we had BMW jet propulsion power units in production. (By the sleepwalker's orders we couldn't say anything about those, of course; you're the first person I've ever told.) I was there, and in uniform! By 1937 the Junkers company was also experimenting with jet propulsion; and I'll never forget the maiden voyage of a certain immense steel bullet with shark-fins and German designs—swastika on the rudder, black cross on wings and fuselage—my heart glowed even more than the first time I heard the sirens of a *Stukageschwader* 77! When a rocket or anything at all rocketlike soars into the sky, there's a beautiful inevitability to the experience. Gravity has been defeated, overruled, just like that! And how easy it's turned out to be! With that rocket go all of *us,* rising toward our dreams, steel in motion, doing what we've been told all our lives we can't do! And there it went, faster and faster, growing upward, steel fruit of a tree of flame, the flame clinging to earth for a long time, then rising behind the rocket, uprooting itself to go somewhere new, the steel bullet diminishing into a metal speck, then into nothingness; all we could see now was the flame; and then the flame entered a cloud and was gone. Even though the security situation didn't permit us to talk about it, Germany saw it! We saw it in Swabia and we glimpsed it from the Ostmark; we tilted up our heads as we stood in crowds on Hermann Göringstrasse and we saw our dreams arise. Meanwhile, Professor Focke invented the world's first helicopter.

2

In those days I dreamed of nothing but flight. Whenever I was with a woman, her arms around me reminded me of the inverted gull wings of the Ju-87. By the time that the BMW-003 project had begun in 1939, I'd seen it all. Have *you* seen it all? You most definitely haven't unless you've seen the test flight or better still the combat flight of a Me-163B rocket-plane, which deserves its name because it's powered by a genuine Walter rocket. (Walter was a friend of mine.) As with so many other things in life, you have at best five or six minutes in the air in this machine, due to the ferocious rate of fuel consumption; moreover, you need to jettison the undercarriage, which never makes for happy landings; but whether you come back or not, you can dictate your sensations and emotions to the world by laryngophone!

We had T-Stoff and C-Stoff for fuel in those days; I knew it all. Unfortunately I never got to fly a rocket myself, but I stood so close to the action that it seemed to me I could have done it in my sleep: Press the black button so that the hydrazine hydrate and alcohol begin to marry the hydrogen peroxide, then press the red button, and experience the shriek of flame! In a twinkling you've risen past the Ack-Ack Tower; you'll land on a secret runway in Dreamland, then continue on by armored car . . . Stay cool and brave—you'll win an Iron Cross!

3

Rocket-flame is sacred, like a flower placed in the hands of a wounded German soldier. Rockets are sacred because their mission is to approach the ideal. And with each new generation, right up to the V-weapons and beyond, they become more themselves. Their slimness grows more elegant, their tapering payloads more aerodynamic. But now that the war's over and they're perfect, nobody cares. Isn't that sad? That's the reason why I prefer to dwell on maiden voyages. Our rockets were mere prototypes then; our test pilots took risks; nobody knew what might happen. When I go back in time to 1936, before the sleepwalker called Göring on the black telephone, I see squatter, cruder rockets traversing our German skies. That was when we reoccupied the Rhineland. In 1935 the rockets were even wider, almost rectangular. They burned alcohol mixed with liquid oxygen. In 1934, when we purged Röhm and those scum, our flying machines were essentially square in cross-section, and their double wings resembled metallized pages of sheet music. In 1933, when the sleepwalker took power, I happened to be a philosophy student in Freiburg. It was night. We stood in a circle outside the library, waiting. The command came. I was ready; I did my part. Liftoff! And so it rose and flew, gloriously propelled by human force; with indescribable joy I watched it spinning sharp-cornered like some strange new propeller device designed to cut the wires of enemy barrage balloons. I estimated its mass and velocity; I predicted its trajectory; I foresaw the duration of the flight down to the last second; I already knew the combustion temperatures involved. Just before it reached maximum altitude, it vanished for the merest eyeblink in the smoke that rose up all around us; next it entered the zone of pitiless light, first as a silhouette, then, once its descent had begun, it opened, revolving about its spinal axis with the print on its pages stark enough for me to read it, had I wanted to, all the way across the pyre—it was some Jew book, something about pacifism, I believe—and Professor Heidegger, now unanimously elected Rector since his Anglo-Bolshevik predecessor had resigned, was speaking to us, or shouting, I should say, his voice deep, exultant, and more *certain* than it had ever sounded in any lecture I'd ever heard; he was telling us all that this marked a new night for German culture; that the old must burn for the sake of the new. Beside me stood my classmate Edelgard, who would later be killed with both her children in a British bombing raid; and I got excited by the firelit rapture on her face; she was hurling books by the handful, and her hair was more beautiful than fire; so I grabbed the collected works of the Jew Freud and threw them right up into the sky; they reached their apogee just as the first book I'd launched swirled finally down to commit itself to the flames of German summer. ▶

WHEN PARZIVAL KILLED THE RED KNIGHT

'Twas in olden times when eagles screamed . . .

—First Helgi-Song (12th century)

1

When Parzival killed the Red Knight simply because he longed to wear his armor, the King felt sad and the court damsels wept; all the same, one couldn't blame Parzival any more than one can the kitten who proudly slays his first robin redbreast. Action is what it is: scarlet feathers, red blood, grey guts and a stench. Cruel? Yes. Useless? Not at all. That's how they learn.

When a certain sleepwalker liquidated the Brownshirts, don't think he didn't have his reasons! All the same, his heartbeats rushed away like machine-gun bullets, thanks to the novelty. He was just beginning; he was still kittenish.

The telephone rang.

We have Röhm in custody, it said.

Tell me.

Yes, my Führer. We caught him in bed. With a man. They kissed each other goodbye.

The kitten didn't need to think; Parzival saw the red armor and knew in his bones what would make him happy, but the sleepwalker hesitated. Röhm had been his friend. Röhm had helped him—

Well, no damsels were going to weep this time. He mounted the red horse; he slammed on his new armor, which was so red that it made one's eyes red just to see it.

2

He derived himself as perfectly from legend as Parzival ever did. To prove it, let's open his storybook.

If we page through volume five of *Meyers Lexikon* we come in time to *Hakenkreuz,* illustrated with an ancient white pictograph in Sweden, a bronze shield *(Nabel)* with four curly arms each ending in a three-knobbed pommel; then a chandelier *(Gewandspange)* in swastika form, each arm spiraling inward to its candle-socket; then an old pot from Hannover with swastikas marching around its sides; a skeletonized bronze disk from Baden, with a swastika in the center, followed by a longish entry which ends with this quotation from *Mein Kampf*: *And simultaneous with him stands the victory of the reified Idea, which has ever been, and ever shall be, anti-Semitic.*

Now for the full page galleries of black-and-white plates: ADOLF HITLER I and ADOLF HITLER II:—look! His father, his mother, his birthplace! Here he is with his comrades in the World War (there will never be another war); it's a snapshot of soldiers in their uniforms and caps, all sprawled carelessly in front of trees; in the center of the front row, one man has his hands in his pockets, but he's too relaxed; after all, romantic heroes must begin in star-crossed obscurity. So maybe Parzival's the one on the far left, he seems lonelier, as befits that night-born man, foredoomed to sink a hoard of German fighters deep down below the sun; he already wears the moustache. On the next page, in ADOLF HITLER II, we see him going over city plans with Albert Speer; Berlin's roads will now crack apart the whites and greens of our mapped German landscape! ADOLF HITLER II also depicts him receiving flowers from German girls in traditional dress; in ADOLF HITLER II he's embracing a fellow Old Fighter, his head low and sideways against the man's chest as he grips his shoulders.

Do you want to know how modest he is? Although he's already killed the Red Knight and his whole race screams for encores, although he's *Führer und Reichskanzler,* although he's *Gründer und Führer der nat.-soz. Bewegung,* he insists that the curtain fall after ADOLF HITLER I and ADOLF HITLER II. In comparison, GARTEN I doesn't end with GARTEN II (a victory garden, so I recall); oh, no, GARTEN III joins the attack, which successfully terminates with GARTEN IV. And that's nothing! GERMANEN I reaches all the way through GERMANEN VIII—a stretch nearly as vast as Operation Barbarossa itself!

In volume eight, in the National Socialism entry, there he is again, full page and in color, glaring.

3

When Parzival killed the Red Knight, it happened to be 1934, a good year for Käthe Kollwitz's "Death" series. I especially admire Leaf 1, *Frau vertraut sich dem Tod an*: A woman who resembles the artist is holding her child in against her skirts, stretching out her hand to entreat bony Death. But Death follows orders.

In Leaf 4, *Tod packt eine Frau,* one of her most powerful compositions, the skeleton seems to be embracing a woman from behind, biting her in the back of the neck while she turns toward him screaming and the little child reaches up, trying to fight him off. Nor should we forget *Tod hält Mädchen im Schoss* (catalogue number 153): The child's lip draws back as if in a sob as she sits in the lap of maternal Death whose face is black like a veiled Muslim woman's; her face lies against Death's dark head. Oh, and *Tod greift in Kinderschar,* ha, ha! The bony angel with black wings like a paratrooper and wasted flesh around its skeleton comes swooping down to grab wide-eyed, uncomprehending children, just as Skorzeny will seize Mussolini in 1943. By then, we'll all have become characters in Parzival's fairytale.* We could have won the World War! Don't you remember how our three-oh-fives blasted right through the French battery at Verdun? Unfortunately, the Jews got to us. That won't happen again. On every canted, bird-inscribed Iron Cross we wear, the white bird will clutch the white bones of a swastika. We'll become as hard and fundamental as skeletons. And Parzival's most fundamental of all; his skeleton's invulnerable, ceaselessly growing; his heart-pistons pound behind a bridge's steel ribs.

But this is still 1934, when a woman embraces Death and gazes on his dark face as lovers do, drawing his head close to hers. The title: *Tod wird als Freund erkannt,* death perceived as a friend.

4

When Parzival killed the Red Knight, he did it for white-armed Lina and for Freya and Elena, not to mention white-armed Lisca Malbran.

In olden times, wars were waged by heroes who admired one another but found themselves forced by fate or blood revenge to do each other harm. In

*Even Käthe Kollwitz herself copied out in her daybook Nietzsche's letter to his sister rhapsodizing over Wagner's "Parsifal."

our time, we fought for hateful ogres against other ogres equally hateful. From a practical point of view, can't it be argued that nothing has changed?

Parzival killed the Red Knight *for us*. In our name, bloodstained tank treads will soon grind down the corn. *Tod wird als Freund erkannt.*

Don't shun the shock! Grind out more gold for him! He knows how to make it red.

5

What else was happening when Parzival killed the Red Knight? On the far side of Myrkvith Forest, where ogresses ride wolves and use snakes for reins, past Sun Fell and Snow Fell, in Sowjet-Russland, another Red Knight (I mean Kirov) fell to Russia's Parzival, who attended the funeral, called for vengeance, and launched his Great Terror.

It was a year after Erich von Manstein had been promoted to Colonel and a year before Friedrich Paulus would be promoted to Colonel. Captive blacksmiths were forging us red-gold rings. German schoolboys began a new course of study: Knighthood. It was the year that Shostakovich's future wife Irina was born. Our composer, two years married to Nina Varzar, was sleeping in Elena Konstantinovskaya's arms when Irina came into the world. It was for Elena that he composed the romantic Opus 40. Meanwhile, Elena's future husband, good, loyal Roman Karmen, made the film "Kirov."

Parzival killed the Red Knight and became King, all of us now hoping for good harvest years.

6

When Parzival killed Galogandres, the standard-bearer of King Clamidê, the attackers called the battle off. The long dark pipelike barrels of their antitank rifles couldn't frighten him: Parzival had saved Queen Condwiramurs! On the next day, it's true, he had to best King Clamidê in single combat, but, even though at the time it seemed difficult—so difficult, in fact, that the blood gushed from Parzival's eyes—it ended correctly, with the sleepwalker's arm rigidly parallel to the ground as he stood at the reviewing stand, Berlin, noon exactly, 7.6.39, and the returned Condor Legion striding past with their guns straight up. ▸

OPUS 40

There is nothing in you which fails to send a wave of joy and fierce passion inside me when I think of you. Lyalya, I love you so, I love you so, as nobody ever loved before. My love, my gold, my dearest, I love you so; I lay down my love before you.

—Shostakovich to E. E. Konstantinovskaya (1934)

1

Each of Shostakovich's symphonies I consider to be a multiply broken bridge, an archipelago of steel trailing off into the river. Opus 40, however, is a house with four rooms. In front, it's true, there's an ornate golden staircase ascending out of a snowy plain, then ending unconsummated in air. But Shostakovich always liked his jokes—oh, me!

In those years he still resembled a boy. Sweetly gazing at the world through his round dark-framed spectacles, he captivated Elena Konstantinovskaya. That sliver of starched white shirt within his dark suit, she couldn't wait to stroke it with her talented hands. He peered shyly down through half-closed eyes. Then he built Opus 40 for her and him to dwell in, and she led him inside.

They were going to have an apartment with a dark passageway, then steps and halfsteps. They'd live there, deep below the piano keys in Moscow. Nina could stay in Leningrad.

2

It was 1934, the year of Y. Bilioch's immortal elegy "Kirov," with camerawork by R. L. Karmen. But Kirov wasn't yet dead on the white night between May and June when Elena first held Shostakovich's hand. The music festival had ended, and the pale boy, who was newly married, crossed his soft white wrists, gazing rapturously at her through his glasses. Elena, *you're the one for me,* he said. Time for private English lessons! Before he'd even kissed her, his bass- and treble-glands had begun composing Opus 40, which prefigures his most beautiful fugues.

3

Her electric clitoris and the phrase *electric clitoris* were the first two aspects of her to be translated musically—a claim which the translator would have rejected, since right up until his Seventh Symphony he proudly disdained program music; but sometimes the critic's exegesis is wiser than the composer's, for the same reason that in recordings of Opus 40, Emanuel Ax plays the piano part better than Shostakovich; no one who has read the entire case file can deny that Elena Konstantinovskaya's clitoris was electric and that its sweet vibrations sing forever in the cello melody which opens the first movement. The phrase or alias which derives from her clitoris gets expressed in the happy, comic, rocking-horse sexuality of the piano in the second movement, when our young Shostakovich looks self-deprecatingly down between his own shoulders (if you've ever drunk absinthe, you'll understand what it's like to be weighed down by the drug almost to paralysis, and at the same time to exist within an invisible ball of consciousness which hovers precisely halfway between your body and the ceiling); from an eminence which sparkles with dust-motes in the bedroom of that dacha in Luga, the second movement *(allegro)* gazes irreverently down upon its pale and awkwardly ecstatic father, whom I'd rather call a child; groaning for joy, the child is riding his hobbyhorse, Elena. His shoulderblades rise and fall as elaborately as the mechanical arms of a player piano; he's copulating in a frenzy! This brief theme expresses a typical lover's sentiment: Look how ridiculous I am compared to you! Joined to you, I make us both ridiculous! All the same, let's, let's, so to speak, *do it,* my darling little Elenochka, because you're the one for me.

Marry me then, said Elena Konstantinovskaya.

And why shouldn't he marry her? She was the only one he ever found who could have dwelled with him in that four-roomed house within his chest, which they were fully capable of connecting, by means of trumpetlike passageways, with the four chambers of her own heart, so that then they would have had quite the castle together, oh, my, sharing refuges and secrets. And on that very first night he took her inside the world beneath the black keys, whispering: My tonic must have been D minor, when you, you know . . . And she understood him. She always did. She smiled and took him in, just the merest half-step, I actually mean a semitone, which is the space between adjacent notes in this diatonic scale we all live by. She was the only one!

4

Therefore, Opus 40, and in particular the first movement, composed of firelight and kisses, remains the most romantic thing that Shostakovich ever wrote. In the recording which he made with D. Shafran ten years later, he played the piano part and Shafran the cello, the cello as vivid as Elena herself, the piano steady and glittery like Shostakovich; even though I have already stated that Elena's song was more perfectly realized in the recording by E. Ax and Y.-Y. Ma, everything was already there: the piano was the skeleton; the cello was the flesh; he was the knowledge and commemoration; she was the life.

5

Elenochka, Lyalya I mean, or better yet my most perfect of all Russian Lyalkas, you possess all the names! You're my jewel, oh, indeed, and I'm just a, a . . . I want to be a rocket scientist for you; I know you like rockets. Unfortunately, all I can do is, er, you know. This is a very complicated decision for us to make, Elena, with many, many factors, such as, I mean, what if I'm not the one for you? Because if you leave me, I'll never forgive you. I'd rather be the one to, to—aren't I contemptible? Lyalochka, I can't sleep anymore for thinking of you! Please don't leave me for a rocket scientist! And no heroes, either! You'd better not be attracted to brave individuals who like to go places; I'm only a mollusk; I need to hide forever within your lovely shell . . .

6

The red glow of embers seen through her hair as they lay by the hearth in Luga, then her vehement kisses, and his mouth on her cunt (his tongue seeking as tenderly as a true pianist's fingers, obeying the timbre of her sighs, to give pleasure as exactly as he could: in short, her sighs were the score; his kisses were the performance; which is also to say that his kisses were the score, and her sighs the performance, the music of Opus 40 itself); and his mouth on her mouth when he penetrated her, and the unearthly beauty of her face in orgasm, and the way she held him tight for a long long time until they drowsed with his penis still inside her; they were still literally one flesh—all this seems to be grammatically the subject (but please confirm this with Comrade Academician Alexandrov); the verb comes only here; because these various acts, occurrences and results have become, as were their bodies, one thing, a coherent self-sufficiency of being which, like a noun, simply is; what they did is what they were; they were love; when she sighed, she sighed *I love you* and then her soft, smooth arms went rigid so that she could brace herself against the warm hearthstones and the sighs became inarticulate expressions of ecstasy, by which I mean again music.

He said to her: Thank you for all the happiness you've given me.

She kissed him passionately. His music became as heavy-lidded as the eyes of Käthe Kollwitz.

7

He could sight-read her, so to speak; he knew how to make her feel as though an orchestra were playing. (Well, wasn't it?) This facility he lost later in life, around the time that the Berlin Wall went up; women began complaining that this Shostakovich had no erotic empathy—one of the two reasons why G. Ustvolskaya would refuse to marry him in 1954. By then he was talking to himself; after Nina died he used to say, I think to the piano: Oh, me, oh, my, Elena; well, if it's not working as it is, then maybe we should leave it and, you know, avoid our mistakes next time we're each with a, a, I'm sorry. That's just my, how should I say, my *personal* point of view.—But he hadn't lost anything in 1934, neither courage nor confidence, let alone integrity; in 1935 he still sparkled with jokes; Elena never stopped laughing! She counted on him to keep her always highspirited; that was one of the myriad ways he cherished her; he remained untouched by what I'll call history, which is why I assert that foreseeing the future is as worthless as observing that the third theme of Opus 40's fourth movement appears more uneven on the page than does the second theme of the first movement. But imagining the future, then mistaking imagination for foresight, is one of life's luxuries; certainly it seemed to him and her (and how could it have been otherwise?) that whenever they kissed they were drinking the future.

Kissing her again and again, he got drunk. All around them both, the dull grey and pinkish-grey building-fronts of Leningrad angled and articulated in accordance with canal-curves. One more kiss, Lyalochka! When he slowly slid his finger in and out of her, she uttered soft clucking sounds from deep within her throat, her eyes closed in ecstasy.

8

The extent of his infatuation with this young woman (who was still, by the way, a member in good standing of the Komsomol—no matter that she smoked cigarettes) may best be conveyed by noting that three weeks into their affair, in June, he had to leave on a concert tour; in July he met Nina in Yalta, then vacationed with her in Polenevo, where the cellist V. Kubatsky, pitying his desperation, implored him to distract himself by composing a new sonata, and the very next month, within a few days of their return to Leningrad, Nina had already moved out, at which her husband burst into tears and said: It's entirely superfluous to, to, how can I make my point, Ninusha, to take the line of least resistance and . . . Then he rushed off to take Elena Konstantinovskaya to another concert.

9

That was on the the thirteenth of August. He walked down the great avenue of trees in Alexander Park, just so he could, you know, think about Elena. On the nineteeth of September, the fourth movement of Opus 40 was already finished, because he couldn't help, how should I say, bustling about; as a small child he'd never been able to sit still in his chair, so his mother had to, never mind. Elena wept when he played her score on his piano: In affairs of the heart, my friends, considerable weeping tends to go on as part of the, you know, background music. On 10 March 1935, he informed his closest confidant, Sollertinsky, that he might never come back to Leningrad; he could now envision himself in Moscow with Elena, where we'll have a little, you know, with two sets of four rooms. His mother had never liked Nina anyway—not that she liked Elena much better, but his sister Maryusa adored her. In Moscow the two of us can get away from everything; we'll start over and I'll never see Nina again. And indeed it was in Moscow that he showed L. T. Atovmyan his divorce certificate.

10

What about Nina? Well, what about her? The late S. Khentova, in whose *Udivitelyenui Shostakovich* (1993) forty-two of Shostakovich's letters to Elena are published, although not without the excisions of certain intimacies (I have all that right here, but it's going to stay in my secret collection), bequeathed us the following summation of the two rivals: *In contrast to Nina Vasilievna, who was not interested in fashion, she dressed elegantly, cultivating grace, femininity and sensuality.*

All the same, he did come back to Nina—twice.

11

Khentova, whom Shostakovich avoided like death, cannot always be trusted. I'm not saying she was in the hire of any foreign powers; I do maintain that her intelligence service was less reliable than mine. For example, she claims that our composer did not become Elena Konstantinovskaya's lover until the summer of 1934, when one of the private English classes in his apartment *ended with kisses.* But Opus 40 itself proves that their love was consummated in the very first movement, the *allegro non troppo.* No doubt they took precautions on those white nights. He hadn't yet volunteered to leave Nina; nor had Elena become unshakably certain of her love for him. So they hid within their eight-chambered house where even sharp-eyed Khentova couldn't see. They fooled Mravinsky, Glikman, Sollertinsky, Nina unquestionably (come to think of it, perhaps they didn't fool Nina), and most impressively, Shostakovich's mother, who still read his diary whenever she could. Deep down they went, down to the red core that he'd revisit alone twenty-six years later, when he composed Opus 110.

A pianist can sometimes resemble a slow underwater swimmer, and a lover likewise swims within the sea of the other, far down where no waves can reach; overhead, the piano's lid, heavier than a coffin's, shuts out extraneous vibrations, while simultaneously demarcating the boundary between water and air. It's too perfect underwater; that's what kills us, the perfection! (This is not my theory, of course; I don't believe in perfection.) And the addictive poisonousness of this perfection was what flooded Shostakovich with the joy of something illicit, first when he was a boy playing weirdness on the piano when others expected a foxtrot; and now when he was Nina's husband and playing out his passion for Elena. Another English lesson, pretty please, Lyalotchka! Elena is to poor Nina as Opus 110, the Eighth

String Quartet, will be to the First, which its composer dismisses as *a particular exercise in the form of a quartet.* Forgive me, Ninusha!

12

After the divorce went through, he went to his previous muse, T. Glivenko, and said to her with a sad laugh: I have a very clever wife, oh, yes—very clever . . .

13

Because he couldn't stop kissing her, her delightfully puffy lips were the next parts of her to get translated. In the course of translation, he necessarily sucked on them. Private English lessons, oh, me, oh, my! He couldn't stop! And so Elena's lips kiss us all forever in the second movement. Elenka dearest, I'm going to write a, let's see, a Moscow Concerto, so that you and I can go to Moscow! And there we'll do it again, oh, yes, Lyalka, we'll orchestrate something else all over again! Because you're my . . .

Then her hair—oh, her, how should I say, her, well, her long, dark hair . . .

14

Right here in *Sovetskaya Muzika,* number three, a certain D. D. Shostakovich denies translation in any specific sense. He's like one of those wretches I deal with at the office every day; they grovel and admit to being Trotskyites, but then when I demand a detailed confession, with acts and especially names, they try to wriggle out of it. Can you imagine? In that same spirit, Shostakovich says to *Sovetskaya Muzika: When a critic for* Worker and Theater *or for* The Evening Red Gazette *writes that in such-and-such a symphony Soviet civil servants are represented by the oboe and the clarinet, and Red Army men by the brass section, you want to scream!*

Well, at my office we know what we hear. And if Shostakovich wants to argue with us, we'll take him down into the cellars and show him what screaming's all about. He has the impudence to deny her long, dark hair.

15

I promise you that from the first time she took his hand—the very first time!—he actually believed; she was ready, lonely, beautiful; she wanted someone to love with all her heart and he was the man; she longed to take care of him, knowing even better than he how much he needed to be taken care of—he still couldn't knot his necktie by himself, and, well, you know. He believed, because an artist must believe as easily and deeply as a child cries. What's creation but self-enacted belief?—Now for a cautionary note from E. Mravinsky: Shostakovich's music is *self-ironic,* which to me implies insincerity. *This masquerade imparts the spurious impression that Shostakovich is being emotional. In reality, his music conceals extremely deep lyric feelings which are carefully protected from the outside world.* In other words, is Shostakovich emotional or not? Feelings conceal—feelings! Could it be that this languishing longing I hear in Opus 40 actually masks something else? But didn't he promise Elena that she was the one for him? And how can love be self-ironic? All right, I do remember the rocking-horse sequence, but isn't that self-mockery simply self-abnegation, the old lover's trick? Elena believes in me, I know she does! How ticklishly wonderful! Even Glikman can see it, although perhaps I shouldn't have told Glikman, because . . . What can love be if not faith? We look into each other's faces and *believe*: Here's the one for me! Lyalya, never forget this, no matter how long you live and whatever happens between us: You will always be the one for me. And in my life I'll *prove* it. You'll see. Sollertinsky claims that Elena's simply lonely. What if Elena's simply twenty? Well, I'm lonely, too. Oh, this Moscow-Baku train is so boring. I can't forgive myself for not kidnapping my golden Elenochka and bringing her to Baku with me. Or does she, how shall I put this, want too much from destiny? My God, destiny is such a ridiculous word. I'll try not to be too, I mean, *why not*? It's still early in my life. That nightmare of the whirling red spot won't stop me! I could start over with Elena and . . . *She loves me.* Ninusha loves me, but Elena, oh, my God, she stares at me with hope and longing; her love remains unimpaired, like a child's. I love children. I want to be a father. I'll tell Nina it's because she can't have children. That won't hurt her as much as, you know. Actually, it's true, because Nina . . . Maybe I can inform her by letter, so I don't have to . . . Ashkenazi will do that for me if I beg him. He's very kind, very kind. Then it will be over! As soon as I'm back in my Lyalka's arms I'll have the strength to resolve everything. If I could only protect that love of hers from ever falling down and skinning its knee, much less from growing up, growing wise and bitter! Then when she's old she'll still look at me like that; I'll still be the one for her.

It's true that you didn't even tell your mother and sisters when you got married?

My dear Elenochka, that's true, oh, yes, because, you see, I, I *didn't want to.* Let's go to the Summer Garden and . . .

You didn't want to what?

I didn't want to marry Nina! But I couldn't bring myself to hurt her, and she, well.

And do you want to stay married to her?

No, he said steadily.

Whom is it, if anyone, that you want to marry?

You, Elena!

Are you sure?

Yes, I'm sure.

Then she laughed for joy and pounced on him; that was the genesis of the fourth movement (*allegro* again); call it a sprightly yet stately dance in a minor key, a dance not of skeletons—they're too mischievous, too *dramatic* for that!—although for a moment Opus 40 does lapse into what will become Shostakovich's signature greyness. The piano brings it back to life: Elena and Shostakovich are stalking each other like cats! A renowned pianist who has performed this composition argues that *the brilliance here is sinister rather than exhibitionistic;* I disagree; Shostakovich is happy! Here comes the *pizzicato:* Elena is drawing her long fingernails lightly and lovingly down his belly. Then the piano cascades gleefully into a warm bed of strings, where the young couple's bright, brisk, expert lovemaking glitters at us. (Why expert? Because they're expert in each other.—Mitya dear, I'm so happy, I can almost taste gingerbread!) Back to the opening song, the richly Russian tune, which stretches itself in several postcoital variations; then Opus 40 ends in a delicious surprise of snapping teeth: that was when Elena bit him again—a nice mark of ownership, right there on the side of his neck!

16

In Baku the sea-wind covered the grand piano with sand. So many people came to his concert that we requested him to perform again the next day, which he did, because he could never say no to anyone who was nice with him; then he went out to the restaurant "New Europe" to hear gypsy songs. Every time the gypsies sang of love he almost cried, but not quite. He knew now that without Elena he would die. And he was meeting Nina in Yalta. He had headaches; it was all Elena's fault . . .

That love-bite of Elena's, it was itching now. He felt happy when he scratched it. How could he represent it musically? He got drunk and showed it off to the gypsies, who applauded. Well, in the fourth movement, at the very end, I'll, I'll—just wait and I'll show you all! I'm going to make her live forever, because . . . Oh, Lyalya, oh, God. When he thought of Elena he was sure that he could do anything.

17

Since so many souvenirs of her have been found in this sonata—doubtless, many more await the discovery of musicologists—can we speak of a Konstantinovskaya Theme in Opus 40?

First of all, for the benefit of persons such as my good colleague Pyotr Alexeev, who's a musical illiterate, allow me to draw three distinctions: *Motif* is a very nineteenth-century sort of term, which is not the slightest bit applicable to our Soviet music today.* *Leitmotiv,* which we most often find applied specifically to Wagner, is a very short passage relating to a character, object or event: for instance, the Magic Fire music. Leave that to the Fascists, I say! *Theme,* at least in Shostakovich, gets worked out, developed, is longer.

It's now widely agreed in progressive social circles that all humankind constitutes a single superorganism. Extending this correct line to culture, why not consider Shostakovich's body of work as a whole? In that sense, a Konstantinovskaya Theme can be detected from 1934 to 1960. According to Beria, Yagoda and T. N. Khrennikov, its characteristics are rainbow tones oozing unpredictably into puddles of metallic greyness, dance melodies which alternate between ponderous and skeletal, and, most happily, achromatic patterns which soar into regions beyond human comprehension, a perfect example of the latter being the Fugue in A Minor which lives within Opus 87.

---

* The so-called "D-S-C-H signature," which will be discussed later, in my analysis of Opus 110, is by this simple criterion akin to a motif: in other words, it's not relevant to the people. Accordingly, any references to an "E-E-K signature" must be contemptuously dismissed as anti-Soviet provocation. As we like to say, it's *no accident* that even in Moser's *Musik Lexikon,* published in the very first year of the Thousand Year Reich, Shostakovich gets passed over. *Sousa* and *Serbian music* are present; they'll soon be considered enemies. Under *Russische Musik,* Shostakovich's teacher Glazunov receives a nod on page 721, and below him a *Gruppe Glasunow* sits reverentially assembled. Glazunov, you see, was a classicist; Shostakovich is a formalist. Even the German Fascists know poison when they see it.

Loyalty to the state now requires me to step back and take the long view. Can we lay bare the context of the Konstantinovskaya Theme? How shall we define the general character of D. D. Shostakovich's production?

The East German musicologist Ekkehard Ochs, writing after Shostakovich's death in a spirit of appropriately comradely reverentiality, reminds us of the dialectic process: *When the world changes, so does the man, so the composer, and art also.* The same source speaks of his symphonies' dialectic between life and death. In this spirit, we find Shostakovich writing to a certain E. Konstantinovskaya: *I try to stop loving you and instead I love you more and more. There is much sadness and disappointment in my love to you. Very complex circumstances* (how should I write this, so that she'll, you know, not hate me?) *play a very important role here.*

18

Others—optimistic, public-spirited types—have claimed to find in Opus 40 (probably in the second movement) the smell of flowers at Kirov's funeral. Who am I to say that I can't smell flowers? But I can't. When I inhale Opus 40, I scent woodsmoke, wine and Elena's hair.

19

They went to a showing of R. L. Karmen's "Comrade Dmitrov in Moscow," because the film sounded so boring that no one they knew would be likely to go, not even Glikman. When the Kino Palace was dark, she held his hand. From this experience derives the third movement, the *largo* (completed on 13 September), which might sound melancholy to those who don't know Shostakovich, particularly the later Shostakovich; in fact this is his secret bunker, the deepest of his heart's four chambers, whose roof is timbered with regular bass-notes of the piano. Here the piano and the cello sing a duet which might sound sad to the rest of the world, or even (here's Elena's favorite English word) *creepy,* but they've hidden themselves away so safely that there is no one else to hear them, let alone misjudge them; they have shut the Danube's gates! In its darkest corners, the room is irregular, its bass roof-timbers as fantastic as the whalebone beams of an ancient Arctic dwelling; and in this darkness, Shostakovich and Elena Konstantinovskaya fall asleep in each other's arms, her head on his chest, his ankles locked around hers; they're like two vines grown together in an old graveyard.

20

On 1 December, the assassin Nikolayev took the life of our beloved Comrade Kirov—a treacherous blow, for which we set out to make the foreign spies and wreckers pay in full. On 4 December the first death sentences were issued. On 29 December we shot Nikolayev, who double-doomed himself by attempting to implicate the highest circles of our Soviet state. By mid-January we were arresting his accomplices by the tens of thousands. Meanwhile, Shostakovich was living with his darling Ninotchka again! When she returned, he cried: Oh, thank you, thank you, thank you very much!—He wrote Elena that he continued to be so busy nursing his Ninusha through a serious illness that he hadn't found time to telephone her. Please forgive me, my dear Lyalya, because I . . .

Elena declined to answer.

Then he rang her up in terror, whispering: Lyalya, I have a very strange feeling, a very *creepy* feeling as you would probably say . . .

He felt that he was being watched. How ridiculous! Of course he was being watched!

He was still a hero in those days. If I may say so, he didn't have a clue.

He started taking her out to concerts again. He needed more English lessons. (Sollertinsky had gotten nowhere trying to teach him German.) He went home with her (65 Kirovsky Prospekt, number 20). When they made love they were so noisy that the neighbors pounded on the walls. That's the second movement for you! The cellist A. Ferkelman, who performed Opus 40 with Shostakovich in 1939, informs us that *I never succeeded in getting any other pianist to take such fast tempi. His playing was on the dry side, but on the other hand he played extremely loudly, doubtless on account of his great force of temperament.* In short, he still loved her. They played the third movement with diabolical ease; all the same, something wasn't right in Elena's song. He wept and said: Lyalka, I don't believe that I'll be yours and you'll be mine. Sometimes I do; sometimes I don't. Now my mood is such that I find it very difficult to, you know, believe.

Elena was sitting beside him at the Kirov Theater, just before the curtain rose on his new opera "Lady Macbeth." Wordlessly she slipped her coat over her shoulders, rose up, turned away and walked out.

21

He rushed after her; he knelt down in the dirty slush and begged. (I was there, trailing A. Akhmatova; I remember snow on the iron fence around the Summer Garden, snow on the Summer Garden's trees.) And she took him home with her; she knew he loved her! What was he so afraid of? Between the two of them they'd long since determined the way that the second movement begins, with its haunting Russian melody in a minor key, passageways of Rodchenko-like golden scaffolding subsequently connecting it to a merry melody which after a very particular, never to be replicated cello-caress becomes buttery-sweet and brief, because he was on his back and she was astride him, teasing him with the succulent inner lips of her cunt and slowly possessing him, taking orgasm after orgasm, forbidding him to move, pausing whenever she liked, as long as she liked; and all the while he had to keep lying perfectly still like a good boy! Then comes that rocking-horse sequence I've mentioned, which transforms itself into another sweet eternity of melting butter: He'd finished, and Elena was back on top of him again, riding him in just the way she liked until she climaxed with the sound of a honeybee, the bow passing smoothly and shrilly across the sounding board. Returning to the Russian melody, Opus 40 then gives the piano another turn at pleasuring itself, so that a second rocking-horse copulation gallops to a happy ejaculation, at which point the piano sparkles and glows; I have it on good authority that at that point they were making love at dawn, and right before they finished, the sounds of morning began as the sun sparkled and glared most busily upon an upturned water-glass, transforming it into an improbable spider-jewel whose legs were beams of white light.

22

The true story of Opus 40 comes to an end at the end of a certain night in the summer of 1935, when the sleepless woman finally dialed Shostakovich's number. Nina answered and curtly said: He's staying with me.

I kept waiting and waiting by the telephone, whispered Elena, just in case he was going to call.

23

Regarding Opus 40, Shostakovich remained everlastingly coy, no doubt for Nina's sake, but he did state for the record that a certain great breakthrough (or, as the Germans would say, *ein grosser Durchbruch*) took place for him that year in the sphere of chamber and concert platform music. (Shostakovich to Konstantinovskaya: *Why did I meet you? Why did I fall in love? I could have lived peacefully. My life as it was does not exist anymore.*)

The premiere took place on 25 December 1935. Elena Konstantinovskaya was absent. Those who wish us ill would doubtless insist on drawing attention to the fact that, following the line laid down by Comrade Stalin, we'd arrested a few thousand more of those scum by then, including Elena. I'm well aware that in the transit prison she received a postcard from Shostakovich—another black mark against him. Having verified all the documents in this matter, I can assure you that the reorganization of the Komsomol had become urgently necessary by then; every district branch was crawling with class enemies. Nothing definite was ever proved against Elena. All the same, let's not cry crocodile tears over inconveniences suffered by a person who was, like all persons, the legitimate focus of interest of our Soviet state. Far more germane to this study of Opus 40 is the fact that the concert, as I can personally testify, was a success, I might even say a glittering success. So what if she wasn't present? After all, the composer had dedicated it not to her but to his friend V. Kubatsky. ▸

OPERATION MAGIC FIRE

◪

And it's in that vague grey middle ground that the fundamental conflicts of our age take place. It's a huge ant hill in which we all crawl.

—Shostakovich (ca. 1970)

1

The Poles say that life itself is a long smelly train of refugees which travels Europe's slowest tracks, getting shunted aside to make room for military transports and industrial freight; there everyone sits, sweltering, stinking, fearing and grieving. The whistle shouts; time to move again! Here comes the next border, where policemen and plainclothesmen will winnow more of us away (her visa is incorrect; he's actually an escaped Jew). The most laughable thing is that we hated life; we wanted to "get somewhere"; and now that they're taking us somewhere by the truckload, we wish that we were still on that long train where everything stank! Well, that's life, all right.

2

The story goes, and for all I know it hasn't yet been discredited, that a quarter-hour after the best performance of Wagner's "Siegfried" since our German recovery began, a certain sleepwalker retired to Haus Wahnfried, where the composer himself once lived, and as soon as Winifred Wagner had poured the tea and he'd kissed Verena Wagner's wrist, those two ladies withdrew, Göring shut the door behind them, and Colonel Hagen, who'd been waiting in the corridor, led in a German businessman whose financial interests coincided with those of General Franco. This was the summer of 1936, when Franco's cause remained desperate. Indeed, our Foreign Office most earnestly advised the sleepwalker not to involve himself, especially since the rebels needed not only bombs, but money. Herr Schacht at the Reichsbank kept warning that we couldn't afford to rearm ourselves, let alone underwrite other people's adventures. The sleepwalker, however, reasoned as follows: If Franco fails, then the leftist government in Spain will surely become a Communist satellite. And if that happens, France will also go Red, at which point our Reich will be menaced both from the East and from the West.—And wasn't he correct? What brought us down in the end, but a two-front war?—In short, he agreed to help the Falangists. On the desert airstrip, our long line of propeller planes stood ready to stab the air with their needle-noses. (Incidentally, he also dismissed Herr Schacht, thereby saving him from getting hanged by the victors of 1945.)

And so our Condor Legion drew first blood; the Blitzkrieg got worked out. The aerial bombardment of Guernica turned out to be a contrapuntal masterpiece, and our new machine-guns didn't jam, either. We did what we chose to; Mussolini's Blue Arrow troops took up the slack. I think we can all agree that the war advanced rapidly. Three years later, there was Franco in the capital, with his trademark cigarette half burned down between his fingers. Mussolini sent him a bill, but we were more generous; we took the longer view.

The sleepwalker not only initiated this exercise, he also named it: Operation Magic Fire.

3

Now, in point of fact, it's at the very end of "Die Walküre," not in "Siegfried" at all, that the famous Magic Fire music occurs. Traditionally the four operas in the *Ring* Cycle get performed in an afternoon and three evenings; so when Colonel Hagen led in the businessman and Verena Wagner poured tea, it would have been only the previous night that "Die Walküre" was sung. I grant that that's well within the bounds of a memory which was always supposed to be perfect; I'm referring to those statistics on troop dispositions and tank production, eternally ready on our Führer's lips! If anybody on earth knew the *Ring* by heart, it would have been he. That's precisely the reason I want to know why he didn't draw on "Siegfried" when he christened the operation. After all, that opera offers plenty of dramatically appropriate music to choose from: the reforging of the sword, the slaying of the dragon, etcetera.

One of my most plausible speculations (I adore inventing those, since I can't be held responsible for them) is that he'd already made up his mind to aid the Falangists on Valkyrie Night. After all, why would he have troubled himself to meet the businessman at all if he hadn't already made his decision? For he was not exactly the sort of fellow whose conclusions could be altered by discusssion.

But it is also possible that the magic fire in and of itself means something in our Spanish context. Recapitulation: Brunnhilde has disobeyed Wotan by doing what he would have done himself, had he not been constrained by his own resentful promise: she saves Siegmund from death in his duel with Hunding, who's an impure, un-German element. (Our sleepwalker could empathize with Wotan. He got quite angry whenever he had to pretend to endorse this or that non-aggression pact.) Wotan accordingly slays Siegmund for duty, Hunding for pleasure, disowns Brunnhilde, casts her into a supernatural sleep, and finally rings her round with flames which only a hero (Siegmund's son Siegfried, as it will transpire) would dare to cross.

The scene is touching. Wotan, doomed and perjured ever since the very first opera, "Das Rheingold," knows all too well that Brunnhilde is right. This correctness of hers springs from instinct; as such, it's as impossible to "disprove" as Aryan superiority. Brunnhilde *is* Wotan, more than Wotan is himself. This is why he loves her so much.

He rumbles out a lullaby whose last words are: *For so goes the god from you; so he kisses your godhead away.* His voice cherishes and broods. Then it trails off. After a moment of silence, the music becomes tense, imperious. Wotan is now invoking Loki, the amoral fire-spirit. (I seem to see the Condor Legion in a triple line at the edge of their airstrip as a uniformed figure gazes down at them from a hill of flowers and desert shrubs, with their biplanes waiting.) He strikes his staff upon the ground. Instantly the fire springs up, walling in the sleeping woman who was once a Valkyrie. The biplanes take off! Wagner's genius makes the fire music pleasant, not threatening. Loki is all play. He's anything and everything. He eats a bad woman's half-burned heart, gets pregnant, and gives birth to the race of ogres. He saves us from cold and he roasts us to death. His essence dances with equal gusto atop Brunnhilde's mountain and the pyres at Dresden. Probably it is for this reason that when I hear the Magic Fire music I imagine not the rainbow of flame which the motif, played in isolation, might suggest, but the blue and green flames which spring from sea-salted driftwood. Wotan sings no more; the opera is ending now; but I seem to see him, black-cloaked and leaning on his staff, as he stands outside the circle which protects the daughter he has lost.

So let's kiss away democracy from Spain! Let's put her to sleep for a hundred years! Now here comes the wall of flame, flowering up from the metal seeds we've sown; and if you care to know how we planted them, I'll draw you a full-page, double-column illustration of airplane formations: the *Gruppenwinkel:* three V's in a row; the *Gruppenkeil:* three groups of three V's, each of which consists of three machines, with the center one below the other two; meanwhile the centermost of the three groups likewise flies below its neighbors so that this constellation itself forms one more immense V; I should also mention the *Staffelkolonne links,* the *Staffelwinkel.* When we flew to Valencia, our *Gruppenkeil* dropped many seeds at once, each one something between a bullet and a dart, with a stinger on its end; they tumbled two by two through the air.

But now that everything has gone so wrong, I wonder which fairy godmother we forgot to invite to the christening of Operation Magic Fire?

4

One evening almost five years later, Colonel Hagen and I agreed to meet for a steak dinner at the Ausland Club on the Leipziger Platz. I arrived early, so I had a beer and sat reading in the newspapers about the China Affair. Speaking frankly, even though the Japanese were now our allies and had even been labeled "honorary Aryans," until then I had never been very much interested in the atrocities and conquests of the Greater East Asia Co-Prosperity Sphere. No doubt this reveals my own limitations. I don't know why I even remember the China Affair now. After all, I was never in China.—And we were having our own difficulties by then; let's call them harmonic stresses. Austria, Czechoslovakia, Poland, France, even Norway, those operations had all gone satisfactorily (no one would deny that it's healthy for us Germans to try to get what we want), but now the most powerful nations on earth were against us—naturally I didn't count Russia in their number, since the sleepwalker had informed us that we only had to kick in the door and the whole rotten structure would come crashing down; moreover, we'd signed a treaty of near-eternal friendship with those Russians. What next? Our German machine-guns were faster than most other varieties, the French for instance, but a drunken gunner whose legs had gotten blown off in the siege of Warsaw wanted me to tell him whether we could keep making enough machine-guns to take on the whole world.—Absolute confidence, I replied to him, that is our capital. That's what will see us through.

But I wasn't confident myself. I was whistling in the graveyard. For months, British time bombs had been falling in the Tiergarten, and yet the sleepwalker had aborted Operation Sea Lion; he knew he couldn't conquer England. Franco wouldn't help us, either; the sleepwalker had made a personal appeal, which went nowhere; Franco merely smiled and smoked another cigarette; I don't know what to say about a man like that.

And so the sleepwalker occupied himself in covering central Europe with Wagner's melodic castles, which are built up of varied repetitions. But England was getting stronger. The Amis,* manipulated by their Jew President, Roosevelt, were helping them and might enter the war at any time. Meanwhile the sleepwalker was reasoning: Eastern Poland is now a Communist satellite. If we don't step in soon, our own new eastern lands will be imperiled; the Russians can break through the Ribbentrop-Molotov Line before we know it. Reacting to *that* won't be quite as easy as organizing one of our motorcycle parades! In short, everything good was already rationed; everything bad was coming. So what did I care about China? And yet I remember everything about that night so perfectly! Let's not call it a Wagnerian presentiment.

Speaking of presentiments, I now feel confident that Hagen already knew about Operation Barbarossa. We were all going to have to be brave, brutal and loyal.

When he came, he looked grimmer than ever. He didn't want to drink beer, so we ordered a bottle of blackish-red Romanian wine. He said to me: How well do you remember our national epic?

The one that's seven hundred years old, or the one we're writing now?

They're the same. Do you remember how Siegfried bled anew in his coffin when the murderer passed by? That's why I ordered the dark wine.

An ancient German touch! I said to him. But blood is only blood. When Siegfried was killed, his wife wept tears of blood. What did that signify? The poet wrote it in to give us a hint of what's coming. The intention must have been to unify past and future, but to me it's a cheap touch, like your drinking wine to make a point. You don't even like wine.

I stand guilty! he replied with a laugh. But next time we meet at Bayreuth, I expect you to protest those gloomy *leitmotivs* in the *Ring*! Of course, then Verena Wagner won't smile at you anymore . . .

---

*Americans.

5

When I think back on Operation Magic Fire, I seem to see Verena Wagner in her slim-waisted white dress (it was so white that it was really cotton-white, like a puff of antiaircraft smoke); she was pouring tea for her Uncle Wolf, who was our uncle, too *(Meyers Lexikon,* 1938: *He is no dictator, suppressing the disenfranchised, but Führer of a believing people, who fully trust in him and enclose him in their utter love*), her wrist displaying sequence and variation;* and for some reason I also visualize that perfect antiaircraft light on the wall of swastika standards and on the long glittering rectangles of steel men; that was the Berlin Nazi rally of 1.5.36, half a year before Verena Wagner served Magic Fire's tea; Franco remained a nothing then; even after Magic Fire had surrounded Spain, and the sleepwalker shut that case folder for good, life was almost the same; the British still believed in peace in our time! So had Siegfried's wife.

Magic Fire's ambiguous, almost keyless chords have fooled many listeners. The tone color is red and orange; everything seems cheerful; as the Amis say, it's only the hearth fires burning. Condor legionnaires sang round the campfire; Franco handed out medals from a little white-clothed table. Barbarossa beckoned; Verena Wagner wiggled her wrist enchantingly; she poured us a war whose various cases, maneuvers and operations would be as tight as the berets of the clean young men in our Condor Legion. And so the *leitmotiv* was vindicated. ▸

---

*In old days, kings gilded the horns of their favorite cows, and I wouldn't have been surprised if that gold bracelet she wore was from Uncle Wolf.

AND I'D DRY MY SALTY HAIR

And I'd dry my salty hair
on a flat rock far from land.
—Anna Akhmatova (1914)

1

On 23 August 1942, when Air Fleet Four's Stukas and Ju-88s were bombing Stalingrad, our Komsomol members rallied to the assistance of citizens who came out between waves of planes to sort corpses and ruins. Whenever anyone recognized a body, the Komsomols instantly embraced him. This made a valid contribution to our defense; I'm not against using children where they're needed. And the previous September, A. A. Akhmatova had spoken on the radio to extol the bravery of Leningrad's women, who were already dying by the thousands. In light of her fame (the sole reason her punishment had been delayed), this broadcast must be considered the equivalent of ten Stalin tanks sent directly to the front. At least that's what Comrade Zhdanov said to me. From my point of view, the correct thing to do would have been to erase her from the picture and then blame the Fascists. (A German shell landed; brown smoke rose up.) But nobody listens to me. I'm certainly willing to agree that a consistent policy is better than no policy, which is why we demanded that Shostakovich complete his Seventh Symphony, the one now known to the world as the "Leningrad." This task he successfully fulfilled in December. Upon the personal recommendation of Comrade Zhdanov we'd even evacuated the bastard, and his family, too. Akhmatova got the same treatment. As Comrade Zhdanov remarked to me, we could deal with her later.

She was said to be rather freakish, I mean exotic, in bed, probably on account of her well-known talent for hooking her leg behind her neck. What she did with A. Lourie you wouldn't believe. Yet she was equally renowned for her coolly retiring politeness. Oh, ice wouldn't have melted in her mouth! That's why my job is so important; I expose those people! I've seen that drawing of her, the one we should have seized and sold abroad; those libertine Counts they still have in the West would have paid enough to endow an orphanage or a collective farm. Pyotr Alexeev has informed me that it's her souvenir of a rose-strewn tryst with Modigliani in Paris shortly after her first marriage.

We've obtained photographs of her various affairs. She used to be the biggest joke going at our office, a *standing* joke, said Pyotr Alexeev, and I won't tell you what he meant. It's untrue that she was nearsighted, but like most of these so-called "intellectuals," she kept her precious head up her ass, or somebody else's—you can't imagine all the filthy things I've seen her do!—so it proved a simple enough business to keep an eye on her. I for my part enjoy more of a challenge. If I say so myself, I'm very adept at foiling the designs of sneaks. For instance, had he been left to me, Solzhenitsyn never could have smuggled his poisonous *Gulag Archipelago* to the other side. Once it fell into the hands of *The New York Times,* that so-called "history" did us incalculable harm. In time we'll give him what Trotsky got.

One thing I'll say for Akhmatova: She cooperated with us, for the sake of her son. (One of her postwar odes runs: *Where Stalin is, is freedom, / Earth's grandeur, and peace!* What a good little whore!) From our point of view she really did keep her nose clean—as clean as anyone can who sticks her nose up other people's . . . —oh, the things I've seen!

Ignorant people say that she founded a secret society of grief. Take it from me; that never happened. I'm in a position to say so. I know what that woman ate for breakfast for the past thirty years!

I do grant that she had her admirers. The Seventh Northern Elegy is clever enough, for all its unwholesomeness. (To tell you the truth, literature bores me.) The first time I saw her, she was wearing one of her many necklaces, posing in profile, wrapped up in herself, with her eyes slyly half-closed.—Not bad! I said to Pyotr Alexeev.—Amidst the other poets of her time, she stood out as much as E. E. Konstantinovskaya would have if she'd been transported into one of Larionov's paintings of pinkish-purple-fleshed, meaty-thighed dancers.

The Trotskyite N. Punin, who admitted to drinking her urine and whom I myself personally arrested—you'll like this part: We disposed of his predecessor Gumilyev on 25 August 1921, so when we took Punin away,* in '49, we waited until 26 August, just to keep her guessing!—liked to argue, and I've got his exact words somewhere, that art does not so much derive from life as actually change the perception and appreciation of it, casting itself across existence *like a shadow.* Unfortunately, he was correct. Derivative as she was, Akhmatova definitely made her mark—like a bitch in heat. It wasn't just her perverted lovers; it was our Soviet culture that she pissed on.

2

Anna Akhmatova, née Gorenko, is best known for two poems, first and foremost the nasty "Requiem," which attacks the "organs" of state security, and incidentally slanders our prison system. Shostakovich was among that literary effort's admirers; I wish I had enough space to tell you a few things about that cocksucker. (On the other hand, he did make us laugh from time to time; I don't mind telling you that my job has its compensations. In 1953 Akhmatova was trying to impress him with some drivel she'd written about his Seventh Symphony, and he thanked her in his usual insincere fashion, then went to the Hotel Sovietskaya and said to his then mistress, G. I. Ustvolskaya, ingenuously assuming the walls don't have ears: *Basically, I can't bear having poetry written about my music.)* Our line on that so-called "work of art" was this: Since she had the good sense not to make a cause out of it, why not let her live out her pathetic little life? We'd already isolated her. Shooting her might have lost us hard currency in the West. Since "Requiem" accuses us, and we already know ourselves, it's of zero investigative interest.

That leaves the "Poem Without a Hero," whose publication I for my part have always welcomed. Do you remember when Hitler staged that exhibition of degenerate art? Don't get me wrong; every time I see a German I want to string him up by the balls; nonetheless, I'm man enough to say this straight: Hitler wasn't incorrect in that instance. Now, "Poem Without a Hero" is as degenerate as anything the Nazis banned. It portrays the so-called "life" of a clique of a parasites and intellectuals in Leningrad before our Revolution. This was the Symbolist epoch, whose atmosphere N. Berdayev aptly charac-

---

*I quote from his diary: *If I myself don't understand anything in art, what then do I understand? The "living" person and that's all. Keep shooting live people; they get in people's way, in the proletariat's way. Keep shooting.*

terized as *the putrefied air of a hothouse*. My children even studied it in school (I had the teacher arrested). To me the main interest of the poem is this: All the characters are real, in which case have we identified all those bastards and sent them where they belong?

3

Once upon a time I found beauty, but beauty left me. I can't say that I'm the worse for the experience, because it helped me appreciate that pallid, dreamy face, the dark eyes and dark bangs, the shadowy sensuality of Akhmatova. After the war her portrait hung in the Shostakoviches' apartment in Moscow; I know why. That famous regality of hers, which so many found condescending, was a quality entirely lacking in Elena Konstantinovskaya, who was shy rather than retiring, sad instead of grave. Akhmatova's calm was impregnable, thanks to the greatness which she knew herself to possess, or be possessed by; Konstantinovskaya's was a leaden defensive mask. Both women proved extraordinarily selfish in love; but in Akhmatova's case we can speak of a higher fidelity to the Muse; in Konstantinovskaya's, of an irremediable disappointment. In 1934 she sent Shostakovich a one-line note in a cipher all her own, with the attached invitation: *Whoever translates this gets to keep me.* I don't mind informing you that we opened this communication and did our best to decode it; we failed. (Pyotr Alexeev wanted to get her for that, but I was magnanimous; I said: Hands off!) The point is that there was, self-evidently, a key to Konstantinovskaya's inner world, and one other person had it. He allowed the key to fall from his hand; he said to himself: What a, a, I mean, what an *error* I've committed! Oh, my God, Lyalka; oh, my God . . . —As for him, he had his own world beneath the piano keys. He was engaged in what it's now fashionable to call *inner emigration*. At my office we don't much care for that term, and I'll tell you why: Hindemith, von Karajan and Furtwängler make music for the Hitlerites, and then, when it's all over, they have the effrontery to plead: Word of honor, I wasn't really *here*! I couldn't possibly have collaborated, since I was living in my head the entire time!—You know what I say to that? I say: Give 'em eight grams! And if you don't know what that means, believe me, you're better off.

Now, what about Akhmatova? In a sense, everybody who could read Russian was invited into *her* inner world. It's true that many of her most so-called "personal" lyrics remained unpublished in her lifetime, but in our Soviet Union we don't give a shit about individualism anyhow. The half-belligerent, half-adoring mockeries by that suicide to be, Mayakovsky, expressed true love, of course, based on an intimate knowlege acquired only through words: icons and ivy, private kisses, ambiguous embraces behind the shutters of old Saint Petersburg. Mayakovsky dreamed of her, to be sure; once I watched him stalk her through the pavilions of the Tauride Garden; but all he got from her was a yellow dress in summer, blue snow in winter, you know, that kind of thing, which any other also gets—talk about promiscuity! Pyotr Alexeev, who although he'll never admit it is still in love with her, insists that every time he rereads "At the Seashore" he inhales the lilac fragrance of Akhmatova's braids. He, Mayakovsky and dozens more—what's wrong with our Russian men?

Shostakovich's inner world was a bunker in which he lived under constant attack. I have a blueprint of it right here. The fact that at any moment one of their eighty-eights or one of our special detachments was going to break through couldn't help but influence the character of his surroundings.

Konstantinovskaya's world was a walled garden with a dead fountain within. Once the fountain had jetted into the air, and the trees had borne flowers and fruit—only once. After 1935, what grew there but rubble and mummies? Well, but the reason why I admire her is that unlike Akhmatova, she made no career out of feeling sorry for herself. Good girl! That Order of the Red Star she got, why shouldn't I inform you that I had something to do with it?

But Akhmatova's world was the semipublic one of Tsarkoe Selo. In the early years of my assignment, trailing her meant promenading along the long, pale-pillared coast of the Catherine Palace. It used to keep me in shape. As a rule, those scum force us to sit in a chair all day listening in on them, so I can't say I hated Akhmatova. In fact, one time I told her that I was considering reading Pushkin's "Bronze Horseman." I asked for advice. Was it really worth my while? I wanted to know. And in that same uninflected voice in which she recited her poetry on demand, she assured me that it would be a waste of my time. I'll always be grateful to her for that, because I'm a busy man.

Sometimes she took me to the Garden of the Toilers on Uritzky Square, where I could inhale a little sunshine. I'm considered excellent at what I do; she never saw me even when she turned on me that smooth cool face like an enamel icon. For a time the Engineering Academy of the Red Army on Ulitsa Rakova, which she persisted in calling Italyanskaya, was also a favorite destination of hers. I didn't mind that; I know a lot of engineers.

Where do you think she was when the February Revolution broke out? At one of Meyerhold's dress rehearsals! It's true that we did see her gliding from barricade to barricade, but not to participate in our struggle, only to do what poets do: play with fire. And what was she doing when we seized power in the October Revolution? Standing on the Liteiny Bridge. Where might she have been in 1936 when the white-clad Stakhanovite workers came marching toward us on Red Square, with the gigantic white image of Comrade Stalin stretching out his arm toward them from atop his column while R. L. Karmen filmed everything? Where do you think? She was in a certain tree-alley by the Vittolovsky Canal.

That's why it hurts me when ignorant people claim that we "isolated her." In 1918, when she divorced Gumilyev and entered into that so-called "marriage" with V. Shileiko (I've seen the block warden's book, and I can assure you that their union was never properly registered), the happy couple withdrew into the icy labyrinth of the Sheremetev Palace, which always reminds me of Hans Christian Andersen's fairytale of the Snow Queen: walls of ice, frozen puzzle-pieces, silence, deadness, and a woman with an ice-cold kiss! (Don't tell me I'm not poetic.) Meanwhile, I took note of a black ring worn around a departing lover's neck, a poem about weeping, a poem about white crosses. But that's not the point. What caused us concern is that after we'd arrested those snakes who dared to vote against Soviet power at the Constituent Assembly, we found Akhmatova rallying enemies of the people with a poem entitled "Your Spirit Is Clouded with Arrogance."

4

When she was still young and beautiful enough to write that the past's power can fail, she mourned unkissed lips. When our Revolution proved that the past can in fact be broken, what then? Unkissed lips returned to hang eternally over her in the yellow fog over Leningrad. I've seen her linger by a pale archway ornamented with bearded heads; she spent an hour there; my toes were getting cold, I can tell you. She gazed at each effigy as if it were someone she'd loved. Well, with her anything was possible. Unkissed lips! When we were supposed to be building socialism! Each mouth was a noose—oh, she hanged herself a thousand times! But from the beginning she celebrated her mourning in colored icons of words. She *needed* to doom herself within those opened lips. I've uncovered a term for that behavior: sexual asphyxia! Just as the reflections of railings get broken up by ripples, then begin to heal themselves, never finishing, so her pain of love and life pulsated in and out of exaltation.

A kiss, then mourning for a kiss—to know both, one must experience love's end. One summer night in 1935 while Shostakovich lay in Elena Konstantinovskaya's arms, whose arms did Akhmatova rest in? No one's. She lay down in the wet grass, gazing at the Chinese Pavilion's crown. I was there; I saw how her cold lips trembled. Shostakovich found salvation within the curtain of Elena's hair. Akhmatova haunted herself with swans and dead water.

By then she'd begun to learn that even greater than the power of the absent lover is *our* power, Soviet power! We were going to plait her braids more tightly for her . . .

I've seen her at Gumilyev's shoulder, gazing away at right angles to him; he wears a rose above his heart, oak-leaves on chest and sleeve; a sword of moonlight fails to cut deeply the black water behind them; statues spy on them from behind the trees. I have every reason to conclude that at that moment he was dreaming about his own Elena, to whom he gave the name "Blue Star."

In those years it was still believed at my office that her sensibility resembled some rainbow-colored clock whose hands were church-towers creaking round and round Petersburg for the very last time, before we stopped that clock. Nobody could have imagined "Requiem"; we associated her with "At the Seashore."

5

Then, thanks in part to her unhappy marriage, and also to her native disposition, she began to more than express her suffering; in typical Russian fashion she treasured it! Her Muse no longer reassured her: *Your happiness will be guarded by the statues in the Summer Garden*. That was all the same to Akhmatova. Since her suffering was strong, if she could only allow it to define her, why couldn't she be indomitable? As early as 1915, N. Nedobrovo noted *her calmness in confessing pain and weakness.** By then, Marina Tsvetaeva was already writing love-poems to her. In 1916 a lover whom I have identified as B. Anrep caused her a highly specific agony which shone within her like a white stone in a well. (When it came to grieving, she was far superior to Shostakovich, who jittered and went to pieces.) Then Shileiko caused her sorrow in the Sheremetev Palace, and more sadness in the Marble Palace; that was how she

---

*In the interests of justice I'm compelled to remind you of her dismissive cruelty to Nedobrovo's wife, whom she despised for her ignorance of poetry—at least she found the husband to her taste. In the end she left the husband—she abandoned everybody!

passed her time. Petersburg became Petrograd, then Leningrad; it starved and rotted all around her. The shiny dark lips of A. Lourie, the affected gestures of O. Glebova-Sudeikina, the droopy eyelids of that so-called "poet" Kuzmin, that entire pallid rabble of aesthetes at the Stray Dog Cabaret, one by one we made them all irrelevant.

Do you think our Anna learned any lesson from this? Not at all. She "immortalized" all those individuals in "Poem Without a Hero."

6

The introduction to this work bears the dateline of 25 August 1941 from "besieged Leningrad," which really pisses me off. She never fired a shot in our defense. So she was in Leningrad when the Fascists attacked. So was I. I was always against the medal we gave her. But that's not the point. Ever since '48 I've become convinced that there's one person in the poem, a darkhaired woman, whom Akhmatova is shielding with her doubletalk; in other words, this darkhaired woman is still out there; we haven't caught her yet. Late at night when I can't sleep, I read the poem over; I know it almost by heart, which is ironic, because quite a number of the "politicals" I've sent to the Gulag also quote from it; in my own private museum I have a nearly complete copy, written from memory on pages of birchbark. I don't mind admitting that it's got a few nice turns of phrase.

7

On 11 December 1920 our patience ended, so we exposed Akhmatova's suppurating apoliticism for the people to see. That experience became another pearl for her oyster-shell! Bitterness and musings on bitterness became inseparable in her poetry, like the concentric ovals of arched bridges and their reflections upon the Winter Canal. Not long afterward, I saw her praying and weeping at Blok's funeral procession; those tears became new beads on her necklace of sorrows. In our Soviet Russia of today, when art is supposed to be positive and life-affirming, there is simply no place for this kind of person.

When we liquidated Gumilyev in '21, for anti-Soviet conspiracy, another crimson jewel splashed into the well. I was there; I made sure that everything went professionally. At the last moment, he stood as stiff and pale as one of those statues outside the Catherine Palace. I allow that he didn't grovel like the others.

I was there in 1930 when she discovered his grave—two holes for sixty people, because why should these scum deserve tombs of their own? There she was, praying and sobbing again! Had it been up to me, I would have shot her right there. But who listens to me? And so naturally she went home and wrote more anti-Soviet poems.

Long before that, in her odious "When in Suicidal Anguish," she'd already compared Leningrad to a drunken whore. Well, she ought to know. That's why I'd just as soon give her eight grams, although she's so birdlike that seven would suffice.

In 1933, when we arrested her son Lev for the very first time, just to tease him, another jewel of suffering glowed within her poetic well; exegesis reveals it to be a second red jewel. The red dot feared by Shostakovich—it haunted all his nightmares—was death, of course. What was it for her? Stars and water, poison drinks, salt and churches, these very specific entities made up her world, in which everything not only meant what it meant, but existed independently. For Shostakovich, the red dot equaled nothing more than death. For Akhmatova, no matter what else it was, it also became a ruby.

Presumably it is this concretion of treasures to which L. K. Chukovskaya is referring when she writes Akhmatova's fate became *something even greater than her own person*.

All the same, we'd finally begun to make progress with her. The way we educate these people is first to shoot someone they love, so that they realize that this can and will happen to them; next, we *take away* someone they love more than themselves. When we did this to Shostakovich, the results were excellent. In Akhmatova's case we were also quite effective: *Where Stalin is, is freedom*, and you know the rest.

No doubt she suffered other shocks, because our Revolution ripped out almost everything, even the brass plates on the doors of what used to be called Saint Petersburg. I almost laughed at her surprise when she saw Krylov's half-sandbagged statue in the Summer Garden!

In that same year, we banned her so-called "work"—a measure which I'm happy to say remained in force until 1940. Her white face and black braids, like the snow and willows at Tsarskoe Selo, lived on as if they'd been forgotten; in fact no one forgot her, especially not us. She once wrote that death eases thirst—with lye. We said to ourselves: Let her get thirstier first! Kisses and prayers, unanswered knocks, more kisses, boredom, abandonment and death, what did we care about any of that? However, I'm not ashamed to tell you that I enjoyed watching her kissing.

8

By now that tight black silk dress of hers had holes in it, and she'd long since sold the oval cameo in her belt; who among us Russians hasn't been desperate for bread?

Our objective for her: No more summer poems. Give us the greenish skies of Leningrad in autumn. Then we'll know she's where we want her.

In 1937 we fulfilled the Stalin Route, the nonstop flight across the Pole to America, in an ANT-25 with a red star on each wing! You'd think that this event would be worth commemorating. I made a point of attending the ceremony. Elena Konstantinovskaya and Roman Karmen, freshly wed and newly returned from Spain, were also at the aerodrome. Elena failed to recognize me, I'm relieved to say. I've watched Karmen's newsreel half a dozen times. It's quite good, really. But do you think Akhmatova cared to participate in our victory? Instead, she polished another jewel in that poisoned necklace called "Requiem."

In 1938 we arrested her son again and condemned him to death by shooting, but we were still just playing; we were curious to see if that would bring her around. I was one of the ones who recommended that his sentence be commuted to five years, and that's what he got, not that he deserved it; he tried to defy us even after we'd beaten him for eight months.

At this point her persona had assumed certain qualities most convenient to us: resignation, poverty, martyrdom, and the pretense of meekness (not that you can ever trust those bourgeoisie, even when we keep our heels on their necks). Then there were the religious trappings, which I'm personally not averse to in the case of such people; it's to our advantage when a dying class stupefies itself with *the opiate of the masses.* We'd stripped her of her yellow dress; now she was no better than all the shivering men in jackets, the bowed women in shawls, waiting in the sun of searchlights beneath fatality's moon-breath for their turn at the window: Will the clerk take my package or not? If not, the person I meant it for has gone to stay with Lev Gumilyev. L. Zhukova, whose relatives we'd already *sent away,* encountered her one winter's day in the queue at Liteiny Prospekt, number 4, and described her in a letter as *an aloof mannequin.* That was how we liked her! Unfortunately, her presence still electrified any crowd. To me, this proves that we hadn't been sufficiently strict with her. An aloof mannequin she might have been, as still as water under ice; but our task was to freeze her solid. In this we never succeeded: after all, Akhmatova was the poet of "Requiem," which even our yes-man Shostakovich admired and which I'm sorry to say I've heard on the lips of students, prisoners, prostitutes, peasants and kerchiefed factory women. Needless to say, it gets no mention in the *Great Soviet Encyclopedia*. All I can say is that world events have confirmed the correctness of that policy.

9

This was the period when L. Chukovskaya, infatuated by those Russian eyes of hers (grave but not sad, steady but not fixed; aware, capable of gentleness and ruthlessness), became Akhmatova's confidante. In her diary (I've read every page), Chukovskaya insists that *she herself, her words, her deeds, her head, shoulders and the movements of her hands were possessed of such perfection, which, in this world, usually only belongs to great works of art*. Tell me she wasn't in love! Later on, Akhmatova turned against her in Tashkent, for no reason. That's how it is with people like that.

10

I followed them across a stone bridge over a canal, and a stone church-head trembled in the dark water below—not decapitated yet, only reflected.—Anna Andreyevna, what do you think of Shostakovich's music?—Well, of course there are brilliant pages, replied Akhmatova.—Chukovskaya took her arm. Then they turned right. For the sake of inconspicuousness, I stayed behind, smoking my cigarette and thinking about Elena Konstantinovskaya. Pyotr Alexeev was already in position. He enjoyed those outings—although he was much more in love with the two beefy, cheery sisters who'd become the tennis champions of our Soviet land. He got ill-tempered when Akhmatova went to Liteiny Prospekt to send another package to Lev; that was a busman's holiday for him. He informed me that on one occasion, when she came up to the window and spoke her name, a woman in the long line behind her burst into tears. This was unpleasant to us. Whatever our next move against her might be, we had to plan it out. On those afternoons when I stayed behind, I had a very pleasant time arranging Akhmatova's future. When that palled, I thought some more about Elena Konstantinovskaya. Chukovskaya was going to come back late and alone. I waited at the bridge. Then I went home, counting Leningrad's broken windows.

In every way, that period marked the height of my career. The Hitlerites hadn't attacked us yet, so even I of all people still got to embrace an illusion or two about "peace" and "freedom"; meanwhile, we'd finally made an impression on our spoiled darling Anna Andreyevna! In corroboration, N. K. Danchenko, whom we often stationed there, reported to me that Akhmatova appeared malnourished (not that I hadn't seen that for myself) and that her face resembled *the shining of a yellow dress at a window.*

To return to my report, by the time those two relics of bourgeois gentility took off their shabby coats and sat down facing one another at the kitchen table, I was invariably ready for them.

11

Her attempts to deceive us had become desperately pitiful by then. How many times can't I remember Akhmatova handing a new scrap of illicit poetry to Lidiya Chukovskaya, who read it hurriedly and silently, memorized it, then passed it back to her hostess, who burned it over an ashtray? I was flat on my belly on the floor of the apartment above, watching them through a hole in the chandelier.*

How early autumn came this year, said Akhmatova, setting fire to another memorized scrap of "Requiem." I'd already noted it down. Come to think of it, we knew "Requiem" by heart before she'd even finished it; it's fair to say that we wrote it ourselves.

Sometimes Chukovskaya used to beg her to recite something.

It's all the same to me, Akhmatova would reply.—It was all the same to me, too. I'm not claiming that she didn't occasionally achieve certain effects (I'm speaking here as someone who knows art—professionally, of course).

Please don't trouble yourself if you're tired, my dear Anna Andreyevna! How are you feeling?

It's extremely good that I'll be dead soon, said Akhmatova.

Chukovskaya stared at her, her eyes filling with tears. Oh, it was love, all right! As far as I was concerned, they could both go where we'd sent Gumilyev.

In fact, from any practical point of view, they should have ceased to exist. Only the war saved them. Poor Lidiya—when should I bring her in? Poor Anna Andreyevna with her broken heel and missing teeth! I felt as an SS-doctor must when he broods over his collection of Jewish skulls, for these two

---

*It wasn't until 1945, on the day after that foreign snake Isaiah Berlin departed, that we screwed a microphone into her ceiling. We made it visible on purpose; that saved us trouble. Next time he came to our country, she wisely refused to meet him.

women were *ghosts,* gliding over the red velvet carpets of olden times. Sometimes they did nothing but stare into each other's eyes, and then I'd eat my lunch, for there's an ancient Russian custom of meals at a graveside.

Sometimes she recited from *Rosary,* which I have always considered her weakest collection, thanks to its religious trash. I have a copy right here, and according to the title page it was published in March 1914, when I was still in what it's best to call *street business.* I'm not averse to informing you that my life wasn't easy in those days. But who cares about me? In 1914, I hated anybody Orthodox. When we were putting the priests on trial in the twenties, my attitude hardened beyond mere hatred; I argued that possession of *Rosary* should be grounds for a death sentence. But something about the religiosity of those two pathetic women almost disarmed me.

12

When we arrested Gumilyev, we found an old volume by Masaryk in his study. I don't feel embarrassed about informing you that when I was searching it for marginalia, I learned a few things about my country. On the subject of Dostoyevsky he writes: *It is not Christ but rather the Russian Christ who is his idol.* Right away, I understood that this emblematized Akhmatova's position also. And, frankly, even committed Stalinists such as myself are proud to be Russians deep down, although we can't always show it. The world-wide conspiracy of the priests against the people, naturally we have to stamp that out. But if Akhmatova's Christ is a Russian Christ, why not let her kiss Him goodbye a little longer? If she's lucky, she'll die before He does.

Masaryk also argues that Russian atheism *is not positivist agnosticism, but rather a kind of embittered skepticism which revels in the laceration of the soul.* I do admit his point. Whenever I've been working over a priest (lacerating him, let's say), I come home in a particularly foul mood. So even when Akhmatova and Chukovskaya knelt down to pray, I didn't feel as disgusted as I would have expected. This speaks for my fairness and neutrality.

Besides, I'm a lover of the arts.

13

All this is a way of leading up to the fact, which fails to embarrass me in the least, but which for obvious reasons I wouldn't confide to just anyone, that on one freezing December afternoon—dead black by four-o'-clock—when Akhmatova happened to be in a delicately happy mood because on my instructions we'd accepted her parcel that day (it was Pyotr Alexeev's turn to take that one home, not that Akhmatova's parcels ever offered us many treats) and Chukovskaya took full advantage of that success to ask her oracle for an elucidation of "At the Seashore"—she seems to have heard about it from M. Shaginyan, whose file I haven't studied but whose acquaintances seem to place her in suspicious proximity to anti-Soviet circles—a sincere joy overcame me, because that's my favorite poem; and a quarter-hour later, when Akhmatova, shivering there in her black dressing gown with the silver dragon on the back, agreed to recite the poem, I could hardly believe my luck; then she began: *Bays wounded the low shore* and my heart thrilled.

14

In the summer of 1914, as the Romanovs, blinded by mysticism and bad alliances, led Russia ever closer to war's edge, Gumilyev was in the second year of his affair with the young T. Adamovicha, who wanted to marry him and to whom he dedicated his next book of poems, which no one has studied more closely than I. Ever since his voyage to Africa, as I know from reading his diary, he'd had nightmares about the future. In one dream, about which I reminded him at his interrogation, he found himself condemned for complicity in a palace revolution in Abyssinia; after his decapitation, he clapped his bloody hands at the goodness and simplicity of it all. In Tanya's arms, of course, he dreamed other dreams. As for Akhmatova, left alone with their child in Slepnyovo (not that she hadn't begun her so-called "friendship" with N. Nedobrovo), she lay on the couch and wrote "At the Seashore." What a parasite!

The notion that there is a "soul" which can express itself through poetry has long since been ringingly disproven; all the same (doubtless on account of my Russian nationality), "At the Seashore" is sufficiently beautiful to bring tears to my eyes. The first line: *Bays wounded the low shore.*

15

Once upon a time, when the sails all blew away, Akhmatova, or the young braided girl who might have been her, sat naked on a flat rock-island. She'd interred her yellow dress back on the beach so that it would not get wet and no one would steal it. *And I'd dry my salty hair on that flat rock far from land.*

That was what she used to do every day, before she and Russia both changed. She played with the green fish and the white bird. She experienced feelings of one kind and another, not knowing them to be happiness; and as I watched and listened through the ceiling, I wondered whether happiness is invisible until it's been lost, at which point Fate (since like any decent Communist I reject God) hurls it down into a pit (for instance, the mine-shaft into which we tumbled the Romanovs), where it shines in the darkness like a supernatural jewel. "At the Seashore" is actually this sort of jewel; that our Muse of Weeping, who loved winter, could write such a poem remains inexplicable to me; parts of it deserve widespread publication.

Once upon a time, the braided girl rested on a wave as dark and hot as blood; she let herself be carried far away; then she swam back to her flat rock and dried her salty hair. Not knowing that she was happy, she sang to the white bird; she swam around the rock, and the green fish kept her company. The rock was so far out to sea that by the time she swam home it was always dusk and the lighthouse had begun to wink.

She wanted to become a Tsarina who'd defend her bay with six battleships and six gunships. So she rejected the grey-eyed fisher-boy who brought her roses, and waited for the Tsarevich to come. When he came he was dead, drowned; he'd had green eyes like the green fish. Her paralyzed sister-double wept; the church glowed like an island; the bells rang for the Tsarevich's soul.

That was only the beginning and the end of it. (The end, by the way, betrays her attitude of religious submission, which I've already alluded to. We'll need to rewrite that.) I've left out the middle, so that this report won't get too long. And now the braided girl, long widowed of her Tsarevich, lived in a torn dressing-gown and had no sugar for her tea. For a moment—such is the dangerous power of poetry—I even felt sorry for her. But it's important to remember that a personal feeling is merely a personal feeling. I've shot any number of enticing women.

I admit that I was overpowered; it was my Russian blood. For her part, Chukovskaya knelt and kissed what Gumilyev, in one of his saddest poems, memorialized as *your cold, slender hands.*

16

Then what? Then bare trees in the snow on the Moika Embankment.

And that night when I went home, I don't mind confessing that my head was filled with all kinds of ridiculous word-rubbish, such as *the moon and six candles,* and *a kiss upon her eyelashes.* What was I to do? Finally I picked up *The Foundations of Leninism* and read two pages at random. That cured me. I still felt melancholy, and it's possible that I might have been sharp with my wife. But, as Akhmatova bitterly laughs in one of her earliest love lyrics, *I don't cure anybody of happiness!* ▸

CASE WHITE

. . . with the mysterious lens in your eye, you will be master of the thoughts of people . . . If you move freely in the world, your blood will flow more easily, all gloomy brooding will cease, and, what is best of all, brightly colored ideas and thoughts will rise in your brain . . .

—E. T. A. Hoffmann (ca. 1822)

In the sleepwalker's time, there were processions of tanks, ϟϟ-troops and pleading diplomats from England and France while we prepared to push death aside forever and ever. The men who used to leap up in beerhalls and shout about destiny now had regiments at their command. And so the orders for Case White got unsealed, and the regiments learned that they would be going to Warsaw, city of squat, honey-colored churches and blue-grimed cobbles, so that they could look up the pink sweaty legs of Polish women.

Our Russian friends put on "Die Walküre" at the Bolshoi (the production Jew-free, to keep us satisfied). They were looking forward to Case White; we'd agreed to let them eat half of Poland. What would they do then? I seem to see an officer's white glove, discolored by cadaveric fluid, a rusty set of keys, a brass Polish eagle, matted muddy scraps of green canvas; multiplied three thousandfold or maybe twelve thousandfold (for no one ever agrees on numbers) in Katyń Forest. What butchers those Slavs are!

The Austrians were happy about Case White, too. They wanted to show their new Reich what they were capable of. (Take your kinsmen's advice; make good your old losses. That was what we told them.) The Czechs and Romanians had their own hopes. In fact, who *wasn't* caught up by Case White? It opened the most spectacular scenario ever written: Germany can no longer be a passive onlooker! Every political possibility has been exhausted; we've decided on a solution by force!—Have you ever read the supernatural stories of E. T. A. Hoffmann? He's the one who drafted Case White; he dreamed up treasures, magic lenses, monsters! If you want to remind me that Hoffmann died in the nineteenth century, all I have to say to you is: That just makes it better! Our regiments were going to march, with the almost maddeningly monotonous perfection of Hoffmann's handwriting, each line perfectly level and perfectly spaced between the one above it and the one below it, each letter canted at the same angle, the same courtly bow. The sea-waves of Rilke's handwriting, the gentle asymmetries of Mozart's script, the ornate crowdedness of Schiller's penmanship, all these had had their day; now it was Hoffmann's turn again, with musical accompaniment in Beethoven's grandiose scrawl and troop dispositions drawn up in Wagner's surprisingly elegant cursive, stylized and sloped, his *d*'s curled. And all summer, in spite of the diplomats who scuttered across her face, Europe lay as miserably passive as one of Dostoyevsky's women. In the beerhall, a man said to me that of course every woman wants it; every woman craves to be raped by the blond beast. He'd just been accepted into Panzer Grenadier Division Grossdeutschland. He bought me a draft and showed off a photograph of his wife, whom he'd married this very year, on Uncle Wolf's birthday, and when I asked him whether he'd ever raped her, he replied that some women don't need to be raped because they're candles; you light them and they burn all by themselves; they melt and they burn. He asked me if I understood him; he wanted to know if I'd ever been with a woman, and I said that I no longer dreamed of women anymore; when I closed my eyes at night I saw a pyramid of flame. Dismissing women, he announced that Poland would not be enough; one had to consider our people's future. (In Europe everything is a performance; everything gets announced.)

Three years later, the next act would stage itself above the pale faces and frozen hands of the Muscovites who heard on street-loudspeakers that the German Fascists were coming. In Poland, people were going up the chimney by then. But before that, yes, before that, summer made its loving leafy promises. I remember Warsaw quite well; I remember the soft yellow pillars and figures of the Church of the Assumption of the Blessed Virgin. One of those statues, a prophet by the look of him, reached up to caress the pillar which was comprised of the same powdery yellow substance as he; everything was a candle ready to be set alight. ▸

OPERATION BARBAROSSA

Therefore this young god always dies early, nailed to the tree . . . the maternal principle which gave birth to him swallows him back in the negative form, and he is reached by ugliness and death . . . Many at that moment prefer to die either by an accident or in war, rather than become old.

—Marie-Louise von Franz (1995)

The night before the Dynamos game he should have been happy, because soccer was now his only escape except for music itself; moreover, before she went to her room for the night, Nina informed him that Shebalina, whom she'd met in a sugar queue, had whispered that everything would be forgiven; poor Ninusha, who had always been so strong-minded, even believed that; she practically congratulated him; and he would have laughed in her face had she not been so obviously trusting that their lives would finally get, how should I say, better and more joyful; in short, he should have been happy, but that night he dreamed that Nina had no face, or, rather, that her face was a black disk of bakelite, perforated by concentric constellations of perfectly round holes; in effect, his wife had become a monstrous telephone receiver; and he awoke in one of his panics, which never disturbed anyone behind the other door because he didn't cry out, not even a moan. What was that sound? He'd write it into Opus 110. He rose and looked in on his family. What was that sound? With her throat trustingly upturned and the two small heads slumbering upon her chest, she lay snoring piano, *forte,* piano, *forte,* her face joyless, prematurely aged; her breath was very bad; for some weeks she'd been complaining of an infected tooth. He would rather have married E . E. Konstantinovskaya, but now Nina was the mother of his children; and she'd kept faith with him in defiance of his persecutors, who included everyone all the way up to, you know, *that bastard.* It had been going on for five years now. Once they came for him, that alone would give them legal license to return for her. Nina knew that, but refused to divorce him. She loved him without understanding him, which may be the noblest love of all.

Retreating to his bed, he fell back into a nightmare punctuated by electric signals just as his life would very soon be by tracer bullets, and there was Nina again, towering over him, shouting at him in that inhuman electric voice, that singing voice, I mean that music; it must be music which issued from her round, black cruelly birdlike face! But when he woke up, his mood seemed to have been reconfigured by a species of rotary stepping system: He felt that something *tremendous and uplifting* would occur. And something would: the Dynamos game!

It was only at Lenin Stadium that he could open his mouth and scream, really scream—and here I should say that only he would have thought of what he did as screaming; he never let himself go the way that V. V. Lebeyev did; the most he might do was hiss out: *Hooligans!* at some unfair play, but even this brought him extreme pleasure. He favored the Dynamos on account of Peki Dementyiev, whom everyone called "the Ballerina" on account of his grace.

Once upon a time, he'd escorted Elena Konstantinovskaya to a match of Zenith *versus* Spartak, which is to say Leningrad *versus* Moscow; the whole time she kept weeping because he'd just informed her that he must remain with Nina, thanks to what proved to be a false pregnancy. They each wore the white shirt and dark shorts of the Dynamo Club. He, likewise weeping (his glasses were smeared), whispered amidst the shouts: You see, Elena, when I looked into the mirror this morning, I, well, I, I said to myself: *Shostakovich does not abandon his children*. That's the, so to speak, situation. But if you'd rather, I'm ready to, I know a man who has a . . . —When Peki scored a goal, so that everyone around them was screaming and screaming like kulaks being executed, he, feeling sheltered by the high level of the signal, if you catch my drift, fumblingly tried to kiss away her tears, which merely stimulated them; pressing his teeth against her ear so that his own signal would be transmitted by bone conduction, he said: Let's light thirteen candles, Elenka, and drink a toast to, to—you *know* it's you I'd prefer to take with me . . .

Another goal! He couldn't help it; he himself started screaming and screaming! (These soccer stars would soon be employed as policemen, to save them from the front line.)

Elenka, Elenochka, Lyalya Konstantinovskaya, well, she was *finished* now, so to speak: married to R. L. Karmen; to be sure, there'd been that long last night in the Luga dacha, her tears and then his dying down, or as we say in music, *morendo,* after which he'd simply needed to remind himself that the feelings which came over him when he saw her face (I mean his faith in her perfect qualities, not to mention his longing to be in her company always) meant nothing and could be induced to attach themselves to other women, darling Ninusha for instance, no matter that her face was a black disk. In a word, Elena Konstantinovskaya wouldn't be coming with him today.

He actually had two soccer matches to attend. I. D. Glikman, who truth to tell was very bored by athletic events, had agreed to come to the first one, out of hero-worship alone. Where were Glikman's Dynamo shorts? The dear man wouldn't dress appropriately, unfortunately. Like Nina, he didn't actually care about the . . .

Don't look so sad, Dmitri Dmitriyevich! What is it? Did you see *her* somewhere?

You see, I, I, well, that would be, not to put too fine a point on it, *impossible,* he told Glikman contemptuously, because they're in Spain.

Be brave! I thought I'd better tell you! You see, here it is in *Izvestiya,* page seven: *The documentary "Spain," whose remarkable sequences, shot at great personal risk by Roman Karmen in company with Boris Makaseyev, expose the lies of the* . . . Don't worry, Dmitri Dmitriyevich, please, please don't worry! If I see her, I'll tell her to keep away from you—

You're correct! But can we please, if you wouldn't mind, not mention . . . Because Ninusha would, oh, dear, oh, *dear,* we'll be late! There goes the streetcar—

Something inside him was broken. Lyalka, you filled my heart until it was ready to explode, and then, oh, me! He was tired. He knew he would never get over Elena Konstantinovskaya, and therefore assumed that she, or at least her absence, must forever define him more than anything. But that very morning, just as he arrived at the stadium with Glikman, the loudspeaker said: *War.*

And at once he knew, somehow he just *knew,* that war would be the core of his life. ▸

THE SLEEPWALKER

◪

It is generally understood, however, that there is an inner ring of superior persons to whom the whole work has a most urgent and searching philosophical and social significance. I profess to be such a superior person . . .

—George Bernard Shaw, *The Perfect Wagnerite: A Commentary on the Niblung's Ring* (1898)

1

Their slave-sister Guthrún, marriage-chained to Huns on the other side of the dark wood, sent Gunnar and Hogni a ring wound around with wolf's hair to warn them not to come; but such devices cannot be guaranteed even in dreams. As the two brothers gazed across the hall-fire at the emissary who sat expectantly or ironically silent in the high-seat, Hogni murmured: Our way'd be fairly fanged, if we rode to claim the gifts he promises us! . . . —And then, raising golden mead-horns in the toasts which kingship requires, they accepted the Hunnish invitation. They could do nothing else, being trapped, as I said, in a fatal dream. While their vassals wept, they sleepwalked down the wooden hall, helmed themselves, mounted horses, and galloped through Myrkvith Forest to their foemen's castle where Guthrún likewise wept to see them, crying: Betrayed!—Gunnar replied: Too late, sister . . . —for when dreams become nightmares it is ever too late.

When on Z-Day 1936 the Chancellor of Germany, a certain Adolf Hitler, orders twenty-five thousand soldiers across six bridges into the Rhineland Zone, he too fears the future. Unlike Gunnar, he appears pale. Frowning, he grips his left wrist in his right. He's forsworn mead. He eats only fruits, vegetables and little Viennese cakes. Clenching his teeth, he strides anxiously to and fro. But slowly his voice deepens, becomes a snarling shout. He swallows. His voice sinks. In a monotone he announces: *At this moment, German troops are on the march.*

What will the English answer? Nothing, for it's Saturday, when every lord sits on his country estate, counting money, drinking champagne with Jews. The French are more inclined than they to prove his banesmen . . .

Here comes an ultimatum! His head twitches like a gun recoiling on its carriage. He grips the limp forelock which perpetually falls across his face. But then the English tell the French: *The Germans, after all, are only going into their own back garden.* —By then it's too late, too late.

I know what *I* should have done, if I'd been the French, laughs Hitler. I should have *struck!* And I should not have allowed a single German soldier to cross the Rhine!

To his vassals and henchmen in Munich he chants: *I go the way that Providence dictates, with the assurance of a sleepwalker.*—They applaud him. The white-armed Hunnish maidens scream with joy.

2

In an Austrian crowd gathered to celebrate his march into Vienna (triple-angled shadows of bodies on parade, boxy tanks, goosesteps, up-pointed rifles), a woman bays before the rest: *Heil Hitler!* —Children pelt his motorcade with flowers. His tanks fly both German and Austrian flags. He drafts a law to join Austria to Germany within twenty-four hours. He's bringing them home to the Reich, he says, his smile as friendly as when he leans across a desk to sign another non-aggression treaty with the credulous dwarfs of Nifelheim.

Dwarfs indeed! With his hands raised up (he's so pale against his own inkblot moustache), he imparts the following unalterable truth: In this world, there are only dwarfs and giants. And *I* know who is whom!

While the sleepwalker looks on, wolf-hearted Göring, his creation, explains that Czechoslovakia is *a trifling piece of Europe.* (Brownshirts have already appeared on the premises, welcoming the sleepwalker with their chin-straps, banners, wreaths. Soon they will write **JEW** on Jewish windows, and shake their fists. In the next act, as the curtains get drawn up from the stage columns, we'll see police coming metal-headed and rigid in the tumbrils to take Jews and hostages away.) Göring continues: The Czechs, a vile race of dwarfs without any culture—nobody even knows where they came from—are oppressing a civilized race; and behind them, together with Moscow, there can be seen the everlasting face of the Jewish fiend!

And Czechoslovakia vanishes like a handful of books flying into flames by night. Children in England and France begin trying on gas masks in anticipation of the sleepwalker's marching columns.

Now beneath the vast gilded eagle in the Reichstag, he sets herds of tanks browsing on the Polish meadows. Bombs fall like clashes of cymbals; arms swing in unison for his government of national recovery.

3

He hesitates again. He fears what lies before him in Myrkvith Forest. Not that hesitation's practical—hasn't he already accepted the aliens' invitation to the contest? He dreads their spider-holes and deceits, but war's begun; he must roll honorably forth.

He craves to clear his mind. Yes, the curtain's risen, but he needs to lose himself one last time within the curved black *Schalldeckel* which conceals the tunnel to the orchestra pit beneath the stage. From nothingness he came. Would he'd come from a solid wooden hall like Gunnar and Hogni! Well, he'll *dream* Germany solid. Homeless, amorphous, he relaxes into nothingness whenever no one can see. He needs to be a certain velvet-puddled something, but fears that that something might really be nothing. He imagines how Gunnar felt when the Huns buried him alive in the snakepit. In his dreams he sometimes becomes a black bag filled with serpents. He wakes up vomiting, but the serpents will not crawl out his throat.

Gunnar had a harp; he played the snakes to sleep—all of them but one. And the sleepwalker, he masks himself in music.

4

The sleepwalker's minions have built him a dream called Eagle's Nest—an eyrie rightly named, for doesn't he possess the droning eagles of steel which are now preying upon Poland? (Each Stuka's but an emanation of his right arm cutting through the air.) Eagle's Nest is reached first by way of a winding mountain road, which conveys the accolyte to the bronze portal, then by a dripping marble corridor through the rock, and finally by a brass elevator up into the heights; the shaft is a hundred and sixty-five feet—why, that's even taller than the chimney will reach at Auschwitz! Here he can gaze down upon his world of henchmen, kinsmen and foemen. All the way to Poland he can see pale, flashing hands clapping, and frozen, pale faces beneath steel helmets uplifted to seek out his hoarse, loud, bullying voice. Just as at Bayreuth one finds singers and listeners sharing the same darkness, so Hitler and his vassals now dream their way through the great night he's spider-spun out of his own fear, weaving strands of blackness ever thicker across the sky until the lights have dimmed—indeed, indeed, just as at Bayreuth! (Before Wagner, frivolous music-munchers sauntered into an opera house whenever they felt like it, and illumination accommodated them, so that musicians and trappings could be seen, rendering the singers no more than human.) And at his command, liegemen launch eastward his bride-tokens of phosphorus, lead and steel.

5

Shooting down come the Stukas, straight down, Polish streets spreading out before them like bloodstains, then bombs fall; flames take wing; people scream and run right into the machine-guns. The Stukas soar, disdaining now those crooked blackened ruins which foemen deserve, their bridges brokenly dangling in rivers.

6

His pale, alert, immobile face watches the victory parade, his eyes like a bird's. Wagner had steam machines and colored lights at Bayreuth; *he* has the many-plumed smoke of ruined Warsaw. And all is as it was before—the same long columns of listeners at Party rallies, long squares of people, mobile barracks drawn up to hear him shouting, warning and exhorting his children of all ages. In come the Gestapo, drawing up new lists of names, confiscating old ones. In Austria they'd accompanied their sleepwalker's voice less obviously, in much the same way that the Wagnerian orchestra lurks in the darkness past the *Schalldeckel*. They arrested three-quarters of a million people in Vienna on the first day of reunification, but softly. In Poland they need not be soft. They're backed by all good Germans, down to the last *heil*-smiling ladies and girls, each of whom agrees with him that his foreign adventures had better be, in his own terrifying phrase, *sealed in blood*. They seek themselves in the sleepwalker's pale mute face, his wrist clasping wrist as he endures the honors on his fiftieth birthday, sipping at the rasping static of an infinite cheer.

7

On 23.07.40 he meets Kubizek at Bayreuth. Kubizek's his old friend from his student days (if we grant that he ever had a friend). Rejected twice for artistic studies, the sleepwalker had stolen away from the unfated other boy to become a tramp. Years he'd spent then imprisoned within the *Schalldeckel*! His life had supplied him with no indications of scale whatsoever; he could have been a giant or a dwarf depending on the size of the trees in the painted backdrop where the aliens, solid people, applauded far above his head. But then came a magic drumbeat; and suddenly our sleepwalker became one of the soldiers waving from the troop trains of 1914, and very soon he found himself desperately running through sharp-angled trenches, fleeing the gas bombs against which the handkerchiefs tied over their mouths could do far less than Gunnar's harp. Kubizek might have admired him then, for he'd distinguished himself, but . . . Well, now that he's the Führer he need be ashamed of nothing anymore. Troops are waving from the trains again. A huge swastika has overhung him ever since he became legal dictator.

He's already promised to support the artistic studies of Kubizek's children at the expense of the state. He's taken a very kind interest, yes, he has. He's even sent Kubizek tickets to the *Ring*.

Of those four operas, "Das Rheingold" is his favorite. (The dwarfs are starving Jewish children with weary old faces, and men with pipestem arms.) Could it be his fondness for the music which enthralls him too deeply to remember Kubizek here? Actually he's very interested in the directing. Next comes "Die Walküre," where at the Magic Fire music, the self-willed, virginal heroine gets safely walled to sleep by searchlights like the flames inside the skeletons of French and Belgian houses, where weeping, gesturing neighbors bury the dead in deep craters. The sleepwalker has already noted Kubizek's frantic applause during the "Ride of the Valkyries" (a stunning, chilling, remorseless hymn to war, which thanks to the subterranean architecture gets necessarily softened and diffused a little at Bayreuth). Wanting to re-ignite the friendship, he thinks to invite him up to his private box, but just then Frau Goebbels and her husband make a scene about some infidelity . . . Now it's already time for "Siegfried," which he wishes to enjoy almost alone with Speer, so that they can whisper in each other's ears about new buildings.

At last, during the first intermission of "Götterdämmerung," he finds time for the meeting. He dreads it; he wishes he'd never been persuaded into it by his own sentimentality. He has no time for such nonentities as August Kubizek.

Shyly, Kubizek congratulates him on conquering France. He replies: And here I have to stand by and watch the war robbing me of my best years . . . We're getting old, Kubizek.—Kubizek bows and nods, not knowing what to say.

And yet, the sleepwalker says, and yet, *this* . . . You remember how we used to stand for hours on end for Wagner, because we could not afford to sit? You remember how "Götterdämmerung" made us weep?

Yes, my Führer . . .

It's like a bath in steel, I tell you. After Wagner, I feel hardened and refreshed . . .

He returns to his box to sit rapturous until the end of the final act, when the devoted woman sets everything she loves on fire, and buildings collapse like sand castles, windowed facades slowly falling to the street, becoming dust and broken glass.

Kubizek in his humbler box remembers how when they were youths together the sleepwalker once wrote a *Hymn to the Beloved* to a tall and slender fairhaired girl named Stephanie Jansten, but never ever spoke to her. (That is exactly how our ancient heroes fell in love, too. Siegfried and Gunnar hadn't even laid eyes on the princesses they pined for.) O yes, fairhaired! Why, she was as blonde as the smoke which now rises up from all the synagogues! Sometimes the sleepwalker had been resolved on suicide; this mood lasted for hours on end, but the trouble was that Stephanie must be ready to die with him.

To the stage comes torchlight, wavering columns of light. When the sleepwalker shouts, they shout and thunder, their arms flashing up and down while his stiff boys bang drums. The sleepwalker speaks, or Siegfried sings; it matters not to the rigidly attentive faces. Light gleams on the side of his face.

8

In 1941 he attacks his ally Russia. War on all fronts! Now Germany's safely surrounded by a wall of fire! How long will it take to reduce that empire to a smear beneath his boot? Three weeks, probably, but in this world exactitude sometimes fails. At Bayreuth, for example, the "Rheingold" has been performed in two-and-a-quarter hours, but occasionally it can take as long as three.

For this Russian campaign he selects a snippet of Liszt's *Preludes* to be played on the radio as a victory fanfare.

9

The sleepwalker charmingly smiles as with both his hands he clasps the wrist of Wagner's granddaughter Verena.

Yes, Uncle Wolf, she murmurs. I will give orders that no one is to disturb you.

He enters his private box at the rear wall. He gazes down across the empty seats, which resemble the keyboard of an immense typewriter upon which he might compose any musical score he pleases.

I will not allow this war to hinder my objectives, he whispers to himself.

Russia will not die. Russia is coming at him like the dragon-worm which will rise up at the end of the world, bearing corpses in its claws. The aliens have tricked him, as he always knew they would. But he's raised the goblet of promise. He must continue on.

10

Another weakling, another little shirker requests permission to report. The sleepwalker gazes at him with angry eyes.

The shirker complains about certain extreme measures. What a gallows-raven he is! He croaks and croaks. (In the *Ring*, don't even gods have to trick the dwarfish Jewish capitalist and even rob him in order to save the world?) The sleepwalker stares him down, but the shirker will not dwindle. Where's Keitel? Where's Jodl? Someone should show him out! On the conference room table there at Wolf's Lair, the shirker lays out photographs of hungry street-crowds in the Warsaw Ghetto, of children's faces like weeping skulls, pale, immobile bodies on the pavement, skinny, pale people lying in crowds on hay mattresses.

A typist gasps.

The sleepwalker whirls to kiss her hand.—Never mind, child, he comforts her. She smiles, rushes from the room.

The shirker whines on and on. He's sure that this matter was never brought to the Führer's attention before. Of course the Jews are our misfortune, but this . . .

And the sleepwalker? He flicks at one of the photographs with his thumbnail. The mouth tightens.

11

Another general insists on disturbing him with bad news of the Russian advance. He says that conditions are degenerating along the entire front.

Well, let them degenerate! he rages. All the better for me!

Yes, my Führer. But our own troops are freezing to death. Just yesterday I saw—

The sleepwalker covers his ears.—Perhaps I'm too sensitive, he replies.

12

The workers have gathered before him into rectangular armies. Swastika standards begin marching in file down a long well of futurity. They shout; he waits, expressionless and dour. Long before the first Blood Purge of 1934 they'd seen him striding up to the dais of destiny, standing atop an immense dais with a swastika on the wall nearest his feet. Now they must all be conscripted, their factories to become still another front. He needs gold rings and henchmen.

He speaks of spiritual matters. Only they can save his grey cathedrals and greatcoats from the Russian Jews, who return to life no matter how many of them he burns. The workers must build new breastworks. Aren't they all answerable to the war dead? Even women will have to labor now, in spite of all his principles. Emergencies require extreme measures. Didn't Siegmund mate with his own sister to save the blood of their race?

And the workers listen. They honor his sacrifice. They will not bereave him of his war. Like the crowd at the Opera House, they offer him "stormy applause." At his drumbeat comes the gorgeous flash of ten thousand spades raised upon the Labor Front. In his honor, German women have strung buntings upon their gingerbread houses. Soon enemy bombs will tumble upon them, and he'll turn away, his face milkily shining by torchlight.

13

He always attends the first cycle at Bayreuth every year. This time again he comes early. At Bayreuth the stage is roofless like bombarded Stalingrad. The sleepwalker paces unyieldingly in his private box, brooding down the fan-shaped tiers of empty seats. He strokes the Corinthian columns. He unbuttons the collar of his shirt. He can almost hear the breathing of Verena Wagner outside. The *Schalldeckel* gapes before him: music's open grave. Like the bridegroom who longs to meet his bride beneath the linen sheets, he craves this hollow of secret repose. Only there can he hoard himself safe from the others whom he must ever watch with turning head. His magic renews itself there; he sleeps without dreaming.

And so he descends into the *Schalldeckel*. The old floorboards creak beneath his jackbooted tread. Coldheartedly nervous, he grips his sweaty forelock, gibbering softly to himself, wondering where to rest. But this time, beyond the darkness he spies the flickering fires of forecourts! Call him not afraid. He's the blond against the dark. But it's *so* dark, just as it once was during the previous World War when he was young and blinded by poison gas . . . He strides blindly forward. Don't his own soldiers hunker down to run through tunnels in the ruins even though flashes of Russian rocket-light and snakes of flame pursue them?

The flames lunge up. A tall woman stands ahead. He scarcely comes up to her knees. The pupils of her eyes resemble sparks from the spearpoints of Valkyries. Jealously mistrusting, he halts, mistrusting, his own eyes glaring like twin red rings.

She clenches her fist. Then he knows he's on trial. Momentarily he awakes, staring candidly at her with his wide, piercing eyes. He could win her over if he put his mind to it. He thrusts his head back, speaks from the chin. He's somber, godlike, expressionless. Dreaming an answer to what she hasn't yet said, he tells her that in the operas, Wotan's noblest striving is for his own supplanting. He doesn't care if he loses the war, if he can only keep the Jews from getting back the magic ring.

Why, then, it's well for you, she replies.

What do they name you?

Laugh-at-Wailing.

Who gave you birth?

Fire's my father. *Doom* is my mother called.

And why do you await me here?

To tell you what you've always known—that you were born guilty and overmastered, that the nothingness you burn for refuses to receive you, that olden treasures grow corrupted at your touch.

The sleepwalker screams: It's all treason! Now I know why my Russian offensive's failed! That's my justification. If I was fated, then how was I to blame? You Jewish bitches have opposed me at every step, but do you think I care? Go ahead; stab me in the back; I'll annihilate you; I'll exterminate you all! You think you're immortal, but I'll test you with every poisoned acid there is! I've always been too lenient. Well, that's about to change. I'll have you broken without mercy; I know what it takes; I'll wear you down . . .

But *Laugh-at-Wailing* answers with a chuckle like a rattle of futurity, like bones jiggling inside a procession of pale coffins across the scorched earth of liberated Auschwitz.

I won't give up! cries the sleepwalker. I don't care if it's useless!

The Valkyrie stands silent.

So then, in a pleading tone, he whispers: *Why did you make me?* I never wanted to be made . . .

For propaganda, of course. It's all in your own book. How can we persuade others to be good, without evil we can point to?

Mercurially calming himelf, he smiles and remarks: You might as well have spared yourself the trouble. What did you think I'd do—walk sheepishly to the gallows? Do you think I've never been judged before?

I don't need opinions, little man.

And you truly believe I'll deviate one hair's breadth from the course I've laid out for myself? You think you can goad me into doing anything more extreme than I would do in any case? Are you so hopeful? Why, then, *it's well for you.*

He withdraws, escorted almost into the light by goblins like Russian tanks scuttering across ruins. He's in a panic. He rushes home to Berlin, where he can closet himself with Speer and gaze down at the Grand Avenue of postwar Berlin, modeled at one to one thousand scale. Speer's cabinetmakers have built the new Opera House at one to fifty scale, and over here there'll be a cinema for the masses. Every edifice will be the same height.

With deferential formality, Speer asks his opinion on some aspect of the Central Railroad Station. Carefully, the sleepwalker tries out the Valkyrie's phrase: *I don't need opinions.* I already see everything.

Speer stares woodenly. The sleepwalker feels inspired.

14

And now what? The inclined arm replicated a millionfold, the knife-edge hand, the shouting voices of his echoers, his chin-strapped orators, all sing out to stand firm. Germany lies obediently below him, like an aerial view of fields, a corduroy of bodies who soon will fight in Russia, shivering, warmed only by the pain of their own wounds. His swastika banners are grassblades in an infinite meadow of war. Up standards! *Sieg Heil!* He's guarded by grimy soldiers with deep-sunk eyes. Comes the great battle between Siegmund and Hunding; the Nibelungs fight on in the burning hall; then long lines of gravediggers are carting corpses two by two to the open pit; down the chute they go; then we paper them over, and add a sprinkle of dirt, hastily so that we will not get into even more trouble with the Germans who have dressed us in the striped uniforms and pale wrinkles of concentration camp inmates and who are even now building our doom out of squat towers and barbed wire.

15

Italy falls, but the sleepwalker knows how to save her from the Jews. Parachutes as beautiful as white flowers bloom upon the skies which he's now capturing. Black columns of smoke have translated the beaches of Normandy into the stage darkness after an intermission. In the next act he must sing of retreating German troops, of dead horses and throttled light. The inky moustache in his grey face, the black, gaping mouth, and above all the raised hands of him suck new blood down the marching orchard-lanes of swastika standards. Before him, beyond his warriors hunched under their caps, he seems to see a plain of faces and lights. Where might it be? Increasingly golden, this country draws him on beyond himself. Now he comprehends in his soul why Gunnar and Hogni could not resist the Hunnish invitation: Although it meant doom and sister-woe, at least they'd win that brilliant if sinister moment of light when they drew near their foemen's forecourts. Futurity shone like a flame-flicker reflected on gold foil. They knew they'd be greeted by raised arms and by faces, faces more pale and numerous than raindrops. The sleepwalker mutters, as he did on the eve of the Russian campaign: *The world will hold its breath . . .*

16

Soothed by solid rows of columns marching alongside the seats at Bayreuth, he fingers the acanthus scrolls. He helps Verena Wagner and her mother with gifts of munificent gold. Soon his *Ring* will begin again. He'll watch it from start to finish, without fail. He always keeps his promises.

17

A horizontal salute from Hitler in the clouds! The sleepwalker dreams his face away from the long line of German prisoners of war so ragged and dirty, who march off to Soviet Arctic prisons, their jaws bound up in blankets and rags. Meanwhile, his own lines of slave workers march feebly past ruined apartments and railroad sidings. His dreams are shriveling and scorching. His henchmen have given over running across each other's corpses in Africa. Shells and flames, tanks in snow, ice-maned horses, siege guns echoing in the wind, all these assault his dreams as the Russian Frost-Giants come west.

18

Now he dwells within walls of smoke. Flames rush up his staircases; chandeliers transform themselves into scorched spiders. The light excites him. In the distance he can see electric glows of barbed wire. To fight the Jews, his henchmen have built many a city of factories in the snow whose long alleys of barbed wire are signposted by frozen, snowy corpses with outstretched arms. Heaps of jawbones, mountains of pliers mark the spots where his vassals extract gold teeth from the living and the dead. Lives blow away like waves of sand. If he can only dream this dream a little longer, they'll all be safely up the chimney. But where are his muscled heroes with their swords? Are they all dead? Snowy Russian tanks breast bluish flames and bluish snow to conquer Auschwitz, where more than seven tons of human hair await transshipment. A parade of skinny, desiccated corpses comes forth to tell lies and inspire new Jewish conspiracies.

19

When the captive Gunnar told the Huns that he'd only reveal to them the hoard of the Niflungs (whose gold shone even brighter than the vertical gleams of sunlight upon marching ϟϟ boots) on condition that they cut out Hogni's heart, they tried to trick his rich-wrought mind by carrying to him a mere thrall's heart upon a board; but he knew his brother's heart would never quiver in terror as that one did even in death. Helpless before his cleverness, they killed Hogni then, who laughed as he died. Then Gunnar said that since only he remained to tell the secret, he had no more fear, for tell he never would.

When they lowered Gunnar into the slimy dungeon of adders, he played upon his harp so beautifully that all the serpents slept. Yet finally he wearied, and from that ball of reptiles he perforce lay upon rose up one to bite his liver, and so he perished there in the darkness of snakes.

Knowing her duty, valiant Guthrún served up her own sons' hearts to the husband who'd slain her brothers. After that she razed the castle by fire.

The sleepwalker in his pale grey coat (our memories of him have become so grey and grainy) craves to be another Gunnar. Isn't he a harpist, too? Hasn't he always been able to lull all snakes to sleep until now? And his Germany, she shall be Guthrún. Germany must die ferocious, burning down everything . . .

20

On 12.04.45, the Berlin Philharmonic presents Brünnhilde's last aria and the finale from "Götterdämmerung." He's seen "Götterdämmerung" more than a hundred times. Each time, his brain burns anew in flames of salmon-colored gold. Silhouettes of hanged corpses comprise the perimeter of his now minuscule empire. A civilian hostage raises both arms. Where now his cruelly smiling pale young faces under steel helmets? Where now his myriad marchers on a hill, following the swastika flag?—In Siberia, or dead under mud or pale cobblestones!—The radio which once spread his words like epidemics now pulses meaninglessly: *Complete obliteration . . . shameful . . . solemn promise . . .* The Russians have already reached Myrkvith Forest; waves of American Jews hem them in on all other fronts. Verena Wagner decides to plan a *Ring* without swastikas for 1946. Shadowy night-crowds burn what they've worn for a dozen years, their livery sewn and ornamented in his image. Other crowds in striped uniforms begin emerging from the lane of barbed wire. Mountains of shoes which from a distance resemble herrings in a tin memorialize those who will nevermore come forth. And the sleepwalker dreams. He gives orders to execute all the new traitors. Germany will be safe. Smiling at last in his address to the schoolboys who've hopelessly fought for him against the parades of Russian tanks now entering Berlin, he speaks of their common lineage, then hands out tokens like unto the ancient rings of red gold. The boys shout: *Heil Hitler!* Closing his eyes, he remembers how five years ago his long lines of victorious warriors passed through the Arc de Triomphe while he paid homage to Napoleon. But the world of the old gods was corrupt; it had to be smashed. He does not tell the boys this. It is too late for any explanations. A few days later, weird-ringed by Russian flames, the sleepwalker and his secret bride kill themselves.

21

In his very first speech as Chancellor he'd cried: I have steadfastly refused to come to the people with cheap promises!—Then he'd pointed to his heart. But now what promises has Gunnar to harp on for all these ungrateful snakes? He tires now; his music stops. Shyly he confesses: On the day following the end of the Bayreuth Festival, I'm gripped by a great sadness—as when one strips the Christmas tree of its ornaments . . .

His music stops, his Berliners running behind mounds of rubble, flames winging out of windows, for he's lost this game of draughts which the gods once played with golden figurines, but even yet he guards hope, for Roosevelt is dead; Stalin and Churchill are falling out; and that most ancient of all Norse prophecies sighs upon the lips of the moldy, grassy Mother who periodically arises from this grave-infested earth: Someday, perhaps even in the meadows of Poland where his herds of tanks recently gamboled, *the golden figures, the far-famed ones, will be found again, which they possessed in olden days.* And then, beneath an even, searing light, he'll win back his city all of gold, whose monuments and plazas remain unmarred by humanity. ▸

THE PALM TREE OF DEBORAH

You know, to a certain extent I think the formula "the end justifies the means" is valid in music.

—D. D. Shostakovich (1968)

1

Barbed wire like music-lines taut in bunches of five, claimed either by the bass cause or the treble—for there never was nor can be a neutral instrumental zone—now embraced Leningrad, that so-called "cradle of the Proletarian Revolution." The bass command's kettledrum melodies of artillery would be performed by Army Group North: thirty-two divisions, seven hundred thousand German Fascists, Field-Marshal Wilhelm Ritter von Leeb conducting. From within the city (treble, tremolo) arose the countervailing piccolo music of screams. (How could I somehow *possibly,* wondered the nearsighted fire-warden on the Conservatory roof, let alone *passably* represent us *pianissimo,* before the snare drum creeps in? Because we're not *pianissimo* at all. We're, um, you know. That's what they'll expect, even though we also have to be the loudest. They want me to, to, you know, to signify this into something they can feed people instead of sausage! Without formalism while I'm at it! To hell with them. I can hold my own.) In the opening bars of those Nine Hundred Days, the chorus comprised three million Leningraders, but a third of them perished. Too weak to push her way through the bread queue, a widow fell in the snow. A sexless child was chewing on coffee grounds. A family was eating oilcake with celluloid in it. Comrade Zhdanov called Stalin on the VC phone, but Stalin would not answer.

As for the fire-warden, whose name was D. D. Shostakovich, I can hear him drumming out the Rat Theme on the rim of his helmet. Although he wouldn't have confessed it, this war arrived none too soon! The explosion of rapture at his First Symphony so long ago should have warned him, for in our Soviet Union as in any besieged zone it's unwise to stand out despicably or dashingly. But—freakish child molting into feminine-mouthed prodigy, then cigarette-twiddling hero, I mean grain-beetle of subversion—he'd never succeeded in camouflage. (His cue: cymbal-clash—*gnash, gnash.*) Oh, how many times other children had hurt him! Gawky, pale, wary-eyed behind the round spectacles, he watched encirclers with a melancholy consciousness of his own vulnerability, which they frequently took for submission. Indeed, surrender should have been his policy, for he exuded softness, being the larvum of a grain-beetle, which is to say the proverbially pallid intellectual grub. Girls wanted to pinch his cheeks, while most boys despised him before the second beat of the overture. If one believes, as does any true Bolshevik, that the working class, destined to be the victorious class, can send advance detachments to break through the perimeter of the bourgeoisie, why not grant that doomed systems may in the course of their retreat leave behind counterpoised stragglers whose smooth hands and inward aspirations betray them? They'll survive for a few measures yet; the composer need not write them out of his score so long as they keep time, but they're outmoded nonetheless; they're as prehistoric as the Tauride Palace's fabled owl of gold, into which some extinct Imperial craftsman by means of clocksprings and prayers once built sentience sufficient for its eyes to roll on state occasions. (They never move anymore. After the Revolution, their mechanism ran down.) As for the boy, he stared owl-eyed at the world. Why did I ever liken him to an insect? He was a bird, now that I come to think of it; or maybe he was a—call him a formalist. He blinked. Then he sat down at the piano. His fingers, which appeared far more fragile than dragonflies or faraway antique biplanes, commenced their beautiful convulsions. Oh, he got attention, all right . . . —But the music itself? No less a figure than A. K. Glazunov, director of the Leningrad Conservatory, admitted that he couldn't understand such harmonies, although he offered to stand aside for them. Our Mitya, he opined, was undoubtedly the future's darling.

(Shostakovich ducked his head.)

Perhaps it's mere jealousy on my part, Glazunov continued (and the other professors laughed, to imagine that somebody as important as Glazunov could feel jealous of a student), but all the same, I don't like your latest opus! Ha, ha, what am I saying? I know he's sincere—you're not just playing with us, are you, Mitya?—and what he's attempting is so, let's say, *revolutionary,* that it can't be appreciated in the very first instant . . .

The pupil smiled, fiddling with his mittens. In his view, which he would have readily defended in less intimidating surroundings, music ought to remain freely undifferentiated from any but emotional content, and perhaps even from that. This notion might not have been as new as it seemed; nor, perhaps, was Glazunov quite as shocked as he pretended to be. (How natural to patronize youth in the guise of meeting it halfway!—Let the boy overvalue his conceptions a trifle, thought Glazunov. Maybe once he matures he'll come up with something important.) When his teachers cited the program music of Mussorgsky, Wagner, Berlioz and Rimsky-Korsakoff, our tousle-headed young genius argued that these compositions could be peeled away from their supposed subjects without detriment; if they couldn't, they failed as music. Such being the case, why not construct sequences of notes without thematic pretense? Dmitri Dmitriyevich Shostakovich stood ready to improvise using shock units, shock methods!—Still and all, sighed Glazunov, discreetly sucking alcohol through a long rubber tube, you need not be so *irreverent,* Mitya.—The boy twitched apologetically. Although it made him nervous, he needed to be noticed. One of Glazunov's agreeable qualities was an easy tolerance of almost anything. On a white summer's night when the assistant director attacked the boy, Glazunov interposed: Then this is no place for you. Shostakovich is one of the brightest hopes for our art.—Who then dares allege that Mitya's mentors didn't want to help him? In the USSR we practice two kinds of criticism: the merciless denunciation of bourgeois ideology, and the coaxing, comradely criticism of our peers. So long as he continued to follow the well-delineated path which Glazunov had named sincerity, he need anticipate only the second variety, which never stings.

Born in the antediluvian time when Leningrad was still the claustrophobic "Petersburg" of the Symbolists, in whose nightmares fallen leaves whirled in ever-narrowing spirals, and the same red dominoes or red-eyed terrorists hounded aristocrats wherever they turned, he dwelled, like all children, at the heart of the world. I prefer not to brand him a narcissist, but people do take on the characteristics of the places where they live, and Petersburg is as labyrinthine, enigmatic and literally self-centered as her own best poet, A. A. Akhmatova. Would you like more adjectives? Simultaneously ornate and impoverished, like the golden-braided droshky-driver who cannot feed his own family (and, come to think of it, like Akhmatova, too), Petersburg infects her most sensitive children with a desperation as noble as it is impractical. In a city whose rich aesthetes can admire the greenish tint of thawing river-snow, while ignoring the same hue in the faces of the starving, we must expect the red dominoes to triumph sooner or later. For Petersburg remains above all the city of Raskolnikov, who exists only in Dostoyevsky's nightmares but whose crime, murder for the sake of an idea, proves its reality again and again. Faint snare drums sound at the beginning of Mitya's as yet unwritten Rat Theme. Something is coming closer. Mitya reaches for the whirling leaves, and his mittens fall off. Scoldingly, his mother bends down. Time ticks, and the ticking of revolution's murder-bomb can scarcely be heard because it hides so cleverly in the minister's study. Measure by measure, death's overture pulses like the black arch-mouths of Saint Nicholas's bell-tower reflected in the Kryukov Canal, formalism's golden spire swimming like a fish-tail, black orifices contracting rapidly and sexually, more alive in their distorted untouchability than the "real" arches which overlook them. The future's darling gazes down at that trembling goldfish, then reaches. His mother smiles, pulling him away.

He was a year old when Bloody Sunday destroyed the Russian people's faith in their Tsar. When he was nine, his mother began to teach him piano. I've read that she herself had been a credible pianist before her marriage; her shy, skinny son sat down beside her on the mahogany bench reluctantly, if family tradition can be trusted, but—proof that parents always know what's best for their children—at the end of the third lesson, the mother announced to the family that he had "talent." The little owl's eyes rolled.

The actress N. L. Komarovskaya remembers how even when he was "a small pale youth with a disobedient lick of hair on his forehead," his prankishness went against the grain. They would tell him to play a foxtrot, for example, and although he'd try (unlike generations of Party activists, Komarovskaya herself remained sure that he honestly intended to be agreeable), his fingers would soon begin to gallop into an incessance completely removed from zeal; then alien improvisations kidnapped the melody, leaving harsh crazed chittering behind. Didn't he understand his errors? Since he remained too young to be guilty of cynicism, nobody knew whether to call him shy, incompetent or merely bewildered.—His compositions are very good, said Cousin Tania. Of course, some of them one cannot understand from the first hearing.—He looked up, as if he heard somebody calling. In truth, whenever his fingertips settled upon a piano, the white keys took on a brilliance as lovely as icicles on a roof when the late-afternoon sun touches them, while the black keys became slits in the whiteness of the world, holes which gaped from meaning all the way down to pure music. What was he to do? Lost, deliciously dazzled, he played the ineffable.

A month after his eleventh birthday, revolution struck. The minds of the losers learned to duck down behind frozen eyes. In the fourth movement of his life, when the Hitlerites arrived, Leningrad would get indrawn still further, within the barrier of the Circle Railroad. Cigarette-smoking, helmeted Fascists would burn villages all around, kicking Russian corpses in disgust. German shells would scream proudly in, and people were more than willing to stand aside for *them,* but . . . *Boom!* An explosion of rapture set the minister's house ablaze! *Boom!* The conductor's baton came sizzling down . . . —Dmitri Dmitriyevich, you've really won a victory on the cultural front!—Thank you, thank you, the young composer whispered. He crossed his legs and uncrossed them. Uneasy grimaces flittered across his cheeks.

Even in the Conservatory, as I've implied, he'd excited jealousy. Certain other students (epoch-tuned, let's call them) sought to strip him of the stipend which armored him against outright hunger. All the same, they didn't win. His mother tried to fight them when they took away his borrowed piano, but he told her not to worry; he could hear each chord in his head as soon as he wrote it on paper. Beethoven hadn't let deafness stop him, so Mitya himself could still, well, you know. Ever since his thirteenth birthday he'd consecrated himself in our Revolution's unheated classrooms. His mother almost starved to feed him; older girl students in threes and fours protected him, fluttering their fingers around long white cigarettes. The worst taunts of his peers (which is to say, their comradely criticisms) hardly ruffled him. It's easy enough to say that he "believed in himself," but that means nothing; don't we each seek our own interest, and dread being crossed? Or, as Mitya would put it, each one composes his own score, and then we all compare versions. Can't I say that he believed in the power of music? The Civil War meant this to him: Sailors from our Baltic Fleet got serenaded by Beethoven's Ninth, then sailed directly to the front to fight the Whites! He was there on the quay, aged fifteen; he thought that the orchestra handled its task reasonably well, although the chorus was, well, one must make allowances for hungry people. And the sailors, you see, they were more than interested, because some of them even, how can I begin to tell you? For example, he wouldn't forget the grizzled pirate who'd clapped his hands like a child. Some of them were so happy that they cried. Their deputies said it was the first time that anyone had ever, you understand. And we had no bread to give them, not even that! All the same, they, they, how can I put this; they *thanked* us! Then they went off and, I think you can imagine. Many didn't come back.—In short, Shostakovich scorned practicality. The whole

Revolution did, or claimed to; but in this life we find people who, no matter how zestfully they imitate Raskolnikov by murdering the old pawnbroker, only pretend to be, as the Rascal convinced himself he was, one of the gods, the arbiters, the "extraordinary men"; their real motive for murder, as we know quite well, is greedy gain. Shostakovich would never be one of them. Nourished by the melodies he composed, he kept up his fighting strength, such as it was (to look at him, you'd think him far from formidable), his expectations guarded and comforted by the knowledge that should the pressure ever become more than he could bear, the world within the black keys would shelter him.—You're just a masturbator, sneered one of his rivals. The way your music sounds, I'd bet anything you don't come from the working class!—Mitya felt hurt by their malice, to be sure, especially since his grandfather had been a revolutionist in Siberia! Regardless, nobody broke through his defenses. Rapidly wiping his glasses, he faced the other boys down in calm awareness of his own worth.

It began to be said of him that he was an individualist. His allegiance to collective life was only a pretense. He could not overcome his addiction to the transgressive harmonies of the chromatic scale.

At about the time that we won the war, shot Kolchak and those scum, and established Soviet power forever, Shostakovich was playing piano for money at the Bright Reel cinema palace, his fingers rushing ahead of the so-called "action" in those silent movies whose mediocrity oppressed him into a fury; when the hero died he'd tinkle out some merrily banal improvisation; when the heroine got kissed he'd pound out a motif or two from Wagner's "Götterdämmerung," meanwhile trying to stifle his tubercular cough. Oh, he had his fill of playing to order, thank you! It was all the same and it always *would* be the same, so he'd show them! Sometimes the patrons complained; more often they were so busy groping each other, or so, how should I say, *ignorant,* that they didn't notice. At times they even complimented him. One legless ex-colonel who came to each film half a dozen times always shook a finger at him and said: With more feeling, my boy! Make us laugh; make us cry!—But I, yes, yes, *yes*! replied our high-pitched owl. Next time I'll get it right! More feeling; let me just write that down, so that I can, um, you know.—Then he'd regurgitate the tale into the projectionist's ear, laughing and coughing. Every afternoon on the way to work he said to himself: If I'm doing this five years from now, I deserve to be, if you see what I mean, *scorned*. The tiny bare bulb over the piano almost warmed his hands. Here came Lenin to the rescue! He'd played this part forty-two times. At this point he'd really better pay attention, because if you mock Lenin you might be in for it. All right, all right; now Lenin's gone I can cut more capers; Dmitri and Elena are parting forever, so let's play a wedding march! When the management finally let him go, after a whole month, it was a relief.

Before he was even twenty, his First Symphony premiered with the Leningrad Philharmonic. As might be imagined, a faction opposed the debut. Objections of immaturity and grotesquerie he met with his usual implacable courtesy.—A very original approach, said the conductor, N. Malko. From an instrumental point of view, it's as compressed as chamber music. The Philharmonic would be honored to perform this, Mitya.—Our prodigy squirmed, staring rigidly down at the piano.—One small matter, however, Malko continued. Would you mind playing the finale for me again? . . . As I thought. You play very precisely, young man, with consideration for the notes. That's good. But the tempo of the finale is impossibly rapid.—The boy smiled, rolling his owl-eyes.—So you agree to alter that much, at least, Mitya? You see, it's rehearsal time, and . . . —Yes, comrade conductor, I promise to take your advice in my next symphony. . . . —Without difficulty, the musicians played the finale as written.

On the day of the premiere, Mitya did not show any nervousness whatsoever, aside from a tremor in his left leg. He went to the library and read about the sexual habits of insects. To his friend I. Sollertinsky, with that customary half-offensive mischievousness, he proposed orchestrating a "Dance of Shit." At the Lion Bridge he flirted with a girl named Tatyana Glivenko. To be specific, he informed her that she was a pouting-faced lyre with crab-claws, and that he longed for her to pinch him while he tickled her strings—the correct approach, it would seem, for she kept him company all the way to Nevsky Prospect. After three kisses, he checked his watch. They kissed goodbye; then he permitted her to adjust his scarf for him and button his jacket all the way up to his throat. Then he had to run, and I do mean run, to the Great Hall of the Philharmonia (later to be named after him) in order to avoid being late, which would have hurt his dignity. Tatyana looked after him laughing, not quite forlorn. Needless to say, he arrived right down to the minute. Malko, to whom the boy already considered himself superior, now had to lend him his own belt, and whiten up his shoes with tooth powder. Then Mitya rushed to the mirror. He bulged his cheeks out just for fun. Twenty-seven minutes to spare! Malko kept telling him not to be nervous. Actually he was dwelling on Tatyana Glivenko, who was really, truly, you get the idea. Malko adjusted his tie. Twenty-six minutes. Satisfied with the impression he made, he tried to tease the orchestra by pretending that he wanted to speed up the finale even more. (Well, he certainly knows what he wants, remarked the conductor, smiling. I'd have to say that's all to the good! Our rehearsals have confirmed the correctness of his conception.) Then it was time for them all to take their positions.—It's going to be all right, said Malko, and Mitya, suddenly feeling sick to his stomach, nodded expressionlessly.

Ovation followed ovation! I don't know what his mother said, but everybody else was rapturous; they had to encore the scherzo . . .

After that, Mitya's harmonic experiments only grew more daring, almost obscene, as was the case with his first opera, "The Nose" (Opus 15)—"no accident" that *that* got denounced as a piece of formalist decadence. *Boom!* There's the Nose himself, wearing a tophat, singing crossed-legged under a Modigliani-like nude.—Tatyana laughed so hard she almost threw up. Then she pulled Mitya into bed, calling him her little genius. Perhaps she wasn't the only one. But he had to run away now; he had an interview with *Proletarian Musician.* Could he please explain his intentions to the public?—Well, giggled Mitya, but why shouldn't I give them a little, you know? I mean, I, I, well, when you consider Rodchenko's spatial constructions, they're like, um, plywood robots! So why can't I get wacky? *He* didn't experience any repercussions. Those so-called "non-objective sculptures" are really . . . There's one that raises its arm like a railroad signal, which for some reason gives me a, a, so to speak, a hard-on . . . —Long before dawn on a winter morning, Mitya spied them crowding excitedly beneath the stone awning of the Kirov Theater, although naturally it wasn't called that yet; Kirov was still alive: old ladies hobbling on aching feet, tall men in fur caps, students, intellectuals. Gazing at the schedules in the glass boxes, they waited to buy their tickets to "The Nose."—Please forgive me, he said to the activists who tried to point out his errors. "The Nose" was just a, let's call it a mere prelude! Wait till you see my . . . I mean, now that you've enlightened me, I'll follow the Party line more closely in all my subsequent operas . . . —The activists were satisfied. On the other hand, what if he were being sarcastic? Throughout Leningrad (a city riven into semiautonomous zones by its canals) it was said that he and his friends all belonged to that faction which fetishizes the so-called "freedom of the artist." Those were Akhmatova's half-wild days; even Mandelstam was still allowed to sing. But Mitya, permeated with restless vulnerability, appeared so unself-reliant, thanks to his awkwardness, that he *must* be docile. His well-wishers at the Conservatory continued to advise him for his own good, and thought they must be going crazy when each note remained nonetheless his own. Women committed similar errors. Because he loved so passionately, they were sure of bringing him round to fidelity. I've read that he often recollected with longing and regret his summer of free love with the nubile Tatyana Glivenko. Stretching out her arms like the double bars which lock ascending notes into a kindred beat, she called him Mitenka. In her orgasms he heard her moaning *coloratura*. She craved to take him brightly and forever, but, refusing to be trapped in only one key, he equivocated until she'd married somebody else. After that, he kept trying to coax her back. This phase ended only when her husband got her pregnant. Then Mitya tumbled into a confused darkness.

Let's call him a soloist. If he'd only lived in ancient times (and, of course, been blueblooded), what a life he could have composed! Until the end of the eighteenth century, so I've read, any leading symphonist remained free to show off his virtuosity by improvising a *cadenza* near the end of the last movement. Beethoven became the first composer to abrogate this liberty. He wrote all the *cadenzas* himself. Lenin and Stalin composed still stricter rules; for in order to safeguard the Revolution, we needed to consolidate, not deviate. Comrade M. Kaganovich sounded the theme: *The ground must tremble when the factory director enters the plant.* Meanwhile, *Proletarian Musician* said that if Shostakovich failed to admit that he'd taken a wrong turn, *then his work will infallibly reach a dead end.* But he wouldn't understand that, even though in his interviews with the press he dutifully recited: To be sure, I, I, obviously music cannot help possessing a political basis . . . —Dark hair curled down his brow in a sea-wave. The talent which bubbled so purely from his heart intoxicated him. It gave him such joy that he—poor boy!—thought himself entitled to exercise his genius in his own way. But the black court carriages of the old regime had fled, and their red lanterns were dimmed forever. No dissonance before the common chord!

2

Looking out the Conservatory window, he saw a troop of gleeful boys come running up Theater Square, flying a kite which some Komsomols had made for them out of Bible pages (confiscated perhaps from the Smolny Convent) whose illuminated majiscules and heavy dark characters in Old Church Slavonic took on a happy rather than ludicrous appearance in the air, larking about high over those young faces. To Mitya, who'd always considered religion a joke, there was something almost inexpressibly pleasing about this spectacle. He could almost imagine that it was one of his own orchestral scores soaring up there, which would have been quite, you know. Not that he wished to be torn, scattered, cut and then glued into diamond-shapes, not by any means! But why couldn't he compose a diamond-shaped concerto or trio which already flew? Wasn't this the Country of the Revolution, where not to innovate was to desecrate?

In the years when Stalin's accolytes were busily exterminating Ukrainian kulaks by the millions, Shostakovich did his stint at the Leningrad Workers' Youth Theater, trying to create proletarian art. Pale, boyish fingers flowed out of the dark sleeves, touched the piano, and made music happen. He really did mean well. Although he gazed steadily through his round glasses at the score, he never needed it. The musicians around him with their violins wedged like rifle-stocks against their shoulders each gazed into a private pit of suffering, discovery or joy. As for him, he got lost in each world he made. His tuberculosis lasted for a decade, but nobody ever heard him complain. Slender, formal, almost elegant (although he never got the hang of bowing gravefully), he produced his flawless sounds. When others sought to help him, he listened politely.—Dmitri Dimitriyevich, *pizzicato* might be even more effective here, they'd say.—Yes, yes, *yes*! he replied with an ingratiating smile. You're correct! *Pizzicato* would be a tremendous, um, improvement. But please keep it *arco* just this once . . . —*Arco* was the way he'd written it.

In 1929 they buried his score for the silent movie "New Babylon" after only a few performances—not for political or artistic reasons, they assured him, but because it had proved too difficult for the unskilled cinema orchestras to perform. Remembering his own unhappy career at the Bright Reel, he could well believe that the standards in the movie houses were low; moreover, his ego required only that he be able to make love to whatever Muse he liked, in whatever way he liked, not that the world adore his offspring. He didn't care to sell himself. If they didn't understand him, or even spread, how should I say, false impressions, well, Mitya was still free; Mitya was happy! If they rejected "New Babylon," that didn't put him out, because he could have written another score in two hours! Did they want him to do that?—Not exactly, my dear Dmitri Dmitriyevich, because in fact (we're sorry to tell you this) there've been complaints; people prefer N. M. Strelnikov's operetta "The Peasant Girl."—Our boy genius didn't care. To Sollertinsky, who rarely wore a necktie and who was now his best friend, he quipped: Overcoming the resistance of an orchestra is the work of born dictators!—Cocking his cap like a sailor from our Baltic Fleet, Sollertinsky clicked his heels and barked: *Ja, mein Führer!* and then they both got drunk. They agreed to be dictators together; they'd never let anybody change a single note! There was a fifteen-year-old whom Sollertinsky had heard about; she acted older; her name was Elena and she was a real secret weapon, I'm telling you, quiet on the outside and . . . —but just then A. Akhmatova passed by with her nose in the air, and (although they both admired her poems), they had such a fine time making fun of her behind her back that they completely forgot about this Elena.

It is, I am sure, no aspersion on Mitya to remark that for the sake of financial self-sufficiency, prestige, and above all, the leisure to whirl down within the secret well of his own mind's ear, hunting for that Beauty which alone defined his life, he'd kept compromising with the world. For example, he now wrote program music on occasion. How was that any different from playing the accompaniments to silent movies at Bright Reel? Besides, as Sollertinsky loyally pointed out, the employment of a motif was not at all inconsistent with sophistication, or even with the outright obscurity which Mitya still found so hilarious. Even Wagner wasn't bad at times, and if we could take his *leitmotifs* and run rings around them, maybe play a few ventriloquists' tricks so that nobody else could even imagine that this could be Wagner, what a laugh! That was how Mitya looked at it. Although it might be irritating to him to do as others told him to do, as long as he could build secret trapdoors and escape hatches into every score, so that the world beneath the piano keys hadn't been forgotten, he was still living on his own terms. Ancient masons used to wall up a live victim in each temple or bridge they built; when he was much older Mitya would immure himself in just this way in the cornerstone of his Opus 110; but for now there was no need to be as drastic as that. He might not enjoy his audience's full comprehension; but he still enjoyed its indulgence, which, now that I think of it, is not such a bad thing to have. If I bow to Lenin's memory and then create what I please, have I been any more constrained than a poet would be by the arbitrariness of rhyme? And so Mitya could still go on thinking rather well of himself. Moreover, pontificated Sollertinsky while he and Mitya stood drunkenly pissing into the Neva, consider M. Tsvetaeva's "Poem of the End," whose language wheels round and round variations of the word *ruchka,* hand. It was the wheeling-around which impressed him, not the *ruchka*. Didn't Mitya himself believe that content was irrelevant? Hadn't everything already been said? Our task was to say it in a new way, that's all. Now listen! And Sollertinsky recited the first six stanzas, which recapitulated the writer's feelings about getting jilted by some White Guardist in Prague. Forbidden fruit! thrilled Mitya, because if Tsvetaeva had slept with a class enemy then she *was* a class enemy, which made her poems all the more secret, illicit, exciting. Anytime she wanted, he'd certainly grant her a visa to come play with him beneath the piano keys . . . (By the way, she was supposed to be pretty, with half-lesbian tastes.) If it were therefore permissible (I'm speaking in the, the, you know, the highest aesthetic sense) for Tsetaeva to write program music, as Mussorgsky and probably even Shakespeare had also done, then why couldn't our D. D. Shostakovich pick up a few kopeks composing the odd cinema score, or inject a few bars of the Marseillaise into some piece of orchestral hackwork, especially if during the premiere he whispered biting quips into Sollertinsky's ear, to prove that he'd mutilated his creations in full knowledge, in which case it wasn't mutilation at all? Oh, me, oh, dear!

Those nasty fellow pupils who'd baited him in the Conservatory's hallways, Malko's well-meaning, pompous obstructionism, these and other quantities which before now he'd only recognized in isolation now thrust themselves upon him as the warp and woof of society itself, weighing him down like so many sheets of fine muslin which kept falling over his face. He brushed them off, and more came swirling down. Had he allowed himself to dwell overmuch on where they came from, he might have panicked. I for one can only pity him. All he wanted was breathing-space. Nobody thinks it reprehensible to lose time in carrying out the excretory functions of the bodies in which our creativity is for the moment nested; nor do we protest the drudgery of breathing which is usually required to sustain our projects. Wasn't it excusable, then, for Shostakovich to carry out the wishes of others in certain well-delineated respects (especially since he could write music so easily), in order to gain the wherewithal to please himself for the rest of the time? He still believed in himself; indeed, that undistinguished Second Symphony, and the public utterances which it had become advisable to make, testified to his belief: The end justifies the means. Just before he took his bow, he whispered in Sollertinsky's ear: *Ruchka, ruchka*. He was really as pleased as could be. After every concert, there'd be a party in his flat on Nikolayevskaya Street, Shostakovich playing the piano, the guests dancing, shouting out toasts and flirting with his mother, breaking glass, arguing over what was truly Russian, how to salvage something from Mussorgsky (at the end of his life, Shostakovich would re-orchestrate that composer's "Dances of Death"); and while the world whirled on around him, its citizens drinking until the very last tram, Shostakovich arranged a rendezvous with the latest girl, simultaneously trotting out Sollertinsky's skill at creating trilingual puns on demand; Meyerhold dropped by so that his stuck-up wife Zinaida could show herself off; Rodchenko had an idea about a new photocollage; I. D. Glikman was there to offer his starstruck services in adjusting the composer's necktie, and I think that Lev Lebedinsky might have been present, too; his sister Mariya cut up the last smoked fish and begged everybody to eat; Zinaida scolded Meyerhold for taking too big a fillet; Sollertinsky told another Akhmatova joke; Shostakovich cocked his head, blinking from behind his crystal-clean spectacles, and finally they were gone, his mother snoring happily in the armchair. He closed the piano silently. Then his long fingers, which unlike the rest of him remained sober, began to spider across the sheets of music paper. Someday he'd compose a passage that was even better than the "Fate" motif in Beethoven's Fifth; he'd pull himself higher and higher! He didn't know cold musical tricks in those days; music gushed out of his fingertips in orgasms of joy; what a young artist lacks in craftsmanship he often makes up for in sincerity; even when principle demands that he withhold, he can't avoid giving of himself. That's why the early cinema music of Shostakovich often evinces superiority to the later—no matter that neither one achieves parity with the "Fate" motif. In response to the Leninist slogan *Fewer but better* he infused all the major-keyed hum-alongs now upwelling from his grimaces and grins with *over and over, louder and louder.*

Running along like a musical errand-boy to earn his cash, he winked one owl-eye. He'd fooled the world, and how happily everything rushed on! (Mitya to Glikman, with the radio set to maximum blare so that no one could overhear: So Stalin, the Politburo and all the other brass hats are riding down the Volga in a big, you know, steamship, which suddenly, I suppose on account of, er, Trotskyite saboteurs, starts to sink. If it goes down instantly, who will be saved? Come on, Isaak Davidovich, it's easy: The people of the USSR!) Germanic oompahs, marches, good feelings all around, swelling heartbeat-drumbeats sped onto the score-sheets with a newness entirely bereft of self-doubt. Our self-satisfied young composer strutted onto the stage of his own dreams even when he was just sitting in the front row with his arms folded, a shy smile on his face. His mother was still proud of him and his biography was clean. Glazunov, Malko and other luminaries assured him of his virtue. Unmolested yet by what for diplomatic reasons we'll continue to call "the world," he retained such high purity of intention that his secret bunkers of harmony remained unpoisoned by any stray gas cannister. *Boom!* Moaning again, Tatyana Glivenko closed her eyes, hoping that her husband wouldn't find out. As the genius lowered his face onto hers, her long black eyelashes became twelve octaves of piano keys.

3

About "New Babylon" he didn't care, I said. But the following year, his score to the ballet "Dynamiada" suffered an equally premature death. On the verge of exasperation (what an innocent he still was!), he tried to talk back to the activists in their dark, pigsnouted propaganda trucks. Sollertinsky had taught him to smoke fancy "Kazbek" cigarettes. He offered them all around, but the activists frowned and refused to accept them. Why were they like that? He pointed out for the tenth time that his grandfather had been a revolutionist in Siberia, and, moreover, that if his best music was like no one else's, that was all the more reason for it to be cherished by the State. Unfortunately, Comrade Stalin had directed that only material in explicit conformity to the Party line should be published.

4

His friends advised him to safeguard himself. Didn't he want to continue his ascent? They said to him: Throw something to the wolves, even an old bone! Don't worry, Dmitri Dmitriyevich; it'll be a purely rhetorical sacrifice . . .

His former mentor Malko had now emigrated to the capitalist zone. Accordingly, he was beyond reach of the Party. Moreover, Shostakovich had never respected him. Biting his cheek, he wrote that open letter to *Proletarian Musician,* denouncing himself for having permitted Malko to conduct a Shostakovich foxtrot. Such light music (he humbly submitted) ought to be liquidated utterly, for it was a dangerous bourgeois infiltration.

He was ashamed, of course. How could he not be? His well-wishers reminded him that he hadn't done Malko any harm, that Malko (who never forgave him) could not understand current conditions here, and that by submitting to orthodoxy before submission was demanded, he'd avoided the worst.

The worst? he inquired, pursing his feminine little lips. And what would that be?

Don't even talk about it, Dmitri Dmitriyevich! By the way, is it true that Nina Varzar has been casting her gaze at you? She's a very determined girl, I hear. Whatever she sets out to get, she . . .

In spite of such precautions, his Third Symphony, the prudently named "Mayday," sustained an outright attack. Everybody warned him to be careful, but he ran two fingers through his cowlick and laughed. He still possessed deep echelons of self-faith.

In 1931 he composed the music for N. P. Akimov's fast-paced film version of *Hamlet,* from which most soliloquys had been stripped so as to avoid distracting the masses. They say that it came to him so easily that he composed most of it at halftime at Lenin Stadium. Once, when the Dynamos made some especially spectacular play, he jumped up and down so crazily that the score blew out of his pocket! He wrote it all over again in a twinkling. The phallic satire of the flute scene—a brainchild of the composer, it's said—became notorious. To amuse himself, he told *The New York Times: Thus we regard Scriabin as our bitterest musical enemy. Why? Because Scriabin's music tends to an unhealthy eroticism.* Then he rushed off to bed with Tatyana Glivenko.

We dynamited the Cathedral of Christ the Savior—another victory against reaction. We put more Mensheviks on trial and demanded that they be shot; it was in all the newspapers. Counterrevolutionaries made confessions in court and then disappeared.—Well, well, said Shostakovich's friends, maybe they're guilty after all.

That same year saw the premiere of his ballet "Bolt," which dealt with the theme of industrial sabotage. A critic in *Rabochii i Teatr* wrote that the reaction of the people to such misguided entertainment *should serve as a last warning to its composer.*

5

The most infallible source on this period is of course our *Great Soviet Encyclopedia,* which states: *In the 1930s, Soviet musical culture made notable advances. Its restructuring was essentially completed.* Even now, Shostakovich refused to comprehend that he must get restructured. Against the best advice he persisted in pretending that the judgment in *Rabochii i Teatr* had been only a critic's grumble, not a hint from the "organs" of the state. After all, how could he bear to go on living, if he couldn't keep hooting his own owl-songs? (Meanwhile, Akhmatova was writing in her forbidden lyrics that *in this place, peerless beauties quarrel / for the privilege of wedding executioners.)* Time to nest! At the center of the Conservatory's square spiral, where in the past he'd studied and in the future he'd teach, our pale grub enthroned himself behind a piano, sheltered on all sides by the barrels of outward-pointing tubas, trumpets, French horns; their practitioners dwelt in turn within the collective porcupine whose quills were the bows of violinists. Then came the grey four-storey walls, decorated with bas-relief wreaths and the occasional lyre. Next, the hedges. Around them, the tilted diamond of Theater Square defined its outline-segments with edifices: the Kirov Theater, of course, where his infamous "Lady Macbeth" would soon premiere; the blocky mazes on the way to Rimsky-Korsakoff Prospect, the canal-curving apartment-fronts, and finally the walled courtyards of the Yusupov Palace, where Rasputin had met his quadruply hideous end. But all these comprised merely the inner defenses of D. D. Shostakovich. Theater Square lies at the southwest extremity of a long island surrounded by the intersections of the Moika River, the Griboedova Canal, and then the Kryukov Canal, which strikes the Moika again. Nor is this all, for the island lies within the greater one formed by the confluence of two watery arcs: the Neva and the Fontanka Canal (the latter of which will take you to Akhmatova's residence). Here is the center of Leningrad itself. The city encircles and protects us here. Someday there will be still another circle, whose inward-pointing evil causes us to black out our windows. Their four-hundred-and-twenty-millimeter railroad guns will enjoy a range of seventeen miles. They'll erect posters: **HITLER—THE LIBERATOR**. The front line will be death's ballroom, where besiegers and besieged get frozen into a stale *contredanse*. But these precognitions, which carry with them the sensations of perishing in an airless room, remained beyond the pale to Shostakovich. In other words, both the music which he loved so much and the utilitarian melody-silk which he spun out as easily as a spider still seemed to him to coexist within the same wholeness. In his nightmares he got glimpses of things; and the music itself (the purest music, at least) enkindled itself with sadness. No matter. Such was his nature. Although it got ever more frequently said that this precocious intellectual with his elitist pretensions enjoyed no hope of composing songs with the mass appeal of, for instance, K. Ia. Listov's "The Machine-Gun Cart," in 1932 Shostakovich's "Song of the Counterplan" (Opus 33) sounded continually on the lips of the people. Hearing them hum his melody on the trams made him as happy as if he were rolling his tongue to yell in concert with his cronies at football games. Ponderous, happy, military-march-ish, the "Counterplan" hallooed and hurrahed as if we were all really going somewhere, sentimental woodwinds alternating with delightfully pompous brasses. The same busybodies who were always admonishing him to be careful now told him that he'd scored another victory on the cultural front! Even the capitalists liked it; they appropriated it for a Hollywood movie.*

That was the year he married the physicist Nina Varzar. (Even then he desperately sought to persuade Tatyana Glivenko to run away with him.) To Nina, who tried throughout her life to protect him from the world, he sang a lukewarm Eroticon.

She herself had been an amateur singer. He quickly broke her of the habit of uttering imperfect noises in his presence. They were not happy. His soft, pale face had plumped out a trifle by then, and in it there shone more confidence and purpose than ever. His eyes, magnified by the lenses of the dark round spectacles, absorbed their surroundings with a nervous awareness which sometimes reeked of sadness.

Shortly after the wedding, we find his sister Mariusa writing to their aunt: *Our greatest fault is that we worshiped him. But I don't regret it. For, after all, he is a really great man now. Frankly speaking, he has a very difficult character . . .*

In 1934 he was elected deputy of the October District of Leningrad. He dreamed that he'd been called to Moscow.

Near the end of that year, Comrade Kirov got assassinated by the internationalist Trotskyite bloc (or, according to capitalist historians, by Comrade Stalin), and the great show trials commenced. Our newlywed still believed that if he only stayed away from politics, nobody would touch him. But in spite of his naive fantasies, Soviet musical culture continued to make notable advances. The poison tide was at his feet.

6

He was marked now, although he could not perceive it. His precious vanity sunken down into a secretive spitefulness, he went on struggling to secure himself. Through his heavy spectacles he watched and watched. I've read that his baby fat protected him yet a little longer, mitigating his most sarcastic grimaces into a pallid blur, so that nothing could be proved against him. Beneath that snowy flesh-armor, he further fortified his innocence within the sandcastle walls of dissonant abstractions. With women he continued to (so Sollertinsky phrased it) *play the octave,* meaning that he could sound the same note in the hearts of several conquests, just as a pianist simultaneously

---

*The title of the American film says it all: "Thousands Cheer."

touches two F-sharps eight notes apart. But he did that just to, how should I say, get by; because the secret place he lived in chilled him with its loneliness; not even Sollertinsky understood this; Glikman and Lebedinsky, who became his closest friends after Sollertinsky's death, never even imagined that the world beneath the black keys existed. At one point he tried to make love with as many mezzo-sopranos as he could; their luxuriant moans nourished his music into special richness. How does that Baudelaire poem go? Because I, you know, since Elena and I went our separate ways I couldn't really, since I can't read French, while she, anyhow, there was a rhyme, I think it was *measure* and *pleasure,* something very calm, slow, sensuous and, and, I don't know how to, I guess it was just full of itself, like Elena's hand gliding slowly down my back. *Calm, luxurious, voluptuous,* I think I remember those words, also, but nowadays it feels too, I mean I'd rather not verify it; I suppose I feel, what's the right word, disillusioned. In short, Shostakovich fell out of step with the times. His compositions weren't very, you know. Nina, who for all her violent temper would never give up loving and forgiving him, warned him of the bad impression he made, but he really could not control himself! A melody exploded in his head, you see, and he had to write it down! His reconnaissance-notes of alienness infiltrated the staffs of score-sheets like flat-capped, rifle-pointing silhouettes creeping through gaps in barbed wire. Of the songs which everyone else was being compelled to sing he persisted in retaining only the vaguest idea. Anyway, hadn't his "Counterplan" won a victory? Surely they'd remember that!

In 1935, when Comrade Stalin made twelve-year-olds subject to the death penalty, and Akhmatova was writing that *without hangman and gallows a poet has no place in this world,* his Cello Sonata in D Minor (Opus 40) provoked the authorities' wrathful puzzlement. All the same, Glikman's brother Gavriil was commissioned to sculpt a bust of Shostakovich for the Leningrad Philharmonic. That being the case, the model reasoned, why should he get, you know, especially since it wasn't as if he'd never experienced insomnia anyhow. They called him music's Kandinsky; they named him music's Rodchenko. Nina made a point of withholding from him the most frightening rumors that she heard at work; in too many respects, he'd never grow out of his frail childhood. Sollertinsky warned her that he was drinking heavily, and she said: You're telling me!

About Opus 40 we might note that it was written during the months of his adulterous passion with the translator E. E. Konstantinovskaya, and that its melodies reflect those emotional and sexual vicissitudes. (She slept in his arms. He lay listening to the wind.) Elena loved him without hope, although he'd already obtained his divorce from Nina. He wavered and trembled. Now for another English lesson; let's play the kissing game; let's pick linden leaves on the paths in Tsarkoe Selo. All this is extremely . . . She gazed at him with huge dark eyes. She made him feel, how should I say, anyhow, it was irrelevant; this should never have happened, because . . . The more he saw her, the more painful it became and the more he longed to see her, although of course there would be other women; he had to, so to speak, follow the score. Meanwhile he soon remarried Nina, for the sake of the unborn child.

His music to the ballet "The Limpid Stream" got singled out for denunciation in *Pravda*. By then, forty thousand Leningraders had already been arrested in reprisal for the Kirov affair. Old Bolsheviks, engineers, generals, commissars, peasants, artists, doctors, students, whole families disappeared into the Black Marias. It was better not to ask about them. Glikman took him into the water closet, turned on the taps, and whispered into his ear that he'd seen four Black Marias in a row driving off in the direction of the marshes where Comrade Kirov used to go duck-hunting. The road dead-ended there. Shostakovich cupped his hands around Glikman's ear and replied: That's called, you know, dialectics.—Truth to tell, he couldn't believe what he'd just heard. It didn't make sense that anybody could be so, you know.

Elena Konstantinovskaya got taken for a ride in a Black Maria, and no one ever knew why. She was fantastically lucky; they released her after a year. In his nightmares, she screamed and screamed, contralto.

7

At the beginning of 1936 he was called to Moscow to appear at a performance of his opera "The Lady Macbeth of the Mtensk District." Such a summons could signify nothing less than the presence of Comrade Stalin. Shostakovich ran two fingers across his cowlick. He kissed his pregnant wife goodbye, took his briefcase and boarded the Moscow Express. Electric wires silhouetted themselves against snowdrifts as the train clanked southeast. The clanking could almost have been represented by padded drumbeats. His mouth twitching with enthusiasm, he thought to himself: What hilarious stupidities I'm going to hear! Those, those *hacks* who name themselves art gods, they . . . —He could hardly wait to be back in Leningrad, telling everything to Sollertinsky. After all, there was every reason to expect his reward at last. Earlier that very month, his colleague I. I. Dzherzhinsky (we needn't say his rival, for Shostakovich, always generous, had helped with the orchestration) suddenly found himself at Stalin's side in the middle bars of the decidedly mediocre "Quiet Flows the Don." Stalin congratulated him. And now nobody dared refrain from giving Dzherzhinsky whatever he wanted! Nina had opined that if Dzherzhinsky had any gratitude at all, he must have put in a good word. And why not? "Lady Macbeth" had premiered in Leningrad two years earlier, to more than half an hour of "hysterical applause"; eighty-three performances had sold out. It had even been performed in capitalist countries.—That means nothing, he'd joked to Nina, they're just hoping to, to, see if it measures up to my greatest work, "The Song of the Counterplan" . . . The musicologist D. Zhitomirsky, who'd attacked "The Nose," was compelled to applaud "Lady Macbeth"'s brilliant depiction of "the despair of the lost soul," although he prudently kept his praises unpublished until 1990.

In fact, our naive, self-satisfied Mitya, finally beginning to realize what we wanted of him, was trying to be a better artisan! That secret world of chromatic dissonance which everybody called "formalism," he'd always live there and love it; he still didn't swallow the notion that music must be fettered to any "content," but since his well-wishers kept reminding him that he didn't eat the people's bread merely in order to exist for himself, he sincerely aspired to be ideological, to invest his talent with feeling, and to the very end, or at least until he composed Opus 110, he would remember with haunting vividness the purity of this project: create beauty *and* be useful. Beethoven for the Baltic Fleet, who was anyone to say that that hadn't helped win the Civil War?

When we first begin to awake from the stupor of youthful egotism, we try to negotiate with the world, trusting that with our health and strength we can do what we wish while carrying out the world's demands. When will full communion with the world begin? We are ready. Is the world?

Shostakovich had himself already met Comrade Stalin once—just last November, in fact, at the Congress of Stakhanovite Workers. Under the chandelier sat eponymous Stakhanov, that miner who'd overfulfilled his daily quota fourteenfold. Beside him sat Lyudmilla, the champion fish-canner; maybe she deserved to be in an opera. In any case, perhaps she might be willing to, you know. All those heroes and heroines were dressed in white as if to celebrate some bridal, but Comrade Stakhanov appeared particularly snowy. He gave Shostakovich a freckled smile and wished him full glory on the cultural front.—Thank you, thank you, Comrade Stakhanov! That is to say, I'll do my best.—At the same moment, Comrade Stalin himself, who appeared to be surprisingly short, sent the two of them a darkly complex look from across the hall. Wondering what this might signify, Shostakovich saved himself with the logical thought that, after all, a look meant nothing. Moreover, a brown-eyed young comrade who'd previously crossed and uncrossed her legs for a dazzling multiplicity of music-measures now laid her hand on his and whispered that she'd heard extremely promising gossip about him. When was he going to join the Party? Oh, my, she was quite the . . . And so Shostakovich was in thrall to certain hopes as the eight organ-pipe columns of the Bolshoi Theater loomed before him.

He entered the vestibule in company with several anxious music apparatchiks. (What a great chance for you, Dmitri Dmitriyevich! said the director.—Shostakovich grinned inappropriately and stared away.) Chandeliers glared sickeningly down on the black and white tiles, which glittered with that harsh light, glittering doubly with the melting snow which had slid off people's boots like dirty tears. They led him past the piano in the main lobby, his footsteps *pianissimo,* then backstage so that he could inspire the orchestra. His mouth was dry; he could scarcely swallow. He peered up at the State Box, which for all the world resembled a gilded four-poster bed; the seats of course were still empty beneath the red canopy. The crowd had begun coming in. The tiers of seats around him, which comprised a curving scarlet cliff, darkened with humanity. Music-loving seagulls, feathered in wool and furs, were settling into their nests. Shostakovich took his own red seat, surrounded by obsequious dignitaries, and awaited the rising of the red curtain.

All went well from the very first. Around him, the audience gazed with titillated horror upon the squalors of pre-Soviet Russia: a rotting house, with the onion domes of reactionary superstition bursting up behind it like toadstools. He'd refused to compose any overture; in the midst of revolution, who had no time for that? Moreover, revolutionary musicologists kept telling him that overtures, being free of content, were but formalism, which the people would not understand. He didn't want to be a formalist, did he? And so the soprano began to sing, and Shostakovich's music fell down upon everyone's shoulders like a snowstorm of gloom.

All his life, he retained an empathy for the situation of women. This Russian Lady Macbeth of his—really, I should say, of the nineteenth-century fabulist N. Leskov's—had been an adulteress, thrice a murderess and finally, spurned by the villain she'd done it all for, a suicide. To Leskov she was a predator. To Shostakovich she was beautiful, intelligent and doomed. In Tsarist times, when girls could be sold to be the toys of brutal old merchants, how could such a person as Katerina Izmailova hope for happiness? This was why the libretto contained scarcely a word that wasn't vulgar, nasty or bullying. The choruses of the workers had to be melodious and ugly at the same time—for example, in their farewell song to Katerina's husband, whose cadences he'd composed to convey that their sorrow was the merest pretense, derived from intimidation; how could any of them really miss their dull, cruel master? It was, in short, the opera's ideological content, not the composer's soul, which required that "melody" be permitted to shine only briefly, and then only in epiphanies of eroticism dragged down immediately afterward by the piglike gruntings of the brasses. (What a cultural soldier our Shostakovich! Throughout his life, his music would remain admirably *unrelieved.*)

Burning with enthusiastic pity, he'd already planned a cycle of operas about women. (And just what do you know about us? drawled Nina with a kiss and a laugh.) He'd brought his Katerina Izmailova to life and to death. His next heroine would be a brave terrorist of the "People's Will" movement. (She also must die, he feared.) Then he'd tell the story of a woman in the 1905 Revolution. Would her tale be tragic or not? It all depended. The final opera must of course be set in our Soviet Russia of today, when, as Comrade Stalin so aptly coined it, **LIFE HAS BECOME BETTER, COMRADES; LIFE HAS BECOME MORE JOYFUL**. The heroine of that work would no longer be an individual at all, but a stylized collective female comrade—woman cement worker, woman teacher, woman engineer all rolled into one. (Do those shockworker girls really dance when they jump off their tractors at night? That's what it says right here in *Izvestiya*. It sounds, so to speak, idiotic. They'd better not make me try to write *that* into my . . .) He could almost see a stern young Russian girl in red at the wheel of a combine, with yellow wheat all around her. (Better yet, proposed Sollertinsky, how about a parade of female fencers on Red Square, showing *lots* of leg?) To the press he announced: I want to write a Soviet *Ring of the Nibelung*!

He loved Katerina, perhaps because she didn't exist. Far more patient with this heroine than with anyone, even Elena Konstantinovskaya, he'd explained to Nina, who was disgusted by Katerina: All of her music has as its purpose the justification of her crimes.

So you're writing program music after all, she drily said, and he tumbled back into confusion.

Listening carefully to the bitter fartings of the trumpets, the defiant clashings of the brasses in Act I, he knew that he had truly conveyed the benightedness of prerevolutionary, vegetative Russia; and, moreover, that he'd carried the audience with him. The mezzo-soprano Nadezhda Welter, who sang

Sonetka the Whore's part in that "Lady Macbeth," later recalled that *sometimes one was overcome with a feeling of cold fear and horror at Shostakovich's brilliant manner of offsetting the eternal themes, good and evil, the striving for freedom and the struggle with brutality.* Now the workmen had trapped the cook in a barrel and were running their hands over her, singing out: Give us a suck! as she transchromatically wept: *Ay! ay! ay! ay!* Twisting anxiously in his seat, he read on all the listeners' faces what he had hoped to find: not amusement, nor even disgust, but outraged pity. In that shocking third scene, as Katerina Izmailova slowly stripped, letting down her long hair and crooning out her yearning for a man who'd caress her pale breasts or at least smile at her, he saw tenderness in his neighbors' gazes—yes, he'd shown them all!

There is a term called *portamento,* which refers to the sliding or changing of the musical voice. That was coming, but Mitya didn't hear it yet, for the strings grew sweet and heavy just as they should, gorgeously perfumed with amorous "exoticism." Came the seduction, half a rape—cold, angry and brassy, with jeeringly lascivious oohs and ahs from the brasses, until Sergei had finished, and Katerina's desperate boredom returned with an ugly wilting glissando.

Meanwhile, the music was *beautiful*—as smooth as the hollows of Elena Konstantinovskaya's neck—

At the end, he supposed, there'd have to be an encore, and then he'd be led up to the State Box. He could not for the life of him figure out what to say. Nina had told him to smile, bow his head and murmur soft thanks.—Do you have everything you need? Stalin would ask. Shostakovich needed any number of things, but Sollertinsky, Glikman, his mother and Nina had all advised him to reply that he possessed absolutely everything. That would please Comrade Stalin . . .

Shostakovich waited patiently through the pseudo-Wagnerian farewell of the illicit lovers in Act II, and still there was no summons, which he found odd. In the very first words of the third act, Sergei seemed to be directly addressing his creator when he sang to Katerina Izmailova: Why do you stand there? What are you gaping at?—She for her part kept staring at the cellar where her husband's corpse hid. And Shostakovich kept twisting in his seat, trying not to gaze at the State Box.

At the end of the third act, Stalin, Molotov and the other luminaries arose from the State Box, then withdrew in an ominous silence. Sickened, Shostakovich waited out the final act, composed his face into the deathmask serenity required by the times, and even took his bow when called upon to do so by the rapturous audience—for public opinion, reader, has its own inertia; and the opera's successes in Sweden, America, Czechoslovakia could not be instantaneously undone. He went backstage to thank the musicians—who recoiled as if he were a leper. His mouth twitched crazily. He took up his briefcase in silence. No one saw him out. He descended the portico into the blue pallor of another snowy night, then stopped. He gazed up at the rearing horses of Apollo above the colonnade—frozen horses. During the Civil War the lucky souls had eaten horseflesh. Oh, yes; that's why our sailors had eaten Beethoven. Yielding himself to the streets, he passed a policeman whose greenish shoulders were obscured by snow. A few hours before, he would have smiled at the man. Now he dared not look into his face. He boarded the Archangel-bound train, his fingertips tapping out the rousing, crazy, drunkenly leering march which seizes hold when the ragged peasant, having discovered the husband's stinking corpse, rushes off to the police station to denounce Katerina and Sergei. And Shostakovich's compartment clitteryclattered *allegro* as he rode away into the oddly tender lavender of a Russian winter dawn.

Two days later, *Pravda* unmasked the opera's bourgeois obscurantism. Expressing a quiet, well-mannered defiance, he continued the tour. Everyone was beginning to recoil from his guilt.

8

The Leningrad Union of Composers summoned him to a discussion of the charges against him, but he refused to attend. This, too, was remembered against him as evidence of unyielding individualism.

Within the week, *Pravda* exposed his collective farm comedy "The Bright Stream" as "Ballet Falsity." His coauthor Piotrovsky was ostracized and eventually liquidated. Shostakovich never wrote another ballet.

As for all who'd ever praised "Lady Macbeth," they found themselves in much the same position as those two female parachutists, Tamara Ivanovna and Liubov' Berlin, who'd been so desperate to best each other in the recent All-Soviet competition that neither one pulled her rip cord in time. What would the praisers do in this turnaround race? *Pravda* had denounced their "fawning music criticism." To save themselves, they must leap as far and fast as possible, leaving Shostakovich alone in the stormy skies of formalism. (And he knew that; he knew the rules. He'd done it to Malko. From Archangel he sent Glikman a telegram: Please send all the press clippings immediately, dear Isaak Davidovich! He wanted to hear each individual note in the symphony of denunciation.) They must rush to earth. They must exclude him from friendship, charity, memory. Ruthless seclusion in private, ruthless conformity in public—those were the two wires they must pull, to steer themselves safely down to obscurity. Now and again one of them got taken, and the rest turned pale; but because it was dangerous to comment ever again on those who had been devoured, let alone wonder whether they themselves might be arrested at the next tick of the metronome, they struggled to prove their faith in the dictum **LIFE HAS BECOME BETTER, COMRADES; LIFE HAS BECOME MORE JOYFUL**, because who wouldn't want that to be so? Some comforted themselves that Comrade Stalin did not realize what was being done in his name; for if that were only true, then they might not be utterly lost. Those afflicted with more knowledge than that still hoped that in regard to his growing collection of victims, Comrade Stalin resembled some bygone Russian *boyar* who, living luxuriously removed from the operation of his own vast power, needed to ask his stewards should he ever for some unlikely reason wish to find out how many villages, serfs and greyhounds he possessed. The truth, of course, was that night after night, Stalin sat up in the Kremlin with Molotov, tallying everything, commanding everything, initialing long lists of names to which they mutually added the prescription: *All to be shot.*

Shostakovich secluded himself. He kept saying to Nina: I don't understand.

On the tenth of February, P. Kerzhentsev, who directed the All Union Committee for Artistic Affairs, publicly urged and exhorted this Shostakovich to redeem himself by studying tuneful folk music from each Soviet zone. Because only the first few bars of this comradely criticism had been orchestrated, there remained at this juncture, like a canal-reflection of the **BETTER-JOYFUL** slogan itself, a trembling image of hope for the composer, who might yet be proved to be no worse than an egotist who'd committed careless errors. Sing an oratorio of contrition; perform the penance demanded; carry out any subsequent expiations, and his greying life might yet again become candy-striped like the tallest dome of the Church of the Savior of the Blood (one of Leningrad's more picturesque edifices, which our Party has now transformed into a Museum of Atheism). Several individuals, who so far forgot the common decency and their own security as to wish him well, remarked that the energy which he must now spend to clear himself would distract him from his apprehensions. If he only did as he'd been told, they said, the next few measures might be sunnier.

Shostakovich was silent, then humbly ambiguous. He requested a meeting with Comrade Stalin. Unfortunately, Comrade Stalin did not seem to be so disposed.

9

Whispering every night with Nina, he tried to determine what had offended *that bastard*. Then he got out of bed; he could hardly get to sleep anymore even if he got drunk. What was that sound? He sat on the piano bench shivering, his shirt buttoned up to the neck, staring downward through his thick glasses as if a score-sheet lay virgin-ready in his lap. Loneliness had penetrated through his egotism first. Next he began to feel the fear.

I'm trying, you see, he whispered, to, to maintain a philosophical attitude, but at the same time it would help if I knew *why*. I was wondering if you'd heard anything new . . .

Just take it as a joke! rejoined his wife with a stinging laugh. What does it matter? Anyhow, the joke's on both of us, I can tell you.

I . . . What do you mean?

Are you really such a child? Asking if I've heard anything *new*! Who's even going to talk to me? I don't have the nerve to borrow a cup of sugar anymore . . .

He tried to be funny. He said: This is only the first movement, Ninochka. In the finale they'll have to shoot me, so I keep saying, come on, let's, let's at least get to the recapitulation, but it's still only the development . . .

Keep laughing. I wonder if a person can laugh when they blow his head off? You are really beyond everything.

Well, well, well, well. Perhaps we both . . . But I really . . . Anyway, their speeches make my ears vomit.

Lower your voice, Mitya!

Tell me one thing, please. "Otello" is still my favorite opera of all time, and don't you still enjoy Verdi also?

What are you getting at?

Because "Lady Macbeth" happens to be dedicated to you, I thought, well . . . do you like it?

Slowly she came to stand beside him, resting one arm upon the upturned piano lid. Her belt was level with his face. Her pregnant belly touched his cheek, and he, he, you know. She said: Mitya, darling, you know I was very flattered.

That's not what I was asking. I wanted to do something *important.* If it's only art, in which case I didn't get it right then, maybe I, I, . . . you see, Lady Macbeth's crimes are a protest against the life she's trapped in, the suffocating existence of the merchant class of the last century—

You haven't said a thing. What's your question, exactly?

Can music attack evil? If I were to try, really sincerely, and perhaps to suffer, and to seek out the sufferings of others, or—

How could it do that?

The Baltic Fleet—

Go take a hike, said Nina. You don't think they would rather have had bread?

So you're saying that what I wanted to do was really, you know, *impossible.*

Who cares about whether it's impossible or not? You love to torture yourself with these abstract questions. In fact, you're so busy torturing yourself that you'll never—

Then they won't need to—ha, ha!—do it for me . . .

Please be careful, Mitya, oh, my God! What are you saying?

I do for some reason, you know, pity Katerina. As if she were actually . . . And if I could have made other people pity her also—

Enough with the past tense!

Then maybe somebody would even, you know, come to the rescue of some woman somewhere who happens to be as trapped as she is—

Stupidity!

And Sergei, you see, my music strips him, so to speak, naked. (I'm out of cigarettes.) Through his air of slick haberdasher oozes the future kulak who, if he hadn't been sentenced to hard labor, would have become a merchant exploiter—

Where do you get all this from? You're talking as if we're in public!

No, no! And stop interrupting me! I sincerely—

They keep telling you to apologize and apply for membership in the Party. Maybe you should just do it. Hold your nose and do it, Mitya! Never mind about me, but you'll soon be a father, remember.

I'm going to, I, well, I'm going to make a stand. When we're all dead they'll see. My music will—

Mitya, listen. I allow you your mistresses and your antisocial games, which might even be crimes. Haven't I done enough? Do I have to let you commit suicide, too?

Anyway, said he, feebly cleaning his glasses, they can threaten me as much as they like. Perhaps they won't actually—but regardless of their threats I'm going to keep on writing the music I please.

Very noble, she said, gazing down at his twitching hands. And what about your family?

Ninusha, you know I didn't mean it like that.

What's that book you keep hiding under the cushion?

Oh, it's—you see? Just an album of press clippings. Glikman was obliging enough to, well, I, I started keeping it last month, to see where my fault lies, so to speak. But, you know, I can't find it.

And he stutteringly commenced yet again to run through everything in the opera which might have been considered incorrect. (Nina's double shadow terrified him upon the ceiling.) Was it the police extortion in Act III, which could have been construed as a dig against our security organs? Then again, Comrade Stalin, being a busy man, might have overlooked the irony of the *Amen* sung by the workers when Katerina's father-in-law, poisoned by her, gives up his nasty ghost. (It might well be, given the earnestness of our anti-religious campaign nowadays, that one should *never* say *Amen* even in jest. This thought just now occurred to him. Mitya had grown up at last.) Turning to the music itself, he worried about the sadistic-sardonic music of the lashes striking Sergei's back while Katerina, watching helplessly from her window, shrieks in perfect time with each stroke. Someone might misconstrue that. Perhaps the abstract chromatism of the first entr'acte should have been toned down—

Are you kidding? said Nina. It's the entire opera that they take issue with! But I'm glad you see (she went on sarcastically) that the "organs" may not appreciate your denunciation of police corruption, and that maybe, just maybe, in this day and age, the vanguard might not be thrilled that you put in two priests and a ghost . . .

Glikman and his wife want to pay us a visit. Do you think that you can prepare something, if it's not too much for you in your, you know? I was hoping that perhaps—

You haven't even heard my argument, and I'm going to bed. You think you know what I'm saying, so you don't even listen. I'm not against you, Mitya, you know that. But just because everybody keeps telling you to toe the line just a little . . .

But—

Oh, Mitya, please, please be careful. What would I do without you?

He dreamed that men in high, shining boots came calling for him in the night time.

10

His former mistress Konstantinovskaya had just come home from the unmentionable regions. He went to congratulate her. (When he departed, she turned her face to the wall.) He said: Well, Elena, you see how lucky it is that you didn't marry me . . .

But she didn't care to talk about that. She merely said: I'm so very sorry about "Lady Macbeth."

May I please tell you something, dear? In fact, I—well, of course you didn't have a chance to attend my opera when you were in *that place*. So you may not be familiar, if I may say so, with the final act. The adulterous lovers are in prison, and . . .

She had been gazing so lovingly into his face; he knew that she loved him, which he would always know; she loved him more than anyone, so naturally circumstances prevented him from marrying her, not that he hadn't, so to speak, considered the possibility of—well, the truth was that every night he'd tried to, so to speak, compose the score of his life, which bifurcated unyieldingly between Elena and Nina, so that he'd frequently dreamed that an upper tooth was loose, and in the dream he kept wiggling it indecisively, until suddenly it came out in his hand, and with it a long strange bone which terrified him—oh! he didn't dare wiggle that tooth anymore!—and now she rose, naked from the waist down, and stood at the frosty window, lighting another cardboard-mouthpieced "Kazbek" cigarette.

And you see, I thought of *us*. That's why I wanted to remind the audience that prisoners are wretches to be pitied, and you shouldn't kick somebody when he's down. I was thinking of you, Elenka, oh, yes, I was—

Don't cry, Mitya. It's much too late for that. Anyhow, it's not my own suffering, but your own grief that you're afraid of—

What do you mean?

Stay the night with me, Mitya. Please. Nina won't care.

But—

He sat down and fiddled with his briefcase. He couldn't stop thinking of a certain violin theme.

She knows. You told me she knows!

If they're watching—

Of course they're watching. But I'm just back from *there,* and you're probably (I hate to say it), on your way *there,* so don't you want one more fling together? How can Nina begrudge us that? She's got everything else! By the way, are you shaking from nerves, or are you angry on account of what I've just said?

No, no, he replied, *decrescendo,* and then: I feel cold . . . Don't you think we both need some vodka, and maybe a little smoked fish? In my briefcase I've got five hundred grams of—please, not a word; it's a present! And I also wanted to say . . . Shall we each have a sample? Well, to be sure, they're all waiting for my bad end. It's . . . Here, Elenochka, do you see what I have with me? Sollertinsky gave me this sturgeon. I don't know where he got it—

I'll make up our bed now, Mitya, she said quietly.

But I can't stay all night. I—

11

Pitying his dear friend Sollertinsky, who was being hounded for his loyalty (and already lay under suspicion in any event, on account of his fluency in more than two dozen foreign languages), Shostakovich gave him permission to vote appropriately. Sollertinsky thanked him in a trembling voice. Thus the resolution of the Leningrad composers to condemn the opera in accordance with the line laid down by *Pravda* was carried "unanimously" (for they dared not report the abstention of the modernist V. Shcherbachov).

In Moscow, his colleague V. Y. Shebalin was twice "invited" (in accents of the utmost menace) to speak against him. Rising at last, he said: I consider that Shostakovich is the greatest genius among composers of this epoch.—As a result of this, Shebalin's music could no longer be performed.

Gorki himself petitioned in favor of Shostakovich, but without success. He would soon die mysteriously—poisoned, so they say, by order of Comrade Stalin.

Disregarding the peril to his famous theater, V. E. Meyerhold, who'd employed him back in unconsolidated days, defended the composer publicly and passionately, insisting: *Experimentation must never be mistaken for pathology.*—Shostakovich hung his head fearfully then, wiping the sweat from his forehead. Doubtless in consequence of this and other crimes that Meyerhold was arrested two years later. He disappeared forever. His wife was found dead at home, with her eyes sliced out.

From these events, Shostakovich was forced to form certain conclusions, one of which had to do with "Lady Macbeth": Comrade Stalin, it seemed, preferred the musical "Volga-Volga."

12

At the corner table of a certain glamorous bar on Gorki Street where he used to wait for Elena, there'd once sat a man in smoked glasses and raspberry boots who slowly drank beer and stared into his face. Pretending that he didn't exist, Shostakovich ordered a vodka. As soon as she came running in, her whole face already smiling with love, the man paid, rose and strode out, gazing over his shoulder at them. And *she*—no, better not to talk about that! What had it meant? Nothing. She'd been taken, but not then, nor with him; so it couldn't have been guilt by association. He couldn't be responsible. Or had her arrest been intended simply to frighten him?

He wondered whether he should avoid her completely from now on, for the sake of his wife and the child in her belly. It was, so to speak, a sad situation, really, one might say almost a desperate one but I, you see, I exaggerate. Once he told Glikman, who was one of the few people not to shun him in those days: The things you love too much perish, my dear Isaak Davidovich. That's why it's necessary to, well . . . —Evidently he hadn't loved this E. E. Konstantinovskya too much, or he would have, you know. Elena, you see how lucky it is that you didn't marry me. So he didn't have to worry; she wouldn't perish if he failed to keep her at arm's length. He decided to visit her again, just to, you get my drift, but a familiar-looking man boarded the streetcar behind him and got off when he did, so . . . Actually it was just as well, because . . .

13

The cliché runs that there are no atheists in foxholes, but in our Soviet Union, where anyone who refuses to be an atheist is either a counterrevolutionary or an idiot, the inhabitants of pits tend to call upon that living God, Comrade You-Know-Who. Who else could intercede? Summoning his courage, Shostakovich prevailed upon himself to disturb Marshal Tukhachevsky, with whom he'd been acquainted for more than ten years. Scourge of Poland, butcher of Kronstadt and Tambov (his maxim for eradicating anti-Soviet banditry: *One should practice large-scale repression and employ incentives*), proponent of mechanization, mobility and operational shock, Tukhachevsky had attended four performances of "Lady Macbeth." His favorite passage is said to have been the bewitching yet snaky string music when Katerina Izmailova promises to live openly with her lover. (Well, Elena, you see how lucky it is that you didn't marry me.) Rapid-spoken, cleanshaven almost like a schoolboy, our Red Army's strategic genius was himself an amateur violinist and violin-maker. Moreover, he and Shostakovich both admired the ballerina Olga Lepeshinskaya's legs. What fun they always had together!—The legs, I mean.—Well, Tukhachevsky had fun, anyhow; Shostakovich for his part never got over a certain fear of, well, of Tukhachevsky's eyes . . .

He arrived exactly on time, wearing his best suit, in the desperate expectation, which can hardly be named confidence, that if he supplicated punctually and receptively, then this pain which goaded him to rush about as if his very flesh were on fire surely *must* be put to rights, simply because it felt so terrible that he could continue living only by believing in its imminent cessation. And who hasn't felt the same way? The punished child, the one whose lover has just kindly, gravely announced that she's leaving him forever, the Arctic explorer perishing for want of food, how can they not keep faith with the proposition that undeviatingly following a given method will save them? Tukhachevsky, then, was the shaman from whom rain is expected.

In the sitting room, all windows remained flagrantly uncurtained. It was almost like dwelling in the drowned dream-days of Petersburg with her many lamps, ballrooms, mazurkas and gallant cavalrymen. Akhmatova was reciting poems at the Straw Dog; everybody was having orgies, in which poor Mitya was too young and studious to join. Then the red spiral exploded: *Boom!* A quarter-century from now, he'd represent that explosion in Opus 110. But where was the Marshal's family? Had Shostakovich become so unclean that they disliked being present, or . . . ? He dared not ask. Jigging his foot and grimacing in a thousand ugly contortions, he gazed down at his clenched hands, ashamed of himself while striving to pretend that Tukhachevsky noticed no sign of it.—I *expected* you'd get in some fix! the "Red Napoleon" was saying in a pleasant baritone, but Shostakovich felt so asphyxiated by his own terror that he understood nothing.

He had imagined that his host's official car would be waiting. They'd ride out to the woods, or to the exhibition halls of the Hermitage, and then they'd stroll almost side by side, this tall, ingenuous-eyed patron half a measure ahead, talking to Shostakovich over his shoulder exactly as he always did on their accustomed outings when rattling off his theories about cinema, French impressionism, German prison camps and the most effective way to execute hostages. But the car was not there. Well, the family must have taken it, or . . . This divergence from the score threw Shostakovich off. And Tukhachevsky looked so strong and handsome in that new suit . . .

Play me the first movement of your new symphony, Mitya. I want to hear it again because there's something in the tempo which (with all respect) deserves criticism. You haven't been criticized enough yet, they say. What a world!

I—

Why don't you join the Party?

You see, I—

Don't be bashful. The piano's right there. It just got written up in *Pravda.* Do you know why?

I beg your pardon—

Ha, ha! Because it's *mine*! When I was in London last month, a certain music-lover asked me: Marshal Tukhachevsky, if you had to represent the sounds of war by a single musical instrument, which would you choose? And I chose the piano, mainly to annoy him, because he was expecting me to light on something more percussive, but I do stand by the fact that there's an inhuman quality about the piano, elegant and cold at the same time, like an operational plan which will result in thousands of enemy casualties . . .

Mikhail Nikolayevich, he blurted out, please understand me. I'm not here for myself. I've come to realize that I'm not deserving—

No need to feel shy around old friends, Mitya! You know how much I admire your work. Especially since they're all complimenting you now. I especially like this one: *He ignored the demand of Soviet culture that all coarseness and wildness be abolished from every corner of Soviet life.* When I read that in *Pravda,* I laughed so hard my wife almost called the doctor! Will you autograph that one for me? *All coarseness and wildness!* I've memorized it, you see! Remember the time you forced that Elena Whatshername to drink half a liter of vodka? That was wildness, to be sure. Whatever happened to her?

I—

She *took a holiday,* didn't she? Well, no harm done. But from now on she'll have to be more careful in her associations, if you get my drift . . .

I understand, Shostakovich dully whispered.

But of course you want to make Nina Vasiliyevna's life a trifle easier. That's natural. How is she, by the way?

Nina? Oh, extremely well, thank you, except that she—

And when is she expecting?

Shostakovich was thinking to himself: No matter what the outcome of all this, even if I'm completely rehabilitated someday, I'll never be what I was. When Father's hair turned grey all at once we didn't understand how that could happen; Mariya kept saying it was like some kind of spell. Why can't I concentrate? Is he asking me something right now? But I know myself now, and I, well, I don't *like* what I know! He's staring at me! But maybe that's a normal symptom of youth's end, to feel that the sky's greyer and that most of what I used to call beautiful isn't more than glitter. I . . .

The two men disappeared into the Marshal's study, to sit beneath a lamp which curved like a medical instrument. (His host shut off the telephones, and they spoke in low voices, just in case.) When Shostakovich emerged, he was smiling. He rushed home, sat down at the piano and began to improvise expressions of his tremulous happiness. For Tukhachevsky had promised to write a letter—direct to Comrade Stalin! Tukhachevsky had said: We'll solve this question *correctly.*—Tukhachevsky had assured him: Don't worry, Dmitri Dmitriyevich. I always get whatever I ask for.

He waited. He aimed to retreat from his apprehensions into his prior innocent state, which Leskov would have called *Russian boredom.* He rushed off with Glikman to watch another Dynamos game. Peki Dementyiev made a kick which was really . . . Nervously his hands sketched bars on sheets of paper, then gave birth to music-notes which peered from and clung to those bars. Tukhachevsky had said . . . Thus almost before he knew it he'd completed his Fourth Symphony, the one in C Minor (Opus 43), but the unalloyed congratulations of that capitalist lackey Otto Klemperer, then visiting Moscow and Leningrad on a Beethoven tour, only increased his peril. The next day, Nina gave birth to their first child Galina. Klemperer's name headed the telegram of congratulations. That would surely be remembered against him—none of which is to imply that he didn't like Klemperer, who'd drunk vodka with him in his flat and for whom he'd played the piano, Klemperer leaning back with a rapturous expression, Mitya dreaming that it was 1932 or '33 again and he was still the boy genius of our Soviet Union, whose song would be sung more joyfully. So what about Rodchenko? What about Dziga Vertov's experimental blendings of water-sounds, machine-noise and speech? (Tukhachevsky had clapped his hands and laughed.) What about Akhmatova, Mandelstam, or for that matter a certain D. D. Shostakovich? Dear Marshal

Tukhachevsky had brought them all back; for he was one of them—an unnerving man, it's true (Elena would have used her favorite English word, *creepy*), but all the same a, a, how should I say, an innovator who admired novelty and brilliance, and didn't he still get whatever he asked for? Oh, dear, oh, my, Elena, you should most definitely have married me! Because then, you and Ninusha and I could have . . . He cocked his head, offering and receiving confidences about the compositional secrets of Mussorgsky. Klemperer was almost drunk. Mitya was almost ready to confess which chord it was which actually caused him to see rainbow icicles. Soon they'd toast him so loudly that his mother would wake up; V. V. Lebedev would order everybody present to acknowledge the perfection of his own favorite team, which also happened to be the Dynamos; Glikman sat in the corner, nourishing Shostakovich with that hero-worshiper's gaze; Nina was still in love with him, I mean *really* in love; he approached the verge of his very first encounter with Elena Konstantinovskaya, not that she would exactly, how should I make myself clear? And then it genuinely became just the way it used to be, with the guests gone (Klemperer had caught the penultimate tram), and he was alone, writing music which was perfect as it came. He believed in himself again. Beneath the piano keys there was a luminous white place with ebony shadows where, you know, and I suspect that right about then someone's long dark hair kept him warm and someone's white face outshone the moon and someone's red lips spiraled inwards.

In this spirit he reread the score for the Fourth Symphony and found nothing to correct, which was precisely why at rehearsal the scared musicians played badly, fixing on him the sad and angry eyes of Russian icons, for this composition reeked so stiflingly of formalism that their own participation might be considered provocation. And so he was summoned to the director's office.

What kind of silence could have been silenter than the noiseless fear which oozed out of his orchestra at that moment, the musicians lighting cigarettes alone, shying away from their own instruments as if from something dangerously electrified? When he returned downstairs, sweaty and ashen, he announced that he had made a personal and entirely voluntary decision to withdraw it from the program. It would not be performed until the end of 1961.

He went home to tell Nina. Although she hadn't changed face when her own mother rode away in a Black Maria, she exploded into tears.

14

He dreamed that he was walking alone down a snowy street in Moscow. Perhaps it was Gorki Street; there was a fancy bar there where he used to drink with Elena Konstantinovskaya. Before him, a heavenly light shone through a windowpane. Suddenly the glass shattered terrifyingly, and light and warmth dribbled into his face.

He and Nina went to the polling place to vote for the candidate for Supreme Soviet. There was only one name on the ballot.

On the sixth of December, during the celebrations in honor of the new Stalin Constitution which guaranteed the rights of all peoples, he whispered to Glikman: If they chop off both my hands, I'll keep writing music with the pen in my teeth . . .

15

He was now in what might be called his life's first *entr'acte,* when the orchestra of compulsion laid down its poisoned violin-bows, and the audience, namely Shostakovich himself and all who cared for him, were momentarily permitted to leave their seats for a moment, descend the marble steps, and stand by the open window smoking cigarettes. What would happen next? Comrade Stalin had written the program, but the program was nowhere distributed. Bribe the usher as many rubles you liked; you still couldn't get a glimpse of what was coming. The bell rang. Everyone rushed back. The monsters resumed singing.

They arrested his brother-in-law. They carried off his NKVD contact V. Dombrovsky and liquidated him. A Black Maria came for one colleague after the next. They exiled his elder sister in Central Asia. He went to the NKVD office on Liteiny Boulevard to plead for her, but without success. He barely had time to buy her warm felt boots . . .

He toed the line. He went to Lenin Stadium, leaped up and opened his mouth to cheer for the Dynamos, although no sound came out. (What's that sound? he asked himself. I mean that, that sound that didn't . . . Where is it? When I hear it will I scream?) Glikman rang him up to invite him to go see R. L. Karmen's newsreel "On the Events in Spain," because that might give him ideas. Poor Glikman—which is to say, what a thought! All the same, he went, just to, to, you know. As a direct result, he wrote an uplifting score for the play "Salute, Spain!" He also wrote music for the movie "The Return of Maxim."

A Black Maria came for Tukhachevsky. They tortured him and put him on trial. (He is said to have asked one of his desperately self-incriminating co-defendants: *Are you dreaming?)* In the interests of all peace-loving peoples, they liquidated him and buried him in a construction trench. They also shot his wife, his mother, one of his sisters and both of his brothers. His daughter and the remaining three sisters went straight to prison camps.

Not long after these events, Shostakovich was summoned to the offices of the NKVD to inquire into his connection with the traitor Tukhachevsky.

16

Our composer was punctual throughout his life. On the rare occasions when he was a minute late, he apologized in anguish. By the same token, if a singer or musician did not show up on time, he grew enraged. What intimidated him the most, therefore, was the way that the secret police kept him waiting hour after hour. It was a large old prewar office, with rococo walls from the time when Leningrad had still been Petersburg, with papers everywhere, even on the floor, and the smell of freshly oiled boots. All the people who had not yet been called were required to stand. Smiling, he mopped at his forehead.

There was a window through which he gazed, just to look at something, at another demonstration, dark-clad people clumped together in a long rectangle beneath the wires and bullhorns, some banners straight and crisp, some sagging. He was almost in sight of the former Army and Navy Club, where Kussevitsky had conducted Scriabin just before the Revolution; his mother had liked the performance; they'd played the "Extase." Her tastes were, you know. But then two Chekists shoved him, literally shoved him away from the window, and one of them said: Don't bother jumping, chum. You kill yourself, and we'll take it out on Nina. We know just what to do with Nina.

He started to faint, I mean really, so they dragged him into a chair and left him there for four more hours.

All right, Shostakovich, wake up and go in that office. Don't be slow about it, either.

They wanted to know whether it was true that he'd played violin duets together with the enemy of the people Tukhachevsky. He confessed that it was. They inquired into the matter of musical codes. What messages might be transmitted by a violin? (It's rumored that at the very end, the condemned man had remarked: I would have been better off as a violinist.) The composer replied: Well, comrades, I, I, which is to say, by training I'm not a cryptographer, you know—

Stick to the point, you shit!

Which favors precisely had that enemy of the people done for Citizen Shostakovich? And why was that enemy of the people's portrait still hanging on the wall in Citizen Shostakovich's flat?

They asked him what he knew about Tukhachevsky's plot to kill Comrade Stalin. He said he didn't know anything. They said to him: Today is Saturday. We'll sign your pass and let you go home. But on Monday you'd better be here, and you'd better remember something. This is very serious.

He rushed home. Thank God Nina was at work, because if she could see his face right now she'd, you know . . .

All that saved him was the arrest of his interrogator.

17

He stayed at home until he had stopped vomiting. (To Nina he whispered: No, no, it's nothing but a mild case of operational shock.) Then, biting his lip, he returned to Liteiny Boulevard.

In the doorway, the two sentries with fixed bayonets sneered and insulted him yet again. Never mind; he wanted to see what he could do to help his exiled sister.

What the hell do you think you're doing coming back here? shouted the prosecutor. Watch out, or you'll be next. I don't give a rat's ass for your so-called "musical accomplishments"—

Again he requested a meeting with Comrade Stalin, but received no answer.

18

Subtitled "A Soviet artist's creative reply to just criticism," and ending as it did *fortissimo* in a major key, the Fifth Symphony premiered to stormy ovations in 1937, but Party investigators accused him of planting applauding stooges among the audience. In Leningrad, the third movement's *largo* literally excited tears. People rushed to the stage like accolytes. The conductor Mravinsky waved the score in the air. Shostakovich grew pallid and weak as the defiant applause continued. Such expressions were an insult to Comrade

Stalin . . . In that same year we find him writing a jazz suite part of whose melody was prudently derived from Stalin's favorite song "Suliko."

He'd retreated somewhat, to be sure; he'd fallen back to his inner line. If you didn't know, you might call it, well, an agreeably stereotyped situation: children and all that, I mean. For instance, Galina, Galya, Galotchka, Galisha, what a girl she was! Her second birthday had been a star performance, although for some reason Nina had been very, never mind. From her he learned that to a child all things are pure. He envied her and felt ashamed. As for Maxim, that red-faced creature, nicknamed Opus 2, wasn't quite six weeks old. Sollertinsky said . . . Shostakovich knew that a father was supposed to get involved with his offspring. Well, why get overly specific? He wasn't going to wash his hands of anything. As far as his so-called "career" went (don't make me, you know, laugh), his hope was that he could still write the music he chose, but only on occasion and only if he presented it obsequiously enough. Glikman advised him to write more movie music, with lots and lots of upbeat chorus numbers; we all knew who'd like that! And if he could, so to speak, keep from being affected personally . . .

Although he was now officially known as "the enemy of the people Shostakovich," the "organs" nonetheless permitted him to rent a dacha near Luga, because it wasn't their way to strike always the same chord; and it was there that he slept in Elena Konstantinovskaya's arms for the very last time. It was July, so I've been told; he rose in the humid white morning to watch sun-play and leaf-play, which Lebedinsky later claimed to find in his Sixth Symphony; when he came back to bed, she was awake and almost dressed.—Did I tell you, Elena (it's really quite hilarious) that, that Glikman tried to persuade me to write an opera, well, more likely it would be an operetta, about a Red Army man and a priest's daughter in Spain? Because Spain, you see, is, well, with the civil war and all, it's a crucible of world struggle; Glikman hypothesizes that Comrade Stalin might, so to speak, *like* that. Have you seen "Salute, Spain"? I won't see it. Sometimes Glikman is very . . . Then I could put "Lady Macbeth" behind me. That's his notion, and—Elenka dearest, why are you crying?—I'm going to Spain, and I'll never come back, she said. And I've drawn a heart on the wall, behind the head of the bed where they'll never see, and in the heart I wrote our initials. I don't want you to look at it. And I won't kiss you again, not ever.

In the autumn of 1938, not long before the first snowfall, he announced that his next symphony would be dedicated to Lenin. Thin, anxious, pale, distinguished by a knife-sharp profile, he promised to include folk songs, too.

But at the premiere, not a single reference to Lenin could be found. The critics sneered that the finale of this Sixth so-called Symphony was nothing more than the recapitulation of a football match; he never to the end of his life forgot *that* humiliation, but at least his life did not feel threatened. For some reason there was a lull in the terror. Indeed, by 1941 his Piano Quintet in G Minor (Opus 57) had in spite of several secret denunciations received a Stalin Prize, category one.

In the press he read that the volume of production in Leningrad was now 12.3 times higher than it had been in 1913. He read that the Kirghiz composer A. Maldybaev's "Aichviek" (The Lunar Beauty) was now considered "a Soviet classic." This last item reminded him of his sister Mariya, still languishing in Middle Asia.

He lurked out of sight with his family, which *The Soviet Way of Life* defines as *a socio-biological community of people characterized by matrimonial or kindred relations, living together and having a common budget.* He and Nina sat in silence together, reading the *Red Evening Gazette.* To Glikman, who saved all his letters and from whom he concealed much, his voicelessness was almost literally godlike: Nothing perturbed the great Shostakovich! But they kept the curtains drawn. Whenever anyone knocked on the door, Nina gasped. He tried not to betray any emotion, but his fingers remained uncontrollable. He rose to clasp Nina tight against his terrified heart. He pretended to be kissing her, so that he could whisper in her ear: This is our life . . . —Sometimes late at night they could hear faint volleys from the Peter and Paul Fortress. Who was dying in the cellars? Galisha woke up and tried to hide; Nina worried that she would smother herself beneath the pillows. Oh, what a comic life we lead! I hold Galya in my arms and I feel better; then I'm ashamed of feeling better, because she's going to grow up alone. Well, well, I love my daughter; no doubt that fact speaks for itself. Shunned by the righteous and the prudent, he expected that midnight knock, followed by the one-way trip in a Black Maria. Elena had told him how it went. No wonder the celebrated "horror" of his Fifth Symphony, which in the words of S. Volkov *expressed the feelings of the intellectual who tried in vain to hide from the menacing outside world.* And now from that outside world came bombs, murk, lights and tanks.

19

Although it was the program music of the Seventh Symphony which would make him famous, the course of the war is better symbolized by the first three movements of his incomparably greater Eighth Symphony in C Minor (an unwholesome work, to be sure, for its pessimism deviates from the Party line). The opening theme truly does bear comparison with the "Fate" motif of Beethoven's Fifth, but whereas the urgency of the German melody is tempered by its composer's autumnal mellowness, Shostakovich's version strikes us as harshly as a Russian winter. The apples have fallen, snow is here, and destiny holds out no possibility of anything but evil. The deep, thrumming resonance of the very first chord evokes a community united only by sleep. Wickedness hovers outside the frosty windows of Leningrad. This wickedness is on the march; and the Eighth Symphony, compressing time like the walls of a condemned cell, hastens its arrival. In my own dreams on the nights before the anniversaries of bad days, I sometimes see my death as a tall shadow bending over me, warning in a soft baritone voice that I'd better rise up and get ready, for it's time to leave my warm bed forever. But it's still night, and it's so cold outside; I don't want to wake into that dream! And who is this shadow? It can't really be death; how could I possibly die? Russia for her part couldn't perceive even the outlines of the figure which menaced her, thanks to the Nazi-Soviet Pact which Comrade Stalin had so wisely signed in 1939. No longer could we denounce Hitler as a Fascist. We'd united with him against the imperialist Franco-British bloc.* When Germany swallowed western Poland, the Soviet Union upheld the interests of the oppressed proletariat and overran the east. Now only rivers and barbed wire stood between us. Diplomats called this expedient partition the Ribbentrop-Molotov Line, and in military maps it was black with swastikas and arrows on the left, blood-red with stars and arrows on the right. Every general who dared to warn of military preparations on the German side, of tanks and planes massing, got threatened with death.

In Berlin, that other composer, Adolf Hitler, was putting the final dispositions on the score of his Thirteenth Symphony: `Skizze B: Heeresgruppe Nord. Eigene Lage am 22.6.1941 abds. Operation` "BARBAROSSA." Roman numerals, an hourglass flag, checkerboard flags, numerals inside circles and semicircles, all of these stood dark upon a pale grey map of western Russia. The plural of *staff* is *staves*. His General Staff were all staves and knaves stacked

---

*As the *Great Soviet Encyclopedia* explains: "The Communist Party and the Soviet government foresaw the possibility of an armed struggle with the forces of imperialism, and, in the years of peaceful socialist development, adopted all the necessary measures to strengthen the country's defensive abilities."

one above another in parallels on the music paper. His score had no end. Shostakovich, it's said, could write twenty or thirty pages a day when well engaged upon a symphony, and *Heeresgruppe Nord,* Army Group North, would make similarly rapid progress across the pale grey flatness en route to Leningrad. The other two Army Groups proved equally exemplary. Before their symphony was done, they'd kill almost as many high-ranking Russian officers as had Comrade Stalin himself.

As any Conservatory student is aware, the staves for higher-pitched voices possess the royal privilege of slithering above their lower-pitched kinsfolk on the orchestral score. In Soviet prison camps the same rule gets followed, with our full-voiced thieves occupying the higher, warmer bunks, while the dying "politicals," almost too weak to utter a sound, stretch themselves out below them on icy planks or, if their voices are *really* low, on the dirty, frozen floorboards by the piss bucket. The German conductor likewise honored this principle. All of his generals who survived would later remember his shrill abuse, singing unceasingly above them. He, their sleepwalker, was the only soloist. Composer, conductor and mezzo-soprano, he made the music of his dreams.

Needless to say, the pages of a score are subdivided not only horizontally by the staves, but also vertically by the partitions between measures which assure that every voice will sing to the same beat. In the symphony called "Barbarossa," these bar lines were provided by a double file of tall German executioners aiming their rifles at an evenly spaced line of civilian hostages who stood facing a stone wall.

20

So came the night of 21–22 June 1941, when the stern, dignified melancholy of the Eighth Symphony's opening rapidly shrills into outright alarm. After a grim stretch of strings, it rises even higher into stridency, this time with a martial component. Drumbeats like distant bursts of machine-guns announce full war, and horns scream like air raid sirens. Barbarossa begins: ten contrabasses, twelve violincelli, twelve violas, thirty violins of two types, four trumpets, four flutes, two oboes, an English horn, two clarinets, bass and piccolo clarinet, and twenty-two other instruments across a front forty-five hundred kilometers long. The Soviet sentries come running from their pillboxes; they're machine-gunned down. Russia awakens far too early on that black morning, sundering herself into the brassy urgency of multiply solitary fears. A crazy, lumbering, hideous march brings the murderers closer: The

Panzergruppen have crossed the bridges. Now here come the planes. In two days, two thousand of our aircraft will be destroyed. In a week, Minsk will surrender (a crime for which Comrade Stalin will shoot eight more of his generals). The symphony wails on. Not a note but reeks of gloom and horror. A terrifyingly idiotic fanfare proclaims an enemy beachhead—they've taken Riga—or is this fanfare in fact to be taken literally as a Soviet call to arms?—or does Shostakovich hope that the "organs" will take it literally when it's actually excoriation of Stalin himself? Well, it's only music.

Suddenly we're illuminated by a hauntingly clarion thrill of trumpets. It sounds all the more genuine because it's so sad, almost hopeless.

The second movement, about which one critic says that *any attempts at jollity are quickly squashed and metamorphosed into irony and causticness,* could almost be movie filler music, sarcastically excreted by the young Shostakovich during his stint at the Bright Reel. (Once he'd almost got fired for his deliberately absurd music for the film "Marsh Birds of Sweden.") Throughout his career, ballet and movie scores were his bread and butter. When it came to his own work, he continued to expressly reject any claim to programmatic representation: Red Army men were *not* brass instruments, he said.—I do not believe him.—His trademark ambiguity infests this second movement. Does Galisha smile and try to dance? Then I've failed. I need her to, to, God forgive me, not that I believe in God! He made it loud; he made it angry, leaving in a half-cheerful bustling quality which alternated with marching dismalness. Then came the snake-rattle of death at the end.

The third movement, the *allegro non troppo,* begins in flight, the score itself, that pale flat sheet of endlessness called the Ukrainian steppes, being half obscured by burning fields and towns whose doom has been translated musically into low strings. It's July. Their Panzers will soon be here. Black tank-smoke's already on the horizon; the hot sky's black with burning. And we, imprisoned by Shostakovich's genius within the fear-poisoned heart-thumps of bass viols, must impotently witness all. Children scream like piccolos. That's also how they'll scream in Leningrad. I hear us running over the plain, passing abandoned villages whose huts and tractor stations will soon serve enemy battalions. Our footfalls are violas and violins. Burned-out oil lamps hang from whitewashed walls. New fires will come; summer is already scorching the edge of the music paper. Now they're all gone east, the ones who will get there; the rest of us are dead or hiding. Dimming down into sick expectancy, Shostakovich's symphony half-illuminates sorrow's carpet: unburnt earth, which soon will drink in blood and groaning. It's a near-blank page now, a plain of trodden grass scattered with the clothing of the fled. With evil speed the last rest expires. Then what? Ask D. D. Shostakovich that question, and he'll drunkenly reply: He who has ears will hear. So wait for death. Horns proclaim that *here they are,* crawling over a low golden ridge with their guns aimed at us. Run, run, run! Now they see us! Run, run! We hide! They come. We run. They come! Very suddenly, *we're them,* and it's all so cheery like the grin of a corpse.* We Nazis are rolling forward and shooting. (But call it a Slavic dance if you will; call it Stalin in peacetime, murdering Ukrainian peasants by the millions.) Ha, ha, ha, ha, ha! *Sempre cresc. sin'al.* With woodwind flourishes we're burning every house in Vitebsk; Smolensk lies afire as in Napoleon's time; smoke the hue of pure light boils out of windows. Their T-34s have all run away. With violin flourishes we speed eastwards through the golden grass. Crossing that same low ridge we'd watched from the far side in that primeval epoch when we'd been us, we spy the Reds fleeing toward the horizon. Never mind; our strafing planes will finish most of them. We're on the frictionless flatness of the score sheet now; with oompapahs and oompapahs our tanks cavort across this dance floor of gratified ambition, driving toward Moscow and Leningrad as easily as if we were skating. When the Russians do form up their troops at last, they're as feebly translucent as rainclouds on a horizon of *pianissimo* violins. Never mind their so-called Stalin Line, or their Luga Line; we'll grind right through both of those, hardly noticing their defensive drumbeats. We kill everything, machine-gun every last charging wraith. And the Ukrainian steppes roll happily on. A crazy old Cossack comes galloping at us, and we blow his head off! He careens; he's a fountain of blood, horse-waltzing ludicrously gruesome until he tumbles. Now the music tilts again like the upswung heads of hanged Ukrainians and again *we're us,* running, running before those brassy baying horns. But *here they come,* running us down . . . We should have known that the only reason that Shostakovich's nightmare restored us to ourselves was so we'd be compelled to drink the cup of anguish. It's not that we've run out of room on the page; we could flee eastward forever, the Soviet Union being infinite, but the Panzers overtake us in less than three dozen measures. Then . . . *Victory! Victory!* They're themselves, mercilessly. As gong, snare drum and cymbals sound a triumphal fanfare of evil, they crush us under tank treads; they toast themselves by upraising our decapitated heads . . .

---

*It is perhaps this part which most influenced Martinov's characterization of the third movement as a "Toccata of Death."

21

On 20 August, the Germans closed the ring around their flank objective, Leningrad. On 4 September, Field-Marshal von Leeb raised his baton: Air raids and bombardments began.—Don't worry, comrades, said our radio, we've halted them at the Ligovo-Pulkovo Line . . . —On 6 September, an enemy communiqué announced that encirclement was "progressing" toward a victory, and two days later Leningrad's last railway connection was lost. On 22 September, Hitler the Liberator with his usual kindness issued the following "Directive on the Future of the City of Petersburg": *The Führer has decided to wipe the city of Petersburg off the face of the earth . . . After the defeat of Soviet Russia, there is no interest in the further existence of this large inhabited area.* (In his favor, we ought to note that he was worried about exposing his soldiers to epidemics.)

Within this killing-zone remained two hundred thousand ill-equipped Red Army men, and three hundred thousand citizens hardly trained or armed at all, but gloriously enrolled in the People's Militia. Pale, weary women toiled with their hair tucked up, packing explosives into the shell casings which stood in rows before them like immense metal bottles. Their counterparts in Moscow were doing the same. Everyone was ready for the future, for death.

Comrade Zhdanov summoned the activists to a meeting and announced with his usual melodrama: Either the working class of Leningrad will be turned into slaves, and the best among them exterminated, or we shall turn Leningrad into the Fascists' grave.

The Party promised to be merciless against deserters. The Party warned that no selfish individualism would be tolerated. Shostakovich had heard it all before.

22

His Seventh or so-called "Leningrad" Symphony was by some accounts already underway before the invasion. In August 1939, when the faithful demanded to know why in defiance of all his promises that undistinguished Sixth Symphony had failed to memorialize Lenin, Shostakovich twitched, slid his spectacles up his nose, smiled to the utmost of his cunningly hidden spite, and announced poker-faced that the Seventh would be program music of a wisely sycophantic species at last: *First movement—Lenin's youth. Second movement—Lenin leading the October storm* . . . These words got eagerly reproduced in *Leningradskaya Pravda, Moskovskii Bolshevik* and suchlike organs of our trusting Soviet press.

The joke went further: The capitalist publication *Current Biography* proclaims in its last number to be published before the Hitlerites attacked Russia that *early in 1941, Shostakovich completed his Seventh Symphony, dedicated to the memory of Lenin.*

I've also read that it was not until July, by which time Army Group North had already overrun all the pillboxes of the Stalin Line, that the actual composition commenced. (The Fascists are cutting all the wires! cried his colleague Yudina, but when he asked which wires and with what result, she wasn't sure; she'd heard it from a loudspeaker.) Meanwhile, a certain Comrade Alexandrov has assured me that Shostakovich accomplished nothing before August.—The more one studies these various assertions, the more peculiar they become; it's as if on a summer's night the many canals of Leningrad were to join together and rearrange themselves into a spiral!—According to the next revision of his biography, by the end of July he'd completed only the first movement, which he provisionally re-entitled "War."

Does it matter which version is true? Musicologists tell me that it does. What, then, do we mean by "already underway?" I myself credit the formulation of that sad and angry torchbearer N. Mandelstam, based on what she'd learned from her martyred poet-husband and his muse, her rival, A. Akhmatova, that *the whole process of composition is one of straining to catch and record something compounded of harmony and sense as it is relayed from an unknown source* . . . Let's suppose that her description applies to music as well as it does to poetry. Whom did Shostakovich hear calling him? A certain woman with long dark hair comes to mind (you're so lucky you didn't marry me), but I ought to suppress this fantasy, which shows utopian individualism at its worst. The allegation that during this period he was wounded by a German shell fragment which, taking up residence within his brain, gifted him with sublime melodies whenever he tilted his head, is an equally colorful falsification.—Why not grant that harmony and sense descended upon him by grace alone? The pen flickered down the staves of his score-sheets, vivifying everything. Behind the blackout curtains, the candle kept shining every night in Shostakovich's study. Chords and motifs trolled between his ears like tank-silhouettes probing the dark teeth of antitank concrete.

Establishing the date of inspiration for the first movement is particularly crucial, since its infamous Rat Theme, the marionette in eleven variations, evokes the madness of German Fascism. What indeed might it represent, had its conception occurred while we were still friends with Hitler the Liberator? (Here's a hint: In the Rat Theme some critics claim to find a mixture of "Deutschland über Alles" and the "Merry Widow"; but there may also be a trace of Tchaikovsky's Fifth.*)

Whatever conclusion we penetrate to, there will always remain deeper levels of meaning, undiscovered bunkers, within the Seventh Symphony. Shostakovich escapes us; he'll die free. The conductor Mravinsky once wrote of him that *everything has been heard in advance, lived through, thought out and calculated.*

23

He dreamed that a bomb was singing to him. From far away, the bomb was coming to marry him. The bomb was his destiny, falling on him, screaming.

24

In August, the leaflets raining out of enemy airplanes advised women to wear white so that they'd be recognized as noncombatants. In spite of our loudspeakers, some of them believed. Their white dresses as they shoveled in the brown antitank trenches made them perfect targets. But then, so did the any-colored dresses of the housewives, who got blown to bits while they waited in bread queues. Fortunately, his wife had paid attention when he'd warned her: Ninotchka, their promises may be new, but their tricks are old. They're Fascists!—And Nina, wearing earth-brown, got passed over, although she came creeping home that night with her face spattered with other women's blood. History repeats itself. For instance, Comrade Stalin promised me the moon, but right after that he kicked me, metaphorically, you know, on my ass! Wasn't that a joke? And just when Elena finally felt ready to marry me, Nina announced she was pregnant, when actually . . . That was *her* joke. So that's how it is. Life calls for the highest order of deafness; then we can be, so to speak, happy. It's actually almost more than I can take. Why wasn't I, you know, born deaf? From his rooftop post, Shostakovich could hear the strafing and the screaming, with our loudspeakers trying to shout it out. Crash and

---

*One critic has even read into this symphony a two-note "Stalin motif" which first appears in bars four and five.

crash! The linden trees on Nevsky Prospect were falling. The screaming was new to his experience. Back in peacetime, when he and Nina had sat at home in terror, waiting for the knock on the door, they'd heard the shots across the city, but the screaming had been muffled under stone. It was now that he began to entertain the thought that a ringing shriek was at least more free than murder overmastered by silence. His music, how should I say, developed accordingly.

The Seventh's opening movement, which some believe shows indebtedness to Sibelius, does not scream at first. Major-keyed, yet "dramatic," it resembles a sunny forest dappled with bass motifs. It doesn't develop a theme as much as gambol in one. All in all, it's a pleasant, vegetative sort of melody, eminently forgettable. As he explained in a cabled dispatch to *New Masses*: The first part of the symphony tells of the happy, joyful life of a people confident in themselves and in their future. Elena, you're so lucky that you didn't marry me. It is a simple life, such as was enjoyed by thousands of Leningrad's Popular Guards . . . —Glikman wrote this for him, and he signed it. **LIFE HAS BECOME BETTER, COMRADES; LIFE HAS BECOME MORE JOYFUL.** (Glikman was extremely useful.) It broke his heart to remember the Leningrad days when Sollertinsky used to ask him what he wanted to be, how he wanted his music to turn out. Because at that time he had, you see, aspirations. Well, well. (Sollertinsky had just been evacuated to Novosibirsk.) Even Stalin likes art; he enjoys choral singing. And I, I . . . He contemplated what it meant to be walled in. Elena once whispered in his ear how it had been to be forced into a suffocating little compartment in the back of a Black Maria, with nothing for company but the groans of unseen fellow sufferers, each crouching in a dark and airless room. And then someone would vomit, she said, and it had already been so difficult to breathe. No one knew where the Black Maria was going, whether to another transit prison or to a pit in the forest. He clasped her in his arms and his mouth trembled; he longed to scream. Now he intended to make his symphony scream, because it may be true, even though Nina wouldn't believe it (let it be true!), that through music one can denounce evil and thereby, so to speak, accomplish something; naturally many people will disagree with me on this point, but the Party's with me. And so he'd compel brass to howl defiance, woodwinds to sob in despair. Why not? Nothing couldn't be turned into music! For instance, the sirens of the Stuka divebombers illustrated the concept of *portamento*, which, as we know, is the glide from one note to another on a woodwind . . . Late at night came the high-pitched insect-songs of approaching bombers, then antiaircraft guns roaring until the apartment trembled, and finally the bombs themselves whistling and exploding, the sounds of breaking glass, the screams, oh, God, Galya and Maxim screaming in Nina's arms.

But now Nina was on civil defense duty. His mother was taking care of the children. He wrote seven or eight arrangements for frontline concerts . . .

25

He volunteered for the People's Militia. When Nina heard, she screamed.

26

Gazing in bemusement upon those round spectacles, that pale, schoolboy face encircled by dark hair, the tiny, slightly effeminate mouth, our Party activists understood quite well that if they sent him to the front, he'd be dead in a week. Had he been anybody else, any other corpse, they wouldn't have cared. But even then there was talk of his Seventh Symphony. Capitalist intellectuals liked him. We needed the capitalists now. We needed them to open up the second front.

Don't waste time, they said to him. What is it that you want?

I, I, well, only by fighting can we save humanity from destruction . . .

Look at him! He even believed it!

Just as so many "politicals" sentenced under Article 58 were now being let out of Arctic prison camps in order to fight German Fascism, so Shostakovich found his previous artistic mistakes glossed over. They politely told him: You will be called to the front when you're required.

Naturally he had to utter a speech expressing gratitude for the forgiveness of his myriad errors. Indeed he did, cocking his head with a curiously mechanical motion. (An unholy light over the Gostinyy Dvor resolved into new corpses and a wall of smoke.) No formalism ever again, he promised. He assured everyone: There can be no music without ideology, comrades! Music is no longer an end in itself, but, how should I say, a vital weapon in the struggle. And I myself, having overcome my, you know, anti-people tendencies . . .

Having convinced himself that these words were but the tongue-tip's articulation of lung-pressure in a wind instrument (*fluttertongue,* they call it), he gave his performance, *allegro,* and afterward tried to forget about it. Nina was kind or tired enough not to ask him anything. They weren't at all hard on him. They had far more important things to do than crush a certain D. D. Shostakovich—

They called him. At first he dug antitank ditches, just as Heidegger would soon be doing in Germany. He was in the Conservatory shovel-brigade. Sometimes he worked in the same trench as the director of the Hermitage. Strung on wires like decapitated heads, the loudspeakers shouted out every clause of the Stalin Constitution. If Gogol were only alive to satirize *that*! Then the experience would certainly be more, you know. I'm not very heartened. In fact, all this is really, oh, well. Watching his fellow musicians roll up the sleeves and trousers of their suits (the only working clothes they had), then commence with great sweat and impracticality to move dirt, he thought to himself: If they hadn't shot Tukhachevsky, this would have been done earlier, not to mention more, so to speak, professionally. We ourselves are not professionals. This is absurd.—Trying sincerely (he really did want to do something), he dug as frantically as the others, his wide grey face locked up in smiles. Finally the Party assigned him to a rooftop fire brigade . . .

A portrait by Sovfoto displays him on the Conservatory roof, dressed in the pale slicker of a fire fighter, his hands mittened in the same shiny material, a double-belted sash around his waist, a shoulder-strap emerging from beneath his collar. Beneath the pale and shiny hat his delicate face half-gazes at us through the round spectacles. The roof has a strangely confused appearance, like the set of a surrealistic ballet. From the roof of the Conservatory he surveys the domes of Saint Nicholas, which were once pale and rare in their gildedness, and are now grey like every muddy day. By then our Alpinists had also ascended the Admiralty Tower and camouflaged it with grey paint. He'd asked Nina where she thought they'd stop. Would they grey down our piano keys next? It certainly seems as if they're getting, you know, carried away. And here comes another German shell; oh, me, oh, my, they're playing their *études* . . .

Between air raids he sat working on his score. On other roofs he could see the antiaircraft guns vertical like contrebassoons. Leningrad's streets were now mostly as empty as the music paper on which his notes, conjoining into chords or beats, resembled insects scuttering over the wire. Sometimes these dying bugs possessed but one leg to which a head, a thorax and an abdomen yet clung; sometimes blank stretches of wire emblematized perfect lethality; often he made evil, manyheaded bugs with bristling legs *(poco animato)*. His few friends not yet rendered hostile or absent congratulated him on the important work with which he'd been entrusted. Lowering his head, he replied with his parody of a smile: I, I, I want to write about our time.—Their praise only agitated him all the more, because he'd kept finding out that he was mistaken about people; he'd thought that this friend or that mistress could be trusted, only to learn that nobody was good; he couldn't rely on anyone except perhaps for Glikman, Sollertinsky, who was far away and who'd soon die in an accident), Lebedinsky, Elena Konstantinovskaya, who liked to be called Lyalya and whom it was best not to see anymore, because . . .

One day, three well-fed NKVD men in tall shiny boots came to his rooftop to visit. That was fine; he had nothing to do right then but gaze through borrowed field glasses at the approaching bombers. In the streets below he could see people preparing pillboxes in the manholes and corner buildings. It was time for the daily scherzo; the loudspeakers, which were our final defense within the walls of concrete and steel, began to shout out orders to take cover. But the men in raspberry-colored boots didn't seem at all anxious, for which he admired them. They questioned him about this prospective symphony of his. Where did he keep the score? He told them that it remained in his head, if one didn't count these scribblings in his pocket, and they threatened him with punishment, at which he almost laughed; they were so, so, well. To be sure, he could increase the tempo of his . . . And now below them the round-faced factory girls with handkerchiefs tied around their heads were running past Lenin's statue, which they really should have done ninety seconds ago, and the antiaircraft guns began to fire, and one of our boxy-angled tanks, which had been proudly lettered **DEATH TO THE GERMAN INVADERS**, attempted to upraise its guns in a Hitler salute, but just then the planes were overhead, bombs whistled down, and that tank exploded. Brown smoke! How should I represent *that* musically? That's what these bastards want. I'll just write them a happy, you know, crossword puzzle.—They didn't act afraid, so neither did he. The planes flew away; from the direction they turned he couldn't tell if they were going back to Siverskaya or Gatchina, which now were properties of Hitler the Liberator; he would have made small talk about that to the NKVD men, but it never did one any good to make conversation with them and anyhow they started threatening him again, or at least two of them did, and probably they weren't even threatening, just trying to milk more music out of him in their professional way; meanwhile the third leaned over the roof-edge and spat. People were coming out of their holes now. How many dead? Usually he tried to count, but right now he was, well, distracted. Even when they reminded him that he was a former enemy of the people, he didn't care, at least not then; every night he faced the same nightmare—a long line of helmeted Germans crawled toward him through a slit they'd made in the earth—so how could he fear *these* idiots? (But that night he told Nina that he'd been visited, and she trembled.) They "invited" him to play for them downstairs on one of the Conservatory pianos, the implication being that if he hadn't composed his quota of chords, he could expect the front line, prison or the nearest wall. Well, well; even in his student days he'd never failed an impromptu examination, so to hell with them. They went downstairs, past the broken window which looked out on a half-destroyed wall where a poster said: **DEATH TO THE CHILD-KILLERS!** They made him go first. Why not? He knew these stairs better than they. Now which piano should he . . . ? Not that one; that was the one on which he'd played Opus 40 for Elena. He'd rather . . . They lit their cigarettes and sat there yawning while he played the first five hundred measures of his Seventh Symphony. Interrupting him, they demanded to know: Was there any residual formalism in it?

Shostakovich swore that he no longer committed that error.

Dmitri Dmitriyevich, can you put in a little more self-sacrifice? And maybe—

Don't worry, don't worry, I'll do what I can, the composer murmured wearily.

And heroism? Listen up! We want to get the message across that anyone can be a hero.

I really love, so to speak, heroism. I'm going to squeeze some in this very instant.

(Far away, our Black Sea fleet was firing. Glikman's brother Salomon had just been killed. Nearer at hand, Field-Marshal Ritter von Leeb sounded the timpani. Across the street, a stinking, shadow-cheeked man clutched his handful of bread. He was there every day. If only he could write *him* into his symphony. He'd find a way.)

I was saying, maybe more optimism.

Well, it would seem that—

We don't believe you've taken note of how optimistic Leningraders are. After all, thousands starved here during the Civil War, but that didn't keep Leningrad down!

You don't remember that, do you, Dmitri Dmitriyevich? You were too protected by your *privileged* background.

Please excuse me, but in fact I, well, my grandfather—

We know all about that grandfather of yours. You're lucky he's dead.

For example, if you rewrote a few measures in a major key . . .

I understand, said Shostakovich with a coiled smile. That would certainly improve it immeasurably, although perhaps in this case—

And then that so-called Rat Theme or Fascism Theme or whatever it is, well, frankly, Dmitri Dmitriyevich, there's been some concern. How long is it?

How *long*? Let's see, let's see; I believe it's two hundred and eighty bars. What does the length have to do with anything?

No wonder Konstantinovskaya left him! Shostakovich, have you ever once satisfied a woman? I know why they call you a masturbator!

No, that's all fine, Dmitri Dmitriyevich. That's irrelevant. Our concern is that it begins too melodiously, which might mislead the masses into believing—

That I like rats?

Always the joker!

That I'm a, a, so to speak, a *Hitlerite*?

Out of your own mouth! You ought to be extremely careful. So if you could . . .

I appreciate your criticism. He who has ears will hear. I can see I'll have to think deeply about this, Comrade Petrov . . .

But, please, Dmitri Dmitriyevich, none of this is meant to detract from the majesty of your symphony. (What crap! put in Comrade Alexandrov.) It's truly very striking, especially the loud parts.

I'm very grateful—

But you need to work faster. Can you finish it in a week?

A week, perhaps, is, so to speak, somewhat—

It's quite good, really. There's hardly a drop of your old individualism in it—

Thank you, thank you, my dear friend. Well, our life is so full of brilliant themes just now . . .

They recommended that he follow the example of his colleague Khrennikov, who'd always persecuted him, who would persecute him to the very end, and who for that reason among other reasons of a similar kind got to be present at the capitulation of Berlin. Shostakovich accordingly promised to let himself be guided by this genius. (As I used to tell Elena, I am a person with a, how shall I describe myself? With a very weak character. I am not certain that I can achieve happiness.) The third man spat on the floor. Thanks again for that, *dear* friend. In every way that he possibly could, he acted as though they had triumphed over him, that he'd actually swallowed all their filth. Could any of them even name the dominant of any scale? Well, well;

technical knowledge is surely, how should I say, overrated, especially when all you need to know is—ha, ha!—how to break bones.

They reminded him, as if he could possibly forget with the loudspeakers screaming it every day, of Comrade Stalin's decree that any soldier who surrendered deserved the supreme punishment. He didn't want to surrender to defeatism, did he? Then they appointed him chairman of the Home Guard Theater, and in an instant he'd composed twenty-seven popular songs.

By the end of the week, nearly everybody in Leningrad was humming his "Oath to the People's Commissar," which was actually very, how should I say, complicated, because the scoring, well, it only pretends to be idiotic. The "organs" were happy with him for that; his song ended by praising the generalship of Comrade Stalin. As he peered down from the Conservatory roof, he saw a troop of Komsomol boys marching off to mine more factories and bridges. Someday his son would be doing that, if he lived. They were singing "Oath to the People's Commissar" in two-part harmony.

In the era of total war, coddling musicians might appear to be a weakness. But our apparatchiks knew better. Music inspired harder work and distracted the toilers from dangerous thoughts. Besides, music was all we could offer just now. The Seventh and Seventy-third Armies of the Northern Front, the Eighth, Eleventh and Twenty-seventh Armies of the Northwestern Front—thirty-nine divisions and two brigades in all—they held the line against the Fascists, but they were dwindling by the thousands. (Many had been liquidated by the ϟϟ Death's-Head Division.) And those squat, propeller-driven MIG-3s in formation over Leningrad, they weren't ready just yet; first we had to relocate our airplane factories out of Hitler's reach, and then we'd need to, so to speak, you know. Where were the T-34 tanks? Wait two years; we had no tank armies yet. That was why loudspeakers chanted from every street corner (Akhmatova was on the radio); that was why even along the White Sea Canal, on whose construction a hundred thousand people died, there'd occasionally been convict orchestras huddled on concrete slabs, their horns drooping down like the beaks of perishing ravens as they played inspirational melodies.

But you have to appeal to a larger audience this time, Dmitri Dmitriyevich.

That goes without saying, comrades! I, I, I'll follow your fraternal guidance . . .

(Late that night, when he saw Nina, he whispered that phrase into her ear, and she laughingly pretended to slap him. Then she leaped up to see if anybody might have been listening at the door.)

So that was how it was. Thirty years later, he told his treacherous disciple Volkov: I wrote my Seventh Symphony very quickly. I couldn't not write it. War surrounded us; I had to be with the people . . .

But by then he scarcely remembered how he had really felt. After thirty years one becomes sentimental.

27

On 1 September, we find Shostakovich on the radio, claiming to have finished the second movement of his symphony *just an hour ago*. He continues: We are all at our battle stations . . .

At first sight this claim of his appears propagandistically fantastic. What a coincidence! He just happened to finish that movement an hour before going on the official radio! Especially since our dear little Galisha was playing with his glasses and hid them for twenty minutes. Still, it's not entirely out of the question, even though he'll later write Glikman that he completed the first movement on the third of September, the second movement on the seventeenth. Even if he did stretch the truth a little, in order to make the Party happy, I'm sure that he was *almost* finished. The conductor G. V. Yudin remembers a certain examination day at the Conservatory, twenty years before the siege. With tension and anticipation seething together in his stomach, Yudin joined his fellow students by the closed door after Shostakovich had been summoned. *After a short pause while he was being told what to play, the silence from behind the closed doors was suddenly broken by a cascade of chords played at* prestissimo *speed. This tempo was so fantastic that we were left suspended in disbelief and awe.* From 1921 to 1941, Shostakovich could only have improved his craft. Why not then suppose that he could compose a symphony at the same *prestissimo* pace? We have, moreover, the example of the infamous Twelfth Symphony. According to Lebedinsky, this supposed ode to Lenin was actually an angry satire against the founder of our Soviet Union. Realizing three or four days before the premiere that this music was practically a death sentence for his entire family, he sat down and wrote a complete new score—no matter that, in Lebedinsky's words, the music was *frightening in its helplessness*. In short, our Shostakovich was a rapid worker, his Seventh was coming along just fine, and its second movement, "Recollection," might well prove the most pleasing of all, thanks to its summery lightness.

28

On 2 September the bread ration was reduced for the first time (to a fourth of its previous level). On 4 September the first German shells exploded in Leningrad. On 6 September came the first bomber attack. He had never before seen any, let's call it a, you know, *exercise* involving aerial explosives. Did you know that under ideal conditions bombs can express all eight degrees of the diatonic scale as they whistle down? Sometimes even the full chromatic scale can, well, anyhow it distracts me from the fear. Nina was still preparing earth walls, antitank ditches, barbed wire emplacements, pillboxes. Every morning he said goodbye to her forever. His mother was too old and sick for anything. The bones in her face, my God, and the way she coughs . . . On 8 September the Badyaev warehouses were destroyed by incendiary bombs. The German tanks were now within ten miles of the city center.

On 9 September, during one of the worst raids, Shostakovich invited his friends and a few of their friends to his fifth floor flat on Bolshaya Pushkarskaya Street so that they could hear (no matter that our composition dates still don't agree) the first two movements of his symphony, played on the piano. Nina was away digging trenches; his mother had the children; anyway there couldn't have been any tea. A kilo of horsemeat for a bottle of red wine, that's how it was. Well, Glikman had brought wine. He was very . . . They sat choking on brick-dust while loudspeakers shouted outside.

A bomb fell, and instantly afterward they all heard piccolo-notes screeching from the victims, but no one mentioned the air raid shelter. One scream lasted for a quarter-hour.—Poor tone, thought Shostakovich, lack of breath support; or perhaps the, well, the embouchure's too large now. I, I do hope it's not Elena.

Sighing, he rose, peered through the blackout curtain and sat down again. He still couldn't tell where that scream was coming from. It went on and on. He was sure that it was Elena now. He got up again. The piano had gotten filthy with brick-dust. He went to the bathroom to find a damp cloth, well, actually, you see, to compose himself, because . . . —Excuse me, everybody, he said. I apologize for this, this, you know.

Sitting down again, he polished each key clean. In the streets of Leningrad, Elena Konstantinovskaya was screaming and screaming.

Well, well, he cheerfully announced. One just can't get away from death. These keys, for instance, they're, how should I say, black and white, like a clothed corpse half covered in snow. I don't know if we should even . . . Anyway they're clean now.

Never mind all that! We're ready, Dmitri Dmitriyevich!

Oh, well, oh, well, let's get on with it. That's the spirit. Now, what do you really think of this? he asked his guests. Because we have to go on as if our suffering isn't meaningless! Do you see my point? Because otherwise . . . This is the first movement, and I, well, here it is.

And he played a theme like a field of tall flowering grass in which consciousness and premonition browsed together like wild deer. Then his hands rushed up from the piano, the fingers twitching out the beat of silence as he played a rest as black and square as the silhouette of a pillbox, and then came what in the orchestral version would be faint snare drums, and the Rat Theme commenced.

At this juncture it could have been the motif of a lover or a muse—a light, flirtatious knocking, as if a certain someone whose initials were E. E. K. had come to awake him for an hour of erotic delight in the Astoria Hotel; but what if it were the NKVD, who knocked in that same coaxing fashion out of sadistic fun, so that he smilingly opened the door, dressed in his very best underpants, when he should have leapt out the window? When he stroked that first go-round out of the white keys and black keys and spaces in between, he employed all the artifices of his trademark sarcasm, which, after all, is *their* sadism once removed, so that it beautifully expressed ugliness, in much the same way that "Lady Macbeth"'s most gruesome and sinister passages always occurred in a major key, or, for that matter, exactly the same way that for the rest of his life he'd refer to informers and police spies as his *dear, dear friends,* precisely the same way that when he eulogized the perfect military genius of Comrade Stalin, he meant exactly the opposite. How gently he plucked it! And the Rat Theme's second iteration was still more open, sweet and beautiful. But when it came around again, a woodwind lurked dissonantly beneath the high sweetness. The Rat Theme now assumed a brassy life, shrugging off its former tentativeness, with celli, horns, piccolos, clarinets, brasses and xylophone creeping in en route to the *ostinato*. And you must believe me when I tell you that even though he had no orchestra on that day, only an out-of-tune piano whose cover had been nicked by shell fragments, he played in such a way that it was all there; this was the true premiere even though hardly anybody was there to hear it. And now the snare drum stiffened the Rat Theme into martialness. The fifth repetition was like the second but much louder, more confident. The Pied Piper had entered his stride (and for the sake of our lives, to say nothing of our musical careers, we'll call him Adolf Hitler, because otherwise we'd, you know). Now in came the orchestra's processional drums, the Rat Theme going national-patriotic, and in the seventh go-round it was positively stern with the snare drum sounding like a rattlesnake. Next it was childishly inane with loud xylophones, then cunningly impressionistic, aping Debussy with vague wavish loudness; but in its tenth incarnation it grew creepy and horrid, with the moaning dissonance of air raid sirens and U-boat alarms; and in the eleventh it marched and bayed in a full-throated major key which might have seemed no worse than pompous in another context (Shostakovich said to Glikman: I suppose that critics with nothing better to do will, so to speak, damn me copying Ravel's "Bolero." Well, let them. You see, my dear friend, that's how I hear war!); the twelfth round changed key, because the Rat Theme, more determined and unstoppable than ever, was already beginning to break up into its own chaos. Fragments of it thrashed in frenetic confusion, wallowed crazily, came back to major-keyed life again, but only for a moment, then flaked, flakked, shredded, collapsed and died. From the "Lady Macbeth" affair he'd learned that we never know when death will come; from those corpses on Nevsky Prospect, with their outflung arms and clenched fists, or their indrawn arms, or missing arms, he'd learned that how death comes is equally secret. Now a slow Sibelius-like dirge returned, mirroring the opening theme of the movement, until once vigilance had slipped the Rat Theme cunningly resurrected itself in an innocuous sort of mountain climber's accompaniment, brave and sporty. Cymbals clashed and gnashed like monster-teeth; the Rat Theme, already very far from what it had been before, scuttled back into anti-programmatic formalism. Sad, slow, near silent contemplation drew wisps of music-consciousness through ruins, mournful woodwinds drifting smoke-like across the creeping blows of the bass. Then a reprise of the opening theme, sweet, melancholy yet unafraid, seemed to securely close the movement. At the very end, however, amidst more creeping thumps and the rattlesnaking of the snare drum, the Rat Theme came back, as it always has and always will, on this occasion disguised as "Taps."

He played utterly by memory, committing no errors. And his friends sat listening and silently weeping. So many tears! And at the end, a man he scarcely knew said to him: Thanks to the war, Dmitri Dmitriyevich, and thanks also to you, for the first time we can cry openly. Not one of us here hasn't lost somebody, somebody killed by the Fascists or else *before*—

My God! cried Glikman in terror. Please watch what you're saying, Ivan Borisovich!

No, I'm sorry, everybody. Of course I didn't mean it like that. Forgive me, Dmitri Dmitriyevich . . .

29

There was a lot of shelling later on that day, and the shells seemed to go right past his ears. Around the corner was a so-called "factory" where pale skinny boys stood shaking and assembling the round magazines of machine-guns; all right, so the Fascists knew about that and were shelling it. It's a shame that those boys were probably, so to speak, well. He'd advanced the thesis to Glikman that a person owns many different sorts of courage stored up within himself like fats; most of them can be exhausted, at which point a man becomes a coward; one must feed one's bravery; it's all a matter of chemicals. His friend gazed at him with huge sad eyes and said: For your own sake, I beg you, try not to get cynical, Dmitri Dmitriyevich!

Oh, I'm not cynical. I merely, I, well, I wonder how all this will affect us in later life. If we're allowed to have a later life . . .

He peered over the edge of the Conservatory roof. We were trying to regain command of Pulkovo Heights, and the loudspeakers were shouting. To the left, women with suspicious eyes stood around a lake of blood. To the right, a pretty, baby-faced girl in a woolen cap was wrapping up the head of bleeding boy who kept scratching at his chest, his rifle flung down on the broken bricks beside him. Suddenly he stopped moving. Sighing, the nurse rose and turned away.—Now do you see? Shostakovich muttered to himself, not even really knowing what he was saying.

30

On 10 September General Voroshilov was removed for "passivity" and General Zhukov arrived in Leningrad with an express directive from Stalin to hold the front line *no matter what the cost.*—Well, and why not? said the fire warden when he heard. Nina was too tired to reply. He said to her: Come on into the bathroom so I can tell you a joke. Don't worry; we'll turn the water up loud . . .

Go to hell, Mitya.

Our history books will show Zhukov's solid, close-shaven head sternly tilted as he listens to his strategic Muse: Stalin will be the savior of Europe. That was the day that a shell landed on Liteiny Boulevard, and Shostakovich could hope that the NKVD headquarters had been hit. He was full of optimism, actually, or maybe it wasn't exactly optimism but some manifestation of concentrated anger such as one frequently hears in the second movement of his Eighth Symphony; it definitely wasn't optimism, which might well have been impossible under these conditions. On 12 September the bread ration was reduced again. Hunger came as slowly as an *adagissimo*. Shostakovich had nothing to say about that. But soon people would be wearing gas masks against the cold and eating library paste. And the children, you see, Maxim was already crying in the night because his stomach was empty, well, can I somehow put that into the Rat Theme, so that they'll . . . ? Nina doesn't believe in this, but I have to believe, to, to, do you understand? When his son wept, he most frequently uttered a highly specific sound in A-flat minor. Can one do anything with this? It hurts me, of course, not that I have anything to say about it, because, because, but the real point is that if it didn't hurt me it would be unconscionable to build it into my music, but since I, my God, how can I *not* weep when my children suffer? And therefore, it would be unconscionable not to use that A-flat minor, when it might somehow, well, it's important to remember that each one of us has his work.

Glikman had already sampled cottonseed cake. He said that it tasted pretty foul, but with a little vodka, you know, some in the glass and just a splash on the cake itself, anyhow, that was how Glikman's wife liked it. (She was already getting weak.) Oh, our fine Russian proverb: *to make a cake out of shit*. That's what I'm doing with this symphony. And Glikman said . . . (Nina whispered that she'd heard the Fascists had just taken Kiev; even General Vlasov had barely escaped.) Then someone knocked on the door, two light taps; first he thought it was the NKVD and he vomited, but it was only that maddening Akhmatova coming around again, with her hands melodramatically bleeding from sewing sandbags, as if other people didn't also, you get the picture; she'd always thought she was really something, and now she was on the radio all the time. I personally prefer to, how should I put, to listen to the metronome. He granted that she was graceful, a genius, and all that. She certainly knew it, too. Anyhow, she promised that she'd use her pull to try to get him out of here, and he replied: My dear Anna Andreyevna, there's no need. I'm where I should be, so to speak. I draw strength from, I—who was that Greek protagonist who, you know—wait! it's coming to me; I mean Antaeus! Or do I mean Lenin? The one who, so to speak, got stronger whenever they threw him down to the ground. There's something about this Russian earth, and when they throw me in it, I'm going to take a big bite . . . By the way,

Anna Andreyevna, you and I had an encounter when I was very small. You probably don't remember it but . . .

Akhmatova closed her eyes and very slowly shook her head. She looked so engaging at that moment, so, how should I say, erotic, that he couldn't help but wonder how it would be to, well. She was only seventeen years older; that was nothing. But he pressed on: There's someone who, well, this is in a sense a, a delicate matter, but, you know, someone who, someone who, I'd have to say someone far more worthy of being evacuated than I—

Than your own family, Dmitri Dmitriyevich?—Akhmatova smiled and said: This must be love!

Oh, *please,* he whispered in an agony, peeking around his shoulder to make sure that Ninochka hadn't come in.

Shall I guess who it is? giggled Akhmatova.

There's no need, dear Anna Andreyevna, no need and no reason to be overly, how shall I say, specific—

I understand, said Akhmatova. In Pushkin's day one did not expose everything about oneself.

Thank you for that; thank you, *thank* you! Because—

I believe she's already on the list, so don't worry. But what do you *see* in her, you grey-eyed prince? She's nothing to me.

Has she . . . is she—

She's surviving. Roman Lazarevich is taking good care of her, from what I hear. Why didn't you marry her? You were very foolish.

My *dear* Anna Andreyevna—

And now I must go.

On 25 September, when shrapnel killed many citizens who were queueing by number for graves, he celebrated his birthday by candlelight, with black bread and potatoes instead of cake. (Nina was angrily, proudly announcing to the guests: He refused to be evacuated!) Four days later, he completed the third movement of his symphony.

For those of you who may still wonder how the so-called "creations" of this formalist intellectual could possibly be as useful as, say, the circus acrobatics of the Kokh Sisters, who in 1943 distracted the masses from wartime cares with their famous Great Semaphore Act, I want to discuss this sweet and brilliant third movement, the *adagio,* which contains traces of that last spring before the invasion, when Shostakovich was in the Crimea picking juniper berries with Shebalin's wife Alisa, a woman who personified Leningrad for him now that Elena Konstantinovskaya was gone; with Alisa he lived, at least for a day or two, in a world as long gone as the hand-kissings of counts and countesses. How she laughed at his owlish little eyes! And he . . . Well, but it was also difficult in a way, since in the nighttime he woke up thinking about Elena. Never mind; we all have our, so to speak, sorrows. Not that there's any call to be sentimental, especially about Elena, who wasn't exactly; never mind; I'm thinking for instance of, of Nina. In fact, if the forest were music, we'd hear a tranquil major key theme—say, this third movement, which he had originally entitled "The Open Spaces of the Heartland," and whose cathedralesque quality is reminiscent of Rimsky-Korsakoff's ode to Easter. Nina had said to him: Don't fuck her so much that you forget to bring *me* any berries.—It was Nina's fate to always give, but hurriedly and quick-temperedly, so her gifts were not received with gratitude. He for his part was a generous man without anything to give. Well, he filled up Alisa's apron with berries (I mean, my dear, dear lady, which is to say . . .) They marinated the berries in vodka, but found the result too strong; they got so drunk and their tongues burned so much that they were laughing and almost missed the train home because Alisa lost an earring and then the taxi kept getting flat tires on the boggy, stony road, so that Shostakovich became nervous unto sickness, especially because he'd confided to her: We all have somebody to, to, you know, cry over . . . —and that night after playing a round of cards with him the violinist P. returned to his first class compartment and died in his sleep, as a result of which Shostakovich was interrogated and almost arrested, which definitely took his mind off Elena. And here the "Pacques" theme of that third movement gave way to a minor-keyed Slavic dance, a wild one which suddenly took on the tramp of avengers' boots. Then the dreamy melody alit again, as beautifully as the four-stranded bundles of tracer bullet light arising from the Maxim guns of Leningrad.

31

I fear that I have not really described this third movement very well. Let me try again. It opens, as I've said, with a stately joy equivalent to that of Rimsky-Korsakoff's "Grand Pacques," then dims down to a frame of sternness to introduce one of the most purely beautiful themes Shostakovich ever wrote, which will be reiterated with an Asian tinge. Then comes a sort of rising, spiraling music as if we were in a plane circling up over the mountains. Shostakovich had not flown very often in those days; nor is the area between Moscow and Leningrad mountainous; but when the plane which was bearing Nina,

Galya, Maxim and himself out of the besieged city (naturally Nina won that argument in the end) had bored through the black cloud-edges and the white fog, they all cried out, because before them lay a perfectly flat rainbow over cloud-edges the length of the horizon, muted by the clouds; this rainbow formed one of the most beautiful lines any of them had ever seen, the sky lavender above it, the sky below diffusely luminous with all colors from electric blue to yellow to peach. And when Shostakovich saw this sight, he heard again within himself those "spiraling" measures of that already completed third movement, which quickly grows more stern and gloomy, suddenly forceful and mechanical in a positive, martial sense, like truckloads of soldiers rolling west out of Kazakhstan, approaching the Stalingrad front—and we might note that on the Conservatory roof in Leningrad he'd listened carefully to the defenders' medium and heavy mortars, trying to decide how they could best be represented. For Leningrad's sake he was willing to make it simple, comprehensible, even vulgar. When I listen to the later Shostakovich, the real Shostakovich, whose melodies are almost completely lightless, I don't know what to believe about this Seventh Symphony.

32

When he clambered down from the Conservatory roof, so faint with fatigue and hunger that he was almost blind, a child grabbed him by the hand, whimpering that it didn't have enough strength to go home.—Don't worry, don't worry, replied Shostakovich. From his pocket he pulled out a scrap of bread. Later he felt guilty, because he should have saved it for his own children.

33

In October, the month of wet winds which thicken a sick man's cough, the Fascists were bombing promptly at seven each evening. Like Shostakovich, they adored punctuality. October was when the potatoes ran out. It wasn't until November that people started feeding on a jelly made from leather straps. October was the merest overture to the time of wide white streets slippery with packed ice, when men wrapped in scarves and hats, women in shawls and hoods, bulky bear-people all of them, and Leningrad began to be mounded here and there with the dead. In September the organs of our civic body still functioned well enough for corpses to get hauled away, but now our task required other measures. Those thirteen-year-old boys assembling artillery shells in each factory's frozen darkness, they couldn't be spared to clean the streets, not in October. October was *pianissimo* at first. Somewhere in the freezing darkness came the downbeat of the conductor's baton: `Skizze B: Heeresgruppe Nord`, as performed by Field-Marshal Ritter Wilhelm von Leeb. The first measure commenced. Here came their whistling woodwinds, and then the first cymbal-clash struck Leningrad's stage. Pale, drooping-headed women shivering inside an unheated bakeshop, waiting to take their bread rations into a purse or a coat pocket, got illuminated into nonexistence by a million mirrors of breaking glass. Some screamed soprano, but there was one bass bray which went on and on—a husband, he conjectured. If only he would please, please, you know . . . Then the loudspeaker was screaming encouragements, first screaming and then *really* screaming; for an instant it sounded almost like, er, you know who, but he had to stop believing that. Late in life he told S. Volkov: Fear of death may be the most intense emotion of all.—But in those days it wasn't true; or at least he didn't most intensely fear his own death; he was terrified that harm might come to the woman he loved, not that he actually loved her anymore, because all that would have been, so to speak, well . . . The next shell killed a family on the second storey of the apartment building across the street. He saw it happen. And what was there to say? Perhaps music could say it. Falling walls applauded. Siege guns are nothing more than, so to speak, brass instruments—specifically, "Wagner tubas," which are what we hear in the *Ring* Cycle . . . I refuse to fear them. I may be a preposterous, useless person; no doubt I should have, you know; but I won't fear them; and if I do fear them, I'll pretend to be brave even if I have to hide the fear inside me where it can poison my life—what life? For an encore, the German cymbals dropped death upon a furcapped man who was shivering and blowing on his hands as he toiled at the roofless munitions plant, and Shostakovich saw that, too; he was longing for a Ju-88 to come and strafe him as he stood in furious anguish there upon the roof! Had he succeeded? Did the Rat Theme say everything yet? (What about the sound of planks getting wrenched out of buildings in Okhta so that somebody would have firewood? He left that out; someday he'd squeeze that into Opus 110.) Oh, my, those screams! And then when I come home, Nina will, she'll, and my children's eyes are already dead; I predict that Maxim will die first. As for me, art, if there's even such a thing, won't suffer if I . . . But Nina wants me to . . . —Snare drums rattled across the trenches, and more people fell dead, gushing from scarlet holes.

Now let's repeat the measure, *da capo*. It's all program music. Entering the scratched oak doors of the Conservatory, Shostakovich ascended the half-dozen steps, passed through the turnstile, and then came inner doors and inner doors until he felt safe. The rooms were cold and dark again, just as they'd been in his Civil War boyhood. He didn't care about that. He was home beneath the piano keys. Hunching down, he gnawed on a scrap of oilcake until his mind cleared. Glikman said that sometimes soldiers gave him sauerkraut or other food; their rations were better. Shostakovich was rarely that lucky. How could he possibly, possibly end the Seventh hopefully while remaining true to it? Actually, he knew that he could; there was no fear of his betraying the music he loved so much, although life was certainly different from what he had expected. Music not only could save him; it (or she, as I should say) already had. He knew that he could die for her and was living for her; therefore everything had become strangely simple and good. She could speak to him through his own skinny nervous fingers, which alone expressed her. A brilliant clean burst of shell fragments, now, if I were a visual artist I might express them kaleidoscopically, because they're so, how should I put it; anyhow a glockenspiel might convey that sparkling tinkling scattering, a steel rainbow coming apart and, and, especially since a glockenspiel is such a, you know, *German* instrument. And if I specified that the orchestra use metal mallets . . . Smiling in utter happiness, he ascended to the roof, wondering whether he would die today.

The German Fascists had been dropping incendiaries all month; the optics factory (which now made grenades and bayonets) caught fire three hundred times on a single night. If anything landed on the Conservatory, he was supposed to, to, never mind; it was preposterous. Not far away he heard machine-gun fire and then the scream of sirens. No, no; Leningrad's mist and stone would hide him. And all the while his brain was organizing the opening of the fourth movement. When a bluish tint came into Maxim's face, he went out by night and bought a kilogram of some unknown illegal meat from a Tartar horse-butcher who crouched amidst many dead below a brick wall. How did buyer and seller find one another? Well, let's just call it a, a, a typical incident. Later he was appalled at the risk that he had taken—thank God Nina never found out; she thought that once again Glikman had played the patron. He could have been shot! And that meat, well, he just hoped it didn't come from the graveyard; in the market there was said to be a sausage made from human flesh. Never mind. It's always easier to believe what we want to believe, much easier. The mentality of a chicken, his mother always used to say, and now she kept prating about our imminent victory over the Fascists. Correct, Mama, one hundred percent, so to speak, correct! We'll be in Berlin tomorrow, and then that bastard in the Kremlin's going to retire! Ha, *ha*! Why be serious? Elena, you see how lucky it is that you didn't marry me.

On the thirteenth of October, his colleague A. D. Kamensky performed Tchaikovsky on the radio. He wanted to hear it, but he had his duty on the roof. Peering over the edge, he watched nine-year-old girls dragging firewood on sledges. Are they too young to be afraid? he wondered. Or are they heroic as the radio says? They look hungry and that's all. My own children are afraid. It must simply be that I'm too far away from these girls to, to, well, after all, I have binoculars.—So he tracked them with those miraculous military-quality lenses which they'd lent him for the Sovfoto portrait, and he saw that they were indeed afraid, which both saddened and comforted him. But he was not afraid. Closing his eyes, he imagined Elena walking safe and radiant along the long shining walkway to the Smolny Institute; his fondest hope was that she could become Zhukov's mistress, or, since he was dreaming, Comrade Stalin's, but on second thought, Comrade Stalin might be more perilous to her than any German tank.

On the fourteenth, which happened to be the eight hundredth anniversary of the Azerbaijani poet Nizami, the first snow fell. People were already eating dogs, cats, laboratory guinea pigs. A crazy woman spread the rumor that the Germans' delayed action bombs were full of sugar, and dozens died hoping to prove it. In the morning he caught Nina in the bathroom eating hair oil. That day it was sunnier and when the shelling began he could see quite readily those dark crowds on the far side of the street, the safe side, whose building-fronts were multiwindowed and white. Everything was black and white, black and white, like piano keys, like a clothed corpse half covered in snow.

The shelling stopped. The Conservatory hadn't caught fire this time, either. Now here came our tommy-gunners who in the white winter uniforms resembled desert Arabs, especially since so many grew beards now, for warmth. And a white-wrapped corpse swam by, dragged down the white streets. Maybe it was one of those old women in shawls who'd been set to digging antitank trenches; it was too big to be a child. Amidst the cemetery drifts, the coffined and the coffinless awaited this new arrival, but then right across the street two women with snow on their shoulders stopped to gaze listlessly upon a third who'd just fallen dead. He heard the roar of a T-34 engine, and farther away he heard the MG-34s being fired by the German Fascist batteries, and then shells began to fall upon Leningrad again. Dark-clad human bundles scuttled into doorways.—Shostakovich, he said to himself, I will die today.—

He tried to be, let's say progressive, philosophical, realistic, even—why not try again to use this word?—optimistic (for instance, the streetcars fortunately still moved; they weren't yet frozen to the streets); and what must have been in all probability an essentially, you know, unfounded feeling armored him against the fear, at least for now; while flame-walls as jagged as broken windowpanes sprang up around him and he activated the alarm. Years later he remembered flames reflected in puddles of melted sugar, but that must have happened during the previous month, when the Badayevskiy warehouses won the lottery.

On the seventeenth he was on the Conservatory roof when a black bundle fell in the street. For a long time he avoided looking, and later he thought to himself, if only I could have thought more clearly, I never, I, I, but hunger lowered my guard, so I, well. I'm sorry. That shouldn't have . . . It was my task right then, for the sake of the symphony, to seek out grief. I know that.

After several hours, he peered down through the field glasses at that Leningrader's closed eyes, the lips pursed almost coquettishly, the ice on the chin. Those details pressed him to alter a chord in the second movement.

On the nineteenth, Moscow was officially declared to be in a state of siege. Nina asked what would happen. He cleaned his glasses and said: I'm sure they'll, which is to say *that bastard,* you know the one I mean, he'll save us all—tomorrow! He'll lead the, so to speak, cavalry charge. He'll choke with his, his . . . —and he looked right and left, then whispered hideously in her ear: His *Constitution.*—Well, what do you know? As soon as he'd croaked that out, the radio announced a victorious counteroffensive! Then, as ever, it fell silent except for the feeble ticking of a metronome. Nina felt dizzy; she had to lie down. As for him, he, well, can't you guess?

From the window he watched a mother dragging her son to the cemetery on his little sled. Some shivering schoolgirls were trying to drag an antitank hedgehog across the ice; one girl fell down and lay there quite awhile before she got up again. The others stood blankly round, not trying to help her. Finally they'd pulled their hedgehog all the way to the corner, passing the corpse with dried blood-bubbles on its lips which had lain there for two weeks; thank God the snow hid it now. It made the children afraid. And Galya said: Papa, I'm hungry.

Now it was night. In that chilly darkness behind the blackout curtain, Maxim was lying on the sofa, his face more pallid than before, his arms and legs as limp as the down-swinging golden arcs and crescents on the stage curtain of the Kirov Theater where those failed ballets "Dynamiada" and

"Bolt" had both premiered so long ago. Why was I thinking about "Bolt" just now? My ballets nauseate me. I'll never write another one, I promise. I'll certainly never write another opera, because I'll be (why not joke about it?) *dead.* But Maxim's going to feel better tomorrow. The news from Glikman was that people had started eating cooked glue. Soon our Red Army engineers would begin dynamiting the frozen ground at Volkovo Cemetery to make mass graves.—Maxim, shall I read you a story?—The boy opened his eyes, but did not answer. Well, but after all, the terrified father tried to reassure himself, children, especially small children, get more quickly debilitated (not that this situation doesn't bear watching), but they also recover more quickly than we do, which isn't to say that I shouldn't somehow prepare, or, or, or, but for instance, and here's just one of, oh, a hundred examples: When I get a chest cold I'm miserable for ten days, whereas Galya and Maxim are as good as new after three. Therefore . . . —And he cleaned his glasses on his sweater, wiping away the tears, but all he did was smudge them. From the Conservatory roof that day he'd seen them take another cart of corpses to Volkovo, reflections of the cartwheels shining in a pool of melting ice, and he remembered the Tartar horse-butcher. Well, well. No doubt that's commonplace in our times. But I, I, to me I, well, I'd simply not pursued such considerations.

Gazing on his wife and children, he saw as if for the first time long starving necks rising out of sweater-collars, and winter was just beginning. The Rat Theme rose up in him like vomit. This situation needs watching, he said to himself. Ha, ha! Hitler the Liberator means to, to, slim us down. Last month Akhmatova had confided that the city's art treasures were being shipped out by train. But that news must now be, so to speak, superseded, because the Fascists had cut all our railroad lines. Perhaps to Elena this wasn't new. The Black Maria had taken her to *that place,* where the wash-water was always frozen, and flat-chested, wrinkled girls prostituted themselves for half a kilo of bread. Why had they let her go? It must have been a random decision; perhaps her prosecutor got arrested. And now she's . . . Anyhow, history can't be undone. The clock winds down and you wind it up, but when the spring, you see, gives way . . . I'm not talking about myself now; I'm talking about something else. You're so lucky I didn't . . . If Maxim died, why then, he'd . . . Galisha would probably . . . What could he do now? He could tell them uplifting lies as the radio did; perhaps he could smuggle home a little more food; but . . . Our snowy-camouflaged men on each tank, pointing black guns across the snow, they might save Leningrad but they couldn't save his children. No one could save anyone, which is why this will someday be, how should I say, the best page of my memoirs: sincerity, self-sacrifice, a common enemy whose name we don't have to whisper, so when Galya dies I can borrow Litvinova's sled and . . . No one can do anything. That motif, like letters from a soldier which keep arriving for weeks after his death, would infect his music for the rest of his life.

But that very month, despite his murmurous protests, Shostakovich and his family got flown out by special plane! The activists said: No more objections, Dmitri Dmitriyevich! Not unless it's true that you're waiting for the Germans. We've heard that you admire the fugues of J. S. Bach . . .

The "Muse of Leningrad," which is to say Akhmatova, had already been evacuated. It's said that she carried the original piano score of the Seventh on her lap, as precaution in case his plane were to be shot down. As for Shostakovich, he had the orchestral score, as well as his much-loved child, "Lady Macbeth." Romain Rolland had liked that opera. Save us from these humanists! Glikman's wife was already dying by then. And where were Sollertinsky, Lebedinsky, and, and, you know? Get over it! His mother, his sister and his brother-in-law had to stay behind.—In short, the authorities agreed with his mother, who'd written that if the roof fell in and she had to choose whom to save, the answer would be *of course Mitya—for this would be the duty of everyone to society, for the sake of art—disregarding all personal feeling*. He said to himself: If I ever forget that I was spared, I'll be as evil as, you know, *that bastard*. The last thing he saw in the city of his birth was a half-melted machine-gun barrel in the snow, snake-twisted like the mouthpiece of a bass clarinet.

34

The fall of Moscow appeared imminent. Vlasov and those other generals hadn't yet turned the tide. How should I put it? We were gloriously falling back. Everybody was shivering except for the NKVD men in their jackets trimmed with lambskin. It was a new era, an era of specialists. Certain people specialized in, you know, keeping warm. Those non-specialists the Shostakoviches couldn't decide whether to continue all the way to Tashkent as Akhmatova had (he'd been informed by Glikman that Elena Konstantinovskaya was there, too), or to stop at the new de facto capital of Kuibyshev. Late at night they arrived at Kazan Station, where women lay sleeping on every bench with their mouths open, breath-steam jetting from their faces like visible snores, Kazakh men pacing, menacingly tall in their cylindrical fur hats, shouting in deep voices, while Russian grandfathers pointed and fussed, scared children coughed, teenaged girls sat on the floor holding each other's hands. Poor Galochka kept whimpering, red in the face. Every time the Fascists launched a shell, she'd scream. Nina didn't know what to do with her. As for our composer, he'd kept his sense of humor. A fat woman farted, and he said in Nina's ear: A bit of, um, artillery preparation, so to speak.—Wide-eyed and silent, Maxim clutched a piece of oilcake.

They embarked at last. And so, comrades: "The Open Spaces of the Heartland!"—Russia is actually as blackly untidy as a page of a Dostoyevsky manuscript, with its excisions, spearpointed insertions, doodled bearded saints.—Shostakovich couldn't help remembering his optimistic journey six years ago from Leningrad to Moscow within the streamlined metal of the express train, with its blind bulbous nose, adorned with a star; one could have likened it to a certain kind of mole, but naturally that trope wouldn't be correct in this epoch of perfect vision; better to conceive of it as an immense bullet inset in a jointed steel phallus which ejaculated low V's of white steam on either side as it clittered down the tracks. "Lady Macbeth" was going to win him the permanent patronage of Comrade Stalin. The way it turned out was actually, how should I say, educational. On another occasion he had boarded this same train to propose to Elena Konstantinovskaya, who'd accepted with sweet hope and joy; that might have been the last time he'd ever seen her smile—probably not, however, for most of us can't stop smiling meaninglessly. Oh, me, the way she moaned that first time! An ocean of ghostly, uprising moans, each one similar to the sound which children make by racing their fingertips across the taut and slender wires within a piano, going up the octaves in a thin metallic music of echoing ghostliness; that was how Elena had moaned, exactly that way, *presto appassionato*. His fingers drummed softly against the steel wall for days as he smiled desperately into space, pressing his greying hair against Nina's greying hair. He was working out the fourth movement of his new symphony.—A symphony! That was nice, but that was nothing; it was only when he was kissing Elena or deep, deep inside her that he'd felt solace, gratitude, fulfillment, absolute peace, which he had never felt before and never would again—no, no, that's another exaggeration; life isn't as fancy as that; we have to, you know, eat whatever food gets set before us, even if it's only oilcake—anyhow, at first he couldn't accustom himself to that feeling which Elena gave him; he distrusted it because, well, he distrusted everything, but *she* was real and steady from that very first night when she unsmilingly invited him into her bed; she didn't merely "give herself" to him as other women did, she gave him a home within her heart, a sweet strong house in which they both could have dwelled until they died, if only the roof hadn't gotten blown off; and afterward, when she stood naked at the hotel window to smoke a cigarette, he felt even closer to her than he had when she was on top of him; usually when the act was finished he felt, so to speak, alone, especially when the woman gazed away; truth to tell, right now Elena wasn't looking at him at all, but the curve of her back, which still glittered with sweat, remained aware of him, and loved him. I've read that he truly *was* a superb lover, and for the same reason that he was a musical genius: he gently intuited harmonies and spaces; the ecstatic droop of a woman's eyelid expressed as much to him as that black piano key he'd half depressed; his body and hers became instruments on which he could play a duet for both of them; in later years, crowds of Muscovites and Leningraders wept at premieres of his "death symphonies," and Elena likewise wept whenever he made love with her; she sobbed with happy lust, wept for love, then cried out, her cry a peculiar chord dominated by B-sharp, and that became his treasure, which he reverently secreted in his own greying heart, never allowing it to shine forth in any of his music. One December night deep in the postwar decades, when Lebedinsky, a little drunk, dared to ask him what it was that he loved so much about her, he might have been remembering that chord, that secret, magnificent sound, when he answered: He who has ears will hear. Or it might have simply been her that he meant; she remained, as she forever would, within his hiddenmost soul, emblem of his youth, strength and bravery, not to mention the goodness he'd separated himself from, his fading prehistoric consecration. He who has ears will hear. No sense in thinking about that! And precisely because he who has ears will hear, he wanted to ensure that each passage of each movement would be as well wired as a German Fascist entrenchment. They needed his symphony without delay, just as they needed the new Katyusha rockets. Could he still remain unerring? Why not? They'd drafted him in advance to oversee the rehearsals of the NKVD Song and Dance Ensemble. Meanwhile he'd lost his two suitcases; A. I. Khatchaturian had to give him some of his clothes. Then he lost the score of the Seventh itself, which Nina had wrapped up in a quilt, but V. Y. Shebalin found it for him. He forgot to eat; he was worried about his mother. Nina begged a smoked fish from D. B. Kabalevsky, which he in his shyness could never have done; throughout his life he requested favors only for others; and while he was munching at it, absently swallowing the bones, he said: You know, Ninochka, I'm not completely sure, but, since Isaak Davidovich has . . . —You want to join him in Tashkent, said Nina flatly and loudly in everyone's hearing. You want to join him in Tashkent because your *other woman* is waiting for you there with open arms and open legs, which is why I can't imagine what her husband sees in her; but he's away a lot, isn't he? Maybe your plan is simply to moon outside her window, which will have a blackout curtain anyway, so why bother?—On 22 October they arrived in their haven, which was named after the moderate Politboro man Kuibyshev, whose mysterious heart ailiment in 1935 had been so convenient for Comrade Stalin. The train stopped, recapitulating the half-strangled violin of the first movement. A beggar with a baritone voice sang a song about our Red Army.

35

A lamp's snow-white incandescence, his own pale, pudgy reflection-silhouette upon the piano lid, his score glowing like a slab of light, the long white jawbone of piano keys which sang to him who caressed it, so ran his world which was guarded to a precarious security by the outward spiralings of squat little bombers with red stars at flank and tail, twelve planes to a squadron, three squadrons to a regiment, four regiments to a division, two divisions to a corps. The children were asleep. Nina came to the piano and laid her hand upon his shoulder. He gazed out the window.

Since the Fascists had come, the coldness between her and him no longer mattered, so perhaps it was not even coldness anymore, this dissonance, chemical incompatibility; they rarely quarreled now for much the same reason that they almost never slept together; necessity discouraged it, and Leningrad's agony chilled their selfishness and anger.

In November, three thousand inhabitants of that city starved to death from sunrise to sunrise. They'd cut the rations for the fifth time by then. Moscow was badly off too, of course . . . Haunted by thoughts of his mother cutting a hole in the frozen street to find water, of puffy-eyed children, crazed old ladies shivering, he gorged himself with semi-secret statistics which were meaningless and already obsolete: three hundred barrage balloons, nine hundred tons of burnt sugar. He had thought that music was the most important thing in the world, but now he realized that he would do almost anything, even compromise his talent, to help Leningrad, formerly known as Petrograd, and before that Saint Petersburg, which is to say City of the Periodic Table—city of Glinka, Mussorgsky, Tchaikovsky, Stravinsky, Prokofieff, Shostakovich! So what if he wrote bad music? No, he'd never . . . It could still be his, given sincerely and unstintingly, and also something they could use. In short, if they wanted program music they'd get program music. He'd make it good in spite of itself. Convenient and effective was what they wanted; all right, but he actually, excuse me for saying so, loved Leningrad, so what they were also going to get in that symphony was, you know, *Leningrad*.

Lev Oborin, who seemed very tired, came by unannounced for an hour of four-handed piano. He was smiling; not only had he tracked down five hundred grams of horsemeat sausage, but we'd just liberated Kalinin! Galya jumped up and down, screaming: *Kalinin, Kalinin!* It was past her bedtime, actually. And she couldn't get over that cough, the "Leningrad cough" they called it. Kalinin, so now I'll have to compose a . . . What's that sound? Oh, it's only . . . Moreover, said Oborin, at Leningrad we'd now gained an ice-bridge across Lake Ladoga; refugees went out and food came in, a little, not enough, and sometimes the Fascists strafed our trucks, but Shostakovich couldn't help wondering at the pride and hope he felt, when he read the confirmation in *Pravda*. Years later, when he returned to Leningrad, just to visit (he never lived there again), his friends told him that on some occasions people had torn bread from each other outside the bakeries, but usually they starved in silence. They didn't want to compromise either, you see. And when he heard that he, well, he grew emotional.

There were many new common graves now in Piskarevskoye Cemetery. In December it got worse. Some calculated that six thousand perished every day of that month; others said four, or ten. No one had the strength to count. Like ripe pears falling off trees, frozen bodies dropped out of windows into the snowy streets. Cannibals were said to be killing stray children every day; steak-meat was cut from the shoulders, thighs and buttocks of corpses abandoned at the cemetery. On 17 December the radio announced that the Volkhov Front had been formed under General Meretskov, but even the announcer failed to express much hope. Now back to the ticking of a metronome; that was all Leningrad had the strength to broadcast. Children's sleds kept getting dragged to the cemetery, with dead children on them. Poets collapsed and died from the exertion of standing upright to read their verses on Radio Leningrad. Then came the metronome again. That was why he wanted to build his symphony not out of music, but out of snow and explosions.

It's almost finished, he told his wife.

Then you'll have accomplished a great thing. And you'll tell me everything you've been thinking, or at least your music will tell me. You have so much to tell me and you never say anything.

But it's the war, Ninochka, just the war. And Maxim never lets go of you—

I know, darling. After the war we'll be freer—

Don't create illusions.

Leaning out the window, he heard two drunken Red Army men bellowing Blanter's song "In the Frontline Forest."

36

At the beginning of December, the defenders of Moscow regained the offensive and began to drive the enemy back; but the siege of Leningrad went on and on. Thirty degrees of frost was as warm as it got there; so he heard. He tried not to, to, you know. In his heart he could see the Philharmonic's raspberry, gilt and white. That was where his symphony must be performed, for his sake and he hoped for theirs. Screaming patriotic slogans, wounded Red Army men crouched in their spider-holes, hoping to kill just one more German Fascist. He wrote that into the third movement, beneath the floor, so to speak, where his chords took snipers' aim and fired before the ear knew they were even there. Cossacks with upcurved sabers threw themselves at bullet-rain. Homes became stage-sets more avant-garde than the long-suppressed theatrical productions of Meyerhold and Shostakovich, walls and bodies getting slashed away from bedrooms in which every knickknack remained in place; women and children hunkered there, waiting for the iron frost to fall on them. (Their men were at the front.) Bundled-up women belly-crawled through the snow between frozen tramcars, hoping to find a frozen rat or a scrap of oilcake which would give them the strength to rise. Shostakovich had nothing to give them except his symphony, whose fourth movement glittered as brilliantly as the nickel-plated door handles of the late Marshal Tukhachevsky's automobile.

37

The last note of the Seventh Symphony was written on 29 December 1941, in tired, crowded Kuibyshev. On the radio, Comrade Stalin said slowly: *Death to the German Fascist invaders. Death, death, death.* And Shostakovich arose from the music bench. A number of his well-wishers, the same who wondered why he hadn't yet hung Comrade Stalin's portrait above the piano, advised various mutually contradictory alterations to the finale, all of which he promised to insert in the Eighth Symphony. Nina had to run to the toilet to conceal her laughter; he heard the water come on. Again they urged him to join the Party, because doing so would help the Seventh to be more widely understood. And Comrade Alexandrov said . . . He agreed to take that under advisement. Maybe after he'd achieved a better comprehension of, of, you know, Leninism . . . He was a bigshot again; he could stall them forever! Anyhow, they owned a more important triumph to report: The bread ration in Leningrad had just been doubled.

On 5 March 1942 the first performance was broadcast by radio. Although the concert took place in Kuibyshev, the announcer followed orders and pretended to be at the Bolshoi Theater in Moscow. (Other sources claim that this first performance took place in Novosibirsk.) We see Shostakovich cross-legged and nervous in the sixth row, with his arms tightly folded in, his suit wrapped tight around him, his dark necktie almost hidden. Nothing but reflections can be seen within the lenses of his round spectacles. The music stands of the orchestra appear as dazzling squares of blankness in this photograph; they might as well be bomb-flashes. At home, number 2a Vilonovsky Street, Nina sits with the children and the neighbors, listening in utter silence. She knows that Glikman and the other members of the Leningrad Conservatory are listening in Tashkent. She supposes that Elena Konstantinovskaya is listening, too. Now here comes the Rat Theme; at the fifth iteration she hears Panzer IIIs surging up riverbanks. Strange to say, on most days, and even most nights, she bears the other woman no ill will. Didn't she make Mitya happy, and even inspire his music?

Nina knows her husband better than Elena ever could. She knows his selfishness, his ugly spitefulness, his narcissism. Elena only knows his penis. She may believe she knows his genius, but no one does, not even Mitya himself; he doesn't even know what makes him happy! He's not very self-aware, actually. (Now he lights up another "Kazbek" cigarette.) For instance, when he used to come home with Elena's perfume all over him, he had no clue that she noticed anything. And when Nina herself steps out, he doesn't catch a thing! Once he wore a purple lovebite on the side of his neck; for days he kept scratching at it. Mitya, you idiot child, if only I could keep you safe . . . In short, he needs her far more than he knows, and that's why she's ready for anything. *Of course Mitya—for this would be the duty of everyone to society, for the sake of art—disregarding all personal feeling.* Then there are the children to consider.

Akhmatova is also tuned in; she's sure of it. Akhmatova's sweet on Mitya. Well, what woman wouldn't be? And Nina's got him, lucky Nina! His grip on her life is clammy. Maybe his soccer player pals from the Dynamos have tuned in, too, if any are still alive. And of course, who knows what Comrade Stalin hears? Two violinists, seen in profile, grip the bows of their instruments determinedly, pointing them outward like bayonets. It's a grey and dreary picture.

In Leningrad, the poetess Olga Berggolts, who in due time would find herself reciting Stalin odes to her fellow prisoners, proclaimed of Shostakovich: *This man is stronger than Hitler!*—Stalin himself is said to have commented that the Seventh was of as great striking power as a squadron of bombers. *Pravda* called it *the creation of the conscience of the Russian people*. Shostakovich's fame was as blinding as the snowdrifts iced over against Leningrad walls. (I seem to see his whitish, half-boyish face blazing awfully close to pretty B. Dulova's, both of them rapt in their concert seats in 1942.) Toscanini conducted the Seventh in Radio City, New York. The director of the Boston Symphony proclaimed: *Never has there been a composer since Beethoven with such tremendous appeal to the masses*. The émigré Seroff, who seems never to have met him, rushed out a biography, which begins with this justification: *Today the "average" American can not only pronounce that name but even spell it*. Bartók parodied the Seventh with bitter disgust—a compliment of sorts. The British *Dictionary of Musical Themes* quoted no less than eleven of its motifs. The bourgeois critic Layton denounced the Rat Theme, insisting that *this naive stroke of pictorialism reduces the Seventh to the impotence of topical art*. In the postwar era, other intellectuals who'd never been compelled to pitch their tents in necessity's winds would soon disdain the Seventh Symphony more loudly, hearing in it a musical battleground occupied by two utterly irreconcilable antagonists: Shostakovich's desire to express reality, and his need to please his masters. Reader, which would you choose?

38

Although D. D. Shostakovich was neither a Jew nor a Pole, Comrade Stalin himself has stated that the very concept of nationality is but a smokescreen used by the capitalists to prevent us from seeing class differences. As for the Party's dictum that art must be national in form, socialist in content, that's a mere transition scheme to wean the people gently from their hidebound categories. Therefore, I make no apologies for ending this fable with an extract from the sixteenth-century musings of a Warsaw Kabbalist named Moses Cordovero. In his *Tomer Devorah*, commonly translated as *The Palm Tree of Deborah*, it is written: *God does not behave as a human being behaves. If one person angers another, even after they are reconciled the latter cannot bring himself to love the one who offended him as he loved him before. Yet if you sin and then return to God, your status is higher. As the saying goes, "Those who return to God occupy a place where even the completely righteous cannot stand."* And so it came to pass that on 11 April 1942, Shostakovich received the Stalin Prize, First Class.

39

At seven-o'-clock in the evening of 9 August 1942—the day that we lost the battle of Maikop—the Seventh Symphony was performed in Leningrad. How should I tell that tale? Adoring Glikman has left us a full account of his ten-day train journey from Tashkent to Kuibyshev, subsisting all the way on twenty insect-ridden meat pies; apparently there was no easier way for the refugees from the Leningrad Conservatory to obtain a copy of the score than to send him personally. Shostakovich met him at the station and then they walked home because the trams were infested with typhus. To Glikman, it was all, as usual, perfect, right down to the *decent-sized divan on which I slept very comfortably for a month . . . I was happy just to be sitting near him and to be able to shoot covert glances at his handsome, animated face.* Several days later, his hero played the Seventh on the piano, just for him, then said: You know, Isaak Davidovich, to be sure, on the whole, I, I'm happy with this symphony, but . . . —Glikman gazed at him in astonishment. Clearing his throat, the host refilled both glasses and murmured (Nina and the children had already withdrawn behind their curtain for the night): I believe that Elena Konstantinovskaya has been, you know, evacuated to Tashkent. Perhaps you could greet her for me. Sometimes her, um, friends call her Lyalya. Perhaps you also—no, forgive me, forgive me; that would have been personal. But do send her my respects, you understand. Just my . . . Actually, on second thought, it might be better not to. You're very . . . But do send everyone my best wishes, and express my, um, apologies for the fact that this symphony isn't more, you know, optimistic . . . —By the middle of May, the score was safely in Tashkent. (That was when Shostakovich was finally beginning to hear which of his colleagues in Leningrad had died.) In June, while the German Fascists launched Operation Blau (Kharkov had already fallen), our countervailing musicians learned their parts.

They arrived in Leningrad just as the first assault on Stalingrad began. In fact, the news could hardly have been worse. During rehearsals the audience-seats had been empty like rows of tombstones, because who could possibly be excused from digging antitank ditches? Secondary musicians were now brought back from the front, and the score (hand-copied by Glikman, runs the legend) flown in by an Li-2 airplane from Vnukovo Airport. High-ranking Party members began to appear, in obedience to the will of Comrade Stalin. Radio broadcasters ran their cables between the bas-reliefed pillars. This was by no means our first such spectacle. To celebrate the anniversary of the October Revolution we'd held a military parade in Moscow in the darkest moments of that city's siege. Such spectacles educated the world, said Comrade Stalin, who as always proved to be correct; even the Americans were impressed. Why not repeat the lesson in Leningrad? Still and all, how strange it was that our slender, treacherously brilliant Mitya, whose fingers never stopped trembling like jellyfish tentacles, whose wife refused to sleep with him, whose mistress had married someone else and whose outlook had been convicted of the crime of formalism, should have been thus elevated, when we'd all long since agreed that his destiny was as worn as the Conservatory's tiled floors, that his next premiere would take place in the Lubyanka's cellars, that his so-called "musical voice" meant no more than the echoing farting of a tuba down the corridor! And it seemed stranger still that Leningrad, that city as mysterious, subtle and narcissistic, hence as distrusted, as her own poet, Anna Akhmatova, should be allowed so much radio time! But this only confirms our faith in Comrade Stalin, whose genius can build socialism out of the most unlikely bricks. (The reactionary critic Wolfgang Dömling has remarked, apologetically in my view, that *it is because of this historic aura and the immense moral stature of the work that discussions about its aesthetic value appear of secondary significance.)* Anyhow, for reasons best known to the "organs" Mitya did not attend his own performance.

The German Fascist High Command now stripped away most of Eleventh Army from an attack upon the Caucasian oil fields and sent it north to break Leningrad. Field-Marshal von Manstein himself was coming—a sure sign that the sleepwalker in Berlin had actually started to wake up. Field-Marshal Ritter Wilhelm von Leeb had resigned seven months ago; he'd been unable to raze the city as ordered, and our counteroffensive had neutralized a hundred thousand of his men. Three years from now this old gentleman would be squatting in the Mannheim prison yard, tracing in the dirt each bygone trench and disposition to prove to his fellow Field-Marshals, Vlasovites and ϟϟ-men that in 1941 he could have rolled into Leningrad with ease, had it not been for Hitler's dilettantish meddling. That might have been true. Anyhow, he'd been replaced first by Field-Marshal Busch, then by Colonel-General von

Küchler, neither of whom was in von Manstein's class, although the latter seemed to be a fair enough conductor, beating out many a military tattoo upon the half-broken city, which nonetheless stood firm. As our new slogan went: *Leningrad is not afraid of death; death is afraid of Leningrad!* All the more reason for us to shake Shostakovich's Seventh Symphony in their faces!

Artillery pieces on loan from Moscow (oriented at forty-five-degree angles like bassoons) would hold the Fascists in check for the duration, so that they couldn't destroy the Great Philharmonic Hall. This proved to be a useful precaution, because General Friedrich Ferch, Chief of Staff of Eighteenth German Army, actually ordered a cannonade when he found his men listening on the radio; the cannonade failed, thanks to us. I've read that General Ferch also listened to the radio, sitting quite still as if he were awaiting some announcement. Von Küchler for his part grew very melancholy on that day, and the remainder of his war, not to mention his life, would not be happy, either. And so the Fascists hunched down in their trenches beneath the golden grass, with tiny sun-glitters adorning their dark helmets as they watched the sky blacken with smoke from the Soviet tanks they'd killed. Their mortars fell silent; they were low on ammunition.

And it came out of Leningrad, spiraling out and out, our transmitters artificially increasing its inductance to decrease the attenuation, transforming it into pure electricity so that it might as well have been a single human voice (for instance, Comrade Stalin's) whose harmonic components had been entirely converted to analogue signals, dominating over all enemy cross-talk by thirty-five decibels or more! The Great Hall Philharmonic, that dull yellow, not particularly ornate building, with its white-on-yellow rococo decorations sparse and faded, this was now the brain of our national telephone; and Shostakovich had braided the sub-waves of his immense signal so as to most beautifully and loudly carry the commands of the automatic central office in a rhythm as reassuringly steady as Red Army men with up-pointed rifles filing past our trapezoidal shelter for the Bronze Horseman. The first movement, which is rather idyllic and slight until the Rat Theme, with here and there a reverie which recalls for me Novgorod's ancient towers silhouetted against the evening sky, reminded the German Fascists of their own landscapes, since after all it was meant to speak to them, its softness being akin to the silence on the telephone after it has rung late at night—Elena, is it you?—No, that pealing shrillness within the telephone's black face means that the secret police are verifying one's presence preparatory to making an arrest. It's already too late.

Shostakovich sat in Kuibyshev listening to the broadcast. Nina was holding his hand. His silent tears were heavier than bullets. On the floor, their children played very, very quietly. In his heart he felt a crushing dissonance, or as I should say an *acciaccatura*.

The announcer crooned: *Listen, comrades . . .*

Many wept. Leningrad was transformed into gold.

40

The grim, stern fanfares of the fourth movement (which is called "Victory") gave way first to a requiem, then bits of sunshine flickered through the clouds, like earth beginning to appear beneath melting snow. It faded back into the Easter theme of loss and resurrection, returning full-fledged in strings; then, as so often happens with Shostakovich, it greyed and dulled back to the beginning major theme, again brightened and dulled until the *attacca* into the finale.

41

On 23.8.42, Hitler the Liberator sent out new orders from Headquarters Werewolf: STAGE 1. MAKE A JUNCTION WITH THE FINNS. STAGE 2. OCCUPY LENINGRAD AND RAZE IT TO THE GROUND. But on the morning of 2 January 1943, our Red Army launched Operation Iskra. Six days later the Nazi blockade had been penetrated five miles to the southeast of Petrokrepost. On 27 January the siege was lifted, the Nine Hundred Days ended. Now that city which Dostoyevsky likens to a consumptive girl blushing into beauty briefly and inexplicably was free again, free to devour herself in secret claustrophobic maelstroms of fear.

As for the secret German military maps, they found themselves compelled to sing: *Dislokation Heeresgruppe Nord nach Lage Ost Gen St d H OpAbt/IIIb.* Those crisp black pen-lines superimposed on the map of the Russian landscape which in its faint grey rivers, place-names and junctions over whiteness most resembled traceries of dirt on snow on a dreary winter's dawn, these lines could not be made to lie outright to the Führer, but the *Heeresgruppe* flags and ϟϟ pennants which once had massed together in baying chords of hunting-horn themes were now bleeding pale, black notes fading self-evidently into weary white quarter-rests which clung in frozen weariness to the music-staves within their trenches until Soviet scouts came creeping with wirecutters and Operation Iskra blared.

On 31 January, the Fascists surrendered at Stalingrad. Even von Manstein couldn't turn our magic back. Hitler the Liberator kept chanting: *The Russians are dead!* but all that summer and much of the next, his soldiers kept running away through sunflower-fields, hunched low. And then they had run entirely out of our Soviet land—those who lived. By the middle of '44, we'd established a solid national-democratic bloc in Romania . . .

So who dares disbelieve in happy endings? In 1945 the productive capacity of Kuibyshev was five times greater than it had been in 1940.

42

Along with ninety-three thousand others, Akhmatova got her Medal for the Defense of Leningrad, although we've already mentioned that she had been compelled to pass most of the Nine Hundred Days elsewhere. It goes without saying that she'd written a poem in praise of Operation Iskra, and many other martial odes besides; but no one ever said that her talent was as powerful as the gun of a Josef Stalin tank. Now that we didn't need the Anglo-Americans anymore, it was high time to bring up her past. In August 1946, we expelled her from the Leningrad Union of Writers. Comrade Zhdanov had a hand in this. Digging up her old epitaph, *half nun, half whore,* he spread the word that she was a real *chéstnaya daválka,* a woman who likes to fuck. He himself died under mysterious circumstances in August 1948. We should probably blame the Fascist-Trotskyite bloc. Thousands would be executed or imprisoned for their part in this so-called "Leningrad Affair." For in Stalin's symphony, we'd now reached the passage marked *a battuta,* which means a return to strict tempo.

As for Shostakovich, as I said, he did quite well. His hair had begun to go white a year or so before the siege was broken. Liver spots burst out on his cheeks, as if he were a very old man. These marks or stains or images, whatever one wants to call them, what are they but reminders of how the flesh must someday corrupt within the coffin? (And Shostakovich, now he too is gone, like the German-killed lime trees of the Peterhof.)

It was in his Eighth Symphony that he first began to articulate the various *danses macabres* which he could no longer prevent himself from hearing. Bones, murdered or merely perished, ought to stay silent. That's the law. But, quick and shrill as a violin-screech, *they come back,* to the terror of all who stand guilty of living, and then they dance, playing on their tomb-lids as lightly as cats—but the game's evil, hateful, angry; there's no fun in being a skeleton!

He dreamed that Elena Konstantinovskaya was calling out to him. Her face was milky with fear. They were taking her away and she was screaming and then a bomb began to whistle down upon the Black Maria and she was screaming, screaming! In time, these hauntings within his ears would evolve into the terrifying Opus 110. For now, the music still had an object other than Death itself: he could blame the Germans. Maybe they'd even make him a Hero of the Soviet Union. Keeping all secrets hid within his maggot-writhing fingers, he crossed his legs, huddling against Aram Khatchaturian's deliciously braided wife while the three of them—that is, Shostakovich and the two Khatchaturians—went over the score of the Eighth Symphony. He smiled anxiously. His glance hid within the sockets of his wounded eyes. ▸

UNTOUCHED

Freed from the constraints imposed by the policy of adventure of your intellectual governing classes, you will fulfill your duty of working to the best of your ability, and you will fulfill it under the powerful protection of Great Germany. All will earn their bread by working under domination; that will be fair. On the other hand, there will be no place for political agitators, dishonest profiteers and Jewish exploiters . . .

—Governor-General Hans Frank, to the Poles, 1939

1

At fifteen-o'-clock a *Kampfflieger* bestowed gifts upon Warsaw, the bulky-shouldered pilot's beret askew, his head sunk deep down into his neck as he hovered within an immense wheel through which the close-packed, steep-roofed Polish houses began to go up in smoke; at the center of the wheel hid an inner wheel dissected into quadrants; that was the sight of his strafing-gun. The wheel was Poland's clock from which bullets ticked, each bullet not a moment but a moment's end for another Pole bewitched into a blackened, grimacing corpse face-down in the mud beside its scorched rifle or pram.

At sixteen-o'-clock the *Kampfflieger* sported over a river and magically created from nothing a canted Polish cruiser (the magic enacted by the pull of a black lever), by which time Case White had been nearly accomplished, with mushroom-headed Germans planting the swastika flag atop the ruined bunkers of Westerplatte.

Ceasefire, armistice, Frank's proclamation, the first "Jewish action," each of these marked another hour on the great clockface. At twenty-one-o'-clock a reconnaissance plane passed by and with all cameras clicking harvested aerial views of the brown smoke which was Warsaw; by twenty-two-fifteen the most perfect exemplar of these, still moist from the last darkroom tray, arrived by special courier in Berlin, so that it too could be counted, recognized, preserved. (In the official military history of our Polish victory, one finds this very photograph, which depicts ruins from edge to edge, with the pious caption: *The church is untouched.*) At twenty-three-forty-five the Russians finished eating their half of Poland. Ten minutes later to the second, the Ribbentrop-Molotov Line had been demarcated all the way to East Prussia. How many crossings were there? That's top secret! But, needless to say, each checkpoint was instantaneously manned by one of our field policemen in his black-and-white-striped sentry box; and a hundred meters away, more or less, one of *their* sentries watched him, smoking a mahorka cigarette. That was the Ribbentrop-Molotov Line. By twenty-three-forty-seven the cleansing of our respective sectors had begun. So-called "national politicians," bourgeois democrats, Polish chauvinist elements, intellectuals, kulaks, officers and Jews were rendered harmless. Then with a ringing chime came midnight, and the thick folder which still lay open on the sleepwalker's desk, a folder ominously snow-hued like forthcoming Russia, received its last checkmark and eagle stamp: Case White was closed.

Next came the folder for Operation Barbarossa. One of his secretaries laid it timidly on the edge of that great desk.—Thank you, my dear Trudl, said the sleepwalker, offering her a little round cake.

The folder was still quite thin at this stage. Its only document was an architectural drawing, very correctly rendered yet not without a certain mood, which conveyed a notion of how Europe Central might be altered into a courtyard of cobblestones as white as light, with a rigid double line of black, black silhouettes waiting to enter a black doorway two by two; they'd never come out.

After all, said the sleepwalker to himself, I'm compelled to act decisively. I've got to make it all tank-proof. A lunatic or a Jewish cancer cell could eliminate me at any time. And then who knows how all this would turn out?

And so Operation Barbarossa was opened, with our nightmares all double-censored like the postcards home of Death's Heads. The telephone rang, requesting verification from the field echelon of Section L. Steel began to clitterclatter from Germany into Russia.

2

Leningrad remained almost untouched, unfortunately. Army Group North had nibbled her around the edges—the best that we could do.—We've got to get hold of this rail junction, muttered the sleepwalker, glaring at one of his maps.

The folder for Operation Barbarossa was thicker now. It would soon be infinitely large, which is to say exactly the same size as Russia; already it came up to the sleepwalker's head; all his secretaries together couldn't trundle it about, even in a ten-shelved cart. Just as an iceberg calves off towering chunks of itself into the deep, so Operation Barbarossa spawned Operations Blue, Wilhelm, Shark, Edelweiss, Fredericus, Heron, Sturgeon, Winter Storm, Thunderclap, Northern Lights . . . These folders with their accompanying sub-folders had now formed themselves into rows of bound volumes on tiers of steel library shelves whose aisles receded infinitely. As for the fundamental issue, Barbarossa itself, no matter how much he hacked off he couldn't touch it; it kept swelling like a gravid corpse. Long past midnight, when the chattering of his fellow Old Fighters had sunk deep down into dreams, the sleepwalker sat alone in the Chancellery, unrolling those white maps of Russia, on which he sought to overlay his own blueprints. Draw another spearhead up here! The emblem of our Fourteenth Panzer Division is the arrowheaded rune Ogal, which means *Possession*. Superstitiously, the sleepwalker always aimed it eastward. And Nineteenth Panzer, that we indicate by reversing the lightning-rune Yr, *Death*, and slashing it with a horizontal line. Death to all of them! He longed to incise it into the whiteness multiply, but resisted. Seventh Panzer is a Y, a vulva; keep that close to home. Twenty-third and Twenty-second are both arrows; we'll aim them each at Moscow. Now tie off another satellite territory down there; that's right, tie it off with ligatures of barbed wire. Cauterize its ghastly red blood vessels; weigh it down with edicts and triumphal thoroughfares. Subdivide it into German farms. Now it's been neutralized; this little matter of operational command is something that anybody can do. All the same, it didn't seem to matter how immense he made his reinforced quadrangles, how elongated his arteries; Barbarossa surpassed them. He massed armies and injected them into Barbarossa, where they expanded into rectangles, arrows and artillery-bristling hedgehogs; Barbarossa diluted them into linelets more insignificant than eyelashes on the white maps. He ran out of space on his desk, so he had to unroll more maps on the floor. He tried to paper them over with all the documents he had. These pages gave off a chill and made him sleepy, a state which he feared more than anything.

Here came the courier now, bearing more bad news about Operation Barbarossa. He steered his motorcycle between the long double line of shiny beetle-backed limousines on the Wilhelmstrasse (another diplomatic reception was in swing) and showed his pass to the guards. It was already seventeen-o'clock. The courier must be in the Mosaic Hall now. Soon he'd be in the Runde Saal. No, already the sleepwalker could hear his jackboots echoing louder and louder as he came down the Marble Gallery.

The sleepwalker wanted to be at Wolf's Lair. He was returning there tomorrow. Then it would be more difficult for bad news to reach him.

He rose, walked to the door, where the two sentries clicked their heels, and he said to them: I mustn't be disturbed. Don't let anybody in, unless it's for the Anti-Comintern Pact.

Yes, my Führer.

Turning his back on them, he closed the door. The Russian army was essentially annihilated. He sat down at his desk and waited for the telephone to ring.

3

At twenty-o'-clock precisely we buried the Panzers in straw-colored holes at Millerovo, so that they'd stay untouched by Russia's freezing cold; but mice ate the wires. Operation Barbarossa had burst out of its folder in a great white explosion, and now those snowy pages began to swirl down out of the sky, burying us alive in maps. We couldn't understand them.

At twenty-ten I caught hold of a top-secret Soviet document whose nested hexagon diagrams and inverted-Y insigniae strangely resembled the sketches of the abstract sculptor Rodchenko; it might have explained everything, so I delivered it to Headquarters with my own hands; unfortunately the courier plane which was supposed to convey it from Headquarters to Wolf's Lair got shot down, so . . .

At twenty-twenty, the sleepwalker sent us a message by teleprinter from Wolf's Lair. He said: The attack's not as serious as all that. I'm definitely keeping these forces right here. If we could just be certain that the Westfront would stay untouched for six to eight weeks . . .

4

He'd promised us that the Reich would never be touched, but after Dresden, Berlin and all the rest, what were we to make of that? By twenty-one-o'-clock, the Foreign Office (number seventy-six, Wilhelmstrasse) was a war-gnawed shell whose facade had been death-licked here and there right down to the white-dusted skeleton and whose serene, round, curly-haired stone face above the double doors would soon be punched out by a Russian rocket; on the other hand, even the Russians would prove limited in what they could touch: even after we'd lost everything, that stone face's twin would still gaze meditatively out on those of us who survived to walk with downcast heads along the ruler-straight wormtracks between rubble piles.

From the sleepwalker's point of view, everything remained untouched and perfectly proportioned, at least in the universe of potentiality. (Dr. Morell prescribed two tablespoons of Brom-Nervacit before bedtime.) Decades ago he'd memorized the map of Vienna's Ringstrasse. Berlin's triumphal arch and Nazi meeting hall would dwarf all that. Göring's new ministry would get what Göring longed for: the greatest staircase in the world. He'd better lose a few kilograms if he wanted to climb it! Dr. Goebbels would get a new ministry, too. (I'm told that he was still intimate with the Czech movie actress Lida Baarova.)—Unrolling Speer's latest blueprint and pinning down its corners with antitank shells, the sleepwalker knelt over his Soldiers' Hall, which would house Germany's greatest treasures: the crypts of our Emperors, Führers, Field-Marshals. Meanwhile, the plaza of the nascent Central Railroad Station would be adorned with captured enemy weapons. His cinema, opera houses, hotels and electric signs already existed as cabinetmaker's models. They'd be ready for the World's Fair of 1950. Himmler guaranteed to supply the granite blocks for everything.

Oh, but the sleepwalker built well! In the Occupation years, our Zoo Flak Tower would defeat the British victors: They planted twenty tons of TNT beneath it, and it was still untouched! They had to drill it full of thermite charges! Or what about Berlin Cathedral, where Hermann and Emmy Göring got married? An honor guard of two hundred war-planes flew over their heads at the end of the ceremony. Berlin Cathedral was certainly still undamaged; it wouldn't be firebombed until 1945. Meanwhile, and we're back in wartime now, the tall windows of the Schauspielhaus, the coffeehouses of the Kemperplatz, the stone eagle and twin sentries of the Chancellery, weren't they all still there?

At twenty-one-forty, an aerial bomb set the cupola of the French Cathedral on fire, but by twenty-two-forty-five Berlin was back in operating condition. At twenty-three-fifteen the Russians still hadn't overrun Wolf's Lair. Until nearly midnight Dr. Goebbels's Propaganda Ministry remained untouched . . .

At one minute before midnight, I myself was saved by a woman whose pubic hair was as soft as the reddish brick-dust upflung in the Tiergarten's very last explosions when the Reich came to an end. She let me hide inside her womb, and the Russians never found me. As for the sleepwalker, some say he closed the hatch upon himself and vanished forever. This reminds me of the Norse legend of the Serpent of Midgaard, who swallowed his own tail. I myself tend to suspect that he's waiting it out inside that cuckoo-clock over there. A Russian bullet stopped its hands at ten seconds to midnight. ▸

FAR AND WIDE MY COUNTRY STRETCHES

Seeing this film, involuntarily one clenches one's fists in wrath . . . This film incites one to fight and inspires one with the certitude of victory.

—Roman Karmen (1942)

1

Europe is Europa; Europe is a woman. Europa's names are Marie-Luise Moskav and Berlin Liubova; Europa is Elena Ekaterinburg and Constanze Konstantinovskaya, not to mention Galina Germany, Rosa Russkaya; Europa encompasses all territory from Anna to Zoya, not omitting the critical railroad junctions Nadezhda, Nina, Fanya, Fridl, Coca (whose formal name was Elena), Katyusha, Verena, Viktoria, Käthe, Katerina, Berthe, Brynhilda, Hilde and Heidi; above all Europa is Elena.

She was as delicious as the white Viazma gingerbread which they used to sell during Palm Week in old Petersburg, and she almost remembered the taste of it; thanks to her police file, I'm aware, as she would never be, that until she was three years old, and our Revolution ended Palm Week, her mother used to break off a piece and put it in her mouth. That is why sometimes when she was very happy she could almost taste gingerbread. I repeat: She was as delicious as white Viazma gingerbread and she didn't even know it! Nor did so many others. No exegesis of her exists but mine. No matter what they say, she wasn't blonde; she had dark hair. She died in 1975; I do agree with that. She was too modest to wear her Order of the Red Star very often. The apparatchiks for whom she interpreted failed to recognize her face if they passed her in the street. Her colleagues ignored her; her students never saw beyond her spectacles. Search the index of any Shostakovich biography (Khentova's excepted) and you'll find the meagerest references to her, never a photograph. And yet she was the most perfect of us all, as white and sweet as gingerbread! In Shostakovich's illicit operas she was the flash of light in the troubled skies of chromatism.

It was R. L. Karmen who got her next. Born in the same antediluvian year as Shostakovich, he was the one who even in his youth had a habit of standing with his legs apart like a heavy old man, the one who summed up his lifelong role: *We were soldiers, armed with a camera.* Unlike Shostakovich, his disposition was fundamentally cheerful, forward-looking. A laughing man dances, clutching at the bottles on a rope ladder, while an accordionist gazes lovingly up at him; thus runs one famous sequence of the movie "Volga-Volga," which derives from Comrade Stalin's favorite musical; more than one of us, particularly women, have compared Roman Karmen to that laughing man. Auntie Olga down the hall used to tell me that something about his likeness, which occasionally appeared in *Izvestiya,* used to make her feel *resolute.* (For good reason, she dropped dead of liver failure in 1964.) Karmen really must be considered an outstanding example of our successful Soviet man. He received the State Prize of the USSR in 1942, 1947 and then again in 1952. Oh, he knew how to smile and laugh!

That smile of his, and the equanimity with which he agreed to commence, abandon or alter his projects as we suggested, gave rise to the supposition (highly beneficial to his career) that he accepted his place in a world whose cinema is as blandly necessary as the long petrol hoses entering the shiny square hoods of cars.

Roman Karmen has been called a great artist. And was he? In the year 2002, when I telephoned the University of Chicago film expert Yuri Tsivian, the following verdict came down: *He's, well, let's say he's an official classic, but he's not remembered as a great filmmaker. If he filmed the surrender at Stalingrad, that wasn't because he was a great artist, but because he was a trusted official. He was brave and reliable, but not anyone I would admire.*

Poor Karmen! And yet, what if Professor Tsivian were wrong? For that matter, even if he were right, how was Karmen supposed to act? All we can do in this life is our best. And if we believe in ourselves, if our best pleases us, haven't we followed the correct line? And who's to say that cinema isn't gasoline? I know a lady who decides which movie to see as a result not of the subject matter but of which time is most convenient for her. Somebody's got to pump her gas. Somebody's got to defend her mind. *We were soldiers, armed with a camera.*

Aged not quite fifteen, he arrived in Moscow in the same year that Lenin suffered his first two strokes and Comrade Stalin became General Secretary of our Party. His most treasured possession was the camera bequeathed to him by his martyred father.

He sent photographs to *Ogonyok* magazine, and received his first press card in 1923, when we find him interviewing Vassil Kolarov, the Bulgarian hero. In his anxiety and inexperience he used too much magnesium oxide; the flash filled the room with black smoke. The negative was blank, so he went back to Kolarov's hotel in the morning. Perhaps it was his smile, perhaps his honesty or simply his desperation. In any event, the young photojournalist succeeded in getting both picture and caption published. For years he was haunted by the ironic gentleness of Kolarov when he granted the youth another chance. With his customary readiness to reveal himself, he told this embarrassing story to Elena Konstantinovskaya, who laughed lightly. For some reason all his embarrassment flooded back; he couldn't understand why; he'd issued this anecdote so many times that it was scarcely new-minted; it was not until he was old that he understood not only why the tale humiliated him before her, but also what had brought it out of him in the first place: her gentleness, oh, her gentleness.

He photographed Lenin's corpse lying in state, and captured many emotion-laden scenes, but the full power of images first impressed itself upon the young Roman Karmen later on in that same year, 1924, when he passed by an exhibition of German art arranged by Otto Nagel. Amidst the other flotsam hung "The Sacrifice" by Käthe Kollwitz. How can I describe this woodcut? The mother's black cloak is open to reveal her breasts as she offers up her baby to death.

In the same folio, which was called "War," Karmen, stunned and riveted, saw "The Parents," a black woodcut of a man mourning, supporting the hand in which his face is buried upon the back of his wife, who mourns in his lap; this couple comprise a dark mass of mourning, silhouetted against a white background and their outlines printed negatively in white.

These two prints moved him to tears. But when, now scanning the walls almost ferociously in his determination to find every scrap of paper by this artist, he discovered "Hunger," which would become leaf number two of most versions of her great "Proletariat" folio of 1925, the emotion which overcame him was *anger*—anger against an order which made people suffer in this way. And how strange it was that he was moved! For he had known hunger himself; and his father had suffered at the hands of the White

Guards. This was the moment when he understood that the representation of reality can be more real than reality itself.

I've seen a photograph of Karmen in a cocked sailor's hat, smiling sweetly, his white teeth peeking up around one edge of that accordion-like instrument his father left him; it is 1926, and he stands before a banner for the cause of the German workers. A moment before the picture was taken, he had just praised Kollwitz's "Hunger" once again.

In 1927, when an exhibition specifically of the works of K. Kollwitz took place in Moscow, Karmen succeeded in photographing the artist, but by then she excited him somewhat less. He was living across the street from a billboard designed by Rodchenko; it advertised macaroni for Mosselprom. He used to study this billboard every day. It seemed to him that in this image every element was perfectly synchronized. Rodchenko not only conveyed information, he also *defamiliarized* it in the manner of the Russian Formalists (who had not yet been ruled alien to our Soviet culture). Furthermore, without in any way distracting us from his mission of selling macaroni, Rodchenko added whimsicality, even humor—a quality which our dear friend K. Kollwitz lacked.

At the end of the decade we find him in every periodical from *Prozhektor* to *Vsyermirnaya Ilustratsia* to Mayakovsky's *Lef*. He'd begun with a still camera, but it was really *motion* which seduced him. Rodchenko would have been content to photograph a single shorthaired Moscow athlete whose Red Star badge proclaimed her **READY FOR WORK AND DEFENSE**; Roman Karmen showed us walls of athletes' legs actually flashing beneath icons to Lenin and Stalin on Red Square!

He captured Dmitrov, Gorki, Alexei Tolstoy, the interplanetary enthusiast-theoretician Tsiolkovsky and even the first American Ambassador, William Bullitt. In his inspirational films of this period, long tables of children bow over their studies; smokestacks vomit blackness above banner-hung posters, Mongolian-looking men in their autonomous folk costumes blow abnormally long horns which resemble the smokestacks.

Thanks to the benevolence of our Soviet state, he'd succeeded in attending the State School of Photography in the malachite-columned hall of the former Yar Restaurant. Among his talents was the supernatural one of meeting all the people he needed to meet, and avoiding the unwholesome. Eisenstein himself is said to have gazed upon him brightly, all the while clutching a briefcase in his armpit. But a canniness entirely alien to, for instance, Shostakovich, kept the young man from accepting too many blessings from this god whom one would have thought to be eternally anchored to his pedestal. Instead, he became a protégé of the rival Pudovkin. He became friends with L. O. Arnshtam, who'd left Meyerhold's theater at the last possible moment; in '37, when Meyerhold and his wife *disappeared,* Arnshtam not only didn't get taken but kept right on making movies for Lenfilm! He and Karmen were inseparable.

From Dziga Vertov, who was already suspect on account of the formalism in his "Man with the Movie Camera," Karmen kept personally clear, although he is known to have seen a number of the man's newsreels. This scrupulous neutrality undoubtedly served him well in his later years, when he taught at the All-Union State College of Cinematography.

In the cutting room, even the scratches on film leaders enthralled him, wiggling past his eyes like the light-streaks of Moscow trams in the night. Soon we began to associate him with the neoclassical pillared facade of Lenfilm Studio in Leningrad. One catalogue gushes: *Unusual angles, the most incredible positioning of the camera, the play of light and shade, compositions—it was all new, unheard of and unique.* The curator had evidently never heard of Rodchenko.

In 1930, when his future with Elena was as tiny as a bomb which is still far overhead and he hadn't even graduated from the State Institute of Cinematography, Vladimir Yerofeyev invited him to be assistant cameraman on our first Soviet sound film, "Far Away in Asia." And so far away in Asia we find him, in collaboration with the renowned and slender Edward Tissé, recording the Kara-Kum expedition. Our new Soviet trucks will pass the test! The temperature reaches one hundred and sixty degrees Fahrenheit. Karmen films the last drink of water. Here's a photograph of Karmen on a camel's back, with a turbaned guide behind him; he's wasting no time; he's filming!

In China, wading a river with his cine-camera lashed to another camel's back; in the ice-covered rigging of the *Sedov* with his camera clutched against the breast of his parka; in besieged Leningrad, leaning over the hood of a ruined truck to establish his position; with his camera at his eye in a New York penthouse; panning the Kino-Eye across a long S-shaped column of captured French soldiers in Vietnam; that was how he would spend his life. A film every year and often more! Simonov remembers him as always working, even bandaged, sick or exhausted, no matter what his mood or how dangerous the conditions.

He sincerely tried to film not only the essence, but the hope. When he produced his sound newsreels about the exemplary shock workers Nikita Izotop and Ivan Gudov, Gudov he filmed at his lathe; Izotop he filmed trying to study geometry. Did Izotop become a geometer? Not exactly. But thanks to his dedicated productivity he'd won the chance to try, as he never would have under capitalism. Now any worker had that chance. This is what Karmen wished to show us. Can such a strategy be called "art"? Roman Karmen didn't care. He was no formalist, not he!

In 1933 he made a film called "Parade on Red Square in Moscow." In 1938, he made "Mayday." In 1948 and 1952 he made two films each of which was called "Mayday on Red Square." No one can say he neglected the home front.

In 1938–39 we find Karmen shooting the newsreel series "Embattled China," his sheepskin collar opened, his sheepskin hat high on his forehead so as not to occlude visibility, aiming a cine camera which curiously resembled a metal butterfly or perhaps the wind-up key of a clock at a burning tower. He repeatedly advised his colleagues to *link all points in any temporal order,* a credo which he had long since forgotten that he'd derived from Vertov. But no harm done! After this bow to dynamism, Karmen invariably linked all points in the order A., B., C. More impressive than the arrangement of points is the undisputed fact that the film team traveled twenty-five thousand kilometers. Upon his return, he wrote *A Year in China,* which—measure of his industriousness—he both started and finished in November 1939. This book achieved immediate publication. Its author was accepted into the Soviet Writers' Union.

2

In 1936 he lay flat on his back during an Italian air raid and filmed straight upwards, with Ethiopian women and children dying all around him. He was always lucky, if you want to call it that. The resulting documentary, "Abyssinia," undercut and embarrassed the Fascists. Almost immediately he began to film the twenty-two installments of our newsreel "On the Events in Spain."

I've been told that it happened like this: Karmen wrote a personal letter to Comrade Stalin, took it himself to the guards at the Kremlin gates, and waited a week—it's like some old parable!—and then he and his fellow cameraman Boris Makaseyev got called to Central Board of Cinematography. Next morning they were both on a plane to Madrid. Roman Karmen had all the luck! On the same day, Shostakovich trembled at home in Leningrad, waiting to be arrested . . .

Two Panzertroopers with cocked berets roll toward Madrid, the great gun between them pointing up at the sky. Somehow, Roman Karmen is hiding in a trench and filming them! In the words of K. Simonov: *As we watched the films sent in by Karmen from far off Spain, we young poets were consumed with a burning envy of that man we did not know, that man with the camera who was now on the front line of the fight against Fascism.*

Street fighting in San Sebastián and Irún; women building fortifications on the outskirts of Madrid, as they would soon be doing on the outskirts of Moscow; a bullfight in Plaza de Torres of Barcelona, after which the bullfighters and spectators went straight to the front—and here's our clean young man, his dark beret not covering his ears, gripping the long lever of his cine-camera, leaning forward and down in the direction of its snout. (Dziga Vertov: *The filmings in Spain represent an indisputable achievement of Soviet cinematography and reflect the great efforts of Makaseyev and Karmen.* No matter that Makaseyev has been listed first. *Their lens is now focused on the real, the direct and heroic aspect of the struggle.*) In each of those twenty-two newsreels he warned us that this was merely the beginning of Fascist aggression, that another great war was coming.

The most dangerous and terrifying sequences of the documentary "Spain" were shot by him alone; for when it came time for Madrid's fiery doom, even Makaseyev departed; Roman Karmen was the only cameraman brave enough to stay.

One of his newsreels from 1936 really got to her: the famous one with the closeup of the resolute young girl who raises her clenched fists; other youths behind her stand up for Spain with their hands and their rifles. And so Elena went to Spain. That was brave, absolutely. Of course I've also heard that she was experiencing some kind of love trouble at that time.

What was going on inside her? None of us will ever know Elena; she's as closed to us as any German. But she must have been captivated not only by the brave passion of these films, but also by the man himself. Sergei Drobaschenko remembers him as *a man filled with energy and elegance*—the antithesis of the helpless, rumpled Shostakovich.

3

Back at home, Shostakovich and Glikman went to see every installment of "The Events in Spain," watching the Loyalists smile proudly beneath their triangular caps which resembled folded cloth napkins. Shostakovich was anxious about something—oh, me, very anxious!—From the screen of the Kino Palace, the Loyalists stared out at them, gripping their rifles; and Shostakovich, whose smile was somehow as irregular as the icy streets of Leningrad would be during the siege, said that he was very, you know, *happy* for Elena.

No doubt he wasted many nights wondering how it must have been for Elena Konstantinovskaya and Roman Karmen in Spain. I know I have. Of course I've seen that photograph of Elena wearing her Order of the Red Star.* She always achieved whatever she set out to do—except in one case, of course. So she got Karmen. It's possible that she had set her sights on him years earlier, when he made that gripping newsreel of the Arctic pilot Farikh, shot at the snow-covered airport. Elena always liked fliers and rocket-men. All the same, anyone who writes about her quickly finds himself at a loss. She's unknowable.

What about Karmen? He said little about their time together, perhaps because, as a certain classical slaveholder once wrote, nothing is more painful than days of joy recollected in days of misery. So we'd better limit ourselves to external evidence, by which I don't mean official photographs: We see him smiling mirthlessly and boyishly beside the American bourgeois-romantic writer E. Hemingway, both of them wearing the dark Basque fighter's caps. He clutches his camera in his lap. Hemingway looks bored.—This I will say: Roman Karmen always meant well, and his films praised and elevated us in

---

*Simonov, whose testimony is unreliable since he seems to have also been in love with her, remembers seeing her going into the Palace Hotel in Madrid, now converted to an orphanage, and always bringing something for the children. On 24 October 1936, when the first Soviet tanks went into combat in the vicinity of Aranjuez, Elena was there in the midst of a detachment of Komsomol volunteers. Karmen saw her and was captivated. He believed her to be as attracted as he was to the Spanish carelessness for death. I'm informed that her Komsomol training stood her in good stead; the TASS journalist Mirova, who unfortunately *disappeared* on her return to Moscow in 1937, is said to have been drawn to her and often expressed admiration (although not to Karmen, who instinctively kept his distance from this individual as he did from the equally unlucky Koltzov of *Pravda*). However, what Mirova read in Konstantinovskaya as cool effectiveness, and Koltzov as a secret rage, Ehrenburg of *Izvestiya*, one of the few journalists to survive the purges, considered to be a calculated determination to get back in the Party's good graces so that her spell of imprisonment in 1935 would not haunt her anymore. In his private letters, Ehrenburg writes about her with a venom akin to a rejected suitor's. In any event, Konstantinovskaya fought bravely, winning her Order of the Red Star in the useless Brunete counteroffensive of July 1937.

all sincerity; his anger on our behalf was a loving, constructive anger, like Lenin's; he raged against the Fascist murderers; he hated ignorance, exploitation, poverty; his heart was good. The most wonderful aspect of the Revolution was that we felt impelled to do things which were really beyond us—take the Revolution itself!—and every so often we succeeded. Shostakovich's experiments, and Rodchenko's, Vertov's, Tsiolkovsky's, were all of a piece. We were dreamers together, within the grand red dream of Comrade Stalin. And Karmen went beyond himself! Is it cruel to call him a mediocrity? I don't think so. A man without legs is a legless man, and it's never unfair to say what's simply true: He's not to be blamed for lacking legs. And is it Karmen's fault that he's not listed more prominently in the *Great Soviet Encyclopedia*?

Now to Spain: There's a certain sequence in his newsreels, a shockingly powerful sequence which shows an old lady in black with her child, who's also wearing black, held in against her lap like something out of K. Kollwitz; the child looks sideways, the old lady looks straight at us with a scared expession; then a boy gazes at us from farther away; nearer, a young woman sits sideways on a blanket, gazing inscrutably at us; they are all sitting on the ground; and in the foreground lies a figure on its side, facing away from us, outstretching its white hands at these others; there is a bundle beneath its head, and at first we cannot tell whether it is living or dead. (In another print of the same film, our Kollwitz mother and child aren't black at all. We can see more detail. Everything's lighter and greyer.) These people are refugees; the Fascist bombers are coming. And here Karmen has somehow found the ability to do artistic justice both to his subjects and to his heart. Why now? Perhaps because he is in love.

It is at precisely this juncture in his career that we discover Karmen gradually moving from shots of groups to shots of individuals. Again I wonder why; the same answer comes to mind: The feelings he had for Elena were such that he finally understood with all his soul that one of us can represent us all just as well as the all contains the one. No doubt it was their passion, which rapidly flowered into marriage, which distracted him from filming the departure of Madrid's gold reserves for Moscow, or our just and necessary liquidation of the Trotskyite Andrés Nin while he sat in his Spanish prison.

Another sequence from "The Events in Spain": a long line of helmeted soldiers with crossed bandoliers, some with binoculars, munitions at their feet; they gaze rigidly ahead. Suddenly the camera zooms in on a woman with long dark hair.

4

He was in Spain for eleven months. Within days of his return to Moscow, he flew to the Arctic in search of Levanevsky's plane, that relic of the failed Polar flight to America. He then spent a year in the Arctic, on what the Germans call Rudolf-Insel. That same year he took the responsible step and joined the Communist Party of the Soviet Union.

By that time we trusted him sufficiently to give him the resources to direct his own films: "The *Sedov* Men" in 1940 and "In China" a year later. "The *Sedov* Men" was his respite; the stranded crewmen lined nicely up for him against their ship's patchwork of black-and-white frozen steel; but he could feel the evil rising up everywhere, even out there in the Polar Sea. He could hardly sleep; he had to get to China! Long after it's all over, K. Slavin will define Karmen's credo thus: *I must always be there, whenever fighting breaks out.*

And so I see him lurking with two Chinese insurgents in a cleft in a boulder, the soldier ahead sighting in, ready to snipe at the Japanese Fascists while Karmen very carefully begins to upraise the movie camera over the man's shoulder, careful not to let the sun glint on the lens. (Touching Elena was far more difficult than this.) Through eleven provinces, and I've already cited that figure of twenty-five thousand kilometers, he recorded for all time the fraternal heroism of the Chinese workers, peasants and fighters.

In the happy time of the Molotov-Ribbentrop Pact, we find him at ease amidst his team as he films the Ukraine's streets, always leaning forward, ready for something sensational to happen. The camera pans across skinny, grinning worker-boys who bear a strange resemblance to Karmen himself. They are clutching shiny silver cylindrical items which might be mechanical parts, shell casings, or trophies. A Ukrainian engineer weeps for joy! He's just been given a job in our Soviet Union. And Roman Karmen is here to film it. This film, "A Day in the New World," employed not only Karmen but ninety-six other cameramen. I proudly inform you that it won the State Prize of our USSR.

5

No footage seems to be available of Comrade Karmen's married life, not even a framed photograph of the young couple together. I do have a copy of that famous image of him posing in a line with five other war correspondents, all in uniform, some holding cigarettes, and behind them a plane whose tail boasts the white-bordered red star of our Soviet Air Force. The date was 1943. I am informed that Elena kept this picture with her throughout her life. Public-spirited Soviet woman that she was, she preferred to see her husband in the company of his peers.

In the autumn of 1940, Elena discovered that she was pregnant. She continued to work at the Leningrad Conservatory as well as in Moscow. Karmen left Moscow to join her in Silver Grove, on the day that she was due to give birth: 22 June 1941.

6

Unlike the rest of us, when Karmen heard the news on the radio, he believed it instantly. He rushed back to the studio. We find him on a military train two days later, bound for the front in company with his favorite cameramen, Lytkin and Scheer. At Velikije Luki the train was halted by a German Fascist attack. His very first footage of the war, shot from a machine-gunner's trench, recorded how our troops fell and died in the hopeless counterattack. (By field telephone in that ruined city he was informed that Elena had given birth to a daughter.) Following Akhmatova's songs, we called ourselves a "family in grief." Roman Karmen panned across a line of dead horses who lay against a brick wall . . .

A Soviet cavalry division galloped crazily on white horses, with their sabers upraised against machine-gun fire. They all fell. Roman Karmen was there filming it.

Lytkin shouted. A bullet had passed through his shoulder. Trying to comfort him, Karmen said: How precious this footage will be for all of us, these first images in the chronicle of our Great Patriotic War!

And he aimed his lens at Lytkin, who grinned back as bravely as he could. There was no doctor.

7

Our nervously smiling Russian boys in the greatcoats they'd now wear winter and summer for half a decade, they were truly his heroes. His "News of the War" features for *Sovkinozhurnal* singled out ordinary people, compelled by emergency and coercion into laying down their lives, and transformed them into volunteers! Well, weren't they? He heard through Elena that even Shostakovich had volunteered . . . He filmed our retreats and did his truehearted best to portray them as victories. (We see him wearied and pale, yet still cheerful as he stands in a forest clearing on our western front, resting one hand on his tripod, glancing at us engagingly while beside him a pair of soldiers offers an opened map to our gaze; Karmen touches a point on its blankness, all the while continuing to look with sweet earnestness at us.) Shostakovich made us hear corpse-sleds scraping across the ice of the Kirovsky Bridge, with whited-out smokestacks in the distance; Comrade R. L. Karmen showed us new T-34s creaking and rasping down the white streets, turrets open, guns straight ahead! He posed us in indomitable lines, holding our rifles. On the radio he heard that anguished lyric of Akhmatova's—*The Leningraders, my heart's blood, march out even-ranked, living and dead; fame can't distinguish them!*—and at once he decided to make a feature on the women tram-drivers of Leningrad so that the whole world could love and admire them. What is truth? Plato says that *the actor's mask becomes his face*. Our squeamishnesses differ as do our necessities. An act which one of us defines as the crowning proof of love another rejects with the words: If you love me, you won't make me do this. And each lover's conception of devotedness remains unassailable, at least to himself.

Whatever Karmen's definitions might have been, they hardened when he saw the gallows at Volokolamsk. It is one thing to film violent death in China or Spain. It is quite another to record the invasion of one's own homeland, and still another to witness the mass torture and murder of innocents, some of whom might be one's friends. I have not been able to ascertain whether he saw the famous corpse of Zoya Kosmodemyanskaya with his own eyes, but he was acquainted with the photojournalist Lidin—Karmen knew everybody!—and it was Lidin who made her death famous. Now his desire to serve humanity exploded into vehemence, and he understood with his whole heart, not merely intellectually, what Gorki had meant when he spoke of the love which created and sustained Lenin's hatred for class enemies. The Germans must not be regarded as human anymore! Remembering those women and dead children by whom he'd been so moved at the Käthe Kollwitz exhibition so many years ago, he now vindictively delighted in their suffering. If only he could have killed every German man, woman and child . . . !

In a single night he sketched out his own screenplay portrait of Alexei Surkov's "Scout Pashkov," who gets caught by the Fascists, tortured, shot and buried, then comes back to us and leads us behind the lines to blast them down! He bent over the field-desk. There'd be a nurse named Lyuba, whose long dark hair would resemble Elena's; a Kazakh camel would pull the artillery wagon. His aspirations were as long as the thirty-seven-millimeter cannons of our Shturmoviks.

Stalin ordered Comrade Voronov to rename his antitank artillery battalions into regiments, for the sake of morale and authority. Roman Karmen captioned his newsreels appropriately. The snowy feet of a corpse in Leningrad, what would Käthe Kollwitz have done with those? Roman Karmen knew what to do; he had neither doubt nor time for doubt.

Even then there remained in his work something of the spatial constructions of Rodchenko, the pathos and occasional sentimentality of Kollwitz. Just as in Shostakovich's view the science of pitch demands the notation of every scream between the two barbed wire zones, so for Roman Karmen objective cinematic work requires depiction of the strange angles which appear in starving faces.

He was with Boris Makaseyev again, shooting "Defeat of the German Fascist Armies Near Moscow," leaning on the panning lever as naturally as does a workman on his shovel. How he longed to see us deal the enemy a crushing blow! He caught a pale worker in a hard hat who was snarling with hate at the next oncoming Fascist salvo, and he filmed that man; he rescued him forever. Then he told another joke to Makaseyev, next to whom he always looked especially dapper and well turned out.

An enemy shell screamed toward him. Laughing, he stood up and lit a cigarette. Makaseyev had to drag him down to safety there amidst the sandbagged bookstalls of Kuznetsky Most. His lens isolated a schoolgirl among schoolgirls in a half-dug antitank trench, saw her better than she saw herself, remembered her forever, and gave her back to us as an angel of victory.

In 1944 he was in the Ukraine, whose Nazi Gauleiter had proposed killing every male over fifteen and keeping the females solely for breeding stock. As evidence of his presence I submit that jolly photo of the Kinogroup of the Second Ukrainian Front; a thatched hut is their backdrop; they're all smiling, posing around a jeep, with R. L. Karmen at the wheel, and beside him (but standing, not sitting actually at his side), a hardfaced brunette whose uniform is buttoned up to the throat. And here's his closeup of the dead German Fascist soldier who's curled around a dictionary of Russian verbs, as if something between Aspektverhältnis and Zeichen will save him. *Die vollendeten und die unvollendeten Formen der Verben . . .*

He was the first journalist to film an extermination camp: in this case, the facility of Majdanek. *Save for 1,000 living corpses saved by the Red Army, no inmate escaped alive,* he informed the world. His footage was admitted as evidence against the chief war criminals at Nuremberg, and I once heard him say that what he was most proud of in his career was his contribution to getting those men hanged. *Link all points in any temporal order,* advises Dziga Vertov, so I'll now project for you the dark sequences of R. L. Karmen's "Judgment of the Peoples" (1946), the Fascist war criminals whispering with their lawyers, surrounded by white-helmeted military policemen as they sit awaiting doom beneath the war-damaged columns; it is those white helmets, which from this angle and distance are almost the size of the faces, that we notice first and last; the Fascist faces are a dull, feeble mid-grey; the columns are darker; the recess of the open door within them is pitch-black. I was there; I saw Karmen and his assistant cameraman standing in the shadows, each of them touching the tripod as if it were something magic, Karmen leaning against a blackened pillar with his other hand as he gazed into the courtroom, waiting for the next sensation to happen. He later told me: Since everything in that court followed a strict consequential logic, the final version of my film expressed the same unyielding logic of life.

8

Some of his most suicidal footage was shot in 1943, when we smashed the enemy's Operation Citadel. K. M. Simonov, who was one of his few frontline colleagues still alive at this period, reports seeing Karmen rise coolly out up from one of our deep antitank ditches, which had been camouflaged by grass, and a Tiger tank instantly fired a shell directly at him! Karmen ducked, then rose up again; upon viewing "Battle of the Oryöl," we learned that he had continued shooting as he fell backwards into the trench, so that there's a crazy, grainy lurch of sky, with the shell speeding across it all! The Tiger roared closer; Karmen filmed it head on; and when one of our hundred-and-twenty-two-millimeter howitzers took it out, Roman Karmen got that on film! After that, we regarded him with awe; at the same time, a few of us wondered if he might be unhappy, to use his life so recklessly. It was one thing to receive an order and charge into certain death, as our soldiers did, but Karmen was never given any such order.

At the same time, we were well aware that his senses were acute and his abilities to interpret, organize and improvise were simply expert. He could tell from a great distance whether our Katyushas were loaded with M-13s or M-30s. When the German Fascists opened up with their eighty-eights, his prescience about where the shells would fall was astonishing. Once I asked for his secret, and he said: It's all in the sound, Comrade Alexandrov! Of course, he went on, and his modestly joking grin strangely resembled a grimace, I don't have the acoustical abilities of a Shostakovich . . .

He was in the subterranean brick bunkers of Poznan; he filmed the crazy old men of the Volkssturm and the Germans hiding in haystacks as we came; finally he was in besieged Berlin itself, which, in V. I. Chuikov's words, *rained rivers of red-hot steel on us.* He filmed the capture of the Reichstag.

On Adolf-Hitler-Platz there was a scorched flat filled with books which our healthy-minded Red Army men were busy trampling on and tearing into bits. Karmen took a leather-bound volume from the shelf, opened it, and read aloud in an ironic tone of voice: *One day he heard tell that in Burgundy there dwelt a maiden of ideal beauty, and from her, as it happened, he would gain both great joy and great sorrow.*—What perverted bourgeois trash! Let me dispose of it, Roman Lazarevich!—And the healthy, tanned young cadre began ripping all the leaves out of that bad old book, laughing like a child at play. Karmen knelt down, rescued a torn page and read to himself: *They improved the time with any number of entertainments, although, truth to tell, again and again he was stung by the love with which that princess had afflicted him, and which would eventually drag him to a sorry doom.*—He felt very uncomfortable; he didn't know why. All the same, this was more interesting than filming the mechanized food preparation procedures of our Giant State Farm.

9

Now for his best known accomplishment: When the battle of Stalingrad began in the summer of '42, Roman Karmen, characteristically, longed to go there.—To see the defeated Paulus! he kept laughing. That's every Russian soldier's dream . . .

Strange to say, although he shot the most crucial parts of Varlamov's seven-reel documentary "Stalingrad," this achievement receives no mention in the *Great Soviet Encyclopedia,* which pays tribute to his existence in volumes eleven, twelve and nineteen.—Run to the warehouse! shouted the staff officers, who were all his friends. And so he managed to be the person with the camera in the doorway when Field-Marshal Paulus surrendered (or, as I should say, when the surrender got officially reenacted). He had already distinguished himself by taking innumerable risks during the course of Stalingrad's defense, and we did not overlook this. Every day he had a new joke on his lips: Did you hear what Rokossovsky said? *We'll let you be the first one to photograph Paulus if you're the one who captures him!* Grinning, he aimed his camera at oncoming tanks! He liked what Germans call the *heisse Punke,* the hot spots. (We see him from the side, wearing a Red Army uniform and beret, raising his Argus-eyed machine-pistol of a camera to his eye and aiming it upward into the distance in parallel with the long gun of the T-34 tank beside him; behind him stand the ruins of the Krasni Oktiabr' Stalingrad Metallurgical Works.) Although the enemy advance (mated in the soundtrack to the Rat Theme of Shostakovich's Seventh Symphony) appears mainly through the medium of captured German footage, much of the most daring footage in "Stalingrad" is Karmen's: the soldier's mouth gaping in a toothy shout as wide and round as his helmet, the dark-clad woman standing over snowy ruins, the blurred Red Army soldiers waving their bayonet-fixed guns, and then the enemy coming straight toward us, closer and closer, until the mouths of their gunbarrels take up the entire frame. Little wonder that a fellow traveler calls this film *simple and heroic in the finest sense of the word.*

It was to Roman Karmen that all the film cannisters got entrusted on that special flight of 2 February 1943. It was still dark when the Shturmovik took off; in the northern pocket, the starving Fascists of Eleventh Corps wouldn't surrender until 1600 in the afternoon, but it was definitely over. Karmen couldn't stop smiling! It was his intention to kiss and hopefully make love with Elena in the grey blush of a Moscow winter noon, but Elena wasn't there. So he celebrated with his colleagues at Central Newsreel Studios, all of whom embraced him. (At the studio we see him posing with many reels of film, frowning abstractedly into the bouquet of film-frames he grips with both hands, while gleaming stacks of reels tower before him and behind him.) Why then was he omitted from the credits? Fifteen other cameramen got listed. Had the notorious vanity of Varlamov written Karmen out? In any case, no one ever heard Karmen complain. No doubt he knew he was luckier than his colleague V. Grossman, who was retained in the credits but whose commentary was deleted on account of its ideological deviation.

Unlike Dziga Vertov, he does not appear in Wakeman's *World Film Directors.* I'm pleased to report that the *Great Soviet Encyclopedia* entry on filmmaking does give him two respectful nods, one for his prizewinning "Tale of the Caspian Oil Field Workers," made the year of Stalin's death, and the other for "Flaming Continent" (1972), which (I haven't seen it, so I'm relying on my colleague Pyotr Alexeev's description) *depicts the struggle with imperialism.*

10

Elena accompanied him neither to the Caspian nor to the flaming continent. They were divorced by then. His famous photo of Paulus, rigid and pale at the surrender at Stalingrad, reminds me of Karmen himself on the day that Elena left him. It was probably all over (although who can measure that?) on the day that she informed him that his various projects and dreams—oh, if there only weren't a war he'd take her to Siberia and shoot a film just about the colors of the ice; he'd find a rainbow in the ice for her; he wanted to ride with her in a bathysphere all the way to the bottom of the ocean, accompanied by luminescent fish; he wanted her at his side when he documented the forthcoming revolutions of Latin America (which wouldn't take place for decades, but when they did he was truly going to be there); he tried to describe his longing to accompany her to the deserts of Turkestan—and here I might mention that long ago, so long ago that it had been peacetime, the sleepwalker hadn't even come to power, once upon a time when Roman Karmen was writing in his diary on that hot summer in the Kara-Kum Desert with Yerofeyev and Tissé, what gave him the most joy was imagining that someday he would return here with a woman who loved him! Oh, he was passionate; he was romantic! It was the first of his three desert trips. He'd returned in 1936 with his own car; in 1950 he would shoot "Soviet Turkestan." Elena was silent, so he said that he also wanted to be with her on a secluded tropical beach, or if she didn't like beaches they could float side by side down a wide warm river—a project which would be excellently realized in his lovely and politically reliable travelogue "Our Friend India" (1954)—all this he proposed on a summer afternoon, trying to bring them closer; first he'd asked what dreams *she* had and she didn't answer, so he told her, yes, the moon and the North Pole and the South Sea; he'd love to bring her with him; he wished to be with her forever and ever—these fantasies struck her as either isolating—and after her relationship with Shostakovich she never wanted to be isolated again—or frightening. In a deep low croon which he meant to be reassuring, he tried to explain; she thought he was being defensive and said: I feel very uncomfortable. Your tone of voice is creepy . . . —He was hurt then; he didn't want anyone to think that he was creepy. On the contrary: He was cheery, brave, wholesome! Oh, he was really hurt.

Perhaps in compensation, after that he was always promising to bring her to Odessa, where he was born. Then they stopped talking about going places.

11

It was she who'd returned his manhood to him. A previous relationship had ended so disastrously that he had been impotent, desireless, for more than a year. He threw himself into his work in Spain; he almost hoped to get killed. The first night he was with Elena he'd apologized and warned her, smiling in embarrassment (he never in his life learned that his embarrassed smile was the same as the cheerful one he put on for journalists and opening nights) that he might no longer be a man; he was very afraid, but with her it all came back, not just once but twice and three times, and it was not just delicious but it was tender from the very first; sentimental as such things sound when they are spoken of, it was the most romantic lovemaking that he had ever known, especially when she was riding on top of him, not rapidly and ruthlessly the way many women did (not that he didn't like that, too), but with extreme concentration and grace, riding him very very slowly so that he almost couldn't bear it, gazing at him, sometimes teasing him, sometimes concentrating very carefully on her own pleasure, taking her time, stopping sometimes or just barely moving, clenching and contracting herself around him with extreme deliberation while his desire and sexual suspense rose up like the smoke from her half-extinguished cigarette in the ashtray behind them. Even when her own orgasm was upon her she didn't ride much faster, although she flung back her head at the last moment and her mouth opened and she uttered a high-pitched cry.

When she lay underneath him she had a way of gripping the headboard when she was coming, or sometimes simply raising both hands above her head. After they had been together for a few months she began to lay her wrist across her eyes right before she climaxed. He didn't think anything of it at first. But then, more and more, that wrist was there across her face whenever he tried to kiss her.

One morning they lay just awoke and he rolled over, took her in his arms, and started to kiss her, but she averted her mouth. She said that his breath wasn't good. He felt hurt, but said nothing.

After that he began to notice that she almost invariably turned her face away when they were making love and he wanted to kiss her, or else her hand was there between their faces, keeping him a little away. Perhaps it was his beard. One time at breakfast she remarked that she thought that moustaches made men look stupid, so he shaved off his moustache, but that night when they made love her hand was there, gently pushing his face away from hers, so all he did was kiss her fingers. Sometimes when she was on top of him, she still kissed him, never as deeply as he would have wanted, never the way she used to; he learned to be passive at those moments, to let her kiss his lips in the gentle, shallow, half-nibbling licks that she liked; he didn't want to frighten her away.

It wasn't at all, or at least not exactly, that she was withdrawing from him, or didn't want him to see her. In her way she was actually a bit of an exhibitionist. She loved herself at the same time that she didn't. She liked him to photograph her nude, but when she picked the pose, it was of herself lying on her stomach, averting her face, offering her buttocks. If he had seen any such image of another person, he would have thought: Here's somebody who doesn't want to be photographed. And yet she had asked him to photograph her.

12

That was the crux of it; that was how he would have told the story if he were making a newsreel about his life: First she used to squeak like a mouse when she came, then she grunted, finally she made no sound at all!

He told her how when they made love he felt connected to her, soul to soul, and she gazed at him in silence.

Isn't it that way for you, Elena?

I don't want to hurt you.

That shot away his confidence, so from then on he thanked her with weepy gratitude every time she made love with him.—Don't thank me, she'd sadly whisper.

I love you, he said.

I love you, too, very very much.

I need you.

No you don't! she cried in a panic. You don't need to need anybody. You love me. That's enough. It makes me happy to think of you being strong and going to Spain or China by yourself, being self-reliant. That's why you're my hero.

And then, raising herself up on one elbow, she said: I want you to be happy for me. I think of you as that laughing man in "Volga-Volga."

13

He often dreamed of seeing Elena through a window. He wondered whether Shostakovich, who they said had been extremely attached to Elena, had ever had such dreams; the only reason he hadn't left his wife for her, it seems, was the man's weak character. Hopefully he'd managed to forget Elena by now. Elena's present husband had no intention of forgetting her; quite the opposite; but even in his dreams he no longer succeeded in being quite present with her. They quarreled in bed; she turned her back to him; miserably and tediously he fell asleep. Where was he now? In this other world, everything went on forever. He hovered and shimmered, not even knowing that he existed. Then through the window he saw Elena, naked, receiving the face of another naked woman against her own; she was reclining with her head bent a little forward, cradling the other woman's head in her hands, her fingers buried in the other woman's hair; and the other woman had closed her eyes in ecstasy, almost crying out, her mouth wide open and her tongue coming out; while his wife, whose eyes had also closed, nuzzled gently at this other woman's upper lip almost like a baby sucking at a nipple, her lips tranquilly parted. It was the other woman, whom he'd never before seen, who was the active, eager partner, gasping with need for his wife, who so sweetly held her and offered herself; and yet, although she was the passive one, the giver, not the taker, there was a sense of indescribably sweet exploration in the way that Elena nuzzled the other woman's mouth; the stunning, perfect tenderness between them bereaved him into agonizing insanity, because nowadays even when Elena allowed him to make love to her, she hid her face behind her hand, especially when she climaxed; she hadn't yet forbidden him from looking her in the face but he knew for a certainty that his looking irritated her; everything about him irritated her. When they'd first become lovers he used to be the one to close his eyes; the intensity of her scrutiny as he neared his climax made him feel shy; she'd been *so* present then that it was almost too much, but that hadn't meant that he didn't love her, only that giving himself to her would be an irrevocable step. Perhaps she now felt the same; at any rate, he sought out her face because he was losing her; for exactly the same reason that he needed to have his camera with him when he saw "history," so that none of it would get lost, he needed the little bits of Elena which remained available to him. And she interposed her hand between her mouth and his whenever he tried to kiss her! Yet she loved him; she attempted to be understanding (she was always saying: *I understand*); she admitted that she didn't know how to be reassuring—she'd chosen to live with him, after all! She could have been living with a woman instead, not to mention with D. D. Shostakovich.

Elena had telephoned him once from Leningrad, very cheerfully, so that he felt nothing amiss, to say that all was well. She'd chatted with him about nothing; he had glowed to hear her voice. Then she telephoned him right back and said: I was unfaithful to you last night.

With whom?

Dmitri Dmitriyevich. He was drunk and he came into my room; he started crying and I felt sorry for him; oh, Roman, I'm sorry, I'm sorry . . .

And then what happened? he said wearily.

There's not much to tell you. He and I, we—we . . . He was so drunk he couldn't do as much as he wanted. And he kept crying. It was awful. Afterward I told him that we couldn't ever do this again, because I felt bad about betraying you. I told him it was over, and he got really sad. I'd rather not talk about it anymore unless there's something you really need to ask me. And I promise you that it will never happen again.

Karmen knew that she needed him to forgive her then; he was grateful that she had confessed on the morning after it had happened; on the other hand, and this is what truly hurt him, there'd been that previous telephone call, which retrospectively horrified him with its cheerfulness because it had cheered *him*; he'd *believed*. That was why he understood that he would never, ever know if Elena were lying to him.

He was a tolerant person, really, and not merely in his own estimation. As many itinerant professionals do, he had enjoyed his share of interludes; he'd found stability in several mutually non-monogamous relationships, in obedience to A. Kollantai's *sex-equals-a-drink-of-water* theory; but that these relationships were honest. If from the very start Elena had told him: Roman, I'd like to be with you, but I'm going to go on sleeping with Dmitri Dmitriyevich, then he could have accepted or rejected her proposition; he would have known what he was getting into. Had he accepted it, her nights with Dmitri Dmitriyevich might have hurt him a little, but that would have been *his* pain, inflicted by him upon himself. The pain which Elena had inflicted upon him was not his. This is why it comprised (and she had used the word) betrayal.

Later, what had happened kept returning to his mind. He wished that he had asked: Did Dmitri Dmitriyevich stay the entire night in your bed, or did he go after you'd completed the sex act? Did he want to stay but you sent him away because you were already remorseful, or did you figure that since you had just copulated with him he might as well stay through the night and maybe you would do it with him one more time?

Such questions as these seemed highly important to his understanding of her behavior, but were they actually important? Didn't he already know everything that he needed to know? This other man, Dmitri Dmitriyevich, had penetrated Elena, with her consent, while she was supposedly with him. How many times had he penetrated her? Had he entered her slowly? Had he been gentle and careful; had her pleasure been one of his considerations, perhaps even the primary point, in which case the emotional connection between them must be still more dangerous? Or had Dmitri Dmitriyevich simply been intent upon his own need? Had Elena climaxed? In the course of the sex act, had she thought about, and better yet, had she pretended that she was with, a certain Roman Karmen? If she hadn't, that was very damaging. On the other hand, if she had, then what did *that* say about her?

He never asked her any of these questions, because he feared hurting her with a lengthy interrogation. He knew all too well how necessary it was to him both in his life and in his work for him to visualize all factors, right down to the smallest detail; in the case of Elena's infidelity, his reconstruction would always remain far more incomplete than any on-the-spot documentation; he'd never know enough! Let it go.

14

He kissed her nipples. He wanted to tell her that her breasts were as white and sweet as Viazma gingerbread, but he was afraid that if he did, she would fear all the more that he wanted to consume her.

It's just a compulsion, Roman, that's all it is. I've thought about myself as you asked me to do, and I've even talked with others. I've established that I'm normal and you're abnormal.

But other women never said that about me—

Don't compare me with other women.

I'm sorry.

Elena looked at him in her gently terrifying way, lit a cigarette and said: You know, when I was a girl I used to be a compulsive masturbator. I was addicted to it. If I didn't have an orgasm every few hours I couldn't stand it. I used to spend all my time scheming out another fifteen minutes to be alone. And it was terrible. I finally broke myself of that habit. And I don't ever want to go back!

I want you to need me the way I need you.

What you want is for me to be unhappy again, the way I was with Vera. I was weak, I was jealous, I was dependent. Whatever she did, it wasn't enough. She couldn't make me happy.

But she was unfaithful to you right and left! She was mean to you! And I'm not that way.

I promised myself I'd never go back to that, Elena said. I made progress. I got over being that way. I'm proud of myself for that. And you want me to go back to that. I'm sorry, Roman, but I'll never, ever go back.

15

On her desk he saw an opened envelope to his wife from Vera Ivanova. Jealous suspicions crawled all over him. He longed more than anything else to read the letter and learn whether Vera and Elena had maintained their sexual relationship. He actually held the envelope in his hands. Then he said to himself: My God, what am I doing? Don't I love her? Don't I trust her?

Elena, he said that night at dinner, have you heard any news from your friend Vera?

Elena lit a cigarette and said: As a matter of fact she invited me to a party but I don't think I'll go. I'm feeling tired.

He believed her; he was happy now; he changed the subject.

16

Every time he begged her to say just once that he was the one for her, Elena flew into a rage. She didn't want to be pinned down like a butterfly! She kept saying: What if someday you turn into a monster?

You're the only woman I've ever been with who won't say I'm the one for you.

Maybe I'm the only one who's honest, Elena replied.

17

I know it's unfair, she whispered softly. I know I'm being selfish. I'm sorry . . .

Love, agony, and strangely erotic pain detonated inside him. This was what she so often said, and whenever she did, he always felt the same.

I know it feels a little unequal, Elena whispered. I'm sorry . . .

I know it's hard, Elena gently said.

I can see that you're sad, Elena said in a beautifully consoling voice. But I know you're strong.

And Karmen, suffering intensely, longed for the next time that he would speak with Elena and she would reject him.

18

A certain Comrade Alexandrov, the one who'd brought them together, in fact, took him aside one day and said: I'll put it to you straight, Roman Lazarevich. Well, maybe I shouldn't tell you. It's a secret. Do you want to know or not?

What kind of secret?

It's about Elena Evseyevna. You should leave her. Forgive me for saying this.

What do you mean?

You must promise to keep the secret. You can't tell her. Do you promise?

Of course I promise, said Karmen numbly.

There's a certain individual at the Conservatory who—look, I don't know how to say this, but in November your wife was seen with him at a party. She was all over him, Roman Lazarevich! I'm very sorry.

I see.

And then last month we saw them together again, drinking. You know, your wife has, how should I say, *flirty eyes*. I mean no disrespect; that's her nature; I mean, that's how she appears, and it's a charming, engaging quality, especially in a pretty young woman such as she is. So our first inclination was simply to assume—

Who are these others who were with you?

That's not the point. Anyhow, we watched them, and unfortunately there was more to it than that. The way she was kissing him, and her hands were . . .

I understand.

But you're not to betray me to her.

Can I ask why?

It has to do with protecting my career. That's all I can tell you.

All right, but then what can I do?

Divorce her. That's what you have to do.

But it's not fair! cried Karmen. She can't confront her accuser; she can't know the grounds on which I'm to leave her; she can't refute these charges—

Do you want the man's name?

I—

He's a certain composer. That first time, last November, she wouldn't take her hands off him, so he actually had to leave the party. I know it's an ugly story. He was upset; he complained about her to a friend who told me; the friend was supposed to keep his secret, because, you see, he depends on Elena for a recommendation. That's why you can't mention his name. Do you believe me?

Karmen sat very still. Finally he said: Of course I believe you, Comrade Alexandrov. But if I'm not allowed to approach him or mention his name to her, then I'll have to go on acting as though I believe her.

19

Then a month later when he was in the Ukraine (and he knew full well that by being so far from her he was abandoning and disappointing her, that what he should have done was keep shooting documentaries about local collective farms for *Sovkinozhurnal*) she telephoned him and he said:

So what did you end up doing last night?

Actually, I didn't stay home. A friend called me, and we went out for a drink . . .

Oh, really? Which friend? he casually asked. He had never asked that before.

There was a silence, and then she said in a very low voice: Shostakovich.

He felt as if she had kicked him in the stomach.

Oh, he said.

You sound upset, came Elena's voice.

Oh, not at all. I'm not upset. So how often do you see him? I don't believe you've mentioned him lately.

He's a . . . a fairly good friend.

Oh, he said again, and changed the subject.

Of course she's unfaithful to you, Roman Lazarevich. (This was the opinion of all his friends.) A man doesn't take a woman out to dinner on a regular basis unless he's getting something from her, especially if she's a married woman.

I know, I know.

Well then?

I guess I really don't care. If she'd only tell me, then I—

Now you're speaking in incomplete sentences, just like that Shostakovich.

The thing is, I think about her all the time.

Work harder, Roman Lazarevich! That's the best cure!

I know. But the odd thing is, my work doesn't matter to me anymore. I know it's ridiculous, but I sometimes feel that my love for her is the only thing that's genuine about me.

20

Standing leftwards of the desk where her husband worked by lamplight, with a canteen beside him, his daybook on one side, and his light meter holding down one corner of the paper, Elena smiled at him lovingly.

Do you think there's any hope at all? he asked.

I can't honestly say that I do feel any hope, she said gently.

But still they stayed together.

And now the war had come, and whenever he got to see her, which was far more often than most husbands got to see their wives, he felt claustrophobic; he couldn't forget how she had called him *creepy* for wanting to be all alone with her in isolated places.

I've already told you how during the Nazi-Soviet idyll he'd gone in the icebreaker *Josef Stalin* to film the rescue of the *Sedov* with her crew of thirteen. This vessel had been icebound for eight hundred and twelve days. Karmen would never forget the magnetic storms, the cold, the silence. And yet none of it had depressed him; he was an adventurer; he truly loved the experience! (Shostakovich would have killed himself.) Of course, what's worst about being icebound is the solitude, but a gregarious man is armored against that. Roman Karmen never ran out of jokes. He'd bunked with his cameraman V. Shtatland and his sound engineer Ruvim Khalulashkov; if either man turned morose, Roman Karmen knew how to make him laugh.* Defeatism is a

---

*In a photograph in an East German retrospective catalogue, we see Karmen in Loyalist uniform, but hatless, standing happily amidst his colleagues, shouldering his camera as they shoulder their rifles, with sandbags and a doorway behind them. He is the happiest man in the picture; for him, Spain seems to be a lark. His colleagues in their berets will stay and die, or else at the war's sad end flee into internment camps in France. But this cruel and ignorant interpretation of a brave man's smile neglects two facts: First, while he was with them, he ran at least as great a risk as they; secondly, he believed, and rightly, that only by inflaming the world, for instance through the camera-propaganda of R. L. Karmen, could the Spanish cause hope to triumph.

crime. They recorded the repair and reassembly of the *Sedov*'s engine. The engine started; the *Sedov* was saved; one more Roman Karmen film ended happily! But now when he was with Elena he was back in the cold; they sat miserably together in the captain's icy cabin.

21

He asked her whether she was sure that the problem was him, not her, and she said that she was sure.

Was it like this with Shostakovich?

Never.

22

They invited him to film the premiere of Shostakovich's Leningrad Symphony, but he didn't want to see Shostakovich; even though Arnshtam scolded him, he said he didn't have time. Instead, he requested a transfer out of the Central Frontline Kinogroup and filmed "Leningrad Strikes Back!" (A titanic poster of D. D. Shostakovich in a fire-helmet gazed shyly down on him.) He crawled with his camera over the ice of Lake Ladoga to film the agony and encourage the defenders, almost getting killed four times.

Two lost soldiers, with frost on their machine-pistols, huddle over their truck's frozen engine as they try to read a map. Ruins stretch behind them and before them. Perhaps they'll die today, but Roman Karmen has photographed them; he wants them to live forever. We see them for a single long instant in his newsreel, and we feel for them; we want them to get safely to Leningrad. Roman Karmen is a man who cares! He stands in the same fur-lined greatcoat in which he filmed "The *Sedov* Men," knee deep in Leningrad snow, with the skeleton of a wrecked bus very black behind him. Throwing back his head and shoulders, yet continuing to gaze levelly ahead, he braces the cine-camera against his heart.

The half-blacked-out eyes of supply trucks creep darkly through the white fog and ice of Lake Ladoga. He leaps to one side, films it, gets back in another truck which turns out to be filled with sullen soldiers he's never met; in thirty seconds he gets them grinning at his imitation of the laughing man in "Volga-Volga."

He came home and she was sitting by the gramophone, listening to

Shostakovich's Cello Sonata in D Minor (which is Opus 40, I believe). He sat down beside her and she gazed at him in annoyance.

23

He had just found that his application to speak at the Conference on American and British Cinema had been accepted. Everyone would be there, even Eisenstein, since his name was familiar to the Americans; he was supposed to read a paper on feature films. It meant good cheer and good food, neither of which was in great supply in those war years, and he had thought that Elena would be coming with him; actually he had applied for her sake. But now they had what's called *a little talk,* which is to say a talk in which she gradually, carefully expressed more and more how hopeless she felt, all the time watching him to make sure that no one dose was lethal. It was like the time that a nurse he cared for had been killed by a Fascist barrage, and they sat him down and said first: Roman Lazarevich, we have some very bad news, and then: We're very sorry, but something has happened, and so on and so on, *und so weiter* as the German Fascists would say. In this spirit, Elena asked him what he thought about their life together, what he thought, what he thought, always what he thought! Eventually, he comprehended: She wants me to do the dirty work!

This isn't fair! he cried weakly.

I understand, said Elena, evidently willing to be infinitely agreeable as long as her object could be obtained. Usually she got angry the instant he accused her of being unfair.

Do you ever think about it? she kept asking him.

After awhile he felt like a character in a silent film—a half-silent film, I should say, for he could still hear and remember her words, but everything he said might as well have been silent.

I tried to let you see that it was all right for you to be happy, she was saying. You deserve someone better than I am.

You've been a pillar of strength to me, she said. I don't know what I'll do without you.

I know I'm letting you down, sobbed Elena. I'm really, really sorry. I hate to lose you.

That's all right, said Karmen wearily.

He threw on his oilskin jacket and went out. She had asked him to telephone her so she wouldn't worry about him, but he didn't. She knew where he would be staying: at the studio, naturally. Two days later she rang him up, and he burst out crying. Elena had that effect on people.

He sobbed: When it happened, I was sure it was a mutual thing, but today it isn't. Every time the phone rings I hope that it's you, and now that it's you I'm hoping that you'll say, *please take me back. You're the one for me.*

There's a large part of me that hates to lose you, Elena said consolingly.

24

That would not happen until the summer of 1943, shortly before Operation Citadel. In 1942 he collaborated on "Defeat of the German Armies near Moscow," and directed "Leningrad in Combat." I've told you how I saw him at Stalingrad, eagerly photographing the captured German Fascist Field-Marshal, a certain F. Paulus, who, like a recently dead person, hadn't entirely shed his former grandeur; in another week he'd be a convict, a nothing, but for now he still remembered how to sit up straight and proud in his uniform. All the same, he stared so woodenly into space! He reminded Karmen of someone, but he didn't know whom. Unfortunately, the light wasn't good enough for cinematic work. I've seen footage of him at Vyazma, standing between his fellow camera-soldiers K. M. Simonov and B. Tseitlin. In his bulky coat and fur cap he looks strangely gamin-like, smiling a slightly buck-toothed smile; yes, he resembles a lost French child. Simonov, who puffs at his pipe, seems the most genuine of the three. Tseitlin's pale grin is tense beneath the cap, and Karmen's smile is cautious. Behind them are ruins and dirty snow.

25

He performed all the trickiest camerawork for L. Arnshtam's 1944 film "Zoya," with a musical score by Shostakovich: Zoom in on the Nazi officer gazing into the slender lamp, losing the battle with himself; now pan to Zoya herself, beautiful, bruised and angry, standing upright before him in her quilted jacket; she's ready to take her medicine, resolute to die without mercy for herself. Cut to closeup of her bloody lips saying: You can't hang all hundred and ninety million of us.

Shostakovich had a question about whether the pacing of a certain long shot on the gallows was to be altered, because it would affect the tempo of the, you know. No one else happened to be in the studio. Arnshtam had rushed off to the Ministry for another argument. Zoya had just wiped the makeup off her lips and stood behind the half-opened lavatory door, flirting with the Nazi officer.* The technician had gone into the darkroom to drink vodka.

Karmen laid his hand on Shostakovich's shoulder and said: I hope it doesn't make you sad to work with me, given the circumstances.

That's not the point, Roman Lazarevich, oh, no, not at all! You know, you were born the same year I was, almost the same day! Three weeks apart—what a narrow frontline trench! That makes us, so to speak, contemporaries. Evidently she likes older men. Because we, I, you know. Well, that's another matter. The point is, the point is that here, you see, in our Soviet homeland, for us . . . —and here Shostakovich's lips fleered out and flittered into a spitefully sarcastic smile—*film* is the most important art form, not music.

My dear Dmitri Dmitriyevich!

No, *nein, nyet, noch nie!* That bastard Dmitri Dmitriyevich is not my concern at the moment. Film is the most . . . As you know, Lenin himself said so. Who can argue with Vladimir Ilyich? *She* wouldn't, because she's been, you know. The results are known—

The results of arguing?

Are you, how should I put it, crazy? screamed Shostakovich in terror. Of course I didn't mean it like that! When she was, no, no! She never even . . . The results of, of, I'm implying of Soviet *film* in our Soviet homeland today! And Comrade Stalin confirmed Lenin's profound and just thought and put it into, so to speak, *execution.*

What Karmen did next exemplified why we like him. (He found himself thinking, as he so often did: One of this person's mannerisms is actually mine, but I don't know what it is.) Squatting down in front of Shostakovich, rocking on his wiry little knees, he said: There's no need for hard feelings on that score, Dmitri Dmitriyevich, absolutely none. I think you know why.

---

*How far should one go with the enemy? Zoya herself will tell you: Not one inch! But G. Vodyanischkaya, who played Zoya, was certainly willing to follow Arnshtam's script; isn't one of the qualities we most prize in an actress acquiescence? Several reels of Karmen's private footage disappeared immediately after his death in 1978, but I have it on good authority that he persuaded two starlets to let him film them kissing; this footage he reviewed over and over late at night at the Studio of Documentary Films, trying to accept Elena for who she was. Long after they'd separated forever, he would experience occasional flashes of rage when he happened to see two women sitting alone at a table in a restaurant, gazing into each other's eyes.

Shostakovich was silent; Shostakovich looked away. And this infuriated Karmen inexpressibly. He did not smile much nowadays. A year later, with a white bandage dividing his head into three zones, the boyish look would be entirely gone as he filmed the ruins of Berlin steadily and without pity. He was with the Second Guards Tank Regiment by then. Toward Shostakovich his anger was no less than toward the enemy. All the same, something inclined him to be gentle. Oh, the gentleness of her that was somehow sweet like milk!

He rose, smiled and said: Do you remember what they said to Robespierre at the end? I'm sure you do.

You mean when they wrenched the, the, his bandage off? And he—

Your education was better than mine. I'm just a gutter-rat from Odessa. Before his arrest, he was calling them all kinds of names, and they said, why should the people's business be thrown out of joint for the sake of one man's wounded self-esteem? You and I should both try to be more optimistic, Dmitri Dmitriyevich.

Shostakovich stared at him. He gaped his mouth as if to scream.

26

In 1945 he directed "Berlin." (Balding and bulky, jovial in his big suitcoat; he took home a bulletholed Unter den Linden sign for a souvenir.) Somehow, he simultaneously found time to collaborate with Troyanovsky on the production of "Albania." The next year he directed the Soviet documentary about the Nuremberg Trials.*

Whitehaired, he filmed Ho Chi Minh in 1954, leaning alertly on his elbow as the Vietnamese leader raised an arm in salute. (That was the year that the formalist Dziga Vertov, long excluded from our national life, died from cancer.) In 1955 his "Vietnam" was released to considerable official acclaim. Even the American monopoly-propagandist Burt Lancaster was forced to recognize (although perhaps not in the context of this anti-American film) his *passionate love for life and people, but also an irreconcilable hatred for war, violence and fascism*. Karmen's working conditions in North Vietnam had been perilous, but at the reception after the premiere he scooped caviar on a biscuit

---

**The New York Times* calls it *grimly gratifying*, but adds: *Except for an obvious partiality toward the Soviet prosecutors, the film might have been assembled by any competent craftsman among the Allies.*

and said: My father died at forty-four, thanks to the White Guards. I turned forty-four in 1950. So whatever happens, I'm ahead!—Then he threw back his head and laughed, just like our favorite actor in "Volga-Volga."

An essay I found in the library basement cites his "Far and Wide My Country Stretches" (1958) as being the first film to use the Kinopanorama system of the wide curved screen, complete with nine tracks of stereophonic sound (and we're glancingly informed that the countervailing American system used only seven). Unfortunately, the difficulty in getting the three projectors to overlap precisely proved to be most annoying, and so, the *Great Soviet Encyclopedia* informs us, Kinopanorama came to be *used increasingly less frequently after 1963.*

He was a delegate of the Twenty-fifth Party Congress in Moscow. I've seen him smile resolutely at the East German leader, Honecker, whose returning smile seems more strained, more like Hilde Benjamin's; Karmen for his part remained *natural* all his life. That is why we all liked him: Dolores Ibarruri, head of the Spanish Communist Party, praised him and smiled eternally; Castro said of him: In the name of our people we thank you for your free and deep friendship for us; Salvador Allende mentioned *my friend Roman Karmen.* For the same reason, at the Moscow Academy of Film he was renowned for his easy closeness with the younger students, men and women both. But these details shunt his story away from its true end.

In 1965 "The Great Patriotic War" appeared under his name. Two famous shots: A haunted old man clutches his hat to his chest; a calm old soldier salutes.

In 1966, shortly before returning to Spain as a tourist, he was named a People's Artist of the Soviet Union. (I remember how he used to be dark and skinny like a French *gamin* as he stood at the panning lever of his cinematic camera in 1933, shooting "Moscow–Kara-Kum–Moscow.") That year's edition of the Moscow *Kinoslovar* describes the character of his films as *strikingly emotive, but the feelings are faithfully bright,* which is to say *remarkably dramatic, but always in a public-spirited context.* Drobaschenko names him in the same breath as the great Dziga Vertov.

In 1968 he co-directed "Granada, Granada, My Granada"* with K. M. Simonov, with whom he'd always got on well. One shrouded female figure halfway through the first reel, some of whose archival footage dates from 1936, is rumored to be Elena Konstantinovskaya. ▸

---

*The Russian title, *Grenada, Grenada, Grenada Moya,* sounds even more like a love song.

BREAKOUT

With few, but courageous allies . . . we must take upon ourselves the defense of a continent which largely does not deserve it.

—Joseph Goebbels (1944)

1

Until July 1942, Lieutenant-General A. A. Vlasov, Commander of the Second Shock Army of the Volkhov Front, remained one of those heroically immaculate men of Soviet marble, each of whom bears a glittering star centered in his forehead like an Indian woman's caste mark (why didn't German snipers shoot at it?), each holding his gleaming black gun in white hands, aiming with confidence. So the old photographs portray them, all highlights bleached into blank purity. Vlasov cannot be descried among them now. Nor has he been found deserving of a citation in the *Great Soviet Encyclopedia*. There is, indeed, an angry entry about "Vlasov Men." That befits, for the crime which Vlasov committed was of a collective nature: He organized an army of traitors to fight against their own motherland.

He is said to have been both brave and coolheaded in the foredoomed defense of Lvov. In a series of energetic attacks, he led a breakout right through the German pincers, saving his troops for future fighting. Repeating this dangerous and thankless accomplishment when the enemy took Kiev, he preserved the remnants of Thirty-seventh Army. (No doubt he was aided both times by the rumors, each day less deniable, that the Fascists were machine-gunning prisoners by the thousands.) He reached Moscow shortly before that city came under siege. The people around him were as faint and intermittent as his reflection in the broken, blacked out windows. Most of them had never even thrown a hand grenade. Vlasov visited his wife and tried to prepare her for the worst. On 10 November 1941, he was summoned beneath the five-pointed Kremlin stars of ruby glass (each of which weighed one ton, and each of which was illuminated from within by incandescent lamps), and so he came into the presence of Comrade Stalin himself. It was literally the stroke of midnight. Rigidly polite, he awaited honor or death.

Stalin demanded his opinions on the protection of Moscow. Vlasov gave them without mitigation but without defeatism, either, recommending a deeply echeloned defense to delay the Fascist Army Group Center until winter. In particular, the Mozhaisk defensive line should be strengthened. Ground might be given, in Kalinin for instance, but it must be contested. Meanwhile, it was essential that we use the time purchased with the lives of a few more hundred thousand peasant boys to form up the Siberian reserves.

Stalin raised his haggard head. He asked: Where will the enemy break through?

Vlasov rose, approached the situation map, and said: I've already mentioned Mozhaisk. Generally speaking, the Iartsevo axis will soon be endangered.

Speak the truth, like a Communist. Will we lose Moscow?

I think not. By the end of this month they'll start freezing to death, and then we can counterattack . . .

With what?

Well, Comrade Stalin, as I said, with the Siberian reserves.

Anybody can defend Moscow with reserves.

Vlasov nodded obediently.

Nevertheless, your analysis is correct, Comrade Vlasov. I'm going to give you fifteen tanks. As for this echeloned defense, you'll present your diagrams to Comrade Zhukov in one hour's time . . .

And that very day, the four hundred and fifty thousand shivering, famished Muscovites who'd been mobilized (three-quarters of them women, for all conditionally fit men had been sent to the front long ago) began reifying the Mozhaisk defensive line with their shovels. Mozhaisk fell. The survivors regrouped to dig more trenches according to Vlasov's specifications: deep and narrow, like the corridors of the Lubyanka. Within hours there were blanket-wrapped corpses in one ditch—magnified representations of the worms which would eat them come summer. Firepoints of concrete blocks sank down into place like tombstones. As for the still-immaculate man, he went to take command of Twentieth Army with his fifteen shopworn tanks. The night sky was already turning pink under Fascist artillery fire. This time he had no chance to say farewell to his wife, who, white-faced in her dark winter coat and shawl, too sick to dig trenches, sat against her cold samovar, hugging herself for warmth with her hands inside her coat-sleeves, the apartment lightless but for a candle. Soon she'd be sleeping underground with the others, beneath the arched roofs of the Metro station. Somebody in raspberry-colored boots was asking a railroad man which train for Kuibyshev would be the last. As for Vlasov, he expected to be dead within a week at most.

In December, Twentieth Army and First Shock Army launched successful counterblows against the German Fascist command. Solnechnogorsk was liberated; the enemy had already set fire to Volokolamansk in preparation for retreat. And so the commissar called upon the soldiers of Twentieth Army to increase their efforts. He pointed out that thanks to Comrade Stalin we now had fifty-four tanks. He invoked the neck-high pyramids of antitank traps made entirely by girls in Leningrad. Vlasov, who'd been studying the strategic maxims of Napoleon, emerged from his dugout, at which the commissar's speech got routed by many cheers. Vlasov smiled shyly. That night he led them back into battle, showing admirable contempt for his own safety. Abnormally tall, he stood out above the other shapes of men bulked and blocked by winter clothes, heads swollen and flattopped like immense boltheads, shoulders swollen and squared. They conquered Volokolamansk. General Rokossovsky sent a radio message of thanks and congratulations; the commissar for his part warned the security "organs" that A. A. Vlasov might be an unreliable element.

By New Year's Eve, when his photograph appeared in the portrait-gallery of prominent generals in *Izvestiya,* they'd recovered ground all the way to the Lama-Riza line. More than half a million Germans died in the snow. Their corpses were often found clad in clumsy straw overshoes, for the Fascist high command had not issued them any winter supplies. The liberation of Mozhaisk was imminent. On 24 January 1942, Vlasov received the Order of the Red Banner.

He was now a Lieutenant-General. Throughout those years of pale men staring down at maps there were many careers of a meteoric character—instant promotions and executions, loyal initiatives, heroes' funerals—but none more dramatic than his. He was a modest, bookish sort who knew well enough when to leave politics alone—namely, always.* Until now, to be sure,

*In our Soviet Union, of course, one may only be apolitical in the most enthusiastic and even militant fashion. It's said that on one occasion Vlasov, having just denounced the brutal, hypocritical murderousness of a certain article in *Pravda,* was interrupted by the visit of a Party apparatchik. Quickly he began to praise the selfsame article. When the guest had gone away at last, Vlasov's wife, standing numbly in the kitchen doorway, said to him, "Andrei, can you really live like that?"

that abstinence had been a virtue. In meetings with his staff officers he was less inclined to cite the inevitability of a Soviet victory than to bring to their attention some brilliant field maneuver of Peter the Great's. From somewhere he'd obtained a treatise by the executed Tukhachevsky. Later it was also remembered against him that he'd dared to praise the operational genius of the Fascist Panzergruppe commander Guderian. Vlasov felt that knowing the enemy well enough to steal away his science was sufficient; he need not squander time in detesting him. Priding himself on his rationalism, which was truly a species of courage (indeed, it bears comparison with the noble atheism of the true Bolshevik, who fights and dies without hope of any unearthly reward), he failed to foresee how weak a perimeter it might prove against the spearheads of an alien will.

At the end of February he embraced his wife for the last time. The hollows beneath her eyes were yellow and black like snow-stains where a German *Nebelwerfer* shell has exploded. She whispered goodbye almost with indifference; he couldn't tell whether she'd decided to endure.

In March, shortly before the premiere of Shostakovich's Seventh Symphony, Comrade Stalin appointed him Deputy Commander of the Volkhov Front. The strategic aim: to break the siege of Leningrad. Of course the assignment was impossible, but at this stage of the war, what wasn't?—Vlasov said: Comrade Stalin, I accept the responsibility.

That night they airlifted him into a sinister taiga zone beset by snow. Two divisions of nearly prewar strength awaited his command. No retreat would be tolerated. Nor could anyone allow himself to be captured by the Fascists; for that meant collaboration. Vlasov therefore had every motivation for success.

He is said to have infused his sector with an almost monastic resolution. His untrained, half-starved Siberians adored him. (In our memory, why not depict them with the scarlet cloaks and haloes of Russian icons, the forest darkness between their faces traced with capillaries of gold?) Mild whenever possible, yet plain-speaking always, getting his point across with common proverbs (he was, like any Communist hero, the son of poor peasants), he reminded them that in victory lay their only hope of delaying death. Some of them were equipped with antitank rifles. Every other nation had long since given these up, for the man who fights a tank can hardly hope to win the contest, but in those days the Soviet army had no other recourse.* The Siberian

---

*Here we might as well insert another allegory. The metal of the day was steel. Hitler and Mussolini had their Pact of Steel, "Stalin" is a quite literally steely pseudonym; all hearts

riflemen smiled at Vlasov, smoking their mahorka cigarettes. Then they went and died for him. The arc-welder's glare whenever a tank was hit became their own eternal flame. Nonetheless, our attack faltered and froze.

They dwelled in a pocket shaped like a hammerhead, its neck crossing the front line between Novgorod and Spaskaya Polist, then widening to a rounded flatness on the west side of the Luga River. German tanks pointed guns at them, although the tanks were frozen and the gunbarrels filled with snow. As long as the cold endured, Second Shock Army was safe. (Ranged against him: Eighteenth German Army's two hundred tanks and twelve hundred self-propelled guns.) Sleeplessly poring over that static gameboard, Vlasov reread the essays of Guderian. A certain reference to the errors of military traditionalists haunted him: *These men remain essentially unable to break free of recollections of positional warfare, which they persist in viewing as the combat form of the future, and they cannot muster the required act of will to stake all on a rapid decision.* Guderian's criticism rang true. The only question was in what wastes of operational philosophy he, Vlasov, remained frozen. Positional warfare had superseded cavalry charges because a single machine-gun nest could decimate the bravest, most inspired brotherhood of horsemen. What could warriors do but dig themselves into trenches? Then came tank and plane, the Panzer group, the Blitzkrieg. Positional warfare was obsolete forever. And yet the very success of Blitzkrieg had already afflicted it with its own traditionalists. Panzer warriors charged ahead with the same recklessness as their cavalrymen fathers. Supply lines lengthened; the Fascist machine had run out of fuel before Moscow. How could this phenomenon be exploited across the map?

Disobeying the commissar's recommendation, he reread Tukhachevsky, who insisted that Blitzkrieg could be defeated through planning, determination and operational reserves. Of these he could call upon neither the first nor the last. He said to the commissar: If we only had a hundred tanks . . .

He reread Caulaincourt's account of Napoleon's defeat at Moscow. Time, space and weather had worn Napoleon down.

---

were supposed to be hardened and armored. But it remains a sad fact that in our Soviet smelting plants we most often find steel being alloyed against corrosion by means of neither that utopian substance platinum nor even the perfectly adequate nickel; rather, manganese gets pressed into this role, because it's abundant and cheap in the USSR. So it is also with our weapons and even our fighters . . .

Once in a great while, his sentries at the rear might see a truck convoy's many furry eyes of light in the night on the ice-road. The Fascists rarely shot at it. Sometimes an airplane landed, bearing emissaries of Comrade Stalin whose task it was to brief and debrief him. Ensconced in a ring of minefields, he was now full Commander. They'd promised to send him Sixth Guard Rifle Corps, but it didn't happen. They assured him that First Shock Army would rejoin him before the thaw, and then he could outflank the Fascists at Lyuban, save Novgorod, liberate starving Leningrad. They demanded to know why he hadn't already broken through. His appearance deteriorated rapidly. He knew very well that Second Army could expect nothing other than what the enemy called *Kesselschlacht,* cauldron-slaughter. Meanwhile he ate no better than his infantrymen, and never hesitated to expose himself to enemy fire. Call it emblematic that beside the dugout which served as his command post that spring, a corpse's frozen hand was seen upraised from a heap of ice and steel.

2

By 24 April, General K. A. Meretskov, Vlasov's erstwhile superior, was more than anxious about the situation of Second Shock Army.—If nothing is done then a catastrophe is inevitable, he said to Comrade Stalin.—Stalin shrugged his shoulders.

This Meretskov had already been arrested once on suspicion of anti-Soviet activity. The fact that no evidence of guilt was ever found only made the case more serious. At the very least, he could be convicted of defeatism. Like far too many commanders, he kept demanding reinforcements and begging permission to withdraw. (There were no reinforcements; and any further withdrawals would mean the fall of Moscow.) That was why Stalin had dismissed him from the Volkhov Front just yesterday. He was lucky. Several of his colleagues had been shot for losing battles. On 8 June, this roundfaced, curving-eyebrowed Hero of the Soviet Union would be restored to all his dignities, with Stalin's apologies. Indeed, he'd outlast Stalin himself. Assistant Minister of Defense, Deputy to the Supreme Soviet, seven-time recipient of the Order of Lenin (Vlasov had received it only once), he lived to be buried honorably in the Kremlin wall.

Meanwhile, Vlasov's infantrymen kept sighing to one another: If Comrade Stalin only knew to what extent his policies are being sabotaged!

A black cloud hovered above a tank for a photographic millisecond, soft, almost like an embryonic sac, but then it fell, comprised of earth, rubble and steel beams.

Vlasov was summoned to speak with Comrade Stalin on the V-phone.

What's your objection to continuing this offensive, Comrade Vlasov?

We can hold the sector for a few days longer, but deep enemy penetration has compressed our bridgeheads.

Explain this failure.

Well, their tanks aren't frozen anymore. The Fascists have regained their mobility . . .

For a moment Vlasov could hear nothing but heavy, weary breathing, and then the metallic voice said: We can spare you no reinforcements.

Perhaps if First Shock Army—

Impossible. Northwest Front would be endangered.

Then Sixth Guard Rifle Corps—

No.

In that case, I request permission to break out immediately.

Your analysis is incorrect, Stalin replied. You will hold the line at all costs.

The connection ended then. Vlasov sat mournfully in his candle-lit dugout. Holding the receiver against his ear for a moment, he nodded. He even smiled. He remembered a sentence: *These men remain essentially unable to break free of recollections of positional warfare.*

Well, Comrade General? said the commissar.

Withdrawal is premature, he says.

I understand how you must feel. Still, once Comrade Stalin has laid down the line, there's nothing for us to do but follow it.

Then we're doomed. Within a week, they'll enfilade us with artillery fire—

In an exasperated voice, the commissar replied: Everything you say may be correct from the military viewpoint, but politically speaking it's quite incorrect. You'd better be more careful. I've heard that your eldest brother was shot for anti-Bolshevik activity during the Civil War . . .

There came the "general alarm" signal.

Telephone communications are broken, sir!

Send me the liaison officer.

He's dead.

On 24 June, the German pincers having long since squeezed shut, Vlasov informed his soldiers that no further hope remained unless they could break out in small groups. This having been said, he wished them good luck, and Second Shock Army disbanded into fugitives.

3

That twenty-day interval when Vlasov dwelled between the Soviet and the Nazi systems was, as biographers love to say, "crucial to his development." In the first stage, he continued in all good faith to discover a gap in the Fascist lines, so that he could repeat the near-miracles of Lvov and Kiev. This period came to an end on the day after he, the lieutenant-colonel and the scout had eaten a family of drowned fieldmice somewhere near Mostki. The scout was already through the barbed wire and the lieutenant-colonel was holding two corroded strands apart for Vlasov to crawl between when the upraised needle of a distant tank-gun began to move. When he'd returned to his body, he found himself covered with blood, but it wasn't his. Sun-flashes on German helmets and German guns sought him out. Rolling down into the shell crater where his companions lay, he closed his eyes, but could no longer remember his wife's face. In good time, when the artillery explosions seemed to be growing louder to the east, he dodged south, into the swamps. He continued to seek a way back to immaculateness, but he'd lost confidence, and the sounds of motors harassed him almost as much as the flies on his bloodstained uniform. Silver streams and silver skies, sandy ooze, immense trees, and every now and then a uniform containing something halfway between flesh and muck—this taiga bogscape, shrinking limbo of Soviet sovereignty, remained as blank on both enemies' maps as a hero's forehead.—Should Vlasov have entombed himself there? Ask Comrade Stalin.—In any event, hunger flushed him out.

He was well into the second stage when just off the Luga road, not far from where Pushkin had fought his fatal duel, he came across the bodies of fifty peasant women in the open air by their ruined hearths. They'd perished variously, as people will, some ending face-down in the dirt, others on, say, their left side, legs twisted in a final spasm, and one even lay inexplicably on her back, with her hands folded across her heart, as if somebody who loved her had laid her out for a funeral. What welded these manifestations of individualism into an enigmatic parable of universal fatality was the fact that each victim had been shot in the base of the skull—a method of execution which the German language, so capable of inventing words for all eventualities, names a *Nackenschuss*. Cartridges glittered in the bloodstained grass. I suspect that not even Vlasov himself could have described his feelings at the moment, although he'd seen as many horrors as any other military man, especially during the fall of Kiev. On the battlefield, corpses tend to clump randomly together, their nested kneescapes and elbowscapes resembling mountain ranges photographed from high altitudes. Vlasov had taught himself to look upon such deaths as accidents. But these women lay in an evenly spaced line, like deserters after the commissar imposes sentence. It may not be out of place to mention that in the course of Thirty-second Army's retreat to Moscow, certain secret dispatches inadvertently left behind (orders to hold the long since overrun Stalin Line) had given Vlasov occasion to return to a village they'd evacuated an hour before. I am sorry to say that he found the peasants, with utter contempt for Soviet power, already preparing the bread and salt of traditional welcome, which they clearly meant to offer to the oncoming Fascists. Not without difficulty, Vlasov prevented his machine-gunner from feasting those traitors on lead. Perhaps this inaction is something to reproach him for. Indeed, his aversion to murder was the very reason he'd requested permission to withdraw from the Volkhov pocket. What was the use of allowing Second Shock Army to be slaughtered without hope of any operational or tactical breakthrough? But Comrade Stalin had replied: You will hold the line at all costs.—These fifty corpses (fifty exactly) proved the correctness of Comrade Stalin's order. Had the collapse of Second Shock Army been prevented, these women would still be alive. Exhausted by heartache, anxiety and guilt, Vlasov came near to regressing to the first stage. But then he heard engines. Scavenging through the ashes of the nearest hearth, he found a few charred potatoes, tumbled them into his coat pockets and ran across wet, sandy ground, circling the village until he reached the place where he could hide. He thought of Zoya the Partisan's last words (as reported by the *Pravda* journalist Lidin): *You can't hang all hundred and ninety million of us.* Closing his eyes, he seemed to see that photograph of her frozen, mutilated breasts. It was not strange that that image could still cause him to feel wounded in his own heart, for he still retained his immaculateness. Like Zoya, who perhaps had wept quietly before the Fascists executed her, he could be enveloped and annihilated, but no one could break through the impregnable marble of his convictions. Not long after he'd crawled into the tall grass to eat his potatoes, a line of mobile assault guns came grinding up the Luga road, their barrels and tank treads shining, and helmeted German boys were sitting on top, half-smiling into the lens of history. What had Second Army ever possessed to oppose them? A few Sokolov Maxim 7.62-millimeter machine-guns, which resembled farm machinery with their two wheels and towing yoke, their fat barrels pointing backwards as if to drop leaden seeds into the fields (five hundred per minute of them)—how ludicrous!—And with this reflection, he entered the third stage.

All this time he'd kept one of the cartridges from the massacre clenched in his left hand so tightly that the fingers bore greenish stains. When the Fascists had gone, he brought it close to his spectacles, to read the marking: Geco, 7.65 millimeter, of German manufacture.

4

The fourth stage in General Vlasov's development followed inescapably from the third, given his logical bent. The intellect which read Napoleon, Caulaincourt, Guderian, Tukhachevsky and Peter the Great with fairness to all prided itself on its willingness to admit the sway of physical laws, even and especially if those laws operated to its own disadvantage. He who says *I have failed* is more likely to be sincere than he who declares victory. Datum: The Fascist invaders outnumbered the Soviet military forces by a factor of 1.8 in personnel, 1.5 in medium and heavy tanks, 3.2 in combat planes, and 1.2 in guns and infantry mortars. Leningrad must fall this summer, and likewise Moscow. The enemy would soon control the oil fields of the Caucasus. They could not be defeated. This was the fact. Therefore, any attempt to defeat them was absurd.

(He remembered the lieutenant-colonel's last words: I don't understand how the Fascists were able to cross the Stalin Line . . .)

Here, in the roofless ruin of the dacha he hid in (on the wall behind the bed's skeleton, someone had drawn a heart with the initials E. K. and D. D. S.), other facts and memories seemed to linger like his wife's miserable face peering around a half-lifted blackout curtain whenever he left her. So many sad chances faced him now! General Meretskov had whispered in confidence that *ten thousand lives* were lost in the evacuation of Tallinn alone. How many of these could be ascribed simply to numerical inferiority, how many to incompetent leadership, and how many to madness beyond cruelty? (Andrei, said his wife, how can you live with yourself?)

Consider the case of the *Kazakhstan*'s Captain Kalitayev. (Meretskov had told Vlasov that tale, too.) Knocked unconscious by a German shell, he fell into the water. The *Kazakhstan* sailed on without him. After his rescuers carried him to Kronstadt, he was shot for desertion.

For that matter, everybody knew that Stalin and Beria had shot Army Group General Pavlov, then Generals Klimovskikh and Klich, for the crime of defeat. Their understrength, untrained battalions had rushed into action with a few bullets apiece, commanded to hold the line while the Fascists got vanquished by half a dozen tanks "donated" by some collective farm. No enemy breakthrough could be permitted. The last thing those dying soldiers heard was a metallically amplified speech of Comrade Stalin, played over and over again, reminding them of the virtues of the new Soviet Constitution.

Vlasov had known all these things, but in the interests of that certain kind of "realism" which allows us to live life, he'd never *confessed* them until now. Now he shuddered. He saw into himself. He grew more rational than ever before.

(Two days before he dissolved Second Shock Army, with the pocket already nearly as narrow as a corridor of the Lubyanka, the Supreme Command had sent a Lavochkin SFN fighter to fly him out. Vlasov refused, preferring to remain with his men. Was he brave? Everybody said so. But Comrade Stalin had told him that no retreat would be tolerated. He preferred not to share the doom of Generals Pavlov, Klimovskikh and Klich.)

Munching on a handful of bog billberries, he heard artillery bursts from the direction of Leningrad. How many ditch-digging schoolgirls were dying there today? Supposing that their bravery equaled, since nothing could excel, that of the pair of Russian soldiers at Smolensk who'd hid for ten days in a tank's hulk beside the decomposing corpse of their comrade, radioing the positions of the German victors who passed all around them, what then?

(What must have happened to those two soldiers in the end?—Discovered, shot.)

5

Directed by German fires shining between roof-ribs, he found an old peasant who fed him. The peasant said: When there is no more Red Army, the Germans will give us our land back.

Mutely, Vlasov held up the Geco 7.65-millimeter shell.

The peasant said: Excuse me, Comrade General, but in the last war the Germans behaved very correctly.

Vlasov had his own memories of war. They resembled the hardened blood on his uniform, mementoes of the lieutenant-colonel and the scout.

6

On 12 July 1942, round about the time that Stalin issued Order Number 227 ("Not a Step Backward"), Lieutenant-General Vlasov was captured by the Fascists. He'd been betrayed yet again, this time by a village elder of whom he'd begged a little bread. How did he feel when the lock-bolt clicked behind him? Let's call his night in the fire brigade shed the fifth stage of his political development. Nobody brought him even a cup of water. Late next morning, when he'd begun to swelter, he heard the growl of a vehicle, probably a staff car, coming up the bad road. He heard the hobnailed footsteps of German soldiers. The bolt slammed back. Through the opening door he saw two silhouettes with leveled machine-guns, and then a voice in German-accented Russian shouted: *Out!*

Don't shoot, he murmured, exhausted. I'm General Vlasov . . .

For the moment they allowed him to keep everything except his pistol. (In the pocket of his greatcoat was a shell: Geco, 7.65 millimeter.) Perusing his identification papers, which were bound in the finest morocco leather, they lighted upon the signature of none other than Comrade Stalin himself, and stroked it in a kind of awe. Just to be sure, they made him show them his gold tooth, which had been mentioned in the "wanted" messages.

Strangely enough, they did not place him within one of those open boxcars already crammed with Russians packed and stacked vertically—still alive, most of them (soon they'd commence eating each other). Nor did they give him unto those German murderers straight and clean whom archivists and war crimes prosecutors would later spy in photographs, lightheartedly posing halfway down the slope of the newest mass grave. Instead, they took him to the frontline Stalag to be classified.

Their field police recognized him immediately. They said to him: Don't worry, General. You're a politically acceptable element.

Vlasov kept expecting to be shot. But instead they conveyed him respectfully to the headquarters of a German general in a field-grey greatcoat. The name of the German general was H. Lindemann. He commanded Eighteenth Army. And General Lindemann said to Vlasov, with exactly the same gentleness as he would have bestowed upon one of his own wounded soldiers: Well, your war's ended. But I must say you fought with honor. Upon my word, dear fellow, you gave us a devil of a time—

Vlasov bowed a little, sipping the tea which General Lindemann's orderly had poured out for him.

If you'd ever gotten the reinforcements you deserved, you just might have outflanked us! Ha, ha, look at this map! Do you see that break in my line down here just behind Lyuban? Every day, oh, until almost April, I should say, I used to tell my staff officers: Gentlemen, we'd better pray that Vlasov doesn't get reinforced . . .

General Lindemann, would a German officer in my place have shot himself?

Heavens, no! Capture's no disgrace for someone like you, who's fought with his unit up to the very last instant . . . Why do you look at me that way?

I beg your pardon, General Lindemann. I'm a little tired . . .

We are not the monsters your Premier Stalin makes us out to be. We are human beings.

Vlasov smiled drily, waiting to be shot.

I suppose you've wondered why we came, said Lindemann. Personally, I was against it, but personal opinions are of no importance nowadays. Fate has sent Germany a great genius: Adolf Hitler. We must obey his will.

Vlasov was silent.

Now let me tell you something, continued General Lindemann with the utmost kindness. To my mind, Bolshevism is a crime inflicted against the world in general, and Russia in particular. You Slavs are perfectly capable of ethical conceptions, as I know from Dostoyevsky and—hm, Tolstoy's not really manly—and yet you've allowed yourselves to be tricked into following these, well, excuse me, these *murderers*.

On that subject I can hardly begin to answer you, General Lindemann.

Both of them heard the scream of the incoming shell, but that meant nothing. Then the adjutant rushed in with a dispatch, stood a little foolishly, then slowly backed out, still holding that piece of paper which after all must not have been so important. The Russian shell continued overhead and finally exploded dully somewhere to the west.

Very well, General Vlasov. What if it's not true? What if we are in fact monsters? Tell me why that should invalidate our critique of *your* monsters. Think about that. And now I'm afraid our lads in Military Intelligence must impose on you a little . . .

And so he was swallowed up by Germany. Germany was a monster of rubber, oil, gold, steel and chromium ore.

7

The man behind the steel desk offered him a cigarette. A blackout curtain covered something on a wall, perhaps a military map. The man said: Don't think I approve of all these measures.

Which measures?

And now he talks back to me, the man said. Imagine that. It's 1942, and I have to tolerate a Slav talking back to me. I don't give a shit what the General says. This must be happening in another country. This must not be Russia. What do you think, Slav? You think that explains what's going on here?

Vlasov waited to be tortured or shot.

Where were you?

I was captured in Tukhovetchi Village.

We know that. Now tell me why it took so long for us to catch you.

I never stayed in one place.

Who hid you?

I've heard about your Barbarossa Decree, said Vlasov, expecting to be shot.

So you don't want your partisan friends executed. Your little Zoya took care of you, eh? Well, we can understand that. We'll get their names and locations out of you later. But maybe you have incorrect ideas about us. We don't mind working with people who admit their mistakes in full.

I've made mistakes, said Vlasov palely. Otherwise I wouldn't be here.

Well, think about it, said the man behind the desk. You have all the time in the world.

How much time?

The rest of your life.

8

They all kept telling him to think about it. General Lindemann, who was an extremely handsome man, and rendered still more resplendent by the black cross at his throat, the glittering metal eagle, the row of six buttons each as glowing and glaring as the sun, had advised him to consider the issue of moral equivalency. Vlasov was compelled to remind himself that such arguments were not in the least objectively motivated; nevertheless, they might be true. He thought about it. Even when they asked him how many tanks and artillery pieces he'd commanded in the Volkhov pocket and he told them, they asked him to reconsider, just in case he might be forgetting something. When they asked him about Meretskov's new divisions, he told them (his head awkwardly bowed just as it would usually be in the official photographs of the propagandists, his dark strange new uniform—plain and brown, not German—too big for him, enwrapping him like bends of sheet-metal) that his soldier's honor prohibited him from any comment, and they said that they understood. Then they suggested that he contemplate the matter further. Pale and anxious, he traced invisible arcs on a map with his forefinger while General Lindemann looked on. Their typist recorded everything. They thanked him for his information, which they said was very helpful and important. Half-guilty now, he wondered what he'd given away, or whether that was just one of their tricks . . .

But he said to himself: I need to be realistic. I need to save what can be saved.

A military intelligence officer poured out two glasses of cognac from Paris. Vlasov was shocked by his own gratitude. The officer remarked: I admire your fanatical determination. The Polish campaign won't get more than a paragraph in the history books. But we're going to have to write an entire chapter about you Slavs! Do you know what I told my wife last summer? I told her what my commanding officer promised me. Don't worry, I said. The Russian question will be solved in six weeks.

Vlasov laughed a little, not disliking the man. Outside an amplified voice sang almost pleasantly: *Jews and commissars, step forward!*

Nonetheless, with our new eighty-eight-millimeter guns, your tanks won't have a chance.

Anyway, said Vlasov with a sad smile, we've already lost twenty thousand tanks.

9

After a thorough but correct interrogation at Lotzen, they sent him to Vinnitsa in the Ukraine, where a comfortable prison camp awaited him—a really nice one, in fact, where each of the reprieved lay licking up sleep as a cat does drops of milk. It was a hot journey, but the Fascists kept him in a special train-car where he could stretch his legs, in company with some perfectly correct S.D. policemen.—Don't be alarmed, said the captain, but before crossing into the Reich, every Russian must be deloused at Eydtkuhnen Station . . . —Composing his face into an aloof smile, Vlasov awaited developments. His former life's freedom of action now seemed wondrous, but he reminded himself that it had hardly been his choice to get inserted into the Volkhov pocket to fight there uselessly. What if something good could come of all this? Certainly when Comrade Stalin had dispatched him to China, he hadn't known what to expect, and yet he'd been able to do his duty there without disappointing anyone; he'd even been awarded the Order of the Golden Dragon by Chiang Kai-shek, although as soon as he reentered the Soviet Union, the secret police confiscated it, for reasons of state. His wife had been disappointed; she'd wanted to see his golden dragon . . . Hoping and believing that he could break out of his new difficulties, he replied courteously but not obsequiously to the small talk of the S.D. men, who wanted to know which features of the Crimean landscape he considered most beautiful. (He'd fought there with distinction in 1920, against the monarchists.) After that, the S.D. captain told him about a certain sailing excursion he'd once taken on the Bodensee, seven years ago it was, when his lucky number came up, thanks to the Führer's "Strength Through Joy" program. Had General Vlasov heard of the Bodensee? Vlasov nodded, clearing his throat.

Seeing that he made no attempt to escape, they finally told him where he was going.—Yes, Vinnitsa, he replied with one of his meaningless smiles. I remember when that was General Tyulenev's headquarters . . .

(Over one-third of the people's armed forces were already out of commission—if we didn't count all those schoolgirls now dying for the sake of useless antitank obstacles. That figure kept exploding within his forehead, malignantly trying to break through.)

Although their conveyance passed several of the newborn concentration camps in which Russians huddled in bare fields sealed off by barbed wire, thirsting and sickening, digging up mice and earthworms with their bare hands so as to extend the term of starvation, Vlasov is said to have seen nothing. After all, window-gazing is not one of the pastimes permitted to prisoners-of-war. Nor would it have been fair to impute any evil to the German administration on the basis of those camps, for it takes time to put conquered dominions in order. Soon, when these zones were better Germanized, the survivors, the one-in-ten, would be inducted into striped uniforms. They'd wear a red triangle superimposed with the letter **R**.

10

Vinnitsa, where in the words of a German policeman-poet, *we saw two worlds, and will permit only one to rule,* had only recently been cleansed of Jews. Nowadays we'd probably label it a "strategic location," for it was rapidly becoming a junction for military traffic of all kinds. From behind barbed wire, the prisoners could often see processions of armored troop carriers cobblestoned with German faces and helmets. (Yes, it's all true, a grief-crazed major muttered into Vlasov's ear. At Smolensk alone, they caught a hundred thousand of us . . .) Long hospital trains clanked rearward; truckloads of ammunition and jaunty dispatch riders went the other way. Just a couple of weeks ago the

Führer had established his latest military headquarters on the edge of town, in a discreet little forest compound called "Werewolf." Precisely because Werewolf was such a secret, even the inmates of the prison camp knew all about it. It was said that the Führer wanted to give the drive against the Caucasus oilfields his personal direction. Stalingrad wouldn't halt *him* for long! Nobody knew when Moscow was slated to fall at last, but the drama of approaching victory excited everyone into a rage of impatience at considerable variance from the resignation one might have expected; for the "Prominente" could not help but feel that six months from now, when the war was over, it would be too late to prove themselves to their new masters. As for Vlasov, his unexpected proximity to the head of the German government gave him hope. (Every wall regaled him with posters which said **HITLER—THE LIBERATOR**.) He sufficiently understood his own worth to be aware that rationality itself required the Führer to redeem him into usefulness. At this point, he still didn't know what he wanted. He remained determined to ensconce his own integrity within the deepest, most concentrated defenses. But on his face he felt the seductive breath of opportunity.

A photogenic old peasant, magnificently muscled and bearded, kept saying to everyone: As soon as the Communists are finished, we can all go back home.

You see my face, General? said a Polish colonel . With all due respect, when your Red Army captured me back in '39, they knocked half my teeth out. I wouldn't sign anything, so they propped my eyelids open on little sticks . . .

Frankly, I'm surprised to see you here, Vlasov replied. I was under the impression that the Fascists were liquidating the Polish officer class.

It's not so simple. In fact . . . But there's a compatriot of yours in our barracks; his name is Colonel Vladimir Boyarsky. He can explain it all to you . . .

Although it was this Boyarsky whose assurances finally persuaded Vlasov to sit down for discussions, first with the diplomat Gustav Hilger, then with Second Lieutenant Dürken direct from the OKW Department of Propaganda, and ultimately with Captain Wilfried Strik-Strikfeldt, without whom there might well have been no Vlasov Army, Boyarsky remained no more than the doorkeeper of fate.* Much the same can be said of Hilger. But less than a week after that interview, Vlasov was summoned into Second Lieutenant Dürken's presence. A guard led him toward the commandant's office.

---

*Accounts of his fate vary. The reader is invited to select one element from each of the following pairs: a bullet or a noose; the Germans or the Russians.

And now from across the parade ground he already spied a man, a man pale and slender, sunken-eyed, narrow-lipped, with the white death's head on his black collar-tab and an Iron Cross just below the throat; a man with a swastika on the breast-pocket, a man whose dreamily quizzical expression proclaimed him master of the world. Vlasov thought him one of the most sinister individuals he'd ever seen. During his various battles, breakouts and evacuations, he'd spied the corpses of Waffen-ϟϟ-men, and only those; they never permitted themselves to be taken alive. There was a certain deep ravine near Kiev, called Babi Yar. Vlasov remembered it very well. He'd read in *Izvestiya* that a week or two after the zone fell into Fascist hands, Waffen-ϟϟ-men had machine-gunned thirty thousand Jews there, but the tale seemed implausible. He'd said to his wife: That sort of conduct would only interfere with the German war effort by turning people against them. Besides, what threat would unarmed Jewish families pose to the Wehrmacht? You know, when I was in Poland I found out that most of what *Izvestiya* said about class exploitation there was lies. The peasants eat better than we do . . .

I believe you, Andrei, she'd wearily replied. You don't have to argue the matter with me. But please lower your voice; somebody might be listening . . .

No, General, they have their honor, Boyarsky had insisted in turn. There's a positive mist of propaganda in this war; it obscures everything! I won't deny that reprisals were taken against a few Yids right here in Vinnitsa, but their cases got thoroughly investigated beforehand. I've been told that they were all Stalin's hangmen.

But women and children—

It wasn't like you think. They're all partisans! And it was humanely done. When the Jews saw how easy it was to be executed, they ran to the pits of their own free will. After all, have *you* been tortured here? If not, then how can you assume that they were coerced in any way? Just think about that. And these ϟϟ whom everybody keeps complaining about, they're actually quite noble in their way. You know how an ϟϟ-man takes out one of our K.V. II tanks? I've seen it myself. First he shoots off a tread. Then he charges right up and plants a grenade inside the muzzle of the cannon! You have to admit—

Let's be rational, Vlasov interrupted him. Nobody runs to get shot unless—

I know it's hard to explain. So let me ask you something else: *Do you want to live without hope?*

I beg your pardon?

General Vlasov, until the war's over we won't be able to calculate the number of victims on both sides. But think back on the purges of '37—

But—

Excuse me, General! Think back on the mass arrests, the horrors of collectivization, the disastrous and utterly unnecessary casualties of the Finnish War. How would you sum all that up?

In a quiet earnest voice Vlasov replied: *Lack of realism.*

(And indeed, it had always struck him as not only unrealistic but unreal. He seemed to see his wife, brown-eyed queen of his integrity, feebly rising up from her bed of illness to say: Can you be sure? Andrei, did you *see* Stalin's men murder all those millions? Can you live with yourself if you're wrong?)

All right, Boyarsky was insisting. And wouldn't it be *realistic* to hope that the other side might be better? Because the side we come from is so impossibly evil—

As it turned out, the man with the white death's head wasn't Second Lieutenant Dürken at all, only a sort of doorkeeper. He inspected the pass which the guard presented, signed a receipt for Vlasov, and led him into a waiting room, where he indicated a bench. Both of them sat down. Feeling intimidated, Vlasov would not have launched any conversation, but his keeper kept looking him up and down with bemusement and finally said: General Vlasov, we have something in common. You survived and defended yourself in the Volkhov pocket. I myself was surrounded by your armies at Demyansk!

That would have been our Eleventh, our Thirty-fourth, and then our First Shock Army . . .

That's correct. You commanded Second Shock Army, I believe?

I—yes.

Fanatical fighters! laughed the ϟϟ-man. You put a lot of pressure on us even after we forced you to the defensive!

Thank you . . .

Don't be despondent, General. You may be a Slav, but I respect you as a man. Care for a smoke?

Yes, please.

I'm curious. A shock army is what exactly?

An instrument of breakthrough, Vlasov replied a little stiffly.

Ah. The Lieutenant is almost ready to see you. He didn't have time to finish reading your file until now. He feels that preparation is especially important in a case like this.

What exactly do you mean?

The Lieutenant will see you now.

And he led Vlasov into a room which was painted white.

Second Lieutenant Dürken did not rise. Smiling, he said that he was quite ready to grant Vlasov's men the status of *semi-allies.*

I must request that you clarify, said Vlasov, feeling all his apprehensions return.

In due course. I see here that you joined the Communist Party in 1930, General. Did you take that step out of political conviction?

At that time, yes.

In other words, your present attitude may or may not be different. All right. We'll get to that. I'm very interested in Communism as a phenomenon. How about you, General?

I don't know what you mean.

Your form of rule was discredited long ago by Plato. In the *Republic* he points out that true democracy is mob rule. And that's what you Slavs have. Why do you think we were able to conquer you so quickly? Because mob rule purged the best thinkers in your officer corps!

I beg to disagree, Vlasov replied. Those purges were organized by the Soviet leadership—

That's not important. The point is that unlike our system, Communism leaves no place for individual merit. I've heard that you admire General Guderian. Well, we Germans also give credit where credit is due. Some of us don't mind calling your Tukhachevsky a genius, even though—well, it was out of *fear* of his genius that you shot him. We would have made him a Field-Marshal!

I myself have often wished we'd followed his line with respect to tank development—

Ah, you use his name, General Vlasov, but can you quote him? No doubt the tyrannical Jewish-Bolshevik regime—

With an ironic smile, the Russian recited: *It is necessary to observe the promise of privileged treatment to those who surrender voluntarily with their arms.*

Oh, he said that? Hm. Perhaps he wasn't ruthless enough for today. Anyway, you shot him.

Lieutenant, it wasn't I who pulled the trigger!

Of course it's *never* anyone in particular! But does Stalin really exist, or is he just the convenient projection for a hive of Jews?

He exists, all right. I've met him. These are very peculiar things you're saying, said Vlasov in a tone of exasperated pride. And, if you don't mind my saying so, you haven't conquered Russia as of yet.

Oh, come. Leningrad and Moscow may hold out another six months, but what then? You've been known to say that yourself! Most of your high-quality elements were destroyed long before we came. Consider yourself fortunate, General, that you were captured in time to be saved . . .

What do you truly want?

We want a democracy of the best, a society in which all aristocrats are free and equal, so that they'll give their best to the State. Imagine an officer corps with free rein! No more purges . . .

And everyone else?

Serfs, of course. For now, we need them for their productive value. Later on, when robots can take their places, we won't require them for anything.

You'll exterminate them?

Of course not. We'll let them share in our accomplishments, as long as they obey us unconditionally. The measures which we're obliged to take in wartime are simple self-defensive necessity.

Is it true that you're shooting all the Jews?

Propaganda! They're all being resettled in labor camps to help the war effort. But let's not waste time talking about those vermin—

Vlasov hesitated. Then a bitter smile traversed his face. Between thumb and forefinger he began turning and turning a certain memory-token: Geco, 7.65 millimeter.

In the end, he could not bring himself to cooperate with Second Lieutenant Dürken, whose attack upon his moral defenses had lacked depth and evinced a vulgarly linear character. But at the urging of Colonel Boyarsky, he wrote a letter directly to the Reich, requesting permission to establish an autonomous Russian National Army. It's said that when the authorities received it, they adorned its margins with exclamation points.

11

At last the enigmatic organization Fremde Heere Ost dispatched one of its own, a certain Captain Wilfried Strik-Strikfeldt, who was to play a crucial role in the Vlasov game—indeed, he might have been more important than Vlasov himself. As it happened, Strik-Strikfeldt was a Baltic German who'd been to university in Saint Petersburg. Our Führer teaches that blood calls to blood; and in this case racial kinship did facilitate the project. With his wry, half-ruthless smile, his merrily narrowed eyes and clean high forehead, his military crewcut and naked ears, Strik-Strikfeldt achieved a dashing appearance. Vlasov liked him at once.

Sitting alertly in chairs made of crooked birch-limbs, enjoying the July days on the dusty plain of Vinnitsa, they faced one another across the long table. Beside each of them sat German officers with their military caps on, and then at the next table, which was well within earshot, a German in dark glasses pretended to be reading a newspaper while a female stenographer typed everything. Behind her, the log cabin barracks lay sleepily silent, and trees rose all around.

Strik-Strikfeldt had already begun to feel like a new-made American millionaire. This Russian general was decent, intelligent, capable, and ready to be guided by somebody who didn't make Dürken's mistakes. *Vlasov spoke openly,* he remarks in his memoirs, *and I did also, insofar as my oath of service permitted me.*

How peculiar life is! he remarked. I fought in the Imperial Russian Army and now I'm serving on the German General Staff. Sometimes I can hardly catch my breath—

Vlasov smiled sadly, eyeing the lyre-like decorations on his dark collar, and the German eagle below.

Not really disconcerted, Strik-Strikfeldt continued: My dear fellow, do you think Stalin would have allowed me to enlist as the lowest private in the Soviet Army? *Eight grams* was what he would have fed me. Eight grams of lead—

I suppose you've seen my memorandum, said Vlasov, a little impatiently.

To be sure. A number of us have studied it. Have I mentioned that before the war I used to run a business in Riga? Don't think I'm indifferent to Mother Russia! And let me tell you something. *Now is the time,* when the territorial situation is so fluid, to push through certain measures. I swear to you, we can make good all Russia's losses . . .

Clasping his hands, Vlasov replied in a harsh voice: Only if I put human values before nationalist values would I be justified in accepting your aid against the Kremlin.

My, my, but he goes straight to the point! I admire your earnestness, General. Well, we have several issues to discuss, but it's not impossible that I can help you.

Vlasov waited, perceptibly anxious.

First of all, we need to know your attitude on the subject of the Stalin government. I suppose you've suffered—

The Soviet regime has brought me no personal disadvantages, said Vlasov flatly.

Ah.

The tall Russian sat glowering at him, so Strik-Strikfeldt, who was very cunning in such situations, said: And doubtless you were given every assistance and reasonable orders in carrying out your command—

Wilfried Karlovich, at Przemysl and at Lvov my corps was attacked, held its ground and was ready to counterattack, but my proposals were rejected. At Kiev we were commanded to hold almost to the last man, to no purpose except to hide the vanity and incompetence of our leadership; you know as well as I how many thousands died as a result. When they refused to allow Second Shock Army to pull out of the Volkhov pocket while there was still time, that decision murdered more and more and *more*—

It was as if Vlasov could not stop talking now. Strik-Strikfeldt gazed unwaveringly into his anguished eyes as he spoke of collectivization, purges, murders, arrests. The man was truly pitiful.

Well, my dear fellow, don't worry, for we'll be able to put everything to rights within a few months—or do you think that Stalin has any chance of escaping defeat?

Vlasov fitted his fingertips together and said: Two factors must entail our loss of the war: first, the unwillingness of Russians to defend our Bolshevik masters, and second, the inadequacy of a military leadership debilitated by interference from the commissars. That was what I wrote in my memorandum.

Yes, of course. I merely wanted to make sure you hadn't changed your mind. You told Dürken that we haven't conquered Russia as of yet—

Well, this Dürken—

Say no more. He just doesn't realize . . .

12

Once, not too long ago, I was lying in the arms of a woman who'd explained that she still loved me but could no longer endure to go on in the dishonest, enervating, frightening, exhilarating and unspeakably sad way that we'd gone on. She, the one who for years had always clung to me, wheedling just a moment more and then a moment more in my embrace, now grew restless there on the bed. She'd already refused to make love with me one last time, because it would be too pitiful and she didn't know how one ought to go about lovemaking for the last time. Should she put her all into it, or . . . ? Then I too agreed that doing that really would have been too sad. I kissed her once, desperately, then lay back with her still in my arms, her body, having determined that mine was now inimical, trying politely not to squirm away from mine.—But putting it this way is so unfair to her! She really did still love me, you see; it wasn't that I bored her; it was simply that everything was over.—I wondered whether I should stop calling her darling now or next time we met. I knew that as soon as I stood up, everything really *would* be over forever. But she was still mine for another five minutes, and then another five minutes while she yawned and asked whether we ought to get up and take a drive or play a board game. And it had come to this point between Vlasov and his immaculateness. (She was always far more admirable, sincere, honest and decent than I.) Strik-Strikfeldt was explaining that under the secret direction of the Experimental Formation Center, *a Russian National People's Army had already been formed!*

13

Wilfried Karlovich, said the prisoner in a tone of almost childish eagerness, what did you really think of my memorandum? Was it clear? And has the German leadership made any comment?

Ah, said Strik-Strikfeldt. Well, it's an admirable document, but, as drafted, too Russian. Shock tactics!

Do you know, laughed Vlasov irrelevantly, once I gave my parents-in-law a cow, and in consequence they got punished for being kulaks!

14

My friend, if you don't mind me asking you, what are you doing with that spent cartridge?

It's a souvenir, he replied in a suddenly lifeless voice.

May I have a look at it? Why, it's a Geco, 7.65 millimeter. I'm told that the Führer himself carries a Walther pistol of that caliber. Good for close work, they say. Does it have some sort of sentimental value, or am I getting too personal?

Awkwardly stiff, roundfaced, his hair receding, Vlasov watched everyone through round heavy spectacles which gave him an impression of half-comical surprise. Even his mouth was round. Round buttons descended from the sharp triangular points of his collar. He said: It reminds me not to make any commitments I might later regret.

Hmm. Well, that's a worthy goal, to be sure, remarked Strik-Strikfeldt in a tone of brooding alertness. I wonder if there's something you're trying to tell me? But no, you didn't call attention to . . . Well, let me rephrase the question. Is there something that you disapprove of, or that perhaps worries you a trifle?

Vlasov was silent.

Strik-Strikfeldt sighed.—I beg your pardon if I've inadvertently offended you. Well, well, here it is, and may it bring you good luck.

Wilfried Karlovich, if I told you that I found this in a burned village, about ten days before my capture, would you understand me?

Of course. Now it's quite clear. I'm sure you saw something regrettable. But *there was a reason* . . .

What reason? No, I—

When Stalin purged the officer corps, did you see what happened to the men who disappeared?

No.

And, you know, we never want to admit the invincibility of death. I myself, well, once I was at the front with some colleagues who'd become dear friends, not too far from here actually, in this same forest terrain, and partisans ambushed us—the spawn of Zoya herself! I was the only survivor. Well, well, Vlasov, I'm sure you've seen worse; the point is that even though they were both quite obviously, you know, *dead*, and I was even drenched with their—

Vlasov was staring at him.

As I was saying, the point is that I couldn't have forgiven myself if I hadn't rushed them to the field hospital, just in case. But they were *dead, dead, dead.* But what if they weren't? So I understand your position perfectly, my dear fellow, because it's so difficult to believe in death. So you can't be *sure* that Stalin's actually committed atrocities, whereas what you saw when you picked up this bullet—well, what exactly did you see?

Nothing important, said Vlasov in a strangled voice. A few corpses—

Listen to me. You've assured me that you believe in rationalism. There's always a reasonable explanation. You don't know who killed those people or why. Now I'm going to tell you something. This is top secret, so if it ever gets out that you heard it here, it's the concentration camp for me. But I'm trusting you. When our forces entered Poland, the *casus belli* was an attack by Poles upon a German radio station at the border. Well, that attack was faked. The propaganda organs supplied the bullets, the uniforms and the bodies. They were *dead*. But how and why they died, and who they were, well, death doesn't always play a straight hand—

I know that, Wilfried Karlovich.

Good. Just give everyone the benefit of the doubt. That's all I ask. Don't be hindered by unverifiable assumptions. I grant that thousands of Russian prisoners may have died from hunger and cold. But let me assure you, my dear General Vlasov, that our own soldiers froze to death on hospital trains last winter! Just consider the conditions under which both of our armies must fight! If anything, the suffering we share should bring us together . . .

Vlasov longed for Strik-Strikfeldt to think well of him. They had to trust one another. Here was Vlasov's chance to fight for something he believed in. (Where he came from, one was free to choose: Death at the hands of Fascists, or death in our execution cellars.) He couldn't demand too many conditions. When he expressed uneasiness about the way that so many Russians were being treated, his new friend replied: Some of that might well be true. But I swear to you, the Führer's a flexible man. We can persuade him to change his mind.

Vlasov was easily led to assume that Strik-Strikfeldt would never have said such words had they not been authorized at the highest level. In fact, the latter belonged to the category of what Khrushchev privately called "temporary people"—rich and powerful serfs whom their master could cast into the pit at any moment. (Khrushchev, of course, was talking about the minions of Stalin. In our Greater Germany, no such perils exist.)

In fact, many of us disagree with Berlin on a number of important points! And I want you to think about that, General Vlasov. If I were a Russian and I announced that I disagreed with Moscow, what do you think would happen to me?

And so his scruples were crushed by concentric attack.

That evening, the musically talented inmates organized a serenade for Vlasov, on balalaikas provided by the Germans.

15

He dreamed that once again he was standing over the massacred peasant women in the burnt weeds where the Geco cartridges glittered, but this time he understood enough to bend down and gently cleanse the blood from their faces with a black scarf dipped in the river; and as soon as he had done this he realized that the blood wasn't even theirs; unwounded, immaculate, they opened their eyes, sat up and kissed his lips in turn.

16

Summoning him back to the commandant's office, Second Lieutenant Dürken invited him to sign a propaganda leaflet calling upon Soviet troops to surrender.

Vlasov replied: As a soldier, I cannot ask other soldiers to stop doing their duty.

Then we'll take out the part asking them to desert, Dürken replied eagerly.

Vlasov signed.

On 10.9.42, just as General Paulus's Sixth Army began to run into trouble at Stalingrad, the Germans dropped leaflets on the Red Army, inviting them to desert. These leaflets bore Vlasov's name.

17

On 17.9.42, thanks to a word from Second Lieutenant Dürken, the Fascists installed him in the Department of Propaganda on Viktoriastrasse, Berlin. (Reader, think of them as the mechanized corps of the third echelon, meant to exploit breakthroughs.)—You may feel a bit fettered here in the Old Reich, Strik-Strikfeldt had warned him. There's more legalism here than in the occupied territories—more obstructionism, I should say. As for the men in the office, I don't really know them that well. If you have any problems, just ring me up, old fellow. I won't desert you . . .

When will I meet Hitler?

Oh, right now he's busy trying to decide how quickly our Tiger tanks ought to be fitted with the new eighty-eight-millimeter cannons—

Vlasov's new offices were brightly lit, if windowless, and the administration gave him plenty of liquor. On the wall glared the face of **HITLER—THE LIBERATOR**. Sometimes there were hilarious drinking parties with the secretaries, who almost seemed to have been selected for their voluptuousness (if I may be permitted to employ that word to describe creatures of the Slavic racial type). Sitting back on a faded green sofa, he smiled a little awkwardly while a drunken Cossack poet whose parents had been shot by the Bolsheviks back in '21 declaimed strophes pertaining to *this antipodal realm / where summer burns eternal.* (You're quite the relativist, but I don't blame you! laughed a lieutenant-general who hailed from the coldest part of Siberia.) A German girl was desperately kissing a Russian girl in the corner.—Well, let them all take their pleasure where they can, thought Vlasov with an impersonally pitying affection. Soon enough they'll be fighting for their lives.—Perhaps because he himself had become a little drunk, they reminded him of the mahorka-smoking troops he'd commanded during the battle of Moscow. Bivouacking under the snow (for the Fascists had burned down all the peasant huts), they too got tipsy, sang songs *(I'm warm in this freezing bunker / thanks to your love's* *eternal flame!*), played chess, crushed lice, cleaned their weapons and prepared to die. At those times Vlasov found his war stories much in demand. Pouting, a typist named Olenka demanded to know why he hadn't saved his Chinese Order of the Golden Dragon for her.—I would have worn it around my neck, Andrei Andreyevich, I really really would. And do you know what else? Every night I would have *kissed* it . . . —Vlasov chuckled and pinched her, his face relaxing into goodnatured ugliness.

It was on this very same green sofa that in company with a certain M. A. Zykov (soon to be liquidated on account of his Jewish antecedents) Vlasov wrote the famous Smolensk Declaration, which begins: ***Friends and brothers! BOLSHEVISM IS THE ENEMY OF THE RUSSIAN PEOPLE***. Their colleagues toasted them with vodka and then again with schnapps. It was signed on 27.12.42 and published on 13.1.43, one day after having been approved by the Führer. Although it was meant for the Red Army, Reich Minister Rosenberg arranged for it to fall on the occupied territories, where, in Strik-Strikfeldt's words, *one could come across grey wraiths who subsisted on corpses and tree-bark.*

By then the Germans had already lost the strategic initiative. Rommel was in trouble at El Alamein; then came the landing in French North Africa; Stalingrad was encircled.—Even the Führer kept saying now: The Russians will break through somehow. They always do.—As the Barons of the East began to perceive an alarmingly fluid operational situation, they cast about for a way to redirect policy. Maybe their fiefdoms could still be saved, if somebody like Vlasov . . .

And so Vlasov felt that he had somewhat reestablished himself in the world (or, if you prefer, that he'd stabilized his defensive front). This new life offered no "security," it's true, but nobody had been secure under Comrade Stalin, either. Nor had he stained his conscience in any way. To be sure, all of our decisions, even self-destructive ones, contain opportunistic elements; but really the safest, most comfortable thing would have been to ensconce himself in that office on Viktoriastrasse and sign leaflets dictated by his German masters. He refused to do that. He wanted to fight for the liberation of Russia. And so the propaganda officers, promising him an imminent escape from this pleasant limbo, photographed Vlasov in his new regalia, raising his right hand in a sort of Indian salute, with smiling German officers at his side as he paced down the wall of imaginary volunteers.

Listening to Liszt on the gramophone in his new quarters at the Russian Court Hotel, he continued to believe in a German victory, if only because any other kind would have such evil consequences for his dreams. (What *were* his dreams? He lay down, his feet hanging off the edge of the bed, and dreamed that his wife was embracing him, but she was a six-armed monster with a face of brass and she was choking him and he could not break free. He woke up gasping, and for the remainder of the night lay staring up at the ceiling in infinite bewilderment and distress.) Europe was becoming (to appropriate Guderian's words) *a fortress of unlimited breadth and depth,* and there was no reason why that fortress could not thwart any breakthrough. The disaster at Stalingrad gave him pause, but in the end he merely thought it all the more urgent to return to the front line and apply his talents, instead of signing his name to other people's propaganda. His colleagues kept invoking the Führer with such reassuring conviction that the forthcoming meeting would obviously settle everything. And Strik-Strikfeldt rang him up again with the news that he'd now obtained the support of a powerful faction in the Supreme Command . . .

Indeed, our merry Balt, whose motives gamboled within an inviolable perimeter of goodness, continued to do whatever he could to set up his friend on what he called "solid foundations." If his influence was not quite as powerful as Vlasov imagined, it remained nonetheless considerable. He wrote poems and plays about the misery which Germany had brought to the East. He sent them to a winnowed list of Wehrmacht officers, many of whom were quite moved. To his more immediate colleagues he insisted: We cannot alter policy. But in the name of improved security for our combat troops, we can introduce a new factor which may persuade Berlin to reconsider policy.— And to a third constituency he proved capable of speaking still a third language. Thanks to the war, staples, goods and even luxuries kept flowing from the occupied territories into the Old Reich, where (as seemed only right) they sold for more than they had cost, which was nothing. Strik-Strikfeldt happened to be in touch with certain sources of supply. All he needed to do was bring them into contact with some factory owner, general's nephew or bored actress in order to retain his financial freedom. So when he became Vlasov's partisan, he got in touch with a few well-chosen individuals and said, putting the case in their language for the sake of courtesy: Gentlemen, it's like this. Since the Slavic-Asiatic character only understands the absolute, disobedience is non-existent among them. They'll follow our orders blindly, don't you see? We'll require Vlasov to do the impossible, and there'll be no complaint—

Allow us to ask just how you think we're supposed to accommodate ourselves to such a shameful alliance. *They're Slavs!*

That's just a trifle! Think of all the blood they'll cost Stalin! Don't worry about that. And afterwards we can . . .

He did his best, he really did. Slipping on his glasses, he wrote many a memorandum. The Russian National People's Army now comprised more than seven thousand paper volunteers. But General Keitel, who reported directly to Hitler, had already ruled out any *Wlassow-Aktion*.

As for Vlasov, he played patience alongside Zykov, who was excellent at all card games. He rolled another cigarette from last week's German newspaper. He reread Guderian: *These men remain essentially unable to break free of recollections of positional warfare.* What could better sum up the mistakes of the German leadership at Stalingrad? He wondered why Guderian had not been consulted there. (He didn't know that Guderian had been relieved of his command in disgrace long ago for seeking to contract the defensive line during the battle of Moscow.) He asked for Napoleon's memoirs, but they told him that that sort of thing wasn't considered very uplifting. Olenka made him dance with her. Through his dreams the following words writhed in vain attempts at alignment: *operating, fortified, undefended.*

By now the Soviet propaganda machine, which had first kept silence, then insisted that he was either dead or an immobilized object of Fascist propaganda, had begun to take note of his charismatic appeal. Denouncing him as a Trotskyite, it now connected his stale life with the counterrevolutionary conspiracy launched by that exterminated snake Tukhachevsky. It revealed him to the peace-loving toilers of the Soviet Union as a Hitlerite, an imperialist henchman, a traitor to the motherland.

These compliments were timely, for on 1.3.43 the Propaganda Department opened Dabendorf Camp, where under the rubric of paper fantasias real Russian soldiers began their training at last. (The German inspection report concluded: *Discipline: Slack. Men do not rise to their feet on the entrance of a German officer.)* A captive Russian artist prepared no fewer than nine sketches of a proposed insignia, each one of which got returned by the authorities, each one defaced by the prohibitory "X." Vlasov is said to have remarked: I'd really like to leave it that way—our Russian flag crossed out by the Germans because they fear it.

Finally they were allowed to utilize the Cross of Saint Andrew, blue on a white field.

The next step was to actually start fighting. That was bound to happen any time now.

18

Strik-Strikfeldt said: Unfortunately, he didn't agree. But I have a friend who often goes hunting with none other than Obergruppenführer Friedrich Jeckeln—

Very slowly Vlasov raised his head from the row of cards which he was turning over as industriously as the woman who rolls muddy corpses face-upward until she can verify the particular death which will permit her to grieve. Then his crude, almost simian face sank back between the nicotine-stained thumb and forefinger of his left hand. He crossed his long, long legs. He yawned. He said: You can't even give me a suit that fits, and you want to conquer the world!

Don't get bitter, my dear fellow. After all, this is wartime, and you have a peculiar build.

Listen to me, Wilfried Karlovich. I want to go back to the prison camp. This feels like being half awake all the time. It's . . .

The Führer is always convinced by results. Your Smolensk Declaration had more impact on the occupied territories than a hundred anti-partisan detachments! Once he understands that the only possible way for us to keep our territorial gains is to give your Russian National People's Army something to do—

But—

Isn't that the reality of the situation?

And so once again the bolt clicked shut, and Vlasov found himself back inside his sweltering conceptual prison, the notion that logic, limitation and *realism* informed the doings of influential men.

19

Let's say for the sake of argument (although it's really not credible) that even then he didn't know about the bloody-beaten boys wrist-tied together in pairs for easier shooting, the bandaged girls led off to be shot against a wall, the schoolteachers clambering obediently up onto barrels while the noose was tied, the families noosed and then thrown off their own balconies, the young men lined up against the wall for the double-rowed firing squad.—We'll bypass that for now, as Strik-Strikfeldt would say. No, he knew; he groaned in his sleep; awaking once and twice, he'd drink away his pangs, struggling through the logic (which he stubbornly defended) of *Stalin is worse* to overtake his ideal, his love, his eastern objective; and from a sufficiently distant aerial perspective he comes to resemble the German soldiers straining eight on a side to move a truck through kilometer after kilometer of knee-deep mud whose shining puddles proclaim their ever so beautiful reflections of birch-trees. On the night table beside the almost empty bottle of schnapps there stood upended, now tarnished green by much finger-oil, a certain cartridge, Geco, 7.65 millimeter. (Call it his defensive front.) But to claim on Vlasov's part more *knowledge* than that (and without knowledge it may well be that there's no responsibility) would be as simplistic and old-fashioned as Stalin's cordon strategy of defense. Strik-Strikfeldt insists in his postwar memoirs that it wasn't until he was a prisoner and an American sergeant assaulted him with photographs of Dachau that he learned that *in German concentration camps there had been bestialities such as in no other camps in the world.* The sergeant, he indignantly writes, refused to pay credence to his cries of ignorance. But then, after all, *the world still does not believe that these thugs managed to conceal their crimes from a great part of the German people. The Western world refused to believe it—just as we, at that time, refused to believe in the betrayal of freedom by free America.* There you have it, and from a figure who always spoke as openly as his oath of service permitted him.

20

Vlasov's integrity, then, or, if you will, his wife, had shielded herself from him behind a wall of curving steel plates; through the little bulletproof window he could see her smiling lovingly and mercifully; she was ready to talk to him; she would do whatever she could to help him; but she would never embrace him again—she who had been so weak, she who had sobbingly clung to him, seeking to prolong if only by a few instants their time together in the dark and gentle room; he'd caressed her lovingly, wondering how soon without hurting her he could rise and pull on his boots. How laughable, to think that he couldn't hurt her! All she wanted was to stay with him forever. But *he* had things to do. Let's say that there was a war on. Or let's say that he was, like so many of us, "creative," or "married," "drafted," "politically involved," "uncommitted," "busy," "distracted," or otherwise engaged and compromised. For one reason or another, he'd made the war his war. She implored him not to go, and maybe he even had to go (let's say that a certain Adolf Hitler had invaded the country), but no, let's say—let's say nothing for a line or two except that of course we wouldn't want to "trivialize" World War II by extruding its gruesomeness through the star-shaped cookie dough gun of some allegory or other—but integrity *is* love, and love of two entities, faithfulness to them both, may comprise betrayal of them both. (If only the pain in her eyes had killed me!) He had to go. It was like that every time until he expected it and began to manage it; it was like that every time; perhaps it even flattered him, once he became accustomed to what originally afflicted him with dread and guilt; every time it was like that, with this real and intelligent woman who loved him, I mean this allegory, mythic goddess of moral rectitude, no, I mean someone who wasn't perfect but who loved him, someone who was better than he was, someone who said to him: Andrei, can you really live like that? He had to leave her, and hated to do it, but he promised to be right back. *It is well known,* explains the *Great Soviet Encyclopedia, that the structure of emotional life changes from one historical epoch to another. Consequently, the feeling of love also changes, since it is influenced by class relationships, by changes in the personality and by changes in value orientations.* Changes in value orientations, that's it! Her eyes, her big brown eyes so often swollen from weeping, launched reproaches his way, sometimes scared ones, often angry ones; sometimes she wasn't quite fair, but she was his integrity. She warned him: I don't know how long I can do this, and then: I don't think I can do this, because he was, let's say, fighting on the side of someone who'd murdered so many millions. After his actions in that world, he kept coming back to her. His integrity said: I don't think I can do this right now. I feel as if I need to get to know you again first.—His integrity said: Is your mouth clean? You don't taste clean.—She said: You know I'm very delicate down there. I'm just not up for it right now. She said: Please don't go. She said: That feels so *perfect.* She said: Oh, sweetheart.—She was crying when she said: Don't go. Next time he saw her, she was crying, and she said: I can't do this anymore.—After that she stopped crying. She became very calm and gentle.

When the one I loved finally left me, it didn't hurt too much at first, but then my own heart, not yet killed, began to sicken with drop after drop of her poisonous absence. Then all my friends seemed to fall away, which simply means that they didn't seem like friends anymore, being no substitute for her; and with each moment that I could no longer expect to see her, my heart grew a little more inflamed with grief. As yet it was still strong, for our love had been strong (at least I thought so); therefore the death-agony must expand, elongate, and wriggle endlessly like a parasitic worm. A strong organism can't die. And so Vlasov still clung to the past time when he'd been intimate with his integrity. (She'd said to him: We can lie down together for a minute if you need to, as long as it's not too intimate. I can't do that anymore, or I'll get confused . . .)

She was a statue now, safe from him behind that thick glass. She wanted to be his friend. Merciful and distant, she pitied him. He was free now. He must make his own way in life.

21

They sent him on a tour of the occupied territories to drum up support. On 28.2.43 he arrived in Smolensk, where he spoke to the helots to great acclaim. (This man led the Fourth Mechanized against us at Lvov! Strik-Strikfeldt was explaining to everybody in a reverential voice.)—Russia must be independent, Vlasov kept saying.—Standing on a scorched and icy plinth which had once been burdened by a marble titan, he gazed down at his audience: shivering old men unfit for labor service, displaced peasant women in dark headscarves, hungry office workers who'd been given Vlasov in lieu of a more expensive treat. To these people, who even yet hadn't entirely abandoned their hope that the Germans might bring something good, his speech was electrifying. That one of their own—a famous general, no less—would be permitted to say anything at all, much less shout out a call for a Russo-German alliance against Stalin, while Wehrmacht officers stood around smiling indulgently, was a sign that some middle path, however provisional and solitary, to the salvation which most of them after more than two decades of reeducation continued to cast in religious terms, might be more than a tragic figment. (We told you so! the old men whispered. What with the partisans, and Stalingrad, and that breakout at Leningrad, Adolf can't be so arrogant anymore . . .) Vlasov's right arm rose high in salute to forthcoming Russian victories. Then he was photographed again, at attention in a file of Fascist officers each of whom was wearing shiny knee-length boots. He toured the newly reopened cathedral: Hitler the Liberator was bringing back religion! (But wily Stalin had begun reopening churches, too.) That night, he addressed a full house at the state theater, standing room only. As yet, his sponsors dared not permit him to broadcast on the radio. He propagandized here and there for three weeks, calling for volunteers. The first Vlasov Men already stood on parade for his inspection. (Let's assume that he didn't know about the Russian prisoners of war who were being gassed at Auschwitz, shot at Dachau and Buchenwald. At Smolensk alone the death rate was hundreds per day.) Insisting that he was no puppet, he quoted the old peasant proverb: *A foreign coat never fits a Russian.* (The uniform they'd fashioned for him was brown like a Storm Trooper's.) To hostile questioners he replied: The Germans have begun to acknowledge their mistakes. And, after all, it's just not realistic to hope to enslave almost two hundred million people . . .

(*You can't hang all hundred and ninety million of us,* Zoya had said.)

His erstwhile captor General Lindemann came to congratulate him, and they clinked glasses.

I must say, that was a riveting speech! These people believe in you, there's no doubt about it . . .

Frankly, I'm in despair, said Vlasov, for he'd just learned that the formations of Russian volunteers had all been broken up and distributed among German units.

Upon my word now, what kind of thing is that for a military man to say? Just be patient a little longer, and Berlin will come around, I promise you!

You see, it's not just the war crimes, it's the *absurdity.* How can your leadership fail to understand that by alienating the masses, they're obstructing their own purpose?

The German general sighed and said: Never mind, my dear fellow. The East and the West are two worlds, and they cannot understand each other.

On his return to Berlin, the spring mud of the Reich now mouse-green like Hitler's field jacket, he sent another memorandum admonishing the Reich government: *The mass of the Russian population now look upon this conflict as a German war of conquest.* (Zykov lost at solitaire and recited another stanza from Pushkin.) He advised his masters that even now it might still be possible to regain good relations with the people, so terribly had they suffered under Communism, but it was essential to make immediate changes in occupation policy.

Olenka the typist had disappeared, but her replacement, a Latvian brunette named Masha, was an even more fun-loving girl.* One morning he awoke at the Russian Court Hotel with her still sleeping in his arms. Gazing

---

*Here we might note that in several accounts, Vlasov is said to have fallen into German hands in the company of a certain Maria Voronova, whose husband was being reeducated at the expense of the state, in a certain unknown location in Siberia. To make ends meet, she cooked for the Vlasov family. At Vlasov's wife's behest, Maria Voronova supposedly made her way to the Volkhov pocket. In a photograph commemorating their capture, the pair sit in a military vehicle whose machine-guns face the sky. Vlasov's taut, exhausted face can be seen only in near-profile. His glasses have slipped halfway down his nose. In his hand he clutches a tapering object which might well be a German cartridge, Geco 7.65 millimeter. Maria Voronova, if indeed this pallid, kerchiefed young woman is she, has managed to retain some of her attractiveness. She sits at his side, almost smiling.

into this gentle face, he seemed to see the closed eyes of his broken wife. (And I myself, I see the big brown eyes of the woman who finally left me, the one who would have stayed with me forever if I'd only made a certain promise. She was my integrity.)

22

I repeat: Thus far, the assault on Vlasov's character had accomplished only a limited tactical breakthrough. The attackers did not know how to achieve operational shock. As Strik-Strikfeldt so wisely aphorized: *Too much propaganda is merely propaganda.*

And so he found himself back at work. Coolish and warmish Berlin spring days, cloud-sogged skies and linden-shade, these exudations transfused themselves most pleasantly into his bones. He sat wondering what to do. Zykov had not yet gone missing. One wall of his shabby little office was stacked up with bales of a colleague's literary production: *And this underworld of the Untermensch found its leader: the eternal Jew!*

He received a warning from the Gestapo that the USSR had sent a certain Major S. N. Kapustin to infiltrate his army and assassinate him. He didn't care. Drunkenly he told a bored file clerk of the female gender: I remember when I counterattacked at Nemirov. Tank fighting for four days—

Just as a shattered concentration of troops tends to polarize around the towns or command posts it knows, which is why the attacking enemy will tend to close lethal circles around those very points, so Vlasov couldn't help but be obsessed by that Geco cartridge of his, which he turned round and round between his fingers, trying to steel himself against the next offensive. Zykov laughed at him. Masha once stole his toy, just for fun, but he became very angry until she begged his pardon and blushingly dropped it back into his hand. There always seemed to be so much schnapps on hand that he stopped writing manifestoes. Indeed, he soon became so listless that he scarcely bothered to chat with the man from the Office for the Germanization of Eastern Nations. A. A. Vlasov might as well have been one of Berlin's time-smoked building-stones crowned by winged figures, figures with crucifixes or figures with lances, all time-blackened into their own silhouettes. The Germans grew concerned about his health. Moreover, another proclamation of his phantom army had just come out and they didn't want to make him into too much of a one-man show. Why not let him disappear for a bit? So, with Strik-Strikfeldt as chaperone, they sent him on a rest cure. Oh, yes; they permitted him to tour the Rhine, whose coils sometimes nearly complete a circle, their aquatic thumbs and forefingers squeezing various peninsulas of forest and slate-roofed houses into almost-islandness, while summery leaves strain outwards. He visited Köln, Frankfurt, Vienna . . .

What a sight they are! cried his best friend, merrily squinting his eyes. Look quickly, my dear Vlasov! No, no, over there! Why, they practically take my breath away . . .

In a park, rows of German girls stood with outstretched arms and breasts, mimicking their stiff wax-doll *Lehrerin* who stood above them on the monument's steps, calling out: *One—two—three—four! All together!*

Vlasov continued to drink. After considerable efforts (none of which his ward seemed to appreciate), Strik-Strikfeldt obtained permission to take him to a convalescent home for ϟϟ-men in Ruhpolding, Bavaria. It was there that Vlasov met his German wife.

23

If you have ever happened to see Adolf Ziegler's "The Four Elements," which hangs over the fireplace of our Führerhaus in München, you may remember, in the middle panel of that triptych, a slender, small-breasted blonde who sits nestling against her darker-haired sister, staring modestly at the checkerboard floor while her elbow guards the junction of her chastely clenched thighs. There is something absurd (or, as Vlasov would say, unrealistic) about the poses of the other three nudes, especially the darkhaired one who daintily pulls a bit of drapery across her lap while clasping a harvest sheaf in her right hand. The blonde's compact, withdrawn posture appears at least natural and comfortable. The relentless tidiness of the room which that painting dwells in, the drollness of the little round table between sofa and hearth, the fresh-scrubbed bricks of the hearth, and, above all, the insistently allegorical quality of Ziegler's work, all work together to sugar-coat its lewdness into a veritable pill of propriety. And the ridiculous gestures of those Aryan goddesses double-coat the pill. Nobody would ever hold her arms so, or tilt her head so, unless perhaps a machine-gun blast had caused that effect when it tumbled her into the mass grave! But the seated blonde (if we disregard the empty bowl which Ziegler directed her to hold) could almost be a figure out of "real life."

Have you guessed that Heidi Bielenberg was an athlete? She'd been one of those blondes with braids, those blue-eyed blondes who, screaming with crowd-happiness, outstretch their white-sleeved arms in salute behind a protective wall of expressionless ᛋᛋ-men whose helmets are adorned with swastikas within red shields; so that everything everywhere grows white, black, grey, red and blonde. We first see her in a wall of German girls in tight-fitting undergarments, raising globes above their heads: *One—two—three—four! All together!* Heidi's instructor told her that she might be capable of excellence, if she worked hard and governed herself *with inflexible harshness.* That was easy for her. She'd always been like that. Her mother was the same. Heidi wanted to be in the 1936 Olympics, but that proved impossible. Fortunately, in our Reich there were many other exciting things to do. She became a crack shot with a revolver, and got licensed to keep a pistol (I think a 7.65-millimeter Walther). Her pretty face, which specialists had measured with calipers from nose-bridge to chin, and her hair, matched against various reference-rectangles of tinted glass, both passed muster, scientifically validating her as Aryan. At a regional competition, she stood atop a rolling hoop, outstretching a swastika flag in each arm. Then they'd invited her to take part in the Nuremberg Rally, where she shared a tent with two other girls and got to see the Führer with her own eyes! (She'd kept in touch with her tent-mates. One had already given birth to a pair of Aryan twins at a *Lebensborn* facility. The other was now making eighty-eight-millimeter shell fuses, in order to do her part for total war.) Shortly after the Röhm purge, Heidi won the Reich Sports Medal, whose possession is required on the part of any girl who aspires to wed an ᛋᛋ-man. Himmler himself, who knew perfection when he saw it, had already entered her into the topmost classification in the card indexes of the ᛋᛋ Head Office for Race and Settlement.

She met her first husband at the 1938 Yuletide bonfire. Everything about him felt right to her, from his agility when he danced, to the strangely tender gaze of his skull-emblem's baby-eyes. Everything happened in a rush. Holding his arm, clutching the bouquet in the crook of her elbow, she passed beneath the arch of saluting hands as the wedding guests chanted: *Sieg Heil! Sieg Heil!* Germany was already at war then, so she'd hardly seen Otto after the honeymoon. Two years later (it was by one of those swinging-door coincidences the time of Vlasov's capture, one husband out, the next one in), Heidi received and immediately framed the regimental telegram, which proclaimed OUR PROUD SORROW. His commanding officer also wrote her a letter, assuring her that it had been both heroic and instantaneous. Heidi framed that, too. She retained an almost virginal conviction that since she had suffered, fate was unlikely to require any further sacrifices from her. It was only at the vigil over his swastika-draped coffin, with her mother clasping her hand and so many of his comrades at attention, holding wax torches, that Heidi realized the seriousness of this struggle against Jewish bandits. Slowly she commenced to understand certain remarks and silences which she had hitherto dismissed as fruitlessly enigmatic or even defeatist. Her mother, who continued to trust in a good resolution of everything, did her best to draw Heidi back up into the mirror-pure realm of faith, and succeeded even more rapidly than she had anticipated; for the widow needed, in the spirit of the times, to give herself unendingly, and show that she could be strong unto death. Every day she went to pistol-practice. In spite of maternity, she continued to possess the streamlined body and frank appetites of a *Sportfräulein*. She loved hiking, skiing and other exercises in keeping with that wise Nazi adage: *The javelin and the springboard are more useful than lipstick for the promotion of health.* To Vlasov it was an immense pleasure merely to see her eat: white German bread slathered with sweet butter (not even apparatchiks could dine like that in Russia), great draughts of German Pilsbier, half a roast chicken at a go. At such times her face shone with such utter engrossment in her own enjoyment that he could hardly help being carried out of his gloom. If his admiration of what he thought of as her innocence might have had a patronizing quality, well, patronization is kin to the voyeurism of an old man, who wants to do what he no longer can. The sad pale face of his own immaculateness had withdrawn forever behind the blackout curtain. He was tainted now; he was mature. Why not look with pleasure upon the antics of somebody who was still fortunate to be in her moral childhood? Moreover, Heidi had a stunning chest.

I don't know whether I love you or not, he told her with his accustomed frankness. But after all this time I, I have very strong sexual feelings . . .

Smiling, the young widow recited: *The healthy is a heroic commandment.*

24

She felt dreary most of the time. Oh, yes, she was dead, desolate, cut off; what she loved was far away beneath the Russian earth. (No name on the grave, they said—only his helmet.) As long as she could remember, she'd hated to be alone. Sometimes there was nothing to do except flip through *Signal* magazine. What she admired the most about this General Vlasov was that he owned a dream for which he was willing to fight fanatically to the end. (This fellow led the main attack on our Army Group Center during the Battle of Moscow! crowed Strik-Strikfeldt with loving exaggeration.) She had heard so much about his qualities—his unshakeable will, his charisma with subordinates, his intelligence and above all (for we Germans believe that strength forms its own justification) his prowess on the battlefield. She knew about his Order of the Red Banner, and the medal he'd received in China. (You really admire him, too, don't you, Herr Strik?) She even knew about the wife in Moscow. It was said that he hadn't yet cooperated with Germany a hundred percent. Who can blame Heidi for hoping to smash his defensive front?

Andrei, you're a biologically valuable man, she said, crossing her muscular thighs. You're a fighter, a son of the soil. You *deserve* to have two wives. The Führer needs your children . . .

Vlasov laughed in embarrassment.—The Führer doesn't know he needs me—

Well, then he hasn't been informed. But didn't he approve your Smolensk Declaration?

He needs to act on it, or the Ostfront cannot be held! I'm getting worried about that. Moreover, the number of tank battalions in each Panzer division must be increased. Fortunately, Guderian's been appointed Inspector-General of Armored Troops—

Heidi rose and touched his hand.—I think you're a real Nazi and you don't even know it. Tell me this. What's your heart's desire?

To fight for the liberation of Russia.

That's exactly what my husband said. Do you find me beautiful?

Scarcely knowing what he was saying, Vlasov muttered: Heidi, when I look at you my heart beats fast . . .

Since you're ready to die for the Führer, I'm ready to give you what you want.

25

Of course she couldn't believe that in this Slav's arms she'd be able to breed an Übermensch, but at the beginning it wasn't even about breeding. (Vlasov is said to have played a guitar when he wooed her. He was always sweet with her little daughter Frauke.) The blond, blue-eyed ϟϟ-men who came here to recover and then went back to the Ostfront to die, she'd had as many of them as she liked. Perhaps she wanted a change from bread and butter.

A little later, with what Himmler used to berate in Heydrich as "cold, rational criticism," she began to brood on the lesson of Stalingrad. Her convalescents (the lucky few who'd been airlifted out of that so-called "fortress") couldn't help telling her how it had really been, especially when they lay weeping in her arms. Nearly everyone except General Vlasov was getting cold feet now!—They promised Paulus full supply by air, so he wasn't permitted to break out even when the Panzers still had enough fuel. So we kept starving, and the Russians kept shooting and tightening the ring . . . (What else did her charges mention? Probably not the German prison cages, nor the Russian epidemics cured with flamethrowers.) And so Heidi unrolled the map, and her pet Slav, whom they jokingly called *the democratic people's Jew,* held down the furling corners like a good doggie. Below Leningrad crouched the flag comprised of four squares, two white, two black: 18. Bolshevo; then clung Korück 583 below that, Span. Legion to the west of it, ᛋᛋ Nordlund in between, all of them seemingly sheltered by that black front line which ran east along the gulf shore below Leningrad, then curved by fits southeast and southwest, down toward Moscow. But her soldier-boys had whispered to her that the Russians were beginning to introduce homogeneous tank armies, hundreds and then thousands of those terrible T-34s. They could break through anywhere, at any time. What if the war were really lost? Maybe even then Heidi could be First Lady of the new Russia if she married General Vlasov and he . . . —Like everybody associated with the ᛋᛋ, she'd grown accustomed to dreaming magnificent dreams. Besides, her mother insisted on marriage to legitimize the relationship.

Andrei darling, what do you think of what I just said?

Looking at the map, not at her, he replied with a sad little grin: Oh, well, in Moscow I had to haul everything on sleds attached to tanks. The struggle for life—

She flung her arms around him. She said: I understand you with all my heart.

The hostility of her friends, and especially of her mother, who could hardly have imagined her to be capable of committing racial disgrace with a Slav, was painful, to be sure, but not unexpected. Moreover, there comes a moment in almost everyone's life when fate (as our Führer would call it) summons us to cross the gulf of change, and reestablish ourselves in an antipodal world. At such a time, even the most earnest protestations of those who love us dwindle into the merest formalities of departure.

And perhaps it enhanced Heidi's self-confidence that in every true German sense she was better than the man she'd agreed to marry. Oh, she could admit that without pity toward herself! (Allegations that Strik-Strikfeldt, whom everyone considered to be sunnily indispensable, had loaned her a copy of Vlasov's Gestapo file, need not be entirely ruled out.)

He was stroking her hair. He seemed constrained or worried about something.

She murmured: Andrei, darling, I know you will always be grateful to me, and give me whatever I wish . . .

26

Wilfried Karlovich, whatever happened to Masha?

My dear fellow, I don't have enough grey cells to remember every skirt you've—

She was a typist at Viktoriastrasse.

A typist, you say? Probably an illegal element. Here, have a look for yourself; there's nobody by that name on the roster. Come, come, why are you glaring at me in that way? Do you really think that here in the Reich people simply disappear without cause? In Stalinist Russia, now, that's a different matter—

She—

Our faithful advocate of the *Wlassow-Aktion* raised a finger for silence. Far away, they both could hear the short blasts of the early warning siren. Then he shrugged and said to Vlasov: I fear that certain assumptions are obstructing you again. Think about it. Would it be rational to harm anybody who can contribute to the war effort?

No. Not rational—

Did you really care for her all that much? If so, perhaps I can—

She was the merest flirtation, replied Vlasov in his flat way. But I'm concerned for her as a human being.

Most likely she's working in an armaments factory. Meanwhile, how do you feel about Heidi? I want you to know that in recognition of your hard work, certain regulations have been waived. Your union with Heidi has been sanctioned *at the highest level.*—Or is there some obstacle? By the way, what are you playing with in your pocket?—Oh, I see, it must be that stupid cartridge of yours . . .

27

On 22.3.43 we find him presiding over the graduation of the first officers' class at Dabendorf. He was very happy with his Russian Liberation Army cockade, which made use of the same three colors as the French *tricouleur* and the American stars-'n'-stripes. Gripping the lectern, which barely came above his waist, he continued the commencement speech: I expect each of you not only to take a stand, but to be a fanatical fighter for our ideal. What do I mean by fanaticism? Well, let's momentarily consider the logic of this war. Logically speaking, we are incapable of forcing the Bolsheviks, with their incomparably greater forces, to withdraw. Logic compels us to abandon our struggle. Therefore, I call on you to abandon logic. When I led the Fourth Mechanized at Lvov, we attacked Sixth Army—long before Stalingrad, you understand, so they were close to full strength, while we hardly had any tanks (Kroeger, stop filling up my glass!)—and so logically speaking we shouldn't have hoped for any success. But that was when General von Kleist himself paid me a real compliment. He said . . .

Let's hope he can pull this off, one officer muttered to another.

Anyhow, better here than in a camp!

What if he's been tricked?

The Führer says . . .

At her own request, and against the wishes of her mother, who'd warned: *Liebchen,* stay out of politics. It's not healthy for a woman!, Vlasov's fiancée attended the reception. I've read that she was wearing her German National Sports badge, whose interlocking letter-tendrils had been encircled by a wreath whose fruit was a single swastika. A Russian prisoner-of-war complimented her on it, with what might have been an ironic smile. Heidi said to him: I have to pass a test every year, or they'll take it back.

28

On the morning of 13.4.43, a few hours before Radio Berlin made a spectacular announcement to the world, launching what Goebbels would call *a hundred-percent victory for German propaganda and especially for me personally,* Vlasov was sheltering listlessly in the arms of Heidi Bielenberg, enduring her endearments (the only Russian words she was ever to learn), when the telephone rang. Praying that it be a summons to command, execution, or anything other than more of this, he reached for the receiver. It was Strik-Strikfeldt.

My dear Vlasov, am I disturbing you? Listen, I have some extremely important news. I'll be over in a quarter-hour.

Ya tebya lyublyu, his wife was saying.

I love you, too, he said mechanically. Rising, he began to dress.

Andrei, be prepared for everything. Be ready; be healthy—

(He was choking within his tightly buttoned collar.)

Andrei, did you hear me?

The buzzer assaulted him. He went downstairs.

Well, well, Vlasov, and have you been keeping busy?

I've been making up a list of words which are considered to be obscenities in both Germany and the USSR. Want to hear a few? *Internationalism. Cosmopolitan. Plutocracy. Intellectual. Softness. Weakness. Mercy.*

And what would you expect, my dear fellow? We're at war with each other, so it's natural that both our systems would get a trifle hardened and bunkered down . . .

That's good, murmured Vlasov, that you always show respect . . .

And how's your pretty wife?

She's pretty, and she's my wife.

I take it she's *en déshabillé,* or you'd have invited me up . . .

Wilfried Karlovich, I'm the son of peasants. I don't understand French.

Let's take a walk, said his jocular genius, and before Vlasov knew it, they'd passed the Zeughaus and were crossing the river by means of the dear old Schlossbrücke whose wrought-iron horses Strik-Strikfeldt rarely failed to caress in a triply echeloned offensive. This time, however, he denied himself the snaky fish, the martial seahorse and even the cheerfully grotesque merman whose tail transformed itself into horse-legs. He was very excited. Beneath a winged Victory who proudly watched them from her pink-granite pillar he paused and said: I wanted to be the first to tell you . . .

I'm listening.

Although I flatter myself that I've become your friend, of course there are certain aspects to your situation here that . . . well, you haven't always been fairly treated. I admit that, and I'm sorry. But there's one matter very dear to my heart in which you've never quite believed: *the honor of the German soldier.* To get right down to it, Germans really are honorable people. They don't murder women and children. I don't deny that there's been occasional wartime harshness, but not—not what you think.

So? said Vlasov.

Well, the news is going to be broadcast this afternoon. Lieutenant-Colonel Ahrens of our Five Hundred and Thirty-seventh Signal Regiment first made the report last month, but it was classified top secret until the forensic teams had made a complete investigation.

Vlasov stared at him.

It seems that a wolf was nosing around in the forest near Smolensk, and uncovered bones. Some Hiwis on work detail found the pit. They erected a cross. In due time Ahrens was notified.

You love to spin out a story, don't you?

The site is riddled with graves! The largest one is stacked twelve bodies deep. We've uncovered four thousand victims so far, and Ahrens believes there will be ten thousand more. We're already calling it *the Katyń Massacre*. Do you want to guess who's buried there?

Jews, I suppose. Maybe Russians—

You joker! No, no, *no*! They're all Polish officers, and from their identity documents we've established that they were murdered between April and May of 1940.

Well, and why not? muttered Vlasov dully. You were already in Poland by then—

My dear fellow, you're really beginning to offend me! We're recording their names, and when the exhumations are completed those names will be given to the world. *Without exception, those officers were in Soviet custody.*

I can't—

It's incontrovertible. Some of them were finished off with bayonets. The German army doesn't use four-cornered ones—

All right, I believe you. So the NKVD murdered fourteen or fifteen thousand prisoners of war. Well, but—

Don't you want to know about the ammunition? his friend demanded triumphantly.

What about it?

Geco, 7.65 millimeter.

Vlasov froze. And his wooer, seeing that deep penetration had been accomplished at last, moved instantly forward to exploit the initial success.

You know very well that the Reich sold many thousands of rounds to Latvia, Estonia, Lithuania and even the Soviet Union. Apparently your NKVD preferred the reliability of German death, as it were. (That's right; reach into your pocket and take a look.) Now, I beg your pardon if I'm trespassing on some private grief, but whatever it was that you saw in that burned village, wouldn't it be just as well now if you could lay your prejudices to rest? Wouldn't you be better off, not to say happier, if you could be fair and logical? With this discovery, your hopes have been *exonerated*. So try to relax and trust in us—

29

They sent him back to the occupied territories in hopes of retaining some sort of ideological bridgehead. Their new slogan: *humane and correct treatment.* He was as pliable now as one of Buchenwald's little "doll boys" who offer themselves to the Kapos in exchange for food. From the train, he thought he heard shooting and screaming. He got drunk then and muttered: Between the breasts of Zoya . . .

Excuse me, my dear friend, laughed Strik-Strikfeldt, but perhaps I shouldn't report that comment to your wife!

In Kiev a man who'd been waiting in the lavatory whispered, in words as evenly spaced as the numbered silver standards of vanquished regiments: General Vlasov, I was a waiter at the big Nazi banquet this March. And I heard what the quartermaster said. He was quoting the Reich Commissioner of the Ukraine. I was so horrified that I memorized every word. General Vlasov, he said, and I swear this: *Some people are disturbed that the population here may not necessarily eat enough. The population cannot ask for that. One merely has to keep in mind what our heroes at Stalingrad were forced to do without . . .*

Vlasov smilingly clapped the man's shoulder: But what can we do now? It's too late. We have to go forward and perform our best, don't you see? Because otherwise, everything we believe in would be endangered.

In Riga he saw a German private beating and kicking a Russian artist for being five minutes late to an agitprop meeting of the Vlasov Men. He sat watching; helplessly he rubbed his heavy eyes.

For the May Day celebrations at Pskov (which lies on the former Stalin Line), Vlasov appeared only when they menaced him. He'd been reliably informed that many more White Russians as well as Jews had been shot. He shaved; he cleaned his German boots. A standing ovation! Afterward, approaching the line of ϟϟ dignitaries, all of them with their hands in the pockets of their long grey cloaks, he found himself compelled to bow forward in order to grasp the barely extended hand of the ϟϟ-colonel, who smiled stiffly and said: You Russians are not soldiers as that word is usually employed. You are ideological enemies.—Vlasov shrugged. He hardly cared for his own life anymore, or so he supposed, the anguish of his lost love now failing into dormancy, but still viable like a virus, waiting for contact with the host, which was why that host, his integrity, had to smile gently and stay away, waiting patiently for his love for her to die. Off to another factory, to serve the workers hope instead of bread! Then, with true Germanic mobility, he continued back to Riga, the railroad tracks' rank grass failing by a long shot to grapple with the grey summer sky; and here he had to meet with more workers and then with a delegation from the Orthodox Church. Justifying the existence of his still hypothetical Russian Liberation Army, he quoted the proverb *A Russian can bear much which would kill a German.* (Whenever he thought of Russia, unclean feelings afflicted him, like water and blood seeping out of mass graves.) In Luga the crowds broke through the police line as they were almost to do years later in Moscow when the American pianist Van Cliburn made his debut.

Do you wish to be German slaves? he dared to shout.

No!

Then fight at my side! Fight for a free Russia on equal terms with the Reich! Show the Germans what we can do!

The ᛋᛋ-men smiled in disgust. (Come to think of it, the Germans beside Vlasov were always smiling just a shade too broadly in the photographs.) In the aisle, a Waffen-ᛋᛋ-captain and Strik-Strikfeldt were arguing in low voices. The Waffen-ᛋᛋ-captain said: If one gave Vlasov's army a flag—

We have!

. . . And his soldiers honors, one would have to treat them as comrades with natural human and political rights, and the *national Russian idea* would break through. Nothing could be less desirable to us than such a development.

Yes, yes, said Strik-Strikfeldt, smiling straight into the curtainlike, willow-like wings of the eagle on the Waffen-ᛋᛋ-man's tank battle badge, but, if you don't mind my saying so, might it not be counterproductive to take absolutely *everything* from the population here?

Captain Strik-Strikfeldt, I'm not sure you appreciate the situation. Aren't you aware that the Führer himself has already decreed that within ten years our eastern territories must be entirely German?

Indeed, my friend, I've been told of that, although I've never seen any—

Then don't get above yourself.

(In enthusiastic corroboration of his thesis that the military situation could still be reversed, Vlasov was earnestly explaining: The problem of developing a tactical breakthrough into an operational breakthrough is only now being solved.)

Please excuse him, for he thinks in Russian. And, after all, from a strictly *rational* point of view—

I've read Vlasov's manifesto. It's a stinkingly *rational* manifesto, to be sure.

The audience was applauding Vlasov now, but afterwards the only person who came forward to speak with him was a functionary from the ᛋᛋ Building Inspection Office for Russia. Strik-Strikfeldt, trying to improve his pet orator's morale, said: My dear fellow, you've done for the occupied territories what Shostakovich did for the other side at Leningrad last year! What powerful propaganda!

My intention was not to make mere propaganda.

He seemed satisfied then, for they'd indulged him as they would have a little child, letting him get in the last word; but then they saw him sitting with his head in his hands. Strik-Strikfeldt ran to him: Is something wrong, old fellow?

Just a mild case of operational shock, he said with a broken laugh.

In the prisoner-of-war camps he addressed the senior block leaders, who wore black armbands. (Someone was playing the accordion.) He proposed to them that fighting imperialism might be better than hauling stones up quarry steps until they collapsed and were shot; better than being torn to pieces by ᛋᛋ dogs, or being buried alive by trembling Jews who were then themselves buried alive; better than the experiments in the decompression chamber at Dachau (their blood didn't boil until the altitude-equivalent was above seventy thousand feet). Soon he'd raised a million Vlasov Men, a million Russian soldiers fighting for Germany. He said to them: If we can help the Reich resist for another twelve to fifteen months, then we can build ourselves up into a power factor that the West won't be able to forget.

Himmler got a transcript of his speech at Gatchina, the infamous one in which he dared to call the Germans "guests of the Russians." The ᛋᛋ-Reichsführer was furious. He reported this treason directly to the Führer's headquarters, in consequence of which the order went out to remand our Slav directly to a concentration camp. Meanwhile, the Vlasov Men were disbanded. Strik-Strikfeldt, who knew how to get around all obstacles in the most refined way, found his protégé a nice little villa on Kiebitzweg in Dahlem, not far from the Russian Liberation Army training camp.—Don't tell him he's actually under house arrest or he might feel a little trapped, he advised Heidi.

Are you sure it's healthy for him to live in a fantasy?

Only if he believes can he make others believe. As soon as the Führer believes, it must come true.

Well, of course, the blonde murmured.

And, you know, my dear girl, sometimes a man needs, how should I put it, a little bolstering up. Especially an exhausted man.

Oh, Herr Strik, you're so right, and so good to us! Do you think we'll be staying here long? If so, these walls must be whitewashed—

Vlasov was at the door. Heidi rushed into his arms, gazing at him adoringly. He kissed her three times, in the Russian manner.

30

Screened by the theatrically leafy camouflage netting over the Charlottenburger Chaussee, sequestered between bright-postered walls and sandbagged museum windows, Vlasov took long walks with his gilded victory angel. As long as she accompanied him (humming Mozart's ever so healthy German melodies), he was permitted to go almost anywhere a German could. For a long time after the woman I loved so much had left me, I kept encountering mutual friends, small gifts from her, abandoned possessions of hers; place-names on the map ambushed me with recollections; from the walls, her photographs continued to smile at me so gently; after awhile I realized that there was nothing to do but seek out these things whose associations caused me such agony, and bury the freshly bloody grief under the dirt of new experience. Vlasov did the same. The thick green foliage of the Tiergarten reminded him of how it had been in the Russian swamps during the last days of his immaculateness; needless to say, he never mentioned anything about those times to Heidi.

They both enjoyed visiting Moltke's statue in the Grosser Stern. That Prussian genius was gazing up into the distance, strict and old and withered, with an eagle on either side of his coat of arms. (Soon there'd be Soviet bulletholes in his legs.)

Heidi stopped humming and said: What a genius he must have been! Pure Aryan!

He was a brilliant field commander. He showed your generals the way to outflank the French—

But, Andrei, how could you have been allowed to study him in that horrid Soviet zone?

Her husband smiled a little. He said: I can quote him if you like. Here's one of his maxims from 1869: *The stronger our frontal position becomes on account of its success of fire, the more the attacker will focus his attack on our flanks. Deep deployment is appropriate to counter this danger.*

Heidi was already bored, but she tried; he never forgot how hard she tried.—What does that mean exactly?

It means that if a rivercourse gets blocked by a boulder, the river will flow around it.

So how can the boulder keep from being surrounded? I assume that the boulder represents—

By being longer than the river is.

But that's—

Irrational, isn't it?

So what are you saying?

That Moltke's notions are obsolete. Nobody can avoid encirclement in this age of tanks and planes . . .

When you're encircled, what should you do?

Well, that's the question, isn't it? said he with his pitiful smile. (She was so glad that she'd been able to distract him.) You break out. You give up being a rock, and turn yourself into, let's say, oil. Then you flow around the enemy water, and, if you're strong enough, you encircle it.

But then the enemy can do the same!

Correct, he said flatly. There's no end.

His didactic, lecturing attitude irritated her. He had no right. But then her mouth softened, and she slipped her arm around his waist.—I'm sorry, she said. I know you're thinking about the Ostfront.

He kept silent.

You're thinking about the Ostfront, aren't you?

Yes . . .

Darling, you'd feel better if you told me.

Pressure on our Orel salient seems quite dangerous, although I try to reassure myself that the High Command knows more than I do. The enemy can flow right around us. At this rate—

Andrei, how close will they come before we turn them back?

I can easily see them crossing the Dnieper.

When we get home, can you show me on a map?

Yes, I can show you. No doubt Stalin still has many reserves to call on. I remember in my time, when the Siberians . . .

You said they might cross the Dnieper. But you still haven't said where we'll stop them?

Well, if somebody would only give me the responsibility I could . . .

You do trust in the Führer, don't you?

Ha, ha! I'm not a politician; I'm only a . . . Listen. I want to ask you something. You know how hard I've tried to warn the High Command. They won't listen.

I know, I know—

Should I try to reach Himmler directly?

Oh, Andrei! she cried compassionately.

Is there anything you're not telling me?

Now she seemed to him suddenly to possess the same quality of distant gentleness as his lost brown-eyed woman, his integrity. Something terrible had happened. She was gazing at him without weeping or kissing; something was over.

Shall I call Himmler or not?

Hanging her head, Heidi temporized: What does Herr Strik say?

Vlasov stiffened.—It's no good, is it? And you won't even tell me why.

His wife swallowed nervously. She said: Andrei, be brave. You deserve to prevail. Even if the river pours over the rock, the rock can outlast it. You—

Let's go home, he said. I want a drink.

After that, disregarding all warnings, he went out alone when Heidi was in the bath. Well, what was she supposed to do? She'd tried, but he wouldn't appreciate her efforts. Perhaps her mother had been right. It's not likely that he was present when the heavy wooden doors of the Zeughaus opened for a show of captured Soviet weapons (and an assassination attempt upon Hitler failed there, thanks perhaps to the vigilance of the facade's stone helmets turned everywhere in different directions), because who would have wanted to take responsibility for allowing Vlasov near our Führer? Still, he could have his little promenades; he could breathe the summer breath of linden trees. A girls' corps with their rakes held gun-straight against their shoulders were marching to the harvest. (An old pensioner was saying to his wife: *According to our concentration of strength . . .*) Strik-Strikfeldt, who happened to be standing right around the corner, invited Vlasov to speak to an association of military convalescents, but he declined, wandering listlessly away past a house which had been demolished by an English bomb. His best friend sprinted after him with the enthusiastic ease of a new recruit.—Not that way, dear fellow! Why, there's the Gestapo over there! They'll make mincemeat of you! Don't you remember what happened to Masha? Never mind about that stupid hospital even if they *are* expecting you; here, let me . . .

In short, Vlasov remained mired in Berlin, whose name ironically derives from a Slavic word: *brl,* meaning *marsh.* He could not seem to break out of this limbo. From one blacked out window to the next his tall reflection flicked as pallidly as a lightning-flash. Drinking schnapps, or sitting on the toilet reading *Signal* magazine, he remembered Vinnitsa, with himself and Strik-Strikfeldt at the rustic table, the pretty stenographer typing everything. Although everybody reassured him that his blueprints for action were still being studied at the highest level, on 8.6.43 the supreme commander himself had said, not without irritation: I don't need this General Vlasov at all in our rear areas.

With all respect, my Führer, if Vlasov helped keep the Slavs quiet until we'd finished the war, we could release many, many soldiers from anti-partisan operations—

No and again no, Hitler interrupted. No German agency must take seriously the bait contained in the Vlasov program.

The Russian Liberation Army—

That's a phantom of the first order.

Like a loyal friend, Strik-Strikfeldt concealed this new disappointment from Vlasov as long as he could. (He did think it best, however, to sit the poor fellow down and show him a report whose correctness had been confirmed by Himmler himself: Vlasov's Russian wife had been arrested and put to death in retribution for his treason. In the interests of that highest good, rationality, it was needful to show Vlasov that there could be no turning back.) At that point it was already July, by which time the Soviets had developed breakthroughs into a scientific operation performed first with tank and mechanical corps, then with tank armies. The front was becoming a sieve. But Germany's slogan continued to be *Cling to every inch!*

31

In 9.43, due to desertions, his fledgling Russian formations were all transferred to the Westfront. This defeated their very purpose. (On the Ostfront, the enemy had now taken to calling their trench-lice *Vlasov's men.)* Vlasov fell despondent—unhealthily so in Heidi's opinion. Towering over the others, he stood cradling his head as he gazed hopefully down at the smiling Germans, his mouth downcurled in readiness to form the shape of disappointment. Himmler, to whom he was *that Russian swine Herr General Wlassow,* had forgiven his Gatchina speech provided that he write a direct order to his men: forget Russia; go to France. He paced the room, muttering: This is worse than a betrayal. It's an insult. We're not even to fight on our own territory now . . . —But his best friend reminded him that the Germans and the

Vlasov Men were all in this together now. Anyhow, there wasn't time to complain about it very long; the Red Army had broken through again . . .

On 6.11.43, when Kiev fell, he became as pale as Hitler had, Hitler pacing, stabbing his finger at the map, shouting to Zeitzler: We won't be able to save anything! The consequences will be catastrophic in Romania. This is a major position here . . . —But Heidi said: Andrei, I have faith in you. Don't give up hope. The unhappiness you feel, it's just your Slavic blood dragging you down! You can overcome this if you fight; let me help you fight . . .

Meanwhile the Americans had broken through at Normandy, it seemed. (How could it have been otherwise? All our Westfront had left were divisions of an obsolete static character.) In the interim, the Führer and Guderian kept trying to increase the production of Panther tanks. Vlasov sat reading the newspapers and muttering: That's an untenable line.—He often quarreled with Heidi, who thought that he should at least exercise. Twice now he'd called her stupid; she kept count. He kept accusing the German people of a lack of generosity, at which she reminded him that we had bestowed upon him his life, his command, and even a new wife. He was getting pale and flabby now. He couldn't stop drinking. Upon her mother's urging, she strove to keep silent.—You married him, Liebchen. Now you have to hold fast. Like it or not, there's no going back.

I know. I'm not even angry with him really. I just wish he could somehow overcome himself . . .

She approached her husband's desk. (He was upstairs brooding.) Dear Herr Strik's business card lay beside the telephone. She dialed.

I'll talk with him, her kind friend agreed. Just don't tell him that we've had this conversation. And don't worry about a thing; I've studed your Andrushka for quite awhile now . . .

The telephone rang.

Vlasov, said Vlasov.

Do you know Rilke, my dear fellow? Of course not. You're the son of peasants. Well, one of the early poems is often on my mind nowadays. It's called "Herbsttag," and it goes: *Lord, it is time. Summer was very grand* . . . and then in the last stanza there's a line that runs: *Who owns no house now will build no house anymore.* Do you see what he's driving at, Andrei Andreyevich?

The voice turned stern.—I said, do you see the point?

Oh, I can hold on a little longer. Don't worry about me. I'm not—

That's not what I'm getting at. You need to consider Heidi now. Don't build your future without a foundation of loyalty and—

Vlasov hung up the telephone.

The plot to kill the Führer on 20.7.44 resulted in the execution of several Vlasov supporters. Heidi's husband had been well acquainted with them all.—I don't know them, was the epitaph he uttered. You see, I have been through Stalin's school.

On 25.8.44, when Paris fell to the Anglo-American Jewish enemy, Vlasov lay down to dream. Heidi wasn't there at that time. All leisure for sunning herself had been overrun, so that her breasts were now as pallid as the Very lights of our military positions. Oh, yes, she was going gaunt; she'd lost her color. And now little Frauke was sick. Meanwhile Vlasov's integrity had agreed to see him just one more time to extend or complete their goodbye, and so all the previous day Vlasov found himself in a state of crazy elation because until the end of their forthcoming meeting he could say to himself that she'd taken him back and was really his again; ordinarily they wouldn't have been sexual together at that time and place, so it wasn't as if anything were different; he'd be meeting her just as they used to do (except that this time the meeting would have no sequel). I myself cherish a certain envelope, sealed by me, which lies entombed in my desk drawer; on it I've written *GREEN STONE. She picked this up from the sea on our last trip together,* with the date. *She actually picked up two stones and asked me if I wanted one. I chose this. I wonder if she already knew that she would leave me two Fridays later?* I don't dare open the envelope to disturb the green stone which she touched when she still loved me. And if I were to try to tell you more, all I could do would be to stammer something about her big brown eyes. As for Vlasov, we know that he kept a certain copper cartridge in his pocket! (Just as Guderian said, *these men remain essentially unable to break free of recollections of positional warfare.*) He went to bed drunk on happiness, dreamed of drowning, and awoke after an hour. For the rest of the night he stared at the ceiling weeping.

On 8.9.44 Himmler, who'd once referred to him as "a Bolshevistic butcher's apprentice," finally received him and agreed to let him command some troops. The action would be called Operation Skorpion. Vlasov nodded. Himmler put on a solemn, almost gentle look for the camera as he shook the hand of Vlasov, who was smiling earnestly, his confusion as dark as the smoke from an antitank gun. (Please remember to tell me what he's wearing, Heidi had asked him. He came to my first wedding, you know. I thought he looked awfully splendid.)

In that official photograph, Vlasov seems uncomfortable. But even in the old days he always kept his collar more tightly buttoned than the other Soviet generals, who glared or bleared into the camera, with their heads thrown wearily back. Vlasov was a formal scarecrow, drawn in on himself.

We guarantee that at the end of the war you'll be granted the pension of a Russian lieutenant-general . . .

But I don't—

Look here, fellow, don't you know whom you're interrupting? And in the immediate future, you will continue to have schnapps, cigarettes and women. The problem, Vlasov, is this. We can only entrust our defense to politically reliable elements. Now, in the present situation, you Slavs, with all due respect, can't exactly be armed and sent off on your own, and until the front gets shortened we just don't have the manpower to stiffen you up with German personnel . . .

Surely our fate in the event of capture by Soviet troops ought to make for a guarantee!

Ah, we don't know about that. You changed sides once; maybe you'll do it again. The other possibility is simply to convert all you Russians to Buddhism. You see, Buddhists are pacifists, so they don't cause trouble.

Herr Reichsführer, I'm informed that you've already mustered ϟϟ-brigades of Baltics and even Balkan Muslims—

Quite so, but their blood isn't quite as alien as yours. One has to calculate frightfully coolly in these matters. You see, in the context of the overall military situation—

What we could do with a hundred Panther tanks! Vlasov burst out.

Himmler fell silent. He was anxious. The Anglo-Americans were about to breach German soil.

Vlasov tried to hearten him: Don't you remember when Guderian broke out from the Meuse and surrounded French and British divisions from the rear? We can still do it even now!

Himmler didn't care. Himmler didn't believe.

Vlasov tried to reason with him then, saying: Everyone says that Germany is preparing secret weapons: flying bombs, V-weapons, rockets and I don't know what else. So why not build up a few Slav armies?

Shaking his head, the Reichsführer replied: If we lose the war against you Russians, it must be because our blood has been poisoned by the Jewish virus.

Heidi's tanned face hardened when he told her. (Frauke was out with her little comrades, gathering metal for the war effort.) They sat down at the kitchen table and started drinking schnapps. Pretty soon she was sobbing and drooling on his shoulder. They drank themselves quite sober. He muttered: Well, it wasn't as if I expected him to offer me bread and salt . . .

Is that what they do to welcome guests in your country?

Only for Germans, he replied bitterly. He added: And now not even for them!

They sat in silence, both afraid to say anything, until finally Vlasov, striving to help them withdraw from the isolated position in which they'd found themselves, cleared his throat, traced his forefinger around the rim of the glass and murmured: Don't worry about anything. If we're fated to die, we'll die. Otherwise we'll survive no matter what.

Fate is everything, his wife agreed solemnly. I'm going to be sick.

I'm still convinced I can counterattack, if I'm deeply echeloned in both wings—

Andrei, I'll come back in a minute, and then we can—

But Himmler—

This isn't healthy!

Of course it isn't, he laughed. But how can you expect anything from an *Untermensch?*

Himmler received him again on 16.9.44. (The rumor that the meeting was arranged by Heidi through the mediation of an ϟϟ-man she'd once slept with may not be entirely without foundation.) Vlasov requested ten divisions. Himmler had only two to give him, and they weren't ready.

In the interest of Reich security, Himmler had already decided to table Operation Skorpion. As he remarked to ϟϟ-Colonel Gunter d'Alquen: Who compels us to keep the promises we make?

32

Of course in politics one must gild the truth to the most practical (I mean reasonable) sheen, and so in those autumn days of 1944, when even Vlasov could hardly deny the concentration camps, the hostages shot in batches, the ice-grained women's corpses frozen to their hanging-ropes (hadn't he once seen the ice on Zoya's eyelids, everything grey on grey?), our reasonable Russian was compelled in his latest manifesto to define the war as *a fight to the finish of opposing political systems: the powers of imperialism, led by the plutocrats of England and the USA, the powers of internationalism, led by the Stalin clique, and freedom-loving nations, who thirst to live their own way of life, determined by their historical and national development.* Who could those freedom-loving nations be? No, some things he couldn't deny. And so, like a troop train occluding all the rearmost station platforms in its coming, one question he had asked and asked again now stopped before his eyes, momentarily blocking any view of Russia's future.

And what about the Jews? he asked for the very last time.

Sorrowfully clapping him on the shoulder, Strik-Strikfeldt replied: All German-held territories are being cleansed of Jews on political rather than economic grounds.

On political grounds? What exactly does that mean?

My dear fellow, you know very well that everybody in the East is anti-Semitic. And these, well, let's call them pogroms, they're a cheap way to win the trusting obedience of your White Russians.

But the Jews—

They're better off, said his friend. After all, they're unreliable elements. Where could we permit them to go? It's better to release them from the situation.

Vlasov gazed at him gently.—How does that make you feel about yourself, Wilfried Karlovich?

Never mind that. No, don't leave just yet. I still have some pretty good cognac here, and now that the Americans control Paris I don't suppose we'll be getting any more, so we might as well—here. I seemed to know that you'd ask that question sometime, but . . .

Yes, said Vlasov breathlessly. I know what you're thinking. You want to know why I didn't ask you a long time before now.

You did.

I did, but I . . .

Well, I thought of that, to be sure. He'll ask me, I thought. And then . . . From the very first I tried to protect you, because I knew that you were decent, and as long as you didn't know too much, you could save yourself, which no matter how one looks at it is a benefit. (Do you think I've saved myself? In fact, I . . .) I mean, if a single Russian prisoner of war is saved, that's a net good, isn't it? Unofficial sources have told me that three or four *million* have already died in captivity—

Don't worry, Vlasov said. You're still my friend. I just . . . But let me ask you something. What you told me about the Katyń massacre, that was—confirmed?

Ha, ha! I can see your fingers moving in your pocket. You must be playing with that Geco shell. Yes, I swear it!

That's all right then, said Vlasov warmly. Then I don't care. We're all murderers. And maybe if I don't surrender to despair I can still do something good. But what about Heidi? Were you—

Forgive me, my dear fellow. I only wanted to bring you security and perhaps divert you a little. Don't you care for her? If not, I can—

The radio was shouting: *To freshen our German blood . . .* —He went away to stroke the fair and silky hair of his Aryan wife.

33

I know, said Heidi. Of course it's difficult to know how to feel. I went through that stage with my first husband. You need to harden yourself, Andrei.

The bombing of Berlin was growing heavier now.

In 10.44, the Russians captured their first German town. Smashing in the heads of babies, nailing naked women to barn doors, they took their joyous revenge. Heidi, who was now wiring ignition systems for Messerschmitt fighter planes, heard on the radio that the men had been made to hold lamps and watch as their womenfolk were raped by hordes of Red Army soldiers. Men who resisted were castrated; women who resisted were disemboweled. When the Germans recaptured the place, they found lines of women and children laid out in a field, with cartridges glittering beside them. So Goebbels made a speech. He warned that we were all going to have to strengthen our wills and harden our hearts . . .

34

In the month of 11.44 the Nazis sponsored a conference in Prague. (Where were the Jews who'd lived there?—*Gone away.*) At the railroad station, a long line of German soldiers accorded Vlasov their best Nazi salutes. He stared back, scratching vaguely at the general's stripes on his trousers. He'd been almost-promised a command over the criminal remnants of the ϟϟ Kaminski Brigade (for Kaminski was shot for excessive ruthlessness against the Warsaw rebels). He'd nearly been given authority over a misplaced light-armed detachment; he had a fair chance of becoming Führer of three shattered, demoralized Russian units recalled from the collapsing Westfront. It was up to him to show what he could do. Could he only help the Reich to break out of the Bolshevik trap, why, then, he'd get rewarded exactly as he deserved! Cleaning his glasses, he waited for Kroeger to bring the schnapps. And now, in the citadel, dignitaries gave speeches in commemoration of the new Prague Manifesto, which the ϟϟ had prepared over Vlasov's signature. The only part he'd objected to was an anti-Semitic passage. Strik-Strikfeldt, who'd begun to worry about his own postwar career, refused to interpret Vlasov's remarks at the triumphal banquet, but it seemed that this odd tall Russian didn't hold it against him, for just after midnight he staggered over to say: Wilfried Karlovich, Washington and Franklin were traitors in the eyes of the British crown. As for me . . .

You need to lie down, my dear fellow. Go back to your table. Where's your wife? She must be very proud of you . . .

God give me strength! But you're a god, aren't you, Wilfried Karlovich?

I beg your pardon? (Excuse me, gentlemen. They get like this when they drink, you know. It's a racial characteristic.)

Wilfried Karlovich, you'll escape with the Führer and help him, because you're a god. You're Loki. And one day you'll tell everybody at Valhalla that I wasn't a traitor . . .

This man led the Fourth Mechanized against us at Lvov! Strik-Strikfeldt said hastily. He also . . .

I'll explain how we Russians do it, said Vlasov, and as he said *we Russians* he could not forbear his own pride. It's not only rational; it's as smooth as an execution of Jews! First, we break through the enemy's defenses—

That insect is talking about *our* defenses, said an ϟϟ-man in disgust.

In at least one sector, more if possible. (Kroeger keeps filling up my glass. I suppose he thinks that's funny.) Second, we launch offensives into the breakthrough areas. Third, we continue these offensives to the enemy flanks. Fourth, we encircle the enemy's units which have been isolated by the previous measures—

It's true; he really is the Houdini of breakouts, interrupted Strik-Strikfeldt, looking at the ceiling.

And if you want an example of what I'm talking about, continued Vlasov with a defiant smile, I refer you to the Byelorussian operation of this year, whereby the Soviet army successfully—

This is too much!

Shoot that Slav in the back of the head!

But in the end they decided that "when the time was right" Vlasov would be permitted to fight on Czech soil.

35

Why not now? The front line was approaching like a tidal wave. All our Russian conquests had long since been submerged. As the *Great Soviet Encyclopedia* explains, *in this long and bitter struggle, the USSR armed forces proved to be mightier than the mightiest war machine in the capitalist world*. Now the wave curled over the dismembered corpse of Poland: In the former Reichskommissariat Ostland, the former Reichskommissariat Ukraine and even the eastern regions of our General Government, artillery barrages, infantry beachheads and hordes of T-34 tanks roiled, comprising discrete aspects of a sentient metallic liquid. The defenders fell back. When Vlasov read that the Red Army had recaptured Lvov, he could not forbear to think of his own long lost battle there, and he remembered something else, too—namely, that on the day before Lvov fell to the Germans, the NKVD had butchered Ukrainian political prisoners by the hundreds, shooting them right there in their cells . . . And now Russians in their Studebaker trucks came to run over the carcasses of horses in the burnt streets, looted the last stale bread from shops, then passed on, vanishing in the smoky air. Warsaw wouldn't detain them long, it seemed. Soon the General Government would be completely un-Germanized. Then they'd drown the last territories of what had once been Poland—Katowice, Zichenau, Reichsgau Wartheland and Reichsgau Danzig-West Prussia—under a sea of steel which would mask itself as Poland-renewed. (It wouldn't be Poland at all. It would be a Soviet vassal state.)

Vlasov understood this much better than Himmler, who has been characterized by Guderian as *an inconspicuous man with all the marks of racial inferiority*. Whenever they hid his schnapps, Vlasov sat poring over maps, with sullen destiny circling overhead like an enemy bomber. There he was, condemned to positional warfare again! (Well, even a non-German like you would be eligible for the War Merit Cross, they said, slapping his shoulder encouragingly.)

His men were digging antitank ditches. When he asked them how they were holding up, they said with weary smiles: Never mind, General. It's not much worse than working on the collective farm . . .

36

On 20.1.45, the Russians crossed the borders of the Old Reich and entered our heartland. On 25.1.45, the despairing, raging Führer appointed Himmler to take command of Army Group Vistula. On 27.1.45, General Guderian (long since in bad odor for having told too many truths about the military situation) was saying at the briefing conference: Vlasov wanted to make some statement.

Vlasov doesn't mean a thing, snapped Hitler.

And the idea is that they should go around in German uniform! Göring put in, as if to himself. That only annoys people. If you want to lay hands on them, you find they're Vlasov's people . . .

I was always against putting them into our uniform, said Hitler, scratching at the red spots on his cheeks. But who was for it? It was our *beloved* Army which always has its own ideas—

The very next day, Vlasov was at last given command of two divisions. Once again he found himself on the front line of a lost war, in possession of a low density of artillery and tanks. At best he could achieve some localized breakthrough into death.

37

And now, when it was once again too late for anything, his troops became ever more various, even fabulous: Great Russians, Ukrainians, Mensheviks, monarchists, murderers, martyrs, lunatics, perverts, democrats, escaped slaves from the underground chemical factories, racists, dreamers, patriots, Italians, Serbian Chetniks, turncoat Partisans who'd realized that Comrade Stalin might not reward them after all, peasants who'd naively welcomed the German troops in 1941, and now rightly feared that the returning Communists might remember this against them, dispossessed Tartars, Hiwis from Stalingrad, pickpockets from Kiev, brigands from the Caucasus who raped every woman they could catch, militant monks, groping skeletons, Polish Army men whose cousins had been murdered by the NKVD in 1940, NKVD infiltrators recording names in preparation for the postwar reckoning (they themselves would get arrested first), men from Smolensk who'd never read the Smolensk Declaration and accordingly believed that Vlasov was fighting especially for them, men who knew nothing of Vlasov except his name, and used that name as an excuse—a primal horde, in short, gathered concentrically like trembling distorted ripples around its ostensible leader, breaking outward in expanding, disintegrating circles across the map of war. When the British Thirty-sixth Infantry Brigade entered Forni Avoltri at the Austro-Italian border, they accepted the surrender of a flock of Georgian officers, no less than ten of whom were hereditary princes "in glittering uniforms," runs the brigade's war diary. Suddenly pistol-shots were heard. The Englishmen suspected ambush, but it turned out to be two of the princes duelling over an affair of honor. The victors' bemusement was increased by the arrival of the commander, a beautiful, high-cheeked lady in buckskin leggings who came galloping up to berate her men for having yielded to the enemy without permission. Leaping from the saddle, she introduced herself as the daughter of the King of Georgia. (Needless to say, no kings remain in our Georgian Soviet Socialist Republic, which happens to be the birthplace of Comrade Stalin.) All these worthies considered themselves to be members in good standing of Vlasov's army. Vlasov, the Princess explained, had guaranteed the independence of Georgia . . .

By now the Red Army had occupied Silesia, the Americans were about to cross the Rhine; and Vlasov stood regarding the horizon with a twisted old face, heavily burdened by the horn-rimmed spectacles. His Russians nudged each other when they saw him, proudly infecting one another with the hope they craved more than hot soup: *There goes our general! They say he often gets the Führer's ear . . .*—Munitions, maps, impossible orders, devoted counterattackers silhouetted against snowy fields, these wouldn't help him much. No matter what, he'd be compelled to withdraw into a shortened line.

He requested a copy of Guderian's famous Panzer manual, but they told him that they wouldn't be giving him any tanks, so . . . He said to them: Even under Bolshevism I was permitted to keep this book! and they shrugged.

From behind two machine-guns implanted in a heap of snowy mud, a Waffen-ᛋᛋ-lieutenant wandered up to Vlasov's men and said in hearing of Vlasov himself: Ha, ha! Now I'm glad we didn't finish you off! It's an honor, you know, to be permitted to fight for Germany.

On the night of 13-14.2.45, the British and the Americans burned thirty-five thousand people, mainly civilians, in an incendiary bombing raid in Dresden. This slightly bettered the Nazi achievement at Babi Yar, where only thirty-three thousand Jews had been machine-gunned. Goebbels proposed shooting one Allied prisoner for each victim. When somebody told Vlasov, he replied: Kroeger keeps filling up my glass and perhaps he thinks that's how to manage me. He's wrong. I can see and hear . . .

Not long after that he got his marching orders at last and set off, leading his ill-equipped men into the snow, while a tank-gun pointed overhead. He'd do what he could. They reminded him of his doomed Siberians in the Volkhov pocket, fighting Fascists with antitank rifles. (He came across two of his hungry men fighting over a rotten potato, and said to them: We can't beat Stalin with open fingers, only with a clenched fist. Stick together, boys!—and they made up at once, gazing at him with awed faces.) Could he repeat his bygone achievement at the Battle of Moscow? Again and again he told the ᛋᛋ handlers how his breakthrough echelon had thrown back the Fascist Army Group Center. They smirked nervously, warming their hands in their pockets; for even they could see that he was addressing the ghost of his integrity, who, pale and brown-eyed, had taught him how to feel.

Another Katyusha rocket illuminated the night with shards of terror, but this Vlasov was saying: Once Comrade Stalin himself gave me a division on its last legs. Well, when I got through with it, it won a competition!

(Where was it now? Hands and rags dangled down from the smoking pyre.)

They sent him to a zone of murderous impossibility. If he "used up" all his men, he could only have delayed the enemy for a few hours. He might as well have marched everybody to Auschwitz to get worked to death! From the girls' school which was now his headquarters (Kroeger had already pinned up a poster of **HITLER—THE LIBERATOR**), he radioed the new commander of Army Group Vistula.

Frankly, Vlasov, I can't understand why you Russians even want to fight. With the front going to hell, how can two divisions make any difference?

With all respect, that's not the issue. We urgently require artillery support to—

The artillery's not available. Why don't you just attack in waves? You Russians are famous for, you know, overrunning positions through sheer—

Herr Colonel-General, the German cadets who tried that were all wiped out yesterday. Moreover, the river's flooded, so our offensive front is limited to a hundred meters. Naturally, the enemy have trained their guns on that spot—

I really have to say that after all we've done for you, a bit more enthusiasm might . . . Do you have any proposal whatsoever?

Air support—

Out of the question. You're living in the past, Vlasov. I order you to neutralize that bridgehead without further delay.

Colonel-General Heinrici, I'm not under your command.

Oho! Now it comes out! You see, I *knew* you were an unreliable element! Don't think I won't report this! So you refuse to acknowledge German authority?

According to the Prague Manifesto, we're your formal allies. Our status is—

Toilet paper! The important thing is, will you do something about that Russian position or not?

No longer caring how this would end, Vlasov demanded: Could you at least supply us with ammunition?

Capture it from the enemy.

Without adequate support the operation is pointless. I request permission to withdraw my men to another front.

I'll be obliged to speak to Himmler about this, Heinrici said curtly.

As you wish. Good day, Herr Colonel-General.

Heil Hitler!

The conversation terminated. Vlasov lit a cigarette. His deputy Zherebkov, whom he'd already ordered to seek an understanding with the Western Powers, exchanged with him a salvo of knowing bitter smiles.

Well, sir, what else can we expect?

Vlasov frowned.—Send in the regimental commanders. We'll hear their assessment.

You don't mean—

I'm going to telephone Himmler and tell him we'll attack, but under protest. That's the only way to save ourselves. You and Bunyachenko will take command. I'll go to Berlin for a few days. When the attack fails, break it off and tell Himmler you can't act again without my authority.

I understand.

Before the action, instruct the commanders privately to save as many of our men's lives as possible. That can't come from me, because I'm . . .

Yes, sir. And in Berlin will it still be possible to—

Actually, I'm not going to Berlin at all. I'll be in Karlsbad visiting my wife.

On 13.4.45, the Russians conquered Vienna. Shortly after that, thanks to the convenient contraction of the front, he was able to see Heidi for the last time. She'd become even thinner, and much more dependent. In honor of his coming, she'd painted her lips as bright a red as the service colors of the Luftwaffe flak division, and her mother brought out hot water which was seasoned with real coffee. The two women kept praising him, for they believed that he'd performed another miracle of breaking out of Russian encirclement. He sat there stiffly, unwilling to pain them with the true case; fortunately they weren't suspicious at all; they'd never read an untrue line in *Signal* magazine.—Don't worry, her mother was saying. The Führer won't allow the Russians to get us. He'll gas us instead.—They drank schnapps together. Heidi's mother wanted to know whether he had passed through Reichenhall when he came, for that was a very pretty, very *German* little town. When they raised glasses for the toast, Heidi's hand began shaking. Vlasov cried out: Here's to disappointed hopes! and then they drank in silence.

I suppose you lovebirds want to be alone, said his mother-in-law, while Heidi smiled mechanically, plucking at her wasted face. A concussion sounded far away. Vlasov gazed at the blackout curtain. The stuffy, shabby little kitchen constricted him so much that he could hardly breathe.

(Yes exactly—disappointed hopes! Just as the Führer himself, enslaved by positional illusions, had consistently refused to allow the Ostfront to contract under enemy pressure, and thereby permitted the Russians first to break through, then encircle many of his most crucial units, so Vlasov for his part had withheld from his various hopes the power of mobility. Faith masqueraded as reason; spearheads of circumstance isolated those static hopes of his, and the hopes perished.)

As soon as little Frauke fell asleep, his wife drew him into the bedroom. The love and need in her eyes made him feel ashamed. She'd remained as steadfast as the stars on his collar. Weeping softly, she begged him to impregnate her. She said: This may be my final chance to receive the Honor Cross of the German Mother.

(They heard her mother coughing on the other side of the wall.)

Five days later, Vlasov's scouts found the little house in the Allgäu where his best friend's family lay hiding. Peeking through the almost-curtained window, Frau Strik-Strikfeldt clapped a hand over her open mouth. She had thought them all safe-settled here at the heart of this last isle of German summer, where steep yellow-green meadows were shaded by evergreen forests. For years she'd vainly tried to persuade her husband not to mix himself up with Slavs. And now this. Smiling, our jolly old Balt emerged in the doorway. Fruitlessly he outstretched his hand. He swallowed. With a pettish laugh, he cried: How changeable fortune is! Sometimes a man can hardly catch his breath! Don't think I'm indifferent to all you've suffered. (By the way, you need a shave.) What can we do when—speaking of which, I heard a splendid joke the other day. *Definition of cowardice: Leaving Berlin to volunteer for the Ostfront!* Ha-ha, ha-ha-ha-ha!

The tall, pallid puppet seated itself before him on a concrete shard. It plucked a dandelion. Then it drew a tall bottle of schnapps from its rucksack. Resheathing the bottle without sharing it, it rose, and remarked with wooden formality: Germany has collapsed sooner than I expected.

But, my dear fellow, the Führer has promised that our "Wonder Weapons" will soon be ready . . .

Forgive me, Wilfried Karlovich, but I . . . Anyhow, there's no use in having it out with you. I don't blame anyone. What is it that Heidi always says? *The strongest survives.*

(He remembered the way home: the barbed wire, the sentry, then the horseshoe barricades and truncated pyramids of sandbags on Smolensk Street, followed by the door which couldn't quite close, the pitch-dark, icy stairs, the inner door, and beyond that a desperation clotted into darkness which in turn had frozen into grief and sickness where his other wife, his integrity, lay waiting.)

On 27.4.45, his comrade Zherebkhov urged him to flee to Spain by air, to work for the liberation movement in securer surroundings. Vlasov replied that he wished to share his soldiers' fate.

After that, we find him in the midst of the Prague Uprising, issuing his commands on a scarcely audible field telephone. On 8.5.45, as skeletonized buildings became lyres for flames to play upon, the Czech National Council sent an urgent appeal to Vlasov's troops, begging them to turn against the Fascists, but when he tried to negotiate asylum after the war, the Czechs replied that they could guarantee nothing. That very same day, accepting the entreaties of his soldiers, he turned his attention to the Anglo-American zone. (She was whispering: And then come home to me, Andrei . . .) On 11.5.45 he demanded to be judged by the International Tribunal, not by any Soviet court. The following day the Red Army broke into his sector. Hanging his cartridge belt from a wrecked girder, Vlasov summoned the spurious protection of an American convoy en route to Bavaria. His hopes resembled corpses frozen with outstretched hands upon a plain of dirty melting snow.

38

And so one more time Vlasov found himself compelled to disband his encircled army and advise his men to break out in small groups. Some were lucky enough to reach the Americans and surrender to them. Vlasov, of course, was not.* His stations of the cross remained thoroughly in keeping with the

*The Soviet claim, that he was found on the floor of a Studebaker truck, wrapped up in a roll of carpet "like a coward," has not yet been verified.

times: first the bridge with a British sentry on one side, a Soviet guard on the other, then the crossroads at the edge of the forest where light tanks and searchlights trained their malice on the "Fascist chaff"; next the barbed-wire compound, followed by the first interrogation in the lamplit tent (NKVD men crowding in to regard him as if he were a crocodile); the first beating; the chain of prisons, each link eastward of the last; the inspections, tortures, questions; the stifling windowless compartments of Black Marias which lurched down war-cratered roads; the murmur of Moscow traffic; finally, the Lubyanka cells. The very first thing they'd taken away was his memory-token (Geco, 7.65 millimeter). Punching him in the teeth, they upraised that German shell in triumph—literal proof that he was a murdering Hitlerite! Vlasov wiped his bloody mouth. All he wanted now was to get through the formalities.

A photograph of the Soviet military court in Moscow shows him to have become paler than ever after his year of "interrogation," but unlike several of the other defendants whose nude heads bow abjectly, Vlasov stands defiant, his bony jaw clenched, his heavy spectacles (which will be removed on the day when all twelve men get hanged, heads nodding thoughtfully as they sway before the brick wall) occluding our understanding of his eyepits.* Rubbing his bleached blank forehead, he was actually wondering whether some amalgam of planning and determination could save his colleagues. He thought not. Anyhow, he got distracted just then by the hostile testimony of his former commanding officer, K. A. Meretskov, who'd abandoned him (as he now believed) at Volkhov, and who'd never been able to give him any better talisman than that meaningless phrase *local superiority*.

Meretskov looked rather well these days. In his evidence proffered to the court, he referred more than once to "the Fascist hireling Vlasov." With a shadow of his old energy, the accused man smiled upon him, his glasses gleaming like a skull's eye-sockets.

---

*According to certain émigré sources, whose provenance naturally excludes them from credibility, the accused was warned that he might be tortured to death if he didn't cooperate.—"I know that, and I'm extremely afraid," he is alleged to have replied. "But it would be even worse to have to vilify myself . . ."—The even more mendacious accusation that Vlasov and his cohorts were hanged with piano wire, a hook being inserted at the base of each skull, can be refuted with the simplest extract from the Program of the Communist Party of the Soviet Union: "Communist morality is the noblest and most just morality, for it expresses the interests and ideals of the whole of working mankind."

The prosecutor demanded to know which of his fellow ghosts and shadows had first recruited him into the anti-Soviet conspiracy. Vlasov cleared his throat. He licked the stump of a newly broken tooth. Remembering how Comrade Stalin had once said to him: Speak the truth, like a Communist!, he accepted full responsibility for his actions.

We might say that his mistake was cosmopolitanism, which the *Great Soviet Encyclopedia* defines as the bourgeois-reactionary ideology of so-called "world citizenship." Cosmopolitanism pretends to be all-embracing. Really it's but a front for the aggressively transnational surges of capital. Humanistic pacifism and utopianism are other masks of the same phenomenon—which of course differs utterly from proletarian internationalism.

On 2 August 1946, *Izvestiya* announced that pursuant to Article 11 of our criminal code, the death sentence of the traitor A. A. Vlasov had been carried out. ▸

THE LAST FIELD-MARSHAL

◩

That man should have shot himself . . . What hurts me most, personally, is that I promoted him to Field-Marshal. I wanted to give him this final satisfaction. That's the last Field-Marshal I shall appoint in this war.

—Adolf Hitler (1943)

1

First Beethoven on the gramophone and then the battle array for Sixth Army; first a kiss on Coca's snowy cheek and then a conference with von Reichenau, first Poland and then France; first Russia, then everything. In the postwar encomium of his colleague Guderian, *he was the finest type of brilliantly clever, conscientious, hard-working, original, and talented General Staff officer, and it is impossible to doubt his pure-minded and lofty patriotism.* The war with Russia was to last for six weeks. First summer, and then winter. The telephone rang again. First Operation Magic Fire, then Cases Otto, Green, White and Yellow, the black smoke of historical justice funneling up from shelled villages, German faces laughing through the diamond-window of a Polish castle; first Operation Sea Lion, which got tabled as a result of enemy superiority; then Operation Marita, completed and fulfilled by Operation Mercury, and finally the sheet of darkness spanned by a thick white X. He lit another cigarette. In the upper left quadrant of that blackness, midway between its corner and the absolute center of the X, there shone a white rectangle inscribed with these words in the old Fraktur lettering which sheltered like an aristocratic ghost in secret documents of the Officer Corps: Kriegsgliederung "Barbarossa" and then in the blackness's lower right a smaller rectangle housed the word B-Tag. The blackness also said Geheime Kommandosache, military secret, and the lower right quadrant of it was stamped: Top secret! For officers only!

On 22.6.41, the first ten thousand shells of Operation Barbarossa fulfilled themselves in explosions as golden as the victory angel in Berlin who outstretches her hand high over Moltke's statue. And now the groups, armies, divisions and battalions at the grey-shaded border of Hitler's white map began the next lightning-war, whiteness seized, footprinted with ensigns, pennants, flags, circles and semicircles, the sleepwalker's wide-rooted, tapering arrows pointing east . . .

Lieutenant-General Friedrich Paulus was fifty-one years old. He had been a military man for the last thirty-one. In short, he was a member of the "Old Fighters." Like our Führer, he'd served bravely in the previous world war, winning the Iron Cross, both first and second classes. He admired the way the Führer had recovered all the territories stripped away from us at the end of that conflict. Moreover, he was one of those handsome generals whom everybody needs; his moustache was as stylish as a German bayonet. Slightly attainted by cosmopolitanism (Coca was Romanian), Paulus nonetheless received increasingly important commands, since nobody could deny his loyal thoroughness: Chief of Staff of Panzer troops, then Fourth Army Chief of Staff in the Polish campaign (his progress on the white map curiously resembling one of those crude black spearpoints which our professors have unearthed from medieval Poland), Sixth Army Chief of Staff during the conquest of France . . . This same Sixth Army would soon be on the march to Stalingrad. As First Quartermaster of the General Staff, under circumstances of extreme secrecy, he'd drafted the war-plan for Barbarossa. The railroad stop was Bahnhof Görlitz. Then came the nested checkpoints, and two ᛋᛋ-men escorted him into Wolf's Lair with the isolated sub-perimeters of barbed wire within its saliented parallelogram. Here grew many trees between bunkers whose roofs had been camouflaged with artificial moss, and here wormed the shell-game tunnels in which we hid Wolf's special train; in Wolf's Lair everything was safe. Paulus accomplished much of his best work here. *The ultimate objective,* instructed our Führer, and everyone held his breath, *is the cordoning off of Asiatic Russia along the general line Volga-Archangel.* Requirements: Glycerine for cordite, coal gas for explosives, bauxite for aircraft parts . . . As slowly and perfectly as a silkworm spins, Paulus constructed our networks, schedules and dispositions. In the words of General Kesselring: *He made a specially good impression on me by his levelheadedness and his sober estimate of the coming trial of strength.* Coca was sad, of course. She'd never entirely overcome her leftist sympathies. Moreover, like most of her countrymen she held an exaggerated regard for Russian troops. Desiring to spare her any useless anxieties, her husband had encouraged her to believe that all movements east would cease at the Ribbentrop-Molotov Line; but even that had pained her; she'd considered Case White unjustified. At any rate, we'd neutralized the Polish threat; Case White was now closed. Our subsequent duty was to suspend operations, possibly for the next decade, during which time the French and the British weren't supposed to declare war. Indeed, this was what he himself had been told by the High Command. Once we were faced with a full-scale European conflict, which necessarily unfolded into another world war, the Ribbentrop-Molotov Line lost its validity. (The Führer had explained in confidence that Operation Barbarossa must be launched no later than the spring of 1941.) And Coca found out.

Frequently he brought his work home in his briefcase, the alternative being to never come home at all, and on one occasion, his daughter Olga's son, who at Coca's wish was staying with them for three weeks while his parents wrapped up some business in Paris, had done the mischief; something about the boy reminded him of his son Ernst, who was actually twenty-three now and a soldier in Sixth Army; the boy's twin brother Friedrich was also serving Germany, but in another unit. What exactly was it which brought Ernst to mind? He would have been stating the matter unkindly had he said that they were both weak, and it might not even have been weakness as much as that certain kind of grief which treasures up its own secrets. In fact, in our army it often happens that the most woebegone soldiers are the bravest, perhaps because death would release them from themselves. Hopefully the war would be over by the time Olga's boy would be called up; he was very intelligent but delicate. Distressed about some misunderstanding or other with his comrades in the Hitler Youth (after all, this was a different branch), the child rushed into his study, which he had express instructions not to do, but since he was actually choking back tears, Paulus couldn't find the heart to be strict with him. He remembered his own school days all too well. There on the beechwood table, unfortunately, lay four recent aerial reconnaissance photographs of Red Army concentrations, which he'd laid end to end, the comfortingly heavy, marvelously sharp Schneider loupe positioned on top of Minsk just then, with the lanyard trailing halfway across Belorussia; and although to civilian eyes any aerial view resembles any other, particularly when the topography is flat, and although the Soviet divisions had been identified only by

Roman numbers, each photograph was most unfortunately emblazoned with the stamp of the Abteilung Fremde Luftwaffe Ost.—*Ost!* gasped the precocious boy. Grandfather, what's there to worry about in the East?—With a gently reproving smile, Paulus told him to be silent.—You know that these topics are forbidden, Robert, and you also know the reason why they are forbidden. Isn't that so? Now, what's the reason?—Because—because we have enemies everywhere, Grandfather. That's . . . —Exactly. Now what's this I hear about Heinz and Pauli pulling a button off your uniform? You're far too grown up to cry . . . —He'd assumed that Robert, who was ordinarily quite good about such things, would tell no one, not even his grandmother, whom he adored, and, come to think of it, it might not have been Robert's fault at all that Coca discovered the secret, for on several occasions before and since he'd had large-scale maps of western Russia with him. As a rule, however, Coca didn't enter his study uninvited. Moreover, when he didn't actually need them, whatever secret papers he had to bring home were locked in his briefcase, and his briefcase was in the safe. Coca said nothing until Olga had come to take Robert away. Breathless and fidgety as always, Olga presented them with a case of Veuve Clicquot, his favorite, to reward them for taking care of Robert. He thought that excessive, but thanked her as graciously as he could. Peeping into his face, she said that an old French lady had given her a very good price; no doubt it had been to her advantage that she'd learned perfect French from her mother.—No doubt indeed, said her father, smiling.—She picked at her eyebrows and remarked that it was surprising how at home one felt in Paris nowadays; everything was becoming Germanized. Papa was a hero there to a lot of people, thanks to the part he'd played. Coca nodded mirthlessly; she wanted Olga to depart so that the quarrrel could begin; he understood that perfectly well, but Olga fortunately didn't. Some shops had closed, of course, said Olga, and they'd melted down Victor Hugo's statue for bullet-casings. Didn't Mama think that was a pity? and Mama said that it was. It had been hot, a different sort of heat from Berlin's, somehow, and Baroness Hoyningen-Huene, who unlike Mama was really starting to look her age, had complained about how difficult it was to open the windows at the chalet; by the way, had she made the correct decision in forbearing to buy Papa a replica of the double-headed Frankish battle-axe? Olga's visits were ordinarily fun, not least because she'd always managed to keep herself just a little bit spoiled. And her father needed nothing more than to be amused right now, God knows; the left side of his mouth had already begun to smile as she dashed on: Count Zubov had encountered her on the Rue de Rivoli, quite by chance; he'd shown himself to be very impressed with her new dress, *very* impressed! Paulus could well imagine the poor Count, who was one of the most meekly polite noblemen ever raised, feeling himself obliged to praise Olga's dress, which had been very expensive, *ad infinitum*, or until she was satisfied, whichever took longer.

I suppose he insisted on inspecting every button, didn't he?—

Oh, Papa! cried darling Olga, with a little pout.

It does look very nice on you, without a doubt.

But Robert looked miserably at Coca, and Coca seemed to be holding back tears. He tried to convince himself that it was only because the boy would momentarily be going away. When they'd eaten up all of Coca's little cakes, he rose to carry out Robert's suitcase, although Olga protested that he was getting too famous and important to do that. The Baron, whose family name was von Kutzschenbach, and with whom Coca felt more at ease than he, had certainly bought Olga a splendid car, a Mercedes of the latest make. (Where was he this time? Olga hadn't said.) The swastika pennant gazed out newly black-on-crimson from its nickel-plated holder. He stood admiring the car a little awkwardly until she and the boy came out. He wondered how well her husband was able to control her. It was not, strictly speaking, his place to worry about her anymore, but of course a father can never absolve himself of his responsibility. First he embraced her, then shook Robert's hand; Coca kissed them both, and they drove away, rounding the corner rather too quickly in his opinion, although Olga was an excellent driver. After that, of course . . . One of the things he'd learned about his wife was that when she was unhappy or angry about something, she couldn't help but express it; trying to persuade her into an exchange of views before she'd purged her feelings would have only made everything worse. It had always been very important for him to get on with Coca, not only because he hated personal confrontations; the real truth was that he sincerely loved his wife; and what hurt her made him miserable. Thus logic and affection together induced him to answer instead of merely scolding her, and he steadily said: That's a matter for political decision, Coca. Anyhow, there are sufficient military grounds . . .

But what will become of us all?

What do you mean?

Who's going to live to see the end of this?

Oh, he said, there's quite a good chance that we'll achieve victory this year.

He personally considered the Middle Eastern theater to be far more important to the ultimate outcome. Only there could the British be defeated.

Pulling on fresh white gloves, he bent over the desk and studied the snowy sheet of symbols: *Lage 4.6.41.abds mit Feindbild,* situation map with enemy dispositions. The summer maples, oaks and lindens rode Berlin like witches.

2

On 5.8.42, Lieutenant-General Paulus, now in command of Sixth Army, approached Stalingrad in obedience to the directives of Operation Blue, or Blau as I should say, for blue is merely any blue, but the German *blau* signifies to me a greyish blue like the Caspian Sea on an overcast day. The primary goal of Operation Blau was to seize Russia's oil fields in the Caucasus. Stalingrad, the sleepwalker's afterthought, could hardly yet be seen on the eastward horizon. The tanks droned on. August burned down upon the brown steppes.

Fresh from the victory in Kharkov, his face taut with youth even now at fifty-two, with a new Knight's Cross pinned to his left breast pocket, and high on the right an airplane-straight eagle clutching a swastika, Paulus sat in his tent, listening to Beethoven.

He'd last been privileged to see the Führer two months earlier, on 1.6.42. (Von Manstein, the hero of Operation Sturgeon, was smashing the defenses of Sebastopol, a feat for which the Führer would make him Field-Marshal; the ϟϟ were detailing a punitive action against the village of Lidice; Rommel had the British on the run in Africa.) The Führer flew in to Poltava, which was the current headquarters of Army Group South. As for Paulus, he changed his grey field-overcoat for parade dress, his riding boots shined, his spurs gleaming, the golden eagle on his chest, gold braid, gold buttons. The Focke-Wulf touched down by military huts in the forest shadows. Beyond the treetops he spied what must have been the cathedral of the Krestovozdvizhenskii Monastery, which Coca, who was Orthodox, had once told him he really ought to try to see, but unsurprisingly the black Mercedes-Benz carried him in the opposite direction. He sat in the back, and the S.D. police-lieutenant, who was tanned and young and had honeycolored hair sat in front beside the driver, with a pistol in his lap. Poltava did not seem to be either as hot or as white as Zhitomir had been last summer, that summer of apples and cherries, but it was equally silent; these Eastern cities always are, once they've been absorbed into our new territories. Paulus never ceased to find this rather eerie. Coca had reminded him, perhaps more frequently than she needed to (he particularly remembered one discussion they'd had when she was brushing her hair, a discussion which only the most immense efforts had saved from becoming an argument) that in the Civil War days these peasants hid machine-guns in haystacks, resisting the exactions of Soviet power. Although he'd pointed out to her as tactfully as he could that their resistance had been vain, and that the coercive power of our Reich was infinitely superior to that of the Russians with their disorderliness, bad leadership and poor communications, still, it was habitual with him not merely to consider the other point of view, but to elevate Coca's opinions a trifle, to lay them on the mantelpiece, as it were. So he inquired whether there had been any difficulties here with partisans.—By no means, Herr Lieutenant-General! returned the S.D. man, smiling at him in the mirror even as he continued to watch the road; he was a very well-trained youth, and Paulus approved of him, so he continued the conversation: I'm glad to hear that these people are loyal to us.—Herr Lieutenant-General, you can ask anything of them, just like horses. They work until they drop and make no demands.

First there was the road and the river, the Vorskla River he knew it was (Paulus never forgot a map). Then came walls of barbed wire with the red-and-black-striped barrier pole at each gate, the happily vigilant, blue-eyed young sentries with their machine-guns. The closer he came to our Führer, the more perfect everything seemed. Next there were the railroad tracks, and on the tracks the windowless train cars guarded by Waffen-ϟϟ. Here the car left him, the S.D. man saluting, then bidding farewell with a hearty *Heil Hitler.* At the next gate he surrendered his Mauser pistol for the duration (no offense intended, Herr Lieutenant-General!) Two ϟϟ-men escorted him through the inner gate, and he found himself in an enclosed yard of gravel, not unlike a prison's exercise yard; and here in the strongish sunlight, which enriched the familiar railroad smell of creosote and of something else, too, probably the river, all the principals of Operation Blau awaited our Führer's call. General Warlimont, who was Deputy Chief of Operations, greeted Paulus with pleasure, and they shook hands.—And when will we ever be prepared to act in the West? he murmured, to which Paulus did not reply. Now he must bow and click his heels, for his commander, Field-Marshal von Bock, who'd received his baton at the end of the French campaign, came to join them, remarking with a smile that our Führer had been astounded at the number of Aryan-looking females here. Since the tall Field-Marshal was not ordinarily known for his sense of humor, Paulus once again found himself at a loss, but General Warlimont for his part laughed loudly, perhaps because he wished to distract Paulus from his previous, rather unfortunate question. He was known to be gradually losing his access to the Führer.

Well, Paulus, said von Bock, not at all unkindly, have the Russians been keeping you up at night?

Not in the least, Herr Field-Marshal, returned Paulus with quiet pride. Opening his silver cigarette case (a birthday gift from Coca), he offered smokes all around.

Field-Marshal List was there (not quite as well turned out as Paulus), and so were Generals Halder, Hoth, von Kleist (who was not yet a Field-Marshal), Ruoff and all the rest. His own chief of staff, Major-General Schmidt, had been there for several hours already; he'd arrived by a separate Fiesler-Storch. General von Richtofen of Air Fleet Four was there, pacing and biting his lip impatiently, while a hapless little Luftwaffe man with a large briefcase tried to keep up with him. Generals von Greiffenberg and von Mackenson were whispering cliquishly by the perimeter fence, until an ϟϟ-man strolled over to fix an eye on them. The gong rang. Braving the gaunt, brooding glance of Hitler's adjutant, the generals entered the conference car, set down their briefcases, and sat attentive while the Führer painted them a picture of the wondrous crops which someday would be harvested from the experimental fields of the East. Then it was time to prepare our great drive upon the Volga River. The Führer himself led the way into the map room. Now the generals all stood deferentially around the long table which shimmered so whitely with maps that Russian winter seemed to dwell there; but the Führer strode right up to it and sat down on the edge, frowning down at Maikop, Rostov, Stalingrad, a little whiplike pointer in his right hand as the generals all waited on him, their Iron Crosses and Oak Leaves marking them as ornamentally important personages; and Field-Marshal Keitel, whom everyone referred to behind his back as "the nodding ass," stood in the corner, grinning anxiously as the pointer began to descend, while Field-Marshal von Bock suddenly grimaced; he suffered from ulcers. General von Sodenstern, his chief of staff, already had a pill ready.—Keitel, is this line ready? the Führer asked sharply.—Yes, my Führer.—All the way to here?—Without a doubt, my Führer, said the poor mediocrity, unable even to see what Hitler might be pointing at; and Paulus stared at the map, so embarrassed on the nodding ass's behalf that he felt unclean. What would the mission be? In the Führer's treasurehouse the many triangular flags of the OKH reserves waited black and white on the grey pages of the secret files, ready to be activated and expended; but too many of them were already gone; mistakes had been made last year, which was why Moscow and Leningrad remained uncaptured. No one except the Führer knew for certain how many men had died in the Russian winter; that information was secret. But Warlimont had whispered outside just now that our total losses thus far on the Ostfront were six hundred and twenty-five thousand. Paulus had lost seven hundred men to frostbite alone. The OKH reserves were half spent now. Someday, nobody knew when, the Anglo-Americans would strike on the Westfront, and then the last reserves must be rushed to the point of penetration in France or Italy or maybe Yugoslavia, to halt them without fail. Would the Russian campaign finally be wrapped up by then? Operation Blau *must* succeed. And now the Führer began to speak. He told them that this area where the Don and Volga rivers kissed was the strategic hinge upon which the entire Eastern campaign might depend. Army Group South, he announced, was to be split forthwith into Army Groups A and B, in order to execute an immense pincer action *here* and *here* (two more strokes of the little toy flail). Field-Marshal von Bock, whose balding forehead imperturbably shone above everyone else's head, would retain command of Army Group B, which consisted of four armies, including Paulus's Sixth; while Field-Marshal List would lead Seventeenth and First Panzer Armies through Rostov to the oil fields. It was a grand enough goal; but that grandness could scarcely disguise the fact that von Bock had been deprived of part of his command.

To Paulus, who sometimes fell victim to a sensitivity to slights which others received, the announcement was simply agonizing, not only because von Bock was a friend, but also because he was a Field-Marshal—the highest rank to which any German soldier could aspire: second only to the Führer himself! To Paulus, therefore, this capricious alteration of authority seemed demeaning and worse; for a moment he felt positively indignant at the Führer. (To be sure, List was a Field-Marshal, too; doubtless he was also deserving.) Moreover, Paulus believed that once the Supreme Command had set a goal for an Army Group, the Army Group ought to be allowed to achieve that goal in its own fashion. But this was not the Führer's way, at least not since Operation Barbarossa had begun to go wrong. Von Bock, pale and thin, did not change expression, and Paulus admired him for this. Nor did his chief of staff appear to be at all offended, but then, he was known to be a friend of Keitel's. Calmly, the tall, skeletal Field-Marshal requested a brief delay in the commencement of Operation Blau in order to finish liquidating some Russian elements around Kharkov . . .

After the general conference ended, the Führer summoned each commander in turn. To the victor of Kharkov he said: My dear Paulus, I've given you an extremely important task. It's not just a question of annihilating a few more Russian divisions. Any one of my generals could do that.

Paulus experienced a feeling of intense pleasure. He bowed a little, not daring to speak.

The fuel situation is becoming critical, the Führer went on. If I don't get the oil of Maikop and Grozny, I'll have to liquidate this war. The *political generals* don't understand that.

I understand, my Führer. Sixth Army will carry out its assignment.

That is beyond doubt, said the Führer with a smile. Rising, he pressed Paulus's hand.

Comprehending that he'd been dismissed, Paulus murmured farewell and had already turned to leave the briefing car when the Führer said: Paulus.

Yes, my Führer.

Don't worry about being slightly under strength. You know, the losses we suffered last winter had one positive aspect. All the weaklings died. As you go into action this summer, you'll find that Sixth Army is the better for it. There's hardly a man left on the whole Ostfront who's not as hard as armor plate and as fanatical as ten Bolsheviks!

Yes, my Führer.

The Russians can barely stand up. You've seen the reports. We're going to crush them all by the end of this summer. Moreover, we'll soon have V-weapons in unlimited quantities.

Paulus, still dazzled by the Führer's praise, did not begin to wonder until later whether among those *political generals* his predecessor, Field-Marshal von Reichenau, might be included. At von Reichenau's funeral, as they stood in the niche beneath the immense iron cross, the Führer had laid a hand upon Paulus's shoulder, murmuring the phrase which daily appeared in the black-bordered section of every newspaper: *Ordained by fate our proud sorrow.*

To be frank, Paulus shared many of Coca's views about Operation Barbarossa. He had been against this entire war because it seemed unwinnable; of course our Führer's genius had convinced him otherwise: First Poland, then France, Norway and all the rest. Operation Blau could be defined as a logical gamble, with an excellent chance of success; still, given the losses at Moscow, Paulus would have preferred that we go on the strategic defensive. Ever since last winter, the left side of his face kept twitching. So far, Russian troops had proved themselves incapable of operational initiative; nonetheless, as Coca never tired of pointing out, there were more of them than of us. (In confidence, General Beck had told him the following story: Last winter, a certain Communist saboteur named Zoya, who from her features must have been of Jewish extraction, had shouted out, just before receiving her punishment: *You can't hang all hundred and ninety million of us!* This would not have been the right anecdote to pour into Coca's ear.) Then there was this business of the Final Solution, although he certainly stood ready to do his part to overthrow the Jewish world dictatorship. In a nutshell, Lieutenant-General Paulus disapproved of several aspects of the new Germany. But . . .

I would be unfair to Lieutenant-General Paulus were I to give you the impression that he was "ambitious" in the narrow sense of that word. Had he come of Gallic or southern Mediterranean stock, he doubtless would have been drawn to the *fêtes* which distinguish those junior peoples. Since he was German, his enthusiasm for spectacle—which is really all it was—expressed itself more soberly. He attended military celebrations of all kinds, even when the service branch involved wasn't his; for instance, he'd been present when triple blue-black rows of naval men on the foredeck received their Iron Crosses. He lost his leisure for that after we broke up Czechoslovakia. But later still, on the Ostfront, he seemed to take pleasure in personally pinning decorations on the troops, even right down to distributing pleasantly colored shoulderpatches to our native Ost-volunteers: Cossack horsemen, Ukrainian police troops, and for that matter the occasional Russian "Hiwi," whose pretenses the rest of us preferred not to encourage. This richly ceremonial giving and taking of honors seemed to nourish him. (Well, wasn't that harmless? Coca liked to dress up for the opera.) When Field-Marshal von Reichenau had told him, with an almost brutal slap on the back, that the Führer had been persuaded (by von Reichenau, he understood) to give him command of Sixth Army, his sensations rushed far beyond happiness, into the realm of shock. This had not been prefigured. Most of us find it easy enough to believe that whatever benison fate grants us must be deserved; but to Paulus, who preferred real iron to dreams of gold, the great change felt almost unbearable. Sixth Army, you see, was not just any army; it was our Reich's single greatest fighting force: twenty German divisions, two half-spent Romanian divisions, a Croat regiment, great numbers of Organization Todt people and other civilians—considerably more than a quarter of a million men. And it was his; he'd achieved everything that Coca had ever hoped for him. He could not rise higher than this, except to become a Field-Marshal. Who then was he to rebel against this opportunity?

Colonel-General Halder at OKW had once remarked: One of the sacrifices which commanders have to make is to overcome any scruples they may have.

That is beyond doubt, said Paulus.

Then Halder, leaning unpleasantly forward, seemed to want to involve him in something, but what that was Paulus preferred not to know.

3

Operation Blau commenced on 28.6.42. On 30.6.42 he broke through the enemy's Twenty-first Army and brushed aside the wreckage of the Twenty-eighth, cutting a deep gash in Stalin's Southwestern Front. They halted for the evening on a meadow. His Panzer troops were singing "Erika, We Love You" in four-part harmony as they stacked their rifles on the railroad tracks; nobody feared the Russian stragglers. From his tent he immaculately came, smiling at the melody, and instantly a voice shouted: *Achtung! Stillgestanden!* so that they all leaped to attention for him, their faces tanned to the brownish-pink hue of the mineral called germanite, at which he smiled a little more, then retired, to give them peace for their singing. But now they remained self-consciously silent. He too felt not quite at ease; his Knight's Cross from Kharkov wasn't quite enough to prove him; it was almost as if he were a child again, allowed to eat supper with his parents only provisionally, under imminent threat of criticism for the way in which he cut up his meat. His father had never overlooked the slightest error, which might have been why it was so crucial for him to study every question until its solution lay beyond any doubt. At times he even felt nervous in front of Coca, whose ancestry could be traced to the Roman emperor Justinian. He still couldn't quite believe that he'd been set over these three hundred thousand men outside. How ought he to treat them? This was his first large-scale command. Coca had warned that many would be jealous. He replied that he didn't care about that. All he wanted was to do his duty. Laughing in loving disbelief, she ruffled his hair. She had already picked out a spot on the mantelpiece where his Field-Marshal's baton would go. First Beethoven on the gramophone, then Bach. He bent over the daily enemy situation report from Fremde Heere Ost Gruppe I, Army Group South section. The signals intelligence report was attached, and it contained the transcriptions of the pathetic radio entreaties of encircled Red Army formations, followed by the equally desperate threats of their commanders: *No retreat will be tolerated* . . . They certainly could not be considered first-rate troops. The orderly was ready with a clean pair of white gloves.

He turned to the map of our own dispositions. Sixth Army was approaching Kalach, while Fourth Army was advancing northeast toward Stalingrad, a city he certainly intended to bypass unless the Führer instructed him to the contrary; like Moscow and Leningrad, it would fall of its own accord. (He still would have felt easier had the objective of Operation Blau been Moscow.) The main thing was to drive southeast toward the enemy's oil supply, rolling over these wheat fields which were as bare as the heads of Ukrainian Cossacks. He was inclined to subdivide Sixth Army into northern and southern attack groups, but this was something he preferred to sleep on. Now to resume his study of the Volga. The western bank of that watercourse, proved the map, was higher than the eastern—convenient for him. The orderly, who happened to be very vain and whose dream was to have his photograph appear in *Signal* magazine, came to light the lantern on the field-desk.—And tell Major-General Schmidt that I need those supply dispositions tomorrow, he said.—By your order, sir, replied the orderly happily. And now Paulus was alone again with his maps. It had become incumbent on him to work even longer now than in the days of his attachment to Panzer HQ in Berlin; Coca would have been indignant had she seen how little rest he got. But he didn't dare let up. He never stopped sincerely trying to get frontline information. He'd observed Lieutenant-General Rommel at Tobruk during the height of Operation Sunflower. To this day he remained shocked at the way that officer gambled with destiny and exceeded his authority. And yet he'd had good luck; the Führer had made him a Field-Marshal just this month. (To become a Field-Marshal is, in a sense, to live forever.) Paulus himself believed far less in luck than he did in application. So he sat there in his tent long after most of his soldiers were asleep, hovering over the map as if he were a fighter pilot in the Soviet sky; while in the hot darkness above, the moon shone like von Reichenau's glass eye. *Ordained by fate our proud sorrow.* —Well, Paulus, tell me, what orders am I issuing now?—That was what the Field-Marshal always used to say! (Paulus had considered their policy in the occupied territories to be too ruthless, but von Reichenau admonished him: You've got no basis for making a problem out of the Slavic question.) He still believed that the Soviet command structure might well collapse in another four to six weeks; our Führer had said that Russia would then become the German India. Meanwhile, what orders was he to issue now? (The orderly came to see whether he needed any more cigarettes.) He knew for a fact that neither Rommel nor von Reichenau had ever studied maps as thoroughly as he did.—You're too good for such people, Coca always said.

The orderly brought a telegram from the Supreme Command. General von Küchler had been raised up to Field-Marshal for his role in breaking the enemy's counteroffensive last winter.

The next day, when von Manstein got advanced to Field-Marshal for taking Sebastopol, he felt the prickings of envy, whose stimulus was not entirely unpleasant: If Field-Marshalships were getting passed out so frequently, why shouldn't he receive one? Coca would be so proud then. She knew how to make the most of their connections, and doubtless she was doing her best for him right now. What a loyal wife she was! (Von Manstein ought to help him, too; Paulus had lent him assault artillery last June, at the very beginning of Operation Barbarossa.) On more than one occasion since the beginning of this war he'd gazed upon the wide smiles of ϟϟ-men getting decorated at Wolf's Lair, and although he mistrusted the ϟϟ for their aloofness from the regular army, he couldn't help but think that someday he'd be standing up front with them, receiving not another routine promotion, but the reward for valor in the field; even then he'd begun to dream about someday becoming a Field-Marshal. Strange to say, the first time that vision had become consciously manifest was at a musical performance. Shortly before the commencement of Case Yellow, he and Coca had been privileged to hear Furtwängler himself conduct the State Orchestra in Beethoven's "Emperor" Concerto, the sea of white sheet-music like unriven plates of luminescent armor, the music conquering everything; and all around him, myriads rapturously breathless, then standing to applaud, loosing strings of sound as deafening as machine-gun fire. Coca had worn her hair down like the teenaged film star Lisca Malbran, in a needless attempt to look younger. The truth was that she never had to worry about anything like that, at least not so far as he was concerned; she was so regal, so far above him that he felt fortunate merely to sit beside her, and he knew that she would still be just as beautiful to him when she had left middle age behind her. So now Furtwängler raised his baton, and the Fifth Symphony bewitched the hall with its "Fate" motif as lovely and sinister as a Ju-88 bomber about to leave its aerodrome at night, its propeller-shadows long black whirling stripes upon the runway's glassy luminescence. He had been imagining that he was Furtwängler, the Führer of the music, whose melody now came streaming into everyone's hearts; when suddenly he realized that after all he *could* be this; he too could own a baton encrusted with precious stones like Göring's; and he began to see war somewhat as our Führer must, which is to say not as the implementation of preconsidered operations, but as music in and of itself, pulsations of godlike creativity whose patterns are their own harmonies. And when his tanks clanked down the tree-lined streets of Kharkov (a feat which triggered a message of congratulations from prominent Ukrainians), he felt as if he were truly at the conductor's podium. What must it be like for the Führer on the reviewing stand at Nuremberg, when a hundred thousand Nazis chanted his name and anti-aircraft beams swiveled across the night? And now von Manstein had been elevated almost to that plane—not that he didn't deserve it. That made twelve already. How could he, Friedrich Paulus, become the thirteenth? After the reduction of Stalingrad, if the Führer did want that city, Sixth Army would press on to the Caspian Sea. Possibly, were his progress sufficiently rapid and his prisoners numerous enough, the Führer might remember him . . . Sitting down to his field-desk, he composed a message of congratulations to Field-Marshal von Manstein.

4

Running low and fast, with their guns pointed ahead like steel phalli, his men conquered more and more of Russia. That sullen land, raped by Cossacks Red and White, neighbor against neighbor, then scientifically starved by Comrade Stalin's dekulakization program, wanted only to sleep and quietly grow its buckwheat, but now Sixth Army was here and the Reds kept sniping and dying behind every ruin; somebody kept talking about roast chicken. The interrogated civilians denied that anyone here had ever been a commissar but pointed out all the Jews; these were instructed to go home and wait for the Einsatzgruppen, who'd arrive soon. He and Coca agreed that the Jews needed to be excluded from our national life; he accepted her assurances that in Romania the situation might be somewhat different. Coca had a wonderful power of making one feel the complexities of everything; on their honeymoon her soul had grown and budded around them both until he'd felt as if he were in a cherry arbor in summer, a deliciously stifling sensation of being overwhelmed; he had always longed to let himself go, sinking and spinning into something greater than himself; and his mind quite naturally worked to consider every facet of every question; so when he was with Coca, who transformed twenty facets into twenty thousand, he could get dizzy if he weren't careful; so he always avoided drawing her into his own perplexities; what he wasn't too proud to name her superiority would only have multiplied them. He abstained; he went forward, just as he had done last summer in Zhitomir and Kiev; he absorbed more of Russia under his tank-treads, and the enemy radio transmissions said: *Comrade Commander, I am asking for help!* or *Comrade General, what should we do now?* Up until now, their weakness had been that they kept going over to a rigid defensive. Now they'd finally learned to run away.

On 5.7.42 our forces began to enter Voronezh, while Paulus for his part rolled through Ostrogorzhsk. In effect, he'd smashed the Southern Front of General Timoshenko, whom he almost pitied. Phase I of Operation Blau had nearly been completed. The day before yesterday he'd taken another forty thousand prisoners. To the rear, a line of German soldiers lay dead and tumbled between their burning tanks. They would be buried, each one under a cross, and after the final victory our subject peoples could tend all the cemeteries. As for the dead Russians, the peasants would take care of them or not. A week from now there'd be crosses of lashed saplings, some of them even fashioned into spearheads, and kerchiefed old babushkas would come to pray over them, at least until the Einsatzgruppen detachments scared them off.

They encircled and annihilated two more enemy armies—a gain for which more Germans died. Three old women sat watching from a ruined house. In the long run, he was well aware, our manpower problem must become insoluble, but for now, Sixth Army still had many soldiers to spend.—Somehow we'll manage, Herr Lieutenant-General! That was what Major-General Schmidt always said. This Schmidt had been his chief of staff since June, and his energetic optimism made a favorable impression. Nonethless, how many more Soviet armies remained? On the eve of Operation Barbarossa, Fremde Heere Ost Gruppe I had calculated that there were no more than eleven of them in European Russia. The others—nine or ten, perhaps—wouldn't ever be moved into the zone of engagement, because Stalin feared a Japanese attack. So how many armies did that work out to? **Special formations: Numbers unknown,** concluded Fremde Heere Ost. **The clumsiness, schematism, the avoidance of decision and responsibility, these have not altered since the Finnish campaign.**

Stalin seemed to be withdrawing his forces. Perhaps he still imagined that Operation Blau was a feint. In any event, there was no decisive encounter, not yet, even as we launched Phase II.

On 6.7.42 we crossed the Don. On 9.7.42 our forces finally crushed all resistance in Voronezh, which is a very important railroad junction, and more flatcars heaped with Russian prisoners rolled westward to the concentration camps, thereby wrapping up Operation Wilhelm; but since that battle took four days, the Führer, so Paulus heard, expressed vehement displeasure with Field-Marshal von Bock. He was watching the calendar as much as everyone. After the misery of the Moscow campaign, everyone had learned better than to squander Russia's golden summer days. That was why Operation Blau needed to be completed by the end of October at the latest. Paulus could hardly contest that the Führer held every right to be exasperated. The enemy had used the delay to withdraw eastward in good order, so the capture of Voronezh, necessary as it surely had been, left a sour taste in Germany's devouring mouth. Kalach might not fall easily, either. According to Fremde Heere Ost Gruppe I, Army Group South, the enemy still had twelve infantry divisions and five armored brigades there. Although he was alone in the staff car, an embarrassed smile came to his lips. He did not want to be known as the man who couldn't take Kalach. Major-General Schmidt had already volunteered that in his opinion the soldiers of Sixth Army stood ready for even greater exertions. Uncertain whether to approve the man's zeal or rebuke an insinuation, Paulus replied, after a pause and perhaps a trifle drily: Sixth Army's willingness to make efforts lies beyond a doubt. That will be all for now, Schmidt.—He began to visit the front line more often than before, although, not being a grandstander such as Field-Marshals von Manstein and von Reichenau, he tried not to let his soldiers see him. He remembered his father overwatching everything he did; he refused to distrust people in that fashion. His biographer Goerlitz describes him as frequently looking exhausted and dusty during this period. He was in the midst of preparing Operation Fredericus II, which would obliterate the enemy strongpoint of Kupiansk. Coca would have worried about him, although she ought to have known how it was; two of her brothers had been officers. Sometimes Sixth Army was fired on from one of those Russian peasant huts ringed with earth, and rather than accept more delay, Paulus adopted the extravagant solution of an antitank round, because in war as in any other endeavor one must spend something to get something; in this case one spends time, manpower or materiel. Of these, time, golden time, was currently most precious. The slave laborers of the Ostlands could always produce more tank shells, but summer was going, going.

On 15.7.42, the Führer made an alteration in Operation Blau. He'd removed Field-Marshal von Bock from command of Army Group A on account of timidity and insubordination. (In my opinion, sir, said Major-General Schmidt, there was always something half-hearted about him.) But this was really a *pro forma* decision; von Bock's disgrace had actually occurred, as

Paulus remembered all too well, during that conference back in Poltava, on that hot creosote-scented day when everyone gathered around the snow-white map—and here Paulus suddenly recalled that his wife, who was really very well read, possessed a uniform edition, in similarly snow-white bindings, of the complete works of Pushkin; and one of these volumes (he could almost see it) was entitled *Poltava*. His memory for details approached the photographic: When he overgazed a map of, say, Stalingrad, various topographic features would recall to his mind the enemy troop concentrations at each strongpoint and the dispositions of Sixth Army which would be required to reduce them; in the case of *Poltava*, which remained literally a closed book to him (although he enjoyed it when Coca read to him, he'd never found much leisure for poetry, even in peacetime), his recollections had to do with mild German sunshine, whose bygone character invested it with more plenitude than it ever could have carried at the time; in that lost and now languorous-seeming epoch before our Führer came to power, those white volumes had spanned a bookshelf in their bedroom, and what he must be remembering, he supposed, was one of those summer mornings when Coca lay sleeping on his shoulder, and he with his far-sighted eyes picked out the title gilt-lettered on the spine of each white book, not in German; unlike most of us, he could sound out the Cyrillic alphabet, and although he didn't know what the words meant it was surprising how often this capability of transliteration taught him something useful, particularly nowadays, of course, when he inspected captured enemy documents; very likely he'd been a trifle bored but hadn't had the heart to wake Coca; where were the children? They must have been very little then. Ernst in particular always used to want to come into bed with them; the poor child suffered from nightmares. In fact, he'd once come in early one morning when he and Coca were making love; at first neither of them had noticed the slowly opening door; then the plump little face was looking up at them, woebegone and bewildered; thank God they'd had the sheet over them; that memory distressed him. And then another time he'd been making love with Coca and it had been a very rich time; he felt that her moans were a boat which was carrying them both slowly down some broad wide river of sunlight; then they were finished and Coca was kissing him, weeping with happiness; she was a very emotional woman; while he for his own part, gripped by the extreme clarity which often takes over a man in the very first instant after orgasm, lay fixing his eyes upon the bookshelf, where he saw the word ПОЛТАВА, Poltava. How many times in those years had he read the lettering on that particular volume without ever once troubling to open it? Often books of that nature contained frontispieces of old wars and such; it would have been interesting, come to think of it, to learn more about the history of this region. First invasions, then rebellions; he knew that much from military college. While Coca lay with her long soft hair across them both, sleepily licking his nipple, he deciphered ΠΟΛΤΑΒΑ again. Just then the door slowly, silently opened: Ernst was peeking in. Why was he remembering that now? He hadn't thought of those Pushkin volumes in years; where had Coca hidden them? It seemed as if so much had happened during that one instant when the strengthening sunshine happened to strike that particular book that the moment had been practically infinite; he almost supposed that he could see and feel every strand of Coca's hair that had been so warmly caressing them when Ernst crept in; and now, although his mind ranged over these details with a voluptuous completeness which itself approached infinity, all of this happened in the time it took to light another cigarette; then the orderly brought in the tray, polished like a mirror, upon which the communications of the day had been arranged, first the enemy situation report, then the signals intelligence report, both of them courtesy of Gehlen at Fremde Heere Ost, Gruppe I, Army Group B; but before he got to either, the orderly carried in a decrypted announcement from OKW at Poltava: The Führer had decided to strip him of Fourth Panzer Army, whose support thus far had greatly facilitated his lightning advance. Apparently someone had convinced OKW (he hoped it wasn't "the nodding ass") that Fourth Panzer should participate in the vast pincer movement against Rostov. This decision troubled Paulus; he'd already been sorry enough to see First Panzer go; without their help it would have taken him much longer to tie off the Barvenko salient, and now, with less manpower at his disposal, everything would be still more protracted; but orders are orders. Some of his officers complained; even Major-General Schmidt looked glum; but he had made up his mind to treat them all as we treat our Romanian allies—namely, with tactful firmness. He broadened his bridgehead at Kalach, which fell easily. The Führer was pleased; so he gathered from General Warlimont's signal. Now that he had a moment, he sent a message of friendship and commiseration to Field-Marshal von Bock, whose command had now been turned over to Colonel-General von Weichs; within two hours the Field-Marshal replied: *My dear Paulus, the important thing is to keep calm.* Evidently he would be assigned to Führer Reserve, God help him. Weary and dusty from another inspection of the front line, he wrote a quick note to Olga, enclosing greetings for his grandson and son-in-law; he advised her to get her Mercedes serviced sooner rather than later, in case there were problems in obtaining spare parts. Then he returned to the business of constructing and guiding his spearheads. On 23.7.42 we finally captured Rostov, after beating down vicious enemy resistance. (Kerchiefed old Russian women were struggling on either side of a bicycle to which buckets of water had been strapped; they staggered slowly through the volcanic dust between the ruins, then vanished. Why hadn't their High Command evacuated them? This negligence on Premier Stalin's part seemed contrary to the basic conduct of humanitarian operations.) Congratulating all of us on the successful fulfillment of Operation Blau, Phase II, the Führer canceled Phase III and commenced Operations Edelweiss and Heron. Operation Heron was a lightning attack on Stalingrad, and the man charged with that operation was Lieutenant-General Paulus. Operation Edelweiss was the continuation of our drive infinitely southeastward, for whose sake Paulus was now commanded to give up fifty percent of his ammunition and fifty percent of his fuel. No matter: Panzergruppen were on the way to help him! Whose would they be? Probably Colonel-General Hoth's. He had full confidence in that man. Unfortunately, aerial reconnaissance indicated that the enemy was taking full advantage of the delay (eighteen days) to regroup on the Volga, in that city called Stalingrad.

5

The *Great Soviet Encyclopedia* informs us that the city of Stalingrad, formerly Tsaritsyn, was founded on an island sometime in the sixteenth century, and this fairytale isolation and encirclement could not be more fitting. *During the seventeenth and eighteenth centuries,* we learn, *Tsaritsyn was a major center of the struggle of the people against feudal exploitation.* So far so good; and it gets better, for during the Civil War the defense of this place devolved on, among others, Comrade Stalin himself, and in the natural course of things his role there became retrospectively magnified, which is why it got named after him.— The forces of Adolf Hitler, having in the meantime destroyed two more Russian armies, now drew near the City of Stalin. Therefore, what was about to happen had to happen.

6

Lieutenant-General Paulus was not a cruel man, as may be proved by the fact that the Soviets never charged him with any war crimes. Immediately upon succeeding to command of Sixth Army, he'd canceled our late Field-Marshal von Reichenau's order of 10.10.41 to proceed with extreme measures against subhumans. Nonetheless, Lieutenant-General Paulus esteemed the effectiveness of terror raids: They broke an enemy population, and thereby ended war, more rapidly than other, supposedly more lenient measures. By the beginning of August he was fully engaged against First and Fourth Soviet Tank Armies on the Don River bend. His advance grew delayed; he found the so-called "annihilation battalions" especially troublesome. He shuffled maps and regiments, the long swastika flag hanging down above his headquarters there at Golubskaya-on-the-Don. The enemy proving superior in numbers if nothing else, our Führer sent Fourth Panzer Army back to Paulus's aid; they were approaching in good order from Kotel'niko. He drafted a friendly welcome to their commander, Colonel-General Hoth. Meanwhile, the orderly came in and refilled his silver cigarette case. Actually he wasn't feeling very well; for some weeks now he'd suffered from "the Russian sickness." No matter; he'd had dysentery in the last war, too. It was better not to inform Coca. At 0430 hours on 15.8.42 he commenced his offensive, shattering Fourth Soviet Tank Army. The Italians were showing a bit of funk; he sent Lieutenant-General Blumentritt over to regroup them. He advised Headquarters of the weakness of his northern flank, but they told him to press on without making demands. This hurt his feelings slightly, but he remembered what Field-Marshal von Bock would have said: The important thing is to keep calm. First Bach, then Mozart. Coca liked Mozart's operas more then he did; he preferred the instrumental music. On 22.8.42, he enjoyed a light moment with the officers when the radio announced that Brazil had declared war on the Reich; somebody remarked that Field-Marshal von Reichenau had always expressed a desire to visit Rio de Janeiro, and Paulus, wishing to deflect them from thoughts of the dead, whom they surely all missed (von Reichenau had never failed to remember Paulus's birthday), replied with a pleasant half-smile: Gentlemen, without a doubt the Brazilian campaign will have its compensations!—Major-General Schmidt laughed twice, *ha, ha,* while the others laughed longer; then the orderly poured Veuve Clicquot all around, in tiny little glasses of Bohemian crystal, after which they all went to bed early, because the next morning would be hectic; the twelve hundred bombers and strafing planes of Fourth Air Corps were scheduled to arrive at Stalingrad; and when they did, they killed forty thousand people, leaving skeletonized apartments in a red mist, oh, yes, as red as Cossack trousers, those corpses on broken plinths of ferroconcrete. The enemy radio was shouting: *Vokzal'naia Square, Deomstratsii Square* . . . Meanwhile, Sixth Army was already shelling the office of the District Soviet.

7

By 31.8.43, the city was nearly encircled. He'd already cut off most of Sixty-second Soviet Army. It was merely a question of time and manpower. General von Wietersheim, however, for some reason advocated withdrawal from Stalingrad. There was no need even to speculate on what the Führer would have said about that. Lighting a cigarette, assuring him that he was sorry, he relieved General von Wietersheim of his command at once, replacing him with Colonel-General Hoth. At the next staff conference his sleek and handsome officers sat reading newspapers together, their caps crisp and new, their sleeves perfectly creased as they awaited his instructions; on the matter of General von Wietersheim they all kept silent, excepting only Major-General Schmidt, who approved of the decision and tried to express his approval publicly and at length, until Paulus said: No doubt he was doing his duty as he saw it, Schmidt. That will be all.—His spearheads breached the enemy's front in the sector Vertyachii-Peskoravka, with Stukas screaming and bombing just forward of each assault. On 2.9.42, the Führer decreed that upon his entry into this troublesome city, all the males must be liquidated, presumably by shooting, and all females deported. Paulus was not in sympathy with this order. In any event, it could not be carried out immediately. That day a far more pleasant message entered on the silver tray; his old friend Colonel Metz wrote him (belatedly, it seemed, and then the card must have been held up by censorship and routing errors): *Let me congratulate you on your Knight's Cross—and it won't be long, sir, before the Field-Marshal's baton follows.* On 3.9.42 he crushed the feeble counterattack of Moskalenko's First Guards Army. He beat them back again on the fifth. Continuing enemy pressure compelled him to divert some of his troops to the northwest, among them his son Ernst, who was acquitting himself well in his tank regiment, he'd heard. He had ground down Sixty-second and Sixty-fourth Soviet armies almost to extinction. They said to him: Herr Lieutenant-General, sir, Yeremenko's digging in to resist us on Line G . . .

On 9.9.42, when the Führer forced Field-Marshal List to resign command of Army Group A for having gone over to the defensive, Lieutenant-General Paulus was perfecting the details of his all-out attack. At 0630 hours on 13.9.42, the assault on Stalingrad began: First Line O, the outermost defense perimeter; next, in concentric succession, Lines K, S and G, which was the innermost, the final bastion. His orderly kept wondering when *Signal* magazine would send their photographer; but there'd already been a nice spread on our resolute young Panzergrenadieren in their grey-green, holding up endless necklaces of bullets for the camera.

He intercepted requests from Sixty-second Soviet Army to withdraw to Line G.

First our Panzers penetrate the enemy's front; then they wheel round to encircle him. (He was almost entirely recovered from "the Russian sickness.") Next we strengthen the ring with infantry. We Germans have coined the perfect noun for this formation: a *Kessel,* a cauldron in which the enemy now begins to boil. If need be, which is to say, if the enemy retains any capability for breakout, we'll construct an inner ring out of more soldiers whose guns and ideology point ever inward. Bereft of supply, our victim must begin to perish now. Since every cook knows that meat stews faster in smaller chunks, we now inject spearheads of Panzers and infantry to subdivide the *Kessel* into mutually isolated zones, houses sliced open to reveal the people's soul. Each such concentric attack, successful or not, further wounds the enemy. His men are starving; his ammunition's almost gone. We slice him right down into tidbits, which we'll then devour. This comprised the working basis of Operation Heron.

Although the arrows of his advance were as shiny-perfect as the rivers of tank ammunition which still flowed from Germany's conveyor belts, it did not go quite as easily as usual, perhaps because the Führer had sent Panzer Grenadier Division Grossdeutschland away to the Westfront. That must have been why it took days instead of hours to wipe out the Red remnants who kept resisting in that grain elevator. Major-General Schmidt wondered aloud whether General von Wietersheim had spread defeatism among our troops before he'd been relieved. Paulus told him, perhaps a little sharply: You'd do better to worry about our supply situation. In an hour I'll expect your report.—If he could only disrupt their ferry system, that would be the end! They made their crossings at night, unfortunately, which put Air Fleet Four to far too much trouble. But anyway, what was night in Stalingrad, where the sky was black without surcease, the sun gone like last year's summer, black sun, black rain, moonlessly black sky of day and night, everyone coughing, the red gleam of reflected fire on the Volga as planes swooped down on the ferries at midnight, Russians screaming, Germans cursing, sirens sobbing, machine-guns marking time just as the broadcast metronome did in besieged Leningrad, long cattails of black smoke hanging as soft and fluffy as an opera diva's boa?

Fremde Heere Ost, Gruppe I, Army Group B intercepted another of Premier Stalin's midnight directives: Stalingrad was to be held at all costs. (Stalingrad was already smashed, of course, just like Leningrad's Warsaw Station.)

First air attack, then ground attack. Our Air Force supported him with heavy strikes on the south-central sector. He'd reduced Sixty-second Soviet Army to one percent of strength. But new enemy troops kept coming from Kotel'niko.

By your order, Herr Lieutenant-General, if we break through right here at Pavlovsk-Serafimovich—

Yes, he explained to them, but unfortunately, they have a hundred and sixty thousand men over there. That's two armies, gentlemen!

Herr Lieutenant-General, said Schmidt, I believe that between Kletskaya and Verkno-Kurmoyarskaya—

Unlike Field-Marshal von Rundstedt, who enjoyed dressing in a colonel's uniform for a lark, Paulus guarded his dignity. He didn't always reply to their suggestions. Just as we take a street in the daytime and the Russians take it back at night, so the forward zone of his own consciousness alternated between confidence and disappointment. The exhilaration of power which he never could have known in peacetime, the power to compose a few lines and ring for the orderly to take them away on the silver tray, or, if the case was urgent, to utter a dozen words into the field telephone, and then to lift his binoculars and *see* those words incarnated into bullets and bombs, what he felt then he hardly even could have confided to Coca, although as soon as they were together again she'd know; they shared everything. Meanwhile, he found himself in complete agreement with the aphorism of Field-Marshal von Manstein that *the safety of a tank formation operating in the enemy's rear largely depends on its ability to keep moving*. They could not keep moving in Stalingrad.

In fact, this urban fighting might well be considered a misuse both of his own abilities and of the army he commanded. To Paulus, who could not help but feel apprehension as well as resentment about the way the summer was spending itself, it would have been a comfort, to say the least, to leave these ruins behind him and rush again east or southeast across the golden steppes (whose most common herb seemed to be *Artemisia pauciflora)*, liquidating enemy troop concentrations in fair and open combat. And to think he could have gone to Africa instead! (Keep your fingers out of that pie, Coca had said with the look he dreaded.) Personally, he preferred to tread a fine line between Field-Marshal von Kluge, who liked to keep his Panzer corps on a short leash so that they could liquidate any encircled concentrations, and General Guderian, who would rather send them ahead to shatter Russian fronts into morsels for our infantry, for our blond, tanned boys to eat for breakfast.

Lighting a cigarette, he broke the seal of the enemy situation report. Ten meters away lay, God alone knows why, the corpse of a Ukrainian official in old-style velvet trousers. First Beethoven, then Bach. Fremde Heere Ost Gruppe I, Army Group B advised him that while an assault against his deep flank could not be ruled out, or perhaps the odd attack on our allies' weakly held bridgeheads, the Russians' winter offensive would occur, if it occurred at all, far to the north, in Army Group Center's zone—most likely in the vicinity of Moscow. This information had been confirmed by the Abwehr, whose Max Organization in Sofia had full access to enemy signals. He didn't believe it or disbelieve it.

On 12.9.42, accompanied by General Weichs, he fully expressed his worries regarding the narrowness of his front to the Führer himself, who'd now moved headquarters eastward from Wolf's Lair to Werewolf, just north of Vinnitsa on the Berdichev road. Unfortunately, he could hardly ask to be given priority just now, not only because, as he knew quite well, he was liked rather than loved by the Führer, but also because the entire Eastern campaign had become, as Warlimont whispered, stalemated. He didn't want to give anybody, neither his subordinates nor the Führer, the impression that he took matters too seriously, because that would only weaken the esteem in which he was held; nonetheless, Operation Northern Lights, as probably even Field-Marshal Keitel must admit, had failed to subdue Leningrad, which we'd besieged for a year now; and the results of his own effort, Operation Heron, remained inconclusive; finally, Operation Edelweiss had stalled in the Caucasus. The greatest victory of that offensive thus far, namely the conquest of Maikop, had melted away in our mouths because when Army Group A rolled and clattered into that city, they'd found its refineries utterly wrecked by the retreating Jewish Bolsheviks. The Führer was said to have been seriously disappointed, given our growing petroleum requirements. Still, the enemy must be worse off than we; they'd now lost eighty percent of their oil. First disruption, then dispossession; that was the program of Operation Blau.

Like all of us, Lieutenant-General Paulus retained a certain basic confidence in his own acumen. Back in December 1940 his war-games had predicted our exact troop dispositions around Moscow in October 1941. He'd been complimented for his accuracy by Field-Marshal von Reichenau personally. Surely this counted for something. Then there was his Iron Cross, both First Class and Second, from the previous world war, his Knight's Cross of the Iron Cross from Kharkov and his position as commanding officer of Sixth Army. In December 1940 he had also predicted that Operation Barbarossa might last longer than a single summer. The Führer had flown into a rage and shouted: There is not going to be a winter campaign!—So that was a sore point between them. Paulus could never mention winter campaigns now.

Werewolf, that long, perfect rectangle oriented southeast, was subdivided by inner fences into three controlled zones. He doubted that they'd had time to lay thousands of mines around it, as they'd done at Wolf's Lair; anyhow this was not something which one asked. So many of these secret headquarters he'd visited now—the steep high roofs of Wolf's Gorge in Belgium, the damp bunkers of Tannenberg in the Black Forest, then Wolf's Lair, Werewolf, and how many more? Everything was concrete and welded steel plate, the curtains of the rare windows always drawn. At his side, General Weichs swallowed nervously. There was a barber shop here at Werewolf and a sauna, he'd heard; he'd hoped to have time to refresh himself there before meeting with the Führer; he tried to learn from the S.D. man in the front seat how much time he might have, but the latter smilingly replied: They tell me nothing, Herr Lieutenant-General! And perhaps it's better that way; the less I know, the less I can fail!—Paulus laughed a little, but didn't care for the man's cynicism. The central zone, the one deepest inward, now swallowed up the car; and General Weichs was led off to obey a surprise summons from the nodding ass, while Paulus left his dagger and pistol with the S.D. man, following his ᛋᛋ conductors through the barbed wire to the second checkpoint, and then they led him between the trees to the teahouse, where he was coolly greeted by Martin Bormann. Everything possessed an oily gleam, like the leather saddles of our cavalry.—If the General would kindly wait a moment, said Bormann, the stenographers have almost completed their change of shift. You're welcome to gamble in the casino.

I don't gamble, returned Lieutenant-General Paulus.

I might have known, said Bormann. By the way, when the Führer's finished with you I'll need to ask you a few questions about your wife Elena, *Coca* I believe you call her . . .

He requested permission to use the lavatory. There he quickly checked the fineness of his shave and pulled on fresh white gloves. The 1:300,000-scale map of the enemy railroad system, stamped **Geheim**, with annotations in his own hand (written very largely, for our Führer's ageing eyes), was still where it should be, in the outermost pocket of his briefcase, which he unlatched so as to get at it more easily when the Führer's eyes would be on him; thinking better of this, he closed the briefcase again, for the sake of a smarter appearance. As always when he was about to enter our Führer's presence, he felt so nervous that he nearly vomited. He really wished that General Weichs were here. Bormann's mention of Coca, which was the sort of ploy that man was infamous for—what could he have against her? she was Romanian; our Romanian allies were received practically as equals!—had further unnerved him; he scarcely knew what was appropriate in such circumstances, not being a *political general.* Had he not been surprised in that way, he would definitely have replied with something biting. A protective rage began to rise up within him, and he resolved to ignore Bormann's demand. This made him feel better. (What precisely was the difficulty? Was it that she was Greek Orthodox?) Now that he'd turned Bormann's words over and over, he'd fully realized that there was nothing to fear from this brute, who would never have dared to be so rude to Field-Marshal von Reichenau—why, he would have gotten throttled! Paulus smiled palely. The ᛋᛋ-man was waiting in the corridor outside. He must assert himself; he'd do his utmost to make the Führer realize—

Do come in, Paulus, said the Führer, rising to shake his hand. Have you eaten?

Not yet, my Führer.—He bowed and clicked his heels.

Well, don't worry; they'll lay a place for you. It'll be vegetarian, I'm afraid. Is this your first time in Vinnitsa?

Once, before the war, my wife and I—

Well, it's a filthy city, said the Führer, his voice rising.—The Ukrainians, yes, a thin Germanic layer, and below that, dreadful material. The Jews: the most horrible thing imaginable. The towns choked in dirt—oh, I've learned quite a bit in these few weeks! If Slavs had ruled for a decade or two over the Old Reich, everything would be lice-infested and decayed . . .

Without a doubt, said white-gloved Paulus.

They're holding Vlasov over there, the Führer went on. You know Vlasov, don't you?

Yes, in fact I fought against him at—

Right over there, on the other side of town! And they tell me I have to make use of him! Can you believe it?

No, my Führer, I hadn't heard.

Thank God you're not one of those *political generals*! All right, then, Paulus, here's the map. Does this line accurately lay out your position?

Just a moment . . . Yes, my Führer; it's entirely correct.

That's good. I had to ask, because one can't trust anyone these days. You wouldn't believe how my orders get misconstrued! And then they try to hoodwink me. They try to force false information down my throat. But do you know what, Paulus? I'm going to give them all something to choke on!

By your order, my Führer.

Well. We have to hope that Stalin can't repeat his counterattack of 1920, remarked our Führer, who was a military genius. After all, you're quite right. Keitel! Where the devil is Keitel?

Here I am, my Führer—

And now he realized that General Weichs hadn't been allowed in. The nodding ass probably didn't even realize why he'd been told to call Weichs here and then send Weichs there. Well, it wasn't as if Weichs were needed, exactly; it was just that when one was alone it seemed more difficult to hang on to oneself in the Führer's presence . . .

Lieutenant-General Paulus is concerned about his front, Keitel. Do you see on this map how shallowly he's echeloned?

Yes, my Führer—

My dear Paulus, if even Keitel can see the danger, nothing more need be said. Keitel, fetch me my eyeglasses over there.

Crimsoning, Paulus bowed and clicked his heels.

Now, that's all very well, and I'll send help in good time, but for now you'll just have to make do. How are your sons, by the way?

As far as I'm aware, they both continue to do their duty to their country and to you, my Führer.

I've heard great things about Friedrich. When the time comes, perhaps he'll take part in the conquest of England. I'm expressing myself openly on this point. And Ernst is under your command?

Yes, he is, my Führer.

An officer?

Yes, my Führer, with a tank regiment—

He's very lucky. I hope he won't get a swelled head!

My Führer, I assure you that he receives exactly the same treatment as any other soldier, and to spare him any unpleasantness among his comrades I make a point of never—

That's very wise and cautious of you, my dear Paulus. Yes, yes, it's always better to keep one's distance. Where he is now?

Right here on the map, my Führer, about four kilometers from the Mamayev Kurgan. He's been assigned to the—

I envy you, Paulus, for having two fine boys who are ready to spend themselves for Germany. They're twins, aren't they?

They are, my Führer.

When a woman bears twins, that's pure heroism! Your Coca is fine breeding stock!

Thank you, my Führer—

Quite stylish, also. You made a good choice. Don't worry about either one of your sons. Warlimont complained to you that we're eighteen percent understrength, didn't he? You see, I hear everything; I have my feelers out! Well, the troops will be found when we need them. We don't need them now. But as soon as we've choked the life out of Leningrad . . .

Yes, my Führer, said Paulus. He longed to point out the enemy antitank positions along the Mechetka-Volga axis; where they were, the Führer's map showed only whiteness. Moreover, Sixth Army's flanks were screened with inferior satellite troops.

Frankly, said the Führer with an abrupt change of tone, I'm disappointed that Stalingrad's still on the map. In a couple of weeks I'm going to make a speech at the Sportpalast. What shall I tell them? Will you have cleaned up Stalingrad by then?

If the Air Force had only—

My dear Paulus, we're in complete agreement about that, the Führer said. Not one of us has been tough enough. The cowards and bleeding-hearts will never understand us . . .

With a loving smile, he clapped Paulus on the shoulder; and Paulus experienced what Major-General Schmidt liked to call *the greatest happiness any of our contemporaries can experience—that of serving a genius.*

8

He stood on a plain of rubble and discussed the situation with Lieutenant-General Pfeiffer. Schmidt was at his shoulder listening. His assault of the thirteenth had won Sadovaya Station and the edge of Minim. It had, in fact, been a perfect attack, and if Coca were here he would have told her exactly how he'd arrayed his divisions and why he'd closed his pincers where he did;

after the war it would be pleasant to give a lecture about it to the officer cadets. The next stage was to take the summit of the Mamayev Kurgan. He'd achieved multiple penetrations along the entire Red front, his spearheads swelling outwards like the arms of an Iron Cross, then linking up to encircle the enemy in convenient-sized strangleholds. Now the enemy was Thirteenth Soviet Guards; they were harassing him from the eastern bank. Very well; he would take Stalingrad inch by inch and never let it go.

Hatchcovers up, his tanks paraded down the ruined streets, crushing rubble which sparkled blindingly under the dusty white sky. Whiteness glared through the hollow vertebral columns of charred buildings. White dust marked their footfalls.

Not much to report, Herr Lieutenant-General. We've captured the Univermag department store. And we've killed Fedoseyev and his staff—

Good. Were there any maps?

I'll check with Section Intelligence, Herr Lieutenant-General.

Report back to me.

Herr Lieutenant-General . . .

What is it?

They keep digging in their tanks so we can't see them, and then—

I'm aware of that. Would more ammunition make a difference?

Yes, sir.

I'll do what I can for you. Now, which group liquidated Fedoseyev?

Here are their names, sir.

I'll put them all in for decorations.

By your order, Herr Lieutenant-General!

A soldier screamed, and blood came beautifully from his heart. The rubble clinked faintly. It was no use trying to find the sniper.

On that same day, 21.9.42, he destroyed two hostile brigades and a regiment, razing the enemy strongpoints with his tanks, crushing those screaming Russians under his treads. He instructed Major-General Schmidt to put more pressure on Headquarters about our ammunition situation. He sent a postcard to Field-Marshal von Reichenau's widow, the Countess von Maltzan, assuring her that her husband's name remained on Sixth Army's lips. And now he must prepare to attack the Red October Tractor Works.

Two nights later, he celebrated his birthday with a few of his staff officers while a counterattack of Siberians wrested a few meters of Volga frontage out of his hands. He obliterated those Siberians, of course. Until he had the Volga he couldn't split the Reds' defenses. He had repeatedly drawn everyone's attention to that fact. But his exhausted men couldn't recover the ground they'd lost. (Somehow we'll manage, sir, Major-General Schmidt consoled him.) He understood, forgave; he permitted them to remain in place, with their weapons at the ready. Had he acted any differently, the way that the Field-Marshal von Reichenau, for instance, would have acted, let alone Schörner or those other hatchet-men, they'd have been quite shocked. But they were not even thankful; whatever fate sends us quickly becomes us, and we grow blind to what we might otherwise have been. And how else should it be? If we could see ourselves as capable of being different, then how resentful, or else in the opposite case how fearful that would leave us!

He took the long view. He felt extreme apprehension about the future security of his deep northern flank. It was unwise for us to rely upon the Romanians. He couldn't explain that to Coca, of course.

First the birthday cake from OKW, then toasts all around. Retiring to his quarters, he lit a cigarette and began reading through the signals reports. Later on he'd open the card from Coca, which had actually arrived on last week's airlift. Apparently the Russians were now digging in seventy rifle divisions and eighty armored formations, although where they'd gotten them nobody knew. To wipe them out, he might have to draw further manpower from his already attenuated flank troops. His vision blurred; his ageing eyes were having trouble focusing on the dispositions. Our Führer had demonstrated to him how necessary it was to complete Operation Heron soon, in order to link up with Army Group A before winter. And doubtless the Führer was receiving records of his behavior! For all he knew, Schmidt was one of the people reporting on him. Moreover, that annoying Colonel-General Richtofen at Air Fleet Four, a man he'd always treated decently, kept ringing up to advise him: Just one more push, my dear Paulus.—One more push! What did he know about it? And why wasn't Air Fleet Four darkening the skies of Stalingrad as much as they used to? Nonetheless, on 29.9.42, lighting another cigarette, he sent in Thirty-eighth Infantry, One Hundredth Infantry, Sixtieth Motorized and his best-rested regiments of Sixteenth Panzer, hoping to choke off the enemy's Orlovsky salient, which he did on 7.10.42, spending lives by the thousand in order to achieve this necessary result: He'd now compressed the Russians' front to a maximum depth of twenty-five hundred meters. They were truly finished now.

The aerial reconnaissance report informed him of a large enemy ammunition dump on the east bank of the Volga, just opposite the Red October Works. He requested that the Luftwaffe excise it, and there were two bombing raids, but no one could tell him whether it had been wiped out; it might have been camouflaged.

Again the Romanians warned him that they were not receiving full supplies. Evidently they counted on his sympathy, since Coca was a countrywoman of theirs. He promised to inform OKW (and did in fact inform Schmidt). Resupply, unfortunately, did not lie entirely within his power. Moreover, he was well aware that OKW was naturally inclined when resources were scarce to favor us over our allies, due to a certain variation in the latters' fighting qualities.

He spied new enemy antiaircraft regiments near the Volga islands . . .

He was not a *political general,* but he'd heard secretly through a subordinate of Warlimont's that the Führer meant to give him General Jodl's position as soon as he'd taken Stalingrad.

9

The second assault likewise went badly. The enemy repelled him with machine-guns and Molotov cocktails. But his spearheads reached the Volga. This really meant the end for the Red Army; he was thrilled when he thought of what Coca would say. She, who'd grown up with only the best opportunities and possessions, deserved this triumph now. In six weeks at the outside he'd be telling her all about it; that was beyond doubt; and Coca, whose reflected movements in the mirror when she was brushing her hair still took his breath away, would understand and approve of all that he'd done. Major-General Schmidt stopped by to express his congratulations in advance, as he put it. Sixth Army had cleared its name! Paulus made a note to ask the orderly whether there would be enough Veuve Clicquot for every officer in Sixth Army to have a glass. Next he resolved the case of Private Dietrich, who'd been condemned to death by shooting because he'd feigned a leg injury. Paulus ordered X-rays; much to Dr. Braunstein's amazement the tibia was actually fractured; with Bach on the gramophone he cleared all charges against Private Dietrich, considered, smiled a little, and remanded the boy home for six weeks, so that he wouldn't develop bitter feelings against Sixth Army. That night as he closed his eyes to sleep he could see again those brilliant white-skinned volumes of Pushkin on the bookshelf, with the sun glancing in on *Poltava,* and once more he wondered where she'd hidden them, and then for the first time he wondered whether she'd ever read any of them, and just before he fell asleep he glimpsed Ernst's sad, scared, grubby little face peeping in. Ernst was probably grubby again now, like all the other frontline men. Awaking suddenly, Paulus offered up a soundless prayer for the safety of both his sons. Then he ignited the lantern and bent over the enemy situation map (1:300,000 scale). On the sixteenth, as his columns whipped south in an attempt to encircle Sixty-second Soviet Army, an ambush of sunken, camouflaged T-34 tanks blew them to bits. He sent in the five new Pioneer battalions which the Führer had given him. Most of those boys died, unfortunately. On 18.10 his infantry captured the Tramvayna street line. On his inspection tour he spied one of his soldiers twirling round on his finger the blue and red cap of an NKVD officer, doubtless "sent to the rear." In some jurisdictions those caps were green, he believed. The design was, in his opinion, garish. For some reason, he was unable to put Olga's new dress out of his mind. The letter from Coca had said: *Olga seems to be in good health, although I gather she is having financial troubles. No more trips to Paris for her! Prices are going up everywhere. You wouldn't believe how much butter costs. The only good news is that Robert has won a prize for his part in the anti-Jewish pantomime. He is such a good child, so intelligent and so willing to please. I hope he won't get dizzy with success! Frau Reiting has just come to me in tears; apparently her son fell in action at Leningrad. How do you think I can comfort her? She has always been so nice to us, especially to Olga. I will add her to my prayers. I have heard nothing from Friedrich, and am quite worried. Has he written to you? Yesterday a short letter came from Ernst; he says it's been a long while since he's seen you.* The left side of his mouth twitched a trifle. *Surely you could ask someone to find out if he is all right. I still pray for you every day and every night. Has it snowed there yet? All my kisses to you. I continue to believe in you and in our Führer* (the last four words he knew she'd written for the censors). Not making his presence known, he ordered that congratulations and cigarettes be distributed all around. His order of the day explained that everything would proceed more smoothly now that the Tramvayna line was in our hands.

On 21.10 he sent in Seventy-ninth Infantry against the Red October and Barrikady factories. What he really needed to do was shore up General Dumitrescu of Third Romanian Army, but our Führer still had not responded to his request for reinforcements. For now he had to neglect Third Romanian, since the battle on the threshold of the Red October Works required full attention. Specifically, his boys were dying in unusual numbers—as were the Reds, of course. The orderly brought him fresh white gloves on the silver tray. Major-General Schmidt came just to say: We all believe in you, sir.—They were now approaching that moment in any close battle when the wills of attackers and defenders alike have been nearly broken, so that one great effort on one side or the other will suffice to decide the struggle. It was now that he especially regretted the loss of those forces which the Führer had redirected to the Caucasus. But Lieutenant-General Paulus was not a quitting sort of man. Opening his silver cigarette case, he lit a match, trying to work out everything thoroughly, keeping close account of frontage and distribution. It was quite complicated, actually; he almost called in Schmidt to help him. The Dzherzhinskii district was now essentially in our hands; the Red October Works couldn't resist any longer; that day he called in seven hundred dive-bombing attacks on it; Spartanovka was about to cave in. In that month we find him writing to his old comrade Lutz: *The great thing now is to hit the Russian so hard a crack that he won't recover for a very long time.* The sentiment was banal, the goal practical. Of such stuff are effective soldiers made. To Coca he wrote that Ernst's tank regiment was performing very creditably; unfortunately, there was no time to pay the lad a visit, but she needn't worry about him; if anything had happened he would have heard. He asked her to send Olga his kisses; he felt it incumbent on him to advise that young lady one more time of the dangers of exceeding one's resources. To Friedrich, the other son, he wrote a brief letter of love and encouragement; Friedrich was in Africa now with Field-Marshal Rommel. First Beethoven on the gramophone, then a cigarette, then the enemy signals report, courtesy of Fremde Heere Ost, Gruppe I, Army Group B. He had to smile; Major-General Gehlen was so good at being plausible. The analysis of Red Army signals bore out Gehlen's assertion that the productive capacity of what remained of Russian Europe had been essentially obliterated.

Shooting rockets out of windows, the Soviet enemy, their ammo belts slung across broken girders, popped up to hurl stick-grenades, then ducked back into jagged-toothed caves. Soviet factory workers charged with guns in their hands, dying almost uselessly, but not quite, because every time three or a dozen of them fell, a German did, too. There were always more Russians; his prisoners now everlastingly quoted to him the words of Zoya the Partisan, whom we'd executed for sabotage last winter: *You can't hang all hundred and ninety million of us!*—There were only eighty million Germans. Last week he'd pointed that out to Schmidt, who merely smiled and replied: I'm sure we'll manage one way or another, sir.

First the daily enemy situation report, then the signals intelligence report. Unfortunately, we no longer possessed enough Heinkel-IIIs to continue aerial reconnaissance on as frequent a basis as before. The enemy radio was saying: *Keep a tighter grip on your tanks.* But what tanks did they have? Toward the end of September, their transmissions had begun very occasionally to refer to some far-off Operation Uranus. Paulus, who had been justly credited for the complete success of Operation Shark, the plan which had tricked Russia with a buildup of forces on the western front just before we launched Barbarossa (even Coca had been impressed), scented danger, not on his own sector, to be sure, but it might well prove to be a threat to Army Group Center. Field-Marshal von Reichenau would have let Group Center take care of itself; Field-Marshal von Reichenau for that matter would not even have bothered to study those enemy transmissions, but Lieutenant-General Paulus, ever considerate and conscientious even to his own detriment, sent a message in cipher to Fremde Heere Ost Gruppe I, Army Group B, to warn them about it. They never replied, which first bewildered, then offended him. He knew that behind his back many generals called him "the office assistant." They found him womanish; they equated him with that laughably fat and bustling Field-Marshal Keitel at OKW; they said he had no dash, no experience, no right to command Sixth Army. Their opinions shamed him more and more. Nobody except Coca had ever expressed any appreciation for Operation Shark, although it must have saved thousands of German lives. Well, that was their business, but they really ought to be more careful. When Russians are involved, reconnaissance in force will invariably escalate into a general offensive if it succeeds. No one seemed to comprehend this, not even Schmidt. Anyhow, all mentions of Operation Uranus soon faded from enemy communications. Lighting another cigarette, he made a note to query Major-General Gehlen directly about it, just as soon as—

Mamayev Kurgan back in enemy hands, Herr Lieutenant-General!

Connect me with Air Fleet Four, please.

By your order, Herr Lieutenant-General!

He called in another bombing attack, but the bombs didn't dislodge them. He stared at the map.

He changed his mind now almost as often as the railroad station changed hands.

The next day they excitedly told him: Attack, Herr Lieutenant-General! About two divisions, with one or two tank brigades—

On the Mamayev Kurgan?

Yes, Herr Lieutenant-General. They're pushing us back—

They're T-60s and T-70s, aren't they?

I'll check, sir.

No, take me there.

By your order, Herr Lieutenant-General . . .

No, we'll send in armored support, he decided. And please tell Schmidt to report to me immediately.

Herr Lieutenant-General, what should we tell the men?

To press on toward the final victory, he replied, putting on his glasses.

In confidence, a certain Lieutenant-General asked him in a whisper whether he himself remained certain of this final victory.

So long as the Führer is kept precisely informed, he replied.

10

Silhouettes on the dark front struggled with one another in hatred, grief and anguish, while munitions rushed overhead like glowing planets. At 0800 hours on a morning as cold and damp as a trench, the third assault failed. The left side of his face twitched. Some of his officers dared to imply that he should have led the charge, as Field-Marshal von Reichenau would have done; he coldly remarked that the commander of an army can accomplish more with maps than by dancing like a madman in the forefront. (Major-General Schmidt smiled politely but did not laugh.) He'd injected eleven divisions and eighty tanks into the battle; now these were bent and blunted: His running low-bent troops ran no more. His duty at the moment was to restore confidence to the front line. Soon winter would come, and then they would be filling the radiators of their vehicles with alcohol as they had done last year outside Moscow. First Stalingrad, then Baku. They would be shivering; they would be wrapping socks around their woolen gloves. There was no hope for Germany if she failed to continue forward in every direction. No doubt at OKW they were now murmuring in the Führer's ear: Before he got Sixth Army, he never even commanded a regiment!—But Lieutenant-General Paulus was too well bred to speak ill of anyone, no matter what he might think. In Colonel Heim's assessment, he was *a slender, rather over-tall figure, whose slight stoop seemed somehow to be a gesture of goodwill toward those of lesser stature*. This was true, and so was Coca's eternal characterization: Sweetheart, you're simply too good for those people.

He didn't swim rivers, the way von Reichenau used to in Poland. Perhaps that was why they didn't respect him.

They said to him: This defensive mission is contrary to the German soldier's nature.

He explained that Sixth Army was still making progress, although, to be sure, that progress had become as slow as a charge through heavy snow. From the east bank of the Volga, enemy artillery kept murdering his troops. The bombers couldn't do anything about that.

General von Schwederer sought to argue with his strategy. Paulus relieved him of his command.

He pointed out to Schmidt that the ammunition situation might soon get urgent. Schmidt replied, reproachfully smiling: I telephone them about it every day, sir, and all they ever say is, *when will you fellows take Stalingrad?*

First Beethoven, then a cigarette. He composed another message to the Führer, warning of Sixth Army's declining infantry strength. The front was now very sparsely manned; he thought it best to consolidate the positions of Army Group B against the human vectors of that Bolshevist ideology which had the power to corrode and decompose everything.

11

Thanks to our Führer's standing orders he could prepare no defense in depth; the front line could never be abandoned, so practically every man had to hold the front line. One enemy breakthrough anywhere, and his forces could be encircled. And such breakthroughs were inevitable. A German general who survived the war and found haven in the apartheid of South Africa has recalled: *Practically every Russian attack was preceded by large-scale infiltration, by an "oozing through" of small units and individual men. In this kind of warfare the Russians have not yet found their masters.*

What was he supposed to do? At last he was summoned again to the presence of the Führer, who would surely give him the appropriate operational recommendation.

12

In the first and most glorious year of Operation Barbarossa, Paulus, then Deputy Chief of Staff for the Army High Command, found himself flown to Wolf's Lair, which was then, as it was now and would again be intermittently, the Führer's headquarters. I have already told you that Wolf's Lair was a series of clammy concrete bunkers, sometimes four of them, sometimes ten, all half-sunk in the earth of East Prussia, their interiors softened with wooden paneling. Wolf's Lair smelled of cooking and of boots. With its thirty-odd antiaircraft guns and its arsenal of light machine-guns, antitank guns, smart new flamethrowers of the latest make, Wolf's Lair was very, very safe; they even had guards at the private cinema. Wolf's Lair was, in a very real sense, the soul of Germany.

On several occasions, Paulus had met with General Warlimont and Colonel von Lossberg to plan what should be seized after the capture of Moscow. It was generally agreed that the bulk of our armed forces could then be withdrawn from the Ostfront, for deployment in Africa or England. Afterwards, he'd been invited for an evening of listening to records in the tea-house car, the Führer calling: "Siegfried," first act! He'd seemed to enjoy almost everything in those days; it wasn't just all the not yet undone victories, but he hadn't yet suppressed the Austrian in him, the charming compliments, the hand-kissing of women, etcetera. Paulus, expecting another uncomfortable evening of being slighted, had fallen in love with the man's self-confidence, which Field-Marshal von Reichenau had also possessed, to be sure, but in a lesser allotment; for when the Führer began speaking about the future, whatever he described seemed to come close and embody itself into something far more alluring than our sweetest fantasy; Moscow *would* be captured; we had both the will and the superiority; therefore, Moscow was nearly, in effect, captured. Only through the Führer could any of this come into being.

But now he'd begun to be afraid, and so he relied all the more upon the Führer to set him right, to help him see how in fact these conquests could still be accomplished. Without the Führer, it was hard to imagine that we would ever, for instance, take Moscow.

This time there was no SS escort; instead, they gave him a day pass, and a single S.D. man led him around the casino to make a right turn at Martin Bormann's bunker (whose blinds writhed slightly as he passed; he saw an eye staring angrily at him out of darkness), but then it turned out that the S.D. man had made a mistake; our Führer expected him at the communications center. There'd just been a practice gas alert, which hadn't gone well; the gong failed to ring on time.

They permitted him to freshen up in the bathhouse, where he met Field-Marshal von Manstein. With the water-pressure as loud upon the concrete as an artillery barrage, the other man whispered in his ear: Paulus, it's hopeless here, unfortunately. Don't expect to find any real discussion. He no longer shakes anyone's hand . . .

Terrified, Paulus replied: And he won't permit me to withdraw! If I'd at least receive the reserves I've been promised!

Ah, whispered Field-Marshal von Manstein with a compassionate smile, this policy of covering everything and surrendering nothing usually leads to the defeat of the weaker party.

But don't most strategies lead to the defeat of the weaker party?

If that were true, strategy would be no science. There's the soap.

Now for the bowing and the clicking of heels, the gaggle of generals waiting to see the Führer—first greetings, then lies.

All of us who survived the winter of '41 learned the hard way that any caliber smaller than a hundred and fifty millimeters is ineffective, because snow will absorb all the shell fragments!

And then I made them stand at attention all night! I said to them, look me in the eye, you cowards! I told them that next time they'd better stand fast! I . . .

. . . in a ghetto now, at least in Warsaw. We'll soon find it necessary to . . .

Fortunately, our V-weapons are nearly ready for deployment.

As he spoke with them about his own situation, Paulus found himself striving to imitate the grey dignity and half-shut eye of Field-Marshal von Manstein.

Let's turn to the cardinal problem, gentlemen. After the USSR is defeated . . .

Halder had been replaced by Zeitzler, who was pontificating and puffing himself up: Once we've erased Leningrad and Moscow from the map, and seized all the oil reserves of the Caucasus, the Führer intends if possible to construct a gigantic line of defense and let the eastern campaign rest there.

Warlimont rolled his eyes. Taking Paulus aside, he murmured that he was very concerned about the way that the Führer had dispersed Sixth Army's forces.

We must accept that risk to the full, said Lieutenant-General Paulus.

First Warlimont, then Bormann; first another identification check, then another conference with the Führer, whose eyes were now as sinister as the black crosses on our airplanes' wings.

Paulus, I'll never forget that time back in '21 when the Communists tried to break up my speech at the Hofbräuhaus! I made it clear to my Brownshirts that today they'd have to show their loyalty to the bitter end. I said that not a man of us would leave that hall unless we got carried out *dead*! I warned them that if I saw anybody play the coward, I myself would rip off his armband . . .

Yes, my Führer.

The Russians are finished.

Paulus went whiter than a German tank.

13

Swiveling arrows on the military map led his aspirations this way and that. Sixth Army's three assaults had failed to seal off the enemy forces; that was beyond a doubt. Meanwhile, trapped and concentrated in the ruined city, his troops continued to suffer terribly as a result of direct fire from massed enemy guns. The attrition shocked him. The enemy had now begun to challenge his Romanian flank troops; by 4.10.42, while he was still trying to crush Sixty-second Soviet Army once and for all, they'd already seized ground along the axis of the lakes Barmantsak-Tsatsa-Sarpa. Worse yet, those Romanians had permitted their artillery to be captured! As much as it humiliated him, there was nothing for it now but to ask the Führer for new operational and tactical reserves—an innovation for which we must credit Julius Caesar; so Paulus had learned at the General Staff Academy. But where were the reserves? Couldn't he at least get a few ϟϟ-troops to stiffen the line? (He shared Field-Marshal von Manstein's high regard for the march discipline of the Death's Head Division.) Oh, the outcome now seemed as inky as the smoke from burning oil as his young Germans in their wide-flaring helmets peered ever more anxiously around the broken walls. The main thing was to press on. He really had to lean on Schmidt now to keep things rolling; nor did the other officers seem to appreciate how bad it was. Peering anxiously through his field-glasses, he spied a silhouetted swirl of Russian greatcoats and rifles as their infantry ran to the attack; and then, precisely at his signal, our machine-guns and flamethrowers obliterated them. First defense, then counterattack: Here we came, running low, crouching over ridges in the smoky ruins, aiming into the smoke at the half-obscured bones of the city where enemy vermin also waited; his son Ernst never knew that Lieutenant-General Paulus was following the progress of his tank through his field-glasses; a certain corporal whose hobby was committing Bach's cantatas to memory had confided that Ernst was one of the bravest soldiers he'd ever seen.—For him it's a question of honor, the corporal said.—That night he wrote down those words in a letter to Coca. Persons unafflicted with his knowledge of the finitude of the triangular flags still shiny and unworn in their boxes in the OKH reserves—and among those unafflicted persons he counted Major-General Schmidt—might well assume, on the basis of, say, the Nuremberg rally back in 11.9.38, when the Führer spoke to a hundred and twenty thousand Storm Troopers, whose tombstone shoulders and metal mushroom necks dwindled symmetrically and forever all the way to the concrete island on which our faraway

Führer stood, with three titanic swastika banners at his back, towering much higher than the trees, that more men and more men could eternally be found; but so many men lay dead now! We *needed* the shaveheaded Cossacks on our side; we had some of them but we needed all the rest, and every Ukrainian male sixteen years and older; all the females had better dig ditches; we needed to take our reserves where we could find them, but unfortunately the Führer said . . . Paulus remembered how the medieval streets of Nuremberg had been literally paved with marching helmeted men for the rally of '36; he'd been there; Coca had been at his side, dressed in velvet; he'd pridefully heard the horns and watched the upraised rifles of that perfect column ten abreast whose steel-shod footfalls clinked as melodiously as Wagner's Siegfried forging his sword; he remembered the grand cavalry parade of '35, and where were those men now? First Warsaw, then Moscow; first the Black Sea, then the Caspian; first Rostov in the summer, then the snowy filth and lunar ice of Mamayev Hill; first mechanized columns in perfect order, then broken men and broken engines, tanks with red flags on them, snow-gushes of explosions; and Lieutenant-General Paulus sat gazing downward, his gloved hands folded in his lap.

A million Volga Germans had been deported last August by none other than Comrade Stalin, in order to prevent them from aiding us. If only they were here now! (Where were they? Siberia, he believed, and maybe Kazakhstan . . .)

Major-General Schmidt advised him to place more trust in Sixth Army's will to victory.—Unfortunately, he replied coldly, I cannot act as you suggest.

On 3.11.42, right when Field-Marshal Rommel communicated to OKW that superior enemy forces were driving him out of El Alamein, Lieutenant-General Paulus uneasily realized that the enemy seemed to be fortifying villages to the south and west, as if for protracted defense. But one grows accustomed to everything. It had become normal for him first to be conquering cities and armies in France, and then to be fighting in Stalingrad, endlessly. Coca was still waiting for him to bring home his Field-Marshal's baton. (No one had been made Field-Marshal since the elevation of von Manstein back in July.) He was now under such great strain that he tried not to think of anything but the next attack, the next diminishment of Sixth Army's men, and just as we all spend moments and years counting ourselves wise in the spending of them and hopeful almost to certainty that today's temporary difficulties will be stabilized tomorrow and then there will come no new misfortunes, not ever, so he believed, and avoided weighing that belief, that after he'd dispatched to their deaths a few thousand more of Sixth Army's men,

Stalingrad would be won. In truth, the management of Sixth Army's affairs now fascinated him less than he had expected. Well, after all, he wasn't so young now; it would really be delightful to take a long rest with Coca. His letters to her became more ardent and sensual than ever before. Although he knew that the censors read them, a fact of life which used to inhibit him, he didn't care about that so much now; he often fell asleep imagining himself at home with her: first dinner, then Coca in bed, and then they'd drowse away the night until that beam of morning sunlight sped in like a tracer bullet to strike the white volumes across the room; Coca's slip would be hanging on the chair and she would be sleeping with her face turned so lightly and gently in against his shoulder.

On 8.11.42, when the Anglo-Jewish coalition landed in French Morocco and Algeria, he knew that Rommel was finished. He lit a cigarette. All around him, Stalingrad was quiet. Beyond their lines came the eternal Russian accordion-songs and those purposeless, barbaric gunshots; couldn't their commanders enforce any sort of discipline? Whenever we took them prisoner, they were always unshaven and smelly—perfect Slavs. What were they doing? A thousand hypothetical cases unfolded behind his eyelids. They continued to enforce radio silence. Schmidt advised him not to worry; Schmidt said that he was looking extremely tired.

On 11.11.42, Fremde Heere Ost Gruppe I, Army Group B reported that the Red Army had created a new Don Front. The signals reconnaissance report warned him of increasing night traffic along the railroad axis Urbakh–Baskunchak–Akhtuba. This probably meant nothing more than defensive enemy behavior. The prisoner-of-war interrogation reports contained nothing but empty pleas for mercy. ᛋᛋ-Einsatzgruppeführer Weiss brought him documents seized from the person of a Jewish Bolshevist whose purport indicated large scale entrainments along the Stalingrad axis; unfortunately, this Jew, whom Paulus wished to question further, had already been "sent to the rear"—that is, neutralized. Paulus rose in silence and bowed a trifle, smiling pleasantly at the Einsatzgruppeführer, who after all had only been doing his job. Then he held a little exchange of views with his officers, none of whom seemed to be nervous about the future, provided that Sixth Army was brought back up to strength. He was compelled to inform them that as a result of certain developments, their "provided that" could not be relied upon. They sat silent. (Perhaps he wasn't at his best. Ernst had been wounded quite badly in the thigh; technically speaking, his case was not too serious for a frontline hospital, but he sent the boy back to the Reich to convalesce, not for his sake but for Coca's, a decision which ultimately saved his son's life.) Assembling them around the map, he pointed to the Soviet bridgehead which now menaced Romanian Third Army. That, he explained, was a symptom of our weakness; nobody could neutralize it. They stared back at him, most of them unshaven and grim, and he told them that he was strongly considering informing OKW that he wished to withdraw to the Don and the Chir before winter locked them in. They replied to him with silent contempt. He said: Gentlemen, if you disagree with me, you must express yourselves more clearly. We all want to lay Stalingrad at our Führer's feet . . . —Then they expressed themselves; they most certainly did. Not one of them wanted to go on record as saying that Sixth Army lacked sufficient fanaticism to finish the job. Major-General Schmidt brightly said: Well, sir, it seems to be unanimous!—Paulus, smiling compassionately, said that in that case he would defer his recommendation of withdrawal for the present. The next day's signals intelligence report confirmed that there seemed to be abnormal railroad activity approaching Stalingrad. He queried Führer Headquarters, but received no answer. (Somebody there ought to be sent before a military tribunal.) Fremde Heere Ost Gruppe I, Army Group B reassured him that the new enemy troop concentrations remained much too weak for far-reaching operations.

Suddenly half-impaled by fear, he conceived that something was happening, and at 0630 hours on 11.11.42 launched his final attack upon Sixty-second Army, hoping to shatter them at last and dominate the Volga. How hard it was now to present himself before his officers, his judges, whose men he'd decimated and whose self-confidence, what was left of it, trusted in his! He did take Red October, mostly; Barrikady could really be called finished; another Soviet division got encircled, although it kept firing stubbornly at him from behind the snow-skinned teats of Cossack burial mounds. If he could only annihilate Thirteenth Soviet Guards . . . But they were forming beachheads and strongpoints again.

At 1617 hours on 18.11.42 he intercepted an enemy signal: `Send a messenger to pick up the fur gloves.` No one could tell him what it meant. Should he ask Schmidt to come over? But what could Schmidt say? He listened to Beethoven on the gramophone, then lay down, sleeping poorly. At 0240 hours he rose, lit the lantern, and gazed at the map, longing to see the disposition of his forces which would allow him to destroy Thirteenth Soviet Guards. The front line was always drawn in blue on Major-General Gehlen's maps, with the Soviet order of battle in red. That blue border like one of summer's rivers, the way it meandered to make almost-islands, no longer seemed to him, as it did to his staff officers, emblematic of a lethal stasis; no, it was literally fluid, like war, life, destiny—a viaduct, not a barrier. Drowsing off, he seemed to be boating on the Spree with Coca, Olga, Friedrich and Ernst. **Übersicht über sowjetrussischen Kräfteeinsatz**, the legend ran. If only we could persuade the Japanese to attack in the Far East! Then Stalin would be compelled to disengage from this dank desert of ruins, title to which we'd surely earned. By 0330 he was exhausted. Out with the light. He dreamed of his father, who'd been a civil servant just like our Führer's; he dreamed that his father was giant and perfect as he used to be; nothing happened in that dream except that he gazed on his father's face with awe. At 0730 hours, the orderly awoke him with an urgent telegram: He was under artillery attack along a wide front.

Then came the teeming red arrows of Russian advances, the tiny blue circles of German, Romanian and Italian divisions overwhelmed by vast new tank armies.

Our defensive line is broken, Herr Lieutenant-General!

He touched his cheek in disbelief.

Romanian Third Army's on the run, sir!

Inform the OKW, said Paulus.

Herr Lieutenant-General, the Führer has personally ordered Forty-eighth Panzer to stabilize the line . . .

They all looked away, for an order like that was an insult to him, a vote of no confidence. He was thinking: Poor Coca must never know of this.

Good, he quietly said. I'd like you to send a message to General Heim . . .

By your order, Herr Lieutenant-General!

Where's Seventh Romanian Corps right now?

At Pronin, Herr Lieutenant-General.

So if they link up with Twenty-second Panzer—

Sir, Perelazovskii has fallen!

I don't understand why we failed to hold Perelazovskii, said Paulus. Try again to reach General Heim.

Herr Lieutenant-General, Twenty-second Panzer's falling back—

But Seventh Romanian should have—

Excuse me, Herr Lieutenant-General, but here's a message from Army Group B Headquarters . . .

Well, well, said Paulus, putting his glasses on. Evidently we're expected to take radical measures.

Herr Lieutenant-General, Sixth Romanian Corps has surrendered.

All of them?

Herr Lieutenant-General, I—

Herr Lieutenant-General, we've positively identified Thirteenth Soviet Tank Corps coming north—

They weren't supposed to be in our sector at all, he lectured them, and they fell silent.

Where's our Twenty-ninth Motorized? Not far from Nariman, I suppose . . .

We've lost contact, Herr Lieutenant-General.

Herr Lieutenant-General, the Romanians refuse to—

Herr Lieutenant-General, what should—

Where's Schmidt?

Sir, he's—

Herr Lieutenant-General, contact broken with—

Herr Lieutenant-General, Sixty-fifth Soviet Army has sliced open our flank!

He opened his silver cigarette-case and told them: Keep calm, please.

But, Herr Lieutenant-General, we're being pushed back over here!

Said Paulus: Against all your objections I speak two words: *Adolf Hitler.*

14

According to the *Great Soviet Encyclopedia,* whose thirty-one volumes contain the entire sum of useful knowledge, *encirclement is most often achieved when the enemy defense is broken through in two or more sectors of the front and the attack develops along converging axes. As a result, a solid internal front and an active external front are created, cutting the surrounded grouping off from the remainder of its forces.* The Soviet tank brigades, shock armies, cavalry corps and ski battalions had accomplished this, and now the ring was hardening just as ice does: a delicate skin at first, as easy to crack as sugar-glazing. Paulus, his eyes now sunken deep behind the thick, almost Slavic brows, realized that the enemy spearheads would probably meet at Kalach. He possessed no reserves to stop them. On the other hand, they'd already lost a hundred tanks. Perhaps they were finished.

On 21.11.42 the encirclement of Stalingrad was complete. He calmly requested two Fiesler-Storch airplanes to convey himself and Major-General Schmidt to Nizhne-Chirskaya, where General Hoth would be instructed to meet them. He instructed his aides to begin burning documents. Then he ordered Eleventh Army Corps to retreat across the Don into the center of the pocket, which they did, using Russian prisoners to pull the ammunition-carts and shooting them when they could pull no more. According to his reports, more Russians, white-clad Russians, were already running across the black-smeared snow, five armies of them; and they had linked up at Sovietsky and were digging in. Soon it would be too late. A bluish-jawed Russian with a star on his cap opened his mouth in a scream of joyous hatred as the Katyushas went off . . .

As the plane became airborne, he gazed out the window and saw Russian troops attempting with laughable fanaticism to bring him down with small arms. Their muzzle-flashes winked like mica. Major-General Schmidt shook a finger at them and winked. Then a zone of yellowish cloud took Stalingrad away, and Paulus closed his eyes, pretending to sleep so that he would not need to look at Schmidt. He could not help remembering that June day in Poltava when he'd promised the Führer that Sixth Army would carry out its assignment. He'd never become a Field-Marshal now.

At Nizhne-Chirskaya, pensive R-maidens, whose hair was as delicious as the Ukraine's flax and buckwheat, took his spare uniform away to be pressed, and when he had finished his bath they brought freshly laundered white gloves for him to wear for when he bent over the conference table, overgazing the most recent aerial reconnaissance photographs from Fremde Heere Ost Gruppe I, Army Group B. After awhile, he realized that the photographs were old and out of date. There was no indication at all of the enemy troop movements, not even any prefiguration of it, although that might have been due to their excellent winter camouflage. At the far end of the room, Major-General Schmidt was on the telephone to Eighth Air Corps, demanding resupply. And now Paulus rose to exchange greetings with General Hoth, wrinkled, shaveheaded General Hoth whose oakleaf collar was always buttoned up tight.

Our main task, instructed Paulus, must now be to destroy the opposing tanks.

But that was already long past possible, due to the Russians' superior capacity for tank production.

He asked General Hoth what he could do, but General Hoth could do nothing.

What about Sixteenth Motorized?

Didn't you hear? They buried their tanks for warmth, and fieldmice ate all the wires!

Everyone advised him to recommend a breakout to the Führer, before it was too late.

In that case, he said to them, more than ten thousand wounded and most of our heavy weapons would have to be written off. And then what? First we give up Stalingrad; then we recapitulate Napoleon's retreat. Surely you remember your history, gentlemen. He started with four hundred thousand men. When he left Moscow he had a hundred thousand. That's attrition for you. Then the retreat. He got to Poland with ten thousand . . .

We're supposed to counterattack, they insisted.

Who told you that?

I heard that our Führer himself—

But Major-General Schmidt was on the telephone again. Army Group B no longer possessed any force for counterattack.

General Hoth wondered aloud whether Army Group A could relieve them, at which Paulus was compelled to indicate in a single sweep of his map-hand the breadth of the Kalmyk Steppes.

The bitter facts which were pressing in on him from all sides could not be gainsaid, although he'd spoken against retreat, partly because so drastic a decision must first be considered at length and partly in order to express his confidence in our Führer, who was already accusing *him* of cowardice for flying out, so he'd heard. His immediate return to Sixth Army was demanded. He was to organize a hedgehog defense and await further orders. Field-Marshal von Manstein was to command the new Army Group Don. (Coca rather liked his wife Jutta-Sibylle.) For now, any breakout was forbidden. Voronezh and Stalingrad were our two strongpoints in this zone. Both of them must be held to the death. They said to Paulus: The Führer's instructed the Ministry of Aviation to supply you with all resources . . . —General Heim, who'd done no wrong, was arrested and condemned to death, although his colleagues later saved him. Incensed and shamed by these imputations—in fact he felt like one of those medieval criminals who'd been condemned to being pulled apart by four horses; which way could he go? what could he do?—but betraying nothing, if we exclude the twitching of his face, Paulus strapped himself into the Fiesler-Storch, accompanied by a present from General Hoth: red Romanian wine and a case of Veuve Clicquot from Paris. He was too good for these people.—Are you ready, Herr Lieutenant-General? Evasive action time! It may be a bit bumpy . . . —These Luftwaffe pilots certainly deserved the green ribbon for bravery! He wished that he could decorate them all. Seeing into the future as effortlessly as ever, he worried about Sixth Army's long-term fuel situation: Petrol gives us not only warmth, but mobility. Schmidt was staring at him; he turned away. Now here came the river Aksay's long, narrow valley-lips, the river itself frozen over, then the four-meter snowdrifts he knew so well, the yellow-grey sky, the lengthy black lines of frozen trucks in the whiteness of Gumrak's runway, grey tents in the snow, the railroad station which was now Stalingrad HQ (for Golubinskaya, the headquarters he'd flown out of yesterday, was now in enemy hands), the encircled army frozen in time like silver-armored knights in a museum, all knight-flesh long since rotted away from inside the armor. The ᛋᛋ surgeon said that several dozen men had developed frostbite gangrene in the folds of the eyelids.—Thank you, said Paulus. You may go.—He summoned all his staff officers to analyze the dispositions of the enemy's strike groups. After that, they pored over the perfect black glossiness of Paulus's formations superimposed on the half-real grey map, which never depicted enemy troops. First defense, then preparations for breakout; that was how it had to be done. The outer line was to be forward of Kotel'niko. As soon as it became clear what he must do next, he'd have to exert himself to the utmost. His fingertips felt very cold within the white gloves, and his mouth was dry. He needed to save himself for the moment of decision, but when would that moment come? For the sake of his own evenness of mind, on which the outcome depended, he tried to repel all recollections of our Führer's criticism, but then it came back, the filthy shame, as if he were a boy again and his father the bookkeeper had caught him masturbating; all he could do was try to convince himself that very likely the Führer hadn't given his own accusations any further thought; everybody knew that the Führer's temper had been growing worse ever since Moscow.

Paulus felt unsure of himself. But Sixth Army was still conditionally fit. The air stank of cigarettes.

After all, said Major-General Schmidt, it was the Romanians who let the enemy break through. What can you expect from that Slavicized trash? The Führer's expecting us Germans to step in and do our duty.—In fact, there was not much to do but wait for our Führer and Field-Marshal von Manstein, and they all knew it.

Never mind, they kept telling each other, trying to maintain the correct attitude. Every cadet knows that defense is the strongest form of fighting.

Our will—

But where did all those operational groupings come from?

What do you mean, where did they come from? Russia's infinite, you idiot!

If we only harden ourselves enough—

. . . Or else the enemy will break through to Europe!

. . . Struggle as the precondition of higher development . . .

As soon as von Manstein—

He doesn't care about us.

Who doesn't?

You know.

On the contrary, I can assure you that he cares almost too much. *Mein Kampf* proves it beyond any doubt. It's because he has a horror of witnessing your suffering—

They sincerely tried to be brave, in much the same way that a meager-faced ϟϟ-man awaits his capture and murder at the hands of cigarette-smoking Kazakh horsemen.

Reddish clouds of sunset dirt settled over the frozen ruins. He served the champagne all around. This was now Fortress Stalingrad, our Führer said. It would be their destiny to recapitulate the suffering of the Russians at Leningrad. They invoked the German cornfields, coal mines and refineries which would soon rise out of this barrenness, all bunkered behind a massive Ostwall, in the service of which he raised the matter of village-based strong pockets. Now, the bubbles going to their heads, they cried that they wanted to break out at once, but Lieutenant-General Paulus made it clear that he accepted the Führer's decision.—I can't give up, he said in one of his rare, gentle jests. You see, I'm as stubborn as a Westphalian!—The Führer had doubted his bravery, and so he could never break out now. If we want to understand the sort of person he was, we might compare him to Field-Marshal von Brauchitsch, who in Field-Marshal von Manstein's opinion was *not belonging to quite the same class as Baron von Fritsch, Beck, von Rundstedt, von Bock and Ritter von Leeb.*

15

At 2215 hours that same dreary night, a radio transmission came from our Führer: Sixth Army is temporarily surrounded by Russian forces. I know Sixth Army and your Commander-in-Chief, so I have no doubt that in this difficult situation you will stand bravely fast. You must know I am doing everything possible to relieve you. I will issue my instructions at the proper time. A D O L F H I T L E R.

Then he was happy again. Our Führer still believed in him. Our Führer's confidence was as vital to him as is gasoline to our troops at Stalingrad.

They asked him what they should do.

The left side of his face twitched.

They looked at him.

We must convince each soldier of his superiority, said white-gloved Lieutenant-General Paulus.

16

Another Ju-52, black cross visible on the canted wing, came hurtling downward, wheels already extended, black smoke spreading crazily from the cockpit; then came the crash, the explosion, the red flames in the snow. His soldiers groaned.

Standing fast is all very well, he remarked to no one, but not for inadequate forces deployed on excessively wide sectors.

Yes, sir, said Major-General Schmidt. Did you see this dispatch? The Führer's just come back to Wolf's Lair. He says he's confident about our situation.

17

They preserved themselves quite well and cheerfully until Christmas, each of their *Nebelwerfer* shells as heavy as a half-grown child. Comrade Stalin is said to have been quite astonished at the effectiveness of their defense. For this we must credit Paulus, at least in part, for it was he who kept studying the situation maps, drawing up defensive concentration points for each subsector. Eleventh Corps and Fourteenth Panzer would be drawn in *here* and *here,* on the east bank of the Don. The west bank he'd relinquish, for now. The men believed in him; they trusted that he would get them out. He who had always been cursed by his ability to foresee the murkiest potentialities of every move on the chessboard now found himself not yet checkmated but checked, to be sure; he was a white king thinly screened by pawns. He told his officers: Don't worry. I'll assume full responsibility.—Truth to tell, he still thought that he could hold, given sufficient exertion. Soon he'd be granted permission to initiate Operation Winter Storm, followed by Operation Thunderclap. (He longed for the privilege of one last conference at Headquarters Werewolf or Headquarters Wolf's Lair; he longed to fall down on his knees, upraise his arms, and cry out: Without you, my Führer, there's no hope.) His triumph at Kharkov last spring now seemed to him to have been the result of fanatical steadfastness pure and simple: He'd said no to Twenty-eighth Soviet Army, and Twenty-eighth Soviet Army had stopped dead. It was then that he'd injected his tanks into the bleeding enemy wound at Balakleya. Why hadn't he been made Field-Marshal after that? (Superior will, he'd once been instructed by Field-Marshal von Reichenau, is as effective as a pistol held to an R-girl's head!) And now the enemy concluded Operation Saturn against Rostov and Millerovo.

First the maps, then a cigarette, then Coca. He wrote her another of his rare letters, saying: *At the moment I've got a really difficult problem on my hands, but I hope to solve it soon.*

Just then he heard a melody. On the icy street, a soldier was playing Beethoven on a grand piano which someone had trundled out of a destroyed house. He played quite well; it was the Fifth Piano Concerto, the dear old "Emperor." A hundred soldiers stood around the pianist listening, with blankets wrapped around their heads against the cold. They were his young girl-faced boys whose belts of creaking leather had frozen to their uniforms. Some were smiling. The chords echoed like a fusillade, then flew away into the snow-choked ravines of Stalingrad, and as they flew they became even lovelier than the multicolored fireworks of the enemy rockets. Paulus could hear them three blocks away. He longed to come and stand in the crowd with the others, but feared to destroy their pleasure. The field telephone was already whispering like Ukrainian cornfields; there'd been an incursion on his southeast perimeter.

Nowadays he counted a great deal on Field-Marshal von Manstein, who'd installed himself at the emergency headquarters at Novocherkask. Under his command, General Hoth and the surviving Romanian formations were partitioning off some of the Russian attacks. He'd heard it said that von Manstein was one of the few who could still keep the Führer's mind on course. Like Paulus, he'd faced difficulties, but in the end he'd won out; he'd penetrated Fort Stalin, which was why the Führer had made him Field-Marshal. As for his whispered words in the shower at Wolf's Lair, well, we all have our bad days. In Gehlen's assessment, he was *one of the finest soldiers of this century.* That was why Operation Thunderclap would surely succeed. In the meantime, one did what one could.

His officers unanimously (if we exclude the pointed abstention of Schmidt) begged him to request a withdrawal, so he did; it would have to be to the southwest, which meant weakening his northern perimeter in preparation. If they did get out, vastly superior enemy forces would be waiting to engage them on the snowy plains. Not minimizing these disadvantages, he presented the proposal to our Führer, who of course withheld permission for any breakout. Paulus felt married to Stalingrad now.

He extracted Fourth Corps of Fourth Panzer Army from its now untenable position and regrouped it along the southern line in preparation for Operation Thunderclap. First defense, then counterattack, just as soon the Luftwaffe could supply us. He had also begun waiting for the convoy troops of the Rollbahn to send us sheepskins, portable heaters and above all gasoline; first reinforce the perimeter, with tanks or else the snow-covered wreckage of tanks; then . . .

The signals intelligence report said that the Reds no longer troubled to use even their two-digit cipher, so contemptuously sure were they of the outcome. No fewer than twenty-four formations had closed in. By the end of November, Army Group Don warned him that one hundred and forty-three formations were now in the zone. Field-Marshal von Manstein scolded him by teleprinter: `The best chance for an independent breakout has already been missed.` But Paulus, now promoted to Colonel-General, improved his strongpoints to perfection. Wherever they could, the soldiers of Sixth Army built ring-mounds around themselves, even if only of rubble; thus they emulated the fashion of the Russian peasant houses. Upon learning of each incursion (and he was kept very well informed; he retained visual command of his front), he dispatched reserves pulled from other sectors, and off they went to die, gripping the stanchions of their open lorries, guns beside them and pointing upward. The enemy, leaping through snowy gaps in ruined walls, kept getting likewise annihilated. Soon all that would be left of them were snapshots of young men in summer, inanely waving from atop their planes or tanks. In the small hours of those December nights the teleprinter at Gumrak chattered `S E C R E T` and, for instance, `No. 421026/42`, and `PERSONAL & IMMEDIATE`; often it was our Führer himself, commanding: `will be held and kept in operation at all costs and to the last man.`

Generals must obey orders just like any other soldier, our Führer had said.

After teleprinter consultations with Field-Marshal von Manstein, he marked the map: First Fourth Panzer Army and Forty-eighth Panzer Corps would rip open the enemy's siege lines, right here where just today through his field-glasses he'd seen breath-smoke rising from frozen trenches like dreams (dreams of what? of holding hands with an R-girl?); then he'd pull everyone together for the counterstrike; we'd flee toward Donskaya Tsaritsa . . . Dreading the look in Schmidt's face when he mentioned withdrawal, he interred the map in a black folder whose center was stamped Geheime Kommandosache, military secret, and whose lower right quadrant of it was stamped: Top secret! For officers only!

He summoned his adjutant, Colonel Adam, to take dictation.—Please lock the door, he said.

By your order, Herr Colonel-General!

Where's that OKW liaison fellow?

He's in Major-General Schmidt's office, sir.

Those two are quite friendly, without a doubt, he said, and Colonel Adam made no reply.

Very good. This is for Field-Marshal von Manstein's eyes only. Are you ready?

Yes, sir.

Dear Field-Marshal, he began, *I beg permission to acknowledge your signal of 24.11.42 and to thank you for the help you propose giving.* Do you have that down?

Yes, sir.

In the entire zone between Marinovka and the Don there are nothing but flimsy German protective screens. The way to Stalingrad lies open to the Russian tanks and motorized forces.

My God, sir! I—

In this difficult situation I recently sent the Führer a signal asking for freedom of action should it become necessary. I have no means of proving that I should only issue such an order in an extreme emergency and can only ask you to accept my word for this.

Yes, sir.

I have received no direct reply to this signal.

Yes, sir.

As I see it, the main assaults on our northern front have still to come, as the enemy has roads and railroads to . . .

Yes, sir?

To bring up reinforcements. I still believe, however, that the army can hold out for a time.

Heil Hitler! Yes, sir!

As I am being bombarded every day with numerous inquiries about the future, which are more than understandable, I should be grateful if I—

Do you need to rest, sir?

Could be provided with more information than hitherto in order to increase the confidence of my men.

Yes, sir.

Allow me to say, Herr Field-Marshal, that I regard your leadership as a guarantee, and can you finish it, please, Adam? You'll know how to end it properly . . .

Yes, sir.

Are you finished? Then bring it here for my signature. You know, Adam, sometimes you remind me of my son Friedrich. He's a very brave and energetic young man. Doubtless we'd better add an apology for its being in longhand. All right, seal it up. Find a trustworthy officer and have him fly this out to Army Group Don Headquarters.

By your order, Herr Colonel-General! Shall I take it to Major-General Schmidt?

What for?

To be approved, sir.

I believe I told you that this is for Field-Marshal von Manstein's eyes only.

Yes, sir.

You may go.

He tried to close his eyes, but a quarter of an hour later, Lieutenant-General Jaenecke, who was not only a loyal subordinate but a friend, was already knocking on his door yet again to plead for a breakout, insisting: We'll go through the Russians like a hot knife through butter!

That is beyond doubt, but we must follow the Führer's word, he replied.

It was only natural that men such as Jaenecke romanticize what lay ahead. (What actually did? Alimentary dystrophy, also known as starvation.) Field-Marshal von Reichenau's ghost overhung them all. He'd reminded Paulus somewhat of his own father, who could have done almost anything. Who could forget the way that von Reichenau had literally led our charge at Kiev? Still, charges, splendid as they are, only succeed when one has reserves—not to mention a place to charge to.

Von Reichenau, Rommel, and even von Manstein, of them he now heard it said that they would simply have gone ahead, evacuating Stalingrad before the Führer could have forbidden it. Even Jaenecke had implied this in their little talk. Well, that might be so, but didn't they care about the charges of disloyalty which had already been directed at the leaders of the German Army?

Bormann and the others were just looking for an excuse to abolish the General Staff and Nazify everything. And where did Schmidt fit in with all this? He trusted nobody anymore.

A deputation of his officers came to plead with him to initiate Operation Thunderclap, which was supposed to be top secret and which was on every soldier's lips; and when he replied that for the time being no breakout could be authorized, they practically exploded around him, just as ice-boulders come dancing up from frozen Russian rivers when we get them under shellfire; he explained to them that this topic no longer lay under discussion, because they themselves had resisted withdrawal to the Chir when he'd broached the matter with them last month; he would therefore be obliged to them for not raising it without his prior authorization. General von Hartmann looked the saddest, so Paulus invited him to stay after the others. Clicking his heels and bowing, the guest assured him of the continuing loyalty of everyone concerned.—Of course one must be loyal, Paulus replied. That's not even a question, Hartmann. A soldier without the justification of obedience is the merest murderer.

Yes, Herr Colonel-General. I keep wondering how all our struggle and grief will appear as viewed from, say, Sirius.

Doubtless the answer will be different depending on whether one puts the question before or after our conquest of the Sirians! Would you like a cigarette, Hartmann?

Thank you, sir. So you believe that obedience justifies this campaign?

It's incumbent on you to be more careful, Hartmann. I wouldn't repeat what you just said in front of, say, Major-General Schmidt. You may go.

Lighting a cigarette, he sadly confirmed a death sentence for cowardice. Private Vogel had shot himself in the left hand, hoping to get invalided out of Stalingrad. First Beethoven on the gramophone, then another cigarette, then that letter to Coca: *At the moment I've got a really difficult problem on my hands, but I hope to solve it soon.* She would understand; she was a German officer's wife; after all these years what she most expected of him was that he do his best. When he thought of her nowadays, he felt as if he were trapped within a multifaceted crystal vessel which blinded him with sunlight. As for Private Vogel, he was lashed to the perimeter wire now, ankles joined, knees joined, wrists joined with leather straps buckled tight, a cardboard sign already hung around his chest, to instruct his former comrades that at the convenience of the officer in charge this boy was destined for death by shooting. First administrative matters of this kind, which one gets through as calmly as one can; then another cigarette. It was not yet time to give Coca any grounds for apprehension; doubtless she appreciated his situation quite well. In fact, life in Fortress Stalingrad had become normalized. (This was Fortress Stalingrad: double walls of dirty snow around the railroad tracks, frozen bloody bandages on the dugout floors.) He kept her photograph on the field-desk, the photograph of her with her hair down like the actress Lisca Malbran.

He received Field-Marshal von Manstein's Chief of Staff and assured him that Sixth Army could hold out, if we were only adequately supplied as per agreement. He anxiously awaited the order to commence Operation Thunderclap. The two men toasted one another. Then they drank another toast to Sixth Army. The Chief of Staff flew out, and Paulus never saw him again.

On 11.12.42, when the enemy overran the Italian sector, Paulus told the director of the Luftwaffe Air Supply: Your airlift has failed us. We've received only one-sixth of the supplies you promised. With this, my army can neither exist nor fight.

Herr Colonel-General, Reich-Marshal Göring himself has promised us—

We could have broken out before, Paulus interrupted. But the Führer believed the Reich-Marshal. What am I supposed to tell my soldiers now?

Major-General Schmidt was loudly humming "Erika, We Love You."

Enemy pressure was increasing on our Chir front. He issued an order that henceforth we would follow the same security procedures that they did at Wolf's Lair: A violet flare, for instance, would indicate that we'd come under paratroop attack. He prepared to form alarm units from volunteers among his B-echelon troops; their task would be to lurk outside the perimeter, sacrificing themselves if need be to give warning of surprise incursions. He began to write a letter to Ernst, but couldn't find the right words. As Field-Marshal von Bock always used to say, the important thing was to keep calm. He completed a letter to Olga advising her to be more careful with money. He sent Friedrich his best hopes.

On 18.12.42 he received Field-Marshal von Manstein's intelligence officer, a certain Major Eismann, and regaled him with a slice of frozen horse. Major Eismann brought him the latest report from Fremde Heere Ost Gruppe I, Army Group B; and this report suggested that the situation of Stalingrad might well be serious. Major Eismann also brought a case of schnapps. They made a toast to victory. Major Eismann warned him that once Operation Thunderclap commenced, Sixth Army would have to press on considerably beyond Donskaya Tsaritsa in order to link up with our relieving forces. Paulus's face fell, and he began rolling a pencil between his fingers. He began to speak, but Major-General Schmidt, whose soul was as powerful as one of our Führer's 7.7-liter cars, interrupted: Sixth Army will still be in position at Easter. All you people need to do is supply us better. Don't you agree, sir?

Paulus nodded. Then he said: At any rate, under current conditions a breakout would be impossible . . .

With all due respect, Herr Colonel-General, a breakout is your army's sole chance.

That's treason-talk! said Major-General Schmidt.

My dear Major Eismann, said Paulus, perhaps you don't have a full appreciation of our position. Only a hundred tanks remain operational, and the petrol situation will only allow them to go thirty kilometers at best.

Yes, Herr Colonel-General, but once Thunderclap is in progress, air supply should become increasingly more practical.

That is without a doubt, said Paulus graciously, nodding and nodding his head.

Herr Major-General, may I please have a word with Colonel-General Paulus alone?

Impossible, explained Major-General Schmidt.

As you wish. Herr Colonel-General, we understand your moral position. Technically speaking you are the subordinate of Army Group Don, but the Führer has given you a direct order to hold Stalingrad, and so you may feel that Operation Thunderclap would contravene this. Under the circumstances, Field-Marshal von Manstein is prepared to absolve you of your responsibility—

To whom?

To OKW.

To the Führer, you mean.

Smilingly flicking something from his silver assault badge, Major-General Schmidt remarked: Major, I've met quite a few men like you.

Well, well, said Paulus into the silence. The Field-Marshal's suggestion is, to say the least, unexpected. And just how would he go about absolving me?

He would issue a direct order that you initiate Thunderclap. As your superior officer, he would then take the consequences upon himself.

I see, said Paulus. Major, this conversation has been extremely interesting.

On 19.12.42 he dispatched a warning to Army Headquarters that the maximum range of his Panzer tanks had now dwindled to twenty kilometers. The Bolshevists were pressing him hard at the Myshkova River. Field-Marshal von Manstein had just issued a top-secret order to launch Operations Winter

Storm and Thunderclap at the first possible instant. On 23.12.42 the teleprinter chattered: `Good evening, Paulus.` It was Field-Marshal von Manstein. `The day before yesterday, you reported that you had sufficient fuel for a 20-km sortie. Zeitzler asks, would you please re-check and confirm this?`

Dread began to pulse in Paulus's guts.

`Now, if during the next few days we could fly in a limited amount of fuel and supplies, do you think that if worst came to worst you could launch Operation Thunderclap? I don't want an immediate answer. Think it over and get in touch with me again, please, at 2100 hours.`

Staring at the wall above the head of the military typist, who in turn stared nowhere, his bluish white fingers obediently convulsive against the teleprinter keys, Paulus paced and dictated: *Thunderclap has become more difficult than before, because during the last few days the enemy has been digging in on the south and southwestern front, and according to wireless intercepts, appears to have concentrated six armored brigades behind these new positions.*

Now, shockingly, the typist was gazing full into his face, and the gaze was pleading.

Preparations, he continued, *would take*—let's see—*six days. It will be a very difficult operation, unless Hoth manages to tie down really strong enemy forces outside. Am I to take it that I am now authorized to initiate Operation Thunderclap? Once it's launched, there'll be no turning back. Over.*

The typist was praying.

`I can't give you full authority today,` replied the teleprinter, and a single tear began its progress down the typist's white, white face. Paulus pretended not to see; that would be kindest. He himself felt nothing but relief. Whenever he thought about breaking out, a horror which seemed somehow *dirty* burst out like sweat; he knew to his bones that the thing was impossible; as long as he could hang on here, there'd be no further shame. And he felt that our Führer far away at Wolf's Lair understood him. If he only continued to do his best here at Stalingrad for as long as he could, our Führer would forgive and preserve him. Certainly, nobody who stayed here could be called a coward . . .

By Christmas, although they informed him that the ϟϟ Viking Division would soon arrive at Salsk, which might to some degree stabilize the defense of the western Don, he decided to cut the bread ration to fifty grams per day. (He did not yet know that as a result of other enemy incursions Field-Marshal von Manstein would be unable to spare ϟϟ Viking when it did come.) He remarked to no one: It's different from fighting in France, I'll tell you! . . . — But the relieving forces fought their way closer; their forward corps actually came within sight of the gunfire at Stalingrad. Field-Marshal von Manstein called upon him to attack. That would have been impossible, of course.

On Christmas night, the Russians took the ruins of the Shestakov Bridge, in obedience to one of his aphorisms: *The whole thing is a question of time and manpower.* The manpower question explained why they were now making Russian girls wash the surgical instruments. He was still hoping to be allowed to commence Operation Thunderclap, even though his enfeebled men might well be decimated in the attempt. But no word came from Wolf's Lair. First reliefs, then distribution of fuel and ammunition, then breakout; he knew how it should be done. A breakout to the southwest was the theoretically correct solution. *Can aircraft still take off safely from Tatsinskaya?* Schmidt was loudly dictating to the teleprinter clerk, not the one who had cried, but another one who reminded him a little of his son Friedrich. Paulus wished his staff officers a merry Christmas, and they toasted Sixth Army. That night, his face greyish-white like the element germanium, he went out amidst the skeletons of devoured horses to inspect the positions as quietly as he could, so as not to disturb or exhaust the men with false hopes. The rescue force was retreating now, driven back to the Aksai, then to Kotel'niko. Within the skeleton of an apartment tower, a chaplain was conducting a service on an altar comprised of an ammunition box. The congregation prayed fervently, some of them weeping. Trotting at his side, Major-General Schmidt said: Well, sir, on the positive side, these privations will strengthen our racial hatred.

18

Major-General Schmidt had begun to create special units out of our reserves, the *Aufgreifkommandos* they were called. Their task was shooting deserters.

Do you approve these measures, sir?

I prefer to make long-term policy recommendations, Paulus replied.

Yes, sir. Do you approve these measures?

To be sure. Every soldier must follow orders. You have authority to act as you see fit—

Since the tanks were now almost entirely out of fuel, he commanded that they be dug in at the front line, as deeply and permanently as possible, so as to support the infantry in the capacity of pillboxes. If nothing else, the sentries would have a place to shelter from this killing wind, which felt worse than it had last year at Moscow, although naturally it wasn't; it only seemed that way due to the nutritional deficit.

A corporal said: I always knew I should have studied Russian! . . . —and Major-General Schmidt personally shot him in the head, one-two. Paulus lit a cigarette.

Skirting his Germans lurking in their snowy trenches, his Germans babying their siege guns, which were now anti-siege guns, against the cold, he went out to the front line with Colonel Adam. It was very dark. He was halfway hoping to see the muzzle-flashes of our relieving forces, even though he knew that was impossible now. Colonel Adam implored him to turn back, on account of the danger. Suddenly the enemy began to shoot at them. He sat down in the snow so relaxedly that Colonel Adam was sure he must have been hit, but he only smiled and lit them each a cigarette.

19

Field-Marshal von Manstein's messages seemed less urgent now, less encouraging. He was trying to get command of a largish battle group near Millerovo, but the Führer hadn't yet ruled on that.

Paulus sent him a radio signal: `Army can continue to beat off small-scale attacks for some time yet, always providing that supply improves. Only 70 tons were flown in today. Some of the corps will exhaust bread supplies tomorrow, fats this evening, evening fare tomorrow. Radical measures now urgent.`

Field-Marshal von Manstein, however, hoped to recapture the airfield at Tatsinskaya. He was doing his best to persuade the Führer to allow Sixth Army to break out, although by now, of course, only a few remnants could possibly make it through the enemy ring.

The winter days dwindled behind Sixth Army as steadily as the frozen horse-legs stuck in the snow for road markers. Paulus was almost out of cigarettes. *Christmas, naturally, was not very happy,* he wrote to Coca. *In times like these, it is better to avoid celebrations.* First the screaming of the enemy's Katyusha rockets, much shriller than the sirens of Wolf's Lair; then the explosions, followed after an interval by the crystal-clear cracklings of frozen rubble shivering to fragments, the cries of the survivors, each cry utterly sincere and wrapped up in itself, as if its own pain were the first pain which had ever come into this world; it always surprised him how many of his soldiers called for their mothers at the end. First assault, then defense, each time at the price of a further weakened perimeter; first Stalingrad, then everything. He talked with officers of all ranks, hoping to establish the working basis of a real plan. Sixth Army needed to be echeloned in depth, he explained. He didn't bring any pressure at all to bear upon them; they voluntarily accepted his proposals, smiling vacantly, probably as a result of hunger. His friend Karl Hollidt at XVII Corps continued to believe in him. And Major-General Schmidt still thought it entirely possible that the Russians might surrender. When Paulus asked him on what considerations he based this opinion, Major-General Schmidt replied: We can live without the Jew. In fact, we'll be better off. But he can't survive without us. He's a parasite.

Lieutenant-General Jaenecke proposed a breakout yet again.

To where? asked Paulus.

To Voronezh. That's the *real* fortress—

And then?

It's for the Führer to decide.

But he's decided that we're to hold fast right here. You know that.

Herr Colonel-General, if we broke out to the southwest—

That's an extreme solution, said Paulus disapprovingly.

In 1928, a certain Count Hermann Keyserling wrote an essay entitled *Das Spektrum Europas*. Nowadays such endeavors as his would be decidedly out of fashion, for this European mirror endeavors to reflect, chapter by chapter, the lineaments of national character; moreover, our Count adheres to a sternly abstract style whose pretensions to rigor sit uneasily on this reader. Nonetheless, *Das Spektrum Europas* makes many interesting observations about Germans, of which the following may perhaps apply to Colonel-General Paulus: *To regard the fulfillment of duty rather than personal responsibility as the highest virtue, indicates a primal need for yielding oneself up.*

20

After New Year's, not so many of the unshaven, straw-shod members of Sixth Army believed in final victory. They didn't even long for OKW's operational reserves to come and save them. All that had become as far away as Kharkov's snow and wrecked machines. Somewhere in Kharkov there were sheds of blankets and sheds of food, sheds filled with the yellow ointment for frostbite; and there were sheds heaped with ammunition, and sheds full of "Spandau" machine-guns, and sheds of petrol, sheds of chocolate, sheds of fur coats confiscated from Jewesses who wouldn't need them anymore, sheds of submissive U-girls and R-maidens to comfort the doomed, sheds of warmth, sheds of life; but as for the reserves, there would never be any more soldiers to save Sixth Army.

But why not? In June they'd called up the class of '23. What if they . . . ?

What about our Hiwis?

They won't let the Germans down!

But they're Slavs!

So what? If the Reds break in here, all Hiwis will wind up in the very first ditch! They *know* that—

But maybe they'll—

Schmidt says—

Shoot them is what I say. We can't feed ourselves, let alone that Russian trash.

That's exactly what I'm thinking. Maybe, to forestall a revolt, we'd better take measures.

Don't we have other worries? They're no more dangerous than cockroaches; they're only Hiwis!

I could eat a cockroach right now.

Zeitzler's put himself on Stalingrad rations. He wants the Führer to see how desperate our case is . . .

Where does he get his two hundred grams per day of horsemeat? murmured General von Hartmann with a poisonous smile. Probably kills a horse every day just to make the point, or some Jew does it for him. Those rear echelon bastards . . .

Somewhere, in the world where our Führer lived, there would always be more reserves, and these reserves now came out of their boxes so that the fighter squadrons all in a line now loaded themselves with new men already sitting in the cockpits, a swastika on every Messerschmitt's tail, a triangle and a white-oulined black cross on each Messerschmitt's thorax, all the propellers pointing precisely up; and the telephone said: *A severe but just punishment* . . . and steel began to move, ever more rapidly, the reserves shooting forward toward Stalingrad, accelerating faster than any Russian shell. Paulus knew that if he could only be shown in to Wolf's Lair one more time, Wolf's Lair at the hub of its railroad spiderweb, Wolf's Lair with its four outer checkpoints and one inner checkpoint to serve the purpose of airlocks between this rapidly Russifying Europe and the Reich, the real Reich where everything was still possible, Wolf's Lair, Wolf's Lair where there was good coffee and he could change into white gloves and the military typists complained of feeling "too warm," if he could stand again outside the welded steel door to the room where the Führer was expecting him, then, if he could assert and express himself properly, it would all be over because the Führer knew the deep picture; he could see deep down into the earth. That was how everybody in Sixth Army felt. Operation Thunderclap wouldn't have been called off if that had happened. Just as our flatcarloads of Russian prisoners shelter themselves from the wind behind walls of their own dead, so Paulus's soldiers hid behind their belief in the Führer as long as they could, pulling mortars on sleighs, their eye-sockets as white as winterstruck shellholes. Jealous of the lush-furred Russian mitts, for they themselves were warmed now only by the hellish orange winds of enemy flamethrowers which leaped across wrecked buildings, they washed their frostbitten hands in alcohol pilfered from the radiators of their useless tanks. The squat black helmets, modeled after medieval German armor, froze miserably upon their heads.

The compiler-biographer Goerlitz believes that the order to issue rations only to the healthy fighters was given not by Paulus, who suffered whenever his men did, but by General Roske, the final commander of Seventy-first Division. If this is so, then it would seem that Paulus had lost touch with his own subordinates—a palpably absurd idea, given that we know he kept doing his duty, peering blankly at his maps, mechanically opening the lid of his empty cigarette case, searching for the magic disposition of forces which would allow him to take the offensive against these Red Army criminals, isolating and destroying them in detail, after which it might still be possible to master the Caspian basin. Therefore, I for my part prefer to believe that the order in question was never issued, that nothing incorrect was done; for to hold any other opinion is to slander this very intelligent, thorough man: Paulus the Logician.

On New Year's Eve he is reported to have said to Zitzewitz (who was haunted by these words forever after): Everything has occurred exactly as I foretold. It's all in writing in that safe.—Heim had long since seen in him the face of a martyr.

21

His men had begun to resemble concentration camp Jews. When would they be permitted to join hands with Field-Marshal von Manstein's troops? Their heroism moved him almost to tears. Now more than ever he revered the memory of his mother, who'd never complained about her many illnesses. On one of nights when everyone at headquarters sat listening to the whines of the Ju-52s, wondering what they'd bring (the temperature must have been twenty to thirty degrees of frost), he lectured Colonel Adam, who also still believed in him: That dirty secret, the superiority of the T-34 tanks to our own Panzers, helps to explain the failure of our operations here. You see, Adam, since tank production is dependent on electro-steel, it would help us to prepare a more realistic operational plan for the spring if we knew the figures on Russian steel production . . . —At 0200 hours, he and Major-General Schmidt were playing war-games on sheets of Sixth Army stationery. Major-General Schmidt was the Red Army and Paulus was the Wehrmacht. Over his white gloves he wore Russian fur gloves, and so did Major-General Schmidt, because headquarters was heatless; Paulus had ordered that in the interest of simple fairness, until we had petrol to warm the men on the front line, the gas heaters here must not be activated. After twenty-seven turns, he'd maneuvered Major-General Schmidt into abandoning Moscow to our forces, although not without high casualties; all this was provided that Paulus enjoyed centralized control of operations. (He could not help but remember a certain assessment of our Führer's gamesmanship, which General Warlimont had literally whispered into his ear: *Strategically he does not comprehend the principle of concentrating forces at the decisive point.)* After the twenty-ninth round, Major-General Schmidt resigned the game, saying: You certainly haven't lost your touch, sir!—And he lit his commander's cigarette. No, they still weren't quite out of cigarettes; there were always reserves.

Paulus and Colonel Adam walked out to the front line, stepping over the grey tussocks of German corpses. It was all quiet.

22

On 4.1.43 the daily briefing to the Führer, which encompassed the entire world situation on a single page, allotted this paragraph to Stalingrad: **6 Armee, Heeresgruppe Don: Powerful enemy tank attack against N.W. front repelled after temporary break-in. On the army's S.W. front, strengthening enemy artillery fire.** Schmidt carried out that operation; he was the one who saved our northwestern front. Colonel-General Paulus was sitting in the basement, turning the leaves of a book he'd found in a shellhole, and he was still sitting there on the following day, which marked the first anniversary of his appointment to full command of Sixth Army; it was a very yellowed nineteenth-century volume, all in Cyrillic, of course, which he could transliterate but not interpret; and it opened naturally to an engraving of a sad-eyed bearded man who wore a squarish wool cap: ПУГАЧЕВЪ, which was to say Pugachev, the illiterate Don Cossack and pretender to the throne who abolished serfdom, attacked Orenburg, burned Kazan, took Saratov, and besieged Tsaritsyn, which is to say, Stalingrad, where Suvorov's army defeated him; he was transported to Moscow and executed there in 1775. Paulus had studied his rebellion many years ago, back at Staff College. The Russian soldiers of Pugachev's epoch had worn Iron Crosses as we do nowadays, although theirs sported striped ribbons, it seemed. They kept staring at him as he ranged at will through picturebook Russia, forgetting cowardice, "conscience," Jewish trade unions, and all the other filth of so-called "civilization"; now he found himself on a single-sailed boat on a wide, calm river which could have been the Don or the Volga, low mountains all around, grasping trees, sunbeams gushing strangely through the aquatinted sky; and the pallid, moody immensity of Russia hypnotized him; aside from the fact that he couldn't stop shivering, he might have been on holiday with Coca at Baden-Baden, sitting beside her in the sand, rereading *War and Peace;* he'd just reached the section about Napoleon's retreat, which as a result of his own research he could confirm had been very accurately written; it was all foregone, deliciously perilous as Coca held his hand, sunning herself in the bathing-chair, while Ernst built a sand-castle with Friedrich and Olga went to try on her new swimming-suit, and he luxuriated in the German summer, lighting another cigarette. He turned the page, but the book sprang back open to Pugachev.

On 9.1.43, in accordance with our Führer's instructions, he rejected the enemy's demand for capitulation. (After all, said our Führer to Field-Marshal von Manstein, there's no point in surrender. What do you think would happen to them? The Russians never keep any agreements.)

On 10.1.43, the Russians commenced Operation Ring. Our Marinovka salient began to collapse. Paulus awarded the Iron Cross for bravery to all his soldiers. He urged them to exert themselves toward the final victory.

On 13.1.43, Fortress Voronezh, which was our last remaining strongpoint in the vicinity of Stalingrad, came under attack; and it would fall soon; that was beyond any doubt. How could there be any relief now? Field-Marshal von Manstein had hinted to him that even if Sixth Army's position might possibly be, in the long run, hopeless, Sixth Army still had a world-historical task:

to tie up the Red Army as long as possible, which might buy Army Group South sufficient time to consolidate its defenses in southeast Russia. He was no longer optimistic about Operation Thunderclap.

On 15.1.43, when news came that the enemy had broken through our pincers at faraway Leningrad, Paulus fell silent. With his adjutant, Colonel Adam, he ventured out of his headquarters, and together they trod Red Square's wide sweep of rubble, Paulus turning back from time to time to gaze at the place they'd just come from, where the swastika flag still flew from the charred balcony's outcurve and the sentry on duty (One Hundred and Ninety-fourth Grenadiers) stood shivering.—Are you well, Herr Colonel-General?—Paulus did not reply. They clambered as high as it was safe to go within the skeleton of a certain half-shattered apartment building (had we or they destroyed it?), and here Paulus raised his field-glasses to his eyes, surveying his southwestern front, which was quiet. Three soldiers he didn't recognize were shoveling snow on the runway.—So it's over at Leningrad, after nine hundred days of sustained effort. You know, Adam, in a way that clears my mind.—Yes, Herr Colonel-General . . . —Paulus made an impatient gesture, and they returned unspeaking to the Univermag Department Store. That very same day in his own sector, the Russians utterly shattered Hungarian Second Army. His staff officers, as if for the first time, whispered that Sixth Army really ought to fight its way out . . . —Paulus rose, his face ghastly, and said to them all: I expect you as soldiers to carry out the orders of your superior officers. In the same manner the Führer, as my superior, can and must expect that I shall obey his orders.

In retrospect we can't really say that he was as brave and inspiring as Field-Marshal Model, nor that he stopped the Russians as had Field-Marshal von Küchler, that he enjoyed the combination of decisiveness and luck which Field-Marshal Rommel for a time possessed; that he was as cruel as Field-Marshal Schoerner, as zealously officious as fat old Field-Marshal Keitel, as effective as Field-Marshal von Reichenau (who was lucky to die before the Allies could hang him), as treasonously decent as Field-Marshal von Witzleben (whom our Führer hanged for being so), as aloof as Field-Marshal von Leeb, as competent in defensive operations as Field-Marshal von Kleist. What was he, then? I see him as the central figure of a parable, and therefore apathetic in spite of himself; in his long leather trenchcoat, his gloves and collar perfectly white even now, his loyalty gleaming, he was brought into the story of our Reich to illustrate a principle, to carry out a function, to think and suffer while things were done to him. (What's your operational strength? he asked General von Hartmann, who replied: Sir, just count the crosses at Gumrak!) We National Socialists know that the best defense is counterattack; but Colonel-General Paulus was not allowed the forces and mobility to do that. He was nothing but a playing-card soldier, a character in a book. He sat very still in his tent and listened to Beethoven on the gramophone; his gloves were already soiled again. Did he have an inkling yet what he would be forced to suffer? Probably, since by then more than one man heard him say: History has already passed its verdict on me . . . —Stalingrad would be called "the turning point." After Stalingrad, and as a result of Stalingrad, the mastery of central Europe would pass from Germany to Russia. And all because of him! If he had only . . . —or if the Red Army had accidentally . . . —The downfall of our Reich can therefore be blamed on Colonel-General Paulus. After all, it would never have happened, had everything been left up to the sunblown, tousleheaded, adorable Luftwaffe boys in *Signal* magazine.

We still have a mortar and fifteen shells, Herr Colonel-General—

Very good, he replied.

On 16.1.43, the day that Iraq declared war on the Reich, the daily briefing said: **6 Armee, Heeresgruppe Don: On the W. and S. fronts the enemy has reestablished pressure on our positions. N. of the Don, enemy advance over the Kagalnik. Attacks on the N.E. and N. fronts were repelled.** That was the day that we lost the airstrip at Pitomnik.

A Luftwaffe major came to brief him on the strategic situation of Army Group Don. Paulus replied: Dead men are no longer interested in military history.

On the nineteenth, half choked by the yellow smoke of Russian aerial bombs, he wrote his farewell letter to Coca, keeping it brief for both of their sakes. Within the foldings of the thick Sixth Army stationery he enclosed his wedding ring, signet and military decorations. The prudent soldier leaves his original medals at home, and wears authorized copies to guard against loss or frontline rust. He had not done this. Such behavior on the part of a high-ranking officer might have been construed as timidity. As soon as he had sealed the envelope, he felt better. All he wished for now was that the plane which carried these tokens back to her not get shot down.

On 22.1.43, the last airstrip in Stalingrad fell to the Russians. Paulus again requested permission to surrender. The Führer replied: You must stand fast to the last soldier and the last bullet.

23

Now they'd split us into two mutually isolated sub-fortresses, with Paulus in the southern pocket, and grey groups of soldiers crawled across the ruins in search of bread and warmth, mimicking the grey squadrons of lice which abandoned the bandages of the dead. The Romanians were worse off, of course; our Germans must be fed first.

General von Hartmann, he was informed, had exposed himself to the enemy until they shot him in the head. General Stempel did the same. He therefore issued an order forbidding suicide.

He took his daily constitutional to the front in company with Colonel Adam, who supported his staggering steps and who whispered in his ear: I can speak Russian if the need arises, sir.—It will not, replied Colonel-General Paulus.

On 24.1.43 he considered visiting the dressing station in the cellar of the former NKVD headquarters, to encourage the wounded, and Major-General Schmidt gave him permission to do so, but on reflection he began to fear that the sight of him might instead enrage them, and he did not want to add to their suffering. So he paced outside for a turn or two, circling the mountain of frozen bandages and amputated limbs around which the snow was rose-pink, like the tunic facings of a Waffen-ϟϟ antitank unit. Then he returned to headquarters and dictated the following signal to OKW: `No basis left on which to carry out mission to hold Stalingrad. Russians already able to pierce individual fronts, entire sectors of which are being lost through men dying. Heroism of officer and men nonetheless unbroken.`

On 25.1.43, General von Seydlitz granted his own men freedom of action to surrender. Paulus removed him from command. His replacement was General Heitz, who coined the slogan *We fight to the last bullet but one.*

The enemy now began to bombard Red Square.

24

On 27.1.43, when the American Air Force dropped its first bombs on our Reich, more Russian attacks were repelled at Fortress Stalingrad (Paulus in his greatcoat staggering, his head down); and the next day the enemy launched such a powerful artillery barrage that some of his men's eardrums literally burst. The officers sat smoking cigarettes; they'd found a few more of those.

I once heard Field-Marshal von Manstein declare that he'd never be taken alive by those torturers, said Lieutenant-General Jaenecke.

General Pfieffer, who'd been infected with the defeatist virus for quite awhile now, told them what German captives had faced during the previous war: the wounded lying groaning in Panje wagons, the floggings with a seven-tailed *nagaika,* the frozen puddles of urine in Siberia, the men dragged away to death. No doubt it would be worse this time, he said.

Major-General Schmidt reminded them all how in '39, when the Russians had marched in to seize their half of Poland, back in the days when we and they were friends, General Timoshenko had issued a proclamation to the Polish soldiers, calling on them to murder their officers. Imagine what the Reds would do to *us,* said Major-General Schmidt.

They started looking at each other speculatively.

Paulus for his part remembered an incident which had occurred when Field-Marshal von Reichenau was still alive.

In 7.41, Sixth Army had been stationed at Zhitomir, where the Jew Isaac Babel, while taking notes for his horrific "Red Cavalry" stories, discussed and disputed with his co-religionists about the ethics of the Communist revolution which would shoot him in 1940; it was in Zhitomir at the height of that first summer of apples and cherries and of corpses floating down the Teterev River that by Field-Marshal von Reichenau's order we hanged a Soviet judge and rendered the Jews harmless, getting the job done in batches because it was just a question of time and manpower, one marksman per Jew, repeated four hundred times; some marksmen proved incompetent, which merely meant that they were nervous virgins, Operation Barbarossa being less than a month old: the Jews either failed to perish instantly or else splattered the firing squad with brains, which happens when one works at overly close range. (*I am happy,* Babel had written in his diary, *large faces, hooked noses, black, grey-streaked beards; I have many thoughts; farewell to you, dead men.* The year was 1920.) The following month, our German summer still hot and golden, Sixth Army was in Kiev, and after a few hundred more full-grown Jews and Jewesses had been neutralized, their offspring, numbering about ninety, were left alive for a day or two: squeamishness again. Some of our troops complained, because the children weren't given any food or water (the cries of the infants were especially upsetting), and finally two military chaplains became involved. Their report actually equated these necessary operations with the atrocities being committed by the enemy. Field Marshal von Reichenau, always exasperated by any interference, wrote a memorandum in triplicate to Army Headquarters, stating: *I have ascer-*

tained in principle that, once begun, the action was conducted in an appropriate manner. The report in question is incorrect, inappropriate and impertinent in the extreme. Moreover, this comment was written in an open communication which passed through many hands. It would have been far better if the report had not been written at all. It was at this juncture precisely that Paulus had flown in from OKW to inspect Sixth Army. He told Coca a little lie; he said that it was the dysentery, "the Russian sickness," which made him look so ghastly on his return. He'd tried ever since then never to think about the anti-Jewish measures.

But those measures, with which he had had nothing to do—indeed, he'd rescinded them as soon as he took command—might well be blamed on him. It went without saying that the enemy were all Jews. They were bound to be vindictive. He decided that he, too, would never be taken alive.

25

He sat slowly reading an old issue of *Signal* which had come in with God knows what mail drop, probably back during the fall. The Russian mortar fire hurt his ears. His forehead was bandaged; both he and Colonel Adam had sustained skull wounds during the last air raid. In a full-page color photograph, a man and a boy, their reddish-blond heads touching, admired a green and red model submarine which sported the swastika flag of our Reich, the man holding the toy in his arms (he wore an Iron Cross, First Class), the boy so dreamily happy, his lips parted. The man was in fact an admiral whom Paulus had met socially several years ago, at a huntsmen's banquet at Göring's. Yet somehow his likeness reminded Paulus of himself, and the boy of Ernst. Although Ernst and Friedrich were twins, the father had always felt closer to his namesake than to Ernst, who'd been involved in this or that sordidness at school; he often had to speak to him sharply, saying: You are the son of a German officer!—Despite that or because of it, it was Ernst whom he thought of now. At that moment the tableau in *Signal* did not seem at all sentimental or false. He believed in it.

That was when the teleprinter began to chatter. It was 30.1.43. A bluefaced shock troop leader staggered over to see what it might command. Then he stared and stared.

Our Führer had promoted Paulus to Field-Marshal.

26

This then was the climax, the personal victory which Coca had always wanted for him. She'd never asked for very much of him; after all, any soldier's wife knows that she'll very likely be a widow whether her husband gets killed or not. She had loved him, helped him, bearing his absences without reproach. Now they were getting old, and in the thirty-one years since their marriage how many nights had she slept at his side? And all that she had ever wanted in return for her loyalty was a few tokens of success, public honor, for her to be proud of. In a sense, everything he'd done in Russia he'd done for her. To be sure, he could have stayed at home with her, but would she have wanted that of him? When he pulled on his fresh white gloves, lit a cigarette and bent over a map, that was when he could give his best; and the fact that he was far away from her, while regrettable, could not occlude his perfect love for her. He wondered whether she had been informed. He could see her there in the living room, gazing at the mantelpiece where his Field-Marshal's baton would go. Without a doubt it would go right beside the silver-framed photograph of him bending attentively over Colonel-General von Reichenau, who was not yet Field-Marshal on 28.5.40, as the King of Belgium's surrender was accepted; pan-Germanism had won the victory at last. Then there was a replica of his Iron Crosses from the previous war, first and second class; then the small photograph, also framed in silver, of himself with Coca and the children when they were all much younger, everybody in focus except Ernst, who typically enough was fidgeting and looking away; why had Coca framed that picture? Something about it must have pleased her, and, after all, it never did to argue with Coca. Oh, but she'd been so very, very beautiful then! She was still beautiful, of course, but the young lady he'd married in 1912 had been perfect beyond description, her warmly white face shining out upon the world beneath her coils of hair, a slightly exotic fashion which she had renounced after Friedrich and Ernst were born. The instant that her brothers had introduced him to her, she'd shone upon him with a brilliant light. He would literally have set the world on fire for her. This photograph had been taken in 1920, shortly after the Kapp Putsch, which he'd supported so passionately at the time and which no one even remembered now. And all three children were grown and gone. These days Coca must dye her hair, although he'd never caught her at it. That dusty golden summer of theirs, where had it gone?

He presented himself to receive the congratulatory murmurs of his bandaged, frostbitten men. And now, like someone limping, a thought crept slowly into his skull—was it even a thought? It was merely what people always said: *No German Field-Marshal has ever in history fallen alive in enemy hands.*

27

Was the price of his triumph really that he must become another one of those corpses whose flesh was as perfectly white as the walls of Chemnitz barracks?

Pulling on his fresh white gloves, he thought: One might as well be a professional to the end.

In German the compound word for suicide may be disassembled into "free death."

Were he captured after all this, it would naturally be a great disappointment to the Reich.

And to Coca, too, of course . . .

28

She was the wife of a German officer, so she would not flinch; the worse the situation of Stalingrad became, the prouder he grew of her and of himself. Bit by bit he was overcoming his awe of her, which had never come oppressively between them; he'd worshiped his votive goddess for all these years, offering up the best of himself to gain her loving pride in him, which lay upon him as sweetly as her hair across his face when they lay in each other's arms; but now his suffering and that of this army whose soldiers he'd always felt, as any good general must, to be his own extension, had grown so undeniable to all parties, including the enemy, that his fortitude shone undeniably, too; and each day that he held the perimeter was as much of an achievement as his victory at Kharkov; that was why he now possessed more pride and satisfaction in himself than ever before. He knew that he could hold on until death. He'd always been brave; he'd endured many discomforts; but this miserable and quite possibly hopeless struggle had stripped away everything but truth: He was ready; he was worthy; he believed fully in himself. How grateful he felt to Coca for believing in him all these years! He had needed her faith; if this beautiful, passionate woman of royal blood stood willing to be his comrade for life, then his rejection by the Navy, his father's dreary career, his own reserve in friendship, could be regarded with the smiling tolerance with which a man remembers the missteps of boyhood. He'd won the prize! And now he'd grown beyond that. He loved her even more than before, but as an equal at last, as a woman with whom he shared a deep understanding, a person who could be imperfect, even childish at times, as childish as their children; whose various frailties he could now admit, support and even love, because he was not frail anymore. No one could say he hadn't done his duty, even though the Russian mortars boomed on and on. He wished he'd been more strict with Olga and Friedrich, less strict with Ernst. Well, all that was past now.

29

On 29.1.43, a signal rushed to Berlin: `To the Führer! The Sixth Army greets their Führer on the anniversary of your seizure of power. The swastika yet flies over Stalingrad. Heil mein Führer! PAULUS.`

On 30.1.43 the daily briefing said: **6 Armee, Heeresgruppe Don: More Russian attacks against the N. and S. fronts of the southern pocket. 3 enemy tanks destroyed by shooting.**

In the official Soviet accounts, he was captured by Sixty-fourth Army, under General M. S. Shumylov. He surrendered on 31.1.43, the day after the Führer had promoted him to Field-Marshal. (To General Pfieffer he is alleged to have treasonously said: I have no intention of shooting myself for this Bohemian corporal.) Then he withdrew into a private room while his underlings negotiated the surrender. When that was completed, he ascended the stairs, flanked by a line of grinning Slavic boys in hooded white jackets. A German eyewitness writes: *Sorrow and grief lined his face. His complexion was the color of ashes.* Outside, the Allied press was ready, and photographed Field-Marshal Friedrich Paulus in his greatcoat plodding neatly through the snow. Major-General Schmidt was whispering in his ear: Remember that you are a Field-Marshal of the German army.—He didn't have to go very far. They directed him to his own staff car, which carried him to headquarters, after which the car, a Mercedes just like his daughter Olga's, was confiscated in the name of the people. Gunshots popped as gaily as champagne corks; they were shooting his Hiwis as they found them. In the Pioneer barracks they were already incinerating the wounded.

Paulus was now a slender, grey-stubbled cipher, his hat low over his downcast eyes.

He found himself in a peasant house. There was a warm fire. The enemy generals inspected him with self-congratulatory curiosity while he bowed and clicked his heels. In the doorway, a big bald Russian was filming him with a movie camera. The Russian's jacket was filthy, oil-stained from the look of it. For some reason, this was particularly horrible to him. On the other hand, his own gloves were dirty. He stared at the wall.

First they demanded to know why Hitler hadn't flown him out. They said that none of *them* would ever have been left to an enemy's mercies.

I believe you've forgotten General Vlasov, he told them. He's been working with us since last July.

That louse!

Doubtless you know him better than I, he said.

Anyhow, you still haven't explained why your so-called "Führer" abandoned you.

It's the tradition in our army, he patiently explained, for the officer in command to share the fate of his troops.

Well, we appreciate that inspiring lesson, Herr Field-Marshal! And you deserve our gratitude on another score, too. Thanks to you, we now have great and priceless experience of defensive fighting here on the banks of the Volga; rest assured we'll put it to use!

Realizing that they mocked him (which indeed was no less than he had expected), he kept silent.

They instructed him to order the remainder of his army to surrender.

Calmly he replied: That would be unworthy of a soldier!

They laughed their ugly Russian laughs, and one of them, a particularly nasty Slav who looked as if he were ready to spit in Paulus's face, grinned and grinned, his teeth stained brownish-yellow like a Jewish corpse, and then this Slav demanded: How can it be possible to claim that saving the lives of your subordinates is unworthy of a soldier, when you yourself have surrendered?

I did not surrender, he corrected them. I was caught by surprise.

Well, well. Anyhow, we are speaking of a humanitarian act.

Even if I did sign any such order, they would ignore it, since by surrendering I have automatically ceased to be their commander.

Such logic, Herr General Field-Marshal!

They were exactly as his nightmares had depicted them: insolent, menacing, unswayed by argument. (We'll find a way to deal with him, said Comrade Stalin.) One of them, a rather woebegone little lad, seemed dreamily familiar. Just as the German face is thinner and more expressive than the Slavic, more sensitive, so Paulus could not help but let his soul shine through, his inner anxiety, the desire to maintain a decent appearance which he'd always had. And he understood all too well that as of this instant forever afterwards he must hide his pain away, out of loyalty to himself; that in place of his white gloves he could only don a stony look; he'd freeze; he'd harden himself; he'd show them nothing. Wishing that he had fulfilled the Führer's final expectation, Paulus told them: I must reiterate my refusal.

And I in turn must inform *you,* Herr General Field-Marshal, that by your refusal to save your own soldiers' lives you are incurring a grave responsibility toward the German people and the future of Germany.

Turning his face back to the wall, he once again became as silent and stiff as a corpse caught in electrified wire.

The hold-outs in the northern pocket (Eleventh Corps) surrendered anyhow, of course, on 2.2.43; and we next see them in their frostbitten hordes, stonefaced, despairing or shyly smiling at the Soviet supermen in white who hurried them on to Siberia, shooting stragglers on either side. For years, long dark double lines of them remained at work in Stalingrad's ruined squares. They learned to be very good at burying corpses. Almost all would perish from exposure, starvation, typhus, neglect and cruelty. (I've lost track of what happened to a certain Schmundt, who'd kept advising him: We must become more fanatical, sir. Major-General Schmidt, however, remained loyal to our Führer to the very end, which is why he got twenty-five years in a labor camp.) If they had anything at all to look forward to, it would have been the brisk, commanding, yet not entirely compassionless behavior of the Slavic female, especially of the woman official. Even Paulus clicked his heels, kissed the woman doctor's hand. (Socialism would obliterate all such national traits, but of course that would take time.) A few of them, the strong, technically inclined workers already preconditioned to obedience, did rather well as foremen in the Arctic construction battalions.

Paulus, weary and thin, joined the anti-Fascist Union of German Officers. Why not? The Führer had already said: That's the last Field-Marshal I shall appoint in this war.*—Gazing down at the brass pen-stand in his interroga-

---

*He kept this promise as perfectly as all the others. On 1.2.43, which is to say the day after Field-Marshal Paulus's surrender, Generals von Weichs, von Kleist and Busch all attained to the selfsame dignity. On 1.3.44, "Hitler's fireman," the brave General Model, got elevated in recognition of his defensive excellence, which bought us time to gas the Hungarian Jews. The truly final Field-Marshal was Schoerner (5.4.45), a man whose commendably hysterical brutality made him long to do to the defeatists of the German General Staff what he'd already done to Russian civilians; it seems more than befitting that he received his baton from the hands of our Führer himself.

tor's office, trying not to think of what Field-Marshal von Manstein would say, he joined the National Committee for a Free Germany. They were correct with him, for they respected his talents. Some of them even congratulated him on having once bested General Timoshenko at Kharkov. Clicking his heels, he bowed, smiling woodenly. They were very gentle with the former Field-Marshal Friedrich Paulus. He wondered how he ever could have believed that anybody might defeat the Soviet Union, which stood for the people. (Two months after his surrender, the Stalingrad Tractor Works had already been reconstructed sufficiently to commence tank repair operations.) Soon he'd become a committed Marxist-Leninist. He now saw that national questions, if indeed they were not entirely spurious, should always be subordinated to more general social questions.

They paraded him for more journalists. The *London Sunday Times* correspondent A. Werth wrote: *Paulus looked pale and sick, and had a nervous twitch in his left cheek. He had more natural dignity than the others, and wore only one or two decorations.*

In Moscow there were photographs of Stalin and Beria in the interrogation room, Bokhara rugs on the floor. They gave him a whole pack of cigarettes. He sat at the little table screwed to the floor in his cell in the Lubyanka and earnestly thought through the best way to do as he had been told. For this reason, and because of his value as a captured chessman, he never had to discover very much about the Kolyma gold mines, the quarries where German prisoners got worked to death, the three ration categories, the pleasures of logging fir-trees in exchange for squares of dirty bread. They put him and twenty of his generals on a special train which carried them to a very soft camp in Krasnogorsk. This train, well, it wasn't quite as nice as the Führer's, which is completely composed of welded steel; on the other hand, it was warm. For the time being, he even got to keep his silver cigarette case. Later he was sent to Susdal, then to Voykovo Camp Forty-eight. A wise old convict said: Even a miserable life is better than death—but nobody ever said that to the last Field-Marshal, who was treated even better than a high status *urka* criminal. (Our Führer promised to court-martial him after the war, because he hadn't shot himself. Our Führer said: What hurts me the most personally is that I went on and promoted him Field-Marshal. Our Führer said: So many men have to die and then a man like this comes along and at the last moment besmirches the heroism of so many others.)

Had he been anybody else, they would have torn up Coca's photograph in one of the searches; and had he protested, a guard would have chucklingly twisted his ear and said: Nice-looking woman! Don't worry. Russians have already had her.—As it was, he got to keep her likeness until the very end, although it's true that he never saw her again. They informed him that the Gestapo had invited her to divorce him and change her name; but she'd remained true to him; she'd chosen the concentration camp. (No doubt they'd hinted at the other choice she should have taken, the one which would have pleased the Führer, who always admired our proud German women to whom honor remains more important than existence. Anyhow, she was only a Romanian.) The NKVD officers expressed satisfaction that Coca had followed the correct line. They had no information as to whether she was still alive.

They photographed him shaking hands with a Siberian ballerina who'd flown parachute troops behind his lines at Stalingrad. This is my fate, he said to himself. They photographed him addressing the Union of German Officers, whose members are now as irrelevant as those eighteenth century German princes with curled and powdered hair.

In February 1946 we find him sullen-eyed and pale, pretending with convict's craft to gaze as openly as in the days before his ruin, when really his stare is pacing within the prison of his own skull, circumnavigating itself as he hunches there in the witness box at Nuremberg, gripping the headphones tight against his shriveled temples. The Russian prosecutors laughingly called him their *secret weapon,* so much did his sudden appearance astonish the court. (The others called him *the Ghost of Stalingrad.*)

Lieutenant-General Roman Rudenko demanded of him which of his former comrades (now glaring at him from the dock) had been active participants in initiating the war of imperialist aggression against the USSR (or, as his former employer would have called it, the Jewish-Asiatic Power). Calmly, unhesitatingly, Paulus named them all.

(I always took his side with the Führer, whispered "the nodding ass," Field-Marshal Keitel, who was soon to be hanged.—What a shame for Paulus to be testifying against us!)

Rudenko next inquired, eager-eyed: Have I rightly concluded from your testimony that long before 22 June 1941 the Hitlerite government and the Supreme Command of the Armed Forces were planning an aggressive war against the Soviet Union?

Paulus stared at Rudenko's two rows of shining buttons. He replied: That is beyond doubt according to all the developments as I described them and also in connection with all the directives issued.

In the back of the courtroom, his son Ernst, who looked very thin, was staring at him shyly and wretchedly.

The defense attorney, remembering Göring's instructions *(Ask that dirty pig if he's a traitor! Ask him if he's taken out Russian citizenship papers . . .)*, cleared his throat and inquired: What about you, Field-Marshal Paulus? If the aggressive nature of this war was beyond doubt, why did you participate?

Folding his head down against his chest, drawing in his shoulders like the wings of a bird at evening, the last Field-Marshal replied: I didn't come to a full understanding of this issue until after Stalingrad, because, like most German officers, I saw nothing unusual in basing the fate of a people and a nation on power politics. As I conceived it, I was doing my duty to the Fatherland . . .

They escorted him out, and he pretended to gaze straight ahead but once again inturned his sight so as not to see those doomed defendants in the double-rowed dock, walled in by rigid, white-helmeted agents of victors' justice. Had he won the battle of Stalingrad, he would have been sitting there, too; for any war against our Soviet Union must be a lost war. (That man is finished, remarked the Foreign Minister, Ribbentrop. He has disgraced himself.—Of course, said General Jodl, who had once yawned during one of Paulus's presentations at Wolf's Lair. Coca had advised her husband to cut him dead.—He is all washed up, continued Jodl, but I can hardly blame him; he needs to save his neck.—Both defendants lost theirs.) Past the wavy, roofless facades of destroyed German houses, past the fragments of the city wall he floated, back to his Russian prison.

First Hitler, then Stalin. He remained honest to the working class which had forgiven and adopted him. After Stalin died in '53, they let him go to Dresden, which was just beginning to establish its prestige in the electrical and optical industries.

On his first day of liberty there, he was walking with his now pronounced stoop, and he came to a concert in a bombed-out hall whose sooty and dismembered rococo nymphs clung to the walls as faithfully as corpses frozen into Russian roadways; and here, in a huddle of black dress suits, the musicians were playing a string quartet by a certain D. D. Shostakovich, said to have been a great favorite of the late Comrade Stalin's. The last Field-Marshal stood politely smiling as he listened. He hated the dissonant harmonies, which reminded him less of melody than they did of war. The scores gleamed all the whiter against the players' dark attire, like Alpine snowfields interrupted by rock-silhouettes; but the audience around them were grey and feeble, and across the street a dog's carcass stank in a burned house. Eight years since the firestorm it had been, but in our Deutsche Demokratische Republik time passes more slowly, change being released in controlled and minuscule doses for the sake of our delicate personalities soon to be protected by the Berlin Wall. Every now and then, the rebuilders still came across relics which resembled Berlin's time-blackened statues of Silesian sandstone. Over the musicians hung a sign adorned by a red star: **LANG LEBE STALIN!** and now the authorities dared neither to remove nor retain it; they must wait on Comrade Khruschev's word.

They gave him a villa and allowed him to serve the people as a middle-ranking police inspector. To the extent that the postwar situation permitted, he bore out Colonel Heim's characterization of him from the lost days: *Well groomed and with slender hands, always beautifully turned out, with gleaming white collar and immaculately polished field-boots.* About his villa, which at his preference and theirs was set apart in the Platteleite district on a hill above town, I can tell you (for I've seen it) that from its windows and verandas one can look down deep into the sumacs, and, beyond them, still deeper down into a mysterious gulf of trees: the central European forest. When health and leisure permitted, the old man descended sunken steps, then passed through a concrete arch to the lower lookout, comforted by the balconies, round turrets, porches and decks which overhung him. An old reddish-haired lady was gathering flowers in the weeds. Coca would have loved it here; she'd died back in '47, in Baden-Baden, they told him. His son Ernst was allowed to visit him from time to time, probably because the Nazis had put him in a concentration camp for awhile, which made him an anti-Fascist. The other twin, Friedrich, dwelled farther away now: killed in action in Anzio in '44. As for Olga, she never came; Ernst said that she was well, although that Baron of hers had lost a great deal of money during the war; he didn't know why she refused to write. With palsied fingers, the father wrote her a note of congratulations upon her forty-second birthday. Ernst promised to carry it back to the other side of the Iron Curtain. He was a very loyal son, really. I've heard (although this cannot be verified) that in his bedroom, in that revanchist puppet state called West Germany, he kept, in defiance of "denazification," a photograph in a silver frame of that Poltava conference back in '42 when Operation Blau began: There was Heusinger with his fist on the edge of the map table, and Ernst's tall, handsome father stood between Heusinger and our Führer, somewhat to the rear of them both, with his hands locked behind him; while von Weichs of Second Army gazed genially down into the white winter of the map-world, whose border the Führer was gripping with both hands, as if he were about to rip it apart. Ernst could never decide whether or not to have his father's likeness isolated and enlarged.—The two men lit cigarettes and gazed down into Europe. It was very humid that afternoon; they had to contend with the sagging summer clouds of Saxony. Ernst's wound, his souvenir of Stalingrad he called it, annoyed him at night sometimes, he said. He seemed to be letting himself go. He was flabby now, and he shaved imperfectly, and there were always dark circles under his eyes. Once he said: You'll never know how happy I was, father, when I heard about your Iron Cross. I saw you from a distance once, during the fighting at Kharkov . . . —You may have it if you like, said Paulus with a little smile. I sent it to your mother in a letter, just before we lost the Stalingradsky airstrip. She would have kept it to the end, without a doubt. I also . . . —Oh, so that's why you no longer wear your wedding ring, said Ernst with indescribable bitterness. Mama never received any such letter.—Paulus sat rigid, the left side of his face twitching like a heartbeat. On another occasion, perhaps to torment him, or so he suspected, Ernst brought him, he couldn't imagine how he'd gotten it in these times, a copy of the Führer's testament, after which they sat there in that villa behind closed doors, the last Field-Marshal and the ex-Captain, smoking cigarettes and gazing at the wall, with Beethoven on the gramophone, while the document lay between them: . . . `and therefore to choose death of my own free will` . . . After Ernst departed for West Germany, he tore it to shreds and burned it. `May it be one day a part of the code of honor of the German officer, as it already is in our Navy, that the surrender of a district or a town is impossible, and that in this respect the Leader above all should give a shining example of faithful performance of duty unto death.` He'd become very fond of the white and purple clover which came out every spring. First the clover, then the smell of trees and leaves; the heavily jeweled sumacs were July's trees; from the balcony of his ship-breasted house he kept track of each summer's progress down there in the dark gorge. In winter he listened to Beethoven on the gramophone, not Shostakovich. Nobody ever asked his address; if anyone had, he'd prepared the answer: Lausitzer Street. First right, then left—left straight on to the end. When Hilde Benjamin, nicknamed "the Red Guillotine," became Minister of Justice, she made the correct decision, preserving and even promoting him, for Friedrich Paulus was a painstakingly accurate subordinate.—One has to be on the watch like a spider in its web, the Führer used to say, staring and glaring into Paulus's face, searching for something evil.—Thank God I've always had a pretty good nose for everything. I can smell things out before they happen . . . —The Red Guillotine had much the same nose. She was a grey-haired troll with pouches under her eyes—not much of a looker, opined her male colleagues, but if this were '45 she could still have served the turn of a dozen Russian boys. Inspector Paulus, of course, never joked in any such fashion. Nor did the other policemen make remarks in his presence; they felt uncomfortable around him; it wasn't that they didn't trust him (he'd been neutralized long since, rendered harmless), but they didn't know how to take him. Why, for instance, did he punctiliously attend not only military parades, which one would have expected, but every other event, too, right down to the most tediously insignificant celebrations of the working class, which made even Stasi operatives yawn? There he stood, all alone, watching them march beneath Dresden's half-wrecked, green-bronzed domes and cupola'd towers. He lacked what a far abler Field-Marshal (I mean of course von Manstein, who was presently serving time in a British jail) practically embodied; modestly calling it the "Prussian tradition," as if it were just a procedure which he followed without especial credit to him; von Manstein, in short, was an officer who knew how to be close to his men. Did this Inspector Paulus think that he was too good for his colleagues? No matter. Sometimes without notice the Red Guillotine visited Dresden in her shiny black car, and on those occasions she invariably entered Paulus's neat little office, where portraits of Marx, Lenin and Stalin hung all on a level, and she'd look at him, just look at him, as if he had a spot on his collar, at which he'd raise his head from his papers and gaze back at her without defiance or even blankness; he was ready for anything. Then she drove back to Berlin. It was as if he fascinated her. She often praised the clarity and completeness of his reports, and why not? He'd certainly worked everything out thoroughly; his logic was as rigorous as the solution to some problem of crystal chemistry. That must have been why he never got into trouble for his prewar associations with Coca's aristocratic friends: Count Zubov, Baroness Hoyningen-Huene, the exiled prince and princess . . . Unlike poor dead Coca, the Red Guillotine enjoyed full access to his prewar service reports, one of which read: *Modest, perhaps too modest; amiable, with extremely courteous manners, and a good comrade.* (Many citizens, all too many, discovered something in her eyes like the light of a burning gasoline depot, but Paulus never saw it; she smiled upon him.) According to her own assessment, which has been preserved forever in the Stasi archives, Inspector Paulus was *an innocuous representative of the former military-*

professional caste. Until more specialists rise up from the ranks of the people, we should make use of him. He is cautious, discreet, industrious, punctual, intelligent and lacking in all personal ambition. Sometimes, it's true, he gave lectures at the military college, but these presentations, which he invariably cleared with the Stasi beforehand, were nothing more dangerous than an old man's self-justifications. Their topic: Stalingrad. The theme: I predicted the outcome, but the Fascist High Command didn't listen. These lectures were permitted because they offered still another example of how Hitlerism, which is essentially monopoly capitalism, misleads the people. I'm told that even the Red Guillotine attended one or two of these events, smiling rather ironically at him from the very back row. When he saw her, his heart leaped up thrillingly in his chest; he couldn't have said why; it was almost as if he'd received a visitation from Coca. The left side of his face twitched, but he continued: At the same time, particular attention was invited to Sixth Army's inadequate stock of supplies . . . —Other than this hobbyhorse of his, and Ernst's intermittent visits (they now reminisced quite pleasurably together about Stalingrad; Ernst had encouraged him to expand his typewritten notes), he caused no trouble at all. Lighting one cigarette after the next (he'd developed a taste for Russian mahorka), he remained faithfully at his desk while the June Uprising got put down by the tanks of the people's armed forces; he could hear them outside, ranging through the tight-cobblestoned streets, old T-34s by the sound of them. As the great Moltke used to say, *Genius is diligence.* First investigation, then conviction and its sequel in the cellars of the yellow-ocher castles. In a magnificent victory for the working class, they liquidated the Gehlen Organization. He remembered Major-General Gehlen very well. It was above Gehlen's signature that those reports used to come, those misleadingly optimistic daily enemy situation reports of Fremde Heere Ost Gruppe I, Army Group B. Ernst, who seemed to be rather well connected nowadays, told him that Gehlen was now boasting: My department predicted ten days in advance precisely where the blow would fall at Stalingrad! The show trial came off perfectly, although Gehlen wasn't in the dock; we couldn't get to him in his lair in West Berlin. No matter: five hundred and forty-six spies arrested! As he used to say in the old days, *it's just a matter of time and manpower.* On Münchner Platz, where the electric guillotine used to cut off Jews' and defeatists' heads at an optimum rate of one per two minutes, we were now guillotining drunks for singing Nazi songs.

He passed away in 1957, the year after "de-Stalinization" began and the year before Field-Marshal von Manstein published *Lost Victories*; this death rather fittingly resulted from a progressive sclerosis which allowed his mind to contemplate its hopeless situation up to the last moment, increasing the impairment on all sides while his body became unable to move, even to twitch, until even the heart got overwhelmed. He is said to have borne this agony with the utmost patience. Thanks to bureaucratic difficulties at the border, Ernst arrived too late to say goodbye. I think he might have borne his father back to Baden-Baden, to place him at Coca's side; on the other hand, I've also read that he was buried in Dresden. Doubtless both accounts are true; I've seen with my own eyes that Christ possesses two tombs in Jerusalem. Creepers and wistaria overswarmed his grave, then red sumac berries burst out in triumph. He was the last Field-Marshal. Not for him had any mausoleum been assigned: neither pillar nor crypt, no granite eagles, no sad sooty knights killing snakes of stone. But he perished lucky; they'd granted him the slate-roofed heaven of a Saxon summer, lazy linden-games of light, clouds sweating rain. They'd given him that house which resembled an attempt to construct a breast out of plane surfaces. Later the Stasi took it over, for the furtherance of democratic police power.

In 1960, the very year when Shostakovich visited Dresden and, evidently feeling stifled by the dreamily mysterious forest all around, composed his unhappy Opus 110, Paulus's memoir *Ich stehe hier auf Befehl* saw the light; but by then Liddell Hart had already published *The German Generals Talk,* so nobody paid much attention to this secondary effort, which was, after all, no more than the self-justification of a bookkeeper's son. Thanks to the Cold War, Stalingrad had become an embarrassment to everyone concerned. Nonetheless, some of the victors conceded that this Paulus hadn't been half bad at certain tactical operations involving armor. His son faithfully preserved, revised and elaborated these various defensive writings, but Dresden's maples and lindens grew over the father's memory like monuments. First the will, then the deed: In 1970, when the Stalingrad Tractor Works (now called the Volgograd Tractor Works) rolled out its one-millionth tank, Ernst Paulus followed our Führer's wish at last, blowing off the skullcap in a grey and crimson shower. The last thing he saw, or seemed to see, was an army of white skeletons on that black day. ▸

ZOYA

The essential thing about anti-guerrilla warfare—one must hammer this home to everybody—is that whatever succeeds is right.

—Adolf Hitler (1942)

1

Zoya's story has no beginning. Defined only by its end, which takes place not far westward of Moscow, in a village called Petrischevo, the tale projects itself backwards through predictable and possibly fallible contrasts into the sunny prewar collectivity for which Zoya chose to give her life. But what if she didn't choose? The crime for which the Fascists condemned her—setting fire to a stables, in obedience to Comrade Stalin's scorched earth policy—would surely have been followed up by grander salvoes had luck permitted. In brief, Zoya didn't mean to die—at least, not then, not for a stables! But then, to how many has it been given to reckon at all, let alone to conclude: *My death is a fair price to pay for this objective*? The July Twentieth conspirators might have been thus satisfied, had they succeeded in their intention of assassinating Hitler. They didn't, and got hanged with piano wire. General Vlasov, who fought first against Hitler, then against Stalin, met a kindred death. Was that "worth it"? What about the Berliners and Leningraders who died in air raids, or the soldiers on both sides who perished merely because their respective Supreme Commands from fear, vanity or incompetence forbade retreat? Or, to take the case still further, what about the random deaths that we die in peacetime? Looked at in this light, Zoya's fate becomes supremely ordinary.

2

In those days, neutrality meant friendlessness at best, while allegiance to either side invited a capital sentence from the other. Moreover, these punishments usually visited themselves upon the innocent. For every German soldier killed by the Partisans, between fifty and a hundred civilian hostages got stood against the wall. Accordingly, it was no "traitor," but a reasonable conclave of the villagers themselves, who went to report Zoya Kosmodemyanskaya, member in good standing of the Moscow Komsomol, to the Field Police. If somebody had to go to the gallows for what appeared to have been a rash, even absurd action, then why not the perpetrator, who'd endangered them all without their consent? Indeed, they were just in time. The S.D. lieutenant sat looking out the window of what had once been the school. (He'd had the teacher hanged in the very first batch of hostages. One of her high heels fell off at the very end; he remembered that.) Making a vague gesture at the huts across the street, he said: Arrest all that scum.—Just then the delegation of villagers came in.

In a photograph which a peasant soldier, hopeful of sausage or a wristwatch, found on the body of a battle-slain Fascist, we see Zoya (whose *nom de guerre* was Tanya) with downcast head as she limps through the snow to her execution, wearing already the self-accusing sign around her neck. It is 29 November 1941. Her eighteenth birthday was in September. A crowd of young Germans escort her, gazing on her with the sort of lustful appraisal which is common currency in a dancehall.

Now she has arrived. The snow is hard underfoot. A dark oval wall of spectators—Fascists whose double columns of buttons gleam dully on their greatcoats; kerchiefed village women, whose faces express the same pale seriousness their grandmothers would have worn for any camera or stranger; small, dark, hooded children in the front row—encloses the scene. Beside the sturdy, three-legged gallows, which rises out of sight, a pyramidal platform of snow-covered crates allows one party, the hangman, to ascend, while a tall stool awaits the other. Zoya stands there between two tall soldiers. Clenching her pale fists, shaking her dark hair out of her eyes, she swings her head toward one of the soldiers, who draws himself up stiff and straight to accept her gaze. She says: You can't hang all hundred and ninety million of us.

Some say that it was General Vlasov's soldiers who found her at the beginning of the Moscow counteroffensive the following month. I myself can hardly credit that, for Vlasov, who commands my sympathy, if not my imitation, would surely have hesitated to collaborate with the Fascists had he found such early and striking proof of their cruelty. No doubt he saw the final photograph (taken, so I've read, by the *Pravda* journalist Lidin), the one which presents to us her naked corpse in the snow, her head arched back as if in sexual ecstasy, her long-lashed eyes frozen tightly shut, her lips clenched, as if to protect her broken teeth, and that noose, now hard as a braid of wire cable, still biting into her neck, her face swollen with blood into a Greek mask. Perhaps Vlasov convinced himself that this image was a propaganda fake, or even that she could by some sufficiently draconian interpretation of military law have been construed to be a fifth columnist worthy of death.

It was the night before they retook Solnechnogorsk. Vlasov was pacing a riverbank like the frozen, snow-crusted defile between Zoya's breasts. Beside him strode a scout who'd just returned from the Fascist lines. The two men had finished discussing the enemy dispositions. Now they were talking about Zoya.

What they did to her will make us all fight more fiercely tomorrow, I guarantee it, Comrade General.

So would you say that she distinguished herself?

Why, she's a national heroine!

And that's what's strange. Why on earth would the Fascists want to give us a national heroine?

They returned to camp in silence. Vlasov was still considering how best to deploy his three hundred and eleven mortars and heavy guns. Back in '36 he'd attended a lecture given by the late Marshal Tukhachevsky, who'd aphorized that *the next war will be won by tanks and aviation*. He was correct, and Vlasov possessed neither. What could he do, but expend men like bullets?

His Siberians were waxing their skis with plunder taken from a half-burnt beehive. They'd already masticated every trace of honey from the comb. The antitank riflemen in the breakthrough echelon were lubricating their rifles one last time, and two beardless boys were singing in a loud pretense of bravery: *Into battle for our nation, into battle for our Stalin*. On the radio, Beria and Zhukov were threatening all defeated generals with death. At the edge of the sunken, snow-rimmed fire, the commissar was scribbling out a speech of which Zoya would be the subject, reminding everyone that the goal of partisan activity was to do *anything*, however much or little, which might hinder the movement of enemy reserves toward the front line. By this rather lenient criterion the girl had succeeded; and the restive troops, who longed to believe in something, would be, he hoped, inspired into emulation. *He* knew that every Soviet battle-death was worth it! Who am I to call him stupid, cynical, incurable? Most of Vlasov's men would end up killed or in the German prison camps, where they could look forward to being the subjects of experiments involving poisoned bullets, Zyklon B, decompression or freezing. (When Russian inmates died, no death certificates were required.) Well, if murdering them delayed a few thousand Fascists from manning the front line, then one had to keep calm and—

General Vlasov stood gazing down at the frozen river. The pincers of despairing, hopeless responsibility gripped his heart until he almost groaned. But suddenly peace came to him, and he muttered, not quite knowing what he was saying: Between the breasts of Zoya.

3

Here is what I imagine he meant by these words.

Because he was an outstandingly charismatic commander who never failed to make his men feel that they were brothers, and because he did everything honestly, we can assume that Vlasov already possessed the sense, which for the past quarter-century Communism had done everything possible to destroy, that the Soviet Union really *was* a union, that it comprised a single desperately embattled organism whose long chance for survival could be improved only through a selfless coordination *(Gleichschaltung,* his Fascist counterparts called it) of every cell, tentacle, cilium and internal organism, that the overstimulated endocrine secretions of hatred which had half poisoned and half crazed the organism for so long could now finally be usefully concentrated in fangs and stingers to be discharged against Germany, whose defeat, because Germany had struck first, could even be called a noble purpose.

As for the masses, they needed Zoya's dead breasts to drink from. They drank. Then they became likewise poisoned with resolve.

Zoya's fate stained and hardened the women night bomber pilots who laughed and smoked cigarettes, the peasant boys who shot rifles at the Fascist tanks, and even Comrade Stalin himself, whose speeches now invariably ended: *Death to the Fascist invaders.* Zoya's frozen blood, darker than steel, strengthened the upraised sabers of Cossacks galloping into the heavy grey photographic plates of myth. Her death became a movie ("Soyuzdetfilm," 1944), with a score composed by Shostakovich. Decades after the war, memories of Zoya reincarnated themselves in the witch Loreley, who sings an irresistible song of suicide in the same composer's "Death" Symphony. By then,

Zoya's corpse had become the Russian landscape itself, and I don't just mean that streets and tanks were named after her, which they were; Russia actually became Zoya, and when General Vlasov studied the map, preparing to thrust his breakthrough echelon against the Fascist Army Group Center, he seemed to see the body of a young giantess lying there beneath the snow, her arms and legs the ridges whose loved and familiar contours would help him, her thousand lips the antitank ditches which were delaying and exhausting the Fascists, her womb, silvergold with the sparkling sheen of snowy trenches, a bunker from which unending new divisions, airplanes and T-34 tanks would be born—yes, she'd died a virgin, but she was now literally the Motherland!—her hair the frozen thickets from which the partisans could ambush the enemy forever and ever, her breasts the points of strategic concentration whose investiture would save the Red Army—and between the breasts, between the breasts of Zoya, there lay the valley of perfect whiteness and smoothness; it was here, when Vlasov's striving finally ended, that he could lay his head. ▸

CLEAN HANDS

◩

. . . every attempt to present altruism as a route to the transformation of an antagonistic society on nonegoistic principles leads ultimately to ideological hypocrisy, masking the antagonism of class relations.

—Great Soviet Encyclopedia

1

They said to him: An idealist like you should make a fanatical Party member.

He smiled quickly, a smile which lacked three teeth. Rage outstretched its wings within his chest.

So he became a Nazi. He raised his right arm. The next step was to apply to the ϟϟ. That too went as smoothly as rounding up the nearest Jew. Everybody welcomed Kurt Gerstein. Blond and blue-eyed both, this young man also received perfect marks for his genealogical chart: one hundred percent Aryan! Moreover, he was educated (a mining engineer), quiet-mannered, and accustomed to working in organizations. Until we coordinated all groups, clubs and affiliations into a single expression of our Führer's will, Gerstein served on the national council of the Young Men's Christian Association, a position simultaneously responsible and harmless. Although he'd lacked occasion thus far to demonstrate the "cadaver obedience" of our Old Fighters, he was more than just another cigar store clerk.

So he trod the road of fate whose pavement consists of standing bodies; he joined the hundreds repeating the oath. Torches and arches inspired the night. His squat dagger was engraved: MY HONOR IS MY LOYALTY. From a distance Himmler smiled upon him, and in the darkness that smile resembled sunlight on a murderer's shoulder, a blotch of brightness on a fat, shrugging, wool-skinned shoulder with an eagle and a swastika on it; sun on the diamond shoulder-tab, sun on the pale, cruel cheek of the chinstrapped, helmeted face.

They couldn't have imagined what impelled him: His sister-in-law Berthe had been euthanized at Hadamar. He wished to discover what else was being done in the Führer's name; he desired the power to open those dark folders stamped with the word **Geheim**, which means *secret*; he longed to read the documents whose circular stamps bear swastika-gripping eagles.

Ironically, they placed this impure element in the Department of Hygiene. No one disliked him. He improved procedures for disinfecting soldiers and prisoners-of-war.

2

On 17.8.42, three months after the assassination of Deputy Reich Protector Heydrich, Gerstein stood before the desk of Hans Günther, who was assistant to Adolf Eichmann himself. It was time to write a new chapter in each and all of those multitudinous books entitled *Historia Polski*. "Clever Hans" Günther was one of those people who never stop believing that pure energy will solve the question of the day. When this method fails, the optimist turns angry. Such bosses are feared and respected. Our Führer loves them.

Gerstein, do you like to travel?

I'm ready, Herr Captain.

That's the answer I like! We're going to Poland tomorrow. Are you acquainted with Dr. Pfannenstiel?

Of Marburg? Naturally, Herr Captain. He's a professor of hygiene; we've corresponded—

Good. He'll also be taking part in this. Get a hundred kilograms of prussic acid without fail. Do you need a requisition?

No, Herr Captain, I have that much in stock.

It's best to deliver it directly to this office. My orderlies will load it onto the baggage car.

By your order, Herr Captain.

That's all. Here's your ticket.

By your order, Herr Captain.

One more thing, Gerstein. Listen carefully. This is one of the most secret matters, even the most secret. Do you understand? Anyone who talks about it will be shot immediately.

I understand, Herr Captain.

Heil Hitler!

Heil Hitler, said Gerstein, and he clicked his heels.

In their compartment of the Warsaw Express, a beautiful, placid dark-haired Polish girl sat ever so slowly turning over the leaves of her illustrated German magazine; the skin of her naked throat was as perfect as a political idea. She might have been a woman of pleasure. Presently a middle-aged Wehrmacht officer came and sat beside her. At his breast he wore a Knight's Cross which he kept fingering nervously. Gerstein leaped to his feet and saluted; the lieutenant waved him down, his small eyes swimming ceaselessly in his exhausted, desperate face. Then he whispered something to the girl. Strangely enough, although she now awarded him the first of several cursory smiles, it was Kurt Gerstein whom she seemed to look upon. The young man lowered his eyes.

Dr. Pfannenstiel drummed his fingers on the windowsill. Finally he indulged himself to the point of remarking: As the Führer says, after so many generations we Goths are riding again!

No doubt, said Captain Günther.

The lieutenant grinned mockingly at this (for, in truth, poor Dr. Pfannenstiel was as heavy as an Opel-Blitz truck). The girl also smiled, stroking her lover's sleeve, but the smile sank away at once. Turning to Kurt Gerstein, as people so often did, the lieutenant inquired: Where might you Goths be riding to?

Warsaw, the young man lied pleasantly. And yourself, Herr Oberstleutnant?

I'm taking Basia to her parents. Then it's straight back to the Ostfront!

With a self-important air, he adjusted his Knight's Cross. Gerstein thought him rather pitiable.

And when will you come back for me? asked the girl in a weak and listless voice.

Don't worry, darling; there will be plenty of passes given out as soon as we take Stalingrad.

The summer-green forests were growing crazily, nourished by atrocity. It seemed to Gerstein, such was the profusion of foliage, that the train was now passing into the earth itself, and through some illusion the shimmering of the leaves resembled veins of crystalline chalcedony. After all, it was now evening, the sky turning Prussian blue in the train windows. Ahead lay the still richer summer leaf-darkness of the Polish countryside. (But Poland, of course, had ceased to exist.) Although Basia suffered the lieutenant to hold her hand, she never stopped looking at Gerstein. Unable to control himself any longer, he allowed his eyes to find her eyes. At once, doubtless through some peculiarity of lighting, her face seemed to take on the features of his murdered sister-in-law, and she said in a voice which only he could hear: Be brave, Kurt Gerstein. I am your conscience. When you walk the dark way, remember me, and always do your best.

He had, perhaps, been in love with Berthe. Her smile was always grave approaching sadness, and the more sweet for that. She had deep brown eyes with rich lashes, and brown hair which waved so graciously across her forehead before, caressing her rich eyebrows, it curled back against her temples and then flared down all the way to her shoulders. Her lips were both full and delicate. There had been something Jewish-looking about her.

Gerstein did not even feel frightened. Perhaps he was dreaming, for the others in the compartment continued to notice nothing. Ever since his childhood, strange enthusiasms and hallucinations had attacked him. His late mother had always worried about his susceptibilities, and used to keep him away from military uniforms and memorabilia inasmuch as she was able—not merely because any reminder of her other son's death grieved her, but also since she feared, not without foundation, that any passing whimsy might induce him to sign up for dangerous adventures. In adolescence he used to dream of a pale face, neither male or female, which hung over his and kissed him all night. Sometimes it had seemed more than a dream, as did this apparition.

He tried to cobble together some reply, but now already Berthe's face was melting back into Basia's (for a moment, when it was neither one or the other, it almost seemed to take on the appearance of a skull); then Dr. Pfannenstiel took out his pocket watch as the train entered a zone demarcated by searchlights and barbed wire: the former frontier. The lands ahead had all been annexed into our Reich. And out the window they saw a helmet on a cross, a flower-bush on a mound of earth. Gerstein and the other two ϟϟ-men rose and rigidly saluted the corpse. The lieutenant stared at them with twitching lips. As for Basia, she had returned to her German magazine.

3

On the silent weed-grown tracks of Rzepin, a long black windowless train basked beside them in the dusk. The lieutenant and his mistress disembarked here without any farewell. The whistle screamed. Then came small houses whose roof-tiles partook of the color of earth. Big-breasted Polish girls were lounging in a brickwork doorway, smiling at the train and smoking cigarettes. One of them laughed aloud, and her mouth glistened poisonously. After more brown-green grass and shunted trains, they passed bullet-riddled hulks of engines at the yard at Posen. Gazing through the window at the dim platform crowded with Poles, Gerstein wondered who Basia had really been. A real German woman needs no makeup, but *she* had painted her lips as carmine-red as the service colors of the Polizei fire brigade. Neither his father nor his wife would have liked her.

They paused at the next station for a long time. No one disturbed them. Dr. Pfannenstiel snored, then awoke with a gasp. Captain Günther was so still that he might as well not have existed. As for Gerstein, he stared wearily out the window. Tired S.D. men were checking documents, their jackbooted feet wide apart on the dirty concrete. The train began to move again at last, very slowly now, and after an interminable time reached the new frontier. They stopped once more for nearly an hour while the police inspected everyone's papers. Then they crossed into the General Government.

So it's sprayed directly on the clothes? inquired Dr. Pfannenstiel. I'm not personally familiar with this substance.

Correct, said Gerstein. It comes highly recommended by the Sanitation Office.

In Berlin?

Berlin, yes, answered Gerstein with a vacant smile, that smile which lacked three teeth.

Changing trains in Warsaw, they rode across the Vistula bridge and arrived in Lublin.

Gerstein, I've heard that there are some outstanding Ruthenian-Byzantine frescoes in that Dominican church over there. You're a Catholic, I believe?

No, Herr Captain, an Evangelical.

So. I'll do my best to overlook that. Do Evangelicals cross themselves?

No, Herr Captain.

All the same, don't start crossing yourself in public! The Führer has said that after Jews, Slavs and Freemasons, the churches are Germany's most dangerous enemies.

By your order, Herr Captain.

I'm afraid you won't have time to see your little frescoes, Gerstein. But we may be able to visit Lublin Castle. Quite a number of prisoners being kept on ice in the cellars . . .

4

What's your opinion of the castle, Gerstein?

Well, from the outside it seems—

The Führer has said that everything Polish must be erased from the world.

Heil Hitler! cried Gerstein at once.

The railroad tracks were the same color as the evening sky.

5

They went by car to Lvov, which our forces had captured a year ago from that Slavic general, Vlasov. (Vlasov would soon begin working for us.) Lvov was now called Lemberg. In the windows of all the nice restaurants, neat signs warned: *GERMANS ONLY. NO POLES ADMITTED.*

You're a quiet young man, Gerstein. I commend that.

Thank you, Herr Captain.

You haven't been in Lemberg before.

No, Herr Captain.

I'm happy to say that Lemberg was a very anti-Semitic city long before we arrived here. Even the Polish students used to . . .

Gerstein smiled on him with hatred.

Hidden beyond the greatness and greenness of Polish summer trees, past tallish rounded Polish haystacks like ancient tumuli, a railroad spur ran to the secret place called Belzec, which would sometimes appear in his nightmares as a negative image, white on black, the Nazi eagle-stamp a white blotch on the document with the swastika black; sometimes eagle and swastika went completely white together, becoming a winged bomb falling in prefiguration of our V-2 rockets: GEHEIM. And then that file was opened; the secret of Belzec opened unto him in typed and numbered paragraphs, the numbers centered, the section titles underlined after the fashion of legal contracts. It was all for the best; thus the lesson he'd been meant to learn. Once the zone was clean and clear, there'd be happier scenes: Volksdeutsche receiving farmhouses, identification cards and framed photographs of the Führer as they entered their new inheritance.

Gentlemen, I'd like you to meet ϟϟ-Brigade Chief Otto Globocnik. Chief, I believe you've already met Professor Dr. Pfannenstiel, our Waffen-ϟϟ hygienist. And this fresh-faced young man is our delousing expert, ϟϟ-Obersturmführer Kurt Gerstein.

Heil Hitler! Yes, Dr. Pfannenstiel and I exchanged ideas just two weeks ago, in Lublin.

Heil Hitler!

Heil Hitler!

Brigade Chief Globocnik has been entrusted with organizing the actions against the Jews in Lublin District. And how's the good work coming?

It's a cesspool here, Günther. No matter how hard we work, there's more shit and more shit! *Jewish* shit. Hopefully we'll be able to clean it up faster—

That's your task, Brigade Chief.

Of course. But they keep dumping more Jews on me. Just when I got Lublin nearly cleaned up, they sent me Jews from Austria. Last week I got a shipment from the Old Reich, and they're all pretending to be war heroes!

What scoundrels!

They've all gone *to the bathhouse* now! Do you understand me, Gerstein?

No, Brigade Chief.

Well, you'll learn. Now, you're going to have two jobs at Belzec. First of all, you'll develop a procedure for disinfecting clothing. We have mountains of it piling up, all used, and crawling with God knows what sort of vermin from Russians, Poles, Jews and all that riffraff . . .

By your order, Brigade Chief.

Secondly, we need a faster working gas than diesel exhaust. That's where your prussic acid comes in.

Gerstein trotted after them, smiling woodenly as he waited to be enlightened. Dr. Pfannenstiel already knew. Dr. Pfannenstiel horrified him.

Gerstein, meet Kripo Chief Herr Christian Wirth. Wirth, this is ϟϟ-Obersturmführer Kurt Gerstein, who's a very ingenious and reliable young man, I've heard . . .

Heil Hitler, Captain Wirth!

Heil Hitler! You'll get used to the smell, Gerstein. Haven't you ever passed by a rendering plant? Even paper-mills stink. Now, this here is the dressing hut. Do you see that window to turn in valuables? It's surprising how many of them actually do it. We find that it reassures them. Moreover, it saves work for the Sonderkommando later, although our regulations do require us to inspect every body cavity.

That was when Captain Günther said: You're not going to disappoint us, will you, Gerstein?

By your order, sir—

Next I'll take you to the barber room, where we shave the heads of the women. We actually turn quite a profit on haircloth. Jewesses in particular seem to pamper their hair. I suppose it's a racial characteristic. Then that lane over there with barbed wire on both sides, that leads to the baths, which is where you come in.

By your order, Captain Wirth—

A naked blonde Jewess, smiling at Gerstein without hope or shame, raised her hands one by one above her head and mopped her sweating armpits with a rag which had not yet been taken from her. The hair of her axilla resembled golden wire. Seeing how he looked at her, Captain Wirth shook his head.

Nature is inherently cruel, Gerstein, explained Captain Günther.

6

Gerstein, start your stopwatch.

In a fury, Captain Wirth was whipping Heckenholt's Ukrainian assistant.

After two hours and forty-nine minutes, Heckenholt got the diesel motor working. Thirty-two minutes after that, all the Jews were dead.

Gerstein said to nobody in particular: The Führer himself has stated that Madagascar would be an acceptable residence for the Jews.

As a matter of fact, replied Captain Wirth in a monitory tone, the wishes of the Führer on this matter are top secret. Just remember this: The Final Solution is the only way we can reduce the danger of epidemics.

I understand, Herr Captain.

Now what? he was wondering. The answer proved logical: iron hooks in the mouths, then Captain Wirth gloating over his jam-box filled with the gold teeth of dead Jews. (The Ukrainians had made off with a golden mace from the sixteenth century, some coins, an ivory figurine of some saint.)—Into the mass grave! Now for petrol and match!

Dr. Pfannenstiel approached the pit rather gingerly and said: These bodies have not been completely burned.

So what, man? They're only Jews!

Dr. Pfannenstiel cleared his throat and reproachfully explained: That's not the issue. The whole procedure is not entirely satisfactory from the point of view of hygiene.

Gerstein was sure that he must be wearing his horror as conspicuously as an Iron Cross, but down sank another of his illusions. Everybody smiled at the handsome young blond man. Captain Wirth slapped him on the shoulder and said: There are not ten people alive who have seen, or will see, as much as you.

7

There is a roster of good souls. Open the dark grey folder and read: The names and identification numbers of these righteous have been typed in the lefthand column, followed by other boxes which contain in turn the dates of service, the methods employed and the numbers of people saved. To tell the truth, I had imagined that this roster resembled one of those Greek codices with golden anchors and crowns in the margins; but the practice of virtue is such a dreary, low-paying business that it's all that the angels can do to hire a military typist; not even alphabetical order can be respected here, which is why on one of the loose sheets we find, in this order, Dr. Hermann Maas of Heidelberg, who helped many Jews get safely to England and Switzerland (he got sent to a labor camp in 1944, but survived the war despite his advanced age); Pastor Erik Myrgren of Berlin, whom the Israelis have designated one of the Righteous Among Nations; and Dr. Elisabeth Abegg, also of Berlin, who sold her jewelry in order to finance the escapes of Jews.—The name of Kurt Gerstein is not here.

There is another register, much more voluminous than the first; it's an old book on whose title page, above the single red Cyrillic word, hangs an immense bar of darkness with white gratings, then spiderwebs surrounded by a cross. This book is as tall as a gravestone; its covers are cast out of lead; it takes six strong men to carry it. At Nuremberg the prosecution caused it to be brought into the courtroom as evidence against each of the major war criminals; the appearance of the defendant's name on any one of its pages sufficed to ensure conviction, unless he was a rocket scientist. Once West Germany became a crucial Anglo-American ally in the Cold War, this volume was deposited in the National Archives in Washington, D.C., and subsequently misshelved. This is why most of its inmates lived out prosperous postwar lives. In its pages have been been written forever the names of Captain Günther, Dr. Pfannenstiel (whose indictment got dismissed), Captain Wirth, Brigade Chief Globocnik, and ever so many others—my random gaze uncovers ϟϟ-Personalakte Hellmuth Becker, commander of the ϟϟ Death's Head Division, who liked to rape Russian women in the streets.—But Gerstein's name is not here, either.

What then is Gerstein? Wherein should he be inscribed?—Geheim.

His story is as rare, and hence as shocking, as full-figure reliefs of the saints on otherwise featureless walls.

Now that story started to run in earnest, like rope hissing out from greased coils as the gallows-trap drops. He was falling; he was free to make something of himself between beginning and end. On the train from Warsaw to Berlin he met a Swedish attaché and told him what he had seen at Belzec, whispering in his ear all that hot and ghastly night. Soon he'd lapsed into the present tense: *The people stand together on each other's feet. Seven hundred, eight hundred people in an area of twenty-five square meters!* At his side, Baron von Otter stood rigidly there in the corridor of the sleeping car, turning his face away from the blond man's breath. It was pitch-dark in the General Government. Soon, thank God, they'd have passed through Radom Station, and then the Reich frontier would come; not long after that he could get away. He lit another cigarette. When he couldn't bear to listen anymore, he kept politely nodding, his lips moving in what Gerstein must have assumed was a prayer for the dead Jews but which was actually nothing more than a list of all the names he remembered from a recent visit to a Romanian cemetery: Ecaterina, Eufrosina, Maria, Gelu, Andrei, Gheorghe, Nicu, Leni, Ionifia, Elena, Eleffenie, Melinte. Languages were his hobby. He meant to learn Romanian someday. For a Latinist, it surely wouldn't be difficult. Elena, Eleffenie, Melinte. Then the light came on, glaring on all the naked blue bodies, and one of them was still moving; she stretched out her hands toward the window, so they turned the light back out and Eleffenie, Melinte. He wished to know how accurately Gerstein had counted these alleged victims. The blond man choked out: *My stopwatch has registered everything faithfully. Fifty minutes seventy seconds—the engine still has not started! The people are waiting in their gas chamber. You can hear them crying, sobbing . . .* —In short, he'd fallen prey to the dangerous capability of the *Untermensch* to mask itself behind a human face (his sister-in-law's, for instance), and thereby excite pity.

Baron von Otter sent a report to his government, but this report must have been stamped GEHEIM, for it remained unpublished until three months after the war's end.

8

As for Gerstein, he opened the New Testament and read: *Leave the dead to bury the dead.* Then horror came upon him like a sickness.

9

It's natural to believe, or want to believe, since inertia is self-preservation, that once we have opened the vault, the dark grey file, and read some stupefying secret, we've learned *the* secret, in which all others, if in fact there are any others, must be contained; hence we need not go to the dangerous trouble of digging anything else up. The allurements of ease, which kept most Germans from doing what Gerstein tried to do, encourage us to say: In any event, I've done my duty now. The rest is up to others.

Ever since he was a child, he'd been afflicted by what his father called *evil thoughts,* meaning an introspection of the melancholy, isolating sort. If only he had not had those thoughts! Then he would not have been obliged to cause himself and others so much pain . . .

The working capacity of Belzec was fifteen thousand murders per day. That meant (he made the calculation on a sheet of stationery of the Deutsche Gesandtschaft Budapest, with the Nazi eagle on it; then he tore the page into pieces and burned it) four hundred and fifty thousand Jews gassed every month, or *five and a half million Jews per year,* under ideal conditions of course. This was shocking enough that on that first time at Belzec when the bright light came on in the chamber, he thought that he knew the worst. But the next day, after parting from Captain Günther at Lemberg with a loud *Heil Hitler!* (Captain Günther was required on secret business, in a place called Chelmno), the blond man found himself riding in a French-made lorry beside his intimate friend Dr. Pfannenstiel, Captain Wirth at the wheel, to a second extermination camp, called Treblinka, whose eight gas chambers could kill twenty-five thousand Jews per day; and in due course Gerstein's various liaison and inspection duties would bring him to the virgin facility of Maidanek, whose greenish barracks could devour only two thousand Jews per day, but the place produced luscious cabbages which were manured with the snow-white ashes of Jews; and Captain Günther had mentioned Chelmno, while Captain Wirth with a wink admitted to him knowledge of Sobibor (capacity: twenty thousand per day), where German engineers had invented a special mill for grinding Jews' bones to powder. As the Scripture says, *my house has many mansions.*

The joke at Sobibor (Gerstein was really going to split his sides at this one, Captain Wirth promised) was that our very first gassing there—forty-odd screaming naked Jewesses; you should have seen how they . . . —was accomplished by means of a two-hundred-horsepower petrol engine of *Russian* manufacture! If only those Bolshevist kikes could see how we used their technology!—Dr. Pfannenstiel was the one who laughed; Dr. Pfannenstiel was the one who remarked that Captain Wirth's point, namely, the ironic justice of our appropriation of captured matériel, would make for an excellent column in *Signal* magazine. Too bad that it was GEHEIM!

Gerstein, mechanically smiling, a smile which hid the missing three teeth, had just worked out the total for these facilities: more than twenty-two million Jews per year, excluding Chelmno and ignoring human or mechanical failures—how many Jews were there in Europe? Did he dare ask Dr. Pfannenstiel? How many Jews remained above the ground in Europe? How many were there in the entire world? What if his estimates were faulty? Suppose that in fact no more than, for example, two million Jews per year were put to death? And how many other camps might there be? Two million, five million or twenty-two million—he was a mining engineer. He could comprehend large figures.

At Treblinka the ϟϟ held a banquet for them, and after a *Sieg Heil!* for our Führer and a hearty if not entirely tuneful singing of "Deutschland über Alles," Dr. Pfannenstiel, flushed with Polish wine, rose to give an impromptu speech which concluded: When one sees the bodies of these Jews, one understands the greatness of the work you're doing!—Gerstein laughed in a great shout, raising his goblet for the toast. Dr. Pfannenstiel sat down. It was late afternoon. From outside came women's screams in a quick-ceasing chorus; was that an action, a general action, or a total action? Dr. Pfannenstiel refilled Gerstein's glass with a little bow. Gerstein thanked him.—I *like* you, you blue-eyed Goth! chuckled his colleague; so wide a chuckle it was that Gerstein could see down his throat.—Then Captain Wirth beckoned.

Gerstein, you've seen for yourself that we run a good operation here, he began, embarrassed, and Gerstein, smiling disarmingly, nodding at him like a schoolboy, thought: This monster wants a favor!

You won't mention the engine problem to Berlin, will you?

Of course not, Herr Captain! That sort of thing can happen anywhere—

You're a very understanding young man, and I won't forget that. Now I want to ask you something else. What do you intend to do with the prussic acid?

As you advise me, Herr Captain, returned Gerstein in the most ingratiating tone he could wring out. Actually, this wasn't so bad. Anything was better than sitting next to Dr. Pfannenstiel.

You'll appreciate my motives in putting this to you: Heckenholt and all the others depend on me for their livelihood. As for Globocnik, well, between you and me, he's been in trouble before, and he doesn't want to get sidelined. None of us want to be sidelined here, Gerstein. Do you see what I mean? Now, here's what I want you to do.

By your order, Captain!

I want you to tell those people in Berlin that we don't need any modifications, at least not at Belzec (about Treblinka I don't give a shit). Thanks to their interference, we've already been made to give up bottled gas, which worked perfectly well, believe me, back at the start of all this. They can complain all they like about supply problems. Well, in this life we all have supply problems. Bottled gas is what we used to carry out T-4, after the bleeding hearts decided that shooting wasn't good enough for Germans. Well, they can all go to hell. Tell those assholes in Berlin that based on your technical expertise, diesel is more sensible than prussic acid—more rapid or more safe or whatever. Get those bureaucrats to leave us in peace. They're not living in the real world. Do we have a deal?

Gerstein, knowing that every hour Heckenholt's engine broke down was an hour when Jews would escape murder at Belzec, also knowing that the lethality of his sky-blue prussic acid crystals was far superior to that of carbon monoxide, smiled at Captain Wirth with charming frankness and said: I'm afraid the prussic acid has deteriorated in transit. It's quite unstable, actually. I fear that we have no alternative but to bury it—

Good man! Gerstein, I'll cut you in. Do you see that Ukrainian over there? I'll make sure he has something for you.

Herr Captain, that's not necessary—

But now Captain Wirth began to worry that Gerstein was holding out for more than a one-time payment in Jew-gold. All the prostitutes of Poland, so it seemed, had set up shop just beyond his railroad siding, not at all put out by the stinking black fog which overhung Belzec rain or shine; and his liaison officer Oberhauser, who enjoyed the occasional tryst with any Aryan-looking P-maiden, had reported to him that they kept raising their prices, doubtless because the treasures of Belzec were, at least from the standpoint of such sports, inexhaustible. (Captain Wirth had himself seen a blondish wench leading two of his Ukrainians into a sort of cave she'd made in the mound of Jew-clothes behind the locomotive shed. He'd had to punish her for that.) In his fear, Captain Wirth became grotesquely confiding, and soon, just for laughs, he was telling Gerstein all about Hadamar, *my God, he's talking about Hadamar,* and later, when Captain Wirth kept telling him to take a few pounds of butter at least, not to mention a suitcase of "Wyborowca" vodka (in the end, Dr. Pfannenstiel was happy to relieve him of that), he kept staring as he smiled, like someone dazed by a glaring light, because Captain Wirth had told him how back in the glory days of Operation T-4—a very necessary endeavor, as he was sure that Gerstein knew, a challenging project, to get right down to it, a rewarding time, a procedure which, in spite of being classified Geheim, had been exposed and interrupted by those Christian swine whose fat asses we were saving in this war—he used to personally shoot mental defectives in the back of the head with his service revolver, because it wasn't until '41 that a genius thought up the system of false showerbaths. Gerstein, sympathetically astonished, wondered why an officer of his rank and quality hadn't been assigned more help in the performance of this duty, to which Captain Wirth laughingly replied that in such close quarters, and considering that the targets were merely peaceful mental patients, not hardened Jews, one shooter was better than two, because two in the head is too much; two will practically tear the head off; and that was when it occurred to Gerstein that Captain Wirth, who was pale, bespectacled, and pinchfaced except when he explicated Operations T-4 and Reinhard, that Captain Wirth, who wore an Iron Cross, a metal sunburst and a death's head cap, had in all likelihood killed everybody at Hadamar himself—which is to say, he was the one who'd murdered Berthe.

10

To his friend Helmut Franz he once said in his typically didactic fashion: The times leave me no choice but to seek knife-edge paths and live dangerously.—That was in the golden summer of '41, when we were rushing deeper and deeper into Russia, and, following closely behind our soldiers, the colleagues of Kurt Gerstein were marching Jews on a one-way trip out of town. Gerstein didn't yet know anything apodictically; he hadn't been invited to Belzec. But he was an SS-man; he was on the knife-edge path. Futurity became a black tomb with an iron ring.

So now he'd pulled the iron ring; the pleasure wasn't his.* He dreamed that its blackness came off on his hands, and then . . .

---

*As we read in Gottfried's *Tristan*: *What harms love more than doubt and suspicion? . . . Yet it is far more remiss in a man to reduce doubt and surmise to certainty; since when he has gained his object and knows that his doubts are justified, the fact which he was at pains to track down becomes a grief surpassing all others.*

He went home, to his father's house. His wife was waiting for him. She offered her waxen cheek to be kissed. His father came slowly downstairs, greeting him with a sleepy *Heil Hitler.* The children were long in bed. There was dinner, a good dinner under the circumstances; Elfriede had done the best she could; and he wondered what the poor thing would have thought of him had she known that he'd turned down all that Jewish butter.

11

Below the portrait of his eldest brother, whom he scarcely remembered (fallen on the Westfront back in 1918), his father sat in the armchair, frowning at a feature in *Signal* magazine about three winsome young workers from the East (R-maidens from the look of them) who posed in knee-length skirts on the summer lawn of the Potsdam Palace, giggling. *They have already adopted European fashions and have quickly learned the Western European style of hairdressing.* On the facing page was another color photograph of tanks rolling onto an Italian freighter, the picture saturated with the Mediterranean hues of ocean and earth, everything summery. The caption read: "Supplies for Tunis."

Ha! said the old man suddenly, remembering. I forgot to write you this, Kurt. Another Yid tried to steal our name! Another *Goldstein.* But this time they caught up with him. Do you remember when I complained about the last case back in '33? And my complaint went unanswered. Well, this one they smoked out, thanks be to the All-Highest. Shipped him off!

Where did they catch him, father?

At the Technical University, right in Berlin if you can believe it! He was a cheeky one, not wearing the yellow star. His first name was something Russian. I suppose they'll have to make an example of him. The things that go on nowadays! Although I remember another case, in which a certain Richard Goldstein of Hamburg . . .

Father, you've told us that story many times.

Ludwig Gerstein stared at his son. Then he rose, departing like a dark planet falling silently to one side.

Kurt, why couldn't you have let him have his say? It's harmless, and it makes him happy. Now he'll worry that you think he's senile . . .

He used to say that he regretted what was being done.

Of course you don't care that he'll avenge himself on me after you leave.

But Kurt Gerstein gazed at her with sternness as ungiving as his father's.

12

She could never understand why he wouldn't allow her and the children to come to Berlin.—Father needs to be cared for, was all he said. And in times like these, if we give up this house, we'll never get it back again.

We'd all rather be with you, Kurt. But I suppose you prefer those widow's sons you've taken in.

You've seen for yourself how poor Frau Hedwig is!

To be sure, that was a perfectly executed charitable maneuver, said Elfriede with a nasty smile. Meanwhile, you leave your own three children alone with me.

He said nothing. Tübingen was the city of his childhood, the place where he'd failed his theological studies. He'd been someone else here. Thank God for the blackout curtains! He hated the sight of Tübingen.

Well, his wife pursued, and how are they doing now?

Who?

Who's under discussion? Hedwig's boys.

Feeling as if they were speaking of people whom neither of them had ever met, he cast about for something to say, and finally told her: They're in the Hitler Youth, of course.

They must look stunning together, in their matching uniforms. Twins, yet!

What are you implying?

Nothing. I'm going to bed.

God keep you then, he said.

When he was courting her, they used to pretend together that he had saved an enchanted castle from ogres, thereby winning its beautiful mistress. Elfriede had long since grown beyond such foolish games.

13

In spite of his good manners and magnificent pedigree, Obersturmführer Gerstein remained less popular with his ᛋᛋ-comrades than anyone would have expected.—He found God, they said of him. We would have liked him better if he hadn't.—Or, to tell the tale more positively, no friendships distracted him from his official duties. Accordingly, Gerstein's professional life became as pretty as the mountains one sees to the south on the way to Auschwitz. His service record from this period reads: *G. is especially suitable for all tasks. Proficient and sure. He is disciplined and has authority.* Gassing van inspectors learned to come to Kurt Gerstein whenever they wanted to complain about inappropriate procedures. They'd sink into the low leather sofa, reach for the latest issue of *Signal* magazine from the coffee table, bored by the very first full-page photograph (the shining metal grillework of a Ju-52 transport plane being swabbed clean by our tanned blond soldier-boys in Africa), say sugar or no sugar to the alert schoolmarm of a secretary-typist, and then they'd wait until the man on the far side of that immense office finished roaring into the telephone: *You tell them they'd better finish by noon tomorrow, or they're up the chimney! Did you hear me? You'd better have heard me. Heil Hitler!* and he'd clang the heavy black receiver down into its cradle, "like a swordsmith with hammer and anvil," the poets among them thought, and none of them ever caught on that the person to whom he'd been shouting (and for that matter the shouter himself) did not exist. Now here he came, lopsidedly smiling because those three missing teeth humiliated him; they leaped up for a *Heil Hitler!* and then ᛋᛋ-Obersturmführer Gerstein, dear blond Kurt Gerstein, his hair combed back, was asking what he could do for them.—The operators keep calibrating the engines incorrectly, Herr Obersturmführer, and it doesn't do any good to bawl them out! It's not very nice for the cleaning crews, I'll tell you! The Jews shit and puke all over the floor before they . . . —And smiling, blond Kurt Gerstein, the one man in the ᛋᛋ who understood them, agreed that this was unseemly, promised to request an investigation, asked for details as to the quantities of Jews being killed, the locations of the temporary extermination centers, the widths and depths of the mass graves, etcetera, which, these matters being Geheim, they really shouldn't have revealed, but if one can't trust an ᛋᛋ-man, it's hopeless! In fact, working methods throughout our Eastern territories gradually did improve as Auschwitz came up to capacity. Some of them thanked Kurt Gerstein for that.

Have you ever seen our tank parks and artillery parks all arranged in neat squares upon the green grass of Germany? (If you have, I hope they won't shoot you!) ᛋᛋ-Obersturmführer Kurt Gerstein's office was laid out in just that orderly fashion, with every stack of files compulsively squared up, as if he feared inspection, and that latest issue of *Signal* centered on the coffee table, all the file cabinets locked, half a dozen framed portraits of our Führer marching around the walls according to size; and the pens and pencils absolutely vertical, crammed in the holder like Jews in a gas chamber—well, you get the picture. Gerstein was always helpful and correct with his colleagues, no matter that he did pray. An old pensioner named Greisler, who if you ask his former occupation mutters something about being a diesel mechanic, sings Gerstein's praises to this day: He helped my nephew get into an Adolf Hitler School!—We must not over-emphasize the testimony of Frau Alexandra Bälz, who remembered visiting him at summer's end '42; after sobbing that he couldn't go on, he poisoned her life forever with his horrid secret. (If the ϟϟ had heard, he would have been shot immediately, and his family all sent to Dachau.) On the very next evening, Obersturmführer Gerstein was dining quite merrily with "Clever Hans" Günther in one of Prague's subterranean restaurants—an establishment so deep and dim, in fact, that both men had the feeling of being inside a wine cask. Abstaining from the wine, he assured his superior that he longed only to be of use to our Reich. How could he best further the completion of Operation Reinhard?

Gerstein, I had doubts about you at first, but now I can see you're as firm as iron! I'll bring you to Theresienstadt tomorrow morning. Captain Seidl is Austrian, like our Führer himself. A real iron man! I think you'll be impressed by the way he hoodwinks the Bohemian Jews. Even the Red Cross swallows the bait! It's time to teach you his system, because we have to get ready for Hungary.

By your order, Herr Captain! Thank you for your confidence in me . . .

Nor should we allot exaggerated importance to the recollection of Pastor Otto Wehr that at his final rendezvous with Gerstein, in the fall of 1944, the latter told him: Every half hour, those trainloads of doomed Jews come chasing me . . . —He gasped out to Bishop Dibelius, who'd officiated at his wedding: *Help us, help us! These things must become the talk of the world*— . . . —Why dwell on sad and secret matters? After all, the General Plan for the East was being fulfilled!

To be sure, the Plan's very success had impelled us out of sight of those easy days when the very heart of the Reich had still been full of Jews who, ripe for the harvesting, offered their hunters not only the currency and valuables which any city dweller, even the poorest, is practically bound to have, but also the shared language so convenient for torment (spit in the face of the quarry's Aryan wife and call her *Jew's whore*; no fear that the husband won't understand!). But now the hunters were compelled not only by the scarcity of game in the homeland but more so by the continuously increasing magnitude of the hunt to forage in the alien preserves of the General Government, the Reichskommissariat Ukraine (where Gerstein could have helped himself to a golden tankard with an eagle on the lid), the Reichskommissariat Ostland, the widening strip of unincorporated Soviet territory behind the eastward-rushing front, not to mention Romania, Croatia, Bulgaria, Greece, Hungary, where in many cases the Jewish peasants, already accustomed to centuries of beatings, confiscations and pogroms, clumped silently together when the hunters flushed them out of their already blazing huts; and when the hunters cursed them the Jews gazed back wide-eyed as though they comprehended nothing even when the Einsaztgruppen men, in between reading advertisements for Rosodont, which is to say ***Bergmann's Solidified Toothpaste***, shot the old ones and the sick ones right there; even when they took the strong young males away to dig the pit, the hunters' domination seemed to make no mark upon those faces pale as writing paper; worse yet, what was there to pilfer except a few gold teeth? Of course the Jews of Holland, Belgium, Italy and France were richer, but they tended to get stripped by the police of their own countries. So the German hunters felt that everything was diminishing now. Sometimes there weren't even gold teeth. Ebbing Jewry might dry up completely, as it continued to seem, yet profitlessly, rustling and dying, draining into each new earth-pit, its blood absorbed, its memory walled off like the festering heart of Shostakovich's still unwritten Eighth String Quartet (Opus 110), the charred smears of Jewish villages quickly overgrown with grasses golder than guilt. The hunters still believed in the hunt (after all, in our Ukraine there remain compliant U-maidens, in Russia R-girls, and so on). But they'd begun to feel as if they were shooting fieldmice instead of deer.

Until the Ostfront stabilizes . . . Captain Günther kept saying now. He had begun registering Jewish property in the last marches of Bohemia. The former owners marched past Prague's powder-tower, whose bas-reliefs of matronly virgins and froglike knights were all black and old. Then off they went to Theresienstadt, to wait until Auschwitz's ovens had room for them. As for Gerstein, he grew haggard trying to learn the contents of more secret documents. This was his honor, you might say. His comrades were disappointed, because he couldn't find time to accompany them to the cinema to see Lisca Malbran. Mostly he shuttled between Prague and Berlin, but I seem to see him at Dachau, where Russian prisoners got frozen for experimental purposes, their falling body temperatures being measured with rectal thermometers; and he was likewise at Birkenau, where his SS comrades collected the most interesting skulls of Jewish-Bolshevik commissars, coding them, then affixing labels as colorful as Mussolini's decorations. (There was Berthe again. Her eyes resembled those of the Italian princess who died in the brothel of Buchenwald.) I find him pacing the sidewalk below the Deutsches

Haus in Prague, with wreaths and swastika buntings fading moment by moment above his head; now here came the transport: fifteen Green Minnas whose barred high windows showed him only darkness; he knew from experience that as many as fifty prisoners could be packed in, if their packers didn't care about a few suffocations, so that meant that a possible seven hundred and fifty more victims of Hitler had just now (at 1145 hours) passed this street corner and vanished while he'd pretended not to count them; they must be bound for the Petschek Palace, where the Gestapo operated; his quest called him there to observe the incoming traffic, but moderation forbade him. Traversing and transecting Europe Central with his top-secret manifests for the delivery of Zyklon B, he sometimes had time to inhale the gloomy yet somehow satisfying smell of old church-stone soaked with five hundred years' worth of incense, breath, and the steam from fresh-baked sacred bread. Instead of relief, his prayers brought him only desperation. How could he deny that with knowledge came sin and death, that his quest to learn the truth had infected him with horror, that he was now an accomplice until he saved the Jews?—But he had clean hands.

In 8.42, his horrid visions like heel-claps echoing in an old church, he sought out the Papal Nuncio in Berlin to bear witness. Monsignor Orsenigo would not see him, perhaps on account of the ϟϟ *Siegrunen* flashing on a shield on the side of his dark helmet. Leave bad manners to their own quarrel, his father always used to say, but Kurt Gerstein, who still had much to learn, persisted until they begged him to go away in God's name. When he emerged from the legation, pale and twitching, a policeman began to follow him, and then another policeman on a bicycle came after the first. He changed direction, ducking around a wall whose poster, a little torn and grimy, for it was last month's "Word of the Week," displayed the compulsory Jewish star, with the explanation **Who wears this symbol is an enemy of our people.** The two policemen continued to follow him. His first thought was to knock on Bishop Dibelius's door, but he disdained implicating anybody in his own doom. (What I can do is almost nothing, Dibelius had said.) Desperately he leaped aboard a tram and rode three stops toward Wannsee; that was how he shook them. (Captain Wirth dined with him at Auschwitz and said: You need stronger nerves, my friend.)

He paid a call on the Swiss press attaché, who sniffed at him and said: Of course I'll relay your story to the bureau, Herr Gerstein. But in the first place, it's unbelievable; and in the second place, if you take a look at the map of central Europe, you'll see that Switzerland is not a very large country, but the Reich is growing all the time, so please don't expect to read your anecdote in the newspapers tomorrow.—Gerstein turned on his heel.

Once more he attempted to meet with Monsignor Orsenigo, but that gentleman, they told him, was away at the Vatican. So at extreme peril to himself he conveyed a note to Dr. Winter, legal adviser of the Archishop of Berlin. There came no answer.

Day after day, dangerously neglecting his own duties, he paced before the gates of the Swedish embassy until he saw Baron von Otter emerge. Frau Hedwig's twins expected him to come and speak to their Hitler Youth chapter on the topic of German chivalry, but he was going to be late. At the corner, two Gestapo men sat in a Mercedes-Benz watching. Gerstein rushed at his acquaintance, wrung his hand, asked in a quivering voice whether anything had come of the story he'd told.—Of course I made a report, his acquaintance replied, glancing at the Mercedes uneasily. It has already had a great influence on the relations between Sweden and Germany.

Thanks be to God!

And now please excuse me, Obersturmführer Gerstein. I must attend to my official duties . . .

Baron, I beg to inform you that they're now opening all the mass graves in the East, to destroy the evidence. Write this down, please: ᛋᛋ-Standartenführer Paul Blobel is their incineration expert—

Herr Obersturmführer, are you insane? Those men over there—

That winter they were in a broken-windowed, sandbag-walled nightclub in Minsk, a city now belonging to our Reich, which was why with the exception of certain specialists who were needed for the war effort the Jews there had already been apprehended and rendered harmless, and Gerstein, who to the astonishment of his comrades had just declined the present of a huge glass jar of malt syrup, which his wife would have gratefully received, was thinking: What is my life? A lovely blonde R-girl who's so slender I could wrap my arm around her waist twice, she lounges against the wall or carefully squats down to pass tiny cold transparent glasses of "Kazakhstan" vodka to the Wehrmacht officers who are playing billiards in the sunken room; she is glowing with her youth, burning her youth instant by instant, wasting it here. What should she be doing with it? What should I have done with mine? Mine is gone, burned out. And she is as slender and blonde as this candle she's lit for me, the candle with its slender blonde flame which ever so gently sways as her head does, its expression as unreadable as hers. She's Aryan; she's one of us; she's beautiful; she should be *with* one of us. That's what they say. But the flame eats the candle whether it touches another wick or not. (Don't you want to watch the show, Gerstein? We're just about to cram the gas chamber full of naked women!—But they seem so innocent!—Ha, ha! How sly they are!—And his heart screamed out; far away, in Kuibyshev, Shostakovich heard the scream in his nightmares and saved it for Opus 110.) She squats down, and places another vodka glass on the ledge by the billiard-players. The liquid trembles. It's clearer than ice, more silver than water. Her face is blank. Is she bored or afraid? She wants to go home. If she had enough to eat I suppose she wouldn't be here. Then what would she do with her beauty? Does she even know? It's night, and the snow is dark and dirty outside—snow in the shell-cratered streets, dark houses plastered with tattered eagle-and-swastika announcements of regulations and reprisals, then more snow, frozen garbage, swastika buntings flapping and creaking unseen in the night wind, and somewhere, probably in a narrow alley heaped roof-high with rubble, Berthe's ghost glides, forever invisible to those shivering, blue-faced German soldiers who await another grey dawn. She's not Berthe; I know that. She lays her hand upon her cheek. She gazes down at the billiards. I expect her to yawn. Her hips barely bell out. Her legs seem to come all the way up to her chest. Her breasts are modest but firm. She's streamlined like a German airplane. This blonde woman-metal shoots through the air, consuming itself with a magnesium flame. The flame is steady. She faintly smiles. A player whirls his billiard stick like a propeller; he would fly, too, if he could, but he's too fat and old. Youth will win. Youth is her firm, almost flat buttocks which swell out from her only with the most subtle and aerodynamic roundedness. And her face—a fully perfect blank blonde stone! Those Greek caryatids, they're female without being human. That's what she is. Maybe I don't want to be human. I want to be her. I want to eat her like caviar. But if I could eat her goodness, it would only melt away on my tongue.

Across from Gerstein sat another SS-man, watching him searchingly. At last this comrade said kindly: Never mind, Gerstein. I myself vomited after my first execution.

14

His wife implored him to resign from the SS, for her sake and the sake of the children. She took him by the hand and drew him to a mirror, murmuring: Look at yourself, Kurt! Look at what this is doing to you!

Proudly he said: I myself have chosen this road.

Then she said: How can you, a man of honor and a sincere Christian, stand by and watch these things?

His face hardened into helmet-flesh and he replied: I am glad to have seen these atrocities with my own eyes, so that one day, God permitting, I may be able to testify about them.

She laughed at him.

Then he swung round as though he were about to strike her; and he said: Perhaps I ought to sue for divorce. What do you think? That would save you, should anything happen to me . . .

No, Kurt, no—

Very well then. We mustn't just think of ourselves.

But wasn't that precisely what he was doing? The next time he went to Theresienstadt, on another secret mission for "Clever Hans" Günther, there weren't as many boxcars as usual so he completed the registration early. Detraining at Prague, he thought to buy something for his family. He was an ᛋᛋ-man; he could go anywhere he chose! Czechs and Germans alike, everyone gazed at him with fear, which made him long to scream. Smiling coldly, he flicked an imaginary granule of dust from his death's head cap. He called himself *a spy for God.* In those curving streets walled high with watchful windows, swastika banners hung down on either side with perfect regularity just as in Berlin, so quite often he could see three ahead on his left, three more on his right, until the street arrived at a squat black archway like a grave. Following a stone bridge across the Vltava, the Moldau we call it now, he came to a street where an old woman was selling honey. She was sitting on the cobblestoned curb, drowsily humming to herself. Something about her face reminded him of the Catholic nurse who'd cared for him in his childhood; she was the only one who'd been kind to him. When his shadow fell on her, she looked up and screamed.

15

The Anglo-Jewish Bolshevists label us "totalitarians," and it's true that all over our Reich, even at Wolf's Lair itself, we express ourselves by means of the same signals; for example, the preliminary end of an air raid alert is represented by three high-pitched sounds within a one-minute interval; then, once the cessation of the enemy threat has been verified, a tone of the same pitch shrills out steadily for one minute; we have found this consistency to be quite convenient. I'd be surprised if the enemy didn't have their own equally "totalitarian" system! For much the same reasons, we've elected to school every German boy, every decent one, that is, in the Hitler Youth; so that his response in these times of racial threat can be relied on.

Frau Hedwig's twins, Erich and Edmund, were among the decent ones. They had just been studying the Teutonic Knights. When he entered the room, Edmund was reading aloud: *Long and wide went the forest through which he must make his way were he not to shun the combat to which, through no fault of his own, he had been called.*

Laying his hand on the boy's shoulder, Gerstein asked him how he understood what he had just read. Edmund replied: **Hard times, hard hearts!** That's our Word of the Week. When a war gets foisted on us by international Jewry, we don't have a choice. We have to fight. That's what it means for us today.

Correct! laughed good blond Kurt Gerstein. By the way, have you dreamed about that dark forest?

Never, said Edmund.

Erich?

No, Herr Gerstein. Perhaps we don't understand your question. It's about good *versus* evil, isn't it?

Clearly. Now read it again.

Long and wide went the forest through which he must make his way . . .

Would you boys like to be knights?

Oh, yes! Like you, Herr Gerstein!

Continue.

Were he not to shun the combat . . .

Against whom?

The Jews, Herr Gerstein.

And who else?

There is no one else! cried the handsome boy, proud to have solved the trick question. *The Jews are our misfortune.* The Slavs and Anglo-Americans merely follow them. Isn't that right, Herr Gerstein?

That's right, he said gently, remembering that time back in '35 when the Hitler Youth insulted our Lord in their performance of *Wittekind* by Edmund Kiss. When the blond young actor on stage jeered: *We'll have no Savior who weeps and laments!* Kurt Gerstein had stood up to shout: We shall not allow our faith to be publicly mocked without protest!—They kicked him to the floor, and kept kicking. That was when he'd lost three of his teeth.

Hadn't he done everything he could? Wasn't he still doing it? He told the boys the tale of Simple Hans, whose princely brothers despised him for a fool but who won the princess in the end because he saved the ants, ducks and bees from harm, a favor they requited by coming to his aid when he was set humanly impossible magic tasks in the castle of stone effigies: The ants gathered up and counted all the scattered pearls, the ducks dove down to find the lost key, and the bee queen tasted the lips of each sleeping princess to find out which girl was the most charming.

16

Once more he succeeded in meeting the Swiss consul, Hochstrasser, and furtively spewed out his disgusting secret, while Hochstrasser gazed upon him with resentment.—I'll pass on your story to Berne if you insist, Herr Obersturmführer. But you continue to require that it remain unattributed!

For the love of Christ, sir! Don't you comprehend the situation of my wife and children?

As you prefer, then. But unattributed rumors of this kind, well—

What do you want me to do? Must I bring you a trainload of corpses?

Herr Obersturmführer, good day.

17

Again the prussic acid has decomposed! reported Obersturmführer Gerstein. There is nothing to do with it now except bury it.

It seems to decompose awfully frequently these days, said "Clever Hans" Günther.

There's wartime quality for you! his ϟϟ-man replied with a ringing laugh. I've complained to the factory in person several times.

Someone should be shot.

Naturally they use Jews and Slavs on the production line! But for the sake of our transportation personnel—

18

Your father hasn't yet forgiven you, reported his wife the next time he visited; and even though he didn't know what he hadn't been forgiven for, the knowledge of being in the wrong came as easily as ever. Towering over her, he shot her that look which she would never see as anything other than stern; and then he waited.

For cutting off his little story, she explained.

Oh, said he, placing another log upon the fire. The one about the Jew they caught.

He knew how it must have been for that Jew, because it had already happened to him twice, the first time back in 1936, that time he'd sent out the seven thousand anti-Nazi religious pamphlets and then they took him away in one of the Green Minnas, where through a small square barred window on the righthand side he saw clouds, darkness and windows; then it was right face and forward march with the others into Columbia House where the Blackshirts tortured him with wet horsewhips. In 1938, because they absurdly suspected him of monarchism, another Green Minna carried him to a concentration camp, where he quickly learned to tell the smirking doctor: I fell downstairs.—In short, he overcame all his previous ideological errors. A certain Gestapo man had gotten him out, but his father had also helped by insisting that Kurt Gerstein had always been a sincere anti-Semite. He'd never forget those weeks at Welzheim, his vacation they called it; and in particular the thing which he'd never tell anybody about, the thing that the ᛋᛋ-men had done to him. Of course all this had taken place back in the days when we still played around, when we beat them instead of liquidating them. Once upon a time, Röhm's portrait still hung in all our concentration camps. Then we shot Röhm and got serious. We commenced Operations Reinhard and Barbarossa, and set up shop at Belzec.

His wife said: You really ought to apologize.

As you wish, Friedl, he said, and he went up to Ludwig Gerstein's room. Didn't he owe his life to his father twice over?

Ever since he was a little child, his father's presence had always reminded him of Berlin's Zeughaus, which is square and reddish-tan, an immense stern cube studded with figures.

The old man was lying down. Half-opening his eyes, he gazed at his son with wolfish hostility. There was nothing to do but kneel down, kiss the father's hand, and beg his pardon: You know I've always been a bundle of nerves, and what with the war . . .

His father gazed at him stonily.

Inspired, the blond man leaned over and whispered: Not to mention my *secret work* . . .

This won the day. His father said: I do forgive you, Kurt. And now we'll never talk about it again.

Thank you, father. Once again, I'm sorry I—

Nowadays people are trying to accomplish so much. I trust that you also are doing your utmost.

Yes, father.

For whoever desires the Grail must approach that prize with the sword, his father recited, and Kurt Gerstein nodded submissively.

And have you been traveling? What do they tell you about the situation on the Ostfront?

Shall we talk about it by the fire, father? Friedl's soup should be ready about now—

Just tell me this, Kurt, before we go down to the others. From what you've heard, will Paulus be able to hold out?

I can hardly say, said Gerstein, and then at once, perceiving the ghastly fear upon his father's face, he amended himself: The Führer has promised us that Fortress Stalingrad will never be conquered.

You're right, his father said after a pause. That's the only way to think about things now. Now we'll go down to the others.

Seeing them descend the stairs together, his father's arm around his shoulder, Elfriede smiled with gladness, and he suddenly thought: Why, how much like Berthe she looks!

(Well, but after all, Berthe was her sister.)

His three children, pale and dispirited, ate their soup in silence. Friedl said: Now you must tell us where you've been, Kurt.

Minsk. Did you get my letter?

Not yet, she said steadily

Is it pretty bombed up? asked his father.

I'm afraid so. There's not much good to say about that place.

Well, after all, it was under Jewish domination for so long. Have all the Jews fled, or are they still causing trouble?

They've been evacuated, he said bitterly. This is excellent soup.

His son Christian said: Vati, I've heard there's a lot to eat in Prague. You go to Prague, don't you?

Yes.

Did you bring us anything from Prague?

Let your father eat, said Elfriede. Can't you see how tired he is?

Vati, someday will you take us there?

After the war, he replied with his head in his hands.

How many castles do they have? And what colors are on their flag? I'm doing a project about flags for school.

Their flag is the swastika now, of course. What on earth have your teachers been telling you?

He didn't bring home good marks this time, Elfriede announced harshly, and Gerstein knew that he, the absent man, was failing all of them. Charity begins at home, runs the proverb, and he was spending his charity far, far away, on a race whose extinction no one would even remember! *Leave the dead to bury the dead,* as Scripture says. For a moment he imagined bringing his family to Prague on a holiday, or taking Christian at least, so that the boy could see the ornate towers, the curving stone balconies flying our long crimson buntings whose swastikas make us all proud; it wasn't Germany, but those devils who—

Vati, next time you go to Prague will you please bring us something really good to eat?

Christian, said Elfriede, but not as sharply as she might have, you know better than to speak to your father that way! Say you're sorry!

Sorry, Vati. Vati, what do they have to eat in Prague?

He wanted to please them. He said: Well, sometimes there's roast duck.

With red cabbage?

That will be enough, said Ludwig Gerstein. Try not to be angry at him, Kurt.

I'm not angry, father. Why is it so dark in here?

It's not dark. The fire's very bright.

No, it's those blackout curtains. What a ridiculous regulation! The Allies have devices with which they can pinpoint their targets in the dark . . .

Don't be a defeatist, Kurt!

Nobody said anything until the soup was gone, and then Christian asked in a low shy voice: Vati, may I please see your cap?

Smiling with relief, Gerstein took it off and passed it across the table. He remembered seeing soldiers as a small boy, and longing to be one.

I like that death's head! laughed the child.

Silly! You've seen it before!

Please, Mama, let me look at it just a little bit more!

Let him, Ludwig Gerstein decreed. It won't do the lad any harm.

Vati, when I grow up can I be in the ϟϟ like you?

Surely, said Gerstein, trying not to burst into tears.

19

In 11.42, they closed Belzec, having liquidated half a million Jewish-Polish bandits. They burned the bodies, shot the work-Jews and burned them, too, demolished the installations, and interred their final report in a folder stamped with the invocation GEHEIM. Then they motored back to Lemberg to celebrate in one of the restaurants for *Germans Only. No Poles Admitted*. Truth to tell, Belzec had never been any more than a fifty-mile practice march, so to speak; the real campaign must be waged at Auschwitz, whose public name is Camp A. Good blond ϟϟ-Oberstrumführer Kurt Gerstein was in on it from the first; with his colleagues he sang "Erika, We Love You," a melody very popular with our Panzer troops at Stalingrad; and this Gerstein had a beautiful voice; he was said to have been a Christian youth leader once, so doubtless he'd led many a choir in his time. Come to think of it, he resembled a choirmaster with his strangely delicate eyes and fine lips like a girl's, his face almost as fair as the twin lightning-bolts like pallid gashes in the darkness of his right collar-tab; he cut a very dashing silver-and-black appearance; the way he carried himself, with his head thrown back, seemed confident at first, but then the backflung head began to strike any thoughtful observer (fortunately for him, in this world there are few of those) as the sort of stance which might be taken by, say, a Polish hostage standing before the firing squad; in our experience it is rather surprising how frequently such racial chaff actually tries to be brave; well, brave or not, they know the bullet will enter the forehead—if they're lucky—so while the eyes gaze at us levelly, and sometimes the mouth can even *smile* (no matter that the smile lacks three teeth), the head creeps backward, unknown to itself, striving in its primitive way to gain another inch of distance from fate.

With his fine comrades he marched down Krakow's streets, all of them singing "Erika, We Love You" in perfect time, accompanied by the pleasing clink of their steel boots on the cobblestones, and at that moment only he of all of them remembered the pits full of dead Jews stinking and brownish-yellow like the earth which rains back down upon the snow after another mortar explodes at Stalingrad. Siegfried the bankrupt tavernkeeper's son was out of cigarettes (he'd just completed two weeks' "sharp arrest" for smoking in the motor pool); Kurt Gerstein gave him a whole pack of them. Albrecht the former assistant cashier wanted to send his mother some gold bars which he'd providentially found; Kurt Gerstein telephoned Captain Wirth, and it was arranged. Handsome Heini and Karl, who'd first met in prison back in

'32, were sulky because instead of having more fun with P-girls, they must now deliver some documents all the way to the Central Office for the Jewish Problem in Bohemia and Moravia; dear blond Kurt Gerstein offered to make the journey himself.

He was trying to read the newspaper, whose front page presented Ribbentrop jutting out his chin in imitation of the statues in his renovated Foreign Office; that meant that there was no news at all, no good news at any rate. He wanted to finish the article about Ribbentrop, but they wouldn't let him. They were his children. Heini, who'd grown newly enthusiastic about our national literature, kept hounding him about *Tristan*, which to save time the boy was reading in a modern German version. He'd finally gotten as far as the verse where Tristan the Amorous sets out to help Dwarf Tristan regain a mistress raped away into a foeman's castle. They slay the evil knight, along with his six brothers; that part's all right, but Dwarf Tristan dies in the process, and Tristan the Amorous gets wounded in the groin with a poisoned spear. Only Isolde can save Tristan, and she won't arrive in time. Handsome Heini wanted to know the significance of the poisoned spear. Why did it have to be in the loins? What was all that about? Perhaps, wondered Handsome Heini aloud in an innocent tone, Kurt Gerstein could explain something about knights who'd been wounded in the loins.—Instead, Kurt Gerstein led them in "Three Riders Rode Out to the Gate," after which they decided that Kurt Gerstein was really very nice; they got drunk and embraced him, the way our truehearted soldiers do. They drew their revolvers and clattered them down on the café table, laughing at everybody's terror. Then they swore blood brotherhood with each other, sweet blond Kurt Gerstein included: they all pricked their fingers with their SS daggers and mixed their blood with his!

In our medieval romances, brother battles brother because identity's hid behind each closed visor. But these young men all wore the same armor as he; their honor was their loyalty. He pretended to be their brother, and they didn't see his face. As long as it was dark he couldn't see their faces; he prayed that Captain Wirth wouldn't turn on the light. And he wished that he knew how to play cards, because that would have made them happy. They murdered innocently, because they'd been told to murder and because they were stupid. How could Christ Himself blame their bloody hands? They invited him to drink beers with them and watch leg shows at the Wintergarten as soon as the war was over. They asked him which film actress he preferred, Ingrid Lutze or seventeen-year-old Lisca Malbrum, and he smiled and said there was a certain Berthe whom he never stopped thinking about; when they asked who she was, he sang one more round of "Erika, We Love You." He led them in *Heil Dir im Siegerkranz*. They thought he must have lost those three teeth in a street fight; they knew he'd been with the Brownshirts, just like the legendary Barricade Otto. And that made them love him all the more.

Now, across the tanned skull of a shaveheaded Pole, he spied an ϟϟ-man slipping his arm around a U-blonde as they passed down the angling twisting street to get swallowed by a bar's awning. He laughed, his eyelid twitching, and muttered: **Geheim**!

Finally he got away from them. (As Friedl kept telling him, your fanatical convictions are making you unhappy, Kurt.) He was very sorry, but now he must answer the call of duty. They thought him a sanctimonious ass; he never knew how to have fun.

In the town of Oświęcim he met Captain Wirth, who was drinking beer from a dead family's soup tureen which was a conch shell inset in herringbone-patterned silver; and Captain Wirth told him, "between you and me," how the new crematoria, built with truly Germanic perfection by Topf und Söhne, were nearly doubling their rated capacity of four thousand five hundred and seventy-six corpses (Captain Wirth had memorized this figure), at which Gerstein (already calculating: eight hundred a day makes twenty-nine thousand two hundred a year, excluding the occasional open pyres of two thousand a day, which makes . . .) laughed and shouted: Serves those Jews right!—then his eyelid twitched, which did not make Captain Wirth suspicious in the least because our huntsmen do develop mannerisms indicative of the stress of the heroic work.—Remember to keep this close to your chest! sniggered Captain Wirth. After all, even the Russians seal their radio equipment before a secret offensive . . .

And then we turn on the light—

What's that? Now, have you met Haupsturmführer Professor August Hirt? I don't give a shit about most of those eggheads, but Professor Hirt is a real down to earth, Volkish sort of fellow. Just duck when he shoots his jargon at you. You should meet him, Gerstein. He's just started a Jewish skeleton collection . . .

20

After the collapse of Fortress Stalingrad, the mood became even fiercer, the zealots more numerous, just as in the course of certain diseases the blood's thrombocyte content actually increases after bleeding. It was necessary to proceed with the most radical measures. Those who knew us best, namely, our fiendish enemy on the Ostfront, characterized the German temper as wandering between the antipodes of *bitter resistance, bordering on unthinking rashness; and timidity shading into morbid cowardice.*

The way I look at it, said ᛋᛋ-Obersturmführer Kurt Gerstein, leniency in dealing with the Jews would be as fatal as hesitation in eliminating a Russian bridgehead.

Well spoken, young man!

As a matter of fact, no matter how eloquent this Gerstein might be, some of us were beginning to follow a different line now. Exterminate the Jews? By all means! But first let's squeeze some cash out of them. Soon Auschwitz would begin to turn a profit.

It was at this time that the Dutch engineer H. J. Ubbink visited Gerstein's apartment in Berlin and took the tale of Belzec to London. No one would believe it. Even Ubbink himself no longer believed it and took to referring to Gerstein as "the holy fool." So another German summer came unmolested, and the holy fool, whom "Clever Hans" Günther now dispatched on an inspection tour of Chelmno, escaped by the slenderest margin being compelled to take his place on the wide-spaced line of ᛋᛋ-men shooting down Jews, while sunshine consecrated the shooters' toadstool-helmets. Thanks to their hard work, there'd never again be a Poland.—This mass butchery is against German tradition, said Dr. Pfannenstiel, who was there for his own research. Thank Heaven for the gas chambers!—The shooters narrowed their eyes at that. The gas chambers were out of order that day, and they felt overworked. One fellow named Sorli had to make do with a misfiring Nagant; he could have done the job faster with his leather whip! Dr. Pfannenstiel exasperated him. He didn't much like the look of Kurt Gerstein, either, not that Gerstein had even said anything, but when there's a war on one gets pretty good at sizing up one's fellow man: Is he steely enough for our time? Sorli told Gerstein right to his face that he must be one of those rear echelon assholes who expect other people to get their hands dirty. (Dr. Pfannenstiel was of a similar opinion, but the way he put it was more literary: In our national epic, Siegfried won Brunhilde for Gunther and some say even deflowered her for him, so weak was the latter king. We truehearted workers are Siegfrieds, not Gunthers! Isn't that correct, my dear Gerstein?) By then the entire squad was of the opinion that maybe Eichmann should be informed about Kurt Gerstein's attitude. With healthy fanatical race-hatred, Gerstein, laughing as loudly as he could, started kicking the face of a dead Jew. He said: Looks like that Yid fell downstairs!—That appeased them; he'd kept the faith. Sorli liked him then. They all drank schnapps afterwards. Sorli bragged about this and that—more grist for Gerstein's indictment. Sorli was also a man of culture; he couldn't stop talking about the time he'd seen Lizzi Waldmüller back in 1930; it had been "Traum einer Nacht" at the Nollendorfplatz. Then it was time to shoot another batch of Jews. Surely this time at least Kurt Gerstein would show his truehearted metal! . . .

How could Gerstein go on? And yet the blond man is said to have secretly flown to Finland to inform people there of the Final Solution. He returned exhausted and terrified to that office of his with Hitler's likeness on every wall, *Signal* magazine on the coffee table, and on his desk a small photograph, inscribed by its subject to *Kurt Gerstein, in brotherhood,* of ᛋᛋ-Oberdienstleiter Viktor Brack, whose grey, abnormally lean face displayed both the misery of old age and a certain native stoniness; Brack was a very decent man, really, a correct man, and a go-getter, too; he if anyone was the genius of Operation T-4, which was why the Americans would hang him on 2.6.48; Gerstein had told him once, at crazy, suicidal risk to himself: Herr Oberführer, something about you, your smile actually, reminds me of my late sister-in-law . . .

The telephone was about to ring. The telephone would send him off to Auschwitz. He opened the new issue of *Signal* and read an article about conditions in America: Negro schoolchildren were intimidating their teachers in several larger cities. Even the Americans were beginning to see that measures might be necessary. In the courtyard, ᛋᛋ were shouting and then another truckload of prisoners went clattering away over the cobblestones as the typist from the motor pool brought him his ersatz coffee. There was no air raid today. Right there in front of her, he prayed.

He tried to telephone Baron von Otter, who was in Romania again, they said. What about Bishop Dibelius? He was a moderate man; he advocated only the exclusion of the Jews from our economic life. Trembling, Gerstein ran downstairs.

He must have looked a sight, but the swastika-lapeled porter opened the door for him with an imperturbable *Heil Hitler!* Where could he go? He needed to walk and walk, to cool his head . . . On the Kurfürstendamm, a reddish-blonde woman on a bicycle was pedaling with long pink legs; everything about her was pink; that reddish-blonde hair of hers resembled the "good red gold" which ancient Norsemen prized. Why wasn't she working in a munitions factory? She must be the wife of someone important. Nothing was wrong. In the Tiergarten, a policeman on a brown horse passed slowly by, half visible between trees . . .

The telephone rang. It summoned him to Bohemia. Clever Hans had some surplus Jews.

One eyewitness claims (this I can hardly believe) to have seen him enter the Castle of Prague, residence of our Reich Protector of Bohemia and Moravia, where under the guise of inter-district cooperation, he is supposed to have questioned ᛋᛋ-Oberstgruppenführer Daleuege's personal staff about certain secret actions carried out against the Czechs in revenge for Heydrich's assassination. A parade of Nazi nurses was passing outside. Through the open window he heard them screaming: *Sieg Heil, Sieg Heil!* Daleuege's assistant was saying: Something about you smells, Herr Gerstein. I'm going to report you.—Gerstein stood up tall, slapped his face, smiled (deliberately showing off the missing three teeth), and said: Go ahead and report me, you pasty-faced little kike! Now, Berlin wants to know whether this office has been *hard* enough, whether measures have been taken. For instance, it's alleged that the female inhabitants of Lidice are still alive. I'm going to tell Berlin that you're not men here, that you're just a bunch of soft-shelled Jewish creeps.—In the end, because he acted so crazy that he must really be from Berlin, they allowed him to read the file on Lidice: one hundred and seventy-three men shot in the village, nineteen more liquidated in detention, seven women rendered harmless, two hundred and three others sent to concentration camps, a hundred and five children either deported or Germanized, the village razed, all with the approval of our Führer himself. To Gerstein that was the next horror, the next iron-ringed vault now opened within him: He had always known that the sleepwalker knew, but that knowledge had been kept secret from himself, like a skeleton in a forest, like something silver on black.

He went back to Berlin and from memory wrote down the statistics on Lidice. American bombs were falling on the Reich Chancellery again. Someone he'd never met was shouting; he was supposed to go to the air raid shelter. Coldly, he replied that he was busy. At that moment, the Kaiserhof Hotel got smashed by the planes. He heard our antiaircraft guns firing, and then the all-clear. Then he tried once more to telephone Baron von Otter. The line was out. When service was restored, he telephoned three half-strangers, all of whom hung up quickly and quietly. Then the typist from the motor pool came in with ersatz coffee. Very gently she said to him: Excuse me, Herr Obersturmführer, but what you are under the uniform is nobody's business.

21

He dreamed that he was digging in the earth, and turned up a golden skull with rubies for eyes—a death's head both beautiful and terrifying, like the uniform he wore; as he awoke he had a dissolving vision of holding the skull up to the sunlight.

22

Prague called him once again on the telephone; he took the express. "Clever Hans" Günther was waiting at the office.

More secret business for you, Gerstein. Most secret.

By your order, Herr Captain.

Take this suitcase to Herr Lang at the Reichsbank and tell him that this is from me. You're not to ask for a receipt. Do you understand?

It's all clear, thank you, Herr Captain.

Gerstein, I'm very pleased with your work. You're an outstanding young man. That's all. Heil Hitler!

Heil Hitler!

What a heavy suitcase! He knew all too well what was in it; Clever Hans's trust in him was now proven. He sat gazing out the window of the Berlin Express, watching the summer scenery. Hour upon hour the other passengers in his compartment sat in silence, too terrified to look at him. An old woman coughed. Flicking a fingernail across the death's head on his cap, Gerstein turned slowly toward her, fixing a stony expression on his face. The woman lowered her head. Then the conductor came. Gerstein thrust out his ticket, staring the man down. He lit a cigarette. Now came the long tall facade of the Reichsbank, with its swastika banners and its five rows of rectangular window-pits which resembled the slits from which the defenders of medieval castles used to discharge their arrows. Herr Lang was expecting him. Together they weighed the gold: twenty-two kilos. To Gerstein there was something terribly unclean about that brownish-yellow mass: was it the fact that it came from dead peoples' mouths, or did its Jewishness defile it? This is one of the most secret matters. He closed his eyes, turned out the gas chamber's light.

Are you unwell, Herr Obersturmführer?

No, I was just trying to calculate how many Reichsmarks it comes to.

Quite so. Well, in round numbers . . .

A month later he was summoned back to Prague, to receive another suitcase. He had two hours before his train. (There went his colleagues, marching in a light as straight and grand as the Doric columns of Schinkel's Neue Wache.) This time his footsteps guided him to an antique store's ticking clock, bare-breasted porcelains, fake pearl necklaces and dead women's black gowns. Something for his wife . . . He allowed himself to imagine how Christian's face would have lit up had he dropped around his neck that eighteenth-century Cross of the Order of the White Eagle which Captain Wirth had forced on him; boys always love militaria, and this was an eight-pointed star of *gold,* garnished with silver and diamonds! Actually, what he should have done was to sell it and feed his family. Instead, he buried it in the Polish earth, praying softly for its former owner, the grey-green trees going ethereal beyond his tears as they would have done in any rain. Rain of blood, rain of steel, rain on the rich green grass of Auschwitz! Tears and prayers are both supposed to refresh one's soul.

23

Like Himmler, he now secreted a cyanide capsule on his person; I believe he kept it beneath the signet stone of his ring. Just as in the beech forests of Lower Saxony, the shadows of converging autumn-bare trunks project like guns into the darkness they're made of, so his own thoughts led him deeper and deeper into despairing confusion: Here comes Kurt Gerstein, who since his adolescence has always rejected the impurity of this earthly existence, inspecting another extermination camp! *One is tempted to dismiss Gerstein as a romancer,* writes the historian-ethicist Michael Balfour. *He must have realized that his actions were having no result.*

He compelled himself to witness everything now; maniacally he counted strands in the barbed wire of a transit ghetto: another footnote in his not yet written affidavit. He stood over the dark huddle of Polish Jews who sat in the marketplace of their town; they were waiting for the ϟϟ and police who ringed them round to escort them to death. While his colleagues guarded them, Gerstein counted them: seven hundred and twenty-four more crimes for his affidavit. And then—because his pass, stamped by Eichmann's office, allowed him to come and go almost at will—he went with the trucks, to see where the mass graves were. He was present, trying to laugh with his comrades, when they stripped the Jews naked, beat them and shot them. An old man, needing to relieve himself, squatted down in the bushes and got overlooked by his murderers. Gerstein whispered in his ear, urging him to hide in the forest.—

No, thank you, Herr Obersturmführer, the Jew said coldly, in perfect German. I prefer the company of my wife and children.—And then he pulled up his pants and joined the next batch of lean, yellow-faced Russian Jews with upraised hands, bearded, kneeling, while the Order Police stood smiling easily, posing for pictures beside their bagged quarry. They were so at ease that they could have been Sunday equestrians in the Tiergarten. In the town, the churchbell under its cross-roofed platform stayed silent, dangling between massive wooden legs.

24

Evening, and he strolled around the grounds of the old palace. By seven it began to grow cool, and the fountains were delightful. A mosquito bit his neck. Beneath the honeysuckled arch, the ticket girl chain-smoked cigarettes, launching quips at all the German officers. Then came Berthe, simultaneous with the pure, rather thin bell-tones of seven. He remembered a passage out of *Tristan* which he had helped explicate for Handsome Heini: *Whoever gazes into Isolde's eyes feels both heart and soul refined like gold in the white-hot flame*—the flame of the crematorium, of course.

She took each of his fingers in turn into her hand, reminding him of his arrest back in '36, when they'd made him "play the piano," which means to be fingerprinted. The Storm Troopers had been gentle with him then, because he was no Jew and because he could sing.

He said: Do you remember how you told me to go down the dark way?

Of course. And I know what wrings your heart now. It's long, isn't it, this dark way? And you're losing heart, aren't you?

Never, he whispered.

Look at your hands, crooned the dead woman. They're so soft and white. There's no blood on them.

Thank you, Berthe. Thank you for saying that . . .

He kissed her Jewish-looking eyes. Then she led him into the church. The sacristan came trembling forward.

Open the crypt at once! ordered ᛋᛋ-Obersturmführer Kurt Gerstein. Now leave me. Wait outside.

Shiny black marble steles, old white granite tombs, wooden crosses, a rusty iron box with a cross on it, that was the place where Berthe had led him. Do you want to know how to get through life? At the base of a wooden cross, burn a candle.

25

And now, a note for those of you who consider this a vulgarly supernatural tale: It may well be that ambitious people of any stripe find themselves compelled to schematize the subjects of their solicitude into, say, Jews to be liquidated, or Jews to be saved. There might not be time to learn the name of every Esther or Isaac who falls within Operation Reinhard's purview. And the further those subjects (I mean objects) get altered in accordance with the purpose, the more problematic it becomes to perceive their irrelevantly human qualities. I quote the testimony of Michal Chilczuk, Polish People's Army (he'd participated in the liberation of Sachsenhausen): *But what I saw were people I call humans, but it was difficult to grasp that they were humans.* What did Chilczuk mean by this? To put it aphoristically, a human skeleton is not human. It frightens us because it proves the truth of that gravestone epitaph so common in the age of Holbein: *What I once was, so you are. What I am now, so you will be.* The gaze of those dark, sharp-edged eye-sockets seems implacable, and the many teeth, which haunted Edgar Allan Poe, snarl much too nakedly, bereft of those festive pink ribbons of flesh we call "lips," whose convolutions and involutions can express mirth, friendliness, even tenderness. A human skull's smile is as menacing as a crocodile's. Since death itself is nothing, the best our minds can do to represent it is through that expressionless face of bone which one day will be ours, and to which we cannot help imparting an expression. Under such circumstances, how can that expression be reassuring? This is why SS-Obersturmführer Kurt Gerstein cannot help clothe the skull in beloved Berthe's image.

On Ash Wednesday of that year, he'd been present when those few pastors of the Prussian Confessional Church who dared read a sermon about the commandment *Thou shalt not kill.* Even then his SS colleagues failed to suspect him, such was their own confidence in themselves.

Following the collapse of the Ostfront on a secret map, he shouted: *Christ will overcome those devils!* The neighbors must have heard, but no one ever reported him. Every evening he read from the Bible, then prayed aloud, lying weakly in bed.

Next came the Warsaw Ghetto uprising, which struck everybody as no less viciously, ruthlessly useless than the way that encircled Russians will fight to the death.

Why wouldn't the Allies do anything? They must dread the responsibility for sheltering so many millions—or were they themselves anti-Semites?—

He stood between the columns of the church nave, trying to ask. Glaring arches of candle flame replied. What was the use? He might as well have kept on bowing and clicking his heels to Berthe's ghost.

Helmut Franz whispered into his ear that the British, who alone could have done it, had deliberately refrained from bombing the gas chambers of Auschwitz. Switzerland refused to grant asylum to Jews. Only Kurt Gerstein was willing to act!

26

We now see him alone and impeccably uniformed, silver on black, his face as resolute as the death's head on his forehead as he sped down the road from Warsaw to Krakow in a military truck, with a spade and six fifty-kilogram cannisters of sky-blue Zyklon B crystals under a tarpaulin in the back, and around him the wet and gentle crests of Polish fields in summer rain, tall flowers behind house-fences, wet roads, lush trees bearing white stars for blossoms, and on the far horizon ahead of him stood other trees as grey as the North Sea. At each checkpoint they clicked their heels, saluted and gestured him through. If they could have seen within his soul, they would have shot him, shot him, *shot him*!

Tall, blond SS-Obersturmführer Kurt Gerstein rushed on toward Auschwitz. Soon now he'd arrive at the black-and-white signal barrier, the sign ARBEIT MACHT FREI, and it would be too late. (He'd just told Helmut Franz about the female victims of medical experiments in Nr. 1 Block.) How many cannisters could decompose in transit? Quick, into the slender-trunked, green green forest shining with new rain! Were there any partisans here? Let them kill him. Screened by trees, sweating and trembling, he began to dig a grave for the prussic acid: two cannisters' worth today, a hundred kilograms. In theory, he was saving a hundred thousand lives. Out it came into the pit, glittering, celestially beautiful; he retched at the fumes. They'd shoot him, shoot him, shoot him! Why didn't he just stuff a handful into his mouth and be done with it? *Give 'em something to chew on!* That was what Sergeant Möll always said, when they swished it down the distribution cones into the gas chambers at Auschwitz. And Gerstein *laughed;* he actually *laughed* so that they'd leave him free to fulfill his pledge . . . Afterwards he'd spend the night in Krakow. He usually managed a visit to Saint Mary's Basilica, the terrorized crowds rushing aside to let him through to lurk within that dark wooden labyrinth smoothed by many hands, gazing emptily at dark candelabra, darker portraits, windows as deep as a skull's eye-sockets. Their pale Christ had risen, but, alas, risen nailed to His cross. There He was, hovering helplessly in the high blue firmament of the groined ceiling with its golden stars.

27

By 31.1.44 the front line had broken into segments of flotsam on an ebbing wave.—They'll never breach our Atlantic Wall! cried his father loyally.

How could they? agreed ϟϟ-Obersturmführer Kurt Gerstein. He was the perfect picture of our Aryan race; quite obviously he possessed a firm resolve to harshly but fairly enforce German authority.

Kurt, old as I am, I feel I should be doing something.

Look at you, father! You can scarcely walk!

That's all right. Give me a shovel, and even if it takes me all day I can still dig my meter of antitank trench!

That's commendable, father.

Recently I had a nightmare. I dreamed that the Slavs were in Berlin! You don't suppose they'll ever come here?

God will do what's best.

What exactly does that mean? In the name of the All-Highest, do you support our Führer or not?

You see the uniform I wear, said Kurt Gerstein through clenched teeth.

I see what you think of that uniform. Even your children see that. And Elfriede! What that poor girl suffers on your account you'll never understand. If you want to live a worthy life, Kurt, you must never treat a woman badly. A woman, you know, bears no weapons in her hands. Your duty—

Excuse me, father, but how do you define your *Christian* duty?

Did you mean to criticize me just now, Kurt? Was that your intention?

No.

Well, then what were you trying to say?

Father, I . . . To me, the worship of Our Lord means nothing unless it's expressed in practical acts of charity.

But that in and of itself is impractical, because if each of us decided to express his Christian love in the way he thought best, no one would do his duty. The truth is, we're all selfish, and we all look for excuses! You know, Kurt, in the course of my career I often had to condemn some poor wretch to the gallows. From an individual, human point of view, he might not have done anything wrong, and nobody will ever know how much I sympathized. For example, one fellow's mother was dying an agonizing death of cancer. They could do nothing for her; on account of those damned Versailles sanctions, the pharmacies didn't even carry any opiates to reduce her pain. And so he suffocated her with a pillow—purely out of love, do you understand me, Kurt? But one has to do one's duty.

Suppose you'd refused to convict . . .

First of all, I might have faced disbarment, and I don't know what would have become of your mother and all you children in those years. We were already poor enough, not to mention the disgrace. One must not lose sight of such things. But setting aside my obvious family duty, the larger principle is this: If the man who suffocates his mother for love gets acquitted, then you may be sure that the man who suffocates his mother for hate will seize on that fact!

But there's a distinction, after all—

And you continue arguing against me, your own father! You stand against all of us. Just what do you stand for?

Forgive me, father, but this distinction—

We see a distinction only because we're abstracting the two cases of matricide; we're letting them be hypothetical, so that we can play God and peer into the defendants' hearts. But in real life we'll never know.

But *you* knew.

Yes, I do *believe,* I'm humanly *certain,* that the man whom I sentenced to death was a mercy-killer; and the current law of our land might well allow his mother to be released from her agony, provided that it was the Reich itself which—

Speaking of such things, father, I've obtained proof that Berthe was euthanized at Hadamar.

You're interrupting me. What if she was? Poor girl, she's better off! Have you forgotten how she used to touch herself in church? I hope you'll show the decency never to tell Elfriede. The point is, we shouldn't have the impertinence to play God. It's not up to us to decide who should live and who should die.

Father, said Kurt Gerstein desperately, if I had been you I should have resigned my office.

For shame! To think that I would ever hear my own son . . .

Forgive me, father. I don't mean—

Then why don't you resign yours?

I won't lay down my responsibility, the blond man steadily replied, and then, in an effort to defuse this conversation: By the way, where is Friedl?

Shopping, shopping, said the old man with an indulgent wave of the hand.

Gerstein smiled, trying to hide his rage. Friedl was probably standing in a queue to buy watered-down milk.

Unlike you, his father continued (Ludwig Gerstein never got distracted from a topic), I'm not a quitter. When I was a magistrate *I did my duty,* no matter how painful it was. I also fought on the Westfront in the last war, Kurt; you can't imagine the things I saw . . .

The son almost laughed.—No, father. I can't imagine.

I did my duty, and I never played God. I kept to the humility that befits a human being.

And you don't think we ought to choose for ourselves?

As Adam and Eve chose, against the commandment of God? As the Bolshevists continue to choose today? Have you forgotten that Katyń Forest massacre? That's their bloody, bloody work, which our Führer would save us from—

Kurt Gerstein whispered: We need to choose as Jesus chose.

No, said his father, that's perfect fantasy. You're not Jesus. What you imagine is impossible.

His father, who believed in the growing might of our Reich's air defenses, had never been like him: From birth Kurt Gerstein had always been as fearful as a Jew.

28

In 7.44 a Swiss newspaper printed an article about the situation of the Hungarian Jews, the headline being: **People Are Disappearing**. An anonymous friend slipped a clipping of the story under Gerstein's door. His heart began to pound so fiercely that he feared he might vomit. Collapsing on the bed, he read it through, hoping not to be implicated. Fortunately, *Die Ostschweiz* credited the Polish Government-in-Exile. Then of course Gerstein felt disappointed.

That was when the Second Guards Tank Army of the USSR liberated Maidanek concentration camp. They found the mounds of clothes, the shooting room. The documentarist Roman Karmen, stern and correct in his army cap and uniform, filmed the grubby captured Nazis in front of Block 2, his camera pressed in against his body as if he didn't want it to get too close to them; they were us; he was shooting us from underneath, aiming up at our stubbled chins to make us look even uglier than our souls. He filmed the giant cabbages; he zoomed in on the human ashes which fertilized them. And thousands of Russians saw that newsreel, maybe hundreds of thousands. The Soviet press organs printed extensive accounts. As yet, however, the Western Allies still refused to believe. Gerstein was in despair. As for his colleagues, they'd begun to look over their shoulders a little, almost as if they could see the Russians coming.

Captain Wirth, who for some reason always tilted his head back when saying *Heil Hitler!*, just as our Austrians do, poured him a drink and said: To get right down to it, that Günther of yours, they don't call him Clever Hans for nothing. All this time he's been complaining about being Stahlecker's subordinate! You don't report to Stahlecker, do you?

No, Herr Captain.

Cut the phony formality with me, Gerstein; we're in this together. Here's the way I see it: Stahlecker's going to be the fall guy. You mark my words, Gerstein. If this war keeps going to shit, Clever Hans will be sitting pretty, and all the world's going to hear about Major-General Walther So-and-So Stahlecker, who committed all these crimes against the Yids! But you know what, Gerstein? Hey, are you drunk? I said, you know what? I'm not going to be the fall guy. Now listen. Here's what you and I have got to do . . .

But Gerstein was not listening at all.

He kept haunting churches, adventuring like a knight, approaching any pastor who preached sermons against killing; he showed almost every guest those red-edged dark grey folders which read SECRET REICH MATTER and GEHEIM; and his colleagues went marching triple file along the right-hand edge of a barbed wire lane, their Death's Head insigniae baby-white against their tanned baby faces and dark uniforms; they were not all blond like Gerstein, but they marched in step, chins up, gazing straight ahead; they were as reliable as Panzer tanks. Now here came Commandant Rudolf Höss, en route from the department "Canada" with his head up and his benignly stupid eyes a little worried while helpful Kurt Gerstein, ᛋᛋ-Obersturmführer Kurt Gerstein I mean, trotted alongside, bending down to murmur into the Commandant's ear that some of the Zyklon B had been decomposed in transit and would need to be buried to avoid any risks to the health of the gassing detail.

But what's Himmler going to say? And this has happened before. It seems as if you're always trying to take away my prussic acid, Gerstein! Ha, ha! Is the substance really that dangerous?

I'm afraid so, Herr Commandant.

Well, this will affect our efficiency! Tell me, Gerstein, can't you improve the reliability of the transportation process? As I understand it, the prompt and safe delivery of this essential neutralizing agent is really in your sphere of responsibility.

By your order, Herr Commandant!

I understand that you observed those preliminary *ad hoc* operations at Treblinka and Belzec. That is correct?

Yes, Herr Commandant.

At that time, you supported Captain Wirth's argument in favor of diesel exhaust as opposed to Zyklon B. I've read your report. Frankly, I'm surprised that you could have expressed those views. Is that what you still maintain?

Herr Commandant, as you yourself remarked just now, Zyklon B suffers from a tendency to spoil. In my opinion, it's better to resettle fewer Jews per day in a *reliable* fashion than to gamble with an extremely dangerous and uncontrollable toxic agent—

I see your point, but I disagree with it. We have to forge ahead. Unfortunately, we just don't have the manpower to shoot them . . . Well, I understand that this is not your worry. We each of us work toward the Führer in the best way we can. But I must warn you, Gerstein: If this happens again, and we have to resort to diesel engines again, or, God forbid, to small-caliber weapons, I'll file a report. Do you understand?

Absolutely, Herr Commandant, and once again I assure you that it's not my—

Do you know what I find very strange? Most of our Zyklon comes from Dr. Mryugowsky's hygiene service. And his gas never seems to spoil. Who's your supplier?

A Dr. Peters, at the Degesch Company. Herr Commandant, I want you to know that I have already been following up this matter with him. Apparently the most microscopic impurities in the tin cannisters may cause—

All right, all right, sighed Commandant Höss. We don't want any impurities . . .

Sorry about the inconvenience, Herr Commandant.

Don't worry, Höss said calmly. Had you inconvenienced me, I should certainly have filed a report. As it is, Gerstein, the quantity you're able to supply is so negligible in comparison to Dr. Mryugowsky's that these interruptions don't impede our operations here. Will you be staying for lunch?

With pleasure, Herr Commandant. I—

That's enough now. Don't worry. Nobody's going to file any report at this stage. I'll expect you at 1315 sharp. Heil Hitler!

Heil Hitler!

What a goodlooking boy! Höss was thinking to himself as he continued on to the crematorium.

29

Now he no longer dared to destroy the prussic acid. Therefore he became an accomplice, history said.

Suffering from diabetes, he frequently blacked out. His ϟϟ-brothers also lost heart; they got drunk more often than ever, saying to one another: If only I'd known how everything was going to turn out . . . —In his dreams he saw Berthe's skull, which wept, the tears drying, leaving a whitish crust on the verdigrised bell-dome of her skeleton-church. Just as trenches grow shallower as they approach the front line, so his own defenses against what he had seen, and the secret life he led, sheltered him less and less. Another way of saying it is that culture gets cruder, life less valuable, as we go East: Prague's baroque decorations, for instance, are heavier and squatter than the fluid marble nudes of Vienna. By the time we get to Leningrad, there's nothing at all, only a smoking mass grave bereft of any adornment but snow and rubble—pure proof of Slavic subhumanity. On Kaprova-Josefov Street in Prague, not far from "Clever Hans" Günther's office, a tall, skinny, mummylike bas-relief flexed its skinny arms upon a corner wall; adorned with chains and fishes, it was a harmless Christian symbol, but to Gerstein it was a dead Jew hanging there and haunting him. (Don't be a coward! Captain Wirth would have said.) In Berlin, thank God, no bookstores assaulted him with the word **SLAVISTIKA**; but other items frightened him unpredictably. His depositions against the Hitler regime were now as white, regular and endless as a German cemetery in December at Stalingrad. If the Gestapo found those, he'd be lucky if they did nothing worse than shoot him and his family . . . In his office the telephone rang and said: . . . *A block raid, to catch suspects* . . .

He sought out Monsignor Orsenigo again, to try to reach the Pope, but once more got turned away. In anguish he cried out to his wife: What action against Nazism can anyone demand of an ordinary citizen when the representative of Jesus on earth refuses to hear me?

Listen to me, Kurt! Please, please listen! Nobody demands of you what you're doing!

Our Lord Jesus Christ would have done this much and more, he said to her.

Elfriede wrung her hands, but in fact she'd become very bitter against him. Every other ϟϟ-wife she knew lived well, but Kurt never brought anything home, not even Bohemian honey anymore, no matter how hungry the children became. He was an egotist, she told everybody; he didn't care about anybody but himself. And those Yids he went on and on about, they made her ill. Didn't he remember that our people were suffering, too? In fact, our Führer had said . . . She longed to command her husband, as her father-in-law could: *And now we'll never talk about it again.*

The truth was that Kurt had never been normal. Even before the war he'd been so highstrung; she wondered what could have possessed her to marry him.

Frau Hedwig's twins, considering him odd, had returned to their mother, for which he blamed himself. Edmund grew up to be more reserved than Erich, who in later life was known to say: My brother and I both saw it coming. (Summer is always pregnant with winter, of course, and when September arrives, Berlin is positively gravid, her heavy white clouds about to burst with rain, her yellow leaves ready to descend like paratroopers from the maternal stem.) The blond man became a patient at various ϟϟ hospitals, muttering like so many other shellshocked men: What does God think of me?—In those places there was nothing to read but *Signal* magazine: *"I'll have the second from the right," says Hilde as she admires the new handbag which has just been placed in the repaired shop window. "I don't care how many bombs they drop," says old Mayer. "Germany will keep right on working!"*

30

He entered a church's open door and heard: *We admonish our German folk to stand by the doctrine of blood and soil.* Then he went out to the beerhall with ϟϟ-man Müller, "the crematorium clown." It was Müller who first told him about the malaria experiments of Dr. Klaus Schilling at Dachau.—Commendable, said Gerstein gravely, realizing that now he would have to add an entirely new section to his war crimes affidavit.

Commendable nothing! cried Müller, who now was very drunk. I've got a comrade in the S.D. You know what he likes to do, just for laughs?

What?

Make the Jews kneel down and beg for their lives, and then—

And then?

Don't be stupid. You know the rest. But first he . . .

And Müller whispered something really obscene into Gerstein's ear. And the blond man laughed. He *laughed*! He had to.

31

Baron von Otter had been transferred to Bucharest, they told him, but he managed one last secret interview with Consul Hochstrasser, telling him: I've checked this information personally. The code name for Hitler's special train has been changed from "Amerika" to "Brandenburg." He rarely takes one of his cars anymore, but if he does, it's worth knowing that he's had the bulletproof tires removed for the sake of his queasy stomach. The thickness of the rear steel plate is eight millimeters . . .

Herr Obersturmführer, this is outright provocation. Do you realize what would happen to my country if Berlin had any suspicion of—

I'm telling you, even as we speak, people are being stripped naked and forced into gas chambers all over Central Europe! You can hear them screaming . . .

I do believe that you have, said the Consul as graciously as he could.

And I am grateful for your belief, said Gerstein a little stiffly. Now shall I go on? The side-plates are only four millimeters thick; therefore—

Herr Obersturmführer, your own security, and that of your family, is your business. I myself—

If Hitler should lose, he'll slam the door behind him with such force that the earth will shake. Can't you imagine what he's preparing for all of us?

As I said, I myself refuse to be compromised, replied the Consul with a stony thick-lipped smile not unlike the one eternally carved on Bacchus's face; I've seen him grinning and glaring at me above an archway of the Palais im Grossen Garten in Dresden. You had warning. I intend to give orders that you never again be admitted to this office.

His inspection tours of the shrinking Eastern territories, if they continued at all, went entirely unwitnessed; however, I do have at hand fairly reliable evidence of his having visited the camps at Oranienburg (where they clapped his shoulder and said: Gerstein, what you see here makes you either brutal or sentimental!) and Ravensbrück, the latter being particularly upsetting to him since its inmates were females. The ϟϟ-women there (so I'm told) were quite struck by tall, handsome Kurt Gerstein. One in particular, a bisexual opera singer who had a different Frenchwoman served up to her every week, a crime for which she later become a prisoner herself, had a scheme involving the disinfection of the ϟϟ laundry, which would have brought the blond man to Ravensbrück quite often; pretending to be interested in her, Gerstein was able to hear from her own lips about the secret "Night and Fog" Gestapo stamp in certain prisoners' dossiers; he also learned from her that since the Hungarian Jewesses weren't dying rapidly enough, other measures were in preparation. Ravensbrück was a pretty soft camp, with only one crematorium, and Gerstein fairly quickly realized that he had seen far more than ϟϟ-Aufseherin Luise. I think it unlikely that she told him about the young Polish girls whose legs were slit open and injected with gangrene, to simulate war wounds.—They all whine and pretend to be specialists! giggled Luise, pinching his arm. But enough about them! Would you like me to sing the "Liebestod" from "Tristan"? It's said I can move a man to tears. Are you ready? Kurt, I said are you ready?

Rage's beak drilled at the back of his skull. Rage's claws grubbed in his guts, piercing and digging.

32

"Clever Hans" Günther called for his advice as to whether it would be practical to liquidate the remaining Jews of Theresienstadt all at once if we herded them into open ditches and then sprinkled them with Zyklon B. The always clean and pleasing look of Kurt Gerstein's face came into play when the blond man lied and said that it was utterly impossible. That was the last time he succeeded in saving anybody. As it turned out, those Jews got murdered anyway, by shooting.

In his flat he frequently committed the capital crime of listening to BBC broadcasts; moreover, he increased the volume until the neighbors could hear it through the walls. He lay in bed thinking what his father always called his evil thoughts; he scribbled additions to his indictments: During the French campaign they'd murdered British prisoners-of-war in the village of Le Paradis. He even tuned in to Radio Moscow. Field-Marshal Paulus was speaking on the Freedom Broadcasting Station, offering to fight for a "democratic order" in Germany. When his increasingly rare visitors taxed him with giving in to suicidal impulses, the blond man stubbornly insisted that he was doing this only so that the neighbors could have access to these broadcasts without any risk to themselves. He defended this absurd position so loudly that guests sometimes feared for his reason. Then, in a sudden fury, he began to describe to them the way Jew-brains explode high into the air when we shoot at close range. He couldn't stop seeing that, he said.

Herr Gerstein, forgive me for asking this, but have you ever personally taken part in the actions against the Jews?

I have clean hands, he replied through clenched teeth.

33

His father came for a visit, and Kurt Gerstein, summoning up all his courage, began with a dry mouth to hint at some of the things which were occurring in the East. (Anyone who talks will be shot immediately, "Clever Hans" had said.)

Hard times demand hard methods, said his father with a shrug.

But what would Christ say about those methods?

I still believe in Hitler, his father replied. But there's something I want to ask you.

Yes, father?

Why don't you carry a riding-crop?

Excuse me?

Well, I often see ϟϟ-men with riding crops. I think that it looks quite stylish. Would you like me to buy you one?

That's very generous, father, but riding-crops are reserved for members of the permanent staff, at Belzec, for instance—

Well, why don't you get yourself appointed to some permanent staff? Seriously, my boy, I'm worried about you. You seem as though you've lost your way.

34

You seem as though you've lost your way, his father had said, but Berthe whispered her pride and gratitude that he'd been faithful to her. . . .

Ha, ha! You should have seen the way we killed the—

Better not tell your wife!

Trudchen? She's such a little prude-chen she'd never—

Now it's your turn, Gerstein! Are you one of us or not? Tell us a story.

What kind of story?

Don't play coy! Come on, now! Are you going to participate in our fellowship?

Very well, said racial comrade Kurt Gerstein with a carefree laugh. (Oh, his candid eyes and firm lips!)—Now, this anecdote goes back to the summer of '40, when I first heard about the T-4 operation. In retrospect, I think it was providential that my sister-in-law Berthe—

They were staring at him.

Was gassed, or more probably shot in the back of the head with a small-caliber revolver. She was deranged, you see. Incurable. And that was when I realized that hard times demand hard measures. And so I joined the ᛋᛋ.

We know you're an idealist, Gerstein. We were merely hoping that for once you could—

To hell with it, Franz. He's never going to come down to our level.

You know what, Gerstein? Sometimes I find your patently Christian attitude offensive. In our line of work, there's nothing wrong with a laugh now and then. In fact, it's good for us.

The truth is—

We all have to get our hands dirty from time to time. We don't get to sit at a great big office like you. We're nobodies. We didn't have bigshot fathers like you, so we have to eat our lunches there in the crematorium, day after day, with dead Jews stinking and burning and ashes falling on our sandwiches. What do you think about that?

Tell us the truth, Pastor Gerstein—

Rabbi Gerstein, you mean!

When was the last time you personally sent a Jew to the Promised Land?

To get right down to it, Gerstein, what's your stance on the Jewish question?

Franz, *I'm a specialist in cyanide disinfectants*. Don't you understand what that means?

Then they had to laugh. Blond Kurt Gerstein was one of them after all, in spite of his perpetually inappropriate half-smile—

Late in '43, I can't tell you exactly when, an old friend paid a visit to his office. Gerstein was sitting at his big desk, doing his accounts—Auschwitz's current tally, he calculated, was two million victims—when he saw the big Mercedes with the swastika pennant. He thought it was the Gestapo, but it was only Dr. Pfannenstiel. He wanted Gerstein to go to Poland with him, for the pleasure of his company, of course, and also to inspect some new technical developments relating to Operation Reinhard.

If you can get me a sleeping car! laughed Kurt Gerstein, knowing that he couldn't.

That's hardly a Gothic demand, my young friend—

But if there's anything you need—

Well, after all, since you're the man who invented the gas chamber—

Excuse me?

No false modesty, please! It was you who brought the Zyklon B to Belzec. Then you wrote up your report.

Correct, said Gerstein. However, what I actually said—

I have it on reliable authority from Clever Hans himself, who adores you, that without you the entire operation would have—

Tell me something, Herr Doktor, and without any Jewish subtleties, please: In your medical opinion, when those dead Jews at Belzec lay staring at us all in a heap, what was the *expression* on their faces?

Dr. Pfannenstiel looked at him severely and said: I noticed nothing special about the corpses, except that some of them showed a bluish puffiness about the face. This is not surprising, since they died of asphyxiation.

Gerstein said: I take it you haven't yet been invited to Auschwitz, Herr Doktor, because they're employing Zyklon B over there, which makes them pink!

You don't say! But that's the merest curiosity, Gerstein. The relevant question is this: Can science devise a way to render this process of exterminating human beings devoid of cruelty?

35

It's for your wife, said Captain Wirth, smiling. You're so impossible about accepting gifts, I finally said to myself, I said, hit the armored man in his wife-spot!

Thank you, said Gertstein, stroking the soft supple leather of the handbag a little absently.

Human skin, said Captain Wirth. Don't worry; it's not Jewish. A good Russian peasant-boy; I picked him out myself.

36

When he was still a schoolboy, before he'd even passed his *Abitur* exam, in fact, his friend Helmut Franz had shown him a reproduction of Käthe Kollwitz's famous chalk drawing entitled "The Volunteers," which depicts young, young men with gaping, hypnotized faces marching off all in row, with a skeleton leading them. Well, but after all, that image, made in 1920, in no way corresponded to the realities of our current world-historical situation, which can be easily represented by the empty acorn-caps and squashed chestnuts one sees in the gravel alongside the Landwehrkanal.—Neither he nor Helmut Franz had liked "The Volunteers." They'd found it anti-German.

Helmut Franz had elaborated: Yes, I grant that a skeleton led us last time, but there will never be another World War!

Naturally not, said Gerstein. Anyhow, it's up to all of us to will the best for Germany, not the worst.

For a long time he had continued to believe this, and in a sense he continued to believe it. He wanted to be Hagen, standing up for Germany in the world. When the sleepwalker became Chancellor in 1933, he granted that the man had faults, but Helmut Franz reminded him that if each of them, and every German, simply and unceasingly willed his goodness, then the sleepwalker would become good. This meant volunteering in the highest sense, intuiting and working toward what our Führer would want, setting aside any flaws in the leadership.

And so, when he told his friend of the crimes he had seen in the huge industrial green of Birkenau with its many strands of barbed wire bent over curving concrete light-poles, Helmut Franz, who'd been shocked to learn the secret of Belzec, now warned him: It's better not to investigate evil things too deeply, Kurt, not only for your safety and ours but also because evil deserves to be respected! Would you strip a leper of his clothes and expose him? Would you call attention to the ugliness of someone who owns the power to do you harm?

I reject that! Gerstein replied. Parzifal's sin was *not* asking, *not* inquiring into evil's source. That's why he became accursed and lost the Grail.

You're too much the mystic. Nowadays, the only hope for us Germans is to forge our own Grail. If it's not perfect, may our loyalty make it so!

Loyalty? When Dr. Mengele stands whistling a tune as he points with his thumb, left or right! And then they—

Where's your own evil in this, Kurt?

What do you mean? I bear no responsibility.

All your life, you've been the martyr. You've suffered the strictness of your father, but bearing it never brought you any peace. You stood up to evil and got your teeth knocked out. You warned us all of evil and went to a concentration camp. When all of us helped you get rehabilitated—and you know, Kurt, it wasn't just your father; it really *was* all of us—you promptly did everything you could to get sent to Belzec, and now you have nightmares! I can't help wondering whether you're bringing your own fate upon yourself.

Are you claiming that I want to suffer? That's—

No. You're not a masochist in the clinical sense. These terrible things keep happening to you because you insist that you're not evil like everyone else.

What specifically is my sin?

Pride, Kurt, or willed blindness. You think that you're better than we are. So you attempt the impossible. Of course you'll get punished.

Perhaps that's so. But in that case, your sin is relying on impossibility as a shield against any kind of commitment.

In other words, Kurt, you accuse me of standing still while you rise up and volunteer. But who's your leader?

I follow our Lord Jesus Christ, he replied through clenched teeth.

You think you are. But what if you're in that Kollwitz drawing, following the skeleton?

They parted coldly. The subway was crowded with invalids and old women. He remembered how back in '32 it would have been packed with Storm Troopers who sang rude songs and threatened everybody in their goodnatured way; then the Führer had liquidated Röhm, and after that one saw mainly ᛋᛋ, steady and professionally cool; now the folders for Case White and Operation Barbarossa had sprung open, and men got swallowed up in the war. He missed the Storm Troopers. In those days he'd still believed in victory. Thrilled by the phrase *radical measures,* he'd almost joined the Steel Helmets.

Helmut Franz was partly correct about him; Kurt Gerstein had always been a volunteer. The first time he joined the Party, it was out of true German ardor; Berthe was still alive. Then he'd volunteered to be a spy for God.

Helmut Franz was also, perhaps, jealous. For one thing, he would never look as wholesome as Kurt Gerstein.

37

Down the dark way! Berthe lay under the earthen mound into which a path led, underneath the tall, tapering brick chimney. Hadn't he won the right to love her as he did her sister? Let gape the gates! The Commandant's watch-dogs howled; the ᛋᛋ formed up in a double line with rifles raised; they were an honor guard; MY HONOR IS MY LOYALTY. What would happen next? **Geheim**.

He could no longer imagine what would have happened next. He was finished; he'd done everything; it was over.

38

Yes, it was over. Soon the hunters would have to hide whatever they could. Like Kurt Gerstein, they must take the knife-edge path. For Operation Reinhard was approaching its close! In the official records, Captain Wirth was murdered by Jewish-Bolshevik partisans in the autumn of '44, while Brigade Chief Globocnik, in despair at the way that the armed forces kept betraying our Führer, shot himself in the head with his Walther pistol (Geco, 7.65 millimeter). Their bodies were never found. The Jewish gold was already entering Switzerland, in accounts classified GEHEIM. Division 1005 (corpse obliteration) had almost wound up its work throughout the Eastern territories we still controlled; they'd slipped up at Majdanek, unfortunately; they'd left traces in Lemberg, which was already Lvov again; but at Auschwitz the gas chambers and crematoria stood ready to be blown up when the time came, so that nothing could be proved against us. Naturally, Division 1005 kept requisitioning large quantities of methanol. Gerstein did the little he could, which was nothing, to impede the work. He'd tried to tittletattle again to Baron von Otter. For the convenience of some postwar prosecutor whose existence he no longer imagined, he recorded the locations of the pits and the approximate volume of the matter within, the tight-packed mass I should say, whose shape partook of the same irregularity as the fireball which blossoms from an airplane after a direct hit; this thing, which Division 1005 had to pickaxe apart into its component members before they could burn it, infested Gerstein's nightmares to the point of literal stench; he woke up choking, with the reek of Belzec in his mouth. Needless to say, the instant that the war ended, he'd draw up all his affidavits and get free.

As for the hunters, they didn't give a hang about Division 1005. Demobilizing against (I mean in advance of) orders, they planned to buy tiny white houses on various meadow-cliffs. Their pasts remained, it's true, like rocks bony under the lushness, but, saying to themselves, just as they'd always done, *we need to face facts,* they'd remove a few photographs from their wartime albums; they'd plan new careers in the surprising stillness of the Swiss Alps, the moist warm summer silence. Just as Swiss mountains open out into wide steep valleys of green and grey across which time passes disguised as clouds, so "the postwar era," which our Führer would have called *the interval between two wars,* would expand before them, bordered not by prison walls but avalanche fences and terraced vineyards. In the guest room, or maybe in the closet, but most likely in a safe deposit box they'd keep that shirt of golden armor from Transylvania. Every Christmas and every Easter would be often enough to break out that wine cup comprised of an immense snail shell (or was it a chambered nautilus?), whose base was a golden woman, naked save for a loincloth, standing on a gasping golden fish; somehow she reminded them of Poland's blonde fields. But all that was half a year away. Until the last minute they kept shooting intellectuals, Jews and more Jews, Communists, Polish and Russian soldiers, hospital patients and lunatics. (Naturally, they did it out of sight of the generals, according to a procedure stamped GEHEIM.)

As for Gerstein, he continued to hold his dangerously illegal gatherings, seeking always to warn about and learn about the Third Reich's latest crimes: the mass hangings at Plötzensee, the reprisals in Slovakia, Dr. Brachtl's liver puncture experiments, Jewish hands in the air, Jewish eyes looking desperately away, ᛋᛋ-men and Order Police looting the silent houses, army trucks shuttling convenient batches of Jews to the antitank ditches in the forest. At the office he kept doing his accounts. "Clever Hans" Günther, for instance, seemed to have murdered about two hundred thousand people. Gerstein tried and failed to compute subtotals from Bohemia and Moravia. His mind rode on through the dark forest. Afterwards he lay weak in bed, awaiting his final arrest.

In 8.44 we find him writing to his father: *You are wrong about one thing. I never participated in any of this. Whenever I received orders, I not only didn't follow them, but made sure they were disobeyed. For my part, I leave all this with clean hands and a clear conscience.* At terrible risk, he had misdirected a few more shipments of Zyklon B. He also modified the formula to make the deaths less excruciating. Why not call him as heroic as ᛋᛋ-Obersturmführer Michael Wittmann, who won the Knight's Cross for destroying sixty-six Soviet tanks singlehanded?

On 25.5.45 he turned himself in to the Americans, presenting them with detailed and incriminating documents against Wirth, Pfannenstiel, Günther, Eichmann, Brack, Höss, and all the rest, each paper adorned by the swastika-clutching eagle within its circle. He told his wife: People will hear about me, you can be sure of that! You will be astounded to learn all the things I have done . . .

She and the children were living on stale breadcrusts by then, "Stalin tarts" we'd already learned to call them. When summer came, they might be able to pick a few gooseberries.—Your father says we'll be astounded, she said to Christian with a weary laugh.

But the Americans sent Kurt Gerstein home. So he went to pledge himself to the French.

They imprisoned him in Paris with other ϟϟ-officers. On 10.7.45 they commenced proceedings against him for the crime of genocide.

39

When Parzival was dishonored for not questioning the evil which infested the Grail Castle, he set out to cleanse his name. In due course he met his piebald brother, redeemed himself, converted his brother and became King. Unfortunately, Kurt Gerstein could not follow any of these measures once he'd been dishonored, because on 25.7.45, the turnkey looked into his cell and found his corpse hanging there.

In 1949 the Denazification Council of Tübingen refused to rehabilitate his memory, calling him a "petty Nazi." He was no comrade to us.

A court in 1955 noted regretfully: *It may be that the mere fact of making such efforts, associated with a constant risk of death, had been sufficient to persuade him that his conscience and his hands were unsullied. But this conviction does not indicate whether those efforts always achieved the desired success.*

On 20.1.65 he was in fact rehabilitated. By that time, anti-Semites around the world were already denying that anything untoward had happened. After all, as Göring laughed during his own trial for war crimes at Nuremberg: *Anybody can make an atrocity film if they take corpses out of their graves and then show a tractor shoving them back in again . . .* ▸

THE SECOND FRONT

All the faces seem familiar, even those I never met: probably because we were all soldiers fighting for the common victory.

—V. Karpov, Hero of the Soviet Union, ca. 1987

1

V. I. Chuikov, Marshal of the Soviet Union, twice Hero of the Soviet Union, and not incidentally "the hero of Stalingrad," writes surprisingly lyrical prose in his memoirs. Guderian, Paulus, Rokossovsky, Meretskov, even von Manstein—the other generals all fall short in this respect. Chuikov's career is blemished by several failures, not least his incorrect deployment of Ninth Army during the Finnish War. But now that everything has ended, with the Fascists blotted out, Germany sundered into a pair of nearly harmless bookends, and the Finns, as it just happens, anxiously subservient to us, we can afford to praise his literary efforts. He takes time to mention *the black humped shapes, like camels on their knees, of dead enemy tanks.* He has a way of bringing alive for us Fediuninskii with his pencil-written order to take command of Forty-second Army—what was Forty-second Army then? nothing but skinny men, many of them without weapons and uniforms, who shivered as they crouched shoulder to shoulder—of showing us the human being within the ruthless Rokossovsky, whose prior arrest and rehabilitation were now state secrets; of leading us dangerously close to Zhukov's pale, pouchy face (Zhukov was the one who eternally warned: *I'll have you shot!* or *I'll court-martial you!*) Less prominent individuals also get their due. A certain Russian woman whose initials are E. E. K. receives warm mention; Chuikov seems to have been especially captivated by her long black hair. From reliable third parties I've learned that their relationship was platonic, that indeed he never saw her except in a photograph; she seems to have been the wife of a documentary cameraman who was temporarily attached to his staff. Discretion prevents me from recording the cameraman's name. The story goes that the cameraman, who succeeded in filming at extremely close range the first interrogation of the captured German Fascist Field-Marshal Paulus, obtained his vantage point only through bribery: someone, we needn't say who, gained possession of the photograph of the mysterious E. E. K., who was actually, so I've heard, rather plain. Not long after this episode, the cameraman and E .E. K. divorced. This tale may well be a fabrication, and I report it only for the sake of completeness. Certainly you won't find any but the most elliptical allusion to it in Chuikov's account, whose optimism, by the way, takes on an almost individualistic taint after the surrender of Paulus. About our massive offensives after Stalingrad he writes: *The spring was with us, but behind the enemy's lines it was autumn.* Well, he was right about that! I'm happy to say that in spite of such embellishments his book never fails to hammer home the political lessons of the war, which we all know was foisted on us by the predatory interests of the international bourgeoisie. What you shouldn't expect from this general is an overall strategic perspective. Europe, the Central Front, the Voronezh Front, with the Steppe Front as a strategic reserve, all these integers and quantities have already been tabulated for us in the equations of a far greater mathematician (of course I mean Comrade Stalin); nonetheless, Comrade Chuikov makes sure we remember what's what. In particular, *this long delay in the opening of the second front causes us to understand the actions of our Western allies much more correctly than the way they're represented in those soothing messages.*

2

The tale goes that Chuikov, who as I said was "literary," happened to be studying the enemy troop dispositions on an evening between the battles of Stalingrad and Kursk. Discovering some flaw in the German array, he smiled, showed the commissar, and recited this stanza from Marina Tsvetaeva: *You can't withstand me, for I'm everywhere / at dawn, beneath the earth, in breath, in bread! I'm omnipresent. That's how I'll win / your lips!*

The commissar laughed. He liked Chuikov, admired his achievements, and saw no reason to report this weakness for an unwholesome poet (a suicide at that). A more germane concern was: How had Tsvetaeva infected him?

Elena Konstantinovskaya, so I'm told, happened to hear the *I'll win your lips!* although once again, how seems to be the issue. In fact, what was she doing there at all? Granted, she was a professional translator; could she have been employed in the interrogation of captured Fascists? One can't assume that her husband's assignment had corrected itself to include her—spouses lived and worked apart in those war years. On the other hand, why not assume it? The husband, R. L. Karmen, did have power, which the phrase *documentary cameraman* understates, and he would have pulled any string for her. He would have had her sent for in a white Zis limousine.

3

Outside, steam ascended from the porridge on the massive wheeled stove. Two soldiers were shaving one another in a pan of dirty snow-water. The tank commander with the pet porcupine was dreaming an erotic dream about Elena Konstantinovskaya. Elena herself had almost finished verifying her translation of an intercepted message from Ninth German Panzer Division. Her husband was away, interviewing a woman from our Forty-sixth Guards Night Light Bomber Regiment; she would make a perfect heroine for a *Sovkinozhurna* newsreel, and he told her so, with his ingenuous crooked grin. The pilot giggled shyly. She was having the time of her life. Elena sealed translation, original and all her notes in an envelope, which she then signed across the flap, smoked a German cigarette, buttoned up her jacket, put on her fur hat, checked her hair, drew back the flap of her tent, and set out to deliver her work to a very friendly communications officer who insisted that Elena call her Natalya Kovalova, not Lieutenant Danchenko. Natalya Kovalova was of course a representative of "the organs," so everybody shunned her. Undoubtedly she knew that Elena had been *taken away* back in 1936. Elena hated her.

Just as she passed General Chuikov's tent, she heard a happy voice, obviously his, sing out: *I'll win your lips!*

She had already met him several times. What she remembered most was his exhausted face.

4

We each had some special prize we were hoping to seize in Berlin. In Karmen's case, it was the sleepwalker's desk at the Reich Chancellery. It was supposed to be inlaid with Medusa's head. He would have loved to put his feet up on it as he planned out films about our victory.—What he actually ended up with was a street sign for Unter den Linden. Doesn't that say something about life?

(Truth to tell, in keeping with his profession he was fascinated by signs, and often collected them. One specimen he'd remark upon to the end of his career stood in the ruins of a village we were to liberate in 1944. The enemy would leave that sign with two arrows especially for him:

◄ TO THE HOMELAND: ORSCHA–MINSK–WARSCHAU

and

TO THE FRONT: WJASMA–MOSHAISK–MOSKAU ►

It was a marker to be moved at will, as the enemy homeland moved. By the time Karmen added it to his collection, the Reich's border had already shrunk back past Warsaw.)

The troops were dreaming of Nazi gold. They'd heard that it came from Jews' teeth, but they didn't care about that; they just wanted to get home alive and rich.

Chuikov, so I'm informed, dreamed of a week of nights with Elena in a lavish apartment, perhaps Göring's or Ribbentrop's. He was a surprisingly sentimental man. When Klavdia Sulzhenko sang "The Blue Kerchief," he wept. His designs on Elena partook of this same romantic character. She was married, but why not? His orderly had laughingly reported finding a nurse's fur-lined mitten on the floor of Karmen's tent; that had been the day before E. E. K.'s arrival. Stocky, slab-faced and poorly educated, Chuikov had no particular illusions about his desirability; on the other hand, the prestige he'd earned at Stalingrad allowed him to help himself to a good many things he wanted.

As for Elena, she could almost see herself stroking Chuikov's dark hair (he was only forty-three), but not quite, for she was really more interested in women than in new men, and she had no expectation of being in Berlin anyhow. That self-satisfied, catlike sensuality of hers, which in my opinion (Comrade Alexandrov speaking) is highly becoming in a woman, had lured any number of adventurers to heartbreak, but it could also make do quite well with itself. She had once made a remark which crushed her husband for a long time. But it was all his fault. Self-pityingly, and for exactly the same reason that decades after she'd divorced him he would return, whitehaired but still slim, to raise the cine-camera to his face in Toledo—he wanted to record every place he'd ever been with her!—he sometimes insisted on expressing his version of their past. It was one of his follies that there was an old Elena and a new Elena: the old one had been loving and ardent; the new one wasn't. This comparison invariably exasperated Elena into an icy rage. And now he was talking on and on about the nights when they used to make love. Elena smiled, staring into space. In despair he described the *deep connection* which he could have sworn they'd shared at those moments. He wanted to know—he needed to know!—whether she'd felt it, too.

I don't want to hurt your feelings, replied Elena calmly.

But I need to know!

No. I've never felt what you describe. For me it's just a bodily sensation.

But don't you—

It's just manipulation, said Elena indifferently.

5

On the next day, Roman Karmen and his wife were invited to dinner with Chuikov. The commissar was there; so was the tank commander who kept the pet porcupine. The porcupine was unfortunately absent.

Not everyone gets to dine in a general's tent! But since a commander must occasionally show himself to his frontline troops, we have a high regard for cinema and its associated apparatchiks—R. L. Karmen, for instance. As a matter of fact, we liked this loyal Soviet artist. In peacetime he had recorded the inauguration of the very first blast furnace in our Soviet land—the great facility at Krasnogorsk. *There were tears in the men's eyes when that first fiery stream of liquid metal came pouring out. Karmen was there and recorded it all on film.* He was sufficiently confident in himself to refrain from filming the official ceremony, his ostensible subject. Our verdict: highly effective. We'd been similarly impressed by Karmen's incredible images of our silhouetted troops leaning forward, distorted like evening shadows or Rodchenko sculptures, black-on-white by the thousands as they swarmed to complete the ring and finish off Paulus in Operation Saturn.

As for the wife, she also made an impression. She wore the Order of the Red Star.

They all knew the brave cameraman Pogozelyi, so they talked about him. This led Karmen to tell the tale of the woman sniper at Stalingrad, in the Orlovka sector, to be precise, who'd taken a bullet to the heart, coughed, slowly raised her rifle and sighted through it, squeezed off one more shot (which, however, flew wild), and fell back stone dead. Was it true? Why shouldn't it be true?—She had long dark hair like Elena, said her husband, and Elena can do anything.

Elena smiled and stared at the wall.

Whereas all the Fascists are cowards, said the commissar. You witnessed Paulus's interrogation. How I wish I could have been there! Did he break down immediately?

Well, said Karmen thoughtfully, it's true that when he lit a cigarette his hand was shaking.

That made the commissar happy; Roman Karmen always knew how to please us.

No one wanted to stop talking about Stalingrad. Our victory was less than a month old. With cheerful eagerness, Karmen told how it had been on that first cold night—oh, it was very, very cold!—when the German Fascists marched into captivity by the thousands.—You know, that crunching sound hovered in the air! he said with a smile. It reminded me of an enormous waterfall over the meadows of Privolskye. Did you have the same reaction, Comrade General?

Chuikov nodded tolerantly, staring at Elena.

6

Roman Lazarevich, said the commissar, I've heard that last year you spoke at the Conference on American and British Cinema.

So I did, said Karmen. That would have been in August.

And what did our *Allies* have to say?

I'm sure you can imagine, said Karmen with a smile.

The cone of lamplight brought Chuikov's decorations to a soft white sheen. I've heard it said that he was now one of Comrade Stalin's favorite generals.—Please eat, he said.

As a matter of fact, aside from the tea and the bread it was all American food: G-rations, to be exact, which Lend-Lease had brought us. There was even American butter! And so the conversation naturally turned to various presents received from the Allies. They'd sent us hand-me-down Aerocobras and Spitfires; the Aerocobras weren't so bad. Their tanks were useless, especially the kind the British gave us, which we called *tombs for seven brothers.* The jeeps were better than anything we could have imagined.

And didn't you also film Churchill last year? asked the commissar.

Yes, at Vnukovo Airport. He and Harriman were in Moscow to negotiate the second front.

Elena laid her hand on his in proud encouragement, so he went on: I filmed him close up as he reviewed his honor guard.

What did Churchill say, Roman Lazarevich?

Oh, that he was *fully resolved to continue the struggle* . . . Then he raised his fingers in that *V-sign* of his.

Karmen's ingenuous crooked grin had never seemed so charming as in that instant. Everybody burst out laughing at Churchill and the Allies.

7

The spring thaw was just beginning. We had straightened out our front, excepting the Kursk Salient, whose bulge ran favorably westward. When the snow had finished turning to mud, and the mud to dust, then our Southwestern and Southern Fronts were to liberate Slavyansk and Mariupol, thereby positioning us to destroy the German Fascist Army Group Center. But it was hard, so hard to shatter that German magic which turns villages into mud and corpses! Last month we'd liberated Kharkov, and now the Fascists had gotten it back again.

No, he's *von* Paulus, the commissar was insisting. All of those people are.

Chuikov sat morose and weary. Elena drank her tea. It felt very late.

The commissar was acquainted with Boris Sher, who had been Karmen's assistant cameraman at Stalingrad. They also both knew a woman named Ekaterina at Moscow Newsreel Studio. Neither Elena nor Chuikov knew her.

The most important thing is not to forget any detail, said Karmen. At Stalingrad I tried to remember everything—not simply to record it, but to remember it! And I know that once we get to Germany I'll do the same.

In that case, be sure and remember the second front! replied the commissar with a horrid chuckle.

Startled, Karmen blinked. He seemed to see a frozen, grimacing corpse in the snow, with a dead tank on the horizon.

8

Chuikov, pale and ghastly with fatigue, asked his guests to excuse him; he had to take some rest.—In other words, he added, I'm fully resolved to continue the struggle!

Everybody laughed, and Karmen made that hilarious *V-sign*.

9

A few days later, Karmen set out with a small detachment, including the tank commander who kept the pet porcupine, so that the remnant of a Panzer group which had been hiding in the woods amidst the shells of their own broken tanks—fifty men at most—could be captured and their capture recorded. Log barricades on those snowy Russian roads, frozen bodies, it was all old news. But Roman Karmen would make it significant. Moreover, he'd meet his deadline.

He'd been hoping to film Chuikov himself, but that individual seemed overtired. It would be easier to film the Front commander, Malinovsky, whom Karmen already knew from the defense of Madrid. And the commissar, who seemed exceptionally friendly, had promised to introduce him to one of Chuikov's most photogenic subordinates: Major-General N. F. Batyuk, Seventy-ninth Guards Rifle Division.

He longed for Chuikov's approval. He worshiped him, really. He'd dealt the Fascists an unyielding blow! Leaping, running at a crouch, Karmen would spend the war trying to live up to men such as Chuikov. Have you ever seen Dziga Vertov's seven-reel declaration of love for the women of our Soviet military forces? Roman Karmen wanted to create something like that. And if he couldn't make seven reels, he'd make one. Soon he'd begin work on his film "The Battle of Orlov." (New T-34s swarm over the curving streetcar tracks, while civilians run between them; they're all aimed for the front!) His newsreel from Operation Citadel would explain both in words and in a shockingly dangerous camera sequence how the enemy's vast eight-wheeled "Ferdinand" tank-destroyers were effective at frontal assaults with their eighty-eight-millimeter gun, but vulnerable to being attacked from the side or swarmed by our Red infantry. He was one of us; he actually flew aerial missions against the enemy. He filmed; he released the bomb-release lever with his own hands.

The tank commander with the pet porcupine told him a story about something horrible which had happened in '41, amidst the giant caltrops in the snow around Moscow, and Karmen pretended to listen as he stared ahead, remembering how Elena had told him in her soft voice of perfect gentleness: I can't honestly say that I do feel any hope.—He couldn't stop hearing that. And all the time she was so gentle with him; her gentleness was as unreal as the second front.—And so they came into the woods.

Combat! The gun lunged forward, replicating the flash of a concert pianists bow. Fascists in the round turrets popped their heads out; they were centaurs. The tank commander with the pet porcupine was almost killed, but we rescued him. Roman Karmen filmed it.

10

Meanwhile, Chuikov, gripping the corner of the map table between thumb and forefinger, kept thinking about Elena.

She came to him with a gramophone record of Shostakovich's Opus 40, which Chuikov found mostly romantic and pleasant, although some passages of the third movement were beyond him.

What was it about her? He could have had one of the laughing, big-breasted nurses anytime he wanted . . .

There in his secret world, which resembled one of those stove-warmed boxes on sleds which keep our wounded alive on the way from the front line to the dressing station, she might possibly have given herself to him, but her effect on him made him uneasy; he couldn't take her all in at once; just as the weak glare of the hanging lamp illuminates the center of the map, our immediate battle zone, more than it does the corners, so he perceived and experienced her, wanting to know her entirely, but only one man had ever been able to do that. There's something about her, he kept thinking, but he didn't know what it was.

He was only lonely and tired; that's all. He almost never got to rest! Stalingrad had failed to break his health, but even now he desired sleep more than anything. And soon the ground would have thawed sufficiently to resume serious operations. Von Manstein had deflected our spearheads from the Dnieper and recaptured Kharkov; we'd have to rectify that. On 17 July, he'd take part in the Izyum-Barvenkov operation to assist our Voronezh Front's southern flank against the German Fascist Operation Citadel.

He asked her how she won her Order of the Red Star, and she smiled with her red, red lips, lit a cigarette and said: It's a secret. He liked that. She asked him about his own Order of the Red Star, and he said: I won it on the second front! She smiled again. She reached for another cigarette, and he leaned forward to light it for her. And that was all that happened between them.

Her hair was as dark as the lamp-wire on the pallid tent-wall.

11

Karmen had come back looking cheerful and pleased with himself; he had German tobacco for Elena and a pair of black Zeiss binoculars for the commissar. Moreover, on the way back he'd shot footage of another indomitable peasant grandmother in her ruined house, baking bread in a tin made from a piece of a German airplane's wing. He took off his jacket; he hung up his grubby astrakhan hat. Then, his smile already becoming uncertain, he took a step toward her. But Elena was as silent as a steppe pony.

It did not do to transgress Elena's silences. For instance, where had she been before they met in Spain? Her taciturnity about that contained within its snowy forests palisades and watchtowers, chains and gangways glimpsed through the gaps in its steel fences. Elena's silences were warnings all the more fearful for their steadiness, I'd almost say tranquility. Oh, her beautiful face with its gentleness, its unmoving gentleness!

Once upon a time, R. L. Karmen, just back from filming a sports parade on Red Square—young women in lyotards hoisting giant Cyrillic letters over their shoulders, and overtopping them Comrade Stalin's portrait (the women's white shoes flashed when they marched; his lens had caught that)—took his wife to an art exhibition in Leningrad, not the retrospective of 1932, for he hadn't even known Elena then; all the same, one artist who figured importantly on the walls, through the efforts of a certain Otto Nagel, was the woman whom he had photographed at the Belorussian-Baltic Station, hoping that her portrait would be published in *Vsyermirnaya Ilustratsia*. Oh, yes, our hopes! All the same, he still admired this K. Kollwitz; even today he thought that her monumental group portraits might afford new ideas for camera angles. (An example from 1965: One of our Red Army men feeds a smiling little Russian girl in "The Great Patriotic War," directed by R. L. Karmen.)

Elena had already gone over to a corner of the room to browse through the monographs. Karmen followed her. Just as he came up to her, he saw her gazing calmly and beautifully at a page which quoted the artist as saying: *I believe that bisexuality is almost a necessary factor in artistic production*. Karmen felt a sensation of such extreme pain that he could hardly speak. Elena was conscious of him, of course; she knew that he was reading what she was reading; but later on, years later, he suspected that she had been oblivious of his pain; for who are we to think ourselves of such interest to others, even to our spouses, that they can truly read us? At the time it seemed to him that she was perfectly aware of his feelings, whose existence must naturally have been unpleasant to her, and that she calmly continued to be exactly what she was, knowing that this hurt him, distantly sorry for that, but certain above all that her nature neither could nor should be changed. He admired her steadiness; he hated and adored her; meanwhile he longed for each of them to be what neither could be; and all this happened in an instant, as they stood side by side reading *I believe that bisexuality is almost a necessary factor in artistic production*. That was how she was. That was *who* she was. And there was nothing he could do to satisfy her need for women.

But it wasn't that at all! He really imagined that he could accept her being with any and every woman she chose, if only she were also fully present with him. That was what tortured him.

And at that moment he'd believed that Elena wasn't bisexual at all, that her professed desires for other women were simply a smokescreen for her feelings for Shostakovich.

But maybe even that he didn't believe; it might have been interpolated later; all he knew was that he and Elena, who now diverged so greatly in their desires to make love that the topic was agonizing for both of them, were standing side by side, reading something which reminded them both of that difference. Then Elena walked outside to smoke a cigarette. He did not follow her. Most likely she'd forgotten the moment immediately.

He never forgot. He remembered it now in this tent at Sixty-second Army Headquarters. His wife's silence brought it back.

Elena went outside to smoke. Karmen leaning on his elbow as he sat at his desk, still wearing his jacket, looking pale and weary, preparing the shooting script.

12

After Stalingrad, the system of dual command had supposedly been abolished to reward the army: No longer would commissars dog our every breath. Epaulettes were introduced; there was even talk of allowing the troops to edit their own frontline newspapers. All the same, anyone who thought that the commissars were no longer dangerous was an innocent. (For instance—Comrade Alexandrov inserts this—all I had to do was pick up the telephone and two SMERSH operatives would be right over.)

And so perhaps the commissar was merely feeling bilious, or perhaps he was playing politics, but he was the one who told Karmen that his wife had visited Comrade General Chuikov, and there'd been music.

Karmen and the commissar were two men of the same breed. Their function was identical: to mobilize, encourage, strengthen, hearten. To do that, they had to portray things as they ought to be. And sometimes this made them very tired. We should not be surprised that they understood each other.

Where was Elena? Oh, she was over in Natalya Kovalova's tent, translating something to do with the ϟϟ Panzer Division "Adolf Hitler," something top secret. And Karmen thought: Very possibly she prefers Natalya Kovalova.

He sat with the commissar, getting drunk.—I remember what she used to do and what she won't do now, he said.

The commissar slapped him on the back, poured him another glass, and said: Don't let her get to you, Roman Lazarevich! As Comrade Stalin says, *feelings are women's concern*. Is it true that you've been to Comrade Stalin's dacha?

Last summer, said Karmen wearily. At Zubalovo.

You're a very lucky man, Roman Lazarevich. And did Comrade Stalin drink with you?

No, but the light was on in his study.

So. Well, all the same, I don't mind saying I envy you for that. By the way, what did Elena Evseyevna win her Red Star for?

Oh, bravery. She's very brave, very honest. But at the same time . . .

Finally, to distract him, the commissar tried to inspire him with our forthcoming victory, which would surely occur by the beginning of 1944 at the latest—or would if our so-called "Allies" would only open the second front.

Sulkily, Karmen muttered that the Allies reminded him of Elena, who kept always saying *I understand* while making no move to do anything about the situation.

13

Then came Kursk, Maidanek, Bucharest, Poznan. Every bullet bounced off Karmen's creased and oil-splotched fur-lined jacket.

Elena never got to Berlin of course; she never saw her former lover, Lina, not to mention the misty ruins and rusty steel beams along the Teltowkanal. Whatever became of her? Her story ended in the same soft secrecy as Barcelona used to hide in on nights that the Condor Legion was coming—all dark, except for little blue nightlights! That was the heart of Elena Konstantinovskaya.

As for the second front, by the time our Allies finally opened the second front, who cared? It's true that they died by the thousands on the beaches of

Normandie. But we'd already died by the hundreds of thousands. Moreover, it's objectively clear that their only reason for invading France at that late date was to deny us total victory in Germany.

Subsequent to the Fascist capitulation, which is to say some three weeks after Chuikov had been named a Hero of the Soviet Union for the second time, we immediately expropriated all items of value in our sector—machine tools, wristwatches, window-sashes, and of course whichever women our Red Army men fancied (an incendiary shell usually brought them out of their cellars). We even took the street signs—why not? So it went, right through the first winter. In February 1946 a great wind blew through the rubble, after which one of us found a page of a letter lying in the snow, or perhaps it wasn't a letter at all, just a sheet of paper with crazy Russian words on it, especially the name Elena written over and over—oh, it was so crazy!—and because he could not read, he brought it to Headquarters just in case it might be some anti-Soviet provocation. Comrade General Chuikov never saw it, of course. He was much too important for such trifles. But many of us did turn it through our scarred hands. Only our commissar was shrewd enough to recognize Roman Karmen's writing. ▸

OPERATION CITADEL

The German method is really rooted in the German character, which—contrary to all the nonsense talked about "blind obedience"—has a strong streak of individuality and—possibly as part of its Germanic heritage—finds a certain pleasure in taking risks.

—Field-Marshal von Manstein (1958)

To be a German means to do a thing for its own sake.

—Concentration camp commandant (1933)

1

From beneath the filigreed gates of Prague, triple columns of us came marching, with our rifles pointing upward and our faces as hard as the eagles carved on the Moltke Bridge. From Berlin we came, passing through the Brandenburg Gate; behind us, the victory angel atop the Siegessäule cast golden light upon our helmets. (Have you ever seen her, with her great fluted axeheads of wing, her raised scepter, billowing dress, and outstretched garland, everything of gold? She's our queen of eagles.) From Warsaw we also came, not so many as were needed, for an uprising had broken out in the Jewish ghetto and we had to neutralize that; nevertheless, some of us did come from Warsaw, others from Budapest and Bucharest; many came from reserve pools north and south by the front line; from everywhere in the Reich we came, and off we all went to Kursk. Goebbels had just introduced the slogan *Total war, the shortest war,* because death was coming back to us, singing in the East with the wailing voice of a Katyusha rocket. Our only hope lay in the sleepwalker, who'd already assumed full responsibility for the disaster at Stalingrad.

Grave as the loss of Sixth Army certainly is, said Field-Marshal von Manstein very carefully, lacing his fingers together, it still need not mean that the war in the East is irretrievably lost. We can force a stalemate even now—if we adapt to such a solution.

Whenever I consider this offensive, said the sleepwalker, not listening, my stomach turns over.

As for me, I felt uneasy, too, because even though we kept capturing them by the thousands and the tens of thousands, sending them back to the rear areas to be disposed of (at the military rifle range outside Dachau, we shot them in lots of five hundred), there were always more Russians! Everyone I knew had bad dreams. That enemy salient within which Marx and Engels had solved the national question, that salient at Kursk, how many Russians did *it* hide? We ourselves were fifty divisions, two tank brigades, three tank battalions, eight artillery gun battalions: nine hundred thousand men! But what's any number, compared to infinity?

That's why so few of us supported Operation Citadel. After all, we should have been easier on ourselves: it wasn't our task to win; no one expected that of us. It was only our job to take the blame.

The day we unsealed our orders the sun was lemon yellow, like the armband of a Waffen-ᛋᛋ signals man. We came with our horses, tanks and motorcycles on the muddy roads; we assembled, waiting to hear the latest bad news. The smell of enemy wheat put us in mind of summer. Maybe the sleepwalker had dreamed up some way to reorganize our Kampfgruppen. Or could the V-weapons be ready at last? Rüdiger, who was from my home town, didn't think so. Sometimes he sat beside me in our trench, rereading last month's *Signal* magazine and shaking his head while I made sure that all my wires were nicely wound on their spools. The only feature he ever approved of was the double-page spread on Lisca Malbran. But what good would *she* have been in a trench? That was what Dancwart wanted to know. As you can imagine, Rüdiger had an answer. He'd seen her in "Young Heart," which is a politically reliable E-film. He would have done anything to see her in "Between Two Fires," but that film came and went while we marked months in the slaughter-field. Well, well; we were out of the trenches now; we'd reached jumpoff position, and the sleepwalker's long-range guns peered over our tents.—It'll be hot tomorrow, remarked our Rüdiger, shaking his head.—Then we invoked our bitter German idealism, such as it was, and came to attention, *Achtung! Stillgestanden!* The orders, which contained the words *total* and *unparalleled,* warned that the Red Army had deployed against us fifteen hundred antitank mines and seventeen hundred antipersonnel mines per kilometer of front, not to mention one point three million men. So now we knew exactly how large infinity was. In short, we must anticipate substantial counterattacks. Never mind. The new Tiger tanks would save us.

That was when the old war cripple came in from nowhere, begging to fight beside us; he remembered the days of horse-drawn guns under snowy trees—lost days, the days of '41! It was summer now; we'd bought summer at the price of Sixth Army and four allied formations, not to mention the various lands we'd gained in 1942—all turned to ice! Well, so what? It was still summer.

Honestly, I don't know how that far-faring cripple got through without movement orders. But, come to think of it, we weren't even calling up fifty-year-olds yet, because Operation Citadel would set everything right. He was an old, old man, maybe seventy or more, blind in one eye, but he traveled fast on his crutch. When I think back on it now, it's like a dream. And why did he choose us in particular? I was in Ninth Army, Forty-seventh Panzer Corps, Ninth Panzer Division, which by then was hardly winning any prizes. We were all of us as gaunt as antitank rounds in our field-grey cloaks and hats, our striped belts pulled tight, our grey helmets transforming our heads into bullets. We were hungry and sullen, doing little without direct orders, knowing that we would leave another forest of neat crosses here, with helmets hanging on some of them, and triangular roofs over a very few, all destined to be wrenched out of the mud once the Slavs took over. Even Private Volker, who'd sedulously tried to improve his mind by sightseeing in the various uncanny places we went, cranked up no enthusiasm for Kursk, which is noted primarily for its State Bank and the palaces of the Romodanov boyars. I remember how at the beginning of Operation Barbarossa he used to peer into every cottage before we torched it, hopeful to see evidence of anything beyond what we politely referred to as *a certain form of existence*. Rüdiger used to tell him: There's no point. What could a Red possibly have that one of us would want? Even their Natashas are hideous! Do you want to see German beauty? Here's my daughter's photograph . . . —But Rüdiger didn't understand. Volker wasn't a souvenir hunter; he shared few qualities with Corporal Dancwart, who once crammed an entire tank full of embroidered peasant blouses. Volker—why am I talking about Volker? He's dead. The last time I saw him get excited was months before Operation Citadel, when a direct hit from a Katyusha sent up our ammunition dump in beautiful fireworks. The boy often entertained me. His guidebook devoted two chapters to Moscow.

The second chapter was all churches, so given what I know about Reds I can promise you that it was out of date; a couple of lines would have exhausted that topic after Stalin took over! Well, what's the difference? Going to church won't save you. Volker wanted to set foot in Saint Basil's Cathedral not to be saved, but because its dome reminded him of a painted wooden top which he and his brother used to play with. That brother caught a bullet in the throat at Sebastapol. He died for our Reich. Did Volker want to pay back any Slavs for that? In my opinion, that wouldn't have accorded with his nature; he was more interested in music. Once he remarked that he would have liked to be at the siege of Leningrad, just to hear Shostakovich's new symphony! Such idealists aren't long for this world. By the way, he was a very brave man, and in hand-to-hand combat the Reds avoided him; they feared his face. It's a pity he never visited Moscow, which enjoys many amenities, so I've heard; Rüdiger spoke incorrectly; their Natashas aren't trollish at all. And the Kremlin is adorned with red glass stars; I'd take one home if I could find the right sort for my Christmas tree. So why not Moscow? As soon as we'd tied off the salient and clanked into Kursk, no doubt we'd get there, because with the destruction of the Central Front and the Voronezh Front, only the Steppe Front and an infinite number of other Fronts would stand in our way.

Now I wonder if Dancwart wasn't correct. At least he got something; those embroidered blouses transformed themselves into schnapps, cigarettes and new Natashas (P-girls and U-maidens, I should say). But he bored me. His favorite proverb was: *Keep riding until daybreak*. And now Volker bored me, too. All he longed for was to get wounded again, as who didn't?

Not this cripple! He wanted to be a hero. Can you imagine? In our national poem, when second-sighted Hagen warns Gunther not to ride to the country of the Huns, they name him a coward, so he angrily insists on sharing their doom. My psychoanalyst would call that compensation. The sleepwalker would call it a noble sacrifice. It might have been either or both, because the cripple was now informing us: You might not know it to look at me, but I was accepted into Panzer Grenadier Division Grossdeutschland!

Rüdiger shook his head, Gernot was as silent as a Russian civilian, while Dancwart, who'd once had a Slavic wife but did the right thing, looked up from the raw potato he was cutting rotten spots out of, and with genuine amazement inquired: Why in the world should we care?

Anyhow, chuckled the cripple, here I am. I've been fighting for Germany ever since we Aryanized the Hermann Tietz department store. Here we go again!

I remembered him then.—How's your wife? I said.

He started wiping his eye then, and we got disgusted.

I was a telephonist; I sat there cranking my grey box. Operation Citadel was Operation Suicide, and I sincerely tried to warn him of that fact. Consider the enemy salient—half the size of England! They should have taken my discouragements into account when I came before the Denazification Court, but there's another tale. Yes, I tried to weaken Hitler's army—I was practically a member of the Resistance!—for I told the old man: Watch out for those T-34 wolfpacks!

Believe it or not, he replied, I can stand my ground as well with one leg as you can with two.

What could I say to that? The T-34s comprised my own worst fear. They came in daylight or darkness, with their headlights continuously on. And how many Tiger tanks do you think we had in Ninth Panzer? Not one. So how could we hope to stop the Slavs? To get right down to it, my hope was for something both more private and more realistic: a moderate wound. I was moderate in everything. A soldier hunching low and weary in a narrow mud trench, that was me. In those days, when a soldier went on leave from the Ostfront he got a special Führer-parcel of sausage, butter and chocolate. That's all I was wishing for. But Rüdiger sighed that there might not be any leaves from now on, no more ever.

The cripple said, and I'd forgotten that he was even here: It's no use denying it. There was an air raid. That was her end.

Gernot rolled leaves into a cigarette. Gernot didn't care. Gernot's wife had already burned.

The cripple said: The Amis did it, but I don't mind revenging myself on Russians. Besides, I'm a former athlete. I like exercise. I believe in physical culture.

Well, I don't know why I troubled myself, but I led him to Sergeant Gunther, who said: We need every man we can get. He can draw Schnelling's rations; the dead list hasn't gone through. If he's thickskulled enough to volunteer, maybe the Russian shells will bounce off his head . . .

2

Operation Citadel commenced at 0430 hours on 5.7.43. It concluded on 19.7.43, after seventy thousand of us were dead. Well, from the very beginning we'd known that it was no use; as I've just told you, it was up to us as frontline soldiers simply to obey orders and bear the responsibility. Nobody was singing "Erika, We Love You" anymore. And all that time the air burned with the sound of metal screaming; and after we'd failed on the Ol'khovatka axis, the sky grew light grey, like the service colors of an ᛋᛋ-general; and after Ninth Army lost two-thirds of its tanks on the Ponyri axis the sky became as brown as the service colors of an ᛋᛋ concentration camp guard; and finally, after we'd lost on the Oboian' and Korcha axes it was as black as an army engineer's armband. The Prokhorovka axis was where we were truly beaten. Stalingrad had been the end, but Kursk was really the end; two years after Operation Citadel I saw a Russian with his German girl in Berlin; they were playing with his pistol, shooting it at the sun, and he was kissing her and she was kissing him and she wore a blood-red rose in her hair.

3

As for us, no Russians had tasted our girls yet; we still bore arms, and on command we disguised the X of our divisional emblem with a V overhung by a horizontal bar. We didn't want to make it easy for those Slavs to know who we were, see.

It's said that Freissner's Twenty-third Corps struck first, but I'll never believe that we didn't earn the prize! At 0500 hours we came forth from the Butovo-Gerzovka Line, with the long guns of our Tiger tanks pointing the way far above our heads; I won't forget how those great steel nursemaids rolled calmly at our side, comforting us in our triple line of march. So far, our formation was still as perfectly spaced as the eyelashes of Lisca Malbran. I didn't feel unsteady. You see, I hadn't spied any T-34s yet. When the Tigers began to pull away (they all belonged to the bastards in Twenty-first Panzer), it was as if someone were holding my head underwater and I had to accept my first breath of fatality; but although I choked, it didn't kill me; death was in my lungs now and soon would be in my blood, but I just went on choking; thus my German fortitude. Once upon a time, a woman loved me and I loved her and everything was perfect; then she stopped wanting to sleep with me quite so much and I panicked, which drove her farther away; eventually I learned to hide my anguish from her, to delay the final disengagement; in short, I believed in magic; if I only concealed my need for the Tigers to stay, they'd keep me company for a half hour longer! But there they went now; the shadows of their eighty-eight guns passed over me and cooled me; a grenadier, standing in his open hatch, waved at me, and his tank groaned and clattered onward; then they were all roaring ahead out of sight, and we remained alone.

Rüdiger shook his head. I liked him because he always expected the worst.

We had six command tanks, thirty-eight Panzer-IVs, thirty-eight Panzer-IIIs, which at this stage of the war were scarcely better than bicycles, and one repainted Panzer-II, whose crew regarded themselves as already buried. There you have the tale of us in Ninth Panzer. We were skinny soldiers marching out of order, with cigarettes drooping in our mouths as we stared anxiously ahead. Twenty-first held only half as many tanks, so they had the cheek to envy *us*; we would have been happy to trade them two for one, as long as we got Tigers! That woman I mentioned (Lina was her name), when she wasn't there I missed her so much I thought I'd die; when I was with her the knowledge that I'd soon lose her poisoned everything; that was how I felt now, seeing the Tiger tanks go away. There went another of our mortar platoons with their eighty-ones; my God, were we really going to be left without help on our assault front? Those seventy-fives that our Panzer-IVs were saddled with, well, I'll complain about them later. At least Army Groups Center and South were both engaged today, and that was comfort of a sort: strength in numbers, as they say. Unfortunately, the salient was so vast that Army Group South remained an infinite distance away! On the bright side, South faced ten thousand Russian tanks, while we in Center faced only three thousand—excellent news for me. No doubt our dedication would produce decisive results. At least that was what the cripple said, and so did our commander, Lieutenant-General Scheller.

The enemy had beset our way with many tank traps, especially in the Gerzovka lowlands, but we broke through the outer Russian line. That wasn't pleasant. We waited a moment, to let them finish shooting their own wounded before we moved in. Nobody can say we're not humane.

By 0900 hours we had reached our first objective, Point 237.8, which lay westward of Cherkasskoye. You can take it from me that it wasn't in Private Volker's guidebook. And beside me, excellent Rüdiger, still young but powder-burned, his blond hair cropped, watched ahead, his neck pulsing, his right hand ready on the trigger; he searched for death with his bitter, wary eyes. Oh, that was Rüdiger for you! And Rüdiger shook his head. *Action!* We now faced a heavy aircraft assault, and by 0915 hours our regimental bomb station had received a direct hit. Among those killed were my friend Regimental Adjutant Hauptmann Hildebrand. (He was the one who always used to say: It could have been worse! We could have been at Stalingrad!) His pale head met the dirt; dark blood crept from his mouth. Well, so what? It could have been me. Somebody I didn't know was already blubbering about the betrayed offensive, and the officers were all shouting, far too late: *Set up defensive positions!* after which the roaring of our eighty-eights silenced everything human.—At 1000 hours we achieved our second objective, Point 210.7, where First and Second Battalions joined us. Here we were delayed by more tank traps.

Rüdiger, soulful Rüdiger was now in the truck ahead of me and Volker was behind. According to his guidebook, the Tverskaia quarter of Moscow is supposed to be very nice; Stalin widened the streets just for us! As for the old cripple, I initially supposed that he was with Sergeant Gunther, which couldn't have been the case; to tell you the truth, I couldn't have cared less about him right then. We could almost hear the breathing of the Slavs all around us in the wheat fields. That made me sick with fear. And here I want to state that the sleepwalker made sure that the best new assault guns went to his pets in the Waffen-ᛋᛋ; we were under strength and certainly didn't get to ride in armored half-tracks, I can assure you! As I've already inserted into the record, I was only a telephonist; I had to ride in an open truck. I kept saying to myself: If there's only something I can do; if I can only reason it out! I'm not a good person but I'm not such a monster, either. I've never shot a civilian except when under orders. I deserve to live. What measures can I take? Hermit crabs become all helmet whenever they want to; smugglers invent a hiding place that no one has ever thought of before; tank crews get themselves transferred into Tigers. And tanks protect themselves with antimagnetic paste, so that Russian mines can't—

Then suddenly from somewhere within a dense tall forest of sunflowerstalks rose a metal thing which resembled a cup on a stick; this innocuous object whirled through the air, landed on the engine cover of the Panzer-III on our left flank, which was Dancwart's, and blew it up, just as I'd expected; that was the end of Dancwart. To the sleepwalker, all this was merely reconnaissance in force.

At 1100 hours our engineers had completed their bridge over the Gerzovka lowlands, and even I, who knew better, almost convinced myself that we would actually break through and shatter these supernatural enemy concentrations, because an illusion was better than the nastiness of Sergeant Gunther, who'd said: Whoever doesn't get killed is going to be called a traitor for losing, so you might as well give it your all! And don't think about getting captured, either. Slavs drink from the skulls of their enemies.—At 1300 hours a Russian tank attack toward Korovino was halted by us, we destroying all seven tanks. But then came more tanks in squares of a hundred and two hundred.

Well, we kept doing what we could. Our wills were armored, like our Führer's heart, train and automobile. Volker said: There's nothing we can do, so we may as well roll on and find out what's going to happen to us . . .

By the end of the second day we'd achieved a breakthrough to the depth of fifteen kilometers. After that, everything got impossible. By the fifth day we'd penetrated deeper, to be sure, half a dozen more kilometers; our wills might have been armored, but the enemy's armor was thicker. We tried to be cautious; we raised our binoculars and peered through holes in every wall; but dead men, black with flies, lay in the killing zones between barbed wire. Even if only one in four was German, we'd still lost, because there are so many Russians, you see!

Our planes kept rising overhead, screaming and screaming, but there were more Russian planes than I had ever seen, sometimes ramming ours in mid-air. Sergeant Gunther ordered me to contact Europe Central at once.

I unrolled my telephone cable and listened to the skeleton-clicks, but all I could learn was that our FREYA network had gone deaf. No instructions! Then the signal hushed: I received an implication of T-34s ready to burst out of nowhere in vast secret concentrations.

Here came another flock of Shturmoviks!—Take cover! shouted Sergeant Gunther.—I prayed that they weren't piloted by the "night witches"; those were the most terrifying women on earth! Back in '41, when Operation Barbarossa began, we could have shot them all down with our magic eighty-eights. The eighty-eight is an antiaircraft gun; it's a perfect gun, really, but now we needed the eighty-eights to save ourselves from those T-34 tanks! If anyone ever tells you that a seventy-five will do the job, don't believe him. I've seen too many of our Panzer-IVs score direct hits and still lose out. You can shoot a vampire with a machine-gun, but if none of your bullets are silver you might as well use them on yourself.—Remember, Sergeant Gunther used to say, aim for the rear on those T-34s. Send 'em to Commissar Heaven on a pillar of flame!—But I never succeeded in killing one, since I was only a telephonist. It's a wonder that they didn't kill *me* a thousand times over.

Dying, we penetrated a few centimeters deeper into their defenses, refusing to acknowledge the stepped silhouettes of more tanks on the horizon. Beware of being too wise, it's said. I was glad to lose sight of them in the brownish-black smoke which rose diagonally from the engines of our murdered Panzer-IVs.

In Berlin our sleepwalker was surely opening a new case folder, a green one or a grey one, whose operational rescue plans interlaced in pincers as effective as Wagner's dovetailing leitmotivs: Citadel would achieve the objective! But what if he were actually at lunch? We ducked down; smoke arose from the village across the wheat field. Penetrations made, waves of Russian planes, so sped our lives. Fifteenth Rifles had already been forced back to the western ridgeline; the Reds were shooting at us with their fourteen-point-five-millimeter antitank guns; then our eighty-eights went off and killed them; thank God for eighty-eights!

By 9.7.43 we couldn't progress any further. We were almost across what was surely the final sunflower field when we encountered a line of Red Army riflemen all firing at us from their trench. Then a Slav ran forward, pulling the pin on a grenade.—In that case, laughed Rüdiger, I wish I'd never tried to reason with you.—His bullet struck home before mine did. But here came twenty more Slavs!

Have you ever through ignorance or stubborn carelessness worn down a drill bit? Perhaps it was meant for wood, and you need to bore a hole through a steel plate. The metal's not awfully thick; why shouldn't the drill bit last? But it gets hot, and you lean on your drill, until the bit is ruined and you haven't punched through. That was why Rüdiger had learned to express a certain knowingness without even moving his eyes. Not only had the friction of enemy counterattacks blunted us, but from the heights ahead, deep within the salient and out of our range, Russian batteries blasted us. Why couldn't the Luftwaffe take them out? Nor did we have enough flamethrower teams; we'd even run out of jellied petrol. Still we struggled to fulfill this new fairytale held together with anti-magnetic paste and adorned by the red-enameled tin stars which we'd stolen from Soviet graves; it was a fine fairytale about green-and-yellow-camouflaged German tanks; but on 11.7.43, enemy spearheads broke through our Orel salient, and Colonel-General Model, who wasn't yet Field-Marshal, had to call some of us off the assault to meet that threat. To get right down to it, we were getting smaller while infinity was getting bigger.

4

In the old legend, when Kriemhild sets the palace on fire, Hagen advises his companions to cool themselves by drinking the blood of the slain. But when their artillery opened up at our marsh-trapped and mine-maimed tanks, how were we supposed to cool ourselves then? I remember that four-day battle along the ridgetops, when Russians kept popping out of the straw-packed earth like cardboard cutouts, all of them wearing berets and aiming long or short guns at us, while FREYA never answered me. As soon as we called our tanks back to help us, the Reds hid again. Oh, we were fine fellows. Send us Teutonic Knights off to storm another castle! Our *Nebelwerfers* against their Katyushas, what an unresolved problem! I wore a white bandage around my forehead by then; a mortar shell had exploded in the sunflowers to my left. Sergeant Gunther was already dead. Within five minutes his corpse had turned as yellow as Ribbentrop's fancy office on the Wilhelmstrasse. Now the old cripple could draw *his* rations, too.

That was when a T-34 reared upward at me at full speed, its proboscis stabbing the air; it overhung us for an instant, then tilted horrifyingly down, grinding us under its treads.

I know I must have screamed; I wish I knew why that thing has always terrified me so much; it's as if its designers knew exactly what I most dreaded and hated; they'd created exactly what I didn't want them to. (Meanwhile, everything that I *didn't* fear was embodied in the shape of the Tiger, at which I swear I'd smile even if I knew it were coming to crush me.) This T-34 roared so loudly that I couldn't hear my comrades' shrieks. It left crimson ruts in the grass. Then it charged on toward our rear and was soon out of sight; I don't know how it finally met its end, because just then another Katyusha killed six of us.

That was when we got ordered forward to exploit the capture of Soborovka Village, which also wasn't in Volker's guidebook. By your order, sir! Forward it was; we ran ahead as if we hoped to overtake the speeding shells fired by our own eighty-eights. Gernot clapped his hand to his face in screaming desolation when death took him by the testicles. Then he fell. Oh, I forgot; he was already dead. Somewhere a telephone rang.

5

Before the war I suffered from nightmares, so I went to a psychoanalyst who explained to me: Wherever the unconscious gets rejected, it forms battalions to counterattack somewhere else. You can reject *them* as much as you please; if you're strong enough, you can even wipe them out, but it will be self-defeating. The unconscious will mobilize more battalions. And they'll attack the conscious until they break through. In my opinion, this is what's happening to you.

Well, he was correct. The machine-guns had begun picking us off, and if we tried to duck down into any gullies for cover, it was a sure bet that those places had been booby trapped with Russian mines. That was what befell Private Volker. He flew straight to Moscow—in a thousand pieces. Don't say we don't get what we wish for. The rest of us advanced toward the final victory, which we might even have achieved with the help of a few more *Nebelwerfer* brigades. If we could only establish a bridgehead; if only we could dig ourselves in within a circle of dug-in Tigers! There unfortunately weren't enough Tigers to be everywhere; years later I learned that Ninth Army in its entirety had only thirty-one of them; when I'd seen Twenty-first Panzer grinding optimistically off toward their assault front on that first day I certainly didn't suspect that there went every single Tiger we possesssed on our side of the salient; Army Group South had all the rest! Can you believe it? Their task was to be the point of the wedge, and the wedge was wearing down; the enemy kept shooting at our tanks with their Zis-3s.

How many more thousands did we have to kill? Wheat rose up to the shoulders of our steel horses, then drowned us. Our assault guns were running out of fuel, and I still couldn't achieve contact with FREYA. So I dialed the emergency frequency, and guess what signal I received? Europe Central commanded that we tighten up our assault front! Maybe they expected me to scratch runes on the back of my hand. Why even expend saliva on a curse?

Rüdiger shook his head once more; in the next instant, all that remained of him was a white face torn open, its red insides already black. He used to share his parcels with me; once he gave Gernot a very pretty dagger that he'd picked up somewhere. Decisive results, why not, so we struggled forward until an enemy tank brigade drove us back; we dug in and waited for our self-propelled guns to clear the way; then by your order we went forward again until we met something almost as terrible as the T-34s: a bank of Katyushas, aimed not at our tanks but straight at *us*, screaming over the earth as they sped from open sights! Even if I'd had a whole ᛋᛋ division to protect me, even if the sleepwalker himself had pulled me under his magic blanket, I wouldn't have survived that, and yet somehow I did continue to exist; I was almost the only one; the other one was that old cripple.

6

The worst thing I have ever seen was not the annihilation of men I lived and fought with; after all, they comprised an insignificant part of Ninth Panzer Division, which was but one of many units of Ninth German Army, which continued to advance upon Olkovatka after Rüdiger and the rest of us disappeared, and, moreover, could in turn have been extinguished, just as Sixth Army had been at Stalingrad, without negating the existence of its Army Group. For that matter, had Army Group Center vanished, the military forces of our Reich would have continued to function to the end! Rüdiger, to be sure; I missed Rüdiger; but precisely because I identified with him so perfectly, his death was no more tragic than mine would have been. What actually crushed me was when a fifty-seven-millimeter Russian gun opened up on one of our Tigers and punched right through it. That time I did hear the crew screaming. And it burned, calmly and spectacularly, from the inside out. Until then I had truly believed that Tigers were safe.

The cripple croaked in my ear: Tungsten-cored ammunition. That's their secret. Don't worry. We'll take vengeance on those Slavs.

Have you ever seen an injured bird at the seashore? Here come crabs from nowhere—they wait under the sand—and ring it round, cautiously at first; before you know it, the first crab has leapt onto the broken wing and pinched off a morsel. The bird struggles, but here come other crabs in a rush. That's how it is when T-34s surround a Tiger or a Ferdinand, probing with their seventy-sixes until a close-range shot gets through; if that doesn't work, the Russian infantrymen, who ride on the backs of those tanks like eggs glued down to a mother beetle's shell, board us and shoot into every ventilation slit, or pour in gasoline and light it—oh, there's nothing those Slavs won't do! Then what? From a hole in a Panzer a hand dangles, half connected to a black puzzle of bones.*

*Why couldn't the human factor have been eliminated entirely? World War III, which I expect Germany to win, will be fought with robots. Then we can all hide in deep bunkers; we'll be invulnerable. On the first afternoon of Operation Citadel, our Goliath radio-controlled explosion machines broke through at Maloarkhangelsk, but One Hundred-and-Twenty-ninth Soviet Armored Brigade defeated further penetrations. Does that fact invalidate our Goliaths? Not at all. It's merely that we didn't have enough of them.

7

My existence had become as heavy as a Stalinets S-60 tractor. What could I do but drag it forward? A line of Russians stretched behind me now; I didn't dare raise my head to look at them, but they were laughing. Forward toward the final victory; that remained my direction and theirs.

The sun winked at me from the moles on an SU-152's face. I ducked down, crawled through the sunflower stems beneath the great proboscis, avoided the blind square face of that evil thing which killed our Tigers. It didn't see me.

The old man was right behind, dragging his crutch. Then he was beside me. Then he was ahead of me. We crawled and crawled. He never got tired.

At 2200 hours, with the night sky spider-legged by artillery fire, we stopped. Where we were remains disputable—between the second and third of the enemy's defensive lines would be my guess. I longed to telephone Headquarters and give them our position report; they might even have had some use for that information. Whenever I got isolated on the Ostfront, which happened more often than you might imagine, I used to calm myself by visualizing myself amidst the switchboard operators all in a row; they sat facing the wall so that all any third party could have seen of them was their uniformed backs and cropped heads, a black phone dug in against each left ear, a bank of narrow metal shelves sprouting cables and wires like ivy; to me they represented consciousness itself; each one of them was a thought wired into other thoughts; together they comprised a brain, safely hidden under the earth, blind to the enemy outside: nothing could frighten them. Like any child, I used to will away monsters under the bed by shutting my eyes. This might not have been rational, but it was better than smoking cigarettes with Rüdiger, sitting in the dirt.

The old man said in my ear: Do you want me to show you how you can live?

I didn't like him anymore. I would have preferred Volker, who was always loyal and volunteered for the night watch. He'd passed his life sitting on the grassy lip of a trench-womb, writing letters home which would never get there. That species of futility I respected.

Disdaining to answer, I started to crawl again, gripping my helmet-strap in my teeth, and I kept on until I found shelter behind the hulk of a burned Tiger tank, whose gun-turret went twice as high as I could stand. Now they were shooting at us with their antitank rifles, but blindly. If Dancwart were here, he would have opened up with his eighty-eight! The old man stayed right behind me. We hid there together, observing the hopeless seeking of our long white rays of antiaircraft light in the enemy darkness. When they stopped shooting, we kept hiding, because as Sergeant Gunther used to brilliantly remark, you never know.

Dawn came at 0300 hours. The old man repeated: Shall I show you how you can live?

I wouldn't answer. Off to the north, I could see half a dozen Tigers locked in position against a pack of T-34s. All at once the sun glinted on their gun-barrels, and our Tigers began to fire. They killed every T-34, whose shots in turn bounced off the Tigers. I wanted to cheer, but didn't dare. What if the Russians heard?

I'll have to hang you for awhile, the cripple said.

Now I know who you are, I told him. You're Wotan. Well, I don't want your knowledge. Don't you remember how Siegfried shoves Wotan out of the way? I'm Siegfried.

That's only in Wagner, he said wearily. That's incorrect.

We started to crawl eastward. I couldn't shake him, which was in character for me; never would I have any chance of being Siegfried! "Between Two Fires," that was I. What a perfect E-film! Lisca Malbran would have had more hope of representing German manhood than Siegfried the telephonist—how Rüdiger would have shaken his head at me!

After half an hour we rested in a Russian spider-hole, the dead Russian still in it below the waist, the rest of him sprawled out on the trampled wheat; he hardly stank yet, and his forage cap was pulled down over his eyes, so we didn't need to enter into any relationship with him.

Doom never dies, said the old man.

I wouldn't answer. We sucked in our cheeks beneath our helmets and off we went.

In the next trench lay one of our own dead, and beside him, a communications outfit! Longing to escape my hopelessness, I found myself trying to speak to FREYA on the muddy telephone; needless to say, the enemy had snipped the wire.

I understood all too well what the cripple expected of me. He wanted to place me in anguish, suspended between the zones until I could grow. But I was determined not to change in any way; that would have been disloyal to my own sufferings.

8

Let me expand on this point: Perseverance is eternally correct, even when it inflames the other side. I remember from the fairytales that Grandmother Elsa used to tell me that it's necessary to follow without the slightest deviation the advice of the fox, fish, sleepwalker, raven, telephone, ragged dwarf; moreover, this advice grows all the more valid as it disguises itself as nonsense: When stealing the golden horse, saddle him up in the worn tackle, not the jeweled harness which hangs on the other peg. When stealing the Golden Princess, who offers to come with you willingly on condition that you permit her to say goodbye to her parents, you must forbid her precisely this. Be firm; let her weep! In other words, the reward will fall only to him who obeys blindly and faithfully.

Now, I have always been willing to submit myself, particularly to women. Nonetheless, in my weaker moments, further weakened by the treasonous insinuations of Rüdiger, it had begun to seem to me that unthinking obedience, "cadaver obedience" we called it, had lost us Moscow and Stalingrad; it hadn't yet won us Leningrad; nor could Operation Citadel be said to be progressing happily. In short, my belief in the sleepwalker had died. But *he* believed! He held Europe Central together in his sleep! FREYA would have short-circuited herself without him. My field telephone buzzed out code-clicks of another impending victory: He'd force the enemy to fall back . . .

Once upon a time, when Fremde Heere Ost cautioned him that the Russians were deploying seven hundred new tanks against us every month, the sleepwalker replied: *The Russians are dead!*

What if saying so could make it so? What if throwing away Sixth Army at Stalingrad corresponded to saddling the golden horse in ragged leather? What if Operation Citadel would win us the Golden Princess if and only if we threw ourselves away?

When the four dozen ebony men in chains appear, you must not reply when they ask who you are. You must allow them first to beat you, then to cut off your head. When T-34s converge on you, you must gaze steadily up their snouts. Don't yield a single square centimeter to them! If you follow these orders faithfully, then the talking serpent will change back into a princess for you to marry, and you'll become King of the Golden Castle.

I wish I could marry the Golden Princess, I thought, and it turned out that I'd thought aloud.

The old man replied: Those are the first sensible words you've spoken.

Unfortunately, there's no Golden Princess.

In fact there is.

Perhaps on top of the Siegessäule in Berlin . . .

No, she's straight ahead, just past the Thirty-eighth Defensive Construction Directorate! However, the Russians aren't going to make it easy. They don't like you.

Well, to be sure, they have good reason for that, I said. But they were doomed to lose their lands. It's the will of history. They ought to love us now, for what they had will never come back.

Then show them the will of history! Or are you afraid of a few Slavs?

What could I reply? As I keep saying, I'm only a telephonist. I don't mind admitting to being a timid sort. Back before my Lina left me, or I her (I forget which came first), we used to sit on a bench overlooking the Landwehrkanal, and in September the acorns struck the ground like gunshots; sometimes they rang off the backs of neighboring benches; I freely confess that I felt anxious; one reason that she left me was because she wanted a hero when I reminded her of a Jew.

So what *did* I reply?—I'll keep on! I shouted.

A headless Russian, dripping with worms, burst out of his grave and advanced toward me, clawing at the air as he came. I blew him up with a hand grenade.

9

When I refused his help for the third time, the old man vanished. He went up in smoke; he was *gone*, just like Rüdiger, Dancwart, Gernot and Volker. I was glad; I didn't want to be in his fairytale. Somewhere there had to be a garden of golden pears where I could waylay the Golden Princess or at least steal the golden horse and ride away to Baden-Baden. That was the fairytale I preferred to be in, the one which ended with my delicious Führer-parcel. As it was, I couldn't get out of this fairytale spoken by Russians, whose mouths were Degatyarev DP machine guns, which we called record players because of their disk-like magazines. FREYA tried to whisper-click secrets to me on the field telephone, but the Russians shouted her down. Oh, this was becoming a nasty story; how I longed to fall back into Europe Central! But first I was going to have to overcome homogeneous forces in concentration, echeloned defenses in depth, hermeneutically endless layers of tank traps, ditches, spider holes. And those T-34s, my God! Sergeant Gunther used to make us aim for the reserve fuel tanks which sat squarishly behind the hulls, but you know what happened to Sergeant Gunther.

I'll fight to the last man! I cried, at which ten dead Russians exploded out of the ground and began marching toward me, grinding worms between their teeth. Even the sleepwalker would have screamed. I dodged around them. They kept trudging blindly on toward our lines; the worms had eaten their eyes.

If only we'd had more Tigers! Granted, they weren't invulnerable, but when they traveled in packs, the T-34s didn't dare fire at them; then the T-34s dug in and hid like me.

Ammunition, like all life-force, is heavy; a man can carry only so much of it. I didn't dare to count my rounds. This I did know: The weaker I got, the stronger they got. Here came more Russians! I sent them to their second death or got away from them; then their brothers sprouted up, new shoots from moldering onions. I still had my cartridge belt, with a few cartridges ready.

Here came a Slav as evil-looking as Rasputin, with stars on his shoulder-tabs, and I was all alone! He saw me; he stretched out his arms to me. And this Russian tried to kiss me on the mouth, which I knew would have been my death, so I blew him up with my last grenade, but here came more Russians. As the sleepwalker had insisted, *the Russians are dead!*

Once upon a time I'd been an invulnerable constituent of our herds of armored personnel carriers gouging their way across the wheat fields of the Kursk salient. The Germans are dead! If I'd only had something or someone to sell to the devil, you can be sure that I would have done it, for I was in difficulties!

10

The next thing that happened was that, miraculously overcoming the incessant pressure of the unconscious, I penetrated one more enemy line. Well, so what? A stereoscopic rangefinder was gazing at me like the uplifted heads of two cobras, and then I saw a Russian hiding in the sunflowers; I shot him with my very last bullet! This act freed the way for me to encounter an old lady in a hut on chicken legs; she was weaving something out of worms. Was that supposed to scare me?

I know how my psychotherapist would have categorized her: an angry feminine principle, which is to say (just in case I'd missed the point) an angry woman, a furious woman. But I myself happen to believe that she was simply an old lady in a hut on chicken legs. There's no such thing as magic, Tiger tanks excepted.

Have a bowl of soup, she said, but I refused. Never eat anything in the other world! Persephone nibbles six pomegranate seeds and finds herself compelled to live in Hades for half the year. That was why for security reasons the Führer caused to be destroyed all the candy and caviar which Marshal Antonescu sent him.

What is it that you want? she demanded. She kept nodding and nodding.

Nothing, really, I replied. I'm only a telephonist.

Well, you must be here for something.

That's precisely what I used to say to Rüdiger.

I made soup out of his eyes. And now you're here.

I quoted her something I'd heard somewhere: *To be a German means to do a thing for its own sake.*

She stood up from her loom, waddled over to the hearth and stirred her blackly bubbling broth with a ladle made out of an airman's goggles. Oh, how Rüdiger would have shaken his head! As for me, I couldn't help but feel anxious. Was that news?

All this time you've been hunting for the secret of life, said the witch. Well, you won't find that here. But I have something more important—the secret of death.

I confess that her offer tempted me for an instant. People will tell you that the darkness needs to be faced; that's why we had to attack in the East to begin with! And if I only possessed the secret of death, I could have fulfilled Operation Citadel all by myself, applying what von Manstein calls *a clear focal point of effort at the decisive spot.* Then FREYA would love me. But what if knowing that secret changed me? I was determined not to change. To get right down to it, I wasn't here by choice; I was only a telephonist.

Forgive me, I told her, but I'm afraid of death. For that matter, I wouldn't even have accepted the secret of life from you. How can knowledge be anything but death?

You're going to be sorry! she replied. I think she felt rejected.

Rejected content will come out somewhere else. That's what my psychotherapist kept saying. I know, I know. And I was out of bullets.

11

So I'd rejected knowledge. Forward to the final victory!

What I longed for was to get back in touch with the big black telephone at Europe Central, where true knowledge lived, the kind which was both lifeless and deathless. I'd been trained to will myself inside the telephone, and gaze up at the underside of the black bakelite pan at the constellations of signals and connections as bright as the sparks on Valkyries' spearpoints. Then I could guide myself; then I'd know where to go, what to do.

Oh, I was so lonely, so lonely! Just as a burning tank roars blindly about until it blunders onto a land mine and perishes, so I was; I tried to regroup and reinforce, but hopelessly. And the sky was always dark. Around me, T-34s kept pouring endlessly toward every operational objective. And FREYA had left me! FREYA was Lina, whom from now on I would think of as LINA. To speak more correctly, FREYA and LINA were sisters. I should have understood that before. Some things we're blind to until it's already too late. For instance, the Reds' thrust against Twenty-third Panzer Corps prevented Division Grossdeutschland from participating in the drive on Kursk. Who knows? If Grossdeutschland had been there, Citadel might have succeeded. If LINA had loved me, what might my possibilities have been?—FREYA and LINA were both as pretty as the globs of molten metal which sometimes spew from a burning plane.

In a sunflower field, a cloud of fire idled like a swarm of flies over a dead Tiger. Then came broken carapaces crazy in the mud, doughnut-shaped trenches in the scorched sand, twin wires twitching in a skull, an induction coil spiraling infinitely in someone's eye-socket: sufficient for me to finally raise FREYA!

I gave the password; that was why she let me touch her. Then I signaled: What must I guard against?

Sixteenth Russian Air Army . . . said FREYA. Her voice was warm and cold at the same time in that spectacular metallic fashion of gold.

Pillboxes and mortar positions . . . added LINA. I'd loved her the best. But it was now my duty to win the Golden Princess.

And then I lost them both; I'd been cheated out of that endless moment, sentimentalized by the etchings of Käthe Kollwitz, when a woman bids her soldier-boy goodbye.

12

I went on deeper and deeper into my own loneliness. (As I'd learned from my total education, *the object must be fanatically pursued*.) Soldiers and machine-guns lurking in the corn, soldiers hiding in river-grass as they awaited their turn to wade across the water in single file, they were all behind me now; it was rare that I came across the ruins of tanks canted in the mud; once I bypassed a gun which was camouflaged with wavering black stripes, almost like the facade of a Swiss cuckoo-clock house; this was an anomaly; I'd crept beyond almost everything. In other words, I was deep in the unconscious now, and thereby increasingly vulnerable to armored attacks on my lengthening flank.

So I took up the black mouthpiece, sucker of wounds, and dialed Allfather in Berlin! I wanted to tell him that there was an enemy awaiting outside, a giant in a helmet; his mouth was as vast as the gunbarrel of an SU-152; above all, I wanted to confess that the unconscious was too much for me, but I didn't dare, so when the sleepwalker came on the line I merely asked him whether I should move forward in support of our left flank or attack out of my position. This was the sort of question that Allfather liked. (It wasn't true that he only had one eye. Like me, he refused all knowledge which might infect him with death.)

You want me to concern myself with this very particular question? he shouted. When the Jewish wirepullers have already wormed their cables into my telephone? You scoundrel!

Yes, my Führer!

Give me your commanding officer at once. I'm going to order you to be *shot*!

Yes, my Führer. He's dead, my Führer.

So you're the only one?

Yes, my Führer.

And you stand prepared to carry on the reconquest of these lost territories?

Yes, my Führer!

He lowered his voice and whispered: You'll need to be very careful. There are Jews all around you. And the farther east you go, the closer you'll get to those yellow Asiatics. Stalin's one of those. Spare no one, do you hear me? Be fair, but ruthless!

Yes, my Führer! But I have no more bullets!

He might have slammed down his black telephone, but I'll never believe it. Allfather was my loving Uncle Wolf! In any event, once again the line had gone dead.

What to do but soldier on? All I could do was my best. At any moment now, I said to myself, I'd see more giants and dragons, not to mention a castle with a red flag where an ogre would be raping Aryan girls. And then what? A magic weapon of some kind, or . . .

13

Now I was coming into autumn. In September those gracefully bullet-shaped acorns in the Tiergarten, shiny as fingernails, begin to fall to the ground and decay inside, so that when Lina and I break them open they seem to be filled with rich black gunpowder. That's autumn for me. When the leaves turn yellow and spin down into the Landwehrkanal, they're more vividly golden than ever before, since not only can we see through them as if they were lantern slides—after all, they've hung between us and the sun—but they're now also in irrevocable motion; they shift, showing us the sun on one edge or the other, then fall full on like paratroopers, and it's all so fast; they speed downward, meteors, liquid globs of gold; but once in that water, which is green-brown in the light, green-blue in the shade, they're nothing but debris; they're dirt. That's how autumn is, that sad golden instant. Autumn is No Man's Land.

Nourishing myself on ammunition from dead men, I passed tank-herds rolling evenly across the meadow toward the forest of smoke-plumes on the horizon, but they had nothing to do with me. They got devoured by hungry clouds which resembled the semicircular connectors between notes in a Shostakovich score. I can't say I hadn't expected that, because by now the weather was getting very gloomy. Meanwhile a flock of Shturmoviks, staggered line abreast, came croaking through the sky; with the red stars on their sides, they resembled September's maple leaves caught in a gust. Oh, but what if they saw me? I hid in one of the many white-rimmed craters left by their bombs and kept steadily on; my psychotherapist, not to mention Sergeant Gunther, would have been proud. After that, a talking skull in a bunker wanted to tell me something or give me something, but, frankly, I didn't care to be enlightened. A raven croaked at me: *Bring the shadow back to the Germans!* I shot at it and missed.

An enemy armed car! That was serious. But I dodged it; I also escaped the witches in the sunflower fields. Bursting through a ruined palisade, with my gun high in the air, and running across a burning field whose crops were dead tanks, toward a destination utterly obscured by smoke, I felt so frightened that I wasn't even scared.

14

After a long time I saw light on the horizon, a hellishly familiar light, but it wasn't from tracers or explosions; when I got closer I saw that it was metal; to be exact, it was a wall of metal plates—hatchcovers, shields or battleship decking. And this wall was polished so that it shone like fire.

Well, I was a telephonist; nobody could fool me; I knew about this sort of signal. Even if I hadn't seen it, I'd read about it. There'd be a sleeping Valkyrie on the other side. All I had to was unhelm her and . . . But what did I care? Every Valkyrie flies away someday, even if she's been a loving wife for seven years. She craves war. Even if I knew how to make jewels for her, she'd leave me. They always leave me, because I'm nothing but a telephonist.

Straining to encode myself into something, I became prescient. I could almost feel the fingers of their reconnaissance goblins on the back of my neck. Now I could receive the signals of a nearby cave of monsters! Here came the first of them, a T-34 with its round twin hatch-covers open to vertical like astonished crab-eyes. And I knew that it was expected of me at Europe Central that I brave these T-34s in order to win the Golden Princess, and I even had some notion of how to go about it (first, get the command tank, the one with the radio transmitter; the other tanks can only receive), but hadn't I already done enough? So I ran forward toward the wall, which shone ever more brightly, like a mountain of snow. Really I was running away from the T-34s, but when you flee one menace for another, the world will call you brave.

Oh, it was getting icy all around me! That armored car was chasing me again, but it skidded on the ice and overturned; the last I saw of it, it was spinning round and round on its back, until a great steel eagle with Klieg lights for eyes came speeding down and carried it off. Now what about those T-34s? Better not to look!

I see you shining, my beloved, chaotic, all-knowing, heartless Russia. Stalin's daughter Svetlana wrote that. She was referring to this wall.

Cubes of concrete half-sunk into prisoner-dug hills of ice gave me magic lurking-places as I made my serpentine way forward; I didn't want to be the *enemy in the open,* the one which Comrade Bukharin unmasked. Meanwhile, the wall had grown so bright that I no longer needed to open my eyes to see. At last I understood what it must be like to be a sleepwalker.

The wall was guarded by a man made of steel; he was as stern as Colonel-General Hoth, whom I'd once seen, maybe in *Front,* maybe in *Signal;* as I recall, he was peering through a twin-necked rangefinder at the Slavs although there were probably no Slavs in sight; I experienced the pleasure of watching Rüdiger shake his head over that color picture of Colonel-General Hoth, whom we never met. As for this other man of steel, he resembled a Teutonic knight and was sitting with his metal hands between his knees; the ankles of his steel boots were glitteringly articulated like a nickel-alloy shower hose; our time gave birth to men like that; in future decades I was going to keep seeing more and more of them. I don't mind confessing that he was too fearsome for me!

He saw me. He came striding forward. If I'd had a grenade I would have thrown it at him.

Fortunately, there happened to be a mucky bloody hole under the wall—perfect for a wretch of a telephonist!

So I wormed myself under and now I stood in front of the castle, which rose as infinitely high as the black smoke which boils up through the hatch of a dying T-34.

I should have asked someone what to do next. But whom? Not that old cripple who knew everything and kept insinuating that I just had to trust him; not the old witch or the talking skull. I'd tried to ask Allfather, but you know how that turned out. LINA might have known. Once she even took a trip to the East; she'd been studying linguistics. But LINA and FREYA were both out of commission now. In short, I had nothing; I was nothing.

All the same, my Golden Princess was waiting for me in the doorway, alone.

Why? Why does a woman ever do anything for a man who's not a hero? Because she was sorry for me.

15

When one gazes up at the victory goddess atop the Siegessäule one perceives her graceful femininity; the way she outstretches the golden garland is simultaneously tender and regal, but what's the expression on her golden face? She's too high, too far away. That's how I've felt about each woman in my life. For their part, women have tried to understand me, but what is there to understand? I am nothing more than I am. When on a windless Sunday in the Tiergarten sunlight moves like flames through the leaves of a seemingly motionless oak, there's no explanation. Why can't I feel the wind? Why can't I see the leaves twitching? With women and me it's exactly the same. Rüdiger, my double, never knew women, either. That's why femaleness summed itself up for him in the semi-masklike face of Lisca Malbran. Lisca Malbran in "Young Heart," smiling directly at me, with white, white speckles of glare on her glossy grey lips, wasn't she the Golden Princesss? Lisca Malbran's soft and naked shoulders, Lisca Malbran leaning demurely forward, gazing at the cinema hero with her chastely alert eyes; Lisca Malbran in yet another calm, half-smiling, semi-formal embrace with Harald Holberg in "Between Two Fires" (Rüdiger used to say that he hated Harald Holberg more than the Slavs, because it wasn't right that any man should touch her); Lisca Malbran in *Signal* magazine, wearing a pretty white sailor miniskirt which I myself for all my lack of masculinity longed to rip off of her—she held a coil of rope in her right hand while nipping at her lower lip with a smile of sweet determination—seventeen-year-old Lisca Malbran was certainly a victory goddess, a *Goldelse,* I should say, for that is the nickname of the golden figure on our Siegessäule. Lisca Malbran used to get mentioned almost every hour, back when Rüdiger and Volker and I were standing in the road in our shiny boots, smoking real tobacco or singing songs as we watched another village burn.

16

Well? said the Golden Princess, with her hands on her hips.

No doubt I should have asked her to give us a V-weapon so that we could end the war on our terms, preserving all victories and triumphs. At the very least I should have saved Berlin. (But what *is* Berlin supposed to be, but cobwebs and chestnuts?) Any decent German would have wanted that. But I wasn't decent. I don't believe that Rüdiger would have wished for a V-weapon, either; his heart's desire would have been some kind of carnal knowledge. (Her hair was as dark as the Vltava River on a cloudy spring day.) But I wasn't even man enough for that; I was only a telephonist!

How could I bring her back to the Reich? What would FREYA and LINA say, not to mention my father? Wouldn't ordinary life disappoint her? No, let me say it straight: Wouldn't *I* have disappointed her? I was so accustomed by then to receiving and transmitting the messages of others that when I dreamed erotic dreams about anybody, even LINA, I found myself watching private film of her when she was young, I mean really young like Lisca Malbran, and she was sitting pale, soft and perfect with her thighs spread and her eyes closed and her neck-tendons straining but her lips almost parted as her thumb pressed down on the base of her belly and her other fingers worked frantically to bear her to orgasm. Where was I while she was doing that? Plugged into a telephone bank! Perhaps she might have saved me with her love, but that was crazy, too, because if she made too much of me, I'd fail to live up to her; how could I be a Golden Prince? I wasn't better or worse than everyone else, and everyone else was getting slaughtered, so how could I possibly be saved? In short, what would I do if she placed me, or I placed myself, in a position of trying to be supernaturally noble? I'd only kill myself.

So I wished my own wish, the coward's wish, which was to be every morning sitting in a Biergarten under the trees with the old widows who didn't have to worry because they'd already lost so much; they touched their cups of ersatz coffee or gripped their glasses of wartime Rheinwine; they whispered in each other's ears about whose grandsons had fallen on the Ostfront, which Jews had been taken away; even if their houses got bombed away they were still the lucky ones. That was the life I wanted. I wasn't pushy; I didn't even request creamcakes. Aching bones and loneliness, dead friends, the Golden Princess didn't have to change any of that. She didn't even have to pour coffee into my cup. Oh, I was an easy man; I was wishing for trifles! And if I couldn't have those, I'd settle for lurking once more with Rüdiger in my zigzag trench, with a Tiger tank guarding me on the horizon.

17

I made my wish. I knelt down at the knees of my darling Golden Princess. When she forbore from slaying me, I dared to rise. I took a deep breath. *Happily ever after?* I prayed.

When I kissed her it suddenly came true that none of this had ever been real, and that what I'd taken for enemy tank-herds was but a grand formation of leaves scuttering all together across the sidewalks by the Siegessäule.

18

On 9.7.43, when the ᛋᛋ Death's Head Division seized Red October Village, which lay on the innermost defensive line before Kursk itself, goal of Operation Citadel, our sleepwalker must have thought that the Golden Princess couldn't get away from him now; but on 17.7.43 he had to cancel Citadel, in order to solve the new Anglo-American threat in Italy. Field-Marshal von Manstein served him with a writ of I-told-you-so. In the spring of 1944, the sleepwalker relieved him of his command, which, considering how the war turned out, was just as well for that gentleman. Good Prussian that he was, he bore his retirement and subsequent prison sentence with proud restraint. In *Lost Victories* he writes about Citadel: *And so the final German offensive in the East ended in fiasco, no matter that the enemy opposite the two attacking formations of Army Group South suffered four times their losses in prisoners, dead and wounded.*

I was never in Army Group South, of course. That must be why the achievement which consoled von Manstein leaves me cold. I was with Dancwart, whom I often saw clothed in Russian blood; Volker, who always insisted on taking his turn in the most dangerous spot; Gernot, who always enjoyed fighting in the open; Rüdiger, who was generous even to enemies. We were all excellent Panzer grenadiers with straps around our helmets. Well, after all, what's the difference?

The engagement at Prokhorovka (12.7.43) is usually considered the precise locus of our defeat in the Kursk Salient. I'm told that this was the greatest tank battle in history, but I can't confirm it; I was sitting on a park bench at that time, kissing Lisca Malbran on the mouth. Somewhere north of Bjelgorod, in a place where the fields had been deeply cut by our dark tank-tracks whose shadows were darker than blood, our Tiger tanks crushed the grass and wheat, the black crosses on them as dark as their ruts in that glaring summer light. But T-34s sucked the life out of them. Stalin gloated: *If the Battle of Stalingrad signalled the twilight of the German-Fascist Army, then the Battle of Kursk confronted it with catastrophe.*—In short, he agreed with von Manstein. Well, who says that Citadel wasn't worthwhile? Our withdrawal enabled those Slavs to execute many of our collaborators.

After Operation Citadel came Operations Kutuzov and Rumiantsev, each of which ended badly for us. It was all as rapid as the westward recession of summer greenness; winter was coming from the east again, but in the west the moist emerald fields still insisted that it was July; the green shadows of the oaks and lindens were as warmly humid as the sweat from my Golden Princess's armpits. We'd already withdrawn to the Hagen Line. I think I must have been there; I almost remember screaming: *Run for your life! It's T-34s!*

They took Orel away from us, but not before we'd blown it up and killed more Slavs. There they discovered the mass graves and began making propaganda against us. By the end of August, Kharkov was lost. Then they launched Operation Suvorov . . .

So we retreated, laying down land mines like metal suitcases, and next to me a shellshocked colonel with sunken eyes kept saying over and over again: My name is Hagen. My job is to take the blame. ▸

THE TELEPHONE RINGS

As a general rule, writing for two voices is only successful . . . when discords are prepared by a common note.

—Rimsky-Korsakoff, Principles of Orchestration (draft, 1891)

1

He dreamed that the big black telephone rang and the voice in his ear was hers; that was when he thought that he was going to incur a heart attack. She wanted him to visit her, but he didn't think he could bear it. In that agonizingly beautiful voice of hers, she said that she needed him to come. So he went to her, at which point she said that what she actually needed was for them to be friends. That, he answered, he definitely couldn't bear; so long as he didn't see her, ever, then what they had been to each other could stay frozen just the way it was, but as soon as they began to be "friends," the thing he refused to let go of would really be *over, over.* He was weeping when he stood up to leave her and she, refraining of course from approaching him, was gazing at him with implacable gentleness. So he faced away from her and began to go out; he did in fact go out of his dream, awaking with tears on his cheeks and the old longing poisoning him to the very bones; it was all he could do not to go to her right then, or at least telephone her; but, after all, everyone should do his own work all the way to the end. All the while, the familiarity of his anguish was such a comfortable old trick; it did, so to speak, comfort him in a way. The reformed addict who feels the craving almost believes in it, then merely smiles; that was the sort of fellow he was now; he'd never get rid of it now, but after all it was better than the other feeling, the fear which also lived in his bones, year by year eating away his skeleton from the inside out. As for Elena Konstantinovskaya, he remembered for a fact how jealous she had been—why, she'd never trusted him even with his male colleagues, Glikman especially. What was it about that man? Their friendship wasn't as close as Glikman thought; for that matter, anyone who presumed on a, a, well, an *intimacy,* let's say, with Dmitri Dmitriyevich Shostakovich was welcome to dream whatever liked; he himself didn't mind armoring himself in irony if that would, well, the point is that every instant he'd spent away from Elena embittered her to a more fantastic degree; because the way she quite reasonably looked at it, he was still living with Nina, wasn't he? And he was never going to leave Nina, never. Therefore, he had no right to further subdivide his heart even for innocuous friendships, did he? Did he? He'd been so often afraid of Elena! Oh, the times when she threw a plate against the wall simply because Sollertinsky had telephoned, or snatched up one of his scores, threatening to tear it up for absolutely no reason that he'd ever comprehended—how he'd hated her, really! Or at least, how he'd feared her . . . ! Why then had she so deeply wounded him by walking out? Well, it had certainly been a shock. He needed to analyze this shock without delay.

I must have been in love with, I mean, an *illusion,* he thought, which sounded so trite that he wondered in which bad novel he'd read it. But it was true. And he still was. He loved her to the point of agony. And it was worse than hopeless; he could never . . .

Remember, said Glikman, trying to console him, it wasn't as if she left you. Be logical, Dmitri Dmitriyevich! Why feel abandoned? She offered to marry you, but you went back to Nina. Doesn't that make it better? *Elena never left you.*

Grinning malignantly at his *dear friend,* Shostakovich replied: That makes it worse, you, you, you sonofabitch—no, forgive me, Isaak Davidovich, I . . . My word, what a rude thing I've just said! Put it out of your mind, I beg you; it was just a . . . You see, I prefer to think she left me, because in that case I had no choice. I didn't have a, a *choice* which I—

The telephone rang. It was not Elena Konstantinovskaya.

2

Our so-called "Allies" had finally launched Operation Overlord against the Fascists; they'd established a beachhead on the French coast, in the locale of Normandy. Can you believe it? We bled ourselves almost to death at Stalingrad, while they, you know. It's like a parody. Their casualty statistics must be exaggerated; I don't believe that France could be all that dangerous. Of course we all try hard; we all do what we can. Who am I to, to, say that Americans shouldn't play second violin? Nina says I don't know anything. He was trying to read about this development in *Pravda,* but Maxim, who hadn't yet left behind that boyhood age of mischief and tricks, kept teasing him by dragging a toothbrush across the wires of the second-best piano; that sound made him melancholy but he didn't know why. Lebedinsky, who'd been raised strictly, was appalled that he didn't beat the child, but he just couldn't.—He's performing the classics! cried Shostakovich with a hideous attempt at a smile; he was afraid that Lebedinsky looked down on him for his leniency. Truth to tell, when he heard that ghostly, almost erotic sound, which resembled a woman's moan, it, so to speak, gave him ideas; he wouldn't mind weaving that chord into his Ninth Symphony, which was almost completed, or perhaps into the Tenth. (Actually, it materialized in the terrifying Fourteenth.)

The telephone failed to ring. Lebedinsky watched him stare at it. Misconstruing vigilance for hatred, Lebedinsky, whose brother-in-law had been taken away after a telephone call summoning him to an important meeting, said: Oh, yes, Dmitri Dmitriyevich, what a pleasure! To wait on the *pleasure* of that thing, so that—

I know, I know, interrupted the host in alarm. Lebedinsky grew embarrassed, discomfited. A quarter-hour later he'd taken his leave. Shostakovich sat alone, drinking vodka and staring at the telephone.

Galya was at the kitchen table doing her homework. The assignment: Write an essay on the subject "Immortal Heroes of the Great Patriotic War." Her chosen immortal hero was liaison officer Putilov, who had been stationed at Stalingrad. The tale goes that under heavy enemy fire he crawled out to repair a communication line. The Fascists machine-gunned him. Clenching the two broken strands of wire in his teeth, he completed the circuit and died. Communications were restored.

Papa, do you think it happened just like that?

I think it's quite interesting, Galisha, and, you know, quite, quite educational. Could it actually have happened? I mean, whether or not the electrons . . . Ask your mama; she's a physicist. You're lucky she . . . By the way, your hair looks extremely, you know, *pretty* pulled back like that. How I love you, dear child! Is that a new style? And that red ribbon is very . . . But it's not fastened properly. Oh, me! Come here, please, you pretty child, and I'll . . .

The days went by. The telephone never rang.

There was a scene from a certain Roman Karmen newsreel: A dead streetlamp bulb hangs like a translucent olive from its metal stem; unshoveled snow reaches almost all the way up to heaven. Which one was that? Maybe "The Men of the *Sedov.*" Curious how that snow made him feel! Because snow, you see, signifies waiting—not that I believe in program music. If only the telephone would, you know, *ring*! Well, well, and now our busy little German Fascists were launching V-weapons against England. Sometimes he had to laugh—

That night he dreamed about a monstrous idol whose face was a black telephone, then woke up gasping. It was not much after four. Hours to go before dawn, but not enough hours to give him any hope of falling asleep again. Tomorrow he was going to be worthless. Fortunately, the dance music they'd demanded wasn't complicated; he could score it awake, asleep, or in between. Send me out, and I'll take the wires in my teeth; who cares what happens after that, as long as their signal goes through? This is my life; this is my life. It's a very, how should I say, typical situation. And the longer Galya believes it's wonderful, the better for her.

He was composing his Second String Quartet when the telephone rang. It shrieked with the same brassy shrillness that it had had when it rang last year to announce that Comrade Stalin had rejected the national anthem he'd composed with A. Khatchaturian. This time it was merely the storeman of the NKVD Ensemble, informing him that if he brought a can around it would be filled with jam; Nina had been begging for that, less for Maxim's sake than for Galya's. The girl seemed to have stopped growing, although she no longer complained of hunger. He understood that this condition was now prevalent, unfortunately. And Nina had told him (somewhat sharply, in fact) that the least he could do was beg a few grams of something for his children, given all the favors he did for strangers. She refused to believe that he loved Galya as much as Maxim. In fact, every time he laid eyes on that girl he remembered holding her when she was a baby; he remembered the first time she'd said his name; he'd gladly chop himself into pieces if that would in any way, you know. He said to Nina: Maybe they ought to add a trumpet or two, so that—

What on earth are you talking about?

The *telephone,* you imbecile. So that we really can't escape it. And then accent the—

I don't have time for this, Nina said, as she always did. Well, he shouldn't have called her an imbecile, but on the other hand he frequently felt that he could hardly—

The telephone rang. His heart exploded sickeningly. He lifted the receiver and heard nothing but an evil silence. This was what they sometimes did to make sure you were home, when they, you know. What he really wanted was to find a nice rabbit-fur coat for Galisha while he was still *here*, because . . . Very quietly he reinterred the receiver, took up his briefcase, which contained a toothbrush, clean underwear, and a few scraps of music paper, and then he went out to the landing by the elevator, waiting very quietly for an hour, so that the children would not have to see him being arrested.

3

The day after he'd persuaded the jury to award Rostropovich the first prize in the All-Union Competition, the telephone rang. It was, well, you know. This was the worst, even worse than being arrested. She wanted to know how he was. She was very gentle. He couldn't speak with her, unfortunately; he actually could barely even, well, I'm sure you get the point. Some things are infinite. Fortunately, Nina and the children weren't home. Elena would have known that; that was why she'd . . . He doubled over and burst into tears. ▸

ECSTASY

Another quality of the Poem: a magic potion being poured into a vessel suddenly thickens and turns into my biography, as if seen by someone in a dream or in a row of mirrors . . . Sometimes it looks transparent and gives off an incomprehensible light (similar to light during the White Nights, when everything shines from within) . . .

—Anna Akhmatova (1961)

She once told that him he was lucky and he said yes, thinking: I am lucky because I sometimes get to see you, which was not what she had meant.

He once wanted to tell her that she was lucky, too, because two men loved her very very much, but he caught himself: His loving her wasn't lucky for her at all, because she and the other man were so much better than he.

It was understood that he could never touch her.

Once in a letter he asked whether there was really no hope, and she wrote back promising him that there was absolutely none. So he asked again. She told him firmly, sadly and not without affection that there would never, ever, ever be any hope. She felt sorry for him. As for him, he continued right on hoping, firstly because she kept seeing him, sometimes without the other man's knowledge, secondly because even though she used to murmur *don't say that* when, unable to control himself, he repeated that he loved her, by the second month she no longer objected, merely looked at the restaurant table or into his face with an indecipherable expression which made him want to lay his life down at her feet since like a divinity she heard, even though she did not grant, his prayer; thirdly because when he glancingly mentioned that he'd written and destroyed a diary of the imaginary years they'd dwelled together in one of those houses like narrow white islands in the rectangular oceans of pear trees—a very particular house, the one with the windowed tower which gazed over the levee—she'd remarked that she wished she could have read that diary; fourthly because she told him of her own volition that had she not met the other man first they could have been very happy (although she subsequently began to wonder aloud whether she would in fact have been the right woman for him); and fifthly because it would have been too unbearable for him not to hope. Needless to say, he couldn't divorce Nina.

She was always good to him. She smiled silently upon his worship. When he asked what she was feeling, she replied: I feel that you already understand everything.

His hope made him happy, and their meetings mostly made him very happy, although sometimes the fact that he could never marry her nor even take her in his arms stiffened his chest with such agony that he fell silent and only with the greatest effort could avoid tears. At those times he always remembered to smile at her, who truly wanted the best for him and whose goodness vastly overtowered the pain which he kept ridiculously inflicting on himself.

She said: There's no point in waiting for me.

He said: Do you know, Elena, I, I think I'll wait.

She said: Don't wait.

He asked whether he would see her that afternoon.

About this matter of taking her in his arms I should explain that a few times they had embraced hello and that once she had embraced him goodbye for a long time, tightly and tremblingly, which had convinced him that she didn't want to see him anymore, but that wasn't the case, although it was true, or appeared to be, that from that day on, whenever he tried to embrace her she folded her arms and walked past him, so he, sickened at the thought of forcing himself on her in any way, stopped trying, not knowing for how long he could control himself in this respect and at the same time knowing proudly and ecstatically that he could in fact refrain from this for the rest of his life if that was what she desired or expected. Three or four days later, he got the courage to ask why he couldn't embrace her anymore, and she, smoothing her dark hair, assured him that he could; it had all been a misunderstanding; she'd thought that he hadn't wanted to. I can hardly describe to you how happy he became then. Moreover, that day he received the great fortune of meeting her twice; and on the second meeting he embraced her very tightly; for the rest of the day he was in ecstasy.

Once when he told her how much he loved her, she answered: I'm sorry.

(Usually she just half-smiled and said nothing. She listened to him as patiently and silently as God. But this time he had written to her, and so she replied in writing.)

His idea was that there was a one percent chance that she would leave the other man in ten or twenty years. As long as he could believe in that, he could frequently be happy.

The other man was by definition more loving, honest and decent than he. Had she ever exceeded the limits and given herself to him, how could he have lived up to the standard which the other man had set? Even if he devoted himself only to her, that wouldn't have been sufficient, for the other man was already devoted to her, and the pain which he, the worshiper, would have caused the woman in making her cause pain to the other man would have been unforgivable. So all that remained was to devote himself to her as much as the circumstances allowed. And since those circumstances prescribed that his devotion be carried out more or less in her absence, what he prayed for was to go crazy so that he could live in a world where she would always be with him. Every day his love for her seared deeper into his chest and throat.

It was in writing, as I have said, that they truly communicated during this period, although that communication could not be anything but painful. After she and he were quits, he communicated only through music. In fact he was going to write her a symphony, but she explained that the difficulty was that he had already given her too much of everything except for the one thing that he really should have given her. He wrote her many, many letters, and she wrote him three in return, the last of which she requested that he destroy, and then she accepted but no longer replied to his letters, which after all said only the one thing. Their meetings, infused with her occasional stories and compassionate, half-acquiescent silences, gave him an opportunity to be simultaneously unrealistic and selfish. Sometimes he even forgot the war. When he wasn't too sad or shy, he talked, too much, of course, but only so that he could say *I love you,* since she never would. He gazed into her face in ecstasy. Every time he saw her, the ecstasy increased. Then she looked at her watch and had to go away. He was in agony even though he was exalted to have been with her, and he wondered when he could see her again; oh, he was crazy about her.

He was really quite addicted to her face, and yet for the longest time he could not remember it at all, it being so much brighter than sunlight on a pool of water that he could only recall that blinding brightness; then after awhile, since she refused to give him her photograph, he began to practice looking away for a moment when he was still with her, striving to uphold in his inner vision what he had just seen (her pale, serious, smooth and slender face, oh, her dark hair, her dark hair), so that after immense effort he began to retain something of her likeness although the likeness was necessarily softened by his fallibility into a grainy, washed-out photograph of some bygone court beauty, the hair a solid mass of black except for parallel streaks of sunlight as distinct as the tines of a comb, the hand-tinted costume sweetly faded, the eyes looking sadly, gently through him, the entire image cobwebbed by a sheet of semitranslucent Thai paper whose white fibers twisted in the lacquered space between her and him like gorgeous worms; in other words, she remained eternally elsewhere.

But, again, this was not to say that she was not present, gazing steadily at him from across the table, speaking or listening. She cared for him (and once more I must emphasize that she was not at all remote; it was more than pity which she felt for him). He hoped and imagined that she loved him; if he only could be sure that she did, he could go on easily down the long path of dreams, despair and useless hopes.

Everything she'd ever given him he'd kept, of course. They'd given one another books. At some point he'd begun to lend her some of his own books; needless to say, he would gladly have given them to her to keep, but feared making her uncomfortable by doing that, for she might well have felt awkward about accepting the things he treasured, since that would have deprived him of them (he wouldn't have cared) or perhaps unduly encouraged him (about which he would have cared only too much). Sometimes he could in fact in a politely quiet sort of way give her things he treasured, but this bordered on dishonesty and he didn't want to tell her any untruths. Why then didn't he buy her mint-new copies of those books and be done? Some were out of print, but the main reason was once again that he didn't want to overwhelm her by always giving and giving. She knew how much he loved her. At first she'd disbelieved, but now she believed (so he thought; she said that she didn't believe him but he supposed she had to say this in order to avoid encouraging him). Wasn't that enough? So he lent her books. After all, one of life's best pleasures is reading a book of perfect beauty; more pleasurable still is rereading that book; most pleasurable of all is lending it to the person one loves: Now she is reading or has just read the scene with the mirrors; she who is so lovely is drinking in that loveliness I've drunk.

Amidst the other grey, red, greenish, black and orange volumes of various heights, this white book with the black lettering was perfectly proportioned in every way, neither showy nor insignificant. It was one of his favorite books (we can't say his favorite since his life wasn't over yet). He mentioned it, and she was willing to accept it; she was that kind, to read the book which he loved.

At the moment that it actually passed from his hand to hers they were sitting across from each other in one of the three or four restaurants where they usually met; and she, having gazed into his face with her usual richly intelligent seriousness, studied the book she now held with the same air of happy possession which he would have hoped to find had she been looking over his body before making love with him, which she would never, ever do no matter how long they both lived, a fact which made him want to utter a sound much softer and more leaden than any scream; and then, sitting within touching distance of her beautiful hands which he could not touch, he watched her open the book to the title page with its half-calligraphic brush-rendering by an unknown artist of a Buddhist *pongmalai* garland, probably of jasmine flowers, which was draped across a woman's naked thigh. This was the most intimate moment that he and she would ever have (unless of course his one percent became a hundred, and she accepted him forever). He would not be at her side when she began to actually read the book; but from their frequent conversations he thought he could keep abreast of where she'd arrived each day. She'd promised to begin it that very night, when she was home with the other man, which meant that she would at least cross the frontier of the half-title page, followed by the dramatic double plant-stalks (connected by a leaf), of the initial letter E. And now she saw before her those wide white margins and those generous white lines-between-the-lines which encouraged every word to preen itself like the treasure that it truly was.

I should mention that this beautiful volume, which was such a pleasure to hold, began its tale with a dazzling abruptness, as if the reader had just emerged from a dark tunnel into another world, a perfect world whose ground was a hot white plain of salt upon which the words lived their eternal lives.

I need say nothing about the plot, whose involutions (it's a tale of obsessive love) progressed like the nested terraces on a Buddha-studded tower which narrows perfectly into nothingness. Once I visited a certain *wat* in Bangkok where although the day was exhaustingly hot and bright I grew enthralled by the sensation of wandering on a high place somewhere in the mist, a plateau exploding with ornately weathered crags. There were many towers, just as in this world there are many perfect books.

This book, well, it would be wrong to say that it contained everything, but it did hold a white wall which was frescoed with masked figures, demons and bare-breasted dancing girls all wearing golden-scaled armor. These characters, who presumably represented the various types of being which flourished during the author's epoch, journeyed through strange adventures, of course, and more commentaries have been written about their chapters than about any others in the book, for their encounters with bandit leaders in the jungle, their dialogues with the Prince of Heaven, and their dangerous dives beneath the sea to obtain the One Pearl do not lack in beauty and even philosophical significance, but these personages remained the two-dimensional inhabitants of parables—universal shadows, to be sure, but dependent, imprisoned on that white wall (which was really a double spread of white pages). They won love, power and treasure when they followed the Right Path, but the happiness available to them was founded on an ignorance, mercifully instilled in them by their author, of the fact that they were not real, and that in the realm of the real, where the true forms of love, power and treasure endure forever, their bright flat strivings (imagine the animated lives of Matisse's cutouts) would never, ever, ever find any hope; for the dreams they lived in could be transcended by the book's protagonist alone, whose supernatural perfection began to evince itself in the fifth chapter. For now, he could hardly wait for her to get to the second chapter, whose words, so he had read in one of the antique commentaries, had been syntactically and typographically arranged to replicate heart-shaped lilypads in a vast vase before a golden wall. Between the lilypads, in the complex interstices of the water-mirror, she'd be able to look directly into that pure zone upon which the lines of print had been so evenly superimposed. He comprehended very well that every sentence she read brought nearer that moment when she would have finished the book, that moment when the extremest final tendril of orgasm elongates, tapers and begins to become a memory; but even this he could accept; he passionately longed to follow her from chapter to chapter like a lover hastily stripping off his clothes, seeking laughingly to overtake the one he loves who has already almost finished taking off everything as she stands before him in that small white room.

That week he found himself less often dreaming his way into that place of houses like white islands, which, if one gazes down on it from an airplane, like a reader soaring over an opened book, seems almost bluish-green, with occasional bright yellow rectangles of mustard fields, and cool rivers winding through the flatness, their richly grassy lips studded every now and then with trees. Where the fields shine most greenish, there too one of the rivers sometimes also goes green, but in one spot where the green has gone so rich as to rival blackness, the river retains its original lapis-grey character; and it's there that the windowed tower of that narrow white house rises over the pear orchard to gaze across the levee. This house was empty now. But he wasn't worried; he knew where she was. She was inside the white book. And as long as she dwelled there, she was with him. He was in ecstasy.

(He sent her a telegram to find out whether she had gotten to the lilypad chapter and she had; she'd understood everything; and even though she was busy she telephoned him right back so sweetly and spoke with him for nearly half an hour, after which he begged her to please give him her photograph and she gently replied: No.)

That book which he had entered, now she too was living within it. Now and forever it would be hers.

His love was graced by perfect control. He knew that he would never hurt her or the other man. He could live without asking anything. He loved her so much that he could freely give her up if she asked that of him. His love was far more perfect than he was. We might say that it partook of the same perfection as this white book, whose two-dimensional dancers (brought into being only to emphasize the wholeness of the protagonist) wore golden crowns which tapered into ribbed sequined stingers. Their wrists made slow swimming motions while the devotees knelt before the incense-swirls and the flower sticks. And now in the fifth chapter, the woman of the naked thighs, the one from the title page, emerged from an initial letter E and began to dominate the other characters, who were really no more than the glittering piecemeal reflections of faces on golden tiles.

She was reading the fifth chapter right now. He remembered it so well. He had read it one summer's afternoon, in much the same way that he now gazed so deeply into her face, drinking and drinking of its inexhaustible brightness while she gazed gently back at him and he could not help but smile into her face because he was so happy and she smiled back, her slender fingers sliding up and down the coffee glass. The happiness of knowing that she was now in that particular room with the golden tiles where he had been and could be again whenever he chose, this happiness was so intense that he longed for death. All anguish was gone.

And now in the eighth chapter this protagonist, this woman of the book was accepting a fancy *pongmalai* from somebody; it consisted of two lavender ribbons, each wearing its own string of white buds and green buds and more white buds which then merged into the upturned bowl of an opened rose; then a white banana flower the size of an apple led the eye across the divide to the mirror image, the downturned rose, followed by two more strings of fragrant white jasmine buds each tasseled with banana petals. This was the crucial scene. She was reading it at that moment. And he experienced the ecstasy of knowing that she with her perfect intelligence now knew that the woman in the book was *she,* with every visual element, every typographical atom down to the very final letter a, perfectly representing and adoring her attributes. ▶

OPERATION HAGEN

"I gave her my oath that I'd not wrong her anymore,"
returned King Gunther, "and I mean to keep it forevermore.
When all's said and done, she is my sister."
"Let me take the blame," replied Hagen.

—Nibelungenlied, ca. 1200

1

We obliterated Warsaw block by block; why let the Slavs get it back? We prepared to dynamite Prague, but unfortunately it fell too quickly.

Hagen, more anciently called Hogni, had been opposed to attacking Russia in the first place. But he was too noble to hide his own guilt. I consider him as brave and forward-looking as Rommel. He said: Let me take the blame.

The sleepwalker liked that, I can assure you! And so Hagen got classified as indispensable to the war effort (I've held his identity card in my hand, counting up its various swastikas and eagles)—but in between crises he wasn't even authorized to enter the outer checkpoint at Wolf's Lair. That tells you how the High Command felt about him. A lesser man might have been offended, but Hagen never stopped being realistic. He said to me: I know what I'm here for, and I accept it. Now let's go get drunk at the Golden Horseshoe. Himmler claims that the hostess is the last Negress left in Berlin . . .

He got drunk; I didn't. I watched a single tear creep down his cheek.

In the first winter of Operation Barbarossa, with Moscow unvanquished and our soldiers freezing to death by the thousands, Hagen and I went to Kranzler's for a beer. The place was almost empty, and there wasn't any coffee, either. Hagen murmured to me that the twenty percent wartime surcharge on alcohol might soon be raised; of course he'd bear the blame for that.

The cigarette girl, who looked exhausted, sat slowly stitching up the upholstery of the most tattered chairs with packing twine. German string wasn't strong enough nowadays, being nothing but braided paper; but packages still came from Switzerland; everybody scavenged those. The cigarette girl was bitter against the Jewish agents who'd caused this shocking turn in the war. Winking at me, Hagen said: It's all my fault. I'm the King of the Jews.

She slapped his face.

Hagen laughed and turned the other cheek. A single tear began to swell upon the duct of his bloodshot eye.

On 12.12.42, when the sleepwalker was saying: We must under no circumstances give Stalingrad up. We should never get it back again!, Hagen kept quiet, but afterwards he remarked to me: Don't think I can't see the end. I *know* what's coming.—He saw it, all right. But he never flinched. Isn't that a virtue?

On 19.7.43, when we abandoned Operation Citadel as lost, the sleepwalker sent for Hagen by telephone. I was all the way at the other end of the Marble Gallery when he slammed down the telephone, but the crash was gunshot-loud, so I came running. Then I saw the expression on his face. He could have been an SS-man machine-gunning a truckful of Russian infantry in revenge for the Ostfront's fogs, encirclements, airplane attacks, partisans, suicide charges, winters, swamps. He caught me looking at him and screamed: *Dismissed!* I clicked my heels, saluted and marched away as far as the waiting room, where I'd still be within call in case he needed anything. Another crash! He was trying to slam the telephone down under the earth! But here came Hagen, immaculate, ironic, ready for anything. He should have been a general but he was only a colonel. He winked at me as I opened the door to announce him. Before I had shut it behind him, I could already hear shouting and breaking glass. When Hagen staggered out, he looked as if he'd donated too much blood at a frontline hospital. He sighed: I need some Pervitin to pick me up . . .

We went to watch a newsreel at the Ufa-Palast. The film was out of date; it was all victories. Most of the audience had only come for the feature: Lisca Malbran in "Young Heart." You can imagine them: ancient ladies, legless men, and a few pallid factory workers—but I should also mention that solitary, radiant little boy in a Hitlerjugend uniform; he *Sieg Heil*'d every falling bomb.—My replacement, joked Hagen.

We promenaded on Wilhelmstrasse and counted broken windows; we strolled past the boarded-up shops on Potsdamer Strasse, at which point he laughed angrily: *We must under no circumstances give Stalingrad up.* I felt no need to ask him where it would all end.

By then I was sleeping with the cigarette girl at Kranzler's. She didn't even have enough ration points to buy a new girdle. After her apartment got bombed out, I made the mistake of asking Hagen for advice on where we should live. He said: There are pewter coffins in the crypt.

I wouldn't want you to think that I was angry at him. When all's said and done, he was the best friend I ever had. He never lied to me or put the blame on others.

My cigarette girl got called up to work at an armaments plant where every new bullet was still copper-roofed like the Berlin Cathedral, but the copper ran out, which was all Hagen's fault. Then the British dropped one, ten minutes before the end of her shift. I didn't even get a scrap of her dress to hold onto.

To distract me, Hagen took me to the Bayreuth Festival to see "Götterdämmerung." In the final act, when Gunther sings: *Complain not to me, but to Hagen; he's the cursed boar who slew this hero!* Hagen laughed aloud, then wept again. Because he was in uniform, they didn't dare tell him to be quiet. I glanced up at the sleepwalker's private box, but the curtain was drawn. Sometimes it's better not to know.

2

Here comes Hagen through the Brandenburg Gate, at the head of a long file of anxious women and children. The battle of Berlin has just ended. They say that a hundred thousand civilians died. The survivors are coming back. A woman strides quickly into West Berlin, clutching her buttonless coat. Another woman, a darkhaired beauty, holds her child's hand, her face blank and shocked. Hagen leaps up on a mound of rubble and shouts down at them: I did it! I lost Berlin!

They throw stones at him. But Hagen's invulnerable, like Judas. He's armored with steel-plated guilt.

I see Hagen at Nuremberg—naturally. How could he not be there? He's a principal defendant! They might have let him off, since he was only a colonel, but he insists that he was really a general.

I'll never forget the look on Justice Jackson's face when Hagen rose, stared straight forward, and coolly explained: The function of Germans in Europe, and our duty itself, is to take the blame for everything. We commit crimes so that the rest of you can feel pure.

On 1.10.46 he was found guilty on all counts. General Nikitchenko added: The record is filled with his own admissions of complicity. There is nothing to be said in mitigation.

There he sat, in the very front row, with the worst of those war criminals, some of whom were in uniforms and others in suits; their heads slumped forward, as if the headphones weighed them down, and they closed their eyes, waiting for sentence to be passed upon them. It happened in alphabetical order. As each one's turn neared, he opened his eyes, sat up straight, and braced himself, staring up at the judges. But when the court called upon Hagen to rise, his face became as bright as the lights of the Metropole on that night I'll never forget when the *artistes* Margot and Heidi Hoffner danced nude together, and all of us who saw them felt that we'd been given a secret deep within the embrace of the wartime blackout.

Defendant Hagen, said the President, on the counts of the indictment on which you have been convicted, the International Military Tribunal sentences you to death by hanging.

I knew that, said Hagen.

The prison psychiatrist came on the last afternoon, to record his feelings. Hagen told him: My emotions can be summed up in two words: *Déjà vu*.

Dr. Gilbert wrote down this reply. He seemed irritated.

Everything's my fault, yawned Hagen, blowing a smoke-ring. I killed all those Jews. I saw today coming, too. I foresaw all this back in 1929.

Do you remember the tests I gave you? said the doctor in an angry voice. I learned quite a lot about you. Among other flaws, you're diseased by infantilism. That's why you can't stop playing with people. You've never taken responsibility for anything.

What on earth are you talking about? You can punish me for anything you like! I'm ready. When you have marital problems, feel free to tell your wife it was all my doing. I know how *that* will turn out.

Dr. Gilbert slammed the notebook shut. He rose and banged on the cell door so that the guard would let him out. He refused to look at the condemned man, but when the key began to turn, he hissed over his shoulder: You don't know who you are. Tonight you're going to die without even knowing that much.

Of course I would prefer to be myself, said Hagen. But something always brings me back to take the blame for what God has done. And what if this something is also myself? ▸

INTO THE MOUNTAIN

We have diagrammed the troop groupings as though they were the receding wings of a theater set—1, 2, 3, 4—inwards.

—Sergei Eisenstein, ca. 1942

Before the sleepwalker slammed the door behind him he needed there to be nothing left, not even the door itself; in the old Norse legends great men go into the mountain when they die, and their voices may sometimes be heard where there are hollows in the earth; but the sleepwalker's intention was that there would be no mountain after him, no voices in the ground, no ground, and certainly nobody above ground to listen.

He said: Trudl, bring me the folder for Operation Spiral, would you, please? That's a good child.

(Do you want to know why it was called Operation Spiral? The Midgaard Serpent swallows his own tail, and then what? Where does he go?)

The telephone rang. Four officers had waited too long to blow up the Remagen bridge; the enemy was across the Rhine!

Have them shot, he said.

The telephone rang. The Ruhr basin would soon pass out of our hands.

Flood the coal mines, he said. It will take the Jews twenty years to get them working again!

The telephone rang. The enemy was approaching Düsseldorf.

Then burn Düsseldorf, he said. Do I have to tell you everything?

The telephone rang. Gauleiter Wagner wished to confirm that the waterworks of Baden should be destroyed.

Confirmed, he said. Trudl, child, could you kindly put the tea on?

The telephone rang. Speer had committed treason.

Send him down to me this evening, he said.

When Speer came, the sleepwalker glared at him and said: Bormann has given me a report on your conference with the Reich Gauleiters. You pressed them not to carry out my orders, and even declared that the war is lost. Are you aware of what must follow from that?

Speer, peering up at the concrete ceiling as though he'd spied a crack, insisted that the war *was* lost.

If you could at least hope! the sleepwalker pleaded, for Speer was his architect. That would be enough to satisfy me . . .

Speer remained silent.

You have twenty-hour hours to think it over! the sleepwalker shouted. Get out now; you're ill; you're dismissed from my office!

The telephone rang. Some officer or other wanted to know what to do with the women and children in his sector once their houses had been demolished.

Tell him that the nature of this struggle permits no consideration for the populace to be taken.

The telephone rang. His National Redoubt in the Alps was almost ready. Saying nothing, he hung up.

The telephone rang. Göring wanted to assure him that the Philharmonic would go under with everything else. Meanwhile he heard an explosion far away and aboveground.

He snatched up the telephone at once, demanding to know how the Russians were able to shell Berlin. The telephone explained that they had laid down a heavy and precise curtain of fire on the airfield in Prague, so that our Luftwaffe was helpless.

Then the Luftwaffe is superfluous, said the sleepwalker. The entire Luftwaffe command should be hanged at once!

He slammed down the telephone in a rage.

The telephone rang.—*Mein Führer,* we've lost communication with Wenk. The Russians are—

Oh, I have no doubt that I'm their target, he said.

The telephone rang. Although Wenk still could not be reached, Ninth Army had been encircled, and Heinrici's troops had also fallen out of touch, General Koller was ready nonetheless to start the counteroffensive which would save Berlin. The sleepwalker threatened him: Any commander who holds back his troops will forfeit his life in five hours!

The telephone rang. When would he be coming to the National Redoubt?

Out of the question, he explained. They might catch me through some trick. I have no desire to be exhibited in a Jewish museum.

The telephone rang. His chauffeur, Kempka, had delivered two hundred liters of petrol to the garden upstairs as ordered. The Russians were in the Tiergarten.

The telephone rang. British bombers had destroyed the National Redoubt.

You see? he remarked to his secretaries. I always know what's right.

His bride, Eva, who was as rich and good as Holstein butter, had now swallowed a capsule on his instructions. She lay beside him on the sofa, with her big cowlike eyes filming over. He raised the Walther to his head, then hesitated, lowered it a trifle, and peered into the barrel, to see what he might see within the mountain. First it was dark, then dark, and then far inside shone a pale blue light which must have come all the way from Russia; he thought he could spy the Grand Salle de Fêtes of the Empress Elizabeth Petrovna at Tsarkoie-Sélo, the carpet as vast and multiply monogrammed as a collective farm's sugarbeet field, cartouches of angels dimly hovering on the ceiling, then a casement window opened onto vistas of other castles. Soon he'd take possession of all that.

Just then the telephone rang again, and he knew from the cadence of the ring that it would be bad news.

No regrets now! he said with a smile. ▸

DENAZIFICATION

◩

There aren't bad peoples.
But without mercy
I'll tell you, . . .
each people
has its own reptiles.
—Yevgeni Yevtushenko (1962)

1

A long line of wooden-faced men in steel helmets lowered their swastika standards to the cobblestones. They were the last coins in that hoard of soldiers now vanished like gold thrown into a river. That was where it ended, there in the Tiergarten.

A Werewolf pushed a button, and row upon row of antitank guns hidden in the grass exploded. They'd run out of shells. Then came a shot. The Werewolf had saved the last bullet for himself. He was no longer a factor.

Then they marched out of Berlin in a column, saying farewell to the ruined buildings which so few would see again; you see, they were going east. Soon they'd learn about the whitish secretions of tubercular lungs; they'd grow expert in observing the sharpening of a dying prisoner's face. (They'd observed the deaths of Slavs, but that was different.)

Europe Central, burned clean, could now become as wide and white as Stalin-Allee in the new Berlin of our Soviet zone, whose tiny citizens recede between trees and massive apartment-cubes toward the future's distant tower. With the arrival of the Red Army, Unter den Linden with its cubical buildings and sentinel-like roof-figures had instantaneously become almost perfect, but we wouldn't stop there: Each new skyscraper would be taller and better than any artifacts of the capitalist world. And this really happened, or at least nearly happened, which is the most any offensive can hope for: I remember the new towers and bays of Moscow University, whose yellowish tinge (thanks to the ageing of the blueprints as I study them in 2001) gilded them with a monumentally Roman look. I remember Comrade Stalin pacing the shining wet catwalks of the Kremlin, safeguarding everything in our great Soviet land. (I wasn't there, but Roman Karmen filmed it. I've seen all of his movies.) Sometimes Comrade Voroshilov joined him, bearing huge stars on his red epaulettes. They gazed down at the clean cool factories and apartment-blocks of Moscow, remaining alert, collected and resolute. Now toward them came the line of Fascist prisoners.

2

We journeyed for thousands of kilometers, sometimes in windowless train cars, the rest of the time on foot. Most of us remembered how it had been the first time, with Ivans and Natashas straggling ahead of our Panzers, carrying their belongings on their backs. The sleepwalker had said: Don't forget who the masters are! and Field-Marshal von Manstein had walked beside us smiling and alert, his hands in his pockets. But all victories fell into the Rhine, even though our Pioneers blew up every building that still stood. We slipped west, then east again! Von Manstein was now squinting and craning at his trial . . .

Back in Germany where fog bleeds silver slime upon the willows, chestnut trees and maples, which is to say too far back to be imagined, our sisters were prostituting themselves for chocolate or chewing gum. The sleepwalker was gone—into the mountain, it was said—so we'd been decapitated, like the statue of Mars in the Zeughaus (a direct hit from a Russian gun took care of him). We limped east, and sometimes they clubbed us in the face or let loose a machine-gun burst into our ranks.

Well, they're the victors, so they must be the master race.—This was how we tried to explain it to ourselves. We were wide-eyed corpses, trying to learn the first few lessons of the afterlife. First kilometer by kilometer, then verst by verst we weakened, receding into time, becoming denazified.—I was never a Nazi, we all said.

High on a hill of pines, the broken castle looked blindly down upon a landscape of red roofs and green fields. And here the Russians shot another straggler, who fell still dreaming of a Reichskreuz a thousand years old, of a

Reichskreuz bulging with pearls and jewels. By then we knew how to keep our mouths shut.

The wind began to bite our faces. Mockingly, our captors quoted to us these lines of Akhmatova's: *I smile no more. A freezing wind numbs my lips.*

3

They carried us east in boxcars; we rode railroad tracks as narrow in gauge as the strange note-strung segments which begin in measure ninety-six of Shostakovich's Eighth Symphony; they're for the instruments *Piatti* and *Cassa*. Most of us were bound for the mines, they said. The miners in our German fairytales were rich enough to have golden nails in their boot soles. Well, who knows? Maybe it would be like that. By train and by truck, we rode further east. Then we had to walk for twenty hours straight, without even a drink of dirty water. When they let us rest, which was sometimes just for the night, sometimes for weeks, we looked down at our clasped hands and wondered aloud whether we might have been saved by only one more Teller mine in the Hürtgen Forest.

Next was that parade in Moscow, that ordeal-by-disgrace before they subdivided us into long worms of prisoner columns to burrow into this or that hole in the Russian dirt and work to death; we marched down Red Square and people spat on us; but I'd discovered my trick; I pretended that I was still one of the heroes of the Condor Legion, marching past Franco's swastika-hung reviewing stand in Madrid, with our right arms extended: *Sieg Heil!*

In the courtroom, our guards were replaced every two hours. The telephone screamed like an eagle. Then they sentenced us in batches. But once in the transit prison a Russian woman brought us a pail of hot milk.

After that came the camp, of course, which at first was nothing more than a ring of barbed wire enclosing barren ground; some of us, still bound, gazed exhaustedly down at the dirt; others gaped up at the sky; and still they packed more and more of us in until we were so crowded that we couldn't do anything more than stand; we'd been turned into one of Käthe Kollwitz's etchings of the Kaiser's prisoners! One of us whispered: My wife was a national swimming champion . . . —As for me, I never mentioned my family, who for all I know are still living in their underground cave in Köln.

A shot of adrenaline into the chest can sometimes resurrect a stopped heart. Unfortunately, the camp doctor had no adrenaline. Each corpse turned olive-green like an American troop carrier.

Those of us whose eagles hadn't yet been stripped from our breast-pockets were already laying plans for Operation Volund. One very cold night, one of us began to sing in a stunning tenor: *Wälse! Wälse! Where's your sword, the strong sword I'll swing against fate? Will it break out from my breast, where my angry heart hides it?*

4

And so we denazified them, making possible the following triumphant entry in our *Great Soviet Encyclopedia:*

> **Germany**—A state in Europe (capital, Berlin) which existed up to the end of World War II (1933–45).

Germany was gone forever. The two lapdog states which remained could be tricked into fighting each other eternally, just as we and Germany used to do. As for the old Germany, she reminded us of the bygone days when Moscow was nothing but churches, river-curves and droshkys . . .

Then we returned to our own concerns. We constructed an arc vacuum furnace to smelt titanium ingots. ▸

AIRLIFT IDYLLS

■

For three whole days, during which time did not exist for him, he struggled in that black sack into which he was being forced by an unseen, invincible power.

—Tolstoy (1886)

1

It's nearly impossible to convince my grandchildren that at the beginning the Iron Curtain was just that—although now that I think of it, the material might not have been iron at all. If you've ever inspected one of those pouches of lead foil which protects film from X-rays at airport security checkpoints, you can well imagine the abnormal heaviness, not to mention limp pendulousness (as opposed to flexibility) of that Iron Curtain: grasp a fresh corpse by the knee and raise it; the calf will swing inwards, compelling the foot to describe the same unfailing arc as a grandfather clock's weighted pendulum; but it's a one-way affair; heel strikes buttock or thigh, and that's the end. When we stood our turn in the exit queue of the border station, I sometimes used to bend down and raise the hem of the Iron Curtain, just to peek out at the capitalist side where I was going; nobody was very strict in those days, and obviously I wasn't trying to "escape." Anyhow, the "iron" or whatever it was must have been fifteen centimeters thick; I could only lift it up to ankle height before its weight and the white light blazing in overwhelmed me, so I'd let go, and it would sink silently back into place, momentum so perfectly dampened by deadness that there could never have been the tiniest afterswing. According to an American lecturer, the Eighth String Quartet of Shostakovich (Opus 110) is supposed to represent the Curtain's darkness, but (speaking only for myself), I'd have to say that my sensation on the Communist side was something quite different from melancholy; everything *was* dark, that's true, but it was the darkness of a circus tent, where anything could happen. I'll tell you just how it felt. Drawing the heavy passport from my pocket, already anticipating the treat of winning a new stamp (at that time the visa pictography of Europe Central changed almost monthly, in part as a result of the political situation—any symbol might get infected with enemy connotations—but mainly for security reasons: black marketeers duplicated those stamps easily, so the only recourse of nascent people's power was to change the red star to a blue sickle, or enclose it in a square rectangle), first I'd hear breathing all around me; next, a hand would take my passport; after a long while I'd hear the angry thud of the stamp, and that pallid, hairy hand returned to view, spewing the document back into my possession. I stepped forward. In a sudden dazzle of flashbulbs, secret policemen would photograph me from the side, after which I'd pass beween two soldiers whose fixed bayonets tickled my ears; finally I'd round the last bend where two flaps of the Curtain (try to visualize a woman's slit skirt) had been pulled apart and secured by ceiling-chains to admit a very narrow triangle of breathtakingly beautiful light through which each of us had to struggle, usually not without griming our shoulders with graphite, lead or whatever was actually the substance of the Iron Curtain; now I was free; but what I'll never be able to explain is that at that exact instant my head invariably became heavy; I tasted metal and my lips swelled; a drunken nausea robbed me of my balance; and when I stood up again I thought I'd faint. It happened to all of us. Perhaps some mind-altering chemical had been released by one side against or in collusion with the other. We lurched to the West German checkpoint (Bornholmer Strasse), and the sun scorched our pale skins. If somebody had poured sand inside my head I couldn't have felt any stranger. We'd forgotten everything! It was the taste of sleep that we were all licking off our lips. Here again stood the policeman with the long handlebar moustache; he greeted me by name now, and stamped my passport with extra crispness, because he liked me; the eagle of capitalist Germany was his alter ego. I'd never lost sight of him; the sunlight was harshly perfect on his metal buttons; but what had those two sentries on the other side looked like? Maybe their bayonets had annoyed me sufficiently to distract me from their faces. Behind them there'd been the border guard who'd stamped my passport, this time with the representation of a sledgehammer standing on end and bearing three sharp-pointed stars within its head; the East German official, counterpart to this moustached gentleman of Bornholmer Strasse, had scrutinized me most searchingly from his booth; it was incorrect that I'd glimpsed his hand; I now recollected an angled spotlight just below that window-slit through which documents were given and received; this glaring luminescence, which I'd somehow mistakenly associated with the flashbulbs of secret police, had struck me full in the chin, in order for the border guard behind his wall of dark glass to better compare me to my photograph; actually the glass couldn't have been dark, because I remembered a pale, blurry sort of face, perhaps with more than two eyes; there might have also been an eye in the brim of his cap, because . . . But prior to him there was nothing. I might as well have never visited the world behind the Iron Curtain!

In the onion fields of Europe, translucent-lipped wombs grow concentrically within wombs; and within *them* grows what? I could definitely remember lifting up the Iron Curtain from within, just to see the brightness; I longed to ask the policeman with the handlebar moustache whether he'd allow me to do the same from this side, but then his expression would have altered; he'd realize that his friendly trust should never have touched me; it would be awkward between the two of us forever, because West Germans, who are the only Germans left, follow the rules. What should I do? For I so much wanted to see! Berlin, which in medieval times had resembled a heart carved out of a human carcass, subdivided into seventeen lobes—Wedding, Moabit, Königsviertel and all the rest (no matter that they were each as cramped as a Messerschmitt-109)—Berlin was now a quartered heart, its chambers sealed off from one another by walls of sandbags; and now this Iron Curtain was already in the dreams of Stalinists getting elaborated into the raked sand of slaughter chutes within the complex of the Berlin Wall. (I brought that about; you'll see.) German blood must clot henceforth; it could no longer flow free. In the French sector they sing a little song about something that happens, some pretty little thing, I forget what, my French was never all that perfect anyway, when a blonde dancer from Stalingrad shows leg in the Soviet sector; I think maybe there comes a flash of sunlight in the Communist darkness or something like that. The real issue is: How can the conscious mind know what the unconscious is up to? Chancellor Adenauer in one of his speeches proclaimed that in this scientific (meaning nuclear) age, the metaphor of a heart has become outmoded; it's better to consider Berlin as a brain; and in his, Adenauer's view, what's behind the Iron Curtain is the reptilian brain, the primordial, amoral system of involuntary control which, located at the very base of the skull, can and must be dispatched by

NATO in a surgical, missile-based *Nackenschuss*; only thus may Germany, which is Europe and therefore all of us,* become whole again. (This is also what the Führer used to say.)

2

Unconsciousness can never examine consciousness; but the reverse is possible, for consciousness is *reliable,* like a Ju-52 transport plane. On a sunset as purple as the identity card of an NKVD agent, I passed behind the Iron Curtain once more, and this time I meant to maintain a death-grip upon my impressions. Oh, the mysterious East! I was there for a good long while, I couldn't tell you how long exactly, but I do remember snow and darkness; I think I experienced a symphony which stunned and chained me with chords of steel, although it's possible that I heard not the orchestral elaboration but the core of it, in which case it would have been performed by a bespectacled genius who played by memory for me on a grand piano which was for sale, payment to be made in bread; I remember kissing somebody named Elena, but I'm not certain anymore whether she was named Elena Konstantinovskaya, Elena Kruglikova, or possibly Elena Rosetti-Solescu, with whom I seem to associate the nickname Coca. I'm fairly sure that the pavements were shimmering and shining with ice; I believe that I might have seen children peeping at me from within their fur-ruffed hoods; but I have a West German friend (codenamed HIRSCH) who subscribes to *National Geographic,* and he once showed me a pictorial about Canada, where there are people called Eskimos, in whose existence I disbelieve because they live in conditions which the phenomenon of our Iron Curtain can't explicate: daylight for six months, darkness otherwise; but should there in fact be Eskimos, then the fur-hooded children in HIRSCH's article may be germane; although it's equally plausible that the children I met were Kazakhs; I could have easily gone that far east; I was in a land as deep and broad as the devil's antitank trench; I heard the ticking of a metronome.

Well, was she Elena Konstantinovskaya or Elena Kruglikova? And what was she to me? I've retained an ice-clear memory of the tight black fur caps

---

*Here once again let's quote Count Hermann Keyserling's *Das Spektrum Europas,* which never goes out of date: *Germany is the conscience of mankind . . . the mirror of the world.*

which seem to match Kazakh women's hair, so I must have been in Kazakhstan. I can also recollect blonde Russian girls whose blonde fur shoulders—yes, they must have been wearing fox or maybe white sable, so was I at the opera?—resembled sunlight on the snow. But the rest was dark; that I'd swear to.—What category of darkness, did you ask? Dirt-black like a soldier's hands, iron-black like the Curtain itself—with a taste of blue and grey, as is customary in metals.

That's the sum of all intelligence I managed to gather, which really wasn't bad for a first trip. So I decided to cross back into West Berlin. I yearned to see how successfully I prevent these recollections from effervescing away; and I might have had any number of additional objectives, too, but I can't remember them. When I got up to the Iron Curtain itself, where darkness is particularly dark, the border guard kept his light upon me for a such a long time that I began to wonder whether he had always done this; and then he said: Why are your eyes so shifty today?

Shocked and frightened, trying to formulate an answer, I fidgeted, and then I could actually see him lean forward behind the dark glass, much as if I were looking into the dark water of the Kryukov Canal and then glimpsed the darker darkness of some fish or monster swimming up toward me; yes, he leaned forward and he crooned: *What are you, actually?*

3

I feared that official; so next time I determined to dig my illegal way; in this rubbled earth we all dig like gravediggers, mindful that some fleeing ϟϟ-man might have stopped here to bury a golden coronation sword, or maybe even a suitcase filled with gold and silver spoons from a castle in Krakow; we all hide things when we see death coming, and it may well be that by thus interring our treasures, we prepare our minds for our own entombment. Pharaoh must have been comforted to know that his scepter and his women would sleep forever with him. All the while, to be sure, one longs to believe that it's possible to awake from that sleep, crawl back under the Curtain and reclaim one's property, which remains (another hope!) safely cached away from the expropriations of Commissar Death—aren't human beings absurd?

Lifting up a corner of the Iron Curtain in the vicinity of what would soon be called Checkpoint Charlie, I discovered darkness within, but I was prepared; I had with me the latest "Eagle" electric torch! Now I could see domes, bells, eagles and round windows. My eyes were already getting heavy, but I was ready for that, too; I started pinching myself. This must be Yugoslavia. The edifices of the Austro-Hungarian Empire, shellholed although they might be, spread themselves out before me like the pages of a book, with windows in place of words. What should I have read there? This place (so I've been told—by Yugoslavs, coincidentally) is the soul of Europe, or at least the Slavic soul. But why accept a map drawn by others? As lightly as a soap bubble I sleepwalked farther east. What did I see? Better yet, what *didn't* I see? My tale is cluttered with visual bric-a-brac, none of which matters; it's all rubble, so to speak; and if I lead you down an alley where red stars and red spiders dance on strings, that's mere *reality,* which, being itself instead of ourselves, remains inherently alien, like the pretty flames which ought to be ornaments but betray the child by burning its hand. Actually, nothing's nearly as *real* as a certain old West Berliner lady in black who gazes lovingly at me from deep-set eyes, crouching beside her empty basket; nowadays I see her every morning just before I slip beneath the Wall. She's an operative of the Gehlen Organization, and she's codenamed NEY. She neither alters nor sleeps. And now here I was in Byelorussia; well, well. That must have been why I started to dream of something pale—snow, maybe; well, whatever it was, it was almost as white as the service colors of the Organization Todt Frontline Command . . . so I pinched myself again. And now my flashlight beam picked out a Slavic hero on a rearing charger; the pediment was bas-reliefed with other Slavs; then came the war wreaths, graves and fires, nationalism being kept decently within Communist bounds. I admit that I was definitely getting sleepy by then. The faces of the inhabitants seemed to drift about me like seaweed. I had somehow entered a crowd of them: Slavs or dream-figures; their bony white faces, made terrifying by black mouths and broken black eye-sockets, kept gazing out at me from long black cloaks and dresses which were interrupted only by the white triangles of wrists emerging from dark sleeves and entering black pockets. I thought I heard the name Elena Kruglikova; perhaps it was Konstantinovskaya. Pinching myself as hard as I could, I discovered that a beautiful woman was kissing me. Probably I was on the Tverskaia then, in one of those icy doorways where they sell wooden toys.

4

Everything which has existed will always exist. This is the chief consolation, however spurious, of both religion and mathematics. Somewhere farther back in Russia, Nicholas II's *salon de réception* survived with its gilt-edged screens and chairs, a carpet of dizzying ornamentality, mainly white, like a jigsaw puzzle of ice-floes; and on the wall, a depiction of an immense military column—are they on horseback?—this room's so dim! . . . Someone is saluting; it seems to be sunset—probably this now obsolete receiving area had been transferred, as would have been an entirely correct decision, to an iceberg. And this woman kissing me, whoever she was, I had to believe that even if I lost her she would always be with me. But that won't be true of Shostakovich, because, you know . . . Elena was kissing me, *kissing me*! Now where had she gone? My flashlight battery was dead; I started digging blindly westward. The war between Germany and Russia had been a conflict between lava and ice; ice had won, but everything that the ice had chilled to death, and everything that the lava had seared away, were safe somewhere, meaning Russia, since Adenauer has proved that Russia is the collective unconscious. According to the *Great Soviet Encyclopedia*, volume fifteen, *love for an idea*, which is to say for the no longer consciously "existent," *can take the form of an intellectual ecstasy that may be possible only at certain cultural levels*, each of which must be guarded and demarcated, first by the People's Police, then by the Soviet Military Authority, then finally by home units of the Red Army. This is why the Iron Curtain was in everybody's interest.

But even then, when we couldn't possibly know that it would someday get pulled down and interred in a lead mine in Ekaterinberg, that Europe Central's Bolshevized courtyards of rubble, skulls and boarded-up palaces would either be taken over by crypto-Fascist separatists (among whom I regretfully include the West German NIKA, who compromised Trotskyite organizations from 1951 until he was neutralized in 1974), or else fall into the clutches of the Hotel Astoria, where happy American tourists carried lacework, wooden dolls, absinthe and prewar folios up to their rooms, I could sense that the Iron Curtain would not be eternal. And I freely admit that this saddened me. A pyramid of flame (to pick a familiar wartime example) possesses a specific shape at any given instant, and a general shape over time; we call it a pyramid only for convenience; it's writhing upward, getting nowhere in particular, doomed to subsidence. But an Iron Curtain, if it only lasted, would give us something to navigate us from good to evil and back again, even if we disagreed as to which was which! Well, it's vanished now, it really has, like the prewar icon shops of Saint Petersburg, and I'm now going to tell you exactly how it happened.

5

But first it's necessary to mention that when I came tunneling back into my own zone, yawning and rubbing my eyes, it was blinding daylight, and so they saw me and the sirens went off.

They took me by taxi, not by Green Minna, thank God, to the Gehlen Organization to be interrogated; and in a room without windows, a pale, pale man who wore dark glasses said to me: You've absorbed the Russian mentality.

How can you tell?

There's something of the Russian soul in you, that emotional, sentimental, immeasurable something . . .

He opened a black folder which bore the red-and-white label GEHEIM, and he showed me that my name had been deleted from the list of persons to be trusted. I need not claim that he terrified me even ten percent as much as the the East German border official had done; all the same, whenever authority's representatives define my soul, I can't help but wonder if that clicking sound I hear in the basement is the firing squad cocking triggers; so I asked him, wanting to gain as much information as possible: What do I need to do to be trusted again?

Kill someone.

And then?

We'll forget that you concerned us. We might even pay you.

The desk drawer sprang open, and shoving aside two long heavy pistols and a pair of spurs like silver sun-wheels (they must have belonged to the prewar Polish cavalry), he fished out a brand-new Walther and a box of ammunition: Geco, 7.65 millimeter.

They're special, he said with a strangely shy smile, and I knew then that he had cast the bullets himself. (Those sunken eyes in that pale, puffy face, that even voice; whom did he remind me of?)

I opened the box. The casings were brass, but each projectile was solid silver.

You see, he explained, they're vampires over there. You can only kill a Slav with one of these.

Knowing now that I would betray him for the sake of the beautiful woman who'd kissed me, I said: That's all very well, but how can I stay awake?

Do you swear to uphold the "watertight bulkhead" system of the Gehlen Organization?

Naturally. I mean, I . . .

Yes or no?

I do.

Swallow this pill. You'll never sleep again.

You mean I won't be able to dream?

Dreams are for cowards. Swallow it, and be quick about it, or else I'll have to press this button.

Do you have any liquid to wash it down with?

Liquid's for cowards.

I see, I said, pretending to swallow the capsule. Actually it lay beneath my tongue. Now I really needed to get out of there, because it was starting to dissolve. With every moment, I would sleep a little worse.

Excuse me, I said, but now I need to piss.

Take this pill. You'll never—

But I sometimes enjoy pissing—

You do? I'll note that in your file. All right. Go down the hall, but don't forget that we're watching you. Can you guess what I miss most?

No, I said, fidgeting urgently.

The beech forests of Lower Saxony. They're locked away in Dreamland now. Did you by any chance see them?

No.

Answer just for me. This isn't official at all. You know, there's a certain long line of trees beneath long lines of mist, with the sky between them cut off, strangled you might say, and my father's house stands straight ahead; it has an exceptionally steep roof and it's made of stone. Have you been there?

I go farther east.

Farther east! You really are a natural! he said proudly. You've been codenamed HINDEMITH. Don't worry. We're going to make a man out of you.

Rushing out of his office, I found the lavatory, bolted myself inside a stall, removed the pill, wrapped it up in toilet paper and hid it inside the porcelain tank. Fortunately, it floated. I was already feeling more wide awake than I'd been in years.

Good, he said when I'd returned. This is the one you're going to kill.

He showed me a photograph of a pallid, balding man with thick glasses: the Soviet composer Shostakovich.

He said to me: He's the one behind all this.

Then he said: The birds in the Tiergarten, the green summer light in the Tiergarten, we're going to get all that back.

6

Why yes, said Shostakovich with an inconstant attempt at a witty smile, even in Leningrad, even this far, so to speak, *north,* we did hear something about a, an interruption I guess one ought to call it; I don't know for certain whether it was a *war* exactly . . .

Of course, I said.

They made my little Galisha play the Butterfly Game at school, and that Sunday there was supposed to be a Dynamos match when . . . You think I eat moon mushrooms for breakfast, no?

I unbuckled my Walther and fired a silver bullet into his face. Screeching, he shriveled into a pile of charred music-paper. Then I woke up. I was still in West Germany, with two hours left before they inserted me into my mission zone.

It was a hot afternoon of stinking ruins. Three boys were taking turns swinging from the barrel of a broken antiaircraft gun. The Iron Curtain sullied the horizon with its leaden fog. I walked slowly through the flatness of bomber-cleared lots, wondering what on earth I really ought to be or do.

When you separate from a woman, what you have to do is kill your love for her; you have to blockade it and starve it to death, just as the sleepwalker set out to do in Leningrad; that's the only way. To separate Shostakovich from this world, one must be similarly energetic. Basically, it's a question of time and manpower.

The Gehlen Organization had just finished laying a secret telephone cable in one of the canals which separated East from West Berlin. Fishing the receiver from the water at 2315 hours, I spoke the code word and received the go-ahead. (There was also something about proceeding from Anhalter Bahnhof to Hahenklee, but I've woken up since then; I don't remember that part. I think it happened earlier.) Remembering how it had been once upon a time, when the enemy crept out from between Russian trees to murder us, I felt exactly the way I used to: depressed, yet resolute. So I crossed their canal hand over hand, the cable thrilling me with faint electrical tingles all the way. On the far side, they'd dug in a pole to prop up one pleat in the Iron Curtain for me, to the tune of maybe thirty centimeters. I wriggled under that leaden darkness, kicked down the pole behind me, and was back in Dreamland.

Fleets of narrow windows, perfectly stationed upon each wall's stony sea, deployed their shallow balconies all around the world like guns. Evidently I had breached the Curtain in Prague. A little operative came up to me and made conversation, whispering: You and I both work in the East, so we know what's what. . . . —I nodded, meanwhile shaking the last drops of canal water out of the barrel of my Walther.

The command post is in that cellar, said the little operative, who was codenamed GREINER. Unfortunately, there's nobody left. The Red Guillotine got them all last night . . .

Don't worry, I said, wanting to console him. Everything's just a dream anyhow. Even if the Red Guillotine catches you, you'll wake up before you die. You can't die in a dream.

Unless you really die, he whispered bitterly.

Well, that's just a contingency, I said. I was already getting sleepy, but only slightly—exactly enough to numb that scared feeling. As we humans say, this can't really be happening! Self-deception is a pessimistic definition of optimism. I was confident that tonight I could do the job and get stricken from the list of persons who "concerned" the Gehlen Organization. That was my new goal in life. So I shook GREINER's tiny hand and wished him a long-lasting camouflage. He yawned and crawled into the cellar to sleep, which appeared incautious to me, but in my organization we refrain from advising each other how to live.

My target shouldn't be difficult to locate, they'd told me, because he quote *lives in a fairytale ballet without human context* end quote, so I floated in the direction which seemed most inhuman, proceeding rapidly eastward beneath what a nineteeth-century traveler has described as *a pearl-grey, faintly blue sky which lent a luminous quality to everything except the pale green roofs,* yes, I knew that, everything transparently grey, with lime trees painted on the stage backdrop.

Shostakovich was eating dinner with a younger woman, a certain Galina Ustvolskaya, about whom I'd been given no information; they appeared to be consuming some sort of fat blind white cave-fish which resembled turbot. He looked unhealthy, and she seemed angry about something. Frankly, I didn't like her. Groaning, my host locked the door behind me and hobbled back to the table. When I asked him how he was, he smilingly quoted the poetess Akhmatova: *Call this working! This is the life! To overhear some music, and pretend that it's my own . . .*

Ustvolskaya began screaming when I drew my gun. I shot him in the head five times, after which he said to me: There's a musical term—it's, it's, well, it's Italian actually, which you might not . . . *ma non tanto,* which I think means *but not so much.*

7

Then I woke up in a double bed with starched sheets; on the pillow beside me slept a single long dark hair. That made me very happy, although I wished that I could remember who my co-dreamer had been; on the other hand, if I really chose to know, I could have made inquiries through the Gehlen Organization. Throwing a white bathrobe around my shoulders, I opened the French doors and stepped out upon the terrace, enjoying the sunshine on my bare feet, and the lovely terrace-view of the squat white dome of our Great Hall of the People—how fine it felt to be home again! I let my gaze be carried down the wide white boulevard which passes through the Arch of Triumph (which of course overtowers the French original), then widens, widens again into a perfect white channel in the white maze of Berlin; it becomes a narrow strait between watchtowers, then widens into a horseshoe-shaped courtyard gripped by the rectangular wings of the vast white ministry where our sleepwalker watches over us. Just then my case officers knocked. I rushed back to bed, and hid the long dark hair beneath my pillow just in time. There were three of them—GRAENER, who bore no resemblance to GREINER; HAVEMANN and PFITZNER—and they trooped in almost shyly, because I was their hero, you see; they gathered around my bed, smiling forgivingly. The anti-sleeping pill was working even better than expected, they assured me. I shouldn't feel discouraged. With a wink, GRAENER patted my pillow and added: The German people need romanticism once more. Then PFITZNER raised the syringe: Here we go again! Close your eyes! They re-injected me into the Soviet Zone.

8

This time I was getting better at, at, so to speak—my God! Now I was thought-stuttering like *him*—

I swam through Europe Central, which is an aquarium scattered with the stone shells of ancient Polish institutes. I went to Moscow, which might well have been Leningrad, found Shostakovich, and shot him as dead as I could. That is what I did, more or less. He was alone that time; he must have fallen out with G. I. Ustvolskaya. This time I finished it. I transformed him into a new man. When I'd completed my world-historical mission, he was smashed like the stone lion of Potsdam, and his brains were scattered over three rooms. Since there was one bullet left, I also made sure that his heart had stopped. I repeat: It was only a question of time and manpower. Then I slipped the Walther back into the pocket of my trenchcoat. I was on my way out when he said to me: My heart is actually, so to speak, inside that piano. I wouldn't have minded if you'd actually, er, written me out of the score, but unfortunately you'll have to . . .

How could I bear to look at him? And the timbre of his voice, my God, my God! What was he going to say about me behind my back? I went out into the snowy street, trying not to fall asleep amidst the translucent rushing crowds. Evidently there was more, how should I say, *complexity* to this situation than I'd been informed. Well, that's not uncommon in intelligence work. Was I in over my head? I'd better return straightaway to the office and request a deeper briefing.

L. Moholy-Nagy once wrote: *Penetration of the body with light is one of the greatest visual experiences.* And so I came back into my Germany, the real Germany, where the sunlight was as white as Heydrich's hands.

9

Who moves the mover? inquired the pale man in dark glasses. He seemed far unhappier than I. He longed for the old days when soldiers, not dreams, marched through the Brandenburg Gate. He reminded me of his chief grievance: *They all dance to Shostakovich's tune.*

I felt so ashamed of my failures that I simply bowed my head. HAVEMANN waggled a finger a me.

Somehow the brightness felt less bright. It was doomed since it was already articulated. What if even the pale man were doomed? I'd begun to feel more suspicious of him, although I still declined to fear him, since I had so easily tricked him. Reminding myself that I had often voyaged eastward of my own volition, I shored myself up; wasn't I doing exactly what I wanted?

PFITZNER entered the room, bearing more silver bullets on a tray. GRAENER brought me a ring of invisibility. The pale man, frowning and rising, said to me: You'll be in our thoughts when you're on the other side.

Then I wondered: What *is* the other side?

10

That night I had to meet them on Stresemannstrasse. They injected me into the Russian sector right across from the ruined dome of the Haus Vaterland.

It took six motivated ex-Nazis to lift up the Iron Curtain for me. There was no distinction between them and me, except that they knew who they were. One of them slapped me between my shoulderblades and whispered: Thank God somebody is finally doing something.—Another one slipped an American cigarette between my lips. NEY whispered a report into her empty basket. Then off I went. I felt as lonely as a dispatch rider cycling off into the enemy's field of fire.

I floated around, trying to get my bearings.—We're going to get all that back, the pale man had insisted, but what exactly would we get back? Was he longing for the good old days of Kontroll-Girls in three grades and Bubis in long coats dancing with their Mädis in lesbian bars? The sleepy feeling retreated, leaving me as nauseous as if I'd overdosed ever so slightly on some narcotic.

Location: East Berlin. Russian soldiers were carrying messages in and out of what used to be our Air Ministry, with the Wall before them. I could hardly prevent myself from envying these individuals. They seemed so happy, with their smoke-blackened faces and their looted wristwatches! (Top secret: Their Party already planned to make office blocks out of the Cafe Kranzler.)

This time I had brought with me, disguised as a rolled-up umbrella, one of those old *Faustpatronen* we'd handed out to the old men in the Home Guard at the very end; this one-shot weapon was meant to kill a tank, and my plan was to blast it through both of Shostakovich's pianos, in hopes of finally stopping his heart. The pale man in dark glasses would have been disappointed to be informed, if he hadn't been already, that I'd given up on his silver bullets. As much as I cared to please him, I preferred to be returned to the list of people who could be trusted. The worst part was knowing that I couldn't trust myself.

As for the ring of invisibility, I'd already lost it. Well, in every mission something goes wrong. No doubt there's a scientific explanation for that.

Before I knew it, I was in a wintery sort of place whose frosted icicles reminded me of the snow-white walls and crystal bed of the Cave of Love in Gottfried's *Tristan*. Somebody was kissing me; I'm fairly sure that this time it was Elena Kruglikova. Now here came evenly spaced tanks (three abreast) clanking down Gorki Street. Quick! I dodged out of sight. Elena seemed disappointed, but only for an instant, since I wasn't real; she was already dreaming of someone else, probably a certain, well, you know. Where was *he?* I spied the triple smokestacks of the *Aurora* protruding from the harbor's ice; over there, the Univermag Department Store memorialized Stalingrad; now if only I could see the Bronze Horseman . . . Pretty women from the Home Guard marched past the long facade of the Winter Palace, with their rifles pointed at the sky; they hadn't yet begun to starve. Then I heard the inimitable sound of Shostakovich's fingernails clicking down on piano keys; he was about to play this reduction of the Seventh Symphony; Elena Kruglikova was already beginning to sing. There he was! I could see him perfectly through a frostless circle in the window. What an interesting composition it was, without atonal fallacies; the Rat Theme especially, which made me want to dance. (But I'm positive that had I not been eavesdropping, it wouldn't have appealed to me nearly as much.) I waited until he had finished. He rose from the piano bench, bowing awkwardly, with his fists clenched at his sides, and E. Kruglikova, who in real life might never have met him (I have no confirmed information on this), smiled lustrously; she was wearing a formal black dress and a necklace of frozen tears. Their friends applauded, thereby imitating static on a clandestine radio.

Excuse me, excuse me; it was nothing but a little *nothing,* apologized Shostakovich (who was codenamed ELENKA; I neglected to tell you that.)

Standing on my tiptoes, I fist-rocketed him as planned, following up with light machine-gun fire until everybody was dead, blackened and pockmarked like Saint Hedwig's Cathedral—you can count on it! He was *gone,* just like the Romanisches Café. His severed hands scuttled inside the piano, where they doubtless lived in some sort of nest or spider-hole; but I had *plans* for that piano! Two hand grenades later, I couldn't even have picked my teeth with it, it was so perfectly pulverized. I waited. Very cautiously, blood began to leach out of that pile of sawdust, so I must have gotten his heart at last. Then a sky-blue icicle peeped out, so I stamped on it.

I know I should accept it and simply, so to speak, be, well, *dead,* said Shostakovich, carefully inserting the bloody teeth back into his mouth, especially since not many people listen to music nowadays. It's all very . . . But I *can't.* There's something in me that won't let me accept, how should I say, fate.

I couldn't think of anything to say. I certainly couldn't imagine the report I would need to write. Instantly, I was suffering what we used to call *a crisis of nerve*—bring your own gas mask! And Shostakovich kept pattering on:

Maybe on account of *that bastard,* you know who, that Kremlin mountaineer who climbed up his heap of corpses; I could have been one of them, but somehow I was never able to surrender, musically I mean, since of course I did abase myself in every other way—not that I joined the Party, at least.

Come to think of it, if you want to kill me you're going to have to make me write false music—

Clearing my throat (why not try to be pleasant?), I ventured: What about your "Song of the Forests," Herr Schostakowitsch? Isn't that a bit of Stalinist ass-kissing?

Not at all, my dear friend! I said, not at all! You see, even there, there's parody—not that *that bastard* would ever notice—and it's swollen with self-loathing. But the one I loathe tonight is *you*. Just because you're a monster, do you have to be an idiot?

Herr Schostakowitsch, I'm as tired of this as you are.

Now he could put his spectacles back on, so that he could glare at me. He said: Once or even twice, that's, you know, because I kept saying to myself, he'll learn. But you haven't. This is almost not funny anymore.

11

With perseverance I'd get him. Back in Berlin-West, I took a sleeping tablet and dreamed of Valkyries. When I woke up, I went to the office, where they gave me American instant coffee. The pale man wasn't there, but somebody codenamed LEHMANN told me that they were all proud of me; even Adenauer had been informed. Would I like another coffee? I felt *valuable*. This would constitute the turning point. It had better, since my existence in both zones remained potentially punishable.

I could see a long line of shabby shoes marching eastward under the Iron Curtain, and in a counterattack of self-confidence I told myself: Let those poor dreamers queue up to be examined; as for me, I'll come and go as I please; I work for the Gehlen Organization!

If only I hadn't misplaced that ring of invisibility! (The problem was that I couldn't see it.) At least I had the latest crop of silver bullets; PFITZNER had assured me that they'd been blessed by a Croatian priest. If I failed this time, it would truly be my fault. How embarrassing, that Shostakovich considered me to be an idiot! Once upon a time, in some fairytale or other, I used to think well of myself, but I don't remember when or where. At least I had one thing going for me: I was a realist.

At 0210 hours I breached the Curtain through a cellar in the ruined Kaiserhof Hotel. They had cut a diaperlike flap of grey Ur-metal to hang down across the broken stairs, and it proved more challenging than I had imagined to worm myself underneath, for it was so heavy, cold and dead; at least it wasn't yet poisoned or electrified. Anyhow, up I came. No more dancing with Aryan girls at the Berolina Haus! Smashed tanks around the smashed Reichstag, black marketeers doing business in the moonlit grassy rubble all around (because the People's Police couldn't crack down on everything yet), this was not the Berlin that I could have imagined back in the days when our stone eagles flew. If only LEHMANN were here to repeat how proud of me they all were!

All the same, the instant I reached the East I'd begun to *feel* different, as if I'd escaped from false consciousness. They were marching, or gliding as I should say, beneath a banner which proclaimed their lives better and more joyful; I got caught up in their emotion: Life seemed that way to me. I dreamed about marrying the owner of that long, dark hair, whoever she was, just as soon as the pale man confirmed my presence on the safe citizens' list. Or arguably I'd go into currency speculation. But first I needed to be *vigilant*. Suspecting that once again Shostakovich might doublecross me, I resolved to keep calm no matter what; according to any enlightened calculus it didn't matter if he got to play dead once or twice more. Eventually he'd stay dead. After all, if he didn't, how would I ever get my name moved from the bad list to the good list?

At a café in a ruined courtyard I stopped for a beer. Didn't I have the right? I was an operative in good standing of the Gehlen Organization! On the radio, Klavdia Sulzhenko sang "The Blue Kerchief." The war had died; that song was getting old; then again, so was I. But the beer was good; it actually tasted like something more than dreamwater; night by night I was adopting a more realistic attitude to the East. For instance, the Iron Curtain was better for both sides; I'd realized that now. It used to be that the NKVD drove right into West Berlin to kidnap people they didn't like, and once they were back in the Russian sector there was nothing anybody could do. Now we were safer from them, and they were safer from us; that was why **LIFE HAS BECOME BETTER.** I was also thrilled by the degree to which this zone had retained its infinite character, endlessly bearing dark grey European field-rectangles outlined in white or sometimes silver; this unlimited aspect reminded me of the good old days when we'd dreamed of a summer to which no one else could put a final four-beat rest. When *did* Europe actually come to an end? In the Urals, so I'd been advised, there were places where the map had been crumpled into mountains, that was where the Frost Giants dwelled. But first things first: I'd now perform Opus 110: "The Execution of Dmitri Shostakovich." Poor man! It was nothing personal. Time to fly over ruins, ruins again, orienting myself (assuming that I actually cared to be oriented) by those parallel railroad tracks as multitudinous as the music-lines for a single measure of Wagner's *Ring*; long trains rode them eastward, bearing German prisoners and machine tools.

Someone tried to kiss me, but I'd have none of it; I wasn't about to let myself be caught in an East German honeypot trap. The waitress brought me another beer.

Now where was I? Was I drunk or merely sleepy? How long ago had Klavdia Sulzhenko finished singing? I wanted a warm voice to drink; Elena Kruglikova's would do, but better yet would be that sweetly husky cigarette smoker's voice of Shostakovich's bisexual Muse. Hiding in the oblivion behind a hill of rubble, I spied on a bright-lit doorway which was all that remained of a building; its broken brick edges ended as distinctly as a starfish's arms; they were dead white against the darkness; and within the doorway was also darkness; foregrounded against that darkness stood Elena Konstantinovskaya with her hair down and her brown eyes wide with sadness and love.

Knowing that in Dreamland one meets the anima wherever one goes, I left that incarnation of her to grieve in peace; doubtless she'd just separated from Shostakovich. Verification (achieved through Zeiss lenses): Tears nearly as large as grapefruits were rushing down her cheeks. I've heard from Comrade Alexandrov, who continues to closely follow this case and who's codenamed LYALKA, that the last thing she said to him, or rather called out or sobbed out as she went down the stairs, leaving our composer writhing on the bed like a loathsome worm of agony (she'd kissed his mouth, then his forehead, then one last time his mouth; he'd kept his lips closed) was that she was sorry and that she loved him. He called down that he loved her, too. If this intelligence is true, then what? I theorize as follows: She was *afraid* of being alone with him, isolated, locked into a dark bedroom beneath the piano keys. She screamed an obscenity at him; at least she didn't break dishes. He expected her to *change*, in order to accommodate his desire! (Am I thinking of Shostakovich here or of R. L. Karmen?) That was why she'd left him twice already; and that third time, when it was really him forcing the issue, he asked her to write out on music-paper what she wanted of him; he wrote out what he needed of her; he agreed to everything she wanted of him but now she refused to believe that he could live up to that, and she for her part couldn't do what he wanted, which was to give him ever more of herself; she feared being consumed; and so the last time he'd come to see her they quarreled and hadn't made love at all; then the time after that, which was the absolutely last time, when she'd come to take care of him after the first time I assassinated him, she'd slept with him, but only slept, and with her clothes on; she'd embraced him, but never closely enough to stop the draft which blew in between them, and when he'd begged her to hold him tight she'd angrily refused, and so they were compelled to part forever; it was she who pronounced the sentence, but only when he asked her; and she could have been willing to go on as they were—poor Elena!—she didn't want to lose him or hurt him; she was sobbing and sobbing as she went down the stairs forever, with big tears speeding down her face. I can't say I didn't long to comfort her.

But maybe it never happened like that; maybe she never left him. I was in Dreamland, so I might have been getting Elena mixed up with Lina, who left me before Operation Citadel; I forget why; sometimes we forget in order to, you know.

Well, now that she'd officially left him, I wouldn't be hurting her if I shot him. The theme I meant to instill—renunciation, letting Elena go, helping her find her ideal one, her *true* Shostakovich—could best be played out by liquidating the false one upstairs.

The American bombers had blown off the front wall of this stage set, so I took aim, but every bullet turned into a black music-note that screeched straight into his heart!

I should have known that he wouldn't mind it; he even liked it. After he had popped his eyeballs back in and cleaned his spectacles he even waved; thanks to me he'd now collected new despairing dissonances for Opus 110. What was I doing wrong? Next time I'd figure it out. It was simply a question of time and manpower. But I didn't dare look over my shoulder, in case Shostakovich might be imitating my mannerisms, even sticking out his tongue.

12

In Berlin-West I made my plans all day, although the brightness hurt my eyes; I almost wished for the old wartime blackouts. Or perhaps it was simply that I couldn't bear to stay awake. Could I bear to live this way anymore? Moment by moment I try not to be gruesome. Hospital wards crammed full of soldiers without legs or eyes, never mind! Shostakovich's music, fine. NATO's come to save us from all that. But until we've garrisoned our side of the Wall, I'll dwell in dreams.

First the Iron Curtain, then the Gendarmenmarkt, that was how it would go. Belgian Nazis who survived by selling their memories to both sides advised me to poison his piano; that would get to him; but the little operative codenamed GREINER, whom I was frankly beginning to consider defeatist, insisted that the Soviets had antidotes to everything, even unfortunate facts. I found myself dreading the night; I didn't know why, for I preferred the east side now; I craved the safe and comfortable feeling which always came over me when I saw Stalin's massive, star-topped portrait guarding the Hotel Adlon, which had been more or less burned down by drunken Red Army men in search of wine.

All the same, GREINER had taught me that the Gehlen Organization was in the right to pursue Operation ELENKA: Our target (you know whom I mean) was a pianist in exactly the same sense as were those members of the infamous Red Orchestra, who consorted with innocent German women, sold us black market goods at friendly prices, and carried out orders in our offices across occupied Europe; all the while, these fanatically loyal subordinates, whom we'd trusted in our noble German manner, were playing Hagen's part, stabbing Siegfried in the back with their myriad Judeo-Bolshevik spears. But halt! Our subject was pianists. Oh, yes, they rented flats in Paris, Brussels, even Berlin itself; and at hours and frequencies which their Center, which they undoubtedly called Europe Central, dictated, they hunched over their transmitters (which it sometimes took us great trouble to pinpoint) and played *our* enciphered tunes of troop dispositions for Operation Barbarossa, strategic objectives for Operation Blau, entrainments for Operation Citadel. Gestapo Müller used to be a friend of mine. He said: Think of them all as dark little Jews, bent over their transmitters at night, clicking away all our dearest secrets!—Actually, he was never my friend; I seem to have been dreaming someone else's dream. I couldn't even hum my own songs.

More and more I say to myself: Why bother? Haven't I already failed at everything? Isn't it better that I don't know to whom that strand of long dark hair belongs? Especially since I've long since lost it; I'd tied it to my ring of invisibility for luck . . .

Enough dreaming! In 1950 we'd bored a listening tunnel under the Curtain; that had been Operation Gold. Today was the dawn of Operation Quicksilver. In other words, Operation ELENKA will mutate into its own success. I recited to myself: *We must base our work on the assumption of victory.*

13

Next ploy: I rang up ELENKA on the black telephone.

Crumpling a piece of cellophane up against the receiver all the while, to imitate static, I shouted: Comrade Shostakovich, Europe Central calling! You've been summoned to the Teltowkanal at once.

But this is really, I mean, thank you, thank you!

I crumpled cellophane.

And could you tell me please exactly where the, how should I say it, this *Teltowkanal*—oh, oh, excuse me, someone is knocking now. What if it's, how should I say? Just a moment; just a moment!

And that tricky bastard hung up on me!

Well, never say die. Flashing my passport, I crossed legally behind the Curtain, this time at Friedrichstrasse, because I was now both a foreigner and a diplomat. I was a one-man column of marchers luxuriously flowing in a specific direction.

14

Skipping silently between the land mines, I came to a burned tank, ducked down, caught my breath, and peered carefully around to see East Germans working by torchlight, hauling away limestone from the shell of our Reich Chancellery on their special narrow-gauge railway. Well, why not? It was dead, and its half naked skeleton was flanked by hills of its own gravel and powder. If only they could trundle away my last few vanities and illusions! I wanted to fulfill myself by casting off everything dubious. I wished to become a perfect skeleton. No doubt if I only swallowed the correct pill I'd be able to reach a zone where the Chancellery still stood, and then if I strode down the Marble Gallery, which was as long as a runway for light aircraft, I'd get farther and farther from this brave new night of red-starred constellations. Unfortunately, they were breaking up the Marble Gallery right now. They were using it to make headstones for Soviet heroes. Talk about illusions!

They'd already torn down the American Embassy by the Brandenburg Gate. I had to laugh; it seemed so pointless! They'd reopened the Volksbühne Theater for proletarian shows. They'd renamed everything they could. We'd changed Bülowplatz to Horst-Wessel-Platz, so *they* changed it to Rosa-Luxemburg-Platz. I should have known! Wilhelmstrasse became Otto-Grotewohl-Strasse, and who the hell was Otto Grotewohl? Let's just say that he was no Kaiser. If you don't mind, I'll keep calling it Wilhelmstrasse. They deny the broken earthworks of their war memories by memorializing the future; I do the same by living in the past. Frankly, that's why we'll always need two Germanys.

(But everything's all dreams, all nothingness.) Dorotheenstrasse became Clara-Zetkin-Strasse; well, I can live with that; I'm not against women, even women Communists. If only one of them would kiss me again! But Reds have no time for kisses. Besides, who would kiss me? I'm a traitor to both sides, and I'm long in the tooth; my eyeballs are sinking into my face, so to hell with everything except for that one black hair which can't say no to me. They'd stolen the pearl-studded golden ball with a golden crucifix attached to it by bands of gold; they'd crowned Stalin with our crown of precious stones; they'd given him our crosshatched dagger, our golden scepter. They could shove it up Stalin's ass—oh, I was in a fine mood these days! PFITZNER had informed me that my colleagues were getting disappointed. Well, how was I supposed to neutralize an unkillable target? For that matter, what had PFITZNER done to further our goal? He could at least have obtained the cooperation of a small neutral country. I detested PFITZNER. And these land mines on the Wilhelmstrasse where our Foreign Office used to be, those ruins in the night, their spires and lacunae sweeping up and down like the spans of fancy bridges, all that was enough to irritate anyone.

Over there stood the Schauspielhaus, almost untouched. Why hadn't they demolished it yet? I once saw Marlene Dietrich there in 1927. Now they used it for giving uplifting speeches about work quotas. Never mind. I was used to falling asleep; their speeches wouldn't trouble me. Besides, the pale man at the Gehlen Organization had promised me that we'd get everything back.

I went and hid behind one of those impressive pillars, which were scarcely even scorched, and took my bearings.—No, I'd underestimated those Slavs! The voice of Elena Kruglikova rose into the sky.

15

That was when I realized the following: *I am Shostakovich's shadow.*

But what do we each stand for? We're opposites, granted. So, if his significance gets added to my significance, is the result zero? In that case, why proceed?

I was beginning to wonder if the only way to kill him was for me to kill myself.

That cold night zone opened up before me; it was even wider than the boulevard which the sleepwalker had once planned out for Berlin (it would have put the Champs-Élysées to shame by twenty meters); I sped through space until I met him at the stroke of midnight; he seemed to be expecting me, for just as I floated in through the window, Elena Konstantinovskaya screamed and he feebly raised one hand in front of his eyes.

That was when I discovered that I'd somehow forgotten to load my pistol; I hadn't slept enough lately.

Shostakovich said: You know, my dear friend, there's something you have that I don't. You display, how should I say, *resolution*. To be sure, I stick to my own guns in my music; no one can dictate that, but otherwise I, well.

I told him, and I was being sincere: Actually, Herr Schostakowitsch, I admire you.

That's too kind; that's too kind. Oh, how you've dirtied yourself! You deserve to, well, well, why upset you? I'm willing to agree that something in me has to die. How can we both end this torture? Perhaps poison will . . .

That's just what I proposed to GREINER, Herr Schostakowitsch, but he—

(Where was Elena? She'd dissolved into the air. What if she'd never been here? I was getting very sleepy.)

Do you hate me? he demanded.

Of course not, Herr Schostakowitsch! I just told you how much I admire you.

But I hate *you*. I consider you a wicked, terrible man. The nightmares you've caused my friends, especially, how should I say, Elena . . .

But this is harmless; it's not real!

What can you hope to get out of my death? Money? An Adenauer Prize? It must be money. You love money over there.

Begging your pardon, Herr Schostakowitsch, but I'm on a list.

Oh, he said. So that's how it is. And to save yourself you're willing to, to—

I begged him to forgive me then. I realized that he was correct. In an instant, he'd completely turned me against the Gehlen Organization.

I refuse to forgive you, he said. I feel no pity, oh, not! Because you've been nasty, you see. Let me tell you something: Like all murderers, you're too, how shall I put this, *optimistic*.

In my now habitual state of disgrace and despair (I'll never forget how Elena Konstantinovskaya looked at me before she faded away), I turned away from him, wandering west between various rubble-hills which were stuck through with steel spears. So he hated me! I lost myself in a tumble of bricks, a mass of plinths, iron collars, steel strings, rocky guts all crammed under ruined arches. He hated me! I felt as sunless as Dresden in winter. And I dug my way back under the Iron Curtain and into a blindingly bright afternoon in

West Berlin, the long white boulevard stretching from the Arch of Triumph to the Hall of the People with its knife-winged dark eagle, the only entity which wasn't white; the boulevard was perfect and it was empty; beyond the Hall of the People it articulated leftward into the clouds; white parks and guardhouses surrounded me, and then everything faded into a glare so excruciating that I finally comprehended that I would always be in the dark as to the real strategic purpose of this operation.

16

That meant that I must be awake at last: I knew that I didn't know.

17

As soon as I'd rested, I penetrated beneath the Curtain through a disused S-Bahn tunnel which led to the center of the earth, which I can now assure you is a hemispherical room whose pattern of blue and white tiles have been chessboarded, staired and umbrella'd for centuries. Here I discovered rows of listening devices like pictures in a gallery, each machine affixed to reality by its two wires, each one labeled: **ZOYA, VLASOV, GEHLEN** . . . They went on and on, infinitely. Where was **SHOSTAKOVICH**? But after all, I had to *see* him; I had to face him! In a crypt in Berlin I've spied the effigy of an infant whose hand reaches innocently out at the world which he has been denied, while a stone eagle guards him. I was the child within the tomb! I had nothing, not even an eagle, because he hated me.

But I found resurrection in the delicious moonlight of Berlin-East. And like a champagne cork I popped up into the air, speeding into Europe Central! It was quite gusty; I would have enjoyed carrying my Variometer, to check variations in barometric pressure. But my Variometer was another item I've lost over the years. Prague's hills crowded with trees and towers were all dark; Riga was buried under autumn leaves; and in an empty snowy park in Moscow I found Shostakovich walking round and round.

Smeared with iron-colored grime I interrupted his circles; I blocked his way; I snivelled and insisted: Herr Schostakowitsch, I'm sorry—

Indignantly he interrupted: I must tell you this, my *dear* German friend: I feel it's the worst cynicism to, to, to besmirch yourself with ugly behavior and then speak beautiful words. I, do you know, I think it's preferable to say ugly words and not commit illegal acts . . .

But nothing could take me away from him now! He was everything to me. He—and Elena, of course. (Where was Elena?)

Oh, how cold it was! I had to get down and grovel in the snow. But it paid off; I fulfilled my objective. People rarely choose to accept my apologies. But in the end, Shostakovich did. He's a very nice man.

What I dreamed of by then was inventing a method to bring about a reconciliation between him and Elena (who was codenamed LINA); was I supposed to shoot him before or after that? How about not at all? You see, I'd come to adore the man, and I valued his happiness more than my own. Many's the time I've peeped in on him as he's composing. When he closed his eyes, I saw how happy he truly was; with my Zeiss lenses I was able to obtain a magnified view of the veins in his eyelids, which pulsed in time with what must have been his Fifth Symphony, described by R. Taruskin as *a series of components, gestures or events that are immediately recognizable as signs or symbols whose referents are not specified by any universally recognized and stable code.* Now he was smiling! His fingers spread out on the table and he seemed to be playing a complex chord on the piano, or perhaps milking Elena's left breast—how I loved him for his happiness!

On one of those assassination visits, which now numbered more than the total number of Allied bombing raids on Berlin, he'd confided to me that there was a certain *other world* he sometimes lived in, a world beneath the piano keys; not caring to hurt his feelings by revealing that I already knew that, I calculated the sum instead: Let me keep this all straight; first there's Berlin itself, divided into East and West just as Europe is; second of all, there are the four sectors of Germany; meanwhile, within the Soviet zone, there's this other zone, this place where everything is beautiful and pure (this is why I loved him; this is in fact an extremely Germanic conception); but who can go there? Only Shostakovich himself? Can Elena go there, too? She left him because she didn't want to go there; but what if she'd actually left him because he believed her capable of entering that world and she knew that she couldn't? Whenever I listen to Opus 40 I believe that she can, but if that's the case, where did the operation break down? He'd told me that toward the end she was really trying; she framed the first page of the score to Opus 40, a composition which was truly *her* as he knew her; and she hung it up on the wall of her little flat on Kirovsky Prospekt in Leningrad, to show him that she, that she, you know (these last six words come verbatim from Shostakovich). All right, but could he ever bring her there? Please God, why not?

He'd also told me of a nightmare which had attacked him for years: He tries to make love with Elena but every time he takes her into his arms the telephone rings.

I begged him for the password. I wanted admission to that world east of East, the world beneath the piano keys. If I only had that, I'd be free; I wouldn't need to worry about which list the Gehlen Organization kept me on.

He said: But that's sad, because you're not my, how should I say, I mean, your name's not Lyalka! What's the basis of our relationship? I mean, frankly, you really haven't been very, you know. Moreover, *it's not your world.*

Where is my world then, Herr Schostakowitsch?

Build one, my dear friend . . .

I don't know how.

So much energy, so much, how should I say, aggression, so much talent! No doubt you could make something look good. You've worked hard—

But that's the kiss of death, Herr Schostakowitsch!

I'm sorry; this is all very . . .

I filled his glass with West German schnapps and he cried: Oh, thank you, thank you!

Then I implored him again, so he said: You can get in, but you can't get out.

Whatever do you mean, Herr Schostakowitsch?

Where were you in this war? How can you not understand? Never mind. Listen to this chord!

And he closed his hands around the air. I heard a bell-like sound.

Oh, my God! It was the most beautiful sound that I ever did or ever will hear—and the saddest.

I would have done anything for him then; I would even have stuttered like him.

But there remained what Goethe would have called *the eternal Elena-question,* because, well, how should I say . . . ?

The eternal note! Love Elena or die! Love Elena *and* die! It must be one of the two. Oh, if only I could, well, you know.

18

The next thing I knew, I had fallen for Elena Konstantinovskaya. To hell with Shostakovich! I wanted her for myself. Oh, don't tell me I don't know what Aryan beauty is; I've seen Lisca Malbran posing in a peasant dress. But so what if I never saw another film with Lisca Malbran in it? Elena was the one I loved.

At the office, they most definitely weren't happy. They'd nearly lost their faith in me. I don't dare tell you what HAVEMANN said . . .

They declined to offer me a chair in the outer office where two men sat diagonally at each oak desk, one of them by the telephone, the other at the typewriter; oak filing cabinets rose all the way up to ceiling, and I longed to know which drawer contained me; probably HAVEMANN knew, but HAVEMANN, after administering his reproof, left me alone, after which no one would look at me. I could scarcely stand myself now—oh, how I longed not to exist!

Finally the buzzer rang. GRAENER and NEY escorted me down the corridor of white steel filing cabinets, turned right at the hall of black steel filing cabinets where an operative stood whistling, pretending to study a certain fingerprint record when all the while he was glaring at me over the top of the document, and then GRAENER and NEY abandoned me on the threshold of the inner office.

Stroking the cradle of his black telephone, which curved down as freakishly as the secretary's spectacles—he'd send her away for the duration of our little chat—the pale man demanded to know whether I'd really swallowed that very first pill. I insisted that I had; I, how should I say, stuck to my guns, you know.

You're grimacing, he reproved me. You look as if wild horses are pulling you apart!

It's the times, sir, I said.

Sit down, he said.

I did.

Clearing his throat, he began: The mystery of why Siegfried stole Brunhild's ring and girdle, which laid him open to being proved her deflowerer and therefore hated by her kinsmen, the matter of why he told Kriemhild of his vulnerable spot so that she herself could foolishly reveal it to Hagen, these point at a will to self-destruction. And where does *that* come from?

I replied (and I was proud of my answer, too): Firstly, vanity. Secondly, inability to keep a secret. Isn't all this in the case file, sir? There's every reason to suspect Kriemhild of being a "Juliette" spy. As for Siegfried, he refused to be colorless or self-protective; he was simply *himself,* and he paid the price.

My friend, that's true as far as it goes, but don't you see that it's beauty which causes all evil? Do you remember Hoffmann's tale "Madame de Scuderi"? The demonic goldsmith makes bracelets, necklaces, rings so perfectly that he can't bear to let them go. What can he do but creep out by night, murder his clients, and get his treasures back again? And isn't your Elena also like that?

No. With all due respect, she isn't.

She's warping your reason.

By your command, sir!

Whose hair did you tie to that covert operations ring we issued you?

I don't know.

You didn't lose the ring. We took it to get the hair.

Didn't you plant the hair in the first place?

He chuckled.—Perhaps we did that, too. If so, what would that prove?

I don't know.

Coward! Take this tablet! No, wait. Your responses are extremely revealing. What really happened *before* between Siegfried and Brunhild—I mean, before the legend begins?

I agree that she somehow knows him, since—

You do agree? Good. That's why I need you to tell me the origin of that single dark hair you found on your pillow.

A succubus? I theorized.

Don't be sarcastic with me. I order you to consider your prior, unconscious relationship with Elena Konstantinovskaya, who by your own interpretation of pattern-events is undoubtedly a "Juliette" spy. Prepare a written report by tomorrow. Name every name.

By your command, sir, I said. But Elena was still the one I loved. Knowing that I loved her, I knew who I was.

19

What about Shostakovich? By this question I don't mean, *who is he*? Opus 110 answers that. I mean, *what shall I do about him*? One of the Gehlen Organization's own "Juliette" spies, perhaps NEY if not a high-class torch singer at the Wintergarten, might lure him away from her. I'd certainly given up on silver bullets. Oh, but how could I do even that to him? Well, for Elena, of course. (She would have her own secret world; I could hide there.)

My desire was to bring her under the Iron Curtain and buy her whatever she wanted at the KaDeWe department store. What would make anyone happier than that? If she wouldn't go with me, I wanted to lay at her feet a steel box of contraband! Next dream: Our child would resemble the little East German girl who chalks a sun on the sidewalk and smiles up into the lens for Roman Karmen's "Comrade Berlin" as the sun shines on her pressed-together knees. You see, I was already beginning to think like one of them!

That night I did nothing but float around Berlin-East in a trance, seeing Elena in every window.

I was happy even at dawn when I came home to the West. I nearly kissed the wide, sharp-angled and strangely delicate wings of the stone eagle on the Chancellery's facade.

But when I stopped by the office, I was compelled to turn in my report, an uncompromising one, I'm afraid; and the time after that, they kept me waiting a long while and finally claimed that the pale man was busy. What about HAVEMANN? He was also busy. And PFITZNER? We don't mention him at the office anymore. What if I were on another list now, a worse one? An operative I'd never met (in retrospect I half-believe him to have been the ex-ᛋᛋ-Captain KHANNI, who sold himself to the East, then bored into the Gehlen Organization, recruiting KURT in the process) informed me, not without sympathy, that Operation ELENKA had been downgraded, important as it definitely remained to the ultimate future of Germany, because in preparation for the imminent Cold War, the Amis were now demanding that we devote more manpower to unearthing the final Luftwaffe blueprints of V-weapons, which had been hidden in a coffin in a village graveyard just before the surrender; this was henceforth to constitute our Priority Apple. I said: When Priority Apple has been achieved, I wonder if we'll be told? Everyone still had faith in me, the operative replied, but I'd need to assassinate ELENKA without logistical support.

Take one of these tablets! he added. They're *new*.

New? So what?

They improve concentration. That's what you need now, soldier.

I didn't want to, but his lower lip trembled, so . . .

Then I went out; I went down, and came up one of the marble passageways into the foyer of the Südbahnhof; I came into the sunlight; I descended the steps, which were almost infinitely wide, crossed the street and gazed back at its immense rectangular facade with the two giant clocks and the swastika-gripping eagle; the Bahnhof's windowed stone arms stretched out in either direction as far as I could see. I felt safe; all my powers seemed to have returned to me. If only my dear friend Shostakovich could see this! He'd be proud of me at last.—My speculations grew ever more rhapsodic, until I awoke behind the Curtain, in the former hospital at Berlin-Karlshorst. In case you haven't heard, I'll now inform you that people no longer go there for their health.

Three tall men in blue uniforms sat on an extremely long sofa, comparing scores of Shostakovich and Wagner and making tick-marks with red pencils. Between them slept a woman in a blue smock. When she woke up, I realized that she was Elena Kruglikova, although she actually might have been Klavdia Sulzhenko. At last I saw the light. She was a "Juliette" spy! They meant to distract me from Elena Konstantinovskaya! That must have been the objective all along. Against Kruglikova's charms I safeguarded myself with the cautionary tale of that Romeo spy WALTER, who once upon a time seduced, then married LOLA, who coincidentally happened to be a secretary in the West German Foreign Ministry. Poor LOLA! I even know her real name. One day the Gehlen Organization, or perhaps the Central Intelligence Agency, reeled in her Soviet handler, MAKS, who accordingly defected, exposing both spouses. When she was arrested and shown her husband's confession that he had married her for ideology, not love, LOLA hanged herself in her cell.

A glass of water with my interrogators, a brandy-toast to friendship, a nibble or two of caviar, you know how it goes. These were the people who'd snatched the jurist Walter Linse right out of West Berlin and hanged him in Moscow.

If you work correctly with us, we will always be good friends, promised the tallest man, who was codenamed GLASUNOW.

The woman who might have been Kruglikova opened her eyes, sat up, and smiled at me with a *what's a little sex between comrades?* look. I shook my head, and she vanished into the air.

Then they gave me a nice leather map case with three pencils in its stitched-on pockets, but there was no map in it. Unable to resist stroking it, I knew at once that any rumors of black tears *in der Sowjetzone* were propaganda!

Sometimes, you see, I didn't know who I was without my identification sign! And after all the cutouts and dead letterboxes of the Gehlen Organization, after far too many crossings of that bridge over black satin water, water which was really a black curtain with pleats of grainy yellow light; and then somehow (for I was already getting sleepy), after too many traversals of that broad white wall arched with darkness, with windows and white palaces, I couldn't even be certain what I loved. You see, "Juliette" spies are so treacherous! And alliances can get even more entangling than that. For example, consider this subplot from Case NIBELUNG: When RÜDIGER, once his friend and now by virtue of conflicting loyalties about to become his enemy, offers HAGEN his own shield, the latter fervently swears never to harm him in the forthcoming battle, and keeps his word; instead, RÜDIGER will be killed by the sword which he's presented to his son-in-law GERNOT. What's the use of that? I wish I'd never decrypted it.

What should HAGEN and RÜDIGER have done? The flat clean blankness of the sleepwalker's stone banks and ministries always stood for something unchanging—no matter that the Nazi-Soviet Pact became Operation Barbarossa; that was a superhuman event, occurring so far above me that it failed to twist my integrity. Now that I possessed a choice, I'd tried to act, each time blaming my failures of accomplishment on illusionism of miscast silver bullets; what if there were a better explanation which relieved me from even more responsibility? Oh, how sleepy I was! I could slumber now; I could blame everything on the opportunism of the bourgeoisie; it was as good as having the sleepwalker back.

The shortest man, codenamed RIMSKY, said to me that freedom means understanding our place within the laws of history; we are more free when we acknowledge our submission to the law of gravity than when we foolishly deny it.

And it seemed to me that RIMSKY was as familiar as my own father; he offered me the comfort which my father would have, if he hadn't been gassed at Ypres two wars ago. Laws of history! I could surely find myself if I only obeyed enough laws.

But what would GREINER have said about me then, or the pale man in the dark glasses? Whom would I become if they thought badly of me?

Socioeconomic formations *versus* an officer's heels on a parquet floor, which would I choose?

RIMSKY advised me to *never think backwards.* If I betrayed the Gehlen Organization freely and fully, they'd give me a nice little villa in Trescow-Allee where Elena and I could make little Kruglikovas. Then I'd be safely in the peace camp! Every now and then I'd be called on to speak out *against* remilitarization and *for* reunification on the appropriate terms. Was I ready?

I need to dream about it.

Dreams are for cowards, said the third man, who must have been the East German spymaster, Markus Wolf.

They flew me to a walled villa in the woods outside Moscow, whose grounds were illuminated at night; and here, among the pines and birches of Silverwood, where Elena Konstantinovskaya had given birth on 22.6.41, the Center gave me my chance for happiness.

20

Elena, will you please marry me?

Which intelligence service sent you here? Remember, they're listening.

Elena, if I devote myself to you, will I be able to become myself?

No.

I promise to be very, very loyal. I'll always say yes to you. Please say yes to me—

No. Your eyes scare me. I'm sorry. Try to be strong . . .

21

That was how I learned that no is stronger than yes. (Shostakovich already knew that.) It takes two yesses for I to become we, but only one no for we to break apart, no matter what the other party wishes. Elena Konstantinovskaya's no killed my yes, which fell voiceless into solitude. She did this, and there will never be any remedy.

She said no, in order to be true to herself. In that case, will I find myself if I say no? How can I be any worse off? (I dislike this feeling in my heart; I wonder if I can sleep it off?) From now on, I'll say no to everything.

22

In the next room, Shostakovich sat at the piano. I can't say he was in on what had just taken place; I'll never know how much he knew; I was too heartbroken. Probably he didn't know; he was far too lost in himself, stationed in that windowless chamber day and night, writing passwords and cipher groups into the score of Opus 110.

Patting me on the shoulder, he said: Don't worry, don't worry. There's nothing but nonsense in this world . . .

He was kind to me; he didn't need to be kind! He was the one I loved . . .

23

So I refused to collaborate. I said no. Unfortunately, no means yes, since they'd arranged the meeting with Elena Konstantinovskaya and they must have influenced the outcome. But yes would also have meant yes. In other words, yes is stronger than no. All the same, I insist that I acted upon my convictions. I told them my guilt was too great, not that they cared about guilt. I demanded to be turned over to the Stasi. I confessed that I was even at this very moment a malignantly active member of the Gehlen Organization. Even an interview at the Ministry of State Security didn't change my mind. When they pinched me, I scarcely felt it.

They flew me back to East Berlin; I have always enjoyed airplanes. A stenographer kept me company at my interrogation. Perhaps he liked me for myself. He "played the piano" on a captured "Erika" typewriter. Next they brought me before the Red Guillotine, who condemned me to death, then gave me a fair trial according to all principles of socialist legality. A golden bust of Wilhelm Pieck looked on in sternly loving solicitude. Again I admitted everything. Infected by American gangsterism, I'd conspired to weaken their defensive preparedness. Worse yet, I'd continued to dream of a so-called "German way to socialism." I'd forgotten the greatest ally and friend of the German working class, the Soviet Union. Indeed, I'd thought to rob the Soviet Union of my beautiful Elena Konstantinovskaya. Finally, I reminded the court that my class had already fulfilled its historical mission and no longer deserved to exist. My defense attorney proudly embraced me.

When they shot me, I wasn't worried; I knew that it wouldn't do me any more harm than I had done Shostakovich. What it resembled was getting whirled down the drain of a stained old sink in a communal apartment; I could feel myself getting sucked downward, speeding round and round ever more rapidly until suddenly I was in the leaden pipe which communicated secretly with the West.

I came out, none the worse for wear, and it was night. To die in the East is to live in the West.

24

Now I'd done it! Their black telephones began to toll. My confession had revealed to them the danger in which they stood. Shostakovich was their voice, and Elena their soul. If we could steal her, then we'd have a soul, and they'd have none. I'd now been rendered harmless, by love if not by *Nackenschuss*, but what if GREINER or NEY got through?

They blockaded Berlin. That was Stage One. As soon as they could, they'd reinforce the Iron Curtain. For now, they'd starve us out of Berlin-West. This was precisely what the sleepwalker always used to worry about.

The dreamers who held hands and ran westward through Dreamland's forests every night, trying to get away from the Red Guillotine and come to us, the Iron Curtain already stopped them. Do you remember the last days of Operation Citadel, when we were too weak to break through at Prokhorovka? This was a continuation of that operation; no war ever ends. The lucky ones were arrested in the Restricted Area; they never even reached the Protected Zone.

There remained certain games, ploys, possibilities, as exemplified by Kurt Strübund's maneuver with the leather-bound documents of an erotic club called the Confederation Diplomatique; he smuggled a hundred and eighty East Germans across; the People's Police believed them to be diplomatic passports! But the Iron Curtain, which was as dark grey as the soil of Poltava, jigjagged west across Prinzenstrasse to Checkpoint Charlie, then north along the edge of the Tiergarten to the Brandenburg Gate, bisecting Unter den Linden, grazing the ruined Reichstag, continuing up to Invalidenstrasse and Chausseestrasse, then east past Brunnenstrasse before it whipped north again, enclosing, containing or sealing off sections not all of which any one individual could see (thanks to ideological differences, you know); and they now lowered the Curtain to the very ground, screwed its hem into the ground, then added long bolts! They meant to take us all to the police station, lock us away, and let us sleep off reality forever.

25

Fortunately for the Free World, in Tempelhof Field we'd dreamed up a great ring of hangars and terminals around the circular runway: Tempelhof Airport, with the pair of facing lions in the shadow of the two facing towers! Much of this edifice existed only in the model of the architect Sagebiel, but at least the eagle on the passenger terminal's roof had established itself on earth; I remember seeing Russian soldiers hoist their flag up there in '45; despite their best efforts, our eagle dwarfed them. As for the unfinished bits, no matter; we could always dream them into solidity.

Two Red Army men in forage caps and long greatcoats were clearing mines with circle-headed wands; they wore rifles at their backs, rubble before and around them. What were they really afraid of? Maybe some explosion would wake up the East, and then summer light would rush in! God knows. As it turned out, they were readying the ground for the Wall. It wouldn't be long before the day when reliable Soviet soldiers began unrolling the very first ring of barbed wire, flush up against *their* side of the sign which said **BRITISH SECTOR**.

26

And what about me?

By rights I should have been relegated to the worst list of all, but the pale man in dark glasses was sentimental, I think because I'd told him that I'd once floated past a certain long line of trees in Dreamland where his father's house used to stand; needless to say, I'd never been there, but he believed me. Operation ELENKA had always been a long shot; the Luftwaffe blueprints had been recovered to the satisfaction of the Amis, and countering the Berlin blockade was now Priority Apple. Moreover, precisely because I didn't know who I really was, I had a way with dream-creatures. GRAENER, GREINER; HAVEMANN and PFITZNER all tried to do what I eventually did; none could withdraw the sword from the stone! For my own part, upon receiving my authorization from the highest levels of the Gehlen Organization, I clambered up to the roof of Tempelhof and struck the stone eagle with a stick. Away it flew, screaming!

Roger, Wilco, A-OK! Our airlift idylls began.

27

Here came the *Rosinenbombers,* bearing powdered milk, butter and chocolate from our former enemies, the Anglo-American Jewish plutocrats; today it was clear that our differences had been mistaken, and we all should have united against the Slavs back before Stalingrad fell.

Walls of flourbags, milkbags and sandbags rose in the warehouses! Then we really had to admit that the Amis were good.

Berliners queued up for their turn at the barrel of American milk. Smiling, skinny old men who remembered quite well how to shout *Heil Hitler!* wrapped themselves up in all their clothes, sat on rubble and drank bowls of American soup. One-legged black marketeers offering butter by a ruined wall looked up, while around the perimeter of Tempelhof our Amis kept rolling slowly forward, riding atop their open tanks; they were ready to beat off any monsters who might come sneaking towards us from beneath the Iron Curtain.

Another plane came through Dreamland, keeping our island vigilantly alive! (From the air, Berlin was an immense, intricately ridge-patterned butter-biscuit, whose inviting insets and arcs seemed to be made of hard white sugar; in fact it was all concrete.) More sweets flew to Tempelhof! Children ran to the summit of a hill of broken bricks, waving and waving to the American gods of chocolate.

More body-shaped bags of powdered foodstuffs descended from the bellies of those C-54s, which landed at Tempelhof every ninety seconds. It was like a dream.

We saved the black-aproned fishwives of the Markt-Halle; we allowed currency reforms to continue to incubate beneath the Reichsbank's long square coast. We rescued the Kroll Opera House, where once upon a time the Enabling Act transformed our sleepwalker into absolute dictator. We preserved Tempelhof itself, where Käthe Kollwitz once took her son Peter to see the landing of the Wright Brothers' "White Flame," and the sleepwalker declared war on unemployment.

Do you remember that famous photograph of children perched on rubble and broken steel beams, waving at one of the departing *Rosinenbombers*? Nowadays we call that *disinformation*. We pretend that it was for them, like the sparks which caught them on fire when they tried to run away from Dresden. In fact they were keeping Berlin supplied just for me. I was their hero again, because I kept getting executed. I alone possessed the talent to go East. If I'd only been able to neutralize Shostakovich, then Western civilization would be saved. But since I couldn't, well, you know.

Oh, yes, I hid from the Stasi and the NKVD in various fabulously ruined apartments, which narrowed into peaks as improbable as Gothic spires. It takes time to prove one's unkillability. Sometimes I nightcrawled to the sign **YOU ARE LEAVING THE AMERICAN SECTOR**, and then I did leave it, straight through the Iron Curtain! (Antifascist democratic state power leaked cloudy summer sunshine across the railroad ties. I could feel it, even though just then a rat came out.) I'd shot ELENKA so many times, it was only fair to let them shoot me a few more, too, as the working class demands. And it did, and they did. Sometimes I could hardly stay awake . . .

One occasion, right before they liquidated me (it never even stung), GLASUNOW stood watching, and he shouted: *West Berlin was never a part of the Federal Republic and will never belong to it!*

But we didn't care what GLASUNOW said! We stuck it out until the Soviets capitulated. They withdrew their blockade in the spring of '49. We had a party at the office. After that, the "economic miracle" occupied us; we went from one victory to another. All the same, the Iron Curtain was more adamantine than an old soldier-woman's cheekbones. But we didn't care about that. As Comrade Honecker foresaw, we were already planning a step by step takeover by West German monopolies. On 5.5.55, the Allied High Commission dissolved itself! West Germany, the true Germany, was now once more a sovereign state!

28

What about Shostakovich and Elena? I was now so numb to them that I might as well have been asleep! I'd lost *her,* so why admit her existence? I'd failed either to kill *him* or help him, so why face my shame? I'd found myself; they loved me at the office; I was a symbol of the superhuman. I never woke anymore; I mean, I never slept; and once I enjoyed a waking dream of a dark-haired woman, stark naked, who gazed at me with wide brown eyes, unsmilingly proud; her gaze reminded me of a customs inspector's; I think she might have been Elena Konstantinovskaya, but if not, she was probably Elena Kruglikova. Closing my burning eyes, I heard breathing all around me; in retrospect, I must have been at a movie theater, watching an old print of "Airlift Idylls," starring Lisca Malbran. She wore a snow-white sailor suit but she was actually a paratrooper; they flew her across the lines so that she could singlehandedly save Stalingrad. She was a heroine and I was a hero—a national hero. Every time I received another bullet in the neck, I got another medal, posthumously of course. Oh, I was on the good list now! I rationalized that here in Berlin, the entire world's railroad tracks begin and end in parallels, so I knew that I could get to him or her somehow, or else, they could get to me. The Iron Curtain had never stopped me. Moreover, on July 1961, Comrade Ulbricht announced at a press conference that *no one has any intention of building a wall*!

And so on 13.8.61 Comrade Honecker proudly reported: *At 0.00 hours the alert was given and the action got underway.*

29

Stalinallee, eighty meters wide, had become Karl-Marx-Allee by then. The Wall elaborated itself around the Curtain by the week, until it was even huger than the statue of the Red Army man in Treptow Park. Before the apartments on Bernauer Strasse got sealed off, I still used to see people jump, first out of the first floor windows, then out of the second. Well, they stopped that. Hardly anyone could get across anymore. I remember how the twin stone lions crouched down on their broken Lion Bridge as if they were about to howl at the two stone lions on the other side; I remember the Wall passing in sight of the demolished Potsdam Station; I can't forget anything; my mind's as full of armor as the old Ordens Palace. And now that's gone, just like the Iron Curtain. But in those days, well, you know!

The Red Guillotine busily condemned people to death. Sometimes, when I wasn't being executed myself, I used to watch the executions from one of the twin stone pillars which overlook Tempelhof's circular runway. (I pretty much had my run of Berlin by then.) In Warsaw, a stone head and a stone hand lay separately in the dirt for years. Farther to the East, they still had everything: the straw palliasses in Soviet prisons, the many gold-framed icons on the Empress's blue walls. But the Iron Curtain was shut; and the Wall, watched by long convoys of Ami jeeps with white stars and glaring headlights, killed ever more of its victims; watchdogs snarled in the death zone to defend inevitable upward development against the Teutonic Knights of NATO's Operation Grey; President Kennedy called on the free world to be resolute; Adenauer sent his *brotherly love* to the East Germans *who are still forced to dwell, separated from us, in thralldom and lawlessness. We call to them: you are part of us, and we belong to you*. Hearing this, our truehearted West German women spontaneously presented him with a bouquet!

I wouldn't want you to disbelieve in happy endings, at least not on our side. We'd won the inestimable treaure of democracy: shabby West Berliners lining up to vote, and silver-white summer clouds over everything. The new-planted saplings on Unter den Linden grew taller by the hour. A girl stood on one leg, blew cigarette smoke at me through painted lips, tilted her head and winked. ▸

THE RED GUILLOTINE

◩

More quickly than Moscow itself, one gets to know Berlin through Moscow.

—Walter Benjamin (1927)

1

Once upon a time, although there might have been previous times, the first button glowed; then the telephone began to ring, straight from Europe Central. For the Red Guillotine, herself a member of the Zentralkomitee, and therefore aware of developments before the telephone told her, this was another moment to count up her triumphs and rejoice that her ideals grew more massive with the years. Outside, almost in sight of Berlin-West, our Thälmann Pioneers held hands in a circle, singing on a cobblestoned space which the Rubblefrauen had cleared of ruins. The Red Guillotine almost sang along. She'd been so happy in the Wandervogel when she was fourteen! The words had changed, but many tunes remained the same.

The telephone said: Sentence confirmed for Nellis.

Good, said the Red Guillotine, whom Comrade Sorgenicht has correctly eulogized as *Hilde Benjamin, Communist personality, who personifies the unity of theory and practice.* The so-called "West German" press describes her as *a negroid woman with dark, evil eyes, the female incarnation of Roland Freisler. Defendants know to expect no mercy from this charming individual.* Coming from such a source, this can safely be considered a compliment.

The *Great Soviet Encyclopedia* neglects her in favor of that famous suicide-aesthete whom a weird chance made her brother-in-law. Nor has she been granted any monument in Comrade Honecker's *From My Life*. These silences must not be misunderstood. Does the American Secret Service expose its most effective operatives for the sake of history books? The Red Guillotine remains one of our foremost *zero hour activists,* and in the era of this legend, most of which takes place between the constitutions of 1949 and 1968, we all saw her name if not her face. (Why not her face? We could never be certain that she wasn't peering at us from behind the velvet curtains in the tiny windows of a Russian limousine.) I'm informed that she bore a physical resemblance both to Comrade N. K. Krupskaya, and also, as I said, to our fellow traveler K. Kollwitz, reproductions of whose sorrowful woodcuts we often show our Pioneers, in order to indoctrinate them with the appropriate class hatred. Kollwitz represented *herself.* The Red Guillotine represented all of us. It would be a pardonable error to conflate her with some Rodchenko-like profile of a woman made out of wire.

2

The tale is told that on that *zero hour* day when the victors mobilized our children to carry mirrors, typewriters and other booty out of our flats and to the trainyard where it could wait in the rain to go to Russia, the Red Guillotine strode into the office of the Soviet military commandant—not a place which most Germans visited lightly—and he received her, drunk and wearing four wristwatches.

What you want, Frau? Frau no pretty; Frau get out!

I speak Russian, she answered in that language.

He looked astonished. She stood before him, waiting. Suddenly he peeled off a watch, thrust it at her, and said: Take it.

Thank you, Herr Commandant.

All Germans hate Russians. Do you hate Russians?

No.

I hate Germans.

That's the reality.

Good. Drink with me.

And she did.

All right. Now what do you want?

Then she confided to him her dream. She longed to apply to Germany the progressive legal science of our Eastern mother, the Soviet Union.

3

Go back to 1919, when K. Liebknecht and R. Luxemburg were murdered by rightwing elements. Helene Marie Hildegard Lange, aged seventeen, burst into tears, lost her appetite, and practically stopped speaking to anyone.—But, Hilde, what can one do against such people? demanded her mother. It's not only dangerous to fight them; it's useless.

Frau Lange had much on her side: logic, experience, and, above all, love. But at the very moment when the girl had almost been convinced to "go on with her life," she saw the memorial woodcut to Liebknecht, made by K. Kollwitz from drawings done at the morgue at the invitation of the family. The martyr's head, thrown back upon the white nothingnesss of the paper, is runneled with the shadows of his final agony. Light shines on his chin and cheekbones. The bulletholes in his forehead have been pitiably concealed, or honored, by red flowers. The mouth's final grimace is a downcurving semicircular groove. In the half-dozen sketches Kollwitz made, the face is nothing more than what it objectively was: dull, pale, inanimate. In fact, it may well be less. In the very first drawing the flowers have been omitted. Next comes the charcoal study, which retains detail but now, with the same motive and effect of a woman applying makeup, adds the moody smudginess of the medium to the corpse. Here the artist also introduces a line of mourning workers. Old women need more makeup than young; the dead need more still; so this eager-to-please K. Kollwitz next proceeds to an intaglio etching, darkening Liebknecht's face to such an extent that the ear, eye-socket, cheekbone, hair and forehead are entirely gloomed over. The subsequent lithograph abstracts the scene into lines; the ink wash study, into brush-strokes; finally she settles on the woodcut, whose chisel-marks appear to dissect away every mourner's face into underlying muscles and tendons; they're all pale, sorrowing corpses in the darkness around the dead man's face, a few more planes, crescents and angles of which have been restored to the light but which remain as in those first sketches a portrait of *nothingness,* now solidified into something akin to an ebony idol. What about the most prominent part of the image, the bier itself? It's white nothingness—more exactly, it's a long white mummy-shroud with a few straight ripples of blackness across its edges. In 1960, immediately following the premier of "Comrade Berlin," there was a banquet in honor of the filmmaker, a certain R. L. Karmen, who in between nibbles of our excellent German cheese informed the Red Guillotine that this daring device of blankness in the Liebknecht memorial sheet had inspired him to something similar in his documentary on the opening of our first blast furnace at Krasnogorsk: he'd omitted the ceremony itself!—As for the Red Guillotine, what effect might Kollwitz's graphic starkness have produced on her? (We Communists say, if it has no practically measurable effect, it's not people's art!) Speaking strictly as an aesthetic critic, not as Comrade Alexandrov, I'd have to reply that what this woodcut teaches us is *simplification and abstraction.*

And so Fräulein Lange decided to study law at Heidelberg. Her mother asked why. She replied: I believe I will be able to help the victims of injustice.

Please think better of this, darling. It's one thing to go into law, and entirely another to—

In a steely voice she said: They murdered Liebknecht and his daughter is going into law! That's why *I'm* going into law.

Her mother could do nothing with her.

The legend informs us that she was one of the best students, and perhaps the best of all. She sometimes dreamed of a golden box which could not be opened. She was searching for the key. Someday she would find it, and then . . .

She did piecework in a metal shop to earn her tuition. As the legend tells it, she was practically a member of the working class. Late one night, having finished at the lathe, she locked up and walked to her tram stop, arriving just as a beggar like a troll or kobold, whose few sodden hairs clung to his wrinkled skull, snatched away an old woman's purse. Fräulein Lange looked on silently. Even then she had a reputation for impartiality.

On 27.2.26 she married Comrade Georg Benjamin, a physician, whom the legend is quick to remind us *was also Superintendent of Schools in Berlin-Wedding, a working-class quarter.* In 11.27, finally understanding the maxim of Comrade Ulbricht that *Social Democracy equals Social Fascism,* she joined the only legitimate organization of the proletariat, the Communist Party. Two years later she took on the legal defense of our Red Help organization, to which K. Kollwitz also contributed with her poster-propaganda.

Bourgeois historians, romantics and deviants prefer to remember Weimar Berlin as a concretion of the Princess Café's private niches, where Georg's brother Walter and Walter's poet friend Heinle used to meet prostitutes. They commemorate the old men with canes and tophats at the Prussian Academy, last survivors of a dying class, who considered themselves entitled to "reward" Kollwitz's achievements when objectively speaking they were nothing more than hypocritically rarefied imitations of the lesbians at Schwerinstrasse-13, who couldn't stop dreaming about a certain Lina's pretty knees! Well, let the gentlemen of the bourgeoisie remember Berlin any way they please. As Comrade Khruschev promised us, *we will bury them.*

From our heroine's point of view, Berlin was nothing but one chamber after another of the Imperial Labor Court, where she became one of the fieriest accusers of the bourgeois state, inspired by the memory of Comrade Liebknecht. In those days her love for the future was impatient and angry, like the mother's who brushes her child's curls a trifle too hard, ignoring its screams, so that it will be perfect for school. She proved particularly uncompromising when she defended strikers against trumped-up charges of disturbing the peace. In the Fourth Criminal Senate, she battled year after year against the malignant Dr. Niedner. The more dissatisfied she became with the world around her, the more convincingly she dreamed. That is why she spoke out so effectively at Party rallies, always advising us to fight the capitalists without compromise; she taught us the slogan *Release the proletarian prisoners!* As Comrade Liebknecht had done, she called for the organs of the Prussian-German bourgeois state to be replaced by workers' and soldiers' councils, for the generals and aristocrats to face justice in revolutionary tribunals. Her mother had bad dreams now; she dreaded that Hilde might meet Comrade Liebknecht's fate. Hilde stood ready. The legend informs us that *in that period, Communist Hilde Benjamin was clear that her most important work was the realization of the Party's decisions.*

In 9.30 she defended the worker whom the class-biased legal system of the Republic had seen fit to charge with murdering that Nazi provocateur Horst Wessel. (He *had* murdered Wessel, but that's not the point.) The young attorney made a striking picture in the first row of wax-gleaming defendant's benches in that elegant wood-paneled courtoom, for she was calm, thoughtful and even smiling. The defendant, whose eyes shone with desperation and whose collar was less than clean, whispered another of his anxieties into her ear. Frau Dr. Benjamin's smile elongated slightly. Unkind observers might have described it as a smile of contempt.—Sit up straight, she said from the side of her mouth. Act like a human being. Look the enemy in the face.

Called upon by the prosecutor, Horst Wessel's mother held aloft his bloody uniform. She prayed for the day when Germans would take vengeance on the Jews for this and many other crimes. Frau Dr. Benjamin laughed ironically.

The Fascists did not forget her. Their so-called "Führer" was said to have her name on a list. Frau Dr. Benjamin remarked: There must be so many other names on it, I'll be old by the time he gets to me!—The truth was that every time she saw them marching in the streets, or, worse yet, heard them singing their "Horst-Wessel-Lied," the bottom dropped out of her stomach. But our line in those days was that the quicker those brutes came to power the better, because they would bring capitalism's contradictions to a head.

Whenever she lost a trial, she had one very particular thing to say to her client. It was not the so-called "consolation" with which a bourgeois lawyer seeks to wash his own hands of what the fired trade unionist or the hungry thief must now suffer—or, if it was, it was consolation sharp as a razor. It inculcated hatred; it simplified and abstracted the case to its socioeconomic essentials; it directed energy toward the future. What she said was this: I've come to recognize that questions of law and justice are at the same time questions of power.

4

Like good Communists, we'll pass over the irrelevantly personal aspects of her marriage to Dr. Georg Benjamin. Their son Michael (born when the Reich absorbed Austria) is likewise of no concern to us; we'll merely note that in the end he fulfilled their expectations and studied in Moscow.

As soon as the sleepwalker came to power, she found herself in imminent danger of being *taken away*. All the same, she kept bravely defending the workers, following the maxim of Comrade W. Ulbricht that *the Communists must be the ones who know Fascist labor law the best.* Georg feared for her, but she told him what she used to tell her mother: *I myself have a head to think with!* Naturally she soon lost her right to practice her profession.

Her husband was a Jew, and his fate ordinary: arrested in May 1933, sent to KZ-Lichtenburg, released for Christmas, resumed legal and illegal political work, rearrested in 1936, sentenced to six years' hard labor, which he completed through contact with the electrified barbed wire of Mauthausen.

Do you want to know who stands ready to help us Germans now? There can be but one answer: SMAD, the Sowjetische Militäradministration.

Watching the open boxcars of women, children and old men hoping to escape the Slavs, she bided her time. They had black ruins for their food and grey sky to drink, but they rode the silver rails of hope: If only they could get to the American zone before the Reds crossed the Oder! The widow Benjamin stayed quietly at home.

Then came that visit to the man with four wristwatches, as a result of which (I quote the legend exactly) *she was asked by the commander of the Berlin city precinct Stieglitz to organize the judicial system, and was thus made District Attorney.* That was in May. (She paused to smile on camera for Roman Karmen's new film, "Berlin.") By September she was already Director of Cadre Development. *The radical removal of Nazi and reactionary elements was a main focus of her department.*

5

The plan of the *zero hour activists:* Since East Germany doesn't even have trade unions yet, our first task will be to complete the bourgeois revolution of 1848. Then we'll smash the monopoly capitalists and Junkers who created Nazism.

No elections, of course. Hitler had elections.

Hence we'll fly in the Ulbricht Group* from Moscow, form our working committee of the two proletarian parties, then create a broad-based antifascist bloc, which we'll winnow down bit by bit until only we are included.

Next step: the democratic land reform, commenced in our very first autumn—I mean collectivization, with loudspeakers, searchlights, threats and happy fireworks. After all, the producers of national wealth are the only ones who deserve full citizenship. Whatever mercy we might have possessed was interred beneath the greenish-beige dirt of Auschwitz.

6

A pregnant young woman whose husband SMAD had just *sent East* asked her, perhaps a little wistfully, what she thought of the developments in the American sector, and the new District Attorney contemptuously replied: Over there, it's not creation of the new, but restoration of the old.

7

Almost every other German avoided that barbed-wire-topped fence at Karlshorst behind which General Zhukov operated. Comrade Ulbricht loved to go

---

*Comrade Ulbricht had already proven helpful to us during the Spanish Civil War, when he'd prepared Trotskyite volunteers for liquidation. He declined to smile for R. L. Karmen's cine-camera. From her own experience, Elena Konstantinovskaya knew exactly what he was and avoided him in terror. Comrade Leonhard remembers him as follows: *Being entirely innocent of theoretical ideas or personal feelings, to the best of my knowledge he never failed to carry out the directives transmitted to him by the Soviet authorities with ruthlessness and skill.* This was exactly the sort of person we wanted to run East Germany. Somewhat to our surprise, he survived the death of Stalin by pointing out that if he himself were purged, the criminals of 17.6.53 might be emboldened; and, after all, nothing must accrue to the advantage of these subversive elements. In 1969, A. A. Grechko, Marshal of the Soviet Union, who'd commanded the Soviet Union's fraternal armed forces in Germany from 1953 through 1957, was overheard to say: *The old one isn't worth much anymore.* And indeed, in 1971 Ulbricht was ousted by our new man, Comrade Honecker.

there; only then did we see him smile. (The collectivizers beg him to intercede with the Russians, who keep dismantling everything and shipping it eastward, even the machinery we'll need for collectivization. Comrade Ulbricht replies: *This meeting has nothing to do with dismantling.)* As for the Red Guillotine, she rushed to Karlshorst nearly twice a week. She had a pass. She was pale, shining-eyed, roundheaded—there was something almost deformed about her. She'd come to hasten that decisive moment when the firing squad approaches the stakes, one man bending over each victim with a pistol ready for the *coup de grâce.* Sometimes she failed to get her heart's desire, but at least she could send them forever or almost forever to one of our Eastern zone's jails, which we'd begun to call *the yellow misery.*

The Fascists kept saying, up against the wall, up against the wall, and after a while one wanted to put them up against the wall, or tie them to chairs at the base of some sunny rubble-hill, the firing squad now in position. Instead of feeling sorry for her country, she was sickened and angered by the myriad pale white upraised arms like antennae from each marching caterpillar of German prisoners.

I myself am reminded of the scene in the *Nibelungenlied* when Kriemhild agreed to dry her tears and marry again only when the envoy promised to take upon himself anything needed to avenge wrongs committed against her.

8

We Communists have long since exposed the lie that law can be universally applied. If A. exploits B., then equal freedom for A. and B. means that A. will continue to exploit B.

This is why we require a new socialist legality to overcome bourgeois legality.

Law is the instrument of the working class.

It has not always been this way. It will not always be this way. Socialist legality is dynamic. But in the first stage, removal of the bourgeoisie, law must found itself on dictatorship of the proletariat. After the old regime's exploiters have been rendered entirely extinct, socialist legality will have done with violence and move to the second stage, a single-tiered legality for an entire people, a people now led without question by the working class, as for instance in our beloved Soviet Union.

And how do we achieve this second stage? Comrade Benjamin knows the answer: Develop the best forces of the people.

9

By 1946 she'd become the leading influence in the Central Administration of Justice. She was still slender then. I've seen her gripping the foliage-hung rim of the lectern at a women's conference; she wore a dark dress. Wasting not a moment, she began training people's judges and people's prosecutors—for example, the slender, pale yet steady old man in the leather cap who sat every day on a stool by the courtyard, scraping the dead mortar off salvaged bricks; his workbench was a plank stretched across three towers of bricks, and he never looked up. When we called on him, he looked up then; when we raised the issue of class hatred he began to grin. The Red Guillotine grinned back; she flattered him that he belonged to *the truly revolutionary element.* He didn't need to study the essence of jurisprudence in order to be a people's judge!

She began to be called first *the woman without mercy,* then *the Red Hilde of Wedding,* and soon, *the Red Guillotine.*

Explaining to us that *law must correspond with the progression of civilization,* she began to apply our Constitution's Article Six, Paragraph Two against corporate criminals and imperialist agents.

10

Once upon a time, Comrade Margot Feist, bearing flowers, congratulated the worker Wilhelm Pieck on his presidency, and we progressed happily ever after. The fruit trees of Potsdam were bearing again; the stagnant waters of the Spree Forest were no longer troubled by artillery shells. We'd kept the church at Neuzelle open. A drunk with a beer belly watched it for us. All the same, conditions for building socialism remained sub-optimal. For instance, the Constitution still looked backward, not forward. Moreover, we'd classified eighty-nine percent of the industries of Leipzig as inoperative. *(This meeting has nothing to do with dismantling.)* And the food supply would be erratic for at least the next two years. After all, what had been sown in our fields but land mines and artillery shells? Workers accordingly deserted their places of labor to hunt for something to eat. What choice did we have, but strictness?—A woman gets six years for selling eggs in West Berlin—another victory for Party-minded justice. Spectators dare to express their pity. But the Red Guillotine explains that to achieve socialism we must eliminate so-called "civil rights."

All magic spells fail without belief. We enforced belief. In place of ruins we offered the wide white monumentality of Stalinallee, arched, windowed, black and white, fading magnificently into the East.

11

Thanks to the losses justly inflicted upon German Fascism, in our new zone we found ourselves burdened with a female-to-male ratio of one point three five to one. The result: sexual exploitation. The remedy: uncompromising legal struggle, enacted by our own Red Guillotine, to bring about absolute equality for women. It seemed to her more than ever that the only hope, not merely for her—what did one being matter?—but for all of us, lay in some realm of future dawn, and that to find her way there she must dynamite her way out of the past.

But at a meeting when we were discussing the necessary changes which must be made in the Constitution itself, a delegation of doctors dared to interrupt us with the demand that we permit German women raped by the Red Army to obtain abortions. Comrade Ulbricht replied: The Germans should have thought about that before they launched Operation Barbarossa.

Comrade Benjamin, you're a woman; surely you can understand! We appeal to you!

I stand by Comrade Ulbricht, replied the Red Guillotine.

But, Comrade Benjamin, *you were there yesterday* when those two Mongolians raped Resi Nordlund in the street. We saw you pass by! And you feel nothing?

My *feelings* are of no relevance, said the Red Guillotine contemptuously.

She was only eleven years old! Are you aware that she died? And all that Russian officer did was fire into the air . . .

We brought it on ourselves. I refuse to discuss this case any further.

That child brought it on herself?

I have nothing to say about the individuals involved in this case. As Communists we must be realistic. Legislation follows the Party, *doesn't it?* The Party follows Comrade Stalin, *doesn't it?* Do you think that Comrade Stalin's in a mood to let us accuse the Red Army of anything?

(The Russian officer had run out of bullets, shrugged and turned his back. The Red Guillotine looked on for a moment. She passed the test; she retained her reputation for impartiality.)

And so we stood firm; that was the only practical way to build the future.

Our new zone became a vista of rubble-hills bristling with workers! We organized labor parties; we got the water mains working again. The Red Guillotine spoke at another rally before the bulletpocked pillars of a Nazi shell: a great banner, an upraised hand, the words **FOR FREEDOM AND HUMANITY, AGAINST THE REVANCHISM OF BONN!** Her watchword: *Thorough cleansing of the entire public sphere.*

On 20.9.47, in the German State Opera House, we played Beethoven, and then the Second Party Congress of the Socialist Unity Party commenced. Our future: toasts to international friendship, long lines of flag-armed tractors in our German fields, laughing Pioneers running downhill in triple file, white smoke from our new factories and smiling delegates.

12

In the spring of 1948, our Soviet oracles announced that denazification had been completed in the East German zone. We were happy then! Perhaps the Red Army would go home. But in September, revolutionary realism, explicated by the big black telephone, compelled us to dismiss the pipedream of a so-called *German road to socialism.* Some argued with this just and necessary decision. The Red Guillotine proved them to be implicated in the American-rooted Slansky-Rajk conspiracy. As her legend so prettily puts it, *she showed the ability to continually evolve in accordance with her ever-increasing responsibilities while simultaneously shaping the new judicial system of our socialist state.* And what if denazification hadn't quite been completed after all? Among her circle, love was disdained; at best it expressed itself silently. Georg Benjamin had been a good man; she'd trusted him; he believed in what she did and therefore understood her; wasn't that sufficient? But after they'd reduced him to an inky skeleton which grimaced at the electric wire it sizzled on, he haunted her as one lover haunts another. She could not save him, but she could punish *them.*

She mobilized the Party Control Commissions to sift out traitors: Titoists, revanchists, etcetera. The only ones who weren't traitors were the men with shovels, the women clambering on brickheaps. As the Red Guillotine explained it to her people's judges: *Since man develops his personality primarily in work, in addition to the right to work there also exists the right to a job which corresponds to one's talents and abilities.* Which job might that be? Whichever one we assign to you.

She was closely involved in drafting the criminal legislation of 1948 which protects our economy against all parasites, barterers and investors. Six years for selling eggs? Why not twenty? I see her hand in SMAD's Order 160 against sabotage. After all, as Comrade W. Pieck announced in the Third Party Congress in 1950, *the Socialist Unity Party is a party of legality.*

She instructed her people's judges: *The important thing is to apply the laws in a new democratic spirit.* And so we charged seventy-eight thousand individuals with political crimes in 1950 alone (that was the year our Stasi came into being.) The necessary result: There no longer remained any classes or sections which could live at the expense of others.

13

In the last two months of 1950, eleven spies were shot by SMAD; then six more—Jehovah's Witnesses and other hired killers of the American imperialists—got condemned for American espionage.—That is your signature, is it not? hissed the Red Guillotine.

But even now, too many of our judges failed to understand that every verdict is a political verdict! There can be neutrality, no "objectivity," in a court of law. That is why we now named Comrade Benjamin Vice-President of the Supreme Court. *She proved capable,* says the legend, *of disciplining enemies of the new republic with unrelenting severity.*

Why haven't you admitted that you were in the hire of the British Secret Service? she shouted.

No, I wasn't at all aware that there was anyone there, replied the defendant weakly; I'm afraid that he made a poor impression in our courtroom.

You didn't know that at all, although you did sign this receipt!

But that's merely an everyday business document—

Don't evade in that fashion. Don't put up a front as if you were stupid. You were doing business with monopolists whom we've already arrested. There. I've said it. And you were going to your appointment with the British Secret Service, right? *Yes or no?* screamed the Red Guillotine.

He sought to wriggle out of it; he wouldn't answer correctly. Within the hour came the sentence of death, which she imposed for the unity for the German people and the freedom of the entire world.

14

On 23.5.52, three months after Humboldt University awarded her an honorary doctorate, our Law on the State Prosecution Service finally allowed us to control the decisions of judges and prosecutors directly. Beneath a lamp's white mushroom she signed another death sentence with a gleaming silver pen, her hair braided up on top of her head, books on the shelves in the background, a round stone gleaming in the ring; she signed with drooping eyelids and clenched lips like a woman doing some household task.

As soon as the Anglo-American crypto-Fascist clique rejected Comrade Stalin's moderate proposal for a united neutralized Germany, the Red Guillotine showed them that we saw through their despicable actions. This time she'd surely render harmless her nightmare that there might actually be a nest of Nazis in the ground, some of whom were silently playing Skat in a logwalled bunker, with their death's head caps resting on their knees and their rifles leaning against the wall; one of them hunched over a crystal set with his headphones on and a map on the wall beside him; he was giving away our state secrets to the reactionary Adenauer, the traitor Tito, the traitor Schumacher and the American imperialists. In my opinion she was strangely elegant in her dark suit with the white button shirt beneath, the triangular pin over her left breast; in the name of the people she presided over the trial of the contemptible Wolfgang Kaiser, who'd committed the crime of establishing contact with a so-called "human rights organization" in West Germany. He attempted to justify himself—but not for long. With what we Germans call a *Lustschrei,* a cry of pleasure, she proved that his intention had been to plant bombs and poison cigarettes. We decapitated him on 6.9.52—a natural outgrowth of our democratic antifascist tendencies.

She attended the vast Party Conference in July, when we set out formally to build socialism in our Germany; we also agreed on the necessity of further hardening our line. In this spirit, the Red Guillotine passed our first new constitutional legislation. Then she had to rush off to condemn more saboteurs.

15

Johann Burianek sabotaged a bridge with explosives supplied to him by the American imperialists; we made him memorize his confession before we *sent him where he belonged.* Don't worry; he won't come back.

That fall a West German journalist issued the following verdict: *Who has ever once experienced this woman when she pulls out all the stops of her ice-cold intellect won't soon forget her. She alone is the law.*

16

In 1953, in ungrateful discord with A. Pohl's landmark film "The Invincible Ones," whose protagonist is the German working class, certain enemies of democracy resisted the imposition of labor-norms. For her own part, the Red Guillotine took every rational measure to prevent the forthcoming uprising. For instance, she rendered harmless the electrician Kurt König, who'd carried out military espionage against the Soviet Union on the territory of our own German Democratic Republic! Would Kriemhild ever have forgiven her husband's murderer even had he bent the knee? Not likely, and he knew it. Defiance therefore would have cost this König no portion of his already foredoomed safety, and saved his pride. But now he was exhausted. He begged and pleaded before we guillotined him.

All the same, they dared to carry this banner against us: **WE DEMAND A REDUCTION IN THE NORMS**. The Red Guillotine saw that for what it was: a Fascist provocation. Indeed, within a few instants they'd also begun misleading the masses with the so-called "human rights question." Half the workers were striking at the Bergmann-Borsig Engineering Works! The "Progress" clothing combine also became infected. Soon there were five hundred thousand criminals! The Red Guillotine shook her head in a fury when the telephone informed her of flames and broken windows at the Potsdamer Platz! The telephone commanded: *Declare martial law in a hundred and sixty-seven districts.*

Fortunately for people's power, we still had nineteen Red Army divisions. The stonethrowers at the Potsdamer Platz had no better success against our T-34s now than in 1945.

Our Minister of Justice, Fechner, who'd been foolish enough to support the workers' right to strike against their own regime, was removed on 16.7.53. In his place we appointed the Red Guillotine. And now her legend truly begins.

As the *Great Soviet Encyclopedia* explains it: *The General Prosecuting Authority, headed by the prosecutor general of the GDR, exercises supervision over the observance of socialist legality.* The General Prosecuting Authority now found full and natural expression in the Red Guillotine.

On the Invalidenstrasse, just east of where the Wall would soon rise, the Kaiser-Wilhelm-Akademie für die Ausbildung von Militärärzten, completed in 1905, Nazified in 1933, was now Hilde Benjamin's courthouse, and every morning she arrived at 0800 hours precisely; at 0750 she was joking with the two Rubblefrauen she saw every day on the other side of the street; one of them wore goggles and kept her white-dusted hair up in a bun; the other, who was younger, wore a dark skirt which went not far below the knee; at the recess, the Red Guillotine frequently saw them sitting on bricks, resting their backs against the brickheap they'd built; the Rubblefrau in goggles stared off into space and the Rubblefrau in the skirt read the newspaper. But that was only for a year. Then the rubble near the courthouse had all been cleared. The Red Guillotine missed those two women a little. Sometimes in summer she wandered to the window and gazed westward. She could see the way that the foliage of the Tiergarten paints the summer clouds green. *Her most important trials are known,* runs the legend, *and need not be mentioned further.*

17

We arrested six thousand criminals, Fascists and foreign agents. Soviet military tribunals began shooting the ringleaders in August; we'd already liquidated several others. The Red Guillotine is said to have taken pleasure in being present at these affairs; she particularly enjoyed inspecting the coffin beforehand. In her Stasi file, an evaluation from this period reports that `Comrade BENJAMIN is from the professional and political standpoint an extremely qualified comrade. She works scientifically.` She'd long since added to our penal code the crimes of offense against work discipline, offense against Plan discipline. Scornfully she addressed the defendants: You have the right to strike, yes, but a Fascist *putsch* is not a strike! In the name of the people, I find you *guilty*; you are sentenced to *death*!—and she drank a glass of water.

As we would expect, she never failed to distinguish carefully in her verdicts between misguided workers and provocateurs.

18

What about Fechner? This question remained on the lips of the working class until 1955, when our darling Red Guillotine arrested him. She gave him an opportunity to clarify his attitude, not for his own sake but for the sake of our people who had yet to learn the meaning of vigilance. Then she sentenced him to eight years.

19

She assembled new brigades of instructors in the courts, to command the judges, and further transform them from dupes of bourgeois "objectivity" into uncompromising fighters—a task all the more compelling since she'd now begun to worry that many of her own colleagues might be unsteady, insubstantial in the work. She instructed her minions: *We can show neither softness nor weakness in the confrontation against the adversary of our order. Therefore, hard punishments are correct punishments.*

Marveling at her accomplishments during this period, Comrade Gotthold Bley implicitly compares her to a factory proletarian when he writes that *socialist law and socialist legislation were tools, motors and levers she used.*

She withdrew the new proposed Criminal Code, which wasn't strict enough. (Believe it or not, in many subcategories of law we continued to rely on the Criminal Code of 1871.) Justice now became as neat as the salvaged bricks stacked on carts in Dresden. With a bitter smile, she laced her fingers like scissors, her eyes glittering almost happily as she unraveled another plot. (Comrade Büttner: *She solidified the dialectical interrelation between law and society in the general consciousness.)*

In September she condemned Werner Hoffmann, who'd wormed his way all the way up to the Ministry of the Interior. I'll never forget the way her lips parted like a beak as she clenched the lectern, demanding *death*.

In October, since the purpose of our justice system is to smash the resistance of expropriated monopolists for all time and defend the achievements of the workers against external enemies, we liquidated the engineer Christian Lange-Werner, whose Nazi connections can be proved. I was there when the Red Guillotine cried out: *Only here in the German Democratic Republic have we learned the lessons of the past.*

This wretched Lange-Werner tried to justify himself.—Lies! laughed the Red Guillotine, and the whole world laughed with her.

She proved to all of us that he had attempted betrayal of the Fatherland to the West German agent codenamed SYLVIA, who no doubt worked for British intelligence, the American imperialists, Department K-5 and the Gehlen Organization. While his trial was still in progress, the Red Guillotine commanded: *The sentence is to be carried out immediately after a reprieve has been turned down.*

By the time we had elevated her to full Zentralkomitee status, she was the terror of imperialists everywhere, and her Stasi file accordingly reports that on 28. 1. 54 it came to our attention that the American Secret Service planted an accomplice to carry out terrorist acts against Frau Dr. Hilde BENJAMIN. But we caught him; we guillotined him in secret.

20

The forces of revanchism paid her other compliments. One winter night, unknown persons erected a mock gallows on the roof of her dacha in Brieselang; they even hanged a straw doll from it—an outrageous provocation. We were the ones who informed her; we noticed it at dawn, when she was still sleeping. When the black telephone advised her of the situation, she turned pale, but quickly laughed it off. To soothe her, we arrested four suspicious individuals at once, and it's certainly possible that one of them might have been the culprit.

Ever since we'd taken note of a strange rumor, reported several times by our informants, that she had fled to Switzerland en route to Israel, because she was a Jew. This simply shows how crucial it remains to exterminate the Fascist criminals without mercy. For instance, two workers were drinking at an inn, and one said to the other: *There are three kinds of people here: those who have been arrested, those who are arrested and those who will be arrested.* The black telephone overheard, which meant that so did the Red Guillotine. Leaning forward in her pale grey suit, the light ricocheting off her dark grey hair, she gazed across the thicket of microphones with the same rapt sincerity as a child begging for candy, and her moist little lips parted as she demanded *death, death, death.*

21

She began to say that to achieve the future we needed to study the lessons of the past still more closely. She had herself chauffeured to Dresden to attend another lecture given by the former German Fascist Field-Marshal Paulus, who blamed Hitler, von Manstein and the monopolists for everything—which is the correct line, after all. His glaring white old man's face gaped in what might have been meant to be firmness, his eyes huge as if panicked behind the heavy black spectacles as he stood at the lectern, a glass of water never far away. The Red Guillotine sat in the back row, smiling. On her lap she held a Stasi folder. From time to time, she opened it and peeked humorously at the topmost item, which was a photograph of Paulus in the Nuremberg Palace of Justice eight years before, when Germany remained undivided; he'd resembled a scarecrow in the witness stand; a white helmeted military policeman stood beside him; wires ran from Paulus's earphones; he stared queasily ahead; only the MP was looking back at him. For some reason she could not explain, this image gave her pleasure.

22

In 7.54, thanks to steadily increasing cooperation between the courts and our people's representatives, we guillotined the former Nazi Wilhelm Wolff for causing epidemics in farm animals on our collective farms, and for other equally depraved crimes. I attended his trial; I remember Hilde Benjamin standing at the lectern, digging her fingers into it as she leaned toward the microphone, shouting: *No freedom for the enemies of democracy!*

Called on to defend himself, the Fascist reptile Wolff pointed out that he would have had no motive to cause an epidemic.

Replied the Red Guillotine: Here is your motive—to spread unrest.

And she condemned him to *death, death, death.*

23

By 1955 she was squat and shapeless like a frog; I saw her flashing her crazy teeth at the Albanians. On 8.3.55, not quite a week before we sentenced Paul Köppe to death, the Politbüro confirmed his condemnation (the bourgeois get the order backwards). On the same day, in the Rudloff trial, when the General State Prosecutor proposed leniency, the Red Guillotine stepped in to save society from this four-time murderer.

I've seen her in a short pale trenchcoat, with her head and knees both bare and her hands in her pockets, striding grimly just behind Comrade Ulbricht, whose trenchcoat is much longer and who wears a tophat almost like a capitalist; his right arm is locked in a salute, the knife-edge of his hand is wedged against the brim of his hat as he and the Red Guillotine march down the rain-shiny tarmac of Potsdam, not quite treading on the reflected heads of the rifle-bearing soldiers who face them in a long, long wall; everybody is saluting except for the Red Guillotine.

In 5.55, when we guillotined Karl-Ernst Hahn and Alfred Rzepio for their failed murder of a taxi driver, a crime which had been suggested to them by American gangster movies, the Red Guillotine cried out: *As Comrade Mielke has noted, they have expelled themselves from the working class!* and our democratic jurists, in close cooperation with the security organs of reborn Germany, concurred. With her fingers spread and pointing upward, her lips earnestly parted, she stood before the microphone, utterly sincere as she called for another death, another death.

There was a sleepy aspect to her now, as if she were a well-fed sacred crocodile which could always count on receiving the next human sacrifice. Sometimes she only half-opened her eyes. She yawned at times (poor Comrade Benjamin is getting old after all her sufferings!), cutting off the defendant with an upraised finger instead of an angry word-assault. But if he dared to plead his case instead of confessing, or, worse yet, sought to contradict her, then the Red Guillotine could still snap! On 14.9.55, when we liquidated the former Stasi agents Susanne and Bruno Krieger for espionage against our state, the masses cheered like Arctic workers raising their gloved fists in salute in a Roman Karmen movie. All the same, some were disappointed; for the Red Guillotine didn't give them much of a show. Possibly that was because the Kriegers failed to stick up for themselves. (Susanne Krieger had believed that she wouldn't be guillotined if she incriminated others. There's no reason to keep our agreements with such people.)

That same month, when we disposed of Director Nellis of the J. W. Stalin Electrical Works for sabotage, the technical manageress of the factory stationed herself in the courtroom to bring back reports to all his former colleagues. She was there when the Red Guillotine's round, coarse face grew cheerful, split into smiles, and denounced Director Nellis to pieces. She demanded *death, death, death*. How could we deny her that treat?

In 1.56, we guillotined the Fascist agents of the United States Werner Rudert and Max Held. When the Politburo confirmed their sentences, her smile grew as full of fat and sugar as one of our *intelligentsia parcels*. Then she took a nap at her desk, snoring and grinning.

24

On 4.11.56 she arrived at the courthouse at 0755 hours for the Hagen trial. Nikolai from Stalingrad smiled at her in a sparkle of steel teeth; his greeting always temporarily undid that heavy, pale, somehow distinguished sadness in her head which dragged it down; the dark heaviness of her suit grew bright because his Kalashnikov was shining.

Well, well, Comrade Benjamin, so will another head roll today?

Count on it! laughed the Red Guillotine.

She imagined that he liked her, but he was terrified of her.

And up she went to her office, where a picture-gallery of deceased saints gazed down at her: the pioneer prosecutor E. Melsheimer, the constitutionalist K. Polak, brave G. Dmitroff, who'd defied a Hitlerite court and won, and of course that representative of the international workers' movement, Felix Dzherzhinsky, whose "organs" have liquidated millions of human beings in our beloved Soviet Union.

They brought in the defendant, whose desperate face reminded her of the white-cratered blackness of our opera house's scorched facade. The Red Guillotine was already there; she preferred to have her victims find everything already in place. They'd be marched in, and there sat the Red Guillotine at the center of her long high desk, with a bust of Comrade Ulbricht on her left and a bust of Comrade Stalin on her right. In her signature dark suit, white blouse and black cravat, she surveyed the world, her head held high and her arms folded while she gazed complacently down at our socialist reporters and photojournalists, then slowly, slowly turned her head right to inspect her latest prey, who as he was led to his seat in the dock, hemmed in by secret police and the so-called "defense" attorneys, could scarcely help feeling like a pupil late for school. And that was merely the beginning of what he felt; because it's now time to turn our attention to the dread which her presence somehow injected into people, paralyzing them as if with a spider's poison, so that they grew confused, submissive, silent. Later on, when they were being led to the whitewashed execution chamber, they spent the last instants of their lives seeking in vain to understand how she had entrapped them; the truth is that her mouth was not eloquent (it didn't need to be; it licked its lips with a grey and gleeful tongue); her logic could never be recapitulated—how could it be? For the condemned were innocent, by those "objective" human standards which are now obsolete.

Now, who was *this* one? It seems that when a team of Rubblefrauen were raising up the remains of the gravestones in the Jewish cemetery they heard a noise, so three of them stood round the hole with shovels raised to strike, while the fourth ran for the People's Police. The Fascist war criminal Hagen had ensconced himself there. What a provocation! The Anglo-Americans had pretended to hang him at Nuremberg, and here he was! He had a tunnel and even a crystal set so that he could receive orders from the enemies of our new Germany. It was the Anglo-Fascist Operation Gold all over again. Our brave

People's Police, led by Oberst H. Scholz, ran to give their aid; Red Army men came speeding down Leninallee in their Vopo-Jeeps. And so we captured the imperialist snake Hagen.

First pursing her fat grey lips, then showing her crooked teeth, the Red Guillotine narrowed her eyes at the defendant, who gazed insolently back at her. Oh, she felt a rage coming on! Meanwhile, in the name of East Germany's smiling chemists and laughing athletes, our Young Pioneers (ages six to ten) were already shrieking out *Down with the traitor!* while our Thälmann Pioneers (eleven to fourteen) waved beautifully lettered placards in support of our inevitably just sentence, whatever it might be.

Esteemed comrades and friends! began the Red Guillotine *in the name of the people*; and her wide little eyes and parted little lips definitely stood ready to do justice. Vigilance against the reptiles! Spies beware! We've caught another one!

And still, no matter how she glowered and glared, the Fascist traitor refused to lower his eyes, and thereby revealed his negative attitude. How pale he was! He must have been a long time underground.

All the preparations were ready. His sentence had already been confirmed. She felt that she could hardly rest until he was in the grave, with his head severed from his shoulders.

Confesss your criminal activities, began the Red Guillotine.

Which ones? laughed Hagen.

When Hagen not only refuses to rise for Siegfried's widow, but lays across his lap the jasper-jeweled sword of the man he's murdered, the bard who's made him grows gleeful; what's more manly than open defiance, especially in the presence of a superior host? Hagen knows he's doomed, and shows off his hostility in that sword's beauty and insulting nakedness.

The Red Guillotine gazed back into his defiant face and experienced a hideous sense of familiarity. It had never been her habit to indulge the so-called "feelings," so the sensations of sorrow and repugnance which now assaulted her were overwhelmingingly inexplicable. This Hagen had been, said the indictment, a guard at KZ-Mauthausen. Although Georg's death had been officially judged a suicide, we all know how *those people* do things. It was possible that Hagen had witnessed or even precipitated her husband's death. All the same, a true Communist remains unaffected by such things.

Defendant Hagen, you committed crimes against the people, did you not?

That I did.

Then why did you say to the arresting officers that you had done *nothing out of the ordinary,* when you knew perfectly well that such was not the case?

The accused began to answer: I can't say it any more exactly than this—

In fact, you can say it extremely exactly! laughed the Red Guillotine, and the courtroom laughed with her. But you want to make fools of us.

No, I don't want to . . . he whispered. At least, that is what the others had always whispered. But Hagen didn't whisper at all. In fact, he chuckled: You're not simply a Jew by marriage, now, are you, Frau Benjamin? You're a *blood-Jew.* Do you know what Germans think about blood-Jews?

She went greyish-white.

Of course she condemned him to *death*—one more example of the impartiality of justice in our German Democratic Republic. To us onlookers she explained: This sentence is a warning for all who waver in the defense of our state, for all who fail to press forward for the victory of world peace.

But her round pale face writhed and trembled restlessly.

25

After that she seemed to age ever more swiftly, and the set of her mouth expressed weariness and disgust. Neither torchlight processions in our traditional German manner nor trainloads of glistening coal gladdened her. The smoke of the past hung so gloomily over everything! And that dream she had, the one of the tarnished silver box whose lock she could not master, she could never understand why it caused her such anxiety.

She came into the Stasi office and Comrade Mielke was all smiles; but she wondered whether an instant before her arrival he'd been making anti-Semitic innuendos against her.

In 1956, when we created our National People's Army to counter the increasing threat from the West, the second Five-Year Plan was approved, and Roman Karmen made the film "India's Dawn." Meanwhile, de-Stalinization began. This put the Red Guillotine in almost as awkward a position as Comrade Ulbricht. In any event, it was already being said of her that her energies had slackened. What she used to demand of those within her power was confession. After Hagen, what she longed for more than anything was silence before the quick conviction. Her courtrooms were no longer quite so full of sadistically expectant onlookers. And now, without regard to the very serious internal and external situation we faced in those days, *Neues Deutschland,* following Comrade Khruschev's line, dared to attack her for being *schematic and unbending.*

We retreated; we amnestied twenty-one thousand criminals. Fortunately, the so-called "Hungarian uprising" gave us the excuse we needed to reestablish our standards. On 17.10.56, the Red Guillotine announced: *We cannot permit ourselves to dispense with the death penalty. There have been no unjust sentences in our German Democratic Republic.*

All the same, in 1957 we agreed to punish murder with twenty-five years' imprisonment, not death. I saw her sitting beside the Hungarian Minister of Justice, Ferenc Nezval, each of them isolated, and later that same day she signed this dreadful piece of legislation in a bizarre ceremony of abstruse plainness, while dark-suited figures stood behind them in a line, and behind them hung a huge portrait of a man with white hair: Comrade Ulbricht. Fortunately, treason, espionage and kindred crimes could still be penalized as they deserved.

I'm told that she attended the funeral of the former Field-Marshal Paulus, which for political reasons was a restrained affair. Afterward she sat at the writing-desk of her hotel room, opened her briefcase, removed the Stasi folder, withdrew the second photograph, which showed Paulus in a waist-deep trench at Stalingrad, clasping his wrist and seeming to push away at the enemy as the men in uniform who surround him gaze obediently on; laughing, she tore this photograph to pieces.

She signed another death sentence, and then I saw her speaking earnestly with Erich Mückenberger, her missing and crooked teeth giving her a cheaply monstrous expression; the sentence was not carried out. Meanwhile her Stasi file began to contain complaints of her overbearing, imperious, "uncolleaguish" lapses of temper. It was around this time that we reinvestigated her past record and discovered that the years 1937–39, which her autobiographical statement claimed she'd spent as a retail employee, were in fact passed in a Jewish-owned pastry shop. It's not that we have anything against Jews in *our* Germany. (I won't speak for the West.) All the same, one can't be too careful, given the adventurism of the Zionists nowadays. It's possible that a report was made to Comrade Mielke. On the other hand, I can't believe that anything came of it. The memorial tribute she wrote to Georg Benjamin a few years later was published to careful acclaim.

On 5 December, when we'd passed around cigarettes and schnapps to celebrate Soviet Constitution Day, she tried to ingratiate herself with Comrade

Honecker, who was obviously going to be Number One sooner or later, but he snubbed her.

I've seen her in her fur coat, standing next to SED- Zentralkomitee Secretary Grüneberg in 1958, by which time we had completely liquidated unemployment. That was when peace-loving peoples of the Soviet Union demanded that the Anglo-American imperialists demilitarize Berlin. Needless to say, the imperialists rejected this just demand. No matter. When the time is ripe we will open their eyes.

At another ceremony with Soviet soldiers she was smiling, looking sweet, with her grey hair braided in coils upon the top of her head; and her striped scarf appeared quite stylish within the fur coat. Particularly as she aged, she came to have a strangely sweet meditative face, round and soft as she sat at a white-clothed table with a line of other dignitaries; she could be a Jewish refugee, which by marriage she was, or a Spanish gypsy woman or even Käthe Kollwitz herself with that heavy round face; oh, how odd that she could be Käthe Kollwitz! As the Programmatic Declaration of the State Council so perfectly put it in 1960: *Our laws are the realization of human freedom.*

That same year, when the Stasi expanded its powers and membership in order to better spy on *hostile-negatives;* when we executed the traitor Manfred Smolka; when Roman Karmen directed "Our Friend Indonesia" and Shostakovich composed Opus 110, we resumed our drive for forced collectivization—a task which the drought of 1959 had made doubly urgent. Who was willing to undertake the prosecutions for failure to deliver harvest quotas? Why, our dear Red Guillotine! (Comrade Bley: *Based on the teachings of Lenin, she envisioned a necessary direction for the workers' and farmers' movement in socialist legislation.)* Meanwhile, the Red Guillotine sat frail and uncomfortable in the front row of a gathering, her hand gripping the armrest, her white legs crossed for the hundred and fiftieth anniversary of Humboldt University.

Naturally, our increased efforts to socialize agriculture caused more parasites to flee the nation—two thousand of them a day!—The Red Guillotine sent the ones we caught to prison, crying to the courtroom: *To get a free education and then run away, is that decent?* All the same, more and more of them got away. So Comrade Ulbricht was forced to build the Wall—or, as it's more properly termed, the *anti-Fascist protective barrier.* That worked perfectly. It made manifest to the world the utter divide between our new Germany and what has been aptly called *nazideutscher Faschismus.* The telephone screamed for joy. *Only a shambles was left of Adenauer's "policy of strength,"* Comrade Honecker gloated.

26

She drafted our Family Law of 1966, which protects the property of wives after marriage and requires parents to educate their children with a socialist outlook. How many other countries can boast such progressive legislation? Her head was tilted, showing the part in her hair as she signed; a man from the Zentralkomitee bent over her, while at her right another man was bending over Comrade Ulbricht. They gave her the Service Medal of the National People's Army in gold. But her ideals were already being lost.

Regarding the Volkskammer elections of 1967, it had been arranged immediately before her one-week trip to Bulgaria that she would be put up for candidature as usual; but three days after her return, on 30.5.67, she called her chauffeur and had herself driven to Potsdam in that tiny-windowed limousine so that she could take care of the formalities, only to discover that she wasn't going to be nominated after all; and, in fact, that her term as Minister of Justice was over. A report by Richter Hauptmann of the Stasi describes her as `between astonished and angry`. Her round grey head sank deep between her dark-suited shoulders. And so she found herself obliged to step aside for Dr. Kurt Wünsche. After all, she was now sixty-five.

She took a few mementoes with her, including a folder whose only exhibit now was a grainy photograph of Paulus from the side as he enters his captivity, head up. Now she entered hers, in her two-storey house in the new concrete-walled restricted area between Basdorf and Wandlitz, with its tennis court and shooting range; according to Comrade Ulbricht, the food was far better than it had been at the "reserved" restaurant in Moscow's Hotel Lux. She could walk over to Justice Minister Matern's house whenever she pleased, or even to Comrade Ulbricht's, which boasted Chinese silk hangings. But she didn't like either of them. Sometimes when she went to get a massage she met Comrade Ulbricht doing calisthenics, and she did her best to be polite, but how could she forget that he had not prevented her removal?

In '68, we firmly supported the Soviet Union against the Czech provocateurs. Listening to her radio at home, the Red Guillotine screamed: *Death, death!* The year after that, the Soviet Union sold us out and normalized relations with West Germany! (Look! There's Roman Karmen, smiling amiably at little crewcut children as he films "Comrade Berlin." He'll come back again soon for a retrospective in celebration of his sixty-fifth birthday. But none of this makes the Red Guillotine feel any better.)

That September she attended an international legal conference at Walter Ulbricht German Academy of State and Law, but she was only a lecturer in the history of law; she was no longer allowed to do what she'd been put on earth to do. The lessons of the Hagen case were forgotten. And everything got worse and worse in our ever more advanced socialist society right up until 1989, the last year of her old age, by which time her dark eyes kept looking away from everything, while her drawn mouth showed teeth. A few months after she closed her eyes forever, so did East Germany.

Well, what had she accomplished? By 1967, seventy-five percent of our judges in the regional and district courts derived from the working class. *To be remembered here is her impartiality, as well as her distinct contributions to refining the family law system and conducting cases consistent with the culture of socialist jurisdiction.* Her praises stretch as long as the lines at the Intertank gas station. By the time she retired, ninety-three hundred industrial enterprises had been demonopolized and transferred to the ownership of the people; thirteen thousand seven hundred farms had been confiscated by local agencies of self-government! Much of this vital work was accomplished in the courtroom, for which we must thank our Red Guillotine. The sly cones of the SM-70 automatic shooting devices on the Wall were not in place until the seventies; we can't give her credit for instituting those; but she could be proud of having presided over our new Criminal Code of 1968, which respects Soviet justice even more, and replaces beheading by (I quote the regulations) *an unexpected shot at close quarters in the back of the head.* As Comrade Mielke always used to say: Short schrift to all of them! Because I'm a humanitarian.

27

In the first week of August 1971, Comrade Mielke himself picked up the telephone. The call originated on Majakowskiweg 18/20. The ancient female voice on the line was so hysterical that for a long time he could hardly understand what it was saying.

She had in any case been sleeping very poorly that summer on account of a recurring dream, that dream of the black iron box which none could open; and then the first anonymous telephone call came, very early at morning: *Your coffin is ready, Comrade Benjamin.*

Shuddering, she disconnected the line with a clang almost as loud as the sleepwalker's; and then she sat on the sofa, trembling.

The telephone rang again. *Comrade Benjamin, your coffin is right outside.*

And again, and again! Each time her coffin was coming closer. Finally she called the special number at the Stasi. That was when Comrade Mielke decided to handle this business personally.

Our People's Police have always honorably fulfilled their duty against German Fascists; moreover, she was *one of us*, so they arrested somebody just to satisfy her, but then the telephone rang again. The undertaker was calling for Comrade Benjamin.

It's because I'm a Jew, isn't it? she whispered to Comrade Mielke. Tell me frankly, just because I married a Jew do you consider me a Jew? ▸

WE'LL NEVER MENTION IT AGAIN

Everywhere that Torah is studied at night
one thread-thin ray appears from that hidden light
and flows down upon those absorbed in her.
—Kabbalah (13th century)

1

Every time she said no to him, that no was as perfect as her cheekbones.

There was about her something comfortably immovable, reassuringly merciless—still, silent, slender and incorruptible, hence ultimately fragile; since she was too good to bend, she would have had to shatter if she'd ever said yes; which was why to the very end he remained able to be proud of himself for accepting her refusals with his best if fallible grace, loving and respecting her all the more for not giving him all of herself. He cherished her, so he must cherish the coherence which she'd created with the other man and which his touch would accordingly have broken. He loved her; he would not damage her.

He asked her for her photograph at least and she gazed at him across the table, then said so quietly: No.

Not long after that, his First Cello Concerto in E-flat Major premiered, so there were any number of women, not that at his age he could always, you know, and so, forty minutes after the embarrassing recording session with Rostropovich, there was a woman who pretty soon was kissing him and kissing him, lying on top of him on the big hotel bed, holding him tight so that some of the loneliness oozed away, leaving him sufficiently clearheaded to win some chance of not committing errors if he only considered rapidly and logically what on earth he wanted, this woman, this kind woman who liked him and who had already told him that after the merest four hours of his company, for three hours of which she had seen him only across a loudly crowded room which shone with liquor-glasses (my dear lady, thank you for your, your, you know, but I, I, well, I simply took a simple little theme and I did my simple, *simple* best to develop it!), she now felt jealous of all the other women who might be in his life (he never told her about the one with the dark, dark hair), this woman who was lying on top of him might help him; because what he needed was something sexual so that he could relieve a portion of his desire for the woman with the dark hair and thereby alleviate the nuisance which his passion inflicted upon her, although I don't quite mean nuisance, I mean anguish, misery, outright harm, because she *cared* for him; and since he himself had, so to speak, reciprocal feelings, the something sexual which he now sought from the woman on top of him must not be *too* sexual, for he would not betray, lapse in fidelity to, the woman with the dark, dark hair, whose unmade double bed (at that time she'd still been married to R. L. Karmen) he'd once seen with an agony (not of jealousy, only of a sensation we can't call loss, since he no longer possessed any fragment of her to lose) which for an instant he mistakenly supposed that he couldn't bear. That was before Nina died. And now the darkhaired woman was married to Professor Vigodsky. He bore it; he composed a string quartet. Later he would telephone the darkhaired woman—oh, how much he loved telephones! Then he married Margarita, who did her narrow best to fill Nina's place; she wasn't very, well, you understand what I mean. So he asked the woman on top of him whether she would kindly do him the favor of laying her gentle fingers on his throat, then strangling him just a little and a little more, which between smiles, whispers and long kisses she affectionately did, assuring him that she didn't mind one way or the other if it was what he needed, and because she hadn't been told how dangerous it was, she went farther than Galina Ustvolskaya ever had, farther than his first love Tatyana Glivenko, farther even than the other one, his darkhaired one who'd left him forever and from whose memory a continuing and even now not entirely unrequited love had saved him with shocking power. So the woman on top of him, kissing his mouth again and again, dreamily reached for his throat whenever she felt like it, smiling at his smile of grateful anticipatory happiness; then she laid down her soft hands just below his chin and began to squeeze, *legato, dolce,* her eyes so intent on his eyes as her fingers began to dig into him and take hold of his wildly worthless life which he yearned to lay down at the feet of the darkhaired woman for her to keep or break as she chose, the keeping or breaking equally conformable to his thrilling acceptance because he was hers and if she destroyed him, he would remain hers completely whereas if instead she raised him up to her starshine face for awhile, then he could knowingly be with her that much longer. Elena, you're so lucky you didn't marry me. A red spot was spinning. By now somebody unfamiliar to him was uttering involuntary noises from a throat, deeper than the noises which he himself made in orgasm, yet broken like a scattering of cylindrical beads which had once made up a necklace; these staccato, somewhat unpleasant, not really liquid sounds, neither coughs nor gurgles nor metronome-clicks which he would represent musically in the third movement of Opus 110, seemed to substitute quite well for the breathing which he no longer could or desired to accomplish; he sank into a delightful swoony feeling which should have never ended but always did, at which point his heart broke because he found himself alone, meaning without the darkhaired woman.

Lying alone on that big empty bed with his hands ice-cold and his heart and throat so tight with the tension of waiting for the black telephone to ring or not ring ever again anymore, he eventually realized that it would not ring, because the darkhaired woman must have finished at the Conservatory hours ago, so he dialed the number without worrying about anybody in raspberry-colored boots, not to mention that other man, Vigodsky; when the other man answered he hung up; an hour later he called again, this time succeeding in hearing her sleep-husky voice, a voice *ritenuto,* to which he choked out: I want so much to have you on top of me here on this bed, Elena; I need you on top of me, kissing and kissing and *kissing* me . . .

Then he turned out the light and lay there beginning to taste blood inside his throat. He switched on the radio, just to, you know. It was Klavdia Sulzhenko singing "The Blue Kerchief": *The machine-gunner fights for the blue kerchief those dear shoulders wore.* He silenced her, not that she didn't have a certain something; it was just that he, anyhow, our life is such a comedy. The next morning he put on a highcollared shirt because his neck was bruised by the kind woman's fingers, which had been almost as white and perfect as the darkhaired woman's teeth.

2

Last October, when they'd met around the corner from the Eliseyev department store three hours before the premiere of his Eleventh Symphony, it had been snowing and they were both late. She had adjusted his necktie just like a wife.

He requested her to please leave him gently if she ever left him, to which she replied that they no longer were and never would be together anyway.—Oh, you're a wise one! he laughed. Give me another English lesson!—Then, overcoming his agony, he insisted, *mezzo piano,* that of course they were together. He knew what he knew; didn't she know it, too? Hadn't she herself admitted that she sometimes kept silent instead of saying whatever it was that she might be feeling? Whenever he came to Leningrad, which was often nowadays, there always being something new to rehearse, she saw him either every day or else almost every day, and when she sat across from him at the hard currency bar she nearly always smiled so tenderly! How could she deny that? Therefore, he explained to her, she probably still loved him, at least to a degree, which was precisely why he had telephoned her so late that night to tell her how much he longed for her to be with him now in this hotel room, lying on top of him, kissing him, kissing him, to which on the next day, after Rostropovich had driven him to Komarovo, she had replied by telephoning him there (he'd given her his itineraries, hotels, residences and numbers, especially his sister Mariya's) to declare in her soft firm voice that she didn't want him to whisper any more messages like that into her ear ever again because they were too sad.

The pain which this caused him was nearly beyond expression, but only nearly; musically there's always a way to, how should I say. He could never "have" her in his intended sense of having her lie down on top of him in an empty room and hold him tight, not even for one hour, let alone for ever and ever. Even at the Philharmonic he didn't dare to, if you see what I'm saying, take any chances which might, so to speak, make him noticed. He'd sent her a pair of tickets for the premiere last October. It was nice of them to come; Vigodsky bestowed upon him that strangely French smile of his. If only she could have, well, but he himself had to sit next to Margarita, who'd really tarted herself up, the little . . . Sometimes he hardly knew why he . . . Akhmatova could inevitably be spotted in the audience, usually in the company of her friend Z. B. Tomashevskaya. Was her son still *away*? Poor lady; poor lady! She was extremely, well, you know. He steered clear of both those ladies, fearing that Akhmatova in particular might have learned too many of his secrets. There in the fourth row sat the darkhaired one; she smiled at her husband, impersonally he hoped, then, unfortunately, laid down her head on his shoulder. Why couldn't she at least . . . ? Once upon a time, on a linden alley at Tsarkoe Selo, they'd been kissing on a bench and then she'd rested her head on his shoulder and her hair, oh, my God, her long, dark hair. And now she was doing it with Vigodsky, which he found extremely . . . When he sat alone at these Leningrad rehearsals he always wished that she were beside him, but of course that would have been especially, so to speak, demonstrative. Perhaps if Glikman could act as go-between once again she might at least sort of, I mean, but even that would be impossible; one aspect of her he especially admired was how quietly and immovably she could say no. Nina had also been like that. On the other hand, in every other sense he did have Elena; he could love her; he could think about her; better yet, just as the gentle arch of the Blue Bridge offers us the way to Saint Isaac's domes, so Opus 40 helps us over the cold dark waters of reality to the place where Elena is; Lyalka she liked me to call her, when we still . . . Elena, help me! Elena, I can't bear this! But you're the one person who must never comfort me for the same reason that you're the only one who could. Isn't that curious? I have represented this dilemma many times with *ostinato*. Tonight I'll . . .

I've already said that when he stayed over in Leningrad she met him almost every day, so that he could gaze into her beautiful eyes and sit close enough to touch her, on condition that he not touch her; he could tell her anything; she told him some things; in short, he could go on and on proudly loving her and being with her as long as he could tell her everything. But now she was saying that they had never been together and that he was not permitted to tell her everything. That was why he felt the strangling pain.

3

When the richly plump girl, who was even darkhaired, started kissing him so deeply with her paddle-shaped tongue, he stroked her hair and desired her, which is to say that he didn't desire her in and of herself; he simply needed to sojourn in any woman's body; so he took her into his arms on one of those empty double beds he slept in, but the instant he began to ride her, *prestissimo con moto* if he could say so himself, he saw the face of the woman he loved gazing at him right through the flesh of the substitute, whose whiteness might have been tracing paper, so little did it conceal that intensely looking and listening face of the darkhaired woman with its not quite sad quarter-smile of red, red lips which crazed his desire into something which could be expressed only chokingly, by falling on his knees when she wasn't there to be molested by his prayers; yes, so little could strange flesh conceal the dark, dark hair which glowed through it; and so his hands withered and fell away.

Thus, she, the one he loved, lay, not between them exactly, but beyond them, more real than either he or this other whom he was now inside; even with his eyes shut he could not help but see her face gazing steadily at him through the other woman's flesh; her eyes, unflinching and sad, remained on him; it was just as if she were sitting next to him on the sofa; she'd said that he didn't need to hide anything from her, that he could tell her anything . . .

He made the richly plump girl very happy, grateful even, and that was something, something to solve his own loneliness partially, and something good in and of itself.

Than he went to see the woman with the dark, dark hair.

How's your daughter, Elena?

She's well; thank you for asking—

Then he said to her: I believe you're trying not to, so to speak, love me, but I, I also believe you love me just the same.

What do you want, Mitya? It was so long ago—

And whenever you try to pretend that we're not together now—

We aren't.

Or that we never were together, when in fact—

She was turning away.

In point of fact, you, well. Recently I passed by that dacha near Luga. If you remember, you wrote our initials behind the head of the bed and told me not to look, so this time I, I, it turns out that the heart you drew is also still there; it survived the Germans.

I don't remember. I was never there; I hardly know you . . .

This is precisely what gives me hope, my dear Elena, when you, yes, yes, yes, I'm so sorry that now you're, please forgive me.

The next time he saw her he asked for her photograph again and she said no; the time after that he whispered: Do you have a photograph for me? and Elena *smiled*; she smiled with a lazy smile and said: Maybe.

Night after night he came to know the ambiguous boundary in that photograph between her yellow-ivory face and her hair, her dark, dark hair which framed it to the latitude of her lower lip so that her temples and her cheeks blended into something both gold and black, essence of tiger, while the white light frozen on each upcurling hair on her face's right side made a more zebra-ish contrast. If he could simply, well, or if she could meet him alone at Komarovo, which would have been out of the question, then . . . Margarita wouldn't care as long as he . . . She'd even make the bed afterward! Oh, Elena, you're so lucky you didn't marry me.

She was smiling at him, her dark eyes elongated by that smile, a smile which seemed to see and know him even though she hadn't met him in that year when the photograph was taken; he hadn't yet married Nina, either; the smile seemed to say: I accept your love and acknowledge it although I will never be yours; I will be your sky; you will always be able to look up and see me; I will never stop smiling upon you.

Needless to say, she'd been much younger when she was happily, lovingly, sincerely smiling in that way with her perfect red lips and perfect white teeth—how can a smile be described? Everybody has a mouth, you know! (Lebedinsky would understand. But he couldn't tell anyone, not even Lebedinsky. He'd promised her.) And her hair, her dark hair which she might have started dyeing by now, for she was forty-five, which he could hardly believe, had been just a little lighter in the sunlight of those days; his ballet "Bolt" had just premiered and she was sixteen; her hair had been almost reddish, because it had been so dark that it was almost every color, and every hair of her perfect eyebrows was visible against her fair, fair face; her dark eyes were smiling at somebody else, the unknown photographer; who it was she didn't remember, or said she didn't remember; later she said that it might have been her best friend Vera Ivanova; since then her face had tanned slightly and her hair had darkened.

As she got older, her eyes elongated less often into any smile; they gazed with loving intimacy at the other man, then at the other man after him; her deeply red lips which only the other man would ever taste half-smiled at the other man as they sometimes did at him who now possessed this photograph to be a relic and a comfort to him forever; and that hair, that dark, dark hair, brown or black depending on the light, made a living loving darkness in which the other man could rest.

Whenever he fell into that photograph, sinking far past the way that her face widened at the cheekbones and then, just below the mouth, drew in to make a long chin whose strange grace reminded him of a flute-note in a Haydn sonata, he was able to believe if he could have just waited and been patient for he'd never know how many years, she might perhaps have found herself able to give him more of herself without thereby damaging herself. Until she'd given him the photograph, the difficulty had been that he couldn't be sure that he possessed any part of her at all except for the handshake-equivalent which almost anybody would give almost anybody; for she was correct; that summer morning near Luga had never happened; Glikman was the one who had gone there for him and returned to say: My dear Dmitri Dmitriyevich, I'm sorry to tell you that only one wall is standing. A direct hit from a Tiger tank . . .

One night in Riga, where the connection wouldn't have been very good anyway, he didn't telephone her because, unable to endure his need for her, he'd gone to sleep beneath the kind woman who liked him very much, so that she could half-strangle him again, and the corporeal comfort of that woman's hands upon him, the balm of her liking (perhaps she even loved him now), the knowledge that had he nicely asked her to, she would have strangled him all the way to death—yes, she would have killed him so that he would sleep safely and forever in a woman's hands!—all this was indescribably assuaging at the very same time that it compounded his loneliness because he was quite aware that this woman who liked or loved him was not the woman with the dark, dark hair. So he couldn't telephone that night; that was the first night that he didn't; and in the morning, exhausted and even lower-voiced than usual, she confessed that she'd gotten literally hysterical, so much so that the other man had nearly noticed; and as soon as she had said this he realized that she had now let him inside herself, and then even before he'd laid down the telephone he became selfishly happy, although his happiness knew that the anguish of going back to that place of not being certain would be unendurable.

He knew that he had to be careful now in case his happiness panicked her in the same way that her hysteria had made him happy. Several measures later, as he rode to Leningrad in Rostropovich's car, they were discussing the color of a certain violin tremolo in his Jewish cycle and he was imagining what it would feel like if he could somehow persuade Rostropovich's wife Galina, the eminent soprano, to meet him somewhere and play his throat like a xylophone—an inexcusable fantasy, to be sure, which shamed him and rendered him deserving of punishment, since Rostropovich was as loyal as a leech—and then Rostropovich offered him a shy question about Prokofieff which he seemed to be pondering until Rostropovich, glancing away from the snowy road, saw that he had in fact retreated into the world beneath the black slabs and white snow of the piano keys. Her photograph had become the one place where he could be with her even if she wasn't with him. Her face, which had grown more sad and closed since the days of the photograph (or perhaps it appeared sad only when she was with him), he now knew better than his own. She should have been his.

On a morning as white as the sun-gleam upon her red, red lips in that photograph he was lying on the double bed in Leningrad with the telephone receiver against his face. He heard her usual silence, and then she very quietly said: You know, I'm going to have to ask for it back. I did the wrong thing. I hurt him and me and you. I'm sorry.

Well, that's quite true, to be sure. I fully . . . Maybe you'll change your mind again, Elena; that's my hope.

No. I won't change my mind.

All right.

There was a silence, and she said: We won't talk about it anymore. I won't say anything. Just, next time you see me, you can give it to me without saying anything.

But if you don't say anything I'll, you see, keep supposing that you might have changed your mind.

No. I won't. Just give it back and don't say anything. It was my fault. I'm sorry.

He determined never to ask her why, and in this labor, whose immensity wearied him far more than the construction of a symphony, whose essence is merely communication instead of that greater song called silence, he succeeded, thanks to something which he named, and why not, love, thank you very much. Meet me in the Summer Garden. Oh, take no notice, Elena, take no notice. I'm well aware that years ago I should have, you know. Soon he was going to accompany the orchestra to England and France for performances of the Eighth Symphony. Five rehearsals at least, and then the dress rehearsal; he could hardly . . . He'd also better lay in munitions against loneliness; high time to telephone that richly plump girl with the paddle-shaped tongue. And vodka! T. Nikolayeva would surely stop by and play a duet—good girl! Should he divorce Margarita? He must see Glikman, who was such a faithful listener, and then . . . Well, but why must she take her picture back when it had meant so little to her and so much to *him* to give it to him in the first place? Then he understood: That was precisely why she had to do it.

The next morning his anguish had diminished by the time he awoke because he'd convinced himself that someday she might change her mind again since she had already changed her mind once, and even if she didn't, well, he had once thought that he, speaking frankly, couldn't quite, couldn't, you know, *couldn't keep on doing this,* but now he knew that he could; he could do this forever; he could go on and on.

4

Knowing that he would have to get everything he could out of the photograph now since he'd never see it again (never mind, he told himself; this will just be one more little death), he rememorized that delicately female face, with its smile of youth now replaced by a smoldering look which had borne much and could bear almost anything.

Desperately concealing his desperation (I should say attempting to conceal it) in the garments of a jest, he'd again remarked that he could face the approach of their next meeting, when it was understood that he'd give the photograph back, because his hopes kept expanding, to which she replied in her low and perfect voice: No. I won't change my mind anymore. I don't want to talk about it anymore. I want you to return the photo without saying anything else, and then we'll never talk about it again.

So there was that photograph which he would soon have to honorably relinquish either forever or until she, she, you know, that face in the photograph more beautifully remote from him than ever, shining through the envelope he'd already sealed in token of obedience and fidelity since what it contained no longer belonged to him. Oh, he still had several days left; she wouldn't have blamed him, or at least said anything, or even known, had he kept drinking in the photograph, kissing it and sleeping with it under the adjacent pillow of the empty double bed; but he wouldn't rape; he wouldn't spy; he wouldn't force himself on that to which he had no right.

Closing his eyes, he found her smile more noncommittal now than it had been in the photograph. Oh, yes, her teeth were as crystalline as the Jupiter Symphony! The thrill of waiting for her, of drawing strength from the memory of her voice, was nearly unbearable. That strange way she had of being everywhere untouchable, like the sky, he could almost be instructed by that. Plato says that as one learns to love, the image of any specific beloved can be left behind for knowledge of the Good. This might not have been true in his case, there being nothing more Good or beloved than the darkhaired woman, but because everything she was and did had to be, as I said, Good, then her retraction of the photograph had to be Good, which meant that if he understood and accepted it as he had her every other act, then his faithfulness could only strengthen. He said to himself: What kind of love would it be, if it needed any external image of her?—He had been the merest fetishist. Could he only pass beyond superstition and corporeality, he would love her all the more truly.

(In the street he saw a man slip his arm around a woman and that was extremely painful.)

He tried to understand (which merely means to believe) that what she was really saying was this: I will be your sky; I will never stop smiling upon you; but now you will not see that smile anymore.

And so the very next time he saw her (she'd come from far away to meet him here at the Eliseyev store) he gave her the envelope, murmuring: *I have something that doesn't belong to me.* She accepted it in silence. And after that, neither one of them ever mentioned the photograph again. ▸

WHY WE DON'T TALK ABOUT FREYA ANYMORE

◩

There is something fearful in bearing such a relation to a creature so imperfectly known . . .

—Nathaniel Hawthorne (1846)

1

In the shining cobblestoned darkness of Ernst-Thälmann-Strasse, black crowds stood before the bright and empty shop windows. And Lina was lost among them. Lina had come in memory of her sister Freya, who'd been sacrificed to the firestorm. And Lina was lost everywhere! Once upon a time, the dome, tower and spire of the Frauenkirche rose above Dresden's ancient narrow streets, which were now far more fictional than they had ever been in Hoffmann's fairytale of the Golden Pot. Come to think of it, that strangely flat ornateness of so many edifices in prewar Dresden could have been theatrical backdrops. The play was called "Lina and Freya." The Dresden in the old books never existed except in books, an objective fact, which implies that the ruins in broken waves of brick and stone from that night and morning when all Dresden got shattered open like a pomegranate whose seeds have been plucked from their catacombs *weren't actually there.* Dresden is Europe Central, the walled kingdom in the middle of the past! Every day here begins *once upon a time.* But Barbarossa has withdrawn into his mountain cave to dream new cruel dreams; he's lost to us; he never existed. Just as depressing truths from Stalingrad must be considered Russian propaganda (a mother kneeling over a frozen body, a long, long winding column of muffled, staggering figures vanishing into the fog), so the burning of Dresden was itself nothing more than a nightmare: Wake from it and see our homeland's blond German boys in little uniforms, reaping the harvest with hand-forged scythes! This logic also allows me to say that neither Lina nor Freya ever existed except as acronymic reifications of the black telephone's tentacles. What were they, but literary characters?

But Lina was lost. Once this had been a different street, with a different name. Now it was Ernst-Thälmann-Strasse with its exposed pipes shading the snow.

2

When she crossed into Berlin-Ost at the end of that last year before the Wall, she had been somehow sure that a person would be waiting for her, perhaps one of her parents; she remembered them coming to meet her when she was a child; she expected someone, anyone. Well, wasn't that life? There's never any help, her father always used to say.

Frankly, she had been a little afraid to go. She'd heard what we all had about the other Germany. But she had to respect Freya's memory.

It was like returning ten years to enter this new East Germany. Here, of course, the economic miracle had never occurred. Everyone looked hungry and shabby to her.

From Berlin-Ost she took the train back into our German heartland—dark trees above blonde grass, and clouds over all—where it seemed as if another five years undid themselves! Scorched castles, boarded-up apartments, empty towns. All these stage sets had been shunted from eastward by the machinery of politics, so that the dying fairytale could play itself out to other captive audiences. They passed a poster which no one had troubled to remove: ***LEARNING FROM THE SOVIET UNION MEANS LEARNING FROM VICTORY!*** Ivy had grown across it. Which hero would wake Sleeping Beauty?

At Bahnhof-Dresden her family was not waiting at the platform; how could Lina have predicted when she would arrive? She disembarked with her one suitcase and stood in the cold, dirty station. Here was where she'd once kissed that lieutenant whose name she no longer remembered; he'd spoken in the accents of a Silesian. Where must he be now? East or underground.

3

The love of Lina's life had been a Russian translator named Elena Konstantinovskaya, for whom she had drawn up her white, white knees; she had never done anything like that before with a woman, and it was never the same afterward, not the way it had been with Elena.

It was the very last year for Weimar Berlin: Red-lipped Hansis in long red dresses kept licking their swizzlesticks at Lina. She won the pretty-knee contest at that well-known venue on Schwerinstrasse 13. All the while she had been longing for Elena. At the Verona-Lounge she learned to dance tangos with ripe-breasted Gougnettes who wore men's hats. Freya would have been scandalized. I've seen her wear a Titus-Kopf, for whose snaky coils she paid the hairdresser two days' wages. Gypsy-Lotte at the Topkeller, who was always kind to her, even on Friday nights, fixed her up with Christa, Grete, and then, despairingly, with Red Minna, but Lina never felt, as she had with Elena, that her white thighs were shining.

You never inspect yourself in the mirror, said Lotte. That's a giveaway. Women who don't love looking at themselves don't love other women. You're not actually one of us.

Lina replied: It's just that whenever I look I'm disappointed.

Doubtless *brevity* and *novelty* had contributed substantially to the perfection of Lina's experience, which seemed in retrospect to have lasted longer than one of Leningrad's white nights. She remembered lying on her side gazing down at her lover, until dawn set Elena's throat whitely aglow; now Lina could see her pulse, which was healthy and rapid like someone hurrying away from her. Elena's rich red lips were parted and her cigarette-breath soughed almost inaudibly in and out. When she began to wake, Lina rolled away to save Elena from being haunted by her needy eyes. (This was the curse of Elena's life, that so many people loved her so deeply that she must fail them all.)

What happened to you in Leningrad? Freya asked over and over.

That had been the beginning of the coldness between them.

Then what? A government of national recovery.

After Stalingrad, Lina had been mobilized to insert the fuses into eighty-eight-caliber shells. In 1945 she found herself mobilized again, this time by the Amis, who made us walk the hot stinking meadows where concentration camp corpses had been laid out: stinking, festering matchstick legs, groins prudishly covered by blankets. How could this have gone on? We'd never heard anything about it except a few whispers. The woman in front of her vomited. As for Lina, she looked straight ahead, disgusted but not overwhelmed; for by the time the war ended we'd all seen judgments of one kind or another.

Next came the Cold War. We all got mobilized again.

Lina's eyes were still brown but her hair was grey.

4

Do you remember the line of scurrying archaic figures on the Georgentor? They were following a skeleton, as in Käthe Kollwitz's drawings. And now their skeleton had led them into nothingness. They were gone in the fire.

Her family were all at home. She hadn't seen them since '42. She burst into tears at the sight of their starved submissive faces.

They sat around a white-draped oval table, drinking tea and wine for Lina's birthday; Freya's photograph was on the wall, and a porcelain angel simpered down upon them all in sanitized nudity.

Her father, who was now very, very old, tried to explain to her how it had all happened: We tried to keep them away with a barrage from our eighty-eights, but there were too many planes, flying too fast and too high.

Fortunately, that was dead history. The Anglo-American criminals exercised no jurisdiction over our zone. Dresden had come to know the comforting presence of the Red Army soldier.

She had brought chocolate and coffee. Her mother cried.

And Freya? No one had said a word about her yet. Among us Germans, that's how it is.

5

Had Freya ever existed? Portraits can be faked. Why not repudiate her? To deny the dead is to deny death itself. Why treasure up every grief, as Shostakovich does? Waking from a nightmare of fire, we find counterfeits, improbabilities. Do we even exist anymore? We need a secret mirror—Elena, for instance.

Once upon a time, Lina, whom they called a *slim-hipped Mädi,* went to the Auluka-Lounge to learn from reflecting herself in women which woman she really was. A former Russian prince was playing the piano, but it wasn't he who reminded Lina of Elena; it was the artificial snowballs: how cold, how white, hence how Russian! The truth is that Elena would have preferred the Café Olala on Zietenstrasse, whose dirty windows and scratchy records were more "real," but what's real when we're imprisoned in a fairytale?

My reflection in the shopwindow on Thälmann-Strasse is not me. It is Elena Konstantinovskaya. (We're both so white, aren't we?) I reach out to touch her and find between my palm and hers—the center of Europe. Elena can be my mirror; how I long for her to be! But not Freya—I don't want my reflection to be a skeleton.

6

On the Altmarkt's shining wet cobblestones, dark crowds queued around the glowing lights of the department store "Howa." Inside were glowing triangles, glowing stars, perfect statuettes. And then, beyond the Howa, Ernst-Thälmann-Strasse went off into the darkness.

The dead had lain here, while undernourished Hitlerjugend boys and old men in long tired coats passed through, lifting them one by one by the arms and the legs onto horsedrawn carts to be hauled off to the smoking pyres. It was her cousin Vala who told her this. Vala was greyhaired now, and her front teeth were missing. She kept sighing: Oh, Lina, it's a hard, hard life.

Did they burn Freya here?

Oh, no, said Vala.

Did it happen in the first wave or the second wave? Vala, I have a right. She was my sister.

In the second wave, said her cousin. Let's not talk about it.

7

Once upon a time, a smiling, blonde-braided girl planted a bouquet in a Condor volunteer's buttonhole. Another girl, less blonde and more serious, fumbled over the edelweiss; her soldier looked down at his breast a little anxiously, wondering whether she'd done it right and whether it would be incorrect to say something if she hadn't. This second girl was Freya.

Who was the smiling girl? There's always someone else, someone irrelevant. She's possibly dead herself, and we deny her.

Who then was Freya? She's dead, so isn't that irrelevant?

Of course the entire family had been there. They'd stayed at Lina's flat in Berlin. That must have been in '36 or '37, when the Frauenkirche was still whole, when its organ still sang. That day they'd had the privilege of watching with their very own eyes as the sleepwalker wafted himself by in an open Mercedes-Klemm. And the Condor Legionnaires marched through the Brandenburg Gate . . .

8

The broken castle, then the Kultur Palace, then the Altmarkt, this was what Lina saw every day when she looked out the window. (Where were the Russians? They separated themselves; they had their own place.) At "Honetta Damenmoden" on the Altmarkt, one could buy a long dress, shoes or perhaps a suitcase. These objects seemed more lonely than they really were because Lina and Vala were gazing at them from the outside as they stood in the arcade on that December night.

And right here, whispered Vala, there was a little blonde girl crying by a wagon of corpses, right where that dripping pipe is. The sweetest little girl you could imagine! One hundred percent Aryan. And for some reason I've never stopped wondering what happened to her.

And the two of them stood there, staring wearily at that exposed pipe in the burnt and frozen muck.

9

Freya didn't die in the firestorm, did she? asked Lina.

Vala took her arm and led her into a scene without life, only white footprints in the white snow around the Kreuzkirche, and then she said: Are you certain that you want to know?

Yes.

Well, then, it happened on the anniversary of the Russian Revolution, when Red Army men always get drunk. Now it's better, of course. That was when they came into our houses, year after year.

I've heard about it.

Exactly. Everything we used to be told in *those days* was true. They're not human. For example, Grandmother was in her eighties. Now have you heard enough?

Lina said nothing. They were one of half a dozen black-clad couples walking on the grey sidewalk.

Vala said: They entered the maternity ward at gunpoint and raped the nurse who persuaded them not to rape a mother who'd just given birth. I won't say who it is; you know her. Perhaps she knew what would happen, in which case I admire her sacrifice. Lina, you have no idea what it was like. They raped us on the streets, on the trains, in the fields. They arrested us and raped us. They raped us as we were cleaning their floors. Of course it wasn't quite as bad as at the beginning, when they used to rape us in front of our husbands and then—

And you? Don't tell me if you don't wish it—

Five times, in broad daylight. If you want to know, it was on a dead horse in the middle of Grossenhanter Strasse, right across from Weber's wine cellar—

Vala—

But all they did afterward, probably because I'd been a good girl, was kick me in the face a few times. Heinz was already dead, as you know, so at least he didn't have to witness that . . . Excuse me for telling you.

Lina knew Vala. She knew that it would be best to refrain from comment on what she had just heard, now and forever. Moreover, she knew not to look at Vala, much less touch her hand. So she said only: I understand. And what about Freya?

Mayor Petzold of Saupersdorf used to arrange parties for the Russians, with vodka and young girls. That was how he maintained his position. You can imagine the rest. Shall we go now? I need to buy two loaves at Meyer's, before he runs out.

It comforted Lina to learn that no one had intended to kill her sister; she must have merely been, as Vala put it in regards to their grandmother, *delicate inside.*

Your father did what he could, Vala said. He even went to the colonel to complain, which in those days took courage. The colonel warned him that if he didn't get out, he'd be arrested for slandering the Red Army.

After that, said Vala, all he did was go around whispering *Ivan will never go away.*

10

But this never happened. There never was a Freya. I went to the Albertinium for an exhibition of proletarian painting and sculpture in 1958, and no matter how long I looked, I couldn't find anything unhappy!

Do you want to know what happiness is? Happiness is the absence of unpleasant information. I do my best to live within that definition when I make my reports. What everybody wants to hear is that everything is perfect, happily ever after.

I enjoy gazing at the loaves of bread stacked four high, end out, and the sausages hanging vertically, one per hook, in that clean shop on Postplatz. To me, that's perfection. Herr Meyer also thinks so; he's proud of his establishment. If I wanted to, I could remember November 1945, when the first light came back on in the Postplatz, smokily glowing in the skeletons of buildings; that was a triumph then, but in comparison to the way it is now in 1960, it's sad. Even when I don't want to, I sometimes remember a smashed, burned, dust-sugared skeleton lying on the Postplatz in a scorched Nazi armband, the ruined mouth gaping and the black teeth falling out of it like the bricks of the Lukaskirche; that was a triumph, too, for our victorious enemies.

I enjoy denying Freya's life and death, thereby sparing myself from certain information. And I enjoy gazing at the Dresden schoolgirls in knee-length checkered skirts, their blouses buttoned demurely up to their throats. Isn't that happiness?

Why feel sorry for ourselves, I say? Let's reserve our compassion for the North Korean orphans at the Maxim Gorki Home. Our East German brides hold bouquets; we wish them well from tenement windows.

Our long-skirted Rubblefrauen who dragged four-wheeled boxcars filled with broken bricks down the railroad tracks for twenty years straight, with Dresden's church-bones and tower-skeletons mourning themselves on the other side of the Elbe, they helped get us where we are today, and now that we're here, let's get the Rubblefrauen out of the picture!

11

Her brother Hans was now a tall, pale, grim old man with sunken eyes. He kept his hands in the pockets of his prewar vest. That dark steel skeleton we'd just built across the Elbe, the "Blue Wonder" we call it, Hans had been mobilized to carry beams for that project, and his bad knee hadn't helped him get out of it at all; in fact, since it was a war injury, received on the Ostfront, mentioning it had cost Hans a box on the ear; he was lucky it hadn't been worse. And now his children had to learn Russian in school, he said; pretty soon we wouldn't be Germans anymore. And it was cold in winter now, so cold, he said; the Russians had taken his stove away.

Hans's wife Gertrud had died in the first wave. He'd dug her out himself; he'd carried her in his arms to the Altmarkt. He'd stood there watching when the horsedrawn wagon carried her to the pyre, but they hadn't permitted him to come closer, for fear of epidemics.

He lived with his children in the house of Gertrud's parents, who were still alive. Lina went to visit, and found them sitting around the table with drapes drawn, the older people smiling cautiously, ready for something bad to happen, the boys grinning at the prospect of cake. Stalin's portrait hung overhead, with a wreath of flowers at his throat, because he'd already died and become a god. They seemed relieved when she said goodbye.

I'll walk you back, said Hans.

Across the street, in scaffolding resembling the ghost-rungs attached to whichever music-notes protrude above the staff in Shostakovich's Eighth Quartet, a dozen laborers roosted, passing a bottle of schnapps. One of them shouted an obscenity at Lina.

Say nothing, Hans told her.

When have I ever said anything?

Everyone has bad manners now, even my children. Please forgive them.

The dirty grey snow had been ground down to slime on the cobblestones of the empty streets, and silhouettes passed sparsely through the cold shade, moving as slowly and silently as mourners.

Do you remember Vice-Landrat Beda? he said in her ear.

Of course. Once when we were small he gave us each a chocolate . . .

They indicted him for sabotage, because they didn't like his report on the sowing. He was jailed for ten months; but they didn't like that, either, so they increased the sentence to three years. That was in '46, so he should have gotten out in '49, but he's never come back.

The rubble-piles were heaped neatly around the broken bookends of the Frauenkirche as if in offering; the round window still standing, framing nothing but grey sky.

You're probably wondering why we don't talk about Freya, he said then. You see, the Russians *took her away*. I don't know how to tell you this; it's so shameful.

Ivan will never go away, Lina recited, but in a voice as low as her brother's, because a policeman was blowing his nose on the far side of the street. Three stout women leaned on their shovels, pretending to work.

No, it's worse than that, said Hans. You lived in Berlin; perhaps you've heard of such things, but we . . . You see, Freya—I don't know how to say this—went away with a woman. That's why we don't talk about her anymore.

Lina burst out laughing. ▸

OPERATION WOLUND

Was their ill fate sealed when in they looked.

—Voçlundarkviîa (9th century?)

1

I was the last one, except for Raoul Hillenberg, Raoul Wallenberg and a hundred thousand others. I was the last one I knew about. They'd kept me because of my prior relationship with Colonel Hagen, whom of all the war criminals they loathed most. And while they never feared me (though feared me they should), I'm sure they read the hate in me.

They kept me on an island without a name; at least if the island had a name I never knew it. The last place with a name I ever knew was Shpalnery Prison.

I wrought work for them which only a German could do. Do you want to know what it was? It was rocket work.

They'd shackled and hamstrung me; furthermore, I had to sleep within a web of barbed wire woven by a metal spider whose arms were as long and narrow as that cold-steel Russian sword called the *shpaga*; to get right down to it, I didn't sleep much, on account of the injections. What they longed for was a missile which could fly all the way across Myrkvith Forest and exterminate the West Germans; they also hoped to kill the Amis in Washington. I wished to live, so I told them that I could do whatever they wanted; besides, I actually could do it.

They peered into my toolchest. They photographed my workbench. They knocked on the side of my rocket and it sounded hollow. They didn't understand a thing.

Lieutenant Danchenko always treated me nicely. I'll never forget the red flashes on her blue NKVD uniform. Once when her partner was in the latrine I told her that I could make her something special if that would please her, something beautiful and poisonous which would let her kill anyone she wanted. She got suspicious then. She wondered what favor I wished in return. I whispered that what I wished was her.

She liked that. Soon I was calling her Natalya Kovalova. Then it was Natalka. She came to me within my spiderweb.

One night when we were making love I strangled her. Then I took her keys and found the long sawtoothed one which went inside the spider's belly. I unlocked the spider and came out of the web. *Heil Dir im Siegerkranz.*

Then I cut Natalka's eyes out—beautiful brown eyes!—and bored wires into them, which I hooked up to transistors and diodes. I squeezed the bulb and they opened. Now they were sensors. After all, it's the worker who creates all material values. I installed Natalka's eyes high in the nose of the rocket which was supposed to kill the Amis, and the rocket came alive. It was already a fine rocket, whose shell was magnalium alloy.

I sharpened Natalka's fine white little teeth, which had proved so good at making lovebites, and packed them into grenades which I mounted under my rocket's wings. (I saved her canine teeth for an antipersonnel mine which I wired up against the door.) I cleaned out her skull and filled it full of wires and switches so that the rocket had a guidance system. I filled the fuel tanks with her hot Russian blood! As for the rest of her, oh, she was as soft-skinned as an Ami truck; her flesh was as smoothly sloping as a T-34's breast, which repels our shells as a duck's breast does rain. So the rest of her I reduced to metal-tinned cubes in order to have something to eat on my journey. Then I was ready to fly as high as heaven.

Under other circumstances I would have made jewels for that woman. Poor Natalka! But I was a prisoner and I was in a rage, knowing that there'd never again be children coming to see us off at the train station in Berlin.

Now here they came, shooting through the door. I was in the cockpit of my rocket by then. As they came bursting in, my antipersonnel mine exploded and Natalka's teeth killed half a dozen of them! Laughing, I pulled the switch and blasted right through the ceiling.

Shall I tell you how and why I'd won out? Under my tongue (the one place they didn't search) I kept a splinter of the old Reichscrown, in other words a piece of the True Cross. ▸

OPUS 110

The problem of the "black bread" of culture has now been completely solved, and now is the time to provide society with the "sweet biscuits" of culture.

—The Soviet Way of Life (1974)

1

Best listened to in a windowless room, better than best an airless room—correctly speaking, a bunker sealed forever and enwrapped in tree-roots—the Eighth String Quartet of Shostakovich (Opus 110) is the living corpse of music, perfect in its horror. Call it the simultaneous asphyxiation and bleeding of melody. The soul strips itself of life in a dusty room. When the war's over, when Stalin's dead and for cemetery obelisks Europe sports the orphaned chimneys of firebombed Murmansk, the scorched churches of Dresden, politics spares us for a blink or two, nervously gnawing its own claws. The soldier comes home, pulls off his muddy, bloody uniform and becomes a citizen again. So too Shostakovich. Visitors remark on his success: white and black bread both, cheese, butter, even sausage on the table! Nylon stockings for Ninusha! His children love him, Lebedinsky respects him, Glikman reveres him; Ninusha (Nina Vasilyevna to you!) keeps unwanted visitors away; the Party woos him; Galina Ustvolskaya kisses him. Oh, yes, he's very, how should I say? If I could only . . . Don't answer the telephone! Because it's time to, well, you know. But what's that sound? It certainly wasn't in Opus 40. What key most effectively expresses bereavement? In the darkness, a cello saws out a tune as dry as the buzzing of wasps within a skull. He claps his hands to his ears, but what good will that do? It comes from within! What's that sound? Until now, all that he and *we* could hear was the patriotic clanking of tanks under Leningrad's arches, as translated into my Seventh

Symphony. And I even *believed*! I'm not saying that the others weren't idealists, even fat-chinned Khrennikov, who earned his . . . not that I'd speak ill of a colleague, oh, no, *dear* friends! Did you know that Comrade Stalin praises Khrennikov? Count on it! They're two of a kind. No, it's not I who should be considered the man of our epoch. I get angry when they kick somebody in the teeth and expect me to set it to music. How strange that Roman Lazarevich wants me to write scores for his so-called "masterpieces," when Khrennikov would be more, you know. Of course *she* never slept with Khrennikov, at least not that I . . . Thank heavens that's all over. Isaak Davidovich tells me that she divorced him, so he must be very . . . Not that it's my business. She'll probably find another older man. And, yes, the war's over, too; I wish that Maxim would stop having nightmares about Auschwitz! I mean, in this world we have to . . . And Galisha tells me that the boy won't even . . . Not that she's so lucky herself, to have me for a father. Oh, my! Now Europe is silent—but what's that sound?

It's *himself*, starved, choking and weeping in an airless room. In the wise judgment of *Sovetskaya Musika*: *It is impossible to forget that Shostakovich's work has a certain tendency to close in upon itself, that the popular roots of his music are not deep enough*. His pale and shining face sinks down toward the music-paper, which he's anchored to the desk by his suitsleeves, elbows outward; he doesn't resemble a boy anymore; his hairline's receding; he needs another cigarette. What ought to cause him agony he no longer feels; he's but the catalyst of a biochemical reaction which turns pain into music.—What's that sound? A D-note, probably.—To his right, from the long black jawbone of the best piano, music-teeth grin at him; when the time comes, when Opus 110 is ready for execution, they'll know what to do! Fuzzy fibrous tree-roots will eat his flesh. Right now they're neither popular nor deep enough. No fear; they'll bite deeper. What's that sound? The mournful, sinister groanings of the strings comprise a *largo* of suffocation. Less grisly than the *allegretto* of skeletons when the soul is pursued and caught by death, *that sound* is sadder: Death having done its work, we must now suffer through the dying. Thus Opus 110.

We might note that this quartet opens with the four-note signature *D, E-flat, C, B,* which is to say in inappropriately German notation *DSCH,* and which therefore is also to say *Dmitri Shostakovich*. Assertion of self-characterized Soviet artists who were persecuted for following their private Muses. In the case of Akhmatova, who was proscribed from publishing for many years and who lost both son and lover to prison camps, not to mention that ex-husband whom we'd shot long before, the shrill *I am* approaches megalomania. Had she been, say, an Englishwoman, her egocentricity might have proved insufferable. She versifies about the strophes, streets and monuments which posterity will name after her. But she was *Russian*. She was not free. What could she assert but herself? In the world of *we*, the failing *I* repeated her name, defiant. She became a heroine; her poems were memorized secretly in Black Marias and Arctic camps. She wrote *I*, and Shostakovich wrote *DSCH*.

Not long before Opus 110, she composed a poem to him. She wrote that his music kept her company in the grave *as if every flower burst into words*. Then, slowly, she sank into decrepitude, weeping and drinking tea for years in an airless room.

2

When they heard the hideous news that the Americans had detonated two "atom-bombs" over Japan, killing thousands or hundreds of thousands (as usual, the numbers of the dead varied with the teller), Shostakovich said with a horridly gloomy smile: It's our task to rejoice.

Younger musicians had begun to draw away, on account of that diabolical cynicism of his, which seemed almost to ape Stalin's, swelling until it overshadowed Moscow's new heroic columns; while his own generation, who knew him better, simply worried about his will to live. No need: He'd already survived. To him they were all blue morning shadows on new snow, silhouette-hued people gliding cautiously along the icy sidewalks, an occasional camel-brown or blonde-furred coat like a surprise, a bareheaded woman steaming breath ahead of her; he watched them from his redoubt beneath the piano keys. Peering out and up, ready to duck back behind his glasses, he exchanged courtesies even with the ones in raspberry-colored boots—dear Shostakovich! He was as moderate as Comrade Stalin. Those caustic, hideous things that wailed out of his twitching smile with the suddenness of violin-shrieks *(it's our task to rejoice)*—well, well . . .

As early as 1944, the cellist V. Berlinsky, while praising his astounding musical memory, had felt forced to describe him as *a lump of nerves*. And now, with the Germans crushed under their own rubble, Shostakovich, half-smoothfaced, smoothhanded and perfectly pallid as he sat at the piano with his wrists in corpse-white parallels, listened again and again within his skull-bunker to the Eighth Symphony (soon to be denounced as *repulsive, ultra-individualist*); when he'd arrived at that resolute call to arms of the fourth movement, that tense, sweet thrumming of all-sacrificing sincerity, he bit his lips for self-disgust, to think that he could have believed in anything! He'd stood up to be counted. He'd even hoped. Now he composed fugues (and here we might note that the Latin source-word *fuga* means quite simply *flight*).

We know that Hitler had actually considered sealing off Leningrad with an electric fence. Now the whole country was sealed off, even better than before. Specters whirled through the Summer Garden in ever-narrowing spirals, but it wasn't summer. And Shostakovich, taking his first breaths of peacetime air, found himself in the situation of the shaggy peasant in his banned opera "Lady Macbeth" who breaks into the cellar in search of wine to steal, and staggers out overcome by the stench of a murdered corpse.

In 1945 we find him writing the popular song "Burn, Burn, Burn" especially for the NKVD Ensemble. Even then he still kept a change of underwear and an extra toothbrush in his briefcase, against the eventuality of arrest. Just for, you know, *fun,* he liked to imagine that they'd knock on the door in a 5/4 theme, which would be very . . . Nina likewise had prepared herself. When the children were sleeping he sometimes entered her bed, pressed his lips against her ear and began to whisper curses against Comrade Stalin. Her eyes opened. In a low voice she entreated: My God, what are you saying? Think of what could happen to us!

Could it have always been like this? A nineteenth-century French traveler whose prose was as purple as an NKVD agent's identification card once declared: *The Russians are not ghosts, but specters, walking solemnly beside or behind one another, neither sad nor glad, never letting a word escape their lips.* Those words were written when all the six hundred and twenty-six church-bells of Petersburg still rang. Could they have been tuned? He wished he could have, you know. And now, when Petersburg was Leningrad and the noble-born girls of the Smolny Convent were dead, even silence was unsafe. Everybody had to sing hosannas. D-flat-C-D-flat was how *he'd* sung, ever so nastily, in the *allegretto* of the Eighth Symphony. At the premiere they'd seemed nervous. He'd wanted to blow them all up! He was a loyal citizen of our great Soviet land; he hummed along. Then he went to sleep in the other room.

3

In 1946, Stalin's enthusiastically ruthless shadow Comrade Zhdanov (who was soon to die under peculiar circumstances) announced to the Leningrad

Union of Soviet Writers: *Leninism proceeds from the fact that our literature cannot be politically indifferent, cannot be "art for art's sake."* They got quiet then; they knew what was coming. In truth, the only wonder was that it hadn't come sooner. When the motif has already sounded, how can the opus go on without it? Folding his arms across his massive breast so that he resembled one of our KV tanks, Comrade Zhdanov forthwith demanded that there be no further deviation from the task at hand on the literary front—namely, to create art *to light the way ahead with a searchlight.*

Reading this directive in the pages of *Pravda,* Shostakovich understood that it was only a matter of time before they turned their attention back to music. It would be "Lady Macbeth" all over again.

Nina tried to lay her hand on his shoulder, but he shrugged her off in a terrified rage. What a ridiculous man he was! *With a searchlight.* And in the dark, when everything's frozen, it's not so easy to dig down under the snow and hide before the searchlight comes; I'd probably represent it by a B-flat between two C-notes, in a humming, thrumming base, since that would be very, as Elena used to say in her favorite English phrase, *creepy.*—Oh, dear, oh, me, what brilliant arguments they'll muster against all of us! he muttered, cocking his head like a wind-up owl, drinking vodka until he turned pale.

Slamming the door, Nina went out to her "special friend," the physicist A. Alikhanyan.

He lit another "Kazbek" cigarette, his hair rushing carelessly down his face as he played with his children. Galisha was getting spoiled, but he couldn't bring himself to be firm with the girl; she'd soon enough find out how the world, you know, *operated.* He remembered her as a baby in Leningrad, hungrily sucking on a piece of oilcake. She used to cry and hide her head in his lap when the Fascists let off their eighty-eights. And Akhmatova had said . . . —How would they develop the offensive this time? They'd probably use Khrennikov to denounce him on the radio. The man loved that sort of work. He was perfectly adapted to our time, like one of those blowflies which specialize in, no need to spell it out. Why even . . . ? But I saved Galisha from that—Maxim, too, who by the way needs to write something for the wall newspaper of his Pioneer brigade. He's extremely . . . And even though Nina won't forgive me; she says I didn't do enough for my own family, I never stopped, well, I should have just . . . And all for nothing! The *sincerity* of that Seventh Symphony, whenever I hear it I can hardly bear it! I'm so ashamed of it now. With a, a, a *searchlight,* so to speak; that's how they'll . . . Even though Lebedinsky will say . . . Leo Oskarovich informs me that wherever

Stalin's daughter goes, she has a bodyguard, of course, and this man especially hates concerts! When she goes to the Conservatory to listen to, for instance, compositions by the former and future enemy of the people Shostakovich, this Mikhail Nikiforovich complains: *Begging your pardon, my dear Svetlana Alliluyeva, now they will start sawing up boxes for firewood again.* It must be the string instruments that he's referring to, don't you think? And then Svetlana Alliluyeva replies—what does she reply? It's *hilarious*! I suppose that's what they all think. Then Khrennikov! He knows how to do it—right in the nape of the neck, they say, so that there's no . . . And here come the blowflies. Next they'll shut me out of the cinema, where I make my money. "Zoya" just won a Stalin Prize, so they'll regret that I wrote the music for that monstrosity. I'd better compose one more film score while I still can. Roman Lazarevich might help me, out of pity. He gets invitations to drink with Stalin's children, so I hear. He's quite the . . . If not, I could hope that Leo Oskarovich, or perhaps Simonov, to hell with Simonov.

Maxim kept drawing sailing-ships whose outlines he copied from photographs in the newspaper. The father tried to smile. He attached the best drawings to the wall.

Who was the lead actress in "Zoya"? I can almost remember her name. Was it Galina Vodyanischkaya or Galya Vodyanischkaya? That was when Roman Lazarevich affronted me. He told me to, to, actually I forget what he told me. Had I better telephone him? But he's a good boy. Now that I'm a leper again, he'll keep his distance. That's what he did last time. But last time there was a woman, so to speak, between us, and therefore . . . But she's still between us. Her voice always sounds so sad! If I could only pick up the telephone and, and, you know, she'd be extremely . . .

He was, I swear it, almost ready to divorce Nina, I mean, not next year but this year, and ask Elena Konstantinovskaya to marry him; but he had a nightmare that Maxim was struggling to run to him but Nina wouldn't let the child go; suddenly she became a crocodile who bit off Maxim's arm and Maxim was screaming! Who else screamed like that? My God, it was only a dream! At least it wasn't the dream of the red spot. Sometimes one simply has to . . .

Without warning, his mind rang with a chord as beautiful as a flamethrower's red river gushing into an enemy dugout! Fourteen years later, that sound, which everybody else would find terrifying, hideous, shrieked out of Opus 110. Well, but what is Opus 110 anyhow? It's not the, the so-called *climax* of my life, because that would be very . . .

Nina had urged him not to undertake any new friendships, especially with officials, but he already knew that. In her short skirt and rakish hat, she'd looked quite glamorous at his side in Prague. (Comrade Alexandrov's assessment: *A young, pretty blonde woman with gentle brown eyes and a good figure.)* When he thought about Nina, he experienced his guilt and compassion at a distance, as why shouldn't he, because otherwise they couldn't, you know. When he got sick or sad or, or, that was when he knew that Elena would have been the one. Elena, you're so lucky you didn't marry me. Nina slammed down another bowl of her excellent mushroom soup in front of him; he wondered where she'd found the . . . Maxim was quarreling with Galisha, who said . . . He wondered if they'd ever have another vacation together. It was impossible to predict who'd turn criminal next. That knocking in a 5/4 theme should have come back in '36, and his underwear was still packed! That was why he couldn't stop drinking. It was all part of the, the, you know. Anyhow, he had to; otherwise his colleagues would be, why say it? Apparatchiks, propagandists, chauvinists, functionaries and drones clinked glasses with him; and two bullies of the secret police, languidly unzipping their lambskin-lined jackets, strolled up to the frightened composer and kissed him on both cheeks. The taller one shouted out: Dmitri Dmitriyevich, you're as Russian as red gold!—Perhaps this was meant to warn him away from straying any farther into the illicit darkness of his new project, the cycle entitled *From Jewish Poetry.*

4

What drew Shostakovich to Jewish harmonies? The simplest answer, and the truest, might be *their sadness*. Leave this aside for the moment. Although I cannot forbear to discern insectoid shapes in musical notation, within a score there dwell many human forms. A treble clef, for example, resembles a Muscovite or Leningrader in a bulky hooded parka. A bass clef bends as simply and painfully as a silhouetted widow in Leningrad drawing water from the whiteness of a frozen canal. I myself can't explain why this should be so, unless those figures somehow indicate or represent an underlying content, perhaps the Infinite Cause of Causes. Why not? After all, Kabbalists believe that the very letters of the alphabet are emanations of God; and in our Soviet Union we accept the Marxist conception that art, and indeed all culture, comprises a mere superstructure founded on economic realities. What was the *content* of D. D. Shostakovich? Wherein did his meaning lie? He struggled rhythmically for his freedom, but what would he do with it if he ever got it? Or was there, as the new Existentialist movement implied, no aspect to freedom excepting the struggle itself?

One night, not long after the ruling circles of the reactionary powers set up a separate "West German" state, he had a very strange dream filled with both ominousness and promise. He dreamed that he was once again a pale young student who haunted the halls of the Leningrad Conservatory like his own rapturous ghost. This domain had now become the fabled world within every piano's black keys, the reverberating refuge into which since childhood his soul had always been able to withdraw. Outside, dark boy-figures in wool caps bowed their faces against the blinding snow they stood on; the dreamer understood that this whiteness was the *ostensible world,* where his body, his honors and his persecutors dwelled. Within, he was safe. The piquant vibrations of chromaticism which infused those corridors nourished him as if he were still a baby with his head on his mother's breast, listening to the beating of her heart. Or imagine, if you wish, that these hovering chords resembled dust-motes gilded by a divine tracer-bullet of sunlight, unearthly and untouchable forever. But suddenly it was as if the dust began to whirl about in menacing spirals; the harmonies suffered interruption and distortion, as if someone had clapped a hand upon an ululating mouth for an interval, then released the pent-up sound in a rising while, stopped it again, then freed it, the mufflings of the sound devouring ever longer beats until at last that selfsame choking silence which exists within each note of Opus 110 had conquered the obscurity forever. And in the tunnel, approaching him with a dragging sort of cadence symptomatic of his life's diminished intervals, he now spied a kindred wraith, a tall, bearlike apparition with the beard and sidelocks of a Hasidic Jew. Somehow he knew that this individual's name was Comrade Luria, and that Comrade Luria was angry with him.

Because you betrayed all of us with that facile Seventh Symphony of yours, which wears its own *meaning* on its chest like an idiotic medal . . .

Well, well, well, then I must beg you to forgive me, replied Shostakovich, almost asphyxiated by dreamy dread. You see, I wanted to inspire people, and—well, I mean to say I thought I could make myself useful—

Useful? said Comrade Luria in a rage. You know all too well that utility's the merest pimp for whom true art gets prostituted! Moreover . . .

He took a step closer. Shostakovich trembled.

Moreover, Dmitri Dmitriyevich, it's high time we talk about form.

Another step. Now Shostakovich was touched by the odor of burned hair.

I'm sure you've noticed, continued Comrade Luria, how much aestheticians like to prate about the impotence of form without content, or content without form. But in music, perfect form and content together can remain as stillborn as a law without the seal of Heaven on it. There has to be *emotion* . . .

Excuse me, excuse me; but isn't emotion the same as, er, *content* in this case? Naturally I understand that it's not equivalent to *form,* no matter what our socialist realists preach. For instance, in the right hands an *allegro* in a major key can convey anything, not just happiness—

Exactly, said Comrade Luria, taking another step. You've proved that yourself in "Lady Macbeth."

Oh, well, thank you for that, yes, thank you. But, if I may ask, what *is* musical content if not the feeling of the music?

Comrade Luria smiled, took three more rapid steps, outstretched an arm as if in benediction, and *touched* him.

That touch! It was like entering a darkened room and suddenly getting assaulted by soft, silent, hideous moths whose scales flaked off as they brushed in their dozens across nose, forehead, cheek and eyes, dryly flapping and dying, blindly disintegrating, polluting, attacking, asphyxiating. He reeled. He choked on dust which might have been smoke from all the millions and millions of burned Jews.

Comrade Luria was a charred skeleton. Comrade Luria knowingly said: After somebody's been cremated (no matter whether he was living or dead), his form's his image in your memory. His feeling, his emotional value if you will, is nothing more or less than the feeling *you* have when you remember him. So what's his content?

I don't know.

Is it a handful of ash? demanded Comrade Luria, breathing in Shostakovich's face that terrible breath which stank of roasted flesh.

No, no—

What's your content?

I . . . I have no content; I'm empty.

Then say so in your music.

5

Later, in the course of his Jewish researches, he learned that Isaac Luria had been an eminent Kabbalist.

6

I'm *empty*! he crowed to Glikman and Lebedinsky. I have no, how should I say, no content. If I hummed a few bars of "Suleiko" I'd achieve my dream, because—

Please, Dmitri Dmitriyevich!

No more communitarian exhortations!

We beg of you, please be silent! Who knows who might be—

Their terror that he might say something both forbidden and overheard was hideously apparent in their faces. He studied what he saw, and expertly converted it into a single musical chord, which in due course he'd retrieve from his skull's storehouse and weld into the chassis of Opus 110.

7

The Shostakoviches now lived in Moscow. Too many of their friends had perished in Leningrad; they couldn't bear to go back. (Comrade Alexandrov notes here: *Shostakovich exaggerates. Only eight percent of Leningrad's housing was destroyed.*) Those tan- and earth-hued houses remained windowpaneless, their multiple rectilinear darknesses as strangely inhuman as Roman ruins, with the life within them long gone and carried to the cemetery by Komsomol boys and girls during spring cleanups. In comparison, Moscow remained untouched. The children were less likely to be, I mean, *reminded*. Moreover, Lebedinsky, Glikman and his other friends whispered that the Party had resumed its attacks upon Leningrad intellectuals, not that Nina, who seemed to be getting more fearful with each birthday, believed that Moscow was any safer; but it was preferable to think that one could be safer *somewhere*. Then Comrade Zhdanov had made that speech about his—ha, ha!—*searchlight*! Moreover, E. E. Konstantinovskaya was teaching at the Conservatory, and he didn't want to accidentally, you know. (Her face would have gone cotton-white, like a puff of antiaircraft smoke.) His sister Mariya said that Elena had married a Professor Vigodsky. Better to stay away! Lastly, I mean firstly, the Dynamo Stadium was right here in Moscow, and he'd never grown tired of football.

The composer had two grand pianos in the double flat. He kept them swathed in black cloths whenever he didn't need them. The flat, the pianos, the dacha and everything were a gift from Comrade Stalin. (Keep your eye on that queer, Stalin told Beria. Sooner or later he'll fuck up. Then I want you to hit him hard.)

Shostakovich was ageing fast. Oh, oh, he felt sick! Meaning was departing from him. His best pupil of that period, a reclusive beauty named G. I. Ustvolskaya, sat in an unheated room, literally taking her fists to the piano in an angry struggle to give birth to her Sonata No. 1, which she insisted (to his horror) expressed his influence; well, I, to be sure, perhaps the piccolo did, a trifle, I mean, but this young woman's rage was not bridled as his had eternally been; it discomfited him; why did she jerk her head away like that, gazing at the wall, clenching her teeth? She said that it was the times, which he, well, he certainly couldn't call her foolish, although she wasn't healthy; in spite of her manifest unfitness for life, something about her reminded him of Nina; his dear friend Sollertinsky, now deceased for ever so many years, had once opined that he was attracted to strong women.

The moldy gloomy chords which she wrested from the piano were most appropriate, so she said, for a church. There was that expression of Elena Konstantinovskaya's, oh, yes; once they'd even studied English together: *It gives me the creeps*. Actually, he hadn't thought about that for years. Ustvolskaya's sonata gave him the creeps. So did his nightmares of Comrade Luria, not to mention, er, well, the times, which is to say, you know, *that bastard*. As for Shostakovich himself, struggling to seek beauty in his way, to be true only to the melodies he heard (this being the only loyalty he could not betray), he descended like a spinning bomb toward the tomb of Opus 110. There he could explode all he liked. That would be harmless, there being no air to support combustion . . . Faster and faster, deeper and deeper! By now he'd grown greyer than the walls of the Leningrad Conservatory. The harsh, dry cold of the Russian winter (which meteorologists blame on the Asiatic anticyclone) bit him more deeply than ever nowadays. The only way he could get warm was to drink vodka. But Nina said . . .

He made his students write their scores in ink without exception now, for the sake of his eyes.

8

I. Schwartz, who already showed a certain lyrical talent, could no longer afford to continue his studies. Shostakovich told him: What I've heard is better than anything by Shostakovich! (And he told the same to the other students.) He paid all Schwartz's fees for the next two years, in secret, so that the young man wouldn't feel beholden. But Comrade Stalin probably knew. Comrade

Stalin probably smiled triumphantly to see that Shostakovich was bankrolling characters with German names . . .

People were finally getting tired of whistling Khrennikov's "Song of the Artillerymen." Shostakovich's old "Song of the Counterplan" was coming back. Nina told him that just last week she'd heard a legless veteran singing it near the train station.

He spoke sharply to Nina, and she drew the blinds. In Petersburg, in the room where Paul was murdered in 1801 by an army clique, an edict kept the blinds drawn for more than half a century. Meanwhile, prayers hid themselves away likewise within the star-riddled cupolas of the Ismaelovski, and pretty young noblewomen learned to be ladies behind the high walls of the Smolny. Oh, me, that was back in the opening bars of the overture! And Nina went out; from the way she slammed the door he knew that she was going to come back late.

The next day, two men in tall, shiny boots dropped by to advise him: You're denying yourself true happiness, Dmitri Dmitriyevich. What could make a real Communist happier than expressing himself on the subject of Lenin?

Or for that matter the subject of Comrade Stalin! put in the shorter man.

Yes, yes, to be sure; what an oversight I've committed—

There was an infinite supply of these characters, but the way they spoke never changed. He knew them so well that he could almost laugh! If he were still twenty he could have scored a ballet about them; the dancers would have been cardboard beetles. Because it was all so . . . And yet, strange or not so strange to say, each new assault further abraded his defenses. Nina would have approved of his realism; on the other hand, if Galina Ustvolskaya could have seen how ingratiatingly he was smiling at them, she would have punched her fist through the piano.

You promised us Lenin in your Sixth Symphony. Then you promised him in the Seventh. Not that we have anything against the Seventh, of course, but *when will you get around to Lenin?*

Comrades, you know I try to write sincerely! I don't want to throw away my second-best music on, uh, Lenin. Certainly the Seventh wasn't worthy of him. That was only a . . . To be frank, I'm waiting for—

Yeah, what *are* you waiting for?

Dmitri Dmitriyevich, what comes into your head when you think of Lenin? Answer immediately.

Well, I, I'd have to say a *largo* in *passacaglia* form . . .

Come off it! What are you waiting for, Dmitri Dmitriyevich? You're not against Lenin, are you?

Although his Ninth Symphony had disappointed many critics, his Second Piano Trio won a Stalin Prize! I can almost see him rocking crazily with joy when they told him, like a small boy riding his hobbyhorse, or baby-young Mitya riding Tatyana Glivenko or Elena Konstantinovskaya into the red sunset of, of, whatever; not to mention D. D. Shostakovich on the verge of being summoned by Comrade Stalin to the State Box! The curtain rises; "Lady Macbeth" begins.—No matter about "Lady Macbeth"; at last he was in step! But he wasn't going to unpack his underwear, oh, me! Because it was precisely when they, how should I say, and you thought they loved you and forgave you, that the knock came on the door! And then Nina would be staring in dry-eyed horror when they started dumping his scores and manuscripts on the carpet, looking for that *largo* in *passacaglia* form, and the children, you see, yes, exactly, my children. Which reminds me: I keep meaning to buy some white "Moscow" face powder for Galisha, because . . . And a blue crepe dress; she really wants a new dress. Poor child—with a father like me to, to, am I making myself clear? That's why a Stalin Prize is the highest honor in our great Soviet land, and I'm very, you know. It's said that his expression on that occasion resembled that of a child in a trench gazing up between his fingers at oncoming German bombers. (At that time we didn't have enough one fifty-twos to stop them.) And no wonder! He was chronically afflicted with stage-fright! He went home to Nina and muttered: I'm most upset, I don't know exactly why . . .

Why indeed? For in those days, thanks to Comrade Stalin, Soviet music had become as wide and stable as the treads of a T-34 tank! We felt ourselves to be impelled by the noble Soviet goal of rising above all prior cultural stages, of *planning* culture. There were only a few deviationists left. Well, actually, far too many of the leading composers were deviationists. And so now our new propaganda organ *Culture and Life* began to attack a certain D. D. Shostakovich. By 1948 he was being accused once more of formalistic and anti-democratic tendencies.

9

The Central Committee of the Communist Party singled out him and others as aliens. *Now they will start sawing up boxes for firewood again.* He instantly lost his position in the Composers' Union. When the director called him into his office to inform him of this new promotion, Shostakovich thanked the man, looking far away. He had to clean out his desk right away and go, to avoid contaminating the others. And the way my heart beats, that lurch, almost baroque, if I represented it as a, a, a, bass element then I could put it in my next opus. No, they didn't exactly call him *music's Kandinsky* anymore! Did Elena feel unclean when they called her in to expel her from the Komsomol? I never asked her about that, because . . . And when they took her off in a Black Maria, how vile did she feel then? I . . . There had once been a poster of D. D. Shostakovich in a copper helmet, leading the fire-watch on the Conservatory roof. That poster had been everywhere in Leningrad! Nina kept a copy to save for the children when they were older. If he ever found it, he'd, you know, wipe his asshole with it. Back in '41, Glikman's brother Gavriil had opined that the helmet suited him excellently. It went well with his classic face. (This individual, by the way, was another acolyte. When he received his call-up notice, he spent his last free moments at the Academy of Sculpture, carving a bust of Shostakovich out of white alabaster. Then off he went to artillery school.) Evidently our Great Composer, you know, a certain S——, had once again decided to make life *a battuta:* **LIFE HAS BECOME BETTER, COMRADES; LIFE HAS BECOME MORE JOYFUL.** Why be surprised? Elena had taught him the motto she'd learned in the Pioneers: *Always ready.* He used to whisper that into her ear, right before they, you know. She'd always giggled. My underwear's packed. Come and take me away, you bastards. Or worse yet, march me off to watch Roman Karmen's latest horror. What is it now? It'll come to me. Oh, I know: "Song of the Kolkhoz Fields!" What a . . . Should I compose a "Song of the Forests" or a "Song of the Factories"? Then they can all . . .

In February, much of his work, including that invidious Eighth Symphony, was banned by the organ Glavretkom—a necessary policy, with which no true Communist can argue. E. A. Mravinsky, who'd conducted the premiere of the Fifth a decade ago, under equally foreboding circumstances, had raised the score above his head then, at considerable risk to himself. Now the Fifth was to be outlawed altogether. Mravinsky conducted the final performance, kissed the score, then raised it high . . .

After all, what should this Shostakovich have expected? Refusing to participate in our collective struggle during the war years, he'd removed himself from the Leningrad front.

There was a broad, low snowy mound in the middle of Theater Square. Naked earth glistened darkly in the middle. The mound resembled the areola of a barely pubescent girl. He paced and paced around it, in that intersection of paths bordered by fences and benches. Beyond the fences lay snowy grass. He stopped. He gazed between the pillars of the Bolshoi Theater, remembering that evening a quarter-century ago now when he'd come rushing from the train station, rightly trusting to the curving, glowing tram to preserve his legendary punctuality. He'd had the score of "Lady Macbeth" in his briefcase, in case he might be expected to present it to Comrade Stalin. And then the crowds had come in, the curtain had gone up, and . . .

He trudged round and round the dirt.

In April, summoned to the First All-Union Congress of Soviet Composers to receive further instruction regarding his errors, Shostakovich, unable to further imperil Nina and the children, why did I ever, you know, rose to approach the lectern. His face was more squarish than it used to be. He no longer gazed shyly down at his adorers' feet; instead, he stared levelly through his condemners. He'd cropped his hair a trifle. His mouth was tighter and firmer. Even during the "Lady Macbeth" affair he'd managed to entrench himself out of reach of this special humiliation. But back then there were still Old Bolsheviks to vivisect. Now that Comrade Stalin had won the game, even white pawns such as Shostakovich had to paint themselves black, because the year after "Lady Macbeth," yes, in '37 it certainly was, the composer N. S. Zhelayev had been arrested for, for, what's the difference. He never came back, did he? And Elena had already had her little, how should I put it, *experience*. Thanks to what she'd whispered in his ear, he knew the pitch of a hammer striking a rail on an Arctic winter morning—prison camp reveille. That would be preserved in Opus 110. And what can I glean for my opus now? What's the meaning of, of my so-called, you know; oh, it's funny, really; it's crazy; I want to laugh because it feels just the same as receiving a Stalin Prize! Stagefright, you know, and all that. Should I have worn my Medal for the Defense of Leningrad, or would they have called that a provocation? Everything's a provocation. And the worst of it is . . . Galina must be praying for me; that's something she would do. If they take me away I could see her jumping out the window, and then I'd . . . And Elena must know about this from the newspaper. Elena, you're lucky that you didn't marry me. Ninusha agreed about *that*! He had to do this, for, for her and for the children, after which they'd never talk about it again. When he remembered how Meyerhold had disappeared—my God! The man was never anything but a theater manager!—and how his wife Zinaida had been found with her eyes cut out, why can't I stop thinking about that year after year?

For Mravinksy's grand gesture, as for the other one back in '38, he felt no gratitude, no, no, even gratitude he must dissimulate! Impossible to say what tune the "organs" might play now! And that impossibility haunted him. Every night his terror broke through his sleep.

Yesterday Nina had begged him to apply for membership in the Party. He'd replied (it was night time, and of course their quarrel took place in hideous whispers): I, I, I'll go there and shit all over myself, but I'll never do *that,* never, not even if they take us all away! I won't join the Nazi Party, either!

Gripping the podium with both hands, he stared into the first face he saw, a face as smug as some Stakhanovite cement works wristwatch-winner, exemplar of overweening productivity. The face bared its teeth at him quite suddenly, in *scherzo*-like aggression.

Shostakovich cleared his throat. He said: Comrades, it's all true. I'm—I'm a formalist alien . . . —Frowning uneasily, he scratched at his mop of fading hair, his face's ageing skin unable to avoid wrinkling itself up in a thousand new grimaces. All around him he seemed to see the double grins of Nazi caps above Nazi faces. He thought to himself: *the whipping rack at Buchenwald.* But how could he have gone off the track? Why not just imagine himself as being one with those pallid figures of acrobats glaringly illuminated in the darkness of the Moscow Circus? Why be gratuitous? People were going to call him gratuitous anyway, because he, well. They were waiting, and not very nicely, either.

He said, straining not to explode in laughter or tears: Every time I turn on the radio and hear Klavdia Sulzhenko sing "The Blue Kerchief," I realize the depths of my, you see, well, I mean to say, I, I, certain negative characteristics in my musical style prevented me from reconstructing myself . . .

Beneath the gigantic likenesses of Lenin and Stalin he confessed all his crimes, his anti-democratic, neurotic erotic tendencies. This way Nina wouldn't have to, you know. It's not real. Not even music is real. That's why I reject program music, because it pretends to be real. And Galisha, darling little Galisha who had just yesterday tossed her head at him so pertly with her braids dancing across the shoulders of her flower-striped sweater; he'd been helping her with her homework when she, she, anyway, how could he have ever thought of harming his own daughter?—Why can't I get wacky?—That's what he'd actually used to say; he'd compared himself to Rodchenko, back in the years when, hell. And Meyerhold had said . . . Meyerhold never came back either. And what they did to his wife, it makes me want to . . . What's that sound? That's what the neighbors heard when they started in on her left eye. Remember it, please, for Opus 110. Then he expressed his total faith in the wisdom of the Party.

Darling Mita, you've united the left and right! For at the same time your equally endangered colleagues spurn you—some of them are as endangered as you, but they haven't recanted yet—spontaneous representatives of the Soviet people threaten Nina and shatter your windows.

10

August was when they hanged the Fascist collaborator A. A. Vlasov. That's how we light the way ahead *with a searchlight*. The way the rope creaked, can I put that in Opus 110? In September, while Comrade Stalin's cadres began rounding up Zionist conspirators, Shostakovich was stripped of his teaching jobs at the Leningrad Conservatory and the Moscow Conservatory alike.—Give him eight grams! somebody screamed out. (That was a bullet's weight.)—Thank you, thank you, he replied, rising from his seat. I was never here, so how can I feel humiliated? They think they've won a so-called "victory," but I'm not here; I'm under the piano keys, in my, my . . . That's where I want to rest. Are my lips still moving? I feel extremely . . . And if only she could have . . . In which case, it would need to be sixteen grams!—Then he walked out, blinking steadily through his glasses. Call it a down cadence; it wasn't despair. No one dared say a word of comfort to him, certainly not his students, who that very day had been standing respectfully behind him as he played another theme for them at the piano; well, could he blame them? I'm only a, a, whatchamacallit. Of course they wanted to be progressive; they didn't want to be eradicated. It was very . . .

Poor Maxim, now ten years old, found himself required to denounce his father during an examination at music school.—Smiling when he heard, Shostakovich stroked the boy's hair.

I'm sorry, Papa. Don't be angry. They made me do it, but I love you—

Of course, of course, laughed Shostakovich. I know you're loyal to me. After all, dear boy, we cannot help but put ourselves at the service of our own, um, class. Now why are your socks so dirty? Come here a minute. Oh, dear, oh, my—

What were his sensations at that moment? Within Maxim's eyes, something screamed and screamed; that was the thing that agonized him, or, to be specific, the sound (what's that sound?); his soul knew what it ought to sound like, and it became another note of Opus 110! Well, well, and Lebedinsky informs me Akhmatova's also had her moment of fame, in *Leningradskaya Pravda*. "Poetry Harmful and Alien to the People." That's really very . . . To think she carried my Seventh Symphony out of Leningrad on her lap. Poor lady, poor lady! I'd better keep my distance. Someday I'll have to set one of her poems to music, just to kind of, you know. Glikman assures me that in "Poem Without a Hero," the words *my seventh* are a reference to, to . . . What's that sound? Oh, it hurts; it hurts; *it hurts*!—What was it like for Shostakovich, and was it the same right then, when it first exploded within his skull like a cerebral hemorrhage, as it would be twelve years later when he locked himself up in the spa town above Dresden and flicked down the notes of that very chord onto the music-paper? How can I tell you? Well, during the war years, the inborn secrecy behind his shyness, which our Revolution's communal character and his own ideals had besieged, had actually been temporarily breached, such was the emergency. Instead of hearing only his own music, he sometimes had to listen to people, whose various sorrows and aspirations could not but affect him. In particular, he could not get away from soldiers, because nearly every man was one. There'd been a certain Red Army man in Leningrad, whom he'd met only once, and only for an instant, yet whom he could never forget, whose entire family died an instant death that first August, courtesy of a shell dispatched to their apartment under authority of Field-Marshal Ritter Wilhelm von Leeb; this soldier had been wounded shortly thereafter, and he adored his wound as if it were his child; he was proud of it; it was his, and it was all he had. A German Fascist had bayoneted him in the forearm, but he'd killed the bastard; he'd cut his soft white throat! Drunk, perhaps absent without leave, with nowhere to go, the Red Army man literally grabbed Shostakovich in the street, increasing the latter's natural anxiety to a level approximating *fortissimo* because he was supposed to take his fire-warden station on the Conservatory roof in seventeen minutes; but the Red Army man, who was very tall and whose sour-sad breath and red-rimmed eyes haunted him forever, didn't understand that at all. First he told Shostakovich how in his opinion each member of his family must have died; of course he hadn't been there or he would have been dead, too; he'd been on the front line, which was not many blocks from here; and the activity of his imagination (Mama, you see, she likes to sit right at the window when she sews, 'cause her eyes ain't so good for detail work now; she's farsighted, so I figure she must've seen it coming; that's what gets to me) was his organism's way of resisting the shock; after he'd told the story over and over—and Shostakovich felt nothing toward him but a compassion which was itself an agony; perhaps he never experienced such closeness with any other soul in his life, except when he and Elena were, you know—the Red Army man rolled up his sleeve to thrust the wound, the hideous wound, which he'd refused to allow any nurse to bandage and which was accordingly infected, into Shostakovich's face, lovingly recounting how he got it, how honored he was to carry its half healing, half putrefying scar with him forever; and he said that sometimes he kissed it and pretended that it was his dead wife's lips; sometimes he pretended that it was a very young girl named Natalka, a girl with long black hair whom he'd loved even more than his wife but whose father, unfortunately, had been an enemy of the people (and Shostakovich was thinking: my God, oh, dear, what are you saying?); sometimes he pretended that our Motherland was this young Natalka, and that when he was kissing his wound he was kissing her; then he got nasty and started asking Shostakovich what *he,* an obvious stinking intellectual, had done for our Motherland; at which point Glikman helped him get away. Each note of Opus 110 would be a wound like this, a wound which the composer cherished and prepared to spitefully thrust up everybody's ear—

But at the same time he *detected* this feeling and expertly reduced it to its component metals, in order to trim it into artful strips and weld it onto the most strategic chord-walls of Opus 110, he couldn't feel it. It possessed no reality.

Good Communists wrote him letters saying that he ought to be exterminated. Well, weren't they correct? Wasn't he a formalist, an American lapdog, a Vlasovite? They mentioned his thick black glasses; they categorized him as a bourgeois decadent aesthete, a Zionist apologist.—He winked at Nina like a sad old crow when he heard this last, and then he whispered in her ear: That makes me, so to speak, proud. Because, you see, do you know what Comrade Hitler said? *Conscience is a Jewish creation.* —And Nina jerked away from him as if she'd been burned. His suicidal cynicism appalled her.

Comrade Khrennikov had long since labeled him "alien to the Soviet people." They destroyed his recordings and scores wherever they could . . .

11

In that same year, just when Comrade Stalin began sealing off Berlin against the capitalists,* Shostakovich finished his cycle *From Jewish Poetry,* which, of course, given that second word, could never be publicly performed so long as Comrade Stalin was alive, and maybe not afterward, either. When his friends

---

*As the *Great Soviet Encyclopedia* explains, "the Western Powers . . . increasingly sabotaged the work of the Allied Control Council, and in March, 1948, wrecked it completely."

expressed determination to find a venue, he said: Why waste our efforts? This is our life . . .

His besieged hopes, like semi-skeletonized buildings glimpsed through the smoke of burning tanks, secreted themselves deeper and deeper behind his tics and his meaningless murmured assents to everything.

Activists said to him: Dmitri Dmitriyevich, we thought you'd learned your lesson in 1936, when we exposed the errors of "Ledi Makbet."

Yes, yes, exactly.

But we'd hoped you'd taken your punishment to heart! Certainly in your Seventh Symphony you placed your art in the service of the people.

Thank you, thank you—

It wasn't meant as a compliment. Frankly, you're not living up to your own former ideals.

I appreciate your valuable critical observations, he said to them humbly, comforted only by the thought of Nina's pillow-choked laughter tonight when he whispered all this mummery to her. Oh, he was a clown, wasn't he? They could never breach *his* defenses!

Do you understand the sanctions you face?

Naturally, comrades, and I'm sure those sanctions will, mmm, to speak, inspire me to, to (Ninusha will love this!) future creative work and provide, er, *insights*—

Dmitri Dmitriyevich, you're in grave danger of becoming an enemy of the people again!

I appreciate the warning, comrades. But don't worry about me; please don't worry. Rather than take a step backward I shall take a step, so to speak (Ninotchka will die laughing; actually Ninotchka will be terrified) *forward*—

Actually he didn't care anymore; he almost wanted them to shoot him, as long as Nina and the children wouldn't be harmed. Galina Ustvolskaya, well, she wasn't as close to him as Elena had been, and . . . Although her compositions were very . . . Do you remember Dziga Vertov's *heart of machines* sequence in "Stride, Soviet"? That must have been in 1926, because it was right before my Second, you know, Symphony. A fine filmmaker, really, although he was also very, well, like Roman Lazarevich, he was too much the true believer. I wonder if Vertov's still alive. I suppose he's *disappeared.* Roman Lazarevich would know, but I don't dare ask him. I want a *heart of machines* for Opus 110. It'll be a machine for, I don't know, let's say for pulverizing human bones; Roman Lazarevich filmed that; I remember that for some reason I was in the Kino Palace with Ninusha, who cried—very unlike her, if I may say so. Give me eight grams! Or is it nine? Then they can pulverize my . . . He'd never felt *that* way before! When would he need that underwear in the suitcase? Back in '37 they liked to leave a disgraced man at liberty for weeks or months, to wear him out with worrying until the Black Maria came. Now life was more confusing, comrades, **LIFE HAS BECOME MORE JOYFUL.**

But, Mitya, wailed his wife, they're reaching out their hands to you! Please join them! I've never begged anything of you before—

Oh, me, oh, my! But a hand can also, you know, *grab* you!

There he was, almost rigid in the chair, anchored by his pear-shaped flesh, his white fingers outspread on the piano while G. A. Ilizarova stared worshipfully at him, her dark hair tucked back around her pale face like a helmet of chastity.—Dmitri Dmitriyevich, don't ever join the Party! she whispered. We're so proud of you! Keep fighting!

What if someone were listening? Quickly (but winking at Ilizarova) he began praising the ever brilliant victories of our Soviet people.

12

At this very same moment, his "Song of the Forests" (Opus 81), which celebrated Soviet labor (and incidentally praised Comrade Stalin), resounded in almost every factory of the USSR. Ninusha loved it, she actually loved it! That was the worst. He could hardly . . . Whereas "Lady Macbeth," which he'd dedicated to her, well, the point is that Ninusha now got her hair waved and smiled like a chiseled image above her starched white collar, seated compactly in the velvet padded box beside her husband, who might be arrested this very instant and who'd just won the Stalin Prize: ten thousand rubles! Poor woman, didn't she deserve her moment of fame?

Opus 81 was, from an artistic point of view, the opposite of conspicuous. Don't you remember how Saint Isaac's Cathedral used to be visible all the way from Finland, thanks to its golden dome? That was why we'd had to grey it down during the Nine Hundred Days—a very dark grey, as he remembered, which made the victory garden of cabbages all the greener. Opus 81 was good music greyed down for the sake of survival—greyed down to gaudy gold. And Nina didn't even care. But what was he saying? Nina loved him; she wanted him to succeed and thrive; as for the ten thousand rubles, she knew how to get through those; it's only a question of time and manpower. Now he could go out, get drunk and, you know. He'd also like to send some money to Elena

Konstantinovskaya, who Glikman said had been impoverished ever since she divorced Roman Lazarevich. This Professor Vigodsky didn't earn much, and they had a daughter now. Elena had a child! Imagine that! How time, you know, *flies*. He only hoped that she never heard "Song of the Forests." Oh, me! How could she not hear? And I used to tell her that I'd never . . . Well, we were young. But it's really, I mean I'm not too thrilled about this.

After the premiere in Leningrad, he rushed to his hotel room, accompanied by his pupil-mistress Galina Ustvolskaya, and hid his head beneath a pillow. Then he began weeping wretchedly with shame and self-disgust.

13

Ustvolskaya stood at the side of the bed. She knew him so well. Trying to suppress the loathing which rose up between her ribs like nausea, she said: You're being unfair to yourself. So what if you have to throw them a bone once in awhile? Don't forget your genius. You've accomplished so very very many of your dreams . . .

Thank you; thank you. But how can you love me now?

She hesitated.

Don't say it, he said, fearing the answer. Now let's talk about you. I fear you haven't been composing enough—

Dmitryosha, I'd rather keep worrying about you—

His lips vibrated like a brass player's. He finally said: Don't throw away your efforts.

14

He went home, and instantly got into an argument with his wife. (Someday she too would be a skeleton.) She said that she was sick and tired of his moping about the success of "The Song of the Forest." He didn't see what she was driving at. He said so. She said:

Did you really not think, or do you enjoy being self-destructive? When you make a mess, you ought to sweep up after yourself.

Ninotchka, don't be harsh, no, no, no, no, not now—

No! Stay there and listen. You look just like a cheap bourgeois in the movies; it's almost comical. You can't hide your secrets from me, Mitya. When you were sleeping with that slut Elena I could literally smell her on you. That cheap, catty smell of her—ugh! You're a man who has to have affairs. Maybe I would have preferred to love somebody different, but that's how it is, right? Well, are you going to answer me or not?

I, I don't see what this has to do with—

Maybe the only person that an artist can be faithful to is himself. Maybe he's got to betray everybody else. Will you kindly get that martyred look off your face? That's just how it goes. Sometimes I think you're not even conscious of it. A pair of dark eyes comes floating toward you, and you can't help yourself; you follow them like a sleepwalker—

Nina, you're *killing* me, that's what you're doing. Not that you even—

I'm not complaining. I knew what I was getting into. As soon as you married me you had to step out. *That bastard* tells you to zig; he even warns you in *Pravda,* and so you zag. All that trouble we got into over "Lady Macbeth," you *knew* you were bringing it on us! Oh, I'm not saying it was anything personal—

Nina!

Nina, what? You're a genius and all that, but you don't know the first thing about yourself. You're always looking for a Muse to follow, and she's got to be a dark-eyed Muse from someplace else. Any other Soviet composer would be thrilled by the success of "The Song of the Forest," but *you*—

I can see it's no use continuing with this talk, no, no, no. I'm going round to see Lebedinsky . . .

Mitya, stop acting childish. You know that I love you. Hopefully you're aware that I even respect certain things about you. I'm only the slightest bit angry with you; I'm not asking you to change your ways. After all, you're going to sleep with whomever you sleep with.

Excuse me, but what's the purpose of this conversation?

I don't know. As you always say, why waste one's efforts? And yet, when you come back all rapturous from your little Galisha, who by the way is never going to marry you, and you think that you're hiding it from me even though she *studied* with you for ten bloody years, and your other little Galisha, the one you and I are raising together, knows perfectly well what's going on, as does Maxim, and meanwhile you feel angry that I'm me and not her, so you get all strict and silent with me, why, then I guess I want to tell you what you are.

Very well then, he cried, so pale and agonized that she couldn't decide whether to slap his face or burst out crying, what am I?

You're a—well, well, you don't follow the Party line, that's for sure! My God, but you're a free spirit, Mitya! You're a *formalist.*

15

Dmitryosha, would you like some tea? I could make it for you very quickly. A nice, hot cup of tea—there's comfort in it, especially on a cold dark night . . .

She had served in a military hospital during the war. She knew how to tend the sick even when she felt very angry.

He said to her: Can music attack evil or not?

Certainly not. All it can do is scream.

He laughed gruesomely.—You *formalist,* you! But still, I wonder what it all means, if there's no, so to speak, no purpose in—

Ustvolskaya's face wore an expression of pity, irritation and perhaps repulsion; he couldn't make it out. She said to him: Please don't cry anymore, Dmitryosha. You'll suffer much less when you stop hoping for the impossible. There's no hope for any of us, whether they shoot us or not.

But illusions don't die all at once—

I never had any.

It's a long process, like a toothache. And then the illusions rot and stink inside us, like—

You've told me all that before. Drink your tea now.

I've seen you hold your teacup when you compose, and I've seen you wrap your long white fingers around the warmth.

Whenever she had an orgasm, her mouth reminded him of a certain little round window in the Kirov Theater about which he used to have friendly feelings.

16

In January 1949, Comrade Stalin finally began his campaign against Jewish influences. Maybe it was only now, with the distractions of the war years more or less mastered, that he'd found the time to read *Mein Kampf.* In February, Galina Ustvolskaya completed her Sonata No. 2, whose dreary fetters of quarter-notes left her lover almost beside himself with gloom. In March, at *that bastard*'s express wish, Shostakovich was sent to New York as a member of the Soviet peace delegation. All his works had been un-banned four days before. (We'll take care of that problem, Comrade Shostakovich.—This was exactly what Stalin had said on the telephone. Oh, me, oh, my, he'd, so to speak, authorized the operation!) And the composer, who'd forgotten nearly everything except how to be most vigilantly afraid, suddenly began to hope that if he only acted sufficiently obedient and broken, maybe his music might be performed again.

Meanwhile, what was he supposed to play? Probably not the incidental music to "Lady Macbeth"—*that* would be a joke! And Opus 40 would only make me sad and get Elena in trouble. What about my crowd-pleaser? But you-know-who is taking measures, so *Pravda* informs me, to transform the Soviet sector of shattered Nazidom into an All-German Republic subservient to the needs of, how shall I put this, history. Therefore, my Seventh Symphony might have, er, outlived its *usefulness,* you see. Because we need Germans again! Time to renew the, how shall I say, the Nazi-Soviet Pact! Ha, ha! Ninusha, don't glare at me with your mouth open like that, because it makes you, um, but seriously, in these *happy, happy* times, wouldn't it be better to forget about the siege of Leningrad? And Vlasov never existed, either. If only I'd composed a fluffy little trio or something in honor of Operation Citadel! Because that would be really, really . . . Please don't look at me like that, Galina!

To be sure, our *Great Soviet Encyclopedia* continues to state that the Seventh *played an important role in rallying the world against fascism.* But encyclopedias are subject to revision. Thus we find Shostakovich playing the second movement of his less famous Fifth Symphony at Madison Square Garden, his dark-suited shoulders squared as he sat at the piano, his face hunching forward, his mouth stiffly downcurved: First a chord as warm as the streak of white foam in a *café au lait,* and then, you know. He couldn't understand the simplest things Americans said, even though he'd once taken English lessons with Elena Konstantinovskaya. *It gives me the creeps.* That was all he remembered. How many years ago was that?—I don't feel much enthusiasm, he said to himself as his widespread fingers began to hurtle down on the piano's white-and-black terrain. Somebody in the front muttered: That guy looks like a weirdo.

Afterward, there'd be more reporters, insinuations and petty-bourgeois stupidity, when all he cared about was keeping his family out of, why say it? America being a capitalist country, the various civic choirs sing *a cappella* there, meaning without instrumental accompaniment. In a well-ordered zone, such license would never be tolerated. High time to harden our line against the Americans! They're very . . . Oh, me! Anyhow, why the Fifth? Because we're on Fifth Avenue, stupid! That symphony got me in trouble, too, because the audiences applauded too loudly when I was officially a, a, what was it, oh, yes, a cultural alien. Elena had already been taken to the, you know.—Second movement. An hour more; then I can sit in a corner and drink champagne. Maybe some American woman will consent to, you know, pop out the cork! The shot heard round the world . . . *Pizzicato*.

The Fifth was hardly his, so to speak, favorite—I mean, to hell with it. It was subtitled *a Soviet artist's creative reply to just criticism*—precisely the motif he sought to sound today.

He played adequately. We all did, or else. Even Akhmatova wrote her chirpy odes in praise of *that bastard*. Well, not everyone: Brave Tsevtaeva had actually, I don't need to say it. He'd heard that it didn't hurt, unless they were doing it to you and they used piano wire. Vlasov must have . . . But we don't talk about that. In one of her last poems, written when the sleepwalker's army marched into Prague, Tsevtaeva had written, "in anger and in love," *I refuse to be*. That sentiment would be mortared into the grey chamber of Opus 110.

Decrescendo. The Americans applauded—hypocritically, he thought. His foot kept jerking sideways when he bowed. They say that you keep twitching for a long time, even after you, well. Then he read out denunciations upon command, all the while twisting an unlit "Kazbek" cigarette. He attacked among others a certain D. D. Shostakovich, who'd committed various errors. His mouth grew dry, and he could not finish the speech. A pleasant male voice completed it for him.

17

Yes, he grew pale when he drank vodka. He grew paler when he drank the future. To be sure, it wasn't as bad as those Moscow nights at the beginning of '45 when there was no electricity from six in the morning to six at night, so that by three in the afternoon, when the winter sun failed, he'd had to sit in cold darkness, unable to compose by that pale kerosene-light; later on he'd be tense, unable to sleep before midnight, awaking in the dark with his heart stuttering like a machine-gun. Now he . . . In fine, his major task nowadays consisted in preparing responses to various foreseeable criticisms. Once in awhile he got the odd job: Now, Dmitri Dmitriyevich, there's going to be a twenty-four-gun salute in Moscow for the liberation of each capital, so the world will know that it wasn't just Leningrad, that it was Minsk, Kiev, Stalingrad and all the rest! We've decided, and no doubt you'll agree, that your fanfare ought to consist of twenty-four-note chords, which will undoubtedly create an impressive tonal effect, much wider than the bass theme which you'll be called upon to write to symbolize the Fascist German command. Then it was time for another dream of leaving home on a rainy night, Nina screaming and shaking her fist at him through the glass of the front door, Maxim and Galya silently mouthing *Daddy, Daddy, Daddy!* as he went through the darkness to Elena's house where she let him kiss her through the window but didn't allow him in.

How long could he remain in step? A hundred times a night he'd torture himself with his fears. Glikman dragged him off to see Roman Karmen's "Soviet Kazakhstan," which was reliably spectacular. Naturally he dreaded to find Elena at the Kino Palace; he felt crushed not to find her.

In 1950, shortly after the reactionary powers defeated our blockade of Berlin, he wrote a soundtrack for the film "Belinsky," scoring the orchestration with the same confident rapidity in which the former German Fascist Field-Marshal Paulus once drew up his orders of battle: a row for each subunit, motorized or not, each division assigned its own measure, then those measures clustered together into corps which he indrew to make his armies; the armies coalesced into *Heeresgruppen*; and the apparatchiks loved it. Much the same happened with *Hamlet*. The black telephone rang; Roman Karmen wished him to know that his scoring was perfect, superb.

But Karmen sounded sad! His voice was very . . . He was still, perhaps, getting over Elena, just like the rest of us—oh, me! But it wouldn't do to, well, especially given that he and I, er, and besides, I need him to call Arnshtam for me; I need work; I need a favor, dear Leo Oskarovich! Because all that "Zoya" money's gone. The children are so . . . By the way, whatever became of your actress Vodyanischkaya? An excellent Zoya! She reminded me a little of Elena. But what does this apparatchik *want* from me? Why won't he get off the line? Especially when I'm starting to feel a bit, you know, *panicked*? My dear Roman Lazarevich, if I'm permitted to, to—ahem!—to use a musical metaphor, not that I, well, one gets, so to speak, *tuned* to the person one loves. And then even though one clings to any stranger, or even takes her to bed and then, you know, all to, just to block that artillery barrage of, how should I say, loneliness, one feels bored and, and—a proxy just can't carry the tune! That's why I *do not like* too friendly or too antagonistic relationships between people. Or even if a proxy manages to carry the tune after all, a different key has a different, I don't know. So one says goodbye. But the instant one's alone again, the craving for the person one's tuned to comes back and then, don't think I don't know! How can I say any of this to you, my dear, *dear* Roman Lazarevich? By the way, next time you happen to see Leo Oskarovich, please do greet him for me and ask him if he has any, er, you know. And that child-actress who played Zoya when she was a little girl, what was her name? It'll come to me. Was it Katya Skvortsova or was it Elena Skvortsova? Elena is such a common name; it keeps coming up.

He composed the music to that cinema spectacular, "The Fall of Berlin," whose protagonist was Comrade Stalin. Roman Karmen wasn't involved, he claimed, because he was too hard at work on "Soviet Turkmenistan," but it might have been because he'd fallen out with the bastards at Mosfilm, because I've heard that what you say is not what we want to hear, so he said, and Karmen replied, after which they both fell silent; well, so kind of you to trouble yourself, my dear, *dear* Roman Lazarevich! Thank you for speaking with Leo Oskarovich on my behalf, even though, well. Does he still play the piano? And how is—never mind, I just wanted to, to, and please accept my very best wishes.

He agreed with the wise decision to withhold his new Fourth String Quartet from publication, due to its Jewish intonations.

18

They sent him to East Germany as the principal Soviet delegate to the Bach Festival. He didn't want to go, but he was on the jury. (He thought he heard somebody calling.) A Russian would win. He'd already promised to take the appropriate "class approach."

His escort of German Communists clicked their heels and saluted him. They asked if he needed anything.—Thank you, thank you, but please don't trouble yourselves, he replied. The other jurors called him *esteemed comrade.* He remembered Nazis tall and grinning. He remembered white blurred faces in the winter twilights of Leningrad, dark eye-sockets of starvation. He remembered all the newsreels he'd seen of milk-pale children getting hanged, the German Fascists fussily adjusting each noose beforehand to get it perfect. Luckily, Comrade Stalin had liquidated their state apparatus.

East Berlin remained much damaged, thanks to the senseless resistance of the Hitlerite remnants. Laughing, somebody remarked that Dresden looked worse. Comrade Alexandrov wanted to know why the Bach Festival was in Leipzig when Leipzig was the city of the proto-Fascist Richard Wagner. Shostakovich kept silent, feeling worms crawling in his heart. He decided to avoid Dresden forever. He didn't want to see any more, you know. About Berlin, which was, after all, merely our transit point, he didn't care. Years ago, his teacher Glazunov had praised the city's stone gates, but their grandiosity had long since tarnished into something like earth. Was the western sector any less ruined? Well, why shouldn't it be? How close was it?—Right over there!—And had they . . . ? Better not to ask. He felt as if he were suffocating and bleeding at the same time. What was that sound? He wanted a piano to compose on. What was that sound? On the windowsill of the car, his fingers began to tap out the *allegro molto* of Opus 110.

He didn't care about Bach, either, not then; over the decades he'd tried to learn what he could from Bach the craftsman, who put one note after the other, then fitted the third note perfectly into place; but this innocuously banal observation proved to be the spearhead of something inimical which now breached his mind's defenses, namely, the axion of that Nazi mediocrity Paulus, who if you don't keep up with such things was the Field-Marshal we'd captured at Stalingrad; apparently he used to aphorize: *It's merely a question of time and manpower.* That was how Bach must have built his compositions; it's what we all do, and when I myself, when I . . .

The next time he saw Glikman, he asked whether we'd shot Paulus; Glikman wasn't sure; he might have missed the announcement in *Pravda*. It's just a question of . . . and for the rest of that day, Bach was spoiled for him. What if there were no difference between people who created bit by bit and people who murdered piece by piece? Nobody would agree, of course; anyhow it was better to think of something else, Elena Konstantinovskaya for instance. Her hair was fire and her skin was milk. What if she'd been in Dresden when the Anglo-Americans came? Why had she divorced Roman Lazarevich? Glikman said . . . Actually, he probably shouldn't think about Elena.

Intermission! Time to write a postcard to Glikman: *Everything is so fine, so perfectly excellent, that I can find almost nothing to write about.*

After they gave him a tour of Stalin-Allee he asked for permission to return to the hotel to rest, because thanks to his Leningrad education he already possessed an intimate comprehension of the way that the corners of bombarded buildings, being stronger than the rest, survive to form grisly spires whose churchlike effect is accentuated at night when the stars delineate the nave of an immense cathedral of niches, crypts, galleries, freestanding stone doorways in which one half expects to see a Russian icon, a marble likeness of a German Catholic saint, a Kaiser's sarcophagus; but there is nothing to make an offering to, no reason to lay down even a withered flower in memory of Europe Central's dead. Now a whitish-yellow light comes glaring: a military patrol. This is closest we can come to gilded grillework, comrades! Save your gold for Opus 110.

Please, Comrade Schostakowitsch, a German woman begged in secret, my little brother's being denazified because everybody in his school had to join the Hitler Youth. It wasn't his fault; what was he supposed to do? This letter, I received it last month, it says that his apartment got taken away and since then I haven't . . .

To be sure, to be sure. Dear lady, I'm very sorry. That is the reality . . .

And a train bore him away across the flat green of the German heartland.

19

In Leipzig he stood beside the pianist T. P. Nikolayeva, who was fresh from Moscow.

Would you like to tour Dresden, Dmitri Dmitriyevich? inquired an individual in raspberry-colored boots. We're quite close. It's good for the Russian soul, actually, to see it so smashed up. I hate all these Germans. You do, too, don't you? You haven't forgotten Leningrad, have you?

Comrade Alexandrov, you're completely on the mark, so to speak, and if I have time after the competition—well, well, who's to say how long it'll last?

And then they all went into the Thomaskirche, where Bach's remains had just been reinterred.

Nikolayeva waited rigidly; she must have been nervous. Although since '45 he'd passed her many times in the half-real darkness of the Conservatory, his own weariness, which breeds narrowness, and the various persecutions raining down on him like sizzling steel fragments, had isolated him; this young woman might as well have been a stranger; after all, she'd studied with Goldenweiser, not with him. His eyes were dull, round-cornered triangles of light splayed out upon his spectacles. He'd better not flirt; he was getting too old! A long, long time ago, once upon a time, in fact, Akhmatova had licked her lips, and he'd laughingly cried: Very good, Anna Andreyevna, yes, very good. The embouchure *must* be kept wet, since you're about to play my French horn . . . —No, those days are buried. This fine young Nikolayeva, far too lively to be homely, maybe it actually wasn't too late to, never mind, smiled beside him, showing her upper teeth. What sort of person was she? Another devotee of white keys and black keys who knew her in childhood remembers her as *this typical Russian girl, with her two braids, always serious, friendly and neat.* Nationals of the capitalist powers make each other's acquaintances (at least, so I'm told) by asking how they prefer to spend money: Do you collect stamps? I like to watch war movies. But to know somebody in our Soviet land, which now includes half of Germany and will in the measurable future include all of it, one need only learn what form her suffering happened to take during the Great Patriotic War (husband hanged in Minsk, sister starved to death in Leningrad, all four sons killed in battle at Stalingrad); however, since such communications are painful both to transmit and to receive, it's better that we all share a tacit commonality of horror, speaking only with our eyes or by means of music. So again, what sort of person was she? When she began to play, she did not fill the Thomaskirche with soulful gloom; instead, something light, distinct, aloof constructed itself: a castle, not a fountain, an artifact whose tessellated surface possessed a precise and nearly perfect geometry of notes; her rendition contained no chiaroscuro, only skill. Without haste or melodrama, with the seemingly simple harmony of a Roman inscription, she built her castles in the air, nakedly showing herself, unashamed and unafraid as he could never be; even in his youth, when he'd been the future's darling from whom all misfortune would forever withhold itself, his nature had tended to express itself extravagantly—hence the mischievous grotesqueries of "The Nose," the rapid fire of "Bolt," the complex dissonances of "Lady Macbeth," none of which were strained or "wrong," simply hyperactive, a trifle anxious, maybe; this was D. D. Shostakovich, to be sure; this was "honest," but, but, how should I say? Nikolayeva made music as a Tsarina must have carried herself, with calmly unhurried grace. It was as if she were saying to him: All that's happened is inconsequential; it cannot hurt us anymore; there's only music, which lives within us and beyond us, needing us to express it but capable of surviving forever between expressions. Castle succeeded castle.

The jury had instructed her to play whichever one of Bach's forty-eight preludes and fugues she'd best prepared; she played them all. Shostakovich lost himself. He no longer saw the grey heads like eggs in the wooden pews. He felt, how should I say, quite heartened, because . . . Actually (I hope it's appropriate to reveal his secret), he felt as if he'd found a new companion to dwell with him in the secret world beneath the piano keys! Not that he and she could ever . . . Besides, he'd never let himself be caught again. Because after Elena, with all that, you know, it was better not to even . . . She's Elena Vigodsky now, imagine! And how could I hope for anything? At least I can . . . And so Tatyana won the competition. Flowers for her! More flowers for Bach's grave . . . His spectacles kept slipping down his nose. He felt very . . . Then and there he resolved to compose a cycle of preludes and fugues (Opus 87), dedicated to her and arranged in ascending fifths. The brief, happy flame of the Fugue in A Minor, which he'd write the following year, became his special homage to her soul.

Esteemed comrade . . . said a German, but already Shostakovich's inner life was winging away with careful subtlety, in just the same way that the first prelude, the *moderato* in C major, begins with the very notes of Bach himself, sweet and melodious, classical, like a good Communist composer following the correct harmonic line; and then comes a dissonance. The melody returns, but muted and misted by chromatism. The prelude begins to soar farther and farther into the sky of absolute music, until that ordered landscape has been interred beneath clouds, and we rise beyond atonality into a sacredness beyond comprehension. Flashes of green and golden orderedness reveal themselves far below, then vanish because we are in the sky. We have escaped. We are beyond them. We have died.

20

In 1951 he was elected deputy to the Supreme Soviet of the Russian Federated Soviet Republic. Taking his bench, he felt the gaze of the pale, titanic Lenin behind him. Lenin was stone. He was stone. They asked him when he would consecrate his symphony to Lenin, and he muttered something. His thoughts were as dull and brittle as war-metal. On the way home he took a detour toward Lebedinsky's to pay him back for the bottle of vodka he'd borrowed last week, and a few old women, members of the former possessing classes who'd somehow escaped prison camps, were huddled against an icy wall, begging. With a shy grimace, Shostakovich approached them. He gave the nearest crone a few rubles, his face flushed with embarrassment, and rushed away, trying not to hear the others' imploring cries. And then on the other side of the street, in a nice coat with a silver fox–fur collar, *there she was,* Elena Konstantinovskaya I mean, her hair now grey but only the more, what can I say, I'm afraid to say beautiful, because, well, she was as perfect, and as unlikely for being so, as a gold-framed prerevolutionary icon; and she saw him but both of them had been educated by those niches in corridors in which passing prisoners can be placed, faces to the wall, so that they won't recognize each other. He hoped that she was better off with this, this, whatshisname, this Vigodsky; their daughter must be very, well, he could ask his sister Mariya. Anyhow, hadn't he possibly glimpsed her at the premiere of Roman Karmen's "Soviet Georgia"? Because nowadays one's eyes, you know, were not so very . . . He rushed home and collapsed. Thank God Ninusha was out! He sobbed for his life and for himself. He tried to keep silent at all times, but every now and then they gave him a speech to read, and he had to stand up and mumble it. In musical language, the phrase *da capo al segno* means *repeat these measures until you reach the sign S*. The sign S was Stalin. It was for D. D. Shostakovich to repeat and repeat what he'd been told.

He sat down. He reassured himself: There is no form. There is no content. No words mean anything.—His foot twitched, and his face erupted in grimaces.

He could not forget that time when the NKVD had interrogated him about his connection with Marshal Tukhachevsky. Down the hall he'd heard somebody screaming—very pure screams mostly in B-flat; in due time he'd wring them into Opus 110. Now he was a deputy to the Supreme Soviet. Tomorrow he'd be lying next to Tukhachevsky if that was what they wanted. How did that jingle go? *It's not enough to love Soviet power. Soviet power also has to love you.*

He drummed his fingers on his knee, working out the cadences of his preludes and fugues, for which the Union of Composers would denounce him again as a "formalist." At his summons, Nikolayeva came rushing to his flat to hear each composition as he completed it: Do have some more pancakes, darling. Ninusha really knows how to, that's right, with sour cream. Sometimes she sat at the other piano and watched his flickering fingers; sometimes she sat on the sofa beneath Akhmatova's portrait. When it was just him and her he was always able to play *con fuoco*, with fire.

The very first time she came, he'd finished the C major pair, which he played quite boldly, she thought; and then without a pause, gazing into her eyes, he commenced the Prelude in A Minor. When he played the accompanying fugue for her, richly *allegretto*, a deep flush began to ascend from the base of her neck. She understood that this music signified *her*. Even now, after Stalin and Zhdanov, no deficit barred him from the perfect world within the black keys, the chromatic world of sharps and flats and skittering celestial evasions, the place between yes and no. Needless to say, this piece got singled out for special criticism at that recital in the Union of Composers, whose flowerbeds are planted so that the blossoms form likenesses of Lenin and Stalin.

I absolutely reject such music, began our Union Secretary, a certain malignant S. Skrebov. And in my view, the A minor fugue sounds distorted and false, erroneous in its modulations and chords. As for the G major prelude . . . —

Nikolayeva turned the pages for him as he played.—Thank you, Tatyana, he whispered, his new spectacles sitting more heavily than ever on his flesh which was now of grandfatherly coarseness. In consequence of his anxiety he played extremely badly.

Dmitri Dmitriyevich needed to remember (his colleagues explained, as he sat at the piano with his head between his knees) that the intelligentsia no longer existed for itself; it was only an advance detachment of the working class. He was making the same errors he'd made with "Lady Macbeth" back in 1936. He was running a serious risk of being considered a deserter from the cultural front.

Dmitri Dmitriyevich, not only did you play atrociously, but the works are so gloomy that they're going to impede your creative rehabilitation.

You're absolutely correct, of course, replied the composer, while Nikolayeva stood comfortingly beside him, as if she were about to turn another page. You need, how should I put it, loyal lyrics and sanitary symphonies, people's preludes and, and—let's see now—

At least he understands that much.

If you don't mind my saying so, you ought to listen to your own Seventh Symphony, Dmitri Dmitriyevich! There you succeeded in drawing your music from the life of the masses. I'm told that you based the third movement entirely on indigenous folksongs of our fraternal peoples. Isn't that so?

Yes, yes, I assure you, whispered Shostakovich. He smiled faintly, and his spectacles flashed. He tried to light a cigarette, but his trembling fingers kept breaking the matches.

Now, this formalist trash you've just subjected us to, this is, well—why can't you be guided by Party spirit?

I much appreciate your guidance, comrades. You certainly know how to, um, *to light the way ahead with a searchlight*. And what luminescence! It's very . . . Could you recommend—

If you keep it simple you'll never go wrong, Dmitri Dmitriyevich. For instance, do you know that song "Chapaev the Hero Roamed the Urals"? That's a real Soviet classic.

Oh, yes, oh, *oh*, yes, I've heard that on the radio. There seems to be quite a demand for it.

Or Pokrass's ditty—you know, "The Red Army Is Most Powerful of All."

Perhaps Dmitri Dmitriyevich should also pay more attention to the heroic epics of oppressed Slavic peoples.

We already told him that, comrade. And, to give him his due, that Seventh Symphony does, after all—

Thank you, thank you!

We're all in favor of internationalism, Dmitri Dmitriyevich, but there's a difference between internationalism and *cosmopolitanism*, if you see what I'm saying. You're playing into the hands of the Zionists!

The Zionists! But I never—I mean, in that case what a terrible, er, *error* I've committed!

He sat there at the piano bench, smiling at them over his shoulder, and his fidgety hands trembled over the keys with the fingers dangling down, each hand like the burned half-skeleton of a warstruck bridge, until Nikolayeva finally laid her hand on him and whispered in his ear. He leapt gratefully up and found a chair in the corner of the stage.

And he keeps himself aloof from us. He won't apply to the Party—

Succeeding at last in lighting a cigarette, Shostakovich admitted the absolute justice of all their criticisms. Then he went home with Nikolayeva.

She said to him: How are you feeling, Dmitri Dmitriyevich?

Agitato, he laughed, writhing his fingers.

When no one could see, she took his face in her hands and kissed him, *affettuoso.* But it wasn't, you know.

21

Nearly despairing of his unteachability, they nonetheless assigned him an old tutor to come to his home and quiz him on his knowledge of the works of Comrade Stalin. The tutor was horrified to find no portrait of Comrade Stalin in his study. Shostakovich stammered and apologized, behind his back all ten fingers lashing like the tentacles of a fresh-caught cuttlefish; beneath the flurry, with a cool cruel humorousness, his defensive apparatus was already preparing sentences of insidiously mocking abnegation: To be sure, Comrade Ivanov, I must have been asleep all these years, but it's only because I, well, you see, I knew that Comrade Stalin had worked everything out, so I thought that he, I mean, I suppose I've been lazy (if I could simply make it up to him and be his, his—ha, ha, ha! percussion instrument!), so now it's time for this old fool to *learn*; and since everything has been analyzed for all time by Comrade Stalin's genius, perhaps if you taught me the high points, I could, so to speak, take three steps forward instead of two steps back, because it's all a question of time and manpower, and then once I understand the subtleties my music will doubtless attain, um, perfect *melodiousness.*

Glikman prepared cribs of the odious volumes, so he didn't have to read them. The tutor was astounded at his progress. He promised to hang a portrait of Comrade Stalin just as soon as he found the right one, *to hang him, I said,* he whispered that night to Ninusha, chuckling so helplessly that she feared he might choke. *Oh, that, that murdering bastard.*

He wanted the whole cycle to be played together—everything from scherzo to sarabande—but didn't dare to do it himself. The devoted Nikolayeva did. He dreamed that she was summoning him to her side.

In 1952, the year of Roman Karmen's classic "Aerial Parade," he won another Stalin Prize, category two, for his choral work "Ten Poems on Texts by Revolutionary Poets" (Opus 88). Meanwhile he finished his Fifth Quartet, wearing his heart on his musical sleeve by quoting from the Trio for Clarinet, Violin and Piano of his beloved Galina Ustvolskaya.

22

What are you dreaming about now? asked his wife.

You might better ask me what I'm hearing. I can't get the third movement of my Seventh out of my head. Well, well, excuse me, my dear, take no notice . . .

It's those pastoral passages that you're ashamed of listening to on the sly—

How on earth did you know?

Because you have to compose them to keep the apparatchiks off your back and so you write ugly music all the time just to protest, but deep down you'd rather—

Untrue, untrue, he sighed, lighting up a "Kazbek" cigarette. I always preferred ugly music! Even "Lady Macbeth" wasn't diatonic at all, and that was before I felt compelled to be anything in particular—

Then why do you hear that third movement now? You told me at the time that you wrote it just so the masses would—

And that's why I can't bear to listen to it now, don't you see? I'm getting tired of—

Oh, I think you rather like it.

23

In 1953, the Jewish composer Weinberg was arrested. With almost suicidal courage, Shostakovich opened his desk, withdrew a single sheet of music-paper as thin as that with which we blacked out windows back in Leningrad, turned it over and wrote a letter directly to Comrade Beria on his colleague's behalf. Something sealed off the tunnel between face and soul—something did, surely, like an impermeable steel cofferdam on a petroleum freighter. Because the spouse of an enemy of the people automatically became an enemy, too, Weinberg's wife Natalya would be arrested next—at dawn, no doubt;

Lebedinsky whispered to him that that was the fashion now.—I'm sure that he'll take a "camp wife," sobbed poor Natalya; he'd gotten her drunk, not knowing what else to do for her.—Of course not, my dear lady. You're far too beautiful for him ever to, you know. Don't worry, don't worry . . . —And probably all this time he was on a slave ship bound for, say, Kolyma. Or had they shut down Kolyma?—Shostakovich made quiet arrangements to adopt the couple's seven-year-old daughter Vitosha. A man in raspberry-colored boots advised him to let the matter go, and he said: Oh, me! What a, a *preposterous* error I've just committed!—at which the apparatchik understood all too well that this unmanageable Shostakovich would never alter, would never stop doing whatever he could to save Vitosha.

No wonder it was so cold in here! The paper around the windows had started to crack. I'll have to be sure and remind dear Ninusha to glue down some new strips of *Isvestiya;* that hot air should keep us warm! And if not, let's send for Rostropovich and his cello. *Now they will start sawing up boxes for firewood again.* What a joke—oh, me! Have I already told Mstislav Leopoldovich? Nina thought it was stupid. Nina's ready, thank God; she's always been brave. Let them open up with their eighty-eights!

Then, trembling with terror (he wouldn't have felt alive without that), he began to make, so to speak, inquiries, very tactfully, of course, so that they wouldn't, I think you understand, and Comrade Alexandrov dropped by to inform him with an evil smile that that shit he'd interested himself in was still in transfer prison, Nizhnegorodsky Prison it turned out to be, not Lefortovo, thank God, Who according to the *Great Soviet Encyclopedia* is *an imaginary figure of a powerful supernatural being;* Nizhnegorodsky is not as bad as, say, Kresti in Leningrad; and Comrade Alexandrov even explained how Natalya could send parcels.—If I had my way, he added, I'd give him nine grams of lead, right in the kisser! As for you, Dmitri Dmitriyevich, guess what color your file is now? Want a hint? Try shit-brown. As for that Zionist scum, he'll never, ever get out. If you really want to help that kike family, tell Natalya to divorce him and change her name. She'll pull through; she's not bad looking, for an old bitch. In your opinion, are women sufficiently intelligent to play chess? Because if she isn't, she's going to be checkmated! I don't mind telling you that you've made a serious mistake this time. The only reason I'm sticking my neck out for you is that you were in Leningrad when it mattered . . .

Fortunately, Stalin now shook his fist at the sky, fell back into bed and died; and a month afterward Weinberg found himself released.

Shostakovich sat at home. He'd grown as fat as one of the pillars of Saint

Isaac's church. His flesh was bluish-grey like the Neva in the dank days of November, when the gilded dome of Kazan Cathedral pales into irresolution. Many white hands like milk-puddings spilled on his piano. A cluster of souls clung around the score of his symphony, far below V. I. Lenin's portrait. His good friend Denisov had somehow obtained five hundred grams of pure Caspian caviar, the black variety, whose globules burst between the teeth like ripe grapelets. (Give him nine grams!) Glikman was absent. He'd had to do something with his wife. Shostakovich had always tried to help Glikman. Upon learning of his second marriage, he advised him: If you ignore the feminine, then you'll, how should I say, well, you yourself will suffer.—Weinberg and Natalya were hovering over Nina, whispering something in her ear as the radio said: *a fearless officer and a Communist.* Nikolayeva was on the sofa humming sadly to herself. Ustvolskaya had declined to come, but the downstairs neighbors were there. At their request he played one of his preludes, *moderato no troppo,* his hands sure today, his skill perfect because the music was perfect with that selfsame liquidlike streaming of metal particles from an explosive charge, no melting involved, only controlled superstress which empowers the shockwave to penetrate anything from a ribcage to a steel tank. When he finished, all was silent; two of the women were crying, but Nikolayeva was smiling like a cat who'd just caught a mouse.

Clasping his hands to his knees, looking *sportif* as he leaned against pretty I. Makharova, he tossed down another vodka while A. Khatchaturian looked on with a gaze whose jealousy was only emphasized by noble renunciation. Was Makharova willing to have her buttock squeezed? The left one, of course, only the left one! Our composer withdrew his hands, both corners of his mouth twitching *allegro* when the conversation turned political. The guests all seemed hopeful, now that the Stalin chord was at last dissolved back into its arpeggio.

But, Dmitri Dmitriyevich, surely there will be improvements now!

Edik, said Shostakovich, the times are new, but the informers are old.

This new Tenth Symphony of his, which capitalists had the impudence to call his "masterpiece," was of course attacked in the home country for dissonance and pessimism. Moreover, it contained an offensively erotic element. The second movement teemed with his musical signature intertwined with the musical initials of his latest unrequited love, the young pianist E. M. Nazirova. He hastened to apologize for all this in *Sovietskaya Muzyka.*

In August we find him writing the loyal Glikman, begging him to find out the whereabouts of a certain G. I. Ustvolskaya, with whom he had many matters to discuss; the next day he wrote: *Dear Isaak Davidovich: Please forget my request. I have received a telegram and no longer have any cause for concern.*

We see his pale, bespectacled face shining wearily over Prokofieff's bier. He made many good-faith efforts to get the widow released from the concentration camp where she'd been since 1948. He also intervened for the Leningrad conductor Kurt Sanderling. When Nina, distraught with fear, warned him of the possible consequences, he said: Don't worry, dear, don't worry; they won't do anything to me.

He was willing to denounce Beria in private, but apathetically. He'd been half poisoned by the humiliation of being given all those public librettos to sing. In *Pravda,* denunciations of class enemies appeared regularly over his signature. At official functions he pretended to write down the insightfully correct remarks of other comrades, so that he could at least refrain from applauding.

24

It's said that shortly after Stalin's death a guest discovered Shostakovich reading the monster's official biography, but in secret, as if it were shameful. Why, millions had read that book (or at least bought it)! Just as *Mein Kampf* had been on practically every German family's bookshelf during a certain period, so in the days of the "cult of personality" Stalin's life had sold rather well—even better, perhaps, than Stalin's *Foundations of Leninism.* No Soviet citizen could get away from it. And *now,* only now, Shostakovich was reading it—and now he was *hiding* it! It was all so strange . . .

Soon afterward he was honored by the Italians.

25

The brief winter's day was nearly done. Peering between the curtains of his hotel room, he gazed into the sky, which had turned the dark, warm reddish-black of tea infused with raspberry jam. He remembered the delicious somberness of Tatyana Glivenko's menstrual blood one morning on the white sheets—well, that had been forty years ago now, which must have been why his recollections were tainted by less erotic crimsonness, like the image he could not forget of that woman right outside the Conservatory who'd lost her face to a German shell. Letting the curtains close, he drummed out a cadence from Opus 40 on the writing-desk. (Never mind; these others would never recognize it.) A subsequent hour found him sitting very silent in his chair with his head bowed, listening to the rhythm of faint footsteps far down the hall. The ringing metronome-like clicking of high heels reassured him, for it was feminine and it hid nothing. It was the muddier sounds of soft squishy boots, or muffled steps, or the steady yet under-obvious drumbeats of men's heels which pierced him like pins. He could hear speech in the next room. He could hear water running. He heard the weary cadence of a toilet-flush.

Trembling, he opened the door of his hotel room and found the floor lady watching him. He tried to smile at her. Then he rushed to the elevator.

Two men in dark ankle-length coats and shiny boots stood in the lobby, gazing at themselves in the mirror. After awhile one yawned, unfolded his hands from behind his back, and leaned over the counter. Something about those hands reminded Shostakovich of the alabaster inkstand in his room upstairs. The terrified reception girl offered up the register. Meanwhile the other man turned and said: Why, if it isn't Dmitri Dmitriyevich! Congratulations on your rehabilitation.

Thank you, thank you . . .

The man with the alabaster hands yawned, let the register fall out of his hands, strolled up to Shostakovich and said: Almost a decade between symphonies, isn't that so? You're not exactly a shock worker!

Because my hand gets tired, comrades, even when I . . . It, so to speak, *subverts* me. But I'm only a worm, and my symphonies are mere, uh, so it's no loss to, to . . . I do apologize.

Take a vodka with us. We've been meaning to have a talk with you.

Oh, how very, but my friend, unfortunately, is—

Comrade Ustvolskaya has been delayed. Come over here, you.

They sat at the bar, and Shostakovich clutched the little glass of vodka in his trembling hands.

They asked him if he knew that M. Weinberg had been approached by an agent of British intelligence. They wanted to know when his Lenin Symphony would be finished. They demanded that he join the Communist Party, which is the only true party of the working class. He preferred to be associated with the working class, didn't he? They kept referring to *your obligation to the people.*

Yes, yes, *yes,* he replied with a smile as otherworldly as the gleaming of golden church-domes across a canal.

26

In the winter of 1954, not long after reactionary circles in the USA formed the SEATO aggressive bloc, Nina died suddenly. After that, he dreamed that she was calling him. His other nightmares resembled groups of Red Army men and women in uniform, posing in fading photographs. And so he proposed to Galina Ustvolskaya. But she had long since been imprisoned by her awareness that just as in winter the cobalt blue of the Russian atmosphere so quickly greys into darkness, so within him and all his projects any instant of brightness inevitably faded into dreary obscurity. He knew many jokes, to be sure, but in truth it was not very much fun to be around D. D. Shostakovich! That was why she refused him, he supposed. Not that she herself was exactly, how should I put it, fun-loving. All the more reason for her to seek a man who could, well, you know. I'm not saying he wasn't hurt. But whatever he might have felt or experienced in this regard, let's just say that it happened in another cadence, a *down* cadence, naturally, but I, I, anyhow, what's the point?

He married M. A. Kainova, Komsomol functionary. Well, didn't Elena used to belong to the Komsomol? (They'd expelled her before they'd arrested her.) Although the main purpose of this union was to gain a mother for his two half-wild children now being brought up after a fashion by the maid Mariya (you see, I endanger everybody, their father used to say, I *attaint* everybody, and so, so, so, therefore . . .), his friends suspected that he'd rushed into this wedding because solitude frightened him almost as much as his own compositions which were now invariably as thick, wide and grey as battleships. But talk about brightness! Everybody he knew was gloomy, or else accused him of being so (Elena, you're lucky you didn't marry me); hence why not commit a different error? Now we'll find out if brightness actually suits D. D. Shostakovich, or whether he's better off, you know. Margarita, inspired, so she said, by the boats and shining water of Roman Karmen's "Our Friend India," which they saw together at the Kino Palace, wanted to go someplace warm for the honeymoon—a beach on the Black Sea, for instance. He almost panicked, and they hadn't even . . . I've read that when Glikman came to pay a formal visit to the new couple, everybody was silent except for the bride, who proudly announced that she understood nothing about music.—And that's all to the good, Isaak Davidovich, because I'm going to make Mitya concentrate on important things. Do you know what he's promised me? He's agreed to join the Party as soon as the time is right!—Shostakovich hung his head miserably. He sat down at the piano and played a chord which resembled a cold blue September Sunday morning in Prague. When they'd drunk up all the vodka, he walked Glikman out.—Keep him in hand, Isaak Davidovich!—Goodnight, and all my respects to you, Margarita Andreyevna!

Out of pity, the guest had decided to say nothing to his friend, but Shostakovich, trembling and stuttering as they stood in the snowy brightness of the tram stop, cried out to him: Oh, I'm such a bastard, and now I've, I've, so to speak, disgraced myself before you because I, she drove you away, I realize that, and when I'm with her all I want to do is sit in the corner and not even write music anymore, because she, you see, taunts me; I think she does it on purpose! Don't you agree? Why didn't I listen to you, dear Isaak Davidovich? I know you didn't approve. You probably think I married her just to get a young, so to say, a youngish piece of ass, but it's the *nights,* you see, not that Nina and I ever slept in the same bed after Maxim was born, well, hardly ever; there were, if you understand me, moments when we, when, you know, but she mostly left me alone, which was what *I* wanted; you saw how it was when you stayed with us in Kuibyshev back in, when was it now, in '42 it must have been, because you'd come for the score of my, my, Seventh Symphony, which was nothing but an, I, I, an *intermezzo.* Those nights when . . . I could give you any number of sad examples. Do you remember those years, Isaak Davidovich? If only a German shell had—but at least I got to dream out my music, and she never treated me with indifference.

Of course she didn't, said Glikman, laying a hand on his arm. Nina loved you.

Yes, oh, yes, she did, my dear Isaak Davidovich, while all the time I . . .

Glikman, who knew him so well, murmured thoughtfully: That's right. Last year, when Nina died, that made twenty years exactly, didn't it?

Shostakovich flushed. (The sickening compassion in his friend's eyes, he'd write *that* into Opus 110, too, oh, yes he would!) Then, slowly drawing a line in the snow with his foot, he said: Nina was still alive when it, I mean to say, the anniversary fell, technically speaking, in May. Twenty years! And she herself was twenty. That's the magic number. Isaak Davidovich, you're absolutely correct. I don't suppose you ever hear from, from *her.* If you did, would you tell me? On second thought, please don't, because that would be, you know.

As you wish.

I've heard it said, hissed Shostakovich in very low voice, that he courted her in a *suit.* He had a suit even on the front line in Spain. He looked quite dashing then. I think it was the same suit he wore when he photographed Dmitrov—

You own plenty of suits, Dmitri Dmitriyevich.

On the other hand, Lebedinsky says she looks a bit, how should I say, *in need,* and if I could do anything to . . . I even know the day in May, and if I ever forget it I still have (I took it with me when we got evacuated from Leningrad) the program from that music festival, when we, it was when I played my piano concerto that I met her; she, she remarked that my music reminded her of the white nights . . .

With all due respect, you could have married her, Dmitri Dmitriyevich.

Yes, but unfortunately—

Excuse me, but I disagree. *She was the one for you.* Even after Nina told you she was pregnant you still could have gone through with it. Please forgive me, Dmitri Dmitriyevich, I'm speaking only as your friend—

You're right, of course. I've always been such a coward—

Don't say that, I beg you! cried Glikman in agony.

You were there, weren't you? I seem to remember you dancing with her . . .

I'm sorry, Dmitri Dmitriyevich, but I wasn't there.

Are you quite sure? Denisov tells me that she wears her hair in a knot now. And that very first night I felt—oh, my God!

Perhaps it's not too late even now. I could make inquiries—

Everybody knows, isn't that so? Nina knew, Tukhachevsky knew; my children know all too well; whenever that sonofabitch Comrade Alexandrov drops by he likes to twit me about it. Well, well, let all their actions speak for themselves! It hurts to remember. And I, maybe she's not, I, I, please tell me what I should do, Isaak Davidovich! Please—

Marry her.

She's married. To Vigodsky.

Marry her.

Even Galina Ustvolskaya, do you know what she said? I wanted her for a, so to speak, a substitute. I calculated that if I couldn't have Elena, at least she might . . . And needless to say I tried to be smart about it. In these times one gets experienced at hiding things! Because I admire her, her, her *mind.* What a formalist! I mean, a revisionist; that's how they come after us now. Well, I still know beautiful music when I hear it, thank God. And she . . . And I also . . . Well, she laughed in my face! You don't know what a spiteful one she is! It was quite a situation. We were in bed when I proposed, at which point she—

Are you sure you want to tell me this, Dmitri Dmitriyevich? Perhaps tomorrow you'll feel embarrassed.

Don't interrupt me; I can't bear it! She got out of bed, stark naked as she was, turned her back to me and started dressing. When she'd buttoned up her coat, she faced me again and said: *You had your chance on 26 May 1934!* You see, even she had the date memorized, that first time that Elena and I . . . But I swear I never told her! (By the way, have you met this Vigodsky?) That date will never stop being, you know, although naturally it sometimes makes me unhappy, which also speaks for itself. What you said, Isaak Davidovich, it's one hundred percent correct. And then Galina said, and the way she said it, oh, she's cold! She said: *I'm not her and I don't want to be her.* I'd committed a major error! Although it's not my concern to . . . And then she . . .

Don't say it, Dmitri Dmitriyevich!

And then she spat on me.

Mitya, pull yourself together . . .

And I—

Please, please, for your own sake—

I can't help myself. Do you know what I *ask* women to do?

Dmitri Dmitriyevich, I—

Do me a favor, my dear Isaak Davidovich. The next time you see me, and the time after that, and every other time until we die, please be so good as to, you know, to, to—

I understand. We'll never mention this again.

Thank you, thank you!

Not unless you wish it. But shall I—

Not another word, Isaak Davidovich, I'm begging you!

But you won't join the Party? Please promise me.

When Margarita gets to insisting on that, I, well, I can't help what she says. Those Party texts of Dolmatovsky's were, um, actually, when Margarita rang up Dolmatovsky himself and told him I'd agreed to, to, at that point I couldn't say no, so that was Opus 98. But join the Party? Not if they pull my teeth out! I promise I'll never cave in on that.

That means so much to me, said Glikman, and here came his tram.

Misunderstanding him, hating him at times, Nina had cared for him to the end, tolerating his poses, sharing his perilous disgrace. Margarita for her part seemed to be always with him in a rather different way, dragging him to official functions, reminding him of his duty to the masses. Long buried now those days of Shostakovich sitting alone in a wilderness of dark chairs, his mouth pressed against his hand as he listened to the rehearsal of his Seventh! He'd believed then that music could be *good.* Now he . . . Was he to listen to nothing, then?—You made us late again! Margarita was snarling through her little white teeth.—He and she were soon divorced, and he lurked at Lebedinsky's flat, waiting for her to finish disappearing. Here was a film magazine; he paged through it over and over. In a photograph, old Roman Karmen was holding his camera as casually and expertly as a soldier does a gun, smiling flirtatiously down at a Viet Cong girl with a submachine-gun; she was in a line of fighters; they were always in a line; and Shostakovich waited and waited until the telephone rang; Maxim had done the deed; Margarita was gone; she had subsumed herself forever within the auto-beams and sign-reflections upon the cold wetness of Moscow's streets. I'm told that she allied herself with a better man. Why not say that this, this, you know, this *Vigodsky* now has two wives? He takes in my cast-offs. Oh, I'm such a bastard, such a . . . Life is nothing but trouble. I wonder if Elena still has that saffroned handbag I bought her in Turkey? It was very good quality. Hopefully Nina never found out, because . . . Meanwhile the apparatchiks proclaimed him a People's Artist of the USSR; Sweden awarded him honorary membership in the Royal Academy of Music. Everybody advised him to take out that opera of his, that "Lady Macbeth" or whatever it was, and polish it up, to bring it up to date with the times. For instance, with all due respect, how would it sound transposed into a major key? Then there was the matter of his bits of melody borrowed from the reactionary Mussorgsky. To this accusation he readily confessed: All those musical quotations, well, they're just a way for me not to be myself.—Oh, those bastards! If they'd only . . . —On the other hand, his interest in the situation of women was certainly appreciated, they said. "Lady Macbeth" might serve to show how greatly the lives of our female citizens and comrades had been advanced by the Revolution. Perhaps if he made the heroine into more of a victim, so that she wouldn't be misconstrued . . . —"Interest," oh, me! He could coax their clothes off as gently as he'd charmed M. Meyerovich into rewriting his Gypsy Rhapsody—although that had happened ten years ago already. All right, that was over. Time, how should I say, passes.

Falling snow dimming the white streets, trees transformed by snow into thickened negative images of themselves, soft beige slush, white snow falling on women's fur-clad shoulders, white outlines of once-black railings, Russian caps and Kazakh fur hats wide as tree-crowns, all was as all-or-nothing as the notes he inked onto his score-sheets; and peering timidly between the curtains of his flat he spied before the speckled, soft-stained building-fronts a living note of music; she was dressed in a white fur jacket, and her long hair spilled blackly from beneath her hat like a downward-stemmed A-sharp—

only a dream, but, oh my God, that long dark hair! She didn't dare to approach more closely, it seemed. Well, no wonder; twenty paces away from her stood a man with snow on his dark moustache, snow on his dark fur cap and coat; he was wearing tall shiny boots and he kept staring up into Shostakovich's window. Isn't he the one who's always following Akhmatova? Now I'm glad it's only a dream, because . . . At least everything remained white and black; it was nearly the same as his true home beneath the piano keys. When will this dream end? I want to wake up now. There's something about it I don't like, and I don't know why. Two longhaired girls came walking under a red umbrella. The redness interrupted and assaulted him. Now it was ubiquitous in troops of little girls with red balloons, troops of Pioneers with red flags. But I'm not anti-Communist. It's just that red spot which I . . . What's that sound? And how can I preserve it musically? There's a high B-sharp in it that chills me, but it also contains dry bass elements. Akhmatova has a good ear. I wonder how she's . . . The sounds of shelling she characterized in her poem "First Long-Range Firing on Leningrad" as a kind of *dry thunder.* But that's not precisely what this is. I'm going to wake up now and . . . There it is again. What's that sound? Oh, my, how I hate that sound. And it's closer; they must have have gotten the range. I think that sound lives inside the red spot. Do you know, I think I must have seen something when I was young, which . . . Maybe a drop of blood on my father's lips when he, no. Or something which, which, what's that sound? It's not dry thunder at all, because that B-sharp . . .

Poor Glikman, who always meant well, drew his attention to a film about the female workers who'd reconstructed Stalingrad, sleeping in wrecked German planes because there were no other quarters; he thought that their heroism might be a fitting subject for Shostakovich's next symphony.—To be sure, Isaak Davidovich; I'll have to consider that topic extremely, how should I say, *carefully.* Anything *female,* of course, has its so-called "advantages." For example, that factory worker who flirts with you, Vera Ivanovna, you know, when I walk you to the tram stop at night, I've seen her put on purple lipstick first, and then her hard hat. Now, that's actually rather . . . —And he wrenched his head away, so that Glikman wouldn't see his angry smile.

And yet why be so, so, you know? Glikman had once taken him to the Kino Palace in about '32 it must have been, before he'd even kissed Elena for the very first time; he had just begun composing "Lady Macbeth" and cared about the situation of women, or thought he did; Nina already complained that he'd never cared about *her,* but that was, how should I say; the point was that the Kino Palace was showing a Roman Karmen documentary about the collective farm shock worker Yevdokia Yermoshkina; when she'd begun teaching illiterate women, pointing to the blackboard and making them all chant the lesson: *We are not slaves, no slaves are we,* a thrill had passed over Shostakovich. He'd been, um, *young,* you see. Oh, and Karmen, too! Was our *dear* Roman Lazarevich still a true believer? Eighteen years a Party member; eighteen years of kissing assholes; no wonder Elena couldn't face him; I hear she's very, very . . . I suppose he's proud. When will he make a sequel about Yevdokia Yermoshkina? She probably got drunk and wrecked her tractor, because that's how we . . .

Oh, Shostakovich smiled! He slobbered poison. Anything *female,* of course—in my very next symphony! Even the stern middle-aged dragon-ladies in our Soviet hotels who keep everything in order, he charmed even them. (Gazing out the window late on those "white nights," he sometimes saw Black Marias carrying away enemies of the people as usual, but now they pretended to be bread trucks. The pitch of their tire-squeals he'd glean for Opus 110.) His music was becoming a vast orbit around the planet of the twelve-tone scale, the orbit slowly decaying.

27

In 1955, when the ruling circles of the USA had just begun to suppress the national liberation movement of Vietnam, his song-cycle *From Jewish Poetry* premiered at last (in cosmopolitan Leningrad, of course.) We forgave him this Zionist provocation, in spite of the fact that he still held back from joining the Party. Even when he used his growing prestige to help effect the posthumous rehabilitation of V. Meyerhold, we continued to forbear. Oh, he was a real internationalist, a neutral element! Unfortunately, our Soviet Union still has need of such people. So we sat in the back row, yawning and rubbing our raspberry-colored boots together. Then we told the critics what to say about those Jewish songs (which after their long suppression, nearly a decade now, seemed as dismal and ancient to him as Kirov's obsequies in the Tauride Palace), and they said it. But the audience applauded him. Wearied by another nightmare's flank attack, he bowed and bowed, clutching at his throat as if his necktie were too tight for him. Afterward he sat down on the edge of the bed in the room she'd taken in her name at the Sovietskaya Hotel; we see him peering timidly down through the curtains at those few blocky, dark cars in the slush-shining streets; here came a bright red tramcar;

there was a red pennant on a Ministry's facade; here came another Moscow sunset, *adagio*. Soon she'd arrive, if the floor lady didn't, so to speak, well, in point of fact he worried about the floor lady. (Oh, my dear friend, those floor ladies oversee every room and elevator! With quasi-comradely vigilance, you understand. Noiseless and watchful; they're old or young, but always on the job; turn your key in the lock as quietly as you please, open the door, and step out into the hall, and you'll find one of them watching, to make sure that you're you. Nonetheless, they're Slavs like us; moreover, they're women, so they can at times be, how should I put it, extremely understanding.) Now she was late. When he closed his eyes, he could literally see her in her dark coat and dark shoes, ascending the worn steps of the Leningrad Conservatory. Had she changed her mind? The night was as black as an ᛋᛋ-man's uniform.

You know, Galisha, I'd never say this if I hadn't—this vodka's quite—but your face, you resemble—

I wish I could send her to hell, she said flatly.

How did you know?

You once said her name in your sleep. That's why I'll never marry you.

You're always angry! And I, I—

But Ustvolskaya had already run away, slamming the door behind her.

He telephoned T. P. Nikolayeva and summoned her to the hotel room to drink the remainder of the vodka.—Yes, Mitya, I'll come, but I can't—

Don't worry; don't worry. I'm not asking for that.

Two hours later she arrived in a rush, bearing a packet of deliciously greasy sausages, and he realized that she'd been alarmed on his behalf, not that he . . . He lit up a cigarette and said: Tatiana, sometimes I feel that, well, I'm not a poet, as is, for instance, Blok, but do you ever feel that there's a *woman* somewhere at the center of things, a goddess, let's say, or does a woman perceive the same thing as a male principle?

You're talking about your music.

Yes, in a way, although I—

I suppose that when one dedicates oneself sincerely enough to anything, one personalizes it.

I knew you'd understand me! Being faithful to an idea is like being faithful to a woman. I've never betrayed my own music, not yet. I've written money-makers, oh, yes, for films and what not. Even Akhmatova for all her regal pride had to kiss *that bastard*'s ass in the end because she—

Mitya, please be careful!

Don't worry; they can't hear us with that radio blaring out Khrennikov's latest monstrosity. Music certainly reveals its composer's soul, don't you think? When I encounter this, uh, this musical turd, I, I don't even pity Khrennikov. Did I tell you that he's still trying to suppress me on the cinematic front? What a trooper, what a bulldog!

Sometimes you're like a child . . .

Forgive me, forgive me! But to get back to Akhmatova, the essential point is that she chose to save her son's life instead of keeping pure, and to me she, she . . . Do you remember when they shot her first husband?

I wasn't born.

Excuse me, my sweetest little Tatianochka, sometimes I forget how time ticks! Well, they shot him and not her. In your opinion, which of them was luckier?

What a question!

At least tell me this much, and as honestly as you can. Elena told me—she heard for herself!—that they recite her poems even in the Gulag. So she's a . . . But did she damage her life's work when she wrote that other trash?

Not at all. If anything, she safeguarded it. Otherwise they would have—

To be sure! Oh, you angel! But that's not my only point. You do that so they don't shoot you, and then you . . . Well, to grieve is also a right, but it's not granted to everyone! So I haven't, I repeat, I *haven't* done anything to . . . And music is like a, well, at any rate, no one's solved the woman question yet, have they, Tatiana? Not even Lenin himself! You strange creatures! I—

Everyone knows whom you love, Mitya. Why don't you marry her?

Oh, I'm not good enough for . . . You see, I mainly write quartets instead of symphonies now. I'm getting impotent.

He sat up all night getting drunk with her. They never touched each other. The next morning he felt pretty awful. Maxim, who was mooning around the flat these days, waiting for the Composers' Union to call on him, wanted to go see the film "Vietnam," by a certain R. L. Karmen, but his father didn't have time, because he was very, you know. It was really terrible that he didn't have a secretary. It used to be that Nina always picked up the telephone and said that he was away for two months. Well, well, time to be philosophical!

Next his mother died. At the side of her deathbed he found a volume of Chekhov's tales turned open to *Isn't our living in town, airless and crowded—isn't that a sort of case for us?* This gave him a horror; he didn't know why. He'd write that airless crowdedness into Opus 110.

28

In 1956, the year of Khruschev's "secret speech" denouncing the Stalin cult, the Eighth Symphony was rehabilitated; and an editorial in the journal *Voprosy Filosofii* decried the repression of "Lady Macbeth" twenty years ago. Colleagues, musicians and conductors leaned self-satisfiedly against his two pianos. As for him, he smiled as angrily as if he could already see the way everything would be for the rest of his life. (Who says we can't foretell the future? If that German shell whistles, it'll miss us. If it *sizzles,* then watch out!) Actually the anger was the easiest part; what he couldn't stand was the fear. Under the piano he still kept his suitcase packed, with two changes of underwear. He'd heard that no matter what, one got lice-infested. Elena had had to shave her head after her release; she really resembled a convict then! And she had always had such long, beautiful hair. He wondered what she looked like now. His sister said that Elena's daughter was very quick with languages. Once or twice he'd dreamed, well, fine, it might have been half a dozen times, that from the Conservatory roof he powerlessly watched a shaveheaded Russian sniper being frisked by two Germans, his face black with dirt, despair staining him; he'd be liquidated; and then when the Fascists stood him up against the wall he suddenly realized that they were about to shoot Elena, whose Red Army uniform had disguised her; he tried to cry out but then the nightmare rolled over his chest, and it was as heavy, broad and metallic as tank-treads. Fortunately, such disturbances had now been almost entirely eradicated. Why couldn't all the toadies and screws watch *her,* not him, and give him a daily report? Perhaps she . . .

The Ministry of Culture had organized this audition. Oh, he'd slaved; he'd prepared; he'd eliminated many a measure which might be construed as erotic, let alone anti-Soviet; here was the revised libretto, definitive now, tamed and trimmed like a bathing beauty's bikini line, perfect indeed, which is to say, one note forward and ten notes back, everything better and more joyous; so his persecutors grinned like crocodiles right there in his apartment (number 87, 37–45 Mozhaiskoye Shosse), when he seated himself at what he called *the other piano* and played the opera through by memory, thinking to himself: He who has ears will hear.

Afterward, Comrade Kabalevsky remarked: In spite of a few pretty passages, and I certainly don't wish to demean you as a musician, my dear Mitya, it's still an apology for a debauched murderess!

Comrade Luria was also there, and he gave off a stink of burning. Stroking his beard, he contented himself by reminding us all that even the émigré Martynov had summed up Shostakovich's opus as *a warning of harmful deviation*.

Yes, to be sure, my *dear* friends, because I myself am nothing but a, you know.

And you seriously intended to compose an entire cycle of these so-called "feminist operas," Dmitri Dmitriyevich?

I'm afraid so, he whispered triumphantly. When you, er, buy little boys in ancient China they're *little hands*; little girls are just *cocoons*. Which makes me feel . . .

What a disgusting piece of nonsense!

Comrade Khubov inserted the third dagger, saying: The real point is that the "Muddle Instead of Music" article in *Pravda* has never been retracted. Therefore, it's still in force.

In a rage, Glikman shouted at them: But Stalin is *dead*!

That's as may be, Isaak Davidovich. But, when all's said and done, Comrade Stalin remains a genius. He was the head of the Party at that time. And it's just not done to go against the Party. Don't you agree, Mitya?

Correct, correct, correct! cried Shostakovich in a trembling voice. It's just a question of—I mean, I've evidently failed to overcome my age-old errors!

Ah. Well, I'm glad you see that much. Keep toeing the line, Mitya, and we'll do what we can. Maybe in another ten years the time will be right. As for you, Isaak Davidovich, speaking as your colleague, if not quite your friend, I'd advise you to be very, very careful. Needless to say, nobody's remarks will go beyond this room. All the same, don't you see that your misguided counteroffensive could actually hurt Mitya?

Don't worry, don't worry, whispered Shostakovich. I'd like to thank you all for your helpful criticisms . . .

Mitya, don't take this so much to heart! Nobody's calling you an enemy of the people yet! Just calm down and remember that we're only interested in your good—

Thank you for that, Comrade Khubov. Thank you, thank you!

And now for a technical question. Don't worry, Comrade Alexandrov; it won't be *too* technical. What I want to know, Mitya, is this: What key is this opera in?

Well, I—

I want you to know that this morning we all listened to your music to "The

Fall of Berlin." Parts of that movie are dated now, obviously, but in my opinion what you did there is your best work.

Thank you, thank you!

It's what the Americans would call *feel-good music,* if you follow me, Mitya. It sends us out into the world with a song that we can whistle! In essence, we begin in a major key, then after some dramatic strife, in the course of which we win our victory against international Fascism, we return to the tonic, the harmonic base. We're back in that same major key, following the correct line. What key *is* that, by the way?

In fact—

Never mind. Mitya, you obviously understand the concept of the tonic, and in this case you succeed almost as well as Blanter or even Khrennikov.

(Shostakovich ducked and smiled his gratitude, twiddling his fingers as frantically as Scarlatti.)

Unfortunately, this opera of yours lacks a tonic. It's lost its way. It ventures out behind enemy lines and gets cut off.

Comrade Kabalevsky, you've exposed the, the, how should I say, central error of my career. I'm only a . . . Lost, that's exactly it. You've not only exposed me, you've, um, *lighted the way ahead with a searchlight.* You see, I lost the tonic in 1935 or thereabouts. Maybe it was 1934, or 1936. It was . . . Do you believe that each composer's soul (well, I don't mean soul, which is, is, let's say personality, a word more suited to our, so to speak, modern Soviet epoch) is best suited to working in a certain key, or, or, even . . . ? My tonic must have been D minor, which sometimes reminds me of the maples and limes of the Summer Garden, because I . . . But then I, um, misplaced it.

What nonsense!

You see, I'm confused. I confess to that. At least it wasn't malicious. I'm, I'm, there's something wrong. And "Lady Macbeth merely reflects . . .

What I can't imagine is how your poor wife must have felt when you dedicated this obscene trash to her.

She was actually my, so to speak, fiancée at the time, Comrade Alexandrov—

But you did dedicate it to her?

Unfortunately I did; that can't be washed away, but Nina always had a very healthy proletarian sense. She never liked it—

Where is Nina right now, by the way?

She—

It says right here that you claimed that your opera was about *love*. Is that true?

It's about, I, I, how love could have been if the world weren't full of vile things . . .

Which vile things exactly?

Uh, Hitlerism for instance.

Don't get smart with us, Mitya! When you signed off on that lump of formalist drivel, the Fascists hadn't invaded yet.

Well, then, let's say proto-Hitlerism. Because of course, the Reichstag fire and all that, you know, Dmitroff's trial . . . And you're absolutely right; I see now that "Lady Macbeth" is and always will be nothing but a disgusting muddle; thank you for helping me to see that—

They kept talking; their skull-jaws moved; but all he could hear was his own Rat Theme reiterating itself louder and louder.

29

He was completely rehabilitated at the Second All-Union Congress of Soviet Composers in the spring of 1957. Galina Ustvolskaya had just completed her Sonata No. 4, which consisted of four *attacca* movements, so he'd heard; she hadn't found time to play it for him, but Glikman, who seemed to get around, had already heard it and pronounced it extremely depressing.

Photographs from this period often show him leaning his hand against his forehead, staring at the whiteness of a score in the recording studio. When he was alone he laughingly choked out: Oh, yes, my tonic must have been D minor! That was perfect! Even Glikman didn't know what I was . . . — He continued to be as productive as those Stakhanovite coal mine workers who overfulfill their norms by a factor of fourteen. His chords paraded across each score like some exercise march of suntanned girls in Red Square, each in a white tank top and grey shorts. Sometimes they were even happy; sometimes they resembled rainbow flower-explosions made of arrows. At a gathering of his friends he drank too much and began singing: *Burn, candle, burn bright, in Lenin's little red asshole,* which could have gotten him ten years. That fall his Eleventh Symphony, which had already achieved immense success in spite of its secret references to the Soviet tanks now crushing the Hungarian uprising (Maxim had whispered: Papa, what if they hang you for this?), won a Lenin Prize—which after Khruschev's secret speech could not be called a Stalin Prize anymore, you see. The capitalists dismissed it as program music.

Pale cold lights, arising diagonally from the wet pavement, diffused into the darkness like jet trails. Patches of wet light, flat zones and darkness, and then the pallid welcome of lights in the porticoes of official buildings besieged the celebrations. Far, far within, Shostakovich paced tremblingly from handshake to handshake, smiling in a flutter, drinking too much vodka. Oh, what a smile! He hid within it; he actually believed that it protected him. (*The Russians,* wrote a German, *are masters in the construction of shellproof wooden field fortifications.*) He smiled. People thought him as stiff as a frozen corpse.

In 1958, when he won the Sibelius Prize, the Central Committee passed a resolution partly denouncing the Zhdanov Decree of 1948, but only partly. They called it the Decree on the Correction of Errors. Shostakovich smiled venomously when he heard. Well, what's the difference? Not even Nina believed in me, even when I thought that my Seventh Symphony could, you know. Maxim was crying for hunger and I actually thought I could make art out of it! I . . .

That was the year when Pasternak was forced to decline his Nobel Prize, the year when a Soviet selection of Akhmatova's verses appeared in print, inscribed *to Dmitri Dmitriyevich Shostakovich, in whose epoch I dwelled on earth.* Oh, I know precisely what you mean, my dear, *dear* Anna Andreyevna! In my epoch. My stinking epoch of . . .

We see him pale and weary in a dress shirt and necktie, his arm around A. Mravinsky, who will soon betray him out of fear, and who folds his own arms, as gaunt and indifferent as a wounded soldier. We hear him whispering to his young friend E. Denisov: When I look back on my life, I realize that I've been a coward, a coward. But if you'd seen everything I have, Edik, perhaps you too would have become a coward. Can you imagine? To, to, you know, to accept the invitation of a friend, and when you arrive at his flat to discover that he's *disappeared,* with all his books and clothes thrown into the street, and some new *comrade* already living there! I . . .

The telephone rang. His *dear* friend Leo Oskarovich, who'd tried to console him after he divorced Margarita, was inviting him to a party at Leningradskoe 44-2, you know, the Kino House; he could bring anyone he liked; Roman Lazarevich was going to be there, and there might be work if our trustworthy Dmitri Dmitriyevich could whip off something anti-formalist in a major key—nothing like your Eleventh Symphony, please forgive me for saying that, but we only want to help you—for the soundtrack of the world's first Kinopanorama film, "Far and Wide My Country Stretches." Roman Lazarevich wants you to know, Dmitri Dmitreyevich, that he's very . . .

That was the year that they appointed him Chairman of the Organizing Committee for the First International Tchaikovsky Competition (the prize went to a tall young American named Van Cliburn); that was the year that the arthritis or whatever it was began to settle in his wrists, the year that the municipality of Moscow held a special unveiling of memorial plaques to Prokofieff. Plaques and prizes, it's all so . . . Take for instance that Order of the Red Star over her right breast; my sister says that she wears it whenever Vigodsky wants to go out in public, and, and you know . . . Prokofieff's first wife used the occasion to create a scandal against the second. And why should I even care? It wasn't as if Prokofieff and I were even, you know; but since I've dispensed with feeling certain other feelings, why not gratify my, my *ugliness*? Because that makes me all the more ready for Opus 110! Will it actually be Opus 110 or Opus 111? I'm shooting for 110, which will be a quartet, something intimate, so that everybody can hear the, the, whatchamacallit. As if Prokofieff's wife were even a, a . . . Trembling with rage, Shostakovich inhaled vodka, railing against the foulness of women. When the musicologist M. Sabinina objected in a tentative voice that after all, she herself was a woman, he backed water a trifle, then confessed that, like Prokofieff with the second wife, he himself was now entirely impotent.

Between himself and Galina Ustvolskaya there was no longer a consonance. Mutual friends warned that she tirelessly denounced both his music and his person. (I've read that she'd fallen in love with Y. A. Balkashin.) Trying not to think about her, he sat dreaming about the young girls at the Conservatory, with their violin-cases over their shoulders. He muttered to Lebedinsky: Pushkin said it! *There's no escaping one's destiny!*

He had to go to Leningrad for a concert. He dreaded to go. At every street, he was afraid he'd see Ustvolskaya. He dreaded her more than anything, because she had left him and she . . .

He had a sudden irrational idea (he knew that it was irrational) that if he only killed himself before tomorrow it wouldn't be too late, and then she'd know he loved her and take him back.

All the while he knew very well that it was Elena Konstantinovskaya whom he loved. Elena, you're the one for me. Oh, why didn't I say it? Just as in winter we frontline men dread abandoning our dugouts, because it's so difficult to dig new ones in the frozen ground, so he did not want to give up Ustvolskaya, especially now that his penis could no longer perform its world-historic task; there was nothing more to it than that. She was his outer perimeter and Elena was the inner. He missed her music, of course.

In 1959, when Lunik landed on the moon (another Soviet victory on the scientific front), his daughter married. Blindly, like a doomed soldier throwing grenades from his foxhole, Shostakovich composed myriad smiles, wishing that he were alone and away; but he pretended that Nina was holding his hand. They'd asked him to play something but his wrists hurt. Galya looked so joyous as she stood beside that new husband of hers, in whose presence he felt awkward, that all he wanted to do was sit in the corner, for fear that he might cast his stinking shadow on her happiness. Solicitously, Glikman filled his vodka glass to the very top and whispered that it was all going well.

As for this music she wants, whispered Shostakovich, instead of me, it should have been the master composer sitting here, the great man himself, you know whom I mean, the, the, that bastard.

My God, Dmitri Dmitriyevich! I implore you, please be careful! That fellow over there, what's his name?

Why, that's our fine, so to speak, *friend* Comrade Alexandrov. Don't you admire the sheen of his boots? He always puts the welfare of the proletariat at the very—

Dmitri Dmitriyevich, he's trying to listen! Shall I take you home?

By no means, my dear Isaak Davidovich. I only wanted to remark that Comrade Stalin was a brilliant composer of orchestral fugues. And you know which instruments he played them on? Why, the, the, the *organs,* of course! Isaak Davidovich, I'm sorry; I shouldn't be saying such things; I'm just a sonofabitch—

Elena Konstantinovskaya had told him that during her time "away" her sleep had been continually troubled by the clicking, scraping and shrieking of steel loops along the perimeter-wire as chained watchdogs ran back and forth, lunging at prisoners. He had never been able to forget this detail. It was this which had suddenly invaded his mind as he sat there at Galina's wedding. Right then he started working out how to transmute it into music, because . . . Well, how could he say why? That clicking, scraping and shrieking, he'd find a way to include them in Opus 110.

Afterwards, half-drunk or perhaps merely quarter-drunk, he approached the elegantly squarish shaft of the Leningradskaya Hotel (built 1948–53), with its belfry on top, and on the steeple no cross, of course, but a star. He paced slowly round and round.

Dmitri Dmitriyevich, so happy you got our invitation! said the men in raspberry-colored boots. Have you met Comrade Alexandrov? We wanted to talk to you about joining the Party.

Ah, to be sure, yes, yes, Shostakovich replied in a voice as waxen as a corpse's toes, I *promise* to apply just as soon as I finish my symphony about Lenin. That way I'll, so to speak, have something to offer. And maybe I ought to compose a few bars about the German-Polish question. Right now I'm only a worm, you know, only a—so to speak—a worm. But . . .

Wasn't your Seventh Symphony supposed to be about Lenin?

Oh, dear, the Seventh, I mean, but at the time I wasn't *ready*. Lenin is, well, I myself intend the fullest preparation, in order to do full justice to this topic. For example, the liquidation of classes ought to be expressed *pizzicato*—

Let's quit clowning around. We're more aware than you might imagine of your real attitude toward Soviet power. All things considered, Dmitri Dmitriyevich, you've been lucky. We continue looking into your case. Back in '36, for instance, the only reason you weren't dragged down with Tukhachevsky was that your interrogator got arrested. Well, guess what? He's been rehabilitated!

Posthumously, right? Or have you been, so to speak—

The jokes you allow yourself, Dmitri Dmitriyevich! Really, sometimes it almost makes one believe that somebody's holding his hand over you! Well, think about what we've said. We expect your full collaboration. And remember: The "organs" aren't going to forget you—

This was the time that his First Cello Concerto in E-flat Major premiered. In the last movement was a parody of Stalin's favorite tune "Suleiko"—so deeply buried, to be sure, that not even Rostropovich, to whom the concerto had been dedicated, could have ever sniffed it out—no matter what the fellows in raspberry-colored boots said, Shostakovich valued his head, oh, *yes*, good friends!—but when they were all alone, with vodka in their glasses, the composer hummed it out like a furious hornet, and how could they *not* all hear it then? *Su-lei-ko!* Rostropovich burst out laughing, but Shostakovich already felt faint and was biting his nails and peering all around him. Rostropovich poured out vodka. Then Shostakovich set out with the Soviet cultural delegation to tour American cities.

30

In April 1960, when in token of his impending elevation he found himself elected First Secretary to the RSFSR Congress of Composers, Khruschev was there, booming away with his inimitable vulgarity about the good music that any proletarian could hum along with, as opposed to the bad music, the intellectual kind that sounded like "the croaking of crows." Everyone within reach was compelled to play the sycophant, of course. The luckier ones lurked in darker corners of the reception hall. Shostakovich, of course, clung to that darkness, hiding amongst his colleagues, gazing blankly through his spectacles while a thousand tortured or malignant smiles successively devoured one another upon his lips.

A man in a dark suit was taking photographs. His flash resembled the blinding night-lights of Butyrki Prison. Why not imagine that he resembles this Professor Vigodsky of Elena's? I must send Glikman over there so that he can tell me what the man, you know. I want to kill him! And they have a daughter now, so it's . . . Meanwhile, the blackest vacuum must be conquered; the mission of the cosmonauts was to prevent American astronauts from overcoming our leading position. (At that very moment, the Americans were threatening us in Cuba.) While all the opinions on this matter were enthusiastically the same, the cacophony of untuned voices represented the intonation discrepancies of valve instruments. Now they had spied him out and were spiraling in upon him. When they inquired whether he supported the total Sovietization of space, he nodded obediently. Truth to tell, the planets unnerved him. For some reason he was frightened by the Great Red Spot of Jupiter. No doubt we'd get to Jupiter eventually; our cosmonauts would, so to speak, force the Vistula . . . The sad, subtle music of "Lady Macbeth" was sounding between his ears—doubtless the only performance in all Russia. That bully Khruschev, he could see him right now singing the part of those workmen who'd thrown the fat cook in a barrel and were feeling her up, pinching her tits and shouting: *Give me a suck . . . !* He'd find a way to concentrate the venom of those measures and inject it into Opus 110. And now Comrade Alexandrov was saying . . .

He hated them. He hated them all.

Suddenly Khruschev's forefinger came lunging at him. Shostakovich smiled in alarm.

Now, Dmitri Dmitriyevich here, Khruschev was shouting out, he . . . well, he saw the light right at the beginning of the war with his whatchamacallit, his symphony.

Shostakovich thought to himself: He speaks with a mixed cadence—no, a deceptive cadence . . .

That's right, comrades! cried an apparatchik. Nikita Sergeevich has hit it right on the head! Our Dmitri Dmitriyevich might have brought some unpleasant times on himself, but he's seen the light!

Khruschev strode up to him and extended his hand. Bitterly, Shostakovich permitted him to shake it. (His arm was troubling him especially today. After 1964 he would be compelled to forgo public performances.)—Why, Dmitri Dmitriyevich, they told me you were as skinny as a rail, and here you are, a regular barrage balloon! You must have been eating your share and more of our fine Russian bread!

Excuse me for that, esteemed Nikita Sergeevich, please forgive me—

Just a joke! Let's get down to business. When are you going to come around and join the Party?

Khruschev smelled of sweat. His own belly was as big as the rotunda of the Kirov Theater.

Oh, dear, oh, me, sighed Shostakovich. The difficulty is, I mean, not to put too fine a point on it, Nikita Sergeevich, I never could understand the, the, you know, when they talk about surplus value—

Leave that crap to the intellectuals! shouted Khruschev. Just tell me you're a Party man. Are you a Party man?

I, I support the Party with all my—

Now the epigones all applauded, and the people's composer L. Lyadova, a woman not exactly his type, rushed over and kissed him. . . .

Lyadova wanted to give him some comradely criticism, to help him write more correct music. She thought his music should be more clear. In one of their final quarrels, Galina Ustvolskaya had told him that he'd betrayed his music because he was willing to *pretend* for these murderers that it meant whatever they wanted it to mean. And then she'd, I, I mean to say that after that she'd . . . Whereas this Lyadova was as busy as a stream of eighth-notes! There might be something cheerful about her. Might it be that she actually, you know? After all, was he condemned to live out his years in a, so to speak, cemetery? He couldn't decide whether her stupidity would be safe or merely unendurable. She'd painted her lips as red as rocket flares. He wondered what it would be like to, to, oh, forget it. Stroking his grey and greasy hair, puffing out her mouth at him in a dazzling crimson spot, she whispered: Don't you want to foil the designs of the imperialists, Dmitri Dmitriyevich? When will you join the Party? That will send a very—

What he wanted was to get drunk. He wanted to pass out. He dreamed that a skeleton was beckoning to him. **LIFE HAS BECOME BITTER, COMRADES.** How long can a soul struggle and strain?

He sat there with his expressionless look, which was often, thank God, taken for dazed, and folded in his arms as tightly as he could, sitting motionless on the dais as the musicians played his "Song of the Forests."

31

Fat and pale, in a heavy dark suit, he smiled over his wine with the other grinning functionaries. Soon, with his discreetest sarcasm, he'd send all his friends congratulatory postcards on the anniversary of the glorious October Revolution. To Glikman he wrote: *Life is far from easy. How I long to summon the aid of the Old Woman so inspiringly invoked* (how Glikman would laugh! how Nina would have snorted! he himself was laughing and sobbing as he deepened the joke; listening to himself, he heard a three-toned keening like an air raid siren) *by the poet in his* Horizon Beyond the Horizon, *published in* (Glikman would split his sides at this next pomposity) *the Party's Central Organ* Pravda *on 29 April 1960*. Forty-one years later, when Glikman finally published the correspondence of Shostakovich, he added a special footnote to explain, for the benefit of those of us who don't possess the "Enigma" decoding device, that the Old Woman personified death. *I kiss you warmly,* the letter went on. *Be well and happy.*

Upon receipt of this greeting, Glikman, overcome by eeriness, actually made efforts, so I'm told, to visit Elena Konstantinovskaya, who was now the chairwoman of foreign languages at the Leningrad Conservatory, but she repulsed his approaches, remarking: Look, I'm already forty-six years old, and Mitya is what? Fifty-four? It's too late for both of us. And I'm married. And my daughter would never understand; she hates Mitya! More to the point, since you've come to me behind Mitya's back, he's obviously not interested. You may think he needs me, but what am I? and her cigarette mysteriously went out. She threw it on the floor, lit another, and went on: I'm not just someone to be *needed;* I, I—now you've got me talking like him! So please give Isaak Davidovich my best respects, and there's no message for Mitya since he sent none to me, and now would you please please, please get out?

Mitya imprisoned his cigarette in a sybaritic clutch. Although his Seventh String Quartet proved as nervously beautiful as his memories of Galina Ustvolskaya gnawing her snow-white knuckles back in 1951, he himself was reverting to earth. Still he sat straight at the piano, his hands flat enough for a parade of toy soldiers to march over, but the use of his limbs grew increasingly painful, the doctors couldn't say why. He hid from the world in his shabby dacha in Komarovo, out of sight of Moscow, where the reflections of white-limed trees resembled bones on the wet brown streets. When visitors came, he took them on long walks and talked about the weather. Sometimes he sat down on a bench, folded his arms, and glared until they went away. He wanted to, well, I don't know. Maybe I should ring up Roman Lazarevich for advice. Because he . . . Far away, some little peasant child was droning in a voice as highpitched as a German bomber over Leningrad. It was all very, how should I say, pleasant. But then money worries would draw him out, or he'd get a craving to hear his latest music performed. Addicted to the voices of young sopranos, he could no longer hold himself back from writing textual parts for them to sing. He was now flirting with a quiet married woman named I. A. Supinskaya. Elena, you see how lucky it is that you didn't marry me. His passion resembled the healthy blonde upleaping of flames in a stoveful of taiga logs, but Irina was so much younger that he had no heart to, you know. As a general rule he loathed the sight of his own round, pale, weary face. How could he inflict himself on anyone? As Lebedinsky kept telling him, You don't have much luck with women, Dmitri Dmitriyevich! Or maybe it's more accurate to say that you've racked up your share of failures.—Thank you, thank you! he bitterly replied. Fundamentally he was as solitary as a mollusk. But whenever he got summoned to perform, he couldn't get out of it. That is why we see him nervously sitting in a factory, his arms tightly indrawn as all the babushkas and peasant girls who worked there applauded on command. He needed a woman to, never mind. He was an asset to his country now—no matter that his music had failed to rid itself entirely of undesirable elements. In the Central Committee they put him forward as proof that we could hold our own against the Americans, at least on the cultural front.

When he held her hand for the first time, Irina told him how much his Leningrad Symphony had always inspired her.—He pulled his hand away. He said: Actually, I'm not against your calling the Seventh the Leningrad Symphony, but it's not about Leningrad under siege. It's about the Leningrad that Stalin destroyed and Hitler only, so to speak, finished off.

Please be careful what you say, Dmitri Dmitriyevich!

Oh, please, oh, please, call me Mitya—

Somebody might be—

That's exactly what I, so to speak, mean, he replied, with a smile of self-satisfied grief. He knew that he was being very hateful then. At the same time, something was hanging on this moment. Now she understood why they used to call him *the enemy of the people Shostakovich.* If she refrained from snubbing him now, why then . . .

She wore her hair pulled tight back from her forehead into a prudish little bun which he found erotic. She was as earnest as any choir girl—oh, how sweetly they open up their black scores, gazing into the conductor's eyes just as a certain D. D. Shostakovich's children used to do when he read them stories! Between her legs his fat old fingers would soon come to life, expressing the most crystalline *glissandos*. She had very intelligent eyebrows which could rise at any untoward word. Sometimes when she looked at him she rested her face upon her delicate fingers. Looking away, he felt the same despairing craving for salvation which had driven him to appeal to Tukhachevsky back in '36. But this time it was not life, but only order that he longed for. If Irina accepted him, she'd be kind to him. She'd lower him gently into his grave.

He summoned Lebedinsky over to his flat to drink vodka. Frowning down at the piano, tickling the black keys most silently, he invited the guest to speak about women. Lebedinsky laughed and called him a hard case. Time for the caviar! One more little bitty, you know, cucumber, and then a gulp of, of, because, you see, it was very cold today. Lebedinsky didn't mind; he liked vodka quite well. They say it's good for you, because . . . Oh, my head! I need more vodka. When he'd swallowed down enough to make his face go pallid, he began to whisper that it was fortunate that Stalin had squashed "Lady Macbeth" so that his perhaps unknowingly ambiguous indictment of repression had never been soiled by a pro-Soviet counterpart.

But you're so cynical, Mitya! How can you twist yourself around so masochistically like that? It almost makes me sick to hear you—

Don't worry; don't worry. It's, so to speak, *irrelevant* when the earthworm twists on the hook. And you know what? I don't care about myself anymore.

What do you mean, you don't care?

I'd sign anything even if they shoved it at me upside down. All I want is to be left alone . . .

He switched on the radio, and Comrade Khruschev was demanding to know: Plainly speaking, why do the United States of America, France and the United Kingdom need West Berlin? They need it as a dog needs a fifth leg. By the way, no one encroaches on West Berlin.

Just then the telephone rang. He began to shake; he didn't want to answer it, but Lebedinsky was looking at him, so he pretended to be brave; and it turned out to be nobody worse than our esteemed Comrade Karmen, who had just won a Lenin Prize for his two gripping films about Caspian oil workers, and was now, I don't *believe* this, ringing him up to advise: Perhaps you should join the Party, Dmitri Dmitriyevich. Let us help you! You know, I've been a member ever since '36, and it's definitely smoothed my way. It makes me very sorry to see all your needless struggles . . .

Thank you so much for your suggestion, my dear, *dear* Roman Lazarevich! Perhaps after my next, you know, symphony . . .

Buttering another slice of thick black bread, Lebedinsky chuckled, not so loudly that the big black telephone could hear: That's the way, Mitya! Keep stalling the sonsofbitches until you're dead!

My *various needless struggles,* he says. And when I think of him, you know, running his hands over Elena . . . Congratulations on your, so to speak, your fine work, Roman Lazarevich! A Lenin Prize, just imagine! I'm extremely . . .

You can count on me to put in a good word for you with the Party.

Roman Lazarevich, that's very . . . I'll never forget your kind wishes.

Thank God I got ride of that sonofabitch, not that I believe in God, nor should I completely shut Roman Lazarevich out (Lebedinsky refuses to understand this), because *he was there,* and for once I don't mean with her, not at all; I mean Leningrad, oh, yes, my friends, when we . . . ha, ha! That snow and still more snow and corpses frozen to the sidewalk and Maxim begging me for food, but *we* didn't have to go through *anything,* thanks to the wonders of my, of my so-called "symphony." The ones we left behind covered up their faces and then they . . . fortunately, *dear* Roman Lazarevich recorded that winter for me, so I can feel guilty forever! Galisha's still not the way she, I mean, a sustained scream, perhaps in the key of B-flat, is what I should, you know. In Opus 110. Those ice-white windows, and then the, the, but those sleds were the worst. With the little dead children on them. And Maxim, I've got to do something for Maxim. I wonder how he's, anyhow, it's a mercy he gets on better with Irina than he did with Margarita. She's so good to me! As for Galisha, now that she's married I can't, why complete that thought? I need to . . . What's that sound? Something under the piano. It must be a (Lebedinsky will like this!), a rat from my Rat Theme.

Lebedinsky had to go soon after that because, well, you know. But Shostakovich didn't want to be alone! Irina was with her husband, so Nikolayeva was with *him,* sitting beneath Akhmatova's portrait. They no longer held hands. Well, it was for the best, because she had a somewhat, how should I say, *cowlike* appearance; this thought made him crumple up his grey face in a crackle of laughter, not that he could tell Glikman, who . . . He adored her; she was very . . . I have my own ideas about Russian women.

Comrade Khruschev was on the radio again. He said to her: Listen to that bully. He denies it now, but of course he was cutting throats right next to Comrade Stalin . . .

Hush, Mitenka! Are you out of your mind? Why, somebody could be—

You're right, of course. I mean, you and I are both very well taken care of. But his voice, you know, Shostakovich droned on, well, it's gone *flat,* just like mine. Even Comrade Khruschev needs a rest! Tatiana, my little angel, do you remember much about the brass instruments? You see, at the Leningrad Conservatory I learned from Glazunov himself that there are two kinds—

Live bells and dead bells, put in Nikolayeva, who could not bear to have anyone think her stupid.

Exactly. And a live bell—correct me if I'm mistaken, dear girl—well, the heaviness and the temper of its metal give it a, well, which is to say, a *ringing* tone. I still have a great deal of music to write, but I'm the merest dead bell now, like Nikita Sergeevich there on the radio. Everything I used to compose—

You're drinking too much, Mitya.

No, no, no, it's just to warm me up. Dear girl, please why don't you . . . ? Well, dead bells, you know, they're made of *soft* metal. The dark tones they're capable of, like, like, well, as if somebody were playing a trombone in a catacomb—

The preludes and fugues you wrote for me weren't at all like that, said Nikolayeva earnestly. They make me *happy.* I intend to perform them all my life . . .

There may be a few good notes in those, yes, yes, yes, my dear, said the old man with some satisfaction. And I'm not saying there won't be more. The *allegro molto* in the, you know, the D-flat major fugue is rather—well, you know it, and I'm sorry it didn't quite . . .

So even that doesn't make you happy? What about your Seventh Symphony? At least it rallied people. Once you told me how alive you felt then; you said you gave it your all—

Didn't you learn in school, he demanded in a hateful voice, that Ivan the Terrible, having coaxed his architect into, so to speak, putting the very best of himself into building Polrovsky Cathedral, afterwards *put out his eyes*? Anyway, things are so much easier in our century. **LIFE HAS BECOME MORE JOYFUL!** Although Meyerhold's wife, you see, they cut her eyes out, too, as I recall. With a—ha, *ha*! That was extremely . . . She must have been a real anti-Soviet element, don't you think? Nowadays we're more enlightened. An extremely beautiful woman, by the way, although she might have been slightly, so to speak, plump, in our Russian fashion. Not that I mean any . . . Well, once I'm blinded and gelded and all the rest, then I . . . Do have a little more vodka, Tatianochka. It keeps, you know, it keeps out the *chill.*

In June he somehow found himself in company with some unknown persons who wore tall shiny boots. They were very friendly and came right into his home so he had to give them vodka. One of them, whom he seemed to have met before, was named Comrade Alexandrov, and he persisted in hoping that on account of this prior acquaintanceship, which he couldn't quite recollect, they'd go easy on him, that the finale would end on a, so to speak, major key, since by the law of averages he ought to succeed in avoiding further misfortunes, although that notion might simply prove to be (how should I put this?) stupidity on his part. Now the vodka was all gone, but they must have brought vodka of their own, as it seemed, because they kept filling his glass.

They wanted him to play the piano, but he didn't want to. He wasn't a, a, you know, a trained seal.

They shoved their chairs right up against his and spoke into his face.—We will open your eyes, they said.—Clenching his fists, he smiled down at his knees. Where was Maxim? If only Maxim would come home right now! Pretty soon they were talking about Mother Russia, and he said: Honestly, I, I, there are times when I just want to get down on my knees and kiss the dirt! at which they chuckled and nudged each other, not at all put off by the loathsome sadness of his eyes. He'd meant every bit of it; he was actually thinking of a phrase he'd heard somewhere—it must have been in that Roman Karmen movie when Vlasov whispers *the breasts of Zoya* and starts to kiss a little snowhill in the forest—but my God, it couldn't have been Vlasov, because Vlasov had been, you know. Maybe Marina Tsvetaeva had written something about, um, *I set my lips to the breast of the great round battling earth,* but Tsvetaeva had tied a knot around her throat and, I mean, why go on, it was best to say nothing. They kept looking at him so that he stammered to deprecate himself, longing to be dead so that they couldn't catch him, although then he'd scarcely see Elena anymore.

They filled his glass again until he commenced certain stereotyped and futile gestures of resistance, more or less the same as when an old white-shawled babushka throws up her hands in horror once after days of searching she's finally found her grandson's corpse, its ankles crossed, its hands up-flung like hers as if to stop the Nazi bullet. Well, but vodka's harmless; it's even a, you might say, a sort of medicine! Although it does make you, well, you understand—especially in June, because that's when the "white nights" come to Leningrad. Those were the nights when I first lay in Elena's arms. Did I say that or just think it? Why do they keep grinning at me? What *did* I think? Think about it, they said. We can be good friends, but we can also be tough.—I'm thinking; I'm thinking! Should I ring up Glikman? But that would compromise him. How about Lebedinsky? Or even Roman Lazarevich! Is he in

Cuba or Indonesia now? Honestly, I can't keep track; I'm old. I can hardly stand this; it's going to kill me! But I do have to, um, so please, if you would excuse me for just three measures, *prestissimo,* I promise! All I want is breathing-space. While he went to the toilet and vomited, they turned over his volume of Dostoyevsky which was lying facedown on the second-best piano and discovered that he'd underlined this passage: *Why do even the finest people always seem to be hiding something from others and keeping quiet about it?* All they had to do was stand there when he came back; they smiled and pointed at the book.

After that, he lacked any defensive front. He tried to become as flat as a cockroach so that he could hide between the piano keys, but they gripped him until his fingers commenced palely trembling just like those dancers of the Musical Comedy Theater in Leningrad back in '41; dear me, he'd never forget how during the rehearsals several of them had dropped dead right there on the stage, due to (how shall I put it?) hunger. He jittered and trembled, jittered and almost broke; then he was lying on the sofa while they bent over him. When he sobered up, he found he'd signed an application for membership in the Communist Party.

He went to pieces. Had his blunt-speaking Ninotchka still been alive, she would have kept them away! Lebedinsky would have barred the door!

He boarded the "Red Arrow" midnight train from Moscow to Leningrad, pretending like a child that this stratagem would protect him from them; Maxim and Galya were old enough to care for themselves; he'd never return to Moscow! So he sped deeper into darkness, quipping to himself: *All railroads lead to Auschwitz!*

Irina would have kept him company if he'd asked; she was ready to leave her husband, who seemed to be very, how should I say. But right now, just in case he couldn't hold firm about the Party, the thought of how she'd stare at him with her almost abnormally expressive, hyperintelligent eyes, well . . . — Lebedinsky and Glikman met him at the platform. They promised to secrete him here so that he'd miss the Moscow convocation. He was sick, they'd announced. They'd telephone the Party for him. But this was only a postponement.

32

It was the *personal wish* of Comrade Khruschev that he join the Party, they'd said. Many changes had been made. He'd find that it was really a very nice Party now, a lovely Party, really.

He rushed off to his sister Mariya's flat and hid there. They might not find him here; they'd try the Evropaskaya Hotel. (The worst of it was: What would Elena say?)

Once he'd joined the Party, they'd explained, his way would be clear to become President of the Russian Federation Union of Composers.

Mariya sat him down at her kitchen table and brought him a big bowl of soup. She understood the sonsofbitches quite well. It was she whom they'd once exiled to Central Asia, after the Tukhachevsky affair. That experience might also be the reason she's stayed friends with Elena; those two had a bond; oh, yes.

Is she really as pleased to see me as she pretends? he wondered, or is she pretending, out of pity? My own sister, and yet I'm so . . . And now the telephone will ring. I, I, it feels as if she only gazes on me from a distance, a great distance. I can only, I should have brought her a present! I couldn't even remember to do that. How worthless I am! Why don't they just shoot me? How many years have I kept that spare underwear in the suitcase? Maybe the moths have eaten it. My, oh, me, how old Mariyusha looks! And what if I'm not welcome here? I wonder if her piano's in tune; I see a speck of dust on it. She always used to tell me that I was too proud. Tomorrow I'd best return to Glikman's. And I like the way that Vera Vasilyevna smiles at me when I eat her cooking. He was lucky to marry her! If she'd only have looked at me, then I perhaps . . . —Unimportant!—Lebedinsky would have said . . . I may be proud, but I'd give anything to turn into Glikman and not have to think! I can't help looking down on him, because he loves me. Here at Mariyusha's, well I'm nothing but a, a, you know, an imposition. I don't dare ask her about Elena. How I wish I were deep in the ground, deep in the ground, *tum* ti *tum* ti *tum*, with mountains of black dirt on top of me so that I, so that I couldn't *hear* anything! I really ought to leave Mariyusha's tonight, but I just got here—

You're not eating your soup, Mitya.

Please forgive me. I'm an imbecile, just an—

Shut up and eat.

He raised his spoon almost to his mouth, then said: Do you think that Glikman ever lies to me?

How can you think such a thing? He adores you! He trusts you!

But once you said—

Mitya, your nerves are making you ill. Now go in there and lie down and go to bed. If anybody telephones, I promise I won't say you're here.

Comrade Pospelov from the Bureau of the Central, so to speak, Committee has already rung at Glikman's—

I *promise* you!

Mariyusha, you're an angel! They've completely . . . And then there's a certain Comrade Alexandrov, whom I . . . If only Nina—

Go to sleep now, and don't worry about anything.

But tomorrow I'm going to have to, I, I'm afraid—

Whatever you like, she said with a compassionately distant smile. But you know you're welcome here, Mitya.

Thank you for saying that. And I, you see, do you also think that I should hold out?

You mean, refrain from . . . I'm going to put on the radio. Why, isn't that one of your film scores they're playing? How lucky! I love that song. Now come closer. I'm sure they can't hear us. Cousin Katerina's an engineer, and she said—

But—

The telephone began to ring.

33

Of course you must hold out, Mitya. That goes without saying. How can you even consider joining them? Even if during all these ghastly decades they'd never harmed anybody, not even you, they'd still be evil! Oh, poor dear Mitya, don't cry . . .

34

After all, he whispered *allegro* to Glikman, in whose uncritical love he once again trusted, I mean, *after all,* back in '36 they voted against me, even Sollertinsky did; only Scherbakov abstained, and they flayed him for that! And the wonder is, my opera didn't even impress Scherbakov! But he believed in *truth.* That was really . . . Talk about battles on the cultural front! Speaking of which, have you seen Roman Karmen's latest film? "Our Friend Indonesia," that's what it's called, I kid you not! Our *dear* friend! My children insisted on seeing it; it's really . . . I refused to grovel at that time, but it goes on and on, and I'm not well; when you told them I was sick, it was actually true . . .

Be brave, Dmitri Dmitriyevich! You don't have to join!

You're correct! But, you see, I, I, well, I've become such a bastard . . . My children . . . What's that envelope?

A telegram, said Glikman sadly.

For me?

I'm afraid so.

But Maxim's applying to the Composers' Union, and if I refuse to . . . No, I'll hold out. I'm not going, you see! Let's forget about all this and talk about Tchaikovsky's sex life! Did you know that he loved one lady who, who, let's just say he . . . Forever. It's fantastic, really. She was even willing to, you know. And she would have married him, too, but he said to her: *You're so lucky that you didn't marry me!* They'll only get me to Moscow if they tie me up and drag me there, you understand. They'll have to tie me up—

Please calm yourself, my dear Dmitri Dmitriyevich!

I'd rather kill myself! I won't ever join those murderers—

In July he went to Dresden. The temperate climate of this new German Democratic Republic agreed with him, especially soothing his bones and joints, which were now as rotten as the ancient wooden pavements which dated from the days when Leningrad was called Saint Petersburg. Would he like to see the Georgji Dimitroff Bridge when he got there? They were already advising him that he ought to see it, for the sake of solidarity. He replied that of course he was extremely eager to, you know, see it.

He remembered the premiere of R. L. Karmen's "Comrade Dmitrov in Moscow"; Elena couldn't keep her hands off him; they started kissing even before the lights went out. And now it's Comrade Shostakovich in Dresden! But I'll never be Comrade Shostakovich. I'd rather, you know.

How strange it feels to be in Germany! It's very . . . Gazing out the train window at the rich blonde grass of the German plains, he felt a sense of shame and strangeness, as if he had unveiled the nakedness of some dead woman. Over there, looping as lazily wide as Beethoven's rests and measures, shone the Elbe, where our Allied troops had linked up against the Fascists. Now here came stone arches embellished with figures and rosettes, everything massive yet teeming. Dresden, he'd have to say, felt heavier, less French than Leningrad. Elena wouldn't most likely have . . . My, what a lot of rubbish he saw! Two arched and broken clamshells facing each other across shattered stones; that was their Frauenkirche. Another music-note burst within his head. He wondered whether he were on the verge of having a stroke; when he got back to Moscow he must learn the symptoms. Hadn't Lenin's wife died from something like that? Sometimes it seemed better to just, well.

The guide explained to him that we were now pickaxing down the old chocolate-striped estates of the Junkers and capitalists, to cannibalize them for collective farms.—Very good! laughed Shostakovich. Defensive preparedness! On the, the, the class front, you know . . .

It felt very humid. Fences, tan-colored walls, concrete cracked and white-streaked, then those orange-roofed Saxon houses with broken windows, all the bronze belfries slowly going earth-green, the orange tiles turning earth-black and—look at all those ruins! There were quite a lot of vacant lots in Dresden. Everything had been hauled away in those places. Congratulations. They explained that the statuary in the Grosser Garten had survived; it was basically decadent angels and all that claptrap. He could take a look if he liked, just for fun. Next time he came, it just might be gone, because, well, progress, you know! We're lighting up the way with a *searchlight*. All these little blond children with their first wheelbarrows, learning the dignity of, well, *labor,* it makes me want to vomit. Actually, a lot of the comrades wanted to retire in Dresden when the time came. (What's that sound?) Did he wish to see the spot where R. Wagner had conducted back in the nineteenth century? Unfortunately the American bandits had, you know. And would he care to visit the new Maxim Gorki Home, where East German and North Korean schoolchildren, rescued by us from Anglo-American aggression, had learned to live together in international harmony? To tell the truth, that was exactly what he'd hoped to, er . . . They felt very glad to hear that, because as it happened the schoolchildren were expecting him. He'd be especially gratified to learn that one North Korean boy whose parents had been murdered by the American adventurists wanted to play something on the piano especially for him, a concerto or maybe even a ballad or something, a whatchamacallit. They could guarantee him that it would be uplifting: Art which must fight against what Comrade Ulbricht has wisely termed *the poison of skepticism*.

Regarding the war damage (caused by incendiary bombs), he said to himself: Dresden's wrecked, all right, but I remember how that first shell smashed into the side of the apartments across the street, and *then,* four-beat rest, and *then* from that smoking hole, which was about two storeys wide, I'd say, rubble and corpses began hissing out! A snare drum could recapitulate that sound. It was quite . . . That's what you did to Leningrad. For nine hundred days! *You* did it. With your eighty-eights, I believe. And then you, so to speak, Germanized the Peterhof Palace into a, a, a *skeleton* . . .

No, there'd been a misprint in his itinerary. (They saw him shaking.) He wouldn't be staying in Dresden after all. They'd arranged accommodations for him in the spa town of Goerlitz, which lies in the mountains forty kilometers away. (He was almost ready, his glands secreting music as weird as the steel spiderwebs of the wrecked Dzerzhinsky Tractor Plant.) Comrade Shostakovich (Schostakowitsch was how they said it) ought to remember that he belonged to the people; he must take better care of himself. His visit to the Maxim Gorki Home would be postponed. They knew that he was tired; they wished to create the optimum conditions for his work, which . . .

Thank you, dear friends, thank you, he replied uncertainly. I know I'll have a, so to speak, splendid time—

Above all, he wasn't to worry, they said. They understood that nervous tension had been besieging his health. He'd be given everything he needed. They valued him; they'd made him a corresponding member of the Academy of Arts of the German Democratic Republic, effective as of today. Thank you for that, my *dear, dear,* so to speak, friends. And congratulations on your wonderful Maxim Gorki Home. They'd already arranged a tour of the monuments in Dresden, not to mention the wide *Plätze* and stone lions, the fountains, dead now, the other many-arched old bridges of Dresden (the "Blaues Wunder," too); and he could interview as many of the Americans' victims as he liked. Even former ϟϟ-officers were cooperating with us now, such was their craving for revenge. He'd doubtless find it rewarding to set their stories to music; it was merely a question of time and effort—

But whatever is the matter, Comrade Schostakowitsch?

Well, I, this ringing in my ears, it's always an annoyance now. I'm not expecting to, to, you know, score any great *victories* on the cultural front! It's just as you say, a, a matter of time and manpower. But I, by the way, isn't the dacha of the former German Fascist Field-Marshal Paulus hereabouts? He must have been extremely . . . Yes, yes, I know he just died, three years ago now if I'm not mistaken; I must have read about it in *Pravda* . . .

His interpreter, who was waiting for him in front of an ocher palace, proved to be a darkhaired German beauty, narrow-faced as the Germans often are, who had once been a piano student. Something about the hollow between her shoulderblades reminded him of Elena Konstantinovskaya, I mean Vigodsky, not that he could really, you know. With a modest laugh, she confessed that her teachers had found her devoid of talent. Her brother had fallen on the Ostfront, during Operation Citadel. Her ex-fiancé was in a Soviet prison camp so far as she knew. She'd wisely married someone else. Her mother, father, brothers and sisters had all died shortly before midnight on 13 February 1945. She was there when the Hitler Youth dug away the rubble from their air raid shelter. There was hardly a mark on them, but their skins had been cooked to a golden brown color.

Shostakovich's pale, tired face began to twitch. As gently as he could, he laid his hand upon the girl's shoulder.

There were dead people in all the streets, she went on brightly, but I'd imagine that you saw dead people, too, on your side . . .

Yes, yes, yes, yes, my dear, oh yes, but we might as well spare ourselves the pain of this subject, because, you see—

Excuse me, Herr Schostakowitsch—

Oh, call me Dmitri Dmitriyevich, please.

Dmitri Dmitrijewitsch, I'm sorry, but I just wanted to say that when they took all the corpses to the marketplace and cremated them—

Well, that was the best way perhaps. Well, well, well, well. In Leningrad they dug mass graves once the earth had thawed. But, my dear girl—

And now sometimes I wish I could go crazy. At night I hear the sound of the planes coming. The bombers, I mean.

Well, well, well, well. Never mind. Perhaps we need a bite of something. And have you tasted Russian vodka? No, I see you need to talk about it. Well, can you describe this sound that you hear? Do you possess absolute pitch? A surprising number of people do, you know. And perhaps if you . . .

I'm not sure. Maybe it's a low, vibrating chord in E-flat major.

Why, that's the opening of Wagner's *Ring*, isn't it? "Das Rheingold" begins that way. But I'm not sure that a B-17 wouldn't sing in a higher register, because . . .

I'm very sorry, Dmitri Dmitrijewitsch, but I don't have perfect pitch, and as I said I'm almost talentless.

Never believe that, my dear young, shall I say colleague? We musicians always tend to underrate ourselves! But the actual pitch doesn't matter. The distinguishing feature of Jewish music is the ability to construct a jolly melody on a foundation of sad intonations. And perhaps you Germans do the opposite, which would be, so to speak, *natural* for you, since you don't like Jews, I've heard. Forgive me . . . A major chord, then, shall we call it a major chord? After all, major chords are supposed to be happy. At least that's what my, my, the commissars are always telling me.

He was supposed to be writing the score for the film "Five Days—Five Nights." Instead, he began to compose Opus 110.

35

Of this work he remarked to Glikman: I wrote an ideologically deficient quartet which nobody needs. I reflected that if I die someday, it's hardly likely anyone will compose a work dedicated to my memory. So I decided to write one myself. You could even write on the cover: *Dedicated to the composer of this quartet.*

Officially, of course, he dedicated Opus 110 "to the victims of war and fascism." Why not? Whatever he did made no difference. He, of course, was nobody's victim, because he'd agreed to, you know.

According to the *Great Soviet Encyclopedia,* our planet's most pronounced topographical features comprise an approximate mirror image of the crust's underside. The steppes of the Ukraine thus roof the cratonic platform which replicates them, while the Ural Mountains not only project into the sky, but in equal measure stab down like gunbarrels trained upon the magma on which our continents uneasily slither. To me, the thought that this world is doubled within its own red, liquid hell is a profoundly unnerving one. Chaos seethes beneath my feet. The chaos feels stifled; it wants to breathe. But chaos is by its very nature formalist deviation. I still believe in myself, but only in my own ugliness. Damp it down, comrades! Even in the depths of Soviet coal mines we now insist on the flameless explosion of a Hydrox cartridge, for that reduces danger. Our foreman gives the signal. A muffled crash stifles the stifling darkness, unrelieved by any light. On the official side, a certain D. D. Shostakovich excretes new program music for the masses. And on the mirror-side, where all's presumably flameless (otherwise we'd glimpse red writhings when we gazed down into those bottomless black slits of the piano keys), a counterpart D. D. Shostakovich composes Opus 110.

Roundfaced, staring straight at the piano like an old coachman out of nineteenth-century Saint Petersburg, he watched the sad and angry music ooze out of his fingers. His spectacle-frames had lightened to translucency over the years. Now he was not so much a stern man as a gaping, goggling old fish. His enemies laughed that he'd come to resemble Lenin's widow Krupskaya, who'd been likewise known for ineffectuality and a bulging gaze. (Ineffectuality! Isn't that all that music is? Lebedinsky had told him about that petty Nazi, K. Gerstein, who'd joined the ᛋᛋ in order to reveal its secrets and halt its crimes; the tribunal condemned him for not getting results.)—Operation Reinhard, that's written in now; Operation Blau will be present in the second movement. Can we refer to T-4 in the overture? But it's all got to be *airless.*

Akhmatova insists, correctly in my opinion, that whoever doesn't make continual reference to the torture chambers all around us is a criminal. Under the earth, and then they shoot them! Nina and I used to hear the executions every night. Now Nina's also under the earth, which must be very . . . And then Elena, no. I couldn't expect Nina's sympathy at that time. What's that sound? What a nasty little *allegro,* like a . . . My Rat Theme at least had humor for those who cared to be amused. And I was going to . . . When the Nine Hundred Days began and Maxim was weeping in the night from hunger, I promised I'd write him into the Seventh. And I did; I wrote that for *him.* Now's my final chance to make sure I didn't waste any of his tears, because . . . It was in A-flat minor, I'll never forget that. And my mother said . . . What about Rodchenko? He was an influence, at least a youthful influence. Now that I'm . . . Rodchenko's hollow wooden squares within squares, each figure twisted into a different plane from its neighbor, why, those must be prison cells! More abstract sculpture for my, for my so-called "opus."—Oh, me, oh, dear, I almost forgot Operation Magic Fire! Because that's where Elena met the gallant knight Roman Lazarevich. (Dmitri Dmitriyevich, the knight had condescended to advise, in my opinion the point is to *use* those screams to keep our antifascist hatred in condition, to reject those awful things in the name of peace. It's not good to dwell on the dark side.) And Spain, of course. Where she and Roman Lazarevich . . . We prefer our personal tragedies, because we're all cowards and bastards.

His friends assumed that he was drinking too much. As long as he stayed in East Germany he kept tossing back schnapps, with and without his interpreter. (She smiled at him once, and he remembered the childlike grin of a young woman sniper he'd seen somewhere, maybe in Kuibyshev. Then she stopped smiling. She lowered her softly immaculate face.) Sometimes he drank until he fell asleep. When he awoke, he reached for the tumbler, muttering into the mirror: Generally speaking, I, I'm a degenerate.

It was a cool, humid German summer. He wanted to sit on the grassy bank of the Elbe just to watch the steamboats and to, so to speak, catch his breath, but there wasn't time because they showed him atrocity films all day. Case White couldn't be omitted, but he didn't yet know how to, well, maybe in *largo* form, and if he could squeeze bitterness out of a few more grace notes . . . Then they escorted him back to his hotel. The darkhaired interpreter was ill today. He didn't know whether or not to refer to Operation Citadel. Since her brother had fallen at Kursk, why not? She was a pretty woman, although not quite plump enough for his taste. Let's see, what was I doing during Operation Citadel? I remember seeing Roman Lazarevich's newsreel about it, seventeen years ago it's already been now, in that Kino Palace where Elena and I used to, to, what had it been called? "The Battle of Orel." No, it couldn't have been that Kino Palace, because . . . A Tiger tank snarls through the mud and down into a river; the water sizzles around the treads; it swims like a stately crocodile, grips the mud of the far bank, upraises its gun, and grinds on, with German Fascists standing calmly astride like whale-riders; then Roman Lazarevich, who no doubt was wearing that oil-stained fur-lined jacket of his, pans to show the crew of one of our hundred-and-twenty-twos: Ready, aim, fire! I don't mind admitting he was brave. In fact, I'd rather be him. So what? The bastard, you know, although it was actually I who . . . The Tiger tank explodes, accompanied by music which could have been written by a certain D. D. Shostakovich! How, so to speak, *heroic*! Pan to a wheat field with its hidden strongpoint of antitank guns; pan to mine traps; pan to Red Army generals with their leather greatcoats and binoculars. Later on we'll blow up the evil FREYA network! Had she left him yet? All our planes flying over their tanks, it reminded me even then of a score, but more for orchestra than for a string quartet. So what? I'm going to make sure that Opus 110 contains *everything*, since it's the last time I'll still be, so to speak, me. From a strictly musical point of view, Citadel should be the merest interlude. (On likely nightmare axes he positioned his own thought-traps.) *Allegro* would be too easy. That would resemble letting those ass-lickers in raspberry-colored boots tell me to make everything *happy* and in a major key! There are times when doing the right thing might destroy me, but that doesn't mean it's not the right thing. If Elena were here, or at least Nina . . .

Picking up the newspaper, he read that a traitor named M. Smolka had just been executed for terrorist activities committed at the behest of the American Secret Service. The traitor's last words: *There is no doubt that desertion and treachery to the interests of peace and socialism are the severest of crimes and can only be expiated by the severest of punishments.* It had been an early morning guillotining, no doubt. That was how they did things in Dresden.

Blood raged flamelessly in his windowless heart! He completed Opus 110.

36

About this quartet the most fundamental thing which can be said is that it is too sad even to rise from a moan into a wail at death's uncompassed crescendo. To be sure, the danse macabre of the second movement glows sickeningly vivid as a sodium flare at night (so much for flamelessness!); it's as bright as the electric light which illuminates the gas chamber when it's time to ascertain whether all the Jews are dead; while the menace of the third remains more chilling than those screams of terror in Leningrad when the German bombs come down; they'll never stop coming down. Yet on the whole the effect is of somebody drowning, his most desperate convulsions already behind him; he's begun to inhale water; the green water he sees is going black; and he's settling down into the muck. Some listeners who close their eyes during the second movement claim to perceive a whirling red eyeball or domino, and the more rapidly it speeds, the more balefully it glows. This eidetic image seems to symbolize the approach of something evil. I myself have never seen any red spot, perhaps because Opus 110 already threatens me so perfectly that no kinesthesia is needed to extend or refine the threat. While Shostakovich's music wriggles like the worming of black-gloved fingers clasped behind a policeman's back, the Bronze Horseman sinks down under sandbags and planks. Leningrad strangles in a loop of barbed wire. Meaning dissolves into pure music. (And to think he once wanted to surpass the "Fate motif" of Beethoven's Fifth! When fate and all that are, you know, meaningless!) Hence the opening notes of the first movement as carefully hopeless as men in a snow-trench before Leningrad, resting their machine-guns on blocks of ice.

Western critics claim to find some peculiarly Slavic sorrow which is at least as ancient as the relics of the Volsovo Culture below Riazan. Glikman for his part insists that Opus 110 contains here and there a chord harvested from older ages (for instance, the screams of Peter III after drinking the poisoned wine). This is why it's reductionist to claim that this quartet is merely the corrective to the Seventh Symphony, the distillation of Leningrad's agony with the propaganda decanted off. Anyhow, what *is* Leningrad? Forget the Germans for once. Forget external causes. (Every definition of God leads to heresy, write the Kabbalists.) The foggy, tan-hued tranquility of old Petersburg endures. It's the dead color of a pickled embryo; it's crowned by church-gold and underlined by aquatic mazes of commerce and refuse. Here one finds little Mitya holding his mother's hand; he pulls away to catch a whirling leaf. Here one spies Akhmatova and her first husband Gumilyev (he's the one we'll shoot for counterrevolutionary treason); they're prowling the mists in search of poems!—This part of Opus 110 is not frightening at all, hardly even melancholy, merely Slavic. Well, well, dear friends; you know how things, er, *turn out*. The second movement will be all knives and cadavers, but the measures in which we now find ourselves remain quite silver-on-black, like an ϟϟ badge.—One must understand his character, Akhmatova is murmuring defensively, when Mitya's mother comes running after them: Anna Andreyevna ! Excuse me, Anna Andreyevna; I believe you forgot your scarf.—Extending her hand to receive the trifle (strangers give her flowers all the time), Akhmatova thanks her with that cold politeness for which she's so famous. Then she notices Mitya and says to her husband: There he is! That's my little grey-eyed prince!—The boy doesn't know what she's talking about. He doesn't have grey eyes. He jitters and blushes, crossing his mittened fingers. He understands only this: This lady loves him; she doesn't love his mother or, so it seems, her own husband, who now angrily snatches the scarf: Come on; we'll be late for the masque! Madame, we're much obliged to you . . . They whirl away into a Petersburg the color of catacombs: tan, yellow, brown, all blending, as dead things eventually must, into wet earth. Opus 110 explodes out of it, like metal splinters protruding from broken ferro-concrete.

And the equally broken composer—let's call him a *pechatnik,* the centuries-gone Russian official who keeps the state seal—he remembers, or imagines, the time when Akhmatova was still a goddess, not yet a maimed queen of tears, when we still could go to masques in Russia, before the red domino exploded at the center of Petersburg and turned it into Leningrad. Excuse me, Anna Andreyevna . . . At this point the music, which in this respect oddly resembles some of Scarlatti's harpsichord sonatas, *expands* and *expands,* breaking out of Leningrad's concentric rings of death; it rises like the preludes and fugues which he'd composed for his well-loved T. P. Nikolayeva back in Opus 87, but there is neither joy in it nor even escape; it expands like an ascending aerial view of Dresden's roofless windowlessness and immense fishbones, half-untoothed combs, upon blinding white rubble-gravel, window-holed brickfronts shattered into runes and swastikas, *Strassen* and *Plätze* now utterly sunny and open, sheared-off spicules. As the Führer once said: One can't fight a war with Salvation Army methods! Opus 110 repeats this dictum in the speech of instruments.

What's that sound? The very first moment that Shostakovich arrived in Dresden, music flooded his skull in a hideous scream; he clutched at his chest and the world whirled, but nothing else did: An eighteenth-century maiden outstretched her stone hand, serenely gazing across the brokenness which could be Stalingrad or Leningrad. His interpreter had confided to him that for an instant this cityscape she used to love had resembled a log on the fire-grate, its flesh tortured into cheery cherry-colored facets, and then the crystal shattered, tumbling down between the iron teeth to become grey ash. While it burned, Hitler the Liberator drank in the last warmth he'd ever get from his storehouse of German summers. Then the Grail landscape turned cold, and no *da capo al segno,* no exit. Shostakovich believes this all too well. He didn't escape; he won't get away this time, either; so in Opus 110 he self-loathingly quotes *himself:* the opening motif of the First Cello Concerto, the "Jewish theme" from the Second Piano Trio: Well, Elena, you see how lucky it is that you didn't marry me.—Where's Elena now? Not with me, not with me. (As he scribbled out the chords of the second movement with his quavering, liver-spotted hands, he saw her as a brooding, smiling skeleton in burnt rags, with dust in her long silver hair; her skull was canted almost elegantly, as if in thought, and she gazed sweetly into his eyes; only gradually from her burned eye-sockets did the poison come, that inevitable poison which infects the relations between the living and the dead; there was still something sweet about her and in life she surely wouldn't have meant him any harm, but now the eternal blackness within her smile couldn't help but trap him, weigh him down so that he fell between the teeth and stayed there, wasting away until he died and forever after; he had to get away.) And whenever there's any beauty at all in Opus 110, it's dismembered; it drips with death like shitty guts hanging out of a woman's marble-white torso (thus perish all enemies of Hitler and Stalin's power). And death oozes out of the silences between notes, too, the silences of secret Nazi documents (**Geheim**), the eight-beat rest which hung between himself and Maxim when the boy confessed to having denounced him at school; the suffocating air of a Black Maria with its windowless cages—did I ever tell you that in the Lubyanka prisoners get led in silence, obeying the hand signals of their guards, ready at the appropriate gesture to turn their faces to the wall? He's known that for so much of his life now. **LIFE HAS BECOME MORE,** more, you know . . . Some notes of Opus 110 get coffined up in chords, while others, solo, coffinless, become Leningraders falling one by one into the snow to die.

As for the rhythm, if you've ever been present when our Blackshirts in Berlin or their NKVD cadres in Leningrad are beating enemies of the people, you'll know how it is, the screams alternating with gasps. What's that sound? That's the *allegro molto.*

Of course I've failed to describe Opus 110 just as I've failed to describe death; music remains ultimately indescribable unless Khrennikov and the other artillerymen of Soviet culture compose it for us in pre-measured clips of glittering copper-jacketed mediocrity. And Shostakovich, entering the negative spaces beneath the piano's black keys at last, extends his front line *beyond* music into a perfect hell where his life, dekulakization and Operation Barbarossa become one.

Never mind the second movement, when he really opens up with his eighty-eights! I hear batteries on Pulkovo Heights; the Smolny's now green-blotched, brown-blotched, grey-blotched under camouflage nets; my God, the Fascists have already established a strongpoint in the Leningrad Typewriter Factory! Time to strip the *Aurora*'s old guns . . . Never mind the third movement, even though I myself am all ears. A fireplace like a mouth, and red flames inside it; that's very . . . The brief but tenacious resistance of a sylvan theme in the final movement recalls the patches of green-and-gold melodic ground revealed through the clouds of those high-flying, spectacularly chromatic fugues he'd once made for Tatyana Nikolayeva. But once again the fog has less in common with the obscurity of innovation than with blind melancholy. We fly high, fine, but we don't know to shut off the X-ray beams which shine right through the earth to illuminate the mangled, tortured skeletons; we close our eyes, but can't stop seeing right through our eyelids. According to Lebedinsky, when Shostakovich composed these measures he was remembering the old, verdigrised horses on the bridges of Leningrad, and suchlike frivolities which the Revolution hadn't gotten around to smashing yet. They called him a formalist but he was really a classicist. Let's call that mistake pure comedy. Anyhow, Shostakovich's music always flitters from one mood to another with incredible rapidity, which is to say that he's unstable. That's his, his, so to speak, trademark (isn't that what the capitalists say?). Turn and turn about with the NKVD Ensemble! What's that sound? A quotation from the traditional Russian song "Languishing in Prison" illuminates the airless chamber of the quartet with history's glare, but not brightly enough to show us whose prison or cyanide bath it might be, other than his. In Opus 110, nothing completes itself before perishing. For instance, that flash of prettiness near the end, perfumed by Elena Konstantinovskaya, affords the listener scant relief; rather, it reminds us that D. D. Shostakovich is dying with his eyes open. He knows what happiness is. He knows that he'll never possess it. Hence the sylvan theme is, above all, cruel. Katerina Izmailova, who's the heroine of his ill-starred "Lady Macbeth," sings that same melody to her lover in the final act. The syllables of the tune comprise his nickname, Seryosha—oh, how she adores him! And the other convicts all listen, but . . . What's that sound? Have you ever seen the expressionless faces of people in a queue to send parcels to their spouses in prison camps? They mask themselves out of knowledge that the "organs" are watching. Or perhaps they've developed this habit simply because our Soviet Union is a cold country; one learns to hide oneself simply to, so to speak, stay warm, to, to, to, well. In this opera, however, we're in the ancient times of Russian bear-hunters: Swamps and forests of Russian misery press all around, besieging the walls which jail Katerina. In our time life will be more, so to speak, **JOYFUL:** The walls will grow higher; the Fifth Symphony will end with hordes of perfidiously bristling bug-legged notes and chords strung on the music paper's barbed wire; Opus 110 will scream like invalids in a burning hospital (by the way, screaming is also the task of an intellectual in crisis); unfortunately, "Lady Macbeth" remains trapped in the prerevolutionary era; poor Katerina's on her way to Siberia! But she's *happy,* she sings Seryosha's name. What is it that those idiots always say about Zoya? *Not long but beautifully did she live!* Ha, and then those Fascists hanged her! Beautifully, all right! Sometimes I want to spew. And Katerina's just another, you know. They'll want me to compose her in a major key: *Not long but* **JOYFUL.** What a . . . It might have been well for her had she troubled to consider the studied blankness of her fellow prisoners' faces, because then she might have found the mockery interred so shallowly beneath the twitching earth of their grey lips—buried alive! Well, that's par for the course in Opus 110. On the other hand, why not allow Katerina her little, her, her, you know . . . ? She sings *Seryosha,* each repetition of the name she loves soaring from her throat right up to the heaven of tenderness beyond the prison wall! All this happens in the merest handful of measures. We couldn't allow there to be too much happiness. Seryosha's tired of Katerina. He's found himself a newer convict-slut named Sonetka. With a cruelty which sickened me almost literally when I saw the opera in Leningrad, Seryosha struts around with her at stage right, mocking Katerina to her face. That is why when Katerina sings the sylvan theme, his name defiles it, and his contempt for her, which is visible to us on that stage but not to Comrade Stalin because he withdrew himself two acts ago and not to Katerina because love is truly blind, the murders she's committed for adoration of him, and that selfsame adoration, which empowered her until now to suffer and to endure and even in some measure to remain happy, wavers and beautifully flutters only because a certain extremely cruel God, fate or dialectic, who is not D. D. Shostakovich at all but the unknown suzerain of this known stage we sing our hopes on, wants to exalt her up into sunlight for this instant only so that the shock and depth of her downfall into the uttermost darkness will have been magnified, on exactly the same principle that when Comrade Stalin condemned General Vlasov to be hanged, it was necessary to raise Vlasov somewhat above the dangling noose, in order that the rope be slack enough for convenient manipulation, after which he could be dispossessed from that height either by the operation of a trapdoor in the gallows or else by removing a stool or some other such expedient method; so Shostakovich, seeking even then in that long lost era of his innocent success to give utterance to what must have been his own fundamental, irrevocable despair, wrote that flash of evening sunlight into Katerina's score in order to give her approaching darkness still greater definition, its hideousness being correspondingly enhanced into superior strike depth; and Glikman has personally assured me (not that he's a one percent reliable element) that when Shostakovich composed those measures, hypnotized by the infinite divide between the white and black piano keys, he couldn't help remembering that the German Fascist troops whom we'd cut off at Stalingrad stuck frozen horse-legs in the snow for road markers; those skinny dark posts of flesh must have resembled the black keys, but who played them? Victory did! **LIFE HAS BECOME BETTER, COMRADES.** Life's a transfer prison. Sunlight between two darknesses isn't sunlight at all; it's central Europe herself, which is to say that it's the fourth movement's *largo*, which manages to convey the atmosphere of sickening expectation which overhung Shostakovich at this period; and that feeling is abstracted and generalized to include the naked women standing on a dirt-ledge, facing into the hill so that they won't have to see the pit of white corpses and black blood in which they'll soon lie, for across that pit, two soldiers are feeding a new clip into the machine-gun, waiting for the field telephone to ring. Once we learn that story (Estonian Jews), life alters—doesn't it? Violin, viola, cello, violin! What's that sound? Shostakovich becomes every victim; trembling silently, staring at Nina's black round telephone-face with its perfectly round holes, he writes music which holds its breath, striving not to scream and scream.—In other words, it's all sunlight, white and bright on the cheekbones of the execution squad. A Stuka from the Condor Legion strains up to swallow the sun; the bomber itself resembles a condor, but with whiskers; there it goes! Soon it will dive down and release its seeds, two by two; but in this instant it's still ascending, harmlessly, gloriously. Katerina sings sunlight, then gets immediately assaulted by the fiendish torture of Seryosha mocking her and this new young Sonetka from nowhere also mocking her, and in practically the next instant, she who's poisoned her father-in-law and strangled her husband for love now for the sake of utter and unblinkingly despairing hatred grapples Sonetka into her arms, then leaps into the river (Leskov writes in the nineteenth-century original that she *threw herself on Sonetka like a strong pike on a soft little perch)* so that they both drown. Over their perfect death-embrace the misty sun's out, imparting to the river the warm whiteness of a musical score; it's a summer day over the Elbe, with the skeletons of Dresden's domes still clinging to their bits of brokenness wherever they can; East German schoolboys swim happily by the ruins of the Carolabrücke; the streets are clean and empty around the ruined bookend of the Frauenkirche (there goes the former Field-Marshal Paulus; they're driving him to the office in his official car); the linden trees are in full police-green piping, like the caps of noncomissioned ϟϟ-officers; little East German boys are beating on drums and blowing trumpets to celebrate the impending victory of socialism; that sunlight, the sylvan theme, hangs like a fading rainbow for a duration of several beats (this reminds me of the forest theme's illusory return at the end of the Seventh Symphony's first movement), then loses out forever to the grim seven-note motif* which haunts the prison corridors of the third movement, and then, far past any skeletal rage-clacking or enemy pincer-thrust, which the perceptual filters of hopelessness have already translated from the menacing into the merely ludicrous (so what if that towering yellow skeleton reached down to snatch me into its talons and haul me up into its hard insectoid face as round and yellow and ruthless as the sun, then gnawed me to bloody pieces? So what if that treacherous little white skeleton came scuttling like a crocodile out of the darkness to kill me? I'm already long and uselessly past my own death), recapitulates the opening of the first movement because Opus 110 is no progression, only a prison, and the prisoner (one D. D. Shostakovich) has now paced the walls right back to his starting point. He's at the center of the world, you see. (The center of the world is Leningrad, which is Stalingrad, which is Auschwitz.) Every place leads here. Hence Opus 110's horror as intimate as the throat-slime of music, the strings dripping with bitterness and hate.

---

*The last three notes of this, stressed, sudden and sinister, recall in equal measure the triple knuckle-taps through which Russians in public places warn one another of the appearance of a known police agent, and the three short blasts of the all-clear which in an ominous reversal of their customary meaning admonish good Germans to prepare themselves for a possible air raid.

37

Afterwards his life became as calm as the fading sound of a German bomber which has just released its load. His friends prevented him from carrying out his threat involving sleeping pills. He never frightened them in that way again because, well, it would have been, so to speak, ridiculous. Moreover, Shostakovich does not, you know, abandon his children! Why not continue his work? Sooner or later, death would knock on the door anyhow; Comrade Shostakovich already has his suitcase packed . . . That same year, he whom the capitalists had misnamed "the Mozart of modern Russia" composed his Twelfth Symphony, whose subject at last was Lenin—a hateful, grotesque satire of Lenin. Oh, yes, it was, how should I put it, funny in its way, hilarious, really, almost as humorous as when the NKVD acted out the grovelings of Zinoviev on his way to execution (do it again! Comrade Stalin used to shout, his cheeks all dribbled with laughter's tears). Feculent under-chords tainted the music, which rode over them just the same with businesslike viciousness, like a tank squashing down corpses on the roadside. Lebedinsky talked him out of that suicide attempt, and he completely rewrote it in four days, his normal rate of composition for film scores and other hack work; needless to say, it got praised for its subject (to most of these Soviet critics, music was as obscure as the electrical aspects of bimetallism.)—Dear comrades! he cried in drunken happiness.—Now his Fourth Symphony, which he'd completed in 1936, could finally be performed in public for the very first time. Not long after, our vigilant German allies erected the Berlin Wall.

His old neighbor F. P. Litvinova asked whether his music would have been different without Party guidance, and he replied: You know, my dear Flora Pavlovna, I would have displayed more brilliance, used more sarcasm. I could have, I mean, revealed my ideas openly instead of having to resort to camouflage. I could have written more—how to put it?—more *pure* music.

In short, he'd already succeeded in the most crucial sphere of all: His candidate membership in the Communist Party of our USSR had been ratified in September! I'm happy to inform you that the following year we found him worthy of full membership.—Well, well, he chuckled drunkenly. That was the finale I always had in mind. I know somebody who's very lucky not to have married me!

As for Litvinova, she poured more tea with a bitter smile, straining for the sake of something she would have called decency to conceal her rage, while with spasmodically greedy old hands he spooned more raspberry tea into the cup. Her son, incapable of camouflage, was now in Siberia for having dared to shout that doomed Czech slogan *Socialism with a human face.*

Shostakovich coughed and coughed. Why was Flora Pavlovna so silent? Within his skull sounded a burst of luminous sadness which could be most appropriately expressed in his next string quartet. What was pure music, but formalism? His bones were aching; he wanted to double over like a frontline man (stand straight and a sniper will get you), but Flora Pavlovna might not understand, because she hadn't, which is to say . . . What exactly did she blame him for? It seemed that she blamed him for *something,* and yet he'd always helped her, given her coupons to the GUM department store, listened to her complaints, taught her son music; what did she expect him to do for her son? Comrade Shostakovich was not, so to speak, Comrade Stalin; he couldn't exactly, you know, pull any *strings*; and suddenly his hand began to jerk, spilling tea on his crotch while he observed it in mournful surprise; Litvinova rose to get a napkin. What did she want of him? Was he supposed to apologize to *her* for, for . . . ?

Come to think of it, he'd never trusted that hag anyway. Once he'd encountered her near the Leningradskaya Hotel, where he used to tryst with Elena Konstantinovskaya; and Flora Pavlovna had pretended not to recognize him, he'd never known why. She'd always acted more or less like a neighbor, a friend, but . . . Not that he would have blamed her if she'd, you know, because in our epoch everybody has to, how should I put it, *cooperate.* Meanwhile, everybody blames everybody for what everybody has done! Not that *I* ever . . . Here ran his own slogan, well learned from the late Comrade Stalin: *Never trust anyone. Never say anything*—except musically, of course. Music is safe because nobody understands it. In other words, only in music is everything clear.

Some time ago, about twenty years ago, in fact, we learned to hang clusters of little sandbags on our tanks for protection against those Nazi handrockets called *Faustpatronen,* which resemble plumbers' tools and can shoot through walls a brick and a half thick, and that is just what he did nowadays against people such as Litvinova; he numbed his hide against her wherever he could, so that her anger couldn't sting him. If only he could get as deeply, eternally drunk as Mussorgsky! Then he wouldn't have to, you know. Not that he lived badly; after Opus 110 everything was unreal again. Needless to say, he regretted that Litvinova's son Pavel, who was musically not, so to speak, untalented, had been whisked into the mold and ice of a Kolyma isolation cell; but that happened to all of us! His own sister Mariya had once been exiled, after all, not that I want to face her again after what I've done—oh, dear, how old she is! Every time I see her now, I think the same thing. Her face is as yellow as the Imperial Senate, as yellow as the Admiralty building! I don't want to imagine what Elena looks like now. I certainly don't want to see myself—nor should we omit the case of Akhmatova, and all those, you know; as for E. E. Konstantinovskaya, whom I for one will never call Vigodsky, let's not mention her ever again; it is surely coincidental that she died the same year as D. D. Shostakovich; and Galina Ustvolskaya was out of reach; Tatyana Nikolayeva was, you know; Nina was dead although he still kept a framed photograph of her from when she was still a young girl and cocked her smiling head at him, wearing her flower-blouse (after he married Margarita, it had to disappear from the best piano, but once he'd married Irina it could come back because Irina was tolerantly kind); Tukhachevsky was skeletonized in a construction trench; Leningrad would never be quite the same; Russia and Germany remained rather, how shall I say; and no matter what Litvinova might have suffered, Opus 110 contained it all, in the second movement alone, whose terrifying sounds outclassed the twelve-inch guns of our Black Sea fleet . . .

38

In 1961, when we defended socialism by constructing the Berlin Wall, "Lady Macbeth" got restaged at last, but with the erotic parts excised. Shostakovich didn't give a damn.* That soprano on the stage, what was her name again? It's all getting very . . . I can't hear the high notes anyway; she looks like my idea of, of, let's say lovely, tall Germania, with her sword and her carrion bird! But Irina wouldn't like that comparison. She'd . . .

Meanwhile, Yuri Gargarin became the first human being to visit outer space, and he was one of us; he was a Soviet man, so he sang a Shostakovich song as he orbited the world! Shostakovich didn't care.

Come to think of it, what should Germania look like? This is vexing me! A tall redhaired woman in a robe, with an upright sword in one hand and a banner in the other, or maybe a sheaf of wheat, or something. Needless to say, she's kicking somebody in the face. What's that sound? I forgot to put that sound into Opus 110, and now I've missed my chance. And that book in the

*In fact the word which predominates in "Lady Macbeth" even more than the languorously salivary *tselúy,* kiss me, is—*boredom.*

Nevsky that Galisha found, with that horrifying image of death coming for the children, I forgot that, too! But that's safe from being lost, because it's art, made by a human being, to say *seed corn must not be ground.* Not that they won't keep grinding, but at least somebody is . . . And the suffering *Russian* mother, you know, what about her? An *inostranka,* a foreign woman, will surely be the subject of my next quartet. Maybe that joke is getting . . . What else did I forget to preserve? I'm like Akhmatova with her "Requiem"—I can't let go, because there's always some new, you know. But I'm overwhelmed. Or let's just say I've done my job. As I once said to Elena, very complex circumstances play a very important role here. Now it's better just to, I don't know. I wish I could talk to Irina about this, because she's my angel, but I'm afraid of making her sad. I failed; I was human; I was incomplete. Now Opus 110 is *over*—nothing to scream about anymore! A victory of the . . . What was that bastard Comrade Alexandrov always advising me? Oh, me! *Drown your grief in Red Army power*—hee, hee! And Germania's sitting beneath a tree, marking the place in her Bible with her long sword—very nineteenth-century; Glazunov would, you know; Mussorgsky, too—she's holding a shield adorned with a doubleheaded eagle, with a crown at her feet, and she's . . . Remember when they cut all the children's throats when they were retreating? With her long sword; it's got to be a long sword. They needed blood for their field hospital. Or maybe they used a needle, because Glikman informs me that we saved a few of the children. What's that sound? From a tonal point of view it lights the way ahead with a *searchlight.* An antiaircraft light, let's say. Speer used those at the Nuremberg Rally, right when Elena and Roman Lazarevich were first . . . So Germania has got to have red, *red* lips, with Russian blood running down her mouth. That would be . . . Oh, this opera is endless. What a dull, mediocre composer I am! And to think I used to care whether they played it this way or that way, or left all my notes in! More blood in my next symphony. But I'm almost out of symphonies. The doctor says I have to . . . Poor, dear Irina, to be trapped with me! What a selfish old bastard I am! I should have just . . . Even Margarita didn't deserve what I put her through. If only the plane had crashed! The Fascists could have shot it down. Of course it would have been better if Nina and the children were on another plane. But then . . . A doubleheaded eagle! What's that sound? And she's . . .

He invited Glikman to accompany him to a concert by Galina Ustvolskaya, but at the last moment he didn't have the nerve to, well. Glikman suggested that they attend the premiere of Roman Karmen's new film about the new order in Cuba; it was called "The Blue Lamp," and was supposed to be very, you know, but every time I meet dear Roman Lazarevich I can't help but think of a certain, anyhow, I'm not saying that Shostakovich wasn't busy. Composer and decomposer, he had to go on *al fine,* to the end.

He lived on to 1962, when word got out that his Thirteenth Symphony was explicitly linked to Yevtushenko's subversive poem "Babi Yar,"* and so the district Party secretary cried out: This is outrageous! We let Shostakovich join the Party and then he goes and presents us with a symphony about Jews!—After Yevtushenko caved in and made the changes which the Party required, to deemphasize the Jewish nature of that massacre, Shostakovich got drunk with Lebedinsky, whom he saw less and less these days, and he whispered: I am a Jew! Oh, how I want to be a Jew . . .

Excuse my directness, Dmitri Dmitriyevich, but there's a solution to your troubles.

Well, naturally we'll speak privately about the possibility of a solution, a, a, so to speak, political solution. No, please, please don't smile like that! When I screwed up my courage to divorce Nina, I couldn't face her; I wrote her a letter, but she didn't reply, so Ashkenazi delivered another copy to her. He actually went all the way to Detskoe Selo, where Nina and her mother had already, you know. Sometimes I . . .

Dmitri Dmitriyevich, she's a widow now. I've made inquiries.

Opus 40 was almost finished then; poor Elena was waiting by the telephone. Can you believe it? But *then,* you know . . .

This was the year we find him autographing scores for Young Pioneers who didn't give a shit, the year he married his third wife, Irina, whose smooth round face, round spectacles and glossy hair-knot he loved so well. He secretly apologized to all his friends for her youthful awkwardness. Glikman in particular felt jealous of her. But that's normal. He informs me—can you believe it?—that Roman Lazarevich has also tied the knot this year! I sincerely wish him happiness. This Maya Ovchinnikova, I don't know her circumstances. I hope she likes hunting and fast cars, because otherwise . . . The man's my Doppelgänger! Whatever I do, he copies in his golem-like way. But I only imagine that because of, you know. What would it be like to ring him up and . . . ? Strange to say, although I almost never telephone him, I know

---

*Here we must footnote the dark elegance of "Babi Yar"'s poet, Yevtushenko, who often posed for photographs with his hand on his heart, while Shostakovich smiled beside him anxiously.

his number by heart: *VI, 93, 80*. And if I just said, my dear Roman Lazarevich, come drink vodka with me and we'll talk about the old days, I'm sure he . . . He's a much sweeter person than I—not spiteful. And if I said, Roman Lazarevich, please tell me how it was for you and her in Spain and don't omit anything! I want to know what she said when she first heard that she'd been awarded the Order of the Red Star! I was, you know, *proud*. Whereas I don't give a rat's ass about any of my own decorations. How many people must I invite to my wedding? How I dread such affairs! It would almost be better to, you know.

I meant to write everything into Opus 110, except for Elena; but of course I had to write Elena in, on account of those . . . She, you see, kept screaming and *screaming*. But what I'd rather do is compose something in the style of Opus 40, just a, you know, a simple little something which *adores* her, but even more achromatically, blurring and revealing her the way her hair does, oh, my God, her long hair, it must be grey now, or maybe it's fallen out. What was it she used to, no, I won't admit that I've forgotten her. Just a little something like Opus 40, something which, how should I say, respects her right to *seclude* herself just as the lovely pale pavilion of the Concert Hall veils itself behind the maple leaves of Catherine Park. Should I visit Catherine Park with Irina? She'd surely find that quite, er, *romantic*. Once when I met Elena at the All-Russian Agricultural Museum, we . . .

Laboring with the ruthlessly exemplary dedication of a shock worker, he lived on to 1963, when his friend Marshal Tukhachevsky got posthumously rehabilitated. Let's drink Crimean champagne with R. L. Karmen! Shostakovich wrote the memorial music, feeling (how should I say this?) anxious. No matter that Stalin was dead; it was only habit to, to, you know, well, to expect a hand on one's shoulder. How would the "organs" perceive this? Still, he craved to be a decent person, especially now, since . . .

His silent young Irina stood behind him, with her hair in a double bun. In the raised bell of the stage he could see something flittering behind the tarnished iron leaves of the railing. Elena's skirt had trembled like that, that red skirt she used to wear with the black jacket, and she used to trace patterns with her fingernail upon the glass goblet on the table. As they played on, the bell glowed more and more beautifully against the blue sky which was becoming night, and Elena's skirt, well, actually, it wasn't her skirt at all. Would it hurt me more to know that it was or to know that it wasn't? Oh, me! The lady violinists in white blouses and black shirts, the men in the black and white suits, the cobblestones yellow under the inverted truncated pyramids of the lamps, and the shadows between cobblestones very black, they all added up to something, another composition by another composer, perhaps Haydn, certainly not Shostakovich. These windowpanes curtained or simply black, that's what my music is about. *This* music was very, I mean, he never should have composed it, because first of all it wouldn't bring Tukhachevsky back and second of all, it wasn't, how should I say, healthy to remind the "organs" of their past deeds. Better not to remember the Marshal! *I get everything I ask for!* he used to crow. And then . . . But I'm certainly proud of Irina, who to get right down to it possesses, how should I describe it, an almost serpentine elegance: I *do* adore those pale, slim women! When she puts her hair up in a bun like that I want to sink my teeth into it, it's so delicious! How good she is to me! And how *understanding*. And all the other old men are jealous of me; they don't know I can't even, well, but I wish she'd stop gnawing on her knuckles like that. The poor dear must be nervous. Why bother? It's too late to be nervous! She's already married a former enemy of the people. That was very . . .

When they got home, she wanted to know the wife's fate. He couldn't believe that she didn't know. Of course it was all in Opus 110, but I admit that that's elliptical; all the same, you'd think that, well. Sitting down at the piano bench, resting his aching wrists on the lid which mercifully hid the extended grin of those black and white keys, he told her, watching her reflection in the shiny wood between his hands: The first one, er, *shot herself*. During the Civil War. That must have been very . . . Although I myself—don't look at me like that, Irinochka! They say she was caught stealing bread, and didn't want to disgrace her husband. I never asked him anything, of course. And the second one *disappeared*.

But—

In a poisonous whisper he breathed into her ear: All right, then, *she got liquidated by the "organs."* After they liquidated him, obviously; I mean, you wouldn't want to put a finale before a—

Her eyes became as big as bomb craters.—Mitya, are you sure she wasn't implicated? I don't remember those times, of course, but—

Yes you do! he shouted. We all remember them!

His voice diminished into something as unnerving as a gap in the front line, and he said: But we, we *pretend*, you see . . .

Anyway, said Irina steadily, the performance was very beautiful.

And he shot, I repeat, he shot your own father, yet you're so naive as to maintain—

Be careful, Mitya! Anyhow, my mother said—

To *protect* you, you little fool! Don't you even know that much? And from a Polish father, a Jewish mother, how could you not know *what goes on in this world*? And then what happened to your mother, you, well, that's how it is for all of us. Irinochka, please, please forgive me for my, for, for speaking to you in this monstrous fashion; I know I'm a . . . Poor child! What a lot of pain I've caused you! And you knew it anyway, didn't you?

Breathing heavily, she said: You say all this, and meanwhile you joined the Party.

At this he punched himself in the face again and again with his half-crippled old fist.

39

Well? she said.

It was blackmail, Irinochka . . . If you love me, you won't dig that up . . . Khatchaturian's been a member for years . . .

He lived on to 1964, the thirtieth anniversary of his first meeting with Elena Konstantinovskaya, when the decay of his limbs and joints compelled him to forgo all public performances. (After all, in the Soviet Union aren't old relics an offense against history?) My *dear* friends, are you familiar with that statue who lost his hands in Dresden, from the Allied, you know? That's how it is now, with D. D., how should I say, Shostakovich! Retaining his civic capacities at least, he rose in the assembly hall, panting and trembling a little, splaying his aching fingers like tree-roots, gazing into the socialist horizon beyond the microphone, and expressed his confidence in the future. He was one of our reliable leading cadres. Every time he spied anybody in authority, a policeman or even a janitor, he felt sick with terror. Glaring at the yellow drapes, pretending that he didn't know that this slogan had been discredited, he declaimed to his fellow Party members: **LIFE HAS BECOME BETTER, COMRADES; LIFE HAS BECOME MORE JOYFUL.** People begged him to be more careful.

Anyway, he muttered to his friends, it's over. The second movement was the worst.

Mitya, you're drunk and you really don't look so good. Whatever do you mean?

Opus 110, naturally. That's when we all died. I wrote the second movement like a Katyusha: eight rocket launchers in a go! It was supposed to be horrible. But now they've killed us off, so we don't have to be careful.

This was the year when he publicly denounced the *Soleil des Incas* of E. V. Denisov. The golden sheen of his Medal for the Defense of Leningrad was alive on his breast with armed figurines oriented left, making a wall of guns and bayonets against the enemy; above them, a central tower climaxed in a Soviet star.

Staring as though his features were as terrifying as the bomb-crushed face of some stranger who'd introduced himself a quarter-hour before, Denisov asked why he'd done it. He replied: Well, well, Edik, you know, because I was frightened, of course . . . —(A Party functionary had been there.)—It's, it's, just the same as at movie theaters when we all rise to, to the Horst Wessel Song! Or, or, or *Deutschland über Alles!* I mean, you can . . . In fact, I consider *Le Soleil des Incas* to be a, well, a masterpiece, a real masterpiece. Acoustically speaking, the barbed wire of the second movement is as distinct and cleanly patterned as the concentric polyhedrons of a spiderweb. This is not a work for idiots. I sincerely hope you won't alter a single note . . .

Mitya, didn't you realize that I can't be your friend after this?

Forgive me, I beg of you. I admit that I'm a bastard. But it's our, our, *our life.* Back in '48, or maybe it was '46, when, you know, even Maxim had to . . .

Goodbye, Mitya.

Do you know, do you know, the—the French horn ought to be played, as a general rule, between its fourth and twelfth partials. Well, if somebody who's up to his ears in blood commands that you play it at the seventeenth partial, then a certain degree of distortion—

Denisov was already turning away, now and forever.

Have pity, Edik! Remember the vulnerability of my children!

(To his wife, whose gentleness he valued more and more, he muttered: You see, I'm such an insensitive criminal type! A, a, an enemy of the people, actually. But he'll never . . . Guess what a great comrade said? *Anyone in this world who does not succeed in being hated by his adversaries does not seem to me to be worth much as a friend.* Guess who? He's, so to speak, a German. An Austrian, actually. A late Austrian. My sexy little Irinka, thanks for your . . . But I'll survive. I'll get through this.)

He lived on to 1965, when they made him Doctor of the Arts. *That* honor was truly indispensable!

They urged him to write more popular songs, with civic content. Oh, what patrons of the arts! Now that he was a Party member, which meant that he was truly one of us, he really needed to toe the line a little more exactly. The best reputations require maintenance; even fresh white bricks will slowly tarnish in, for instance, Dresden. They suggested that he use as his templates A. I. Ostrovskii's "Let There Always Be Sunshine," and A. G. Novikov's "March of the Communist Brigades." My, oh, my! They said to him: There's so much filth around us, Dmitri Dmitriyevich! Be careful that you don't get smeared with any of it.—He assented with diplomatic grimaces. Later that day, when his daughter looked in on him, he sat down at the piano and accompanied himself, singing in a crazed cracked voice:

Merry singing makes the heart glow;
merry singing stops the tear-flow!
In the country villages, singing is their meat;
from Moscow straight to Leningrad, singing is their treat!

Do you remember that, Galisha? It was on the radio when you were still a, a little . . . What nice perfume you have on! Is it "Red Dawn," or . . . ? That's what I'm supposed to emulate. The effect is, you know, *enormous.*

She shook her head and said: You're doing this to yourself.

How's married life? Is it true what they say? I've heard that women sometimes . . . never mind. "Let There Always Be Sunshine." By the way, did you hear that your brother's won another award? Will you be attending the ceremony? I'm very . . . Your hair looks extremely, how should I say, effective. Oh, me! Is that a new style?

Meanwhile, Khruschev was removed from power in favor of Brezhnev, who explained to the Twenty-third Congress: Socialist art is profoundly optimistic and life-affirming.—Shostakovich lived on. It's said that he watched R. L. Karmen's new film "The Great Patriotic War" again and again; after awhile not even Glikman would accompany him to the cinema anymore; after all, the man lost his wife in the, so I can see his, his, you know. But Shostakovich couldn't take his eyes off the Leningrad woman in the snowy overcoat who was towing another sled to the cemetery. I could swear she's somebody I know! Because she . . . and her long dark hair. But I can't say that Elena's calling me to lie down beside her, because as far as I know she's still . . . All the same, he avoided more horrors than he sought out. On a rainy afternoon, at a reception for some artist friend of Glikman's, he wondered what he should do, how he should live; what was her name now, he should really, anyhow, it was all oils in gilded frames, flowers, landscapes, fruits, not to mention the occasional, you know, nude. I don't approve of nudes, because then I feel, well. The women were gazing more at each other's smiles than at the art, which was as it should be, but where had Irina slipped off to? Don't leave me here, my God, or they'll all be hounding. All they want is . . . Suddenly he feared that some sneak assault would get through: so many of the individuals he'd cared for, I hope not the majority, better not to count, Denisov makes five, had gone over to the other side, not just Denisov but, oh, me, and especially these snowy landscapes, I don't approve of them, either! What *do* I approve of! Irina, of course. That woman's so good to me! And my children. Why don't they paint something cheerful and *red*? "Let There Always Be Sunshine," and light up the way with a *searchlight;* I know we can do it; it's just a question of, of everything in a major key! Speaking of which, must I congratulate Roman Lazarevich now that he's been named People's Artist of USSR? I have his telephone number right here: *VI, 93, 80*. Leo Oskarovich tells me excellent things about Maya Ovchinnikova. He's got a sweet wife, just as I have; thank God and Soviet power for sweet wives! If I had my own atomic bomb I'd just . . . I wonder if my pretty Irinka would mind sending him a card for me, with greetings to her, so that I could simply . . . I'll bet he still keeps a bust of Stalin at his writing desk! Oh, my, and I also forgot to telephone him when he won his second Order of Lenin last year. When he's always been so, whatever. That's terrible! I have no excuse; it's only . . . One bronze of an absolutely heartbreaking nude, female, bald, with an an almost simian face, brought Opus 110 back; she was halfway between weeping and screaming, with her hands on her hair, and he couldn't bear it, so he turned away and gazed out the window; something dark like rain was cratering the pavement. How can I get out of here? It's so . . . But what's the use? Skyscrapers as blocky and tower-perimetered as castles were going up everywhere, haloed with scaffolding; welders' torches glared on them like unwinking stars (whenever he saw a flame now, he remembered the blistered dead of Dresden, the children who clung to banisters and railings until the fires inhaled them, the screams of the tropical birds getting roasted at the zoo); new trees grew between the communal flats, and airplanes banked protectively over everything. Some of them looked like fighters. Let's see; the German fighters had been based at Gatchina, Siverskaya, Tosna. They bombed Leningrad every day. And Pilutov became a Hero of the Soviet Union when he shot down all those Messerschmitts. That was very . . .

They told R. L. Karmen to film a meeting of the minds between D. D. Shostakovich and A. Akhmatova, with whom he'd never had anything in common anyway, excepting nightmares, so he stood beside her in snowy muck, waiting for the camera to whir, then said: *Eighty-eight, eighty-eight,* an exercise he'd invented for creating the illusion of animated speech by stretching the corners of the mouth; perhaps opera singers might also find it, you know, convenient. Where was Irinochka? She would have been polite; she was so, thank God for that, because at my age, well. Akhmatova stared at him; she was wearing her green-ribboned Medal of Leningrad but he wasn't; the poor woman looked rather stout, because our Russian food, you know . . . All right, so he'd hurt her feelings, but he didn't give a damn, not that he disliked her; the poor woman was looking old and shabby. The only thing he held against her was that she'd carried the score of his Seventh Symphony out of Leningrad, holding it on that promiscuous lap of hers; she thought that made him her soul mate. If she'd only lost the Seventh, and he'd been shot down, then he wouldn't have contributed to that shameful, you know. Not that Nina and the children would have deserved such an ending, even though they might have been, never mind. As for Roman Lazarevich, he seemed satisfied; they shook both hands, and for a moment Shostakovich dreaded that he might utter *her* name; indeed, he feared that more than he'd ever feared anything in this world; he might have screamed.

Karmen's face had become strangely clayey as he aged; it was palish-tan and nude, its white slicked-back hair resembling lines combed into a lump of clay; it was more featureless than it used to be, as if poor Roman Lazarevich were collapsing back into a primordial ball! His lips were two pale bars of clay half-mashed together. To think that he and Elena . . . His head had sunk deeper down upon his clayey neck, settling between the slabs of clay which were called his shoulders. His blank eyes had sunken in a trifle. All in all, he was ready to be taken off the shelf at a moment's notice to have any expression whatsoever painted onto him, and then he could be baked, glazed and finished. But I'm not being very . . . Shooting him a searching look, the director merely said: Much obliged, Dmitri Dmitriyevich! You haven't aged a day! And here's a copy of my new book, just a small gift . . .

The Heroics of Struggle and Creation. Why, thank you, Roman Lazarevich, thank you! In the unlikely event that I myself ever succeed in doing anything, er, *creative,* I'll be sure and send you a copy . . .

And this Dmitri Dmitriyevich, whoever he was, gave speeches on demand, his own gaze expressing that strange dullness of the slaughter-doomed steer which we remember from the former Marshal Tukhachevsky's trial: The Soviet Union fully supports the just position of, how should I put it, Ho Chi Minh.

Elena had told him that in the Arctic camps they split open a corpse's skull before burial, just in case. And that night when those three guards raped her, oh, let's think about something else. So he went everywhere they told him; he trudged the Motherland's icy streets, with Irina juggling two suitcases while holding his arm in case he fell. As soon as they got back to Moscow, he was going to buy her some more "Stone Flower" perfume! The world she lived in he wanted to live in, too (a prosecutor would have pounced on him); he'd been very unfair to marry and drag her into his, his, you get the drift. What was a little more guilt among friends? He'd never even notice. They'd already expelled him from their consideration, just as Shostakovich himself cut out superannuated notes from his scores with a razorblade; as each blade got dull he'd dispatch Glikman or Glikman's brother to go buy a new one for fifty kopeks. Denouncing the continuing Anglo-American aggression in, so to speak, Cuba, deliberately slurring and mumbling each page of typescript, he craned away from the corpselike grins of his audience to stare out the window at the snow on the flat roofs of Soviet Asian cities, snow on the flat roofs of neobureaucratic halls, palaces and apartment blocks. Even Irina had gotten tired of traveling by then. Originally she'd thought, well, he didn't know what she'd thought. Why had she left her husband, anyway? Perhaps neither he nor I can pass for a man. She wants a . . . But how can I please her when I, uh, to counter the unheard insolence of the imperialist camp. We demand the immediate punishment of these, oh, yes, these dangerous enemies of the working class. Those snowy trees, with snow-mountains all around, well, we mustn't, so to speak, exaggerate, but what was the point? He felt as if the music paper had swallowed him up. Whenever people asked him to generalize or pronounce on something, he replied: Ha, ha! My dear lady, in this life we only know our own sector of front, so to speak . . .

Shall we map out the sector assigned to D. D. Shostakovich? His defensive system now consisted first and most fundamentally of Irina (who was very *gemütlich,* I believe), secondly of Glikman, Lebedinsky and his sister Mariya, thirdly of his increasing physical disabilities, which excited compassion and guilt in others, fourthly of his Party membership, which isolated and protected him within what military strategists would refer to as his cutoff and intermediate position; fifthly came the world within the piano keys, the lovely world of pure darkness and white winter icicles, into which he'd once upon a time imagined that he could invite anyone he chose, for instance, the plump girl in the blue dress who sang at the Hotel Sovietskaya; unfortunately, that world's tunnels had suffered many cave-ins since he'd detonated the various Hydrox cartridges of Opus 110; he longed to retreat there and still sometimes did, but it wasn't the same; it was stifling, collapsed, flooded and poisoned, but he couldn't see the point of complaining about it, not even to the, how should I say, people's responsible representatives; sixthly and lastly was his inner line, namely, his memories of Elena Konstantinovskaya, who had always actually been very, you know.

40

The Serbian Academy of Sciences and Arts granted him honorary membership. The rows of seats down the herringboned floor, the stage dissected by chairs and frames, then curtains above everything, it was all quite . . . Weary old owl that he was, he cocked his head, smiled, and tooted out his *thank you, thank you*. The following year, as the new purges of Soviet literature began, he was named Hero of Socialist Labor. By then the infamous dissident A. I. Solzhenitsyn was already referring to him as "the shackled genius." Yet he dared to sign a petition in Solzhenitsyn's favor. I'm told that he'd often stand in the back of a concert hall, listen to the music of other composers, close his eyes and silently weep with emotion. Sweaty, flabby and feeble, he lived on, producing music with an efficiency comparable to that of the SKNK-6 corn-planting machine, which can inseminate 3.5 hectares per hour of ploughed ground. *It's merely a question of time and manpower.* **LIFE HAS BECOME BETTER . . .** *At their best,* wrote the bourgeois critic Layton, *the symphonies have the epic panoramic sweep of the great Russian novels*. To Glikman, to whom everything he wrote was a masterpiece, he wrote: *I have been disappointed in much and I expect many terrible things to happen. I am a dull, mediocre composer.* Ustvolskaya had cut him off forever. Nikolayeva had become very, very busy. Irinushka, who was so good and who forgave everything, would have understood if he'd needed to refresh himself with one of them (not that he could have done anything except with his half-paralyzed hand); she was such a magnificent wife, so loving and respectful of his pain; he even trusted her with his hidden manuscripts. Once she asked him why he hadn't married E. E. Konstantinovskaya, I mean Vigodsky, and he gaily replied: Inferior antitank forces!

She didn't go away, so he cocked his head and said: Irinochka, I, I prefer not to discuss it much. It humiliates me. Well, we, I mean, we tried hard. And, and . . . First and foremost, you musn't think that I don't love you, Irina. Here's the worst of it. She . . . But, you know, what happened to her and me, well, we can't just blame the times and *that bastard*.—Then he lifted the telephone to call Nikolayeva, but the voice on the other end of the wire, a male voice, informed him rather unpleasantly that she was on tour in the Ukraine.—Kindly tell her that I need to talk with her about, you know, about, about Mussorgsky. About the, uh, bass clarinet.—Glikman wrote him again and he began to reply: *Slowly and with great difficulty, squeezing out one note after another, I am writing a violin concerto,* and then such an eerie echo rang between his ears that he had to lay down the pen, because his own phrase, *squeezing out one note after another,* merely repeated the sentiment *it's merely a question of time and manpower.* Oh, those Fascists, they'd been special individuals, all right!

Buried under the rubble of his three Orders of Lenin, his Order of the October Revolution, his Order of the Red Banner of Labor, he lived on to 1968, when Akhmatova died. Her funeral cortège was as steady as the one-track railroad line through Wolf's Lair: Bahnhof Goerlitz, final stop! Now into the hole. He was there, of course. Eighty-eight; eighty-eight. The eighty-eight is the best general-purpose German gun. After all, she'd been in Leningrad when . . . We have a Motherland and they have a Fatherland. Their child is Europe Central. And *I* have Messerschmitts, Heinkels, Junkers, ammunition transported through the sewers, Germans crouching in their snowy trenches, the dark swirl of greatcoats as Red Army men leapt from the earth to charge forward; these comprised his homeland forever, where pale, open-mouthed corpses lay in each other's arms on a street corner in the rain. Here came the Messerschmitts again; she was screaming and screaming.

And his soul was the winter sun of this ghastly dreamland now as bygone as old Petersburg; Elena's screams, which he'd thought to inter in the grey chapel of Opus 110, continued to torture him to the end; they rose and died so nakedly, illuminated by rays of despair. Opus 110 towered above us all; he'd brought a new evil into the world without solving an old one. Supposedly one can actually, so to speak, make a bulletproof wall out of snow, but in this case their artillery can, well, you know. Or had he even done anything at all? Wasn't death always with us? Had he lived five hundred years ago, Shostakovich might have found Opus 110 just as luckily in some deep old well with ferns on the walls and sickly concentric circles of darkness. So let's go down to the Queen of Hell. Then we can come back up and inherit a whole green hill with cemetery ruins embedded in it. Ha, ha! Steep dark stairs burrowing upward through the very stone of the castle walls, chandeliers like spiders, and then if I'm good I'll get to make love with Elena in an ebony bed with snakes carved in it. Glikman encountered them at the spa at Gagra, the

Vigodskys, I mean, not the snakes. He told me they were extremely . . . But what's that sound? And yet in spite of his terrible fear and all the sadness, he even lived on to 1969, when one of his worst tormentors, the musicologist P. Apostolov, was stricken by a heart attack at the premiere of the grim Fourteenth Symphony, whose proclaimed theme was death, and whose melodies (if they can even be called that) were blacker than the smoke from a burning oil depot. Explaining what he required of the orchestra, he said at the first rehearsal: On the left and right flanks, the battalion regions are echeloned to the depth of the, the, you see, the regimental sectors.—But he was only joking. Oh, that hilarious D. D. Shostakovich! To the symphony audience he said: Death is terrifying; there is nothing beyond it. You see, I don't believe in life beyond the grave . . . —Refusing to accompany him into the pit, his old friend Lebedinsky wrote him a letter which severed relations between them; so goes one story, but other people have said that Lebedinsky, like Glikman, was jealous of Irina's influence. The third version, which claims that Lebedinsky dreaded the Party officials and representatives of the "organs" who now frequented the Shostakovich household, may safely be dismissed as an anti-Soviet slander.—Unfortunately, said Shostakovich to his wife, Lebedinsky has grown, how shall I put it, old and stupid.—And he sat down heavily, clutching at his heart. Everybody's equally disgusting. Where are my cigarettes? For instance, here's that war criminal von Manstein; Lebedinsky sent his memoirs when we were still friends; I particularly like this, this, where is it? Here: *It was essential to ensure that,* you know. *Consequently it was now necessary for the Germans, too, to resort to the "scorched earth" policy which the Soviets had adopted during their retreats in previous years.* The worst of it is, the monster's *correct*. He's such a . . . —Back to the Fourteenth, which I myself don't mind confessing has given me nightmares; it really does stink of the tomb; nonetheless, it bears the same relation to Opus 110 as does the postmortem twitching of a dissected frog (a musical twitch, we might as well say, or at least a rhythmic one, for it's brought about according to the quirks of the experimenter, who opens and closes the circuit between flesh and galvanic battery, *prestissimo)* to the actual death-convulsions when we'd placed the reptile in the killing-jar.—My Fourteenth, you know, I've sort of, you know, taken a shine to it, because it's *nasty* and because it reminds me of my past. For instance, the time that Elena, you know, she was having her, her, and then the time when the German Fascists wrecked the Catherine Palace. I forgot to include that in Opus 110 . . . —About this work (ten percussion instruments, nineteen strings, two solo voices), important musical personalities insisted that its symphonic conflict never showed any dialectical resolution—which means that more passages should have been in a major key.

Staring down at the piano keys to which his aching ancient claws of hands couldn't make love anymore, he thanked us for their comradely criticism; oh, yes, he thanked us in words as lucent as the icily sparkling corpses which had once adorned Leningrad.—And in fact, I, well, there's simply no question about it. In my next symphony I'm going to change everything exactly as you advise! If we're fainthearted about carrying out those measures, the ᛋᛋ will step in. That violin section you dislike, I'll tell the orchestra to play it quickly so that the audience won't even hear it! Moreover, I'm going to, er, there'll be dialectical resolution in every measure, I guarantee it! Like a *searchlight*!—But, as usual, he was, how should I say, teasing them. After all, isn't nocturnal antiaircraft fire likewise a song of darkness engraved in pure and delicate lines of light, akin to the rays of twenty-four-carat gold which a bookbinder's heated stylus, if drawn with sufficiently errorless spontaneity across the measured strip of foil, engraves forever in the black leather covers of the Book of Night?

In a grand Hallway of the People with a brass chandelier, he got drunk and whispered into Glikman's face: They talk about this new, this, this cultural exchange! Well, haven't we always had it? We have Black Marias and *they* have Green Minnas!

My dear, dear Dmitri Dmitriyevich, what on earth are you saying? Please be careful—

Or did Green Minnas vanish with the Reich? Maybe they transport them in schoolbuses now—

Them? Whom are you talking about?

Why, I'm talking about all of us. Long live the, so to speak, the, the Fatherland!

Dmitri Dmitriyevich, day and night I worry about your happiness.

Thank you. Thank you!

And I have something important to say to you.

Yes, my friend, said Shostakovich in a panic, his fingers beginning to gallop crazily all over the room. What is it?

Do you remember that many years ago you asked me to—

No, no! Please don't—

And after I saw you last time, when you burst into tears—

I *did not!*

I swear to you—

So you betrayed my confidence, is that what you did?

When you were weeping, you asked me to go to her and—

Did you tell her? How dare you?

She kept asking me, Dmitri Dmitriyevich. So I told her, because—

Because what?

My dear Dmitri Dmitriyevich, I advise you to leave your present situation, because you're not happy. Even now it's not too late to—

Please keep your advice to yourself, my *dear, dear* Isaak Davidovich!

With a despairing and humiliated smile, Glikman said softly: That's how I know you're in love. Because people in love never take the advice of their friends. First they ask for it and don't take it, and then they become quite offended when their friends, who only want to help them and who—

Isaak Davidovich, please forgive me! Oh, I'm a bastard, such a, a, a bastard! And that's why you told her, of course, of course—because I *wanted* you to! How is she? Her hair must be completely white by now. And then I—oh, I'm such a sonofabitch! Galina was right not to marry me!

Never mind her, said Glikman, laying his hand on Shostakovich's shoulder; and Shostakovich suddenly felt that he loved Glikman more than he had ever loved any man or woman on or under this earth, and Glikman tenderly repeated: Never mind her. It's not Galina Ustvolskaya that you love.

Shostakovich lived on to 1970, when he published an article entitled "Lenin's life, an inspiring example to us." He also composed Opus 139, "March of the Soviet Police." I mean, why run ahead of progress? It's better to just, you know. But Irina kept being so kind. The silent tact of the woman who sits on the bench beside the concert pianist, turning pages at just the right moment, and otherwise scarcely existing, that summed up Irinochka, who devoted herself to him so perfectly; how could he possibly deserve her?

He knew that he was ruining her as he'd ruined Tatyana, Elena, Nina and Galina; he was a poisoned bomb who killed all; poor tired Ninusha had suffered the worst, because she'd lived with him the longest. And then he'd . . . Elena, you're so lucky that you didn't marry me. Is the page turner any less important than the concert pianist? First of all, she needs to read music, which is no mean feat in our times. More important still, she keeps me company, knowing me and comforting me. She keeps Opus 110's swarm of sorrows from . . . I, I, the things growing deep within the mass graves! And then . . . From within the great brick arch, the railroad tracks roll toward a stand of trees. I think that's the gas chamber. Wooden watchtowers, A-framed ocher-bricked barracks in rows and rows and rows, the remains of chimneys in the grass, that's my music. Long rows of chords, block after pinewood block of them, long and low with steeper, blacker-roofed chords on the right, it all aims at the same kind of feeling—you know, that feeling of . . . But when she holds me in her arms, Operation Barbarossa never happened! Well, aren't I vile, though, to want to deny . . . ? Do you remember when the American fighter-bombers returned to Dresden for the third raid and began machine-gunning women and children in the grass? Talk about chopping up the melodic lines! The Americans should have, well . . . Some people survived even then. I wonder who was luckier. We can all hope to, to, so to speak, survive. And I myself, although I'm very afraid, I . . .

Time ticked, and he lived on to 1972, when his Fifteenth Symphony premiered; for despite his impairments they still expected him to fulfill his quota of symphonies, just as in the old days they'd demanded that the NKVD chief of some city arrest and shoot ten thousand enemies of the people at once and without fail. Unfortunately, the Fifteenth was no more than a feeble rearguard action, a holding-on behind enemy-occupied lines. Many a chord got borrowed from Wagner, Prokofieff, Mussorgsky and a certain D. D. Shostakovich. On the whole, it was as grey as Tukhachevsky's eyes, as white as Glikman's intentions, as clean as Nina's fingernails, as solitary as Irina's, you know. Elena, you see how lucky it is that, well. I used to be—how should I put it? Conceited. And now, when I hear someone's silly laugh, especially a man's, because women are, you know, I, I can hardly . . . They praised its banality, and his ears kept ringing. He kept expecting to see Comrade Stalin in the back row, or Zhukov, Khrennikov, or anybody else who was unshakably determined *to light the way ahead with a searchlight*. As for our unshakable allies in East Germany, they called it *strangely reserved and introverted*. His attention wandered; his mouth trembled; his coat fell off his lap and Irina picked it for him. The searchlight's on me; it gives me the creeps! His spectacles were now as big as clockfaces. White light gleamed on them, so that it was sometimes difficult for others to read his eyes—thank you, thank you! He sat stiff and frowning, with his useless hands at his sides. Why not cut them off? Then I'd take up less space in this world! That way I could hide from Comrade Alexandrov, who won't leave me alone; he's always around with his . . . Remembering the chord of screams when a German Fascist oil bomb hit a children's hospital, he realized that he'd forgotten to put that sound into Opus 110. Well, well! Should I rewrite it? It would field-strip as nicely as a Nazi pistol, every movement black and silver. And then that one sound—

what's that sound? Because . . . Struggling painfully to his feet to thank the musicians as usual, he found that several shuddered away from his compromised hand. They jeeringly called him *Comrade* Shostakovich. His heart drummed as hellishly as the second movement of Opus 110. The next day, however, an American admirer invited him to her apartment for an intimate breakfast, not far from where the "Spartak" Children's Home used to be. What was her name? It was some, so to speak, *American* name. His memory wasn't always . . . She told him that his Fifteenth was brilliant, and he thought to himself: If I were only fifteen measures younger I could have, I could have, well. Let me calculate it: Fifteen years ago, Nina had just died and Elena would have been forty-three. When did that Vigodsky marry her? After the war; it must have been after the war. She wouldn't have been too old then to, to, how shall I say, but it's better not to think about that because, anyway that's how most meetings go. Besides, for the sake of my so-called "health" . . . He remembered the cries which Elena used to utter: first *appassionato,* almost *con dolore,* then *morendo,* then after a long rigid silence with her face locked away in pleasure, *con brio* for the very finish, not explosively as other women so often did, but as calmly unstoppably as a rocket rising upon its own flame, with superhuman brilliance, really; hence that smooth shrill pass of the cello's bow in the second movement of Opus 40; that was when he'd first known how far above everyone she truly was. Well, that was over. The waffles which this American had made (she seemed to be suffering from a case of leftwing infantile deviation) reminded him of war-skeletonized buildings. It was all a matter of scale. Instead of charred square concrete pits which had once been rooms, square wells of golden starchiness looked up at him, glimmering with melted butter and maple syrup imported all the way from Canada!

Thank you, thank you, dear lady, he said, and now I need to go, for I'm really not well, you see . . . —And he really wasn't well. In fact, I'm so feeble that if Elena were mine I'd drop dead for happiness.

Irina had proposed a visit to Leningrad so that he could see it one last time. And probably he should have gone; Leningrad defined him as much as did Opus 110; Glikman's brother Gavriil, already famous for sculpting the "Apollo Shostakovich," would soon propose setting little stones from Leningrad on his grave, surrounded by metal bars *(Irina Antonova considered my idea to be better than all the others);* we're all sure a tour of that metropolis's socialist reconstruction would have invigorated him. Irina thought it might be nice to promenade on Nevsky Prospect and peer into the shops; somebody had told her (I think it was the singer G. P. Vishnevskaya) that some of the dressmakers there were nearly as clever as the ones in Paris; and there was such a little-girl look in her face when she proposed it, such a smile of anticipated delight, that he realized that she had not been very happy for a long time and so was craving some sort of pleasure, even the most trivial kind; it was that longing for merriment which her eyes so intensely expressed; that was precisely what he found so, how should I say, upsetting, because he was impotent in that department, too. So she wanted to, um, I mean, really, the Nevsky of all places! Not long before the October Revolution, the Symbolist writer Bely proclaimed: *All of Petersburg is an infinity of the Prospect raised to the nth degree. Beyond Petersburg lies nothing.* Nothing but tanks, that is, the T-26s, T-34s, and sixty-ton TVs . . . Oh, my, he remembered quite well, so very, you know, thank you, all the corpses with back-flung faces which used to blow across Nevsky Prospect like leaves, and the living faces the color of dirt, and that severed arm which hung from the garden gate; I would have thought that my Galisha was too young to remember, but even now she has nightmares; I suppose she'll be tortured until she dies. And this child he'd married had no idea! She was simply too young. He remembered especially well the great bundle of guns aiming at the sky in R. L. Karmen's "Leningrad Fights," the Smolny Institute obscured by smoke. Of course he and the family were in Kuibyshev by that time. One had to admire Karmen for, you know. And now that he had wheezed his way to his feet so that he could stand sternly over her like that statue of Lenin which remained before the raised portico of the Smolny throughout the Nine Hundred Days, Irina began to realize that once again she'd offended him, and her face turned red as he ranted: I, I used to gaze at Nevsky Prospect through a jagged hole! And that sound of those Stukas coming, pure *vibrato,* I, I—

And let me guess, interrupted his wife, likewise rising. *She* was standing beside you.

No! he cried, shocked out of his rage. Don't worry, don't worry; that's all garbage. I wasn't even—

Naked, I'm sure. Well, you certainly had your romantic moments, back when you could still—

In a hurried rasp he begged: Don't be cruel, Irina!

I'm sorry! Forgive me, Mitya. I felt jealous for a moment, that was all.

I—

Never mind. Now it's over. Please do forgive me. We won't go to Leningrad.

He lived on to 1973, when he signed an open letter in *Pravda* denouncing the human rights activist A. Sakharov. This servile act cost him several of his remaining friends.* The avant-gardist Y. P. Lyubimov, toward whom he'd always been generous, no longer consented to greet him. So what? Tell it to the the grinning boys of the Condor Legion! His fame was distinct without warmth, like Arctic sunlight on a pavement of soldiers' helmets.

He lived until 1974, when he wrote the spectacular "Suite on Verses of Michelangelo," whose songs are as beautiful as a flock of multicolored fighter planes. Now it had been exactly forty years since that international musical festival in Leningrad when he'd played his piano concerto and then a certain twenty-year-old student had slipped him a note signed with her initials, E. E. K. It was actually Nina who'd wanted the divorce. And Irina had certainly also, you know, but Irina was practically the age of his own daughter; she didn't know what she, anyhow, there were times when she slipped an arm around him and he just laughed to himself: She thinks she's embracing me but she's only embracing my coat! Irina laid her hand on his fingers, which were as soft, fat and white as graveyard-berries. And everywhere he turned he was, you know. For example, and this is just one example, every time Irina turned on the television there was another Roman Karmen program about the fraternal struggle in Latin America, and you know how I feel about dear, *dear* Roman Lazarevich! I wonder how often he gets kissed. He's still in good health, I hear. One's supposed to get kissed farewell three times by our Russian women when one goes off to the front. He's in another of his suits, filming the White House in Washington, D.C.; can you imagine? And now here's Fidel Castro sitting casually in the back seat of a car, chatting with children through the open window (that's a scene in "Flaming Island"), slim, white-haired Roman Karmen stands dreamily beside Castro, who looks very revolutionary and dynamic; pan to children, crowds, old women, militants, parades. And Irina's so gullible; she even thinks these people have now been, you know, *liberated*! Because she saw it on television! She says that just because I'm older doesn't mean I have the right to tell her what to think; she's just as intelligent as I am. What can I say to that? I can't say that Elena would have, well, what do I know? He smiled at Irina; don't think he wasn't, to get right down to it, *grateful*. Nina saw all too clearly that he would have been better off

---

*"I can testify that nobody I knew fought," writes Nadezhda Mandelstam. "All they did was lie low. That was the most that people with a conscience could do—and even that required real courage."

with Elena, but he couldn't go through with it, perhaps exactly because he would have been better off, which he couldn't bear; he trailed after Nina and got her to take him back. He should have believed his heart. And then Elena had said—what had she said?—Bury me in Leningrad, he told Irina.

As a matter of fact, he lived until 1975, when, three-quarters paralyzed and in terrible pain, his masklike face now trembling more than ever, emitting ripples around the blurry reflection of itself, he still managed to create his Viola Sonata (Opus 147), which he himself accurately described as "bright—bright and clear." A month later, lung cancer asphyxiated him.

When his death began, it was as if successive shrouds, each one so gauzy as to be nearly transparent, kept settling over his face, strangling away the breath almost tenderly, with Irina bending over him in the hospital ward, screaming his name like a shrilling telephone. He could hear her longer than he could see her, for the shrouds kept swirling down so that her image steadily greyed into a blackness deeper than meaning, and although for a little while longer he could almost perceive the reflection of her presence swimming on the nightstruck waters, she was fading very rapidly now; indeed, before he had time to mistake her for a certain other woman, she'd vanished with an almost playful suddenness, so that he sank irremediably alone into his velvet agony which drowned and tickled him while a blood-red spot rushed before him in ever-narrowing spirals.

By coincidence, E. E. Konstantinovskaya died that same year.

They buried him in Moscow, of course. Roman Karmen was there, and so were the Glikman brothers, of course; so was the white-uniformed girl in Produce Store Number Thirty-one. Although he was granted a funeral in the Grand Hall of the Moscow Conservatory, and extolled not only as the composer of the Seventh Symphony and the "Counterplan," but also as a good Communist, the "organs" who played all tunes might not have grieved overmuch. A detachment of men in raspberry-colored boots is said to have entered his flat within two hours of his death; they emerged with an armload of private papers, which have never been seen again. The *Great Soviet Encyclopedia* accords him a respectful entry, in keeping with his various honors, medals and decorations (each Stalin Prize tactfully altered to a State Prize of the USSR. Was he ever called upon to return the old trophies to have them re-engraved?) His works, we're told, *affirm the ideals of Soviet humanism.* In the long article on Soviet music, he receives a number of dutiful acknowledgments. The Seventh Symphony, needless to say, is labeled *an immortal monument of the period.* Even his most egregious formalist error, the opera "Lady

Macbeth," now gets called "a Soviet classic." No doubt the castrated revision is being referred to. Now that he was safely dead, there was no need to disgrace him; for that matter, he'd been dead ever since he composed Opus 110.

One might think that his reputation was embalmed as safely as was Lenin in the mausoleum (Stalin, I'm afraid, had been secretly taken out once *his* fame decayed). And yet the regime might have felt some bitterness about his formalist infidelities. I may be imagining things. However, *The Soviet Way of Life,* published the year before his demise, mentions the *interesting results obtained from a poll conducted in industrial enterprises in the Urals.* The workers were asked to name their favorite artists. Of the composers, Tchaikovsky gets mentioned first, and Mussorgsky last, with a couple of foreigners in between. Dmitri Dmitriyevich Shostakovich does not appear. After all, no one individual can be indispensable in our Union of Soviet Socialist Republics, greatest and most perfect country in the world, whose borders touch a dozen seas. ▸

A PIANIST FROM KILGORE

It can't hurt you, so what are you getting excited about? You're a skeleton; nothing hurts a skeleton.

—Jakov Lind, "Soul of Wood" (1962)

In 1958, one year after the launch of the atomic ice-breaker *Lenin,* there was a musical competition in the USSR. Among the gamblers came a young American from Kilgore, Texas, named Van Cliburn.

His playing was as perfect as the stainless steel from the Krasni Oktiabr' Stalingrad Metallurgical Works (now, of course, known as the Krasni Oktiabr' Volgograd Metallurgical Works). And if you wish to know precisely how perfect that would be, I need only tell you that the factory received the Order of Lenin in 1939 and the Order of the Red Banner of Labor in 1948. Shouldn't he have won first prize, then? Well, thanks to the great power chauvinism of the Anglo-Americans, a so-called "Cold War" had developed. (What's cold war, really? We Russians know. It's a soldier's corpse frozen head-first into the snow. Can a piano express this? Yes, under Van Cliburn's hands the piano keys seemed to be made sometimes of ice, sometimes of steel, and sometimes of fragrant toffee. And the notes passed by like summer clouds.) Those who with spurious "objectivism" dare to argue that laurels should get bestowed upon a provincial bourgeois lackey, merely because Moscow audiences shout: *First prize, first prize!* and *Vanyusha, Vanyusha!* miss the point: for the purpose of competitions is not to reward individual "merit," but to educate the masses. Our Soviet Union must be seen as a winner on the cultural front! Nor could some judges and spectators fail to react disdainfully to the way the young fellow craned over the piano, his white-collared neck bent almost horizontal, for he was a full hundred and ninety-three centimeters tall; he had to push back the piano bench; to D. D. Shostakovich, for instance, he resembled an old engraving of a racehorse straining at the gate—which is not to imply that Cliburn's interpretation of the concerto ever sounded strained. The opening's almost military strictness and grandeur were realized with as much control as Operation "Little Saturn" had been at Stalingrad. The *andantino simpico* of the second movement "flowed" in patterns as unpredictable as they were perfectly right, the flow first glittering in a frozen way, like a massive shower of crystal, then lightly fluttering toward something as sweetly unattainable to every listener as a little child's happiness. Wouldn't it be sad if we could actually feel so happy? Van Cliburn kept smiling as if he did. Softspoken but never moody, dressed in the respectful orthodoxy of darkness intensified by narrow slivers of whiteness at neck and sleeves, he must be an innocent. After all, he was American, and moreover had been born too late to get called up for the war. (Good, really very good, said the juror Oborin, but, you know, he's shaking his head a lot, rather sentimentally . . . —Three days later, this very same Oborin appeared in a photograph in the *New York Times,* smilingly gripping the hand of the tall, weary American.)—No question about it: Cliburn was a callow creature, an ignoramus, a pianist from Kilgore, Texas . . . For these and other reasons, several selfless functionaries conspired to give that gold medal, which happened to be accompanied by twenty-five thousand rubles cash, to one of the three Soviet contestants, or, failing that, to the pianist from the People's Republic of China (with whom our differences had not yet become acute); but the distinguished juror S. Richter demanded that this faction be overruled, I think on account of the way Cliburn performed the third movement, the *allegro con fuoco:* Commencing with perfect neutrality (cold in execution, warm in conception), the piano suddenly took on a passion alternating with glissandos of a different sort of neutrality like ripples on a sunny Arctic lake; then came the breathless erotic haste of the finale, which never stopped being clear and careful at the same time, like a lover's deliberate touch.

So much for the Tchaikovsky. Cliburn paused. His hands hovered over the black-striped pianoscape with the same solitary tension which afflicts the pilots of reconnaissance planes when they drone over enemy territory, gathering in the coordinates of railway yards, cathedrals and apartment blocks for the convenience of master bombardiers. A slow, rapturous smile trembled across his face. His hands descended. He began to play the Rachmaninoff. The judges closed their dreamy eyes. The audience wept. An apparatchik rushed to the telephone. Within twenty minutes, militiamen had surrounded the Tchaikovsky Conservatory, holding back the yearning, adoring crowds. What a debacle! In the end, somebody had to call Comrade Khruschev himself. The matter got decided in the American's favor then, I believe because a calculated magnanimity appeared to be the least embarrassing stance. After all, even the jurors were applauding! The bravos lasted eight minutes. Cliburn was embraced by E. Gilels and K. P. Kondrashin . . . —It was the eleventh of April—the selfsame day when, in contradistinction to the American warmongers, we withdrew our last forty-one thousand troops from East Germany. Not long after midnight the sixteen jurors reached agreement (which is to say, they were informed of the decision of Comrade Khruschev). On the thirteenth, a loudspeaker said: *Harvey Lavan Cliburn, Junior.* The crowd screamed: *Vanyitchka, Vanyitchka!*

Oh, dear, oh, dear, said Shostakovich. He was quite surprised, because the paragraph they'd prepared for publication over his signature rhapsodized about "this latest Soviet victory." Already it had come out that Cliburn's father was the hireling of an oil company, and that the son's travel allowance had been provided by a front organization of the international capitalist Rockefeller.

Mitya, please relax, said Oborin. That's not your problem. They'll get you to sign something else. At least he played Russian music . . .

You're correct! the composer replied, much relieved. Oh, dear, oh, dear, oh, dear . . .

He trusted Oborin because he knew him. They'd been evacuated together from the siege of Leningrad, on that long, long train ride which they could never forget, having been accompanied every now and then by the *vibrato* of the Fascist bombers.

Moreover, continued Oborin, it wasn't just the Cliburn kid who played well. The Radio Symphony members truly surpassed themselves . . .

Lev, what did you really think? To be honest, I wasn't exactly, how should I say, listening to the Rachmaninoff, because my son—

Well, I'd have to say the Tchaikovsky concerto was superb to the extent that that's possible with Tchaikovsky, although most of the judges preferred the Rachmaninoff, which I found really cloying. Maybe he laid on the *rubato* a bit thick . . . no, I'm just jealous. The kid's a master.

You don't say! murmured Shostakovich, twiddling his fingers. Who would have thought it? Well, well, well. An American boy from Kilgore, Texas. Can you imagine?

On the eighteenth Van Cliburn gave his first public recital as a winner. (Meanwhile, the United States Navy fired a dummy Polaris warhead from underwater.) Raising his hands and gazing dreamily down at his outstretched fingers as if he'd never seen them before, he repeated the Tchaikovsky concerto, which the *New York Times,* still using the language of war, described as *a big, percussive attack that dominated the orchestra.* While it's true that he peppered the first movement with powerfully booming chords whose metronome-like steadiness overwhelmed the romantic warmth of the strings, he was no war machine. His loudest hammer-blows remained somehow bell-like, controlled. Moreover, that opening thunder soon gave way to crystalline arpeggios, each note of which glittered as distinctly as an ice-crystal. Whenever the score permitted, Cliburn showed a still gentler touch, lingering a little, deviating from the first stern sweetness, confident enough to give the orchestra a place in the sun, sometimes following, sometimes leading, like a dancer showing good manners to his partner. Oh, he was always clear; his every note was glass. They applauded in a frenzy. Then he repeated the Rachmaninoff.—Another ovation! For an encore he played his own composition, "Nostalgia."

And so the time came when Shostakovich had to meet him, at the congratulatory dinner. Come to think of it, he'd already met him twice, first at the opening ceremonies and then when the prize was presented, for, as I may have neglected to tell you, Shostakovich was the Chairman of the Organizing Committee for this First International Tchaikovsky Competition (an appointed position, whose bestowal underlined the Party's confident expectation that his rehabilitation would never be a source of regret), and so it was actually he who'd been required to stand at the podium, praising Van Cliburn, and he who'd transmitted the medal and the envelope of cash into the boy's sweaty hand while newsmen's flashbulbs exploded like antiaircraft rounds. Truth to tell, he was less interested in Cliburn than in the pretty violinist from Volgograd who sat across the table. Something about her lips—well, she wasn't really that young, but Shostakovich had begun to find that every woman now appeared in his eyes a virgin, plus or minus. He couldn't believe how girlish the forty-year-olds had started to look. Yesterday he'd been chatting with E. V. Denisov about what made up a real Russian girl's face: a pleasing prominence of the cheekbones, in youth anyway (or was that just because until just recently Russian children had never gotten enough to eat?); Denisov, less enthralled by this subject, because more concerned about the Central Committee's new Decree on the Correction of Errors, yawned, opened and closed both pianos, ate a herring and directed their mutual consideration to the poor complexions of many Russian females, but Shostakovich counterattacked by praising those wheat fields of hair blonde or auburn or black, not to mention the dark eyebrows which went so well with pale hands (not very proletarian! laughed Denisov).

They'd given Van Cliburn an interpreter of almost intimidating beauty. But Shostakovich noticed that those two scarcely gazed at each other. She kept tapping her hands on the banquet table. (It actually seemed to Cliburn that she was indifferent to him, which gave him a strange feeling, but after all, this was another country, a dangerous country, a Slavic enemy country.)

Mr. Shostakovich, I'd be right honored if you'd call me Van.

But you're too kind! cried the old man anxiously. Dear me! Well, *Van,* thank you, thank you, thank you; and feel free to call me Mitya . . .

He felt almost sorry for Cliburn. The boy was too guileless.

From the next table, the sad young composer S. Gubaidulina was making eyes at him. He knew that as soon as the banquet broke up she'd back him into a corner and begin all over again: Dmitri Dmitriyevich, you're the person our generation depends on to give us answers. Please, I beg of you, don't let them talk you into joining the Party. You can't imagine how many people are counting on you to hold firm . . .

The American boy's blond curls enraged him, he hardly knew why.

Do you know, Van, I myself was once the soloist for this very same Tchaikovsky concerto! It was in Kharkov, in the summer of 1926. Long before all the, the, you know. Hitler took it three times and we took it back twice, after which they . . . three and two, now, how does that work out? But I don't suppose there's much left of the old city. Field-Marshal Paulus had a lot of tanks at first, before we . . . Tree-lined streets. Anyway, nothing lasts. Perhaps a few bricks, or . . . For instance, I was actually young once! You can hardly imagine . . .

He was trying to be kind. As a matter of fact, the nineteenth-century predictability of the composition pained him now. Oborin was correct; Tchaikovsky's music deserved to be parodied.

The boy smiled and started to say something, but Shostakovich, embarrassed and anxious, rushed on with the story, longing to put them both at ease, trying to make it funny: Perhaps you haven't heard of him, Van, but the conductor was, was, he was Nikolai Malko, who's with the Sydney Symphony Orchestra now. He did his best to look after me. Ha! We used to play *billiards* together when we should have been practicing! In 1926 I would have been, excuse me, about the age you are now. Do you play billiards, Van?

Gosh, Mitya, I've never had the time. If you want to teach me, maybe we could try a game . . .

Oborin was already claiming that the only reason the audience had wept at Van Cliburn's performance was mass hysteria

Another Russian girl came with flowers for Vanyitchka. He thanked her shyly, sitting tall and slightly bowed. He didn't seem to know whether or not to rise when he accepted the bouquet. She invited him to escort her to the premiere of "Far and Wide My Country Stretches." Definitely he was blushing now. Everybody looked away, feeling sorry for him. For what reason did his appearance stain Shostakovich with a feeling of peculiarity, almost of horror? He felt as if he'd half forgotten some secret. Then it came to him: the front page of *Izvestiya,* with that portrait gallery of the heroic generals who'd saved Moscow, and among them the favorite of Comrade Stalin (so it was said), tall, thin, anxious Vlasov, who'd peered down at fame through harsh black-rimmed spectacles. Why had Vlasov made such an impression on Shostakovich? No, the impression must have been made later, at the war's end, when the man got hanged for treason and cowardice. There had been no *Izvestiya* photograph then. They'd never met. Nor was Vlasov's fate unusual. But that one image of him, his face already bent as if in anxiety and misery, although the true case must simply have been that he was taller than the photographer, well, there Shostakovich could see himself. As for the American Vanyitchka, he looked nothing like General Vlasov. He was tall, to be sure, and he hunched nervously but . . .

Mitya, I'll tell you something, Oborin had said. Once when I was preparing a concert at the front we drove over a German mine. Everybody except me got killed. In my case it was really just luck, and I . . . Well, anyway, what I remember from that instant is two sharp reports—not particularly *loud,* you understand, but sharp. And sometimes, even now, the sound of a backfiring engine . . .

But Vlasov and this kid, I, there's, there's no—

Look, said Oborin. There's no logical connection between the sputtering of a truck and two land mine explosions. But when you're in danger, you don't have time for logic. Your heart pounds, and you try to save yourself, that's all.

So you're saying that because I might have identified with Vlasov—

Mitya, are you crazy? Don't keep mentioning that name. Who knows if somebody's in the hallway right now . . . ?

Well, Van, it was a remarkable performance, I must say. You ought to feel, how should I say, very proud. I understand that your mother—

My mother was my best teacher. And I played clarinet at Kilgore High, said the boy in a confiding tone.

My mother also taught me well.

I'd be proud to meet her, Mitya.

Unfortunately, she's *dead,* laughed Shostakovich, fiddling with his glasses. And your mother, is she, I mean, is she in good health?

Oh, pretty good, thanks. Mitya, I want to ask you something. Do you think I played the Rachmaninoff too fast? I felt a little nervous—

No, no, *no,* in my opinion your choice of tempo was entirely correct. (Please tell your mother to look after her health.) It was a splendid performance, really, very very talented, and that *moderato* in the first movement, well, the way you played it, it had a steady, you know, tenderness—

Thanks for saying that, Mitya, because I've always been crazy about your Seventh Symphony. When I was playing the *moderato,* as soon as I got through the fast part I tried to slow down into something that would sound like your third movement—

Yes, yes, I think I'm, you might say, *familiar* with that music, said Shostakovich with a wink. How does it go now, Van? The third movement, I mean. Can you carry a tune? Maybe you could—

It always inspired me, continued the boy a little desperately. The part that's called the "Open Spaces of the Heartland"—

Oh, dear, well, perhaps you overrate me. But you certainly put on a fine performance.

Blushing, Van Cliburn listened in his head to the crucial bars of the second movement, the *adagio sostenuto,* just as he had played it. To him this was the most romantic music of all, the piano upholding the sweetness of the strings, then growing as reflective as a Chopin nocturne. Whenever he played it, he felt as though he were walking through a summer pavilion. And the great Shostakovich approved of his performance! He could hardly breathe for joy.

But how's the life for you over there? Oborin wanted to know. Do you serve in your country's armed forces, Van?

They inducted me last year, but I had a blood condition . . .

An East German pianist approached to present his congratulations, and as soon as he was out of earshot, Shostakovich, clutching his vodka-glass, chuckled to Van Cliburn: You know what Comrade Stalin said at the twenty-sixth anniversary parade? I think it was the twenty-sixth. Or was it the twenty-fifth? Never mind. How did he put it? Wait a moment. No, no, now it comes to me!

He said, *Comrades, long live the,* so to speak, *victorious Anglo-Soviet-American fighting alliance. Death to the,* if you get my drift, *German invaders.*

Cliburn blinked and said: Well, thanks for saying that, Mitya. I sure appreciate it.

Shostakovich choked on his vodka.

And now a journalist from TASS leaned across the translator and said with malicious zest: Mr. Cliburn, the Soviet people unanimously demand to know the status of the Negro question in your country.

Gosh, Mitya, said Cliburn, not looking at the journalist at all, I never met a Negro I didn't like. After all, they're Americans, too.

Shostakovich bit his lip to keep from laughing. He could hardly wait to tell Lebedinsky about this! (With Lebedinsky, as with Poe's protagonist, it was the teeth. In '44 he'd seen a Ukrainian village which had just been liberated from the Fascists. All the corpses hung grinning. To him the most menacing thing was their rotting smiles. And now, whenever somebody smiled too widely or too whitely, he longed to scream.)

Hastily, Oborin put in: Van, I imagine that everybody in Kilgore, Texas, must be proud of you today.

A little self-consciously, like his dark bowtie clinging to the tapering slit of whiteness (for I've heard that as a rule they dress casually in America), the boy said: Actually I was born in Shreveport, Louisiana. I don't suppose you know where that is—

No, said Oborin, but I've heard that it's very hot in your southern provinces. Almost like Africa.

Raising his voice, the journalist said: Many Negroes there, laboring in atrocious conditions . . .

Yes, hot, said Van Cliburn in an exhausted voice.

And now Shostakovich began to perceive some haunted and guarded quality about the American's soul. And indeed, the man in raspberry-colored boots who dropped by the next day to drink vodka said with a wink: You see, Dmitri Dmitriyevich, he's a homosexual. We know this irrefutably. It's in his file.

You don't say, returned the composer with a pretense of deep astonishment. Well, well, well, I'm most interested.

What would you expect from such a decadent country? If I had my way (and I'm sure you agree with me, Dmitri Dmitriyevich), I'd smash his smiling American face! I hate 'em all. Remember how they wouldn't open the second front year after year? They wanted the Fascists to bleed us dry—

Yes, yes, yes, yes, said Shostakovich, whose temples had begun to ache from too much liquor. You're absolutely correct, Comrade Alexandrov—

Every time I see an American, it sets me off. I start thinking about that second front, and I . . . Well, at least you're one of us, Dmitri Dmitriyevich. You were in Leningrad . . .

Indeed I was, Comrade Alexandrov, and I, I, I'll never forget what—

My first wife fell into their hands. She was a hostage. In Kiev.

Well, well. She was there on business? If I may say so, my dear friend, sometimes it's better not to—

We'd always believed that the only thing they did was hang her, but do you know what I learned just last year? You know what they did to her first? While those fucking Americans were laughing all the way to the bank! Don't get me started. Who taught him our music?

A Russian. Rozina Levina—

An émigré. Scum.

His mother also taught him, I believe.

That's rich. A mama's boy. No wonder he's a fairy.

She was formerly a concert pianist, he told me—

That just makes it worse.

And it's even worse than that, Comrade Alexandrov. You see, I venture to say that he's—

He's what? We need all the details. Tell me everything you can remember about that bastard—

Do you know, he's—well, I share your feelings of, of, so to speak, betrayal, and yet in this case, well, I truly think he's *not all there.*

How could he say what he truly felt? Perhaps Cliburn knew more than he pretended. But Shostakovich remained convinced that this American was part of the natural process of *forgetting.* Call him a bacterium on the moldering corpse of our war-memories. Soon there'd be nothing left, not even bones. (Of course he was only a little boy, with his hands in his pockets.) When Shostakovich was in Leipzig for the Bach festival, a German Communist, smirking, had quoted him the words of a certain General von Hartmann, commander of the Seventy-first Division of Sixth Army at Stalingrad. A few days before the final surrender, Hartmann had remarked: As seen from Sirius, Goethe's works will be mere dust a thousand years from now, and Sixth Army an indecipherable name, incomprehensible to all.—Then he strode to the top of a railroad embankment, and fired blindly at the Russians until they shot him down. The German Communist continued: I can't deny that these words made an impression on me, Dmitri Dmitriyevich. To get right down to it, his bourgeois-dramatic heroic posture in the service of absolute nihilism—well, that shithead was absolutely correct about Sixth Army. Who cares about it now?—And the German Communist went on laughingly reviling General von Hartmann (of whom Shostakovich had never heard), until it became apparent that the German Communist couldn't stop thinking about Sixth Army and maybe didn't want Sixth Army to become an indecipherable name, because the sufferings which everybody in Germany and Russia had endured had become valuable as the simple result of their own intensity; he dreaded to condemn them to the crematorium of history. What Shostakovich felt (beyond revulsion, which he did his jittering best to mask, that any German should now presume to be his comrade) was something midway between sadness and peace. For didn't he likewise cherish his own hopelessness? And this blond bacterium from America was here on a mission to transform the death which presently characterized all Europeans, and perhaps even vivified them, back into dirt. The bacterium would win.* It would overwhelm him. He did not want to die—which is to say, *he was death;* he could not bear for his death to die . . . ▸

*In fact, within a few years of Shostakovich's death, the New York critics were deriding Cliburn for "superficiality." His repertoire dwindled. In his tour of 1994 he played nothing but Rachmaninoff's Third, and that first Tchaikovsky concerto which had brought him his freakish fame. (The *Great Soviet Encyclopedia*, however, which since the dissolution of the USSR can now never be superseded by a new edition, continues to praise his *spontaneity, straightforward lyricism, exultant sound and impetuous dynamism.*). I am told that he opens every performance with a rendition of "The Star-Spangled Banner."

LOST VICTORIES

◪

And then, as I smoked a cigarette with a tank crew or chatted with a rifle company about the overall situation, I never failed to encounter that irrepressible urge to press onward, that readiness to put forward the very last ounce of energy, which are the hallmarks of the German soldier.

—Field-Marshal Erich von Manstein (1958)

1

In the sleepwalker's time, we took back our honor and issued Panzergruppen in all directions. But when I finally got home, the advance guard of the future had already come marching through the Brandenburg Gate, with their greatcoats triple-buttoned right up to their throats, their hands in their pockets and their eyes as expressionless as shell craters! According to my wife, whose memory isn't bad when she confines herself to verifiable natural events, some of our lindens were in bloom that May, as why wouldn't they be, and the rest were scorched sticks, so she refers to that time as the "Russian spring," which proves that she can be witty, unless of course she heard that phrase on the radio. Anyhow, we got thoroughly denazified. Our own son, so I hear, threw away his Hitlerjugend uniform and sat on the fountain's rim, listening to the United States Army Band day after day. Next the Wall went up, so half of Germany got lost to us, possibly forever, being magically changed into one of the new grey countries of Europe Central, and all our fearfulness of death came back. An old drunk stood up in the beerhall and tried to talk about destiny, but somebody bruised his skull with a two-liter stein, and down he went. When I reached home that night my wife was standing at the foot of the stairs with her hand on the doorjamb, peering at me through the place where the diamond-shaped glass window used to be, and I must have looked sad, because she said to me in a strange soft voice like summer: Never mind those lost years; we still have almost half the century left to make everything right, to which I said: Never mind those eight years I spent in Vorkuta, when they knocked my teeth out and damaged my kidneys, to which she replied: Listen, we all suffered in the war, even me whom you left alone while you were off raping Polish girls and shooting Ukrainians in the ditches; it's common knowledge what you were up to; besides, you're a middle-aged man and, and look at all the beer you swill; your kidneys would have given out on you anyway.—Having reconnoitered her disposition (as my old commanding officer would have said; he died of influenza in some coal mine near Tiflis), I fell back, so to speak; I withdrew from the position in hopes of saving something; I retreated into myself. Let her talk about destiny all she wants, I said to myself. At least *I'm* not tainted by illusions!

As it happened, I'd been saving up a little treat for myself; I'd hoarded it beneath the cushions of my armchair. Right before I went to the hospital, Athenäum-Verlag released the memoirs of my hero, Field-Marshal von Manstein. Although I don't consider myself a bookish person, it seemed befitting to show my support, so to speak, especially since the poor old man had recently gotten out of jail, fourteen years early if memory serves—the only favor I'll ever thank those "Allies" for. For four years I couldn't get to it, on account of the shell splinter in my head, but finally the thing stopped moving, so I got some peace, and there he was, right there on the dust jacket in all his grey dignity, wearing his Iron Cross and his oak leaves. The title of the book was *Lost Victories*.

I've always been of the opinion that had Paulus only been permitted to break out and link up with von Manstein's troops, we could have won the war, and I've proved it to quite a few people, even including one of the Russian guards at Vorkuta. Von Manstein really could have saved us all.

Whenever I think about what happened to Germany, or my own miserable life, or the way my fourteen-year-old niece died, burned to death by the Americans in Dresden, I get so emotional that I start grinding my teeth, and then my wife tells all her friends: *He's in one of his moods again*. She never cared for my brother the former engineer, who's now imprisoned behind the wall of that so-called "German Democratic Republic," repairing sewer mains for the Communists and earning almost nothing, my poor brother whom I'll never see again (although he can still telephone me); he's another victim of our former High Command's deeply echeloned illusions. *She* says he didn't welcome her into the family. As if that were the point! Well, I could go on and on.

But von Manstein was going to take me out of my funk. Von Manstein was going to show me how it should have been done! And I knew from the very first page that he would stand up for the German Army, too. You see, another thing that really pisses me off is the way the whole world condemns "German militarism," as if we hadn't been fighting simply for enough living-space to survive! What would, say, the French have done if they'd lost the last war, and been forced to pay in blood, soil and money, year after year, while all the neighbors sharpened their knives and got ready to carve off another piece of France? They say we went too far in Poland. Well, the Poles would have annexed Germany all the way to Berlin if they could! Von Manstein makes exactly this point in his book, which I really do recommend. He exposes the aggressive power politics of the Poles. Anybody who reads him will never feel the same way about Poland; this I guarantee. To get right down to it, von Manstein knows what's what! The victors may try as hard as they like to bury him, but that only makes me admire him all the more. As a great German said, *the strong man is mightiest alone.*

Well, I hadn't gotten very far in his book, really. I was only about halfway through the Polish campaign. But I could already tell that my faith in von Manstein wouldn't be disappointed, because as soon as the starting gun went off he exploded that lying slander that we meant the Poles any harm; he said—let me find the page—aha, here is how he put it: *When Hitler called for the swift and ruthless destruction of the Polish Army, this was, in military parlance, merely the aim that must be the basis of any big offensive operation.* And how about all those so-called "atrocities" we committed in the process? (Anybody who complains that our army behaved, relatively speaking, incorrectly, ought to spend a few years in Vorkuta!) We brought matters to an end as quickly as we could. The capitulation of Poland, again in von Manstein's words, *in every way upheld the military honor of an enemy defeated after a gallant struggle.* And that's all any good German needs to say about it.

So then what happened? Then those degenerate "Allies," who hanged our leaders for aggressive conspiracy, declared war on *us*!—Well, we did our duty. My best friend Karl, who was with von Richthofen's Eighth Flying Corps and who never in his life told a lie, wrote me in a letter that an eagle flew beside him, just outside the cockpit window, on every sortie against Sedan. I'm not a sentimentalist, but that anecdote does make a person think. Well, Karl got shot down over Stalingrad. He was bringing food and medicine to Sixth Army. Everything wasted! But he wouldn't have wanted my pity. The point is that we followed the only correct line, and our policies remained as generous as they could have been under the circumstances.—Just as a burst or two of light machine-gun fire will usually clear a road of partisans, so von Manstein utters a line, and all objections get blasted away! For instance, *as a result of the impeccable behavior of our troops,* he writes, *nothing happened to disturb our relations with the civil population during my six months in France.* Von Manstein's word is gold. If he says a thing is so, case closed. And yet they punish us for "crimes" against France! That's why sometimes I wake up in the morning all hungover and thinking, what's the use?

My wife was angry again, this time because I'd clogged up the drain by shaving, so her indictment ran, but I bunkered myself down, because right after that part about military honor, *Lost Victories* became especially interesting. I've always had a taste for theoretical issues. In Vorkuta I used to ask the guards how it all would have turned out if Stalin had died instead of Roosevelt; that question cost me those two top front teeth. So you can imagine how excited I felt when von Manstein began to raise theoretical questions, too: What should Poland have done to avoid defeat? To me it's a real exercise in open-mindedness to step into the enemy's shoes just for an eyeblink, and then wiggle one's toes a little, so to speak; it's good preparation for *next time.* Yes, that's the correct way to go about it. And von Manstein, needless to say, had the answer in his ammo clip: Poland should have abandoned the western territories to save her armies from encirclement, then waited for the Allies to come. (Of course, they wouldn't have; they never did. What can you expect from those cowards? Look what Poland is now—a Russian satellite!) I wanted somebody on whom to try this out, but my son, who in the old days would have agreed with everything I said, hadn't shown his face all day; I suppose he was as close as he could get to the Tiergarten, hoping to cadge cigarettes from American Negroes. Anyhow, what would he have cared? When I got back from Vorkuta, he looked at me as if I were a monster. My wife tried to smooth it over by claiming that he didn't recognize me. Well, so what; *the strong man is mightiest* and all that. Next came the question I could really throw my soul into: What ought *we* have done to avoid defeat at Russia's hands? Needless to say, I had this more or less worked out, but only in general terms. So pay good attention, I told myself, because this is Field-Marshal Erich von Manstein speaking! He'd make me *see* the arrows on the maps, the spearheads, the long dotted trails, the ingot-like rectangles of our Army Groups! I was back there now, rushing through all those new states which so came into being on practically every page of *Lost Victories,* with their Reich Commissars pre-assigned by our sleepwalker himself while the Wehrmacht continued forward, its operational area ideally to be (see, I really do understand the theory behind this) not much deeper than the front line itself, in order to avoid interference with our "Special Detachments" in the rear, and about those it's better not to say anything, because they're secret; what I'm trying to get across is that in *Lost Victories* Germany was on the march again, and the farther we went the stronger we got, until we were giants in a land of dreams. I'm a realist, but why can't I visit the past, especially when it's as sweet to me now as that smell of burned sugar that rose up when our bombers hit the Badayevskiy warehouses in Leningrad? About Leningrad von Manstein says (and I agree with him), that back in '41 we could have taken the place if we'd just pushed a little harder, but the sleepwalker wouldn't let us; he demanded Moscow at the same time, which is why he got neither. (In retrospect, he does seem to have been—let's put it kindly—a bit starry-eyed.) We made another thrust in '42, but just when we were getting somewhere, Vlasov's Second Shock Army attacked us, then troops got diverted to the Caucasus; and no sooner had von Manstein straightened out *that* mess when Paulus got into trouble at Stalingrad! So, you see, it was just bad luck that we never got to roll into Leningrad. Burned sugar! I'll never forget that delicious smell. It was as if all the confectioners in Russia were getting busy, baking us a victory cake as big as a mountain; the frosting was all ready; I've always liked caramelized sugar.

Field-Marshal von Manstein closes the first chapter of his memoir: *From now on the weapons would speak.* Soon we would break through the Stalin Line. We would take Leningrad at last. And when we did, von Manstein would be there! He'd raise his Field-Marshal's baton to say *Germany.* At once there would come undying summer.

2

Some of us in that open cage in Vorkuta, with our caps always on and our footcloths and anything else we could find wrapped around our faces against the cold, so that we resembled Russian babushkas, well, to pass the time we used to talk about politics, almost never about love because that would have been too unbearable; it was almost as if we could already see those sleazy smiles on the faces of the Aryan girls we'd given our all for; now they were doing it with American soldiers just to get a little chocolate; when I got home and saw them flashing their teeth at the men who'd burned Dresden, I almost let them have it, I can tell you! As sad and sullen as most of us were at Vorkuta, the woman-crazy ones were the worst off. You can hum "Lili Marlene" like an idiot; you can fantasize about this lady or that until you're as black in the face as a hanged partisan, but you're still here and she's still *there,* beyond the barbed wire; still, even in the Gulag you can advance a theory or an opinion, and precisely because opinions feel, to get right down to it, less real than they do back home, in the barracks or even on the march, why not make the most of them? Headlamps in the forward trench, I always say! You might as well be speeding in dusty convoys of exultation beyond the steppe-horizons, with that growl of tank treads comforting you all the way across the summer flatness; once you've heard that, you'll never stop wanting more. In that frame of mind you can pleasurably debate a question—for instance: Was the Russian campaign aggressive or not? Von Manstein considers the Soviet troop dispositions to have been *deployment against every contingency,* which implies, at least as I see it, that Operation Barbarossa was arguably defensive. Moreover, he writes how on the very first day of the Russian campaign, *the Soviet command showed its true face* by killing and mutilating a German patrol. To me, that's conclusive (especially since von Manstein said it), but in any event you can argue something like that, and polish your opinions until they're as fixed and perfect as diamonds; you might as well, since you're not going anywhere for years and years, if ever.

Right before the sleepwalker married Eva Braun and blew his brains out, he wrote his political testament, a copy of which my paraplegic friend Fritzi somehow got hold of last year. Good thing Fritzi was already denazified! Now, this document makes several statements which I can't entirely support; for example, in my opinion the man was too hard on the Jews, not that they don't need a firm hand. But what did impress me was that he'd made up his mind about everything—*everything*!—back when he was nothing but a hungry tramp in Vienna; in that testament, he insisted that he hadn't altered his conclusions about a single matter in the decades since then. Then he looked around him and said (so I imagine): What are we Germans going to be now? A rabble of syphilitic raped girls and legless men!—So he pulled the trigger. That takes guts. Paulus didn't have the courage to do it at Stalingrad. I would have done it in an eyeblink, if that would have made any difference for Germany. Now, *that's* triumph of the will! So I do still respect him in a way, not least for the fact that he knew what he knew, whether it was true or not. (If only if he'd allowed Guderian's mobile formations to do what Germans do best, instead of adopting that static defense which is more suitable to Slavs!) So why not pass the time deciding what you believed, then arguing for it, being true to it?

Even in those prison days, something in me was getting ready to feel a certain way, like a field-gun zeroing in on the target; I wanted to become something once and for all; strange to say, Vorkuta came back to me as I sat so comfortably at home, reading von Manstein; and they weren't wasted years anymore; they were leading up to something. I wanted to clarify existence, if only for myself, to draw secret and perfect distinctions until my comprehension was a narrow spearhead. (Here's a distinction for you, free of charge: Russians opt for a massive artillery barrage before an attack, while we Germans prefer to trust in our own blood.) It was happening line by line; and I still had hundreds of glorious pages before me, like the Russian steppes in summer '42, stretching on perfectly golden and infinite like all our victories, our lost victories I should say; and as I read I kept notes on the progress of our assault divisions.

3

Don't think I haven't seen it all: the national enthusiasm, the pride, the successes thrown away contrary to the will of Nature, the way our bigshots in their long grey coats used to lean backward and smile like sharks when some Polish dignitary or other would scuttle up to shake hands! In those days the sleepwalker could still dream of cracking Leningrad like a nut, making the Neva run backward, riding on the shoulders of the Bronze Horseman; while I for my part had all my teeth; my dreams swept east like silhouettes of German infantry marching up dusty summer roads. (For laughs we used to tune into Radio Leningrad, because all they broadcast was the ticking of a metronome.) Well, summer's long gone. But I don't care about that, for I've come to recognize something within my soul as titanic as the Big Dora gun which helped us reduce Sevastopol—yes, by now you'll have guessed; I served under *him;* I'm a veteran of von Manstein's Eleventh Army! And I hold the Iron Cross, First Class—no matter that the Americans have decreed that I can't wear it. So I read on and on, *knowing* that I did somehow have a thousand more years ahead of me; and the lindens were shimmering outside the window and German workmen were rebuilding everything. We live not far away from the Landwehrkanal, which was our primary defensive line during the battle of Berlin (it's also where that Jewish bitch Rosa Luxemburg got hers back in 1919). This is where our thirteen-year-old German boys came out in their black school uniforms to die in the struggle against Bolshevism. So much history all around me! And that day I really felt as if I were a part of it, I can tell you, sitting in my armchair finishing *Lost Victories*. Then I got to the part where von Manstein says that Hitler wasn't bold enough to stake everything on success; and that thing that I'd been getting ready for so long to feel, I felt it now. And it was this: *If only von Manstein had been our Führer . . .* ▸

THE WHITE NIGHTS OF LENINGRAD

1

Were this a movie, and in particular the sort of movie which makes people happy in wartime, it would have been set in the famous "white nights" of Leningrad, when Shostakovich lay in Elena Konstantinovskaya's arms. Unfortunately, it isn't. Moreover, summer happens to be a season expressly reserved for Aryans, so this Russian story finds itself compelled to take place in winter, when the nights of Leningrad, like most days, are black, black, black! How about a compromise? We'll tell our tale in grey.

Once upon a time, when it was the twentieth century and my parents were still young, color had yet to enter the world. Light and darkness, black and white, sufficed my poor grandparents; by the time my parents were born, grey had been invented by I. G. Farbenindustrie. At first it didn't seem good for anything except smudgy London fogs, but by the time the Blitz began it could express the smoke of burning cities quite nicely. Three days before the Führer broke off his monumental tank battle in Kursk, the U.S. War Department, having been apprised by a Zeiss defector that Hitler's home movies were now being filmed *in color,* launched the top-secret Taos Project, in the course of which an ingenious boy scientist named Ansel Adams employed a hedgehog formation of photon-guns to fracture the firmament's tonal scale into exactly ten zones, from the primeval black of Zone 0 to the perfect blank of Zone X. Contrast, cloud-cliff relationships, pearly-grey pine trees decked out with recesses of utter black, luminance and detail, mid-range gunmetal rivers banded by wakes of paler grey, these distinctions permitted our universe a greater number of adjustments than the earlier Gutenberg model had enjoyed; but it was not until Operation Polaroid that most citizens got to see colors for the very first time: primary colors in Phase One (we smile now, when we remember that until 1979, high summer foliage could only be yellow or blue); and then, once our American landscape had been suitably conditioned by the Adams Ray, the secondaries, the tertiaries, and finally the various infrared flavors which we enjoy so much in erotic situations. As I said, the Germans had stolen a march on us here, just as the Russians would in outer space; I cannot forbear to quote from the declassified OSS "appreciation" prepared by a certain Frank Voss, our on-the-spot U.S. operative whose real mission is to sniff around for secret weapons here in the ruins of the Führerbunker; this colorblind fellow who is now experiencing color for the very first time (indeed, the only time, since his final reel included capture, torture and liquidation in North Korea) writes that from the heap of steel canisters in the well of rubble at the far end of a dank hall now guarded by no less than three Kalmuck machine-gunners *(they were quite friendly,* he reports, *and also gave me the location of a Werewolf detachment which had created several nuisances in our sector)* there comes a shining more pale than any Zone VII grey, which nonetheless partakes of Zone II's dramatic inevitability; Frank Voss, who at one time was a divinity student, speculates that to the sentries, whose sophistication in his opinion leaves much to be desired (their ideology, he sadly writes, compels them to see in black and white), this indescribable light may be as sacred as the star on the pale forehead of their revolutionary cruiser *Aurora.*—Yes, indescribable!—Defeated, Frank Voss withdraws to safer grey metaphors; reports of the atomic glow over Hiroshima now seem similarly off the mark. Nonetheless, in this episode he wins our hearts almost as much as does that flickering silver eminence, Bing Crosby; indeed, had it not been for the Cold War, our tense young American would probably have received the Order of Kutuzov for bravery, because, without fear or hesitation, he outdoes the daring of his Kalmuck allies: namely, he unscrews the top of the biggest movie cannister! And instantly, for a radius of perhaps twenty feet, the corridor gets colorized not by "red," "blue" or "yellow," for which he would have lacked the words anyway, but by their muted opposites, because the Germans' first experiments with color involved negative film. After following Frank Voss's strangely moving attempts to describe these hues on the basis of their estimated wavelengths, we reach this (partially corrupted) transcript of an attempt to contact HQ: Deeply regret unable to evaluate the phenomenon. Doing all possible. Please confirm immediately on emergency link whether destruction of these objects is advised before Soviet experts arrive. Voss then tries more desperately than ever to describe the magenta blush imparted to the ceiling by several thousand almost identical eight-millimeter frames of Eva Braun's lips, but here the report has been **CENSORED: APPROX. 300 WORDS DELETED**. Well, isn't it better that way? Mystical testimony achieves its maximum propaganda value when it shades off into inchoateness or even darkness. Besides, the Germans never intended for color to be enjoyed by anyone except the elite, and the rest of Europe remained awfully grey in those days, her best Zone 0 being blackout paper, which in museums subject to the penetration of the Adams Ray appears to be a weak greenish-black at best, while her most reliable Zone X can be no paler than a Nazi officer's corpse staring up at the sky. This is the reason why Ansel Adams himself, that true American, never visited Europe until 1974, by which time he'd been projected into his eighth decade of life; he'd calculated that lighting conditions over there would be practically impossible, that high values would be blocked, for beyond Omaha Beach the entire continent remained divided into only two crudely differentiated zones (in which Adams explicitly counted the pearl-grey midnights of Leningrad); but he had to go just the same. In Paris his elongated shadow already lacked even a blue component; and when he got to Arles, on a conveyance whose engineers had advanced far beyond the futuristic blockiness of any armored train, he found himself *lightly charmed by the swift-passing landscape* (leaden-black earth; silver-grey grass-hairs; the Académie Française was now fiercely debating the introduction of certain sepias and russets) *but bored by its rural sameness and the evidence of tired antiquity and modern industrial landscapes.* In a word, *I confess to acute homesickness.*

2

Well, who wouldn't have been homesick, especially during the war years? (Imagine how dreary the spectators must have felt after Comrade Stalin's alpinists had ascended the shining Admiralty Tower of Leningrad and camouflaged it with dull grey paint.) Not only was Europe more higher-contrast and greyer than ever—never mind the broken glass, cold and darkness—but, as period movie footage demonstrates, atomic structures were actually *looser*—hence the stippled grey cheekbones of starving Poles, the fuzzy almost-white of children's skinny legs, the velvety irregularities of what should have been chiseled pillar-grooves in the facades of blurry department stores not yet bombed. The perverse argument of certain liberal "experts" that the film stock of the 1940s was inherently grainier than today's has been disproven by a Central Intelligence Agency study which employed extreme magnification to compare nitrate-based Nazi-Soviet documentaries with today's color features.* As Adams demonstrated, *grain is a fundamental feature of reality itself.*

3

Still and all, one feature must be conceded to the grey old days: coherence. Just as a poem achieves its effect by a narrow application of choice within a wide application of exclusion (the word I need cannot be any of the thousands which fail to rhyme with *grey*), so wartime Europe was perfect in its ghastly fashion, inhabited by beings with coarse-pored silver complexions. What were my parents like when they were young? Their hair is silver now. Of course it always was; they got married before brown was invented. Relatively speaking, they had luck; my father grew up in the ultra-whiteness of Chicago winters; my mother had her grey Nebraska wheat fields. In Europe, the tonal scale remained measurably harsher. What inmate of that continent could hope to be more than a fleeing, slender civilian in an inky-black suit, or one of many snowy-camouflaged men on a tank, pointing black guns across the snow? A few million souls did get to be decorated dull-grey Russian soldier-girls in mid-grey fur hats; we see them marching westward in that propaganda spectacular "The Fall of Berlin," to which Shostakovich wrote the soundtrack. When Khruschev, outflanking Operation Polaroid, introduced the color red into Soviet society in early 1961, it caught on so well that every subsequent decoration had to be either crimson or bloody, but during the war all medals stayed grey, of course, which I actually consider befitting because it was a dreary grey war of frozen corpses; frozen blood goes black; red would have been out of place. The pale skinny boys assembling the round magazines of machine-guns, what color should they have been but dead white? Between the reflections of long white military columns writhing in the Neva and the black trickles of people dwindling day by day on the frozen streets of

---

*The finer detail of our Ortho-Mx projections is the result not only of a higher organized nervous sensibility and improved moral accutance, but, above all, of absolute technological superiority. The millions of colors and tonal zones which we Americans now enjoy look better than ever, thanks to the cooperation of private industry. Digital smoothing is now underway. Before the next war breaks out, we hope to entirely eliminate every intra-atomic space.

Leningrad, only two zones were needed: ultra-field-grey, as exemplified by the squat darkness above the treads of the Panzerkampfwagen (specifically, a Pzkpfw-IIIF), and ice-grey, the color of those Stalinist banners which the Panzers overpassed, the banners which said: **LIFE HAS BECOME MORE JOYFUL.**

4

He rose from the bed and stood lankily naked, watching his breath freeze in the greyish room. He went to the window. Yawning, he scratched a little circle in the window-frost. Through this peephole he saw what he had known he would see: dull grey battleships frozen in the ice.

He saw men in murky greatcoats, with grey wool caps on their heads, hands in their pockets, and rifles wedged under their arms, the barrels aiming straight upwards, every man standing shoulder to shoulder for warmth as the military band played. Then they began to march. White snakes of snow-light flittered across them as they twitched rhythmically out of focus.

He saw the pavements shimmering and shining with ice.

He smiled. (White streaks—scratches in the war film—writhed across his face.) He was as happy as he would ever be, because the woman in the bed was his mistress, Elena Konstantinovskaya, and because after everything she still loved him.

The master composer (which is what he was) does not bemoan the absence of greyness between the piano's white and black keys. Anyhow, he had his greys, three strong, crude Russian shades which sufficed for everything.—Two zones, I've just written, but she brought the third to us. Between black and white lie the following three greys, from dark to light: the charcoal grey of Konstantinovskaya's pubic curls, which corresponds to the shadow which our T-34 tanks cast upon the frozen pavement of Kirovsky Prospekt (let us hereby repudiate the enemy's Pzkpfw-IIIF); the healthy mid-grey of her fingernails, lips and nipples; and the creamy pale grey, not ice-grey at all, of her face, hands and shoulders, which have been tanned by the Russian sun. Underneath her white, white breasts live twin crescent-shadows which crave to express themselves in their own intermediate shade between lip-grey and shoulder-grey, but they cannot, because all greys have been used up. Once the poem has narrowed and thereby deepened itself (for instance, limiting itself to white, black and three greys), it becomes more fully what it is; Konstantinovskaya is perfectly what she is; she is perfect; she saves him who loves her because the white sun of an explosion is a face, Death's face, and

Death's long black tresses are smoke; without Konstantinovskaya, white and black would be only Death; she blessed them into a marriage. Here come more Germans in field-grey; here come NCOs with silver lace on their shoulder straps. Thanks to her, field-grey isn't just an enemy shade; it's lip-grey, too; he kisses it whenever he kisses her mouth . . .

He drinks from her mouth. Her white breath-fog flutters across the blackish-grey swellings of the Neva. That breath will be frozen tomorrow, maning the snow-clods and dirty ice-clods and corpses in new white. Yes, the mud will be frozen silver by her breath, and then it will be dusted white, and the small bomb-smashed houses of Pulkovo will seem cleaner. All will be white on white, even the shy rare smoke which freezes as soon as it's born from chimneys.

5

He said: Well, Elena, how unlucky it is that I didn't marry you—

Don't cry. Stay with me today.

But then I—

And stay the night.

If they're watching—

Of course they're watching, Mitya.

He took heart at that and laughed: Well, to be sure, they're all waiting for my bad end. Here, Elena, do you see what I have with me? I forgot to show you before because I was so excited to be, well, I, I was thinking of you, Elena, oh, yes, I was . . . Sollertinsky gave me this smoked fish. I wish I knew where he got it—

Come to bed now, she said quietly.

6

And it went on, it continued, greyly curving like the triple-railed tramcar tracks of Leningrad which now led directly from Comrade Zhukov's pale, pouchy face to the round bald head and wide round eyes of Field-Marshal Wilhelm Ritter von Leeb; their pearl-grey hours flickered and stuttered past, her white breasts sanctifying by sharing the same unholy light as German munitions coming to kiss the streets newly paved by the corpses they'd made; her eyebrows were a wall of smoke. But it was only a war movie that he dreamed. He was long gone to Kuibyshev by then; he'd been evacuated with his wife and children, because he was valuable. Konstantinovskaya was in Spain; she married and divorced a certain Roman Karmen. And when the last reel flopped and chittered loose, when the projectionist returned them all to ghastly light, then the movie star awoke, rolled away from his wife's snores, rose, fiddled with his Seventh Symphony and later stood with his face sadly and anxiously crumpled as he rested his hands on his two children's shoulders. His glasses kept sliding down his nose. He wanted to take them off. His daughter Galya scratched a circle in the frosty windowpane. Peering through it, he saw the stopped buses, the black, flat-topped Russian automobiles whose fronts sloped doubly down over the wheels like the clasped mandibles of praying mantises, and after he had counted only two shades of grey, his white, white fingers, which in those days were exactly the same shade as piano keys, began to clench like the feelers of an insect drawing up and dying.

7

All right, so he'd known it was a movie all along; he'd rushed to leave her because Nina was pregnant; he'd joined the dark crowds on the far side of the street, the safe side, where building-fronts remained multiwindowed and white. (The stenciled Cyrillic letters, white on grey, said: CITIZENS! DURING ARTILLERY FIRE THIS IS THE MOST DANGEROUS SIDE OF THE STREET.) In the movie he'd finally returned to the side where he was meant to be. The soundtrack was his own. She was on top of him, and he was inside her, and their mouths both opened and then those two pale, open-mouthed Russian corpses formed their own exclusive society on a street corner which shone brilliant silver with rain. ■

SOURCES

These stories are not as rigorously grounded in historical fact as my *Seven Dreams* books. Rather, the goal here was to write a series of parables about famous, infamous and anonymous European moral actors at moments of decision. Most of the characters in this book are real people. I researched the details of their lives as carefully as I could. However, this is a work of fiction. Poetic justice has I hope been rendered, both to them and to their historical situations (which got stripped down into parables, then embellished here and there with supernatural cobwebs). To give one especially glaring example, see my note immediately following this section: "An Imaginary Love Triangle: Shostakovich, Karmen, Konstantinovskaya." I apologize for any offense which I may have given to the living, and I repeat: This is a work of fiction.

Under such circumstances it would be a sterile exercise in didacticism to list sources of anything other than direct quotations. But I've tried to be as accurate in the small details (for instance, "the sound of our footsteps, which I loved, and love still, despite everything"*), and as fair to the historical personages involved as possible. It is probably needless to state that the social systems described here, together with all their institutions and atrocities, derive entirely from the historical record.

The chronology was for the convenience of the reader who may be unfamiliar with some of the names and events mentioned. My publisher persuaded me to cut it, on account of the wartime paper shortage. There is no compelling need to consult it; however, it might have furnished some eerie instances of German and Russian synchronicities.

I prepared the list of patronymics for those of you who have trouble keeping track of Russian names and nicknames.

Military terminology need not trouble the reader overmuch here, especially since its seeming specificity was so often illusory during World War II. The number of soldiers in a divison or a regiment, for instance, varied not only according

*Guy Sajer, *The Forgotten Soldier,* trans. Lily Emmet (New York: Harper and Row, 1971 trans. of original 1967 French ed.), p. 71. The forgotten soldier was Alsatian, and he served with the Wehrmacht. He missed the sound of steel boots on cobblestones, a detail which I have pilfered for "Clean Hands."

to whether that regiment were German, Soviet, Romanian, Italian, etcetera, but also according to how much it had been bled to death. As the war went on, formations tended to become under official strength. (An instance of non-equivalence: When the German attempt on Moscow, Operation Typhoon, was halted in the winter of 1941, ninety-five Soviet divisions—eight hundred thousand men—stopped seventy-seven and a half German divisions—a million men.) After several attempts at drawing up a nice little chart for you, I finally despaired. The relative equivalence of ranks in the armies concerned was less problematical, but often still not exact. The only matter which does require specific elucidation is this: In Axis (and most Allied) usage, the word *front* refers to the immediately contested area between two armies. In Soviet usage, however, a front could be an operational grouping, similar to a Nazi army group. During the Great Patriotic War the Soviet Union formed and dissolved fronts according to the requirements of each situation. There were never less than ten, and never any more than fifteen. To minimize confusion I have capitalized the term when using it in a Soviet sense. Thus, the Volkhov Front is "Volkhov Region Red Army Group," whereas the Volkhov front is the frontline area of the Volkhov area.

Regarding the *Ring* Cycle, *Parzival,* Eschenbach's *Tristan and Isolde,* the *Nibelungenlied* and the Norse songs of the *Poetic Edda,* it should be noted that the names and acts alter in variations of the stories: Hogni is Hagen, and Gunther Gunnar; Brynhild spells her name "Brunnhilde" whenever she finds herself in a Wagner opera. Guthrún may metamorphose into Kriemhild or Grimhild, or vanish entirely. Siegfried wins Brunnhilde for Gunther by riding through a wall of flame, or else he has already done this, awoken her and pledged troth before he ever met Gunther. In either case, the relationship between Siegfried and Gunther is a constant: vainglorious complacency on the one hand, with a hint of illicit intimacy between Siegfried and Brunnhilde, and envious, resentful dependency on the other. I have tried to respect the appropriate consistencies and inconsistencies.

When the plurals of German nouns happen to be identical with the singulars ("Gauleiter," "Nebelwerfer," etc.), I thought it best to Anglicize them with an *s,* especially in such parallelistic constructions as: "Our *Nebelwerfers* against their Katyushas, what an unresolved problem!"

The moral equation of Stalinism with Hitlerism is nothing new. V. Grossman made that point first and best in his novel *Life and Fate.* Here it is merely a point of departure. (What is totalitarianism? In 1945, shortly before his own death in an air raid, the horrible Roland Freisler, judge of the Nazi "People's Court," says to his condemned adversary what a Stalinist could also say: "Only in one respect are we and Christianity alike: We demand the entire man!" —Helmuth James von Moltke, *Letters to Freya 1939–1945,* ed. & trans. by Beate Ruhm von Oppen [New York: Alfred A. Knopf, 1990; orig. German ed. 1988], p. 409.)

A great number of my visual descriptions, both in straightforward prose and in metaphors, derive from the illustrations in Irina Antonova and Jorn Merkert, comp., *Moskva-Berlin Berlin-Moskau 1900–1950* (Moscow: Galart [a supposed coproduction with Prestel-Verlag in Munich and New York; I haven't seen the latter but if it ever comes out it would be preferable for the reader who can't sound out Cyrillic]; 1996). This is a spectacular book.

Descriptions of Third Reich uniforms, weapons and other militaria, particularly on the Ostfront, make occasional reference to Nigel Thomas, *The German Army 1939–45 (3): Eastern Front 1941–43,* illus. Stephen Andrew (Oxford: Osprey Publishing, Men-At-Arms ser. no. 326, 1999); Bruce Quarrie, *Fallschirmjäger: German Paratrooper 1935–45,* illus. Velmir Vuksic (Oxford: Osprey Publishing, Warrior ser. no. 38, 2001); Robin Lumsden, *A Collector's Guide to Third Reich Militaria,* rev. ed. (Surrey: Ian Allan Publishing, 2000 rev. repr. of orig. 1987 ed.); Werner Haupt, *A History of the Panzer Troops 1916–1945,* trans. Dr. Edward Force (West Chester, Pennsylvania: Schiffer Publishing, Ltd., 1990; original German ed. 1989).

Descriptions of the airplanes of all sides are based on the pretty color foldouts in *The Gatefold Book of World War II Warplanes* (New York: Barnes & Noble Books, by arr. w/ Brown Packaging Books Ltd., 1995). For details on the sources of technical specifications to Soviet airplanes, see the appropriate note to "Elena's Rockets."

My occasional descriptions of the handwriting of German and Russian writers and composers derive from the samples which appear in Marianne Bernhard, comp., *Künstler-Autographen: Dichter, Musiker, bildende Künstler in ihren Handschriften* (Dortmund: Die bibliophilen Taschenbücher, Harenberg Kommunikation, 1980). The exception is the handwriting of Shostakovich, which I have described based on facsimiles reproduced in various biographies, etcetera.

◩

ix Shostakovich epigraph: "The majority of my symphonies are tombstones." —*Testimony: The Memoirs of Dmitry Shostakovich as Related to and Edited by Solomon Volkov,* trans. Antonina W. Bouis (New York: Limelight Editions repr. of 1979 Harper & Row ed.), p. 156. (Henceforth cited, for the sake of argument, as Shostakovich and Volkov.)

STEEL IN MOTION

3 Epigraph —Field-Marshal Erich von Manstein, *Lost Victories: The War Memoirs of Hitler's Most Brilliant General,* ed. and trans. Anthony C. Powell (Novato, California: Presidio Press, 1994 repr. of 1958 abridged trans.; original German ed. 1955), p. 22.

3 A German general: Moscow as "the core of the enemy's whole being." —Wilfried Strik-Strikfeldt, *Against Stalin and Hitler: A Memoir of the Russian Liberation Movement 1941–5,* trans. David Footman (London: Macmillan, 1970 trans. of 1970 German ed.), p. 39.

3 "Italy" (actually, Mussolini): "We cannot change our policy now . . ." —Donald Cameron Watt, *How War Came: The Immediate Origins of the Second World War 1938–1939* (New York: Pantheon Books, 1989), p. 200.

3 The sleepwalker (Hitler): "This will strike like a bomb!" —Ibid., p. 462.

4 Marshal Tukhachevsky: "Operations in a future war . . ." —Comrade Stalin: "Modern war will be a war of engines." —John Erickson, *The Road to Stalingrad: Stalin's War with Germany:* Volume One (New Haven, Connecticut: Yale University Press, 1999 repr. of 1975 ed.), p. 5.

5 The telephone: "It was and is Jews who bring the Negroes into the Rhineland." —Adolf Hitler, *Mein Kampf,* trans. Ralph Mannheim (Boston: Houghton Mifflin, 1971; orig. German ed. 1925–26), p. 325.

5 The telephone: "That is precisely why the Party affirms . . ." —J. V. Stalin, *On the Opposition (1927–27)* (Peking: Foreign Languages Press, 1974).
6 Hitler to Paulus: "One has to be on the watch like a spider in its web . . ." —See source-notes to "The Last Field-Marshal" (in that story, an amplified version appears).
8 Telephoned order "Under no circumstances will we agree to artillery preparation," etc. —Gérard Chaliand, ed., *The Art of War in World History from Antiquity to the Nuclear Age* (Berkeley: University of California Press, 1994), pp. 954–55 (Guderian on firepower).

THE SAVIORS

A note on Krupskaya's final years, when I describe her as "writing in support of Stalin's show trials that many of her own former comrades-in-arms deserved to be shot like mad dogs," may be in order. According to one eminent historian of the period, she should undoubtedly be credited with having vainly tried to save a few of her colleagues such as the Old Bolshevik Pyatinsky. Apparently I. D. Chigurin was indebted to her for being permitted to die a natural if wretched death. (See Robert Conquest, *The Great Terror: A Reassessment* [New York: Oxford University Press, 1991 repr. of 1990 ed.], pp. 238, 437–38). In this account, and several others, Krupskaya receives passing mentions, tinctured by sympathy or pity. On the other hand, Solzhenitsyn in his trilogy on the prison system demands to know: "Why didn't Lenin's faithful companion, Krupskaya, fight back? Why didn't she speak out even once with a public exposé, like the old worker in the Rostov Flax Works? Was she really so afraid of losing her old woman's life?" *(The Gulag Archipelago 1918–1956: An Experiment in Literary Investigation,* trans. Thomas P. Whitney [San Francisco: Harper and Row, 1973, 1975, 1978; orig. Russian *samizdat* mss. 1960s], vol. 2, p. 333.)

MOBILIZATION

32 Epigraph —Quoted in Erich Eyck, *Bismarck and the German Empire* (New York: Norton, 1968 repr. of 1950 ed.), p. 239.
32 Bismarck (the Iron Chancellor): "I have always found the word 'Europe' . . ." —Ibid., p. 246.

WOMAN WITH DEAD CHILD

36 Epigraph: "A new bride cries until sunrise . . ." —Russian proverb, quoted to me by a prostitute in Moscow.

Some of my understanding of this artist's character has been informed by Elizabeth Prelinger (with contributions by Alessandra Comini and Hildegard Bachert), *Käthe Kollwitz* (Washington: National Gallery of Art / Yale University Press, 1992).

36 Letter from Kollwitz: "My only hope is in world socialism" —Closely after a letter in *The Diary and Letters of Kaethe Kollwitz,* ed. Hans Kollwitz, trans. Richard and Clara Winston (Evanston, Illinois: Northwestern University Press), p. 184 (21 February 1944).
36 ". . . she stood before a woman whom she'd made out of stone, . . . and stroked the granite woman's cheeks" —Closely after *Diary and Letters,* p. 122 (entry for August 14, 1932: "I stood before the woman, looked at her—my own face—and I wept and stroked her cheeks").
37 The tale of Frau Becker and her children —After Käthe Kollwitz, *Die Tagebücher,* ed. Jutta Bohnke-Kollwitz (Berlin: Akademie-Verlag, 1989), p. 49, entry for 30 August 1909, trans. by WTV.
37 "Peter would have joined them"—*Tagebücher,* p. 379 (9 November 1918, trans. WTV).

37 Kollwitz's family showing the Imperial flag for the first time ever —Large, p. 127.

37 Rumpelstilzchen —Known to Anglo-American fairytale readers as Rumpelstiltskin.

38 "Peter's flag hanging from the balcony" —Described in the *Tagebücher,* p. 170 (10 October 1914, trans. WTV).

38 "Vile, outrageous murder of Liebknecht and Luxemburg" —*Tagebücher,* p. 400 (16 January 1919, trans. WTV).

38 "For Rosa Luxemburg an empty coffin near Liebknecht." —*Tagebücher,* p. 403 (entry for 25 January 1919, trans. WTV).

39 Kollwitz in the morgue: "Oh, what a dismal, dismal place this is . . ." —Large, p. 166, slightly altered.

41 Karl to his wife: "You have strength only for sacrifice and letting go . . ." —*Tagebücher,* p. 176 (27 November 1914, trans. WTV).

41 Käthe's recurring dreams of Peter —*Tagebücher,* p. 193 (end of July 1915, trans. WTV).

Various details on Peter's argument with his parents over volunteering, his death, the condition of his grave and Käthe and Karl's trip to the Soviet Union in 1927 ("Russia intoxicated me") come from the *Tagebücher,* p. 400 (16 January 1919, trans. WTV), pp. 745–47 (Appendix: "Die Jahre 1914–1933 zum Umbruch [1943]". One woman who apparently met Kollwitz claims to have been told by her that "she persuaded him to volunteer for the fighting." But this same woman says that Peter the grandson died "in the Polish campaign." This Peter died in 1942, long after the Polish campaign had ended. (Alison Owings, *Frauen: German Women Recall the Third Reich* [New Brunswick, New Jersey: Rutgers University Press, 1999 3rd paperback repr. of 1993 ed.], p. 311 [testimony of Frau Emmi Heinrich].)

42 "IHR SOHN IST GEFALLEN" —"Your son has fallen."

44 Kollwitz: "Today started work on the sculpture 'Woman with Dead Child' —*Tagebücher,* p. 85 (entry for 9 September 1910, trans. WTV). (Original: *Heut den Beginn gemacht zu der plastischen Gruppe: Frau mit totem Kind.*)

44 Kollwitz on her Russenhilfe image: "It's good, thank God"—*Tagebücher,* p. 508 (entry for 12 September 1921, trans. WTV).

45 Kollwitz to her son Hans: "There are other problems that interest me now . . ." —Christoph Meckel et al, *Käthe Kollwitz* (Bad Godesberg, West Germany: Inter Nationes, 1967), p. 16 (Ulrich Weisner, "On the Art of Käthe Kollwitz"), somewhat altered.

45 "An elegy of the people." —Martha Kearns, *Käthe Kollwitz: Woman and Artist* (Old Westbury, New York: The Feminist Press, 1976), p. 162.

45 The chord *D-D-Sch* —Often so represented in studies of Shostakovich and his later music, especially the Eighth String Quartet. Thomas Melle for his part insists to me: "Inappropriate German notation. The correct German notation would be: d, d, es, c, b."

45 A. Lunacharsky on Kollwitz: "She aims at an immediate effect . . ." —Otto Nagel, *Käthe Kollwitz,* trans. Stella Humphries (London: Studio Vista, 1961), p. 58.

46 Description of Kollwitz amidst the jury of the Prussian Academy —After a photograph in Martin Fritsch (herausgegeben & bearbeitet von Annette Seeler), *Käthe Kollwitz: Zeichnung Grafik Plastik: Bestandskatalog des Käthe-Kollwitz-Museums Berlin* (Leipzig: E. A. Seeman, 1999), p. 37.

46 Professor Moholy-Nagy to Kollwitz: "It is an elementary biological necessity . . ." —Laszlo Moholy-Nagy, *Painting, Photography, Film,* trans. Janet Seligman (Cambridge, Massachusetts: The MIT Press, 1987 repr. of 1927 second German ed.), p. 13. The encounter between these two artists is entirely invented.

46 Professor Moholy-Nagy to Kollwitz: "The traditional painting has become a historical relic . . ." —Ibid., p. 45.

47 The grocer's apprentice: ". . . I would like to stand for something. I would like to be there for something" —After the justification given by Frau Ellen Frey, who defended Hitler decades after the Third Reich; in Owings, p. 181. (Frau Frey said "live for," not

"stand for," but the latter seemed more appropriate in this context, given that the boy is dying.)

47 Description of Peter's hand and body in Kollwitz's recollections —Based on a description in the *Diary and Letters* (p. 115; entry for August 27, 1927) of her doomed grandson Peter: "the frail little hand laid in ours. The beautiful naked little body."

48 Footnote: The role of Otto Nagel —Otto Nagel, *Käthe Kollwitz* (Dresden: VEB Verlag der Kunst, n.d., 1962 or after), p. 41. About the exhibition see pp. 53, 56, 63–64.

49 Letter from Kollwitz to her children about learning Russian —*Diary and Letters of Kaethe Kollwitz*, p. 183 (7 February 1944).

49 Letter from Kollwitz: "The desire, the unquenchable longing . . ." Ibid., p. 187 (13 June 1944).

49 Kollwitz diary entry: "And I must do the prints on Death . . ." —*Diary and Letters*, p. 114 (13 February 1927).

50 Layout of the Kollwitz exhibition in Moscow —After the *Tagebücher*, p. 632 (November 1927). Elena Konstantinovskaya's presence is a fabrication.

51 Grete, Anna and the old proletarian woman —Plucked from the *Tagebücher*.

51 Description of the young Käthe Kollwitz (compared by me to the young Krupskaya) —Based on a photo in David Clay Large, *Berlin* (New York: Basic Books, a member of the Perseus Book Group, 2000), p. 70 ("Käthe Kollwitz, circa 1905." Source: Archiv für Kunst und Geschichte).

51 "They," on Kollwitz: "Her family was involved in the workers' movement" —*Great Soviet Encyclopedia*, vol. 12, p. 586 (entry on Käthe Kollwitz).

51 "The doctor came immediately, and his invoice never" —*Tagebücher*, p. 18 (introduction).

51 Kollwitz: "That's the typical misfortune . . ." —*Diary and Letters*, p. 52 (September 1909).

52 "One young man" to Kollwitz: "The temporal sequence of a movement . . ." —Closely after Ludwig Hirschfeld-Mack, on the subject of his reflected color displays; excerpted in Moholy-Nagy, p. 80.

53 The young man (Comrade Alexandrov): "I used to believe that if I lived out my life . . ." —*The Diaries of Nikolay Punin 1904–1953*, ed. Sidney Monas and Jennifer Greene Krupala, trans. Jennifer Greene Krupala (Austin: University of Texas Press, 1999), p. 51 (entry for 15 August 1917; somewhat reworked).

53 "He wanted to escort her and her husband to a Shostakovich premiere." —There is no evidence that Kollwitz did or did not attend a Shostakovich event. Originally I sentenced her to the rather mediocre Second Symphony simply because its premiere date, 1927, coincided with the year of her visit. In fact, it premiered in Leningrad in November, so Kollwitz had probably come and gone before it arrived in Moscow. For that reason the Scherzo in E-flat Major (1923–24) seemed safer.

54 Kollwitz on Schnabel ("clear-consoling-good") and Beethoven ("the heavens opened") —*Diary and Letters*, p. 115.

55 Kollwitz to Lene Bloch: "Marriage is a kind of work" —*Tagebücher*, pp. 18–19 (introduction).

55 The parade on Red Square —Based in part on the description in her *Briefen an den Sohn*, pp. 201–02 (Moscow, 6 November 1927).

55 The drawing "Listening," later "lithographed . . . as *Slushayuoshchie*" —Kete Kolvitz (so transliterated in Cyrillic) catalogue, *Katalog vystavki proizvedeniy iz muzeev i castnych sobraniy German Demokrat. Republiki* (Moscow: Isdatelstvo Akademii Khudozhest SSSR, n.d. [prob. 1963], no page nos.). This is merely my fabulist's trick. The only reasoning that the name "Listening" got changed to its Russian equivalent was that it so appeared in the catalogue. Of course to Kollwitz herself it remained "Zuhörende," or in some versions "Zuhörender" (catalogue 14, 1927).

55 "Out of Moscow Käthe Kollwitz brought with her a beautiful page . . ." —*Bemerkung*, ascribed to Otto Nagel (op. cit., p. 288; trans. a bit floridly by WTV).

56 Danilo Kiš: "Under my personal supervision a hundred and twenty inmates of the

nearby regional prison camp . . ." —Danilo Kiš, *A Tomb for Boris Davidovich,* trans. Duska Mikic-Mitchell (Normal, Illinois: Dalkey Archive Press, 2001 repr. of 1978 Harcourt ed.; orig. Serbo-Croatian ed. 1976), p. 42. To avoid monotony, I have changed "prisoners in" to "inmates of."

56 Kollwitz: "When the man and the woman are healthy, a worker's life is not unbearable" —*Tagebücher,* p. 49, entry for 30 August 1909, trans, by WTV.

56 "Joy in others and being in harmony with them had always been one of the deepest pleasures in her life." —After *Diary and Letters,* p. 116 (entry for March 1928: "Joy in others and being in harmony with them is one of the deepest pleasures in life.")

56 Kollwitz: "Moscow with its different atmosphere . . ." —*Diary and Letters,* p. 115 (New Year's Eve, 1927).

57 "Frau Kollwitz had taken up etching in order to distribute the maximum number of prints to the working class" —After an assertion in Kearns, p. 141.

58 The meeting between Kollwitz and Karmen I fabricated.

58 Old Reschke in the Cafe Monopol, 1914: "God be thanked that mobilization is happening . . ." —*Tagebücher,* p. 149 (August 1914, trans. WTV, slightly altered). He is not elsewhere mentioned in the diaries, so I don't know whether he was really "old Reschke" (my adjective) or not.

58 Karl: "This noble young generation . . ." *Tagebücher,* p. 152 (10 August 1914, trans. WTV).

59 Description of Peter in the last month of his life —After a photograph in the *Tagebücher,* p. 167 ("Peter Kollwitz, 2. Oktober 1914").

59 Roman Karmen: "How terrible it must seem to be to be a mother who weeps . . . film it!" —K. K. Ognev, ed., *Roman Karmen* (Moscow?: Sovexportfilm, n.d., after 1975), p. 7 (extract from Karmen's daybook while in Spain, presumably in 1936; trans. by WTV).

60 Description of Peter's room —After a photograph in the *Tagebücher,* p. 192.

60 The commentator: "In the diaries one finds . . ." —*Tagebücher,* p. 899 (notes; trans. and slightly reworded by WTV).

60 Hitler's attire in Hamburg, 1928 —*The Infancy of Nazism: The Memoirs of Ex-Gauleiter Albert Krebs 1923–1933,* ed. and trans. William Sheridan Allen (New York: New Viewpoints, a division of Franklin Watts, 1976), p. 155.

60 Käthe to Gorki: "All that I saw in Russia . . ." —*Tagebücher,* p. 899 (notes, trans. and slightly reworded by WTV).

60 "We Protect the Soviet Union!" —This image seems to be rare. I have found it only in Nagel, p. 139 ("Wir schützen die Sowjetunion!").

61 Hitler to his lieutenants: "Speechless obedience" —*Krebs,* p. 189.

61 "And in an instant the bullet struck him!" —Käthe Kollwitz, *Brief an den Sohn 1904 bis 1945,* ed. Jutta Bohnke-Kollwitz (Berlin: Wolf Jobst Siedler Verlag, 1992), p. 91 (19 November 1914, trans. WTV).

61 Description of Hans Kollwitz's bookplate —After Kollwitz, *Brief an den Sohn,* p. 81 ("Das Exlibris, das Käthe Kollwitz 1908 für ihren sechzehnjährigen Sohn entwarf . . .").

62 Description of the Leningrad exhibition —After a photo in Otto Nagel, *Käthe Kollwitz* (Dresden: VEB Verlag der Kunst, n.d., 1962 or after), pp. 66–69. The presence of Konstantinovskaya and Shostakovich has been invented.

62 Footnote: The entry on Kollwitz in *Meyers Lexikon* —Vol. 6, (pub. 1939), p. 1300. *Meyers* lists a few works, such as her "Proletariat" (1925). The implication is that she is a has-been.

62 Footnote: "Oh, Lise, being dead must be good . . ." —*Diary and Letters,* p. 195 (letter of February 1945).

63 Hitler: "The Germans—this is essential—will have to constitute amongst themselves a closed society, like a fortress" —Chaliand, p. 945 (secret conversation of 17–18 September 1941).

YOU HAVE SHUT THE DANUBE'S GATES

64 Epigraph: "At the very point when death becomes visible behind everything . . ." —Kollwitz, *Diary and Letters,* p. 123 (entry for August 1932).

64 *The Song of Igor's Campaign:* "You reign high upon your throne of gold . . ." —*Song of Igor's Campaign: An Epic of the Twelfth Century,* trans. Vladimir Nabokov (New York: Random House / Vintage Books, 1960), p. 55 ("Apostrophe," ll. 523–28; substantially "retranslated" by WTV, less to improve on VN than to avoid permissions fees).

66 Anecdote of the kolkozniks in Moscow —After James von Geldern and Richard Stites, *Mass Culture in Soviet Russia* (Bloomington: Indiana University Press, 1995), p. 184, anecdote.

66 Capture of sixty Soviet tanks by the Condor Legion —Gabriel Jackson, *The Spanish Republic and the Civil War 1931–1939* (Princeton, New Jersey: Princeton University Press, 1965), 401.

66 Akhmatova: "One might say that Leningrad is particularly suited to catastrophes . . ." —Chukovskaya, p. 40 (entry for 27 September 1939), slightly abridged. "The black water with yellow flecks of light . . ." actually was said by Akhmatova, not Chukovskaya.

ELENA'S ROCKETS

68 Epigraph —Lewis Siegelbaum and Andrei Sokolov, ed., *Stalinism as a Way of Life: A Narrative in Documents,* trans. Thomas Hoisington and Steven Shabad (New Haven, Connecticut: Yale University Press, 2000), pp. 395–96 (Document 146, author ["two priggish inspectors"] not cited; State Archive of the Russian Federation [GARF], f.5207, op. 1, d.1293, 11.7–8).

68 Details on Soviet planes, rocket engines, etc. —*Great Soviet Encyclopedia,* entry on aviation; Yaroslav Golovanov, *Sergei Korolev: The Apprenticeship of a Space Pioneer,* trans. M. M. Samokhvalov and H. C. Creighton (Moscow: Mir Publishers, 1975 rev. of 1973 Russian ed.); *Jane's Fighting Aircraft of World War II* (New York: Military Press, 1989 repr. of 1946–47 ed.), entries on Soviet air power and Soviet aero engines.

68 Descriptions (here, in "The Palm Tree of Deborah" and in "Untouched") of Rodchenko's non-objective sculptures —Based on the photographs in Galerie Gmurzynska, *Alexander Rodchenko: Spatial Constructions / Raumkonstruktione* (Ostfildern-Ruit, Germany: Hatje Cantz Verlag, 2002).

68 Assessment of F. Zander: "One of the tragedies of this outstanding intellect . . ." —Golovanov, p. 212.

69 The "forty times forty" churches of Moscow —Marina Tsvetaeva, *Selected Poems,* 3rd ed., trans. Elaine Feinstein (New York: Penguin, 1994 repr. of 1993 ed.), p. 15 ("Verses About Moscow," 1916, stanza 2); slightly "retranslated" by WTV.

69 The "Carpenter" link of the N. K. Krupskaya Brigade —I have invented these names. A Pioneer brigade of forty-fifty member was subdivided into links of ten members each. Each brigade was named after a revolutionary leader; each link was named after tool or field of production. Pioneers were divided by age into Young Pioneers and Little Octobrists. The Komsomol (Communist Youth Organization) kept young people from ages fourteen to twenty-three. Sharpshooting and first aid would indeed have been some of the skills which Elena would have learned there. As mentioned in "Opus 40," she was expelled from the Komsomol in 1935.

69 Details on the Komsomol and the Pioneers —In part from Samuel Northrup Harper, *Civic Training in Soviet Russia* (Chicago: The University of Chicago Press, 1929).

70 "We noticed two black and blue marks on the neck of Elena Konstantinovskaya . . ." —Siegelbaum and Sokolov, loc. cit.; verbatim except that Elena's name has been substituted for that of another girl, and Liza Ivanova has become Vera Ivanova.

71 "Isolde's secret song was her marvelous beauty . . ."—Gottfried von Strassburg, *Tristan;*

with the *Tristan* of Thomas, trans. A. T. Hatto (New York: Penguin, 1975 repr. of 1967 rev. ed.; orig. trans. 1960; Strassburg's poem *ca.* 1210), p. 148, grossly "retranslated" by WTV.

MAIDEN VOYAGE

76 Epigraph: "What child is there . . ." —Hanna Reitsch, *The Sky My Kingdom: Memoirs of the Famous German WWII Test-Pilot,* trans. Lawrence Wilson (London: Greenhill Books, 1991 expanded repr. of 1955 English ed., but [p. 219] "I wrote this book after I had been released from one and a half years as a prisoner in the United States," hence my approximate dating of 1947).

77 Details on German planes, rocket engines, etc. (most of them exaggerated and distorted by me) —Dear and Foot, entry on V-weapons; Reitsch, various minor details on gliders and flight experiences; *Jane's Fighting Aircraft of World War II* (New York: Military Press, 1989 repr. of 1946–47 ed.), entries on German air power and German aero engines.

77 The Geco 7.65 cartridges —Since the plot in part turns on this matter, it may be worth a note. According to Paul (op. cit.), "the Poles" massacred at Katyń "were quickly shot behind the head at close range, probably with a German-made pistol—the light 7.65 mm Walther . . . considered the finest police pistol in the world" (p. 110). "The caliber, Geco 7.65 millimeter, did not fit the Tokarev or Nagan pistols generally carried by the NKVD. It did fit the Walther . . ." (p. 206). Indeed, the Tokarev and the Nagan (often spelled Nagant) were both 7.62 mm in caliber. The table of small arms in I. C. B. Dear and M. R. D. Foot, ed., *The Oxford Companion to World War II* (New York: Oxford University Press, 1995; p. 1016) lists no Soviet 7.65 mm. weapon whatsoever. Inexplicably, that is also the case for German weapons (ibid., p. 1014). The only two German pistols listed, the Parabellum P08 and the Walther P38, are both 9 mm. It would seem, then, that the 7.65 caliber used at Katyń was hardly a favorite with either side. However, the table "Characteristics of German World War II Service Pistols" in Edward Clinton Ezell's famous *Small Arms of the World: A Basic Manual of Small Arms,* 12th ed. (New York: Stackpole Books, 1983; p. 500) has eight entries, the first two being the P08 and the P38 just mentioned, the third being the 7.63 mm Mauser 1932, and the other five *all* sporting the 7.65 mm caliber. These are: the Mauser 1910, the Mauser HSc, the Sauer 38, the Walther PP and the Walther PPK. (It was with one of these latter two models which Hitler committed suicide in 1945.) In the equivalent Soviet table (p. 696), four models of pistols and revolvers appear, including the two already mentioned in Dear and Foot. The remaining two (the Makarov and the Stechkin) are both 9 mm and seem to be largely postwar in any event. In short, on the information at hand, it would seem that Paul's statement is correct: The Poles were murdered with German-made bullets. Large quantities of the Geco 7.65 mm. were sold to the Baltic countries and perhaps even to the USSR during the interwar years. The massacre was certainly committed by the Soviets, not the Germans.

77 Heidegger: "The upward glance passes aloft toward the sky, and yet it remains below on the earth" —Martin Heidegger, *Poetry, Language, Thought,* trans. Albert Hofstadter (New York: Harper & Row / Colophon, 1971), p. 220 (". . . Poetically Man Dwells . . . ," a lecture given in 1951).

WHEN PARZIVAL KILLED THE RED KNIGHT

81 Epigraph: "'Twas in olden times when eagles screamed . . ." —Lee M. Hollander, trans., *The Poetic Edda,* 2nd rev. ed. (Austin: University of Texas Press, 1987 repr. of 1962 ed.), p. 180 ("Helgakvitha Hundingsbana" I, stanza 1, slightly "retranslated" by WTV).

81 "His new armor, which was so red that it made one's eyes red just to see it" —This description of the Red Knight's armor is based on Wolfram von Eschenbach, *Parzival: A*

Romance of the Middle Ages, trans. Helen M. Mustard and Charles E. Passage (New York: Random House / Vintage, 1961; orig. German poem finished *ca.* 1210), p. 81 (Book III). The Red Knight was Ither of Kukumerlant.

82 *Mein Kampf:* "And simultaneous with him stands the victory of the reified Idea, which has ever been, and ever shall be, anti-Semitic" — *Meyers Lexikon,* vol. 5 (1937), p. 711. (I have compressed and added a "stands" to the eye-glazing original: ". . . *und zugleich auch mit ihm den Sieg des Gedankens der schaffenden Arbeit, die selbst ewig antisemitsch war und ewig antisemitsch sein wird.*")

82 The black-and-white plates: Adolf Hitler I and II —Same vol., following p. 1248.

82 Plates on "Garten" and "Germanen" —Ibid.

82 National Socialism entry—Ibid., vol. 8, 1940.

82 Parzival, Galogandres and King Clamidê —Eschenbach, pp. 113–15.

OPUS 40

85 Epigraph: "There is nothing in you which fails to send a wave of joy and fierce passion inside me . . ." —Sofiya Khentova, *Udivitelyenui Shostakovich* (Saint Petersburg: Variant, 1993), p. 117 (2nd letter of 15 June 1934), slightly "retranslated" by WTV.

85 For early Soviet names for Leningrad landmarks, in this story, in "And I'd Dry My Salty Hair" and in "The Palm Tree of Deborah," I have made occasional use of A. Radó, comp. [issued by the Society for Cultural Relations of the Soviet Union with Foreign Countries], *Guide-Book to the Soviet Union* (Berlin: Neuer Deutscher Verlag, 1928), pp. 197–364 (entry on Leningrad).

86 Physical appearance of Shostakovich at this time —After the illustration in Detlef Gojowy, *Schostakowitsch* (Hamburg: Rowohlt, Bildmonographien, 2002 repr. of 1983 ed.), p. 49 ("Porträt Schostakowitschs aus den Jahren 1933 bis 1935").

87 Shostakovich's letters to Elena, and various other background details —Based on Khentova, pp. 114–37, 150–59, 168–70, 245–46, trans. for WTV by Sergi Mineyev (16,746 words at 16.777 cents per word, for a total cost of $2,846.82).

88 Composition dates for various movements of Opus 40 —Laurel E. Fay, *Shostakovich: A Life* (New York: Oxford University Press, 2000), p. 80.

88 Relative evenness of two themes from Opus 40 —Harold Barlow and Sam Morgenstern, *A Dictionary of Musical Themes* (London and Tonbridge: Ernest Benn Limited, 1974 repr. of 1949 ed.), p. 438.

90 S. Khentova: "In contrast to Nina Vasilievna . . ." —Khentova (Mineyev), original, p. 115, Mineyev p. 1.

91 Shostakovich: The First String Quartet is "a particular exercise in the form of a quartet" — *Musik und Gesellschaft,* vol. 34, no. 9 (September 1981), pp. 549–52 (Ekkehard Ochs, "Das Streichquartett im Schaffen von Dmitri Schostakowitch: Zum 75. Geburtstag des Komponisten am 25. September), p. 549 (trans. by WTV).

91 Shostakovich to T. Glivenko: "I have a very clever wife, oh, yes—very clever . . ." —Khentova, p. 131, Mineyev p. 12; Shostakovich-ized by WTV.

91 Shostakovich: "When a critic for *Worker and Theater* or for *The Evening Red Gazette*". . . — Quoted in Richard Taruskin, *Defining Russia Musically: Historical and Hermeneutical Essays* (Princeton, New Jersey: Princeton University Press, 2000 rev. repr. of 1977 ed.), pp. 480–81 (from *Sovetskaya Muzika,* no. 3 [1933], p. 121).

92 E. Mravinsky: "This masquerade imparts the spurious impression that Shostakovich is being emotional . . ." —Khentova (Mineyev), original p. 114, Mineyev p. 1; slightly reworded for contextual clarity by WTV.

92 Shostakovich: "I can't forgive myself for not kidnapping my golden Elenochka and bringing her to Baku with me" and "As soon as I'm back in my Lyalka's arms I'll have the strength to resolve everything" —After Khentova (Mineyev), original p. 116, Mineyev p. 2 (letter from DDS to EEK, 15 June 1934).

93 "The brilliance here is sinister rather than exhibitionistic" —Emanuel Ax, program notes to the CBS "Masterworks" recording of Shostakovich's Trio (Opus 67) and Piano Sonata (Opus 40); produced by James Mallinson (code MX 44664); p. 3.
94 Distinction between *motif, leitmotiv* and *theme* —Based partially on a chat with ethnomusicologist Philip Bohlman in September 2003; after thinking for a moment, Professor Bohlman advised me that "theme" would be the right word to use in connection with Shostakovich.
94 Footnote: Moser's entries on Shostakovich, Sousa, Serbian music, "Glasunow" et al —H. J. Moser's *Musik Lexikon* of 1933 (Berlin-Schöneberg, Max Hesses Verlag, 1935).
95 Ekkehard Ochs on dialectic in Shostakovich —Ochs, p. 551 (trans. by WTV).
95 Shostakovich to Konstantinovskaya: "I try to stop loving you . . ." —Same document, original pp. 119–20; Mineyev p. 4; slightly "retranslated" by WTV.
96 Arrests "by the tens of thousands" —Conquest's figure, in his chapter on the Kirov affair. Kirov was murdered by Stalin.
96 A. Ferkelman on Shostakovich: "I never succeeded in getting any other pianist to take such fast tempi . . ." —Elizabeth Wilson, *Shostakovich: A Life Remembered* (London: Faber and Faber, 1995 repr. of 1994 ed.), p. 105 (testimony of Arnold Ferkelman, slightly "retranslated" by WTV.
96 "I don't believe that I'll be yours . . ." —pp. 122–23, Mineyev, p. 6 (25 June 1934), slightly "retranslated" by WTV.
98 Shostakovich on Opus 40: "A certain great breakthrough" —Ochs, p. 549 (trans. WTV).
98 Shostakovich to Konstantinovskaya: "Why did I meet you? . . ." —Khentova (Mineyev), original, p. 122, Mineyev, p. 6 (1st, short letter of 25 June 1934).

OPERATION MAGIC FIRE

99 Epigraph —Shostakovich and Volkov, p. 94.

Many of my visual descriptions of the Condor Legion and its acts are based on photographs in the Ullstein archive in Berlin.

101 Wotan: "For so goes the god from you; so he kisses your godhead away" —Libretto booklet to the Solti version of Wagner's "Siegfried" (James King, Régine Crespin et al performing; Wiener Staatsopernchor, Wiener Philharmoniker, 1985), p. 130 (Act III, Scene 3; German text trans. by WTV).
101 How Loki gave birth to ogres —*Poetic Edda,* p. 139 ("Voluspá hin skamma," stanza 14).
102 Names and descriptions of various German airplane formations —After a diagram in *Meyers Lexikon,* vol. 4 (Leipzig: Bibliographisches Institut AG., 1938), pp. 193–94: "Fliegen im Verband."
104 *Meyers Lexikon,* 1938: "He is no dictator . . ." —Vol. 5 (1938), p. 1276, trans. and made slightly less ponderous by WTV (end of entry on Adolf Hitler, which then concludes with an encomium from Goebbels).

AND I'D DRY MY SALTY HAIR

105 Epigraph —Combined from *The Complete Poems of Anna Akhmatova,* expanded ed., trans. Judith Hemschemeyer, ed. Roberta Reeder (Boston: Zephyr Press, 1997), p. 521 ("At the Edge of the Sea" 1914), and *Anna Akhmatova: Selected Poems,* trans. D. M. Thomas (New York: Penguin Books, 1985), p. 31 (same poem, trans. as "By the Seashore"), "retranslated" by WTV as "At the Seashore."

For many of the details in Akhmatova's life I've relied on Roberta Reeder's irritatingly reverential *Anna Akhmatova, Poet and Prophet* (New York: St. Martin's Press, 1994). References to Akhmatova's heterosexual affairs are in the main based on the truth as I've understood it; references to more bizarre sexual practices are the fabrication of my narrator, Comrade Alexandrov.

105 "The equivalent of ten Stalin tanks" —An anachronism; Stalin tanks would not have been available at this juncture. But I wanted to mention Stalin's name as close to the opening as possible.
106 "One of her postwar odes": "Where Stalin is, is freedom . . ." —Akhmatova (Hemschemeyer), p. 879 (Appendix, "In Praise of Peace," 1949), "retranslated" by WTV.
107 Footnote: Punin's diary —Op. cit., p. 72 (undated entry for 1921, before 28 July).
107 Punin on art casting itself across life "like a shadow" —Ibid, p. 203 (entry for 24 February 1944).
107 Shostakovich: "Basically, I can't bear having poetry written about my music" —Shostakovich and Volkov, p. 273.
108 N. Berdayev: "The putrefied air of a hothouse" —Quoted in Reeder, p. 25.
111 Gumilyev's affairs with "Blue Star" (Elena Debouchet) and Tanya Adamovich —Reeder, p. 62.
111 N. Nedobrovo: "Her calmness in confessing pain and weakness" —Ibid., p. 88, slightly abridged.
112 Excerpts from "Poem Without a Hero" —All from Akhmatova (Hemschemeyer), pp. 563–64 (I.4.405, 407–11, 415, 418), "retranslated" by WTV.
113 L. K. Chukovskaya: Akhmatova's fate was "something even greater than her own person" —Lydia Chukovskaya, *The Akhmatova Journals*, vol. 1, 1938–1941 (Evanston, Illinois: Northwestern University Press, 2002 repr. of 1994 Farrar, Straus & Giroux ed.; orig. Russian ed. 1989), pp. 6–7.
114 Tale of the "Stalin Route" —Von Geldern and Stites, pp. 258–61.
114 Addresses of main places of detention (mentioned here and in "Opus 110") —Dr. Cronid Lubarsky, ed., *USSR News Brief: Human Rights: List of Political Prisoners in the USSR as on 1 May 1982*, 4th issue (Brussels: Cahiers du Samizdat, 1982), p. 37.
115 Chukovskaya: "She herself, her words, her deeds . . ." —Op. cit., p. 6.
116 Akhmatova: "How early autumn came this year." —Ibid., p. 6.
116 Akhmatova: "It's extremely good that I'll be dead soon." —Ibid., p. 14.
117 Masaryk on Dostoyevsky and on Russian atheism —Thomas Garrigue Masaryk, *The Spirit of Russia* (New York: Barnes and Noble, Inc., 1967; original German ed., 1912), vol. 3, pp. 49, 10.
118 Gumilyev's nightmares —Diary entry quoted in Reeder, p. 61.
119 Gumilyev: "Your cold, slender hands." —Ibid., p. 61 (trans. of "Iambic Pentameter," 1913).

CASE WHITE

121 Epigraph —*Three Märchen of E. T. A. Hoffmann*, trans. Charles E. Passage (Columbia: University of South Carolina Press, 1971), p. 324 ("Master Flea: A Fairytale in Seven Adventures," composed 1822, published 1908).
121 "The most spectacular scenario ever written": "Germany can no longer be a passive onlooker! Every political possibility has been exhausted; we've decided on a solution by force!" —Watt, pp. 514 (Hitler to Sir Nevile Henderson, 29 August 1939), 534 (Hitler's Directive No. 1 for the Conduct of the War, 31 August 1939).

OPERATION BARBAROSSA

123 Epigraph —Marie-Louise von Franz, *Shadow and Evil in Fairy Tales,* rev. ed. (Boston: Shambala Publications [A C. G. Jung Foundation Book], 1995), p. 45.

Some of the technical terms relating to telephones have been extracted (and, I hope, used correctly) from the *Great Soviet Encyclopedia,* vol. 25, p. 476 (entry on telephone communication). These words and information have to a lesser extent also been deployed in "Steel in Motion" and in "The Palm Tree of Deborah"'s description of the Leningrad broadcast of the Seventh Symphony.

125 "Lyalka, you filled my heart until it was ready to explode." —Closely after Khentova, p. 123, Mineyev p. 6 (letter of 25 June 1934).

THE SLEEPWALKER

126 Epigraph —George Bernard Shaw, *The Perfect Wagnerite: A Commentary on the Niblung's Ring* (New York: Dover Publications, 1967, repr. of 1923 4th ed.), p. 2.

126 Gunnar, Hogni and Guthrún —So they are named in the "Greenlandish Lay of Atli" in the *Elder Edda,* from which the *Nibelungenlied* in part derives. In the latter version of the tale, Gunnar is Gunther, Hogni becomes the balefully noble Hagen, and Guthrún, who never wanted her brothers to come to their destruction, is now Kriemhild, who lures them to it in order to take revenge for their murder of Siegfried.

127 Göring: "The Czechs, a vile race of dwarfs without any culture . . ." —Quoted in John Toland, *Adolf Hitler* (New York: Bantam, 1976), p. 646.

129 Hitler's interest in the directing at Bayreuth —Albert Speer, *Inside the Third Reich,* trans. Richard and Clara Winston (New York: Avon, 1970, trans. of 1969 German ed.), p. 185.

131 "We're getting old, Kubizek," &c (conversation at Bayreuth) —After Toland, p. 854 (slightly altered).

131 "Siegfried and Gunnar hadn't even laid eyes on the princesses they pined for" —So we infer from the *Nibelungenlied,* in which Gunnar has actually become Gunther, as already noted; I have kept his Norse name to retain consistency with the opening of "The Sleepwalker."

139 "On the day following the end of the Bayreuth Festival, I'm gripped by a great sadness . . ." —From the "secret conversations," quoted in William Shirer, *Rise and Fall of the Third Reich* (New York: Simon and Schuster, 1960), p. 102.

139 The golden figures, the far-famed ones . . ." —*Voluspá* (The Prophecy of the Seeress"), stanza 60; in *The Poetic Edda,* p. 12.

THE PALM TREE OF DEBORAH

140 Epigraph: Shostakovich on musical means and ends —Fay, p. 258.

140 Russian casualties of the Leningrad siege —Contemporary Soviet sources estimated around 1,000,000 victims. Western figures were substantially lower; usually they claimed 6–700,000 killed. However, as late as the end of Shostakovich's life, the American historian William Craig wrote that "more than a million besieged Russian civilians had starved to death during the nightmarish winter of 1941" alone. —*Enemy at the Gates: The Battle for Stalingrad* (New York: Reader's Digest Press / E. P. Dutton & Co., 1973), p. 18. The *Great Soviet Encyclopedia* [*Bol'shaia Sovetskaia Entisklopediia,* ed. A. M. Prokhorov, 3rd ed. (Moscow: Sovetskaia Entisklopediia Publishing House, 1973)], ed. and trans. Jean Paradise et al. (New York: Macmillan, Inc., 1976), settled on the following statistics: 641,803 people died of hunger and 17,000 of bombings and shellings. The Germans dropped

150,000 artillery shells on Leningrad during the siege, 100,000 incendiary bombs, 5,000 high explosives (vol. 14, p. 383; entry on Leningrad). I decided to use the higher figures for reasons analogous to my use of Gerstein's inflated figures on the Holocaust in "Clean Hands" (see note, below); this is what people would have believed at the time.

142 A. Glazunov: "Then this is no place for you. Shostakovich is one of the brightest hopes for our art" —Wilson, p. 29 (testimony of Mikhail Gnessin, slightly "retranslated" by WTV).

143 N. L. Komarovskaya: "A small pale youth . . ." —Ibid., p. 17.

143 Cousin Tania: "His compositions are very good . . ." —Victor Ilyich Seroff, in collaboration with Nadejda Galli-Shohat, aunt of the composer, *Dmitri Shostakovich: The Life and Background of a Soviet Composer* (New York: Alfred A. Knopf. 1943), p. 102 (letter from Tania to Nadejda Galli-Shohat).

147 N. Malko: "As compressed as chamber music," "he certainly knows what he wants," etc. —Somewhat after Wilson, pp. 48–49. The anecdotes of the shoes and of the mating behavior of insects (the second one slightly altered from what actually took place) have been moved here for the sake of narrative effect. Both events occurred during his later Kharkov recital with Malko.

148 Comrade M. Kaganovich: "The ground must tremble . . ." —Ian Kershaw and Moshe Lewin, ed., *Stalinism and Nazism: Dictatorships in Comparison* (Cambridge, U.K.: Cambridge University Press, 1997), p. 45 (Ronald Grigor Suny, "Stalin and His Stalinism: Power and Authority in the Soviet Union, 1930–53).

148 *Proletarian Musician:* "His work will infallibly reach a dead end." —Fay, p. 55 (slightly altered).

151 Shostakovich to Sollertinsky: "Overcoming the resistance of an orchestra . . ." —Closely after Shostakovich and Volkov, p. 75 (another context).

152 Mitya to Glikman: Joke about Stalin & Co. in the sinking steamship —Von Geldern and Stites, p. 329 ("Anecdotes").

154 Shostakovich to *The New York Times:* "Thus we regard Scriabin . . ." —Seroff, p. 157 *(New York Times,* December 20, 1931).

154 *Rabochii i Teatr:* "A last warning to its composer" —Wilson, p. 90. The 1979 edition of the *Great Soviet Encyclopedia,* which came out after the composer had won several Stalin Prizes and then safely died, confined itself to the dry statement that this ballet as well as "Dyanmiada" "did not remain in the theatrical repertoire."

154 *Great Soviet Encyclopedia:* "In the 1930s, Soviet musical culture . . ." —*Bol'shaia Sovetskaia Entisklopediia,* ed. A. M. Prokhorov, 3rd ed. (Moscow: Sovetskaia Entisklopediia Publishing House, 1973), ed. and trans. Jean Paradise et al. (New York: Macmillan, Inc., 1976), USSR volume, entry on music.

154 A. Akhmatova: "In this place, peerless beauties quarrel . . ." —Hemschemeyer version, "retranslated" by WTV.

156 Footnote on "Thousands Cheer" —This movie played at the Astor in September 1943. Bosley Crowther of *The New York Times* described it as a crowd-pleaser.

156 Shostakovich's sister, Mariyusha, to their aunt: "Our greatest fault is that we worshipped him . . ." —Seroff, p. 180, slightly abridged.

157 A. Akhmatova: "Without hangman and gallows . . ." —Ibid., p. 665 ("Why did you poison the water . . . ," 1935), "retranslated" by WTV.

157 "Music's Kandinsky" —A two-page parallel between Shostakovich and Kandinsky is drawn by Gawriil Glikman (München), "Schostakowitsch, wie ich ihn kannte," in Hilmar Schmalenberg, ed., *Schostakowitsch-Gesellschaft e. V. (Hrsg): Schostakowitsch in Deutschland [Schostakowitsch-Studien, Band I]* (Berlin: Verlag Ernst Kuhn, Studia Slavica Musica, Band 13, 1998), pp. 189–90.

159 D. Zhitomirsky: "The despair of the lost soul" —Wilson, p. 95.

161 Shostakovich to the press: "I want to write a Soviet *Ring of the Nibelung*!" —Seroff, p. 191 (interview with Leonid and Pyotr Tur; exclamation point added).

161 Shostakovich to Nina: "All of her music has as its purpose . . ." —Seroff, p. 252 (actually, from DDS's statement "About My Opera").
162 Nadezhda Welter: "Sometimes one was overcome with a feeling of cold fear . . ." —Wilson, pp. 98–99.
165 Shostakovich to Nina: "Let's at least get to the recapitulation . . ." —Loosely after Shostakovich and Volkov, p. 163 (the original context was the symphonies of Glazunov).
166 Shostakovich to Nina: "Lady Macbeth's crimes are a protest . . ." —Richard Taruskin, *Defining Russia Musically: Historical and Hermeneutical Essays* (Princeton, New Jersey: Princeton University Press, 2000, paperback repr. of 1997 ed.), p. 501 (quoting a "program essay" by Shostakovich).
166 Shostakovich to Nina: "Can music attack evil?" —Shostakovich and Volkov, p. 234.
166 Shostakovich to Nina: "And Sergei, you see, my music strips him . . ." —Loosely after Seroff, p. 253 (from DDS's statement "About My Opera").
168 Shostakovich to E. Konstantinovskaya: "Well, Elena, you see how lucky it is that you didn't marry me . . ." —Wilson, p. 110 (quoted from Sofiya Khentova; slightly altered).
168 Shostakovich to E. Konstantinovskaya: "Prisoners are wretches to be pitied, and you shouldn't kick somebody when he's down" —After Shostakovich and Volkov, p. 110.
169 V. Shebalin: "I consider that Shostakovich is the greatest genius . . ." —Wilson, p. 114 (Alisa Shebalina).
170 Shostakovich to Glikman: "The things you love too much perish" —After Shostakovich and Volkov, p. 78. The composer goes on: "You have to treat everything with irony, especially the things you hold dear."
170 Tukhachevsky: "One should practice large-scale repression and employ incentives" —Chaliand, p. 915 ("Counterinsurgency").
172 *Pravda* editorial on Shostakovich: "He ignored the demand of Soviet culture . . ." —Seroff, pp. 206–07.
173 Tukhachevsky: "I always get whatever I ask for." —Very loosely based on words attributed to him in another context, in Alan Clark, *Barbarossa: The Russian-German Conflict 1941–45* (New York: Quill, 1985, repr. of 1965 ed., with new intro.), p. 33.
176 Tukhachevsky at the time of his arrest and execution: "I would have been better off as a violinist" —Shostakovich and Volkov, p. 97.
176 Shostakovich's interrogation —I have made it far more brutal than it was. One source proposes that it might never have happened: An intensely sensitive man, Shostakovich may have so feared his imminent demise that he lost his ability to discriminate between what happened in fact and what only occurred in his tormented imagination. (This, again, was a common syndrome under the Terror.) —http:/www.siue.edu/~aho/musov/basner/basner.html, 6/20/2002 ("'You Must Remember!'" Shostakovich's alleged interrogation by the NKVD in 1937," p. 3).
177 The Fifth Symphony as "a Soviet artist's creative reply to just criticism" —We're told that this phrase was not Shostakovich's, but he acquiesced in the happy suggestion.
179 Increase in the productive capacity of Leningrad since 1913 —*Great Soviet Encyclopedia*, vol. 14, p. 385. However, the benchmark year was actually 1940, not 1941. I imagine that the accuracy (such as it was) of the statistic is unaffected.
179 "The critics" on Shostakovich's Sixth Symphony: "Nothing more than the recapitulation of a football match" —After Isaak Glikman, *Story of a Friendship: The Letters of Dmitry Shostakovich to Isaak Glikman 1941–1975, with a Commentary by Isaak Glikman*, trans. Anthony Philips (Ithaca, New York: Cornell University Press, 2001; original Russian ed. 1993), p. xxxii.
179 Definition of a family: "A socio-biological community . . ." — *The Soviet Way of Life* (Moscow: Progress Publishers, 1974), p. 347 (ch. 8, "The Soviet Family").
179 S. Volkov: "The feelings of the intellectual . . ." —Solomon Volkov, *Saint Petersburg: A Cultural History*, trans. Antonina W. Bouis (New York: Free Press, 1995), p. 423.
180 Description of the Eighth Symphony —Based in part on my hearing of it, and in part

on the score itself: Dmitri Schostakowitsch, *8. Symphonie Op. 65*, ed. nr. 2221 (Hamburg: Musikverlage Hans Sikorski, Taschenpartitur / Pocket Score; "SovMuz" ["Sowjetische Musik"] ser., n.d., 1991?; orig. comp. 1943).

180 Footnote: *Great Soviet Encyclopedia:* "The Communist Party and the Soviet government . . ." —Vol. 4, p. 334, entry on Great Patriotic War.

180 Hitler: *"Skizze B: Heeresgruppe Nord . . ."* —These maps, and the German military symbols referred to in this story and in "Opus 110," "Breakout" and "The Last Field-Marshal" are derived from the reproductions of orders of battle in Kurt Mehner, ed., *Die Geheimen Tagesberichte der Deutsche Wehrmachstführung im Zweiten Weltkrieg 1939–45* (Osnabrück: Biblio Verlag, 1987).

184 A. Zhdanov: "Either the working-class of Leningrad will be turned into slaves . . ." —Alexander Werth, *Russia at War 1941–45* (New York: E. P. Dutton & Co., 1964), p. 305 (trans. from Pavlov, *Leningrad v. blokade*).

185 *Current Biography*: "Early in 1941, Shostakovich completed his Seventh Symphony . . ." —Vol. 2, no. 5, p. 71 (May 1941, article on Shostakovich).

185 N. Mandelstam: "The whole process of composition . . ." —Nadezhda Mandelstam, *Hope Against Hope*, trans. Max Hayward (New York: Modern Library, 1999, repr. of 1970 trans.), p. 71.

186 Footnote: The two-note "Stalin motif"—Described in Ian MacDonald, *The New Shostakovich* (Boston: Northeastern University Press, 1990), p. 157.

186 Mravinsky: "Everything has been heard in advance . . ." —Wilson, p. 140.

187 Shostakovich to *New Masses:* "The first part of the symphony . . ." —Seroff, p. 237. I have no knowledge that Glikman wrote this, but he did compose such things for Shostakovich from time to time.

188 Party activists to Shostakovich: "You will be called to the front when you're required" —After Seroff, p. 236 (cabled dispatch to *New Masses*, 28 October 1941).

188 Shostakovich to the "Party activists": "Only by fighting can we save humanity from destruction" —Reeder, p. 255 (Shostakovich's written application; abridged and Shostakovich-ized by WTV).

188 Shostakovich's speech of recantation: "There can be no music without ideology, comrades! Music is no longer an end in itself, but a vital weapon in the struggle" —Abridged from Seroff, pp. 160–61 *(New York Times* interview, to which I have added the word *comrades*).

189 Shostakovich: "If they hadn't shot Tukhachevsky . . ." —Loosely after *Testimony: The Memoirs of Dmitry Shostakovich as Related to and Edited by Solomon Volkov*, trans. Antonina W. Bouis (New York: Limelight Editions 2004, repr. of 1979 Harper & Row ed.), p. 103.

190 "I, I, I want to write about our time . . ." —After Shostakovich and Volkov, p. 154.

192 Shostakovich to himself: "I am a person . . . with a very weak character . . ." —After Khentova (Mineyev); original, p. 126, Mineyev, p. 9.

194 Shostakovich to Volkov: "I wrote my Seventh Symphony very quickly . . ." —Shostakovich and Volkov, p. 154.

194 Shostakovich to Glikman: Composition dates for the movements of the Seventh Symphony —Glikman, p. 3 (letter of 30 November 1941). My dates for the completion of the other two movements also follow this source (see p. 6; letter of 4 January 1942).

194 G. V. Yudin: "After a short pause . . ." —Wilson, p. 37.

194 L. Lebedinsky: "Frightening in its helplessness" —Wilson, p. 346.

195 Reduction of the bread ration on 2 September to a fourth of its previous level —*Great Soviet Encyclopedia*, vol. 14, p. 383 (entry on Leningrad).

197 Shostakovich to Glikman: "I suppose that critics with nothing better to do . . ." —Glikman, p. xxxiv, somewhat Shostakovich-ized.

197 "For the first time we can cry openly. Not one of us here hasn't lost somebody . . ." —After Shostakovich and Glikman, pp. 136, 135.

198 Zhukov's strategic Muse: "Stalin will be the savior of Europe" —Actually, Zhukov deplored Stalin's military incompetence.

200 Akhmatova: "In Pushkin's day one did not expose everything about oneself" —Chukovskaya, p. 15; slightly "retranslated" by WTV.

203 Shostakovich to S. Volkov: "Fear of death may be the most intense emotion of all" —After Shostakovich and Glikman, p. 180.

204 Shostakovich: "It's always easier to believe what we want to believe . . . The mentality of a chicken." —Ibid., p. 199.

208 Activists to Shostakovich: " . . . you're waiting for the Germans" —Punin, p. 207 (entry for 30 July 1944, accusations overheard on returning to Leningrad from evacuation; slightly altered). Shostakovich was actually evacuated as early as 1 October, but because I have wanted to associate him with the beginning of a Leningrad winter, I delayed his departure for two weeks.

208 Shostakovich's mother: "Of course Mitya . . ." —Seroff, p. 175 (letter from Sonia Shostakovich to her daughter Zoya, *ca.* 1929).

208 Various information on troop strengths, casualties, military organization, etc. —John Ellis, *World War II: A Statistical Survey* (New York: Facts on File, 1983). Sometimes these figures have been simplified by me for narrative purposes. For instance, when I write in reference to the Red Air Force "four regiments to a division, two divisions to a corps," I omit to state that this was true as of 1943, and that a division might sometimes be three regiments instead of four, a corps anywhere from two to four divisions. Ellis's data make occasional appearances not only in this story but also in "Breakout" and "The Last Field-Marshal."

214 Doubling of Leningrad's bread ration in February 1942 —*Great Soviet Encyclopedia*, vol. 14, p. 383 (entry on Leningrad).

215 Olga Berggolts: "This man is stronger than Hitler!" —Harrison E. Salisbury, *The Nine Hundred Days: The Siege of Leningrad* (New York: Harper & Row, 1969), p. 522.

215 The émigré Seroff: "Today the 'average' American . . ." —Op. cit., p. 3.

215 Quotations from the Seventh in the *Dictionary of Musical Themes* —Barlow and Morgenstern, p. 438.

215 The bourgeois critic Layton: "This naive stroke of pictorialism . . ." —Robert Simpson, ed., *The Symphony* (New York: Drake Publishers, Inc., 1972), vol. 2 ("Mahler to the Present Day"), p. 208 (article on Shostakovich).

215 The disdainful intellectuals —Here is one of them, discoursing on the so-called "masterpiece tone": "Its reduction to absurdity is manifest today through the later symphonies of Shostakovich. Advertised frankly and cynically as owing their particular character to a political directive imposed on their author by state disciplinary action, they have been broadcast throughout the United Nations as models of patriotic expression." —Virgil Thomas, "Masterpieces," 25 June 1944, in Sam Morgenstern, ed., *Composers on Music: An Anthology of Composers' Writings from Palestrina to Copland* (New York: Greenwood Press, 1956), p. 496.

215 Moses Cordovero: "God does not behave as a human being behaves . . ." —Daniel C. Matt, comp. and trans., *The Essential Kabbalah: The Heart of Jewish Mysticism* (San Francisco: HarperSanFrancisco, 1996), p. 83 ("The Palm Tree of Deborah," in "The Ten Sefirot").

216 Glikman: The "decent-sized divan," &c —Op. cit., p. xli. I have changed "steal" to "shoot."

216 Shostakovich to Glikman: "You know, Isaak Davidovich . . ." —Loc. cit., but I have de-Glikmanized this into something much more downcast and hesitant.

217 Wolfgang Dömling: "It is because of this historic aura . . ." —Liner notes to the Sony Classical recording of the Seventh (New York Philharmonic, Leonard Bernstein conducting, recording in New York City, 22–23 October 1962).

219 Hitler's order: "Stage 1, make a junction with the Finns . . ." —General Walter Warlimont, *Inside Hitler's Headquarters 1939–45*, trans. R. H. Barry (Novato, California: Presidio Press repr. of 1964 ed.; original German ed. 1962), p. 254.
219 Leningrad as "that city which Dostoyevsky likens to a consumptive girl blushing into beauty briefly and inexplicably" —Somewhat after Fyodor Dostoyevsky, *Uncle's Dream and Other Stories*, trans. David McDuff (New York: Penguin Classics, 1989), p. 75 ("White Nights").

UNTOUCHED

222 Epigraph —Republic of Poland, Ministry of Foreign Affairs, *German Occupation of Poland: Extract of Note Addressed to the Allied and Neutral Powers* (New York: Greystone Press, *ca.* 1941), p. 80 (Appendix 1, proclamation of October 28, 1939, by Governor-General Frank).
223 Official military history: "The church is untouched" —*Der Sieg in Polen*, herausgegeben vom Oberkommando der Wehrmacht; with a foreword by Field-Marshal Keitel himself (Berlin: Zeitgeschichte-Verlag, 1940), p. 129. The actual word used is *unversehrt.*
224 Emblems of Panzer divisions, 1941–42 —Werner Haupt, *A History of the Panzer Troops 1916–1945*, trans. Dr. Edward Force (West Chester, Pennsylvania: Schiffer Publishing, Ltd., 1990; original German ed. 1989), p. 178.
225 Depictions of runes —Rudolf Koch, *The Book of Signs, Which Contains All Manner of Symbols Used from the Earliest Times to the Middle Ages by Primitive Peoples and Early Christians*, trans. Dydyan Holland (New York: Dover Publications, 1955, repr. of 1930 ed.), pp. 100–04.
226 Various descriptions of Third Reich architecture in Berlin, and its wartime and postwar fate —Based on Speer, chs. 5, 6 and 10; and on photographs and text in Mark R. McGee, *Berlin from 1925 to the Present: A Visual and Historical Documentation* (New York: The Overlook Press, 2002, abr. repr. of 2000 German ed.).
226 Göring: "The greatest staircase in the world" —Speer, p. 192.

FAR AND WIDE MY COUNTRY STRETCHES

228 Epigraph —Louis Harris Cohen, *The Cultural-Political Traditions and Developments of the Soviet Cinema 1917–1972* (New York: Arno Press, 1974), p. 93 (Karmen on Mikhail Slutsky's "One Day of War," 1942).

Some details and dates of Roman Karmen's life derive from the film retrospective catalogue (dedicated to him) published by the Modern Art Museum in New York, 1973. Others come from *Roman Karmen: Retrospektive zur XIV. Internationalen Leipziger Dokumentar- und Kurzfilmwoche* (Leipzig: Staaatliches Filmarchiv der DDR, 1971). I have also made use of the many photographs in the Ognev book, which has been cited already in the Käthe Kollwitz story. No doubt I should have used *Roman Karmen v vospominankyakh sovremennikov* (Moscow: Iskusstvo, 1983), but never got around to it. I am sorry to say that I have also failed to consult the undoubtedly informative *Roman Karmen* by N. Kolesnikova, G. Senchakova and T. Slepneva (Moscow: 1959). Miscellaneous career information on Karmen and L. O. Arnshtam derive from S. I. Yutkevich et al., ed., *Kinoslovar v dvukh tomakh*, vol. 1 (A–L) (no place of publication; prob. Moscow: Izdatelstvo "Sovestskaya Entsiklopediya," 1966), pp. 672–74 and 112–13, respectively.

229 Roman Karmen and Elena Konstanintovskaya seem to have married in Spain sometime 1936 and 1937, since Konstantinovskaya is said to have "brought back a husband from Spain." When they divorced is unknown to me, but it might well have been as soon as 1938 or 1939, given the long trips which Karmen set out on almost immediately

after their return to the USSR. In this book I have imagined that they married in 1936 and divorced in 1943, after Stalingrad and before Kursk.

229 "We were soldiers . . ." —Slightly altered from Roger Manvell, *Films and the Second World War* (New York: A. S. Barnes and Co., 1974), p. 128.

229 *Great Soviet Encyclopedia* references to Roman Karmen —Vol. 11, p. 457 (biographical entry on Karmen himself), vol. 12, p. 368 (entry on filmmaking) and vol. 19, p. 214 (entry on film technology).

229 Yuri Tsivian: "He's, well, let's say he's an official classic . . ." —Interviewed over the telephone by WTV, 2002.

230 Influence of Käthe Kollwitz on Karmen —Invented, as is his attendance at Otto Nagel's exhibition of 1924. "The Sacrifice" would have been a plausible influence, since it not only was made shortly before the show (1922), but was also a very powerful image.

232 "Unusual angles, the most incredible positioning of the camera . . ." —Modern Art Museum catalogue, unnumbered second page.

232 Kara-Kum temperature of one hundred and sixty degrees Fahrenheit (I am skeptical) —Modern Art Museum catalogue, unnumbered p. 9.

233 Vertov: "Link all points in any temporal order." —*Kino-Eye: The Writings of Dziga Vertov,* ed. Annette Michelson, trans. Kevin O'Brien (Berkeley: University of California Press, 1984), p. xxvi ("From Kino-Eye to Radio-Eye," 1929). (Vertov named himself; his original given name was Denis Arkadievich Kaufman.)

234 K. Simonov: "As we watched the films sent in by Karmen [spelled "Carmen" throughout this document] from far off Spain . . ." —Modern Art Museum catalogue, unnumbered p. 11 (slightly abridged).

234 Dziga Vertov: "The filmings in Spain represent an indisputable achievement . . ." —Op. cit., pp. 142–43 ("The Truth About the Heroic Struggle"). These two sentences were widely separated in the original.

234 Drobaschenko: "A man filled with energy and elegance." —*Roman Karmen: Retrospektive,* p. 77 (Sergej Drobaschenko, "Roman Karmen"), trans. WTV.

235 Elena's doings in Spain —All invented (except for her Order of the Red Star), since I could find out nothing definite about her. According to the *Great Soviet Encyclopedia,* vol. 10, p. 603 (entry on Spanish history), more than two thousand Soviet volunteers, mostly pilots and tank operators, fought in Spain.

235 Footnote: Fates of Mirova, Koltzov, Ehrenburg —Burnett Bolloten, *The Spanish Civil War: Revolution and Counterrevolution* (Chapel Hill: The University of North Carolina Press, 1991), p. 308. Mirova *disappeared* on her return to Moscow in 1937; Koltzov was arrested in 1938 and died in the Gulag in 1942; he was eventually rehabilitated.

235 Same footnote: Date of first Spanish combat of Soviet tanks —Gabriel Jackson, p. 319.

236 The departure of Madrid's gold reserves —Martin Blinkhorn, ed., *Spain in Conflict 1931–1939: Democracy and Its Enemies* (London: SAGE Publications, 1986), pp. 228–29. This source gives the figure of 500 metric tons.

236 The liquidation of Andrés Nin —Leon Trotsky, *The Spanish Revolution (1931–39)*, intro. by Les Evans (New York: Pathfinder Press, 1973), pp. 267–68 (no. 66: "The Murder of Andrés Nin by Agents of the GPU," August 8, 1937). Trotsky writes: "He refused to cooperate with the GPU against the interests of the Soviet people. That was his only crime. And for this crime he paid with his life."

237 "I must always be there, whenever fighting breaks out" —Konstantin Slavin, undated Soviet Exportkino book about Karmen, cover missing; in Budesarchiv, Berlin; p. 5.

Information on orders, medals, titles and honors of the USSR (Elena's Order of the Red Star, Chuikov's Order of Lenin, and the Medal for the Defense of Leningrad, which I describe in "Opus 110") —*Great Soviet Encyclopedia,* vol. 9, p. 241; vol. 15, p. 629; vol. 18, pp. 516, 658.

Many details of Karmen's doings during the war years are based on his *Über die Zeit und über mich selbst: Erzählungen über mein Schaffen,* trans. into German by Henschel Verlag, typescript, Bundesarchiv cat. no. 92 28 / 87, pp. 23–37. Very likely this is the same as his *About Myself and the Times,* published in 1968 by the Publicity Office of the Soviet Film Industry. I have not located a copy of this document. Thirty-six hundred words of *Über die Zeit* were translated into English for me (17¢ per word; $613.19) by Elsmarie Hau and Tracy Bigelow. A number of my descriptions, attributions, colleagues and witnesses, etcetera, are entirely invented.

238 Karmen: "How precious this footage will be for all of us . . ." —Somewhat "retranslated" from Ibid., orig. p. 24; Hau-Bigelow, p. 1.
239 Akhmatova: "The Leningraders, my heart's blood, march out even-ranked . . ." —*Selected Poems,* p. 72 ("Courage," 1942), "retranslated" by WTV.
239 The plot of "Scout Pashkov" —Von Geldern and Stites, pp. 338–39.
240 *Aspektverhältnis* and *Zeichen* —Thomas Melle to WTV: "'Zeichen' to me seems too general for a nonphilosophical grammarbook," which was precisely my intention.
241 Karmen to Comrade Alexandrov: "Since everything in that court followed a strict consequential logic . . ." —Slightly abbreviated and "retranslated" from *Über die Zeit,* orig. p. 37; Hau-Bigelow, p. 8.
242 V. I. Chuikov: Berlin "rained rivers of red-hot steel on us." —Op. cit., p. 176 ("raining" in original).
242 The two extracts from the unhealthy old book in Berlin —*The Nibelungenlied,* trans. A. T. Hatto (New York: Penguin, 1969, repr. of 1965 ed.; original German ed. *ca.* 1200), pp. 23, 54 (chs. 3, 5), "retranslated" by WTV.
242 The non-appearance of Karmen in the credits to "Stalingrad" —Very occasionally we do find him listed—once even as codirector of "Stalingrad," in Dr. Roger Manvell, gen. ed., *The International Encyclopedia of Film* (New York: Bonanza Books, 1975, repr. of 1972 Rainbird ed.), p. 174.
243 "A fellow traveller," writing about "Stalingrad": "Simple and heroic in the finest sense of the word" —Thomas Dickinson and Catherine De la Roche, *Soviet Cinema* (London: The Falcon Press, Ltd., 1948), p. 67 (De la Roche writing).
243 Karmen's non-appearance in Wakeman's compilation —John Wakeman, ed., *World Film Directors,* vol. 1: 1890–1945 (New York: The H. W. Wilson Co., 1987), pp. 1122–25.
244 The relationship of Roman Karmen and Elena Konstantinovskaya —Suppose that they had never married. In that case I imagine the following two episodes: (1a) For her birthday he once gave her a long folding screen comprised of still portraits he'd made of peasant women in Kara-Kum. M. Ia. Slutskii, with whom he codirected several documentaries, assured him that the faces were stunning. Of course it was a very large object, an egotistical thing, really, and he would have resented it if anybody gave him something that size and expected him to hang it on the wall; at four meters long, it would certainly dominate a room. So he showed it to Elena first. She told him that she thought it was beautiful. He asked her if she would like to have it. He assured her that if she didn't want it, he wouldn't be insulted; the only reason that he wanted to offer it to her was that he was very proud of it and he wanted to give her something he was proud of. She'd acted happy and overwhelmed; she hung it on the wall of her apartment. And then one day it wasn't there. He didn't say anything about it. The next time he visited, it still wasn't there, and the next time she said casually that she was redoing the wall, and it would go back up eventually. But he knew that it never would. (1b) He truly believed that his images on the screen were beautiful. If they were mediocre, he didn't know better. He only wanted to make Elena happy. Elena loved art. She always said so. She admired visual art especially, although she also enjoyed music; she had quite a few records, many of which he supposed that Shostakovich had given her, and she rarely failed to listen to Shostakovich's latest on the radio. Sometimes that made

him very jealous, but he never said anything. (2) Then there was the time he'd given her a print of an old Kalmuck woman, an image he was particularly proud of; and a month later he found it on the floor of her car, creased and with a footprint on it. She was running him over to Boris Makaseyev's in the car, and he was just about to get out when he saw it. He handed it to her and said: Maybe this could be put in a better place. When she came back to pick him up two hours later it was still in the car, but in the back of the car. Makaseyev's wife saw. She was a very sweet, rather shy woman who was fond of Karmen. She knew that he and Elena were having difficulties.—Why, what a lovely print! she said. May I see it?—Elena handed it to her and said: I feel a little guilty about the fact that it's damaged, because Roman probably thinks I don't care about it.—Karmen said nothing, and Makaseyeva took it in her hands and said: It's beautiful. Elena, don't ever treat his work that way again or I'll slap your face.—Sorry, I was only joking, she quickly said when she saw Elena's expression.

256 Information on the cast, credits, etc., of the movie "Zoya" —Vsesoyuznuii Gospudarstvennui Fond Kinofilmov, *Sovyetksie Khudozhestvennuie Filmui: Annomiyobannui Kamaloy*, vol. 2: "Zvukovuie filmui (1930–1957)" (Moscow: Gosudartvennose Isdatelstvo "Iskusstvo," 1961), pp. 331–32. "Zoya" is item 1789. We find it defined as a drama, released by Soyuzdetfilm on 22 September 1944. Arnshtam listed first and third, Shostakovich listed fourth (as the composer, obviously), Karmen not at all. Zoya was G[alina] Vodyanischkaya; Zoya as a child Katya Skvortsova; V. Podgornui was the German officer; R. Plyatt was the German soldier. (There were far more Russians than Germans in the cast.) "Zoya" won a Stalin Prize in 1946. It got praised in *Pravda* on 22 September 1944, in *Izvestiya* and *Komsomolskaya Pravda* the following day; and two times more in *Komsomolskaya Pravda;* in *Iskusstvo Kino* in 1946, etc. *The New York Times* for its part concluded that Galina Vodianitskaya "plays the heroine elaborately" but that the movie was "tediously constructed"—too many newsreels intercut with too many flashbacks to Zoya's sentimentalized childhood (*The New York Times Film Reviews 1913–1968*, vol. 3 [New York: The New York Times and Arno Press, 1970], p. 2058 [B. C. (Bosley Crowther?)], "Zoya," April 16, 1945, 18:6).

257 "*Film* is the most important art form . . ." —Very loosely after Shostakovich and Volkov, *Testimony*, p. 149.

258 Footnote: *The New York Times*'s opinion of Karmen's documentary on the Nuremberg Trials ("Judgment of the Peoples"), *The New York Times Film Reviews 1913–1968*, vol. 3 (of 6): 1939–1948, p. 2184 (Bosley Crowther, "The Nuremberg Trials," May 26, 1947; 24:2), full sentence substantially abridged by WTV. As for his film on Albania, the *Times* considered that less effective than I. Kopalin and P. Atasheva's documentary about the liberation of Czechoslovakia (p. 2128, "At the Stanley," July 15. 1946, 21:1).

258 Burt Lancaster: Karmen's "passionate love for life and people . . ." —*Roman Karmen: Retrospektive*, p. 78 (Sergej Drobaschenko, "Roman Karmen"), trans. WTV.

259 *Great Soviet Encyclopedia* on "Far and Wide My Country Stretches" —Vol. 19, p. 214. *The New York Times* ridicules this movie for its excess of high-speed automobile driving and the stiffness of the alternating male and female narrators (the former is Karmen himself; the latter is E. Dolmatovsky). All the same, the *Times* enjoys the steel mills of Magnitogorsk, the oil fields of the Caspian and the log raft in the Carpathians. "Far and Wide" seems to be almost all travelogue (*The New York Times Film Reviews 1913–1968*, vol. 5 [1970], p. 3134 [Bosley Crowther, "Great Is My Country," July 1, 1959; 26:1]).

259 Castro: "In the name of our people we thank you . . ." —*Roman Karmen: Retrospektive*, p. 69, trans. WTV.

259 Allende: "My friend Roman Karmen" —Ibid., p. 70, trans. WTV.

259 Moscow *Kinoslovar* on the character of Karmen's films —After S. I. Yutkevich et al., p. 674, trans. WTV. I have somewhat reordered and abridged the items on the original eye-glazing list. In spite of my italics, this is not a direct quote at all, but a second-generation paraphrase.

BREAKOUT

260 Epigraph: "With few, but courageous allies . . ." —Victor Klemperer, *I Will Bear Witness: A Diary of the Nazi Years 1942–1945,* trans. Martin Chalmers (New York: Random House, 1999), p. 287 (entry for 8 January 1944).

262 Footnote: Vlasov's wife: "Andrei, can you really live like that?" —Catherine Andreyev, *Vlasov and the Russian Liberation Movement: Soviet Reality and Émigré Theories* (New York: Cambridge University Press, 1987), p. 39. Vlasov's wife was actually not the allegorical Moscow figurine of my conception, but a doctor from a tiny village in the province of Nizhni Novgorod. She was indeed arrested and executed after his defection. They had a small son, whose fate I don't know.

261 Vlasov's recommendations to Stalin —Not much is known about them, although the two men did have some such conference. Given that Vlasov was in good odor after the Battle of Moscow, I decided to put into his mouth the strategy which actually got followed.

261 Stalin: "Anybody can defend Moscow with reserves" —Harold Shukman, ed., *Stalin's Generals* (New York: Grove Press, 1993), p. 304 (Catherine Andreyev, "Vlasov").

261 Number of Twentieth Army's tanks during the Battle of Moscow —Erickson, p. 534.

265 "What the enemy called *Kesselschlacht,* cauldron-slaughter." Mr. Thomas Melle notes (letter to author, September 2003): "A little semantic confusion crept in here: 'to slaughter' means 'schlachten' (animals, *Slaughterhouse-Five,* etc.); 'Schlacht' means 'battle' or 'fight' and the plural of 'Schlacht' is "Schlachten' —'to slaughter' and 'battles' being the same word in German. I think 'cauldron battle' would be more appropriate. In a dictionary it says 'battle of encirclement and annhilation.'" I myself rest my artistic and semantic case.

265 General K. A. Meretskov: "If nothing is done then a catastrophe is inevitable." —Shukman, p. 305.

266 Guderian: "These men remain essentially unable to break free . . ." —Heinz Guderian, *Achtung-Panzer! The Development of Tank Warfare,* trans. Christopher Duffy (Reading, Berkshire, U.K.: Cassell Military Paperbacks; orig. German ed. 1937), p. 24 ("retranslated").

266 Vlasov's commissar: "Everything you say may be correct from the military viewpoint . . ." —Roughly after Sewern Bialer, ed., *Stalin and His Generals: Soviet Military Memoirs of World War II* (New York: Pegasus, 1969), p. 252 (memoir of Marshal I. Kh. Bagramian).

271 Vlasov's capture —Accurately told, except that he was captured with a woman named Maria Voronova, who was the family servant in Nizhni Novgorod and whom Vlasov's wife actually dispatched to him to take care of him. Since her presence raises several issues not relevant to the parable, I decided to leave her out.

272 Vlasov to General Lindemann and Lindemann's reply: "Would a German officer in my place have shot himself?"—"Capture's no disgrace for someone like you, who's fought with his unit up to the very last instant . . ." —Loosely after an exchange between Vlasov and the German intelligence officer who captured him, Captain von Schwerdtner, indirectly quoted in Sven Steenberg, *Vlasov,* trans. Abe Farbstein (New York: Alfred A. Knopf, 1970 trans. of 1968 German ed.), p. 28.

275 The German policeman-poet: Vinnitsa, where "we saw two worlds, and will permit only one to rule" —Ernst Klee, Willi Dressen and Volker Riess, *"The Good Old Days": The Holocaust as Seen by Its Perpetrators and Bystanders,* trans. Deborah Burnstone (Old Saybrook, Connecticut: Konecky and Konecky, 1991, repr. of 1988 German ed.), p. 123 (my trans.; the English given on the following page differs slightly).

277 Jewish casualties at Babi Yar —Most Western sources estimate that about thirty-three thousand people were murdered. Soviet sources sometimes say seventy thousand. The eyewitness A. Anatoli Kuzentsov gives the figure of one hundred thousand in his "documentary novel" *Babi Yar.*

277 Boyarsky: "When the Jews saw how easy it was to be executed, they ran to the pits of their own free will." —Slightly rephrased from the statement of a German customs official who saw the Jews being machine-gunned in Vinnitsa. The eyewitness estimated that "some thousands" were shot "over the total period" (Klee et al, p. 119).

279 Tukhachevsky: "It is necessary to observe the promise of privileged treatment to those who surrender voluntarily with their arms." —Chaliand, p. 916 ("Counterinsurgency").

281 Strik-Strikfeldt: "Vlasov spoke openly, and I did also, insofar as my oath of service permitted me" —Op. cit., p. 73 (slightly reworded).

281 Vlasov: "Only if I put human values before nationalist values . . ." —Ibid., p. 75 (a little altered).

281 Vlasov: "The Soviet regime has brought me no personal disadvantages," "At Przemysl . . . my proposals were rejected," "Two factors must entail . . . interference from the commissars." —Ibid., pp. 253–54 (Appendix II: "General Vlasov's Open Letter: Why I Took Up Arms Against Bolshevism"; somewhat abridged and altered).

283 Strik-Strikfeldt: "It's an admirable document, but, as drafted, too Russian" —Ibid., p. 76 (slightly altered).

285 Strik-Strikfeldt: "I grant that thousands of Russian prisoners have died . . ." —Loosely after the argument advanced by General Jodl at his war crimes trial in Nuremberg; see Gilbert, p. 253 (10 April 1946).

285 Khrushchev: "Temporary people" —Kershaw and Lewin, p. 51 (Suny).

285 Second Lieutenant Dirksen: "A democracy of the best" —Very loosely based on the views of an S.S. officer in 1937, as remembered by his interlocutor, Eugen Kogon, in *The Theory and Practice of Hell: The German Concentration Camps and the System Behind Them*, trans. Heinz Norden (New York: Berkley Publishing: Berkley Windhover, 1975 repr. of 1950 ed.), pp. 8–9.

286 Vlasov: "As a soldier, I cannot ask other soldiers to stop doing their duty" —Andreyev, p. 44.

286 The song of Vlasov's Russian troops at Moscow: "I'm warm in this freezing bunker / thanks to your love's eternal flame!" —After Antony Beevor, *Stalingrad: The Fateful Siege: 1942–1943* (New York: 1999 repr. of 1998 Penguin U.K. ed.), p. 290 (from the last stanza of *Zemlyanka* ["The Dugout"], "retranslated"). Slightly anachronistic here, since this song was sung in Stalingrad, probably not the previous year at Moscow.

287 Vlasov's Smolensk Declaration: "Friends and brothers! BOLSHEVISM IS THE ENEMY OF THE RUSSIAN PEOPLE" —Andreyev, p. 206 (slightly "retranslated").

287 Strik-Strikfeldt: "One could come across grey wraiths who subsisted on corpses and tree-bark" —Op. cit., p. 49 (which actually reads: "One could come across ghostlike figures, ashen gray, starving, half naked, living perhaps for days on end on corpses and the bark of trees").

288 Guderian: "A fortress of unlimited breadth and depth" —*Guderian*, p. 42 (slightly altered).

288 Strik-Strikfeldt: "Since the Slavic-Asiatic character only understands the absolute . . ." —B. H. Liddell Hart, *The German Generals Talk* (New York: Quill, repr. of 1948 ed., 1979), p. 226 (actually not Strik-Strikfeldt at all but the testimony of General Blumentritt; much altered and expanded).

289 German inspection report: "Discipline: Slack . . ." —Strik-Strikfeldt, p. 256 (Appendix III: "Extracts from Report of Captain Peterson on His Inspection of the Dabendorf Camp, 13 and 14 September 1943").

289 Vlasov on the new flag: "I'd really like to leave it that way . . ." —After Steenberg, p. 85.

290 Vlasov to Strik-Strikfeldt: "You can't even give a suit that fits, and you want to conquer the world!" —"Retranslated" from Steenberg, p. 53.

291 Strik-Strikfeldt's memoirs: "In German concentration camps there had been bestialities . . ." and "The world still does not believe that these thugs . . ." —Strik-Strikfeldt, pp. 242–43.

292 *Great Soviet Encyclopedia:* "It is well known that the structure of emotional life . . ." —Vol. 15, p. 155 (entry on love).

293 Vlasov at Smolensk: "A foreign coat never fits a Russian." —Andreyev, pp. 47–48 (slightly altered).

293 Vlasov at Smolensk: "The Germans have begun to acknowledge their mistakes. And, after all, it's just not realistic to hope to enslave almost two hundred million people . . ." —Loosely after the paraphrase in Steenberg, p. 71.

293 Death rate of Russian prisoners at Smolensk—Strik-Strikfeldt, pp. 49–50.

294 General Lindemann: "The East and the West are two worlds . . ." —Liddell Hart, p. 226 (testimony of General Blumentritt).

294 Vlasov's memoradum to the Reich government: "The mass of the Russian population now look upon this conflict as a German war of conquest" —Alexander Dallin, *German Rule in Russia 1941–1945: A Study of Occupation Policies* (New York: Farrar, Straus & Giroux / Octagon, 1980), p. 567 (slightly reworded and abridged).

295 Strik-Strikfeldt: "Too much propaganda is merely propaganda" —Strik-Strikfeldt, p. 25.

295 "A colleague's literary production" (actually an S.S. pamphlet about the Untermensch): "And this underworld of the Untermensch . . ." —Joachim Remak, ed., *The Nazi Years: A Documentary History* (Englewood Cliffs, New Jersey: Prentice-Hall, Inc., 1969), p. 37 (S.S. Hauptamt-Schulungsamt, *Der Untermensch,* 1942; "retranslated" by WTV).

298 Wise Nazi adage: "The javelin and the springboard are more useful than lipstick for the promotion of health." —George L. Mosse, comp., *Nazi Culture: Intellectual, Cultural and Social Life in the Third Reich* (New York: Grosset & Dunlap, 1966), p. 43 (*Frankfurter Zeitung,* 1937, "The Blond Craze").

298 Heidi Bielenberg: "The healthy is a heroic commandment." —Joachim C. Fest, *The Face of the Third Reich: Portraits of the Nazi Leadership,* trans. Michael Bullock (New York: Ace Books, 1970), p. 392 ("German Wife and Mother," quoting Hans Johnst).

299 Himmler, speaking about Heydrich: "Cold, rational criticism." —Fest, p. 137 ("Reinhard Heydrich—The Successor").

302 Goebbels: "A hundred-percent victory for German propaganda . . ." —Allen Paul, *Katyn: The Untold Story of Stalin's Polish Massacre* (New York: Scribner's, 1991), p. 224 (diary entry of 28 April 1943).

305 The man in the lavatory, quoting the Reich Commissioner of the Ukraine: "Some people are disturbed that the population . . ." —Remak, p. 124 (report of Quartermaster Fähndrich, Kiev, 5 March 1943; somewhat altered).

306 Vlasov at Riga: "A Russian can bear much which would kill a German" —Strik-Strikfeldt, p. 192, slightly changed.

306 The Waffen-S.S. captain: "If one gave Vlasov's army a flag . . ." —Dallin, p. 576 (Erich Koch; verbatim).

306 Vlasov: "The problem of developing a tactical breakthrough into an operational breakthrough . . ." —Partially derived from the *Great Soviet Encyclopedia,* vol. 21, p. 21 (entry: breakthrough).

307 Vlasov: "If we can help the Reich resist . . ." —Loosely after his expressed view as recorded in Strik-Strikfeldt, p. 215.

308 Re: "Mozart's ever so healthy German melodies," Thomas Melle remarks: "You know, of course, that Mozart was Austrian." I do.

308 Moltke's maxim from 1869: "The stronger our frontal position becomes . . ." —Count Helmuth von Moltke, *Moltke on the Art of War: Selected Writings,* ed. Daniel J. Hughes, trans. Harry Bell and Daniel J. Hughes (San Francisco: Presidio Press, 1993), p. 203 (1869 Instructions for Large Unit Commanders," X., "Tactical Considerations," A., "Infantry and Jäger," slightly "retranslated").

311 Hitler: "I don't need this General Vlasov at all in our rear areas," "No German agency must take seriously the bait contained in the Vlasov program," and "That's a phantom of the first order" —Dallin, p. 574 (slightly rearranged).

311 Himmler: "That Russian swine Herr General Wlassow" —Paul Padfield, *Himmler, Reichsführer SS* (New York: Henry Holt & Co., 1990), p. 476 (Padfield spells it "Vlassov").

312 Hitler: "We won't be able to save anything . . ." —Abridged from Warlimont, p. 390 (fragment no. 7, discussion with Colonel-General Zeitzler, 27 December 1943).

312 Lines from "Herbsttag" —*Ahead of All Parting: The Selected Poetry and Prose of Rainer Maria Rilke,* ed. and trans. Stephen Mitchell (New York: Modern Library, 1995), p. 14 (facing German text, trans. by WTV).

313 Vlasov: "I don't know them. You see, I have been through Stalin's school" —Slightly altered from Strik-Strikfeldt, pp. 202–03.

314 Himmler: "We guarantee that at the end of the war you'll be granted the pension of a Russian lieutenant-general," "And in the immediate future, you will continue to have schnapps, cigarettes and women," and "One has to calculate frightfully coolly in these matters" —After Padfield, p. 467.

315 Himmler to Gunter d'Alquen: "Who compels us to keep the promises we make?" —Clark, p. 408.

315 Vlasov's manifesto: "A fight to the finish of opposing political systems . . ." —Severely abridged from Daniels, p. 230.

318 Vlasov: "Washington and Franklin were traitors in the eyes of the British crown." —Strik-Strikfeldt, p. 229.

318 Vlasov: "God give me strength! . . . And one day you'll tell everybody at Valhalla that I wasn't a traitor . . ." —Ibid., p. 230, considerably altered (the original reads: "God give me strength to hold out to the end. But you, Wilfried Karlovich, you will go with Malyshkin and help him. That I know. And one day you will tell the others that Vlasov and his friends loved their country and were not traitors."

319 *Great Soviet Encyclopedia:* "In this long and bitter struggle . . ." —Vol. 4, p. 351 (entry on the Great Patriotic War of 1941–45).

319 Guderian's opinion of Himmler: "An inconspicuous man with all the marks of racial inferiority" —Heinz Guderian, *Panzer Leader,* trans. Constantine Fitzgibbon, abr. (New York: Ballantine Books, n.d.), p. 30.

320 General Guderian: "Vlasov wanted to make some statement," and replies of Hitler and Göring —Warlimont, p. 503 (fragment 24/25, briefing conference on 27 January 1945).

320 War diary of the British Thirty-sixth Infantry Brigade: "In glittering uniforms" —Carol Mather, *Aftermath of War: Everyone Must Go Home* (London: Brassey's [U.K.] Ltd., 1992), p. 70 (embellished a little).

321 Vlasov: "Kroeger keeps filling up my glass . . ." —Strik-Strikfeldt, p. 230.

322 Vlasov to his two quarreling soldiers: "We can't beat Stalin with open fingers . . ." —Loosely after Steenberg, p. 155.

323 Heidi's mother: "The Führer won't allow the Russians to get us. He'll gas us instead" —Ian Kershaw, *Hitler 1936–1945: Nemesis* (New York: W. W. Norton & Co., 2000), p. 762 (the speaker was an anonymous old woman).

324 Strik-Strikfeldt: "Definition of cowardice: Leaving Berlin to volunteer for the Ostfront!" —After Klemperer, p. 313 (entry for 8 May 1944).

324 Vlasov: "Germany has collapsed sooner than I expected." —Strik-Strikfeldt, p. 227.

326 Footnote: Vlasov: "I know that, and I'm extremely afraid . . ." —Andreyev, p. 78 ("retranslated" a little).

326 Same footnote: Program of the Communist Party of the Soviet Union: "Communist morality is the noblest and most just morality . . ." —*The Soviet Way of Life,* p. 316.

327 *Great Soviet Encyclopedia:* Definition of cosmopolitanism —Vol. 13, p. 190 (entry on same).

THE LAST FIELD-MARSHAL

328 Epigraph: "That man should have shot himself . . ."—Alan Bullock, *Hitler, A Study in Tyranny,* rev. ed. (San Francisco: Harper & Row, Harper Colophon Books, 1964), pp. 690–91 (Hitler to his staff officers, 1 February 1943).

328 Guderian on Paulus: "He was the finest type . . ." —*Panzer Leader,* p. 30.

328 Military orders: "Kriegsgliederung 'Barbarossa'" —Mehner, vol. 3, end matter. Untranslated phrases: "War plan 'Barbarossa.' B-Day."

329 Information on enemy strength, dispositions, etc., available to Paulus from Fremde Heere Ost—I have built up much of my imaginary picture from details in David Thomas, "Foreign Armies East and German Military Intelligence in Russia 1941–45," *Journal of Contemporary History,* vol. 22, no. 22 (April 1987).

329 "Fourth Army Chief of Staff in the Polish campaign" —The biographies of Paulus are all in wild disagreement on this as on other issues. (For instance, even the careful Erickson calls him "von Paulus," although Goerlitz makes it clear that our hero was a bookkeeper's son.) Samuel W. Mitcham, for instance, claims in *Hitler's Field Marshals and Their Battles* (New York: Cooper Square Press, 2001; p. 226), that he was actually in Tenth Army then, and that Tenth Army was renamed to Sixth Army.

329 Hitler: "The ultimate objective is the cordoning off of Asiatic Russia . . ." —Directive No. 2 for Barbarossa, as quoted in Walter Goerlitz, *Paulus and Stalingrad: A Life of Field-Marshal Friedrich Paulus with Notes, Sources and Documents from His Papers,* trans. Col. R. H. Stevens (New York: Citadel Press, 1963, trans of 1960 German ed.), p. 96.

329 Kesselring on Paulus: "He made a specially good impression . . ." —*Kesselring: A Soldier's Record* (title page cut away in library binding; published shortly after 1953), p. 52.

330 Paulus's children —Mitcham (p. 224) gives him three: Olga, Friedrich (killed in action in the Anzio campaign) and Alexander. Craig (p. 408) gives him an unnamed daughter, I assume Olga, Alexander (killed at Anzio) and Ernst, and has Ernst commit suicide in 1970. Beevor (p. 427) does not mention Olga, has Friedrich killed at Anzio, and calls the third child Ernst Alexander. So I've settled on Olga, Friedrich and Ernst. Since the circumstances and nature of Ernst's wound have not been specified, I gave him a serious thigh wound which required his evacuation from Stalingrad. Had he not been evacuated, it seems unlikely to me that he and his father would both have survived the Stalingrad campaign. I further imagine that his wounding occurred before the German position at Stalingrad had reached a very desperate stage, since (a) it would have been less likely that he'd be evacuated then and (b) he might have been more inclined to stick it out like his father. All this is the flimsiest speculation, which is God's gift to historical fictioneers.

331 Olga's son Robert —In fact I don't know whether she had any children.

331 Conversation between Paulus and Coca: "That's a matter for political decision . . . a good chance that we'll achieve victory this year" —Somewhat loosely after Goerlitz, p. 28.

334 The S.D. police-lieutenant to Paulus: "You can ask anything of them, just like horses. They work until they drop and make no demands" —Klee, Dressen and Riess, p. 158 (letter from Gendarmerie chief Fritz Jacob, in Kamanets Podolsky, 21 June 1942).

335 Hitler: "Keitel, is this line ready? . . . All the way to here?" —Warlimont, p. 522 (Appendix A: Staff Conference Fragment No. 8, 12 December 1942; actually Hitler and Zeitzler speaking).

336 Warlimont: Total German losses thus far on the Ostfront, 625,000 —Ibid., p. 239 ("War Potential 1942," figures as of 1 May 1942). The reserve situation was actually worse than Paulus might have known. Warlimont writes (p. 240): "At present there are no further reserves available in Germany."

337 Hitler: "The fuel situation . . . liquidate this war" —Kershaw, p. 514 (slightly altered).

337 Hitler and Paulus at von Reichenau's funeral —This never happened. Hitler sent a proxy to the ceremony.

337 Paulus's assessment of Russian troops: "Incapable of operational initiative" —Actually, the assessment of them by Fremde Heere Ost, on the eve of Operation Barbarossa. See Thomas, "Foreign Armies East," p. 274.

339 General Halder: "One of the sacrifices which commanders have to make . . ." —Warlimont, p. 162 (actually, written by Halder in his diary).

343 Fremde Heere Ost: "Special formations: Numbers unknown" —Loosely after the tabulation in Thomas, p. 276.

343 Ditto: "The clumsiness, schematism, avoidance of decision and responsibility has not changed since the Finnish campaign" —Ibid., p. 274. I have added "since the Finnish campaign."

347 *Great Soviet Encyclopedia* on Stalingrad (Tsaritsyn): "During the seventeenth and eighteenth centuries . . ." —Vol. 5, p. 566, entry on Volgograd.

348 "Field-Marshal von Reichenau's order of 10.10.41 to proceed with extreme measures against subhumans" —There were a number of variations of the infamous "commissar order," whose provisions got rescinded at different times and different degrees by different commanders. Regarding commissars, many of the German generals seem to have actually believed, as for instance did von Manstein (p. 179), that since they weren't exactly soldiers, chaplains or doctors; and since their purpose was to encourage "vicious resistance" in the enemy formations, then they didn't qualify as privileged non-combatants; this view, however self-serving, may be faintly arguable. Most of the "commissar" order, however, is sickeningly murderous. In the very first of the numbered "Instructions for the Conduct of the Troops in Russia" we read: "Bolshevism is the deadly enemy of the National Socialist Folk. This subversive world-view and its carriers validate Germany's struggle." The second instruction warns that "this war must be prosecuted ruthlessly against" (and here in the orders the following categories were underlined) "*headmen, fifth columnists, Jews,* and others who stand actively or passively against us." —Mehner. (The German word for "instructions," *Richtlinien,* really means "guidelines," but a more rigid substitution seemed appropriate here. I wanted to literalize it into the cognate *Right Line,* with its even stronger moral tone, but regretfully decided that this had too Stalinist a sound. The excerpts in this note have been slightly abridged.)

348 Some of the military arrows, vectors, etc. for Kharkov and Stalingrad derive from the maps in Günter Wegmann, ed., *"Das Oberkommando der Wehrmacht gibt bekannt . . .": Der deutsche Wehrmachtsbericht* (Osnabrück: Biblio Verlag, 1982).

349 Colonel Metz to Paulus: "Let me congratulate you on your Knight's Cross . . ." —Slightly abridged from Goerlitz, p. 167. This message bears the date of 5 June 1942 and therefore probably reached Paulus much sooner than I have allowed it to.

351 Field-Marshal von Manstein: "The safety of a tank formation operating in the enemy's rear . . ." —Von Manstein, p. 185.

351 Coca to her husband, on Africa: "Keep your fingers out of that pie." —Ibid., p. 32.

353 The Führer: "There is not going to be a winter campaign!"—Ibid., p. 35.

353 The architecture of Werewolf, Wolf's Lair, Wolf's Gorge, and for that matter many of the structural details of Hitler's trains, cars, military headquarters, etcetera, referred to in this story and in "Clean Hands" —Peter Hoffmann, *Hitler's Personal Security* (London: Macmillan Press Ltd., 1979). Hitler was at Wolf's Lair, with many interruptions, from 24 June 1941 through 20 November 1944. Meanwhile came two spells at Werewolf: 16 July to 1 November 1942 (this is the period of greatest relevance here), and 17 February through 13 March 1943. Paulus's final visit to Wolf's Lair, when Paulus goes "whiter than a German tank," is my fabrication.

354 Hitler: "The Ukrainians, yes, a thin Germanic layer . . ." —Kershaw, p. 244 (recollection of A. Rosenberg); somewhat altered; the original was about the Poles rather than the Ukrainians.

356 Hitler: "Once we've erased Leningrad and Moscow from the map . . ." —Warlimont, p. 242, quoting Goebbels, March 1942.

356 Major-General Schmidt: "The greatest happiness any of our contemporaries can experience . . ." —Warlimont; quoting Goebbels's diary, entry for 21 March 1942.

361 Paulus to Lutz: "The great thing now is to hit the Russian so hard a crack . . ." —Goerlitz, p. 169.

363 Colonel Heim on Paulus: "A slender, rather over-tall figure . . ." —Goerlitz, p. 48.

363 "They": "This defensive mission is contrary to the German soldier's nature" —After Newton, p. 63 (Otto Schellert, "Winter Fighting of the 253rd Infantry Division in the Rzhev Area 1941–1942").

364 "A German general who survived the war": "Practically every Russian attack . . ." —Major-General F. W. von Mellenthin, *Panzer Battles: A Story of the Employment of Armour in the Second World War,* trans. H. Betzler (Norman: University of Oklahoma Press, 1956, repr. of 1955 English ed.), p. 185.

366 Field-Marshal von Manstein: "This policy of covering everything . . ." —Walimont, quoting Goebbels's diary entry for 21 March 1942, p. 40.

366 Unnamed officer at Wolf's Lair: "Any caliber smaller than a hundred and fifty millimeters is ineffective . . ." —Loosely after Newton, p. 117 (Gustav Höhne, "In Snow and Mud: 31 Days of Attack Under Seydlitz During Early Spring of 1942").

366 Hitler: "I made it clear to my Brownshirts . . . rip off his armband" —Loosely after *Mein Kampf,* p. 504 ("An Attempted Disruption").

367 "Manstein's high regard for the march discipline of the S.S. Death's Head Division" —Op. cit., p. 187.

369 Fremde Heere Ost, Gruppe I, Army Group report on the Red Army's new Don Front: "Defensive enemy behavior" —Thomas, p. 269. (The source for this erroneous information was actually not the Leitstelle für Nachrichtenaufklärung, however.)

370 Enemy signal of 18.11.42: "Send a messenger to pick up the fur gloves" —Erickson, p. 464.

371 "Übersicht über sowjetrussischen Kräfteeinsatz" and description of the map's colors —*The Service: The Memoirs of General Reinhard Gehlen,* trans. David Irving (New York: Times Mirror, World Publishing, 1972, trans. of 1971 German ed.), frontispiece.

372 *Great Soviet Encyclopedia:* "Encirclement is most often achieved . . ." —Vol. 18, p. 78 (entry on encirclement).

374 Paulus, on a possible breakout: "More than ten thousand wounded and most of our heavy weapons would have to be written off" —Loosely after the sentiment expressed by General Schmidt in Beevor, p. 268. On this same page Beevor writes that Paulus was "haunted" by comparisons with Napoleon's retreat, so I supplied the standard figures on that disaster.

376 Field-Marshal von Manstein on Field-Marshal von Brauchitsch: "Not belonging to quite the same class as Baron von Fritsch . . ." —Manstein, p. 75. About Paulus, Manstein was actually more charitable than this, concluding (p. 303) that "he can hardly have had a sufficiently clear picture of the overall situation."

376 Radio transmission came from our Führer: "Sixth Army is temporarily surrounded by Russian forces . . ." —Moderately altered from the version in Beevor, pp. 269–70.

378 Paulus to Coca: "At the moment I've got a really difficult problem on my hands . . ." —Goerlitz, p. 72 (letter of 7 December 1942).

378 Episode of the grand piano in the street, the ammunition-box altar for Christmas, and a few other miscellaneous details —Loosely based on Franz Schneider and Charles Gullans, trans., *Last Letters from Stalingrad* (New York: William Morrow & Co., 1962).

378 Gehlen's assessment of von Manstein: "One of the finest soldiers of this century." —Gehlen, pp. 153–54. This was actually a postwar evaluation of the man.

379 Field-Marshal von Manstein: "The best chance for an independent breakout has already been missed." —von Manstein, p. 306.

380 Paulus's letter to von Manstein, as dictated to Colonel Adam: Severely abridged,

somewhat "retranslated" and slightly altered from the full version which von Manstein gives as Appendix I (pp. 551–54).

381 Lieutenant-General Jaenecke: "We'll go through the Russians like a hot knife through butter!" —Slightly altered from Mitcham, p. 235.

383 Paulus: "Your airlift has failed us . . ." —Loosely after Craig, p. 234.

384 Major-General Schmidt to Major Eismann: "Sixth Army will still be in position at Easter . . ." —Slightly "retranslated" from von Manstein, p. 334.

384 Paulus to Eismann: "At any rate, under current conditions a breakout would be impossible . . ." —Very loosely after an indirect quotation in von Manstein.

384 The remainder of this conversation with Eismann is fabricated. For evidence that von Manstein was in fact willing to take responsibility for having Paulus disobey Hitler, see his memoir, pp. 341–42.

384 Hitler: "We must under no circumstances give Stalingrad up . . ." —Warlimont, p. 285.

385 Teleprinter conversation between Paulus and von Manstein, 23 December 1942: "Good evening, Paulus . . . full authority today" —Abbreviated and slightly reworded from the original in Goerlitz, pp. 276–77 ("Documents and signals" section).

386 Schmidt to the teleprinter clerk: "Can aircraft still take off safely from Tatsinskaya?" —Teleprinter conversation from Schmidt to his opposite number General Shulz, the Chief of Staff at Army Group Don, 24 December 1942 (Goerlitz, p. 278).

387 Paulus to von Manstein: "Army can continue to beat off small-scale attacks . . ." —Abbreviated and slightly "retranslated" from von Manstein, p. 351.

387 Paulus to Coca: "Christmas, naturally, was not very happy . . ." —Goerlitz, p. 80 (letter of 28 December 1942).

388 Note on German national character: "To regard the fulfillment of duty rather than personal responsibility . . ." —Count Hermann Keyserling, *Europe* (New York: Harcourt, Brace & Co., 1928; original German ed. n.d., *Das Spektrum Europas)*, p. 121.

390 Paulus to Zitzewitz: "Everything has occurred exactly as I foretold . . ." —Goerlitz, p. 43.

390 Heim on Paulus: "The face of a martyr." —Ibid., p. 48.

391 General Warlimont on Hitler: "Strategically he does not comprehend . . ." —Warlimont, p. 244.

391 Daily briefing of 4 January 1943: "6 Armee, Heeresgruppe Don: Powerful enemy tank attack . . ." —Mehner, vol. 6: 1 Dezember 1942—31 Mai 1943, p. 71; my translation and abridgment.

392 Hitler to von Manstein: "The Russians never keep any agreements." —Craig, p. 368.

393 Paulus to his staff officers: "I expect you as soldiers . . ." —Slightly altered from F. W. von Mellenthin, German General Staff Officer. (I presume this is the same Major-General who wrote *Panzer Battles: German Generals of World War II As I Saw Them* [Norman: University of Oklahoma Press, 1977], p. 115. Paulus was actually addressing only one man, Colonel Dingler of the Fourteenth Panzer Corps.)

394 Paulus: "History has already passed its verdict on me" —Goerlitz, p. 72.

394 Daily briefing of 16 January 1943: "6 Armee, Heeresgruppe Don: On the W. and S. fronts . . ." —Mehner, vol. 6, p. 95; my. trans. and abr.

394 16 January 1943 as "the day that we lost the airstrip at Pitomnik" —von Manstein, however, gives this date as the twelfth.

394 Paulus: "Dead men are no longer interested in military history." —Beevor, p. 370.

394 Hitler: "You must stand fast to the last man and the last bullet." —After Warlimont, p. 286; Kershaw, p. 549.

395 "Now they'd split us into two mutually isolated sub-fortresses." —von Manstein (p. 364) writes that there were actually three pockets formed on 24 January, a claim which I have not read anywhere else. Goerlitz asserts that Sixth Army was split into two on 26 January.

395 Paulus to OKW, 24 January 1943: "No basis left on which to carry out mission . . ." —Abridged and "retranslated" from von Manstein, p. 358.

395 General Heitz's slogan: "We fight to the last bullet but one" —Beevor, p. 382.

396 "The Jew Babel" on the Jews of Zhitomir —*The Complete Works of Isaac Babel,* ed. Nathalie Babel, trans. Peter Constantine (New York: W. W. Norton & Company, 2002), p. 380 (diary entry for June 3, 1920).

396 Von Reichenau on the liquidation of the Jewish children: "I have ascertained in principle . . ." —Klee, Dressen and Riess, p. 153 (abridged and slightly altered).

400 Signal of 29 January 1943: "To the Führer! . . ." —After Beevor, p. 379, abridged.

400 Daily briefing of 30 January 1943: "6 Armee, Heeresgruppe Don: More Russian attacks . . ." —Mehner, vol. 6, p. 123; my trans. and abr.

400 Paulus to General Pfieffer: "I have no intention of shooting myself for this Bohemian corporal" —Beevor, p. 381.

400 The German surrender at Stalingrad —The Soviets are said to have captured 2,000 officers and 91,000 thousand men. Very few of those ever came home. In 1958 von Manstein wrote: "Of the 90,000 prisoners who finally fell into Soviet hands, not more than a few thousand can be alive today" (p. 360). The original strength of Sixth Army was about 300,000. Presumably the 200,000-odd men not captured had already been slain in the fighting. Mitcham (p. 239) cites "the commonly accepted figure" of 230,000 Germans killed or captured in the course of the siege, not counting the wounded who were lucky enough to get flown out. Von Manstein (p. 396) estimates that between 200,000 and 220,000 soldiers were in the pocket as of the beginning of the encirclement. "Altogether, the Axis must have lost over half a million men" (Beevor, p. 398). According to Beevor (p. 394), the Russians endured 1.1 million casualties at Stalingrad, 485,751 of which were deaths.

400 Regarding the necessity for Sixth Army's ordeal at Stalingrad, the words of von Manstein (op. cit., p. 354) deserve to be quoted: "Every extra day Sixth Army could continue to tie down enemy forces surrounding it was vital as far as the fate of the entire Eastern Front was concerned. It is idle to point out today that we still lost the war in the end and that its early termination would have spared us infinite misery. That is merely being wise after the event. In those days it was by no means certain that Germany was bound to lose the war in the military sense. A military stalemate . . . would have been entirely within the bounds of possibility if the situation on the southern wing of the German armies could in some way have been restored."

400 German eyewitness: "Sorrow and grief lined his face" —Craig, p. 372.

400 Major-General Schmidt to Paulus: "Remember that you are a Field-Marshal of the German army." —Beevor, p. 388. These words were actually uttered a few hours later, immediately before Paulus's interrogation.

401 Unnamed Russian general, to Paulus: "We now have great and priceless experience of defensive fighting here on the banks of the Volga" —Closely after Vasili I. Chuikov, Marshal of the Soviet Union, Twice Hero of the Soviet Union, *The End of the Third Reich,* trans. Ruth Kisch (Bristol, U.K.: Macgibbon and Kee, 1967; orig. Russian ed. *ca* 1964), p. 17. In the original, Chuikov was speaking neither to Paulus nor sarcastically.

401 Paulus to his captors: "That would be unworthy of a soldier!" and following conversation —After Beevor, p. 390; with some parts verbatim and some parts invented.

403 Paulus's experiences in the USSR, 1943–53 —Based on the occasional mentions of him in Bodo Scheurig, *Free Germany: The National Committee and the League of German Officers,* trans. Herbert Arnold (Middletown, Connecticut: Wesleyan Press, 1969; original German ed. 1961).

403 The *London Sunday Times* correspondent A. Werth: "Paulus looked pale and sick . . ." —Werth, *Russia at War,* p. 549.

403 Hitler on Paulus's surrender: "What hurts me the most personally . . ." and "So many men have to die . . ." —Warlimont, p. 306 (fragment no. 47: midday conference [transcript], 1 February 1943).

404 Field-Marshal Keitel: "I always took his side with the Führer . . ." —Telford Taylor, *The Anatomy of the Nuremberg Trials: A Personal Memoir* (Boston: Little, Brown, Back Bay Books, 1992), p. 310, slightly altered.

404 Rudenko: "Have I rightly concluded from your testimony . . ." and Paulus's reply —Ibid., p. 311.

405 The defense attorney: "What about you, Field-Marshal Paulus?" and Paulus's reply —Loc. cit., somewhat altered.

405 Ribbentrop: "That man is finished . . ." and Jodl's reply —Gilbert, p. 148 (12 February 1946).

406 Colonel Heim's characterization of Paulus: "Well groomed . . ." —Goerlitz, pp. 47–48.

406 Ernst Paulus's postwar relations with his father —The silver-framed photograph from Poltava is, of course, my fabrication. For what it is worth, Ernst Paulus inserted the following into Goerlitz's compilation (p. xiii): "So, in all reverence, I dedicate this book to the memory of Sixth Army."

407 Hitler's will: ": . . . and therefore to choose death of my own free will . . ." Tuviah Friedman, Director of the Documentation Center, *Long Dark Nazi Years: A Record of Documents and Photographs of Adolf Hitler's Final Solution* (Haifa, 1999), testament p. 4 (pages of this book not consistently numbered). This document was discovered in a secret compartment of a suitcase in possession of a Frau Irmgard Unterholzer in Tegernsee.

407 Ditto: "May it be one day a part of the code of honor . . ." —Ibid.; testament p. 6.

407 Hilde Benjamin, nicknamed the Red Guillotine —She makes a few cameo appearances in Richard J. Evans, *Rituals of Retribution: Capital Punishment in Germany 1600–1987* (New York: Oxford University Press, 1996). There is no information available to me that she ever met Paulus in real life.

407 Hitler to Paulus: "One has to be on the watch like a spider in its web . . ." —Slightly altered from Warlimont, pp. 326–27 (fragment no. 5; discussion with Sonderfuuhrer von Neurath concerning Italy on 20 May 1943).

408 Field-Marshal von Manstein on closeness between officers and men as the "Prussian tradition" —Op. cit., p. 207.

408 Paulus's prewar service report (1920): "Modest, perhaps too modest . . ." —Quoted in von Mellenthin, *German Generals*, p. 104.

408 Hilde Benjamin on Paulus: "An innocuous representative of the former military-professional caste . . ." —I have fabricated this.

409 Paulus's Dresden lecture: "At the same time, particular attention was invited to Sixth Army's inadequate stock of supplies" —Goerlitz, p. 219 (memorandum: "The basic facts of Sixth Army's operations at Stalingrad [Phase I]," by Paulus).

409 Gehlen: "My department predicted ten days in advance precisely where the blow would fall at Stalingrad!" —After Gehlen, p. 56. In his memoirs, Gehlen is nearly always right. David Thomas paints a different picture.

409 The show trial of the Gehlen Organization —On 11 November, two ringleaders were guillotined in Dresden between 4:18 and 4:22 A.M., for the crime of industrial espionage.

409 "Five hundred and forty-six spies arrested!" —Number supplied by Gehlen, p. 174, who contemptuously adds: 'A fantastic figure which should itself have sufficed to convince any neutral observer that this was pure propaganda; it reminded me of the RAF and Luftwaffe claims in the Battle of Britain."

ZOYA

As transliterated in the *Great Soviet Encyclopedia* (vol. 13, p. 433), her name is Zoia Anatol'evna (Tania) Kosmodem'ianskaia. In this story I have preferred the looser, less forbidding orthography of World War II Anglo-American accounts. The encyclopedia informs us, in typical fashion omitting any mention of the mundane stables, that "she was captured by the fascists . . . while fulfilling a combat mission."

411 Epigraph: "The essential thing about anti-guerrilla warfare . . ." —Warlimont, p. 289 (Hitler at staff conference, fragment no. 29, evening session, 1 December 1942 in Wolfschanze).

412 Zoya: "You can't hang all hundred and ninety million of us." —Karpov, p. 150. The first two of the three photographs of Zoya are reproduced here.

413 Number of Vlasov's mortars and heavy guns—Erickson, p. 534.

413 Marshal Tukhachevsky: "The next war will be won by tanks and aviation" —After Shostakovich and Volkov, p. 100.

413 The song of the two beardless boys: "Into battle for our nation, into battle for our Stalin" —Alexander Werth, *Leningrad* (New York: Alfred A. Knopf, 1944), p. 33. To follow the meter of the original Russian (which appears on the same page), I've added an "our" before "Stalin" (the original runs *za Stalina)* and accordingly rendered *za rodinu,* "for the nation," as "for our nation."

415 Streets named after her —In addition to a number of Kosmodem'ianskaia Streets, there is a monument to her on the Minsk highway.

CLEAN HANDS

The tale of Gerstein has haunted me for a number of reasons. "At the beginning of Nazism in Germany," writes Marie-Louise von Franz, "I was several times asked by Germans in what respect they were abnormal, for though they were unable to accept Nazism, not doing so made them doubt their own normality . . . misery fell upon people who had done the right thing." —*The Feminine in Fairy Tales,* rev. ed. (Boston: Shambhala, 1993), p. 36. Some of the remarks in "Clean Hands" about the conflicting necessities of parleying with evil and of respecting it by not investigating it are partially indebted to this book; likewise the notion that someone who continues to fight evil and gets victimized is from a psychological perspective complicit. Basically, what von Franz is arguing is that if we repress our own evil side, it will come out somewhere else. My motivation in placing such arguments into the mouths of the other characters is to deepen our sense of what Gerstein's biographer has called "the ambiguity of good." All the same, I firmly believe that there was nothing ambiguous about Gerstein's good, unavailing though it proved to be. He is one of my heroes.

417 Hans Günther: "This is one of the most secret matters, even the most secret . . ." —Nora Levin, *The Holocaust: The Destruction of European Jewry 1933–45* (New York: Schocken, 1973), p. 311 ("retranslated" a little). However, in his own affidavit, which is presumably more accurate, Gerstein assigns these words not to Günther but to S.S. Brigade Chief Otto Globocnik; see Saul Friedländer, *Kurt Gerstein: The Ambiguity of Good,* trans. Charles Fullman (New York: Alfred A. Knopf [Borzoi], 1969), p. 104. For narrative reasons I have employed Levin's version.

417 For a full version of Gerstein's affidavit, see Bundeszentrale für Heimatdienst, *Schriftenreihe der Bundeszentrale für Heimatdienst: Dokumentation zur Massen-Vergasung,* Heft 9 (Bonn: Printed by Oberfränkische Verlangsaft und Druckerei G.m.b.H, Hof/Saale, 1955), pp. 7–16 (affidavit of 4 May 1945).

421 Gerstein's journey to Belzec —In fact, he, Günther and Pfannenstiel traveled together by truck. Since literal faithfulness here would have made it impossible to introduce Berthe's *Doppelgänger,* I gave him a train trip.

422 S.S. Brigade Chief Otto Globocnik: "Now, you're going to have two jobs at Belzec . . ." —Ibid., p. 311 (altered and expanded).

423 Dr. Pfannenstiel: "The whole procedure is not entirely satisfactory . . ." —Closely af-

ter Klee, Dressen and Riess, p. 244 ("'The camp had clean sanitary facilities': Professor Wilhem Pfannanstiel, Waffen-S.S. hygienist, on a gassing at Belzec").

424 Captain Wirth to Gerstein: "There are not ten people alive . . ." —Friedländer, pp. 108–09.

425 Gerstein to the Swedish attaché: "The people stand together . . . You can hear them crying, sobbing . . ." —Abridged from Gerstein's report of 4 May 1945 (presumably to the Americans); in Klee, Dressen and Riess, p. 242. In Friedländer this testimony appears in the past tense.

426 Working capacity of Belzec and other extermination camps —According to Gerstein's 1945 estimate, as reproduced in Friedländer, p. 104. Given the statistics which have since been more or less agreed upon for the number of people murdered in the Holocaust, Gerstein's count is far too high. For instance, based on his figure for Sobibor, the yearly "output" of that camp would be more than 7,000,000 victims. In fact, one of the murderers estimates that a total of "only" 350,000 Jews died there (Erich Bauer, "the Gasmeister"; in Klee, Dressen and Riess, p. 232). The commandant of Auschwitz states that "the highest number of gassings in one day was 10,000. That was the most that could be carried out . . . with modern facilities" (ibid., p. 273). According to the Auschwitz-Birkenau State Museum in Oswiecim, "of the circa 50 million people who died during World War II, around twenty million were victims of the unprecedented policy of extermination of the Third Reich" (p. 11; Franciszek Piper, "The Political and Racist Principles of the Nazi Policy of Extermination and Their Realization at Auschwitz"). In order to better respect and re-create Gerstein's thought processes, I have let his count stand. About Maidanek Gerstein writes only "seen in preparation," so for quantification of its "productivity" I have relied on the 1944 account of Alexander Werth (op. cit., pp. 890–94, which includes that grisly detail about the cabbages). Werth seems to have been the first credentialed Western journalist to see the camp.

427 "How many Jews remained above the ground in Europe?" —The protocols of the Wannsee Conference inform the "Herr Undersecretary of State Luther" that 131,800 Jews remained in the Old Reich, 43,700 in the Ostmark, 2,284,000 in the General Government of the former Poland, around 5,000,000 in the USSR; it all added up to the following total: "*Zusammen: über 11.000.000*" —Peter Longerich, *Die Wannsee-Konferenz vom 20. Januar 1942: Planung und Beginn des Genozids an den europäischen Juden* (Berlin: Gedenk und Bildungsstätte Haus der Wannsee-Konferenz, Band Nr. 7, series ed. by Norbert Kampe; Edition Hentrich, 1998), facsimile p. 6 (also stamped 171), *Besprechungsprotokoll* (with cover letter on SD stationery to Undersecretary of State Luther, dated 16 February 1942, date-stamped by Luther's office 2 March 1942), sec. III.

427 Dr. Pfannenstiel: "When one sees the bodies of these Jews . . ." —Slightly abridged from Gerstein's report (Friedländer, p. 113).

428 Conversation of Wirth and Gerstein: "We don't need any modifications" and "the prussic acid has deteriorated in transit" —Very loosely after Gerstein's report (Friedländer, p. 112), expanded and embellished. Wirth never offered Gerstein an outright bribe.

429 Wirth to Gerstein: "Two in the head is too much; two will practically tear the head off" —Fairly closely after the war diary of Blutenordenträger Felix Landau, in Klee, Dressen and Riess, p. 97 (entry for 12 July 1941; he was shooting Jews).

429 Footnote: "What harms love more than doubt and suspicion?," etc. —Strassburg, p. 223.

430 "They have already adopted . . ." and "Supplies for Tunis." —S. L. Mayer, ed., *Signal: Years of Retreat 1943–44: Hitler's Wartime Picture Magazine* (London: Mayer Hamlyn: A Bison Book, 1979). The issues selected by Mayer were all intended for the Channel Islands and therefore appeared in English. The pages of this volume are unnumbered, so they cannot be cited. I have also drawn on some of the illustrations in *Signal* for "The Last Field-Marshal." Since the dates of the various issues have not been indicated, there may be minor anachronisms.

430 Ludwig Gerstein's tale about the "Yid who tried to steal our name," and subsequent

conversation —Based on the following, written by Ludwig in the family album: "During the 1890s, a Jewish doctor, Richard Goldstein of Hamburg, changed his name to Gerstein. A complaint lodged by my brother Karl with the city Senate was unsuccessful, but he was promised that this would not be allowed to happen again. A renewed complaint on my part in 1933 went unanswered" (Friedländer, p. 10), and then Ludwig Gerstein mentions "an expatriate student" at the Technical University in Berlin. The part about a Jew under an assumed name being discovered and deported is my invention. Ludwig Gerstein closes the album with an exhortation to his descendants to safeguard the purity of their Aryan blood. Since people generally speak more crassly than they write, I haven't hesitated to make him still more fearsomely anti-Semitic than the record proves him to have been.

430 Gerstein on his father: "He used to say that he regretted what was being done" —Closely based on the testimony of the Jewish lawyer R. Coste, in Friedländer, p. 11.

431 Gerstein's service record "from this period": "G. is especially suitable . . ." —Actually, his training report from 5 May 1941, somewhat altered (Friedländer, p. 90).

432 Complaints of the gassing van inspectors: After the statement of August Becker, Ph.D., gas-van inspector (Klee, Dressen and Riess, p. 71). I have not seen any evidence that such people actually went to Gerstein.

433 Recollection of Pastor Otto Wehr: Gerstein: "Every half hour those trainloads of doomed Jews come chasing me . . ." —Very loose rephrasing of Friedländer, p. 134 (Otto Wehr).

433 Gerstein to Bishop Dibelius: "Help us, help us! These things must become the talk of the world—" —Friedländer, p. 136 (testimony of Otto Dibelius, abridged).

435 Ludwig Gerstein: "Leave bad manners to their own quarrel" —Actually, this is part of the advice given to the knight Parzifal by one of his first teachers, Gurnemanz de Graharz. See von Eschenbach, p. 94.

435 "Word of the Week" street poster: "Who wears this symbol is an enemy of our people" —Hans Bohrmann, comp., *Politische Plakate,* with essays by Ruth Malhotra and Manfred Hagen (Dortmund, Germany: Harenberg Kommunikation; Die bibliophilien Taschenbücher, no. 435, 1984), p. 374, item no. 278 (trans. by WTV). The note on p. 643 identifies this item as "Parole der Woche 1942 Nr. 27 (1.–7.7.)," in other words, the "Word of the Week" for the first week of July.

436 Baron von Otter to Gerstein: ". . . a great influence on the relations between Sweden and Germany" —Gerstein believed or wanted to believe that the Baron said this; these are the words of his report to the Allies at the end of the war (Friedländer, p. 124).

439 Edmund: "Long and wide went the forest . . ." —von Eschenbach, p. 214 ("retranslated" by WTV).

439 Gerstein to Helmut Franz: "The times leave me no choice . . ." —Friedländer, p. 91 (recast as direct speech).

439 The Hitler Youth actor in Hagen: "We'll have no Savior who weeps and laments!" and Gerstein's reply: "We shall not allow our faith to be publicly mocked without protest!" —Friedländer, p. 37, slightly "retranslated."

440 Gerstein's final inteview with the Swiss consul Hochstrasser —A fiction, like the first one. According to Balfour (loc. cit.), Gerstein did at some point tell Hochstrasser about the Holocaust, and Hochstrasser passed this information on to his country. I know nothing about his own attitude to Gerstein.

440 Conversation between Gerstein and his wife: "How can you, a man of honor . . . testify about them" —Considerably altered from Friedländer, p. 131 (Gerstein's interlocutor was actually the architect Otto Völkers). According to Friedländer, Gerstein might in fact have tried to protect his wife during this period from full knowledge of what he'd seen at Belzec; but from her testimony (p. 132), it seems clear that she was aware that massive numbers of people were being murdered by the Nazis.

442 Ludwig Gerstein: "For whoever desires the Grail must approach that prize with the sword" —Actually, Eschenbach, p. 269, slightly "retranslated."

442 "His son Christian" —I have not been able to find out the names of Gerstein's children.

443 Gerstein to his family: "The Allies have devices with which they can pinpoint their targets in the dark . . ." —Testimony of Nieuwenhuisen, to whom Gerstein was in fact speaking; in Friedländer, p. 163.

446 Captain Wirth, on the capacity of Auschwitz's crematoria and open pyres: After The Auschwitz-Birkenau State Museum in Oswiecim, pp. 169–70 (Franciszek Piper, "The Mass Extermination of Jews").

447 "Our fiendish enemy on the Ostfront," on the German mood after Stalingrad: "Bitter resistance, bordering on unthinking rashness; and timidity shading into morbid cowardice" —Chuikov, p. 15.

448 Bishop Dibelius, who "advocated only the exclusion of the Jews from our economic life" —Information given in Friedländer, pp. 38–39. This is a heartbreaking datum; Gerstein was so far from Germany normalcy, such a crier in the wilderness, that he had to consider somebody like Dibelius his ally!

449 The typist from the motor pool: "What you are under the uniform is nobody's business" —Actually, this was an old woman whose slightly anti-Nazi son had joined a Nazi group just to get some peace. She is quoted in Karl Billinger, *Fatherland* (New York: Farrar and Rinehart, Inc., 1935; no date given for what must have been the original German publication), p. 243. Billinger was a rather dreary German Communist who was lucky enough to be amnestied after about a year in a camp. I have stolen two or three details from him for my scenes of Gerstein's 1936 arrest and internment.

451 "The historian-ethicist Michael Balfour": "One is tempted to dismiss Gerstein as a romancer . . ." —Michael Balfour, *Withstanding Hitler in Germany 1933–45* (New York: Routledge, 1988), pp. 240–41 (entry on Gerstein).

452 "Whoever gazes into Isolde's eyes feels both heart and soul refined like gold in the white-hot flame." —Strassburg, p. 150, slightly "retranslated" by WTV.

452 Colloquy between Gerstein and Berthe —Very loosely based on the dialogue between Svipdag and his dead mother Gróa in the *Poetic Edda*, pp. 141–43 ("Svipdagsmál," stanzas 1–16). Gróa is giving her son spells and guidance for travel in the other world to win his bride.

453 Michal Chilczuk, Polish People's Army: "But what I saw were people I call humans . . ." —Brewster Chamberlin and Marcia Feldman, ed., *The Liberation of the Nazi Concentration Camps 1945* (Washington, D.C.: United States Holocaust Memorial Council, 1987), p. 38 (slightly "retranslated" by WTV).

454 "In theory, he was saving a hundred thousand lives" —It is unknown how much prussic acid Gerstein destroyed, and exactly by what manner. Friedländer (p. 181) quotes Gerstein as saying in one of his affidavits that "the actual amount involved was approximately 9 tons 7 cwt, enough to kill 8,000,000 people." Of course the Germans used metric measures: 18,700 pounds equals 8,500 kilograms. Since 8,500 goes 941.2 times into 8,000,000, we might as well say that 1 kilogram of Zyklon B can kill 1,000 people; hence Gerstein's desperately theoretical computation that withholding 100 kilograms saved 100,000 people. Like most of Gerstein's computations, this one would have exaggerated Holocaust numbers. According to Commandant Höss, who ought to have known, "five to seven kilograms of Zyklon B sufficed to murder 1,500 people" (The Auschwitz-Birkenau State Museum in Oswiecim, p. 171), so Gerstein was off by a factor of five to seven. Once again, I've thought it best to be faithful to his thought processes, and to the information available to him at the time, rather than give hindsight's corrected statistics.

455 Ludwig Gerstein: "If you want to live a worthy life, Kurt, you must never treat a woman badly. A woman, you know, bears no weapons in her hands" —Substantially "retranslated" and abridged from von Eschenbach, p. 268 (the hermit Trevrizent to Parzifal).

457 *Die Ostschweiz* headline on the Hungarian Jews: "People are Disappearing" —Mentioned by the Auschwitz-Birkenau State Museum in Oswiecim, p. 254 (Henryk Swiebocki, "Disclosure and Denunciation of SS Crimes").
458 Description of Roman Karmen's body language as he filmed the captured Nazis of Maidanek —After a photo in *Ognev*.
458 Details on the suppliers on Zyklon B and Gerstein's own shadowy but probably negligible role in supplying Asuchwitz —Friedländer, pp. 184–88. There is no record of Gerstein's ever having any such conversation with Höss as the one which I have imagined. Presumably he must have had close calls here or elsewhere.
460 Gerstein to his wife: "What action against Nazism . . ." —Gerstein testimony of 1945; in Friedländer, p. 160.
461 *Signal* magazine: "'I'll have the second from the right,'" says Hilde . . ." —Mayer, op. cit. The following sentence, "I don't care how many bombs they drop . . ." is my invention. The repaired shop window through which Hilde is bravely peering was damaged by an Allied air raid.
462 Gerstein to Hochstrasser: "If Hitler should lose, he'll slam the door . . ." —Loosely after Gerstein to Nieuwenhuisen, to whom Gerstein was in fact speaking; in Friedländer, p. 163.
462 "They" at Oranienburg: "What you see here makes you either brutal or sentimental" —Klee et al, p. 163 (letter from S.S.-Obersturmführer Karl Kretchmer, Sonderkommando 4a, 27 September 1942).
463 Details on Ravensbrück concentration camp —Based on Germaine Tillion, *Ravensbrück: An Eyewitness Account of a Women's Concentration Camp*, trans. by Gerald Satterwhite (Garden City, New York: Anchor Books, 1975).
464 Gerstein's father: "Hard times demand hard methods"—Friedländer, p. 203.
466 Dr. Pfannenstiel to Gerstein: "You're the man who invented the gas chamber" —An allegation (not made specifically by Dr. Pfannenstiel or anyone) quoted by Balfour.
466 Dr. Pfannenstiel: "I noticed nothing special about the corpses . . ." —Friedländer, p. 118 (Pfannenstiel's testimony before the Darmstadt Court, 1950, slightly abridged).
466 Gerstein on the pink color of the corpses killed by Zyklon B —Described in The Auschwitz-Birkenau State Museum in Oswiecim, p. 168 (Franciszek Piper, "The Mass Extermination of Jews").
466 Dr. Pfannenstiel: "Can science devise a way to render this process of exterminating human beings devoid of cruelty?" —In his postwar testimony before the Darmstadt Court, Pfannenstiel actually said: "I wanted to know in particular if this process of exterminating human beings was accompanied by any acts of cruelty" (Friedländer, p. 118). I would think that my alteration does perfect justice to his thought processes during the days when he could participate in the Holocaust with impunity.
466 Gerstein and Helmut Franz on Kollwitz's "Volunteers" —Imagined by me. Helmut Franz's views on the need to respect evil and leave it alone are based in part on the argument in von Franz's *Shadow and Evil in Fairy Tales*.
466 The same conversation, on voluntarism and willing Hitler to be good —Somewhat based on Rudolf Hess's notion of loyalty to Hitler, as quoted in Krebs, pp. 206–07. Hess actually does compare himself to Hagen.
468 "Let gape the gates!" —*Poetic Edda*, p. 151 ("Svipdagsmál," stanza 43).
470 "Clever Hans" Günther's victims: two hundred thousand Jews in Bohemia and Moravia —Richard Overy, *Interrogations: The Nazi Elite in Allied Hands, 1945* (New York: Viking, 2001), p. 369 (HQ BAOR, interrogation reports from No. 1 Sub-Centre, 3–10 December 1945).
470 Gerstein to his father: "You are wrong about one thing . . ." —Levin, p. 310; Friedländer, p. 208 ("retranslated" a little).
470 Gerstein to his wife: "People will hear about me . . ." —Friedländer, p. 211.
471 "It may be that the mere fact of making such efforts . . ." —Friedländer, pp. 198–99 (Frankfurt court document, 1955).

471 Göring: "Anybody can make an atrocity film . . ." —G. M. Gilbert, Ph.D., *Nuremberg Diary* (New York: Da Capo, 1995, repr. of 1947 ed.), p. 152 (15 February 1946). Göring was of course sentenced to death. It may be worth noting here that his wife told him: "I shall think you died for Germany!" and "then all suffering vanished from his face." Her verdict: "He was devotion and goodness incarnate." —Emmy Goering, *My Life with Goering* (London: Bruce and Watson Ltd., 1972), pp. 157, 159.

THE SECOND FRONT

472 Epigraph —Vladimir Karpov, ed. [photos; with text by Georgii Drozdov and Evgenii Ryabko, trans. Lydia Kmetyuk], *Russia at War: 1941–45* (London: Stanley Paul, 1987), p. 17.

472 Chuikov's decorations —He also received eight Orders of Lenin and one order of the Red Star. He was not promoted to Field-Marshal until 1955.

472 Assessment of Chuikov's military prowess —After the brief biography by Richard Woff, in Shukman, pp. 67–74. I forgot to mention that during the Nazi-Soviet Pact he'd participated in the heroic liberation of East Poland from the Poles.

472 Chuikov: "The black humped shapes, like camels on their knees, of dead enemy tanks." —Op. cit., p. 18.

473 Chuikov: "The spring was with us, but behind the enemy's lines it was autumn" —Ibid., p. 17.

473 Chuikov: "This long delay in the opening of the second front . . ." —Ibid., p. 20.

473 The stanza from Marina Tsvetaeva: "You can't withstand me . . ." —Tsvetaeva, p. 43 ("Where you are I can reach you" [1923]), "retranslated" and slightly truncated by WTV.

476 "There were tears in the men's eyes . . ." —Modern Art Museum catalogue, unnumbered p. 4.

476 Situation of Chuikov in March 1943 —After Richard Woff, in Shukman, p. 72; John Erickson ("Malinovsky"), in the same work, p. 120; John Erickson, *The Road to Berlin: Stalin's War with Germany*, vol. 2 (New Haven, Connecticut: Yale University Press, 1983), pp. 45–64; *Great Soviet Encyclopedia*, vol. 29, p. 195, which also gives information on Chuikov's various decorations.

477 The trembling of Paulus's hand when he lit a cigarette —*Erzählungen über mein Schaffen*, orig. p. 32; Hau-Bigelow, p. 5.

477 Karmen's simile of the waterfall —After the same document, pp. 32–33, Hau-Bigelow, p. 5.

477 Soviet gratitude for Lend-Lease items —I quote the *Great Soviet Encyclopedia*'s entry on this program: "The deliveries made under lend-lease spurred US production during the war and promoted the enrichment of the monopolies at the expense of the government."

478 Karmen on remembering everything —After *Erzählungen über mein Schaffen*, p. 36, Hau-Bigelow, p. 7 ("Again the ruins of Berlin flash by . . . And again I try not to forget, as I [tried] two years earlier in Stalingrad, not the smallest, not a single detail of this historic event").

479 "Dziga Vertov's seven-reel declaration of love for the women of our Soviet military forces" —Made in 1938, but not widely distributed since by then this filmmaker was getting isolated for his "formalism." As the saying goes, he died in obscurity. I wish I had found time to add a story about the rat-infested basement where the young Dziga Vertov edited *Kino-Pravda*, or the strange coincidence by which his "Three Songs of Lenin" was so well received by the Italian Fascists that it won a prize at the Venice Film Festival of 1935.

479 Karmen's aerial bombing mission —After *Erzählungen über mein Schaffen*, pp. 24–28, Hau-Bigelow, pp. 2–4.

480 Photographs of Soviet prisons from the outside (mentioned occasionally in "The Second Front" and "Opus 110") —Lubarsky, pp. 14–19.

481 Käthe Kollwitz: "I believe that bisexuality is almost a necessary factor in artistic production" —*Diary and Letters*, p. 23 (autobiography).

483 Comrade Stalin: "Feelings are women's concern" —Enzo Biagi, *Svetlana: An Intimate Portrait,* trans. Timothy Wilson (New York: Funk & Wagnalls, 1967), p. 25.

483 Karmen's visit to Stalin's dacha —Ibid, p. 19. According to this source, he and Simonov were present when Svetlana met her great love, the married filmmaker A. J. Kapler, who got *sent away* for five years for his pains.

484 "Their only reason for invading France at that late date was to deny us total victory in Germany" —An actual Communist argument. See Andeas Dorpalen, *German History in Marxist Perspective: The East German Approach* (Detroit, Michigan: Wayne State University Press, 1985), p. 449.

484 Red Army's rape of German women: "an incendiary shell usually brought them out of their cellars." —Information from Clark, p. 417.

OPERATION CITADEL

485 First epigraph —Von Manstein, p. 383.

485 Second epigraph—Billinger, pp. 140–41.

486 Von Manstein: "Grave as the loss of Sixth Army certainly is . . ." —Von Manstein, pp. 289–90, slightly altered.

486 Statistics on troop and mine dispositions at Kursk—*Great Soviet Encyclopedia,* vol. 14, p. 134 (entry on the Battle of Kursk). This engagement is generally considered to have lasted two weeks. Soviet sources, however, concatenate it with other battles, so that it runs fifty days —all the more monumental.

486 Rüdiger's admiration for Lisca Malbran in "Young Heart" —An anachronism. This film cleared the censorship in mid-September 1944 and premiered at the end of November. The Battle of Kursk had taken place in the summer of 1943. "Young Heart" disappeared rapidly because in its second month it had earned only 372 Reichsmarks, ten percent less than the authorities required. It was an E-film ("Erste Grundhaltung latente polit. Funktion"), in other words a "serious" drama with appropriate political nudges. H-films were comic with political nudges. There were also nP-films and P-films (nonpolitical and manifestly political). After Stalingrad, E-films were preferred over H-films, "on account of the seriousness and greatness of our times". Unlike many films, especially P-films, "Young Heart" received no subsidy. Information from Dr. Gerd Albrecht, *Nationalsozialistiche Filmpolitik: Eine soziologische Untersuchung über die Spielfilme des Drittes Reiches* (Stuttgart: Ferdinand Enke Verlag, 1969), summarized for WTV by the delicious Yolande Korb. "Young Heart" must have been dreadful.

487 Various details relative to the weaponry of the two sides at Kursk, especially regarding the numbers and capabilities of Tiger tanks —David M. Glantz and Jonathan M. House, *The Battle of Kursk* (Lawrence: University Press of Kansas, 1999).

487 Some of my visual descriptions of German troops in this operation are based on photographs in the Ullstein archive.

488 Dancwart's favorite proverb: "Keep riding until daybreak" —*Nibelungenlied,* p. 202 ("We cannot bivouc," answered bold Dancwart. "You must all keep riding until daybreak.")

489 The size of the salient: half the size of England —Erickson, *The Road to Berlin,* p. 64.

489 Ninth Panzer Division's experiences at Kursk —Based in part on Haupt, 173–74 (battle diary of Ninth Panzer, Panzer-Grenadier Grosssdeutschland, 6 June 1943, Citadel/ Orel).

490 Ninth Panzer Division's armor strength at Kursk —Glantz and House, p. 349.

490 Twenty-first Panzer Brigade's armor strength at Kursk —Ibid., p. 284.

490 "Well, from the very beginning we'd known that it was no use; it was up to us as frontline soldiers simply to obey orders and bear the responsibility" —After *Hans von Luck, Panzer Commander: The Memoirs of Colonel Hans von Luck* (New York: Random

House / Dell, 1989 repr. of undated Praeger ed.), p. 238 (original reads, in another context: "It sounded to us rather too pathetic, but what was the use? We knew that from now on it was up to us, as frontline soldiers, to bear the responsibility and make the decisions").

490 Emblems of Panzer divisions, 1941–42 —Haupt, p, 178. When I write that "we disguised the X of our divisional emblem with a V overhung by a horizontal bar," I am actually describing the disguise of Fifth Panzer.

490 Number of Tiger tanks assigned to Ninth Army at Kursk —Nik Cornish, *Images of Kursk: History's Greatest Tank Battle, July 1943* (London: Brown Partworks Ltd. / Brassey's, Inc., 2002), p. 135.

493 Sergeant Gunther: "Slavs drink from the skulls of their enemies" —Loosely based on Tsvetaeva, p. 114 ("Bus," 1934–35: "Inside me, warmth and birdsong./You could drink both of them from/the two halves of my skull/[Slavs did that with enemies]").

493 Volker: "There's nothing we can do . . ." —*Nibelungenlied,* p. 215 ("'The things we have been told of will happen irremediably,' said bold Volker the Fiddler. 'Let us ride to court and see what can happen to us fearless men in Hungary.'")

493 "Beware of being too wise, it's said" —Very loosely after the *Poetic Edda,* p. 22 (stanza 54, "Hávamál").

496 "Maybe they expected me to scratch runes on the back of my hand" —"Operation Citadel" has a number of references to the *Poetic Edda,* of which this is a representative example. Brynhild (here known as Sigrdrífa) advises Siegfried, who has just awoken her from her magic sleep, to make his way through life with the help of runes. "On thy beer horn scratch it [the ale rune], and the back of thy hand, and the Need rune on thy nails" (p. 235, "The Lay of Sigrdrífa," stanza 8, interpolated with fn.).

499 "Doom never dies, said the old man" —*Poetic Edda,* p. 25 ("Hávamál," stanza 25, very loosely "retranslated" by WTV).

500 Hitler on Russian tank production figures: "The Russians are dead." —Fest, p. 94.

501 Narrator: "Well, to be sure, they have good reason . . . what they had will never come back" —After the *Nibelungenlied,* p. 215 ("She has good reason for her long mourning," answered Hagen, "but he was killed many years past. She ought to love the King of the Huns now, for Siegfried will never come back—he was buried long ago").

503 Von Manstein: *"A clear focal point of effort at the decisive spot"* — Von Manstein, p. 547 (italics in original, excepting the "a").

504 Significance of the Reds' thrust against Twenty-third Panzer Corps —Described in Glantz and House, p. 161.

507 "First, get the command tank" —Information from Cornish, p. 186.

507 Stalin's daughter, Svetlana: "I see you shining, my beloved, chaotic, all-knowing, heartless Russia" —Svetlana Alliluyeva, *Twenty Letters to a Friend,* trans. Priscilla Johnson McMillan (New York: Avon Books [Discus], 1967), p. 132 (letter 11).

510 Von Manstein: "And so the final German offensive in the East ended in fiasco . . ." —Op. cit., p. 449, "retranslated" by WTV. The translator notes (p. 549) that the chapter on Operation Citadel, from which I've drawn this quotation, is actually an article by von Manstein for the U.S. *Marine Corps Gazette,* which in this English edition has been substituted for the original text's much longer chapter on Citadel, "in order to shorten these memoirs to a size suitable for publication in Britain and the U.S.A."

511 Stalin: "If the Battle of Stalingrad signalled the twilight of the German-Fascist Army . . ." —Quoted in Cornish, p. 216.

THE TELEPHONE RINGS

512 Epigraph —Nikolay Rimsky-Korsakov, *Principles of Orchestration, with Musical Examples Drawn from His Own Work, in Two Volumes Bound as One,* ed. Maximilian Sternberg

[Shostakovich's teacher], trans. Edward Agate (New York: Dover Publications, Inc., 1964 repr. of 1922 Edition Russe de Musique ed.; R-K's draft unfinished in 1891), p. 141 ("Voices related in fifths and fourths"). In these stories I have preferred the orthography "Rimsky-Korsakoff."

512 "Everyone should do his own work from all the way to the end" —After Wilson, p. 288 (testimony of Evgeny Chukovsky: Shostakovich to his son Maxim). The original reads "from beginning to end."

ECSTASY

517 Epigraph—Anna Akhmatova, *My Half-Century: Selected Prose,* trans. Ronald Meyer (Evanston, Illinois: Northwestern University Press, 1997 repr. of 1992 Ardis Press ed.), p. 135 (second letter, Komarovo, August 26, 1861).

521, 523, 524 The three boldfaced letters in the book —I am sorry that these seem obscure to some readers. They are *E, E* and *a,* and they mark the book's beginning, midpoint and ending thus: "**E**lena **E**. Konstantinovskay**a**." (Her name is sometimes more correctly transliterated "**Y**elena," as in Fay's biography of Shostakovich, but out of deference to people who may be unfamiliar with the letter *ye,* I have remained loyal to the more traditional transliteration.)

OPERATION HAGEN

525 Epigraph—"I gave her my oath that I'd not wrong her anymore . . ." —*Nibelungenlied,* p. 148 (ch. 19, "How the Nibelung Treasure Was Brought to Worms"), "retranslated" by WTV.

526 Details about reupholstering the chairs at Kranzler's with Swiss packing twine and the "Negress" at the Golden Horseshoe —Samuel Hynes et al, *Reporting World War II:* Part One: *American Journalism 1938–1944* (New York: Library of America, 1995), pp. 213, 219 (Howard K. Smith, "Valhalla in Transition: Berlin After the Invasion of Russia: Autumn 1941").

527 Günther: "Complain not to me, but to Hagen; he's the cursed boar who slew this hero!" —Libretto booklet to the Solti version of Wagner's "Götterdämmerung" (Birgit Nilsson, Wolfgang Windgassen et al performing; Wiener Staatsopernchor, Wiener Philharmoniker, 1985), p. 206 (Act III, Scene 3, my trans. and alteration of the German libretto, which would literally read: "Complain not to me; complain to Hagen; he is the accursed boar who gored this hero!").

528 General Nikitchenko: "The record is filled with his own admissions of complicity. There is nothing to be said in mitigation" —Uncovered Editions, ed. ("the series has been created directly from the archive of The Stationery Office in London"), *The Judgment of Nuremberg, 1946* (Guildford, Surrey: TSO Publishing; printed by Biddles Ltd., Crown copyright, 1999 abr. repr. of 1946 ed.), pp. 183, 185 (Justice Jackson, judgment of Göring).

528 "The President": "Defendant Hagen, on the counts of the indictment on which you have been convicted . . ." —Ibid., p. 297 (pro forma sentence for each capitally convicted war criminal).

INTO THE MOUNTAIN

529 Epigraph —Sergei Eisenstein, *The Film Sense,* trans. and ed. Jay Leyda (New York: Harcourt Brace Jovanovich / Harvest, 1975 repr. of 1942 ed.; original Russian ed. *ca* 1942; date not given), p. 183 ("Form and Content: Practice," *ca.* 1942).

529 Affair of the Remagen bridge —Speer, p. 562.

529 Plan to flood the Ruhr mines —Ibid., p. 564 (the actual procedure was described by Hörner, assistant to the Gauleiter, and might not have come specifically from Hitler although it conformed to Hitler's general order).

529 Destruction planned for Düsseldorf and Baden —Ibid., pp. 566–67. Again, there is no evidence that Hitler was involved on this minute level.

530 Conversation between Hitler and Speer —Condensed from Ibid., pp. 570–73, with alterations and additions.

530 Hitler to "the officer": "The nature of this struggle permits no consideration for the populace to be taken" —Ibid., p. 577 (this was actually a general order to the commanders-in-chief).

530 Göring and the fate of the Philharmonic —Recounted in Ibid., p. 585.

530 Hitler: "Then the Luftwaffe is superfluous. The entire Luftwaffe command should be hanged at once!" —Slightly altered and abridged from Kershaw, p. 801.

530 Hitler to General Koller: "Any commander who holds back his troops will forfeit his life in five hours." —Bullock, p. 783, citing Koller.

DENAZIFICATION

532 Epigraph—Vladimir Ognev and Dorian Rottenberg, comp., *Fifty Soviet Poets* (Moscow: Progress Publishers, 1974, repr. of 1969 ed.), p. 178 (Yevgeni Yevtushenko, "Snivelling Fascism," my trans. of Russian text. The translation given on p. 179 softens the original).

534 Akhmatova: "I smile no more. A freezing wind numbs my lips" —Akhmatova (Hemschemeyer), p. 175 ("I no longer smile . . .", 1915, from *White Flock)*, "retranslated" by WTV.

535 The German POW: "Wälse! Wälse! Where's your sword," etc. —Libretto booklet to the Solti version of Wagner's "Siegfried" (James King, Régine Crespin et al. performing; Wiener Staatsopernchor, Wiener Philharmoniker, 1985), p. 44 (Act I, Scene 3; German text trans. and slightly altered by WTV; it would more literally run: "the strong sword I'll swing in the storm").

535 *Great Soviet Encyclopedia*, entry on Germany: "A state in Europe" —Vol. 6, p. 340.

AIRLIFT IDYLLS

536 Epigraph —Leo Tolstoy, *The Cossacks and Other Stories*, trans. Rosemary Edmonds (New York: Penguin, 1960), p. 159 ("The Death of Ivan Ilyich," 1886).

537 Various descriptions of Third Reich architecture in Berlin and its wartime and postwar fate —Based on photographs and text in McGee.

538 Description of Hitler's model of postwar Berlin —Large, p. 301 ("Model of Hitler's planned north-south axis, including the Arch of Triumph, and the domed Hall of the People." Source: Landesbildungsstelle.). Various other descriptions of idealized and projected Nazi streetscapes are based on five of Albert Speer's models and drawings reproduced in Antonova and Merkert, pp. 424–25.

539 Footnote: "Germany is the conscience of mankind . . ."—Keyserling, p. 136.

539 Elena Dmitrievna Kruglikova was the soprano who sang the first part of Lyusha in Dzerzhinskii's opera *Virgin Soil Upturned* (1937).

539 Some of my codenames are fictional; some are derived from Christopher Andrew and Vasili Mitrokhin, *The Sword and the Shield: The Mitrokhin Archive and the Secret History of the KGB* (New York: Basic Books / A member of the Perseus Books Group, 1999), pp. 437–59 (ch. 26, "The Federal Republic of Germany"). The sad story of LOLA comes here; of course the dates make it one more anachronism.

542 *Great Soviet Encyclopedia:* "Love for an idea . . ."—Vol. 15, p. 153 (entry on love).

543 The pale, pale man who wore dark glasses: "You've absorbed the Russian mentality. . .

There's something of the Russian soul in you, that emotional, sentimental, immeasurable something . . ." —Closely after Gehlen, p. 127 (Gehlen is speaking about a bilingual colleague-rival).

546 "The poetess Akhmatova": "Call this working! . . ." —Akhmatova (Hemschemeyer), p. 414 ("The Poet," summer 1959), "retranslated" by WTV.

547 GRAENER: "The German people need romanticism once more" —Somewhat after a remark by the composer Paul Graener; quoted in Michael H. Kater, *The Twisted Muse: Musicians and Their Music in the Third Reich* (New York: Oxford University Press, 1997), p. 26.

548 L. Moholy-Nagy: "Penetration of the body with light . . ." —Op. cit., p. 69.

550 "Atonal fallacies" —A phrase in frequent use by Nazi musicians.

559 Shostakovich: "I feel it's the worst cynicism to, to, to besmirch yourself with ugly behavior . . ." —Volkov, p. 243, somewhat altered (originally said in reference to A. Sakharov).

560 The Fifth Symphony as "series of components, gestures or events . . ." —Taruskin, p. 520.

564 Luftwaffe blueprints buried in a coffin —After Otto Jahn, *Twice Through the Lines: The Autobiography of Otto Jahn,* trans. Richard Barry (London: Macmillan London Ltd., 1972, trans. of original 1969 German ed.), p. 223.

565 Some details of the narrator's cloak-and-dagger negotiations with the East German and Russian authorities are pillaged from Jahn, p. 238ff. Jahn was kidnapped (according to his own account; others accuse him of defecting) in July 1954.

565 The kidnapping of Walter Linse took place in 1952, not before the airlift.

569 Kurt Strübund's maneuver —John Dornberg, *The Other Germany* (Garden City, New York: Doubleday & Co., 1968).

571 Frequency of C-54s landings at Tempelhof: every ninety seconds (in spring 1949) —Large, p. 408.

571 "West Berlin was never a part of the Federal Republic and will never belong to it!" —Collective Team," *GDR: 300 Questions, 300 Answers,* trans. by Intertext Berlin (Dresden: Verlag Zeit im Bild, 1967), p. 109.

571 "We were already planning a step-by-step takeover by West German monopolies" —So claimed by Erich Honecker, *From My Life* (New York: Pergamon Press, Leaders of the World Biographical Series, 1981), p. 208.

572 "At 0.00 hours the alert was given and the action got underway" —Ibid., p. 211. Citing the menace posed to Dreamland by Berlin-West's eighty espionage and terror organizations, and, worse yet, by the innumerable currency speculators, not to mention the Anglo-American monopoly capitalists, Honecker demands (p. 209): "Could we afford to look on passively while the open border was exploited to bleed our republic to death by means of an unprecedented economic war?" What to do? Deploy the ghouls of Nightmareland against the capitalists!

573 Adenauer's words to the East Germans (actually spoken in 1955) —Paul Weymar, *Adenauer: His Authorized Biography,* trans. Peter De Mendelssohn (New York: E. P. Dutton & Co., 1957), p. 488.

THE RED GUILLOTINE

574 Epigraph—"More quickly than Moscow itself . . ." —Walter Benjamin, *Reflections: Essays, Aphorisms, Autobiographical Writings,* ed. Peter Demetz, trans. Edmund Jephcott (New York: Harcourt Brace Jovanovich / Harvest / A Helen and Kurt Wolff Book, 1978), p. 92 ("Moscow," orig. written in 1927).

574 Comrade Sorgenicht: "Hilde Benjamin, Communist personality . . ." —[Rolf Steding, ed.], Academy of Political Science and Jurisprudence of the German Democratic Republic, *An Example for Unity of Theory and Practice: On the Occasion of the Eighty-fifth*

Birthday of Professor Dr. Sc. Dr. Hilde Benjamin (Potsdam: Center for State and Justice Information, Department of Publications and Printing, Current Event Articles of Political Science and Jurisprudence ser., no. 345, 1987), translated into English for me (17¢ per word; I now forget how much it all came to) by Elsmarie Hau and Tracy Bigelow; original, pp. 9–17; Hau-Bigelow, p. 5 (Klaus Sorgenicht, "Hilde Benjamin, A Communist Personality Who Personifies the Unity of Theory and Practice").

574 "The so-called 'West German' press," "A negroid woman with dark, evil eyes . . ." —Hilde Benjamin's Stasi file. Stasi Archive copy, obtained September 2003. Kopie BstU, Archiv der Zentralstelle AR 2 E/mi#1.01 [? illegible] 1156/61, 26.4.02. Her file code seems to have been A/27355/15/10/84, Ref. C. All translations, mistranslations and retranslations by WTV. Page BStU 00051 *(Die Welt, 15.8.52,* Wolfgang Weinert, "Ob schuldig oder nicht schuldig"); abbreviated; last two words slightly altered for euphony.

574 Most of my physical descriptions of Hilde Benjamin, and some of my descriptions of the former Field-Marshal Paulus, are based on photographs in the Ullstein archive. One description of Benjamin is after a photograph in Stiftung Haus der Geschichte der Bundesrepublik Deutschland, Zeitgeschichtliches Forum Leipzig (Hg.), *Einsichten: Diktatur und Widerstand in der DDR* (Leipzig: Reclam Verlag Leipzig, 2001), p. 70.

575 Some details of the Red Guillotine's life derive from Hilde Benjamin's Stasi file. A few other biographical tidbits are taken from Marianne Brentzel, *Die Machtfrau: Hilde Benjamin 1902–1989* (Berlin: Christoph Links Verlag, 1997).

575 Benjamin's visit to the commandant with four wristwatches —Some Russian officers did behave this way, but this meeting is entirely imagined. Benjamin herself describes it very differently.

576 Benjamin's associations with Käthe Kollwitz and Roman Karmen are entirely invented.

576 Description of various versions of the Liebknecht memorial image —After the reproductions and text in Prelinger, pp. 51–56.

577 Benjamin to her mother: "I believe I will be able to help the victims of injustice" —Steding (Sorgenicht), trans. Hau-Bigelow, p. 6 (somewhat altered; not said to her mother).

577 Description of Benjamin's life and career before 1945 —In part from her Benjamin Stasi file, pp. BStU 000001–6; p. 786, [?]taaat1.Komitee für Rundfunk, [?]bt. Monitor, 2.1355 (2.135) [handwritten code; some parts illegible], Karl-Wilhelm-Fricke, DLF 21.40 vom 5.2.77, Porträt Hilder Benjamins.

577 Georg Benjamin "was also Superintendent of Schools in Berlin-Wedding, a working-class quarter" —Steding (Sorgenicht), loc. cit.

577 I have drawn some of my inferences about Benjamin's role in the Communist legal arena of the 1920s from Hilde Benjamin, "The Struggle of the Working Class for a New Rule of Law and a Democratic Legal System" (1969), in *Aus Reden und Aufsätzen* (Berlin: Staatsverlag der Deutschen Demokratischen Republik, 1982), trans. for WTV by Pastor Andreas Pielhoop.

578 "The legend": "In that period, Communist Hilde Benjamin was clear that her most important work was the realization of the Party's decisions." —Steding (Sorgenicht), p. 7 (somewhat altered).

578 Description of the courtroom for the Horst Wessel trial —After Benjamin's Stasi file, p. BStU 000229, *Spiegel,* Mittwoch, 18.3.59, p. 30 ("SOWJETZONE: Recht: Zwischen Recht und Rot").

578 Testimony of Horst Wessel's mother, and Benjamin's response —My invention.

579 Benjamin to defendants: "I've come to recognize that questions of law and justice are at the same time questions of power" —Steding (Sorgenicht), loc. cit. (somewhat altered; not to anyone in particular; an official third-person restatement of her views).

579 Comrade W. Ulbricht "The Communists must be the ones who know Fascist labor law the best" —Benjamin (Pielhoop), p. 4.

579 "The legend:" "She was asked by the commander of the Berlin city precinct Stieglitz . . ." —Steding (Sorgenicht), loc. cit.

579 "The radical removal of Nazi and reactionary elements was a main focus of her department." —Ibid., p. 8.

580 "Since East Germany doesn't even have trade unions yet, our first task will be to complete the bourgeois revolution of 1848" —Somewhat after Gareth Pritchard, *The Making of the GDR 1945–53: From Antifascism to Stalinism* (Manchester, U.K.: Manchester University Press, 2000), p. 8.

580 Footnote: Ulbricht's activities in the Spanish Civil War —Robert Conquest, *The Great Terror, A Reassessment* (New York: Oxford University Press, 1990), p. 411.

580 Same footnote: Comrade Leonhard on Ulbricht: "Being entirely innocent of theoretical ideas or personal feelings . . ." —Wolfgang Leonhard, *Child of the Revolution,* trans. C. M. Woodhouse (Whitstable, Kent, U.K.: Ink Links, 1979, repr. of orig. 1957 English ed.; orig. German ed. 1950), p. 288.

580 Same footnote: A. A. Grechko on Ulbricht: "The old one isn't worth much anymore" —Edward N. Peterson, *The Secret Police and the Revolution: The Fall of the German Democratic Republic* (Westport, Connecticut: Praeger, 2002), p. 5.

580 Benjamin: "Not creation of the new, but restoration of the old" —Benjamin Stasi file, p. BStU 000010, p. 4.

581 Ulbricht: "This meeting has nothing to do with dismantling" —Leonhard, p. 343. This source also describes the confrontation with Ulbricht regarding abortion; I have reworded his answer somewhat in the imagined conversation farther on in the text, and entirely invented Benjamin's role.

581 A few descriptions of East German landscapes, and several concepts relating to "socialist legality," are indebted to Arthur W. McCardle and A. Bruce Boenau, eds., *East Germany: A New Germany Nation Under Socialism?* (New York: University Press of America, 1984), pp. 52–79 (Horst Krüger, "Alien Homeland: Sentimental Journey Through the GDR-Province," 1978); and pp. 156–71 (Institut für Theorie des Staates und des Rechts der Akademie der Wissenschaft der DDR, "The Nature of Socialist Legality," 1975). Krüger concludes (p. 73): "Actually the worst thing across the border was this good behavior which bores you to death."

582 Some of the events and statistics I cite from here on are from Gary Bruce, *Resistance with the People: Repression and Resistance in Eastern Germany, 1945–1955* (Oxford: Rowman & Littlefield Publishers, Inc., Harvard Cold War Studies Book Series, 2003). I am also indebted to Angela E. Stent, "Soviet Policy Toward the German Democratic Republic," in Sarah Meiklejohn Terry, ed., *Soviet Policy in Eastern Europe* (New Haven, Connecticut: Yale University Press: A Council on Foreign Relations Book, 1984), pp. 34–41, 47ff.

582 Benjamin: "Law must correspond with the progression of civilization" —Steding (Gotthold Bley, "The Creative Work of Hilde Benjamin in the Formation of the GDR's Legislation and Legal System"); Hau-Bigelow, p. 12 (abr. and reworded).

582 Most of the various East German trials and sentences are from information in Evans's *Rituals of Retribution,* as are a few brief quotations from Hilde Benjamin. From this book I have borrowed, then altered and embellished, various legal phrases and pronouncements to suit the purposes of my American gangsterism. It may be of interest to the reader, as it was to me, to learn that the East German legal system was far, far less lethal than both the Nazi and the Soviet variants. Evans concludes (pp. 864–66) that the GDR executed more than two hundred people, mostly in the fifties. Soviet military tribunals in the GDR executed others. Executions for murder were abolished in 1975; capital punishment was ended entirely a few years later. Evans goes on to call Hilde Benjamin "perfectly capable of mass murder" (p. 869).

582 Sentence of six years for selling eggs in West Berlin —Bruce, p. 227.

584 Benjamin: "Thorough cleansing of the entire public sphere" —Benjamin (Pielhoop), p. 4.
584 "Her legend": "She showed the ability to continually evolve . . ." —Steding (Sorgenicht); Hau-Bigelow, p. 8 (abridged and reworded; she actually proposed, still more radically, that "a law at the time of its enactment would correspond with the progression of civilization").
584 The Red Guillotine: "Since man develops his personality primarily in work . . ." —*GDR: 300 Questions* . . . , p. 62.
585 Benjamin: "The important thing is to apply the laws in a new democratic spirit" —Benjamin (Pielhoop), p. 6.
585 Seventy-eight thousand charged with political crimes in 1950 —*Binsichten: Diktatur und Widerstand,* loc. cit., p. 71. "There were no longer any classes or sections which can live at the expense of others" — *GDR: 300 Questions* . . . , p. 42 (tense altered).
585 "The legend": "She proved capable of disciplining enemies of the new republic with unrelenting severity"—Steding (Sorgenicht); Hau-Bigelow, p. 9 (abridged and reworded).
586 West German journalist: "Who has ever once experienced this woman . . ." —Benjamin Stasi file, p. BStU 00051 *(Die Welt,* 15.8.52, Wolfgang Weinert, "Ob schuldig oder nicht schuldig").
587 Information on the 1953 uprising —Peterson, p. 3.
587 "The General Prosecuting Authority, headed by the prosecutor general of the GDR . . ." —*Great Soviet Encyclopedia,* vol. 6, p. 315 (entry on the German Democratic Republic).
588 "The legend": "Her most important trials are known, and need not be mentioned further." —Steding (Sorgenicht); Hau-Bigelow, p. 9.
588 Stasi evaluation: "Comrade BENJAMIN is from the professional and political standpoint . . ." —Benjamin Stasi file, p. BStU 00055.
589 Comrade Gotthold Bley: "Socialist law and socialist legislation were tools, motors and levers she used" —Steding (Bley); Hau-Bigelow, p. 12.
589 Comrade Büttner: "She solidified the dialectical interrelation between law and society . . ." —Steding (Horst Büttner, "Keeping the Revolutionary Achievements and Experiences of Coming Generations Alive"); Hau-Bigelow, p. 18. (The original, which does refer specifically to her work as Justice Minister in those years, runs: "She solidified the inseparable connection and dialectical interrelation between law and society . . .")
589 Purpose of GDR justice: "Smash the resistance of expropriated monopolists for all time . . ." —Somewhat after Hans Werner Schwarze, *The GDR Today: Life in the "Other Germany,"* trans. John M. Mitchell (London: Oswald Wolff, 1973, trans. of orig. 1970 German ed.), p. 41.
589 Benjamin: "Only here in the German Democratic Republic have we learned the lessons of the past" —Benjamin (Pielhoop), p. 5.
590 "On 28.1.54 it came to our attention . . ." —Benjamin Stasi file, p. BStU 00040.
590 Gallows for Hilde Benjamin —Benjamin Stasi file, p. BStU 0004; newspaper clipping, 3.2.54: "Galgen für Hilde Benjamin."
590 Rumor that Benjamin had fled toward Israel —Benjamin Stasi file, p. BStU 000031 (letter from Breitschneider, Oberkommissar, Leiter der Abteilung VI, to the Stasi, 2.3.54).
590 "There are three kinds of people here . . ." —Peterson, p. 257.
591 Description of Benjamin and Ulbricht at the military parade —Somewhat after a photo in Benjamin's Stasi file, p. BStU 000227, *Spiegel,* Mittwoch, 18.3.59, p. 28 ("SOWJETZONE: Recht: Zwischen Recht und Rot"); the reproduction is poor, and I cannot tell whether the male figure is really Ulbricht.
593 Photographs in Benjamin's office, including the likeness of "that representative of the international workers' movement, Felix Dzherzhinsky" —An accurate list, and F. D., founder of the hated Cheka, is truly described in this way; in Steding (Büttner), original p. 55; Hau-Bigelow, p. 17.

593 Description of Red Guillotine in the courtroom —After Benjamin's Stasi file, p. BStU 000220, *Spiegel*, Mittwoch, 18.3.59, p. 22 ("SOWJETZONE: Recht: Zwischen Recht und Rot"); some details invented (for instance, in the poor reproduction of the newspaper photo I couldn't see whom the busts represented; very possibly Stalin's was gone by this stage; Pieck, Lenin or Marx could have been the subject).

595 Benjamin: "This sentence is a warning for all who waver . . ." —Benjamin Stasi file, p. BStU 000015; p. 10.

597 Programmatic Declaration: "Our laws are the realization of human freedom" —Benjamin (Pielhoop), p. 7.

597 Comrade Bley: "Based on the teachings of Lenin, she envisioned a necessary direction for the workers' and farmers' movement in socialist legislation" —Steding (Bley); Hau-Bigelow, p. 12.

597 Honecker: "Only a shambles was left of Adenauer's 'policy of strength'" —Op. cit., p. 213.

598 Tale of Benjamin's forced retirement —Benjamin Stasi file, p. BStU 000178, Hauptabteilung XX/1/I, Berlin, den 19.6.67.

598 Description of the restricted area where Benjamin, Ulbricht and other privileged Party members lived —Carola Stern, *Ulbricht: A Political Biography*, trans. and adapted by Abe Farbstein (New York: Praeger, 1965; n.d. for orig. German ed.), p. 196.

599 "Seventy-five percent of our judges in the regional and district courts derived from the working class [by 1967]" —*GDR: 300 Questions*, p. 67.

599 "To be remembered here is her impartiality . . ."—Steding (Sorgenicht); Hau-Bigelow, p. 9.

599 Statistics on farms and industrial enterprises confiscated in East Germany (actually by 1974) —*Great Soviet Encyclopedia*, loc. cit., p. 316.

599 The prank calls about the coffin —Benjamin Stasi file, p. BStU 000191, Hauptabteilung XX/1, Berlin 12.8.71. I have altered this incident substaantially.

In Berlin in 2003, Juliane Reitzig, a pretty woman in her twenties, answered my questions about growing up in the DDR as follows: "School was very military-like. You had to show effort, you know. It wasn't like, here's a little book about the bees and you know what. It was very political. In third grade they were already introducing us to the documentaries about the Holocaust. The Americans were our enemies and the Russians were our friends, of course. The Nazis were bad, of course. We the Communists, we were the good people. There wasn't any talk of Eastern Germans being involved in Nazis. It was always the West Germans who were the bad ones . . . They were encouraging us to have pen pals. I was excited, but at the same time they were checking to be sure that we were really writing letters. They would organize holidays if we were making an effort. They would organize trips to Russia . . . There were a lot of people who had more than others, especially those who were in the SED, the Party. Everybody had a job. Everybody had a place to live. But it was a planned economy . . . My parents, they told me that they had applied to leave for the West, they said, don't tell anyone, but I told my best friend, and her grandfather was actually working for the Stasi. There were rumors, and later on they found out he was there for sure. I never really went back to where I used to live. I have a dislike for that man, and also for other people who were very directly involved in that politics . . . Most people wanted the reunification." Juliane did not immediately recognize the name Hilde Benjamin. About the destruction of Dresden she said, "I really don't know all the historic details beyond the bombing, but there was a regime in power that needed to be stopped."

WE'LL NEVER MENTION IT AGAIN

601 Epigraph —"Everywhere that Torah is studied at night . . ." —Matt, p. 90 ("The Hidden Light," from *Zohar* 2, 213–14).

602 "My dear lady, thank you for your, your, you know, but I, I, well, I simply took a simple little theme and I did my simple, *simple* best to develop it!" —Grossly exaggerated from Wilson, p. 325 (testimony of Evgeny Chukovsky: Shostakovich on the First Cello Concerto).

WHY WE DON'T TALK ABOUT FREYA ANYMORE

611 Epigraph: "There is something fearful . . ." —Nathaniel Hawthorne, *Tales and Sketches* (New York: Library of America, 1982), p. 402 ("Monsieur du Miroir," rev. version of 1846).

In various stories, especially this one and "Opus 110," descriptions of Dresden before its destruction are based on the text and photographs (which are labeled with such helpful indicators as *"zerstört, später abgebrochen")* in Fritz Löffler, *Das alte Dresden: Geschichte seiner Bauten* (Leipzig: E. A. Seemann Verlag, 1999, repr. of 1995 ed.). A few details of Dresden in the 1960s derive from Jean Edward Smith, *Germany Beyond the Wall: People, Politics . . . and Prosperity* (Boston: Little, Brown & Co., 1979, rev. of 1967 ed.). This author visited Dresden in 1967.

612 Photographs of Dresden in the first years after the bombing —Christian Borchert, *Zeitreise: Dresden 1954–1995* (Dresden?: Verlag der Kunst, 1996). The window display at "Honetta Damenmoden" was actually photographed in 1956, not 1960, the year of Lina's visit; it probably looked slightly less sparse by then.

613 Photographs of destroyed Dresden, including corpses —Richard Peter, *Dresden: Eine Kamera klagt an* (Halle/Saale: Fliegenkopf Verlag, n.d., *ca.* 2000).

613 Lesbian venues and typologies in Weimar Berlin —Mel Gordon, *Voluptuous Panic: The Erotic World of Weimar Berlin* (Los Angeles: Feral House, 2000).

616 The Russians "separated themselves; they had their own place" —In the interview cited earlier (for "The Red Guillotine"), Juliane Reitzig said the following about the Soviet troops: "I think people were afraid of the Russian soldiers, but at the same time you had to like them. They separated themselves; they were in this airbase; they had their own place. Rarely saw them on the street; there were guards in the separate areas."

616 Information on continuing widespread rape of German women by Russian soldiers in Dresden and other parts of East Germany —Fritz Löwenthal, *News from Soviet Germany*, trans. Edward Fitzgerald (London: Victor Gollancz Ltd., 1950). Bruce (p. 47) tells a nasty story of Red Army men with syphilis who, released from a hospital for a night out, raped East German women in Brandenburg. One reason that so many SED members resisted Russian domination was these rapes. The tale of Vice-Landrat Beda also comes from this source.

OPERATION WOLUND

620 Epigraph: "Was their ill fate sealed   when in they looked." —*Poetic Edda*, p. 164 ("Volundarkvitha," stanza 21).

OPUS 110

622 Epigraph on the "'sweet biscuits' of culture" —*The Soviet Way of Life*, p. 409 (ch. 9: "The Society of Great Culture").

622 Shostakovich's cornucopia of food —G. Glikman (1945), in Schmalenberg, p. 182 (trans. by WTV).

623 *Sovetskaya Musika:* "It is impossible to forget that Shostakovich's work . . ." —Walter Z.

Laquer and Geroge Lichtheim, *The Soviet Cultural Scene 1956–1957* (New York: Atlantic Books / Frederick A. Praeger, 1958), pp. 13–14, citing *Sovetskaya Musika*, 1956, no. 3, p. 9.

624 Akhmatova: "As if every flower burst into words" —Akhmatova (Hemschemeyer), p. 276 ("Music," Zh. 452), "retranslated" by WTV.

624 V. Berlinsky on Shostakovich: "a lump of nerves" —Wilson, p. 244.

624 Eighth Symphony as "repulsive, ultra-individualist" —MacDonald, p. 191. The denouncer was Viktor Belyi, and the setting was, of course, the infamous Union of Soviet Composers' congress in January 1948.

625 A nineteeth-century French traveler: "The Russians are not ghosts . . ." —Dumas, p. 55.

626 Zhdanov: "Leninism proceeds from the fact that our literature cannot be politically indifferent . . ." — Robert V. Daniels, ed., *A Documentary History of Communism in Russia from Lenin to Gorbachev* (Hanover, New Hampshire: University Press of New England, University of Vermont, 1993), pp. 236–37 (Report to the Leningrad Branch of the Soviet Union of Writers and the Leningrad City Committee of the Communist Party, 21 August 1946).

627 Mikhail Nikiforovich: "Begging your pardon, my dear Svetlana Alliluyeva" —Biagi, p. 23. ("Begging your pardon, my dear Svetlana Alliluyeva" was my Shostakovian addition.)

628 Comrade Alexandrov's assessment: "A young, pretty blond woman with gentle brown eyes and a good figure" —Actually, G. Glikman (1945), in Schmalenberg, p. 182 (trans. by WTV). The Shostakoviches had at this time been married for over a decade.

630 Comrade Luria: "As stillborn as a law without the seal of Heaven on it . . ." —This and other aspects of the Jewish creed based on the texts and commentaries in Jacob Neusner, *Introduction to Rabbinic Literature* (New York: Doubleday, 1994).

631 Comrade Alexandrov's note: "Only eight percent of Leningrad's housing was destroyed" —Figure from Werth, *Leningrad*, p. 43.

632 Shostakovich to Schwartz: "What I've heard is better than anything by Shostakovich!" —Loosely after G. Glikman, in Schmalenberg, p. 199 (trans. by WTV).

634 Description of Shostakovich in 1948 —After the illustration in Gojowy, p. 81 ("Im Zebtrum des Kulturkampfes 1948 . . .").

635 The poster of Shostakovich in the copper helmet; Gavriil's reaction to it and his sculpture —G. Glikman, Ibid., pp. 179–80.

637 Shostakovich: "Certain negative characteristics in my musical style prevented me from reconstructing myself" —*New Grove Dictionary of Music and Musicians,* ed. Stanley Sadie (Washington, D.C.: Macmillan Publishing Ltd., 1980), vol. 17, p. 265 (entry on Shostakovich, slightly reworded).

637 Description of Galya Shostakovich as a girl —After the illustration in Gojowy, p. 29 ("Dimitri Schostakowitsch mit seiner Tochter Galina").

638 Akhmatova's denunciation in *Leningradskaya Pravda* —Reeder, p. 296.

640 "Comrade Hitler": "Conscience is a Jewish creation" —The Auschwitz-Birkenau State Museum in Oswiecim, p. 145 (Francizek Piper, "Living Conditions as Methods of Extermination," quotation from H. Rauschning's *Gespräche mit Hitler)*.

640 Khrennikov on Shostakovich: "Alien to the Soviet people" —MacDonald, p. 192.

640 Footnote: *Great Soviet Encyclopedia* remarks on the Allied Control Council —Vol. 13, p. 7, entry for same (slightly modified for context).

641 Shostakovich's doublespeak to the activists: "I appreciate your valuable critical observations . . . I'm sure those sanctions will, mmm, to speak, inspire me to . . . future creative work and provide, er, *insights* . . . Rather than take a step backward I shall take a step, so to speak, forward" —Glikman, p. 27 (letter of 8 December 1943, meant sarcastically in original, further Shostakovich-ized by WTV).

645 Shostakovich to Ustvolskaya: "Illusions don't die all at once—" —Loosely after Shostakovich and Volkov, p. 85.

645 Completion date of Ustvolskaya's Sonata No. 2 —February is my interpolation. I know only that it bears the date 1949.

645 Comrade Stalin: "We'll take care of that problem, Comrade Shostakovich" —Shostakovich and Volkov, p. 148.

647 Marina Tsevtaeva ("in anger and in love"): "I refuse to be" —Op. cit., p. 122 (from "Poems to Czechoslovakia").

648 Shostakovich: "I *do not like* too friendly or too antagonistic relationships between people." —After Khentova (Mineyev); original p. 152, Mineyev, p. 18.

650 Shostakovich to Glikman: "Everything is so fine, so perfectly excellent, that I can find almost nothing to write about" —Glikman, p. 39 (letter of 2 February 1950; this would actually have been written five months before Shostakovich had gone to East Germany, but it's a typical Shostakovich-ism. Glikman notes that whenever his friend wrote such things, he generally meant or at least felt the opposite).

651 Devotee of white keys and black keys: "This typical Russian girl, with her two braids . . ." —Dmitry Paperno, *Notes of a Moscow Pianist* (Portland, Oregon: Amadeus Press, 1998), p. 199.

654 S. Skrebov: "I absolutely reject such music . . ." —Wilson, p. 251 (testimony of Lyubov' Rudneva, slightly altered).

658 *Great Soviet Encyclopedia* on God: "An imaginary figure of a powerful supernatural being." —Vol. 3, entry on God.

660 Shostakovich to Glikman: "Dear Isaak Davidovich . . ." —Glikman, p. 49 (29 August 1953).

670 Shostakovich to Nikolayeva: "Which of them was luckier?" —After Shostakovich and Volkov, p. 98 (here Shostakovich was actually comparing himself to the executed Tukhachevsky).

670 Shostakovich to Nikolayeva: "Well, to grieve is also a right, but it's not granted to everyone!" —After Shostakovich and Volkov, p. 136.

670 Shostakovich: "It was really terrible that he didn't have a secretary. It used to be that Nina always picked up the telephone and said that he was away for two months" —After Gojowy, p. 106 (DDS to Denisov, trans. by WTV).

670 Chekhov: "Isn't our living in town . . ." —Anton Chekhov, *The Tales of Chekhov,* vol. 5: "The Wife" & Other Stories, trans. Constance Garnett (New York: Ecco Press, 1985 repr. of 1918 Macmillan ed.), p. 267 ("The Man in a Case," 1898), abridged by WTV.

671 The difference between a whistling shell and a sizzling one —Werth, p. 55.

672 The émigré Martynov on "Lady Macbeth": "A warning of harmful deviation." —Ivan Martynov, *Dmitri Shostakovich: The Man and His Work,* trans. T. Guralsky (New York: Philosophical Library, 1947), p. 47.

673 Discussion with Comrades Khubov et al about "Lady Macbeth" —Loosely based on the account in Glikman, pp. 261–62.

674 "It's about, I, I, how the love could have been if the world weren't full of vile things . . ." —After Shostakovich and Volkov, p. 108 (the composer was actually speaking of "Lady Macbeth").

674 Shostakovich's song: "Burn, candle, burn bright, in Lenin's little red asshole" —G. Glikman, in Schmalenberg, p. 197 (trans. and slightly altered by WTV).

674 The Eleventh Symphony's "secret references to the Soviet tanks now crushing the Hungarian uprising" —After Wilson, p. 317 (testimony of Lev Lebedinsky: "What we heard in this music was not the police firing on the crowd in front of the Winter Palace in 1905, but the Soviet tanks roaring in the streets of Budapest").

674 Maxim: "Papa, what if they hang you for this?" —Loc. cit.

675 "A German": "The Russians are masters in the construction of shellproof wooden field fortifications." —Steven H. Newton, comp., *German Battle Tactics on the Russian Front 1941–1945* (Atglen, Pennsylvania: Schiffer Military/Aviation History, 1994), p. 127 (Gustav Höhne, "In Snow and Mud: 31 Days of Attack Under Seydlitz During Early Spring of 1942").

675 Shostakovich: "When I look back on my life, I realize that I've been a coward . . ."

—After Wilson, p. 304 (testimony of Edik Denisov). For narrative reasons I have moved this scene from 1957, when it actually occurred, to 1958.

675 Address of the Kino House (Dom Kino) —Dr. Heinrich E. Schulz and Dr. Stephen S. Taylor, *Who's Who in the USSR 1961/62* (Montreal: Intercontinental Book and Publishing Co., Ltd, 1962; printed in Austria; orig. comp. by Institute for the Study of the USSR, Munich), p. 320 (entry on Karmen). Let's hope that the Kino House was in the same place in 1958.

680 Khrushchev and Shostakovich, 1960: Based on a scene described in Wilson, pp. 381–82 (testimony of Sergei Slonimsky).

681 Shostakovich to Glikman: "Life is far from easy. How I long . . ." —Glikman, p. 90 (letter of 30 April 1960).

681 Glikman's secret approach to Elena Konstantinovskaya on Shostakovich's behalf —This is a total fiction.

681 Number of faculty members at the Leningrad Conservatory —*Great Soviet Encyclopedia*, vol 14, p. 396 (entry on Leningrad Conservatory). Since this is a 1972–73 figure, it might be slightly higher than would have been the case a decade earlier.

682 Lebedinsky to Shostakovich: "You don't have much luck with women, Dmitri Dmitriyevich. Or maybe it's more accurate to say that you've racked up your share of failures" —Somewhat after Wilson, p. 352 (testimony of Lebedinsky).

682 Shostakovich to Irina Supinskaya: "Actually, I'm not against your calling the Seventh the Leningrad Symphony . . ." —Closely after Shostakovich and Volkov, p. 156.

683 Shostakovich to Lebedinsky: "I'd sign anything even if they shoved it at me upside down" —Wilson, p. 183 (actually not said to Lebedinsky but remembered by Y. P. Lyubimov, slightly altered).

683 Khrushchev: "Plainly speaking, why do the United States of America . . ." —N. H. Mager and Jacques Katel, comp. and ed., *Conquest Without War: An Analytical Anthology of the Speeches, Interviews, and Remarks of Nikita Sergevich Khrushchev, with Commentary by Lenin, Stalin and Others* (New York: Pocket Books, 1961), p. 99 (at Czechoslovakian embassy, Moscow, quoted in *New York Times* 10 May 1960).

685 Shostakovich on the beauty and plumpness of Meyerhold's wife —Loosely after Shostakovich and Volkov, p. 78.

686 Marina Tsvetaeva : "I set my lips to the breast of the great round battling earth." —Tsvetaeva, p. 20 (from "Insomnia," 1916, stanza 6), "retranslated" by WTV.

687 Dostoyevsky: "Why do even the finest people . . . ?" —*Uncle's Dream* etc., p. 109 ("White Nights").

690 Shostakovich to Glikman: "I'm not going, you see . . . They'll have to tie me up" —Slighly altered from Glikman, p. 92 (Glikman's commentary).

691 German casualties of the Allied bombing of Dresden —Kershaw (p. 761) gives an estimate of "at least 35,000" victims.

692 "Even former S.S. officers were cooperating with us now . . ." —Gehlen (p. 249) names three who worked for East German intelligence in part "to avenge the Allied bombing of Dresden in 1945."

693 Shostakovich: "The distinguishing feature of Jewish music . . ." —Wilson, p. 235 (testimony of Rafiil Matveivich Khozak).

694 Shostakovich to Glikman: "I wrote an ideologically deficient quartet . . ." —Slightly altered from Fay, p. 217.

695 "Akhmatova insists . . . that whoever doesn't make continual reference to the torture chambers all around us is a criminal" —Loosely after Chukovskaya (p. 5), who was actually writing that she herself would be a criminal if she didn't make at least some elliptical record of her conversations with the great poet.

696 Manfred Smolka: "There is no doubt that desertion and treachery . . ." —Richard J. Evans, *Rituals of Retribution: Capital Punishment in Germany 1600–1987* (New York: Ox-

ford University Press, 1996), p. 852. From the context, it is not clear whether Smolka's words were in fact reported in the press.

697 The Kabbalists: "Every definition of God leads to heresy" —Matt, p. 32 (Abraham Isaac Kook, "Pangs of Cleansing," in *Orot*).

697 Shostakovich: "When fate and all that is, you know, meaningless!" —Loosely after Shostakovich and Volkov, p. 17.

701 Conventional wisdom on Zoya: "Not long but beautifully did she live!" —Vsesoyuznuii Gospudarstvennui Fond Kinofilmov, p. 331 (entry on the movie "Zoya," trans. WTV).

703 Leskov on Katerina's final murder: She "threw herself on Sonetka like a strong pike on a soft little perch" —Nikolai Leskov, *The Enchanted Wanderer: Selected Tales,* trans. David Magarshak (London: Andre Deutsch Ltd., 1987, repr. of 1961 Secker & Warburg ed.), p. 50 ("Lady Macbeth of the Mtensk district," 1865).

704 Shostakovich to F. P. Litvinova: "You know, my dear Flora Pavlovna, I would have displayed more brilliance . . ." —Fay, p. 268.

706 Description of Nina's portrait —After the illustration in Gojowy, p. 28 ("Die Ehefrau Dimitri Schostakowitschs, Nina Wassiljewna geb. Warsar").

707 "Seed corn must not be ground." —Title of an image by Käthe Kollwitz, 1941–42.

708 The district Party secretary: "This is outrageous! We let Shostakovich join the Party . . ." —Wilson, p. 359 (Kirill Kondrashin).

708 Tale of Ashkenazi as Shostakovich's divorce intermediary against Nina —Based on Khentova, p. 130, trans. for WTV by Sergi Mineyev.

708 Date of Roman Karmen's marriage to Maya Ovchinnikova, his telephone number and his preference for hunting and fast cars —*The International Who's Who, 1977–78* (London: Europa Publications Ltd., 1977), entry on Karmen. The original says "cars," not "fast cars." But in Karmen's "Far and Wide My Country Stretches" there are a huge number of sequences with fast cars in them.

709 Karmen's private telephone number, *ca.* 1965 —Andrew I. Lebed, Dr. Heinrich E. Schulz and Dr. Stephen S. Taylor, *Who's Who in the USSR 1965–66,* 2nd ed. (New York: Scarecrow Press, 1966; printed in Spain; orig. comp. by Institute for the Study of the USSR, Munich), p. 346 entry on Karmen, whose address was then Polyanka 34. *The International Who's Who* gives him a different number in 1977–78, so it seemed no invasion to publish this one.

711 Shostakovich to his wife: "It was blackmail, Irinochka . . . If you love me, you won't dig that up . . ." —Loosely after Fay, p. 218.

712 Shostakovich to his wife: "You see, I'm such an insensitive criminal type . . ." —Loosely after Shostakovich and Volkov, p. 242 (actually said in reference to the criticisms not of Denisov but of Solzhenitsyn).

712 "A great comrade": "Anyone in this world who does not succeed in being hated . . ." —Hitler, p. 363.

713 The ditty played by Shostakovich: "Merry singing makes the heart glow . . ." —Von Geldern and Stites, p. 234 (Vasily Lebedev-Kumach and Isaac Dunaevsky, "March of the Happy-Go-Lucky Guys," 1934), "retranslated" from the following, which rhymes A B C C in the facing Russian text: "Merry singing fills the heart with joy. / It will never let you be sad. / The countryside and villages love singing, / And big cities love singing, too."

713 Brezhnev: "Socialist art is profoundly optimistic and life-affirming" —Daniels, p. 282 (Report of the CPSU Central Committee to the 23rd Congress of the Communist Party of the Soviet Union, 29 March 1966).

714 The reunion of Shostakovich and Akhmatova ("eighty-eight") —After Shostakovich and Volkov, pp. 274–75. So far as I know, their meeting was not filmed and Roman Karmen was not present.

717 The bourgeois critic Layton: "At their best, the symphonies . . ." —Simpson, op. cit., p. 198.

717 Shostakovich to Glikman: "I am a dull, mediocre composer"—Glikman, p. 140 (letter of 3 February 1967, abridged).
718 Shostakovich to Glikman: "Slowly and with great difficulty . . ." —Glikman, p. 143 (letter of 8 April 1967).
719 Shostakovich to the orchestra: "On the left and right flanks, the battalion regions are echeloned . . ." —After Glantz and House, p. 277 (Stavka Front Directive No. 12248, 8 May 1943, 0429 hours).
719 Shostakovich to the audience: "Death is terrifying . . ." —Wilson, p. 417 (Mark Lubotsky, unpublished memoir).
719 Shostakovich to his wife: "Unfortunately, Lebedinsky has grown, how shall I put it, old and stupid" —Wilson, p. 352, Shostakovich-ized.
719 Von Manstein: "Consequently it was now necessary for the Germans . . ." —Op. cit., p. 470.
722 "Our unshakable allies in East Germany" on the Fifteenth: "Strangely reserved and introverted" —Otto-Jürgen Burba, "Repetitio und Memento: Struktur und Bedeutung der Ostinatoformen bei Dmitri Schostakowitsch," in *Schweizer Musikpädagogische Blätter* (Switzerland), vol. 85, issue 1 (January 1997), pp. 25–30; trans. for WTV by Yolande Korb; "retrans." here and there by WTV; original p. 28; Korb, unnumbered p. 5.
723 Glikman's brother's idea for Shostakovich's gravesite, and his recapitulation of Irina's reaction —G. Glikman, in Schmalenberg, p. 178 (trans. by WTV). In this memoir, Glikman says "Petrograd," not "Leningrad."
724 Bely: "All of Petersburg is an infinity of the Prospect . . ." —Andrei Bely, *Petersburg*, trans. Robert A. Maguire and John E. Malmstad (Bloomington: Indiana University Press, 1978), p. 12 (slightly altered).
724 ". . . and the living faces the color of dirt, and that severed arm which hung from the garden gate . . ." —Punin, p. 191 (entry for Leningrad, 13 December 1941): "For a long time there hung an arm up to the elbow, attached by someone to the fence of the garden of one of the destroyed buildings. Dark crowds of people walk past with faces swollen and earthlike."
725 Nadezhda Mandelstam (footnote): "I can testify that nobody I knew fought . . ." —Mandelstam, p. 307.
727 Non-appearance of Shostakovich's name in the Urals poll —*The Soviet Way of Life*, p. 395 (ch. 9: "The Society of Great Culture").

A PIANIST FROM KILGORE

728 Epigraph —Jakov Lind, *Soul of Wood*, trans. Ralph Manheim (New York: Hill and Wang, 1964; orig. German ed. 1962), p. 46 ("Soul of Wood").
730 Professor Svetlana Boym, who happened to be a fellow at the American Academy during my own brief residence there in 2003, proposes that I've misconceived the Russians' anti-American attitude. In her view they wouldn't have been anti-Cliburn at all. Instead of Cliburn representing something baleful, she says, he would have simply been isolated and forgotten as his Russian colleagues got drunk and chased women.
730 The juror Oborin: "Good, really very good . . ." —Paperno, p. 209.
731 *New York Times:* "A big, percussive attack . . ." —Issue of 11 April 1958, p. 12, col. 5.
732 Sofiya Gubaidulina: "Dmitri Dmitreyvich, you're the person our generation depends on . . ." —Very loosely based on her retrospective testimony in Wilson, pp. 304–05.
733 The premiere of "Far and Wide My Country Stretches" —I am taking a liberty here, not knowing exactly when this film of Roman Karmen's first appeared. The *Great Soviet Encyclopedia* tells me only that it was released in 1958, the year that Cliburn won the competition.
736 General von Hartmann: "As seen from Sirius, Goethe's works will be mere dust . . ." —Craig, p. 373, slightly reworded.

737 Footnote: *Great Soviet Encyclopedia:* "Spontaneity, straightforward lyricism, exultant sound and impetuous dynamism." —Vol. 12, p. 121 (entry on Harvey Lavan Cliburn, Jr.).

LOST VICTORIES

I would have preferred to set this story in 1958, when "Lost Victories" first appeared, rather than in 1962; then the parallelism with "The Pianist from Kilgore" would have been more exact; unfortunately, the Berlin Wall was not erected until 1961. It seemed best to make the events of the story occur a year later, so that the narrator could consider the Wall a settled injustice rather than a brand new outrage.

738 Epigraph —Von Manstein, p. 29.
739 "Had Paulus only been permitted [by Hitler] to break out and link up with von Manstein's troops . . ." —Interestingly enough, Paulus seems to have blamed both Hitler *and* von Manstein. The ambiguously kidnapped Jahn had an opportunity to speak with him in 1954, in the office of Herr Weidauer, the Bürgermeister of Dresden. Jahn describes him (pp. 258–61) as a broken man, talking pitiably about his decorations.
740 "A great German": "The strong man is mightiest alone." —The great German was Schiller, but Hitler loved to quote this aphorism.
740 Speaking of great Germans, here is what the *Great Soviet Encyclopedia* (vol. 15, p. 436, biographical entry) has to say about von Manstein: "an honorary member of a number of revanchist circles."*
740 Von Manstein: "When Hitler called for the swift and ruthless destruction of the Polish Army . . ." —Von Manstein, p. 190.
740 Von Manstein: The capitulation of Poland "in every way upheld the military honor . . ." —Ibid., p. 59.
741 Von Manstein: As a result of the impeccable behavior of our troops . . ." —Ibid., p. 151.
742 Von Manstein: "From now on the weapons would speak." —Ibid., p. 33.
743 "Lili Marlene" —Mr. Thomas Melle would have me write the German "Lili Marleen," but I have never seen it this way in any Anglo-American World War II source, so I fear it would look wrong to my readers.
743 Von Manstein on the Soviet troop dispositions —"Deployment against every contingency" —Op. cit., p. 181.
743 Von Manstein: "The Soviet command showed its true face . . ." —Ibid., p. 180.

THE WHITE NIGHTS OF LENINGRAD

After completing this story I discovered the following footnote in Moholy-Nagy (p. 15): "The interplay of various facts has caused our age to shift almost imperceptibly toward colour-

---

*My own assessment of the man has much to do with the following remark in "Lost Victories" (p. 533): "I can only say that it was not granted to me—as one who had for several years past been engrossed in arduous duties at the front—to perceive Hitler's real nature, or the moral deterioration of the régime, to the extent to which we can obviously do today. Rumors of the kind that circulated at home hardly penetrated to the front, perhaps least of all to ourselves." I can accept this to an extent, but, as the Nuremberg Trial verdicts insisted, blindness at some point becomes culpability. Moreover, what does "moral deterioration" mean? Did he think the Third Reich to be moral at its inception? Did the mass murder of the Brownshirts and the opening of concentration camps at the very beginning not trouble him?

lessness and grey: the grey of the big city, of the black and white newspapers, of the photographic and film services; the colour-eliminating tempo of our life today. Perpetual hurry, fast movement, cause all colours to melt into grey."

748 Ansel Adams: ". . . lightly charmed by the passing landscape . . ." —Ansel Adams, *Examples: The Making of 40 Photographs* (Boston: Little, Brown & Co, 1983), p. 117 (commentary on his photograph of Jacques Henri Lartigue).

AN IMAGINARY LOVE TRIANGLE: SHOSTAKOVICH, KARMEN, KONSTANTINOVSKAYA

For my own narrative purposes I have invented many of the interrelations between these three individuals.

According to Khentova's *Udivitelyenui Shostakovich,* Konstantinovskaya returned from Spain married to Karmen. He was doing documentary work there in 1936 and 1937.

Konstantinovskaya and Shostakovich were intimate for slightly more than a year, from around June 1934 until some time in 1935, probably the late summer or fall, shortly after which she was expelled from the Komsomol and arrested. She seems to have been in prison for a year or less. So I imagine her as having volunteered for duty in Spain in 1936. I have no way of knowing whether she had the gruesome Gulag experiences which I have imputed to her.

It is a fact that she received the Red Star for bravery in Spain. Very likely she was a combatant. Possibly she saw action with a Soviet tank brigade. However, I have been unable to find out any details about her service in Spain. It is the fact of her Red Star which decided me to give her expertise in sharpshooting and first aid while in the Komsomol.

Karmen's memoir *Über die Zeit und über mich selbst: Erzählungen über mein Schaffen* states that his wife was expecting to give birth on 22 June 1941. The portions of the book which I was able to read in Berlin do not state which wife this was. She might well not have been Elena, because almost immediately after the newlyweds returned to the USSR in 1937 Karmen set out on other long journeys, which doesn't imply the closest of marriages; on the other hand, good Soviet citizens were accustomed to putting their families second. In *Europe Central* I have supposed that the expectant mother was Elena.

The International Who's Who, 1977–78 informs us that in 1962 Karmen married Maya Ovchinnikova. So he and Elena must have divorced before then.

Khentova writes that Elena married a Professor Vigodsky, to whom she bore a daughter, but gives no date. Khentova further states that although Elena kept in touch with some of Shostakovich's relatives, particularly his sister Mariya, she saw Shostakovich only once more. All the same, she saved his letters to the end of her life, which she could have done for any number of reasons, but why not suppose that she held a torch for him?

It is unlikely that Shostakovich never got over Elena, as has been imagined in this book. There is equally no reason to suppose that Elena's marriage with Karmen failed because she was still in love with Shostakovich. Moreover, Elena was blonde, not darkhaired, and I have no grounds whatsoever for believing her to have been a bisexual cigarette smoker. Shostakovich held somewhat traditional views about women (for instance, he did not express much respect for female composers, which was a point of contention between him and Galina Ustvolskaya), so I can't be confident that he could have tolerated a bisexual mistress.

When I think of Shostakovich, and when I listen to his music, I imagine a person consumed by fear and regret, a person who (like Kurt Gerstein) did what little he could to uphold the good—in this case, freedom of artistic creation, and the mitigation of other people's emergencies. He became progressively more beaten down, and certainly experienced difficulty saying no—a character trait which may well have kept him alive in the Stalinist years. In spite of the fact that he joined the Party near the end, to me he is a great hero—a tragic hero, naturally. Richard Taruskin writes in *Defining Russia Musically* (p. 537) "How pleasant and comforting it is to portray him as we would like to imagine ourselves acting in his shoes"—in other words, as being a member of some fairytale anti-Soviet Resistance, which would have instantly led him to share Vlasov's fate.

His marriage to Nina Varzar was unhappy in a number of ways, and I wanted to give him, in fiction, at least, a great love—which he might well have experienced with his last wife, Irina. Because in *Europe Central* his passion for Elena dominates his life to the end, including his years with Irina, I beg her pardon, and likewise his children's, for any misrepresentations which this book's objectives required.

Roman Karmen was not a great artist, but he was a brave, adventurous sort whom it would now be all too easy to dismiss as a Stalinist propagandist. He and Käthe Kollwitz may fairly be called fellow propagandists, although to my mind the latter was by far the former's superior from the "aesthetic" point of view. Karmen's documentaries deserve more attention than they have received. I imagine him, plausibly I believe, as a passionate "soldier with a camera" who did his best. I suspect that he was also cheerful and likeable. He very well might have tried to assist Shostakovich as I have imagined in "Opus 110," although here again, by magnifying Shostakovich's obsession with Elena, I have surely exaggerated the number of thoughts which our composer sent Karmen's way. In any event, I respect both men's memories.

What about Elena Konstantinovskaya? She remains an enigma to me. But I certainly love her as much as I can love someone I never knew. I had various reasons for making my version of her to be capable of love for both men and women. One motive was to make her as infinitely lovable as I could. As I've written in this book, "above all Europa is Elena."

ACKNOWLEDGMENTS

I would like to thank my father for our three days in Berlin and Dresden during July 2001. "The Last Field-Marshal," "Opus 110" and "Woman with Dead Child" were the principal beneficiaries. It was wonderful to see both my parents in Berlin in 2003, when I got to take a few more notes.

The American Academy in Berlin very kindly made me writer-in-residence for September 2003, a highly fortuitous, almost voluptuous circumstance which benefited almost all the German stories. The person who made this happen was George Plimpton of the *Paris Review*. Mr. Plimpton died before I returned home from Germany; I wish I had been able to thank him at greater length. I also wish to thank my colleagues at the Academy for their friendship. In particular, the ethnomusicologist Philip Bohlman, professor of music and Jewish studies at the University of Chicago, who was a fellow at the American Academy, helped me considerably, both in translating certain musical terms from East German critica essays on Shostakovich and in answering several of my questions about moti and *leitmotiv* in music. Juliane Reitzig, an intern at the Academy, answered som questions about growing up in the DDR.

Although I paid her well, and I am usually too sour to acknowledge peopl pay, the more I think about the help she gave this book, the more grateful I am Fr. Yolande Korb at the Academy. This research assistant and interpreter beyo dreams took me to Ullstein Bilderdienst and to several other places, got me wh ever library books I wanted, etcetera. She was also very patint with my stu bling confusion (I was on narcotic painkillers the entire me she knew thanks to a broken pelvis).

The photographic archives of Ullstein Bilderdienst, Berlin proved to b rich as the Nibelungen hoard. I hereby express my itude to that estab ment, without which I would never have seen quit many images of the dor Legion, Operation Zitadelle, Hilde Benjamin ich Paulus, Kurt Ger and various German tanks; nor certainly would known such splend the eyelashes of Lisca Malbran.

Dr. Gudrun Fritsch, curator at the Käth tz-Museum in Berlin, with my poor spoken German and gav eful references and adv "Woman with Dead Child."

Mr. Thomas Melle, also of Berlin dly and exactly corrected number of mis-Germanisms, main but once or twice of person well. He also gathered a heavy load of books about Hilde Benjamin for me when I couldn't carry much myself because of my injury. I am extremely grateful to him.

(Now that I have written the previous paragraph, I hereby double and triple it, for Thomas has since read the entire manuscript, patiently saving me from many more of my multifarious ignorances. Thank you so much, my friend.)

I appreciate the last-minute help of Nina Bouis; whose advice about *vruchka* versus *ruchka* I ultimately followed.

Chris Chang of *Film Comment* magazine in New York was very helpful with Roman Karmen contacts and references. He also caught two inconsistencies in ny draft of "The White Nights of Leningrad." Among other favors, he introduced e to University of Chicago film expert Yuri Tsivian, who gave me his views on professional accomplishments of Roman Karmen, and I have accordingly ted this verbatim in "Far and Wide My Country Stretches."

Ir. Heinz Riedel Lehmann of Berlin told me some interesting stories about is in his Soviet captivity; bits of these found their way into this book. In ley, Kara Platoni, whom I hired to do some research on Elena Konstanti- ya, was very efficient and nice; through her I certainly ought to thank Alan , editor of the *DSCH Journal*.

Stein was her usual altruistic self with books and introductions.

l M. Golden was extremely generous with his books, his knowledge laism and the Holocaust, and his time. He even found me three excel- an translators, who were all a pleasure to work with and whom I'd like ere: Pastor Andreas Pielhoop, Elsmarie Hau and Tracey Bigelow, the n put me in contact with Sergi Mineyev, whose rapid translation from of some selections in Khentova's biography of Shostakovich saved rry and strain.

iyeh said nice things about the stories and encouraged me to keep em. I have the happiest memories of our time together. When she ies, that meant the world to me. She kept me company in several s. I wish I could better express how kind and calm and steady she it was for me to rush off another story to her, to share with her bal tic, to search with her for old German newspapers or will always be special to me.

keny, Amel Boussoualim, Moira Brown, Kate Danaher, awai, Paula Keyth, Mayumi Kobana, Mechelle Lee, ferey, Shannon Mullen, Lori Nelson, Ben Pax, Terrie Robinson, Deborah Triesman and Becky Wilson is book and to me, during a difficult time.

vak, Susan Golomb, Amira Pierce, Kim Gold- their work on *Europe Central*. And I am very r for this book. This fine, gentle, intelligent d and confidante for a number of years. ut me.

Lizzy Kate Gray expertly advised me on some matters of musical terminology and instrumentation connected with the Shostakovich stories. I will always be grateful to her for the times we listened together to the selections I was studying of the Seventh, the Eighth, the Fourteenth, Opus 110 and the Preludes and Fugues. Her father Gary and I had a nice chat about the pitch of World War II airplanes.

FOR MORE OF WILLIAM VOLLMANN, LOOK FOR THE 

Argall—Volume Three of *Seven Dreams*
Vollmann alternates between extravagant Elizabethan language and gritty realism in an attempt to dig beneath the legend surrounding Pocahontas, John Smith, and the founding of the Jamestown colony. *ISBN 0-14-200150-3*

The Atlas
Set in locales from Phnom Penh to Mogadishu, and provocatively combining autobiography with invention, these stories examine poverty, violence, and loss even as they celebrate the beauty of landscape. Winner of the PEN/Center USA West Award. *ISBN 0-14-025449-8*

Fathers and Crows—Volume Two of *Seven Dreams*
It is four hundred years ago, and French Jesuit priests are beginning their descent into the forests of Canada, seeking to convert the Huron and courting martyrdom at the hands of the rival Iroquois. Through the eyes of these different peoples, Vollmann reconstructs America's past as tragedy, nightmare, and bloody spectacle. *ISBN 0-14-016717-X*

The Ice-Shirt—Volume One of *Seven Dreams*
A tour-de-force of speculative history, this vivid amalgam of Icelandic saga, Inuit creation myth, and contemporary travel writing yields a new and utterly original vision of our continent and its past. *ISBN 0-14-013196-5*

The Rainbow Stories
Thirteen unnerving and often breathtaking stories are populated by punks and angels, skinheads and religious assassins, streetwalkers and fetishists—people who live outside the law and outside the clear light of the every day. *ISBN 0-14-017154-1*

The Rifles—Volume Six of *Seven Dreams*
As Sir John Franklin embarks on his fourth Arctic voyage to find the Northwest Passage, he defies the warnings of the native people, and his journey ends in ice and death. But his spirit lingers in the Canadian north, where 150 years later, Inuit elders dream of long-gone seal-hunting days and teenagers sniff gasoline. A *New York Times* Notable Book. *ISBN 0-14-017623-3*

The Royal Family
A searing fictional trip through a San Francisco underworld populated by prostitutes, drug addicts, and urban spiritual seekers. Part biblical allegory and part skewed postmodern crime novel, *The Royal Family* is a vivid and unforgettable work of fiction. *ISBN 0-14-100200-X*

Whores for Gloria
A fever dream of a novel about an alcoholic Vietnam veteran, Jimmy, who devotes his government check and his waking hours searching through San Francisco's Tenderloin District for a beautiful and majestic street whore, a woman who may or may not exist save in Jimmy's rambling dreams. *ISBN 0-14-023157-9*

FOR THE BEST IN PAPERBACKS, LOOK FOR THE [illegible]

[illegible]

FOR THE BEST IN PAPERBACKS, LOOK FOR THE 

In every corner of the world, on every subject under the sun, Penguin represents quality and variety—the very best in publishing today.

For complete information about books available from Penguin—including Penguin Classics, Penguin Compass, and Puffins—and how to order them, write to us at the appropriate address below. Please note that for copyright reasons the selection of books varies from country to country.

In the United States: Please write to *Penguin Group (USA), P.O. Box 12289 Dept. B, Newark, New Jersey 07101-5289* or call 1-800-788-6262.

In the United Kingdom: Please write to *Dept. EP, Penguin Books Ltd, Bath Road, Harmondsworth, West Drayton, Middlesex UB7 0DA.*

In Canada: Please write to *Penguin Books Canada Ltd, 90 Eglinton Avenue East, Suite 700, Toronto, Ontario M4P 2Y3.*

In Australia: Please write to *Penguin Books Australia Ltd, P.O. Box 257, Ringwood, Victoria 3134.*

In New Zealand: Please write to *Penguin Books (NZ) Ltd, Private Bag 102902, North Shore Mail Centre, Auckland 10.*

In India: Please write to *Penguin Books India Pvt Ltd, 11 Panchsheel Shopping Centre, Panchsheel Park, New Delhi 110 017.*

In the Netherlands: Please write to *Penguin Books Netherlands bv, Postbus 3507, NL-1001 AH Amsterdam.*

In Germany: Please write to *Penguin Books Deutschland GmbH, Metzlerstrasse 26, 60594 Frankfurt am Main.*

In Spain: Please write to *Penguin Books S. A., Bravo Murillo 19, 1° B, 28015 Madrid.*

In Italy: Please write to *Penguin Italia s.r.l., Via Benedetto Croce 2, 20094 Corsico, Milano.*

In France: Please write to *Penguin France, Le Carré Wilson, 62 rue Benjamin Baillaud, 31500 Toulouse.*

In Japan: Please write to *Penguin Books Japan Ltd, Kaneko Building, 2-3-25 Koraku, Bunkyo-Ku, Tokyo 112.*

In South Africa: Please write to *Penguin Books South Africa (Pty) Ltd, Private Bag X14, Parkview, 2122 Johannesburg.*